Les Misérables
Victor Hugo

CANTERBURY CLASSICS

San Diego

All correspondence concerning the content of this book should be addressed to: Canterbury Classics
10350 Barnes Canyon Road, Suite 100
San Diego, CA 92121

Library of Congress Cataloging-in-Publication Data

Hugo, Victor, 1802-1885.
[Miserables. English]
Les miserables / Victor Hugo.
p. cm. — (Word cloud classics)
ISBN 978-1-60710-816-0 (pbk.)
1. Ex-convicts—Fiction. 2. Orphans—Fiction. 3. Paris (France)—Fiction. I. Title.
PQ2286.A38 2012
843'.7—dc23

2012032493

PRINTED IN CHINA

1 2 3 4 5 16 15 14 13 12

CONTENTS

PREFACE

So long as there shall exist, by virtue of law and custom, decrees of damnation pronounced by society, artificially creating hells amid the civilization of earth, and adding the element of human fate to divine destiny; so long as the three great problems of the century—the degradation of man through pauperism, the corruption of woman through hunger, the crippling of children through lack of light—are unsolved; so long as social asphyxia is possible in any part of the world—in other words, and with a still wider significance, so long as ignorance and poverty exist on earth, books of the nature of *Les Misérables* cannot fail to be of use.

HAUTEVILLE HOUSE, 1862

VOLUME I: FANTINE

BOOK FIRST: A JUST MAN

CHAPTER I—M. MYRIEL

In 1815, M. Charles-Francois-Bienvenu Myriel was Bishop of D———. He was an old man of about seventy-five years of age; he had occupied the see of D——— since 1806. Although this detail has no connection whatever with the real substance of what we are about to relate, it will not be superfluous, if merely for the sake of exactness in all points, to mention here the various rumors and remarks which had been in circulation about him from the very moment when he arrived in the diocese. True or false, that which is said of men often occupies as important a place in their lives, and above all in their destinies, as that which they do. M. Myriel was the son of a counselor of the Parliament of Aix; hence he belonged to the nobility of the bar. It was said that his father, destining him to be the heir of his own post, had married him at a very early age, eighteen or twenty, in accordance with a custom that is rather widely prevalent in parliamentary families. In spite of this marriage, however, it was said that Charles Myriel created a great deal of talk. He was well formed, though rather short in stature, elegant, graceful, intelligent; the whole of the first portion of his life had been devoted to the world and to gallantry.

The Revolution came; events succeeded each other with precipitation; the parliamentary families, decimated, pursued, hunted down, were dispersed. M. Charles Myriel emigrated to Italy at the very beginning of the Revolution. There his wife died of a malady of the chest, from which she had long suffered. He had no children. What took place next in the fate of M. Myriel? The ruin of the French society of the olden days, the fall of his own family, the tragic spectacles of '93, which were, perhaps, even more alarming to the emigrants who viewed them from a distance, with the magnifying powers of terror, did these cause the ideas of renunciation and solitude to germinate in him? Was he, in the midst of these distractions, these affections which absorbed his life, suddenly smitten with one of those mysterious and terrible blows that sometimes overwhelm, by striking to his heart, a man whom public catastrophes would not shake, by striking at his existence and his fortune? No one could have told: all that was known was, that when he returned from Italy he was a priest.

In 1804, M. Myriel was the Curé of B——. He was already advanced in years, and lived in a very retired manner.

About the epoch of the coronation, some petty affair connected with his curacy—just what, is not precisely known—took him to Paris. Among other powerful persons to whom he went to solicit aid for his parishioners was M. le Cardinal Fesch. One day, when the Emperor had come to visit his uncle, the worthy Curé, who was waiting in the anteroom, found himself present when His Majesty passed. Napoleon, on finding himself observed with a certain curiosity by this old man, turned around and said abruptly, "Who is this good man who is staring at me?"

"Sire," said M. Myriel, "you are looking at a good man, and I at a great man. Each of us can profit by it."

That very evening, the Emperor asked the Cardinal the name of the Curé, and some time afterward M. Myriel was utterly astonished to learn that he had been appointed Bishop of D——.

What truth was there, after all, in the stories that were invented as to the early portion of M. Myriel's life? No one knew. Very few families had been acquainted with the Myriel family before the Revolution.

M. Myriel had to undergo the fate of every newcomer in a little town, where there are many mouths that talk, and very few heads that think. He was obliged to undergo it although he was a bishop, and because he was a bishop. But after all, the rumors with which his name was connected were rumors only—noise, sayings, words; less than words—*palabres*, as the energetic language of the South expresses it.

However that may be, after nine years of episcopal power and of residence in D——, all the stories and subjects of conversation that engross petty towns and petty people at the outset had fallen into profound oblivion. No one would have dared to mention them; no one would have dared to recall them.

M. Myriel had arrived at D—— accompanied by an elderly spinster, Mademoiselle Baptistine, who was his sister, and ten years his junior.

Their only domestic was a female servant of the same age as Mademoiselle Baptistine, and named Madame Magloire, who, after having been the servant of M. le Curé, now assumed the double title of maid to Mademoiselle and housekeeper to Monseigneur.

Mademoiselle Baptistine was a long, pale, thin, gentle creature; she realized the ideal expressed by the word "respectable"; for it seems that a woman must needs be a mother in order to be venerable. She had never been pretty; her whole life, which had been nothing but a succession of holy deeds, had finally conferred upon her a sort of pallor and transparency; and as she advanced in years she had acquired what may be called the beauty of goodness. What had been leanness in her youth had become transparency in her maturity; and this diaphaneity allowed the angel to be seen. She was a soul rather than a virgin. Her person seemed made of a shadow; there was hardly sufficient body to provide for sex; a little matter enclosing a light; large eyes forever drooping—a mere pretext for a soul's remaining on the earth.

Madame Magloire was a little, fat, white old woman, corpulent and bustling; always out of breath, in the first place, because of her activity, and in the next, because of her asthma.

On his arrival, M. Myriel was installed in the episcopal palace with the honors required by the Imperial decrees, which class a bishop immediately after a major-general. The mayor and the president paid the first call on him, and he, in turn, paid the first call on the general and the prefect.

The installation over, the town waited to see its bishop at work.

CHAPTER II—M. MYRIEL BECOMES M. WELCOME

The episcopal palace of D—— adjoins the hospital.

The episcopal palace was a huge and beautiful house, built of stone at the beginning of the last century by M. Henri Puget, Doctor of Theology of the Faculty of Paris, Abbé of Simore, who had been Bishop of D—— in 1712. This palace was a genuine seignorial residence. Everything about it had a grand air, the apartments of the Bishop, the drawing rooms, the chambers, the principal courtyard, which was very large, with walks encircling it under arcades in the old Florentine fashion, and gardens planted with magnificent trees. In the dining room, a long and superb gallery that was situated on the ground floor and opened on the gardens, M. Henri Puget had entertained in state, on July 29, 1714, My Lords Charles Brulart de Genlis, archbishop; Prince d'Embrun; Antoine de Mesgrigny, the capuchin, Bishop of Grasse; Philippe de Vendome, Grand Prior of France, Abbé of Saint Honore de Lerins; Francois de Berton de Crillon, bishop, Baron de Vence; Cesar de Sabran de Forcalquier, bishop, Seignor of Glandeve; and Jean Soanen, Priest of the Oratory, preacher in ordinary to the king, bishop, Seignor of Senez. The portraits of these seven reverend personages decorated this apartment; and this memorable date, the

29th of July, 1714, was there engraved in letters of gold on a table of white marble.

The hospital was a low and narrow building of a single story, with a small garden.

Three days after his arrival, the Bishop visited the hospital. The visit ended, he had the director requested to be so good as to come to his house.

"Monsieur the director of the hospital," said he to him, "how many sick people have you at the present moment?"

"Twenty-six, Monseigneur."

"That was the number which I counted," said the Bishop.

"The beds," pursued the director, "are very much crowded against each other."

"That is what I observed."

"The halls are nothing but rooms, and it is with difficulty that the air can be changed in them."

"So it seems to me."

"And then, when there is a ray of sun, the garden is very small for the convalescents."

"That was what I said to myself."

"In case of epidemics—we have had the typhus fever this year; we had the sweating sickness two years ago, and a hundred patients at times—we know not what to do."

"That is the thought which occurred to me."

"What would you have, Monseigneur?" said the director. "One must resign one's self."

This conversation took place in the gallery dining room on the ground floor.

The Bishop remained silent for a moment; then he turned abruptly to the director of the hospital.

"Monsieur," said he, "how many beds do you think this hall alone would hold?"

"Monseigneur's dining room?" exclaimed the stupefied director.

The Bishop cast a glance around the apartment, and seemed to be taking measures and calculations with his eyes.

"It would hold full twenty beds," said he, as though speaking to himself. Then, raising his voice, "Hold, Monsieur the director of the hospital, I will tell you something. There is evidently a mistake here. There are thirty-six of you, in five or six small rooms. There are three of us here, and we have room for sixty. There is some mistake, I tell you; you have my house, and I have yours. Give me back my house; you are at home here."

On the following day the thirty-six patients were installed in the Bishop's palace, and the Bishop was settled in the hospital.

M. Myriel had no property, his family having been ruined by the Revolution. His sister was in receipt of a yearly income of five hundred francs, which sufficed for her personal wants at the vicarage. M. Myriel received from the State, in his quality of bishop, a salary of fifteen thousand francs. On the very day when he took up his abode in the hospital, M. Myriel settled on the disposition of this sum once for all, in the following manner. We transcribe here a note made by his own hand:

NOTE ON THE REGULATION OF MY HOUSEHOLD EXPENSES.

For the little seminary	1,500 livres
Society of the mission	100
For the Lazarists of Montdidier	100
Seminary for foreign missions in Paris	200
Congregation of the Holy Spirit	150
Religious establishments of the Holy Land	100
Charitable maternity societies	300
Extra, for that of Arles	50
Work for the amelioration of prisons	400
Work for the relief and delivery of prisoners	500
To liberate fathers of families incarcerated for debt	1,000
Addition to the salary of the poor teachers of the diocese	2,000
Public granary of the Hautes-Alpes	100
Congregation of the ladies of D——, of Manosque, and of Sisteron, for the gratuitous instruction of poor girls	1,500
For the poor	6,000
My personal expenses	1,000
Total	15,000

M. Myriel made no change in this arrangement during the entire period that he occupied the see of D——. As has been seen, he called it regulating his household expenses.

This arrangement was accepted with absolute submission by Mademoiselle Baptistine. This holy woman regarded Monseigneur of D—— as at one and the same time her brother and her bishop, her friend according to the flesh and her superior according to the Church. She simply loved and venerated him. When he spoke, she bowed; when he acted, she yielded her adherence. Their only servant, Madame Magloire, grumbled a little. It will be observed that Monsieur the Bishop had reserved for himself only one thousand livres, which, added to the pension of Mademoiselle Baptistine, made fifteen hundred francs a year. On these fifteen hundred francs these two old women and the old man subsisted.

And when a village curate came to D——, the Bishop still found means to entertain him, thanks to the severe economy of Madame Magloire, and to the intelligent administration of Mademoiselle Baptistine.

One day, after he had been in D—— about three months, the Bishop said:

"And still I am quite cramped with it all!"

"I should think so!" exclaimed Madame Magloire. "Monseigneur has not even claimed the allowance that the department owes him for the expense of his carriage in town, and for his journeys about the diocese. It was customary for bishops in former days."

"Hold!" cried the Bishop. "You are quite right, Madame Magloire."

And he made his demand.

Some time afterward the General Council took this demand under consideration, and voted him an annual sum of three thousand francs, under this heading: "Allowance to M. the Bishop for expenses of carriage, expenses of posting, and expenses of pastoral visits."

This provoked a great outcry among the local burgesses; and a senator of the Empire, a former member of the Council of the Five Hundred which favored the 18 Brumaire, and who was provided with a magnificent senatorial office in the vicinity of the town of D——, wrote to M. Bigot de Preameneu, the minister of public worship, a very angry and confidential note on the subject, from which we extract these authentic lines:

> "Expenses of carriage? What can be done with it in a town of less than four thousand inhabitants? Expenses of journeys? What is the use of these trips, in the first place? Next, how can the posting be accomplished in these mountainous parts? There are no roads. No one travels otherwise than on horseback. Even the bridge between Durance and Chateau-Arnoux can barely support ox teams. These priests are all thus, greedy and avaricious. This man played the good priest when he first came. Now he does like the rest; he must have a carriage and a posting-chaise, he must have luxuries, like the bishops of the olden days. Oh, all this priesthood! Things will not go well, M. le Comte, until the Emperor has freed us from

these black-capped rascals. Down with the Pope! (Matters were getting embroiled with Rome.) For my part, I am for Caesar alone." Etc., etc.

On the other hand, this affair afforded great delight to Madame Magloire. "Good," said she to Mademoiselle Baptistine; "Monseigneur began with other people, but he has had to wind up with himself, after all. He has regulated all his charities. Now here are three thousand francs for us! At last!"

That same evening the Bishop wrote out and handed to his sister a memorandum conceived in the following terms:

EXPENSES OF CARRIAGE AND CIRCUIT.

For furnishing meat soup to the patients in the hospital	1,500 livres
For the maternity charitable society of Aix	250
For the maternity charitable society of Draguignan	250
For foundlings	500
For orphans	500
Total	3,000

Such was M. Myriel's budget.

As for the chance episcopal perquisites, the fees for marriage bans, dispensations, private baptisms, sermons, benedictions, of churches or chapels, marriages, etc., the Bishop levied them on the wealthy with all the more asperity, since he bestowed them on the needy.

After a time, offerings of money flowed in. Those who had and those who lacked knocked at M. Myriel's door, the latter in search of the alms that the former came to deposit. In less than a year the Bishop had become the treasurer of all benevolence and the cashier of all those in distress. Considerable sums of money passed through his hands, but nothing could induce him to make any change whatever in his mode of life, or add anything superfluous to his bare necessities.

Far from it. As there is always more wretchedness below than there is brotherhood above, all was given away, so to speak, before it was received. It was like water on dry soil; no matter how much money he received, he never had any. Then he stripped himself.

The usage being that bishops shall announce their baptismal names at the head of their charges and their pastoral letters, the poor people of the countryside had selected, with a sort of affectionate instinct, among the names and prenomens of their bishop, that which had a meaning for them; and they never called him anything except Monseigneur Bienvenu. We will follow their example, and will also call him thus when we have occasion to name him. Moreover, this appellation pleased him.

"I like that name," said he. "Bienvenu makes up for the Monseigneur."

We do not claim that the portrait herewith presented is probable; we confine ourselves to stating that it resembles the original.

CHAPTER III—A HARD BISHOPRIC FOR A GOOD BISHOP

The Bishop did not omit his pastoral visits because he had converted his carriage into alms. The diocese of D—— is a fatiguing one. There are very few plains and a great many mountains; hardly any roads, as we have just seen; thirty-two curacies, forty-one vicarships, and two hundred and eighty-five auxiliary chapels. To visit all these is quite a task.

The Bishop managed to do it. He went on foot when it was in the neighborhood, in a tilted spring-cart when it was on the plain, and on a donkey in the mountains. The two old women accompanied him. When the trip was too hard for them, he went alone.

One day he arrived at Senez, which is an ancient episcopal city. He was mounted on an ass. His purse, which was very dry at that moment, did not permit him any other equipage. The mayor of the town came to receive him at the gate of the town, and watched him dismount from his ass, with scandalized eyes. Some of the citizens were laughing around him. "Monsieur the Mayor," said the Bishop, "and Messieurs Citizens, I perceive that I shock you. You think it very arrogant in a poor priest to ride an animal which was used by Jesus Christ. I have done so from necessity, I assure you, and not from vanity."

In the course of these trips he was kind and indulgent, and talked rather than preached. He never went far in search of his arguments and his examples. He quoted to the inhabitants of one district the example of a neighboring district. In the cantons where they were harsh to the poor, he said: "Look at the people of Briancon! They have conferred on the poor, on widows and orphans, the right to have their meadows mown three days in advance of everyone else. They rebuild their houses for them gratuitously when they are ruined. Therefore it is a country that is blessed by God. For a whole century, there has not been a single murderer among them."

In villages that were greedy for profit and harvest, he said, "Look at the people of Embrun! If, at the harvest season, the father of a family has his son away on service in the army, and his daughters at service in the town, and if he is ill and incapacitated, the Curé recommends him to the prayers of the congregation; and on Sunday, after the Mass, all the inhabitants of the village— men, women, and children—go to the poor man's field and do his harvesting for him, and carry his straw and his grain to his granary." To families divided by questions of money and inheritance he said, "Look at the mountaineers of Devolny, a country so wild that the nightingale has not been heard there once in fifty years. Well, when the father of a family dies, the boys go off to seek their fortunes, leaving the property to the girls, so that they may find husbands." To the cantons that had a taste for lawsuits, and where the farmers ruined themselves in stamped paper, he said, "Look at those good peasants in the valley of Queyras! There are three thousand souls of them. *Mon Dieu!* It is like a little republic. Neither judge nor bailiff is known there. The mayor does everything. He allots the imposts, taxes each person conscientiously, judges quarrels for nothing, divides inheritances without charge, pronounces sentences gratuitously; and he is obeyed, because he is a just man among simple men." To villages where he found no schoolmaster, he quoted once more the people of Queyras, "Do you know how they manage?" he said. "Since a little country of a dozen or fifteen hearths cannot always support a teacher, they have schoolmasters who are paid by the whole valley, who make the round of the villages, spending a week in this one, ten days in that, and instruct them. These teachers go to the fairs. I have seen them there. They are to be recognized by the quill pens that they wear in the cord of their hat. Those who teach reading have only one pen; those who teach reading and reckoning have two pens; those who teach reading, reckoning, and Latin have three pens. But what a disgrace to be ignorant! Do like the people of Queyras!"

Thus he discoursed gravely and paternally; in default of examples, he invented parables, going directly to the point, with few phrases and many images, which characteristic formed the real eloquence of Jesus Christ. And being convinced himself, he was persuasive.

CHAPTER IV—WORKS
CORRESPONDING TO WORDS

His conversation was gay and affable. He put himself on a level with the two old women who had passed their lives beside him. When he laughed, it was the laugh of a schoolboy. Madame Magloire liked to call him Your Grace. One day he rose from his armchair, and went to his library in search of a book. This book was on one of the upper shelves. As the bishop was rather short of stature, he could not reach it. "Madame Magloire," said he, "fetch me a chair. My greatness does not reach as far as that shelf."

One of his distant relatives, Madame la Comtesse de Lo, rarely allowed an opportunity to escape of enumerating, in his presence, what she designated as "the expectations" of her three sons. She had numerous relatives, who were very old and near to death, and of whom her sons were the natural heirs. The youngest of the three was to receive from a grandaunt a good hundred thousand livres of income; the second was the heir by entail to the title of the Duke, his uncle; the eldest was to succeed to the peerage of his grandfather. The Bishop was accustomed to listen in silence to these innocent and pardonable maternal boasts. On one occasion, however, he appeared to be more thoughtful than usual, while Madame de Lo was relating once again the details of all these inheritances and all these "expectations." She interrupted herself impatiently, "*Mon Dieu*, cousin! What are you thinking about?"

"I am thinking," replied the Bishop, "of a singular remark, which is to be found, I believe, in St. Augustine, 'Place your hopes in the man from whom you do not inherit.'"

At another time, on receiving a notification of the decease of a gentleman of the countryside, wherein not only the dignities of the dead man, but also the feudal and noble qualifications of all his relatives, spread over an entire page, "What a stout back Death has!" he exclaimed. "What a strange burden of titles is cheerfully imposed on him, and how much wit must men have, in order thus to press the tomb into the service of vanity!"

He was gifted, on occasion, with a gentle raillery, which almost always concealed a serious meaning. In the course of one Lent, a youthful vicar came to D——, and preached in the cathedral. He was tolerably eloquent. The subject of his sermon was charity. He urged the rich to give to the poor, in order to avoid hell, which he depicted in the most frightful manner of which he was capable, and to win paradise, which he represented as charming and desirable. Among the audience there was a wealthy retired merchant, who was somewhat of a usurer, named M. Geborand, who had amassed two million in the manufacture of coarse cloth, serges, and woolen galloons. Never in his whole life had M. Geborand bestowed alms on any poor wretch. After the delivery of that sermon, it was observed that he gave a sou every Sunday to the poor old beggar-women at the door of the cathedral. There were six of them to share it. One day the

Bishop caught sight of him in the act of bestowing this charity, and said to his sister, with a smile, "There is M. Geborand purchasing paradise for a sou."

When it was a question of charity, he was not to be rebuffed even by a refusal, and on such occasions he gave utterance to remarks that induced reflection. Once he was begging for the poor in a drawing room of the town; there was present the Marquis de Champtercier, a wealthy and avaricious old man, who contrived to be, at one and the same time, an ultra-royalist and an ultra-Voltairian. This variety of man has actually existed. When the Bishop came to him, he touched his arm, "You must give me something, M. le Marquis."

The Marquis turned around and answered dryly, "I have poor people of my own, Monseigneur."

"Give them to me," replied the Bishop.

One day he preached the following sermon in the cathedral: "My very dear brethren, my good friends, there are thirteen hundred and twenty thousand peasants' dwellings in France which have but three openings; eighteen hundred and seventeen thousand hovels that have but two openings, the door and one window; and three hundred and forty-six thousand cabins besides which have but one opening, the door. And this arises from a thing which is called the tax on doors and windows. Just put poor families, old women and little children, in those buildings, and behold the fevers and maladies that result! Alas! God gives air to men; the law sells it to them. I do not blame the law, but I bless God. In the department of the Isere, in the Var, in the two departments of the Alpes, the Hautes, and the Basses, the peasants have not even wheelbarrows; they transport their manure on the backs of men; they have no candles, and they burn resinous sticks, and bits of rope dipped in pitch. That is the state of affairs throughout the whole of the hilly country of Dauphine. They make bread for six months at one time; they bake it with dried cow dung. In the winter they break this bread up with an ax, and they soak it for twenty-four hours, in order to render it eatable. My brethren, have pity! Behold the suffering on all sides of you!"

Born a Provencal, he easily familiarized himself with the dialect of the south. He said, *"En be! Moussu, ses sage?"* as in lower Languedoc; *"Onte anaras passa?"* as in the Basses-Alpes; *"Puerte un bouen moutu embe un bouen fromage grase,"* as in upper Dauphine. This pleased the people extremely, and contributed not a little to win him access to all spirits. He was perfectly at home in the thatched cottage and in the mountains. He understood how to say the grandest things in the most vulgar of idioms. As he spoke all tongues, he entered into all hearts.

Moreover, he was the same toward people of the world and toward the lower classes. He condemned nothing in haste and without taking circumstances into account. He said, "Examine the road over which the fault has passed."

Being, as he described himself with a smile, an ex-sinner, he had none of the asperities of austerity, and he professed, with a good deal of distinctness, and without the frown of the ferociously virtuous, a doctrine that may be summed up as follows: "Man has upon him his flesh, which is at once his burden and his temptation. He drags it with him and yields to it. He must watch it, check it, repress it, and obey it only at the last extremity. There may be some fault even in this obedience; but the fault thus committed is venial; it is a fall, but a fall on the knees that may terminate in prayer. To be a saint is the exception; to be an upright man is the rule. Err, fall, sin if you will, but be upright. The least possible sin is the law of man. No sin at all is the dream of the angel. All that is terrestrial is subject to sin. Sin is gravitation."

When he saw everyone exclaiming very loudly, and growing angry very quickly, "Oh! Oh!" he said, with a smile. "To all appearance, this is a great crime that all the world commits. These are hypocrisies which have taken fright, and are in haste to make protest and to put themselves under shelter."

He was indulgent toward women and poor people, on whom the burden of human society rest. He said, "The faults of women, of children, of the feeble, the indigent, and the ignorant, are the fault of the husbands, the fathers, the masters, the strong, the rich, and the wise."

He said, moreover, "Teach those who are ignorant as many things as possible; society is culpable, in that it does not afford instruction gratis; it is responsible for the night which it produces. This soul is full of shadow; sin is therein committed. The guilty one is not the person who has committed the sin, but the person who has created the shadow."

It will be perceived that he had a peculiar manner of his own of judging things; I suspect that he obtained it from the Gospel.

One day he heard a criminal case, which was in preparation and on the point of trial, discussed in a drawing room. A wretched man, being at the end of his resources, had coined counterfeit money, out of love for a woman, and for the child which he had had by her. Counterfeiting was still punishable with death at that epoch. The woman had been arrested in the act of passing the first false piece made by the man. She was held, but there were no proofs except against her. She alone could accuse her lover, and destroy him by her confession. She denied; they insisted. She persisted in her denial. Thereupon an idea occurred to the attorney for the crown. He invented an infidelity on the part of the lover, and succeeded, by means of fragments of letters cunningly presented, in persuading the unfortunate woman that she had a rival, and that the man was deceiving her. Thereupon, exasperated by jealousy, she denounced her lover, confessed all, proved all.

The man was ruined. He was shortly to be tried at Aix with his accomplice. They were relating the matter, and each one was expressing enthusiasm over the cleverness of the magistrate. By bringing jealousy into play, he had caused the truth to burst forth in wrath, he had educed the justice of revenge. The Bishop listened to all this in silence. When they had finished, he inquired, "Where are this man and woman to be tried?"

"At the Court of Assizes."

He went on, "And where will the advocate of the crown be tried?"

A tragic event occurred at D——. A man was condemned to death for murder. He was a wretched fellow, not exactly educated, not exactly ignorant, who had been a mountebank at fairs, and a writer for the public. The town took a great interest in the trial. On the eve of the day fixed for the execution of the condemned man, the chaplain of the prison fell ill. A priest was needed to attend the criminal in his last moments. They sent for the Curé. It seems that he refused to come, saying, "That is no affair of mine. I have nothing to do with that unpleasant task, and with that mountebank: I, too, am ill; and besides, it is not my place."

This reply was reported to the Bishop, who said, "Monsieur le Curé is right: it is not his place; it is mine."

He went instantly to the prison, descended to the cell of the mountebank, called him by name, took him by the hand, and spoke to him. He passed the entire day with him, forgetful of food and sleep, praying to God for the soul of the condemned man, and praying the condemned man for his own. He told him the best truths, which are also the most simple. He was father, brother, friend; he was bishop only to bless. He taught him everything, encouraged and consoled him. The man was on the point of dying in despair. Death was an abyss to him. As he stood trembling on its mournful brink, he recoiled with horror. He was not sufficiently ignorant to be absolutely indifferent. His condemnation, which had been a profound shock, had, in a manner, broken through, here and there, that wall which separates us from the mystery of things, and which we call life. He gazed incessantly beyond this world through these fatal breaches, and beheld only darkness. The Bishop made him see light.

On the following day, when they came to fetch the unhappy wretch, the Bishop was still there. He followed him, and exhibited himself to the eyes of the crowd in his purple camail and with his Episcopal cross upon his neck, side by side with the criminal bound with cords.

He mounted the tumbril with him, he mounted the scaffold with him. The sufferer, who had been so gloomy and cast down on the preceding day, was radiant. He felt that his soul was reconciled, and he hoped in God. The Bishop embraced him, and at the moment when the knife was about to fall, he said to him, "God raises from the dead him whom man slays; he whom his brothers have rejected finds his Father once more. Pray, believe, enter into life: the Father is there." When he descended from the scaffold, there was something in his look that made the people draw aside to let him pass. They did not know which was most worthy of admiration, his pallor or his serenity. On his return to the humble dwelling, which he designated, with a smile, as his palace, he said to his sister, "I have just officiated pontifically."

Since the most sublime things are often those which are the least understood, there were people in the town who said, when commenting on this conduct of the Bishop, "It is affectation."

This, however, was a remark that was confined to the drawing rooms. The populace, which perceives no jest in holy deeds, was touched, and admired him.

As for the Bishop, it was a shock to him to have beheld the guillotine, and it was a long time before he recovered from it.

In fact, when the scaffold is there, all erected and prepared, it has something about it that produces hallucination. One may feel a certain indifference to the death penalty, one may refrain from pronouncing upon it, from saying yes or no, so long as one has not seen a guillotine with one's own eyes: but if one encounters one of them, the shock is violent; one is forced to decide, and to take part for or against. Some admire it, like de Maistre; others execrate it, like Beccaria. The guillotine is the concretion of the law; it is called *vindicte*; it is not neutral, and it does not permit you to remain neutral. He who sees it shivers with the most mysterious of shivers. All social problems erect their interrogation point around this chopping knife. The scaffold is a vision. The scaffold is not a piece of carpentry; the scaffold is not a machine; the scaffold is not an inert bit of mechanism constructed of wood, iron, and cords.

It seems as though it were a being, possessed of I know not what somber initiative; one would say that this piece of carpenter's work saw, that this machine heard, that this mechanism understood, that this wood, this iron, and these cords were possessed of will. In the frightful meditation into which its presence casts the soul the scaffold appears in terrible guise, and as though taking part in what is going on. The scaffold is the accomplice of the executioner; it devours, it eats flesh, it drinks blood; the scaffold is a sort of monster fabricated by the judge and the carpenter, a specter that seems to live with a horrible vitality composed of all the death that it has inflicted.

Therefore, the impression was terrible and profound; on the day following the execution, and on many succeeding days, the Bishop appeared to be crushed. The almost violent serenity of the funereal moment had disappeared; the phantom of social justice tormented him. He, who generally returned from all his deeds with a radiant satisfaction, seemed to be reproaching himself. At times he talked to himself, and stammered lugubrious monologues in a low voice. This is one that his sister overheard one evening and preserved, "I did not think that it was so monstrous. It is wrong to become absorbed in the divine law to such a degree as not to perceive human law. Death belongs to God alone. By what right do men touch that unknown thing?"

In course of time these impressions weakened and probably vanished. Nevertheless, it was observed that the Bishop thenceforth avoided passing the place of execution.

M. Myriel could be summoned at any hour to the bedside of the sick and dying. He did not ignore the fact that therein lay his greatest duty and his greatest labor. Widowed and orphaned families had no need to summon him; he came of his own accord. He understood how to sit down and hold his peace for long hours beside the man who had lost the wife of his love, of the mother who had lost her child. As he knew the moment for silence he knew also the moment for speech. Oh, admirable consoler! He sought not to efface sorrow by forgetfulness, but to magnify and dignify it by hope.

He said, "Have a care of the manner in which you turn toward the dead. Think not of that which perishes. Gaze steadily. You will perceive the living light of your well-beloved dead in the depths of heaven." He knew that faith is wholesome. He sought to counsel and calm the despairing man, by pointing out to him the resigned man, and to transform the grief that gazes upon a grave by showing him the grief that fixes its gaze upon a star.

CHAPTER V — MONSEIGNEUR BIENVENU MADE HIS CASSOCKS LAST TOO LONG

The private life of M. Myriel was filled with the same thoughts as his public life. The voluntary poverty in which the Bishop of D—— lived, would have been a solemn and charming sight for anyone who could have viewed it close at hand.

Like all old men, and like the majority of thinkers, he slept little. This brief slumber was profound. In the morning he meditated for an hour, then he said his Mass, either at the cathedral or in his own house. His Mass said, he broke his fast on rye bread dipped in the milk of his own cows. Then he set to work.

A Bishop is a very busy man: he must every day receive the secretary of the bishopric, who is generally a canon, and nearly every day his vicars-general. He has congregations to reprove, privileges to grant, a whole ecclesiastical library to examine, prayer books, diocesan catechisms, books of hours, etc., charges to write, sermons to authorize, cures and mayors to reconcile, a clerical correspondence, an administrative correspondence; on one side the State, on the other the Holy See; and a thousand matters of business.

What time was left to him, after these thousand details of business, and his offices and his breviary, he bestowed first on the necessitous, the sick, and the afflicted; the time that was left to him from the afflicted, the sick, and the necessitous, he devoted to work. Sometimes he dug in his garden; again, he read or wrote. He had but one word for both these kinds of toil; he called them gardening. "The mind is a garden," said he.

Toward midday, when the weather was fine, he went forth and took a stroll in the country or in town, often entering lowly dwellings. He was seen walking alone, buried in his own thoughts, his eyes cast down, supporting himself on his long cane, clad in his wadded purple garment of silk, which was very warm, wearing purple stockings inside his coarse shoes, and surmounted by a flat hat that allowed three golden tassels of large bullion to droop from its three points.

It was a perfect festival wherever he appeared. One would have said that his presence had something warming and luminous about it. The children and the old people came out to the doorsteps for the Bishop as for the sun. He bestowed his blessing, and they blessed him. They pointed out his house to anyone who was in need of anything.

Here and there he halted, accosted the little boys and girls, and smiled upon the mothers. He visited the poor so long as he had any money; when he no longer had any, he visited the rich.

As he made his cassocks last a long while, and did not wish to have it noticed, he never went out in the town without his wadded purple cloak. This inconvenienced him somewhat in summer.

On his return, he dined. The dinner resembled his breakfast.

At half-past eight in the evening he supped with his sister, Madame Magloire standing behind them and serving them at table. Nothing could be more frugal than this repast. If, however, the Bishop had one of his Curés to supper, Madame

Magloire took advantage of the opportunity to serve Monseigneur with some excellent fish from the lake, or with some fine game from the mountains. Every Curé furnished the pretext for a good meal: the Bishop did not interfere. With that exception, his ordinary diet consisted only of vegetables boiled in water, and oil soup. Thus it was said in the town, when the Bishop does not indulge in the cheer of a Curé, he indulges in the cheer of a Trappist.

After supper he conversed for half an hour with Mademoiselle Baptistine and Madame Magloire; then he retired to his own room and set to writing, sometimes on loose sheets, and again on the margin of some folio. He was a man of letters and rather learned. He left behind him five or six very curious manuscripts; among others, a dissertation on this verse in Genesis: "In the beginning, the spirit of God floated upon the waters." With this verse he compares three texts: the Arabic verse which says, "The winds of God blew"; Flavius Josephus, who says, "A wind from above was precipitated upon the earth"; and finally, the Chaldaic paraphrase of Onkelos, which renders it, "A wind coming from God blew upon the face of the waters." In another dissertation, he examines the theological works of Hugo, Bishop of Ptolemais, great-grand-uncle to the writer of this book, and establishes the fact, that to this bishop must be attributed the divers little works published during the last century, under the pseudonym of Barleycourt.

Sometimes, in the midst of his reading, no matter what the book might be that he had in his hand, he would suddenly fall into a profound meditation, from which he only emerged to write a few lines on the pages of the volume itself. These lines have often no connection whatever with the book that contains them. We now have under our eyes a note written by him on the margin of a quarto entitled "Correspondence of Lord Germain with Generals Clinton, Cornwallis, and the Admirals on the American station. Versailles, Poincot, bookseller; and Paris, Pissot, bookseller, Quai des Augustins."

Here is the note: "Oh, you who are! Ecclesiastes calls you the All-powerful; the Maccabees call you the Creator; the Epistle to the Ephesians calls you liberty; Baruch calls you Immensity; the Psalms call you Wisdom and Truth; John calls you Light; the Books of Kings call you Lord; Exodus calls you Providence; Leviticus, Sanctity; Esdras, Justice; the creation calls you God; man calls you Father; but Solomon calls you Compassion, and that is the most beautiful of all your names."

Toward nine o'clock in the evening the two women retired and betook themselves to their chambers on the first floor, leaving him alone until morning on the ground floor.

It is necessary that we should, in this place, give an exact idea of the dwelling of the Bishop of D——.

CHAPTER VI—WHO GUARDED HIS HOUSE FOR HIM

The house in which he lived consisted, as we have said, of a ground floor, and one story above; three rooms on the ground floor, three chambers on the first, and an attic above. Behind the house was a garden, a quarter of an acre in extent. The two women occupied the first floor; the Bishop was lodged below. The first room, opening on the street, served him as dining room, the second was his bedroom, and the third his oratory. There was no exit possible from this oratory, except by passing through the bedroom, nor from the bedroom, without passing through the dining room. At the end of the suite, in the oratory, there was a detached alcove with a bed, for use in cases of hospitality. The Bishop offered this bed to country curates whom business or the requirements of their parishes brought to D——.

The pharmacy of the hospital, a small building that had been added to the house, and abutted on the garden, had been transformed into a kitchen and cellar. In addition to this, there was in the garden a stable, which had formerly been the kitchen of the hospital, and in which the Bishop kept two cows. No matter what the quantity of milk they gave, he invariably sent half of it every morning to the sick people in the hospital. "I am paying my tithes," he said.

His bedroom was tolerably large, and rather difficult to warm in bad weather. As wood is extremely dear at D——, he hit upon the idea of having a compartment of boards constructed in the cow shed. Here he passed his evenings during seasons of severe cold: he called it his winter salon.

In this winter salon, as in the dining room, there was no other furniture than a square table in white wood, and four straw-seated chairs. In addition to this the dining room was ornamented with an antique sideboard, painted pink, in water colors. Out of a similar sideboard, properly draped with white napery and imitation lace, the Bishop had constructed the altar which decorated his oratory.

His wealthy penitents and the sainted women of D—— had more than once assessed themselves to raise the money for a new altar for Monseigneur's oratory; on each occasion he had taken the money and had given it to the poor. "The most beautiful of altars," he said, "is the soul of an unhappy creature consoled and thanking God."

In his oratory there were two straw prie-dieux, and there was an armchair, also in straw, in his bedroom. When, by chance, he received seven or eight persons at one time, the prefect, or the general, or the staff of the regiment in garrison, or several pupils from the little seminary, the chairs had to be fetched from the winter salon in the stable, the prie-dieu from the oratory, and the armchair from the bedroom: in this way as many as eleven chairs could be collected for the visitors. A room was dismantled for each new guest.

It sometimes happened that there were twelve in the party; the Bishop then relieved the embarrassment of the situation by standing in front of the chimney if it was winter, or by strolling in the garden if it was summer.

There was still another chair in the detached alcove, but the straw was half gone from it, and it had but three legs, so that it was of service only when propped against the wall. Mademoiselle Baptistine had also in her own room a very large easy chair of wood, which had formerly been gilded, and which was covered with flowered pekin; but they had been obliged to hoist this bergere up to the first story through the window, as the staircase was too narrow; it could not, therefore, be reckoned among the possibilities in the way of furniture.

Mademoiselle Baptistine's ambition had been to be able to purchase a set of drawing room furniture in yellow Utrecht velvet, stamped with a rose pattern, and with mahogany in swan's neck style, with a sofa. But this would have cost five hundred francs at least, and in view of the fact that she had only been able to lay by forty-two francs and ten sous for this purpose in the course of five years, she had ended by renouncing the idea. However, who is there who has attained his ideal?

Nothing is more easy to present to the imagination than the Bishop's bedchamber. A glazed door opened on the garden; opposite this was the bed, a hospital bed of iron, with a canopy of green serge; in the shadow of the bed, behind a curtain, were the utensils of the toilet, which still betrayed the elegant habits of the man of the world: there were two doors, one near the chimney, opening into the oratory; the other near the bookcase, opening into the dining room. The bookcase was a large cupboard with glass doors filled with books; the chimney was of wood painted to represent marble, and habitually without fire. In the chimney stood a pair of firedogs of iron, ornamented above with two garlanded vases, and flutings that had formerly been silvered with silver leaf, which was a sort of episcopal luxury; above the chimneypiece hung a crucifix of copper, with the silver worn off, fixed on a background of threadbare velvet in a wooden frame from which the gilding had fallen; near the glass door a large table with an inkstand, loaded with a confusion of papers and with huge volumes; before the table an armchair of straw; in front of the bed a prie-dieu, borrowed from the oratory.

Two portraits in oval frames were fastened to the wall on each side of the bed. Small gilt inscriptions on the plain surface of the cloth at the side of these figures indicated that the portraits represented, one the Abbé of Chaliot, bishop of Saint Claude; the other, the Abbé Tourteau, vicar-general of Agde, Abbé of Grand-Champ, order of Citeaux, diocese of Chartres. When the Bishop succeeded to this apartment, after the hospital patients, he had found these portraits there, and had left them. They were priests, and probably donors—two reasons for respecting them. All that he knew about these two persons was, that they had been appointed by the king, the one to his bishopric, the other to his benefice, on the same day, the 27th of April, 1785. Madame Magloire having taken the pictures down to dust, the Bishop had discovered these particulars written in whitish ink on a little square of paper, yellowed by time, and attached to the back of the portrait of the Abbé of Grand-Champ, with four wafers.

At his window he had an antique curtain of a coarse woolen stuff, which finally became so old, that, in order to avoid the expense of a new one, Madame Magloire was forced to take a large seam in the very middle of it. This seam took the form of a cross. The Bishop often called attention to it: "How delightful that is!" he said.

All the rooms in the house, without exception, those on the ground floor as well as those on the first floor, were whitewashed, which is a fashion in barracks and hospitals.

However, in their later years, Madame Magloire discovered beneath the paper that had been washed over, paintings, ornamenting the apartment of Mademoiselle Baptistine, as we shall see further on. Before becoming a hospital, this house had been the ancient parliament house of the Bourgeois. Hence this decoration. The chambers were paved in red bricks, which were washed every week, with straw mats in front of all the beds. Altogether, this dwelling, which was attended to by the two women, was exquisitely clean from top to bottom. This was the sole luxury that the Bishop permitted. He said, "That takes nothing from the poor."

It must be confessed, however, that he still retained from his former possessions six silver knives and forks and a soup ladle, which Madame Magloire contemplated every day with delight, as they glistened splendidly upon the coarse linen cloth. And since we are now painting the Bishop of D—— as he was in reality, we must add that he had said more than once, "I find it difficult to renounce eating from silver dishes."

To this silverware must be added two large candlesticks of massive silver, which he had inherited from a great-aunt. These candlesticks held two wax candles, and usually figured on the Bishop's chimneypiece. When he had anyone to dinner, Madame Magloire lighted the two candles and set the candlesticks on the table.

In the Bishop's own chamber, at the head of his bed, there was a small cupboard, in which Madame Magloire locked up the six silver knives and forks and the big spoon every night. But it is necessary to add, that the key was never removed.

The garden, which had been rather spoiled by the ugly buildings that we have mentioned, was composed of four alleys in cross-form, radiating from a tank. Another walk made the circuit of the garden, and skirted the white wall that enclosed it. These alleys left behind them four square plots rimmed with box. In three of these, Madame Magloire cultivated vegetables; in the fourth, the Bishop had planted some flowers; here and there stood a few fruit trees. Madame Magloire had once remarked, with a sort of gentle malice: "Monseigneur, you who turn everything to account, have, nevertheless, one useless plot. It would be better to grow salads there than bouquets."

"Madame Magloire," retorted the Bishop, "you are mistaken. The beautiful is as useful as the useful." He added after a pause, "More so, perhaps."

This plot, consisting of three or four beds, occupied the Bishop almost as much as did his books. He liked to pass an hour or two there, trimming, hoeing, and making holes here and there in the earth, into which he dropped seeds. He was not as hostile to insects as a gardener could have wished to see him. Moreover, he made no pretensions to botany; he ignored groups and consistency; he made not the slightest effort to decide between Tournefort and the natural method; he took part neither with the buds against the cotyledons, nor with Jussieu against Linnaeus. He did not study plants; he loved flowers. He respected learned men greatly; he respected the ignorant still more; and, without ever failing in these two respects, he watered his flower beds every summer evening with a tin watering pot painted green.

The house had not a single door which could be locked. The door of the dining room, which, as we have said, opened directly on the cathedral square, had formerly been ornamented with locks and bolts like the door of a prison. The Bishop had had all this ironwork removed, and this door was never fastened, either by night or by day, with anything except the latch. All that the first passerby had to do at any hour, was to give it a push. At first, the two women had been very much tried by this door, which was never fastened, but Monsieur de D—— had said to them, "Have bolts put on your rooms, if that will please you." They had ended by sharing his confidence, or by at least acting as though they shared it. Madame Magloire alone had frights from time to time. As for the Bishop, his thought can be found explained, or at least indicated, in the three lines which he wrote on the margin of a Bible, "This is the shade of difference: the door of the physician should never be shut, the door of the priest should always be open."

On another book, entitled Philosophy of the Medical Science, he had written this other note: "Am not I a physician like them? I also have my patients, and then, too, I have some whom I call my unfortunates."

Again he wrote: "Do not inquire the name of him who asks a shelter of you. The very man who is embarrassed by his name is the one who needs shelter."

It chanced that a worthy cure, I know not whether it was the Curé of Couloubroux or the Curé of Pompierry, took it into his head to ask him one day, probably at the instigation of Madame Magloire, whether Monsieur was sure that he was not committing an indiscretion, to a certain extent, in leaving his door unfastened day and night, at the mercy of anyone who should choose to enter, and whether, in short, he did not fear lest some misfortune might occur in a house so little guarded. The Bishop touched his shoulder, with gentle gravity, and said to him, *"Nisi Dominus custodierit domum, in vanum vigilant qui custodiunt eam."* (Unless the Lord guard the house, in vain do they watch who guard it.)

Then he spoke of something else.

He was fond of saying, "There is a bravery of the priest as well as the bravery of a colonel of dragoons, only," he added, "ours must be tranquil."

CHAPTER VII—CRAVATTE

It is here that a fact falls naturally into place, which we must not omit, because it is one of the sort which show us best what sort of a man the Bishop of D—— was.

After the destruction of the band of Gaspard Bes, who had infested the gorges of Ollioules, one of his lieutenants, Cravatte, took refuge in the mountains. He concealed himself for some time with his bandits, the remnant of Gaspard Bes's troop, in the county of Nice; then he made his way to Piedmont, and suddenly reappeared in France, in the vicinity of Barcelonette. He was first seen at Jauziers, then at Tuiles. He hid himself in the caverns of the Joug-de-l'Aigle, and thence he descended toward the hamlets and villages through the ravines of Ubaye and Ubayette.

He even pushed as far as Embrun, entered the cathedral one night, and despoiled the sacristy. His highway robberies laid waste the countryside. The gendarmes were set on his track, but in vain. He always escaped; sometimes he resisted by main force. He was a bold wretch. In the midst of all this terror the Bishop arrived. He was making his circuit to Chastelar. The mayor came to meet him, and urged him to retrace his steps. Cravatte was in possession of the mountains as far as Arche, and beyond; there was danger even with an escort; it merely exposed three or four unfortunate gendarmes to no purpose.

"Therefore," said the Bishop, "I intend to go without escort."

"You do not really mean that, Monseigneur!" exclaimed the mayor.

"I do mean it so thoroughly that I absolutely refuse any gendarmes, and shall set out in an hour."

"Set out?"

"Set out."

"Alone?"

"Alone."

"Monseigneur, you will not do that!"

"There exists yonder in the mountains," said the Bishop, "a tiny community no bigger than that, which I have not seen for three years. They are my good friends, those gentle and honest shepherds. They own one goat out of every thirty that they tend. They make very pretty woolen cords of various colors, and they play the mountain airs on little flutes with six holes. They need to be told of the good God now and then. What would they say to a bishop who was afraid? What would they say if I did not go?"

"But the brigands, Monseigneur?"

"Hold," said the Bishop, "I must think of that. You are right. I may meet them. They, too, need to be told of the good God."

"But, Monseigneur, there is a band of them! A flock of wolves!"

"Monsieur le maire, it may be that it is of this very flock of wolves that Jesus has constituted me the shepherd. Who knows the ways of Providence?"

"They will rob you, Monseigneur."

"I have nothing."

"They will kill you."

"An old goodman of a priest, who passes along mumbling his prayers? Bah! To what purpose?"

"Oh, *mon Dieu*! What if you should meet them!"

"I should beg alms of them for my poor."

"Do not go, Monseigneur. In the name of Heaven! You are risking your life!"

"Monsieur le maire," said the Bishop, "is that really all? I am not in the world to guard my own life, but to guard souls."

They had to allow him to do as he pleased. He set out, accompanied only by a child who offered to serve as a guide. His obstinacy was bruited about the countryside, and caused great consternation.

He would take neither his sister nor Madame Magloire. He traversed the mountain on muleback, encountered no one, and arrived safe and sound at the residence of his "good friends," the shepherds. He remained there for a fortnight, preaching, administering the sacrament, teaching, exhorting. When the time of his departure approached, he resolved to chant a Te Deum pontifically. He mentioned it to the Curé. But what was to be done? There were no episcopal ornaments. They could only place at his disposal a wretched village sacristy, with a few ancient chasubles of threadbare damask adorned with imitation lace.

"Bah!" said the Bishop. "Let us announce our Te Deum from the pulpit, nevertheless, Monsieur le Curé. Things will arrange themselves."

They instituted a search in the churches of the neighborhood. All the magnificence of these humble parishes combined would not have sufficed to clothe the chorister of a cathedral properly.

While they were thus embarrassed, a large chest was brought and deposited in the presbytery for the Bishop, by two unknown horsemen, who departed on the instant. The chest was opened; it contained a cope of cloth of gold, a miter ornamented with diamonds, an archbishop's cross, a magnificent crosier—all the pontifical vestments that had been stolen a month previously from the treasury of Notre Dame d'Embrun. In the chest was a paper, on which these words were written, "From Cravatte to Monseigneur Bienvenu."

"Did not I say that things would come right of themselves?" said the Bishop. Then he added, with a smile, "To him who contents himself with the surplice of a curate, God sends the cope of an archbishop."

"Monseigneur," murmured the Curé, throwing back his head with a smile. "God—or the Devil."

The Bishop looked steadily at the Curé, and repeated with authority, "God!"

When he returned to Chastelar, the people came out to stare at him as at a curiosity, all along the road. At the priest's house in Chastelar he rejoined Mademoiselle Baptistine and Madame Magloire, who were waiting for him, and he said to his sister, "Well! Was I in the right? The poor priest went to his poor mountaineers with empty hands, and he returns from them with his hands full. I set out bearing only my faith in God; I have brought back the treasure of a cathedral."

That evening, before he went to bed, he said again, "Let us never fear robbers nor murderers. Those are dangers from without, petty dangers. Let us fear ourselves. Prejudices are the real robbers; vices are the real murderers. The great dangers lie within ourselves. What matters is what threatens our head or our purse! Let us think only of that which threatens our soul."

Then, turning to his sister, "Sister, never a precaution on the part of the priest, against his fellow man. That which his fellow does, God permits. Let us confine ourselves to prayer, when we think that a danger is approaching us. Let us pray, not for ourselves, but that our brother may not fall into sin on our account."

However, such incidents were rare in his life. We relate those of which we know; but generally he passed his life in doing the same things at the same moment. One month of his year resembled one hour of his day.

As to what became of "the treasure" of the cathedral of Embrun, we should be embarrassed by any inquiry in that direction. It consisted of very handsome things, very tempting things, and things that were very well adapted to be stolen for the benefit of the unfortunate. Stolen they had already been elsewhere. Half of the adventure was completed; it only remained to impart a new direction to the theft, and to cause it to take a short trip in the direction of the poor. However, we make no assertions on this point. Only, a rather obscure note was found among the Bishop's papers, which may bear some relation to this matter, and which is couched in these terms, "The question is, to decide whether this should be turned over to the cathedral or to the hospital."

CHAPTER VIII—PHILOSOPHY AFTER DRINKING

The senator above mentioned was a clever man, who had made his own way, heedless of those things which present obstacles, and which are called conscience, sworn faith, justice, duty: he had marched straight to his goal, without once flinching in the line of his advancement and his interest. He was an old attorney, softened by success; not a bad man by any means, who rendered all the small services in his power to his sons, his sons-in-law, his relations, and even to his friends, having wisely seized upon, in life, good sides, good opportunities, good windfalls. Everything else seemed to him very stupid. He was intelligent, and just sufficiently educated to think himself a disciple of Epicurus; while he was, in reality, only a product of Pigault-Lebrun. He laughed willingly and pleasantly over infinite and eternal things, and at the "Crotchets of that good old fellow the Bishop." He even sometimes laughed at him with an amiable authority in the presence of M. Myriel himself, who listened to him.

On some semiofficial occasion or other, I do not recollect what, Count and M. Myriel were to dine with the prefect. At dessert, the senator, who was slightly exhilarated, though still perfectly dignified, exclaimed, "Egad, Bishop, let's have a discussion. It is hard for a senator and a bishop to look at each other without winking. We are two augurs.* I am going to make a confession to you. I have a philosophy of my own."

"And you are right," replied the Bishop. "As one makes one's philosophy, so one lies on it. You are on the bed of purple, senator."

The senator was encouraged, and went on, "Let us be good fellows."

"Good devils even," said the Bishop.

"I declare to you," continued the senator, "that the Marquis d'Argens, Pyrrhon, Hobbes, and M. Naigeon are no rascals. I have all the philosophers in my library gilded on the edges."

"Like yourself, Count," interposed the Bishop.

The senator resumed, "I hate Diderot; he is an ideologist, a declaimer, and a revolutionist, a believer in God at bottom, and more bigoted than Voltaire. Voltaire made sport of Needham, and he was wrong, for Needham's eels prove that God is useless. A drop of vinegar in a spoonful of flour paste supplies the *fiat lux.*** Suppose the drop to be larger and the spoonful bigger; you have the world. Man is the eel. Then what is the good of the Eternal Father? The Jehovah hypothesis tires me, Bishop. It is good for nothing but to produce shallow people, whose reasoning is hollow. Down with that great All, which torments me! Hurrah for Zero which leaves me in peace! Between you and me, and in order to empty my sack, and make confession to my pastor, as it behooves me to do, I will admit to you that I have good sense. I am not enthusiastic over your Jesus, who preaches renunciation and sacrifice to the last extremity. 'Tis the counsel of an avaricious man to beggars. Renunciation; why? Sacrifice; to what end? I do not see one wolf immolating himself for the happiness of another wolf. Let us stick to nature, then. We are at the top; let us have a superior philosophy. What is the advantage of being at the top, if one sees no further than the end of other people's noses? Let us live merrily. Life is all. That man has another future elsewhere, on high, below, anywhere, I don't believe; not one single word of it. Ah! Sacrifice and renunciation are

* an official diviner of ancient Rome
** "Let there be light"

recommended to me; I must take heed to everything I do; I must cudgel my brains over good and evil, over the just and the unjust, over the fas and the nefas. Why? Because I shall have to render an account of my actions. When? After death. What a fine dream! After my death it will be a very clever person who can catch me. Have a handful of dust seized by a shadow-hand, if you can. Let us tell the truth, we who are initiated, and who have raised the veil of Isis: there is no such thing as either good or evil; there is vegetation. Let us seek the real. Let us get to the bottom of it. Let us go into it thoroughly. What the deuce! Let us go to the bottom of it! We must scent out the truth; dig in the earth for it, and seize it. Then it gives you exquisite joys. Then you grow strong, and you laugh. I am square on the bottom, I am. Immortality, Bishop, is a chance, a waiting for dead men's shoes. Ah! What a charming promise! Trust to it, if you like! What a fine lot Adam has! We are souls, and we shall be angels, with blue wings on our shoulder blades. Do come to my assistance: is it not Tertullian who says that the blessed shall travel from star to star? Very well. We shall be the grasshoppers of the stars. And then, besides, we shall see God. Ta, ta, ta! What twaddle all these paradises are! God is a nonsensical monster. I would not say that in the Moniteur, egad! But I may whisper it among friends. *Inter pocula.*[*] To sacrifice the world to paradise is to let slip the prey for the shadow. Be the dupe of the infinite! I'm not such a fool. I am a nought. I call myself Monsieur le Comte Nought, senator. Did I exist before my birth? No. Shall I exist after death? No. What am I? A little dust collected in an organism. What am I to do on this earth? The choice rests with me: suffer or enjoy. Where will suffering lead me? To nothingness; but I shall have suffered. Where will enjoyment lead me? To nothingness; but I shall have enjoyed myself. My choice is made. One must eat or be eaten. I shall eat. It is better to be the tooth than the grass. Such is my wisdom. After which, go where I push thee, the grave digger is there; the Pantheon for some of us: all falls into the great hole. End. Finis. Total liquidation. This is the vanishing point. Death is death, believe me. I laugh at the idea of there being anyone who has anything to tell me on that subject. Fables of nurses; bugaboo for children; Jehovah for men. No; our tomorrow is the night. Beyond the tomb there is nothing but equal nothingness. You have been Sardanapalus, you have been Vincent de Paul—it makes no difference. That is the truth. Then live your life, above all things. Make use of your I while you have it. In truth, Bishop, I tell you that I have a philosophy of my own, and I have my philosophers. I don't let

---

[*] between the cups

myself be taken in with that nonsense. Of course, there must be something for those who are down, for the barefooted beggars, knife grinders, and miserable wretches. Legends, chimeras, the soul, immortality, paradise, the stars, are provided for them to swallow. They gobble it down. They spread it on their dry bread. He who has nothing else has the good. God. That is the least he can have. I oppose no objection to that; but I reserve Monsieur Naigeon for myself. The good God is good for the populace."

The Bishop clapped his hands.

"That's talking!" he exclaimed. "What an excellent and really marvelous thing is this materialism! Not everyone who wants it can have it. Ah! When one does have it, one is no longer a dupe, one does not stupidly allow one's self to be exiled like Cato, nor stoned like Stephen, nor burned alive like Jeanne d'Arc. Those who have succeeded in procuring this admirable materialism have the joy of feeling themselves irresponsible, and of thinking that they can devour everything without uneasiness—places, sinecures, dignities, power, whether well or ill acquired, lucrative recantations, useful treacheries, savory capitulations of conscience—and that they shall enter the tomb with their digestion accomplished. How agreeable that is! I do not say that with reference to you, Senator. Nevertheless, it is impossible for me to refrain from congratulating you. You great lords have, so you say, a philosophy of your own, and for yourselves, which is exquisite, refined, accessible to the rich alone, good for all sauces, and which seasons the voluptuousness of life admirably. This philosophy has been extracted from the depths, and unearthed by special seekers. But you are good-natured princes, and you do not think it a bad thing that belief in the good God should constitute the philosophy of the people, very much as the goose stuffed with chestnuts is the truffled turkey of the poor."

CHAPTER IX—THE BROTHER AS DEPICTED BY THE SISTER

In order to furnish an idea of the private establishment of the Bishop of D——, and of the manner in which those two sainted women subordinated their actions, their thoughts, their feminine instincts even, which are easily alarmed, to the habits and purposes of the Bishop, without his even taking the trouble of speaking in order to explain them, we cannot do better than transcribe in this place a letter from Mademoiselle Baptistine to Madame the Vicomtess de Boischevron, the friend of her childhood. This letter is in our possession.

D——, Dec. 16, 18—.

My Good Madam:

Not a day passes without our speaking of you. It is our established custom; but there is another reason besides. Just imagine, while washing and dusting the ceilings and walls, Madam Magloire has made some discoveries; now our two chambers hung with antique paper whitewashed over, would not discredit a château in the style of yours. Madam Magloire has pulled off all the paper. There were things beneath. My drawing room, which contains no furniture, and which we use for spreading out the linen after washing, is fifteen feet in height, eighteen square, with a ceiling that was formerly painted and gilded, and with beams, as in yours. This was covered with a cloth while this was the hospital. And the woodwork was of the era of our grandmothers. But my room is the one you ought to see. Madam Magloire has discovered, under at least ten thicknesses of paper pasted on top, some paintings, which without being good are very tolerable. The subject is Telemachus being knighted by Minerva in some gardens, the name of which escapes me. In short, where the Roman ladies repaired on one single night. What shall I say to you? I have Romans, and Roman ladies (here occurs an illegible word), and the whole train. Madam Magloire has cleaned it all off; this summer she is going to have some small injuries repaired, and the whole revarnished, and my chamber will be a regular museum. She has also found in a corner of the attic two wooden pier tables of ancient fashion. They asked us two crowns of six francs each to regild them, but it is much better to give the money to the poor; and they are very ugly besides, and I should much prefer a round table of mahogany. I am always very happy. My brother is so good. He gives all he has to the poor and sick. We are very much cramped. The country is trying in the winter, and we really must do something for those who are in need. We are almost comfortably lighted and warmed. You see that these are great treats.

My brother has ways of his own. When he talks, he says that a bishop ought to be so. Just imagine! The door of our house is never fastened. Whoever chooses to enter finds himself at once in my brother's room. He fears nothing, even at night. That is his sort of bravery, he says. He does not wish me or Madame Magloire feel any fear for him. He exposes himself to all sorts of dangers, and he does not like to have us even seem to notice it. One must know how to understand him. He goes out in the rain, he walks in the water, he travels in winter. He fears neither suspicious roads nor dangerous encounters, nor night. Last year he went quite alone into a country of robbers. He would not take us. He was absent for a fortnight. On his return nothing had happened to him; he was thought to be dead, but was perfectly well, and said, "This is the way I have been robbed!" And then he opened a trunk full of jewels, all the jewels of the cathedral of Embrun, which the thieves had given him.

When he returned on that occasion, I could not refrain from scolding him a little, taking care, however, not to speak except when the carriage was making a noise, so that no one might hear me.

At first I used to say to myself, "There are no dangers which will stop him; he is terrible." Now I have ended by getting used to it. I make a sign to Madam Magloire that she is not to oppose him. He risks himself as he sees fit. I carry off Madam Magloire, I enter my chamber, I pray for him and fall asleep. I am at ease, because I know that if anything were to happen to him, it would be the end of me. I should go to the good God with my brother and my bishop. It has cost Madam Magloire more trouble than it did me to accustom herself to what she terms his imprudences. But now the habit has been acquired. We pray together, we tremble together, and we fall asleep. If the devil were to enter this house, he would be allowed to do so. After all, what is there for us to fear in this house? There is always someone with us who is stronger than we. The devil may pass through it, but the good God dwells here. This suffices me. My brother has no longer any need of saying a word to me. I understand him without his speaking, and we abandon ourselves to the care of Providence. That is the way one has to do with a man who possesses grandeur of soul.

I have interrogated my brother with regard to the information which you desire on the subject of the Faux family. You are aware that he knows everything, and that he has memories, because he is still a very good royalist. They really are a very ancient Norman family of the generalship of Caen. Five hundred years ago there was a Raoul de Faux, a Jean de Faux, and a Thomas de Faux, who were gentlemen, and one of whom was a seigneur de Rochefort. The last was Guy-Etienne-Alexandre, and was commander of a regiment, and something in the light horse of Bretagne. His daughter, Marie-Louise, married Adrien-Charles de Gramont, son of the Duke Louis de Gramont, peer of France, colonel of the French guards, and lieutenant-general of the army. It is written Faux, Fauq, and Faoucq.

Good Madame, recommend us to the prayers of your sainted relative, Monsieur the Cardinal. As for your dear Sylvanie, she has done well in not wasting the few moments that she passes with you in writing to me. She is well, works as you would wish, and loves me. That is all that I desire. The souvenir that she sent through you reached me safely, and it makes me very happy. My health is not so very bad, and yet I grow thinner every day. Farewell; my paper is at an end, and this forces me to leave you. A thousand good wishes.

BAPTISTINE.

P.S. Your grand nephew is charming. Do you know that he will soon be five years old? Yesterday he saw someone riding by on horseback who had on kneecaps, and he said, "What has he got on his knees?" He is a charming child! His little brother is dragging an old broom about the room, like a carriage, and saying, "Hu!"

As will be perceived from this letter, these two women understood how to mold themselves to the Bishop's ways with that special feminine genius that comprehends the man better than he comprehends himself. The Bishop of D——, in spite of the gentle and candid air that never deserted him, sometimes did things that were grand, bold, and magnificent, without seeming to have even a suspicion of the fact. They trembled, but they let him alone. Sometimes Madame Magloire essayed a remonstrance in advance, but never at the time, nor afterward. They never interfered with him by so much as a word or sign, in any action once entered upon. At certain moments, without his having occasion to mention it, when he was not even conscious of it himself in all probability, so perfect was his simplicity, they vaguely felt that he was acting as a bishop; then they were nothing more than two shadows in the house. They served him passively; and if obedience consisted in disappearing, they disappeared. They understood, with an admirable delicacy of instinct, that certain cares may be put under constraint. Thus, even when believing him to be in peril, they understood, I will not say his thought, but his nature, to such a degree that they no longer watched over him. They confided him to God.

Moreover, Baptistine said, as we have just read, that her brother's end would prove her own. Madame Magloire did not say this, but she knew it.

CHAPTER X—THE BISHOP IN THE PRESENCE OF AN UNKNOWN LIGHT

At an epoch a little later than the date of the letter cited in the preceding pages, he did a thing which, if the whole town was to be believed, was even more hazardous than his trip across the mountains infested with bandits.

In the country near D—— a man lived quite alone. This man, we will state at once, was a former member of the Convention. His name was G——.

Member of the Convention, G—— was mentioned with a sort of horror in the little world of D——. A member of the Convention—can you imagine such a thing? That existed from the time when people called each other thou, and when they said "citizen." This man was almost a monster. He had not voted for the death of the king, but almost. He was a quasi-regicide. He had been a terrible man. How did it happen that such a man had not been brought before a provost's court, on the return of the legitimate princes? They need not have cut off his head, if you please; clemency must be exercised, agreed; but a good banishment for life. An example, in short, etc. Besides, he was an atheist, like all the rest of those people. Gossip of the geese about the vulture.

Was G—— a vulture after all? Yes; if he were to be judged by the element of ferocity in this solitude of his. As he had not voted for the death of the king, he had not been included in the decrees of exile, and had been able to remain in France.

He dwelled at a distance of three-quarters of an hour from the city, far from any hamlet, far from any road, in some hidden turn of a very wild valley, no one knew exactly where. He had there, it was said, a sort of field, a hole, a lair. There were no neighbors, not even passersby. Since he had dwelled in that valley, the path that led there had disappeared under a growth of grass. The locality was spoken of as though it had been the dwelling of a hangman.

Nevertheless, the Bishop meditated on the subject, and from time to time he gazed at the horizon at a point where a clump of trees marked the valley of the former member of the Convention, and he said, "There is a soul yonder that is lonely."

And he added, deep in his own mind, "I owe him a visit."

But, let us avow it, this idea, which seemed natural at the first blush, appeared to him after a moment's reflection, as strange, impossible, and almost repulsive. For, at bottom, he shared the general impression, and the old member of the Convention inspired him, without his being clearly conscious of the fact himself, with that sentiment which borders on hate, and which is so well expressed by the word estrangement.

Still, should the scab of the sheep cause the shepherd to recoil? No. But what a sheep!

The good Bishop was perplexed. Sometimes he set out in that direction; then he returned.

Finally, the rumor one day spread through the town that a sort of young shepherd, who served the member of the Convention in his hovel, had come in quest of a doctor; that the old wretch was dying, that paralysis was gaining on him, and that he would not live overnight. "Thank God!" some added.

The Bishop took his staff, put on his cloak, on account of his too threadbare cassock, as we have mentioned, and because of the evening breeze that was sure to rise soon, and set out.

The sun was setting, and had almost touched the horizon when the Bishop arrived at the excommunicated spot. With a certain beating of the heart, he recognized the fact that he was near the lair. He strode over a ditch, leaped a hedge, made his way through a fence of dead boughs, entered a neglected paddock, took a few steps with a good deal of boldness, and suddenly, at the extremity of the waste land, and behind lofty brambles, he caught sight of the cavern.

It was a very low hut, poor, small, and clean, with a vine nailed against the outside.

Near the door, in an old wheelchair, the armchair of the peasants, there was a white-haired man, smiling at the sun.

Near the seated man stood a young boy, the shepherd lad. He was offering the old man a jar of milk.

While the Bishop was watching him, the old man spoke. "Thank you," he said, "I need nothing." And his smile quitted the sun to rest upon the child.

The Bishop stepped forward. At the sound, which he made in walking, the old man turned his head, and his face expressed the sum total of the surprise, which a man can still feel after a long life.

"This is the first time since I have been here," said he, "that anyone has entered here. Who are you, sir?"

The Bishop answered, "My name is Bienvenu Myriel."

"Bienvenu Myriel? I have heard that name. Are you the man whom the people call Monseigneur Welcome?"

"I am."

The old man resumed with a half-smile, "In that case, you are my bishop?"

"Something of that sort."

"Enter, sir."

The member of the Convention extended his hand to the Bishop, but the Bishop did not take it. The Bishop confined himself to the remark, "I am pleased to see that I have been misinformed. You certainly do not seem to me to be ill."

"Monsieur," replied the old man, "I am going to recover."

He paused, and then said, "I shall die three hours hence."

Then he continued, "I am something of a doctor; I know in what fashion the last hour draws on. Yesterday, only my feet were cold; today, the chill has ascended to my knees; now I feel it mounting to my waist; when it reaches the heart, I shall stop. The sun is beautiful, is it not? I had myself wheeled out here to take a last look at things. You can talk to me; it does not fatigue me. You have done well to come and look at a man who is on the point of death. It is well that there should be witnesses at that moment. One has one's caprices; I should have liked to last until the dawn, but I know that I shall hardly live three hours. It will be night then. What does it matter, after all? Dying is a simple affair. One has no need of the light for that. So be it. I shall die by starlight."

The old man turned to the shepherd lad, "Go to thy bed; thou wert awake all last night; thou art tired."

The child entered the hut.

The old man followed him with his eyes, and added, as though speaking to himself, "I shall die while he sleeps. The two slumbers may be good neighbors."

The Bishop was not touched as it seems that he should have been. He did not think he discerned God in this manner of dying; let us say the whole, for these petty contradictions of great hearts must be indicated like the rest: he, who on occasion was so fond of laughing at "His Grace," was rather shocked at not being addressed as Monseigneur, and he was almost tempted to retort "citizen." He was assailed by a fancy for peevish familiarity, common enough to doctors and priests, but that was not habitual with him. This man, after all, this member of the Convention, this representative of the people, had been one of the powerful ones of the earth; for the first time in his life, probably, the Bishop felt in a mood to be severe.

Meanwhile, the member of the Convention had been surveying him with a modest cordiality, in which one could have distinguished, possibly, that humility which is so fitting when one is on the verge of returning to dust.

The Bishop, on his side, although he generally restrained his curiosity, which, in his opinion, bordered on a fault, could not refrain from examining the member of the Convention with an attention which, as it did not have its course in sympathy, would have served his conscience as a matter of reproach, in connection with any other man. A member of the Convention produced on him somewhat the effect of being outside the pale of the law, even of the law of charity. G——, calm, his body almost upright, his voice vibrating, was one of those octogenarians who form the subject of astonishment to the physiologist. The Revolution had many of these men, proportioned to the epoch. In this old man one was conscious of a man put to the proof. Though so near to his end, he preserved all the gestures of health. In his clear glance, in his firm tone, in the robust movement of his shoulders, there was something calculated to disconcert death. Azrael, the Mohammedan angel of the sepulcher, would have turned back, and thought that he had mistaken the door. G—— seemed to be dying because he willed it so. There was freedom in his agony. His legs alone were motionless. It was there that the shadows held him fast. His feet were cold and dead, but his head survived with all the power of life, and seemed full of light. G——, at this solemn moment, resembled the king in that tale of the Orient who was flesh above and marble below.

There was a stone there. The Bishop sat down. The exordium was abrupt.

"I congratulate you," said he, in the tone which one uses for a reprimand. "You did not vote for the death of the king, after all."

The old member of the Convention did not appear to notice the bitter meaning underlying the words "after all." He replied. The smile had quite disappeared from his face.

"Do not congratulate me too much, sir. I did vote for the death of the tyrant."

It was the tone of austerity answering the tone of severity.

"What do you mean to say?" resumed the Bishop.

"I mean to say that man has a tyrant, ignorance. I voted for the death of that tyrant. That tyrant engendered royalty, which is authority falsely understood, while science is authority rightly understood. Man should be governed only by science."

"And conscience," added the Bishop.

"It is the same thing. Conscience is the quantity of innate science which we have within us."

Monseigneur Bienvenu listened in some astonishment to this language, which was very new to him.

The member of the Convention resumed, "So far as Louis XVI was concerned, I said 'no.' I did not think that I had the right to kill a man; but I felt it my duty to exterminate evil. I voted the end of the tyrant, that is to say, the end of prostitution for woman, the end of slavery for man, the end of night for the child. In voting for the Republic, I voted for that. I voted for fraternity, concord, the dawn. I have aided in the overthrow of prejudices and errors. The crumbling away of prejudices and errors causes light. We have caused the fall of the old world, and the old world, that vase of miseries, has become, through its upsetting upon the human race, an urn of joy."

"Mixed joy," said the Bishop.

"You may say troubled joy, and today, after that fatal return of the past, which is called 1814, joy that has disappeared! Alas! The work was incomplete, I admit: we demolished the ancient regime in deeds; we were not able to suppress it entirely in ideas. To destroy abuses is not sufficient; customs must be modified. The mill is there no longer; the wind is still there."

"You have demolished. It may be of use to demolish, but I distrust a demolition complicated with wrath."

"Right has its wrath, Bishop; and the wrath of right is an element of progress. In any case, and in spite of whatever may be said, the French Revolution is the most important step of the human race since the advent of Christ. Incomplete, it may be, but sublime. It set free all the unknown social quantities; it softened spirits, it calmed, appeased, enlightened; it caused the waves of civilization to flow over the earth. It was a good thing. The French Revolution is the consecration of humanity."

The Bishop could not refrain from murmuring, "Yes? '93!"

The member of the Convention straightened himself up in his chair with an almost lugubrious solemnity, and exclaimed, so far as a dying man is capable of exclamation, "Ah, there you go; '93! I was expecting that word. A cloud had been forming for the space of fifteen hundred years; at the end of fifteen hundred years it burst. You are putting the thunderbolt on its trial."

The Bishop felt, without, perhaps, confessing it that something within him had suffered extinction. Nevertheless, he put a good face on the matter. He replied, "The judge speaks in the name of justice; the priest speaks in the name of pity, which is nothing but a more lofty justice. A thunderbolt should commit no error." And he added, regarding the member of the Convention steadily the while, "Louis XVII?"

The conventionary stretched forth his hand and grasped the Bishop's arm.

"Louis XVII! Let us see. For whom do you mourn? Is it for the innocent child? Very good; in that case I mourn with you. Is it for the royal child? I demand time for reflection. To me, the brother of Cartouche, an innocent child who was hung up by the armpits in the Place de Greve, until death ensued, for the sole crime of having been the brother of Cartouche, is no less painful than the grandson of Louis XV, an innocent child, martyred in the tower of the Temple, for the sole crime of having been grandson of Louis XV."

"Monsieur," said the Bishop, "I like not this conjunction of names."

"Cartouche? Louis XV? To which of the two do you object?"

A momentary silence ensued. The Bishop almost regretted having come, and yet he felt vaguely and strangely shaken.

The conventionary resumed, "Ah, Monsieur Priest, you love not the crudities of the true. Christ loved them. He seized a rod and cleared out the Temple. His scourge, full of lightnings, was a harsh speaker of truths. When he cried, '*Sinite parvulos,* " he made no distinction between the little children. It would not have embarrassed him to bring together the Dauphin of Barabbas and the Dauphin of Herod. Innocence, Monsieur, is its own crown. Innocence has no need to be a highness. It is as august in rags as in fleurs de lys."

"That is true," said the Bishop in a low voice.

"I persist," continued the conventionary G———. "You have mentioned Louis XVII to me. Let us come to an understanding. Shall we weep for all the innocent, all martyrs, all children, the lowly as well as the exalted? I agree to that. But in that case, as I have told you, we must go back further than '93, and our tears must begin before Louis XVII. I will weep with you over the children of kings, provided that you will weep with me over the children of the people."

"I weep for all," said the Bishop.

"Equally!" exclaimed conventionary G———; "and if the balance must incline, let it be on the side of the people. They have been suffering longer."

Another silence ensued. The conventionary was the first to break it. He raised himself on one elbow, took a bit of his cheek between his thumb and his forefinger, as one does mechanically when one interrogates and judges, and appealed to the Bishop with a gaze full of all the forces of the death agony. It was almost an explosion.

"Yes, sir, the people have been suffering a long while. And hold! That is not all, either; why have you just questioned me and talked to me about Louis XVII? I know you not. Ever since I have been in these parts I have dwelled in this enclosure alone, never setting foot outside, and seeing no one but that child who helps me. Your name has reached me in a confused manner, it is true, and very badly pronounced, I must admit; but that signifies nothing: clever

---

* "Suffer the little children"

men have so many ways of imposing on that honest goodman, the people. By the way, I did not hear the sound of your carriage; you have left it yonder, behind the coppice at the fork of the roads, no doubt. I do not know you, I tell you. You have told me that you are the Bishop; but that affords me no information as to your moral personality. In short, I repeat my question. Who are you? You are a bishop; that is to say, a prince of the church, one of those gilded men with heraldic bearings and revenues, who have vast prebends, the bishopric of D—— fifteen thousand francs settled income, ten thousand in perquisites; total, twenty-five thousand francs, who have kitchens, who have liveries, who make good cheer, who eat moorhens on Friday, who strut about, a lackey before, a lackey behind, in a gala coach, and who have palaces, and who roll in their carriages in the name of Jesus Christ who went barefoot! You are a prelate—revenues, palace, horses, servants, good table, all the sensualities of life; you have this like the rest, and like the rest, you enjoy it; it is well; but this says either too much or too little; this does not enlighten me upon the intrinsic and essential value of the man who comes with the probable intention of bringing wisdom to me. To whom do I speak? Who are you?"

The Bishop hung his head and replied, "*Vermis sum*—I am a worm."

"A worm of the earth in a carriage?" growled the conventionary.

It was the conventionary's turn to be arrogant, and the Bishop's to be humble.

The Bishop resumed mildly, "So be it, sir. But explain to me how my carriage, which is a few paces off behind the trees yonder, how my good table and the moorhens that I eat on Friday, how my twenty-five thousand francs income, how my palace and my lackeys prove that clemency is not a duty, and that '93 was not inexorable."

The conventionary passed his hand across his brow, as though to sweep away a cloud.

"Before replying to you," he said, "I beseech you to pardon me. I have just committed a wrong, sir. You are at my house, you are my guest, I owe you courtesy. You discuss my ideas, and it becomes me to confine myself to combating your arguments. Your riches and your pleasures are advantages that I hold over you in the debate; but good taste dictates that I shall not make use of them. I promise you to make no use of them in the future."

"I thank you," said the Bishop.

G—— resumed, "Let us return to the explanation that you have asked of me. Where were we? What were you saying to me? That '93 was inexorable?"

"Inexorable; yes," said the Bishop. "What think you of Marat clapping his hands at the guillotine?"

"What think you of Bossuet chanting the Te Deum over the dragonnades?"

The retort was a harsh one, but it attained its mark with the directness of a point of steel. The Bishop quivered under it; no reply occurred to him; but he was offended by this mode of alluding to Bossuet. The best of minds will have their fetishes, and they sometimes feel vaguely wounded by the want of respect of logic.

The conventionary began to pant; the asthma of the agony which is mingled with the last breaths interrupted his voice; still, there was a perfect lucidity of soul in his eyes. He went on, "Let me say a few words more in this and that direction; I am willing. Apart from the Revolution, which, taken as a whole, is an immense human affirmation, '93 is, alas! A rejoinder. You think it inexorable, sir; but what of the whole monarchy, sir? Carrier is a bandit; but what name do you give to Montrevel? Fouquier-Tainville is a rascal; but what is your opinion as to Lamoignon-Baville? Maillard is terrible; but Saulx-Tavannes, if you please? Duchene senior is ferocious; but what epithet will you allow me for the elder Letellier? Jourdan-Coupe-Tete is a monster; but not so great a one as M. the Marquis de Louvois. Sir, sir, I am sorry for Marie Antoinette, archduchess and queen; but I am also sorry for that poor Huguenot woman, who, in 1685, under Louis the Great, sir, while with a nursing infant, was bound, naked to the waist, to a stake, and the child kept at a distance; her breast swelled with milk and her heart with anguish; the little one, hungry and pale, beheld that breast and cried and agonized; the executioner said to the woman, a mother and a nurse, 'Abjure!' giving her her choice between the death of her infant and the death of her conscience. What say you to that torture of Tantalus as applied to a mother? Bear this well in mind, sir: the French Revolution had its reasons for existence; its wrath will be absolved by the future; its result is the world made better. From its most terrible blows there comes forth a caress for the human race. I abridge, I stop, I have too much the advantage; moreover, I am dying."

And ceasing to gaze at the Bishop, the conventionary concluded his thoughts in these tranquil words, "Yes, the brutalities of progress are called revolutions. When they are over, this fact is recognized, that the human race has been treated harshly, but that it has progressed."

The conventionary doubted not that he had successively conquered all the inmost entrenchments of the Bishop. One remained, however, and from this entrenchment, the last resource of Monseigneur Bienvenu's resistance, came forth this reply, wherein appeared nearly all the harshness of the beginning, "Progress should believe in God. Good cannot have an impious servitor. He who is an atheist is but a bad leader for the human race."

The former representative of the people made no reply. He was seized with a fit of trembling. He looked toward heaven, and in his glance a tear gathered slowly. When the eyelid was full, the tear trickled down his livid cheek, and he said, almost in a stammer, quite low, and to himself, while his eyes were plunged in the depths, "O thou! O ideal! Thou alone exists!"

The Bishop experienced an indescribable shock.

After a pause, the old man raised a finger heavenward and said, "The infinite is. He is there. If the infinite had no person, person would be without limit; it would not be infinite; in other words, it would not exist. There is, then, an I. That I of the infinite is God."

The dying man had pronounced these last words in a loud voice, and with the shiver of ecstasy, as though he beheld someone. When he had spoken, his eyes closed. The effort had exhausted him. It was evident that he had just lived through in a moment the few hours that had been left to him. That which he had said brought him nearer to him who is in death. The supreme moment was approaching.

The Bishop understood this; time pressed; it was as a priest that he had come: from extreme coldness he had passed by degrees to extreme emotion; he gazed at those closed eyes, he took that wrinkled, aged, and ice-cold hand in his, and bent over the dying man.

"This hour is the hour of God. Do you not think that it would be regrettable if we had met in vain?"

The conventionary opened his eyes again. A gravity mingled with gloom was imprinted on his countenance.

"Bishop," said he, with a slowness that probably arose more from his dignity of soul than from the failing of his strength, "I have passed my life in meditation, study, and contemplation. I was sixty years of age when my country called me and commanded me to concern myself with its affairs. I obeyed. Abuses existed, I combated them; tyrannies existed, I destroyed them; rights and principles existed, I proclaimed and confessed them. Our territory was invaded, I defended it; France was menaced, I offered my breast. I was not rich; I am poor. I have been one of the masters of the state; the vaults of the treasury were encumbered with specie to such a degree that we were forced to shore up the walls, which were on the point of bursting beneath the weight of gold and silver; I dined in Dead Tree Street, at twenty-two sous. I have succored the oppressed, I have comforted the suffering. I tore the cloth from the altar, it is true; but it was to bind up the wounds of my country. I have always upheld the march forward of the human race, forward toward the light, and I have sometimes resisted progress without pity. I have, when the occasion offered, protected my own adversaries, men of your profession. And there is at Peteghem, in Flanders, at the very spot where the Merovingian kings had their summer palace, a convent of Urbanists, the Abbéy of Sainte Claire en Beaulieu, which I saved in 1793. I have done my duty according to my powers, and all the good that I was able. After which, I was hunted down, pursued, persecuted, blackened, jeered at, scorned, cursed, proscribed. For many years past, I with my white hair have been conscious that many people think they have the right to despise me; to the poor ignorant masses I present the visage of one damned. And I accept this isolation of hatred, without hating anyone myself. Now I am eighty-six years old; I am on the point of death. What is it that you have come to ask of me?"

"Your blessing," said the Bishop.

And he knelt down.

When the Bishop raised his head again, the face of the conventionary had become august. He had just expired.

The Bishop returned home, deeply absorbed in thoughts that cannot be known to us. He passed the whole night in prayer. On the following morning some bold and curious persons attempted to speak to him about member of the Convention G——; he contented himself with pointing heavenward.

From that moment he redoubled his tenderness and brotherly feeling toward all children and sufferers.

Any allusion to "that old wretch of a G——" caused him to fall into a singular preoccupation. No one could say that the passage of that soul before his, and the reflection of that grand conscience upon his, did not count for something in his approach to perfection.

This "pastoral visit" naturally furnished an occasion for a murmur of comment in all the little local coteries.

"Was the bedside of such a dying man as that the proper place for a bishop? There was evidently no conversion to be expected. All those revolutionists are backsliders. Then why go there? What was there to be seen there? He must have been very curious indeed to see a soul carried off by the devil."

One day a dowager of the impertinent variety who thinks herself spiritual, addressed this sally* to him, "Monseigneur, people are inquiring when Your Greatness will receive the red cap!"

"Oh! Oh! That's a coarse color," replied the Bishop. "It is lucky that those who despise it in a cap revere it in a hat."

---

* witty saying

CHAPTER XI—A RESTRICTION

We should incur a great risk of deceiving ourselves, were we to conclude from this that Monseigneur Welcome was "a philosophical bishop," or a "patriotic Curé." His meeting, which may almost be designated as his union, with conventionary G——, left behind it in his mind a sort of astonishment, which rendered him still more gentle. That is all.

Although Monseigneur Bienvenu was far from being a politician, this is, perhaps, the place to indicate very briefly what his attitude was in the events of that epoch, supposing that Monseigneur Bienvenu ever dreamed of having an attitude.

Let us, then, go back a few years.

Sometime after the elevation of M. Myriel to the episcopate, the Emperor had made him a baron of the Empire, in company with many other bishops. The arrest of the Pope took place, as everyone knows, on the night of the 5th to the 6th of July, 1809; on this occasion, M. Myriel was summoned by Napoleon to the synod of the bishops of France and Italy convened at Paris. This synod was held at Notre-Dame, and assembled for the first time on the 15th of June, 1811, under the presidency of Cardinal Fesch. M. Myriel was one of the ninety-five bishops who attended it. But he was present only at one sitting and at three or four private conferences. Bishop of a mountain diocese, living so very close to nature, in rusticity and deprivation, it appeared that he imported among these eminent personages, ideas that altered the temperature of the assembly. He very soon returned to D——. He was interrogated as to this speedy return, and he replied, "I embarrassed them. The outside air penetrated to them through me. I produced on them the effect of an open door."

On another occasion he said, "What would you have? Those gentlemen are princes. I am only a poor peasant bishop."

The fact is that he displeased them. Among other strange things, it is said that he chanced to remark one evening, when he found himself at the house of one of his most notable colleagues, "What beautiful clocks! What beautiful carpets! What beautiful liveries! They must be a great trouble. I would not have all those superfluities, crying incessantly in my ears: 'There are people who are hungry! There are people who are cold! There are poor people! There are poor people!'"

Let us remark, by the way, that the hatred of luxury is not an intelligent hatred. This hatred would involve the hatred of the arts. Nevertheless, in churchmen, luxury is wrong, except in connection with representations and ceremonies. It seems to reveal habits, which have very little that is charitable about them. An opulent priest is a contradiction. The priest must keep close to the poor. Now, can one come in contact incessantly night and day with all this distress, all these misfortunes, and this poverty, without having about one's own person a little of that misery, like the dust of labor? Is it possible to imagine a man near a brazier who is not warm? Can one imagine a workman who is working near a furnace, and who has neither a singed hair, nor blackened nails, nor a drop of sweat, nor a speck of ashes on his face? The first proof of charity in the priest, in the bishop especially, is poverty.

This is, no doubt, what the Bishop of D—— thought.

It must not be supposed, however, that he shared what we call the "ideas of the century" on certain delicate points. He took very little part in the theological quarrels of the moment, and maintained silence on questions in which Church and State were implicated; but if he had been strongly pressed, it seems that he would have been found to be an ultramontane rather than a gallican. Since we are making a portrait, and since we do not wish to conceal anything, we are forced to add that he was glacial toward Napoleon in his decline. Beginning with 1813, he gave in his adherence to or applauded all hostile manifestations. He refused to see him, as he passed through on his return from the island of Elba, and he abstained from ordering public prayers for the Emperor in his diocese during the Hundred Days.

Besides his sister, Mademoiselle Baptistine, he had two brothers, one a general, the other a prefect. He wrote to both with tolerable frequency. He was harsh for a time toward the former, because, holding a command in Provence at the epoch of the disembarkation at Cannes, the general had put himself at the head of twelve hundred men and had pursued the Emperor as though the latter had been a person whom one is desirous of allowing to escape. His correspondence with the other brother, the ex-prefect, a fine, worthy man who lived in retirement at Paris, Rue Cassette, remained more affectionate.

Thus Monseigneur Bienvenu also had his hour of party spirit, his hour of bitterness, his cloud. The shadow of the passions of the moment traversed this grand and gentle spirit occupied with eternal things. Certainly, such a man would have done well not to entertain any political opinions. Let there be no mistake as to our meaning: we are not confounding what is called "political opinions" with the grand aspiration for progress, with the sublime faith, patriotic, democratic, humane, which in our day should be the very foundation of every generous intellect. Without going deeply into questions that are only indirectly connected with the subject of this book, we will simply say this: It would have been well if Monseigneur Bienvenu had not been a Royalist, and if his glance had never been, for a single instant, turned away from that serene contemplation in which is distinctly discernible, above the fictions and the hatreds of this world, above the stormy vicissitudes of human things, the beaming of those three pure radiances: truth, justice, and charity.

While admitting that it was not for a political office that God created Monseigneur Welcome, we should have understood and admired his protest in the name of right and liberty, his proud opposition, his just but perilous resistance to the all-powerful Napoleon. But that which pleases us in people who are rising pleases us less in the case of people who are falling. We only love the fray so long as there is danger, and in any case, the combatants of the first hour have alone the right to be the exterminators of the last. He who has not been a stubborn accuser in prosperity should hold his peace in the face of ruin. The denunciator of success is the only legitimate executioner of the fall. As for us, when Providence intervenes and strikes, we let it work. 1812 commenced to disarm us. In 1813 the cowardly breach of silence of that taciturn legislative body, emboldened by catastrophe, possessed only traits that aroused indignation. And it was a crime to applaud, in 1814, in the presence of those marshals who betrayed; in the presence of that senate, which passed from one dunghill to another, insulting after having deified; in the presence of that idolatry, which was loosing its footing and spitting on its idol, it was a duty to turn aside the head. In 1815, when the supreme disasters filled the air, when France was seized with a shiver at their sinister approach, when Waterloo could be dimly discerned opening before Napoleon, the mournful acclamation of the army and the people to the condemned of destiny had nothing laughable in it, and, after making all allowance for the despot, a heart like that of the Bishop of D——, ought not perhaps to have failed to recognize the august and touching features presented by the embrace of a great nation and a great man on the brink of the abyss.

With this exception, he was in all things just, true, equitable, intelligent, humble and dignified, beneficent and kindly, which is only another sort of benevolence. He was a priest, a sage, and a man. It must be admitted, that even in the political views with which we have just reproached him, and which we are disposed to judge almost with severity, he was tolerant and easy, more so, perhaps, than we who are speaking here. The porter of the town hall had been placed there by the Emperor. He was an old noncommissioned officer of the old guard, a member of the Legion of Honor at Austerlitz, as much of a

Bonapartist as the eagle. This poor fellow occasionally let slip inconsiderate remarks, which the law then stigmatized as seditious speeches. After the imperial profile disappeared from the Legion of Honor, he never dressed himself in his regimentals, as he said, so that he should not be obliged to wear his cross. He had himself devoutly removed the imperial effigy from the cross that Napoleon had given him; this made a hole, and he would not put anything in its place. "I will die," he said, "rather than wear the three frogs upon my heart!" He liked to scoff aloud at Louis XVIII. "The gouty old creature in English gaiters!" he said; "let him take himself off to Prussia with that queue of his." He was happy to combine in the same imprecation the two things that he most detested, Prussia and England. He did it so often that he lost his place. There he was, turned out of the house, with his wife and children, and without bread. The Bishop sent for him, reproved him gently, and appointed him beadle in the cathedral.

In the course of nine years Monseigneur Bienvenu had, by dint of holy deeds and gentle manners, filled the town of D—— with a sort of tender and filial reverence. Even his conduct toward Napoleon had been accepted and tacitly pardoned, as it were, by the people, the good and weakly flock who adored their emperor, but loved their bishop.

CHAPTER XII—THE SOLITUDE OF MONSEIGNEUR WELCOME

A bishop is almost always surrounded by a full squadron of little abbés, just as a general is by a covey of young officers. This is what that charming Saint Francois de Sales calls somewhere "*les pretres blancs-becs*," callow priests. Every career has its aspirants, who form a train for those who have attained eminence in it. There is no power that has not its dependents. There is no fortune that has not its court. The seekers of the future eddy around the splendid present. Every metropolis has its staff of officials. Every bishop who possesses the least influence has about him his patrol of cherubim from the seminary, which goes the round, and maintains good order in the episcopal palace, and mounts guard over monseigneur's smile. To please a bishop is equivalent to getting one's foot in the stirrup for a subdiaconate. It is necessary to walk one's path discreetly; the apostleship does not disdain the canonship.

Just as there are bigwigs elsewhere, there are big miters in the Church. These are the bishops who stand well at Court, who are rich, well endowed, skillful, accepted by the world, who know how to pray, no doubt, but who know also how to beg, who feel little scruple at making a whole diocese dance attendance in their person, who are connecting links between the sacristy and diplomacy, who are abbés rather than priests, prelates rather than bishops. Happy those who approach them! Being persons of influence, they create a shower about them, upon the assiduous and the favored, and upon all the young men who understand the art of pleasing, of large parishes, prebends, archidiaconates, chaplaincies, and cathedral posts, while awaiting episcopal honors. As they advance themselves, they cause their satellites to progress also; it is a whole solar system on the march. Their radiance casts a gleam of purple over their suite. Their prosperity is crumbled up behind the scenes, into nice little promotions. The larger the diocese of the patron, the fatter the curacy for the favorite. And then, there is Rome. A bishop who understands how to become an archbishop, an archbishop who knows how to become a cardinal, carries you with him as conclavist; you enter a court of papal jurisdiction, you receive the pallium, and behold! You are an auditor, then a papal chamberlain, then monsignor, and from a Grace to an Eminence is only a step, and between the Eminence and the Holiness there is but the smoke of a ballot. Every skullcap may dream of the tiara. The priest is nowadays the only man who can become a king in a regular manner; and what a king! The supreme king. Then what a nursery of aspirations is a seminary! How many blushing choristers, how many youthful abbés bear on their heads Perrette's pot of milk! Who knows how easy it is for ambition to call itself vocation? In good faith, perchance, and deceiving itself, devotee that it is.

Monseigneur Bienvenu, poor, humble, retiring, was not accounted among the big miters. This was plain from the complete absence of young priests about him. We have seen that he "did not take" in Paris. Not a single future dreamed of engrafting itself on this solitary old man. Not a single sprouting ambition committed the folly of putting forth its foliage in his shadow. His canons and grand-vicars were good old men, rather vulgar like himself, walled up like him in this diocese, without exit to a cardinalship, and who resembled their bishop, with this difference, that they were finished and he was completed. The impossibility of growing great under Monseigneur Bienvenu was so well understood, that no sooner had the young men whom he ordained left the seminary than they got themselves recommended to the archbishops of Aix or of Auch, and went off in a great hurry. For, in short, we repeat it, men wish to be pushed. A saint who dwells in a paroxysm of abnegation is a dangerous neighbor; he might communicate to you, by contagion, an incurable poverty, an anchylosis of the joints, which are useful in advancement, and in short, more renunciation than you desire; and this infectious virtue is avoided. Hence the isolation of Monseigneur Bienvenu. We live in the midst of a gloomy society. Success; this is the lesson that falls drop by drop from the slope of corruption.

Be it said in passing, that success is a very hideous thing. Its false resemblance to merit deceives men. For the masses, success has almost the same profile as supremacy. Success, that Menaechmus of talent, has one dupe—history. Juvenal and Tacitus alone grumble at it. In our day, a philosophy that is almost official has entered into its service, wears the livery of success, and performs the service of its antechamber. Succeed: theory. Prosperity argues capacity. Win in the lottery, and behold! You are a clever man. He who triumphs is venerated. Be born with a silver spoon in your mouth! Everything lies in that. Be lucky, and you will have all the rest; be happy, and people will think you great. Outside of five or six immense exceptions, which compose the splendor of a century, contemporary admiration is nothing but short-sightedness. Gilding is gold. It does no harm to be the first arrival by pure chance, so long as you do arrive. The common herd is an old Narcissus who adores himself, and who applauds the vulgar herd. That enormous ability by virtue of which one is Moses, Aeschylus, Dante, Michelangelo, or Napoleon, the multitude awards on the spot, and by acclamation, to whomsoever attains his object, in whatsoever it may consist. Let a notary transfigure himself into a deputy; let a false Corneille compose Tiridate; let a eunuch come to possess a harem; let a military Prudhomme accidentally win the decisive battle of an epoch; let an apothecary invent cardboard shoe soles for the army of the Sambre-and-Meuse, and construct for himself, out of this cardboard, sold as leather, four hundred thousand francs of income; let a pork packer espouse usury, and cause it to bring forth seven or eight millions, of which he is the father and of which it is the mother; let a preacher become a bishop by force of his nasal drawl; let the steward of a fine family be so rich on retiring from service that he is made minister of finances, and men call that Genius, just as they call the face of Mousqueton Beauty, and the mien of Claude Majesty. With the constellations of space they confound the stars of the abyss that are made in the soft mire of the puddle by the feet of ducks.

CHAPTER XIII—WHAT HE BELIEVED

We are not obliged to sound the Bishop of D—— on the score of orthodoxy. In the presence of such a soul we feel ourselves in no mood but respect. The conscience of the just man should be accepted on his word. Moreover, certain natures being given, we admit the possible development of all beauties of human virtue in a belief that differs from our own.

What did he think of this dogma, or of that mystery? These secrets of the inner tribunal of the conscience are known only to the tomb, where souls enter naked. The point on which we are certain is, that the difficulties of faith never resolved themselves into hypocrisy in his case. No decay is possible to the diamond. He believed to the extent of his powers. *"Credo in Patrem,"** he often exclaimed. Moreover, he drew from good works that amount of satisfaction which suffices to the conscience, and which whispers to a man, "Thou art with God!"

The point at which we consider it our duty to note is, that outside of and beyond his faith, as it were, the Bishop possessed an excess of love. In was in that quarter, *quia multum amavit*—because he loved much—that he was regarded as vulnerable by "serious men," "grave persons," and "reasonable people"; favorite locutions of our sad world where egotism takes its word of command from pedantry. What was this excess of love? It was a serene benevolence that overflowed men, as we have already pointed out, and which, on occasion, extended even to things. He lived without disdain. He was indulgent toward God's creation. Every man, even the best, has within him a thoughtless harshness that he reserves for animals. The Bishop of D—— had none of that harshness, which is peculiar to many priests, nevertheless. He did not go as far as the Brahmin, but he seemed to have weighed this saying of Ecclesiastes: "Who knoweth where the soul of the animal goeth?" Hideousness of aspect, deformity of instinct, troubled him not, and did not arouse his indignation. He was touched, almost softened by them. It seemed as though he went thoughtfully away to seek beyond the bounds of life which is apparent, the cause, the explanation, or the excuse for them. He seemed at times to be asking God to commute these penalties. He examined without wrath, and with the eye of a linguist who is deciphering a palimpsest, the portion of chaos that still exists in nature. This reverie sometimes caused him to utter odd sayings. One morning he was in his garden, and thought himself alone, but his sister was walking behind him, unseen by him: suddenly he paused and gazed

---

* "I believe in one God, the Father Almighty"

at something on the ground; it was a large, black, hairy, frightful spider. His sister heard him say, "Poor beast! It is not its fault!"

Why not mention these almost divinely childish sayings of kindness? Puerile they may be; but these sublime puerilities were peculiar to Saint Francis d'Assisi and of Marcus Aurelius. One day he sprained his ankle in his effort to avoid stepping on an ant. Thus lived this just man. Sometimes he fell asleep in his garden, and then there was nothing more venerable possible.

Monseigneur Bienvenu had formerly been, if the stories anent his youth, and even in regard to his manhood, were to be believed, a passionate, and, possibly, a violent man. His universal suavity was less an instinct of nature than the result of a grand conviction which had filtered into his heart through the medium of life, and had trickled there slowly, thought by thought; for, in a character, as in a rock, there may exist apertures made by drops of water. These hollows are ineffaceable; these formations are indestructible.

In 1815, as we think we have already said, he reached his seventy-fifth birthday, but he did not appear to be more than sixty. He was not tall; he was rather plump; and, in order to combat this tendency, he was fond of taking long strolls on foot; his step was firm, and his form was but slightly bent, a detail from which we do not pretend to draw any conclusion. Gregory XVI, at the age of eighty, held himself erect and smiling, which did not prevent him from being a bad bishop. Monseigneur Welcome had what the people term a "fine head," but so amiable was he that they forgot that it was fine.

When he conversed with that infantile gaiety which was one of his charms, and of which we have already spoken, people felt at their ease with him, and joy seemed to radiate from his whole person. His fresh and ruddy complexion, his very white teeth, all of which he had preserved, and which were displayed by his smile, gave him that open and easy air that cause the remark to be made of a man, "He's a good fellow"; and of an old man, "He is a fine man." That, it will be recalled, was the effect which he produced upon Napoleon. On the first encounter, and to one who saw him for the first time, he was nothing, in fact, but a fine man. But if one remained near him for a few hours, and beheld him in the least degree pensive, the fine man became gradually transfigured, and took on some imposing quality, I know not what; his broad and serious brow, rendered august by his white locks, became august also by virtue of meditation; majesty radiated from his goodness, though his goodness ceased not to be radiant; one experienced something of the emotion which one would feel on beholding a smiling angel slowly unfold his wings, without ceasing to smile. Respect, an unutterable respect, penetrated you by degrees and mounted to your heart, and one felt that one had before him one of those strong, thoroughly tried, and indulgent souls where thought is so grand that it can no longer be anything but gentle.

As we have seen, prayer, the celebration of the offices of religion, alms giving, the consolation of the afflicted, the cultivation of a bit of land, fraternity, frugality, hospitality, renunciation, confidence, study, work, filled every day of his life. Filled is exactly the word; certainly the Bishop's day was quite full to the brim, of good words and good deeds. Nevertheless, it was not complete if cold or rainy weather prevented his passing an hour or two in his garden before going to bed, and after the two women had retired. It seemed to be a sort of rite with him, to prepare himself for slumber by meditation in the presence of the grand spectacles of the nocturnal heavens. Sometimes, if the two old women were not asleep, they heard him pacing slowly along the walks at a very advanced hour of the night. He was there alone, communing with himself, peaceful, adoring, comparing the serenity of his heart with the serenity of the ether, moved amid the darkness by the visible splendor of the constellations and the invisible splendor of God, opening his heart to the thoughts that fall from the Unknown. At such moments, while he offered his heart at the hour when nocturnal flowers offer their perfume, illuminated like a lamp amid the starry night, as he poured himself out in ecstasy in the midst of the universal radiance of creation, he could not have told himself, probably, what was passing in his spirit; he felt something take its flight from him, and something descend into him. Mysterious exchange of the abysses of the soul with the abysses of the universe!

He thought of the grandeur and presence of God; of the future eternity, that strange mystery; of the eternity past, a mystery still more strange; of all the infinities, which pierced their way into all his senses, beneath his eyes; and, without seeking to comprehend the incomprehensible, he gazed upon it. He did not study God; he was dazzled by him. He considered those magnificent conjunctions of atoms, which communicate aspects to matter, reveal forces by verifying them, create individualities in unity, proportions in extent, the innumerable in the infinite, and, through light, produce beauty. These conjunctions are formed and dissolved incessantly; hence life and death.

He seated himself on a wooden bench, with his back against a decrepit vine; he gazed at the stars, past the puny and stunted silhouettes of his fruit trees. This quarter of an acre, so poorly planted, so encumbered with mean buildings and sheds, was dear to him, and satisfied his wants.

What more was needed by this old man, who divided the leisure of his life, where there was so little leisure, between gardening in the daytime and contemplation at night? Was not this narrow enclosure, with the heavens for a ceiling, sufficient to enable him to adore God in his most divine works, in turn? Does not this comprehend all, in fact? And what is there left to desire beyond it? A little garden in which to walk, and immensity in which to dream. At one's feet that which can be cultivated and plucked; overhead that which one can study and meditate upon: some flowers on earth, and all the stars in the sky.

CHAPTER XIV—WHAT HE THOUGHT

One last word.

Since this sort of details might, particularly at the present moment, and to use an expression now in fashion, give to the Bishop of D—— a certain "pantheistical" physiognomy, and induce the belief, either to his credit or discredit, that he entertained one of those personal philosophies that are peculiar to our century, which sometimes spring up in solitary spirits, and there take on a form and grow until they usurp the place of religion, we insist upon it, that not one of those persons who knew Monseigneur Welcome would have thought himself authorized to think anything of the sort. That which enlightened this man was his heart. His wisdom was made of the light which comes from there.

No systems; many works. Abstruse speculations contain vertigo; no, there is nothing to indicate that he risked his mind in apocalypses. The apostle may be daring, but the bishop must be timid. He would probably have felt a scruple at sounding too far in advance certain problems which are, in a manner, reserved for terrible great minds. There is a sacred horror beneath the porches of the enigma; those gloomy openings stand yawning there, but something tells you—you, a passerby in life—that you must not enter. Woe to him who penetrates there!

Geniuses in the impenetrable depths of abstraction and pure speculation, situated, so to speak, above all dogmas, propose their ideas to God. Their prayer audaciously offers discussion. Their adoration interrogates. This is direct religion, which is full of anxiety and responsibility for him who attempts its steep cliffs.

Human meditation has no limits. At his own risk and peril, it analyzes and digs deep into its own bedazzlement. One might almost say, that by a sort of splendid reaction, it with it dazzles nature; the mysterious world that surrounds us renders back what it has received; it is probable that the contemplators are contemplated. However that may be, there are on earth men who—are they men?—perceive distinctly at the verge of the horizons of reverie the heights of the absolute, and who have the terrible vision of the infinite mountain. Monseigneur Welcome was one of these men; Monseigneur Welcome was not a genius. He would have feared those sublimities from which some very great men even, like Swedenborg and Pascal, have slipped into insanity. Certainly, these powerful reveries have their moral utility, and by these arduous paths one approaches to ideal perfection. As for him, he took the path that shortens—the Gospel's.

He did not attempt to impart to his chasuble the folds of Elijah's mantle; he projected no ray of future upon the dark groundswell of events; he did not see to condense in flame the light of things; he had nothing of the prophet and nothing of the magician about him. This humble soul loved, and that was all.

That he carried prayer to the pitch of a superhuman aspiration is probable: but one can no more pray too much than one can love too much; and if it is a heresy to pray beyond the texts, Saint Theresa and Saint Jerome would be heretics.

He inclined toward all that groans and all that expiates. The universe appeared to him like an immense malady; everywhere he felt fever, everywhere he heard the sound of suffering, and, without seeking to solve the enigma, he strove to dress the wound. The terrible spectacle of created things developed tenderness in him; he was occupied only in finding for himself, and in inspiring others with the best way to compassionate and relieve. That which exists was for this good and rare priest a permanent subject of sadness, which sought consolation.

There are men who toil at extracting gold; he toiled at the extraction of pity. Universal misery was his mine. The sadness that reigned everywhere was but an excuse for unfailing kindness. Love each other; he declared this to be complete, desired nothing further, and that was the whole of his doctrine. One day, that man who believed himself to be a "philosopher," the senator who has already been alluded to, said to the Bishop, "Just survey the spectacle of the world: all war against all; the strongest has the most wit. Your 'love each other' is nonsense."

"Well," replied Monseigneur Welcome, without contesting the point, "if it is nonsense, the soul should shut itself up in it, as the pearl in the oyster." Thus he shut himself up, he lived there, he was absolutely satisfied with it, leaving on one side the prodigious questions that attract and terrify, the fathomless perspectives of abstraction, the precipices of metaphysics—all those profundities that converge, for the apostle in God, for the atheist in nothingness; destiny, good and evil, the way of being against being, the conscience of man, the thoughtful somnambulism of the animal, the transformation in death, the recapitulation of existences that the tomb contains, the incomprehensible grafting of successive loves on the persistent I, the essence, the substance, the Nile, and the Ens, the soul, nature, liberty, necessity; perpendicular problems, sinister obscurities, where lean the gigantic archangels of the human mind; formidable abysses, which Lucretius,

Manou, Saint Paul, Dante, contemplate with eyes flashing lightning, which seems by its steady gaze on the infinite to cause stars to blaze forth there.

Monseigneur Bienvenu was simply a man who took note of the exterior of mysterious questions without scrutinizing them, and without troubling his own mind with them, and who cherished in his own soul a grave respect for darkness.

BOOK SECOND: THE FALL

CHAPTER I—THE EVENING OF A DAY OF WALKING

Early in the month of October, 1815, about an hour before sunset, a man who was traveling on foot entered the little town of D——. The few inhabitants who were at their windows or on their thresholds at the moment stared at this traveler with a sort of uneasiness. It was difficult to encounter a wayfarer of more wretched appearance. He was a man of medium stature, thickset and robust, in the prime of life. He might have been forty-six or forty-eight years old. A cap with a drooping leather visor partly concealed his face, burned and tanned by sun and wind, and dripping with perspiration. His shirt of coarse yellow linen, fastened at the neck by a small silver anchor, permitted a view of his hairy breast: he had a cravat twisted into a string; trousers of blue drilling, worn and threadbare, white on one knee and torn on the other; an old gray, tattered blouse, patched on one of the elbows with a bit of green cloth sewed on with twine; a tightly packed soldier knapsack, well buckled and perfectly new, on his back; an enormous, knotty stick in his hand; iron-shod shoes on his stockingless feet; a shaved head and a long beard.

The sweat, the heat, the journey on foot, the dust, added I know not what sordid quality to this dilapidated whole. His hair was closely cut, yet bristling, for it had begun to grow a little, and did not seem to have been cut for some time.

No one knew him. He was evidently only a chance passerby. From where came he? From the south; from the seashore, perhaps, for he made his entrance into D—— by the same street that, seven months previously, had witnessed the passage of the Emperor Napoleon on his way from Cannes to Paris. This man must have been walking all day. He seemed very much fatigued. Some women of the ancient market town, which is situated below the city, had seen him pause beneath the trees of the boulevard Gassendi, and drink at the fountain, which stands at the end of the promenade. He must have been very thirsty: for the children who followed him saw him stop again for a drink, two hundred paces further on, at the fountain in the marketplace.

On arriving at the corner of the Rue Poichevert, he turned to the left, and directed his steps toward the town hall. He entered, then came out a quarter of an hour later. A gendarme was seated near the door, on the stone bench that General Drouot had mounted on the 4th of March to read to the frightened throng of the inhabitants of D—— the proclamation of the Gulf Juan. The man pulled off his cap and humbly saluted the gendarme.

The gendarme, without replying to his salute, stared attentively at him, followed him for a while with his eyes, and then entered the town hall.

There then existed at D—— a fine inn at the sign of the Cross of Colbas. This inn had for a landlord a certain Jacquin Labarre, a man of consideration in the town on account of his relationship to another Labarre, who kept the inn of the Three Dauphins in Grenoble, and had served in the Guides. At the time of the Emperor's landing, many rumors had circulated throughout the country with regard to this inn of the Three Dauphins. It was said that General Bertrand, disguised as a carter, had made frequent trips there in the month of January, and that he had distributed crosses of honor to the soldiers and handfuls of gold to the citizens. The truth is, that when the Emperor entered Grenoble he had refused to install himself at the hotel of the prefecture; he had thanked the mayor, saying, "I am going to the house of a brave man of my acquaintance"; and he had betaken himself to the Three Dauphins. This glory of the Labarre of the Three Dauphins was reflected upon the Labarre of the Cross of Colbas, at a distance of five and twenty leagues. It was said of him in the town, "That is the cousin of the man of Grenoble."

The man bent his steps toward this inn, which was the best in the countryside. He entered the kitchen, which opened on a level with the street. All the stoves were lighted; a huge fire blazed gaily in the fireplace. The host, who was also the chief cook, was going from one stew pan to another, very busily superintending an excellent dinner designed for the wagoners, whose loud talking, conversation, and laughter were audible from an adjoining apartment. Anyone who has traveled knows that there is no one who indulges in better cheer than wagoners. A fat marmot, flanked by white partridges and heather-cocks, was turning on a long spit before the fire; on the stove, two huge carps from Lake Lauzet and a trout from Lake Alloz were cooking.

The host, hearing the door open and seeing a newcomer enter, said, without raising his eyes from his stoves, "What do you wish, sir?"

"Food and lodging," said the man.

"Nothing easier," replied the host. At that moment he turned his head, took in the traveler's appearance with a single glance, and added, "By paying for it."

The man drew a large leather purse from the pocket of his blouse, and answered, "I have money."

"In that case, we are at your service," said the host.

The man put his purse back in his pocket, removed his knapsack from his back, put it on the ground near the door, retained his stick in his hand, and seated himself on a low stool close to the fire. D—— is in the mountains. The evenings are cold there in October.

But as the host went back and forth, he scrutinized the traveler.

"Will dinner be ready soon?" said the man.

"Immediately," replied the landlord.

While the newcomer was warming himself before the fire, with his back turned, the worthy host, Jacquin Labarre, drew a pencil from his pocket, then tore off the corner of an old newspaper that was lying on a small table near the window. On the white margin he wrote a line or two, folded it without sealing, and then entrusted this scrap of paper to a child who seemed to serve him in the capacity both of scullion and lackey. The landlord whispered a word in the scullion's ear, and the child set off on a run in the direction of the town hall.

The traveler saw nothing of all this.

Once more he inquired, "Will dinner be ready soon?"

"Immediately," responded the host.

The child returned. He brought back the paper. The host unfolded it eagerly, like a person who is expecting a reply. He seemed to read it attentively, then tossed his head, and remained thoughtful for a moment. Then he took a step in the direction of the traveler, who appeared to be immersed in reflections that were not very serene.

"I cannot receive you, sir," said he.

The man half rose.

"What! Are you afraid that I will not pay you? Do you want me to pay you in advance? I have money, I tell you."

"It is not that."

"What then?"

"You have money—"

"Yes," said the man.

"And I," said the host, "have no room."

The man resumed tranquilly, "Put me in the stable."

"I cannot."

"Why?"

"The horses take up all the space."

"Very well!" retorted the man. "A corner of the loft then, a truss of straw. We will see about that after dinner."

"I cannot give you any dinner."

This declaration, made in a measured but firm tone, struck the stranger as grave. He rose.

"Ah! Bah! But I am dying of hunger. I have been walking since sunrise. I have traveled twelve leagues. I pay. I wish to eat."

"I have nothing," said the landlord.

The man burst out laughing, and turned toward the fireplace and the stoves: "Nothing! And all that?"

"All that is engaged."

"By whom?"

"By messieurs the wagoners."

"How many are there of them?"

"Twelve."

"There is enough food there for twenty."

"They have engaged the whole of it and paid for it in advance."

The man seated himself again, and said, without raising his voice, "I am at an inn; I am hungry, and I shall remain."

Then the host bent down to his ear, and said in a tone which made him start, "Go away!"

At that moment the traveler was bending forward and thrusting some brands into the fire with the iron-shod tip of his staff; he turned quickly around, and as he opened his mouth to reply, the host gazed steadily at him and added, still in a low voice: "Stop! There's enough of that sort of talk. Do you want me to tell you your name? Your name is Jean Valjean. Now do you want me to tell you who you are? When I saw you come in I suspected something; I sent to the town hall, and this was the reply that was sent to me. Can you read?"

So saying, he held out to the stranger, fully unfolded, the paper that had just traveled from the inn to the town hall, and from the town hall to the inn. The man cast a glance upon it. The landlord resumed after a pause.

"I am in the habit of being polite to everyone. Go away!"

The man dropped his head, picked up the knapsack which he had deposited on the ground, and took his departure.

He chose the principal street. He walked straight on at a venture, keeping close to the houses like a sad and humiliated man. He did not turn around a single time. Had he done so, he would have seen the host of the Cross of Colbas standing on his threshold, surrounded by all the guests of his inn, and all the passersby in the street, talking vivaciously, and pointing him out with his finger; and, from the glances of terror and distrust cast by the group, he might have divined that his arrival would speedily become an event for the whole town.

He saw nothing of all this. People who are crushed do not look behind them. They know but too well the evil fate that follows them.

Thus he proceeded for some time, walking on without ceasing, traversing at random streets of which he knew nothing, forgetful of his fatigue, as is often the case when a man is sad. All at once he felt the pangs of hunger sharply. Night was drawing near. He glanced about him, to see whether he could not discover some shelter.

The fine hostelry was closed to him; he was seeking some very humble public house, some hovel, however lowly.

Just then a light flashed up at the end of the streets; a pine branch suspended from a crossbeam of iron was outlined against the white sky of the twilight. He proceeded there.

It proved to be, in fact, a public house. The public house that is in the Rue de Chaffaut.

The wayfarer halted for a moment, and peeped through the window into the interior of the low-studded room of the public house, illuminated by a small lamp on a table and by a large fire on the hearth. Some men were engaged in drinking there. The landlord was warming himself. An iron pot, suspended from a crane, bubbled over the flame.

The entrance to this public house, which is also a sort of an inn, is by two doors. One opens on the street, the other upon a small yard filled with manure. The traveler dare not enter by the street door. He slipped into the yard, halted again, then raised the latch timidly and opened the door.

"Who goes there?" said the master.

"Someone who wants supper and bed."

"Good. We furnish supper and bed here."

He entered. All the men who were drinking turned around. The lamp illuminated him on one side, the firelight on the other. They examined him for some time while he was taking off his knapsack.

The host said to him, "There is the fire. The supper is cooking in the pot. Come and warm yourself, comrade."

He approached and seated himself near the hearth. He stretched out his feet, which were exhausted with fatigue, to the fire; a fine odor was emitted by the pot. All that could be distinguished of his face, beneath his cap, which was well pulled down, assumed a vague appearance of comfort, mingled with that other poignant aspect that habitual suffering bestows.

It was, moreover, a firm, energetic, and melancholy profile. This physiognomy was strangely composed; it began by seeming humble, and ended by seeming severe. The eye shone beneath its lashes like a fire beneath brushwood.

One of the men seated at the table, however, was a fishmonger who, before entering the public house of the Rue de Chaffaut, had been to stable his horse at Labarre's. It chanced that he had that very morning encountered this unprepossessing stranger on the road between Bras d'Asse and—I have forgotten the name. I think it was Escoublon. Now, when he met him, the man, who then seemed already extremely weary, had requested him to take him on his crupper; to which the fishmonger had made no reply except by redoubling his gait. This fishmonger had been a member half an hour previously of the group that surrounded Jacquin Labarre, and had himself related his disagreeable encounter of the morning to the people at the Cross of Colbas. From where he sat he made an imperceptible sign to the tavern keeper. The tavern keeper went to him. They exchanged a few words in a low tone. The man had again become absorbed in his reflections.

The tavern keeper returned to the fireplace, laid his hand abruptly on the shoulder of the man, and said to him, "You are going to get out of here."

The stranger turned around and replied gently, "Ah! You know—?"

"Yes."

"I was sent away from the other inn."

"And you are to be turned out of this one."

"Where would you have me go?"

"Elsewhere."

The man took his stick and his knapsack and departed.

As he went out, some children who had followed him from the Cross of Colbas, and who seemed to be lying in wait for him, threw stones at him. He retraced his steps in anger, and threatened them with his stick: the children dispersed like a flock of birds.

He passed before the prison. At the door hung an iron chain attached to a bell. He rang.

The wicket opened.

"Turnkey," said he, removing his cap politely, "will you have the kindness to admit me, and give me a lodging for the night?"

A voice replied, "The prison is not an inn. Get yourself arrested, and you will be admitted."

The wicket closed again.

He entered a little street in which there were many gardens. Some of them are enclosed only by hedges, which lends a cheerful aspect to the street. In the midst of these gardens and hedges he caught sight of a small house of a single story, the window of which was lighted up. He peered through the pane as he had done at the public house. Within was a large whitewashed room, with a bed draped in printed cotton stuff, and a cradle in one corner, a few wooden chairs, and a double-barreled gun hanging on the wall. A table was spread in the center of the room. A copper lamp illuminated the tablecloth of coarse white linen, the pewter jug shining like silver, and filled with wine, and the brown, smoking soup tureen. At this table sat a man of about forty, with a merry and open countenance, who was dandling a little child on his knees. Close by a very young woman was nursing another child. The father was laughing, the child was laughing, the mother was smiling.

The stranger paused a moment in reverie before this tender and calming spectacle. What was taking place within him? He alone could have told. It is probable that he thought that this joyous house would be hospitable, and that, in a place where he beheld so much happiness, he would find perhaps a little pity.

He tapped on the pane with a very small and feeble knock.

They did not hear him.

He tapped again.

He heard the woman say, "It seems to me, husband, that someone is knocking."

"No," replied the husband.

He tapped a third time.

The husband rose, took the lamp, and went to the door, which he opened.

He was a man of lofty stature, half peasant, half artisan. He wore a huge leather apron, which reached to his left shoulder, and which a hammer, a red handkerchief, a powder-horn, and all sorts of objects which were upheld by the girdle, as in a pocket, caused to bulge out. He carried his head thrown backwards; his shirt, widely opened and turned back, displayed his bull neck, white and bare. He had thick eyelashes, enormous black whiskers, prominent eyes, the lower part of his face like a snout; and besides all this, that air of being on his own ground, which is indescribable.

"Pardon me, sir," said the wayfarer, "could you, in consideration of payment, give me a plate of soup and a corner of that shed yonder in the garden, in which to sleep? Tell me, can you? For money?"

"Who are you?" demanded the master of the house.

The man replied, "I have just come from Puy-Moisson. I have walked all day long. I have traveled twelve leagues. Can you—if I pay?"

"I would not refuse," said the peasant, "to lodge any respectable man who would pay me. But why do you not go to the inn?"

"There is no room."

"Bah! Impossible. This is neither a fair nor a market day. Have you been to Labarre?"

"Yes."

"Well?"

The traveler replied with embarrassment, "I do not know. He did not receive me."

"Have you been to What's-his-name's, in the Rue Chaffaut?"

The stranger's embarrassment increased; he stammered, "He did not receive me either."

The peasant's countenance assumed an expression of distrust; he surveyed the newcomer from head to feet, and suddenly exclaimed, with a sort of shudder, "Are you the man—?"

He cast a fresh glance upon the stranger, took three steps backward, placed the lamp on the table, and took his gun down from the wall.

Meanwhile, at the words "Are you the man?" the woman had risen, had clasped her two children in her arms, and had taken refuge precipitately behind her husband, staring in terror at the stranger, with her bosom uncovered, and with frightened eyes, as she murmured in a low tone, "*Tso-maraude.*"

All this took place in less time than it requires to picture it to one's self. After having scrutinized the man for several moments, as one scrutinizes a viper, the master of the house returned to the door and said, "Clear out!"

"For pity's sake, a glass of water," said the man.

"A shot from my gun!" said the peasant.

Then he closed the door violently, and the man heard him shoot two large bolts. A moment later, the window-shutter was closed, and the sound of a bar of iron which was placed against it was audible outside.

Night continued to fall. A cold wind from the Alps was blowing. By the light of the expiring day the stranger perceived, in one of the gardens that bordered the street, a sort of hut, which seemed to him to be built of sods. He climbed over the wooden fence resolutely, and found himself in the garden. He approached the hut; its door consisted of a very low and narrow aperture, and it resembled those buildings which road laborers construct for themselves along the roads. He thought without doubt, that it was, in fact, the dwelling of a road laborer; he was suffering from cold and hunger, but this was, at least, a shelter from the cold. This sort of dwelling is not usually occupied at night. He threw himself flat on his face, and crawled into the hut. It was warm there, and he found a tolerably good bed of straw. He lay, for a moment, stretched out on this bed, without the power to make a movement, so fatigued was he. Then, as the knapsack on his back was in his way, and as it furnished, moreover, a pillow ready to his hand, he set about unbuckling one of the straps. At that moment, a ferocious growl became audible. He raised his eyes. The head of an enormous dog was outlined in the darkness at the entrance of the hut.

It was a dog's kennel.

He was himself vigorous and formidable; he armed himself with his staff, made a shield of his knapsack, and made his way out of the kennel in the best way he could, not without enlarging the rents in his rags.

He left the garden in the same manner, but backward, being obliged, in order to keep the dog respectful, to have recourse to that maneuver with his stick, which masters in that sort of fencing designate as *la rose couverte*.

When he had, not without difficulty, repassed the fence, and found himself once more in the street, alone, without refuge, without shelter, without a roof over his head, chased even from that bed of straw and from that miserable kennel, he dropped rather than seated himself on a stone, and it appears that a passerby heard him exclaim, "I am not even a dog!"

He soon rose again and resumed his march. He went out of the town, hoping to find some tree or haystack in the fields that would afford him shelter.

He walked thus for some time, with his head still drooping. When he felt himself far from every human habitation, he raised his eyes and gazed searchingly about him. He was in a field. Before him was one of those low hills covered with close-cut stubble, which, after the harvest, resemble shaved heads.

The horizon was perfectly black. This was not alone the obscurity of night; it was caused by very low-hanging clouds that seemed to rest upon the hill itself, and which were mounting and filling the whole sky. Meanwhile, as the moon was about to rise, and as there was still floating in the zenith a remnant of the brightness of twilight, these clouds formed at the summit of the sky a sort of whitish arch, from which a gleam of light fell upon the earth.

The earth was thus better lighted than the sky, which produces a particularly sinister effect, and the hill, whose contour was poor and mean, was outlined vague and wan against the gloomy horizon. The whole effect was hideous, petty, lugubrious, and narrow.

There was nothing in the field or on the hill except a deformed tree, which writhed and shivered a few paces distant from the wayfarer.

This man was evidently very far from having those delicate habits of intelligence and spirit that render one sensible to the mysterious aspects of things; nevertheless, there was something in that sky, in that hill, in that plain, in that tree, which was so profoundly desolate, that after a moment of immobility and reverie he turned back abruptly. There are instants when nature seems hostile.

He retraced his steps; the gates of D——— were closed. D———, which had sustained sieges during the wars of religion, was still surrounded in 1815 by ancient walls flanked by square towers which have been demolished since. He passed through a breach and entered the town again.

It might have been eight o'clock in the evening. As he was not acquainted with the streets, he recommenced his walk at random.

In this way he came to the prefecture, then to the seminary. As he passed through the Cathedral Square, he shook his fist at the church.

At the corner of this square there is a printing establishment. It is there that the proclamations of the Emperor and of the Imperial Guard to the army, brought from the Island of Elba and dictated by Napoleon himself, were printed for the first time.

Worn out with fatigue, and no longer entertaining any hope, he lay down on a stone bench that stands at the doorway of this printing office.

At that moment an old woman came out of the church. She saw the man stretched out in the shadow. "What are you doing there, my friend?" said she.

He answered harshly and angrily, "As you see, my good woman, I am sleeping." The good woman, who was well worthy the name, in fact, was the Marquise de R———.

"On this bench?" she went on.

"I have had a mattress of wood for nineteen years," said the man; "today I have a mattress of stone."

"You have been a soldier?"

"Yes, my good woman, a soldier."

"Why do you not go to the inn?"

"Because I have no money."

"Alas!" said Madame de R——, "I have only four sous in my purse."

"Give it to me all the same."

The man took the four sous. Madame de R—— continued, "You cannot obtain lodgings in an inn for so small a sum. But have you tried? It is impossible for you to pass the night thus. You are cold and hungry, no doubt. Someone might have given you a lodging out of charity."

"I have knocked at all doors."

"Well?"

"I have been driven away everywhere."

The "good woman" touched the man's arm, and pointed out to him on the other side of the street a small, low house, which stood beside the Bishop's palace.

"You have knocked at all doors?"

"Yes."

"Have you knocked at that one?"

"No."

"Knock there."

CHAPTER II—PRUDENCE COUNSELED TO WISDOM

That evening, the Bishop of D——, after his promenade through the town, remained shut up rather late in his room. He was busy over a great work on duties, which was never completed, unfortunately. He was carefully compiling everything that the Fathers and the doctors have said on this important subject. His book was divided into two parts: firstly, the duties of all; secondly, the duties of each individual, according to the class to which he belongs. The duties of all are the great duties. There are four of these. Saint Matthew points them out: duties toward God (Matthew 6); duties toward one's self (Matthew 6:29, 30); duties toward one's neighbor (Matthew 6:12); duties toward animals (Matthew 6:20, 25). As for the other duties the Bishop found them pointed out and prescribed elsewhere: to sovereigns and subjects, in the Epistle to the Romans; to magistrates, to wives, to mothers, to young men, by Saint Peter; to husbands, fathers, children, and servants, in the Epistle to the Ephesians; to the faithful, in the Epistle to the Hebrews; to virgins, in the Epistle to the Corinthians. Out of these precepts he was laboriously constructing a harmonious whole, which he desired to present to souls.

At eight o'clock he was still at work, writing with a good deal of inconvenience upon little squares of paper, with a big book open on his knees, when Madame Magloire entered, according to her wont, to get the silverware from the cupboard near his bed. A moment later, the Bishop, knowing that the table was set, and that his sister was probably waiting for him, shut his book, rose from his table, and entered the dining room.

The dining room was an oblong apartment, with a fireplace, which had a door opening on the street (as we have said), and a window opening on the garden.

Madame Magloire was, in fact, just putting the last touches to the table.

As she performed this service, she was conversing with Mademoiselle Baptistine.

A lamp stood on the table; the table was near the fireplace. A wood fire was burning there.

One can easily picture to one's self these two women, both of whom were over sixty years of age. Madame Magloire small, plump, vivacious; Mademoiselle Baptistine gentle, slender, frail, somewhat taller than her brother, dressed in a gown of puce-colored silk, of the fashion of 1806, which she had purchased at that date in Paris, and which had lasted ever since. To borrow vulgar phrases, which possess the merit of giving utterance in a single word to an idea that a whole page would hardly suffice to express, Madame Magloire had the air of a peasant, and Mademoiselle Baptistine that of a lady. Madame Magloire wore a white quilted cap, a gold Jeannette cross on a velvet ribbon upon her neck, the only bit of feminine jewelry that there was in the house, a very white fichu* puffing out from a gown of coarse black woolen stuff, with large, short sleeves, an apron of cotton cloth in red and green checks, knotted around the waist with a green ribbon, with a stomacher of the same attached by two pins at the upper corners, coarse shoes on her feet, and yellow stockings, like the women of Marseilles. Mademoiselle Baptistine's gown was cut on the patterns of 1806, with a short waist, a narrow, sheathlike skirt, puffed sleeves, with flaps and buttons. She concealed her gray hair under a frizzed wig known as the baby wig. Madame Magloire had an intelligent, vivacious, and kindly air; the two corners of her mouth unequally raised, and her upper lip, which was larger than the lower, imparted to her a rather crabbed and imperious look. So long as Monseigneur held his peace, she talked to him resolutely with a mixture of respect and freedom; but as soon as Monseigneur began to speak, as we have seen, she obeyed passively like her mistress. Mademoiselle Baptistine did not even speak. She confined herself to obeying and pleasing him. She had never been pretty, even when she was young; she had large, blue, prominent

---

* a triangular scarf draped over the shoulders

eyes, and a long arched nose; but her whole visage, her whole person, breathed forth an ineffable goodness, as we stated in the beginning. She had always been predestined to gentleness; but faith, charity, hope, those three virtues which mildly warm the soul, had gradually elevated that gentleness to sanctity. Nature had made her a lamb, religion had made her an angel. Poor sainted virgin! Sweet memory that has vanished!

Mademoiselle Baptistine has so often narrated what passed at the episcopal residence that evening, that there are many people now living who still recall the most minute details.

At the moment when the Bishop entered, Madame Magloire was talking with considerable vivacity. She was haranguing Mademoiselle Baptistine on a subject that was familiar to her and to which the Bishop was also accustomed. The question concerned the lock upon the entrance door.

It appears that while procuring some provisions for supper, Madame Magloire had heard things in divers places. People had spoken of a prowler of evil appearance; a suspicious vagabond had arrived who must be somewhere about the town, and those who should take it into their heads to return home late that night might be subjected to unpleasant encounters. The police was very badly organized, moreover, because there was no love lost between the Prefect and the Mayor, who sought to injure each other by making things happen. It behooved wise people to play the part of their own police, and to guard themselves well, and care must be taken to duly close, bar, and barricade their houses, and to fasten the doors well.

Madame Magloire emphasized these last words; but the Bishop had just come from his room, where it was rather cold. He seated himself in front of the fire, and warmed himself, and then fell to thinking of other things. He did not take up the remark dropped with design by Madame Magloire. She repeated it. Then Mademoiselle Baptistine, desirous of satisfying Madame Magloire without displeasing her brother, ventured to say timidly, "Did you hear what Madame Magloire is saying, Brother?"

"I have heard something of it in a vague way," replied the Bishop. Then half-turning in his chair, placing his hands on his knees, and raising toward the old servant woman his cordial face, which so easily grew joyous, and which was illuminated from below by the firelight,"Come, what is the matter? What is the matter? Are we in any great danger?"

Then Madame Magloire began the whole story afresh, exaggerating it a little without being aware of the fact. It appeared that a Bohemian, a barefooted vagabond, a sort of dangerous mendicant, was at that moment in the town. He had presented himself at Jacquin Labarre's to obtain lodgings, but the latter had not been willing to take him in. He had been seen to arrive by the way of the boulevard Gassendi and roam about the streets in the gloaming. A gallows bird with a terrible face.

"Really!" said the Bishop.

This willingness to interrogate encouraged Madame Magloire; it seemed to her to indicate that the Bishop was on the point of becoming alarmed; she pursued triumphantly, "Yes, Monseigneur. That is how it is. There will be some sort of catastrophe in this town tonight. Everyone says so. And withal, the police is so badly regulated" (a useful repetition). "The idea of living in a mountainous country, and not even having lights in the streets at night! One goes out. Black as ovens, indeed! And I say, Monseigneur, and Mademoiselle there says with me—"

"I," interrupted his sister, "say nothing. What my brother does is well done."

Madame Magloire continued as though there had been no protest, "We say that this house is not safe at all; that if Monseigneur will permit, I will go and tell Paulin Musebois, the locksmith, to come and replace the ancient locks on the doors; we have them, and it is only the work of a moment; for I say that nothing is more terrible than a door that can be opened from the outside with a latch by the first passerby; and I say that we need bolts, Monseigneur, if only for this night; moreover, Monseigneur has the habit of always saying 'come in'; and besides, even in the middle of the night, *O mon Dieu!* There is no need to ask permission."

At that moment there came a tolerably violent knock on the door.

"Come in," said the Bishop.

CHAPTER III—THE HEROISM OF PASSIVE OBEDIENCE

The door opened.

It opened wide with a rapid movement, as though someone had given it an energetic and resolute push.

A man entered.

We already know the man. It was the wayfarer whom we have seen wandering about in search of shelter.

He entered, advanced a step, and halted, leaving the door open behind him. He had his knapsack on his shoulders, his cudgel in his hand, a rough, audacious, weary, and violent expression in his eyes. The fire on the hearth lighted him up.

He was hideous. It was a sinister apparition.

Madame Magloire had not even the strength to utter a cry. She trembled, and stood with her mouth wide open.

Mademoiselle Baptistine turned around, beheld the man entering, and half started up in terror; then, turning her head by degrees toward the fireplace again, she began to observe her brother, and her face became once more profoundly calm and serene.

The Bishop fixed a tranquil eye on the man.

As he opened his mouth, doubtless to ask the newcomer what he desired, the man rested both hands on his staff, directed his gaze at the old man and the two women, and without waiting for the Bishop to speak, he said, in a loud voice, "See here. My name is Jean Valjean. I am a convict from the galleys. I have passed nineteen years in the galleys. I was liberated four days ago, and am on my way to Pontarlier, which is my destination. I have been walking for four days since I left Toulon. I have traveled a dozen leagues today on foot. This evening, when I arrived in these parts, I went to an inn, and they turned me out, because of my yellow passport, which I had shown at the town hall. I had to do it. I went to an inn. They said to me, 'Be off,' at both places. No one would take me. I went to the prison; the jailer would not admit me. I went into a dog's kennel; the dog bit me and chased me off, as though he had been a man. One would have said that he knew who I was. I went into the fields, intending to sleep in the open air, beneath the stars. There were no stars. I thought it was going to rain, and I re-entered the town, to seek the recess of a doorway. Yonder, in the square, I meant to sleep on a stone bench. A good woman pointed out your house to me, and said to me, 'Knock there!' I have knocked. What is this place? Do you keep an inn? I have money—savings. One hundred and nine francs fifteen sous, which I earned in the galleys by my labor, in the course of nineteen years. I will pay. What is that to me? I have money. I am very weary; twelve leagues on foot; I am very hungry. Are you willing that I should remain?"

"Madame Magloire," said the Bishop, "you will set another place."

The man advanced three paces, and approached the lamp that was on the table. "Stop," he resumed, as though he had not quite understood; "that's not it. Did you hear? I am a galley slave; a convict. I come from the galleys." He drew from his pocket a large sheet of yellow paper, which he unfolded. "Here's my passport. Yellow, as you see. This serves to expel me from every place where I go. Will you read it? I know how to read. I learned in the galleys. There is a school there for those who choose to learn. Hold, this is what they put on this passport: 'Jean Valjean, discharged convict, native of'—that is nothing to you—'has been nineteen years in the galleys: five years for house-breaking and burglary; fourteen years for having attempted to escape on four occasions. He is a very dangerous man.' There! Everyone has cast me out. Are you willing to receive me? Is this an inn? Will you give me something to eat and a bed? Have you a stable?"

"Madame Magloire," said the Bishop, "you will put white sheets on the bed in the alcove." We have already explained the character of the two women's obedience.

Madame Magloire retired to execute these orders.

The Bishop turned to the man.

"Sit down, sir, and warm yourself. We are going to sup in a few moments, and your bed will be prepared while you are supping."

At this point the man suddenly comprehended. The expression of his face, up to that time somber and harsh, bore the imprint of stupefaction, of doubt, of joy, and became extraordinary. He began stammering like a crazy man:, "Really? What! You will keep me? You do not drive me forth? A convict! You call me 'sir'! You do not address me as thou? 'Get out of here, you dog!' is what people always say to me. I felt sure that you would expel me, so I told you at once who I am. Oh, what a good woman that was who directed me hither! I am going to sup! A bed with a mattress and sheets, like the rest of the world! a bed! It is nineteen years since I have slept in a bed! You actually do not want me to go! You are good people. Besides, I have money. I will pay well. Pardon me, monsieur the innkeeper, but what is your name? I will pay anything you ask. You are a fine man. You are an innkeeper, are you not?"

"I am," replied the Bishop, "a priest who lives here."

"A priest!" said the man. "Oh, what a fine priest! Then you are not going to demand any money of me? You are theCuré, are you not? The Curé of this big church? Well! I am a fool, truly! I had not perceived your skullcap."

As he spoke, he deposited his knapsack and his cudgel in a corner, replaced his passport in his pocket, and seated himself. Mademoiselle Baptistine gazed mildly at him. He continued, "You are humane, Monsieur le Curé; you have not scorned me. A good priest is a very good thing. Then you do not require me to pay?"

"No," said the Bishop; "keep your money. How much have you? Did you not tell me one hundred and nine francs?"

"And fifteen sous," added the man.

"One hundred and nine francs fifteen sous. And how long did it take you to earn that?"

"Nineteen years."

"Nineteen years!"

The Bishop sighed deeply.

The man continued, "I have still the whole of my money. In four days I have spent only twenty-five sous, which I earned by helping unload some wagons at Grasse. Since you are an abbé, I will tell you that we had a chaplain in the galleys. And one day I saw a bishop there. Monseigneur is what they call him. He was the Bishop of Majore at Marseilles. He is the Curé who rules over the other Curés, you understand. Pardon me, I say that very badly; but it is such a far-off thing to me! You understand what we are! He said Mass in the middle of the galleys, on an altar. He had a pointed thing, made of gold, on his head; it glittered in the bright light of midday. We were all ranged in lines on the three sides, with cannons with lighted matches facing us. We could not see very well. He spoke; but he was too far off, and we did not hear. That is what a bishop is like."

While he was speaking, the Bishop had gone and shut the door, which had remained wide open.

Madame Magloire returned. She brought a silver fork and spoon, which she placed on the table.

"Madame Magloire," said the Bishop, "place those things as near the fire as possible." And turning to his guest, "The night wind is harsh on the Alps. You must be cold, sir."

Each time that he uttered the word "sir," in his voice which was so gently grave and polished, the man's face lighted up. Monsieur to a convict is like a glass of water to one of the shipwrecked of the Medusa. Ignominy thirsts for consideration.

"This lamp gives a very bad light," said the Bishop.

Madame Magloire understood him, and went to get the two silver candlesticks from the chimneypiece in Monseigneur's bedchamber, and placed them, lighted, on the table.

"Monsieur le Curé," said the man, "you are good; you do not despise me. You receive me into your house. You light your candles for me. Yet I have not concealed from you from where I come and that I am an unfortunate man."

The Bishop, who was sitting close to him, gently touched his hand. "You could not help telling me who you were. This is not my house; it is the house of Jesus Christ. This door does not demand of him who enters whether he has a name, but whether he has a grief. You suffer, you are hungry and thirsty; you are welcome. And do not thank me; do not say that I receive you in my house. No one is at home here, except the man who needs a refuge. I say to you, who are passing by, that you are much more at home here than I am myself.

Everything here is yours. What need have I to know your name? Besides, before you told me you had one which I knew."

The man opened his eyes in astonishment.

"Really? You knew what I was called?"

"Yes," replied the Bishop, "you are called my brother."

"Stop, Monsieur le Curé," exclaimed the man. "I was very hungry when I entered here; but you are so good, that I no longer know what has happened to me."

The Bishop looked at him, and said, "You have suffered much?"

"Oh, the red coat, the ball on the ankle, a plank to sleep on, heat, cold, toil, the convicts, the thrashings, the double chain for nothing, the cell for one word; even sick and in bed, still the chain! Dogs, dogs are happier! Nineteen years! I am forty-six. Now there is the yellow passport. That is what it is like."

"Yes," resumed the Bishop, "you have come from a very sad place. Listen. There will be more joy in heaven over the tear-bathed face of a repentant sinner than over the white robes of a hundred just men. If you emerge from that sad place with thoughts of hatred and of wrath against mankind, you are deserving of pity; if you emerge with thoughts of goodwill and of peace, you are more worthy than anyone of us."

In the meantime, Madame Magloire had served supper: soup, made with water, oil, bread, and salt; a little bacon, a bit of mutton, figs, a fresh cheese, and a large loaf of rye bread. She had, of her own accord, added to the Bishop's ordinary fare a bottle of his old Mauves wine.

The Bishop's face at once assumed that expression of gaiety that is peculiar to hospitable natures. "To table!" he cried vivaciously. As was his custom when a stranger supped with him, he made the man sit on his right. Mademoiselle Baptistine, perfectly peaceable and natural, took her seat at his left.

The Bishop asked a blessing; then helped the soup himself, according to his custom. The man began to eat with avidity.

All at once the Bishop said, "It strikes me there is something missing on this table."

Madame Magloire had, in fact, only placed the three sets of forks and spoons which were absolutely necessary. Now, it was the usage of the house, when the Bishop had anyone to supper, to lay out the whole six sets of silver on the tablecloth—an innocent ostentation. This graceful semblance of luxury was a kind of child's play, which was full of charm in that gentle and severe household, which raised poverty into dignity.

Madame Magloire understood the remark, went out without saying a word, and a moment later the three sets of silver forks and spoons demanded by the Bishop were glittering upon the cloth, symmetrically arranged before the three persons seated at the table.

CHAPTER IV—DETAILS CONCERNING THE CHEESE DAIRIES OF PONTARLIER

Now, in order to convey an idea of what passed at that table, we cannot do better than to transcribe here a passage from one of Mademoiselle Baptistine's letters to Madame Boischevron, wherein the conversation between the convict and the Bishop is described with ingenious minuteness:

> This man paid no attention to anyone. He ate with the voracity of a starving man. However, after supper he said, "Monsieur le Curé of the good God, all this is far too good for me; but I must say that the carters who would not allow me to eat with them keep a better table than you do."
>
> Between ourselves, the remark rather shocked me. My brother replied, "They are more fatigued than I."
>
> "No," returned the man, "they have more money. You are poor; I see that plainly. You cannot be even a curate. Are you really a Curé? Ah, if the good God were but just, you certainly ought to be a Curé!"
>
> "The good God is more than just," said my brother.
>
> A moment later he added, "Monsieur Jean Valjean, is it to Pontarlier that you are going?"
>
> "With my road marked out for me." I think that is what the man said. Then he went on, "I must be on my way by daybreak tomorrow. Traveling is hard. If the nights are cold, the days are hot."
>
> "You are going to a good country," said my brother. "During the Revolution my family was ruined. I took refuge in Franche-Comté at first, and there I lived for some time by the toil of my hands. My will was good. I found plenty to occupy me. One has only to choose. There are paper mills, tanneries, distilleries, oil factories, watch factories on a large scale, steel mills, copper works, twenty iron foundries at least, four of which, situated at Lods, at Chatillon, at Audincourt, and at Beure, are tolerably large."
>
> I think I am not mistaken in saying that those are the names which my brother mentioned. Then he interrupted himself

and addressed me, "Have we not some relatives in those parts, my dear sister?"

I replied, "We did have some; among others, M. de Lucenet, who was captain of the gates at Pontarlier under the old regime."

"Yes," resumed my brother; "but in '93, one had no longer any relatives, one had only one's arms. I worked. They have, in the country of Pontarlier, where you are going, Monsieur Valjean, a truly patriarchal and truly charming industry, my sister. It is their cheese dairies, which they call fruitieres."

Then my brother, while urging the man to eat, explained to him, with great minuteness, what these fruitieres of Pontarlier were; that they were divided into two classes: the big barns, which belong to the rich, and where there are forty or fifty cows that produce from seven to eight thousand cheeses each summer, and the associated fruitieres, which belong to the poor; these are the peasants of midmountain, who hold their cows in common, and share the proceeds. "They engage the services of a cheesemaker, whom they call the grurin; the grurin receives the milk of the associates three times a day, and marks the quantity on a double tally. It is toward the end of April that the work of the cheese dairies begins; it is toward the middle of June that the cheesemakers drive their cows to the mountains."

The man recovered his animation as he ate. My brother made him drink that good Mauves wine, which he does not drink himself, because he says that wine is expensive. My brother imparted all these details with that easy gaiety of his with which you are acquainted, interspersing his words with graceful attentions to me. He recurred frequently to that comfortable trade of grurin, as though he wished the man to understand, without advising him directly and harshly, that this would afford him a refuge. One thing struck me. This man was what I have told you. Well, neither during supper, nor during the entire evening, did my brother utter a single word, with the exception of a few words about Jesus when he entered, which could remind the man of what he was, nor of what my brother was. To all appearances, it was an occasion for preaching him a little sermon, and of impressing the Bishop on the convict, so that a mark of the passage might remain behind. This might have appeared to anyone else who had this unfortunate man in his hands to afford a chance to nourish his soul as well as his body, and to bestow upon him some reproach, seasoned with moralizing and advice, or a little commiseration, with an exhortation to conduct himself better in the future. My brother did not even ask him from what country he came, nor what was his history. For in his history there is a fault, and my brother seemed to avoid everything that could remind him of it. To such a point did he carry it, that at one time, when my brother was speaking of the mountaineers of Pontarlier, who exercise a gentle labor near heaven, and who, he added, are happy because they are innocent, he stopped short, fearing lest in this remark there might have escaped him something that might wound the man. By dint of reflection, I think I have comprehended what was passing in my brother's heart. He was thinking, no doubt, that this man, whose name is Jean Valjean, had his misfortune only too vividly present in his mind; that the best thing was to divert him from it, and to make him believe, if only momentarily, that he was a person like any other, by treating him just in his ordinary way. Is not this indeed, to understand charity well? Is there not, dear Madame, something truly evangelical in this delicacy, which abstains from sermon, from moralizing, from allusions? And is not the truest pity, when a man has a sore point, not to touch it at all? It has seemed to me that this might have been my brother's private thought. In any case, what I can say is that, if he entertained all these ideas, he gave no sign of them; from beginning to end, even to me he was the same as he is every evening, and he supped with this Jean Valjean with the same air and in the same manner in which he would have supped with M. Gedeon le Provost, or with the curate of the parish.

Toward the end, when he had reached the figs, there came a knock at the door. It was Mother Gerbaud, with her little one in her arms. My brother kissed the child on the brow, and borrowed fifteen sous, which I had about me to give to Mother Gerbaud. The man was not paying much heed to anything then. He was no longer talking, and he seemed very much fatigued. After poor old Gerbaud had taken her departure, my brother said grace; then he turned to the man and said to him, "You must be in great need of your bed." Madame Magloire cleared the table very promptly. I understood that we must retire, in order to allow this traveler to go to sleep, and we both went upstairs. Nevertheless, I sent Madame Magloire down a moment later, to carry to the man's bed a goat skin from the Black Forest, which was in my room. The nights are frigid, and that keeps one warm. It is a pity that this skin is old; all the hair is falling out. My brother bought it while he was in

Germany, at Tottlingen, near the sources of the Danube, as well as the little ivory-handled knife that I use at table.

Madame Magloire returned immediately. We said our prayers in the drawing room, where we hang up the linen, and then we each retired to our own chambers, without saying a word to each other.

CHAPTER V—TRANQUILITY

After bidding his sister good night, Monseigneur Bienvenu took one of the two silver candlesticks from the table, handed the other to his guest, and said to him, "Monsieur, I will conduct you to your room."

The man followed him.

As might have been observed from what has been said above, the house was so arranged that in order to pass into the oratory where the alcove was situated, or to get out of it, it was necessary to traverse the Bishop's bedroom.

At the moment when he was crossing this apartment, Madame Magloire was putting away the silverware in the cupboard near the head of the bed. This was her last care every evening before she went to bed.

The Bishop installed his guest in the alcove. A fresh white bed had been prepared there. The man set the candle down on a small table.

"Well," said the Bishop, "may you pass a good night. Tomorrow morning, before you set out, you shall drink a cup of warm milk from our cows."

"Thanks, Monsieur l'Abbé," said the man.

Hardly had he pronounced these words full of peace, when all of a sudden, and without transition, he made a strange movement, which would have frozen the two sainted women with horror, had they witnessed it. Even at this day it is difficult for us to explain what inspired him at that moment. Did he intend to convey a warning or to throw out a menace? Was he simply obeying a sort of instinctive impulse that was obscure even to himself? He turned abruptly to the old man, folded his arms, and bending upon his host a savage gaze, he exclaimed in a hoarse voice, "Ah! Really! You lodge me in your house, close to yourself like this?"

He broke off, and added with a laugh in which there lurked something monstrous: "Have you really reflected well? How do you know that I have not been an assassin?"

The Bishop replied, "That is the concern of the good God."

Then gravely, and moving his lips like one who is praying or talking to himself, he raised two fingers of his right hand and bestowed his benediction on the man, who did not bow, and without turning his head or looking behind him, he returned to his bedroom.

When the alcove was in use, a large serge curtain drawn from wall to wall concealed the altar. The Bishop knelt before this curtain as he passed and said a brief prayer. A moment later he was in his garden, walking, meditating, contemplating, his heart and soul wholly absorbed in those grand and mysterious things which God shows at night to the eyes which remain open.

As for the man, he was actually so fatigued that he did not even profit by the nice white sheets. Snuffing out his candle with his nostrils after the manner of convicts, he dropped, all dressed as he was, upon the bed, where he immediately fell into a profound sleep.

Midnight struck as the Bishop returned from his garden to his apartment.

A few minutes later all were asleep in the little house.

CHAPTER VI—JEAN VALJEAN

Toward the middle of the night Jean Valjean woke.

Jean Valjean came from a poor peasant family of Brie. He had not learned to read in his childhood. When he reached man's estate, he became a tree pruner at Faverolles. His mother was named Jeanne Mathieu; his father was called Jean Valjean or Vlajean, probably a sobriquet, and a contraction of *voilà Jean*, "here's Jean."

Jean Valjean was of that thoughtful but not gloomy disposition that constitutes the peculiarity of affectionate natures. On the whole, however, there was something decidedly sluggish and insignificant about Jean Valjean in appearance, at least. He had lost his father and mother at a very early age. His mother had died of a milk fever, which had not been properly attended to. His father, a tree pruner, like himself, had been killed by a fall from a tree. All that remained to Jean Valjean was a sister older than himself, a widow with seven children, boys and girls. This sister had brought up Jean Valjean, and so long as she had a husband she lodged and fed her young brother.

The husband died. The eldest of the seven children was eight years old. The youngest, one.

Jean Valjean had just attained his twenty-fifth year. He took the father's place, and, in his turn, supported the sister who had brought him up. This was done simply as a duty and even a little churlishly on the part of Jean Valjean. Thus his youth had been spent in rude and ill-paid toil. He had never known a "kind woman friend" in his native parts. He had not had the time to fall in love.

He returned at night weary, and ate his broth without uttering a word. His sister, mother Jeanne, often took the best part of his repast from his bowl while he was eating, a bit of meat, a slice of bacon, the heart of the cabbage, to give to one of her children. As he went on eating, with his head bent over the table and almost into his soup, his long hair falling about his bowl and concealing his eyes, he had the air of perceiving nothing and allowing it. There was at Faverolles, not far from the Valjean thatched cottage, on the other side of the lane, a farmer's wife named Marie-Claude; the Valjean children, habitually famished, sometimes went to borrow from Marie-Claude a pint of milk, in their mother's name, which they drank behind a hedge or in some alley corner, snatching the jug from each other so hastily that the little girls spilled it on their aprons and down their necks. If their mother had known of this marauding, she would have punished the delinquents severely. Jean Valjean gruffly and grumblingly paid Marie-Claude for the pint of milk behind their mother's back, and the children were not punished.

In pruning season he earned eighteen sous a day; then he hired out as a hay maker, as laborer, as neat-herd on a farm, as a drudge. He did whatever he could. His sister worked also but what could she do with seven little children? It was a sad group enveloped in misery, which was being gradually annihilated. A very hard winter came. Jean had no work. The family had no bread. No bread literally. Seven children!

One Sunday evening, Maubert Isabeau, the baker on the Church Square at Faverolles, was preparing to go to bed, when he heard a violent blow on the grated front of his shop. He arrived in time to see an arm passed through a hole made by a blow from a fist, through the grating and the glass. The arm seized a loaf of bread and carried it off. Isabeau ran out in haste; the robber fled at the full speed of his legs. Isabeau ran after him and stopped him. The thief had flung away the loaf, but his arm was still bleeding. It was Jean Valjean.

This took place in 1795. Jean Valjean was taken before the tribunals of the time for theft and breaking and entering an inhabited house at night. He had a gun which he used better than anyone else in the world, he was a bit of a poacher, and this injured his case. There exists a legitimate prejudice against poachers. The poacher, like the smuggler, smacks too strongly of the brigand. Nevertheless, we will remark cursorily, there is still an abyss between these races of men and the hideous assassin of the towns. The poacher lives in the forest, the smuggler lives in the mountains or on the sea. The cities make ferocious men because they make corrupt men. The mountain, the sea, the forest, make savage men; they develop the fierce side, but often without destroying the humane side.

Jean Valjean was pronounced guilty. The terms of the Code were explicit. There occur formidable hours in our civilization; there are moments when the penal laws decree a shipwreck. What an ominous minute is that in which society draws back and consummates the irreparable abandonment of a sentient being! Jean Valjean was condemned to five years in the galleys.

On the 22nd of April, 1796, the victory of Montenotte, won by the general-in-chief of the army of Italy, whom the message of the Directory to the Five Hundred, of the 2nd of Floreal, year IV, calls Buona-Parte, was announced in Paris; on that same day a great gang of galley slaves was put in chains at Bicêtre. Jean Valjean formed a part of that gang. An old turnkey of the prison, who is now nearly eighty years old, still recalls perfectly that unfortunate wretch who was chained to the end of the fourth line, in the north angle of the courtyard. He was seated on the ground like the others. He did not seem to comprehend his position, except that it was horrible. It is probable that he, also, was disentangling from amid the vague ideas of a poor man, ignorant of everything, something excessive. While the bolt of his iron collar was being riveted behind his head with heavy blows from the hammer, he wept, his tears stifled him, they impeded his speech; he only managed to say from time to time, "I was a tree pruner at Faverolles." Then still sobbing, he raised his right hand and lowered it gradually seven times, as though he were touching in succession seven heads of unequal heights, and from this gesture it was divined that the thing which he had done, whatever it was, he had done for the sake of clothing and nourishing seven little children.

He set out for Toulon. He arrived there, after a journey of twenty-seven days, on a cart, with a chain on his neck. At Toulon he was clothed in the red cassock. All that had constituted his life, even to his name, was effaced; he was no longer even Jean Valjean; he was number 24601. What became of his sister? What became of the seven children? Who troubled himself about that? What becomes of the handful of leaves from the young tree that is sawed off at the root?

It is always the same story. These poor living beings, these creatures of God, henceforth without support, without guide, without refuge, wandered away at random, who even knows? Each in his own direction perhaps, and little by little buried themselves in that cold mist, which engulfs solitary destinies; gloomy shades, into which disappear in succession so many unlucky heads, in the somber march of the human race. They quitted the country. The clock tower of what had been their village forgot them; the boundary line of what had been their field forgot them; after a few years' residence in the galleys, Jean Valjean himself forgot them. In that heart, where there had been a wound, there was a scar. That is all. Only once, during all the time that he spent at Toulon, did he hear his sister mentioned. This happened, I think, toward the end of the fourth year of his captivity. I know not through what channels the news reached him. Someone who had known them in their own country had seen his sister. She was in Paris. She lived in a poor street Rear Saint-Sulpice, in the Rue du Gindre. She had with her only one child, a little boy, the youngest. Where were the other six? Perhaps she did not know herself. Every morning she went to a printing office, No. 3 Rue du Sabot, where she was a folder and stitcher. She was obliged to be there at six o'clock in the morning—long before daylight in winter. In the same building with the printing office there was a school, and to this school she took her little boy, who was seven years old. But as she entered the printing office at six, and the school only opened at seven, the child had to wait in the courtyard, for the school to open, for an hour—one hour of a winter night in the open air! They would not allow the child to come into the printing office, because he was in the way, they said. When the workmen passed in the morning, they beheld this poor little being seated on the pavement, overcome with drowsiness, and often fast asleep in the shadow, crouched down and doubled up over his basket. When it rained, an old woman, the portress, took pity on him; she took him into her den, where there was a pallet, a spinning-wheel, and two wooden chairs, and the little one slumbered in a corner, pressing himself close to the cat that he might suffer less from cold. At seven o'clock the school opened, and he entered. That is what was told to Jean Valjean.

They talked to him about it for one day; it was a moment, a flash, as though a window had suddenly been opened upon the destiny of those things whom he had loved; then all closed again. He heard nothing more forever. Nothing from them ever reached him again; he never beheld them; he never met them again; and in the continuation of this mournful history they will not be met with anymore.

Toward the end of this fourth year Jean Valjean's turn to escape arrived. His comrades assisted him, as is the custom in that sad place. He escaped. He wandered for two days in the fields at liberty, if being at liberty is to be hunted, to turn the head every instant, to quake at the slightest noise, to be afraid of everything, of a smoking roof, of a passing man, of a barking dog, of a galloping horse, of a striking clock, of the day because one can see, of the night because one cannot see, of the highway, of the path, of a bush, of sleep. On the evening of the second day he was captured. He had neither eaten nor slept for thirty-six hours. The maritime tribunal condemned him, for this crime, to a prolongation of his term for three years, which made eight years. In the sixth year his turn to escape occurred again; he availed himself of it, but could not accomplish his flight fully. He was missing at roll call. The cannon were fired, and at night the patrol found him hidden under the keel of a vessel in process of construction; he resisted the galley guards who seized him. Escape and rebellion. This case, provided for by a special code, was punished by an addition of five years, two of them in the double chain. Thirteen years. In the tenth year his turn came around again; he again profited by it; he succeeded no better. Three years for this fresh attempt. Sixteen years. Finally, I think it was during his thirteenth year, he made a last attempt, and only succeeded in getting retaken at the end of four hours of absence. Three years for those four hours. Nineteen years. In October, 1815, he was released; he had entered there in 1796, for having broken a pane of glass and taken a loaf of bread.

Room for a brief parenthesis. This is the second time, during his studies on the penal question and damnation by law, that the author of this book has come across the theft of a loaf of bread as the point of departure for the disaster of a destiny. Claude Gaux had stolen a loaf; Jean Valjean had stolen a loaf. English statistics prove the fact that four thefts out of five in London have hunger for their immediate cause.

Jean Valjean had entered the galleys sobbing and shuddering; he emerged impassive. He had entered in despair; he emerged gloomy.

What had taken place in that soul?

CHAPTER VII—THE INTERIOR OF DESPAIR

Let us try to say it.

It is necessary that society should look at these things, because it is itself which creates them.

He was, as we have said, an ignorant man, but he was not a fool. The light of nature was ignited in him. Unhappiness, which also possesses a clearness of vision of its own, augmented the small amount of daylight that existed in this mind. Beneath the cudgel, beneath the chain, in the cell, in hardship, beneath the burning sun of the galleys, upon the plank bed of the convict, he withdrew into his own consciousness and meditated.

He constituted himself the tribunal.

He began by putting himself on trial.

He recognized the fact that he was not an innocent man unjustly punished.

He admitted that he had committed an extreme and blameworthy act; that that loaf of bread would probably not have been refused to him had he asked for it; that, in any case, it would have been better to wait until he could get it through compassion or through work; that it is not an unanswerable argument to say, "Can one wait when one is hungry?" That, in the first place, it is very rare for anyone to die of hunger, literally; and next, that, fortunately or unfortunately, man is so constituted that he can suffer long and much, both morally and physically, without dying; that it is therefore necessary to have patience; that that would even have been better for those poor little children; that it had been an act of madness for him, a miserable, unfortunate wretch, to take society at large violently by the collar, and to imagine that one can escape from misery through theft; that that is in any case a poor door through which to escape from misery through which infamy enters; in short, that he was in the wrong.

Then he asked himself—

Whether he had been the only one in fault in his fatal history. Whether it was not a serious thing, that he, a laborer, out of work, that he, an industrious man, should have lacked bread. And whether, the fault once committed and confessed, the chastisement had not been ferocious and disproportioned. Whether there had not been more abuse on the part of the law, in respect to the penalty, than there had been on the part of the culprit in respect to his fault. Whether there had not been an excess of weights in one balance of the scale, in the one which contains expiation. Whether the over-weight of the penalty was not equivalent to the annihilation of the crime, and did not result in reversing the situation, of replacing the fault of the delinquent by the fault of the repression, of converting the guilty man into the victim, and the debtor into the creditor, and of ranging the law definitely on the side of the man who had violated it.

Whether this penalty, complicated by successive aggravations for attempts at escape, had not ended in becoming a sort of outrage perpetrated by the stronger upon the feebler, a crime of society against the individual, a crime that was being committed afresh every day, a crime which had lasted nineteen years.

He asked himself whether human society could have the right to force its members to suffer equally in one case for its own unreasonable lack of foresight, and in the other case for its pitiless foresight; and to seize a poor man forever between a defect and an excess, a default of work and an excess of punishment.

Whether it was not outrageous for society to treat thus precisely those of its members who were the least well-endowed in the division of goods made by chance, and consequently the most deserving of consideration.

These questions put and answered, he judged society and condemned it.

He condemned it to his hatred.

He made it responsible for the fate that he was suffering, and he said to himself that it might be that one day he should not hesitate to call it to account. He declared to himself that there was no equilibrium between the harm which he had caused and the harm that was being done to him; he finally arrived at the conclusion that his punishment was not, in truth, unjust, but that it most assuredly was iniquitous.

Anger may be both foolish and absurd; one can be irritated wrongfully; one is exasperated only when there is some show of right on one's side at bottom. Jean Valjean felt himself exasperated.

And besides, human society had done him nothing but harm; he had never seen anything of it save that angry face, which it calls Justice, and which it shows to those whom it strikes. Men had only touched him to bruise him. Every contact with them had been a blow. Never, since his infancy, since the days of his mother, of his sister, had he ever encountered a friendly word and a kindly glance. From suffering to suffering, he had gradually arrived at the conviction that life is a war; and that in this war he was the conquered. He had no other weapon than his hate. He resolved to whet it in the galleys and to bear it away with him when he departed.

There was at Toulon a school for the convicts, kept by the Ignorantin friars, where the most necessary branches were taught to those of the unfortunate men who had a mind for them. He was of the number who had a mind. He went to school at the age of forty, and learned to read, to write, to cipher. He felt that to fortify his intelligence was to fortify his hate. In certain cases, education and enlightenment can serve to eke out evil.

This is a sad thing to say; after having judged society, which had caused his unhappiness, he judged Providence, which had made society, and he condemned it also.

Thus during nineteen years of torture and slavery, this soul mounted and at the same time fell. Light entered it on one side, and darkness on the other.

Jean Valjean had not, as we have seen, an evil nature. He was still good when he arrived at the galleys. He there condemned society, and felt that he was becoming wicked; he there condemned Providence, and was conscious that he was becoming impious.

It is difficult not to indulge in meditation at this point.

Does human nature thus change utterly and from top to bottom? Can the man created good by God be rendered wicked by man? Can the soul be completely made over by fate, and become evil, fate being evil? Can the heart become misshapen and contract incurable deformities and infirmities under the oppression of a disproportionate unhappiness, as the vertebral column beneath too low a vault? Is there not in every human soul—was there not in the soul of Jean Valjean in particular—a first spark, a divine element, incorruptible in this world, immortal in the other, which good can develop, fan, ignite, and make to glow with splendor, and which evil can never wholly extinguish?

Grave and obscure questions, to the last of which every physiologist would probably have responded no, and that without hesitation, had he beheld at Toulon, during the hours of repose, which were for Jean Valjean hours of reverie, this gloomy galley slave, seated with folded arms upon the bar of some capstan, with the end of his chain thrust into his pocket to prevent its dragging, serious, silent, and thoughtful, a pariah of the laws that regarded the man with wrath, condemned by civilization, and regarding heaven with severity.

Certainly, and we make no attempt to dissimulate the fact, the observing physiologist would have beheld an irremediable misery; he would, perchance, have pitied this sick man, of the law's making; but he would not have even essayed any treatment; he would have turned aside his gaze from the caverns of which he would have caught a glimpse within this soul, and, like Dante at the portals of hell, he would have effaced from this existence the word, which the finger of God has, nevertheless, inscribed upon the brow of every man—hope.

Was this state of his soul, which we have attempted to analyze, as perfectly clear to Jean Valjean as we have tried to render it for those who read us? Did Jean Valjean distinctly perceive, after their formation, and had he seen distinctly during the process of their formation, all the elements of which his moral misery was composed? Had this rough and unlettered man gathered a perfectly clear perception of the succession of ideas through which he had, by degrees, mounted and descended to the lugubrious aspects which had, for so many years, formed the inner horizon of his spirit? Was he conscious of all that passed within him, and of all that was working there? This is something that we do not presume to state; it is something that we do not even believe. There was too much ignorance in Jean Valjean, even after his misfortune, to prevent much vagueness from still lingering there. At times he did not rightly know himself what he felt. Jean Valjean was in the shadows; he suffered in the shadows; he hated in the shadows; one might have said that he hated in advance of himself. He dwelt habitually in this shadow, feeling his way like a blind man and a dreamer. Only, at intervals, there suddenly came to him, from without and from within, an access of wrath, a surcharge of suffering, a livid and rapid flash which illuminated his whole soul, and caused to appear abruptly all around him, in front, behind, amid the gleams of a frightful light, the hideous precipices and the somber perspective of his destiny.

The flash passed, the night closed in again; and where was he? He no longer knew. The peculiarity of pains of this nature, in which that which is pitiless—that is to say, that which is brutalizing—predominates, is to transform a man, little by little, by a sort of stupid transfiguration, into a wild beast; sometimes into a ferocious beast.

Jean Valjean's successive and obstinate attempts at escape would alone suffice to prove this strange working of the law upon the human soul. Jean Valjean would have renewed these attempts, utterly useless and foolish as they were, as often as the opportunity had presented itself, without reflecting for an instant on the result, nor on the experiences that he had already gone through. He escaped impetuously, like the wolf who finds his cage open. Instinct said to him, "Flee!" Reason would have said, "Remain!" But in the presence of so violent a temptation, reason vanished; nothing remained but instinct. The beast alone acted. When he was recaptured, the fresh severities inflicted on him only served to render him still more wild.

One detail, which we must not omit, is that he possessed a physical strength that was not approached by a single one of the denizens of the galleys. At work, at paying out a cable or winding up a capstan, Jean Valjean was worth four men. He sometimes lifted and sustained enormous weights on his back; and when the occasion demanded it, he replaced that implement which is called a jack-screw, and was formerly called *orgueil* (pride), from where, we may remark in passing, is derived the name of the Rue Montorgueil, near the Halles (Fishmarket) in Paris. His comrades had nicknamed him Jean the Jack-screw. Once, when they were repairing the balcony of the town hall at Toulon, one of those admirable caryatids of Puget, which support the balcony, became loosened, and was on the point of falling. Jean Valjean, who was present, supported the caryatid with his shoulder, and gave the workmen time to arrive.

His suppleness even exceeded his strength. Certain convicts who were forever dreaming of escape, ended by making a veritable science of force and skill combined. It is the science of muscles. An entire system of mysterious statics is daily practiced by prisoners, men who are forever envious of the flies and birds. To climb a vertical surface, and to find points of support where hardly a projection was visible, was play to Jean Valjean. An angle of the wall being given, with the tension of his back and legs, with his elbows and his heels fitted into the unevenness of the stone, he raised himself as if by magic to the third story. He sometimes mounted thus even to the roof of the galley prison.

He spoke but little. He laughed not at all. An excessive emotion was required to wring from him, once or twice a year, that lugubrious laugh of the convict, which is like the echo of the laugh of a demon. To all appearance, he seemed to be occupied in the constant contemplation of something terrible.

He was absorbed, in fact.

Athwart the unhealthy perceptions of an incomplete nature and a crushed intelligence, he was confusedly conscious that some monstrous thing was resting on him. In that obscure and wan shadow within which he crawled, each time that he turned his neck and essayed to raise his glance, he perceived with terror, mingled with rage, a sort of frightful accumulation of things, collecting and mounting above him, beyond the range of his vision, laws, prejudices, men, and deeds, whose outlines escaped him, whose mass terrified him, and which was nothing else than that prodigious pyramid which we call civilization. He distinguished, here and there in that swarming and formless mass, now near him, now afar off and on inaccessible table lands, some group, some detail, vividly illuminated; here the galley sergeant and his cudgel; there the gendarme and his sword; yonder the mitered archbishop; away at the top, like a sort of sun, the Emperor, crowned and dazzling. It seemed to him that these distant splendors, far from dissipating his night, rendered it more funereal and more black. All this—laws, prejudices, deeds, men, things—went and came above him, over his head, in accordance with the complicated and mysterious movement which God imparts to civilization, walking over him and crushing him with I know not what peacefulness in its cruelty and inexorability in its indifference. Souls that have fallen to the bottom of all possible misfortune, unhappy men lost in the lowest of those limbos at which no one any longer looks, the reproved of the law, feel the whole weight of this human society, so formidable for him who is without, so frightful for him who is beneath, resting upon their heads.

In this situation Jean Valjean meditated; and what could be the nature of his meditation?

If the grain of millet beneath the millstone had thoughts, it would, doubtless, think that same thing which Jean Valjean thought.

All these things, realities full of specters, phantasmagorias full of realities, had eventually created for him a sort of interior state that is almost indescribable.

At times, amid his convict toil, he paused. He fell to thinking. His reason, at one and the same time riper and more troubled than of yore, rose in revolt. Everything that had happened to him seemed to him absurd; everything that surrounded him seemed to him impossible. He said to himself, "It is a dream." He gazed at the galley sergeant standing a few paces from him; the galley sergeant seemed a phantom to him. All of a sudden the phantom dealt him a blow with his cudgel.

Visible nature hardly existed for him. It would almost be true to say that there existed for Jean Valjean neither sun, nor fine summer days, nor radiant sky, nor fresh April dawns. I know not what vent hole daylight habitually illumined his soul.

To sum up, in conclusion, that which can be summed up and translated into positive results in all that we have just pointed out, we will confine ourselves to the statement that, in the course of nineteen years, Jean Valjean, the inoffensive tree pruner of Faverolles, the formidable convict of Toulon, had become capable, thanks to the manner in which the galleys had molded him, of two sorts of evil action: firstly, of evil action that was rapid, unpremeditated, dashing, entirely instinctive, in the nature of reprisals for the evil that he had undergone; secondly, of evil action which was serious, grave, consciously argued out, and premeditated, with the false ideas which such a misfortune can furnish. His deliberate deeds passed through three successive phases, which natures of a certain stamp can alone traverse: reasoning, will, perseverance. He had for moving causes his habitual wrath, bitterness of soul, a profound sense of indignities suffered, the reaction even against the good, the innocent, and the just, if there are any such. The point of departure, like the point of arrival, for all his thoughts, was hatred of human law; that hatred which, if it be not arrested in its development by some providential incident, becomes, within a given time, the hatred of society, then the hatred of the human race, then the hatred of creation, and which manifests itself by a vague, incessant, and brutal desire to do harm to some living being, no matter whom. It will be perceived that it was not without reason that Jean Valjean's passport described him as a very dangerous man.

From year to year this soul had dried away slowly, but with fatal sureness. When the heart is dry, the eye is dry. On his departure from the galleys it had been nineteen years since he had shed a tear.

CHAPTER VIII—BILLOWS AND SHADOWS

A man overboard!

What matters it? The vessel does not halt. The wind blows. That somber ship has a path, which it is forced to pursue. It passes on.

The man disappears, then reappears; he plunges, he rises again to the surface; he calls, he stretches out his arms; he is not heard. The vessel, trembling under the hurricane, is wholly absorbed in its own workings; the passengers and sailors do not even see the drowning man; his miserable head is but a speck amid the immensity of the waves. He gives vent to desperate cries from out of the depths. What a specter is that retreating sail! He gazes and gazes at it frantically. It retreats, it grows dim, it diminishes in size. He was there but just now, he was one of the crew, he went and came along the deck with the rest, he had his part of breath and of sunlight, he was a living man. Now, what has taken place? He has slipped, he has fallen; all is at an end. He is in the tremendous sea. Under foot he has nothing but what flees and crumbles. The billows, torn and lashed by the wind, encompass him hideously; the tossings of the abyss bear him away; all the tongues of water dash over his head; a populace of waves spits upon him; confused openings half devour him; every time that he sinks, he catches glimpses of precipices filled with night; frightful and unknown vegetations seize him, knot about his feet, draw him to them; he is conscious that he is becoming an abyss, that he forms part of the foam; the waves toss him from one to another; he drinks in the bitterness; the cowardly ocean attacks him furiously, to drown him; the enormity plays with his agony. It seems as though all that water were hate.

Nevertheless, he struggles.

He tries to defend himself; he tries to sustain himself; he makes an effort; he swims. He, his petty strength all exhausted instantly, combats the inexhaustible.

Where, then, is the ship? Yonder. Barely visible in the pale shadows of the horizon.

The wind blows in gusts; all the foam overwhelms him. He raises his eyes and beholds only the lividness of the clouds. He witnesses, amid his death-pangs, the immense madness of the sea. He is tortured by this madness; he hears noises strange to man, which seem to come from beyond the limits of the earth, and from one knows not what frightful region beyond.

There are birds in the clouds, just as there are angels above human distresses; but what can they do for him? They sing and fly and float, and he, he rattles in the death agony.

He feels himself buried in those two infinities, the ocean and the sky, at one and the same time: the one is a tomb; the other is a shroud.

Night descends; he has been swimming for hours; his strength is exhausted; that ship, that distant thing in which there were men, has vanished; he is alone in the formidable twilight gulf; he sinks, he stiffens himself, he twists himself; he feels under him the monstrous billows of the invisible; he shouts.

There are no more men. Where is God?

He shouts. Help! Help! He still shouts on.

Nothing on the horizon; nothing in heaven.

He implores the expanse, the waves, the seaweed, the reef; they are deaf. He beseeches the tempest; the imperturbable tempest obeys only the infinite.

Around him darkness, fog, solitude, the stormy and nonsentient tumult, the undefined curling of those wild waters. In him horror and fatigue. Beneath him the depths. Not a point of support. He thinks of the gloomy adventures of the corpse in the limitless shadow. The bottomless cold paralyzes him. His hands contract convulsively; they close, and grasp nothingness. Winds, clouds, whirlwinds, gusts, useless stars! What is to be done? The desperate man gives up; he is weary, he chooses the alternative of death; he resists not; he lets himself go; he abandons his grip; and then he tosses forevermore in the lugubrious dreary depths of engulfment.

Oh, implacable march of human societies! Oh, losses of men and of souls on the way! Ocean into which falls all that the law lets slip! Disastrous absence of help! Oh, moral death!

The sea is the inexorable social night into which the penal laws fling their condemned. The sea is the immensity of wretchedness.

The soul, going down stream in this gulf, may become a corpse. Who shall resuscitate it?

CHAPTER IX—NEW TROUBLES

When the hour came for him to take his departure from the galleys, when Jean Valjean heard in his ear the strange words, "Thou art free!" The moment seemed improbable and unprecedented; a ray of vivid light, a ray of the true light of the living, suddenly penetrated within him. But it was not long before this ray paled. Jean Valjean had been dazzled by the idea of liberty. He had believed in a new life. He very speedily perceived what sort of liberty it is to which a yellow passport is provided.

And this was encompassed with much bitterness. He had calculated that his earnings, during his sojourn in the galleys, ought to amount to a hundred and seventy-one francs. It is but just to add that he had forgotten to include in his calculations the forced repose of Sundays and festival days during nineteen years, which entailed a diminution of about eighty francs. At all events, his hoard had been reduced by various local levies to the sum of one hundred and nine francs fifteen sous, which had been counted out to him on his departure. He had understood nothing of this, and had thought himself wronged. Let us say the word—robbed.

On the day following his liberation, he saw, at Grasse, in front of an orange-flower distillery, some men engaged in unloading bales. He offered his services. Business was pressing; they were accepted. He set to work. He was intelligent, robust, adroit; he did his best; the master seemed pleased. While he was at work, a gendarme passed, observed him, and demanded his papers. It was necessary to show him the yellow passport. That done, Jean Valjean resumed his labor. A little while before he had questioned one of the workmen as to the amount which they earned each day at this occupation; he had been told thirty sous. When evening arrived, as he was forced to set out again on the following day, he presented himself to the owner of the distillery and requested to be paid. The owner did not utter a word, but handed him fifteen sous. He objected. He was told, "That is enough for thee." He persisted. The master looked him straight between the eyes, and said to him, "Beware of the prison."

There, again, he considered that he had been robbed.

Society, the State, by diminishing his hoard, had robbed him wholesale. Now it was the individual who was robbing him at retail.

Liberation is not deliverance. One gets free from the galleys, but not from the sentence.

That is what happened to him at Grasse. We have seen in what manner he was received at D———.

CHAPTER X—THE MAN AROUSED

As the Cathedral clock struck two in the morning, Jean Valjean awoke. What woke him was that his bed was too good. It was nearly twenty years since he had slept in a bed, and, although he had not undressed, the sensation was too novel not to disturb his slumbers.

He had slept more than four hours. His fatigue had passed away. He was accustomed not to devote many hours to repose.

He opened his eyes and stared into the gloom that surrounded him; then he closed them again, with the intention of going to sleep once more.

When many varied sensations have agitated the day, when various matters preoccupy the mind, one falls asleep once, but not a second time. Sleep comes more easily than it returns. This is what happened to Jean Valjean. He could not get to sleep again, and he fell to thinking.

He was at one of those moments when the thoughts which one has in one's mind are troubled. There was a sort of dark confusion in his brain. His memories of the olden time and of the immediate present floated there pell-mell and mingled confusedly, losing their proper forms, becoming disproportionately large, then suddenly disappearing, as in a muddy and perturbed pool. Many thoughts occurred to him; but there was one that kept constantly presenting itself afresh, and that drove away all others. We will mention this thought at once: he had observed the six sets of silver forks and spoons and the ladle which Madame Magloire had placed on the table.

Those six sets of silver haunted him. They were there, a few paces distant. Just as he was traversing the adjoining room to reach the one in which he then was, the old servant-woman had been in the act of placing them in a little cupboard near the head of the bed. He had taken careful note of this cupboard: on the right, as you entered from the dining room. They were solid; and old silver. From the ladle one could get at least two hundred francs, double what he had earned in nineteen years. It is true that he would have earned more if "the administration had not robbed him."

His mind wavered for a whole hour in fluctuations with which there was certainly mingled some struggle. Three o'clock struck. He opened his eyes again, drew himself up abruptly into a sitting posture, stretched out his arm and felt of his knapsack, which he had thrown down on a corner of the alcove; then he hung his legs over the edge of the bed, and placed his feet on the floor, and thus found himself, almost without knowing it, seated on his bed.

He remained for a time thoughtfully in this attitude, which would have been suggestive of something sinister for anyone who had seen him thus in the dark, the only person awake in that house where all were sleeping. All of a sudden he stooped down, removed his shoes and placed them softly on the mat beside the bed; then he resumed his thoughtful attitude, and became motionless once more.

Throughout this hideous meditation, the thoughts that we have above indicated moved incessantly through his brain; entered, withdrew, re-entered, and in a manner oppressed him; and then he thought, also, without knowing why, and with the mechanical persistence of reverie, of a convict named Brevet, whom he had known in the galleys, and whose trousers had been upheld by a single suspender of knitted cotton. The checkered pattern of that suspender recurred incessantly to his mind.

He remained in this situation, and would have so remained indefinitely, even until daybreak, had not the clock struck one—the half or quarter hour. It seemed to him that that stroke said to him, "Come on!"

He rose to his feet, hesitated still another moment, and listened; all was quiet in the house; then he walked straight ahead, with short steps, to the window, of which he caught a glimpse. The night was not very dark; there was a full moon, across which coursed large clouds driven by the wind. This created, outdoors, alternate shadow and gleams of light, eclipses, then bright openings of the clouds; and indoors a sort of twilight. This twilight, sufficient to enable a person to see his way, intermittent on account of the clouds, resembled the sort of livid light that falls through an airhole in a cellar, before which the passersby come and go. On arriving at the window, Jean Valjean examined it. It had no grating; it opened in the garden and was fastened, according to the fashion of the country, only by a small pin. He opened it; but as a rush of cold and piercing air penetrated the room abruptly, he closed it again immediately. He scrutinized the garden with that attentive gaze, which studies rather than looks. The garden was enclosed by a tolerably low white wall, easy to climb. Far away, at the extremity, he perceived tops of trees, spaced at regular intervals, which indicated that the wall separated the garden from an avenue or lane planted with trees.

Having taken this survey, he executed a movement like that of a man who has made up his mind, strode to his alcove, grasped his knapsack, opened it, fumbled in it, pulled out of it something, which he placed on the bed, put his shoes into one of his pockets, shut the whole thing up again, threw the knapsack on his shoulders, put on his cap, drew the visor down over his eyes, felt for his cudgel, went and placed it in the angle of the window; then returned to the bed, and resolutely seized the object which he had deposited there. It resembled a short bar of iron, pointed like a pike at one end. It would have been difficult to distinguish in that darkness for what employment that bit of iron could have been designed. Perhaps it was a lever; possibly it was a club.

In the daytime it would have been possible to recognize it as nothing more than a miner's candlestick. Convicts were, at that period, sometimes employed in quarrying stone from the lofty hills that environ Toulon, and it was not rare for them to have miners' tools at their command. These miners' candlesticks are of massive iron, terminated at the lower extremity by a point, by means of which they are stuck into the rock.

He took the candlestick in his right hand; holding his breath and trying to deaden the sound of his tread, he directed his steps to the door of the adjoining room, occupied by the Bishop, as we already know.

On arriving at this door, he found it ajar. The Bishop had not closed it.

CHAPTER XI—WHAT HE DOES

Jean Valjean listened. Not a sound.

He gave the door a push.

He pushed it gently with the tip of his finger, lightly, with the furtive and uneasy gentleness of a cat which is desirous of entering.

The door yielded to this pressure, and made an imperceptible and silent movement, which enlarged the opening a little.

He waited a moment; then gave the door a second and a bolder push.

It continued to yield in silence. The opening was now large enough to allow him to pass. But near the door there stood a little table, which formed an embarrassing angle with it, and barred the entrance.

Jean Valjean recognized the difficulty. It was necessary, at any cost, to enlarge the aperture still further.

He decided on his course of action, and gave the door a third push, more energetic than the two preceding. This time a badly oiled hinge suddenly emitted amid the silence a hoarse and prolonged cry.

Jean Valjean shuddered. The noise of the hinge rang in his ears with something of the piercing and formidable sound of the trump of the Day of Judgment.

In the fantastic exaggerations of the first moment he almost imagined that that hinge had just become animated, and had suddenly assumed a terrible life, and that it was barking like a dog to arouse everyone, and warn and to wake those who were asleep. He halted, shuddering, bewildered, and fell back from the tips of his toes upon his heels. He heard the arteries in his temples beating like two forge hammers, and it seemed to him that his breath issued from his breast with the roar of the wind issuing from a cavern. It seemed impossible to him that the horrible clamor of that irritated hinge should not have disturbed the entire household, like the shock of an earthquake; the door, pushed by him, had taken the alarm, and had shouted; the old man would rise at once; the two old women would shriek out; people would come to their assistance; in less than a quarter of an hour the town would be in an uproar, and the gendarmerie on hand. For a moment he thought himself lost.

He remained where he was, petrified like the statue of salt, not daring to make a movement. Several minutes elapsed. The door had fallen wide open. He ventured to peep into the next room. Nothing had stirred there. He lent an ear. Nothing was moving in the house. The noise made by the rusty hinge had not awakened anyone.

This first danger was past; but there still reigned a frightful tumult within him. Nevertheless, he did not retreat. Even when he had thought himself lost, he had not drawn back. His only thought now was to finish as soon as possible. He took a step and entered the room.

This room was in a state of perfect calm. Here and there vague and confused forms were distinguishable, which in the daylight were papers scattered on a table, open folios, volumes piled upon a stool, an armchair heaped with clothing, a prie-dieu, and which at that hour were only shadowy corners and whitish spots. Jean Valjean advanced with precaution, taking care not to knock against the furniture. He could hear, at the extremity of the room, the even and tranquil breathing of the sleeping Bishop.

He suddenly came to a halt. He was near the bed. He had arrived there sooner than he had thought for.

Nature sometimes mingles her effects and her spectacles with our actions with somber and intelligent appropriateness, as though she desired to make us reflect. For the last half-hour a large cloud had covered the heavens. At the moment when Jean Valjean paused in front of the bed, this cloud parted, as though on purpose, and a ray of light, traversing the long window, suddenly illuminated the Bishop's pale face. He was sleeping peacefully. He lay in his bed almost completely dressed, on account of the cold of the Basses-Alps, in a garment of brown wool, which covered his arms to the wrists. His head was thrown back on the pillow, in the careless attitude of repose; his hand, adorned with the pastoral ring, and from which had fallen so many good deeds and so many holy actions, was hanging over the edge of the bed. His whole face was illumined with a vague expression of satisfaction, of hope, and of felicity. It was more than a smile, and almost a radiance. He bore upon his brow the indescribable reflection of a light that was invisible. The soul of the just contemplates in sleep a mysterious heaven.

A reflection of that heaven rested on the Bishop.

It was, at the same time, a luminous transparency, for that heaven was within him. That heaven was his conscience.

At the moment when the ray of moonlight superposed itself, so to speak, upon that inward radiance, the sleeping Bishop seemed as in a glory. It remained, however, gentle and veiled in an ineffable half-light. That moon in the sky, that slumbering nature, that garden without a quiver, that house which was so calm, the hour, the moment, the silence, added some solemn and unspeakable quality to the venerable repose of this man, and enveloped in a sort of serene and majestic aureole that white hair, those closed eyes, that face in which all was hope and all was confidence, that head of an old man, and that slumber of an infant.

There was something almost divine in this man, who was thus august, without being himself aware of it.

Jean Valjean was in the shadow, and stood motionless, with his iron candlestick in his hand, frightened by this luminous old man. Never had he beheld anything like this. This confidence terrified him. The moral world has no grander spectacle than this: a troubled and uneasy conscience, which has arrived on the brink of an evil action, contemplating the slumber of the just.

That slumber in that isolation, and with a neighbor like himself, had about it something sublime, of which he was vaguely but imperiously conscious.

No one could have told what was passing within him, not even himself. In order to attempt to form an idea of it, it is necessary to think of the most violent of things in the presence of the most gentle. Even on his visage it would have been impossible to distinguish anything with certainty. It was a sort of haggard astonishment. He gazed at it, and that was all. But what was his thought? It would have been impossible to divine it. What was evident was, that he was touched and astounded. But what was the nature of this emotion?

His eye never quitted the old man. The only thing that was clearly to be inferred from his attitude and his physiognomy was a strange indecision. One would have said that he was hesitating between the two abysses, the one in which one loses one's self and that in which one saves one's self. He seemed prepared to crush that skull or to kiss that hand.

At the expiration of a few minutes his left arm rose slowly toward his brow, and he took off his cap; then his arm fell back with the same deliberation, and Jean Valjean fell to meditating once more, his cap in his left hand, his club in his right hand, his hair bristling all over his savage head.

The Bishop continued to sleep in profound peace beneath that terrifying gaze.

The gleam of the moon rendered confusedly visible the crucifix over the chimneypiece, which seemed to be extending its arms to both of them, with a benediction for one and pardon for the other.

Suddenly Jean Valjean replaced his cap on his brow; then stepped rapidly past the bed, without glancing at the Bishop, straight to the cupboard, which he saw near the head; he raised his iron candlestick as though to force the lock; the key was there; he opened it; the first thing that presented itself to him was the basket of silverware; he seized it, traversed the chamber with long strides, without taking any precautions and without troubling himself about the noise, gained the door, reentered the oratory, opened the window, seized his cudgel, bestrode the windowsill of the ground floor, put the silver into his knapsack, threw away the basket, crossed the garden, leaped over the wall like a tiger, and fled.

CHAPTER XII—THE BISHOP WORKS

The next morning at sunrise Monseigneur Bienvenu was strolling in his garden. Madame Magloire ran up to him in utter consternation.

"Monseigneur, Monseigneur!" she exclaimed. "Does your Grace know where the basket of silver is?"

"Yes," replied the Bishop.

"Jesus the Lord be blessed!" she resumed; "I did not know what had become of it."

The Bishop had just picked up the basket in a flower bed. He presented it to Madame Magloire.

"Here it is."

"Well!" said she. "Nothing in it! And the silver?"

"Ah," returned the Bishop, "so it is the silver which troubles you? I don't know where it is."

"Great, good God! It is stolen! That man who was here last night has stolen it."

In a twinkling, with all the vivacity of an alert old woman, Madame Magloire had rushed to the oratory, entered the alcove, and returned to the Bishop. The Bishop had just bent down, and was sighing as he examined a plant of cochlearia des Guillons, which the basket had broken as it fell across the bed. He rose up at Madame Magloire's cry.

"Monseigneur, the man is gone! The silver has been stolen!"

As she uttered this exclamation, her eyes fell upon a corner of the garden, where traces of the wall having been scaled were visible. The coping of the wall had been torn away.

"Stay! Yonder is the way he went. He jumped over into Cochefilet Lane. Ah, the abomination! He has stolen our silver!"

The Bishop remained silent for a moment; then he raised his grave eyes, and said gently to Madame Magloire, "And, in the first place, was that silver ours?"

Madame Magloire was speechless. Another silence ensued; then the Bishop went on, "Madame Magloire, I have for a long time detained that silver wrongfully. It belonged to the poor. Who was that man? A poor man, evidently."

"Alas! Jesus!" returned Madame Magloire. "It is not for my sake, nor for Mademoiselle's. It makes no difference to us. But it is for the sake of Monseigneur. What is Monseigneur to eat with now?"

The Bishop gazed at her with an air of amazement.

"Ah, come! Are there no such things as pewter forks and spoons?"

Madame Magloire shrugged her shoulders.

"Pewter has an odor."

"Iron forks and spoons, then."

Madame Magloire made an expressive grimace.

"Iron has a taste."

"Very well," said the Bishop; "wooden ones then."

A few moments later he was breakfasting at the very table at which Jean Valjean had sat on the previous evening. As he ate his breakfast, Monseigneur Welcome remarked gaily to his sister, who said nothing, and to Madame Magloire, who was grumbling under her breath, that one really does not need either fork or spoon, even of wood, in order to dip a bit of bread in a cup of milk.

"A pretty idea, truly," said Madame Magloire to herself, as she went and came, "to take in a man like that! and to lodge him close to one's self! And how fortunate that he did nothing but steal! Ah, *mon Dieu*! it makes one shudder to think of it!"

As the brother and sister were about to rise from the table, there came a knock at the door.

"Come in," said the Bishop.

The door opened. A singular and violent group made its appearance on the threshold. Three men were holding a fourth man by the collar. The three men were gendarmes; the other was Jean Valjean.

A brigadier of gendarmes, who seemed to be in command of the group, was standing near the door. He entered and advanced to the Bishop, making a military salute.

"Monseigneur—" said he.

At this word, Jean Valjean, who was dejected and seemed overwhelmed, raised his head with an air of stupefaction.

"Monseigneur!" he murmured. "So he is not the Curé?"

"Silence!" said the gendarme. "He is Monseigneur the Bishop."

In the meantime, Monseigneur Bienvenu had advanced as quickly as his great age permitted.

"Ah! Here you are!" he exclaimed, looking at Jean Valjean. "I am glad to see you. Well, but how is this? I gave you the candlesticks too, which are of silver like the rest, and for which you can certainly get two hundred francs. Why did you not carry them away with your forks and spoons?"

Jean Valjean opened his eyes wide, and stared at the venerable Bishop with an expression that no human tongue can render any account of.

"Monseigneur," said the brigadier of gendarmes, "so what this man said is true, then? We came across him. He was walking like a man who is running away. We stopped him to look into the matter. He had this silver—"

"And he told you," interposed the Bishop with a smile, "that it had been given to him by a kind old fellow of a priest with whom he had passed the night? I see how the matter stands. And you have brought him back here? It is a mistake."

"In that case," replied the brigadier, "we can let him go?"

"Certainly," replied the Bishop.

The gendarmes released Jean Valjean, who recoiled.

"Is it true that I am to be released?" he said, in an almost inarticulate voice, and as though he were talking in his sleep.

"Yes, thou art released; dost thou not understand?" said one of the gendarmes.

"My friend," resumed the Bishop, "before you go, here are your candlesticks. Take them."

He stepped to the chimneypiece, took the two silver candlesticks, and brought them to Jean Valjean. The two women looked on without uttering a word, without a gesture, without a look that could disconcert the Bishop.

Jean Valjean was trembling in every limb. He took the two candlesticks mechanically, and with a bewildered air.

"Now," said the Bishop, "go in peace. By the way, when you return, my friend, it is not necessary to pass through the garden. You can always enter and depart through the street door. It is never fastened with anything but a latch, either by day or by night."

Then, turning to the gendarmes, "You may retire, gentlemen."

The gendarmes retired.

Jean Valjean was like a man on the point of fainting.

The Bishop drew near to him, and said in a low voice, "Do not forget, never forget, that you have promised to use this money in becoming an honest man."

Jean Valjean, who had no recollection of ever having promised anything, remained speechless. The Bishop had emphasized the words when he uttered them. He resumed with solemnity, "Jean Valjean, my brother, you no longer belong to evil, but to good. It is your soul that I buy from you; I withdraw it from black thoughts and the spirit of perdition, and I give it to God."

CHAPTER XIII—LITTLE GERVAIS

Jean Valjean left the town as though he were fleeing from it. He set out at a very hasty pace through the fields, taking whatever roads and paths presented themselves to him, without perceiving that he was incessantly retracing his steps. He wandered thus the whole morning, without having eaten anything and without feeling hungry. He was the prey of a throng of novel sensations. He was conscious of a sort of rage; he did not know against whom it was directed. He could not have told whether he was touched or humiliated. There came over him at moments a strange emotion, which he resisted and to which he opposed the hardness acquired during the last twenty years of his life. This state of mind fatigued him. He perceived with dismay that the sort of frightful calm, which the injustice of his misfortune had conferred upon him, was giving way within him. He asked himself what would replace this. At times he would have actually preferred to be in prison with the gendarmes, and that things should not have happened in this way; it would have agitated him less. Although the season was tolerably far advanced, there were still a few late flowers in the hedgerows here and there, whose odor as he passed through them in his march recalled to him memories of his childhood. These memories were almost intolerable to him, it was so long since they had recurred to him.

Unutterable thoughts assembled within him in this manner all day long.

As the sun declined to its setting, casting long shadows athwart the soil from every pebble, Jean Valjean sat down behind a bush upon a large ruddy plain, which was absolutely deserted. There was nothing on the horizon except the Alps. Not even the spire of a distant village. Jean Valjean might have been three leagues distant from D———. A path that intersected the plain passed a few paces from the bush.

In the middle of this meditation, which would have contributed not a little to render his rags terrifying to anyone who might have encountered him, a joyous sound became audible.

He turned his head and saw a little Savoyard, about ten years of age, coming up the path and singing, his hurdy-gurdy on his hip, and his marmot box on his back.

One of those gay and gentle children, who go from land to land affording a view of their knees through the holes in their trousers.

Without stopping his song, the lad halted in his march from time to time, and played at knuckle-bones with some coins which he had in his hand—his whole fortune, probably.

Among this money there was one forty-sou piece.

The child halted beside the bush, without perceiving Jean Valjean, and tossed up his handful of sous, which, up to that time, he had caught with a good deal of adroitness on the back of his hand.

This time the forty-sou piece escaped him, and went rolling toward the brushwood until it reached Jean Valjean.

Jean Valjean set his foot upon it.

In the meantime, the child had looked after his coin and had caught sight of him.

He showed no astonishment, but walked straight up to the man.

The spot was absolutely solitary. As far as the eye could see there was not a person on the plain or on the path. The only sound was the tiny, feeble cries of a flock of birds of passage, which was traversing the heavens at an immense height. The child was standing with his back to the sun, which cast threads of gold in his hair and empurpled with its blood-red gleam the savage face of Jean Valjean.

"Sir," said the little Savoyard, with that childish confidence, which is composed of ignorance and innocence, "my money."

"What is your name?" said Jean Valjean.

"Little Gervais, sir."

"Go away," said Jean Valjean.

"Sir," resumed the child, "give me back my money."

Jean Valjean dropped his head, and made no reply.

The child began again, "My money, sir."

Jean Valjean's eyes remained fixed on the earth.

"My piece of money!" cried the child. "My white piece! My silver!"

It seemed as though Jean Valjean did not hear him. The child grasped him by the collar of his blouse and shook him. At the same time he made an effort to displace the big iron-shod shoe that rested on his treasure.

"I want my piece of money! My piece of forty sous!"

The child wept. Jean Valjean raised his head. He still remained seated. His eyes were troubled. He gazed at the child, in a sort of amazement, then he stretched out his hand toward his cudgel and cried in a terrible voice, "Who's there?"

"I, sir," replied the child. "Little Gervais! I! Give me back my forty sous, if you please! Take your foot away, sir, if you please!"

Then irritated, though he was so small, and becoming almost menacing, "Come now, will you take your foot away? Take your foot away, or we'll see!"

"Ah! It's still you!" said Jean Valjean, and rising abruptly to his feet, his foot still resting on the silver piece, he added, "Will you take yourself off!"

The frightened child looked at him, then began to tremble from head to foot, and after a few moments of stupor he set out, running at the top of his speed, without daring to turn his neck or to utter a cry.

Nevertheless, lack of breath forced him to halt after a certain distance, and Jean Valjean heard him sobbing, in the midst of his own reverie.

At the end of a few moments the child had disappeared.

The sun had set.

The shadows were descending around Jean Valjean. He had eaten nothing all day; it is probable that he was feverish.

He had remained standing and had not changed his attitude after the child's flight. The breath heaved his chest at long and irregular intervals. His gaze, fixed ten or twelve paces in front of him, seemed to be scrutinizing with profound attention the shape of an ancient fragment of blue earthenware that had fallen in the grass. All at once he shivered; he had just begun to feel the chill of evening.

He settled his cap more firmly on his brow, sought mechanically to cross and button his blouse, advanced a step, and stopped to pick up his cudgel.

At that moment he caught sight of the forty-sou piece, which his foot had half ground into the earth, and which was shining among the pebbles. It was as though he had received a galvanic shock. "What is this?" he muttered between his teeth. He recoiled three paces, then halted, without being able to detach his gaze from the spot where his foot had trodden but an instant before, as though the thing that lay glittering there in the gloom had been an open eye riveted upon him.

At the expiration of a few moments he darted convulsively toward the silver coin, seized it, and straightened himself up again and began to gaze afar off over the plain, at the same time casting his eyes toward all points of the horizon, as he stood there erect and shivering, like a terrified wild animal which is seeking refuge.

He saw nothing. Night was falling, the plain was cold and vague, great banks of violet haze were rising in the gleam of the twilight.

He said, "Ah!" and set out rapidly in the direction in which the child had disappeared. After about thirty paces he paused, looked about him, and saw nothing.

Then he shouted with all his might, "Little Gervais! Little Gervais!"

He paused and waited.

There was no reply.

The landscape was gloomy and deserted. He was encompassed by space. There was nothing around him but an obscurity in which his gaze was lost, and a silence that engulfed his voice.

An icy north wind was blowing, and imparted to things around him a sort of lugubrious life. The bushes shook their thin little arms with incredible fury. One would have said that they were threatening and pursuing someone.

He set out on his march again, then he began to run; and from time to time he halted and shouted into that solitude, with a voice that was the most formidable and the most disconsolate that it was possible to hear, "Little Gervais! Little Gervais!"

Assuredly, if the child had heard him, he would have been alarmed and would have taken good care not to show himself. But the child was no doubt already far away.

He encountered a priest on horseback. He stepped up to him and said, "Monsieur le Curé, have you seen a child pass?"

"No," said the priest.

"One named Little Gervais?"

"I have seen no one."

He drew two five-franc pieces from his moneybag and handed them to the priest.

"Monsieur le Curé, this is for your poor people. Monsieur le Curé, he was a little lad, about ten years old, with a marmot, I think, and a hurdy-gurdy. One of those Savoyards, you know?"

"I have not seen him."

"Little Gervais? There are no villages here? Can you tell me?"

"If he is like what you say, my friend, he is a little stranger. Such persons pass through these parts. We know nothing of them."

Jean Valjean seized two more coins of five francs each with violence, and gave them to the priest.

"For your poor," he said.

Then he added, wildly, "Monsieur l'Abbé, have me arrested. I am a thief."

The priest put spurs to his horse and fled in haste, much alarmed.

Jean Valjean set out on a run, in the direction which he had first taken.

In this way he traversed a tolerably long distance, gazing, calling, shouting, but he met no one. Two or three times he ran across the plain toward something that conveyed to him the effect of a human being reclining or crouching down; it turned out to be nothing but brushwood or rocks nearly on a level with the earth. At length, at a spot where three paths intersected each other, he stopped. The moon had risen. He sent his gaze into the distance and shouted for the last time, "Little Gervais! Little Gervais! Little Gervais!" His shout died away in the mist, without even awakening an echo. He murmured yet once more, "Little Gervais!" but in a feeble and almost inarticulate voice. It was his last effort; his legs gave way abruptly under him, as though an invisible power had suddenly overwhelmed him with the weight of his evil conscience; he fell exhausted, on a large stone, his fists clenched in his hair and his face on his knees, and he cried, "I am a wretch!"

Then his heart burst, and he began to cry. It was the first time that he had wept in nineteen years.

When Jean Valjean left the Bishop's house, he was, as we have seen, quite thrown out of everything that had been his thought hitherto. He could not yield to the evidence of what was going on within him. He hardened himself against the angelic action and the gentle words of the old man. "You have promised me to become an honest man. I buy your soul. I take it away from the spirit of perversity; I give it to the good God."

This recurred to his mind unceasingly. To this celestial kindness he opposed pride, which is the fortress of evil within us. He was indistinctly conscious that the pardon of this priest was the greatest assault and the most formidable attack that had moved him yet; that his obduracy was finally settled if he resisted this clemency; that if he yielded, he should be obliged to renounce that hatred with which the actions of other men had filled his soul through so many years, and which pleased him; that this time it was necessary to conquer or to be conquered; and that a struggle, a colossal and final struggle, had been begun between his viciousness and the goodness of that man.

In the presence of these lights, he proceeded like a man who is intoxicated. As he walked thus with haggard eyes, did he have a distinct perception of what might result to him from his adventure at D——? Did he understand all those mysterious murmurs that warn or importune the spirit at certain moments of life? Did a voice whisper in his ear that he had just passed the solemn hour of his destiny; that there no longer remained a middle course for him; that if he were not henceforth the best of men, he would be the worst; that it behooved him now, so to speak, to mount higher than the Bishop, or fall lower than the convict; that if he wished to become good be must become an angel; that if he wished to remain evil, he must become a monster?

Here, again, some questions must be put, which we have already put to ourselves elsewhere: did he catch some shadow of all this in his thought, in a confused way? Misfortune certainly, as we have said, does form the education of the intelligence; nevertheless, it is doubtful whether Jean Valjean was in a condition to disentangle all that we have here indicated. If these ideas occurred to him, he but caught glimpses of, rather than saw them, and they only succeeded in throwing him into an unutterable and almost painful state of emotion. On emerging from that black and deformed thing that is called the galleys, the Bishop had hurt his soul, as too vivid a light would have hurt his eyes on emerging from the dark. The future life, the possible life that offered itself to him henceforth, all pure and radiant, filled him with tremors and anxiety. He no longer knew where he really was. Like an owl, who should suddenly see the sun rise, the convict had been dazzled and blinded, as it were, by virtue.

That which was certain, that which he did not doubt, was that he was no longer the same man, that everything about him was changed, that it was no longer in his power to make it as though the Bishop had not spoken to him and had not touched him.

In this state of mind he had encountered little Gervais, and had robbed him of his forty sous. Why? He certainly could not have explained it; was this the last effect and the supreme effort, as it were, of the evil thoughts that he had brought away from the galleys, a remnant of impulse, a result of what is called in statics, acquired force? It was that, and it was also, perhaps, even less than that. Let us say it simply, it was not he who stole; it was not the man; it was the beast, who, by habit and instinct, had simply placed his foot upon that money, while the intelligence was struggling amid so many novel and hitherto unheard-of thoughts besetting it.

When intelligence reawakened and beheld that action of the brute, Jean Valjean recoiled with anguish and uttered a cry of terror.

It was because—strange phenomenon, and one which was possible only in the situation in which he found himself—in stealing the money from that child, he had done a thing of which he was no longer capable.

However that may be, this last evil action had a decisive effect on him; it abruptly traversed that chaos, which he bore in his mind, and dispersed it, placed on one side the thick obscurity, and on the other the light, and acted on his soul, in the state in which it then was, as certain chemical reagents act upon a troubled mixture by precipitating one element and clarifying the other.

First of all, even before examining himself and reflecting, all bewildered, like one who seeks to save himself, he tried to find the child in order to return his money to him; then, when he recognized the fact that this was impossible, he halted in despair. At the moment when he exclaimed, "I am a wretch!" he had just perceived what he was, and he was already separated from himself to such a degree, that he seemed to himself to be no longer anything more than a phantom, and as if he had, there before him, in flesh and blood, the hideous galley convict, Jean Valjean, cudgel in hand, his blouse on his hips, his knapsack filled with stolen objects on his back, with his resolute and gloomy visage, with his thoughts filled with abominable projects.

Excess of unhappiness had, as we have remarked, made him in some sort a visionary. This, then, was in the nature of a vision. He actually saw that Jean Valjean, that sinister face, before him. He had almost reached the point of asking himself who that man was, and he was horrified by him.

His brain was going through one of those violent and yet perfectly calm moments in which reverie is so profound that it absorbs reality. One no longer beholds the object that one has before one, and one sees, as though apart from one's self, the figures that one has in one's own mind.

Thus he contemplated himself, so to speak, face-to-face, and at the same time, athwart this hallucination, he perceived in a mysterious depth a sort of light, which he at first took for a torch. On scrutinizing this light, which appeared to his conscience with more attention, he recognized the fact that it possessed a human form and that this torch was the Bishop.

His conscience weighed in turn these two men thus placed before it—the Bishop and Jean Valjean. Nothing less than the first was required to soften the second. By one of those singular effects, which are peculiar to this sort of ecstasies, in proportion as his reverie continued, as the Bishop grew great and resplendent in his eyes, so did Jean Valjean grow less and vanish. After a certain time he was no longer anything more than a shade. All at once he disappeared. The Bishop alone remained; he filled the whole soul of this wretched man with a magnificent radiance.

Jean Valjean wept for a long time. He wept burning tears, he sobbed with more weakness than a woman, with more fright than a child.

As he wept, daylight penetrated more and more clearly into his soul; an extraordinary light; a light at once ravishing and terrible. His past life, his first fault, his long expiation, his external brutishness, his internal hardness, his dismissal to liberty, rejoicing in manifold plans of vengeance, what had happened to him at the Bishop's, the last thing that he had done, that theft of forty sous from a child, a crime all the more cowardly, and all the more monstrous since it had come after the Bishop's pardon—all this recurred to his mind and appeared clearly to him, but with a clearness that he had never hitherto witnessed. He examined his life, and it seemed horrible to him; his soul, and it seemed frightful to him. In the meantime a gentle light rested over this life and this soul. It seemed to him that he beheld Satan by the light of Paradise.

How many hours did he weep thus? What did he do after he had wept? Where did he go! No one ever knew. The only thing that seems to be authenticated is that that same night the carrier who served Grenoble at that epoch, and who arrived at D—— about three o'clock in the morning, saw, as he traversed the street in which the Bishop's residence was situated, a man in the attitude of prayer, kneeling on the pavement in the shadow, in front of the door of Monseigneur Welcome.

BOOK THIRD: IN THE YEAR 1817

CHAPTER I—THE YEAR 1817

1817 is the year that Louis XVIII, with a certain royal assurance that was not wanting in pride, entitled the twenty-second of his reign. It is the year in which M. Bruguiere de Sorsum was celebrated. All the hairdressers' shops, hoping for powder and the return of the royal bird, were besmeared with azure and decked with fleurs-de-lis. It was the candid time at which Count Lynch sat every Sunday as church warden in the church warden's pew of Saint-Germain-des-Pres, in his costume of a peer of France, with his red ribbon and his long nose and the majesty of profile peculiar to a man who has performed a brilliant action. The brilliant action performed by M. Lynch was this: being mayor of Bordeaux, on the 12th of March, 1814, he had surrendered the city a little too promptly to M. the Duke d'Angoulême. Hence his peerage. In 1817 fashion swallowed up little boys of from four to six years of age in vast caps of morocco leather with eartabs resembling Esquimaux miters. The French army was dressed in white, after the mode of the Austrian; the regiments were called legions; instead of numbers they bore the names of departments; Napoleon was at St. Helena; and since England refused him green cloth, he was having his old coats turned. In 1817 Pelligrini sang; Mademoiselle Bigottini danced; Potier reigned; Odry did not yet exist. Madame Saqui had succeeded to Forioso. There were still Prussians in France. M. Delalot was a personage. Legitimacy had just asserted itself by cutting off the hand, then the head, of Pleignier, of Carbonneau, and of Tolleron. The Prince de Talleyrand, grand chamberlain, and the Abbé Louis, appointed minister of finance, laughed as they looked at each other, with the laugh of the two augurs; both of them had celebrated, on the 14th of July, 1790, the mass of federation in the Champ de Mars; Talleyrand had said it as bishop, Louis had served it in the capacity of deacon. In 1817, in the side alleys of this same Champ de Mars, two great cylinders of wood might have been seen lying in the rain, rotting amid the grass, painted blue, with traces of eagles and bees, from which the gilding was falling. These were the columns, which two years before had upheld the Emperor's platform in the Champ de Mai. They were blackened here and there with the scorches of the bivouac of Austrians encamped near Gros-Caillou. Two or three of these columns had disappeared in these bivouac fires, and had warmed the large hands of the Imperial troops. The Field of May had this remarkable point: that it had been held in the month of June and in the Field of March. In this year, 1817, two things were popular: the Voltaire-Touquet and the snuffbox a la Charter. The most recent Parisian sensation was the crime of Dautun, who had thrown his brother's head into the fountain of the Flower Market.

They had begun to feel anxious at the Naval Department, on account of the lack of news from that fatal frigate, the *Medusa*, which was destined to cover Chaumareix with infamy and Gericault with glory. Colonel Selves was going to Egypt to become Soliman-Pasha. The palace of Thermes, in the Rue de La Harpe, served as a shop for a cooper. On the platform of the octagonal tower of the Hotel de Cluny, the little shed of boards, which had served as an observatory to Messier, the naval astronomer under Louis XVI, was still to be seen. The Duchesse de Duras read to three or four friends her unpublished Ourika, in her boudoir furnished by X in sky-blue satin. The N's were scratched off the Louvre. The bridge of Austerlitz had abdicated, and was entitled the bridge of the King's Garden, a double enigma, which disguised the bridge of Austerlitz and the Jardin des Plantes at one stroke. Louis XVIII, much preoccupied while annotating Horace with the corner of his fingernail, heroes who have become emperors, and makers of wooden shoes who have become dauphins, had two anxieties—Napoleon and Mathurin Bruneau. The French Academy had given for its prize subject, *The Happiness*, procured through Study. M. Bellart was officially eloquent. In his shadow could be seen germinating that future advocate-general of Broe, dedicated to the sarcasms of Paul-Louis Courier. There was a false Chateaubriand, named Marchangy, in the interim, until there should be a false Marchangy, named d'Arlincourt. Claire d'Albe and Malek-Adel were masterpieces; Madame Cottin was proclaimed the chief writer of the epoch. The Institute had the academician, Napoleon Bonaparte, stricken from its list of members. A royal ordinance erected Angoulême into a naval school; for the Duc d'Angoulême, being lord high admiral, it was evident that the city of Angoulême had all the qualities of a seaport; otherwise the monarchical principle would have received a wound. In the Council of Ministers the question was agitated whether vignettes representing slack-rope performances, which adorned Franconi's advertising posters, and which attracted throngs of street urchins, should be tolerated. M. Paer, the author of Agnese, a good sort of fellow, with a square face and a wart on his cheek, directed the little private concerts of the Marquise de Sasenaye in the Rue Ville l'Eveque. All the young girls were singing the Hermit of Saint-Avelle, with words by Edmond Geraud. *The Yellow Dwarf** was transferred into *Mirror*. The Cafe Lemblin stood up for the Emperor, against the Cafe Valois, which upheld the Bourbons. The Duc de Berri, already surveyed from the shadow by Louvel, had just been married to a princess of Sicily. Madame de Stael had died a year previously. The bodyguard hissed Mademoiselle Mars. The grand newspapers were all very small. Their form was restricted, but their liberty was great. The Constitutional was constitutional. La Minerve called Chateaubriand Chateaubriant. That made the good middle-class people laugh heartily at the expense of the great writer. In journals that sold themselves, prostituted journalists, insulted the exiles of 1815. David had no longer any talent, Arnault had no longer any wit, Carnot was no longer honest, Soult had won no battles; it is true that Napoleon had no longer any genius. No one is ignorant of the fact that letters sent to an exile by post very rarely reached him, as the police made it their religious duty to intercept them. This is no new fact; Descartes complained of it in his exile. Now David, having, in a Belgian publication, shown some displeasure at not receiving letters that had been written to him, it struck the royalist journals as amusing; and

---

* A French literary fairy tale

they derided the prescribed man well on this occasion. What separated two men more than an abyss was to say, the regicides, or to say the voters; to say the enemies, or to say the allies; to say Napoleon, or to say Buonaparte. All sensible people were agreed that the era of revolution had been closed forever by King Louis XVIII, surnamed "the Immortal Author of the Charter." On the platform of the Pont-Neuf, the word Redivivus was carved on the pedestal that awaited the statue of Henry IV. M. Piet, in the Rue Therese, No. 4, was making the rough draft of his privy assembly to consolidate the monarchy. The leaders of the Right said at grave conjunctures, "We must write to Bacot." MM. Canuel, O'Mahoney, and De Chappedelaine were preparing the sketch, to some extent with Monsieur's approval, of what was to become later on "The Conspiracy of the Bord de l'Eau"—of the waterside. L'Epingle Noire was already plotting in his own quarter. Delaverderie was conferring with Trogoff. M. Decazes, who was liberal to a degree, reigned. Chateaubriand stood every morning at his window at No. 27 Rue Saint-Dominique, clad in footed trousers, and slippers, with a madras kerchief knotted over his gray hair, with his eyes fixed on a mirror, a complete set of dentist's instruments spread out before him, cleaning his teeth, which were charming, while he dictated the monarchy according to the Charter to M. Pilorge, his secretary. Criticism, assuming an authoritative tone, preferred Lafon to Talma. M. de Feletez signed himself A.; M. Hoffmann signed himself Z. Charles Nodier wrote Therese Aubert. Divorce was abolished. Lyceums called themselves colleges. The collegians, decorated on the collar with a golden fleur-de-lis, fought each other apropos of the King of Rome. The counter-police of the chateau had denounced to her Royal Highness Madame, the portrait, everywhere exhibited, of M. the Duc d'Orleans, who made a better appearance in his uniform of a colonel-general of hussars than M. the Duc de Berri, in his uniform of colonel-general of dragoons—a serious inconvenience. The city of Paris was having the dome of the Invalides regilded at its own expense. Serious men asked themselves what M. de Trinquelague would do on such or such an occasion; M. Clausel de Montals differed on divers points from M. Clausel de Coussergues; M. de Salaberry was not satisfied. The comedian Picard, who belonged to the Academy, which the comedian Moliere had not been able to do, had *The Two Philiberts* played at the Odeon, upon whose pediment the removal of the letters still allowed *Theatre of the Empress* to be plainly read. People took part for or against Cugnet de Montarlot. Fabvier was factious; Bavoux was revolutionary. The Liberal, Pelicier, published an edition of Voltaire, with the following title: *Works of Voltaire, of the French Academy*. "That will attract purchasers," said the ingenious editor. The general opinion was that M. Charles Loyson would be the genius of the century; envy was beginning to gnaw at him—a sign of glory; and this verse was composed on him:

"Even when Loyson steals, one feels that he has paws."

As Cardinal Fesch refused to resign, M. de Pins, Archbishop of Amasie, administered the diocese of Lyons. The quarrel over the valley of Dappes was begun between Switzerland and France by a memoir from Captain, afterward General Dufour. Saint-Simon, ignored, was erecting his sublime dream. There was a celebrated Fourier at the Academy of Science, whom posterity has forgotten; and in some garret an obscure Fourier, whom the future will recall. Lord Byron was beginning to make his mark; a note to a poem by Millevoye introduced him to France in these terms: a certain Lord Baron. David d'Angers was trying to work in marble. The Abbé Caron was speaking, in terms of praise, to a private gathering of seminarists in the blind alley of Feuillantines, of an unknown priest, named Felicite-Robert, who, at a later date, became Lamennais. A thing that smoked and clattered on the Seine with the noise of a swimming dog went and came beneath the windows of the Tuileries, from the Pont Royal to the Pont Louis XV; it was a piece of mechanism which was not good for much; a sort of plaything, the idle dream of a dream-ridden inventor; a utopia—a steamboat. The Parisians stared indifferently at this useless thing. M. de Vaublanc, the reformer of the Institute by a coup d'etat, the distinguished author of numerous academicians, ordinances, and batches of members, after having created them, could not succeed in becoming one himself. The Faubourg Saint-Germain and the pavilion de Marsan wished to have M. Delaveau for prefect of police, on account of his piety. Dupuytren and Recamier entered into a quarrel in the amphitheater of the School of Medicine, and threatened each other with their fists on the subject of the divinity of Jesus Christ. Cuvier, with one eye on Genesis and the other on nature, tried to please bigoted reaction by reconciling fossils with texts and by making mastodons flatter Moses.

M. Francois de Neufchateau, the praiseworthy cultivator of the memory of Parmentier, made a thousand efforts to have *pomme de terre*, pronounced "parmentiere," and succeeded therein not at all. The Abbé Gregoire, ex-bishop, ex-conventionary, ex-senator, had passed, in the royalist polemics, to the state of "Infamous Gregoire." The locution of which we have made use—passed to the state of—has been condemned as a neologism by M. Royer Collard. Under the third arch of the Pont de Jena, the new stone with which, the two years previously, the mining aperture made by Blucher to blow up the bridge had been stopped up, was still recognizable on account of its whiteness. Justice summoned to its bar a man who, on seeing the Comte d'Artois enter Notre Dame, had said aloud, "*Sapristi!*[*] I regret the time when I saw Bonaparte and Talma enter the Bel Sauvage, arm in arm." A seditious utterance. Six months in prison. Traitors showed themselves unbuttoned; men who had gone over to the enemy on the eve of battle made no secret of their recompense, and strutted immodestly in the light of day, in the cynicism of riches and dignities; deserters from Ligny and Quatre-Bras, in the brazenness of their well-paid turpitude, exhibited their devotion to the monarchy in the most barefaced manner.

This is what floats up confusedly, pell-mell, for the year 1817, and is now forgotten. History neglects nearly all these particulars, and cannot do otherwise; the infinity would overwhelm it. Nevertheless, these details, which are wrongly called trivial, there are no trivial facts in humanity, nor little leaves in vegetation, are useful. It is of the physiognomy of the years that the physiognomy of the centuries is composed. In this year of 1817 four young Parisians arranged "a fine farce."

CHAPTER II—A DOUBLE QUARTETTE

These Parisians came, one from Toulouse, another from Limoges, the third from Cahors, and the fourth from Montauban; but they were students; and when one says student, one says Parisian: to study in Paris is to be born in Paris.

These young men were insignificant; everyone has seen such faces; four specimens of humanity taken at random; neither good nor bad, neither wise nor ignorant, neither geniuses nor fools; handsome, with that charming April which is called twenty years. They were four Oscars; for, at that epoch, Arthurs did not yet exist. "Burn for him the perfumes of Araby!" exclaimed romance. Oscar advances. Oscar, I shall behold him! People had just emerged from Ossian; elegance was Scandinavian and Caledonian; the pure English style was only to prevail later, and the first of the Arthurs, Wellington, had but just won the battle of Waterloo.

These Oscars bore the names, one of Felix Tholomyes, of Toulouse; the second, Listolier, of Cahors; the next, Fameuil, of Limoges; the last, Blachevelle, of Montauban. Naturally, each of them had his mistress. Blachevelle loved Favourite, so named because she had been in England; Listolier adored Dahlia, who had taken for her nickname the name of a flower; Fameuil idolized Zephine, an abridgment of Josephine; Tholomyes had

---

[*] Good heavens!

Fantine, called the Blonde, because of her beautiful, sunny hair.

Favourite, Dahlia, Zephine, and Fantine were four ravishing young women, perfumed and radiant, still a little like working-women, and not yet entirely divorced from their needles; somewhat disturbed by intrigues, but still retaining on their faces something of the serenity of toil, and in their souls that flower of honesty, which survives the first fall in woman. One of the four was called the young, because she was the youngest of them, and one was called the old; the old one was twenty-three. Not to conceal anything, the three first were more experienced, more heedless, and more emancipated into the tumult of life than Fantine the Blonde, who was still in her first illusions.

Dahlia, Zephine, and especially Favourite, could not have said as much. There had already been more than one episode in their romance, though hardly begun; and the lover who had borne the name of Adolph in the first chapter had turned out to be Alphonse in the second, and Gustave in the third. Poverty and coquetry are two fatal counselors; one scolds and the other flatters, and the beautiful daughters of the people have both of them whispering in their ear, each on its own side. These badly guarded souls listen. Hence the falls that they accomplish, and the stones that are thrown at them. They are overwhelmed with splendor of all that is immaculate and inaccessible. Alas! What if the Jungfrau were hungry?

Favourite, having been in England, was admired by Dahlia and Zephine. She had had an establishment of her own very early in life. Her father was an old unmarried professor of mathematics, a brutal man and a braggart, who went out to give lessons in spite of his age. This professor, when he was a young man, had one day seen a chambermaid's gown catch on a fender; he had fallen in love in consequence of this accident. The result had been Favourite. She met her father from time to time, and he bowed to her. One morning an old woman with the air of a devotee had entered her apartments, and had said to her, "You do not know me, Mademoiselle?"

"No."

"I am your mother."

Then the old woman opened the sideboard, and ate and drank, had a mattress that she owned brought in, and installed herself. This cross and pious old mother never spoke to Favourite, remained hours without uttering a word, breakfasted, dined, and supped for four, and went down to the porter's quarters for company, where she spoke ill of her daughter.

It was having rosy nails that were too pretty, which had drawn Dahlia to Listolier, to others perhaps, to idleness. How could she make such nails work?

She who wishes to remain virtuous must not have pity on her hands. As for Zephine, she had conquered Fameuil by her roguish and caressing little way of saying "Yes, sir."

The young men were comrades; the young girls were friends. Such loves are always accompanied by such friendships.

Goodness and philosophy are two distinct things; the proof of this is that, after making all due allowances for these little irregular households, Favourite, Zephine, and Dahlia were philosophical young women, while Fantine was a good girl.

Good! Someone will exclaim; and Tholomyes? Solomon would reply that love forms a part of wisdom. We will confine ourselves to saying that the love of Fantine was a first love, a sole love, a faithful love.

She alone, of all the four, was not called "thou" by a single one of them.

Fantine was one of those beings who blossom, so to speak, from the dregs of the people. Though she had emerged from the most unfathomable depths of social shadow, she bore on her brow the sign of the anonymous and the unknown. She was born at M. sur M. Of what parents? Who can say? She had never known father or mother. She was called Fantine. Why Fantine? She had never borne any other name. At the epoch of her birth the Directory still existed. She had no family name; she had no family; no baptismal name; the Church no longer existed. She bore the name that pleased the first random passerby, who had encountered her, when a very small child, running bare-legged in the street. She received the name as she received the water from the clouds upon her brow when it rained. She was called little Fantine. No one knew more than that. This human creature had entered life in just this way. At the age of ten, Fantine quitted the town and went to service with some farmers in the neighborhood. At fifteen she came to Paris "to seek her fortune." Fantine was beautiful, and remained pure as long as she could. She was a lovely blonde, with fine teeth. She had gold and pearls for her dowry; but her gold was on her head, and her pearls were in her mouth.

She worked for her living; then, still for the sake of her living—for the heart, also, has its hunger—she loved.

She loved Tholomyes.

An amour for him; passion for her. The streets of the Latin Quarter, filled with throngs of students and grisettes, saw the beginning of their dream. Fantine had long evaded Tholomyes in the mazes of the hill of the Pantheon, where so many adventurers twine and untwine, but in such a way as constantly to encounter him again. There is a way of avoiding that resembles seeking. In short, the eclogue* took place.

Blachevelle, Listolier, and Fameuil formed a sort of group of which Tholomyes was the head. It was he who possessed the wit.

Tholomyes was the antique old student; he was rich; he had an income of four thousand francs—four thousand francs! A splendid scandal on Mount Sainte-Genevieve. Tholomyes was a fast man of thirty, and badly preserved. He was wrinkled and toothless, and he had the beginning of a bald spot, of which he himself said with sadness, the skull at thirty, the knee at forty. His digestion was mediocre, and he had been attacked by a watering in one eye. But in proportion as his youth disappeared, gaiety was kindled; he replaced his teeth with buffooneries, his hair with mirth, his health with irony, his weeping eye laughed incessantly. He was dilapidated but still in flower. His youth, which was packing up for departure long before its time, beat a retreat in good order, bursting with laughter, and no one saw anything but fire. He had had a piece rejected at the Vaudeville. He made a few verses now and then. In addition to this he doubted everything to the last degree, which is a vast force in the eyes of the weak. Being thus ironical and bald, he was the leader. Iron is an English word. Is it possible that irony is derived from it?

One day Tholomyes took the three others aside, with the gesture of an oracle, and said to them, "Fantine, Dahlia, Zephine, and Favourite have been teasing us for nearly a year to give them a surprise. We have promised them solemnly that we would. They are forever talking about it to us, to me in particular, just as the old women in Naples cry to Saint Januarius, '*Faccia gialluta, fa o miracolo*; yellow face, perform thy miracle,' so our beauties say to me incessantly, 'Tholomyes, when will you bring forth your surprise?' At the same time our parents keep writing to us. Pressure on both sides. The moment has arrived, it seems to me; let us discuss the question."

Thereupon, Tholomyes lowered his voice and articulated something so mirthful, that a vast and enthusiastic grin broke out upon the four mouths simultaneously, and Blachevelle exclaimed, "That is an idea."

A smoky taproom presented itself; they entered, and the remainder of their confidential colloquy was lost in shadow.

The result of these shades was a dazzling pleasure party, which took place on the following Sunday, the four young men inviting the four young girls.

---

* a poem in which shepherds converse

CHAPTER III—FOUR AND FOUR

It is hard nowadays to picture to one's self what a pleasure-trip of students and grisettes to the country was like, forty-five years ago. The suburbs of Paris are no longer the same; the physiognomy of what may be called circumparisian life has changed completely in the last half-century; where there was the cuckoo, there is the railway car; where there was a tender-boat, there is now the steamboat; people speak of Fecamp nowadays as they spoke of Saint-Cloud in those days. The Paris of 1862 is a city which has France for its outskirts.

The four couples conscientiously went through with all the country follies possible at that time. The vacation was beginning, and it was a warm, bright, summer day. On the preceding day, Favourite, the only one who knew how to write, had written the following to Tholomyes in the name of the four: "It is a good hour to emerge from happiness." That is why they rose at five o'clock in the morning. Then they went to Saint-Cloud by the coach, looked at the dry cascade and exclaimed, "This must be very beautiful when there is water!" They breakfasted at the Tete-Noir, where Castaing had not yet been; they treated themselves to a game of ring-throwing under the quincunx of trees of the grand fountain; they ascended Diogenes' lantern, they gambled for macaroons at the roulette establishment of the Pont de Sevres, picked bouquets at Pateaux, bought reed pipes at Neuilly, ate apple tarts everywhere, and were perfectly happy.

The young girls rustled and chatted like warblers escaped from their cage. It was a perfect delirium. From time to time they bestowed little taps on the young men. Matutinal intoxication of life! Adorable years! The wings of the dragonfly quiver. Oh, whoever you may be, do you not remember? Have you rambled through the brushwood, holding aside the branches, on account of the charming head that was coming on behind you? Have you slid, laughing, down a slope all wet with rain, with a beloved woman holding your hand, and crying, "Ah, my new boots! What a state they are in!"

Let us say at once that that merry obstacle, a shower, was lacking in the case of this good-humored party, although Favourite had said as they set out, with a magisterial and maternal tone, "The slugs are crawling in the paths, a sign of rain, children." All four were madly pretty. A good old classic poet, then famous, a good fellow who had an Eleonore, M. le Chevalier de Labouisse, as he strolled that day beneath the chestnut trees of Saint-Cloud, saw them pass about ten o'clock in the morning, and exclaimed, "There is one too many of them," as he thought of the Graces. Favourite, Blachevelle's friend, the one aged three and twenty, the old one, ran on in front under the great green boughs, jumped the ditches, stalked distractedly over bushes, and presided over this merrymaking with the spirit of a young female faun. Zephine and Dahlia, whom chance had made beautiful in such a way that they set each off when they were together, and completed each other, never left each other, more from an instinct of coquetry than from friendship, and clinging to each other, they assumed English poses; the first keepsakes had just made their appearance, melancholy was dawning for women, as later on, Byronism dawned for men; and the hair of the tender sex began to droop dolefully. Zephine and Dahlia had their hair dressed in rolls. Listolier and Fameuil, who were engaged in discussing their professors, explained to Fantine the difference that existed between M. Delvincourt and M. Blondeau.

Blachevelle seemed to have been created expressly to carry Favourite's single-bordered, imitation India shawl of Ternaux's manufacture, on his arm on Sundays.

Tholomyes followed, dominating the group. He was very gay, but one felt the force of government in him; there was dictation in his joviality; his principal ornament was a pair of trousers of elephant-leg pattern of nankeen, with straps of braided copper wire; he carried a stout rattan worth two hundred francs in his hand, and, as he treated himself to everything, a strange thing called a cigar in his mouth. Nothing was sacred to him; he smoked.

"That Tholomyes is astounding!" said the others, with veneration. "What trousers! What energy!"

As for Fantine, she was a joy to behold. Her splendid teeth had evidently received an office from God, laughter. She preferred to carry her little hat of sewed straw, with its long white strings, in her hand rather than on her head. Her thick blonde hair, which was inclined to wave, and which easily uncoiled, and which it was necessary to fasten up incessantly, seemed made for the flight of Galatea under the willows. Her rosy lips babbled enchantingly. The corners of her mouth voluptuously turned up, as in the antique masks of Erigone, had an air of encouraging the audacious; but her long, shadowy lashes drooped discreetly over the jollity of the lower part of the face as though to call a halt. There was something indescribably harmonious and striking about her entire dress. She wore a gown of mauve barege, little reddish brown buskins, whose ribbons traced an X on her fine, white, open-worked stockings, and that sort of muslin spencer, a Marseilles invention, whose name, canezou, a corruption of the words quinze aout, pronounced after the fashion of the Canebiere, signifies fine weather, heat, and midday. The three others, less timid, as we have already said, wore low-necked dresses without disguise, which in summer, beneath flower-adorned hats, are very graceful and enticing; but by the side of these audacious outfits, blonde Fantine's canezou, with its transparencies, its indiscretion, and its reticence, concealing and displaying at one and the same time, seemed an alluring godsend of decency, and the famous Court of Love, presided over by the Vicomtesse de Cette, with the sea-green eyes, would, perhaps, have awarded the prize for coquetry to this canezou, in the contest for the prize of modesty. The most ingenious is, at times, the wisest. This does happen.

Brilliant of face, delicate of profile, with eyes of a deep blue, heavy lids, feet arched and small, wrists and ankles admirably formed, a white skin, which, here and there, allowed the azure branching of the veins to be seen, joy, a cheek that was young and fresh, the robust throat of the Juno of Aegina, a strong and supple nape of the neck, shoulders modeled as though by Coustou, with a voluptuous dimple in the middle, visible through the muslin; a gaiety cooled by dreaminess; sculptural and exquisite—such was Fantine; and beneath these feminine adornments and these ribbons one could divine a statue, and in that statue a soul.

Fantine was beautiful, without being too conscious of it. Those rare dreamers, mysterious priests of the beautiful who silently confront everything with perfection, would have caught a glimpse in this little workingwoman, through the transparency of her Parisian grace, of the ancient sacred euphony. This daughter of the shadows was thoroughbred. She was beautiful in the two ways—style and rhythm. Style is the form of the ideal; rhythm is its movement.

We have said that Fantine was joy; she was also modesty.

To an observer who studied her attentively, that which breathed from her athwart all the intoxication of her age, the season, and her love affair, was an invincible expression of reserve and modesty. She remained a little astonished. This chaste astonishment is the shade of difference that separates Psyche from Venus. Fantine had the long, white, fine fingers of the vestal virgin who stirs the ashes of the sacred fire with a golden pin. Although she would have refused nothing to Tholomyes, as we shall have more than ample opportunity to see, her face in repose was supremely virginal; a sort of serious and almost austere dignity suddenly overwhelmed her at certain times, and there was nothing more singular and disturbing than to see gaiety become so suddenly extinct there, and meditation succeed to cheerfulness without any transition state. This sudden and sometimes severely accentuated gravity resembled the disdain of a goddess. Her brow, her nose, her chin, presented that equilibrium of outline that is quite distinct from equilibrium of proportion, and from which harmony of countenance results; in the very characteristic interval that separates the base of the nose from the upper lip, she had that imperceptible and charming fold, a mysterious sign of chastity, which makes Barberousse fall in love with a Diana found in the treasures of Iconia.

Love is a fault; so be it. Fantine was innocence floating high over fault.

CHAPTER IV—THOLOMYES IS SO MERRY THAT HE SINGS A SPANISH DITTY

That day was composed of dawn, from one end to the other. All nature seemed to be having a holiday, and to be laughing. The flower beds of Saint-Cloud perfumed the air; the breath of the Seine rustled the leaves vaguely; the branches gesticulated in the wind, bees pillaged the jasmines; a whole bohemia of butterflies swooped down upon the yarrow, the clover, and the sterile oats; in the august park of the King of France there was a pack of vagabonds, the birds.

The four merry couples, mingled with the sun, the fields, the flowers, the trees, were resplendent.

And in this community of Paradise, talking, singing, running, dancing, chasing butterflies, plucking convolvulus, wetting their pink, open-work stockings in the tall grass, fresh, wild, without malice, all received, to some extent, the kisses of all, with the exception of Fantine, who was hedged about with that vague resistance of hers composed of dreaminess and wildness, and who was in love. "You always have a queer look about you," said Favourite to her.

Such things are joys. These passages of happy couples are a profound appeal to life and nature, and make a caress and light spring forth from everything. There was once a fairy who created the fields and forests expressly for those in love—in that eternal hedge-school of lovers, which is forever beginning anew, and which will last as long as there are hedges and scholars. Hence the popularity of spring among thinkers. The patrician and the knife-grinder, the duke and the peer, the limb of the law, the courtiers and townspeople, as they used to say in olden times, all are subjects of this fairy. They laugh and hunt, and there is in the air the brilliance of an apotheosis—what a transfiguration effected by love! Notaries' clerks are gods. And the little cries, the pursuits through the grass, the waists embraced on the fly, those jargons that are melodies, those adorations which burst forth in the manner of pronouncing a syllable, those cherries torn from one mouth by another—all this blazes forth and takes its place among the celestial glories. Beautiful women waste themselves sweetly. They think that this will never come to an end. Philosophers, poets, painters, observe these ecstasies and know not what to make of it, so greatly are they dazzled by it. "The departure for Cythera!" exclaims Watteau; Lancret, the painter of plebeians, contemplates his bourgeois, who have flitted away into the azure sky; Diderot stretches out his arms to all these love idylls, and d'Urfe mingles druids with them.

After breakfast the four couples went to what was then called the King's Square to see a newly arrived plant from India, whose name escapes our memory at this moment, and which, at that epoch, was attracting all Paris to Saint-Cloud. It was an odd and charming shrub with a long stem, whose numerous branches, bristling and leafless and as fine as threads, were covered with a million tiny white rosettes; this gave the shrub the air of a head of hair studded with flowers. There was always an admiring crowd about it.

After viewing the shrub, Tholomyes exclaimed, "I offer you asses!" And having agreed upon a price with the owner of the asses, they returned by way of Vanvres and Issy. At Issy an incident occurred. The truly national park, at that time owned by Bourguin the contractor, happened to be wide open. They passed the gates, visited the manikin anchorite in his grotto, tried the mysterious little effects of the famous cabinet of mirrors, the wanton trap worthy of a satyr become a millionaire or of Turcaret metamorphosed into a Priapus. They had stoutly shaken the swing attached to the two chestnut trees celebrated by the Abbé de Bernis. As he swung these beauties, one after the other, producing folds in the fluttering skirts which Greuze would have found to his taste, amid peals of laughter, the Toulousan Tholomyes, who was somewhat of a Spaniard, Toulouse being the cousin of Tolosa, sang, to a melancholy chant, the old ballad gallega, probably inspired by some lovely maid dashing in full flight upon a rope between two trees: "Badajoz is my home, and love is my name. To my eyes in flame, all my soul doth come, for instruction meet I receive at my feet."

Fantine alone refused to swing.

"I don't like to have people put on airs like that," muttered Favourite, with a good deal of acrimony.

After leaving the asses there was a fresh delight; they crossed the Seine in a boat, and proceeding from Passy on foot they reached the barrier of l'Etoile. They had been up since five o'clock that morning, as the reader will remember; but bah! there is no such thing as fatigue on Sunday, said Favourite; on Sunday fatigue does not work.

About three o'clock the four couples, frightened at their happiness, were sliding down the Russian mountains, a singular edifice which then occupied the heights of Beaujon, and whose undulating line was visible above the trees of the Champs Elysees.

From time to time Favourite exclaimed:

"And the surprise? I claim the surprise."

"Patience," replied Tholomyes.

CHAPTER V—AT BOMBARDA'S

The Russian mountains having been exhausted, they began to think about dinner; and the radiant party of eight, somewhat weary at last, became stranded in Bombarda's public house, a branch establishment which had been set up in the Champs-Elysees by that famous restaurant keeper, Bombarda, whose sign could then be seen in the Rue de Rivoli, near Delorme Alley.

A large but ugly room, with an alcove and a bed at the end (they had been obliged to put up with this accommodation in view of the Sunday crowd); two windows from which they could survey beyond the elms, the quay and the river; a magnificent August sunlight lightly touching the panes; two tables; upon one of them a triumphant mountain of bouquets, mingled with the hats of men and women; at the other the four couples seated around a merry confusion of platters, dishes, glasses, and bottles; jugs of beer mingled with flasks of wine; very little order on the table, some disorder beneath it.

"They made beneath the table a noise, a clatter of the feet that was abominable," says Moliere.

This was the state that the shepherd idyll, begun at five o'clock in the morning, had reached at half-past four in the afternoon. The sun was setting; their appetites were satisfied.

The Champs-Elysees, filled with sunshine and with people, were nothing but light and dust, the two things of which glory is composed. The horses of Marly, those neighing marbles, were prancing in a cloud of gold. Carriages were going and coming. A squadron of magnificent bodyguards, with their clarions at their head, were descending the Avenue de Neuilly; the white flag, showing faintly rosy in the setting sun, floated over the dome of the Tuileries. The Place de la Concorde, which had become the Place Louis XV once more, was choked with happy promenaders. Many wore the silver fleur-de-lis suspended from the white-watered ribbon, which had not yet wholly disappeared from buttonholes in the year 1817. Here and there choruses of little girls threw to the winds, amid the passersby, who formed into circles and applauded, the then celebrated Bourbon air, which was destined to strike the Hundred Days with lightning, and which had for its refrain: "Give us back our father from Ghent, give us back our father."

Groups of dwellers in the suburbs, in Sunday array, sometimes even decorated with the fleur-de-lys, like the bourgeois, scattered over the large square and the Marigny square, were playing at rings and revolving on the wooden horses; others were engaged in drinking; some journeyman printers had on paper caps; their laughter was audible. Everything was radiant. It was a time of undisputed peace and profound royalist security; it was the epoch when a special and private report of Chief of Police Angles to the King, on the subject of the suburbs of Paris, terminated with these lines:

"Taking all things into consideration, Sire, there is nothing to be feared from these people. They are as heedless and as indolent as cats. The populace is restless in the provinces; it is not in Paris. These are very pretty men, Sire. It would take all of two of them to make one of your grenadiers. There is nothing to be feared on the part of the populace of Paris the capital. It is remarkable that the stature of this population should have diminished in the last fifty years; and the populace of the suburbs is still more puny than at the time of the Revolution. It is not dangerous. In short, it is an amiable rabble."

Prefects of the police do not deem it possible that a cat can transform itself into a lion; that does happen, however, and in that lies the miracle wrought by the populace of Paris. Moreover, the cat so despised by Count Angles possessed the esteem of the republics of old. In their eyes it was liberty incarnate; and as though to serve as pendant to the Minerva Aptera of the Piraeus, there stood on the public square in Corinth the colossal bronze figure of a cat. The ingenuous police of the Restoration beheld the populace of Paris in too "rose-colored" a light; it is not so much of "an amiable rabble" as it is thought. The Parisian is to the Frenchman what the Athenian was to the Greek: no one sleeps more soundly than he, no one is more frankly frivolous and lazy than he, no one can better assume the air of forgetfulness; let him not be trusted nevertheless; he is ready for any sort of cool deed; but when there is glory at the end of it, he is worthy of admiration in every sort of fury. Give him a pike, he will produce the 10th of August; give him a gun, you will have Austerlitz. He is Napoleon's stay and Danton's resource. Is it a question of country, he enlists; is it a question of liberty, he tears up the pavements. Beware! His hair filled with wrath, is epic; his blouse drapes itself like the folds of a chlamys. Take care! He will make of the first Rue Grenetat that comes to hand Caudine

Forks. When the hour strikes, this man of the faubourgs will grow in stature; this little man will arise, and his gaze will be terrible, and his breath will become a tempest, and there will issue forth from that slender chest enough wind to disarrange the folds of the Alps. It is, thanks to the suburban man of Paris, that the Revolution, mixed with arms, conquers Europe. He sings; it is his delight. Proportion his song to his nature, and you will see! As long as he has for refrain nothing but la Carmagnole, he only overthrows Louis XVI; make him sing the Marseillaise, and he will free the world.

This note jotted down on the margin of Angles's report, we will return to our four couples. The dinner, as we have said, was drawing to its close.

CHAPTER VI—A CHAPTER IN WHICH THEY ADORE EACH OTHER

Chat at table, the chat of love; it is as impossible to reproduce one as the other; the chat of love is a cloud; the chat at table is smoke.

Fameuil and Dahlia were humming. Tholomyes was drinking. Zephine was laughing, Fantine smiling, Listolier blowing a wooden trumpet that he had purchased at Saint-Cloud.

Favourite gazed tenderly at Blachevelle and said, "Blachevelle, I adore you."

This called forth a question from Blachevelle, "What would you do, Favourite, if I were to cease to love you?"

"I!" cried Favourite. "Ah! Do not say that even in jest! If you were to cease to love me, I would spring after you, I would scratch you, I should rend you, I would throw you into the water, I would have you arrested."

Blachevelle smiled with the voluptuous self-conceit of a man who is tickled in his self-love. Favourite resumed, "Yes, I would scream to the police! Ah! I should not restrain myself, not at all! Rabble!"

Blachevelle threw himself back in his chair, in an ecstasy, and closed both eyes proudly.

Dahlia, as she ate, said in a low voice to Favourite, amid the uproar, "So you really idolize him deeply, that Blachevelle of yours?"

"I? I detest him," replied Favourite in the same tone, seizing her fork again. "He is avaricious. I love the little fellow opposite me in my house. He is very nice, that young man; do you know him? One can see that he is an actor by profession. I love actors. As soon as he comes in, his mother says to him: 'Ah! *Mon Dieu!* My peace of mind is gone. There he goes with his shouting. But, my dear, you are splitting my head!' So he goes up to rat-ridden garrets, to black holes, as high as he can mount, and there he sets to singing, declaiming, how do I know what? So that he can be heard downstairs! He earns twenty sous a day at an attorney's by penning quibbles. He is the son of a former precentor of Saint-Jacques-du-Haut-Pas. Ah! He is very nice. He idolizes me so, that one day when he saw me making batter for some pancakes, he said to me, 'Mamselle, make your gloves into fritters, and I will eat them.' It is only artists who can say such things as that. Ah! He is very nice. I am in a fair way to go out of my head over that little fellow. Never mind; I tell Blachevelle that I adore him—how I lie! Hey! How I do lie!"

Favourite paused, and then went on, "I am sad, you see, Dahlia. It has done nothing but rain all summer; the wind irritates me; the wind does not abate. Blachevelle is very stingy; there are hardly any green peas in the market; one does not know what to eat. I have the spleen, as the English say, butter is so dear! and then you see it is horrible, here we are dining in a room with a bed in it, and that disgusts me with life."

CHAPTER VII—THE WISDOM OF THOLOMYES

In the meantime, while some sang, the rest talked together tumultuously all at once; it was no longer anything but noise. Tholomyes intervened.

"Let us not talk at random nor too fast," he exclaimed. "Let us reflect, if we wish to be brilliant. Too much improvisation empties the mind in a stupid way. Running beer gathers no froth. No haste, gentlemen. Let us mingle majesty with the feast. Let us eat with meditation; let us make haste slowly. Let us not hurry. Consider the springtime; if it makes haste, it is done for; that is to say, it gets frozen. Excess of zeal ruins peach trees and apricot trees. Excess of zeal kills the grace and the mirth of good dinners. No zeal, gentlemen! Grimod de la Reynière agrees with Talleyrand."

A hollow sound of rebellion rumbled through the group.

"Leave us in peace, Tholomyes," said Blachevelle.

"Down with the tyrant!" said Fameuil.

"Bombarda, Bombance, and Bambochel!" cried Listolier.

"Sunday exists," resumed Fameuil.

"We are sober," added Listolier.

"Tholomyes," remarked Blachevelle, "contemplate my calmness."

"You are the Marquis of that," retorted Tholomyes.

This mediocre play upon words produced the effect of a stone in a pool.

The Marquis de Montcalm was at that time a celebrated royalist. All the frogs held their peace.

"Friends," cried Tholomyes, with the accent of a man who had recovered his empire, "come to yourselves. This pun, which has fallen from the skies, must not be received with too much stupor. Everything which falls in that way is not necessarily worthy of enthusiasm and respect. The pun is the dung of the mind that soars. The jest falls, no matter where; and the mind after producing a piece of stupidity plunges into the azure depths. A whitish speck flattened against the rock does not prevent the condor from soaring aloft. Far be it from me to insult the pun! I honor it in proportion to its merits; nothing more. All the most august, the most sublime, the most charming of humanity, and perhaps outside of humanity, have made puns. Jesus Christ made a pun on St. Peter, Moses on Isaac, Aeschylus on Polynices, Cleopatra on Octavius. And observe that Cleopatra's pun preceded the battle of Actium, and that had it not been for it, no one would have remembered the city of Toryne, a Greek name that signifies a ladle. That once conceded, I return to my exhortation. I repeat, brothers, I repeat, no zeal, no hubbub, no excess; even in witticisms, gaiety, jollities, or plays on words. Listen to me. I have the prudence of Amphiaraus and the baldness of Caesar. There must be a limit, even to rebuses. *Est modus in rebus.*

"There must be a limit, even to dinners. You are fond of apple turnovers, ladies; do not indulge in them to excess. Even in the matter of turnovers, good sense and art are requisite. Gluttony chastises the glutton, *Gula punit Gulax.* Indigestion is charged by the good God with preaching morality to stomachs. And remember this: each one of our passions, even love, has a stomach that must not be filled too full. In all things the word *finis* must be written in good season; self-control must be exercised when the matter becomes urgent; the bolt must be drawn on appetite; one must set one's own fantasy to the violin, and carry one's self to the post. The sage is the man who knows how, at a given moment, to affect his own arrest. Have some confidence in me, for I have succeeded to some extent in my study of the law, according to the verdict of my examinations, for I know the difference between the question put and the question pending, for I have sustained a thesis in Latin upon the manner in which torture was administered at Rome at the epoch when Munatius Demens was quester of the Parricide; because I am going to be a doctor, apparently it does not follow that it is absolutely necessary that I should be an imbecile. I recommend you to moderation in your desires. It is true that my name is Felix Tholomyes; I speak well. Happy is he who, when the hour strikes, takes a heroic resolve, and abdicates like Sylla or Origenes."

Favourite listened with profound attention.

"Felix," said she, "what a pretty word! I love that name. It is Latin; it means prosper."

Tholomyes went on, "Quirites, gentlemen, caballeros, my friends. Do you wish never to feel the prick, to do without the nuptial bed, and to brave love? Nothing more simple. Here is the receipt: lemonade, excessive exercise, hard labor; work yourself to death, drag blocks, sleep not, hold vigil, gorge yourself with nitrous beverages, and potions of nymphets; drink emulsions of poppies and agnus castus; season this with a strict diet, starve yourself, and add thereto cold baths, girdles of herbs, the application of a plate of lead, lotions made with the subacetate of lead, and fomentations of oxycrat."

"I prefer a woman," said Listolier.

"Woman," resumed Tholomyes; "distrust her. Woe to him who yields himself to the unstable heart of woman! Woman is perfidious and disingenuous. She detests the serpent from professional jealousy. The serpent is the shop over the way."

"Tholomyes!" cried Blachevelle. "You are drunk!"

"Pardieu," said Tholomyes.

"Then be gay," resumed Blachevelle.

"I agree to that," responded Tholomyes.

And, refilling his glass, he rose. "Glory to wine! *Nunc te, Bacche, canam!* Pardon me ladies; that is Spanish. And the proof of it, señoras, is this: like people, like cask. The arrobe of Castile contains sixteen liters; the cantaro of Alicante, twelve; the almude of the Canaries, twenty-five; the cuartin of the Balearic Isles, twenty-six; the boot of Tsar Peter, thirty. Long live that Tsar who was great, and long live his boot, which was still greater! Ladies, take the advice of a friend; make a mistake in your neighbor if you see fit. The property of love is to err. A love affair is not made to crouch down and brutalize itself like an English serving-maid who has callouses on her knees from scrubbing. It is not made for that; it errs gaily, our gentle love. It has been said, error is human; I say, error is love. Ladies, I idolize you all. O Zephine, O Josephine, face more than irregular, you would be charming were you not all askew. You have the air of a pretty face upon which someone has sat down by mistake. As for Favourite, O nymphs and muses! One day when Blachevelle was crossing the gutter in the Rue Guerin-Boisseau, he espied a beautiful girl with white stockings well drawn up, which displayed her legs. This prologue pleased him, and Blachevelle fell in love. The one he loved was Favourite. O Favourite, thou hast Ionian lips. There was a Greek painter named Euphorion, who was surnamed the painter of the lips. That Greek alone would have been worthy to paint thy mouth. Listen! Before thee, there was never a creature worthy of the name. Thou wert made to receive the apple like Venus, or to eat it like Eve; beauty begins with thee. I have just referred to Eve; it is thou who hast created her. Thou deservest the letters-patent of the beautiful woman. O Favourite, I cease to address you as 'thou,' because I pass from poetry to prose. You were speaking of my name a little while ago. That touched me; but let us, whoever we may be, distrust names. They may delude us. I am called Felix, and I am not happy. Words are liars. Let us not blindly accept the indications that they afford us. It would be a mistake to write to Liege 2 for corks, and to Pau for gloves. Miss Dahlia, were I in your place, I would call myself Rosa. A flower should smell sweet, and woman should have wit. I say nothing of Fantine; she is a dreamer, a musing, thoughtful, pensive person; she is a phantom possessed of the form of a nymph and the modesty of a nun, who has strayed into the life of a grisette, but who takes refuge in illusions, and who sings and prays and gazes into the azure without very well knowing what she sees or what she is doing, and who, with her eyes fixed on heaven, wanders in a garden where there are more birds than are in existence. O Fantine, know this: I, Tholomyes, I am all illusion; but she does not even hear me, that blonde maid of chimeras! As for the rest, everything about her is freshness, suavity, youth, sweet morning light. O Fantine, maid worthy of being called Marguerite or Pearl, you are a woman from the beauteous Orient. Ladies, a second piece of advice: do not marry; marriage is a graft; it takes well or ill; avoid that risk. But bah! What am I saying? I am wasting my words. Girls are incurable on the subject of marriage, and all that we wise men can say will not prevent the waistcoat-makers and the shoe-stitchers from dreaming of husbands studded with diamonds. Well, so be it; but, my beauties, remember this, you eat too much sugar. You have but one fault, O woman, and that is nibbling sugar. O nibbling sex, your pretty little white teeth adore sugar. Now, heed me well, sugar is a salt. All salts are withering. Sugar is the most desiccating of all salts; it sucks the liquids of the blood through the veins; hence the coagulation, and then the solidification of the blood; hence tubercles in the lungs, hence death. That is why diabetes borders on consumption. Then, do not crunch sugar, and you will live. I turn to the men: gentlemen, make conquest, rob each other of your well-beloved without remorse. Chassez across. In love there are no friends. Everywhere where there is a pretty woman hostility is open. No quarter, war to the death! A pretty woman is a *casus belli*; a pretty woman is flagrant misdemeanor. All the invasions of history have been determined by petticoats. Woman is man's right. Romulus carried off the Sabines; William carried off the Saxon women; Caesar carried off the Roman women. The man who is not loved soars like a vulture over the mistresses of other men; and for my own part, to all those unfortunate men who are widowers, I throw the sublime proclamation of Bonaparte to the army of Italy: 'Soldiers, you are in need of everything; the enemy has it.'"

Tholomyes paused.

"Take breath, Tholomyes," said Blachevelle.

At the same moment Blachevelle, supported by Listolier and Fameuil, struck up to a plaintive air, one of those studio songs composed of the first words which come to hand, rhymed richly and not at all, as destitute of sense as the gesture of the tree and the sound of the wind, which have their birth in the vapor of pipes, and are dissipated and take their flight with them. This is the couplet by which the group replied to Tholomyes's harangue:

> "The father turkey cocks so grave
> Some money to an agent gave,
> That master good Clermont-Tonnerre
> Might be made pope on Saint Johns' day fair.
> But this good Clermont could not be
> Made pope, because no priest was he;
> And then their agent, whose wrath burned,
> With all their money back returned."

This was not calculated to calm Tholomyes's improvisation; he emptied his glass, filled, refilled it, and began again, "Down with wisdom! Forget all that I have said. Let us be neither prudes nor prudent men nor prudhommes. I propose a toast to mirth; be merry. Let us complete our course of law by folly and eating! Indigestion and the digest. Let Justinian be the male, and Feasting, the female! Joy in the depths! Live, O creation! The world is a great diamond. I am happy. The birds are astonishing. What a festival everywhere! The nightingale is a gratuitous Elleviou. Summer, I salute thee! O Luxembourg! O Georgics of the Rue Madame, and of the Allee de l'Observatoire! O pensive infantry soldiers! O all those charming nurses who, while they guard the children, amuse themselves! The pampas of America would please me if I had not the arcades of the Odeon. My soul flits away into the virgin forests and to the savannas. All is beautiful. The flies buzz in the sun. The sun has sneezed out the humming bird. Embrace me, Fantine!"

He made a mistake and embraced Favourite.

CHAPTER VIII—THE DEATH OF A HORSE

The dinners are better at Edon's than at Bombarda's," exclaimed Zephine. "I prefer Bombarda to Edon," declared Blachevelle. "There is more luxury. It is more Asiatic. Look at the room downstairs; there are mirrors on the walls."

"I prefer them on my plate," said Favourite.

Blachevelle persisted, "Look at the knives. The handles are of silver at Bombarda's and of bone at Edon's. Now, silver is more valuable than bone."

"Except for those who have a silver chin," observed Tholomyes.

He was looking at the dome of the Invalides, which was visible from Bombarda's windows.

A pause ensued.

"Tholomyes," exclaimed Fameuil, "Listolier and I were having a discussion just now."

"A discussion is a good thing," replied Tholomyes; "a quarrel is better."

"We were disputing about philosophy."

"Well?"

"Which do you prefer, Descartes or Spinoza?"

"Desaugiers," said Tholomyes.

This decree pronounced, he took a drink, and went on, "I consent to live. All is not at an end on earth since we can still talk nonsense. For that I return thanks to the immortal gods. We lie. One lies, but one laughs. One affirms, but one doubts. The unexpected bursts forth from the syllogism. That is fine. There are still human beings here below who know how to open and close the surprise box of the paradox merrily. This, ladies, which you are drinking with so tranquil an air is Madeira wine, you must know, from the vineyard of Coural das Freiras, which is three hundred and seventeen fathoms above the level of the sea. Attention while you drink! three hundred and seventeen fathoms! and Monsieur Bombarda, the magnificent eating-house keeper, gives you those three hundred and seventeen fathoms for four francs and fifty centimes."

Again Fameuil interrupted him. "Tholomyes, your opinions fix the law. Who is your favorite author?"

"Ber—"

"Quin?"

"No; Choux."

And Tholomyes continued, "Honor to Bombarda! He would equal Munophis of Elephanta if he could but get me an Indian dancing girl, and Thygelion of Chaeronea if he could bring me a Greek courtesan; for, oh, ladies! There were Bombardas in Greece and in Egypt. Apuleius tells us of them. Alas! Always the same, and nothing new; nothing more unpublished by the creator in creation! *Nil sub sole novum*, says Solomon; *amor omnibus idem*, says Virgil; and Carabine mounts with Carabin into the bark at Saint-Cloud, as Aspasia embarked with Pericles upon the fleet at Samos. One last word. Do you know what Aspasia was, ladies? Although she lived at an epoch when women had, as yet, no soul, she was a soul; a soul of a rosy and purple hue, more ardent hued than fire, fresher than the dawn. Aspasia was a creature in whom two extremes of womanhood met; she was the goddess prostitute; Socrates plus Manon Lescaut. Aspasia was created in case a mistress should be needed for Prometheus."

Tholomyes, once started, would have found some difficulty in stopping, had not a horse fallen down upon the quay just at that moment. The shock caused the cart and the orator to come to a dead halt. It was a Beauceron mare, old and thin, and one fit for the knacker, which was dragging a very heavy cart. On arriving in front of Bombarda's, the worn-out, exhausted beast had refused to proceed any further. This incident attracted a crowd. Hardly had the cursing and indignant carter had time to utter with proper energy the sacramental word, *matin* (the jade), backed up with a pitiless cut of the whip, when the jade fell, never to rise again. On hearing the hubbub made by the passersby, Tholomyes's merry auditors turned their heads, and Tholomyes took advantage of the opportunity to bring his allocution to a close with this melancholy strophe:

"She belonged to that circle where cuckoos and carriages
share the same fate;
and a jade herself, she lived, as jades live,
for the space of a morning!"

"Poor horse!" sighed Fantine.

And Dahlia exclaimed, "There is Fantine on the point of crying over horses. How can one be such a pitiful fool as that!"

At that moment Favourite, folding her arms and throwing her head back, looked resolutely at Tholomyes and said, "Come, now! The surprise?"

"Exactly. The moment has arrived," replied Tholomyes. "Gentlemen, the hour for giving these ladies a surprise has struck. Wait for us a moment, ladies."

"It begins with a kiss," said Blachevelle.

"On the brow," added Tholomyes.

Each gravely bestowed a kiss on his mistress's brow; then all four filed out through the door, with their fingers on their lips.

Favourite clapped her hands on their departure.

"It is beginning to be amusing already," said she.

"Don't be too long," murmured Fantine; "we are waiting for you."

CHAPTER IX—A MERRY END TO MIRTH

When the young girls were left alone, they leaned two by two on the windowsills, chatting, craning out their heads, and talking from one window to the other.

They saw the young men emerge from the Café Bombarda arm in arm. The latter turned around, made signs to them, smiled, and disappeared in that dusty Sunday throng which makes a weekly invasion into the Champs-Elysees.

"Don't be long!" cried Fantine.

"What are they going to bring us?" said Zephine.

"It will certainly be something pretty," said Dahlia.

"For my part," said Favourite, "I want it to be of gold."

Their attention was soon distracted by the movements on the shore of the lake, which they could see through the branches of the large trees, and which diverted them greatly.

It was the hour for the departure of the mail coaches and diligences. Nearly all the stagecoaches for the south and west passed through the Champs-Elysees. The majority followed the quay and went through the Passy Barrier. From moment to moment, some huge vehicle, painted yellow and black, heavily loaded, noisily harnessed, rendered shapeless by trunks, tarpaulins, and valises, full of heads that immediately disappeared, rushed through the crowd with all the sparks of a forge, with dust for smoke, and an air of fury, grinding the pavements, changing all the paving stones into steels. This uproar delighted the young girls. Favourite exclaimed, "What a row! One would say that it was a pile of chains flying away."

It chanced that one of these vehicles, which they could only see with difficulty through the thick elms, halted for a moment, then set out again at a gallop. This surprised Fantine.

"That's odd!" said she. "I thought the diligence never stopped."

Favourite shrugged her shoulders.

"This Fantine is surprising. I am coming to take a look at her out of curiosity. She is dazzled by the simplest things. Suppose a case: I am a traveler; I say to the diligence, 'I will go on in advance; you shall pick me up on the quay as you pass.' The diligence passes, sees me, halts, and takes me. That is done every day. You do not know life, my dear."

In this manner a certain time elapsed. All at once Favourite made a movement, like a person who is just waking up.

"Well," said she, "and the surprise?"

"Yes, by the way," joined in Dahlia, "the famous surprise?"

"They are a very long time about it!" said Fantine.

As Fantine concluded this sigh, the waiter who had served them at dinner entered. He held in his hand something which resembled a letter.

"What is that?" demanded Favourite.

The waiter replied, "It is a paper that those gentlemen left for these ladies."

"Why did you not bring it at once?"

"Because," said the waiter, "the gentlemen ordered me not to deliver it to the ladies for an hour."

Favourite snatched the paper from the waiter's hand. It was, in fact, a letter.

"Stop!" said she; "there is no address; but this is what is written on it: *This is the surprise.*"

She tore the letter open hastily, opened it, and read (she knew how to read):

OUR BELOVED:
You must know that we have parents. Parents—you do not know much about such things. They are called fathers and mothers by the civil code, which is puerile and honest. Now, these parents groan, these old folks implore us, these good men and these good women call us prodigal sons; they desire our return, and offer to kill calves for us. Being virtuous, we obey them. At the hour when you read this, five fiery horses will be bearing us to our papas and mamas. We are pulling up our stakes, as Bossuet says. We are going; we are gone. We flee in the arms of Lafitte and on the wings of Caillard. The Toulouse diligence tears us from the abyss, and the abyss is you, O our little beauties! We return to society, to duty, to respectability, at full trot, at the rate of three leagues an hour. It is necessary for the good of the country that we should be, like the rest of the world, prefects, fathers of families, rural police, and counselors of state. Venerate us. We are sacrificing

ourselves. Mourn for us in haste, and replace us with speed. If this letter lacerates you, do the same by it. Adieu.

For the space of nearly two years we have made you happy. We bear you no grudge for that.

Signed:

Blacheville, Famueil,

Listolier, Felix Tholomyes.

Postscript: The dinner is paid for.

The four young women looked at each other.

Favourite was the first to break the silence.

"Well!" she exclaimed, "it's a very pretty farce, all the same."

"It is very droll," said Zephine.

"That must have been Blachevelle's idea," resumed Favourite. "It makes me in love with him. No sooner is he gone than he is loved. This is an adventure, indeed."

"No," said Dahlia; "it was one of Tholomyes's ideas. That is evident."

"In that case," retorted Favourite, "death to Blachevelle, and long live Tholomyes!"

"Long live Tholomyes!" exclaimed Dahlia and Zephine.

And they burst out laughing.

Fantine laughed with the rest.

An hour later, when she had returned to her room, she wept. It was her first love affair, as we have said; she had given herself to this Tholomyes as to a husband, and the poor girl had a child.

BOOK FOURTH: TO CONFIDE IS SOMETIMES TO DELIVER INTO A PERSON'S POWER

CHAPTER I—ONE MOTHER MEETS ANOTHER MOTHER

There was, at Montfermeil, near Paris, during the first quarter of this century, a sort of cookshop, which no longer exists. This cookshop was kept by some people named Thenardier, husband and wife. It was situated in

Boulanger Lane. Over the door there was a board nailed flat against the wall. Upon this board was painted something that resembled a man carrying another man on his back, the latter wearing the big gilt epaulettes of a general, with large silver stars; red spots represented blood; the rest of the picture consisted of smoke, and probably represented a battle. Below ran this inscription: *At the Sign of Sergeant of Waterloo.*

Nothing is more common than a cart or a truck at the door of a hostelry. Nevertheless, the vehicle, or, to speak more accurately, the fragment of a vehicle, which encumbered the street in front of the cookshop of the Sergeant of Waterloo, one evening in the spring of 1818, would certainly have attracted, by its mass, the attention of any painter who had passed that way.

It was the fore-carriage of one of those trucks that are used in wooded tracts of country, and which serve to transport thick planks and the trunks of trees. This fore-carriage was composed of a massive iron axle-tree with a pivot, into which was fitted a heavy shaft, and which was supported by two huge wheels. The whole thing was compact, overwhelming, and misshapen. It seemed like the gun carriage of an enormous cannon. The ruts of the road had bestowed on the wheels, the fellies, the hub, the axle, and the shaft, a layer of mud, a hideous yellowish daubing hue, tolerably like that with which people are fond of ornamenting cathedrals. The wood was disappearing under mud, and the iron beneath rust. Under the axle-tree hung, like drapery, a huge chain, worthy of some Goliath of a convict. This chain suggested, not the beams, which it was its office to transport, but the mastodons and mammoths that it might have served to harness; it had the air of the galleys, but of cyclopean and superhuman galleys, and it seemed to have been detached from some monster. Homer would have bound Polyphemus with it, and Shakespeare, Caliban.

Why was that fore-carriage of a truck in that place in the street? In the first place, to encumber the street; next, in order that it might finish the process of rusting. There is a throng of institutions in the old social order, which one comes across in this fashion as one walks about outdoors, and which have no other reasons for existence than the above.

The center of the chain swung very near the ground in the middle, and in the loop, as in the rope of a swing, there were seated and grouped, on that particular evening, in exquisite interlacement, two little girls; one about two years and a half old, the other, eighteen months; the younger in the arms of the other. A handkerchief, cleverly knotted about them, prevented their falling out. A mother had caught sight of that frightful chain, and had said, "Come! There's a plaything for my children."

The two children, who were dressed prettily and with some elegance, were radiant with pleasure; one would have said that they were two roses amid old iron; their eyes were a triumph; their fresh cheeks were full of laughter. One had chestnut hair; the other, brown. Their innocent faces were two delighted surprises; a blossoming shrub which grew near wafted to the passersby perfumes which seemed to emanate from them; the child of eighteen months displayed her pretty little bare stomach with the chaste indecency of childhood. Above and around these two delicate heads, all made of happiness and steeped in light, the gigantic fore-carriage, black with rust, almost terrible, all entangled in curves and wild angles, rose in a vault, like the entrance of a cavern. A few paces apart, crouching down upon the threshold of the hostelry, the mother, not a very prepossessing woman, by the way, though touching at that moment, was swinging the two children by means of a long cord, watching them carefully, for fear of accidents, with that animal and celestial expression which is peculiar to maternity. At every backward and forward swing the hideous links emitted a strident sound, which resembled a cry of rage; the little girls were in ecstasies; the setting sun mingled in this joy, and nothing could be more charming than this caprice of chance that had made of a chain of Titans the swing of cherubim.

As she rocked her little ones, the mother hummed in a discordant voice a romance then celebrated, "It must be, said a warrior."

Her song, and the contemplation of her daughters, prevented her hearing and seeing what was going on in the street.

In the meantime, someone had approached her, as she was beginning the first couplet of the romance, and suddenly she heard a voice saying very near her ear, "You have two beautiful children there, Madame."

"To the fair and tender Imogene—" replied the mother, continuing her romance; then she turned her head.

A woman stood before her, a few paces distant. This woman also had a child, which she carried in her arms.

She was carrying, in addition, a large carpetbag, which seemed very heavy.

This woman's child was one of the most divine creatures that it is possible to behold. It was a girl, two or three years of age. She could have entered into competition with the two other little ones, so far as the coquetry of her dress was concerned; she wore a cap of fine linen, ribbons on her bodice, and Valenciennes lace on her cap. The folds of her skirt were raised so as to permit a view of her white, firm, and dimpled leg. She was admirably rosy and healthy. The little beauty inspired a desire to take a bite from the apples of her cheeks. Of her eyes nothing could be known, except that they must be very large, and that they had magnificent lashes. She was asleep.

She slept with that slumber of absolute confidence peculiar to her age. The arms of mothers are made of tenderness; in them children sleep profoundly.

As for the mother, her appearance was sad and poverty-stricken. She was dressed like a workingwoman who is inclined to turn into a peasant again. She was young. Was she handsome? Perhaps; but in that attire it was not apparent. Her hair, a golden lock of which had escaped, seemed very thick, but was severely concealed beneath an ugly, tight, close, nunlike cap, tied under the chin. A smile displays beautiful teeth when one has them; but she did not smile. Her eyes did not seem to have been dry for a very long time. She was pale; she had a very weary and rather sickly appearance. She gazed upon her daughter asleep in her arms with the air peculiar to a mother who has nursed her own child. A large blue handkerchief, such as the Invalides use, was folded into a fichu, and concealed her figure clumsily. Her hands were sunburnt and all dotted with freckles, her forefinger was hardened and lacerated with the needle; she wore a cloak of coarse brown woolen stuff, a linen gown, and coarse shoes. It was Fantine.

It was Fantine, but difficult to recognize. Nevertheless, on scrutinizing her attentively, it was evident that she still retained her beauty. A melancholy fold, which resembled the beginning of irony, wrinkled her right cheek. As for her toilette, that aerial toilette of muslin and ribbons, which seemed made of mirth, of folly, and of music, full of bells, and perfumed with lilacs had vanished like that beautiful and dazzling hoar-frost that is mistaken for diamonds in the sunlight; it melts and leaves the branch quite black.

Ten months had elapsed since the "pretty farce."

What had taken place during those ten months? It can be divined.

After abandonment, straightened circumstances. Fantine had immediately lost sight of Favourite, Zephine, and Dahlia; the bond once broken on the side of the men, it was loosed between the women; they would have been greatly astonished had anyone told them a fortnight later, that they had been friends; there no longer existed any reason for such a thing. Fantine had remained alone. The father of her child gone—alas! Such ruptures are irrevocable. She found herself absolutely isolated, minus the habit of work and plus the taste for pleasure. Drawn away by her liaison with Tholomyes to disdain the pretty trade that she knew, she had neglected to keep her market open; it was now closed to her. She had no resource. Fantine barely knew how to read, and did not know how to write; in her childhood she had only been taught to sign her name; she had a public letter writer indite an epistle to Tholomyes, then a second, then a third. Tholomyes replied to none of them. Fantine heard the gossips say, as they looked at her child, "Who takes those children seriously! One only shrugs one's shoulders over such children!" Then she thought of Tholomyes, who had shrugged his shoulders over his child, and who did not take that innocent being seriously; and her heart grew gloomy toward that man. But what was she to do? She no longer knew to whom to apply. She had committed a fault, but the foundation of her nature, as will be remembered, was modesty and virtue. She was vaguely conscious that she was on the verge of falling into distress, and of gliding into a worse state. Courage was necessary; she possessed it, and held herself firm. The idea of returning to her native town of M. sur M. occurred to her. There, someone might possibly know her and give her work; yes, but it would be necessary to conceal her fault. In a confused way she perceived the necessity of a separation, which would be more painful than the first one. Her heart contracted, but she took her resolution. Fantine, as we shall see, had the fierce bravery of life. She had already valiantly renounced finery, had dressed herself in linen, and had put all her silks, all her ornaments, all her ribbons, and all her laces on her daughter, the only vanity that was left to her, and a holy one it was. She sold all that she had, which produced for her two hundred francs; her little debts paid, she had only about eighty francs left. At the age of twenty-two, on a beautiful spring morning, she quitted Paris, bearing her child on her back. Anyone who had seen these two pass would have had pity on them. This woman had, in all the world, nothing but her child, and the child had, in all the world, no one but this woman. Fantine had nursed her child, and this had tired her chest, and she coughed a little.

We shall have no further occasion to speak of M. Felix Tholomyes. Let us confine ourselves to saying, that, twenty years later, under King Louis Philippe, he was a great provincial lawyer, wealthy and influential, a wise elector, and a very severe juryman; he was still a man of pleasure.

Toward the middle of the day, after having, from time to time, for the sake of resting herself, traveled, for three or four sous a league, in what was then known as the Petites Voitures des Environs de Paris, the "little suburban coach service," Fantine found herself at Montfermeil, in the alley Boulanger.

As she passed the Thenardier hostelry, the two little girls, blissful in the monster swing, had dazzled her in a manner, and she had halted in front of that vision of joy.

Charms exist. These two little girls were a charm to this mother.

She gazed at them in much emotion. The presence of angels is an announcement of Paradise. She thought that, above this inn, she beheld the mysterious *here* of Providence. These two little creatures were evidently happy. She gazed at them, she admired them, in such emotion that at the moment when their mother was recovering her breath between two couplets of her song, she could not refrain from addressing to her the remark, which we have just read, "You have two pretty children, Madame."

The most ferocious creatures are disarmed by caresses bestowed on their young.

The mother raised her head and thanked her, and bade the wayfarer sit down on the bench at the door, she herself being seated on the threshold. The two women began to chat.

"My name is Madame Thenardier," said the mother of the two little girls. "We keep this inn."

Then, her mind still running on her romance, she resumed humming between her teeth: *"It must be so; I am a knight, and I am off to Palestine."*

This Madame Thenardier was a sandy-complexioned woman, thin and angular—the type of the soldier's wife in all its unpleasantness; and what was odd, with a languishing air, which she owed to her perusal of romances. She was a simpering, but masculine creature. Old romances produce that effect when rubbed against the imagination of a cookshop woman. She was still young; she was barely thirty. If this crouching woman had stood upright, her lofty stature and her frame of a perambulating colossus suitable for fairs, might have frightened the traveler at the outset, troubled her confidence, and disturbed what caused what we have to relate to vanish. A person who is seated instead of standing erect—destinies hang upon such a thing as that.

The traveler told her story, with slight modifications.

That she was a workingwoman; that her husband was dead; that her work in Paris had failed her, and that she was on her way to seek it elsewhere, in her own native parts; that she had left Paris that morning on foot; that, as she was carrying her child, and felt fatigued, she had got into the Villemomble coach when she met it; that from Villemomble she had come to Montfermeil on foot; that the little one had walked a little, but not much, because she was so young, and that she had been obliged to take her up, and the jewel had fallen asleep.

At this word she bestowed on her daughter a passionate kiss, which woke her. The child opened her eyes, great blue eyes like her mother's, and looked at—what? Nothing; with that serious and sometimes severe air of little children, which is a mystery of their luminous innocence in the presence of our twilight of virtue. One would say that they feel themselves to be angels, and that they know us to be men. Then the child began to laugh; and although the mother held fast to her, she slipped to the ground with the unconquerable energy of a little being that wished to run. All at once she caught sight of the two others in the swing, stopped short, and put out her tongue, in sign of admiration.

Mother Thenardier released her daughters, made them descend from the swing, and said, "Now amuse yourselves, all three of you."

Children become acquainted quickly at that age, and at the expiration of a minute the little Thenardiers were playing with the newcomer at making holes in the ground, which was an immense pleasure.

The newcomer was very gay; the goodness of the mother is written in the gaiety of the child; she had seized a scrap of wood which served her for a shovel, and energetically dug a cavity big enough for a fly. The gravedigger's business becomes a subject for laughter when performed by a child.

The two women pursued their chat.

"What is your little one's name?"

"Cosette."

For Cosette, read Euphrasie. The child's name was Euphrasie. But out of Euphrasie the mother had made Cosette by that sweet and graceful instinct of mothers and of the populace that changes Josepha into Pepita, and Francoise into Sillette. It is a sort of derivative that disarranges and disconcerts the whole science of etymologists. We have known a grandmother who succeeded in turning Theodore into Gnon.

"How old is she?"

"She is going on three."

"That is the age of my eldest."

In the meantime, the three little girls were grouped in an attitude of profound anxiety and blissfulness; an event had happened; a big worm had emerged from the ground, and they were afraid; and they were in ecstasies over it.

Their radiant brows touched each other; one would have said that there were three heads in one aureole.

"How easily children get acquainted at once!" exclaimed Mother Thenardier; "one would swear that they were three sisters!"

This remark was probably the spark that the other mother had been waiting for. She seized the Thenardier's hand, looked at her fixedly, and said, "Will you keep my child for me?"

The Thenardier made one of those movements of surprise which signify neither assent nor refusal.

Cosette's mother continued, "You see, I cannot take my daughter to the country. My work will not permit it. With a child one can find no situation.

People are ridiculous in the country. It was the good God who caused me to pass your inn. When I caught sight of your little ones, so pretty, so clean, and so happy, it overwhelmed me. I said, 'Here is a good mother. That is just the thing; that will make three sisters.' And then, it will not be long before I return. Will you keep my child for me?"

"I must see about it," replied the Thenardier.

"I will give you six francs a month."

Here a man's voice called from the depths of the cookshop:

"Not for less than seven francs. And six months paid in advance."

"Six times seven makes forty-two," said the Thenardier.

"I will give it," said the mother.

"And fifteen francs in addition for preliminary expenses," added the man's voice.

"Total, fifty-seven francs," said Madame Thenardier. And she hummed vaguely, with these figures, "It must be, said a warrior."

"I will pay it," said the mother. "I have eighty francs. I shall have enough left to reach the country, by traveling on foot. I shall earn money there, and as soon as I have a little I will return for my darling."

The man's voice resumed, "The little one has an outfit?"

"That is my husband," said the Thenardier.

"Of course she has an outfit, the poor treasure—I understood perfectly that it was your husband—and a beautiful outfit, too! A senseless outfit, everything by the dozen, and silk gowns like a lady. It is here, in my carpetbag."

"You must hand it over," struck in the man's voice again.

"Of course I shall give it to you," said the mother. "It would be very queer if I were to leave my daughter quite naked!"

The master's face appeared.

"That's good," said he.

The bargain was concluded. The mother passed the night at the inn, gave up her money and left her child, fastened her carpetbag once more, now reduced in volume by the removal of the outfit, and light henceforth and set out on the following morning, intending to return soon. People arrange such departures tranquilly; but they are despairs!

A neighbor of the Thenardiers met this mother as she was setting out, and came back with the remark:

"I have just seen a woman crying in the street so that it was enough to rend your heart."

When Cosette's mother had taken her departure, the man said to the woman,

"That will serve to pay my note for one hundred and ten francs which falls due tomorrow; I lacked fifty francs. Do you know that I should have had a bailiff and a protest after me? You played the mousetrap nicely with your young ones."

"Without suspecting it," said the woman.

CHAPTER II—FIRST SKETCH OF TWO UNPREPOSSESSING FIGURES

The mouse that had been caught was a pitiful specimen; but the cat rejoices even over a lean mouse.

Who were these Thenardiers?

Let us say a word or two of them now. We will complete the sketch later on.

These beings belonged to that bastard class composed of coarse people who have been successful, and of intelligent people who have descended in the scale, which is between the class called "middle" and the class denominated as "inferior," and which combines some of the defects of the second with nearly all the vices of the first, without possessing the generous impulse of the workingman nor the honest order of the bourgeois.

They were of those dwarfed natures that, if a dull fire chances to warm them up, easily become monstrous. There was in the woman a substratum of the brute, and in the man the material for a blackguard. Both were susceptible, in the highest degree, of the sort of hideous progress that is accomplished in the direction of evil. There exist crablike souls which are continually retreating toward the darkness, retrograding in life rather than advancing, employing experience to augment their deformity, growing incessantly worse, and becoming more and more impregnated with an ever-augmenting blackness. This man and woman possessed such souls.

Thenardier, in particular, was troublesome for a physiognomist. One can only look at some men to distrust them; for one feels that they are dark in both directions. They are uneasy in the rear and threatening in front. There is something of the unknown about them. One can no more answer for what they have done than for what they will do. The shadow that they bear in their glance denounces them. From merely hearing them utter a word or seeing them make a gesture, one obtains a glimpse of somber secrets in their past and of somber mysteries in their future.

This Thenardier, if he himself was to be believed, had been a soldier—a sergeant, he said. He had probably been through the campaign of 1815, and had even conducted himself with tolerable valor, it would seem. We shall see later on how much truth there was in this. The sign of his hostelry was in allusion to one of his feats of arms. He had painted it himself; for he knew how to do a little of everything, and badly.

It was at the epoch when the ancient classical romance that, after having been Clelie, was no longer anything but Lodoiska, still noble, but ever more and more vulgar, having fallen from Mademoiselle de Scuderi to Madame Bournon-Malarme, and from Madame de Lafayette to Madame Barthelemy-Hadot, was setting the loving hearts of the portresses of Paris aflame, and even ravaging the suburbs to some extent. Madame Thenardier was just intelligent enough to read this sort of books. She lived on them. In them she drowned what brains she possessed. This had given her, when very young, and even a little later, a sort of pensive attitude toward her husband, a scamp of a certain depth, a ruffian lettered to the extent of the grammar, coarse and fine at one and the same time, but, so far as sentimentalism was concerned, given to the perusal of Pigault-Lebrun, and "in what concerns the sex," as he said in his jargon—a downright, unmitigated lout. His wife was twelve or fifteen years younger than he was. Later on, when her hair, arranged in a romantically drooping fashion, began to grow gray, when the Magaera began to be developed from the Pamela, the female Thenardier was nothing but a coarse, vicious woman, who had dabbled in stupid romances. Now, one cannot read nonsense with impunity. The result was that her eldest daughter was named Eponine; as for the younger, the poor little thing came near being called Gulnare; I know not to what diversion, effected by a romance of Ducray-Dumenil, she owed the fact that she merely bore the name of Azelma.

However, we will remark by the way, everything was not ridiculous and superficial in that curious epoch to which we are alluding, and which may be designated as the anarchy of baptismal names. By the side of this romantic element which we have just indicated there is the social symptom. It is not rare for the neatherd's boy nowadays to bear the name of Arthur, Alfred, or Alphonse, and for the *vicomte*—if there are still any *vicomtes*—to be called Thomas, Pierre, or Jacques. This displacement, which places the "elegant" name on the plebeian and the rustic name on the aristocrat, is nothing else than an eddy of equality. The irresistible penetration of the new inspiration is there as everywhere else. Beneath this apparent discord there is a great and a profound thing—the French Revolution.

CHAPTER III—THE LARK

It is not all in all sufficient to be wicked in order to prosper. The cookshop was in a bad way.

Thanks to the traveler's fifty-seven francs, Thenardier had been able to avoid a protest and to honor his signature. On the following month they were again in need of money. The woman took Cosette's outfit to Paris, and pawned it at the pawnbroker's for sixty francs. As soon as that sum was spent, the Thenardiers grew accustomed to look on the little girl merely as a child whom they were caring for out of charity; and they treated her accordingly. As she had no longer any clothes, they dressed her in the cast-off petticoats and chemises of the Thenardier brats; that is to say, in rags. They fed her on what all the rest had left—a little better than the dog, a little worse than the cat. Moreover, the cat and the dog were her habitual table companions; Cosette ate with them under the table, from a wooden bowl similar to theirs.

The mother, who had established herself, as we shall see later on, at M. sur M., wrote, or, more correctly, caused to be written, a letter every month, that she might have news of her child. The Thenardiers replied invariably, "Cosette is doing wonderfully well."

At the expiration of the first six months the mother sent seven francs for the seventh month, and continued her remittances with tolerable regularity from month to month. The year was not completed when Thenardier said, "A fine favor she is doing us, in sooth! What does she expect us to do with her seven francs?" and he wrote to demand twelve francs. The mother, whom they had persuaded into the belief that her child was happy, "and was coming on well," submitted, and forwarded the twelve francs.

Certain natures cannot love on the one hand without hating on the other. Mother Thenardier loved her two daughters passionately, which caused her to hate the stranger.

It is sad to think that the love of a mother can possess villainous aspects. Little as was the space occupied by Cosette, it seemed to her as though it were taken from her own, and that that little child diminished the air that her daughters breathed. This woman, like many women of her sort, had a load of caresses and a burden of blows and injuries to dispense each day. If she had not had Cosette, it is certain that her daughters, idolized as they were, would have received the whole of it; but the stranger did them the service to divert the blows to herself. Her daughters received nothing but caresses. Cosette could not make a motion that did not draw down upon her head a heavy shower of violent blows and unmerited chastisement. The sweet, feeble being, who should not have understood anything of this world or of God, incessantly punished, scolded, ill-used, beaten, and seeing beside her two little creatures like herself, who lived in a ray of dawn!

Madame Thenardier was vicious with Cosette. Eponine and Azelma were vicious. Children at that age are only copies of their mother. The size is smaller; that is all.

A year passed; then another.

People in the village said, "Those Thenardiers are good people. They are not rich, and yet they are bringing up a poor child who was abandoned on their hands!"

They thought that Cosette's mother had forgotten her.

In the meanwhile, Thenardier, having learned, it is impossible to say by what obscure means, that the child was probably a bastard, and that the mother could not acknowledge it, exacted fifteen francs a month, saying that "the creature" was growing and "eating," and threatening to send her away. "Let her not bother me," he exclaimed, "or I'll fire her brat right into the middle of her secrets. I must have an increase." The mother paid the fifteen francs.

From year to year the child grew, and so did her wretchedness.

As long as Cosette was little, she was the scape-goat of the two other children; as soon as she began to develop a little, that is to say, before she was even five years old, she became the servant of the household.

Five years old! the reader will say; that is not probable. Alas! It is true. Social suffering begins at all ages. Have we not recently seen the trial of a man named Dumollard, an orphan turned bandit, who, from the age of five, as the official documents state, being alone in the world, "worked for his living and stole"?

Cosette was made to run on errands, to sweep the rooms, the courtyard, the street, to wash the dishes, to even carry burdens. The Thenardiers considered themselves all the more authorized to behave in this manner, since the mother, who was still at M. sur M., had become irregular in her payments. Some months she was in arrears.

If this mother had returned to Montfermeil at the end of these three years, she would not have recognized her child. Cosette, so pretty and rosy on her arrival in that house, was now thin and pale. She had an indescribably uneasy look. "The sly creature," said the Thenardiers.

Injustice had made her peevish, and misery had made her ugly. Nothing remained to her except her beautiful eyes, which inspired pain, because, large as they were, it seemed as though one beheld in them a still larger amount of sadness.

It was a heartbreaking thing to see this poor child, not yet six years old, shivering in the winter in her old rags of linen, full of holes, sweeping the street before daylight, with an enormous broom in her tiny red hands, and a tear in her great eyes. She was called the Lark in the neighborhood. The populace, who are fond of these figures of speech, had taken a fancy to bestow this name on this trembling, frightened, and shivering little creature, no bigger than a bird, who was awake every morning before anyone else in the house or the village, and was always in the street or the fields before daybreak.

Only the little lark never sang.

BOOK FIFTH: THE DESCENT

CHAPTER I—THE HISTORY OF A PROGRESS IN BLACK GLASS TRINKETS

And in the meantime, what had become of that mother who according to the people at Montfermeil, seemed to have abandoned her child? Where was she? What was she doing?

After leaving her little Cosette with the Thenardiers, she had continued her journey, and had reached M. sur M.

This, it will be remembered, was in 1818.

Fantine had quitted her province ten years before. M. sur M. had changed its aspect. While Fantine had been slowly descending from wretchedness to wretchedness, her native town had prospered.

About two years previously one of those industrial facts that are the grand events of small districts had taken place.

This detail is important, and we regard it as useful to develop it at length; we should almost say, to underline it.

From time immemorial, M. sur M. had had for its special industry the imitation of English jet and the black glass trinkets of Germany. This industry had always vegetated, on account of the high price of the raw material, which reacted on the manufacture. At the moment when Fantine returned to M. sur M., an unheard-of transformation had taken place in the production of "black goods." Toward the close of 1815 a man, a stranger, had established himself in the town, and had been inspired with the idea of substituting, in this manufacture, gum-lac for resin, and, for bracelets in particular, slides of sheet-iron simply laid together, for slides of soldered sheet-iron.

This very small change had effected a revolution.

This very small change had, in fact, prodigiously reduced the cost of the raw material, which had rendered it possible in the first place, to raise the price of manufacture, a benefit to the country; in the second place, to improve the workmanship, an advantage to the consumer; in the third place, to sell at a lower price, while trebling the profit, which was a benefit to the manufacturer.

Thus three results ensued from one idea.

In less than three years the inventor of this process had become rich, which is good, and had made everyone about him rich, which is better. He was a stranger in the Department. Of his origin, nothing was known; of the beginning of his career, very little. It was rumored that he had come to town with very little money, a few hundred francs at the most.

It was from this slender capital, enlisted in the service of an ingenious idea, developed by method and thought, that he had drawn his own fortune, and the fortune of the whole countryside.

On his arrival at M. sur M. he had only the garments, the appearance, and the language of a workingman.

It appears that on the very day when he made his obscure entry into the little town of M. sur M., just at nightfall, on a December evening, knapsack on back and thorn club in hand, a large fire had broken out in the town hall. This man had rushed into the flames and saved, at the risk of his own life, two children who belonged to the captain of the gendarmerie; this is why they had forgotten to ask him for his passport. Afterward they had learned his name. He was called Father Madeleine.

CHAPTER II—MADELEINE

He was a man about fifty years of age, who had a preoccupied air, and who was good. That was all that could be said about him.

Thanks to the rapid progress of the industry, which he had so admirably reconstructed, M. sur M. had become a rather important center of trade. Spain, which consumes a good deal of black jet, made enormous purchases there each year. M. sur M. almost rivaled London and Berlin in this branch of commerce. Father Madeleine's profits were such, that at the end of the second year he was able to erect a large factory, in which there were two vast workrooms, one for the men, and the other for women. Anyone who was hungry could present himself there, and was sure of finding employment and bread. Father Madeleine required of the men good will, of the women pure morals, and of all, probity. He had separated the workrooms in order to separate the sexes, and so that the women and girls might remain discreet. On this point he was inflexible. It was the only thing in which he was in a manner intolerant. He was all the more firmly set on this severity, since M. sur M., being a garrison town, opportunities for corruption abounded. However, his coming had been a boon, and his presence was a godsend. Before Father Madeleine's arrival, everything had languished in the country; now everything lived with a healthy life of toil. A strong circulation warmed everything and penetrated everywhere. Slack seasons and wretchedness were unknown. There was no pocket so obscure that it had not a little money in it; no dwelling so lowly that there was not some little joy within it.

Father Madeleine gave employment to everyone. He exacted but one thing: Be an honest man. Be an honest woman.

As we have said, in the midst of this activity of which he was the cause and the pivot, Father Madeleine made his fortune; but a singular thing in a simple man of business, it did not seem as though that were his chief care. He appeared to be thinking much of others, and little of himself. In 1820 he was known to have a sum of six hundred and thirty thousand francs lodged in his name with Laffitte; but before reserving these six hundred and thirty thousand francs, he had spent more than a million for the town and its poor.

The hospital was badly endowed; he founded six beds there. M. sur M. is divided into the upper and the lower town. The lower town, in which he lived, had but one school, a miserable hovel, which was falling to ruin: he constructed two, one for girls, the other for boys. He allotted a salary from his own funds to the two instructors, a salary twice as large as their meager official salary, and one day he said to someone who expressed surprise, "The two prime functionaries of the state are the nurse and the schoolmaster." He created at his own expense an infant school, a thing then almost unknown in France, and a fund for aiding old and infirm workmen. As his factory was a center, a new quarter, in which there were a good many indigent families, rose rapidly around him; he established there a free dispensary.

At first, when they watched his beginnings, the good souls said, "He's a jolly fellow who means to get rich." When they saw him enriching the country before he enriched himself, the good souls said, "He is an ambitious man." This seemed all the more probable since the man was religious, and even practiced his religion to a certain degree, a thing that was very favorably viewed at that epoch. He went regularly to Low Mass every Sunday. The local deputy, who nosed out all rivalry everywhere, soon began to grow uneasy over this religion. This deputy had been a member of the legislative body of the Empire, and shared the religious ideas of a father of the Oratoire, known under the name of Fouche, Duc d'Otrante, whose creature and friend he had been. He indulged in gentle raillery at God with closed doors. But when he beheld the wealthy manufacturer Madeleine going to low mass at seven o'clock, he perceived in him a possible candidate, and resolved to outdo him; he took a Jesuit confessor, and went to High Mass and to vespers. Ambition was at that time, in the direct acceptation of the word, a race to the steeple. The poor profited by this terror as well as the good God, for the honorable deputy also founded two beds in the hospital, which made twelve.

Nevertheless, in 1819 a rumor one morning circulated through the town to the effect that, on the representations of the prefect and in consideration of the services rendered by him to the country, Father Madeleine was to be appointed by the King, mayor of M. sur M. Those who had pronounced this newcomer to be "an ambitious fellow," seized with delight on this opportunity that all men desire, to exclaim, "There! What did we say!" All M. sur M. was in an uproar. The rumor was well founded. Several days later the appointment appeared in the Moniteur. On the following day Father Madeleine refused.

In this same year of 1819 the products of the new process invented by Madeleine figured in the industrial exhibition; when the jury made their report, the King appointed the inventor a chevalier of the Legion of Honor. A fresh excitement in the little town. Well, so it was the cross that he wanted! Father Madeleine refused the cross.

Decidedly this man was an enigma. The good souls got out of their predicament by saying, "After all, he is some sort of an adventurer."

We have seen that the country owed much to him; the poor owed him everything; he was so useful and he was so gentle that people had been obliged to honor and respect him. His workmen, in particular, adored him, and he endured this adoration with a sort of melancholy gravity. When he was known to be rich, "people in society" bowed to him, and he received invitations in the town; he was called, in town, Monsieur Madeleine; his workmen and the children continued to call him Father Madeleine, and that was what was most adapted to make him smile. In proportion as he mounted, throve, invitations rained down upon him. "Society" claimed him for its own. The prim little drawing rooms on M. sur M., which, of course, had at first been closed to the artisan, opened both leaves of their folding doors to the millionaire. They made a thousand advances to him. He refused.

This time the good gossips had no trouble. "He is an ignorant man, of no education. No one knows where he came from. He would not know how to behave in society. It has not been absolutely proved that he knows how to read."

When they saw him making money, they said, "He is a man of business." When they saw him scattering his money about, they said, "He is an ambitious man." When he was seen to decline honors, they said, "He is an adventurer." When they saw him repulse society, they said, "He is a brute."

In 1820, five years after his arrival in M. sur M., the services that he had rendered to the district were so dazzling, the opinion of the whole country round about was so unanimous, that the King again appointed him mayor of the town. He again declined; but the prefect resisted his refusal, all the notabilities of the place came to implore him, the people in the street besought him; the urging was so vigorous that he ended by accepting. It was noticed that the thing which seemed chiefly to bring him to a decision was the almost irritated apostrophe addressed to him by an old woman of the people, who called to him from her threshold, in an angry way, "A good mayor is a useful thing. Is he drawing back before the good which he can do?"

This was the third phase of his ascent. Father Madeleine had become Monsieur Madeleine. Monsieur Madeleine became Monsieur le Maire.

CHAPTER III—SUMS DEPOSITED WITH LAFFITTE

On the other hand, he remained as simple as on the first day. He had gray hair, a serious eye, the sunburned complexion of a laborer, the thoughtful visage of a philosopher. He habitually wore a hat with a wide brim, and a long coat of coarse cloth, buttoned to the chin. He fulfilled his duties as mayor; but, with that exception, he lived in solitude. He spoke to but few people. He avoided polite attentions; he escaped quickly; he smiled to relieve himself of the necessity of talking; he gave, in order to get rid of the necessity for smiling. The women said of him, "What a good-natured bear!" His pleasure consisted in strolling in the fields.

He always took his meals alone, with an open book before him, which he read. He had a well-selected little library. He loved books; books are cold but safe friends. In proportion as leisure came to him with fortune, he seemed to take advantage of it to cultivate his mind. It had been observed that, ever since his arrival at M. sur M., his language had grown more polished, more choice, and more gentle with every passing year. He liked to carry a gun with him on his strolls, but he rarely made use of it. When he did happen to do so, his shooting was something so infallible as to inspire terror. He never killed an inoffensive animal. He never shot at a little bird.

Although he was no longer young, it was thought that he was still prodigiously strong. He offered his assistance to anyone who was in need of it, lifted a horse, released a wheel clogged in the mud, or stopped a runaway bull by the horns. He always had his pockets full of money when he went out; but they were empty on his return. When he passed through a village, the ragged brats ran joyously after him, and surrounded him like a swarm of gnats.

It was thought that he must, in the past, have lived a country life, since he knew all sorts of useful secrets, which he taught to the peasants. He taught them how to destroy scurf on wheat, by sprinkling it and the granary and inundating the cracks in the floor with a solution of common salt; and how to chase away weevils by hanging up orviot in bloom everywhere, on the walls and the ceilings, among the grass, and in the houses.

He had "recipes" for exterminating from a field, blight, tares, foxtail, and all parasitic growths that destroy the wheat. He defended a rabbit warren against rats, simply by the odor of a guinea pig that he placed in it.

One day he saw some country people busily engaged in pulling up nettles; he examined the plants, which were uprooted and already dried, and said, "They are dead. Nevertheless, it would be a good thing to know how to make use of them. When the nettle is young, the leaf makes an excellent vegetable; when it is older, it has filaments and fibers like hemp and flax. Nettle cloth is as good as linen cloth. Chopped up, nettles are good for poultry; pounded, they are good for horned cattle. The seed of the nettle, mixed with fodder, gives gloss to the hair of animals; the root, mixed with salt, produces a beautiful yellow coloring-matter. Moreover, it is an excellent hay, which can be cut twice. And what is required for the nettle? A little soil, no care, no culture. Only the seed falls as it is ripe, and it is difficult to collect it. That is all. With the exercise of a little care, the nettle could be made useful; it is neglected and it becomes hurtful. It is exterminated. How many men resemble the nettle!" He added, after a pause, "Remember this, my friends: there are no such things as bad plants or bad men. There are only bad cultivators."

The children loved him because he knew how to make charming little trifles of straw and coconuts.

When he saw the door of a church hung in black, he entered: he sought out funerals as other men seek christenings. Widowhood and the grief of others attracted him, because of his great gentleness; he mingled with the friends clad in mourning, with families dressed in black, with the priests groaning around a coffin. He seemed to like to give to his thoughts for text these funereal psalmodies filled with the vision of the other world. With his eyes fixed on heaven, he listened with a sort of aspiration toward all the mysteries of the infinite, those sad voices which sing on the verge of the obscure abyss of death.

He performed a multitude of good actions, concealing his agency in them as a man conceals himself because of evil actions. He penetrated houses privately, at night; he ascended staircases furtively. A poor wretch on returning to his attic would find that his door had been opened, sometimes even forced, during his absence. The poor man made a clamor over it; some malefactor had been there! He entered, and the first thing he beheld was a piece of gold lying forgotten on some piece of furniture. The "malefactor" who had been there was Father Madeleine.

He was affable and sad. The people said, "There is a rich man who has not a haughty air. There is a happy man who has not a contented air."

Some people maintained that he was a mysterious person, and that no one ever entered his chamber, which was a regular anchorite's cell, furnished with winged hourglasses and enlivened by crossbones and skulls of dead men! This was much talked of, so that one of the elegant and malicious young women of M. sur M. came to him one day, and asked, "Monsieur le Maire, pray show us your chamber. It is said to be a grotto." He smiled, and introduced them instantly into this "grotto." They were well punished for their curiosity. The room was very simply furnished in mahogany, which was rather ugly, like all furniture of that sort, and hung with paper worth twelve sous. They could see nothing remarkable about it, except two candlesticks of antique pattern, which stood on the chimneypiece and appeared to be silver, "for they were hallmarked," an observation full of the type of wit of petty towns.

Nevertheless, people continued to say that no one ever got into the room, and that it was a hermit's cave, a mysterious retreat, a hole, a tomb.

It was also whispered about that he had "immense" sums deposited with Laffitte, with this peculiar feature, that they were always at his immediate disposal, so that, it was added, M. Madeleine could make his appearance at Laffitte's any morning, sign a receipt, and carry off his two or three millions in ten minutes. In reality, "these two or three millions" were reducible, as we have said, to six hundred and thirty or forty thousand francs.

CHAPTER IV—M. MADELEINE IN MOURNING

At the beginning of 1820 the newspapers announced the death of M. Myriel, Bishop of D——, surnamed "Monseigneur Bienvenu," who had died in the odor of sanctity at the age of eighty-two.

The Bishop of D—— to supply here a detail, which the papers omitted— had been blind for many years before his death, and content to be blind, as his sister was beside him.

Let us remark by the way, that to be blind and to be loved, is, in fact, one of the most strangely exquisite forms of happiness upon this earth, where nothing is complete. To have continually at one's side a woman, a daughter, a sister, a charming being, who is there because you need her and because she cannot do without you; to know that we are indispensable to a person who is necessary to us; to be able to incessantly measure one's affection by the amount of her presence which she bestows on us, and to say to ourselves, "Since she consecrates the whole of her time to me, it is because I possess the whole of her heart"; to behold her thought in lieu of her face; to be able to verify the fidelity of one being amid the eclipse of the world; to regard the rustle of a gown as the sound of wings; to hear her come and go, retire, speak, return, sing, and to think that one is the center of these steps, of this speech; to manifest at each instant one's personal attraction; to feel one's self all the more powerful because of one's infirmity; to become in one's obscurity, and through one's obscurity, the star around which this angel gravitates, few felicities equal this. The supreme happiness of life consists in the conviction that one is loved; loved for one's own sake—let us say rather, loved in spite of one's self; this conviction the blind man possesses. To be served in distress is to be caressed. Does he lack anything? No. One does not lose the sight when one has love. And what love! A love wholly constituted of virtue! There is no blindness where there is certainty. Soul seeks soul, gropingly, and finds it. And this soul, found and tested, is a woman. A hand sustains you; it is hers: a mouth lightly touches your brow; it is her mouth: you hear a breath very near you; it is hers. To have everything of her, from her worship to her pity, never to be left, to have that sweet weakness aiding you, to lean upon that immovable reed, to touch Providence with one's hands, and to be able to take it in one's arms, God made tangible, what bliss! The heart, that obscure, celestial flower, undergoes a mysterious blossoming. One would not exchange that shadow for all brightness! The angel soul is there, uninterruptedly there; if she departs, it is but to return again; she vanishes like a dream, and reappears like reality. One feels warmth approaching, and behold! She is there. One overflows with serenity, with gaiety, with ecstasy; one is a radiance amid the night. And there are a thousand little cares. Nothings, which are enormous in that void. The most ineffable accents of the feminine voice employed to lull you, and supplying the vanished universe to you. One is caressed with the soul. One sees nothing, but one feels that one is adored. It is a paradise of shadows.

It was from this paradise that Monseigneur Welcome had passed to the other.

The announcement of his death was reprinted by the local journal of M. sur M. On the following day, M. Madeleine appeared clad wholly in black, and with crape on his hat.

This mourning was noticed in the town, and commented on. It seemed to throw a light on M. Madeleine's origin. It was concluded that some relationship existed between him and the venerable Bishop. "He has gone into mourning for the Bishop of D——," said the drawing rooms; this raised M. Madeleine's credit greatly, and procured for him, instantly and at one blow, a certain consideration in the noble world of M. sur M. The microscopic Faubourg Saint-Germain of the place meditated raising the quarantine against M. Madeleine, the probable relative of a bishop. M. Madeleine perceived the advancement which he had obtained, by the more numerous courtesies of the old women and the more plentiful smiles of the young ones. One evening, a ruler in that petty great world, who was curious by right of seniority, ventured to ask him, "M. le Maire is doubtless a cousin of the late Bishop of D——?"

He said, "No, Madame."

"But," resumed the dowager, "you are wearing mourning for him."

He replied, "It is because I was a servant in his family in my youth."

Another thing that was remarked, was, that every time that he encountered in the town a young Savoyard who was roaming about the country and seeking chimneys to sweep, the mayor had him summoned, inquired his name, and gave him money. The little Savoyards told each other about it: a great many of them passed that way.

CHAPTER V—VAGUE FLASHES ON THE HORIZON

Little by little, and in the course of time, all this opposition subsided. There had at first been exercised against M. Madeleine, in virtue of a sort of law which all those who rise must submit to, blackening and calumnies; then they grew to be nothing more than ill-nature, then merely malicious remarks, then even this entirely disappeared; respect became complete, unanimous, cordial, and toward 1821 the moment arrived when the word "Monsieur le Maire" was pronounced at M. sur M. with almost the same accent as "Monseigneur the Bishop" had been pronounced in D—— in 1815. People came from a distance of ten leagues around to consult M. Madeleine. He put an end to differences, he prevented lawsuits, he reconciled enemies. Everyone took him for the judge, and with good reason. It seemed as though he had for a soul the book of the natural law. It was like an epidemic of veneration, which in the course of six or seven years gradually took possession of the whole district.

One single man in the town, in the arrondissement, absolutely escaped this contagion, and, whatever Father Madeleine did, remained his opponent as though a sort of incorruptible and imperturbable instinct kept him on the alert and uneasy. It seems, in fact, as though there existed in certain men a veritable bestial instinct, though pure and upright, like all instincts, which creates antipathies and sympathies, which fatally separates one nature from another nature, which does not hesitate, which feels no disquiet, which does not hold its peace, and which never belies itself, clear in its obscurity, infallible, imperious, intractable, stubborn to all counsels of the intelligence and to all the dissolvents of reason, and which, in whatever manner destinies are arranged, secretly warns the man-dog of the presence of the man-cat, and the man-fox of the presence of the man-lion.

It frequently happened that when M. Madeleine was passing along a street, calm, affectionate, surrounded by the blessings of all, a man of lofty stature, clad in an iron-gray frock coat, armed with a heavy cane, and wearing a battered hat, turned around abruptly behind him, and followed him with his eyes until he disappeared, with folded arms and a slow shake of the head, and his upper lip raised in company with his lower to his nose, a sort of significant grimace that might be translated by: "What is that man, after all? I certainly have seen him somewhere. In any case, I am not his dupe."

This person, grave with a gravity that was almost menacing, was one of those men who, even when only seen by a rapid glimpse, arrest the spectator's attention.

His name was Javert, and he belonged to the police.

At M. sur M. he exercised the unpleasant but useful functions of an inspector. He had not seen Madeleine's beginnings. Javert owed the post which he occupied to the protection of M. Chabouillet, the secretary of the Minister of State, Comte Angeles, then prefect of police at Paris. When Javert arrived at

M. sur M. the fortune of the great manufacturer was already made, and Father Madeleine had become Monsieur Madeleine.

Certain police officers have a peculiar physiognomy, which is complicated with an air of baseness mingled with an air of authority. Javert possessed this physiognomy minus the baseness.

It is our conviction that if souls were visible to the eyes, we should be able to see distinctly that strange thing that each one individual of the human race corresponds to someone of the species of the animal creation; and we could easily recognize this truth, hardly perceived by the thinker, that from the oyster to the eagle, from the pig to the tiger, all animals exist in man, and that each one of them is in a man. Sometimes even several of them at a time.

Animals are nothing else than the figures of our virtues and our vices, straying before our eyes, the visible phantoms of our souls. God shows them to us in order to induce us to reflect. Only since animals are mere shadows, God has not made them capable of education in the full sense of the word; what is the use? On the contrary, our souls being realities and having a goal that is appropriate to them, God has bestowed on them intelligence; that is to say, the possibility of education. Social education, when well done, can always draw from a soul, of whatever sort it may be, the utility that it contains.

This, be it said, is of course from the restricted point of view of the terrestrial life, which is apparent, and without prejudging the profound question of the anterior or ulterior personality of the beings which are not man. The visible I in nowise authorizes the thinker to deny the latent I. Having made this reservation, let us pass on.

Now, if the reader will admit, for a moment, with us, that in every man there is one of the animal species of creation, it will be easy for us to say what there was in Police Officer Javert.

The peasants of Asturias are convinced that in every litter of wolves there is one dog, which is killed by the mother because, otherwise, as he grew up, he would devour the other little ones.

Give to this dog-son of a wolf a human face, and the result will be Javert.

Javert had been born in prison, of a fortune-teller, whose husband was in the galleys. As he grew up, he thought that he was outside the pale of society, and he despaired of ever reentering it. He observed that society unpardoningly excludes two classes of men, those who attack it and those who guard it; he had no choice except between these two classes; at the same time, he was conscious of an indescribable foundation of rigidity, regularity, and probity, complicated with an inexpressible hatred for the race of bohemians from which he was sprung. He entered the police; he succeeded there. At forty years of age he was an inspector.

During his youth he had been employed in the convict establishments of the South.

Before proceeding further, let us come to an understanding as to the words, "human face," which we have just applied to Javert.

The human face of Javert consisted of a flat nose, with two deep nostrils, toward which enormous whiskers ascended on his cheeks. One felt ill at ease when he saw these two forests and these two caverns for the first time. When Javert laughed, and his laugh was rare and terrible, his thin lips parted and revealed to view not only his teeth, but his gums, and around his nose there formed a flattened and savage fold, as on the muzzle of a wild beast. Javert, serious, was a watchdog; when he laughed, he was a tiger. As for the rest, he had very little skull and a great deal of jaw; his hair concealed his forehead and fell over his eyebrows; between his eyes there was a permanent, central frown, like an imprint of wrath; his gaze was obscure; his mouth pursed up and terrible; his air that of ferocious command.

This man was composed of two very simple and two very good sentiments, comparatively; but he rendered them almost bad, by dint of exaggerating them, respect for authority, hatred of rebellion; and in his eyes, murder, robbery, all crimes, are only forms of rebellion. He enveloped in a blind and profound faith everyone who had a function in the state, from the prime minister to the rural policeman. He covered with scorn, aversion, and disgust everyone who had once crossed the legal threshold of evil. He was absolute, and admitted no exceptions. On the one hand, he said, "The functionary can make no mistake; the magistrate is never the wrong." On the other hand, he said, "These men are irremediably lost. Nothing good can come from them." He fully shared the opinion of those extreme minds that attribute to human law I know not what power of making, or, if the reader will have it so, of authenticating, demons, and who place a Styx at the base of society. He was stoical, serious, austere; a melancholy dreamer, humble and haughty, like fanatics. His glance was like a gimlet, cold and piercing. His whole life hung on these two words: watchfulness and supervision. He had introduced a straight line into what is the most crooked thing in the world; he possessed the conscience of his usefulness, the religion of his functions, and he was a spy as other men are priests. Woe to the man who fell into his hands! He would have arrested his own father, if the latter had escaped from the galleys, and would have denounced his mother, if she had broken her ban. And he would have done it with that sort of inward satisfaction that is conferred by virtue. And, withal, a life of privation, isolation, abnegation, chastity, with never a diversion. It was implacable duty; the police understood, as the Spartans understood Sparta, a pitiless lying in wait, a ferocious honesty, a marble informer, Brutus in Vidocq.

Javert's whole person was expressive of the man who spies and who withdraws himself from observation. The mystical school of Joseph de Maistre, which at that epoch seasoned with lofty cosmogony those things that were called the ultra-newspapers, would not have failed to declare that Javert was a symbol. His brow was not visible; it disappeared beneath his hat: his eyes were not visible, since they were lost under his eyebrows: his chin was not visible, for it was plunged in his cravat: his hands were not visible; they were drawn up in his sleeves: and his cane was not visible; he carried it under his coat. But when the occasion presented itself, there was suddenly seen to emerge from all this shadow, as from an ambuscade, a narrow and angular forehead, a baleful glance, a threatening chin, enormous hands, and a monstrous cudgel.

In his leisure moments, which were far from frequent, he read, although he hated books; this caused him to be not wholly illiterate. This could be recognized by some emphasis in his speech.

As we have said, he had no vices. When he was pleased with himself, he permitted himself a pinch of snuff. Therein lay his connection with humanity.

The reader will have no difficulty in understanding that Javert was the terror of that whole class, which the annual statistics of the Ministry of Justice designates under the rubric, Vagrants. The name of Javert routed them by its mere utterance; the face of Javert petrified them at sight.

Such was this formidable man.

Javert was like an eye constantly fixed on M. Madeleine. An eye full of suspicion and conjecture. M. Madeleine had finally perceived the fact; but it seemed to be of no importance to him. He did not even put a question to Javert; he neither sought nor avoided him; he bore that embarrassing and almost oppressive gaze without appearing to notice it. He treated Javert with ease and courtesy, as he did all the rest of the world.

It was divined, from some words that escaped Javert, that he had secretly investigated, with that curiosity, which belongs to the race, and into which there enters as much instinct as will, all the anterior traces that Father Madeleine might have left elsewhere. He seemed to know, and he sometimes said in covert words, that someone had gleaned certain information in a certain district about a family that had disappeared. Once he chanced to say, as he was talking to himself, "I think I have him!" Then he remained pensive for three days, and uttered not a word. It seemed that the thread which he thought he held had broken.

Moreover, and this furnishes the necessary corrective for the too absolute sense, which certain words might present, there can be nothing really infallible in a human creature, and the peculiarity of instinct is that it can become confused, thrown off the track, and defeated. Otherwise, it would be superior to intelligence, and the beast would be found to be provided with a better light than man.

Javert was evidently somewhat disconcerted by the perfect naturalness and tranquility of M. Madeleine.

One day, nevertheless, his strange manner appeared to produce an impression on M. Madeleine. It was on the following occasion.

CHAPTER VI—FATHER FAUCHELEVENT

One morning M. Madeleine was passing through an unpaved alley of M. sur M.; he heard a noise, and saw a group some distance away. He approached. An old man named Father Fauchelevent had just fallen beneath his cart, his horse having tumbled down.

This Fauchelevent was one of the few enemies whom M. Madeleine had at that time. When Madeleine arrived in the neighborhood, Fauchelevent, an ex-notary and a peasant who was almost educated, had a business that was beginning to be in a bad way. Fauchelevent had seen this simple workman grow rich, while he, a lawyer, was being ruined. This had filled him with jealousy, and he had done all he could, on every occasion, to injure Madeleine. Then bankruptcy had come; and as the old man had nothing left but a cart and a horse, and neither family nor children, he had turned carter.

The horse had two broken legs and could not rise. The old man was caught in the wheels. The fall had been so unlucky that the whole weight of the vehicle rested on his breast. The cart was quite heavily laden. Father Fauchelevent was rattling in the throat in the most lamentable manner. They had tried, but in vain, to drag him out. An unmethodical effort, aid awkwardly given, a wrong shake, might kill him. It was impossible to disengage him otherwise than by lifting the vehicle off of him. Javert, who had come up at the moment of the accident, had sent for a jackscrew.

M. Madeleine arrived. People stood aside respectfully.

"Help!" cried old Fauchelevent. "Who will be good and save the old man?"

M. Madeleine turned toward those present. "Is there a jackscrew to be had?"

"One has been sent for," answered the peasant.

"How long will it take to get it?"

"They have gone for the nearest, to Flachot's place, where there is a farrier; but it makes no difference; it will take a good quarter of an hour."

"A quarter of an hour!" exclaimed Madeleine.

It had rained on the preceding night; the soil was soaked.

The cart was sinking deeper into the earth every moment, and crushing the old carter's breast more and more. It was evident that his ribs would be broken in five minutes more.

"It is impossible to wait another quarter of an hour," said Madeleine to the peasants, who were staring at him.

"We must!"

"But it will be too late then! Don't you see that the cart is sinking?"

"Well!"

"Listen," resumed Madeleine; "there is still room enough under the cart to allow a man to crawl beneath it and raise it with his back. Only half a minute, and the poor man can be taken out. Is there anyone here who has stout loins and heart? There are five Louis d'or to be earned!"

Not a man in the group stirred.

"Ten Louis," said Madeleine.

The persons present dropped their eyes. One of them muttered, "A man would need to be devilish strong. And then he runs the risk of getting crushed!"

"Come," began Madeleine again, "twenty Louis."

The same silence.

"It is not the will which is lacking," said a voice.

M. Madeleine turned around, and recognized Javert. He had not noticed him on his arrival.

Javert went on, "It is strength. One would have to be a terrible man to do such a thing as lift a cart like that on his back."

Then, gazing fixedly at M. Madeleine, he went on, emphasizing every word that he uttered, "Monsieur Madeleine, I have never known but one man capable of doing what you ask."

Madeleine shuddered.

Javert added, with an air of indifference, but without removing his eyes from Madeleine, "He was a convict."

"Ah!" said Madeleine.

"In the galleys at Toulon."

Madeleine turned pale.

Meanwhile, the cart continued to sink slowly. Father Fauchelevent rattled in the throat, and shrieked, "I am strangling! My ribs are breaking! A screw! Something! Ah!"

Madeleine glanced about him.

"Is there, then, no one who wishes to earn twenty Louis and save the life of this poor old man?"

No one stirred. Javert resumed, "I have never known but one man who could take the place of a screw, and he was that convict."

"Ah! It is crushing me!" cried the old man.

Madeleine raised his head, met Javert's falcon eye still fixed upon him, looked at the motionless peasants, and smiled sadly. Then, without saying a word, he fell on his knees, and before the crowd had even had time to utter a cry, he was underneath the vehicle.

A terrible moment of expectation and silence ensued.

They beheld Madeleine, almost flat on his stomach beneath that terrible weight, make two vain efforts to bring his knees and his elbows together. They shouted to him, "Father Madeleine, come out!" Old Fauchelevent himself said to him, "Monsieur Madeleine, go away! You see that I am fated to die! Leave me! You will get yourself crushed also!" Madeleine made no reply.

All the spectators were panting. The wheels had continued to sink, and it had become almost impossible for Madeleine to make his way from under the vehicle.

Suddenly the enormous mass was seen to quiver, the cart rose slowly, the wheels half emerged from the ruts. They heard a stifled voice crying, "Make haste! Help!" It was Madeleine, who had just made a final effort.

They rushed forward. The devotion of a single man had given force and courage to all. The cart was raised by twenty arms. Old Fauchelevent was saved.

Madeleine rose. He was pale, though dripping with perspiration. His clothes were torn and covered with mud. All wept. The old man kissed his knees and called him the good God. As for him, he bore upon his countenance an indescribable expression of happy and celestial suffering, and he fixed his tranquil eye on Javert, who was still staring at him.

CHAPTER VII—FAUCHELEVENT BECOMES A GARDENER IN PARIS

Fauchelevent had dislocated his kneecap in his fall. Father Madeleine had him conveyed to an infirmary, which he had established for his workmen in the factory building itself, and which was served by two sisters of charity.

On the following morning the old man found a thousand-franc banknote on his nightstand, with these words in Father Madeleine's writing: "I purchase your horse and cart." The cart was broken, and the horse was dead. Fauchelevent recovered, but his knee remained stiff. M. Madeleine, on the recommendation of the sisters of charity and of his priest, got the goodman a place as gardener in a female convent in the Rue Saint-Antoine in Paris.

Some time afterward, M. Madeleine was appointed mayor. The first time that Javert beheld M. Madeleine clothed in the scarf, which gave him authority over the town, he felt the sort of shudder that a watchdog might experience on smelling a wolf in his master's clothes. From that time forth he avoided him as much as he possibly could. When the requirements of the service imperatively demanded it, and he could not do otherwise than meet the mayor, he addressed him with profound respect.

This prosperity created at M. sur M. by Father Madeleine had, besides the visible signs which we have mentioned, another symptom which was nonetheless significant for not being visible. This never deceives. When the population suffers, when work is lacking, when there is no commerce, the taxpayer resists imposts through penury, he exhausts and oversteps his respite, and the state expends a great deal of money in the charges for compelling and collection. When work is abundant, when the country is rich and happy, the taxes are paid easily and cost the state nothing. It may be said, that there is one infallible thermometer of the public misery and riches, the cost of collecting the taxes. In the course of seven years the expense of collecting the taxes had diminished three-fourths in the arrondissement of M. sur M., and this led to this arrondissement being frequently cited from all the rest by M. de Villele, then Minister of Finance.

Such was the condition of the country when Fantine returned there. No one remembered her. Fortunately, the door of M. Madeleine's factory was like the face of a friend. She presented herself there, and was admitted to the women's workroom. The trade was entirely new to Fantine; she could not be very skillful at it, and she therefore earned but little by her day's work; but it was sufficient; the problem was solved; she was earning her living.

CHAPTER VIII—MADAME VICTURNIEN EXPENDS THIRTY FRANCS ON MORALITY

When Fantine saw that she was making her living, she felt joyful for a moment. To live honestly by her own labor, what mercy from heaven! The taste for work had really returned to her. She bought a looking glass, took pleasure in surveying in it her youth, her beautiful hair, her fine teeth; she forgot many things; she thought only of Cosette and of the possible future, and was almost happy. She hired a little room and furnished on credit on the strength of her future work—a lingering trace of her improvident ways. As she was not able to say that she was married she took good care, as we have seen, not to mention her little girl.

At first, as the reader has seen, she paid the Thenardiers promptly. As she only knew how to sign her name, she was obliged to write through a public letter writer.

She wrote often, and this was noticed. It began to be said in an undertone, in the women's workroom, that Fantine "wrote letters" and that "she had ways about her."

There is no one for spying on people's actions like those who are not concerned in them. Why does that gentleman never come except at nightfall? Why does Mr. So-and-So never hang his key on its nail on Tuesday? Why does he always take the narrow streets? Why does Madame always descend from her hackney-coach before reaching her house? Why does she send out to purchase six sheets of note paper, when she has a "whole stationer's shop full of it?" etc. There exist beings who, for the sake of obtaining the key to these enigmas, which are, moreover, of no consequence whatever to them, spend more money, waste more time, take more trouble, than would be required for ten good actions, and that gratuitously, for their own pleasure, without receiving any other payment for their curiosity than curiosity. They will follow up such-and-such a man or woman for whole days; they will do sentry duty for hours at a time on the corners of the streets, under alleyway doors at night, in cold and rain; they will bribe errand-porters, they will make the drivers of hackney-coaches and lackeys tipsy, buy a waiting-maid, suborn a porter. Why? For no reason. A pure passion for seeing, knowing, and penetrating into things. A pure itch for talking. And often these secrets once known, these mysteries made public, these enigmas illuminated by the light of day, bring on catastrophes, duels, failures, the ruin of families, and broken lives, to the great joy of those who have "found out everything," without any interest in the matter, and by pure instinct. A sad thing.

Certain persons are malicious solely through a necessity for talking. Their conversation, the chat of the drawing room, gossip of the anteroom, is like those chimneys which consume wood rapidly; they need a great amount of combustibles; and their combustibles are furnished by their neighbors.

So Fantine was watched.

In addition, many a one was jealous of her golden hair and of her white teeth.

It was remarked that in the workroom she often turned aside, in the midst of the rest, to wipe away a tear. These were the moments when she was thinking of her child; perhaps, also, of the man whom she had loved.

Breaking the gloomy bonds of the past is a mournful task.

It was observed that she wrote twice a month at least, and that she paid the carriage on the letter. They managed to obtain the address: Monsieur, Monsieur Thenardier, innkeeper at Montfermeil. The public writer, a good old man who could not fill his stomach with red wine without emptying his pocket of secrets, was made to talk in the wine shop. In short, it was discovered that Fantine had a child. "She must be a pretty sort of a woman." An old gossip was found, who made the trip to Montfermeil, talked to the Thenardiers, and said on her return, "For my five and thirty francs I have freed my mind. I have seen the child."

The gossip who did this thing was a gorgon named Madame Victurnien, the guardian and doorkeeper of everyone's virtue. Madame Victurnien was fifty-six, and reenforced the mask of ugliness with the mask of age. A quavering voice, a whimsical mind. This old dame had once been young—astonishing fact! In her youth, in '93, she had married a monk who had fled from his cloister in a red cap, and passed from the Bernardines to the Jacobins. She was dry, rough, peevish, sharp, captious, almost venomous; all this in memory of her monk, whose widow she was, and who had ruled over her masterfully and bent her to his will. She was a nettle in which the rustle of the cassock was visible. At the Restoration she had turned bigot, and that with so much energy that the priests had forgiven her her monk. She had a small property, which she bequeathed with much ostentation to a religious community. She was in high favor at the Episcopal palace of Arras. So this Madame Victurnien went to Montfermeil, and returned with the remark, "I have seen the child."

All this took time. Fantine had been at the factory for more than a year, when, one morning, the superintendent of the workroom handed her fifty francs from the mayor, told her that she was no longer employed in the shop, and requested her, in the mayor's name, to leave the neighborhood.

This was the very month when the Thenardiers, after having demanded twelve francs instead of six, had just exacted fifteen francs instead of twelve.

Fantine was overwhelmed. She could not leave the neighborhood; she was in debt for her rent and furniture. Fifty francs was not sufficient to cancel this debt. She stammered a few supplicating words. The superintendent ordered her to leave the shop on the instant. Besides, Fantine was only a moderately good workwoman. Overcome with shame, even more than with despair, she quitted the shop, and returned to her room. So her fault was now known to everyone.

She no longer felt strong enough to say a word. She was advised to see the mayor; she did not dare. The mayor had given her fifty francs because he was good, and had dismissed her because he was just. She bowed before the decision.

CHAPTER IX—MADAME VICTURNIEN'S SUCCESS

So the monk's widow was good for something.

But M. Madeleine had heard nothing of all this. Life is full of just such combinations of events. M. Madeleine was in the habit of almost never entering the women's workroom.

At the head of this room he had placed an elderly spinster, whom the priest had provided for him, and he had full confidence in this superintendent, a truly respectable person, firm, equitable, upright, full of the charity, which consists in giving, but not having in the same degree that charity which consists in understanding and in forgiving. M. Madeleine relied wholly on her. The best men are often obliged to delegate their authority. It was with this full power, and the conviction that she was doing right, that the superintendent had instituted the suit, judged, condemned, and executed Fantine.

As regards the fifty francs, she had given them from a fund which M. Madeleine had entrusted to her for charitable purposes, and for giving assistance to the workwomen, and of which she rendered no account.

Fantine tried to obtain a situation as a servant in the neighborhood; she went from house to house. No one would have her. She could not leave town. The secondhand dealer, to whom she was in debt for her furniture—and what furniture!—said to her, "If you leave, I will have you arrested as a thief." The householder, whom she owed for her rent, said to her, "You are young and pretty; you can pay." She divided the fifty francs between the landlord and the furniture-dealer, returned to the latter three-quarters of his goods, kept only necessaries, and found herself without work, without a trade, with nothing but her bed, and still about fifty francs in debt.

She began to make coarse shirts for soldiers of the garrison, and earned twelve sous a day. Her daughter cost her ten. It was at this point that she began to pay the Thenardiers irregularly.

However, the old woman who lighted her candle for her when she returned at night, taught her the art of living in misery. Back of living on little, there is the living on nothing. These are the two chambers; the first is dark, the second is black.

Fantine learned how to live without fire entirely in the winter; how to give up a bird, which eats a half a farthing's worth of millet every two days; how to make a coverlet of one's petticoat, and a petticoat of one's coverlet; how to save one's candle, by taking one's meals by the light of the opposite window. No one knows all that certain feeble creatures, who have grown old in privation and honesty, can get out of a sou. It ends by being a talent. Fantine acquired this sublime talent, and regained a little courage.

At this epoch she said to a neighbor, "Bah! I say to myself, by only sleeping five hours, and working all the rest of the time at my sewing, I shall always manage to nearly earn my bread. And, then, when one is sad, one eats less. Well, sufferings, uneasiness, a little bread on one hand, trouble on the other, all this will support me."

It would have been a great happiness to have her little girl with her in this distress. She thought of having her come. But what then! Make her share her own destitution! And then, she was in debt to the Thenardiers! How could she pay them? And the journey! How pay for that?

The old woman who had given her lessons in what may be called the life of indigence, was a sainted spinster named Marguerite, who was pious with a true piety, poor and charitable toward the poor, and even toward the rich, knowing how to write just sufficiently to sign herself Marguerite, and believing in God, which is science.

There are many such virtuous people in this lower world; some day they will be in the world above. This life has a morrow.

At first, Fantine had been so ashamed that she had not dared to go out.

When she was in the street, she divined that people turned around behind her, and pointed at her; everyone stared at her and no one greeted her; the cold and bitter scorn of the passersby penetrated her very flesh and soul like a north wind.

It seems as though an unfortunate woman were utterly bare beneath the sarcasm and the curiosity of all in small towns. In Paris, at least, no one knows you, and this obscurity is a garment. Oh! How she would have liked to betake herself to Paris! Impossible!

She was obliged to accustom herself to disrepute, as she had accustomed herself to indigence. Gradually she decided on her course. At the expiration of two or three months she shook off her shame, and began to go about as though there were nothing the matter. "It is all the same to me," she said.

She went and came, bearing her head well up, with a bitter smile, and was conscious that she was becoming brazen-faced.

Madame Victurnien sometimes saw her passing, from her window, noticed the distress of "that creature" who, "thanks to her," had been "put back in her proper place," and congratulated herself. The happiness of the evil-minded is black.

Excess of toil wore out Fantine, and the little dry cough which troubled her increased. She sometimes said to her neighbor, Marguerite, "Just feel how hot my hands are!"

Nevertheless, when she combed her beautiful hair in the morning with an old broken comb, and it flowed about her like floss silk, she experienced a moment of happy coquetry.

CHAPTER X—RESULT OF THE SUCCESS

She had been dismissed toward the end of the winter; the summer passed, but winter came again. Short days, less work. Winter: no warmth, no light, no noonday, the evening joining on to the morning, fogs, twilight; the window is gray; it is impossible to see clearly at it. The sky is but a venthole. The whole day is a cavern. The sun has the air of a beggar. A frightful season! Winter changes the water of heaven and the heart of man into a stone. Her creditors harassed her.

Fantine earned too little. Her debts had increased. The Thenardiers, who were not promptly paid, wrote to her constantly letters whose contents drove her to despair, and whose carriage ruined her. One day they wrote to her that her little Cosette was entirely naked in that cold weather, that she needed a woolen skirt, and that her mother must send at least ten francs for this. She received the letter, and crushed it in her hands all day long. That evening she went into a barber's shop at the corner of the street, and pulled out her comb. Her admirable golden hair fell to her knees.

"What splendid hair!" exclaimed the barber.

"How much will you give me for it?" said she.

"Ten francs."

"Cut it off."

She purchased a knitted petticoat and sent it to the Thenardiers. This petticoat made the Thenardiers furious. It was the money that they wanted. They gave the petticoat to Eponine. The poor Lark continued to shiver.

Fantine thought, "My child is no longer cold. I have clothed her with my hair." She put on little round caps which concealed her shorn head, and in which she was still pretty.

Dark thoughts held possession of Fantine's heart.

When she saw that she could no longer dress her hair, she began to hate everyone about her. She had long shared the universal veneration for Father Madeleine; yet, by dint of repeating to herself that it was he who had discharged her, that he was the cause of her unhappiness, she came to hate him also, and most of all. When she passed the factory in working hours, when the workpeople were at the door, she affected to laugh and sing.

An old workwoman who once saw her laughing and singing in this fashion said, "There's a girl who will come to a bad end."

She took a lover, the first who offered, a man whom she did not love, out of bravado and with rage in her heart. He was a miserable scamp, a sort of mendicant musician, a lazy beggar, who beat her, and who abandoned her as she had taken him, in disgust.

She adored her child.

The lower she descended, the darker everything grew about her, the more radiant shone that little angel at the bottom of her heart. She said, "When I get rich, I will have my Cosette with me;" and she laughed. Her cough did not leave her, and she had sweats on her back.

One day she received from the Thenardiers a letter couched in the following terms: "Cosette is ill with a malady that is going the rounds of the neighborhood. A miliary fever, they call it. Expensive drugs are required. This is ruining us, and we can no longer pay for them. If you do not send us forty francs before the week is out, the little one will be dead."

She burst out laughing, and said to her old neighbor, "Ah! They are good! Forty francs! The idea! That makes two napoleons! Where do they think I am to get them? These peasants are stupid, truly."

Nevertheless she went to a dormer window in the staircase and read the letter once more. Then she descended the stairs and emerged, running and leaping and still laughing.

Someone met her and said to her, "What makes you so gay?"

She replied, "A fine piece of stupidity that some country people have written to me. They demand forty francs of me. So much for you, you peasants!"

As she crossed the square, she saw a great many people collected around a carriage of eccentric shape, upon the top of which stood a man dressed in red, who was holding forth. He was a quack dentist on his rounds, who was offering to the public full sets of teeth, opiates, powders, and elixirs.

Fantine mingled in the group, and began to laugh with the rest at the harangue, which contained slang for the populace and jargon for respectable people. The tooth-puller espied the lovely, laughing girl, and suddenly exclaimed, "You have beautiful teeth, you girl there, who are laughing; if you want to sell me your palettes, I will give you a gold napoleon apiece for them."

"What are my palettes?" asked Fantine.

"The palettes," replied the dental professor, "are the front teeth, the two upper ones."

"How horrible!" exclaimed Fantine.

"Two napoleons!" grumbled a toothless old woman who was present. "Here's a lucky girl!"

Fantine fled and stopped her ears that she might not hear the hoarse voice of the man shouting to her, "Reflect, my beauty! Two napoleons; they may prove of service. If your heart bids you, come this evening to the inn of the Tillac d'Argent; you will find me there."

Fantine returned home. She was furious, and related the occurrence to her good neighbor Marguerite: "Can you understand such a thing? Is he not an abominable man? How can they allow such people to go about the country! Pull out my two front teeth! Why, I should be horrible! My hair will grow again, but my teeth! Ah! What a monster of a man! I should prefer to throw myself head first on the pavement from the fifth story! He told me that he should be at the Tillac d'Argent this evening."

"And what did he offer?" asked Marguerite.

"Two napoleons."

"That makes forty francs."

"Yes," said Fantine; "that makes forty francs."

She remained thoughtful, and began her work. At the expiration of a quarter of an hour she left her sewing and went to read the Thenardiers' letter once more on the staircase.

On her return, she said to Marguerite, who was at work beside her, "What is a miliary fever? Do you know?"

"Yes," answered the old spinster; "it is a disease."

"Does it require many drugs?"

"Oh! Terrible drugs."

"How does one get it?"

"It is a malady that one gets without knowing how."

"Then it attacks children?"

"Children in particular."

"Do people die of it?"

"They may," said Marguerite.

Fantine left the room and went to read her letter once more on the staircase.

That evening she went out, and was seen to turn her steps in the direction of the Rue de Paris, where the inns are situated.

The next morning, when Marguerite entered Fantine's room before daylight, for they always worked together, and in this manner used only one candle for the two, she found Fantine seated on her bed, pale and frozen. She had not lain down. Her cap had fallen on her knees. Her candle had burned all night, and was almost entirely consumed. Marguerite halted on the threshold, petrified at this tremendous wastefulness, and exclaimed, "Lord! the candle is all burned out! Something has happened."

Then she looked at Fantine, who turned toward her, her head bereft of its hair.

Fantine had grown ten years older since the preceding night.

"Jesus!" said Marguerite, "what is the matter with you, Fantine?"

"Nothing," replied Fantine. "Quite the contrary. My child will not die of that frightful malady, for lack of succor. I am content."

So saying, she pointed out to the spinster two napoleons which were glittering on the table.

"Ah! Jesus God!" cried Marguerite. "Why, it is a fortune! Where did you get those Louis d'or?"

"I got them," replied Fantine.

At the same time she smiled. The candle illuminated her countenance. It was a bloody smile. A reddish saliva soiled the corners of her lips, and she had a black hole in her mouth.

The two teeth had been extracted.

She sent the forty francs to Montfermeil.

After all it was a ruse of the Thenardiers to obtain money. Cosette was not ill.

Fantine threw her mirror out of the window. She had long since quitted her cell on the second floor for an attic with only a latch to fasten it, next the roof; one of those attics whose extremity forms an angle with the floor, and knocks you on the head every instant. The poor occupant can reach the end of his chamber as he can the end of his destiny, only by bending over more and more.

She had no longer a bed; a rag which she called her coverlet, a mattress on the floor, and a seatless chair still remained. A little rosebush that she had, had dried up, forgotten, in one corner. In the other corner was a butter-pot to hold water, which froze in winter, and in which the various levels of the water remained long marked by these circles of ice. She had lost her shame; she lost her coquetry. A final sign. She went out, with dirty caps. Whether from lack of time or from indifference, she no longer mended her linen. As the heels wore out, she dragged her stockings down into her shoes. This was evident from the perpendicular wrinkles. She patched her bodice, which was old and worn out, with scraps of calico which tore at the slightest movement. The people to whom she was indebted made "scenes" and gave her no peace. She found them in the street, she found them again on her staircase. She passed many a night weeping and thinking. Her eyes were very bright, and she felt a steady pain in her shoulder toward the top of the left shoulder blade. She coughed a great deal. She deeply hated Father Madeleine, but made no complaint. She sewed seventeen hours a day; but a contractor for the work of prisons, who made the prisoners work at a discount, suddenly made prices fall, which reduced the daily earnings of working-women to nine sous. Seventeen hours of toil, and nine sous a day! Her creditors were more pitiless than ever. The secondhand dealer, who had taken back nearly all his furniture, said to her incessantly, "When will you pay me, you hussy?" What did they want of her, good God! She felt that she was being hunted, and something of the wild beast developed in her. About the same time, Thenardier wrote to her that he had waited with decidedly too much amiability and that he must have a hundred francs at once; otherwise he would turn little Cosette out of doors, convalescent as she was from her heavy illness, into the cold and the streets, and that she might do what she liked with herself, and die if she chose. "A hundred francs," thought Fantine. "But in what trade can one earn a hundred sous a day?"

"Come!" said she, "let us sell what is left."

The unfortunate girl became a woman of the town.

CHAPTER XI—CHRISTUS NOS LIBERAVIT

What is this history of Fantine? It is society purchasing a slave.

From whom? From misery.

From hunger, cold, isolation, destitution. A dolorous bargain. A soul for a morsel of bread. Misery offers; society accepts.

The sacred law of Jesus Christ governs our civilization, but it does not, as yet, permeate it; it is said that slavery has disappeared from European civilization. This is a mistake. It still exists; but it weighs only upon the woman, and it is called prostitution.

It weighs upon the woman, that is to say, upon grace, weakness, beauty, maternity. This is not one of the least of man's disgraces.

At the point in this melancholy drama that we have now reached, nothing is left to Fantine of that which she had formerly been.

She has become marble in becoming mire. Whoever touches her feels cold. She passes; she endures you; she ignores you; she is the severe and dishonored figure. Life and the social order have said their last word for her. All has happened to her that will happen to her. She has felt everything, borne everything, experienced everything, suffered everything, lost everything, mourned everything. She is resigned, with that resignation which resembles indifference, as death resembles sleep. She no longer avoids anything. Let all the clouds fall upon her, and all the ocean sweep over her! What matters it to her? She is a sponge that is soaked.

At least, she believes it to be so; but it is an error to imagine that fate can be exhausted, and that one has reached the bottom of anything whatever.

Alas! What are all these fates, driven on pell-mell? Where are they going? Why are they thus?

He who knows that sees the whole of the shadow.

He is alone. His name is God.

CHAPTER XII—M. BAMATABOIS'S INACTIVITY

There is in all small towns, and there was at M. sur M. in particular, a class of young men who nibble away an income of fifteen hundred francs with the same air with which their prototypes devour two hundred thousand francs a year in Paris. These are beings of the great neuter species: impotent men, parasites, cyphers, who have a little land, a little folly, a little wit; who would be rustics in a drawing room, and who think themselves gentlemen in the dram shop; who say, "My fields, my peasants, my woods"; who hiss actresses at the theater to prove that they are persons of taste; quarrel with the officers of the garrison to prove that they are men of war; hunt, smoke, yawn, drink, smell of tobacco, play billiards, stare at travelers as they descend from the diligence, live at the café, dine at the inn, have a dog that eats the bones under the table, and a mistress who eats the dishes on the table; who stick at a sou, exaggerate the fashions, admire tragedy, despise women, wear out their old boots, copy

London through Paris, and Paris through the medium of Pont-à-Mousson, grow old as dullards, never work, serve no use, and do no great harm.

M. Felix Tholomyes, had he remained in his own province and never beheld Paris, would have been one of these men.

If they were richer, one would say, "They are dandies;" if they were poorer, one would say, "They are idlers." They are simply men without employment. Among these unemployed there are bores, the bored, dreamers, and some knaves.

At that period a dandy was composed of a tall collar, a big cravat, a watch with trinkets, three vests of different colors, worn one on top of the other—the red and blue inside; of a short-waisted olive coat, with a codfish tail, a double row of silver buttons set close to each other and running up to the shoulder; and a pair of trousers of a lighter shade of olive, ornamented on the two seams with an indefinite, but always uneven, number of lines, varying from one to eleven—a limit that was never exceeded. Add to this, high shoes with little irons on the heels, a tall hat with a narrow brim, hair worn in a tuft, an enormous cane, and conversation set off by puns of Potier. Over all, spurs and a mustache. At that epoch mustaches indicated the bourgeois, and spurs the pedestrian.

The provincial dandy wore the longest of spurs and the fiercest of mustaches.

It was the period of the conflict of the republics of South America with the King of Spain, of Bolivar against Morillo. Narrow-brimmed hats were royalist, and were called morillos; liberals wore hats with wide brims, which were called bolivars.

Eight or ten months, then, after that which is related in the preceding pages, toward the first of January, 1823, on a snowy evening, one of these dandies, one of these unemployed, a "right thinker," for he wore a morillo, and was, moreover, warmly enveloped in one of those large cloaks that completed the fashionable costume in cold weather, was amusing himself by tormenting a creature who was prowling about in a ball dress, with neck uncovered and flowers in her hair, in front of the officers' cafe. This dandy was smoking, for he was decidedly fashionable.

Each time that the woman passed in front of him, he bestowed on her, together with a puff from his cigar, some apostrophe which he considered witty and mirthful, such as, "How ugly you are!—Will you get out of my sight?—You have no teeth!" etc., etc. This gentleman was known as M. Bamatabois. The woman, a melancholy, decorated specter that went and came through the snow, made him no reply, did not even glance at him, and nevertheless continued her promenade in silence, and with a somber regularity, which brought her every five minutes within reach of this sarcasm, like the condemned soldier who returns under the rods. The small effect which he produced no doubt piqued the lounger; and taking advantage of a moment when her back was turned, he crept up behind her with the gait of a wolf, and stifling his laugh, bent down, picked up a handful of snow from the pavement, and thrust it abruptly into her back, between her bare shoulders. The woman uttered a roar, whirled around, gave a leap like a panther, and hurled herself upon the man, burying her nails in his face, with the most frightful words that could fall from the guardroom into the gutter. These insults, poured forth in a voice roughened by brandy, did, indeed, proceed in hideous wise from a mouth that lacked its two front teeth. It was Fantine.

At the noise thus produced, the officers ran out in throngs from the café, passersby collected, and a large and merry circle, hooting and applauding, was formed around this whirlwind composed of two beings, whom there was some difficulty in recognizing as a man and a woman: the man struggling, his hat on the ground; the woman striking out with feet and fists, bareheaded, howling, minus hair and teeth, livid with wrath, horrible.

Suddenly a man of lofty stature emerged vivaciously from the crowd, seized the woman by her satin bodice, which was covered with mud, and said to her, "Follow me!"

The woman raised her head; her furious voice suddenly died away. Her eyes were glassy; she turned pale instead of livid, and she trembled with a quiver of terror. She had recognized Javert.

The dandy took advantage of the incident to make his escape.

CHAPTER XIII—THE SOLUTION OF SOME QUESTIONS CONNECTED WITH THE MUNICIPAL POLICE

Javert thrust aside the spectators, broke the circle, and set out with long strides toward the police station, which is situated at the extremity of the square, dragging the wretched woman after him. She yielded mechanically. Neither he nor she uttered a word. The cloud of spectators followed, jesting, in a paroxysm of delight. Supreme misery an occasion for obscenity.

On arriving at the police station, which was a low room, warmed by a stove, with a glazed and grated door opening on the street, and guarded by a detachment, Javert opened the door, entered with Fantine, and shut the door behind him, to the great disappointment of the curious, who raised themselves on tiptoe, and craned their necks in front of the thick glass of the stationhouse, in their effort to see. Curiosity is a sort of gluttony. To see is to devour.

On entering, Fantine fell down in a corner, motionless and mute, crouching down like a terrified dog.

The sergeant of the guard brought a lighted candle to the table. Javert seated himself, drew a sheet of stamped paper from his pocket, and began to write.

This class of women is consigned by our laws entirely to the discretion of the police. The latter do what they please, punish them, as seems good to them, and confiscate at their will those two sorry things which they entitle their industry and their liberty. Javert was impassive; his grave face betrayed no emotion whatever. Nevertheless, he was seriously and deeply preoccupied. It was one of those moments when he was exercising without control, but subject to all the scruples of a severe conscience, his redoubtable discretionary power. At that moment he was conscious that his police agent's stool was a tribunal. He was entering judgment. He judged and condemned. He summoned all the ideas that could possibly exist in his mind, around the great thing that he was doing. The more he examined the deed of this woman, the more shocked he felt. It was evident that he had just witnessed the commission of a crime. He had just beheld, yonder, in the street, society, in the person of a freeholder and an elector, insulted and attacked by a creature who was outside all pales. A prostitute had made an attempt on the life of a citizen. He had seen that, he, Javert. He wrote in silence.

When he had finished he signed the paper, folded it, and said to the sergeant of the guard, as he handed it to him, "Take three men and conduct this creature to jail."

Then, turning to Fantine, "You are to have six months of it." The unhappy woman shuddered.

"Six months! Six months of prison!" she exclaimed. "Six months in which to earn seven sous a day! But what will become of Cosette? My daughter! my daughter! But I still owe the Thenardiers over a hundred francs; do you know that, Monsieur Inspector?"

She dragged herself across the damp floor, among the muddy boots of all those men, without rising, with clasped hands, and taking great strides on her knees.

"Monsieur Javert," said she, "I beseech your mercy. I assure you that I was not in the wrong. If you had seen the beginning, you would have seen. I swear to you by the good God that I was not to blame! That gentleman, the bourgeois, whom I do not know, put snow in my back. Has anyone the right to put snow down our backs when we are walking along peaceably, and doing no harm to anyone? I am rather ill, as you see. And then, he had been saying impertinent things to me for a long time: 'You are ugly! You have no teeth!' I know well that I no longer those teeth. I did nothing; I said to myself, 'The gentleman is amusing himself.' I was honest with him; I did not speak to him. It was at that moment that he put the snow down my back. Monsieur Javert, good Monsieur Inspector! Is there not some person here who saw it and can tell you that this is quite true? Perhaps I did wrong to get angry. You know that one is not master of one's self at the first moment. One gives way to vivacity; and then, when someone puts something cold down your back just when you are not expecting it! I did wrong to spoil that gentleman's hat. Why did he go away? I would ask his pardon. Oh, my God! It makes no difference to me whether I ask his pardon. Do me the favor today, for this once, Monsieur Javert. Hold! You do not know that in prison one can earn only seven sous a day; it is not the government's fault, but seven sous is one's earnings; and just fancy, I must pay one hundred francs, or my little girl will be sent to me. Oh, my God! I cannot have her with me. What I do is so vile! Oh, my Cosette! Oh, my little angel of the Holy Virgin! what will become of her, poor creature? I will tell you: it is the Thenardiers, innkeepers, peasants; and such people are unreasonable. They want money. Don't put me in prison! You see, there is a little girl who will be turned out into the street to get along as best she may, in the very heart of the winter; and you must have pity on such a being, my good Monsieur Javert. If she were older, she might earn her living; but it cannot be done at that age. I am not a bad woman at bottom. It is not cowardliness and gluttony that have made me what I am. If I have drunk brandy, it was out of misery. I do not love it; but it benumbs the senses. When I was happy, it was only necessary to glance into my closets, and it would have been evident that I was not a coquettish and untidy woman. I had linen, a great deal of linen. Have pity on me, Monsieur Javert!"

She spoke thus, rent in twain, shaken with sobs, blinded with tears, her neck bare, wringing her hands, and coughing with a dry, short cough, stammering softly with a voice of agony. Great sorrow is a divine and terrible ray, which transfigures the unhappy. At that moment Fantine had become beautiful once more. From time to time she paused, and tenderly kissed the police agent's coat. She would have softened a heart of granite; but a heart of wood cannot be softened.

"Come!" said Javert, "I have heard you out. Have you entirely finished? You will get six months. Now march! The Eternal Father in person could do nothing more."

At these solemn words, "the Eternal Father in person could do nothing more," she understood that her fate was sealed. She sank down, murmuring, "Mercy!"

Javert turned his back.

The soldiers seized her by the arms.

A few moments earlier a man had entered, but no one had paid any heed to him. He shut the door, leaned his back against it, and listened to Fantine's despairing supplications.

At the instant when the soldiers laid their hands upon the unfortunate woman, who would not rise, he emerged from the shadow, and said, "One moment, if you please."

Javert raised his eyes and recognized M. Madeleine. He removed his hat, and, saluting him with a sort of aggrieved awkwardness, "Excuse me, Mr. Mayor—"

The words "Mr. Mayor" produced a curious effect upon Fantine. She rose to her feet with one bound, like a specter springing from the earth, thrust aside the soldiers with both arms, walked straight up to M. Madeleine before anyone could prevent her, and gazing intently at him, with a bewildered air, she cried:

"Ah! So it is you who are M. le Maire!"

Then she burst into a laugh, and spit in his face.

M. Madeleine wiped his face, and said, "Inspector Javert, set this woman at liberty."

Javert felt that he was on the verge of going mad. He experienced at that moment, blow upon blow and almost simultaneously, the most violent emotions which he had ever undergone in all his life. To see a woman of the town spit in the mayor's face was a thing so monstrous that, in his most daring flights of fancy, he would have regarded it as a sacrilege to believe it possible. On the other hand, at the very bottom of his thought, he made a hideous comparison as to what this woman was, and as to what this mayor might be; and then he, with horror, caught a glimpse of I know not what simple explanation of this prodigious attack. But when he beheld that mayor, that magistrate, calmly wipe his face and say, "Set this woman at liberty," he underwent a sort of intoxication of amazement; thought and word failed him equally; the sum total of possible astonishment had been exceeded in his case. He remained mute.

The words had produced no less strange an effect on Fantine. She raised her bare arm, and clung to the damper of the stove, like a person who is reeling. Nevertheless, she glanced about her, and began to speak in a low voice, as though talking to herself, "At liberty! I am to be allowed to go! I am not to go to prison for six months! Who said that? It is not possible that anyone could have said that. I did not hear right. It cannot have been that monster of a mayor! Was it you, my good Monsieur Javert, who said that I was to be set free? Oh, see here! I will tell you about it, and you will let me go. That monster of a mayor, that old blackguard of a mayor, is the cause of all. Just imagine, Monsieur Javert, he turned me out! All because of a pack of rascally women, who gossip in the workroom. If that is not a horror, what is? To dismiss a poor girl who is doing her work honestly! Then I could no longer earn enough, and all this misery followed. In the first place, there is one improvement, which these gentlemen of the police ought to make, and that is, to prevent prison contractors from wronging poor people. I will explain it to you, you see: you are earning twelve sous at shirtmaking, the price falls to nine sous; and it is not enough to live on. Then one has to become whatever one can. As for me, I had my little Cosette, and I was actually forced to become a bad woman. Now you understand how it is that that blackguard of a mayor caused all the mischief. After that I stamped on that gentleman's hat in front of the officers' café; but he had spoiled my whole dress with snow. We women have but one silk dress for evening wear. You see that I did not do wrong deliberately—truly, Monsieur Javert; and everywhere I behold women who are far more wicked than I, and who are much happier. O Monsieur Javert! It was you who gave orders that I am to be set free, was it not? Make inquiries, speak to my landlord; I am paying my rent now; they will tell you that I am perfectly honest. Ah! my God! I beg your pardon; I have unintentionally touched the damper of the stove, and it has made it smoke."

M. Madeleine listened to her with profound attention. While she was speaking, he fumbled in his waistcoat, drew out his purse and opened it. It was empty. He put it back in his pocket. He said to Fantine, "How much did you say that you owed?"

Fantine, who was looking at Javert only, turned toward him. "Was I speaking to you?"

Then, addressing the soldiers: "Say, you fellows, did you see how I spit in his face? Ah! you old wretch of a mayor, you came here to frighten me, but I'm not afraid of you. I am afraid of Monsieur Javert. I am afraid of my good Monsieur Javert!"

So saying, she turned to the inspector again. "And yet, you see, Mr. Inspector, it is necessary to be just. I understand that you are just, Mr. Inspector; in fact, it is perfectly simple: a man amuses himself by putting snow down a woman's back, and that makes the officers laugh; one must divert themselves in some way; and we—well, we are here for them to amuse themselves with, of course! And then, you, you come; you are certainly obliged to preserve order, you lead off the woman who is in the wrong; but on reflection, since you are a good man, you say that I am to be set at liberty; it is for the sake of the little one, for six months in prison would prevent my supporting my child. 'Only, don't do it again, you hussy!' Oh! I won't do it again, Monsieur Javert! They may do whatever they please to me now; I will not stir. But today, you see, I cried because it hurt me. I was not expecting that snow from the gentleman at all; and then as I told you, I am not well; I have a cough; I seem to have a burning ball in my stomach, and the doctor tells me, 'Take care of yourself.' Here, feel, give me your hand; don't be afraid—it is here."

She no longer wept, her voice was caressing; she placed Javert's coarse hand on her delicate, white throat and looked smilingly at him.

All at once she rapidly adjusted her disordered garments, dropped the folds of her skirt, which had been pushed up as she dragged herself along, almost to the height of her knee, and stepped toward the door, saying to the soldiers in a low voice, and with a friendly nod, "Children, Monsieur l'Inspecteur has said that I am to be released, and I am going."

She laid her hand on the latch of the door. One step more and she would be in the street.

Javert up to that moment had remained erect, motionless, with his eyes fixed on the ground, cast athwart this scene like some displaced statue, which is waiting to be put away somewhere.

The sound of the latch roused him. He raised his head with an expression of sovereign authority, an expression all the more alarming in proportion as the authority rests on a low level, ferocious in the wild beast, atrocious in the man of no estate.

"Sergeant!" he cried, "don't you see that that jade is walking off! Who bade you let her go?"

"I," said Madeleine.

Fantine trembled at the sound of Javert's voice, and let go of the latch as a thief relinquishes the article which he has stolen. At the sound of Madeleine's voice she turned around, and from that moment forth she uttered no word, nor dared so much as to breathe freely, but her glance strayed from Madeleine to Javert, and from Javert to Madeleine in turn, according to which was speaking.

It was evident that Javert must have been exasperated beyond measure before he would permit himself to apostrophize the sergeant as he had done, after the mayor's suggestion that Fantine should be set at liberty. Had he reached the point of forgetting the mayor's presence? Had he finally declared to himself that it was impossible that any "authority" should have given such an order, and that the mayor must certainly have said one thing by mistake for another, without intending it? Or, in view of the enormities of which he had been a witness for the past two hours, did he say to himself, that it was necessary to recur to supreme resolutions, that it was indispensable that the small should be made great, that the police spy should transform himself into a magistrate, that the policeman should become a dispenser of justice, and that, in this prodigious extremity, order, law, morality, government, society in its entirety, was personified in him, Javert?

However that may be, when M. Madeleine uttered that word, I, as we have just heard, Police Inspector Javert was seen to turn toward the mayor, pale, cold, with blue lips, and a look of despair, his whole body agitated by an imperceptible quiver and an unprecedented occurrence, and say to him, with downcast eyes but a firm voice, "Mr. Mayor, that cannot be."

"Why not?" said M. Madeleine.

"This miserable woman has insulted a citizen."

"Inspector Javert," replied the mayor, in a calm and conciliating tone, "listen. You are an honest man, and I feel no hesitation in explaining matters to you. Here is the true state of the case: I was passing through the square just as you were leading this woman away; there were still groups of people standing about, and I made inquiries and learned everything; it was the townsman who was in the wrong and who should have been arrested by properly conducted police."

Javert retorted, "This wretch has just insulted Monsieur le Maire."

"That concerns me," said M. Madeleine. "My own insult belongs to me, I think. I can do what I please about it."

"I beg Monsieur le Maire's pardon. The insult is not to him but to the law."

"Inspector Javert," replied M. Madeleine, "the highest law is conscience. I have heard this woman; I know what I am doing."

"And I, Mr. Mayor, do not know what I see."

"Then content yourself with obeying."

"I am obeying my duty. My duty demands that this woman shall serve six months in prison."

M. Madeleine replied gently, "Heed this well; she will not serve a single day."

At this decisive word, Javert ventured to fix a searching look on the mayor and to say, but in a tone of voice that was still profoundly respectful:

"I am sorry to oppose Monsieur le Maire; it is for the first time in my life, but he will permit me to remark that I am within the bounds of my authority. I confine myself, since Monsieur le Maire desires it, to the question of the gentleman. I was present. This woman flung herself on Monsieur Bamatabnois, who is an elector and the proprietor of that handsome house with a balcony, which forms the corner of the esplanade, three stories high and entirely of cut stone. Such things as there are in the world! In any case, Monsieur le Maire, this is a question of police regulations in the streets, and concerns me, and I shall detain this woman Fantine."

Then M. Madeleine folded his arms, and said in a severe voice that no one in the town had heard hitherto, "The matter to which you refer is one connected with the municipal police. According to the terms of articles nine, eleven, fifteen, and sixty-six of the code of criminal examination, I am the judge. I order that this woman shall be set at liberty."

Javert ventured to make a final effort. "But, Mr. Mayor—"

"I refer you to article eighty-one of the law of the 13th of December, 1799, in regard to arbitrary detention."

"Monsieur le Maire, permit me—"

"Not another word."

"But—"

"Leave the room," said M. Madeleine.

Javert received the blow erect, full in the face, in his breast, like a Russian soldier. He bowed to the very earth before the mayor and left the room.

Fantine stood aside from the door and stared at him in amazement as he passed.

Nevertheless, she also was the prey to a strange confusion. She had just seen herself a subject of dispute between two opposing powers. She had seen two men who held in their hands her liberty, her life, her soul, her child, in combat before her very eyes; one of these men was drawing her toward darkness, the other was leading her back toward the light. In this conflict, viewed through the exaggerations of terror, these two men had appeared to her like two giants; the one spoke like her demon, the other like her good angel. The angel had conquered the demon, and, strange to say, that which made her shudder from head to foot was the fact that this angel, this liberator, was the very man whom she abhorred, that mayor whom she had so long regarded as the author of all her woes, that Madeleine! And at the very moment when she had insulted him in so hideous a fashion, he had saved her! Had she, then, been mistaken? Must she change her whole soul? She did not know; she trembled. She listened in bewilderment, she looked on in affright, and at every word uttered by M.

Madeleine she felt the frightful shades of hatred crumble and melt within her, and something warm and ineffable, indescribable, which was both joy, confidence and love, dawn in her heart.

When Javert had taken his departure, M. Madeleine turned to her and said to her in a deliberate voice, like a serious man who does not wish to weep and who finds some difficulty in speaking, "I have heard you. I knew nothing about what you have mentioned. I believe that it is true, and I feel that it is true. I was even ignorant of the fact that you had left my shop. Why did you not apply to me? But here; I will pay your debts, I will send for your child, or you shall go to her. You shall live here, in Paris, or where you please. I undertake the care of your child and yourself. You shall not work any longer if you do not like. I will give all the money you require. You shall be honest and happy once more. And listen! I declare to you that if all is as you say, and I do not doubt it, you have never ceased to be virtuous and holy in the sight of God. Oh! Poor woman."

This was more than Fantine could bear. To have Cosette! To leave this life of infamy. To live free, rich, happy, respectable with Cosette; to see all these realities of paradise blossom of a sudden in the midst of her misery. She stared stupidly at this man who was talking to her, and could only give vent to two or three sobs, "Oh! Oh! Oh!"

Her limbs gave way beneath her, she knelt in front of M. Madeleine, and before he could prevent her he felt her grasp his hand and press her lips to it.

Then she fainted.

BOOK SIXTH: JAVERT

CHAPTER I—THE BEGINNING OF REPOSE

M. Madeleine had Fantine removed to that infirmary which he had established in his own house. He confided her to the sisters, who put her to bed. A burning fever had come on. She passed a part of the night in delirium and raving. At length, however, she fell asleep.

On the morrow, toward midday, Fantine awoke. She heard someone breathing close to her bed; she drew aside the curtain and saw M. Madeleine standing there and looking at something over her head. His gaze was full of pity, anguish, and supplication. She followed its direction, and saw that it was fixed on a crucifix that was nailed to the wall.

Thenceforth, M. Madeleine was transfigured in Fantine's eyes. He seemed to her to be clothed in light. He was absorbed in a sort of prayer. She gazed at him for a long time without daring to interrupt him. At last she said timidly, "What are you doing?"

M. Madeleine had been there for an hour. He had been waiting for Fantine to awake. He took her hand, felt of her pulse, and replied, "How do you feel?"

"Well, I have slept," she replied; "I think that I am better; it is nothing."

He answered, responding to the first question that she had put to him as though he had just heard it, "I was praying to the martyr there on high."

And he added in his own mind, "For the martyr here below."

M. Madeleine had passed the night and the morning in making inquiries. He knew all now. He knew Fantine's history in all its heartrending details. He went on, "You have suffered much, poor mother. Oh! Do not complain; you now have the dowry of the elect. It is thus that men are transformed into angels. It is not their fault they do not know how to go to work otherwise. You see this hell from which you have just emerged is the first form of heaven. It was necessary to begin there."

He sighed deeply. But she smiled on him with that sublime smile in which two teeth were lacking.

That same night, Javert wrote a letter. The next morning he posted it himself at the office of M. sur M. It was addressed to Paris, and the superscription ran: *To Monsieur Chabouillet, Secretary of Monsieur le Prefet of Police.* As the affair in the stationhouse had been bruited about, the postmistress and some other persons who saw the letter before it was sent off, and who recognized Javert's handwriting on the cover, thought that he was sending in his resignation.

M. Madeleine made haste to write to the Thenardiers. Fantine owed them one hundred and twenty francs. He sent them three hundred francs, telling them to pay themselves from that sum, and to fetch the child instantly to M. sur M., where her sick mother required her presence.

This dazzled Thenardier. "The devil!" said the man to his wife. "Don't allow the child to go. This lark is going to turn into a milch* cow. I see through it. Some ninny has taken a fancy to the mother."

He replied with a very well-drawn-up bill for five hundred and some odd francs. In this memorandum two indisputable items figured up over three hundred francs, one for the doctor, the other for the apothecary who had attended and physicked Eponine and Azelma through two long illnesses.

---

* milk

Cosette, as we have already said, had not been ill. It was only a question of a trifling substitution of names. At the foot of the memorandum Thenardier wrote: *Received on account, three hundred francs.*

M. Madeleine immediately sent three hundred francs more, and wrote, "Make haste to bring Cosette."

"Christi!" said Thenardier. "Let's not give up the child."

In the meantime, Fantine did not recover. She still remained in the infirmary.

The sisters had at first only received and nursed "that woman" with repugnance. Those who have seen the bas-reliefs of Rheims will recall the inflation of the lower lip of the wise virgins as they survey the foolish virgins. The ancient scorn of the vestals for the ambubajae is one of the most profound instincts of feminine dignity; the sisters felt it with the double force contributed by religion. But in a few days Fantine disarmed them. She said all kinds of humble and gentle things, and the mother in her provoked tenderness. One day the sisters heard her say amid her fever, "I have been a sinner; but when I have my child beside me, it will be a sign that God has pardoned me. While I was leading a bad life, I should not have liked to have my Cosette with me; I could not have borne her sad, astonished eyes. It was for her sake that I did evil, and that is why God pardons me. I shall feel the benediction of the good God when Cosette is here. I shall gaze at her; it will do me good to see that innocent creature. She knows nothing at all. She is an angel, you see, my sisters. At that age the wings have not fallen off."

M. Madeleine went to see her twice a day, and each time she asked him, "Shall I see my Cosette soon?"

He answered, "Tomorrow, perhaps. She may arrive at any moment. I am expecting her."

And the mother's pale face grew radiant.

"Oh!" she said. "How happy I am going to be!"

We have just said that she did not recover her health. On the contrary, her condition seemed to become more grave from week to week. That handful of snow applied to her bare skin between her shoulder blades had brought about a sudden suppression of perspiration, as a consequence of which the malady that had been shouldering within her for many years was violently developed at last. At that time people were beginning to follow the fine Laennec's fine suggestions in the study and treatment of chest maladies. The doctor sounded Fantine's chest and shook his head.

M. Madeleine said to the doctor, "Well?"

"Has she not a child which she desires to see?" said the doctor.

"Yes."

"Well! Make haste and get it here!"

M. Madeleine shuddered.

Fantine inquired, "What did the doctor say?"

M. Madeleine forced himself to smile.

"He said that your child was to be brought speedily. That that would restore your health."

"Oh!" she rejoined. "He is right! But what do those Thenardiers mean by keeping my Cosette from me! Oh! She is coming. At last I behold happiness close beside me!"

In the meantime Thenardier did not "let go of the child," and gave a hundred insufficient reasons for it. Cosette was not quite well enough to take a journey in the winter. And then, there still remained some petty but pressing debts in the neighborhood, and they were collecting the bills for them, etc., etc.

"I shall send someone to fetch Cosette!" said Father Madeleine. "If necessary, I will go myself."

He wrote the following letter to Fantine's dictation, and made her sign it:

> Monsieur Thenardier:
> You will deliver Cosette to this person.
> You will be paid for all the little things.
> I have the honor to salute you with respect.
> Fantine.

In the meantime a serious incident occurred. Carve as we will the mysterious block of which our life is made, the black vein of destiny constantly reappears in it.

CHAPTER II—HOW JEAN MAY BECOME CHAMP

One morning M. Madeleine was in his study, occupied in arranging in advance some pressing matters connected with the mayor's office, in case he should decide to take the trip to Montfermeil, when he was informed that Police Inspector Javert was desirous of speaking with him. Madeleine could not refrain from a disagreeable impression on hearing this name. Javert had avoided him more than ever since the affair of the police station, and M. Madeleine had not seen him.

"Admit him," he said.

Javert entered.

M. Madeleine had retained his seat near the fire, pen in hand, his eyes fixed on the docket that he was turning over and annotating, and which contained the trials of the commission on highways for the infraction of police regulations. He did not disturb himself on Javert's account. He could not help thinking of poor Fantine, and it suited him to be glacial in his manner.

Javert bestowed a respectful salute on the mayor, whose back was turned to him. The mayor did not look at him, but went on annotating this docket.

Javert advanced two or three paces into the study, and halted, without breaking the silence.

If any physiognomist who had been familiar with Javert, and who had made a lengthy study of this savage in the service of civilization, this singular composite of the Roman, the Spartan, the monk, and the corporal, this spy who was incapable of a lie, this unspotted police agent—if any physiognomist had known his secret and long-cherished aversion for M. Madeleine, his conflict with the mayor on the subject of Fantine, and had examined Javert at that moment, he would have said to himself, "What has taken place?" It was evident to anyone acquainted with that clear, upright, sincere, honest, austere, and ferocious conscience, that Javert had but just gone through some great interior struggle. Javert had nothing in his soul that he had not also in his countenance. Like violent people in general, he was subject to abrupt changes of opinion. His physiognomy had never been more peculiar and startling. On entering he bowed to M. Madeleine with a look in which there was neither rancor, anger, nor distrust; he halted a few paces in the rear of the mayor's armchair, and there he stood, perfectly erect, in an attitude almost of discipline, with the cold, ingenuous roughness of a man who has never been gentle and who has always been patient; he waited without uttering a word, without making a movement, in genuine humility and tranquil resignation, calm, serious, hat in hand, with eyes cast down, and an expression which was halfway between that of a soldier in the presence of his officer and a criminal in the presence of his judge, until it should please the mayor to turn around. All the sentiments as well as all the memories that one might have attributed to him had disappeared. That face, as impenetrable and simple as granite, no longer bore any trace of anything but a melancholy depression. His whole person breathed lowliness and firmness and an indescribable courageous despondency.

At last the mayor laid down his pen and turned half around.

"Well! What is it? What is the matter, Javert?"

Javert remained silent for an instant as though collecting his ideas, then raised his voice with a sort of sad solemnity, which did not, however, preclude simplicity.

"This is the matter, Mr. Mayor; a culpable act has been committed."

"What act?"

"An inferior agent of the authorities has failed in respect, and in the gravest manner, toward a magistrate. I have come to bring the fact to your knowledge, as it is my duty to do."

"Who is the agent?" asked M. Madeleine.

"I," said Javert.

"You?"

"I."

"And who is the magistrate who has reason to complain of the agent?"

"You, Mr. Mayor."

M. Madeleine sat erect in his armchair. Javert went on, with a severe air and his eyes still cast down.

"Mr. Mayor, I have come to request you to instigate the authorities to dismiss me."

M. Madeleine opened his mouth in amazement. Javert interrupted him. "You will say that I might have handed in my resignation, but that does not suffice. Handing in one's resignation is honorable. I have failed in my duty; I ought to be punished; I must be turned out."

And after a pause he added, "Mr. Mayor, you were severe with me the other day, and unjustly. Be so today, with justice."

"Come, now! Why?" exclaimed M. Madeleine. "What nonsense is this? What is the meaning of this? What culpable act have you been guilty of toward me? What have you done to me? What are your wrongs with regard to me? You accuse yourself; you wish to be superseded—"

"Turned out," said Javert.

"Turned out; so it be, then. That is well. I do not understand."

"You shall understand, Mr. Mayor."

Javert sighed from the very bottom of his chest, and resumed, still coldly and sadly, "Mr. Mayor, six weeks ago, in consequence of the scene over that woman, I was furious, and I informed against you."

"Informed against me!"

"At the Prefecture of Police in Paris."

M. Madeleine, who was not in the habit of laughing much oftener than Javert himself, burst out laughing now, "As a mayor who had encroached on the province of the police?"

"As an ex-convict."

The mayor turned livid.

Javert, who had not raised his eyes, went on, "I thought it was so. I had had an idea for a long time; a resemblance; inquiries which you had caused to be made at Faverolles; the strength of your loins; the adventure with old Fauchelevant; your skill in marksmanship; your leg, which you drag a little—I hardly know what all, absurdities! But, at all events, I took you for a certain Jean Valjean."

"A certain—What did you say the name was?"

"Jean Valjean. He was a convict whom I was in the habit of seeing twenty years ago, when I was adjutant-guard of convicts at Toulon. On leaving the galleys, this Jean Valjean, as it appears, robbed a bishop; then he committed another theft, accompanied with violence, on a public highway on the person of a little Savoyard. He disappeared eight years ago, no one knows how, and he has been sought, I fancied. In short, I did this thing! Wrath impelled me; I denounced you at the Prefecture!"

M. Madeleine, who had taken up the docket again several moments before this, resumed with an air of perfect indifference, "And what reply did you receive?"

"That I was mad."

"Well?"

"Well, they were right."

"It is lucky that you recognize the fact."

"I am forced to do so, since the real Jean Valjean has been found."

The sheet of paper which M. Madeleine was holding dropped from his hand; he raised his head, gazed fixedly at Javert, and said with his indescribable accent, "Ah!"

Javert continued, "This is the way it is, Mr. Mayor. It seems that there was in the neighborhood near Ailly-le-Haut-Clocher an old fellow who was called Father Champmathieu. He was a very wretched creature. No one paid any attention to him. No one knows what such people subsist on. Lately, last autumn, Father Champmathieu was arrested for the theft of some cider apples from—Well, no matter, a theft had been committed, a wall scaled, branches of trees broken. My Champmathieu was arrested. He still had the branch of the apple tree in his hand. The scamp is locked up. Up to this point it was merely an affair of a misdemeanor. But here is where Providence intervened.

"The jail being in a bad condition, the examining magistrate finds it convenient to transfer Champmathieu to Arras, where the departmental prison is situated. In this prison at Arras there is an ex-convict named Brevet, who is detained for I know not what, and who has been appointed turnkey of the house, because of good behavior. Mr. Mayor, no sooner had Champmathieu arrived than Brevet exclaims: 'Eh! Why, I know that man! He is a fagot! Take a good look at me, my good man! You are Jean Valjean! Jean Valjean! Who's Jean Valjean?' Champmathieu feigns astonishment. 'Don't play the innocent dodge,' says Brevet. 'You are Jean Valjean! You have been in the galleys of Toulon; it was twenty years ago; we were there together.' Champmathieu denies it. *Parbleu!* You understand. The case is investigated. The thing was well ventilated for me. This is what they discovered: This Champmathieu had been, thirty years ago, a pruner of trees in various localities, notably at Faverolles. There all trace of him was lost. A long time afterward he was seen again in Auvergne; then in Paris, where he is said to have been a wheelwright, and to have had a daughter, who was a laundress; but that has not been proved. Now, before going to the galleys for theft, what was Jean Valjean? A pruner of trees. Where? At Faverolles. Another fact. This Valjean's Christian name was Jean, and his mother's surname was Mathieu. What more natural to suppose than that, on emerging from the galleys, he should have taken his mother's name for the purpose of concealing himself, and have called himself Jean Mathieu? He goes to Auvergne. The local pronunciation turns Jean into Chan—he is called Chan Mathieu. Our man offers no opposition, and behold him transformed into Champmathieu. You follow me, do you not? Inquiries were made at Faverolles. The family of Jean Valjean is no longer there. It is not known where they have gone. You know that among those classes a family often disappears. Search was made, and nothing was found. When such people are not mud, they are dust. And then, as the beginning of the story dates thirty years back, there is no longer anyone at Faverolles who knew Jean Valjean. Inquiries were made at Toulon. Besides Brevet, there are only two convicts in existence who have seen Jean Valjean; they are Cochepaille and Chenildieu, and are sentenced for life. They are taken from the galleys and confronted with the pretended Champmathieu. They do not hesitate; he is Jean Valjean for them as well as for Brevet. The same age, he is fifty-four, the same height, the same air, the same man; in short, it is he. It was precisely at this moment that I forwarded my denunciation to the Prefecture in Paris. I was told that I had lost my reason, and that Jean Valjean is at Arras, in the power of the authorities. You can imagine whether this surprised me, when I thought that I had that same Jean Valjean here. I write to the examining judge; he sends for me; Champmathieu is conducted to me—"

"Well?" interposed M. Madeleine.

Javert replied, his face incorruptible, and as melancholy as ever, "Mr. Mayor, the truth is the truth. I am sorry; but that man is Jean Valjean. I recognized him also."

M. Madeleine resumed in, a very low voice, "You are sure?"

Javert began to laugh, with that mournful laugh which comes from profound conviction.

"O! Sure!"

He stood there thoughtfully for a moment, mechanically taking pinches of powdered wood for blotting ink from the wooden bowl which stood on the table, and he added, "And even now that I have seen the real Jean Valjean, I do not see how I could have thought otherwise. I beg your pardon, Mr. Mayor."

Javert, as he addressed these grave and supplicating words to the man, who six weeks before had humiliated him in the presence of the whole stationhouse, and bade him "leave the room,"—Javert, that haughty man, was unconsciously full of simplicity and dignity, M. Madeleine made no other reply to his prayer than the abrupt question, "And what does this man say?"

"Ah! Indeed, Mr. Mayor, it's a bad business. If he is Jean Valjean, he has his previous conviction against him. To climb a wall, to break a branch, to purloin apples, is a mischievous trick in a child; for a man it is a misdemeanor; for a convict it is a crime. Robbing and housebreaking—it is all there. It is no longer a question of correctional police; it is a matter for the Court of Assizes. It is no longer a matter of a few days in prison; it is the galleys for life. And then, there is the affair with the little Savoyard, who will return, I hope. The deuce! There is plenty to dispute in the matter, is there not? Yes, for anyone but Jean Valjean. But Jean Valjean is a sly dog. That is the way I recognized him. Any other man would have felt that things were getting hot for him; he would struggle, he would cry out—the kettle sings before the fire; he would not be Jean Valjean, et cetera. But he has not the appearance of understanding; he says, 'I am Champmathieu, and I won't depart from that!' He has an astonished air, he pretends to be stupid; it is far better. Oh! The rogue is clever! But it makes no difference. The proofs are there. He has been recognized by four persons; the old scamp will be condemned. The case has been taken to the Assizes at Arras. I shall go there to give my testimony. I have been summoned."

M. Madeleine had turned to his desk again, and taken up his docket, and was turning over the leaves tranquilly, reading and writing by turns, like a busy man. He turned to Javert. "That will do, Javert. In truth, all these details interest me but little. We are wasting our time, and we have pressing business on hand. Javert, you will betake yourself at once to the house of the woman Buseaupied, who sells herbs at the corner of the Rue Saint-Saulve. You will tell her that she must enter her complaint against carter Pierre Chesnelong. The man is a brute, who came near crushing this woman and her child. He must be punished. You will then go to M. Charcellay, Rue Montre-de-Champigny. He complained that there is a gutter on the adjoining house which discharges rainwater on his premises, and is undermining the foundations of his house. After that, you will verify the infractions of police regulations which have been reported to me in the Rue Guibourg, at Widow Doris's, and Rue du Garraud-Blanc, at Madame Renee le Bosse's, and you will prepare documents. But I am giving you a great deal of work. Are you not to be absent? Did you not tell me that you were going to Arras on that matter in a week or ten days?"

"Sooner than that, Mr. Mayor."

"On what day, then?"

"Why, I thought that I had said to Monsieur le Maire that the case was to be tried tomorrow, and that I am to set out by diligence tonight."

M. Madeleine made an imperceptible movement.

"And how long will the case last?"

"One day, at the most. The judgment will be pronounced tomorrow evening at latest. But I shall not wait for the sentence, which is certain; I shall return here as soon as my deposition has been taken."

"That is well," said M. Madeleine.

And he dismissed Javert with a wave of the hand.

Javert did not withdraw.

"Excuse me, Mr. Mayor," said he.

"What is it now?" demanded M. Madeleine.

"Mr. Mayor, there is still something of which I must remind you."

"What is it?"

"That I must be dismissed."

M. Madeleine rose.

"Javert, you are a man of honor, and I esteem you. You exaggerate your fault. Moreover, this is an offense that concerns me. Javert, you deserve promotion instead of degradation. I wish you to retain your post."

Javert gazed at M. Madeleine with his candid eyes, in whose depths his not very enlightened but pure and rigid conscience seemed visible, and said in a tranquil voice, "Mr. Mayor, I cannot grant you that."

"I repeat," replied M. Madeleine, "that the matter concerns me."

But Javert, heeding his own thought only, continued, "So far as exaggeration is concerned, I am not exaggerating. This is the way I reason: I have suspected you unjustly. That is nothing. It is our right to cherish suspicion, although suspicion directed above ourselves is an abuse. But without proofs, in a fit of rage, with the object of wreaking my vengeance, I have denounced you as a convict, you, a respectable man, a mayor, a magistrate! That is serious, very serious. I have insulted authority in your person, I, an agent of the authorities! If one of my subordinates had done what I have done, I should have declared him unworthy of the service, and have expelled him. Well? Stop, Mr. Mayor; one word more. I have often been severe in the course of my life toward others. That is just. I have done well. Now, if I were not severe toward myself, all the justice that I have done would become injustice. Ought I to spare myself more than others? No! What! I should be good for nothing but to chastise others, and not myself! Why, I should be a blackguard! Those who say, 'That blackguard of a Javert!' would be in the right. Mr. Mayor, I do not desire that you should treat me kindly; your kindness roused sufficient bad blood in me when it was directed to others. I want none of it for myself. The kindness that consists in upholding a woman of the town against a citizen, the police agent against the mayor, the man who is down against the man who is up in the world, is what I call false kindness. That is the sort of kindness that disorganizes society. Good God! It is very easy to be kind; the difficulty lies in being just. Come! If you had been what I thought you, I should not have been kind to you, not I! You would have seen! Mr. Mayor, I must treat myself as I would treat any other man. When I have subdued malefactors, when I have proceeded with vigor against rascals, I have often said to myself, 'If you flinch, if I ever catch you in fault, you may rest at your ease!' I have flinched, I have caught myself in a fault. So much the worse! Come, discharged, cashiered, expelled! That is well. I have arms. I will till the soil; it makes no difference to me. Mr. Mayor, the good of the service demands an example. I simply require the discharge of Inspector Javert."

All this was uttered in a proud, humble, despairing, yet convinced tone, which lent indescribable grandeur to this singular, honest man.

"We shall see," said M. Madeleine.

And he offered him his hand.

Javert recoiled, and said in a wild voice, "Excuse me, Mr. Mayor, but this must not be. A mayor does not offer his hand to a police spy."

He added between his teeth, "A police spy, yes; from the moment when I have misused the police. I am no more than a police spy."

Then he bowed profoundly, and directed his steps toward the door.

There he wheeled around, and with eyes still downcast, "Mr. Mayor," he said, "I shall continue to serve until I am superseded."

He withdrew. M. Madeleine remained thoughtfully listening to the firm, sure step, which died away on the pavement of the corridor.

BOOK SEVENTH: THE CHAMPMATHIEU AFFAIR

CHAPTER I—SISTER SIMPLICE

The incidents the reader is about to peruse were not all known at M. sur M. But the small portion of them that became known left such a memory in that town that a serious gap would exist in this book if we did not narrate them in their most minute details. Among these details the reader will encounter two or three improbable circumstances, which we preserve out of respect for the truth.

On the afternoon following the visit of Javert, M. Madeleine went to see Fantine according to his wont.

Before entering Fantine's room, he had Sister Simplice summoned.

The two nuns who performed the services of nurse in the infirmary, Lazariste ladies, like all sisters of charity, bore the names of Sister Perpetue and Sister Simplice.

Sister Perpetue was an ordinary villager, a sister of charity in a coarse style, who had entered the service of God as one enters any other service. She was a nun as other women are cooks. This type is not so very rare. The monastic orders gladly accept this heavy peasant earthenware, which is easily fashioned into a Capuchin or an Ursuline. These rustics are utilized for the rough work of devotion. The transition from a drover to a Carmelite is not in the least violent; the one turns into the other without much effort; the fund of ignorance common to the village and the cloister is a preparation ready at hand, and places the boor at once on the same footing as the monk: a little more amplitude in the smock, and it becomes a frock. Sister Perpetue was a robust nun from Marines near Pontoise, who chattered her patois, droned, grumbled, sugared the potion according to the bigotry or the hypocrisy of the invalid, treated her patients abruptly, roughly, was crabbed with the dying, almost flung God in their faces, stoned their death agony with prayers mumbled in a rage; was bold, honest, and ruddy.

Sister Simplice was white, with a waxen pallor. Beside Sister Perpetue, she was the taper beside the candle. Vincent de Paul has divinely traced the features of the Sister of Charity in these admirable words, in which he mingles as much freedom as servitude: "They shall have for their convent only the house of the sick; for cell only a hired room; for chapel only their parish church; for cloister only the streets of the town and the wards of the hospitals; for enclosure only obedience; for gratings only the fear of God; for veil only modesty." This ideal was realized in the living person of Sister Simplice: she had never been young, and it seemed as though she would never grow old. No one could have told Sister Simplice's age. She was a person—we dare not say a woman—who was gentle, austere, well-bred, cold, and who had never lied. She was so gentle that she appeared fragile; but she was more solid than granite. She touched the unhappy with fingers that were charmingly pure and fine. There was, so to speak, silence in her speech; she said just what was necessary, and she possessed a tone of voice that would have equally edified a confessional or enchanted a drawing room. This delicacy accommodated itself to the serge gown, finding in this harsh contact a continual reminder of heaven and of God. Let us emphasize one detail. Never to have lied, never to have said, for any interest whatever, even in indifference, any single thing which was not the truth, the sacred truth, was Sister Simplice's distinctive trait; it was the accent of her virtue. She was almost renowned in the congregation for this imperturbable veracity. The Abbé Sicard speaks of Sister Simplice in a letter to the deaf-mute Massieu. However pure and sincere we may be, we all bear upon our candor the crack of the little, innocent lie. She did not. Little lie, innocent lie—does such a thing exist? To lie is the absolute form of evil. To lie a little is not possible: he who lies, lies the whole lie. To lie is the very face of the demon. Satan has two names; he is called Satan and Lying. That is what she thought; and as she thought, so she did. The result was the whiteness which we have mentioned—a whiteness that covered even her lips and her eyes with radiance. Her smile was white, her glance was white. There was not a single spider's web, not a grain of dust, on the glass window of that conscience. On entering the order of Saint Vincent de Paul, she had taken the name of Simplice by special choice. Simplice of Sicily, as we know, is the saint who preferred to allow both her breasts to be torn off rather than to say that she had been born at Segesta when she had been born at Syracuse—a lie that would have saved her. This patron saint suited this soul.

Sister Simplice, on her entrance into the order, had had two faults that she had gradually corrected: she had a taste for dainties, and she liked to receive letters. She never read anything but a book of prayers printed in Latin, in coarse type. She did not understand Latin, but she understood the book.

This pious woman had conceived an affection for Fantine, probably feeling a latent virtue there, and she had devoted herself almost exclusively to her care.

M. Madeleine took Sister Simplice apart and recommended Fantine to her in a singular tone, which the sister recalled later on.

On leaving the sister, he approached Fantine.

Fantine awaited M. Madeleine's appearance every day as one awaits a ray of warmth and joy. She said to the sisters, "I only live when Monsieur le Maire is here."

She had a great deal of fever that day. As soon as she saw M. Madeleine she asked him, "And Cosette?"

He replied with a smile, "Soon."

M. Madeleine was the same as usual with Fantine. Only he remained an hour instead of half an hour, to Fantine's great delight. He urged everyone repeatedly not to allow the invalid to want for anything. It was noticed that there was a moment when his countenance became very somber. But this was explained when it became known that the doctor had bent down to his ear and said to him, "She is losing ground fast."

Then he returned to the town hall, and the clerk observed him attentively examining a road map of France which hung in his study. He wrote a few figures on a bit of paper with a pencil.

CHAPTER II—THE PERSPICACITY OF MASTER SCAUFFLAIRE

From the town hall he betook himself to the extremity of the town, to a Fleming named Master Scaufflaer, French Scaufflaire, who let out "horses and cabriolets as desired."

In order to reach this Scaufflaire, the shortest way was to take the little-frequented street in which was situated the parsonage of the parish in which M. Madeleine resided. The Curé was, it was said, a worthy, respectable, and sensible man. At the moment when M. Madeleine arrived in front of the parsonage there was but one passerby in the street, and this person noticed this: After the mayor had passed the priest's house he halted, stood motionless, then turned about, and retraced his steps to the door of the parsonage, which had an iron knocker. He laid his hand quickly on the knocker and lifted it; then he paused again and stopped short, as though in thought, and after the lapse of a few seconds, instead of allowing the knocker to fall abruptly, he placed it gently, and resumed his way with a sort of haste that had not been apparent previously.

M. Madeleine found Master Scaufflaire at home, engaged in stitching a harness over.

"Master Scaufflaire," he inquired, "have you a good horse?"

"Mr. Mayor," said the Fleming, "all my horses are good. What do you mean by a good horse?"

"I mean a horse that can travel twenty leagues in a day."

"The deuce!" said the Fleming. "Twenty leagues!"

"Yes."

"Hitched to a cabriolet?"

"Yes."

"And how long can he rest at the end of his journey?"

"He must be able to set out again on the next day if necessary."

"To traverse the same road?"

"Yes."

"The deuce! The deuce! And it is twenty leagues?"

M. Madeleine drew from his pocket the paper on which he had penciled some figures. He showed it to the Fleming. The figures were 5, 6, 8½.

"You see," he said, "total, nineteen and a half; as well say twenty leagues."

"Mr. Mayor," returned the Fleming, "I have just what you want. My little white horse—you may have seen him pass occasionally; he is a small beast from Lower Boulonnais. He is full of fire. They wanted to make a saddle horse of him at first. Bah! He reared, he kicked, he laid everybody flat on the ground. He was thought to be vicious, and no one knew what to do with him. I bought him. I harnessed him to a carriage. That is what he wanted, sir; he is as gentle as a girl; he goes like the wind. Ah! Indeed he must not be mounted. It does not suit his ideas to be a saddle horse. Everyone has his ambition. 'Draw? Yes. Carry? No.' We must suppose that is what he said to himself."

"And he will accomplish the trip?"

"Your twenty leagues all at a full trot, and in less than eight hours. But here are the conditions."

"State them."

"In the first place, you will give him half an hour's breathing spell midway of the road; he will eat; and someone must be by while he is eating to prevent the stable boy of the inn from stealing his oats; for I have noticed that in inns the oats are more often drunk by the stable men than eaten by the horses."

"Someone will be by."

"In the second place—is the cabriolet for Monsieur le Maire?"

"Yes."

"Does Monsieur le Maire know how to drive?"

"Yes."

"Well, Monsieur le Maire will travel alone and without baggage, in order not to overload the horse?"

"Agreed."

"But as Monsieur le Maire will have no one with him, he will be obliged to take the trouble himself of seeing that the oats are not stolen."

"That is understood."

"I am to have thirty francs a day. The days of rest to be paid for also—not a farthing less; and the beast's food to be at Monsieur le Maire's expense."

M. Madeleine drew three napoleons from his purse and laid them on the table.

"Here is the pay for two days in advance."

"Fourthly, for such a journey a cabriolet would be too heavy, and would fatigue the horse. Monsieur le Maire must consent to travel in a little tilbury that I own."

"I consent to that."

"It is light, but it has no cover."

"That makes no difference to me."

"Has Monsieur le Maire reflected that we are in the middle of winter?"

M. Madeleine did not reply. The Fleming resumed, "That it is very cold?"

M. Madeleine preserved silence.

Master Scaufflaire continued, "That it may rain?"

M. Madeleine raised his head and said:

"The tilbury and the horse will be in front of my door tomorrow morning at half-past four o'clock."

"Of course, Monsieur le Maire," replied Scaufflaire; then, scratching a speck in the wood of the table with his thumbnail, he resumed with that careless air which the Flemings understand so well how to mingle with their shrewdness, "But this is what I am thinking of now: Monsieur le Maire has not told me where he is going. Where is Monsieur le Maire going?"

He had been thinking of nothing else since the beginning of the conversation, but he did not know why he had not dared to put the question.

"Are your horse's forelegs good?" said M. Madeleine.

"Yes, Monsieur le Maire. You must hold him in a little when going downhill. Are there many descends between here and the place where you are going?"

"Do not forget to be at my door at precisely half-past four o'clock tomorrow morning," replied M. Madeleine; and he took his departure.

The Fleming remained "utterly stupid," as he himself said some time afterward.

The mayor had been gone two or three minutes when the door opened again; it was the mayor once more.

He still wore the same impassive and preoccupied air.

"Monsieur Scaufflaire," said he, "at what sum do you estimate the value of the horse and tilbury which you are to let to me, the one bearing the other?"

"The one dragging the other, Monsieur le Maire," said the Fleming, with a broad smile.

"So be it. Well?"

"Does Monsieur le Maire wish to purchase them or me?"

"No; but I wish to guarantee you in any case. You shall give me back the sum at my return. At what value do you estimate your horse and cabriolet?"

"Five hundred francs, Monsieur le Maire."

"Here it is."

M. Madeleine laid a bank bill on the table, then left the room; and this time he did not return.

Master Scaufflaire experienced a frightful regret that he had not said a thousand francs. Besides the horse and tilbury together were worth but a hundred crowns.

The Fleming called his wife, and related the affair to her. "Where the devil could Monsieur le Maire be going?" They held counsel together.

"He is going to Paris," said the wife. "I don't believe it," said the husband.

M. Madeleine had forgotten the paper with the figures on it, and it lay on the chimneypiece. The Fleming picked it up and studied it. "Five, six, eight and a half? That must designate the posting relays." He turned to his wife. "I have found out."

"What?"

"It is five leagues from here to Hesdin, six from Hesdin to Saint-Pol, eight and a half from Saint-Pol to Arras. He is going to Arras."

Meanwhile, M. Madeleine had returned home. He had taken the longest way to return from Master Scaufflaire's, as though the parsonage door had been a temptation for him, and he had wished to avoid it. He ascended to his room, and there he shut himself up, which was a very simple act, since he liked to go to bed early. Nevertheless, the portress of the factory, who was, at the same time, M. Madeleine's only servant, noticed that the latter's light was extinguished at half-past eight, and she mentioned it to the cashier when he came home, adding, "Is Monsieur le Maire ill? I thought he had a rather singular air."

This cashier occupied a room situated directly under M. Madeleine's chamber. He paid no heed to the portress's words, but went to bed and to sleep. Toward midnight he woke up with a start; in his sleep he had heard a noise above his head. He listened; it was a footstep pacing back and forth, as though someone were walking in the room above him. He listened more attentively, and recognized M. Madeleine's step. This struck him as strange; usually, there was no noise in M. Madeleine's chamber until he rose in the morning. A moment later the cashier heard a noise that resembled that of a cupboard being opened, and then shut again; then a piece of furniture was disarranged; then a pause ensued; then the step began again. The cashier sat up in bed, quite awake now, and staring; and through his windowpanes he saw the reddish gleam of a lighted window reflected on the opposite wall; from the direction of the rays, it could only come from the window of M. Madeleine's chamber. The reflection wavered, as though it came rather from a fire that had been lighted than from a candle. The shadow of the window frame was not shown, which indicated that the window was wide open. The fact that this window was open in such cold weather was surprising. The cashier fell asleep again. An hour or two later he waked again. The same step was still passing slowly and regularly back and forth overhead.

The reflection was still visible on the wall, but now it was pale and peaceful, like the reflection of a lamp or of a candle. The window was still open.

This is what had taken place in M. Madeleine's room.

CHAPTER III—A TEMPEST IN A SKULL

The reader has, no doubt, already divined that M. Madeleine is no other than Jean Valjean.

We have already gazed into the depths of this conscience; the moment has now come when we must take another look into it. We do so not without emotion and trepidation. There is nothing more terrible in existence than this sort of contemplation. The eye of the spirit can nowhere find more dazzling brilliance and more shadow than in man; it can fix itself on no other thing that is more formidable, more complicated, more mysterious, and more infinite. There is a spectacle more grand than the sea; it is heaven: there is a spectacle more grand than heaven; it is the inmost recesses of the soul.

To make the poem of the human conscience, were it only with reference to a single man, were it only in connection with the basest of men, would be to blend all epics into one superior and definitive epic. Conscience is the chaos of chimeras, of lusts, and of temptations; the furnace of dreams; the lair of ideas of which we are ashamed; it is the pandemonium of sophisms; it is the battlefield of the passions. Penetrate, at certain hours, past the livid face of a human being who is engaged in reflection, and look behind, gaze into that soul, gaze into that obscurity. There, beneath that external silence, battles of giants, like those recorded in Homer, are in progress; skirmishes of dragons and hydras and swarms of phantoms, as in Milton; visionary circles, as in Dante. What a solemn thing is this infinity that every man bears within him, and which he measures with despair against the caprices of his brain and the actions of his life!

Alighieri one day met with a sinister-looking door, before which he hesitated. Here is one before us, upon whose threshold we hesitate. Let us enter, nevertheless.

We have but little to add to what the reader already knows of what had happened to Jean Valjean after the adventure with Little Gervais. From that moment forth he was, as we have seen, a totally different man. What the Bishop had wished to make of him, that he carried out. It was more than a transformation; it was a transfiguration.

He succeeded in disappearing, sold the Bishop's silver, reserving only the candlesticks as a souvenir, crept from town to town, traversed France, came to M. sur M., conceived the idea, which we have mentioned, accomplished what we have related, succeeded in rendering himself safe from seizure and inaccessible, and, thenceforth, established at M. sur M., happy in feeling his conscience saddened by the past and the first half of his existence belied by the last, he lived in peace, reassured and hopeful, having henceforth only two thoughts, to conceal his name and to sanctify his life; to escape men and to return to God.

These two thoughts were so closely intertwined in his mind that they formed but a single one there; both were equally absorbing and imperative and ruled his slightest actions. In general, they conspired to regulate the conduct of his life; they turned him toward the gloom; they rendered him kindly and simple; they counseled him to the same things. Sometimes, however, they conflicted. In that case, as the reader will remember, the man whom all the country of M. sur M. called M. Madeleine did not hesitate to sacrifice the first to the second—his security to his virtue. Thus, in spite of all his reserve and all his prudence, he had preserved the Bishop's candlesticks, worn mourning for him, summoned and interrogated all the little Savoyards who passed that way, collected information regarding the families at Faverolles, and saved old Fauchelevent's life, despite the disquieting insinuations of Javert. It seemed, as we have already remarked, as though he thought, following the example of all those who have been wise, holy, and just, that his first duty was not toward himself.

At the same time, it must be confessed, nothing just like this had yet presented itself.

Never had the two ideas that governed the unhappy man whose sufferings we are narrating, engaged in so serious a struggle. He understood this confusedly but profoundly at the very first words pronounced by Javert, when the latter entered his study. At the moment when that name, which he had buried beneath so many layers, was so strangely articulated, he was struck with stupor, and as though intoxicated with the sinister eccentricity of his destiny; and through this stupor he felt that shudder which precedes great shocks. He bent like an oak at the approach of a storm, like a soldier at the approach of an assault. He felt shadows filled with thunders and lightnings descending upon his head. As he listened to Javert, the first thought that occurred to him was to go, to run and denounce himself, to take that Champmathieu out of prison and place himself there; this was as painful and as poignant as an incision in the living flesh. Then it passed away, and he said to himself, "We will see! We will see!" He repressed this first, generous instinct, and recoiled before heroism.

It would be beautiful, no doubt, after the Bishop's holy words, after so many years of repentance and abnegation, in the midst of a penitence admirably begun, if this man had not flinched for an instant, even in the presence of so terrible a conjecture, but had continued to walk with the same step toward this yawning precipice, at the bottom of which lay heaven; that would have been beautiful; but it was not thus. We must render an account of the things that went on in this soul, and we can only tell what there was there. He was carried away, at first, by the instinct of self-preservation; he rallied all his ideas in haste, stifled his emotions, took into consideration Javert's presence, that great danger, postponed all decision with the firmness of terror, shook off thought as to what he had to do, and resumed his calmness as a warrior picks up his buckler.

He remained in this state during the rest of the day, a whirlwind within, a profound tranquility without. He took no "preservative measures," as they may be called. Everything was still confused, and jostling together in his brain. His trouble was so great that he could not perceive the form of a single idea distinctly, and he could have told nothing about himself, except that he had received a great blow.

He repaired to Fantine's bed of suffering, as usual, and prolonged his visit, through a kindly instinct, telling himself that he must behave thus, and recommend her well to the sisters, in case he should be obliged to be absent himself. He had a vague feeling that he might be obliged to go to Arras; and without having the least in the world made up his mind to this trip, he said to himself that being, as he was, beyond the shadow of any suspicion, there could be nothing out of the way in being a witness to what was to take place, and he engaged the tilbury from Scaufflaire in order to be prepared in any event.

He dined with a good deal of appetite.

On returning to his room, he communed with himself.

He examined the situation, and found it unprecedented; so unprecedented that in the midst of his reverie he rose from his chair, moved by some inexplicable impulse of anxiety, and bolted his door. He feared lest something more should enter. He was barricading himself against possibilities.

A moment later he extinguished his light; it embarrassed him.

It seemed to him as though he might be seen.

By whom?

Alas! That on which he desired to close the door had already entered; that which he desired to blind was staring him in the face, his conscience.

His conscience; that is to say, God.

Nevertheless, he deluded himself at first; he had a feeling of security and of solitude; the bolt once drawn, he thought himself impregnable; the candle extinguished, he felt himself invisible. Then he took possession of himself: he set his elbows on the table, leaned his head on his hand, and began to meditate in the dark.

"Where do I stand? Am not I dreaming? What have I heard? Is it really true that I have seen that Javert, and that he spoke to me in that manner? Who can that Champmathieu be? So he resembles me! Is it possible? When I reflect that yesterday I was so tranquil, and so far from suspecting anything! What was I doing yesterday at this hour? What is there in this incident? What will the end be? What is to be done?"

This was the torment in which he found himself. His brain had lost its power of retaining ideas; they passed like waves, and he clutched his brow in both hands to arrest them.

Nothing but anguish extricated itself from this tumult that overwhelmed his will and his reason, and from which he sought to draw proof and resolution.

His head was burning. He went to the window and threw it wide open. There were no stars in the sky. He returned and seated himself at the table.

The first hour passed in this manner.

Gradually, however, vague outlines began to take form and to fix themselves in his meditation, and he was able to catch a glimpse with precision of the reality, not the whole situation, but some of the details. He began by recognizing the fact that, critical and extraordinary as was this situation, he was completely master of it.

This only caused an increase of his stupor.

Independently of the severe and religious aim that he had assigned to his actions, all that he had made up to that day had been nothing but a hole in which to bury his name. That which he had always feared most of all in his hours of self-communion, during his sleepless nights, was to ever hear that name pronounced; he had said to himself, that that would be the end of all things for him; that on the day when that name made its reappearance it would cause his new life to vanish from about him, and—who knows?—perhaps even his new soul within him, also. He shuddered at the very thought that this was possible. Assuredly, if anyone had said to him at such moments that the hour would come when that name would ring in his ears, when the hideous words, Jean Valjean, would suddenly emerge from the darkness and rise in front of him, when that formidable light, capable of dissipating the mystery in which he had enveloped himself, would suddenly blaze forth above his head, and that that name would not menace him, that that light would but produce an obscurity more dense, that this rent veil would but increase the mystery, that this earthquake would solidify his edifice, that this prodigious incident would have no other result, so far as he was concerned, if so it seemed good to him, than that of rendering his existence at once clearer and more impenetrable, and that, out of his confrontation with the phantom of Jean Valjean, the good and worthy citizen Monsieur Madeleine would emerge more honored, more peaceful, and more respected than ever—if anyone had told him that, he would have tossed his head and regarded the words as those of a madman. Well, all this was precisely what had just come to pass; all that accumulation of impossibilities was a fact, and God had permitted these wild fancies to become real things!

His reverie continued to grow clearer. He came more and more to an understanding of his position.

It seemed to him that he had but just waked up from some inexplicable dream, and that he found himself slipping down a declivity in the middle of the night, erect, shivering, holding back all in vain, on the very brink of the abyss. He distinctly perceived in the darkness a stranger, a man unknown to him, whom destiny had mistaken for him, and whom she was thrusting into the gulf in his stead; in order that the gulf might close once more, it was necessary that someone, himself or that other man, should fall into it: he had only let things take their course.

The light became complete, and he acknowledged this to himself: That his place was empty in the galleys; that do what he would, it was still awaiting him; that the theft from little Gervais had led him back to it; that this vacant place would await him, and draw him on until he filled it; that this was inevitable and fatal; and then he said to himself, "that, at this moment, he had a substitute; that it appeared that a certain Champmathieu had that ill luck, and that, as regards himself, being present in the galleys in the person of that Champmathieu, present in society under the name of M. Madeleine, he had nothing more to fear, provided that he did not prevent men from sealing over the head of that Champmathieu this stone of infamy that, like the stone of the sepulcher, falls once, never to rise again."

All this was so strange and so violent, that there suddenly took place in him that indescribable movement, which no man feels more than two or three times in the course of his life, a sort of convulsion of the conscience which stirs up all that there is doubtful in the heart, which is composed of irony, of joy, and of despair, and which may be called an outburst of inward laughter.

He hastily relighted his candle.

"Well, what then?" he said to himself; "what am I afraid of? What is there in all that for me to think about? I am safe; all is over. I had but one partly open door through which my past might invade my life, and behold that door is walled up forever! That Javert, who has been annoying me so long; that terrible instinct, which seemed to have divined me, which had divined me— good God!—and which followed me everywhere; that frightful hunting dog, always making a point at me, is thrown off the scent, engaged elsewhere, absolutely turned from the trail: henceforth he is satisfied; he will leave me in peace; he has his Jean Valjean. Who knows? It is even probable that he will wish to leave town! And all this has been brought about without any aid from me, and I count for nothing in it! Ah! But where is the misfortune in this? Upon my honor, people would think, to see me, that some catastrophe had happened to me! After all, if it does bring harm to someone, that is not my fault in the least: it is Providence which has done it all; it is because it wishes it so to be, evidently. Have I the right to disarrange what it has arranged? What do I ask now? Why should I meddle? It does not concern me; what! I am not satisfied: but what more do I want? The goal to which I have aspired for so many years, the dream of my nights, the object of my prayers to Heaven, security, I have now attained; it is God who wills it; I can do nothing against the will of God, and why does God will it? In order that I may continue what I have begun, that I may do good, that I may one day be a grand and encouraging example, that it may be said at last, that a little happiness has been attached to the penance that I have undergone, and to that virtue to which I have returned. Really, I do not understand why I was afraid, a little while ago, to enter the house of that good curé, and to ask his advice; this is evidently what he would have said to me: It is settled; let things take their course; let the good God do as he likes!"

Thus did he address himself in the depths of his own conscience, bending over what may be called his own abyss; he rose from his chair, and began to pace the room: "Come," said he, "let us think no more about it; my resolve is taken!" but he felt no joy.

Quite the reverse.

One can no more prevent thought from recurring to an idea than one can the sea from returning to the shore: the sailor calls it the tide; the guilty man calls it remorse; God upheaves the soul as he does the ocean.

After the expiration of a few moments, do what he would, he resumed the gloomy dialogue in which it was he who spoke and he who listened, saying that which he would have preferred to ignore, and listened to that which he would have preferred not to hear, yielding to that mysterious power which said to him: "Think!" as it said to another condemned man, two thousand years ago, "March on!"

Before proceeding further, and in order to make ourselves fully understood, let us insist upon one necessary observation.

It is certain that people do talk to themselves; there is no living being who has not done it. It may even be said that the word is never a more magnificent mystery than when it goes from thought to conscience within a man, and when it returns from conscience to thought; it is in this sense only that the words so often employed in this chapter, he said, he exclaimed, must be understood; one speaks to one's self, talks to one's self, exclaims to one's self without breaking the external silence; there is a great tumult; everything about us talks except the mouth. The realities of the soul are nonetheless realities because they are not visible and palpable.

So he asked himself where he stood. He interrogated himself upon that "settled resolve." He confessed to himself that all that he had just arranged in his mind was monstrous, that "to let things take their course, to let the good God do as he liked," was simply horrible; to allow this error of fate and of men to be carried out, not to hinder it, to lend himself to it through his silence, to do nothing, in short, was to do everything! That this was hypocritical baseness in the last degree! That it was a base, cowardly, sneaking, abject, hideous crime!

For the first time in eight years, the wretched man had just tasted the bitter savor of an evil thought and of an evil action.

He spit it out with disgust.

He continued to question himself. He asked himself severely what he had meant by this, "My object is attained!" He declared to himself that his life really had an object; but what object? To conceal his name? To deceive the police? Was it for so petty a thing that he had done all that he had done? Had he not another and a grand object, which was the true one—to save, not his person, but his soul; to become honest and good once more; to be a just man? Was it not that above all, that alone, which he had always desired, which the Bishop had enjoined upon him—to shut the door on his past? But he was not shutting it! Great God! He was reopening it by committing an infamous action! He was becoming a thief once more, and the most odious of thieves! He was robbing another of his existence, his life, his peace, his place in the sunshine. He was becoming an assassin. He was murdering, morally murdering, a wretched man. He was inflicting on him that frightful living death, that death beneath the open sky, which is called the galleys. On the other hand, to surrender himself to save that man, struck down with so melancholy an error, to resume his own name, to become once more, out of duty, the convict Jean Valjean, that was, in truth, to achieve his resurrection, and to close forever that hell from which he had just emerged; to fall back there in appearance was to escape from it in reality. This must be done! He had done nothing if he did not do all this; his whole life was useless; all his penitence was wasted. There was no longer any need of saying, "What is the use?" He felt that the Bishop was there, that the Bishop was present all the more because he was dead, that the Bishop was gazing fixedly at him, that henceforth Mayor Madeleine, with all his virtues, would be abominable to him, and that the convict Jean Valjean would be pure and admirable in his sight; that men beheld his mask, but that the Bishop saw his face; that men saw his life, but that the Bishop beheld his conscience. So he must go to Arras, deliver the false Jean Valjean, and denounce the real one. Alas! That was the greatest of sacrifices, the most poignant of victories, the last step to take; but it must be done. Sad fate! He would enter into sanctity only in the eyes of God when he returned to infamy in the eyes of men.

"Well," said he, "let us decide upon this; let us do our duty; let us save this man." He uttered these words aloud, without perceiving that he was speaking aloud.

He took his books, verified them, and put them in order. He flung in the fire a bundle of bills that he had against petty and embarrassed tradesmen. He wrote and sealed a letter, and on the envelope it might have been read, had there been anyone in his chamber at the moment: *To Monsieur Laffitte, Banker, Rue d'Artois, Paris.* He drew from his secretary a pocketbook which contained several banknotes and the passport of which he had made use that same year when he went to the elections.

Anyone who had seen him during the execution of these various acts, into which there entered such grave thought, would have had no suspicion of what was going on within him. Only occasionally did his lips move; at other times he raised his head and fixed his gaze upon some point of the wall, as though there existed at that point something which he wished to elucidate or interrogate.

When he had finished the letter to M. Laffitte, he put it into his pocket, together with the pocket-book, and began his walk once more.

His reverie had not swerved from its course. He continued to see his duty clearly, written in luminous letters, which flamed before his eyes and changed its place as he altered the direction of his glance, "Go! Tell your name! Denounce yourself!"

In the same way he beheld, as though they had passed before him in visible forms, the two ideas which had, up to that time, formed the double rule of his soul, the concealment of his name, the sanctification of his life. For the first time they appeared to him as absolutely distinct, and he perceived the distance which separated them. He recognized the fact that one of these ideas was, necessarily, good, while the other might become bad; that the first was self-devotion, and that the other was personality; that the one said, my neighbor, and that the other said, myself; that one emanated from the light, and the other from darkness.

They were antagonistic. He saw them in conflict. In proportion as he meditated, they grew before the eyes of his spirit. They had now attained colossal statures, and it seemed to him that he beheld within himself, in that infinity of which we were recently speaking, in the midst of the darkness and the lights, a goddess and a giant contending.

He was filled with terror; but it seemed to him that the good thought was getting the upper hand.

He felt that he was on the brink of the second decisive crisis of his conscience and of his destiny; that the Bishop had marked the first phase of his new life, and that Champmathieu marked the second. After the grand crisis, the grand test.

But the fever, allayed for an instant, gradually resumed possession of him.

A thousand thoughts traversed his mind, but they continued to fortify him in his resolution.

One moment he said to himself that he was, perhaps, taking the matter too keenly; that, after all, this Champmathieu was not interesting, and that he had actually been guilty of theft.

He answered himself, "If this man has, indeed, stolen a few apples, that means a month in prison. It is a long way from that to the galleys. And who knows? Did he steal? Has it been proved? The name of Jean Valjean overwhelms him, and seems to dispense with proofs. Do not the attorneys for the Crown always proceed in this manner? He is supposed to be a thief because he is known to be a convict."

In another instant the thought had occurred to him that, when he denounced himself, the heroism of his deed might, perhaps, be taken into consideration, and his honest life for the last seven years, and what he had done for the district, and that they would have mercy on him.

But this supposition vanished very quickly, and he smiled bitterly as he remembered that the theft of the forty sous from little Gervais put him in the position of a man guilty of a second offense after conviction, that this affair would certainly come up, and, according to the precise terms of the law, would render him liable to penal servitude for life.

He turned aside from all illusions, detached himself more and more from earth, and sought strength and consolation elsewhere. He told himself that he must do his duty; that perhaps he should not be more unhappy after doing his duty than after having avoided it; that if he allowed things to take their own course, if he remained at M. sur M., his consideration, his good name, his good works, the deference and veneration paid to him, his charity, his wealth, his popularity, his virtue, would be seasoned with a crime. And what would be the taste of all these holy things when bound up with this hideous thing? While, if he accomplished his sacrifice, a celestial idea would be mingled with the galleys, the post, the iron necklet, the green cap, unceasing toil, and pitiless shame.

At length he told himself that it must be so, that his destiny was thus allotted, that he had not authority to alter the arrangements made on high, that, in any case, he must make his choice: virtue without and abomination within, or holiness within and infamy without.

The stirring up of these lugubrious ideas did not cause his courage to fail, but his brain grow weary. He began to think of other things, of indifferent matters, in spite of himself.

The veins in his temples throbbed violently; he still paced to and fro;

idnight sounded first from the parish church, then from the town hall; he
ounted the twelve strokes of the two clocks, and compared the sounds of the
wo bells; he recalled in this connection the fact that, a few days previously, he
ad seen in an ironmonger's shop an ancient clock for sale, upon which was
ritten the name, Antoine-Albin de Romainville.

He was cold; he lighted a small fire; it did not occur to him to close the window.

In the meantime he had relapsed into his stupor; he was obliged to make
tolerably vigorous effort to recall what had been the subject of his thoughts
efore midnight had struck; he finally succeeded in doing this.

"Ah! Yes," he said to himself, "I had resolved to inform against myself."

And then, all of a sudden, he thought of Fantine.

"Hold!" said he. "And what about that poor woman?"

Here a fresh crisis declared itself.

Fantine, by appearing thus abruptly in his reverie, produced the effect of
n unexpected ray of light; it seemed to him as though everything about him
ere undergoing a change of aspect: he exclaimed, "Ah! But I have hitherto
onsidered no one but myself; it is proper for me to hold my tongue or to
enounce myself, to conceal my person or to save my soul, to be a despicable
nd respected magistrate, or an infamous and venerable convict; it is I, it
s always I and nothing but I: but, good God! All this is egotism; these are
iverse forms of egotism, but it is egotism all the same. What if I were to
hink a little about others? The highest holiness is to think of others; come,
et us examine the matter. The I excepted, the I effaced, the I forgotten, what
ould be the result of all this? What if I denounce myself? I am arrested; this
Champmathieu is released; I am put back in the galleys; that is well—and what
hen? What is going on here? Ah! Here is a country, a town, here are factories,
n industry, workers, both men and women, aged grandsires, children, poor
eople! All this I have created; all these I provide with their living; everywhere
here there is a smoking chimney, it is I who have placed the brand on the
earth and meat in the pot; I have created ease, circulation, credit; before me
here was nothing; I have elevated, vivified, informed with life, fecundated,
timulated, enriched the whole countryside; lacking me, the soul is lacking; I
ake myself off, everything dies: and this woman, who has suffered so much,
who possesses so many merits in spite of her fall; the cause of all whose misery
have unwittingly been! And that child whom I meant to go in search of, whom
have promised to her mother; do I not also owe something to this woman, in
eparation for the evil which I have done her? If I disappear, what happens?
The mother dies; the child becomes what it can; that is what will take place, if I

denounce myself. If I do not denounce myself? Come, let us see how it will be if I do not denounce myself."

After putting this question to himself, he paused; he seemed to undergo momentary hesitation and trepidation; but it did not last long, and he answered himself calmly, "Well, this man is going to the galleys; it is true, but what the deuce! he has stolen! There is no use in my saying that he has not been guilty of theft, for he has! I remain here; I go on: in ten years I shall have made ten millions; I scatter them over the country; I have nothing of my own; what is that to me? It is not for myself that I am doing it; the prosperity of all goes on augmenting; industries are aroused and animated; factories and shops are multiplied; families, a hundred families, a thousand families, are happy; the district becomes populated; villages spring up where there were only farms before; farms rise where there was nothing; wretchedness disappears, and with wretchedness debauchery, prostitution, theft, murder; all vices disappear, all crimes: and this poor mother rears her child; and behold a whole country rich and honest! Ah! I was a fool! I was absurd! What was that I was saying about denouncing myself? I really must pay attention and not be precipitate about anything. What! Because it would have pleased me to play the grand and generous; this is melodrama, after all; because I should have thought of no one but myself, the idea! For the sake of saving from a punishment, a trifle exaggerated, perhaps, but just at bottom, no one knows whom, a thief, a good-for-nothing, evidently, a whole countryside must perish! A poor woman must die in the hospital! A poor little girl must die in the street! Like dogs; ah, this is abominable! And without the mother even having seen her child once more, almost without the child's having known her mother! and all that for the sake of an old wretch of an apple thief who, most assuredly has deserved the galleys for something else, if not for that; fine scruples, indeed which save a guilty man and sacrifice the innocent, which save an old vagabond who has only a few years to live at most, and who will not be more unhappy in the galleys than in his hovel, and which sacrifice a whole population, mothers, wives, children. This poor little Cosette who has no one in the world but me, and who is, no doubt, blue with cold at this moment in the den of those Thenardiers, those peoples are rascals; and I was going to neglect my duty toward all these poor creatures; and I was going off to denounce myself; and I was about to commit that unspeakable folly! Let us put it at the worst: suppose that there is a wrong action on my part in this, and that my conscience will reproach me for it someday, to accept, for the good of others, these reproaches which weigh only on myself; this evil action which compromises my soul alone; in that lies self-sacrifice; in that alone there is virtue."

He rose and resumed his march; this time, he seemed to be content.

Diamonds are found only in the dark places of the earth; truths are found only in the depths of thought. It seemed to him, that, after having descended into these depths, after having long groped among the darkest of these shadows, he had at last found one of these diamonds, one of these truths, and that he now held it in his hand, and he was dazzled as he gazed upon it.

"Yes," he thought, "this is right; I am on the right road; I have the solution; I must end by holding fast to something; my resolve is taken; let things take their course; let us no longer vacillate; let us no longer hang back; this is for the interest of all, not for my own; I am Madeleine, and Madeleine I remain. Woe to the man who is Jean Valjean! I am no longer he; I do not know that man; I no longer know anything; it turns out that someone is Jean Valjean at the present moment; let him look out for himself; that does not concern me; it is a fatal name that was floating abroad in the night; if it halts and descends on a head, so much the worse for that head."

He looked into the little mirror that hung above his chimneypiece, and said, "Hold! it has relieved me to come to a decision; I am quite another man now."

He proceeded a few paces further, then he stopped short.

"Come!" he said, "I must not flinch before any of the consequences of the resolution that I have once adopted; there are still threads that attach me to that Jean Valjean; they must be broken; in this very room there are objects that would betray me, dumb things which would bear witness against me; it is settled; all these things must disappear."

He fumbled in his pocket, drew out his purse, opened it, and took out a small key; he inserted the key in a lock whose aperture could hardly be seen, so hidden was it in the most somber tones of the design which covered the wallpaper; a secret receptacle opened, a sort of false cupboard constructed in the angle between the wall and the chimneypiece; in this hiding place there were some rags—a blue linen blouse, an old pair of trousers, an old knapsack, and a huge thorn cudgel shod with iron at both ends. Those who had seen Jean Valjean at the epoch when he passed through D——in October, 1815, could easily have recognized all the pieces of this miserable outfit.

He had preserved them as he had preserved the silver candlesticks, in order to remind himself continually of his starting point, but he had concealed all that came from the galleys, and he had allowed the candlesticks, which came from the Bishop, to be seen.

He cast a furtive glance toward the door, as though he feared that it would open in spite of the bolt which fastened it; then, with a quick and abrupt movement, he took the whole in his arms at once, without bestowing so muc as a glance on the things which he had so religiously and so perilously preserve for so many years, and flung them all, rags, cudgel, knapsack, into the fire.

He closed the false cupboard again, and with redoubled precaution henceforth unnecessary, since it was now empty, he concealed the door behin a heavy piece of furniture, which he pushed in front of it.

After the lapse of a few seconds, the room and the opposite wall wer lighted up with a fierce, red, tremulous glow. Everything was on fire; the thor cudgel snapped and threw out sparks to the middle of the chamber.

As the knapsack was consumed, together with the hideous rags that i contained, it revealed something that sparkled in the ashes. By bending over one could have readily recognized a coin, no doubt the forty-sou piece stolen from the little Savoyard.

He did not look at the fire, but paced back and forth with the same step.

All at once his eye fell on the two silver candlesticks, which shone vaguely on the chimneypiece, through the glow.

"Hold!" he thought. "The whole of Jean Valjean is still in them. They mus be destroyed also."

He seized the two candlesticks.

There was still fire enough to allow of their being put out of shape, and converted into a sort of unrecognizable bar of metal.

He bent over the hearth and warmed himself for a moment. He felt a sense of real comfort. "How good warmth is!" said he.

He stirred the live coals with one of the candlesticks.

A minute more, and they were both in the fire.

At that moment it seemed to him that he heard a voice within him shouting, "Jean Valjean! Jean Valjean!"

His hair rose upright; he became like a man who is listening to some terrible thing.

"Yes, that's it! Finish!" said the voice. "Complete what you are about! Destroy these candlesticks! Annihilate this souvenir! Forget the Bishop! Forget everything! Destroy this Champmathieu, do! That is right! Applaud yourself! So it is settled, resolved, fixed, agreed: here is an old man who does not know what is wanted of him, who has, perhaps, done nothing, an innocent man, whose whole misfortune lies in your name, upon whom your name weighs like a crime, who is about to be taken for you, who will be condemned, who will finish his days in abjectness and horror. That is good! Be an honest man yourself; remain Monsieur le Maire; remain honorable and honored; enrich the town; nourish the indigent; rear the orphan; live happy, virtuous, and admired; and, during this time, while you are here in the midst of joy and light, there will be a man who will wear your red blouse, who will bear your name in ignominy, and who will drag your chain in the galleys. Yes, it is well arranged thus. Ah, wretch!"

The perspiration streamed from his brow. He fixed a haggard eye on the candlesticks. But that within him which had spoken had not finished. The voice continued, "Jean Valjean, there will be around you many voices, which will make a great noise, which will talk very loud, and which will bless you, and only one which no one will hear, and which will curse you in the dark. Well! Listen, infamous man! All those benedictions will fall back before they reach heaven, and only the malediction will ascend to God."

This voice, feeble at first, and which had proceeded from the most obscure depths of his conscience, had gradually become startling and formidable, and he now heard it in his very ear. It seemed to him that it had detached itself from him, and that it was now speaking outside of him. He thought that he heard the last words so distinctly, that he glanced around the room in a sort of terror.

"Is there anyone here?" he demanded aloud, in utter bewilderment.

Then he resumed, with a laugh which resembled that of an idiot, "How stupid I am! There can be no one!"

There was someone; but the person who was there was of those whom the human eye cannot see.

He placed the candlesticks on the chimneypiece.

Then he resumed his monotonous and lugubrious tramp, which troubled the dreams of the sleeping man beneath him, and awoke him with a start.

This tramping to and fro soothed and at the same time intoxicated him. It sometimes seems, on supreme occasions, as though people moved about for the purpose of asking advice of everything that they may encounter by change of place. After the lapse of a few minutes he no longer knew his position.

He now recoiled in equal terror before both the resolutions at which he had arrived in turn. The two ideas that counseled him appeared to him equally fatal. What a fatality! What conjunction that that Champmathieu should have been taken for him; to be overwhelmed by precisely the means that Providence seemed to have employed, at first, to strengthen his position!

There was a moment when he reflected on the future. Denounce himself, great God! Deliver himself up! With immense despair he faced all that he should be obliged to leave, all that he should be obliged to take up once more. He should have to bid farewell to that existence, which was so good, so pure, so radiant, to the respect of all, to honor, to liberty. He should never more stroll in the fields; he should never more hear the birds sing in the month o May; he should never more bestow alms on the little children; he should neve more experience the sweetness of having glances of gratitude and love fixe upon him; he should quit that house which he had built, that little chamber Everything seemed charming to him at that moment. Never again should h read those books; never more should he write on that little table of white wood his old portress, the only servant whom he kept, would never more bring hin his coffee in the morning. Great God! Instead of that, the convict gang, th iron necklet, the red waistcoat, the chain on his ankle, fatigue, the cell, th camp bed, all those horrors which he knew so well! At his age, after having been what he was! If he were only young again! But to be addressed in his old age as "thou" by anyone who pleased; to be searched by the convict guard; to receive the galley sergeant's cudgelings; to wear iron-bound shoes on his bare feet; to have to stretch out his leg night and morning to the hammer of the roundsman who visits the gang; to submit to the curiosity of strangers, who would be told, "That man yonder is the famous Jean Valjean, who was mayor of M. sur M."; and at night, dripping with perspiration, overwhelmed with lassitude, their green caps drawn over their eyes, to remount, two by two, the ladder staircase of the galleys beneath the sergeant's whip. Oh, what misery! Can destiny, then, be as malicious as an intelligent being, and become as monstrous as the human heart?

And do what he would, he always fell back upon the heartrending dilemma which lay at the foundation of his reverie: "Should he remain in paradise and become a demon? Should he return to hell and become an angel?"

What was to be done? Great God! What was to be done?

The torment from which he had escaped with so much difficulty was unchained afresh within him. His ideas began to grow confused once more; they assumed a kind of stupefied and mechanical quality which is peculiar to despair. The name of Romainville recurred incessantly to his mind, with the two verses of a song that he had heard in the past. He thought that Romainville was a little grove near Paris, where young lovers go to pluck lilacs in the month of April.

He wavered outwardly as well as inwardly. He walked like a little child who is permitted to toddle alone.

At intervals, as he combated his lassitude, he made an effort to recover the mastery of his mind. He tried to put to himself, for the last time, and definitely, the problem over which he had, in a manner, fallen prostrate with fatigue: Ought he to denounce himself? Ought he to hold his peace? He could not manage to see anything distinctly. The vague aspects of all the courses of easoning that had been sketched out by his meditations quivered and vanished, one after the other, into smoke. He only felt that, to whatever course of action he made up his mind, something in him must die, and that of necessity, and without his being able to escape the fact; that he was entering a sepulcher on the right hand as much as on the left; that he was passing through a death agony, the agony of his happiness, or the agony of his virtue.

Alas! All his resolution had again taken possession of him. He was no further advanced than at the beginning.

Thus did this unhappy soul struggle in its anguish. Eighteen hundred years before this unfortunate man, the mysterious Being in whom are summed up all the sanctities and all the sufferings of humanity had also long thrust aside with his hand, while the olive trees quivered in the wild wind of the infinite, the terrible cup that appeared to Him dripping with darkness and overflowing with shadows in the depths all studded with stars.

CHAPTER IV—FORMS ASSUMED BY SUFFERING DURING SLEEP

Three o'clock in the morning had just struck, and he had been walking thus for five hours, almost uninterruptedly, when he at length allowed himself to drop into his chair.

There he fell asleep and had a dream.

This dream, like the majority of dreams, bore no relation to the situation, except by its painful and heartrending character, but it made an impression on him. This nightmare struck him so forcibly that he wrote it down later on. It is one of the papers in his own handwriting which he has bequeathed to us. We think that we have here reproduced the thing in strict accordance with the text.

Of whatever nature this dream may be, the history of this night would be incomplete if we were to omit it: it is the gloomy adventure of an ailing soul.

Here it is. On the envelope we find this line inscribed: *The Dream I Had that Night.*

> I was in a plain; a vast, gloomy plain, where there was no grass. It did not seem to me to be daylight nor yet night.
> I was walking with my brother, the brother of my childish years, the brother of whom, I must say, I never think, and whom I now hardly remember.

We were conversing and we met some passersby. We were talking of a neighbor of ours in former days, who had always worked with her window open from the time when she came to live on the street. As we talked we felt cold because of that open window.

There were no trees in the plain. We saw a man passing close to us. He was entirely nude, of the hue of ashes, and mounted on a horse which was earth color. The man had no hair; we could see his skull and the veins on it. In his hand he held a switch which was as supple as a vine-shoot and as heavy as iron. This horseman passed and said nothing to us.

My brother said to me, "Let us take to the hollow road."

There existed a hollow way wherein one saw neither a single shrub nor a spear of moss. Everything was dirt-colored, even the sky. After proceeding a few paces, I received no reply when I spoke: I perceived that my brother was no longer with me.

I entered a village which I espied. I reflected that it must be Romainville. (Why Romainville?)

The first street that I entered was deserted. I entered a second street. Behind the angle formed by the two streets, a man was standing erect against the wall. I said to this man, "What country is this? Where am I?" The man made no reply. I saw the door of a house open, and I entered.

The first chamber was deserted. I entered the second. Behind the door of this chamber a man was standing erect against the wall. I inquired of this man, "Whose house is this? Where am I?" The man replied not.

The house had a garden. I quitted the house and entered the garden. The garden was deserted. Behind the first tree I found a man standing upright. I said to this man, "What garden is this? Where am I?" The man did not answer.

I strolled into the village, and perceived that it was a town. All the streets were deserted, all the doors were open. Not a single living being was passing in the streets, walking through the chambers or strolling in the gardens. But behind each angle of the walls, behind each door, behind each tree, stood a silent man. Only one was to be seen at a time. These men watched me pass.

I left the town and began to ramble about the fields.

After the lapse of some time I turned back and saw a great crowd coming up behind me. I recognized all the men whom I had seen in that town. They had strange heads. They did not seem to be in a hurry, yet they walked faster than I did. They made no noise as they walked. In an instant this crowd had overtaken and surrounded me. The faces of these men were earthen in hue.

Then the first one whom I had seen and questioned on entering the town said to me, "Where are you going! Do you not know that you have been dead this long time?"

I opened my mouth to reply, and I perceived that there was no one near me.

He woke. He was icy cold. A wind which was chill like the breeze of dawn was rattling the leaves of the window, which had been left open on their hinges. The fire was out. The candle was nearing its end. It was still black night.

He rose, he went to the window. There were no stars in the sky even yet.

From his window the yard of the house and the street were visible. A sharp, harsh noise, which made him drop his eyes, resounded from the earth.

Below him he perceived two red stars, whose rays lengthened and shortened in a singular manner through the darkness.

As his thoughts were still half immersed in the mists of sleep, "Hold!" said he. "There are no stars in the sky. They are on earth now."

But this confusion vanished; a second sound similar to the first roused him thoroughly; he looked and recognized the fact that these two stars were the lanterns of a carriage. By the light that they cast he was able to distinguish the form of this vehicle. It was a tilbury harnessed to a small white horse. The noise which he had heard was the trampling of the horse's hoofs on the pavement.

"What vehicle is this?" he said to himself. "Who is coming here so early in the morning?"

At that moment there came a light tap on the door of his chamber.

He shuddered from head to foot, and cried in a terrible voice, "Who is there?"

Someone said, "I, Monsieur le Maire."

He recognized the voice of the old woman who was his portress.

"Well!" he replied. "What is it?"

"Monsieur le Maire, it is just five o'clock in the morning."

"What is that to me?"

"The cabriolet is here, Monsieur le Maire."

"What cabriolet?"

"The tilbury."

"What tilbury?"

"Did not Monsieur le Maire order a tilbury?"

"No," said he.

"The coachman says that he has come for Monsieur le Maire."

"What coachman?"

"M. Scaufflaire's coachman."

"M. Scaufflaire?"

That name sent a shudder over him, as though a flash of lightning had passed in front of his face.

"Ah! Yes," he resumed; "M. Scaufflaire!"

If the old woman could have seen him at that moment, she would have been frightened.

A tolerably long silence ensued. He examined the flame of the candle with a stupid air, and from around the wick he took some of the burning wax, which he rolled between his fingers. The old woman waited for him. She even ventured to uplift her voice once more. "What am I to say, Monsieur le Maire?"

"Say that it is well, and that I am coming down."

CHAPTER V—HINDRANCES

The posting service from Arras to M. sur M. was still operated at this period by small mail wagons of the time of the Empire. These mail wagons were two-wheeled cabriolets, upholstered inside with fawn-colored leather, hung on springs, and having but two seats, one for the postboy, the other for the traveler. The wheels were armed with those long, offensive axles which keep other vehicles at a distance, and which may still be seen on the road in Germany. The dispatch box, an immense oblong coffer, was placed behind the vehicle and formed a part of it. This coffer was painted black, and the cabriolet yellow.

These vehicles, which have no counterparts nowadays, had something distorted and hunchbacked about them; and when one saw them passing in the distance, and climbing up some road to the horizon, they resembled the insects which are called, I think, termites, and which, though with but little corselet, drag a great train behind them. But they traveled at a very rapid rate. The post wagon, which set out from Arras at one o'clock every night, after the mail from Paris had passed, arrived at M. sur M. a little before five o'clock in the morning.

That night the wagon, which was descending to M. sur M. by the Hesdin road, collided at the corner of a street, just as it was entering the town, with a little tilbury harnessed to a white horse, which was going in the opposite direction, and in which there was but one person, a man enveloped in a mantle. The wheel of the tilbury received quite a violent shock. The postman shouted to the man to stop, but the traveler paid no heed and pursued his road at full gallop.

"That man is in a devilish hurry!" said the postman.

The man thus hastening on was the one whom we have just seen struggling in convulsions which are certainly deserving of pity.

Where was he going? He could not have told. Why was he hastening? He did not know. He was driving at random, straight ahead. Where? To Arras, no doubt; but he might have been going elsewhere as well. At times he was conscious of it, and he shuddered. He plunged into the night as into a gulf. Something urged him forward; something drew him on. No one could have told what was taking place within him; everyone will understand it. What man is there who has not entered, at least once in his life, into that obscure cavern of the unknown?

However, he had resolved on nothing, decided nothing, formed no plan, done nothing. None of the actions of his conscience had been decisive. He was, more than ever, as he had been at the first moment.

Why was he going to Arras?

He repeated what he had already said to himself when he had hired Scaufflaire's cabriolet: that, whatever the result was to be, there was no reason why he should not see with his own eyes, and judge of matters for himself; that this was even prudent; that he must know what took place; that no decision could be arrived at without having observed and scrutinized; that one made mountains out of everything from a distance; that, at any rate, when he should have seen that Champmathieu, some wretch, his conscience would probably be greatly relieved to allow him to go to the galleys in his stead; that Javert would indeed be there; and that Brevet, that Chenildieu, that Cochepaille, old convicts who had known him; but they certainly would not recognize him— bah! What an idea! That Javert was a hundred leagues from suspecting the truth; that all conjectures and all suppositions were fixed on Champmathieu, and that there is nothing so headstrong as suppositions and conjectures; that accordingly there was no danger.

That it was, no doubt, a dark moment, but that he should emerge from it; that, after all, he held his destiny, however bad it might be, in his own hand; that he was master of it. He clung to this thought.

At bottom, to tell the whole truth, he would have preferred not to go to Arras.

Nevertheless, he was going there.

As he meditated, he whipped up his horse, which was proceeding at tha fine, regular, and even trot which accomplishes two leagues and a half an hour

In proportion as the cabriolet advanced, he felt something within him draw back.

At daybreak he was in the open country; the town of M. sur M. lay far behind him. He watched the horizon grow white; he stared at all the chilly figures of a winter's dawn as they passed before his eyes, but without seeing them. The morning has its specters as well as the evening. He did not see them; but without his being aware of it, and by means of a sort of penetration which was almost physical, these black silhouettes of trees and of hills added some gloomy and sinister quality to the violent state of his soul.

Each time that he passed one of those isolated dwellings that sometimes border on the highway, he said to himself, "And yet there are people there within who are sleeping!"

The trot of the horse, the bells on the harness, the wheels on the road, produced a gentle, monotonous noise. These things are charming when one is joyous, and lugubrious when one is sad.

It was broad daylight when he arrived at Hesdin. He halted in front of the inn, to allow the horse a breathing spell, and to have him given some oats.

The horse belonged, as Scaufflaire had said, to that small race of the Boulonnais, which has too much head, too much belly, and not enough neck and shoulders, but which has a broad chest, a large crupper, thin, fine legs, and solid hoofs—a homely, but a robust and healthy race. The excellent beast had traveled five leagues in two hours, and had not a drop of sweat on his loins.

He did not get out of the tilbury. The stableman who brought the oats suddenly bent down and examined the left wheel.

"Are you going far in this condition?" said the man.

He replied, with an air of not having roused himself from his reverie, "Why?"

"Have you come from a great distance?" went on the man.

"Five leagues."

"Ah!"

"Why do you say, 'Ah'?"

The man bent down once more, was silent for a moment, with his eyes fixed on the wheel; then he rose erect and said, "Because, though this wheel has traveled five leagues, it certainly will not travel another quarter of a league."

He sprang out of the tilbury.

"What is that you say, my friend?"

"I say that it is a miracle that you should have traveled five leagues without you and your horse rolling into some ditch on the highway. Just see here!"

The wheel really had suffered serious damage. The shock administered by the mail wagon had split two spokes and strained the hub, so that the nut no longer held firm.

"My friend," he said to the stableman, "is there a wheelwright here?"

"Certainly, sir."

"Do me the service to go and fetch him."

"He is only a step from here. Hey! Master Bourgaillard!"

Master Bourgaillard, the wheelwright, was standing on his own threshold. He came, examined the wheel and made a grimace like a surgeon when the latter thinks a limb is broken.

"Can you repair this wheel immediately?"

"Yes, sir."

"When can I set out again?"

"Tomorrow."

"Tomorrow!"

"There is a long day's work on it. Are you in a hurry, sir?"

"In a very great hurry. I must set out again in an hour at the latest."

"Impossible, sir."

"I will pay whatever you ask."

"Impossible."

"Well, in two hours, then."

"Impossible today. Two new spokes and a hub must be made. Monsieur will not be able to start before tomorrow morning."

"The matter cannot wait until tomorrow. What if you were to replace this wheel instead of repairing it?"

"How so?"

"You are a wheelwright?"

"Certainly, sir."

"Have you not a wheel that you can sell me? Then I could start again at once."

"A spare wheel?"

"Yes."

"I have no wheel on hand that would fit your cabriolet. Two wheels make a pair. Two wheels cannot be put together haphazard."

"In that case, sell me a pair of wheels."

"Not all wheels fit all axles, sir."

"Try, nevertheless."

"It is useless, sir. I have nothing to sell but cartwheels. We are but a poor country here."

"Have you a cabriolet that you can let me have?"

The wheelwright had seen at the first glance that the tilbury was a hired vehicle. He shrugged his shoulders.

"You treat the cabriolets that people let you so well! If I had one, I would not let it to you!"

"Well, sell it to me, then."

"I have none."

"What! Not even a spring cart? I am not hard to please, as you see."

"We live in a poor country. There is, in truth," added the wheelwright, "an old calash under the shed yonder, which belongs to a bourgeois of the town, who gave it to me to take care of, and who only uses it on the thirty-sixth of the month—never, that is to say. I might let that to you, for what matters it to me? But the bourgeois must not see it pass—and then, it is a calash; it would require two horses."

"I will take two post-horses."

"Where is Monsieur going?"

"To Arras."

"And Monsieur wishes to reach there today?"

"Yes, of course."

"By taking two post-horses?"

"Why not?"

"Does it make any difference whether Monsieur arrives at four o'clock tomorrow morning?"

"Certainly not."

"There is one thing to be said about that, you see, by taking post-horses—Monsieur has his passport?"

"Yes."

"Well, by taking post-horses, Monsieur cannot reach Arras before tomorrow. We are on a crossroad. The relays are badly served, the horses are in the fields. The season for ploughing is just beginning; heavy teams are required, and horses are seized upon everywhere, from the post as well as elsewhere. Monsieur will have to wait three or four hours at the least at every relay. And, then, they drive at a walk. There are many hills to ascend."

"Come then, I will go on horseback. Unharness the cabriolet. Someone can surely sell me a saddle in the neighborhood."

"Without doubt. But will this horse bear the saddle?"

"That is true; you remind me of that; he will not bear it."

"Then—"

"But I can surely hire a horse in the village?"

"A horse to travel to Arras at one stretch?"

"Yes."

"That would require such a horse as does not exist in these parts. You would have to buy it to begin with, because no one knows you. But you will not find one for sale nor to let, for five hundred francs, or for a thousand."

"What am I to do?"

"The best thing is to let me repair the wheel like an honest man, and set out on your journey tomorrow."

"Tomorrow will be too late."

"The deuce!"

"Is there not a mail wagon which runs to Arras? When will it pass?"

"Tonight. Both the posts pass at night; the one going as well as the one coming."

"What! It will take you a day to mend this wheel?"

"A day, and a good long one."

"If you set two men to work?"

"If I set ten men to work."

"What if the spokes were to be tied together with ropes?"

"That could be done with the spokes, not with the hub; and the felly is in a bad state, too."

"Is there anyone in this village who lets out teams?"

"No."

"Is there another wheelwright?"

The stableman and the wheelwright replied in concert, with a toss of the head.

"No."

He felt an immense joy.

It was evident that Providence was intervening. That it was it who had broken the wheel of the tilbury and who was stopping him on the road. He had not yielded to this sort of first summons; he had just made every possible effort to continue the journey; he had loyally and scrupulously exhausted all means; he had been deterred neither by the season, nor fatigue, nor by the expense; he had nothing with which to reproach himself. If he went no further, that was no fault of his. It did not concern him further. It was no longer his fault. It was not the act of his own conscience, but the act of Providence.

He breathed again. He breathed freely and to the full extent of his lungs for the first time since Javert's visit. It seemed to him that the hand of iron which had held his heart in its grasp for the last twenty hours had just released him.

It seemed to him that God was for him now, and was manifesting Himself.

He said himself that he had done all he could, and that now he had nothing to do but retrace his steps quietly.

If his conversation with the wheelwright had taken place in a chamber of the inn, it would have had no witnesses, no one would have heard him, things would have rested there, and it is probable that we should not have had to relate any of the occurrences, which the reader is about to peruse; but this conversation had taken place in the street. Any colloquy in the street inevitably attracts a crowd. There are always people who ask nothing better than to become spectators. While he was questioning the wheelwright, some people who were passing back and forth halted around them. After listening for a few minutes, a young lad, to whom no one had paid any heed, detached himself from the group and ran off.

At the moment when the traveler, after the inward deliberation which we have just described, resolved to retrace his steps, this child returned. He was accompanied by an old woman.

"Monsieur," said the woman, "my boy tells me that you wish to hire a cabriolet."

These simple words uttered by an old woman led by a child made the perspiration trickle down his limbs. He thought that he beheld the hand which had relaxed its grasp reappear in the darkness behind him, ready to seize him once more.

He answered, "Yes, my good woman; I am in search of a cabriolet which I can hire."

And he hastened to add, "But there is none in the place."

"Certainly there is," said the old woman.

"Where?" interpolated the wheelwright.

"At my house," replied the old woman.

He shuddered. The fatal hand had grasped him again.

The old woman really had in her shed a sort of basket spring-cart. The wheelwright and the stableman, in despair at the prospect of the traveler escaping their clutches, interfered.

"It was a frightful old trap; it rests flat on the axle; it is an actual fact that the seats were suspended inside it by leather thongs; the rain came into it; the wheels were rusted and eaten with moisture; it would not go much further than the tilbury; a regular ramshackle old stagewagon; the gentleman would make a great mistake if he trusted himself to it," etc., etc.

All this was true; but this trap, this ramshackle old vehicle, this thing, whatever it was, ran on its two wheels and could go to Arras.

He paid what was asked, left the tilbury with the wheelwright to be repaired, intending to reclaim it on his return, had the white horse put to the cart, climbed into it, and resumed the road that he had been traveling since morning.

At the moment when the cart moved off, he admitted that he had felt, a moment previously, a certain joy in the thought that he should not go where he was now proceeding. He examined this joy with a sort of wrath, and found it absurd. Why should he feel joy at turning back? After all, he was taking this trip of his own free will. No one was forcing him to it.

And assuredly nothing would happen except what he should choose.

As he left Hesdin, he heard a voice shouting to him, "Stop! Stop!" He halted the cart with a vigorous movement, which contained a feverish and convulsive element resembling hope.

It was the old woman's little boy.

"Monsieur," said the latter, "it was I who got the cart for you."

"Well?"

"You have not given me anything."

He who gave to all so readily thought this demand exorbitant and almost odious.

"Ah! It's you, you scamp?" said he. "You shall have nothing."

He whipped up his horse and set off at full speed.

He had lost a great deal of time at Hesdin. He wanted to make it good. The little horse was courageous, and pulled for two; but it was the month of February, there had been rain; the roads were bad. And then, it was no longer the tilbury. The cart was very heavy, and in addition, there were many ascents.

He took nearly four hours to go from Hesdin to Saint-Pol; four hours for five leagues.

At Saint-Pol he had the horse unharnessed at the first inn he came to and led to the stable; as he had promised Scaufflaire, he stood beside the manger while the horse was eating; he thought of sad and confusing things.

The innkeeper's wife came to the stable. "Does not Monsieur wish to breakfast?"

"Come, that is true; I even have a good appetite."

He followed the woman, who had a rosy, cheerful face; she led him to the public room where there were tables covered with waxed cloth.

"Make haste!" said he. "I must start again; I am in a hurry."

A big Flemish servant-maid placed his knife and fork in all haste; he looked at the girl with a sensation of comfort.

"That is what ailed me," he thought; "I had not breakfasted."

His breakfast was served; he seized the bread, took a mouthful, and then slowly replaced it on the table, and did not touch it again.

A carter was eating at another table; he said to this man, "Why is their bread so bitter here?"

The carter was a German and did not understand him.

He returned to the stable and remained near the horse.

An hour later he had quitted Saint-Pol and was directing his course toward Tinques, which is only five leagues from Arras.

What did he do during this journey? Of what was he thinking? As in the morning, he watched the trees, the thatched roofs, the tilled fields pass by, and the way in which the landscape, broken at every turn of the road, vanished; this is a sort of contemplation that sometimes suffices to the soul, and almost relieves it from thought. What is more melancholy and more profound than to see a thousand objects for the first and the last time? To travel is to be born and to die at every instant; perhaps, in the vaguest region of his mind, he did make comparisons between the shifting horizon and our human existence: all the things of life are perpetually fleeing before us; the dark and bright intervals are intermingled; after a dazzling moment, an eclipse; we look, we hasten, we stretch out our hands to grasp what is passing; each event is a turn in the road, and, all at once, we are old; we feel a shock; all is black; we distinguish an obscure door; the gloomy horse of life, which has been drawing us halts, and we see a veiled and unknown person unharnessing amid the shadows.

Twilight was falling when the children who were coming out of school beheld this traveler enter Tinques; it is true that the days were still short; he did not halt at Tinques; as he emerged from the village, a laborer, who was mending the road with stones, raised his head and said to him, "That horse is very much fatigued."

The poor beast was, in fact, going at a walk.

"Are you going to Arras?" added the road-mender.

"Yes."

"If you go on at that rate you will not arrive very early."

He stopped his horse, and asked the laborer, "How far is it from here to Arras?"

"Nearly seven good leagues."

"How is that? The posting guide only says five leagues and a quarter."

"Ah!" returned the road-mender. "So you don't know that the road is under repair? You will find it barred a quarter of an hour further on; there is no way to proceed further."

"Really?"

"You will take the road on the left, leading to Carency; you will cross the river; when you reach Camblin, you will turn to the right; that is the road to Mont-Saint-Eloy, which leads to Arras."

"But it is night, and I shall lose my way."

"You do not belong in these parts?"

"No."

"And, besides, it is all crossroads; stop! Sir," resumed the road-mender, "shall I give you a piece of advice? Your horse is tired; return to Tinques; there is a good inn there; sleep there; you can reach Arras tomorrow."

"I must be there this evening."

"That is different; but go to the inn all the same, and get an extra horse; the stable-boy will guide you through the crossroads."

He followed the road-mender's advice, retraced his steps, and, half an hour later, he passed the same spot again, but this time at full speed, with a good horse to aid; a stableboy, who called himself a postilion, was seated on the shaft of the cariole.

Still, he felt that he had lost time.

Night had fully come.

They turned into the crossroad; the way became frightfully bad; the cart lurched from one rut to the other; he said to the postilion, "Keep at a trot, and you shall have a double fee."

In one of the jolts, the whiffle-tree broke.

"There's the whiffle-tree broken, sir," said the postilion; "I don't know how to harness my horse now; this road is very bad at night; if you wish to return and sleep at Tinques, we could be in Arras early tomorrow morning."

He replied, "Have you a bit of rope and a knife?"

"Yes, sir."

He cut a branch from a tree and made a whiffle-tree of it.

This caused another loss of twenty minutes; but they set out again at a gallop.

The plain was gloomy; low-hanging, black, crisp fogs crept over the hills and wrenched themselves away like smoke: there were whitish gleams in the clouds; a strong breeze which blew in from the sea produced a sound in all quarters of the horizon, as of someone moving furniture; everything that could be seen assumed attitudes of terror. How many things shiver beneath these vast breaths of the night!

He was stiff with cold; he had eaten nothing since the night before; he vaguely recalled his other nocturnal trip in the vast plain in the neighborhood of D——, eight years previously, and it seemed but yesterday.

The hour struck from a distant tower; he asked the boy, "What time is it?"

"Seven o'clock, sir; we shall reach Arras at eight; we have but three leagues still to go."

At that moment, he for the first time indulged in this reflection, thinking it odd the while that it had not occurred to him sooner: that all this trouble that he was taking was, perhaps, useless; that he did not know so much as the hour of the trial; that he should, at least, have informed himself of that; that he was foolish to go thus straight ahead without knowing whether he would be of any service or not; then he sketched out some calculations in his mind: that, ordinarily, the sittings of the Court of Assizes began at nine o'clock in the morning; that it could not be a long affair; that the theft of the apples would be very brief; that there would then remain only a question of identity, four or five depositions, and very little for the lawyers to say; that he should arrive after all was over.

The postilion whipped up the horses; they had crossed the river and left Mont-Saint-Eloy behind them.

The night grew more profound.

CHAPTER VI—SISTER SIMPLICE
PUT TO THE PROOF

But at that moment Fantine was joyous.

She had passed a very bad night; her cough was frightful; her fever had doubled in intensity; she had had dreams: in the morning, when the doctor paid his visit, she was delirious; he assumed an alarmed look, and ordered that he should be informed as soon as M. Madeleine arrived.

All the morning she was melancholy, said but little, and laid plaits in her sheets, murmuring the while, in a low voice, calculations that seemed to be calculations of distances. Her eyes were hollow and staring. They seemed almost extinguished at intervals, then lighted up again and shone like stars. It seems as though, at the approach of a certain dark hour, the light of heaven fills those who are quitting the light of earth.

Each time that Sister Simplice asked her how she felt, she replied invariably, "Well. I should like to see M. Madeleine."

Some months before this, at the moment when Fantine had just lost her last modesty, her last shame, and her last joy, she was the shadow of herself; now she was the specter of herself. Physical suffering had completed the work of moral suffering. This creature of five and twenty had a wrinkled brow, flabby cheeks, pinched nostrils, teeth from which the gums had receded, a leaden complexion, a bony neck, prominent shoulder blades, frail limbs, a clayey skin, and her golden hair was growing out sprinkled with gray. Alas! How illness improvises old age!

At midday the physician returned, gave some directions, inquired whether the mayor had made his appearance at the infirmary, and shook his head.

M. Madeleine usually came to see the invalid at three o'clock. As exactness is kindness, he was exact.

About half-past two, Fantine began to be restless. In the course of twenty minutes, she asked the nun more than ten times, "What time is it, sister?"

Three o'clock struck. At the third stroke, Fantine sat up in bed; she who could, in general, hardly turn over, joined her yellow, fleshless hands in a sort of convulsive clasp, and the nun heard her utter one of those profound sighs which seem to throw off dejection. Then Fantine turned and looked at the door.

No one entered; the door did not open.

She remained thus for a quarter of an hour, her eyes riveted on the door, motionless and apparently holding her breath. The sister dared not speak to her. The clock struck a quarter past three. Fantine fell back on her pillow.

She said nothing, but began to plait the sheets once more.

Half an hour passed, then an hour, no one came; every time the clock struck, Fantine started up and looked toward the door, then fell back again.

Her thought was clearly perceptible, but she uttered no name, she made no complaint, she blamed no one. But she coughed in a melancholy way. One would have said that something dark was descending upon her. She was livid and her lips were blue. She smiled now and then.

Five o'clock struck. Then the sister heard her say, very low and gently, "He is wrong not to come today, since I am going away tomorrow."

Sister Simplice herself was surprised at M. Madeleine's delay.

In the meantime, Fantine was staring at the tester of her bed. She seemed to be endeavoring to recall something. All at once she began to sing in a voice as feeble as a breath. The nun listened. This is what Fantine was singing:

> Lovely things we will buy
> As we stroll the faubourgs through.
> Roses are pink, cornflowers are blue,
> I love my love, cornflowers are blue.

Yestere'en the Virgin Mary came near my stove,
In a broidered mantle clad, and said to me,
"Here, hide 'neath my veil the child
Whom you one day begged from me.
Haste to the city, buy linen, buy a needle, buy thread."

Lovely things we will buy
As we stroll the faubourgs through.

Dear Holy Virgin, beside my stove
I have set a cradle with ribbons decked.
God may give me his loveliest star;
I prefer the child thou hast granted me.
"Madame, what shall I do with this linen fine?"
"Make of it clothes for thy newborn babe."

Roses are pink and cornflowers are blue,
I love my love, and cornflowers are blue.

"Wash this linen."
"Where?"
"In the stream. Make of it, soiling not, spoiling not,
A petticoat fair with its bodice fine,
Which I will embroider and fill with flowers."
"Madame, the child is no longer here; what is to be done?"
"Then make of it a winding sheet in which to bury me."

Lovely things we will buy
As we stroll the faubourgs through,
Roses are pink, cornflowers are blue,
I love my love, cornflowers are blue.

This song was an old cradle romance with which she had, in former days, lulled her little Cosette to sleep, and which had never recurred to her mind in all the five years during which she had been parted from her child. She sang it in so sad a voice, and to so sweet an air, that it was enough to make anyone, even a nun, weep. The sister, accustomed as she was to austerities, felt a tear spring to her eyes.

The clock struck six. Fantine did not seem to hear it. She no longer seemed to pay attention to anything about her.

Sister Simplice sent a servingmaid to inquire of the portress of the factory, whether the mayor had returned, and if he would not come to the infirmary soon. The girl returned in a few minutes.

Fantine was still motionless and seemed absorbed in her own thoughts.

The servant informed Sister Simplice in a very low tone, that the mayor had set out that morning before six o'clock, in a little tilbury harnessed to a white horse, cold as the weather was; that he had gone alone, without even a driver; that no one knew what road he had taken; that people said he had been seen to turn into the road to Arras; that others asserted that they had met him on the road to Paris. That when he went away he had been very gentle, as usual, and that he had merely told the portress not to expect him that night.

While the two women were whispering together, with their backs turned to Fantine's bed, the sister interrogating, the servant conjecturing, Fantine, with the feverish vivacity of certain organic maladies, which unite the free movements of health with the frightful emaciation of death, had raised herself to her knees in bed, with her shriveled hands resting on the bolster, and her head thrust through the opening of the curtains, and was listening. All at once she cried, "You are speaking of M. Madeleine! Why are you talking so low? What is he doing? Why does he not come?"

Her voice was so abrupt and hoarse that the two women thought they heard the voice of a man; they wheeled around in affright.

"Answer me!" cried Fantine.

The servant stammered, "The portress told me that he could not come today."

"Be calm, my child," said the sister; "lie down again."

Fantine, without changing her attitude, continued in a loud voice, and with an accent that was both imperious and heartrending:

"He cannot come? Why not? You know the reason. You are whispering it to each other there. I want to know it."

The servant maid hastened to say in the nun's ear, "Say that he is busy with the city council."

Sister Simplice blushed faintly, for it was a lie that the maid had proposed to her.

On the other hand, it seemed to her that the mere communication of the truth to the invalid would, without doubt, deal her a terrible blow, and that this was a serious matter in Fantine's present state. Her flush did not last long; the sister raised her calm, sad eyes to Fantine, and said, "Monsieur le Maire has gone away."

Fantine raised herself and crouched on her heels in the bed: her eyes sparkled; indescribable joy beamed from that melancholy face.

"Gone!" she cried. "He has gone to get Cosette."

Then she raised her arms to heaven, and her white face became ineffable; her lips moved; she was praying in a low voice.

When her prayer was finished, "Sister," she said, "I am willing to lie down again; I will do anything you wish; I was naughty just now; I beg your pardon for having spoken so loud; it is very wrong to talk loudly; I know that well, my good sister, but, you see, I am very happy: the good God is good; M. Madeleine is good; just think! He has gone to Montfermeil to get my little Cosette."

She lay down again, with the nun's assistance, helped the nun to arrange her pillow, and kissed the little silver cross which she wore on her neck, and which Sister Simplice had given her.

"My child," said the sister, "try to rest now, and do not talk anymore."

Fantine took the sister's hand in her moist hands, and the latter was pained to feel that perspiration.

"He set out this morning for Paris; in fact, he need not even go through Paris; Montfermeil is a little to the left as you come thence. Do you remember how he said to me yesterday, when I spoke to him of Cosette, 'Soon, soon'? He wants to give me a surprise, you know! He made me sign a letter so that she could be taken from the Thenardiers; they cannot say anything, can they? They will give back Cosette, for they have been paid; the authorities will not allow them to keep the child since they have received their pay. Do not make signs to me that I must not talk, sister! I am extremely happy; I am doing well; I am not ill at all anymore; I am going to see Cosette again; I am even quite hungry; it is nearly five years since I saw her last; you cannot imagine how much attached one gets to children, and then, she will be so pretty; you will see! If you only knew what pretty little rosy fingers she had! In the first place, she will have very beautiful hands; she had ridiculous hands when she was only a year old; like this! She must be a big girl now; she is seven years old; she is quite a young lady; I call her Cosette, but her name is really Euphrasie. Stop! This morning I was looking at the dust on the chimneypiece, and I had a sort of idea come across me, like that, that I should see Cosette again soon. *Mon Dieu!* How wrong it is not to see one's children for years! One ought to reflect that life is not eternal. Oh, how good M. le Maire is to go! It is very cold! It is true; he had on his cloak, at least? He will be here tomorrow, will he not? Tomorrow will be a festival day; tomorrow morning, sister, you must remind me to put on my little cap that has lace on it. What a place that Montfermeil is! I took that journey on foot once; it was very long for me, but the diligences go very quickly! He will be here tomorrow with Cosette: how far is it from here to Montfermeil?"

The sister, who had no idea of distances, replied, "Oh, I think that he will be here tomorrow."

"Tomorrow! Tomorrow!" said Fantine, "I shall see Cosette tomorrow! You see, good sister of the good God, that I am no longer ill; I am mad; I could dance if anyone wished it."

A person who had seen her a quarter of an hour previously would not have understood the change; she was all rosy now; she spoke in a lively and natural voice; her whole face was one smile; now and then she talked, she laughed softly; the joy of a mother is almost infantile.

"Well," resumed the nun, "now that you are happy, mind me, and do not talk anymore."

Fantine laid her head on her pillow and said in a low voice, "Yes, lie down again; be good, for you are going to have your child; Sister Simplice is right; everyone here is right."

And then, without stirring, without even moving her head, she began to stare all about her with wide-open eyes and a joyous air, and she said nothing more.

The sister drew the curtains together again, hoping that she would fall into a doze. Between seven and eight o'clock the doctor came; not hearing any sound, he thought Fantine was asleep, entered softly, and approached the bed on tiptoe; he opened the curtains a little, and, by the light of the taper, he saw Fantine's big eyes gazing at him.

She said to him, "She will be allowed to sleep beside me in a little bed, will she not, sir?"

The doctor thought that she was delirious. She added, "See! There is just room."

The doctor took Sister Simplice aside, and she explained matters to him; that M. Madeleine was absent for a day or two, and that in their doubt they had not thought it well to undeceive the invalid, who believed that the mayor had gone to Montfermeil; that it was possible, after all, that her guess was correct: the doctor approved.

He returned to Fantine's bed, and she went on, "You see, when she wakes up in the morning, I shall be able to say good morning to her, poor kitten, and when I cannot sleep at night, I can hear her asleep; her little gentle breathing will do me good."

"Give me your hand," said the doctor.

She stretched out her arm, and exclaimed with a laugh, "Ah, hold! In truth, you did not know it; I am cured; Cosette will arrive tomorrow."

The doctor was surprised; she was better; the pressure on her chest had decreased; her pulse had regained its strength; a sort of life had suddenly supervened and reanimated this poor, worn-out creature.

"Doctor," she went on, "did the sister tell you that M. le Maire has gone to get that mite of a child?"

The doctor recommended silence, and that all painful emotions should be avoided; he prescribed an infusion of pure chinchona, and, in case the fever should increase again during the night, a calming potion. As he took his departure, he said to the sister, "She is doing better; if good luck willed that the mayor should actually arrive tomorrow with the child, who knows? there are crises so astounding; great joy has been known to arrest maladies; I know well that this is an organic disease, and in an advanced state, but all those things are such mysteries: we may be able to save her."

CHAPTER VII—THE TRAVELER ON HIS ARRIVAL TAKES PRECAUTIONS FOR DEPARTURE

It was nearly eight o'clock in the evening when the cart, which we left on the road, entered the porte-cochere of the Hotel de la Poste in Arras; the man whom we have been following up to this moment alighted from it, responded with an abstracted air to the attentions of the people of the inn, sent back the extra horse, and with his own hands led the little white horse to the stable; then he opened the door of a billiard room that was situated on the ground floor, sat down there, and leaned his elbows on a table; he had taken fourteen hours for the journey which he had counted on making in six; he did himself the justice to acknowledge that it was not his fault, but at bottom, he was not sorry.

The landlady of the hotel entered.

"Does Monsieur wish a bed? Does Monsieur require supper?"

He made a sign of the head in the negative.

"The stableman says that Monsieur's horse is extremely fatigued."

Here he broke his silence.

"Will not the horse be in a condition to set out again tomorrow morning?"

"Oh, Monsieur! He must rest for two days at least."

He inquired, "Is not the posting station located here?"

"Yes, sir."

The hostess conducted him to the office; he showed his passport, and inquired whether there was any way of returning that same night to M. sur

M. by the mail wagon; the seat beside the postboy chanced to be vacant; he engaged it and paid for it. "Monsieur," said the clerk, "do not fail to be here ready to start at precisely one o'clock in the morning."

This done, he left the hotel and began to wander about the town.

He was not acquainted with Arras; the streets were dark, and he walked on at random; but seemed bent upon not asking the way of the passersby. He crossed the little river Crinchon, and found himself in a labyrinth of narrow alleys where he lost his way. A citizen was passing along with a lantern. After some hesitation, he decided to apply to this man, not without having first glanced behind and in front of him, as though he feared lest someone should hear the question which he was about to put.

"Monsieur," said he, "where is the courthouse, if you please?"

"You do not belong in town, sir?" replied the bourgeois, who was an oldish man. "Well, follow me. I happen to be going in the direction of the courthouse, that is to say, in the direction of the hotel of the prefecture; for the courthouse is undergoing repairs just at this moment, and the courts are holding their sittings provisionally in the prefecture."

"Is it there that the Assizes are held?" he asked.

"Certainly, sir; you see, the prefecture of today was the bishop's palace before the Revolution. M. de Conzie, who was bishop in '82, built a grand hall there. It is in this grand hall that the court is held."

On the way, the bourgeois said to him, "If Monsieur desires to witness a case, it is rather late. The sittings generally close at six o'clock."

When they arrived on the grand square, however, the man pointed out to him four long windows all lighted up, in the front of a vast and gloomy building.

"Upon my word, sir, you are in luck; you have arrived in season. Do you see those four windows? That is the Court of Assizes. There is light there, so they are not through. The matter must have been greatly protracted, and they are holding an evening session. Do you take an interest in this affair? Is it a criminal case? Are you a witness?"

He replied, "I have not come on any business; I only wish to speak to one of the lawyers."

"That is different," said the bourgeois. "Stop, sir; here is the door where the sentry stands. You have only to ascend the grand staircase."

He conformed to the bourgeois's directions, and a few minutes later he was in a hall containing many people, and where groups, intermingled with lawyers in their gowns, were whispering together here and there.

It is always a heartbreaking thing to see these congregations of men robed in black, murmuring together in low voices, on the threshold of the halls of justice. It is rare that charity and pity are the outcome of these words. Condemnations pronounced in advance are more likely to be the result. All these groups seem to the passing and thoughtful observer so many somber hives where buzzing spirits construct in concert all sorts of dark edifices.

This spacious hall, illuminated by a single lamp, was the old hall of the Episcopal palace, and served as the large hall of the palace of justice. A double-leaved door, which was closed at that moment, separated it from the large apartment where the court was sitting.

The obscurity was such that he did not fear to accost the first lawyer whom he met.

"What stage have they reached, sir?" he asked.

"It is finished," said the lawyer.

"Finished!"

This word was repeated in such accents that the lawyer turned around.

"Excuse me, sir; perhaps you are a relative?"

"No; I know no one here. Has judgment been pronounced?"

"Of course. Nothing else was possible."

"To penal servitude?"

"For life."

He continued, in a voice so weak that it was barely audible:

"Then his identity was established?"

"What identity?" replied the lawyer. "There was no identity to be established. The matter was very simple. The woman had murdered her child; the infanticide was proved; the jury threw out the question of premeditation, and she was condemned for life."

"So it was a woman?" said he.

"Why, certainly. The Limosin woman. Of what are you speaking?"

"Nothing. But since it is all over, how comes it that the hall is still lighted?"

"For another case, which was begun about two hours ago."

"What other case?"

"Oh! This one is a clear case also. It is about a sort of blackguard; a man arrested for a second offense; a convict who has been guilty of theft. I don't know his name exactly. There's a bandit's phiz* for you! I'd send him to the galleys on the strength of his face alone."

"Is there any way of getting into the courtroom, sir?" said he.

---

* face

"I really think that there is not. There is a great crowd. However, the hearing has been suspended. Some people have gone out, and when the hearing is resumed, you might make an effort."

"Where is the entrance?"

"Through yonder large door."

The lawyer left him. In the course of a few moments he had experienced, almost simultaneously, almost intermingled with each other, all possible emotions. The words of this indifferent spectator had, in turn, pierced his heart like needles of ice and like blades of fire. When he saw that nothing was settled, he breathed freely once more; but he could not have told whether what he felt was pain or pleasure.

He drew near to many groups and listened to what they were saying. The docket of the session was very heavy; the president had appointed for the same day two short and simple cases. They had begun with the infanticide, and now they had reached the convict, the old offender, the "return horse." This man had stolen apples, but that did not appear to be entirely proved; what had been proved was, that he had already been in the galleys at Toulon. It was that which lent a bad aspect to his case. However, the man's examination and the depositions of the witnesses had been completed, but the lawyer's plea, and the speech of the public prosecutor were still to come; it could not be finished before midnight. The man would probably be condemned; the attorney-general was very clever, and never missed his culprits; he was a brilliant fellow who wrote verses.

An usher stood at the door communicating with the hall of the Assizes. He inquired of this usher, "Will the door be opened soon, sir?"

"It will not be opened at all," replied the usher.

"What! It will not be opened when the hearing is resumed? Is not the hearing suspended?"

"The hearing has just been begun again," replied the usher, "but the door will not be opened again."

"Why?"

"Because the hall is full."

"What! There is not room for one more?"

"Not another one. The door is closed. No one can enter now."

The usher added after a pause, "There are, to tell the truth, two or three extra places behind Monsieur le President, but Monsieur le President only admits public functionaries to them."

So saying, the usher turned his back.

He retired with bowed head, traversed the antechamber, and slowly descended the stairs, as though hesitating at every step. It is probable that he was holding counsel with himself. The violent conflict that had been going on within him since the preceding evening was not yet ended; and every moment he encountered some new phase of it. On reaching the landing place, he leaned his back against the balusters and folded his arms. All at once he opened his coat, drew out his pocketbook, took from it a pencil, tore out a leaf, and upon that leaf he wrote rapidly, by the light of the street lantern, this line: M. Madeleine, Mayor of M. sur M.; then he ascended the stairs once more with great strides, made his way through the crowd, walked straight up to the usher, handed him the paper, and said in an authoritative manner, "Take this to Monsieur le President."

The usher took the paper, cast a glance upon it, and obeyed.

CHAPTER VIII—
AN ENTRANCE BY FAVOR

Although he did not suspect the fact, the mayor of M. sur M. enjoyed a sort of celebrity. For the space of seven years his reputation for virtue had filled the whole of Bas Boulonnais; it had eventually passed the confines of a small district and had been spread abroad through two or three neighboring departments. Besides the service that he had rendered to the chief town by resuscitating the black jet industry, there was not one out of the hundred and forty communes of the arrondissement of M. sur M. that was not indebted to him for some benefit. He had even at need contrived to aid and multiply the industries of other arrondissements. It was thus that he had, when occasion offered, supported with his credit and his funds the linen factory at Boulogne, the flax-spinning industry at Frevent, and the hydraulic manufacture of cloth at Boubers-sur-Canche. Everywhere the name of M. Madeleine was pronounced with veneration. Arras and Douai envied the happy little town of M. sur M. its mayor.

The Counselor of the Royal Court of Douai, who was presiding over this session of the Assizes at Arras, was acquainted, in common with the rest of the world, with this name that was so profoundly and universally honored. When the usher, discreetly opening the door which connected the council chamber with the courtroom, bent over the back of the President's armchair and handed him the paper on which was inscribed the line which we have just perused, adding, "The gentleman desires to be present at the trial," the President, with a quick and deferential movement, seized a pen and wrote a few words at the bottom of the paper and returned it to the usher, saying, "Admit him."

The unhappy man whose history we are relating had remained near the door of the hall, in the same place and the same attitude in which the usher had left him. In the midst of his reverie he heard someone saying to him, "Will Monsieur do me the honor to follow me?" It was the same usher who had turned his back upon him but a moment previously, and who was now bowing to the earth before him. At the same time, the usher handed him the paper. He unfolded it, and as he chanced to be near the light, he could read it.

"The President of the Court of Assizes presents his respects to M. Madeleine."

He crushed the paper in his hand as though those words contained for him a strange and bitter aftertaste.

He followed the usher.

A few minutes later he found himself alone in a sort of wainscoted cabinet of severe aspect, lighted by two wax candles, placed upon a table with a green cloth. The last words of the usher who had just quitted him still rang in his ears: "Monsieur, you are now in the council-chamber; you have only to turn the copper handle of yonder door, and you will find yourself in the courtroom, behind the President's chair." These words were mingled in his thoughts with a vague memory of narrow corridors and dark staircases which he had recently traversed.

The usher had left him alone. The supreme moment had arrived. He sought to collect his faculties, but could not. It is chiefly at the moment when there is the greatest need for attaching them to the painful realities of life, that the threads of thought snap within the brain. He was in the very place where the judges deliberated and condemned. With stupid tranquility he surveyed this peaceful and terrible apartment, where so many lives had been broken, which was soon to ring with his name, and which his fate was at that moment traversing. He stared at the wall, then he looked at himself, wondering that it should be that chamber and that it should be he.

He had eaten nothing for four and twenty hours; he was worn out by the jolts of the cart, but he was not conscious of it. It seemed to him that he felt nothing.

He approached a black frame that was suspended on the wall, and which contained, under glass, an ancient autograph letter of Jean Nicolas Pache, mayor of Paris and minister, and dated, through an error, no doubt, the 9th of June, of the year II, and in which Pache forwarded to the commune the list of ministers and deputies held in arrest by them. Any spectator who had chanced to see him at that moment, and who had watched him, would have imagined, doubtless, that this letter struck him as very curious, for he did not take his eyes from it, and he read it two or three times. He read it without paying any attention to it, and unconsciously. He was thinking of Fantine and Cosette.

As he dreamed, he turned around, and his eyes fell upon the brass knob of the door that separated him from the Court of Assizes. He had almost forgotten that door. His glance, calm at first, paused there, remained fixed on that brass handle, then grew terrified, and little by little became impregnated with fear. Beads of perspiration burst forth among his hair and trickled down upon his temples.

At a certain moment he made that indescribable gesture of a sort of authority mingled with rebellion, which is intended to convey, and which does so well convey, "*Pardieu!* Who compels me to this?" Then he wheeled briskly around, caught sight of the door through which he had entered in front of him, went to it, opened it, and passed out. He was no longer in that chamber; he was outside in a corridor, a long, narrow corridor, broken by steps and gratings, making all sorts of angles, lighted here and there by lanterns similar to the night taper of invalids, the corridor through which he had approached. He breathed, he listened; not a sound in front, not a sound behind him, and he fled as though pursued.

When he had turned many angles in this corridor, he still listened. The same silence reigned, and there was the same darkness around him. He was out of breath; he staggered; he leaned against the wall. The stone was cold; the perspiration lay ice-cold on his brow; he straightened himself up with a shiver.

Then, there alone in the darkness, trembling with cold and with something else, too, perchance, he meditated.

He had meditated all night long; he had meditated all the day: he heard within him but one voice, which said, "Alas!"

A quarter of an hour passed thus. At length he bowed his head, sighed with agony, dropped his arms, and retraced his steps. He walked slowly, and as though crushed. It seemed as though someone had overtaken him in his flight and was leading him back.

He reentered the council chamber. The first thing he caught sight of was the knob of the door. This knob, which was round and of polished brass, shone like a terrible star for him. He gazed at it as a lamb might gaze into the eye of a tiger.

He could not take his eyes from it. From time to time he advanced a step and approached the door.

Had he listened, he would have heard the sound of the adjoining hall like a sort of confused murmur; but he did not listen, and he did not hear.

Suddenly, without himself knowing how it happened, he found himself near the door; he grasped the knob convulsively; the door opened.

He was in the courtroom.

CHAPTER IX—A PLACE WHERE CONVICTIONS ARE IN PROCESS OF FORMATION

He advanced a pace, closed the door mechanically behind him, and remained standing, contemplating what he saw.

It was a vast and badly lighted apartment, now full of uproar, now full of silence, where all the apparatus of a criminal case, with its petty and mournful gravity in the midst of the throng, was in process of development.

At the one end of the hall, the one where he was, were judges, with abstracted air, in threadbare robes, who were gnawing their nails or closing their eyelids; at the other end, a ragged crowd; lawyers in all sorts of attitudes; soldiers with hard but honest faces; ancient, spotted woodwork, a dirty ceiling, tables covered with serge that was yellow rather than green; doors blackened by handmarks; taproom lamps that emitted more smoke than light, suspended from nails in the wainscot; on the tables candles in brass candlesticks; darkness, ugliness, sadness; and from all this there was disengaged an austere and august impression, for one there felt that grand human thing which is called the law, and that grand divine thing which is called justice.

No one in all that throng paid any attention to him; all glances were directed toward a single point, a wooden bench placed against a small door, in the stretch of wall on the President's left; on this bench, illuminated by several candles, sat a man between two gendarmes.

This man was the man.

He did not seek him; he saw him; his eyes went there naturally, as though they had known beforehand where that figure was.

He thought he was looking at himself, grown old; not absolutely the same in face, of course, but exactly similar in attitude and aspect, with his bristling hair, with that wild and uneasy eye, with that blouse, just as it was on the day when he entered D———, full of hatred, concealing his soul in that hideous mass of frightful thoughts that he had spent nineteen years in collecting on the floor of the prison.

He said to himself with a shudder, "Good God! Shall I become like that again?"

This creature seemed to be at least sixty; there was something indescribably coarse, stupid, and frightened about him.

At the sound made by the opening door, people had drawn aside to make way for him; the President had turned his head, and, understanding that the personage who had just entered was the mayor of M. sur M., he had bowed to him; the attorney general, who had seen M. Madeleine at M. sur M., where the duties of his office had called him more than once, recognized him and saluted him also: he had hardly perceived it; he was the victim of a sort of hallucination; he was watching.

Judges, clerks, gendarmes, a throng of cruelly curious heads, all these he had already beheld once, in days gone by, twenty-seven years before; he had encountered those fatal things once more; there they were; they moved; they existed; it was no longer an effort of his memory, a mirage of his thought; they were real gendarmes and real judges, a real crowd, and real men of flesh and blood: it was all over; he beheld the monstrous aspects of his past reappear and live once more around him, with all that there is formidable in reality.

All this was yawning before him.

He was horrified by it; he shut his eyes, and exclaimed in the deepest recesses of his soul, "Never!"

And by a tragic play of destiny that made all his ideas tremble, and rendered him nearly mad, it was another self of his that was there! All called that man who was being tried Jean Valjean.

Under his very eyes, unheard-of vision, he had a sort of representation of the most horrible moment of his life, enacted by his specter.

Everything was there; the apparatus was the same, the hour of the night, the faces of the judges, of soldiers, and of spectators; all were the same, only above the President's head there hung a crucifix, something which the courts had lacked at the time of his condemnation: God had been absent when he had been judged.

There was a chair behind him; he dropped into it, terrified at the thought that he might be seen; when he was seated, he took advantage of a pile of cardboard boxes, which stood on the judge's desk, to conceal his face from the whole room; he could now see without being seen; he had fully regained consciousness of the reality of things; gradually he recovered; he attained that phase of composure where it is possible to listen.

M. Bamatabois was one of the jurors.

He looked for Javert, but did not see him; the seat of the witnesses was

idden from him by the clerk's table, and then, as we have just said, the hall
vas sparely lighted.

At the moment of this entrance, the defendant's lawyer had just finished
his plea.

The attention of all was excited to the highest pitch; the affair had lasted
for three hours: for three hours that crowd had been watching a strange man,
a miserable specimen of humanity, either profoundly stupid or profoundly
subtle, gradually bending beneath the weight of a terrible likeness. This
man, as the reader already knows, was a vagabond who had been found in
a field carrying a branch laden with ripe apples, broken in the orchard of a
neighbor, called the Pierron orchard. Who was this man? An examination had
been made; witnesses had been heard, and they were unanimous; light had
abounded throughout the entire debate; the accusation said, "We have in our
grasp not only a marauder, a stealer of fruit; we have here, in our hands, a
bandit, an old offender who has broken his ban, an ex-convict, a miscreant
of the most dangerous description, a malefactor named Jean Valjean, whom
justice has long been in search of, and who, eight years ago, on emerging
from the galleys at Toulon, committed a highway robbery, accompanied by
violence, on the person of a child, a Savoyard named Little Gervais; a crime
provided for by article 383 of the Penal Code, the right to try him for which
we reserve hereafter, when his identity shall have been judicially established.
He has just committed a fresh theft; it is a case of a second offense; condemn
him for the fresh deed; later on he will be judged for the old crime." In the face
of this accusation, in the face of the unanimity of the witnesses, the accused
appeared to be astonished more than anything else; he made signs and gestures
that were meant to convey no, or else he stared at the ceiling: he spoke with
difficulty, replied with embarrassment, but his whole person, from head to foot,
was a denial; he was an idiot in the presence of all these minds ranged in order
of battle around him, and like a stranger in the midst of this society that was
seizing fast upon him; nevertheless, it was a question of the most menacing
future for him; the likeness increased every moment, and the entire crowd
surveyed, with more anxiety than he did himself, that sentence freighted with
calamity, which descended ever closer over his head; there was even a glimpse
of a possibility afforded; besides the galleys, a possible death penalty, in case
his identity were established, and the affair of Little Gervais were to end
thereafter in condemnation. Who was this man? What was the nature of his
apathy? Was it imbecility or craft? Did he understand too well, or did he not
understand at all? These were questions that divided the crowd, and seemed to

divide the jury; there was something both terrible and puzzling in this case: the drama was not only melancholy; it was also obscure.

The counsel for the defense had spoken tolerably well, in that provincial tongue, which has long constituted the eloquence of the bar, and which was formerly employed by all advocates, at Paris as well as at Romorantin or a Montbrison, and which today, having become classic, is no longer spoken except by the official orators of magistracy, to whom it is suited on account of its grave sonorousness and its majestic stride; a tongue in which a husband is called a consort, and a woman a spouse; Paris, the center of art and civilization; the king, the monarch; Monseigneur the Bishop, a sainted pontiff; the district attorney, the eloquent interpreter of public prosecution; the arguments, the accents that we have just listened to; the age of Louis XIV, the grand age; a theater, the temple of Melpomene; the reigning family, the august blood of our kings; a concert, a musical solemnity; the General Commandant of the province, the illustrious warrior, who, etc.; the pupils in the seminary, these tender levities; errors imputed to newspapers, the imposture which distills its venom through the columns of those organs; etc. The lawyer had, accordingly, begun with an explanation as to the theft of the apples, an awkward matter couched in fine style; but Benigne Bossuet himself was obliged to allude to a chicken in the midst of a funeral oration, and he extricated himself from the situation in stately fashion. The lawyer established the fact that the theft of the apples had not been circumstantially proved. His client, whom he, in his character of counsel, persisted in calling Champmathieu, had not been seen scaling that wall nor breaking that branch by anyone. He had been taken with that branch (which the lawyer preferred to call a bough) in his possession; but he said that he had found it broken off and lying on the ground, and had picked it up. Where was there any proof to the contrary? No doubt that branch had been broken off and concealed after the scaling of the wall, then thrown away by the alarmed marauder; there was no doubt that there had been a thief in the case. But what proof was there that that thief had been Champmathieu? One thing only. His character as an ex-convict. The lawyer did not deny that that character appeared to be, unhappily, well attested; the accused had resided at Faverolles; the accused had exercised the calling of a tree pruner there; the name of Champmathieu might well have had its origin in Jean Mathieu; all that was true, in short, four witnesses recognize Champmathieu, positively and without hesitation, as that convict, Jean Valjean; to these signs, to this testimony, the council could oppose nothing but the denial of his client, the denial of an interested party; but supposing that he was the convict Jean Valjean, did that prove that he was the thief of the apples? That was a presumption at the most, not a proof. The prisoner, it was true, and his counsel, "in good faith," was obliged to admit it, had adopted "a bad system of defense." He obstinately denied everything, the theft and his character of convict. An admission upon this last point would certainly have been better, and would have won for him the indulgence of his judges; the counsel had advised him to do this; but the accused had obstinately refused, thinking, no doubt, that he would save everything by admitting nothing. It was an error; but ought not the paucity of his intelligence to be taken into consideration? This man was visibly stupid. Long-continued wretchedness in the galleys, long misery outside the galleys, had brutalized him, etc. He defended himself badly; was that a reason for condemning him? As for the affair with Little Gervais, the counsel need not discuss it; it did not enter into the case. The lawyer wound up by beseeching the jury and the court, if the identity of Jean Valjean appeared to them to be evident, to apply to him the police penalties which are provided for a criminal who has broken his ban, and not the frightful chastisement that descends upon the convict guilty of a second offense.

The district attorney answered the counsel for the defense. He was violent and florid, as district attorneys usually are.

He congratulated the counsel for the defense on his "loyalty," and skillfully took advantage of this loyalty. He reached the accused through all the concessions made by his lawyer. The advocate had seemed to admit that the prisoner was Jean Valjean. He took note of this. So this man was Jean Valjean. This point had been conceded to the accusation and could no longer be disputed. Here, by means of a clever autonomasia, which went back to the sources and causes of crime, the district attorney thundered against the immorality of the romantic school, then dawning under the name of the Satanic school, which had been bestowed upon it by the critics of the Quotidienne and the Oriflamme; he attributed, not without some probability, to the influence of this perverse literature the crime of Champmathieu, or rather, to speak more correctly, of Jean Valjean. Having exhausted these considerations, he passed on to Jean Valjean himself. Who was this Jean Valjean? Description of Jean Valjean: a monster spewed forth, etc. The model for this sort of description is contained in the tale of Theramene, which is not useful to tragedy, but which every day renders great services to judicial eloquence. The audience and the jury "shuddered." The description finished, the district attorney resumed with an oratorical turn calculated to raise the enthusiasm of the journal of the prefecture to the highest pitch on the following day: And it is such a man, etc., etc., etc., vagabond, beggar, without means of existence, etc., etc., inured by his past life to culpable deeds, and but little reformed by his sojourn in the galleys, as was proved by the crime committed against Little Gervais, etc., etc. it is such a man, caught upon the highway in the very act of theft, a few paces from a wall that had been scaled, still holding in his hand the object stolen, who denies the crime, the theft, the climbing the wall; denies everything; denies even his own identity! In addition to a hundred other proofs, to which we will not recur, four witnesses recognize him—Javert, the upright inspector of police; Javert, and three of his former companions in infamy, the convicts Brevet, Chenildieu, and Cochepaille. What does he offer in opposition to this overwhelming unanimity? His denial. What obduracy! You will do justice, gentlemen of the jury, etc., etc. While the district attorney was speaking, the accused listened to him open-mouthed, with a sort of amazement in which some admiration was assuredly blended. He was evidently surprised that a man could talk like that. From time to time, at those "energetic" moments of the prosecutor's speech, when eloquence that cannot contain itself overflows in a flood of withering epithets and envelops the accused like a storm, he moved his head slowly from right to left and from left to right in the sort of mute and melancholy protest with which he had contented himself since the beginning of the argument. Two or three times the spectators who were nearest to him heard him say in a low voice, "That is what comes of not having asked M. Baloup." The district attorney directed the attention of the jury to this stupid attitude, evidently deliberate, which denoted not imbecility, but craft, skill, a habit of deceiving justice, and which set forth in all its nakedness the "profound perversity" of this man. He ended by making his reserves on the affair of Little Gervais and demanding a severe sentence.

At that time, as the reader will remember, it was penal servitude for life.

The counsel for the defense rose, began by complimenting Monsieur l'Avocat-General on his "admirable speech," then replied as best he could; but he weakened; the ground was evidently slipping away from under his feet.

CHAPTER X—THE SYSTEM OF DENIALS

The moment for closing the debate had arrived. The President had the accused stand up, and addressed to him the customary question, "Have you anything to add to your defense?"

The man did not appear to understand, as he stood there, twisting in his hands a terrible cap that he had.

The President repeated the question.

This time the man heard it. He seemed to understand. He made a motion like a man who is just waking up, cast his eyes about him, stared at the audience, the gendarmes, his counsel, the jury, the court, laid his monstrous fist on the rim of woodwork in front of his bench, took another look, and all at once, fixing his glance upon the district attorney, he began to speak. It was like an eruption. It seemed, from the manner in which the words escaped from his mouth, incoherent, impetuous, pell-mell, tumbling over each other, as though they were all pressing forward to issue forth at once. He said, "This is what I have to say. That I have been a wheelwright in Paris, and that it was with Monsieur Baloup. It is a hard trade. In the wheelwright's trade one works always in the open air, in courtyards, under sheds when the masters are good, never in closed workshops, because space is required, you see. In winter one gets so cold that one beats one's arms together to warm one's self; but the masters don't like it; they say it wastes time. Handling iron when there is ice between the paving-stones is hard work. That wears a man out quickly One is old while he is still quite young in that trade. At forty a man is done for. I was fifty-three. I was in a bad state. And then, workmen are so mean! When a man is no longer young, they call him nothing but an old bird, old beast! I was not earning more than thirty sous a day. They paid me as little as possible. The masters took advantage of my age—and then I had my daughter, who was a laundress at the river. She earned a little also. It sufficed for us two. She had trouble, also; all day long up to her waist in a tub, in rain, in snow. When the wind cuts your face, when it freezes, it is all the same; you must still wash. There are people who have not much linen, and wait until late; if you do not wash, you lose your custom. The planks are badly joined, and water drops on you from everywhere; you have your petticoats all damp above and below. That penetrates. She has also worked at the laundry of the Enfants-Rouges, where the water comes through faucets. You are not in the tub there; you wash at the faucet in front of you, and rinse in a basin behind you. As it is enclosed, you are not so cold; but there is that hot steam, which is terrible, and which ruins your eyes. She came home at seven o'clock in the evening, and went to bed at once, she was so tired. Her husband beat her. She is dead. We have not been very happy. She was a good girl, who did not go to the ball, and who was very peaceable. I remember one Shrove Tuesday when she went to bed at eight o'clock. There, I am telling the truth; you have only to ask. Ah, yes! How stupid I am! Paris is a gulf. Who knows Father Champmathieu there? But M. Baloup does, I tell you. Go see at M. Baloup's; and after all, I don't know what is wanted of me."

The man ceased speaking, and remained standing. He had said these things in a loud, rapid, hoarse voice, with a sort of irritated and savage ingenuousness. Once he paused to salute someone in the crowd. The sort of affirmations that he seemed to fling out before him at random came like hiccups, and to each he added the gesture of a woodcutter who is splitting wood. When he had finished the audience burst into a laugh. He stared at the public, and, perceiving that they were laughing, and not understanding why, he began to laugh himself.

It was inauspicious.

The President, an attentive and benevolent man, raised his voice.

He reminded "the gentlemen of the jury" that "the sieur Baloup, formerly a master wheelwright, with whom the accused stated that he had served, had been summoned in vain. He had become bankrupt, and was not to be found." Then turning to the accused, he enjoined him to listen to what he was about to say, and added, "You are in a position where reflection is necessary. The gravest presumptions rest upon you, and may induce vital results. Prisoner, in your own interests, I summon you for the last time to explain yourself clearly on two points. In the first place, did you or did you not climb the wall of the Pierron orchard, break the branch, and steal the apples; that is to say, commit the crime of breaking in and theft? In the second place, are you the discharged convict, Jean Valjean—yes or no?"

The prisoner shook his head with a capable air, like a man who has thoroughly understood, and who knows what answer he is going to make. He opened his mouth, turned toward the President, and said, "In the first place—'

Then he stared at his cap, stared at the ceiling, and held his peace.

"Prisoner," said the district attorney, in a severe voice; "pay attention. You are not answering anything that has been asked of you. Your embarrassmen condemns you. It is evident that your name is not Champmathieu; that you are the convict, Jean Valjean, concealed first under the name of Jean Mathieu which was the name of his mother; that you went to Auvergne; that you were born at Faverolles, where you were a pruner of trees. It is evident that you have been guilty of entering, and of the theft of ripe apples from the Pierron orchard. The gentlemen of the jury will form their own opinion."

The prisoner had finally resumed his seat; he arose abruptly when the district attorney had finished, and exclaimed, "You are very wicked; that you are! This is what I wanted to say; I could not find words for it at first. I have stolen nothing. I am a man who does not have something to eat every day. I was coming from Ailly; I was walking through the country after a shower which had made the whole country yellow: even the ponds were overflowed and nothing sprang from the sand any more but the little blades of grass a the wayside. I found a broken branch with apples on the ground; I picked up the branch without knowing that it would get me into trouble. I have been n prison, and they have been dragging me about for the last three months; nore than that I cannot say; people talk against me, they tell me, 'Answer!' The gendarme, who is a good fellow, nudges my elbow, and says to me in a ow voice, 'Come, answer!' I don't know how to explain; I have no education; am a poor man; that is where they wrong me, because they do not see this. I nave not stolen; I picked up from the ground things that were lying there. You say, Jean Valjean, Jean Mathieu! I don't know those persons; they are villagers. I worked for M. Baloup, Boulevard de l'Hopital; my name is Champmathieu. You are very clever to tell me where I was born; I don't know myself: it's not everybody who has a house in which to come into the world; that would be too convenient. I think that my father and mother were people who strolled along the highways; I know nothing different. When I was a child, they called me young fellow; now they call me old fellow; those are my baptismal names; take that as you like. I have been in Auvergne; I have been at Faverolles. Pardi. Well! Can't a man have been in Auvergne, or at Faverolles, without having been in the galleys? I tell you that I have not stolen, and that I am Father Champmathieu; I have been with M. Baloup; I have had a settled residence. You worry me with your nonsense, there! Why is everybody pursuing me so furiously?"

The district attorney had remained standing; he addressed the President, "Monsieur le President, in view of the confused but exceedingly clever denials of the prisoner, who would like to pass himself off as an idiot, but who will not succeed in so doing, we shall attend to that, we demand that it shall please you and that it shall please the court to summon once more into this place the convicts Brevet, Cochepaille, and Chenildieu, and Police Inspector Javert, and question them for the last time as to the identity of the prisoner with the convict Jean Valjean."

"I would remind the district attorney," said the President, "that Police Inspector Javert, recalled by his duties to the capital of a neighboring arrondissement, left the courtroom and the town as soon as he had made his deposition; we have accorded him permission, with the consent of the district attorney and of the counsel for the prisoner."

"That is true, Mr. President," responded the district attorney. "In the absence of sieur Javert, I think it my duty to remind the gentlemen of the jury of what he said here a few hours ago. Javert is an estimable man, who does honor by his rigorous and strict probity to inferior but important functions. These are the terms of his deposition: 'I do not even stand in need of circumstantial proofs and moral presumptions to give the lie to the prisoner's denial. I recognize him perfectly. The name of this man is not Champmathieu; he is an ex-convict named Jean Valjean, and is very vicious and much to be feared. It is only with extreme regret that he was released at the expiration of his term. He underwent nineteen years of penal servitude for theft. He made five or six attempts to escape. Besides the theft from Little Gervais, and from the Pierron orchard, I suspect him of a theft committed in the house of His Grace the late Bishop of D———. I often saw him at the time when I was adjutant of the galley guard at the prison in Toulon. I repeat that I recognize him perfectly.'"

This extremely precise statement appeared to produce a vivid impression on the public and on the jury. The district attorney concluded by insisting, that in default of Javert, the three witnesses Brevet, Chenildieu, and Cochepaille should be heard once more and solemnly interrogated.

The President transmitted the order to an usher, and, a moment later, the door of the witnesses' room opened. The usher, accompanied by a gendarme ready to lend him armed assistance, introduced the convict Brevet. The audience was in suspense; and all breasts heaved as though they had contained but one soul.

The ex-convict Brevet wore the black-and-gray waistcoat of the central prisons. Brevet was a person sixty years of age, who had a sort of business man's face, and the air of a rascal. The two sometimes go together. In prison, where fresh misdeeds had led him, he had become something in the nature of a turnkey. He was a man of whom his superiors said, "He tries to make himself of use." The chaplains bore good testimony as to his religious habits. It must not be forgotten that this passed under the Restoration.

"Brevet," said the President, "you have undergone an ignominious sentence, and you cannot take an oath."

Brevet dropped his eyes.

"Nevertheless," continued the President, "even in the man whom the law has degraded, there may remain, when the divine mercy permits it, a sentiment of honor and of equity. It is to this sentiment that I appeal at this decisive hour. If it still exists in you, and I hope it does, reflect before replying to me: consider on the one hand, this man, whom a word from you may ruin; on the other hand, justice, which a word from you may enlighten. The instant is solemn; there is still time to retract if you think you have been mistaken. Rise, prisoner Brevet, take a good look at the accused, recall your souvenirs, and tell us on your soul and conscience, if you persist in recognizing this man as your former companion in the galleys, Jean Valjean?"

Brevet looked at the prisoner, then turned toward the court.

"Yes, Mr. President, I was the first to recognize him, and I stick to it; that man is Jean Valjean, who entered at Toulon in 1796, and left in 1815. I left a year later. He has the air of a brute now; but it must be because age has brutalized him; he was sly at the galleys: I recognize him positively."

"Take your seat," said the President. "Prisoner, remain standing."

Chenildieu was brought in, a prisoner for life, as was indicated by his red cassock and his green cap. He was serving out his sentence at the galleys of Toulon, from where he had been brought for this case. He was a small man of about fifty, brisk, wrinkled, frail, yellow, brazen-faced, feverish, who had a sort of sickly feebleness about all his limbs and his whole person, and an immense force in his glance. His companions in the galleys had nicknamed him "I Deny God."

The President addressed him in nearly the same words that he had used to Brevet. At the moment when he reminded him of his infamy, which deprived him of the right to take an oath, Chenildieu raised his head and looked the crowd in the face. The President invited him to reflection, and asked him as he had asked Brevet, if he persisted in recognition of the prisoner.

Chenildieu burst out laughing.

"Pardieu, as if I didn't recognize him! We were attached to the same chain for five years. So you are sulking, old fellow?"

"Go take your seat," said the President.

The usher brought in Cochepaille. He was another convict for life, who had come from the galleys, and was dressed in red, like Chenildieu, was a peasant from Lourdes, and a half-bear of the Pyrenees. He had guarded the flocks among the mountains, and from a shepherd he had slipped into a brigand. Cochepaille was no less savage and seemed even more stupid than the prisoner. He was one of those wretched men whom nature has sketched out for wild beasts, and on whom society puts the finishing touches as convicts in the galleys.

The President tried to touch him with some grave and pathetic words, and asked him, as he had asked the other two, if he persisted, without hesitation or trouble, in recognizing the man who was standing before him.

"He is Jean Valjean," said Cochepaille. "He was even called Jean-the-Screw, because he was so strong."

Each of these affirmations from these three men, evidently sincere and in good faith, had raised in the audience a murmur of bad augury for the prisoner, a murmur that increased and lasted longer each time that a fresh declaration was added to the proceeding.

The prisoner had listened to them, with that astounded face which was, according to the accusation, his principal means of defense; at the first, the gendarmes, his neighbors, had heard him mutter between his teeth, "Ah, well, he's a nice one!" After the second, he said, a little louder, with an air that was almost that of satisfaction, "Good!" At the third, he cried, "Famous!"

The President addressed him, "Have you heard, prisoner? What have you to say?"

He replied, "I say, 'Famous!'"

An uproar broke out among the audience, and was communicated to the jury; it was evident that the man was lost.

"Ushers," said the President, "enforce silence! I am going to sum up the arguments."

At that moment there was a movement just beside the President; a voice was heard crying: "Brevet! Chenildieu! Cochepaille! Look here!"

All who heard that voice were chilled, so lamentable and terrible was it; all eyes were turned to the point from where it had proceeded. A man, placed among the privileged spectators who were seated behind the court, had just risen, had pushed open the half-door that separated the tribunal from the audience, and was standing in the middle of the hall; the President, the district attorney, M. Bamatabois, twenty persons, recognized him, and exclaimed in concert, "M. Madeleine!"

CHAPTER XI—CHAMPMATHIEU MORE AND MORE ASTONISHED

It was he, in fact. The clerk's lamp illumined his countenance. He held his hat in his hand; there was no disorder in his clothing; his coat was carefully buttoned; he was very pale, and he trembled slightly; his hair, which had still been gray on his arrival in Arras, was now entirely white: it had turned white during the hour he had sat there.

All heads were raised: the sensation was indescribable; there was a momentary hesitation in the audience, the voice had been so heartrending; the man who stood there appeared so calm that they did not understand at first. They asked themselves whether he had indeed uttered that cry; they could not believe that that tranquil man had been the one to give that terrible outcry.

This indecision only lasted a few seconds. Even before the President and the district attorney could utter a word, before the ushers and the gendarmes could make a gesture, the man whom all still called, at that moment, M. Madeleine, had advanced toward the witnesses Cochepaille, Brevet, and Chenildieu.

"Do you not recognize me?" said he.

All three remained speechless, and indicated by a sign of the head that they did not know him. Cochepaille, who was intimidated, made a military salute. M. Madeleine turned toward the jury and the court, and said in a gentle voice, "Gentlemen of the jury, order the prisoner to be released! Mr. President, have me arrested. He is not the man whom you are in search of; it is I: I am Jean Valjean."

Not a mouth breathed; the first commotion of astonishment had been followed by a silence like that of the grave; those within the hall experienced that sort of religious terror which seizes the masses when something grand has been done.

In the meantime, the face of the President was stamped with sympathy and sadness; he had exchanged a rapid sign with the district attorney and a few low-toned words with the assistant judges; he addressed the public, and asked in accents which all understood, "Is there a physician present?"

The district attorney took the word. "Gentlemen of the jury, the very strange and unexpected incident that disturbs the audience inspires us, like yourselves, only with a sentiment which it is unnecessary for us to express. You all know, by reputation at least, the honorable M. Madeleine, mayor of M. sur M.; if there is a physician in the audience, we join the President in requesting him to attend to M. Madeleine, and to conduct him to his home."

M. Madeleine did not allow the district attorney to finish; he interrupted him in accents full of suavity and authority. These are the words that he uttered; here they are literally, as they were written down, immediately after the trial by one of the witnesses to this scene, and as they now ring in the ears of those who heard them nearly forty years ago: "I thank you, Mr. District Attorney, but I am not mad; you shall see; you were on the point of committing a great error; release this man! I am fulfilling a duty; I am that miserable criminal. I am the only one here who sees the matter clearly, and I am telling you the truth. God, who is on high, looks down on what I am doing at this moment, and that suffices. You can take me, for here I am: but I have done my best; I concealed myself under another name; I have become rich; I have become a mayor; I have tried to reenter the ranks of the honest. It seems that that is not to be done. In short, there are many things which I cannot tell. I will not narrate the story of my life to you; you will hear it one of these days. I robbed Monseigneur the Bishop, it is true; it is true that I robbed Little Gervais; they were right in telling you that Jean Valjean was a very vicious wretch. Perhaps it was not altogether his fault. Listen, honorable judges! A man who has been so greatly humbled as I have has neither any remonstrances to make to Providence, nor any advice to give to society; but, you see, the infamy from which I have tried to escape is an injurious thing; the galleys make the convict what he is; reflect upon that, if you please. Before going to the galleys, I was a poor peasant, with very little intelligence, a sort of idiot; the galleys wrought a change in me. I was stupid; I became vicious: I was a block of wood; I became a firebrand. Later on, indulgence and kindness saved me, as severity had ruined me. But, pardon me, you cannot understand what I am saying. You will find at my house, among the ashes in the fireplace, the forty-sou piece which I stole, seven years ago, from little Gervais. I have nothing farther to add; take me. Good God! The district attorney shakes his head; you say, 'M. Madeleine has gone mad!' You do not believe me! That is distressing. Do not, at least, condemn this man! What! These men do not recognize me! I wish Javert were here; he would recognize me."

Nothing can reproduce the somber and kindly melancholy of tone which accompanied these words.

He turned to the three convicts, and said, "Well, I recognize you; do you remember, Brevet?"

He paused, hesitated for an instant, and said, "Do you remember the knitted suspenders with a checked pattern which you wore in the galleys?"

Brevet gave a start of surprise, and surveyed him from head to foot with a frightened air. He continued, "Chenildieu, you who conferred on yourself the name of 'Jenie-Dieu,' your whole right shoulder bears a deep burn, because you one day laid your shoulder against the chafing-dish full of coals, in order to efface the three letters T. F. P., which are still visible, nevertheless; answer, is this true?"

"It is true," said Chenildieu.

He addressed himself to Cochepaille. "Cochepaille, you have, near the bend in your left arm, a date stamped in blue letters with burnt powder; the date is that of the landing of the Emperor at Cannes, March 1, 1815; pull up your sleeve!"

Cochepaille pushed up his sleeve; all eyes were focused on him and on his bare arm.

A gendarme held a light close to it; there was the date.

The unhappy man turned to the spectators and the judges with a smile that still rends the hearts of all who saw it whenever they think of it. It was a smile of triumph; it was also a smile of despair.

"You see plainly," he said, "that I am Jean Valjean."

In that chamber there were no longer either judges, accusers, nor gendarmes;

there was nothing but staring eyes and sympathizing hearts. No one recalled any longer the part that each might be called upon to play; the district attorney forgot he was there for the purpose of prosecuting, the President that he was there to preside, the counsel for the defense that he was there to defend. It was a striking circumstance that no question was put, that no authority intervened. The peculiarity of sublime spectacles is, that they capture all souls and turn witnesses into spectators. No one, probably, could have explained what he felt; no one, probably, said to himself that he was witnessing the splendid outburst of a grand light: all felt themselves inwardly dazzled.

It was evident that they had Jean Valjean before their eyes. That was clear. The appearance of this man had sufficed to suffuse with light that matter which had been so obscure but a moment previously, without any further explanation: the whole crowd, as by a sort of electric revelation, understood instantly and at a single glance the simple and magnificent history of a man who was delivering himself up so that another man might not be condemned in his stead. The details, the hesitations, little possible oppositions, were swallowed up in that vast and luminous fact.

It was an impression which vanished speedily, but which was irresistible at the moment.

"I do not wish to disturb the court further," resumed Jean Valjean. "I shall withdraw, since you do not arrest me. I have many things to do. The district attorney knows who I am; he knows where I am going; he can have me arrested when he likes."

He directed his steps toward the door. Not a voice was raised, not an arm extended to hinder him. All stood aside. At that moment there was about him that divine something which causes multitudes to stand aside and make way for a man. He traversed the crowd slowly. It was never known who opened the door, but it is certain that he found the door open when he reached it. On arriving there he turned around and said, "I am at your command, Mr. District Attorney."

Then he addressed the audience. "All of you, all who are present—consider me worthy of pity, do you not? Good God! When I think of what I was on the point of doing, I consider that I am to be envied. Nevertheless, I should have preferred not to have had this occur."

He withdrew, and the door closed behind him as it had opened, for those who do certain sovereign things are always sure of being served by someone in the crowd.

Less than an hour after this, the verdict of the jury freed the said

Champmathieu from all accusations; and Champmathieu, being at once released, went off in a state of stupefaction, thinking that all men were fools, and comprehending nothing of this vision.

BOOK EIGHTH: A COUNTERBLOW

CHAPTER I—IN WHAT MIRROR M. MADELEINE CONTEMPLATES HIS HAIR

The day had begun to dawn. Fantine had passed a sleepless and feverish night, filled with happy visions; at daybreak she fell asleep. Sister Simplice, who had been watching with her, availed herself of this slumber to go and prepare a new potion of chinchona. The worthy sister had been in the laboratory of the infirmary but a few moments, bending over her drugs and phials, and scrutinizing things very closely, on account of the dimness which the half-light of dawn spreads over all objects. Suddenly she raised her head and uttered a faint shriek. M. Madeleine stood before her; he had just entered silently.

"Is it you, Mr. Mayor?" she exclaimed.

He replied in a low voice, "How is that poor woman?"

"Not so bad just now; but we have been very uneasy."

She explained to him what had passed: that Fantine had been very ill the day before, and that she was better now, because she thought that the mayor had gone to Montfermeil to get her child. The sister dared not question the mayor; but she perceived plainly from his air that he had not come from there.

"All that is good," said he; "you were right not to undeceive her."

"Yes," responded the sister; "but now, Mr. Mayor, she will see you and will not see her child. What shall we say to her?"

He reflected for a moment.

"God will inspire us," said he.

"But we cannot tell a lie," murmured the sister, half aloud.

It was broad daylight in the room. The light fell full on M. Madeleine's face. The sister chanced to raise her eyes to it.

"Good God, sir!" she exclaimed. "What has happened to you? Your hair is perfectly white!"

"White!" said he.

Sister Simplice had no mirror. She rummaged in a drawer, and pulled out the little glass that the doctor of the infirmary used to see whether a patient was dead and whether he no longer breathed. M. Madeleine took the mirror, looked at his hair, and said, "Well!"

He uttered the word indifferently, and as though his mind were on something else.

The sister felt chilled by something strange of which she caught a glimpse in all this.

He inquired, "Can I see her?"

"Is not Monsieur le Maire going to have her child brought back to her?" said the sister, hardly venturing to put the question.

"Of course; but it will take two or three days at least."

"If she were not to see Monsieur le Maire until that time," went on the sister, timidly, "she would not know that Monsieur le Maire had returned, and it would be easy to inspire her with patience; and when the child arrived, she would naturally think Monsieur le Maire had just come with the child. We should not have to enact a lie."

M. Madeleine seemed to reflect for a few moments; then he said with his calm gravity, "No, sister, I must see her. I may, perhaps, be in haste."

The nun did not appear to notice this word "perhaps," which communicated an obscure and singular sense to the words of the mayor's speech. She replied, lowering her eyes and her voice respectfully, "In that case, she is asleep; but Monsieur le Maire may enter."

He made some remarks about a door that shut badly, and the noise of which might awaken the sick woman; then he entered Fantine's chamber, approached the bed and drew aside the curtains. She was asleep. Her breath issued from her breast with that tragic sound, which is peculiar to those maladies, and which breaks the hearts of mothers when they are watching through the night beside their sleeping child who is condemned to death. But this painful respiration hardly troubled a sort of ineffable serenity that overspread her countenance, and which transfigured her in her sleep. Her pallor had become whiteness; her cheeks were crimson; her long golden lashes, the only beauty of her youth and her virginity that remained to her, palpitated, though they remained closed and drooping. Her whole person was trembling with an indescribable unfolding of wings, all ready to open wide and bear her away, which could be felt as they rustled, though they could not be seen. To see her thus, one would never have dreamed that she was an invalid whose life was almost despaired of. She resembled rather something on the point of soaring away than something on the point of dying.

The branch trembles when a hand approaches it to pluck a flower, and seems to both withdraw and to offer itself at one and the same time. The human body has something of this tremor when the instant arrives in which the mysterious fingers of Death are about to pluck the soul.

M. Madeleine remained for some time motionless beside that bed, gazing in turn upon the sick woman and the crucifix, as he had done two months before, on the day when he had come for the first time to see her in that asylum. They were both still there in the same attitude—she sleeping, he praying; only now, after the lapse of two months, her hair was gray and his was white.

The sister had not entered with him. He stood beside the bed, with his finger on his lips, as though there were someone in the chamber whom he must enjoin to silence.

She opened her eyes, saw him, and said quietly, with a smile, "And Cosette?"

CHAPTER II—FANTINE HAPPY

She made no movement of either surprise or of joy; she was joy itself. That simple question, "And Cosette?" was put with so profound a faith, with so much certainty, with such a complete absence of disquiet and of doubt, that he found not a word of reply. She continued, "I knew that you were there. I was asleep, but I saw you. I have seen you for a long, long time. I have been following you with my eyes all night long. You were in a glory, and you had around you all sorts of celestial forms."

He raised his glance to the crucifix.

"But," she resumed, "tell me where Cosette is. Why did not you place her on my bed against the moment of my waking?"

He made some mechanical reply, which he was never afterward able to recall.

Fortunately, the doctor had been warned, and he now made his appearance. He came to the aid of M. Madeleine.

"Calm yourself, my child," said the doctor; "your child is here."

Fantine's eyes beamed and filled her whole face with light. She clasped her hands with an expression which contained all that is possible to prayer in the way of violence and tenderness.

"Oh!" she exclaimed. "Bring her to me!"

Touching illusion of a mother! Cosette was, for her, still the little child who is carried.

"Not yet," said the doctor, "not just now. You still have some fever. The sight of your child would agitate you and do you harm. You must be cured first."

She interrupted him impetuously, "But I am cured! Oh, I tell you that I am cured! What an ass that doctor is! The idea! I want to see my child!"

"You see," said the doctor, "how excited you become. So long as you are in this state I shall oppose your having your child. It is not enough to see her; it is necessary that you should live for her. When you are reasonable, I will bring her to you myself."

The poor mother bowed her head.

"I beg your pardon, doctor, I really beg your pardon. Formerly I should never have spoken as I have just done; so many misfortunes have happened to me, that I sometimes do not know what I am saying. I understand you; you fear the emotion. I will wait as long as you like, but I swear to you that it would not have harmed me to see my daughter. I have been seeing her; I have not taken my eyes from her since yesterday evening. Do you know? If she were brought to me now, I should talk to her very gently. That is all. Is it not quite natural that I should desire to see my daughter, who has been brought to me expressly from Montfermeil? I am not angry. I know well that I am about to be happy. All night long I have seen white things, and persons who smiled at me. When Monsieur le Docteur pleases, he shall bring me Cosette. I have no longer any fever; I am well. I am perfectly conscious that there is nothing the matter with me anymore; but I am going to behave as though I were ill, and not stir, to please these ladies here. When it is seen that I am very calm, they will say, 'She must have her child.'"

M. Madeleine was sitting on a chair beside the bed. She turned toward him; she was making a visible effort to be calm and "very good," as she expressed it in the feebleness of illness which resembles infancy, in order that, seeing her so peaceable, they might make no difficulty about bringing Cosette to her. But while she controlled herself she could not refrain from questioning M. Madeleine.

"Did you have a pleasant trip, Monsieur le Maire? Oh! How good you were to go and get her for me! Only tell me how she is. Did she stand the journey well? Alas! She will not recognize me. She must have forgotten me by this time, poor darling! Children have no memories. They are like birds. A child sees one thing today and another thing tomorrow, and thinks of nothing any longer. And did she have white linen? Did those Thenardiers keep her clean? How have they fed her? Oh! If you only knew how I have suffered, putting such questions as that to myself during all the time of my wretchedness. Now, it is all past. I am happy. Oh, how I should like to see her! Do you think her pretty, Monsieur le Maire? Is not my daughter beautiful? You must have been very cold in that diligence! Could she not be brought for just one little instant? She might be taken away directly afterward. Tell me; you are the master; it could be so if you chose!"

He took her hand. "Cosette is beautiful," he said, "Cosette is well. You shall see her soon; but calm yourself; you are talking with too much vivacity, and you are throwing your arms out from under the clothes, and that makes you cough."

In fact, fits of coughing interrupted Fantine at nearly every word.

Fantine did not murmur; she feared that she had injured by her too passionate lamentations the confidence which she was desirous of inspiring, and she began to talk of indifferent things.

"Montfermeil is quite pretty, is it not? People go there on pleasure parties in summer. Are the Thenardiers prosperous? There are not many travelers in their parts. That inn of theirs is a sort of a cookshop."

M. Madeleine was still holding her hand, and gazing at her with anxiety; it was evident that he had come to tell her things before, which his mind now hesitated. The doctor, having finished his visit, retired. Sister Simplice remained alone with them.

But in the midst of this pause Fantine exclaimed, "I hear her! *Mon Dieu*, I hear her!"

She stretched out her arm to enjoin silence about her, held her breath, and began to listen with rapture.

There was a child playing in the yard—the child of the portress or of some workwoman. It was one of those accidents that are always occurring, and which seem to form a part of the mysterious stage-setting of mournful scenes. The child—a little girl—was going and coming, running to warm herself, laughing, singing at the top of her voice. Alas! in what are the plays of children not intermingled. It was this little girl whom Fantine heard singing.

"Oh!" she resumed. "It is my Cosette! I recognize her voice."

The child retreated as it had come; the voice died away. Fantine listened for a while longer, then her face clouded over, and M. Madeleine heard her say, in a low voice, "How wicked that doctor is not to allow me to see my daughter! That man has an evil countenance, that he has."

But the smiling background of her thoughts came to the front again. She continued to talk to herself, with her head resting on the pillow: "How happy we are going to be! We shall have a little garden the very first thing; M. Madeleine has promised it to me. My daughter will play in the garden. She must know her letters by this time. I will make her spell. She will run over the grass after butterflies. I will watch her. Then she will take her first communion. Ah! When will she take her first communion?"

She began to reckon on her fingers.

"One, two, three, four—she is seven years old. In five years she will have a white veil, and openwork stockings; she will look like a little woman. O my good sister, you do not know how foolish I become when I think of my daughter's first communion!"

She began to laugh.

He had released Fantine's hand. He listened to her words as one listens to the sighing of the breeze, with his eyes on the ground, his mind absorbed in reflection that had no bottom. All at once she ceased speaking, and this caused him to raise his head mechanically. Fantine had become terrible.

She no longer spoke, she no longer breathed; she had raised herself to a sitting posture, her thin shoulder emerged from her chemise; her face, which had been radiant but a moment before, was ghastly, and she seemed to have fixed her eyes, rendered large with terror, on something alarming at the other extremity of the room.

"Good God!" he exclaimed. "What ails you, Fantine?"

She made no reply; she did not remove her eyes from the object that she seemed to see. She removed one hand from his arm, and with the other made him a sign to look behind him.

He turned, and beheld Javert.

CHAPTER III—JAVERT SATISFIED

This is what had taken place.

The half-hour after midnight had just struck when M. Madeleine quitted the Hall of Assizes in Arras. He regained his inn just in time to set out again by the mail wagon, in which he had engaged his place. A little before six o'clock in the morning he had arrived at M. sur M., and his first care had been to post a letter to M. Laffitte, then to enter the infirmary and see Fantine.

However, he had hardly quitted the audience hall of the Court of Assizes, when the district attorney, recovering from his first shock, had taken the word to deplore the mad deed of the honorable mayor of M. sur M., to declare that his convictions had not been in the least modified by that curious incident, which would be explained thereafter, and to demand, in the meantime, the condemnation of that Champmathieu, who was evidently the real Jean Valjean. The district attorney's persistence was visibly at variance with the sentiments of everyone, of the public, of the court, and of the jury. The counsel for the defense had some difficulty in refuting this harangue and in establishing that, in consequence of the revelations of M. Madeleine, that is to say, of the real Jean Valjean, the aspect of the matter had been thoroughly altered, and that the jury had before their eyes now only an innocent man. Thence the lawyer had drawn some epiphonemas, not very fresh, unfortunately, upon judicial errors, etc., etc.; the President, in his summing up, had joined the counsel for the defense, and in a few minutes the jury had thrown Champmathieu out of the case.

Nevertheless, the district attorney was bent on having a Jean Valjean; and as he had no longer Champmathieu, he took Madeleine.

Immediately after Champmathieu had been set at liberty, the district attorney shut himself up with the President. They conferred "as to the necessity of seizing the person of M. le Maire of M. sur M." This phrase, in which there was a great deal of of, is the district attorney's, written with his own hand, on the minutes of his report to the attorney-general. His first emotion having passed off, the President did not offer many objections. Justice must, after all, take its course. And then, when all was said, although the President was a kindly and a tolerably intelligent man, he was, at the same time, a devoted and almost an ardent royalist, and he had been shocked to hear the Mayor of M. sur M. say the Emperor, and not Bonaparte, when alluding to the landing at Cannes.

The order for his arrest was accordingly dispatched. The district attorney forwarded it to M. sur M. by a special messenger, at full speed, and entrusted its execution to Police Inspector Javert.

The reader knows that Javert had returned to M. sur M. immediately after having given his deposition.

Javert was just getting out of bed when the messenger handed him the order of arrest and the command to produce the prisoner.

The messenger himself was a very clever member of the police, who, in two words, informed Javert of what had taken place at Arras. The order of arrest, signed by the district attorney, was couched in these words: "Inspector Javert will apprehend the body of the Sieur Madeleine, mayor of M. sur M., who, in this day's session of the court, was recognized as the liberated convict, Jean Valjean."

Anyone who did not know Javert, and who had chanced to see him at the moment when he penetrated the antechamber of the infirmary, could have divined nothing of what had taken place, and would have thought his air the most ordinary in the world. He was cool, calm, grave, his gray hair perfectly smooth upon his temples, and he had just mounted the stairs with his habitual deliberation. Anyone who was thoroughly acquainted with him, and who had examined him attentively at the moment, would have shuddered. The buckle of his leather stock was under his left ear instead of at the nape of his neck. This betrayed unwonted agitation.

Javert was a complete character, who never had a wrinkle in his duty or in his uniform; methodical with malefactors, rigid with the buttons of his coat.

That he should have set the buckle of his stock awry, it was indispensable that there should have taken place in him one of those emotions that may be designated as internal earthquakes.

He had come in a simple way, had made a requisition on the neighboring post for a corporal and four soldiers, had left the soldiers in the courtyard, had had Fantine's room pointed out to him by the portress, who was utterly unsuspicious, accustomed as she was to seeing armed men inquiring for the mayor.

On arriving at Fantine's chamber, Javert turned the handle, pushed the door open with the gentleness of a sick nurse or a police spy, and entered.

Properly speaking, he did not enter. He stood erect in the half-open door, his hat on his head and his left hand thrust into his coat, which was buttoned up to the chin. In the bend of his elbow the leaden head of his enormous cane, which was hidden behind him, could be seen.

Thus he remained for nearly a minute, without his presence being perceived. All at once Fantine raised her eyes, saw him, and made M. Madeleine turn around.

The instant that Madeleine's glance encountered Javert's glance, Javert, without stirring, without moving from his post, without approaching him, became terrible. No human sentiment can be as terrible as joy.

It was the visage of a demon who has just found his damned soul.

The satisfaction of at last getting hold of Jean Valjean caused all that was in his soul to appear in his countenance. The depths having been stirred up, mounted to the surface. The humiliation of having, in some slight degree, lost the scent, and of having indulged, for a few moments, in an error with regard to Champmathieu, was effaced by pride at having so well and accurately divined in the first place, and of having for so long cherished a just instinct. Javert's content shone forth in his sovereign attitude. The deformity of triumph overspread that narrow brow. All the demonstrations of horror that a satisfied face can afford were there.

Javert was in heaven at that moment. Without putting the thing clearly to himself, but with a confused intuition of the necessity of his presence and of his success, he, Javert, personified justice, light, and truth in their celestial function of crushing out evil. Behind him and around him, at an infinite distance, he had authority, reason, the case judged, the legal conscience, the public prosecution, all the stars; he was protecting order, he was causing the law to yield up its thunders, he was avenging society, he was lending a helping hand to the absolute, he was standing erect in the midst of a glory. There existed in his victory a remnant of defiance and of combat. Erect, haughty, brilliant, he flaunted abroad in open day the superhuman bestiality of a ferocious archangel. The terrible shadow of the action that he was accomplishing caused the vague flash of the social sword to be visible in his clenched fist; happy and indignant, he held his heel upon crime, vice, rebellion, perdition, hell; he was radiant, he exterminated, he smiled, and there was an incontestable grandeur in this monstrous Saint Michael.

Javert, though frightful, had nothing ignoble about him.

Probity, sincerity, candor, conviction, the sense of duty, are things that may become hideous when wrongly directed; but which, even when hideous, remain grand: their majesty, the majesty peculiar to the human conscience, clings to them in the midst of horror; they are virtues that have one vice: error. The honest, pitiless joy of a fanatic in the full flood of his atrocity preserves a certain lugubriously venerable radiance. Without himself suspecting the fact, Javert in his formidable happiness was to be pitied, as is every ignorant man who triumphs. Nothing could be so poignant and so terrible as this face, wherein was displayed all that may be designated as the evil of the good.

CHAPTER IV—AUTHORITY REASSERTS ITS RIGHTS

Fantine had not seen Javert since the day on which the mayor had torn her from the man. Her ailing brain comprehended nothing, but the only thing which she did not doubt was that he had come to get her. She could not endure that terrible face; she felt her life quitting her; she hid her face in both hands, and shrieked in her anguish, "Monsieur Madeleine, save me!"

Jean Valjean—we shall henceforth not speak of him otherwise—had risen. He said to Fantine in the gentlest and calmest of voices, "Be at ease; it is not for you that he is come."

Then he addressed Javert, and said, "I know what you want."

Javert replied, "Be quick about it!"

There lay in the inflection of voice that accompanied these words something indescribably fierce and frenzied. Javert did not say, "Be quick about it!" he said "Bequiabouit."

No orthography can do justice to the accent with which it was uttered: it was no longer a human word: it was a roar.

He did not proceed according to his custom, he did not enter into the matter, he exhibited no warrant of arrest. In his eyes, Jean Valjean was a sort of mysterious combatant, who was not to be laid hands upon, a wrestler in the dark whom he had had in his grasp for the last five years, without being able to throw him. This arrest was not a beginning, but an end. He confined himself to saying, "Be quick about it!"

As he spoke thus, he did not advance a single step; he hurled at Jean Valjean a glance, which he threw out like a grappling hook, and with which he was accustomed to draw wretches violently to him.

It was this glance that Fantine had felt penetrating to the very marrow of her bones two months previously.

At Javert's exclamation, Fantine opened her eyes once more. But the mayor was there; what had she to fear?

Javert advanced to the middle of the room, and cried, "See here now! Art thou coming?"

The unhappy woman glanced about her. No one was present excepting the nun and the mayor. To whom could that abject use of "thou" be addressed? To her only. She shuddered.

Then she beheld a most unprecedented thing, a thing so unprecedented that nothing equal to it had appeared to her even in the blackest deliriums of fever.

She beheld Javert, the police spy, seize the mayor by the collar; she saw the mayor bow his head. It seemed to her that the world was coming to an end.

Javert had, in fact, grasped Jean Valjean by the collar.

"Monsieur le Maire!" shrieked Fantine.

Javert burst out laughing with that frightful laugh that displayed all his gums. "There is no longer any Monsieur le Maire here!"

Jean Valjean made no attempt to disengage the hand which grasped the collar of his coat. He said, "Javert—"

Javert interrupted him. "Call me Mr. Inspector."

"Monsieur," said Jean Valjean, "I should like to say a word to you in private."

"Aloud! Say it aloud!" replied Javert. "People are in the habit of talking aloud to me."

Jean Valjean went on in a lower tone:

"I have a request to make of you—"

"I tell you to speak loud."

"But you alone should hear it—"

"What difference does that make to me? I shall not listen."

Jean Valjean turned toward him and said very rapidly and in a very low voice, "Grant me three days' grace! Three days in which to go and fetch the child of this unhappy woman. I will pay whatever is necessary. You shall accompany me if you choose."

"You are making sport of me!" cried Javert. "Come now, I did not think you such a fool! You ask me to give you three days in which to run away! You say that it is for the purpose of fetching that creature's child! Ah! Ah! That's good! That's really capital!"

Fantine was seized with a fit of trembling.

"My child!" she cried. "To go and fetch my child! She is not here, then! Answer me, sister; where is Cosette? I want my child! Monsieur Madeleine! Monsieur le Maire!"

Javert stamped his foot.

"And now there's the other one! Will you hold your tongue, you hussy? It's a pretty sort of a place where convicts are magistrates, and where women of the town are cared for like countesses! Ah! But we are going to change all that; it is high time!"

He stared intently at Fantine, and added, once more taking into his grasp Jean Valjean's cravat, shirt, and collar, "I tell you that there is no Monsieur Madeleine and that there is no Monsieur le Maire. There is a thief, a brigand, a convict named Jean Valjean! And I have him in my grasp! That's what there is!"

Fantine raised herself in bed with a bound, supporting herself on her stiffened arms and on both hands: she gazed at Jean Valjean, she gazed at Javert, she gazed at the nun, she opened her mouth as though to speak; a rattle proceeded from the depths of her throat, her teeth chattered; she stretched out her arms in her agony, opening her hands convulsively, and fumbling about her like a drowning person; then suddenly fell back on her pillow.

Her head struck the headboard of the bed and fell forward on her breast, with gaping mouth and staring, sightless eyes.

She was dead.

Jean Valjean laid his hand upon the detaining hand of Javert, and opened it as he would have opened the hand of a baby; then he said to Javert, "You have murdered that woman."

"Let's have an end of this!" shouted Javert, in a fury. "I am not here to listen to argument. Let us economize all that; the guard is below; march on instantly, or you'll get the thumb screws!"

In the corner of the room stood an old iron bedstead, which was in a decidedly decrepit state, and which served the sisters as a camp bed when they were watching with the sick. Jean Valjean stepped up to this bed, in a twinkling wrenched off the headpiece, which was already in a dilapidated condition, an easy matter to muscles like his, grasped the principal rod like a bludgeon, and glanced at Javert. Javert retreated toward the door. Jean Valjean, armed with his bar of iron, walked slowly up to Fantine's couch. When he arrived there he turned and said to Javert, in a voice that was barely audible, "I advise you not to disturb me at this moment."

One thing is certain, and that is, that Javert trembled.

It did occur to him to summon the guard, but Jean Valjean might avail himself of that moment to effect his escape; so he remained, grasped his cane by the small end, and leaned against the doorpost, without removing his eyes from Jean Valjean.

Jean Valjean rested his elbow on the knob at the head of the bed, and his brow on his hand, and began to contemplate the motionless body of Fantine, which lay extended there. He remained thus, mute, absorbed, evidently with no further thought of anything connected with this life. Upon his face and in his attitude there was nothing but inexpressible pity. After a few moments of this meditation he bent toward Fantine, and spoke to her in a low voice.

What did he say to her? What could this man, who was reproved, say to that woman, who was dead? What words were those? No one on earth heard them. Did the dead woman hear them? There are some touching illusions which are, perhaps, sublime realities. The point as to which there exists no doubt is, that Sister Simplice, the sole witness of the incident, often said that at the moment that Jean Valjean whispered in Fantine's ear, she distinctly beheld an ineffable smile dawn on those pale lips, and in those dim eyes, filled with the amazement of the tomb.

Jean Valjean took Fantine's head in both his hands, and arranged it on the pillow as a mother might have done for her child; then he tied the string of her chemise, and smoothed her hair back under her cap. That done, he closed her eyes.

Fantine's face seemed strangely illuminated at that moment.

Death, that signifies entrance into the great light.

Fantine's hand was hanging over the side of the bed. Jean Valjean knelt down before that hand, lifted it gently, and kissed it.

Then he rose, and turned to Javert.

"Now," said he, "I am at your disposal."

CHAPTER V—A SUITABLE TOMB

Javert deposited Jean Valjean in the city prison.

The arrest of M. Madeleine occasioned a sensation, or rather, an extraordinary commotion in M. sur M. We are sorry that we cannot conceal the fact, that at the single word, "He was a convict," nearly everyone deserted him. In less than two hours all the good that he had done had been forgotten, and he was nothing but a "convict from the galleys." It is just to add that the details of what had taken place at Arras were not yet known. All day long conversations like the following were to be heard in all quarters of the town:

"You don't know? He was a liberated convict!" "Who?" "The mayor." "Bah! M. Madeleine?" "Yes." "Really?" "His name was not Madeleine at all; he had a frightful name, Bejean, Bojean, Boujean." "Ah! Good God!" "He has been arrested." "Arrested!" "In prison, in the city prison, while waiting to be transferred." "Until he is transferred!" "He is to be transferred!" "Where is he to be taken?" "He will be tried at the Assizes for a highway robbery which he committed long ago." "Well! I suspected as much. That man was too good, too perfect, too affected. He refused the cross; he bestowed sous on all the little scamps he came across. I always thought there was some evil history back of all that."

The "drawing rooms" particularly abounded in remarks of this nature.

One old lady, a subscriber to the Drapeau Blanc, made the following remark, the depth of which it is impossible to fathom: "I am not sorry. It will be a lesson to the Bonapartists!"

It was thus that the phantom, which had been called M. Madeleine, vanished from M. sur M. Only three or four persons in all the town remained faithful to his memory. The old portress who had served him was among the number.

On the evening of that day the worthy old woman was sitting in her lodge, still in a thorough fright, and absorbed in sad reflections. The factory had been closed all day, the carriage gate was bolted, the street was deserted. There was no one in the house but the two nuns, Sister Perpetue and Sister Simplice, who were watching beside the body of Fantine.

Toward the hour when M. Madeleine was accustomed to return home, the good portress rose mechanically, took from a drawer the key of M. Madeleine's chamber, and the flat candlestick, which he used every evening to go up to his quarters; then she hung the key on the nail from which he was accustomed to take it, and set the candlestick on one side, as though she was expecting him. Then she sat down again on her chair, and became absorbed in thought once more. The poor, good old woman had done all this without being conscious of it.

It was only at the expiration of two hours that she roused herself from her reverie, and exclaimed, "Hold! My good God Jesus! And I hung his key on the nail!"

At that moment the small window in the lodge opened, a hand passed through, seized the key and the candlestick, and lighted the taper at the candle which was burning there.

The portress raised her eyes, and stood there with gaping mouth, and a shriek which she confined to her throat.

She knew that hand, that arm, the sleeve of that coat.

It was M. Madeleine.

It was several seconds before she could speak; she had a seizure, as she said herself, when she related the adventure afterward.

"Good God, Monsieur le Maire," she cried at last, "I thought you were—"

She stopped; the conclusion of her sentence would have been lacking in respect toward the beginning. Jean Valjean was still Monsieur le Maire to her.

He finished her thought.

"In prison," said he. "I was there; I broke a bar of one of the windows; I let myself drop from the top of a roof, and here I am. I am going up to my room; go and find Sister Simplice for me. She is with that poor woman, no doubt."

The old woman obeyed in all haste.

He gave her no orders; he was quite sure that she would guard him better than he should guard himself.

No one ever found out how he had managed to get into the courtyard without opening the big gates. He had, and always carried about him, a passkey which opened a little side door; but he must have been searched, and his latchkey must have been taken from him. This point was never explained.

He ascended the staircase leading to his chamber. On arriving at the top, he left his candle on the top step of his stairs, opened his door with very little noise, went and closed his window and his shutters by feeling, then returned for his candle and reentered his room.

It was a useful precaution; it will be recollected that his window could be seen from the street.

He cast a glance about him, at his table, at his chair, at his bed, which had not been disturbed for three days. No trace of the disorder of the night before last remained. The portress had "done up" his room; only she had picked out of the ashes and placed neatly on the table the two iron ends of the cudgel and the forty-sou piece, which had been blackened by the fire.

He took a sheet of paper, on which he wrote: "*These are the two tips of my iron-shod cudgel and the forty-sou piece stolen from Little Gervais, which I mentioned at the Court of Assizes,*" and he arranged this piece of paper, the bits of iron, and the coin in such a way that they were the first things to be seen on entering the room. From a cupboard he pulled out one of his old shirts, which he tore in pieces. In the strips of linen thus prepared he wrapped the two silver candlesticks. He betrayed neither haste nor agitation; and while he was wrapping up the Bishop's candlesticks, he nibbled at a piece of black bread. It was probably the prison bread that he had carried with him in his flight.

This was proved by the crumbs that were found on the floor of the room when the authorities made an examination later on.

There came two taps at the door.

"Come in," said he.

It was Sister Simplice.

She was pale; her eyes were red; the candle which she carried trembled in her hand. The peculiar feature of the violences of destiny is, that however polished or cool we may be, they wring human nature from our very bowels, and force it to reappear on the surface. The emotions of that day had turned the nun into a woman once more. She had wept, and she was trembling.

Jean Valjean had just finished writing a few lines on a paper, which he handed to the nun, saying, "Sister, you will give this to Monsieur le Curé."

The paper was not folded. She cast a glance upon it.

"You can read it," said he.

She read: "I beg Monsieur le Curé to keep an eye on all that I leave behind me. He will be so good as to pay out of it the expenses of my trial, and of the funeral of the woman who died yesterday. The rest is for the poor."

The sister tried to speak, but she only managed to stammer a few inarticulate sounds. She succeeded in saying, however, "Does not Monsieur le Maire desire to take a last look at that poor, unhappy woman?"

"No," said he; "I am pursued; it would only end in their arresting me in that room, and that would disturb her."

He had hardly finished when a loud noise became audible on the staircase. They heard a tumult of ascending footsteps, and the old portress saying in her loudest and most piercing tones, "My good sir, I swear to you by the good God, that not a soul has entered this house all day, nor all the evening, and that I have not even left the door."

A man responded, "But there is a light in that room, nevertheless."

They recognized Javert's voice.

The chamber was so arranged that the door in opening masked the corner of the wall on the right. Jean Valjean blew out the light and placed himself in his angle. Sister Simplice fell on her knees near the table.

The door opened.

Javert entered.

The whispers of many men and the protestations of the portress were audible in the corridor.

The nun did not raise her eyes. She was praying.

The candle was on the chimneypiece, and gave but very little light.

Javert caught sight of the nun and halted in amazement.

It will be remembered that the fundamental point in Javert, his element, the very air he breathed, was veneration for all authority. This was impregnable, and admitted of neither objection nor restriction. In his eyes, of course, the ecclesiastical authority was the chief of all; he was religious, superficial and correct on this point as on all others. In his eyes, a priest was a mind, who never makes a mistake; a nun was a creature who never sins; they were souls walled in from this world, with a single door that never opened except to allow the truth to pass through.

On perceiving the sister, his first movement was to retire.

But there was also another duty that bound him and impelled him imperiously in the opposite direction. His second movement was to remain and to venture on at least one question.

This was Sister Simplice, who had never told a lie in her life. Javert knew it, and held her in special veneration in consequence.

"Sister," said he, "are you alone in this room?"

A terrible moment ensued, during which the poor portress felt as though she should faint.

The sister raised her eyes and answered, "Yes."

"Then," resumed Javert, "you will excuse me if I persist; it is my duty; you have not seen a certain person—a man—this evening? He has escaped; we are in search of him—that Jean Valjean; you have not seen him?"

The sister replied, "No."

She lied. She had lied twice in succession, one after the other, without hesitation, promptly, as a person does when sacrificing herself.

"Pardon me," said Javert, and he retired with a deep bow.

O sainted maid! You left this world many years ago; you have rejoined your sisters, the virgins, and your brothers, the angels, in the light; may this lie be counted to your credit in paradise!

The sister's affirmation was for Javert so decisive a thing that he did not ever observe the singularity of that candle which had but just been extinguished and which was still smoking on the table.

An hour later, a man, marching amid trees and mists, was rapidly departing from M. sur M. in the direction of Paris. That man was Jean Valjean. It has been established by the testimony of two or three carters who met him, that he was carrying a bundle; that he was dressed in a blouse. Where had he obtained that blouse? No one ever found out. But an aged workman had died in the infirmary of the factory a few days before, leaving behind him nothing but his blouse. Perhaps that was the one.

One last word about Fantine.

We all have a mother, the earth. Fantine was given back to that mother.

The Curé thought that he was doing right, and perhaps he really was, in reserving as much money as possible from what Jean Valjean had left for the poor. Who was concerned, after all? A convict and a woman of the town. That is why he had a very simple funeral for Fantine, and reduced it to that strictly necessary form known as the pauper's grave.

So Fantine was buried in the free corner of the cemetery that belongs to anybody and everybody, and where the poor are lost. Fortunately, God knows where to find the soul again. Fantine was laid in the shade, among the first bones that came to hand; she was subjected to the promiscuousness of ashes. She was thrown into the public grave. Her grave resembled her bed.

VOLUME II: COSETTE

BOOK FIRST: WATERLOO

CHAPTER I—WHAT IS MET WITH ON THE WAY FROM NIVELLES

Last year (1861), on a beautiful May morning, a traveler, the person who is telling this story, was coming from Nivelles, and directing his course toward La Hulpe. He was on foot. He was pursuing a broad paved road, which undulated between two rows of trees, over the hills that succeed each other, raise the road and let it fall again, and produce something in the nature of enormous waves.

He had passed Lillois and Bois-Seigneur-Isaac. In the west he perceived the slate-roofed tower of Braine-l'Alleud, which has the form of a reversed vase. He had just left behind a wood upon an eminence; and at the angle of the crossroad, by the side of a sort of moldy gibbet bearing the inscription Ancient Barrier No. 4, a public house, bearing on its front this sign: *Aux Quatre Vents. Echabeau, Private Café.*

A quarter of a league further on, he arrived at the bottom of a little valley, where there is water that passes beneath an arch made through the embankment of the road. The clump of sparsely planted but very green trees, which fills the valley on one side of the road, is dispersed over the meadows on the other, and disappears gracefully and as in order in the direction of Braine-l'Alleud.

On the right, close to the road, was an inn, with a four-wheeled cart at the door, a large bundle of hop poles, a plow, a heap of dried brushwood near a flourishing hedge, lime smoking in a square hole, and a ladder suspended along an old penthouse with straw partitions. A young girl was weeding in a field, where a huge yellow poster, probably of some outside spectacle, such as a parish festival, was fluttering in the wind. At one corner of the inn, beside a pool in which a flotilla of ducks was navigating, a badly paved path plunged into the bushes. The wayfarer struck into this.

After traversing a hundred paces, skirting a wall of the fifteenth century, surmounted by a pointed gable, with bricks set in contrast, he found himself before a large door of arched stone, with a rectilinear impost, in the sombre style of Louis XIV, flanked by two flat medallions. A severe facade rose above this door; a wall, perpendicular to the facade, almost touched the door, and flanked it with an abrupt right angle. In the meadow before the door lay three harrows, through which, in disorder, grew all the flowers of May. The door was closed. The two decrepit leaves that barred it were ornamented with an old rusty knocker.

The sun was charming; the branches had that soft shivering of May, which seems to proceed rather from the nests than from the wind. A brave little bird, probably a lover, was caroling in a distracted manner in a large tree.

The wayfarer bent over and examined a rather large circular excavation, resembling the hollow of a sphere, in the stone on the left, at the foot of the pier of the door.

At this moment the leaves of the door parted, and a peasant woman emerged.

She saw the wayfarer, and perceived what he was looking at.

"It was a French cannonball that made that," she said to him. And she added, "That which you see there, higher up in the door, near a nail, is the hole of a big iron bullet as large as an egg. The bullet did not pierce the wood."

"What is the name of this place?" inquired the wayfarer.

"Hougomont," said the peasant woman.

The traveler straightened himself up. He walked on a few paces, and went off to look over the tops of the hedges. On the horizon through the trees, he perceived a sort of little elevation, and on this elevation something which at that distance resembled a lion.

He was on the battlefield of Waterloo.

CHAPTER II—HOUGOMONT

Hougomont, this was a funereal spot, the beginning of the obstacle, the first resistance, which that great woodcutter of Europe, called Napoleon, encountered at Waterloo, the first knot under the blows of his ax.

It was a chateau; it is no longer anything but a farm. For the antiquary, Hougomont is Hugomons. This manor was built by Hugo, Sire of Somerel, the same who endowed the sixth chaplaincy of the Abbéy of Villiers.

The traveler pushed open the door, elbowed an ancient calash under the porch, and entered the courtyard.

The first thing that struck him in this paddock was a door of the sixteenth century, which here simulates an arcade, everything else having fallen prostrate around it. A monumental aspect often has its birth in ruin. In a wall near the arcade opens another arched door, of the time of Henry IV, permitting a glimpse of the trees of an orchard; beside this door, a manure hole, some pickaxs, some shovels, some carts, an old well, with its flagstone and its iron reel, a chicken jumping, and a turkey spreading its tail, a chapel surmounted by a small bell tower, a blossoming pear tree trained in espalier against the wall of the chapel—behold the court, the conquest of which was one of Napoleon's dreams. This corner of earth, could he but have seized it, would, perhaps, have given him the world likewise. Chickens are scattering its dust abroad with their beaks. A growl is audible; it is a huge dog, who shows his teeth and replaces the English.

The English behaved admirably there. Cooke's four companies of guards there held out for seven hours against the fury of an army.

Hougomont viewed on the map, as a geometrical plan, comprising buildings and enclosures, presents a sort of irregular rectangle, one angle of which is nicked out. It is this angle that contains the southern door, guarded by this wall, which commands it only a gun's length away. Hougomont has two doors, the southern door, that of the chateau; and the northern door, belonging to the farm. Napoleon sent his brother Jerome against Hougomont; the divisions of Foy, Guilleminot, and Bachelu hurled themselves against it; nearly the entire corps of Reille was employed against it, and miscarried; Kellermann's balls were exhausted on this heroic section of wall. Bauduin's brigade was not strong enough to force Hougomont on the north, and the brigade of Soye could not do more than effect the beginning of a breach on the south, but without taking it.

The farm buildings border the courtyard on the south. A bit of the north door, broken by the French, hangs suspended to the wall. It consists of four planks nailed to two crossbeams, on which the scars of the attack are visible.

The northern door, which was beaten in by the French, and which has had a piece applied to it to replace the panel suspended on the wall, stands half-open at the bottom of the paddock; it is cut squarely in the wall, built of stone below, of brick above which closes in the courtyard on the north. It is a simple door for carts, such as exist in all farms, with the two large leaves made of rustic planks: beyond lie the meadows. The dispute over this entrance was furious. For a long time, all sorts of imprints of bloody hands were visible on the doorposts. It was there that Bauduin was killed.

The storm of the combat still lingers in this courtyard; its horror is visible there; the confusion of the fray was petrified there; it lives and it dies there;

it was only yesterday. The walls are in the death agony, the stones fall; the breaches cry aloud; the holes are wounds; the drooping, quivering trees seem to be making an effort to flee.

This courtyard was more built up in 1815 than it is today. Buildings tha have since been pulled down then formed fortifications and angles.

The English barricaded themselves there; the French made their way in but could not stand their ground. Beside the chapel, one wing of the chateau the only ruin now remaining of the manor of Hougomont, rises in a crumbling state, disemboweled, one might say. The chateau served for a dungeon, the chapel for a blockhouse. There men exterminated each other. The French fired on from every point, from behind the walls, from the summits of the garrets, from the depths of the cellars, through all the casements, through al the airholes, through every crack in the stones, fetched fagots and set fire to walls and men; the reply to the grapeshot was a conflagration.

In the ruined wing, through windows garnished with bars of iron, the dismantled chambers of the main building of brick are visible; the English guards were in ambush in these rooms; the spiral of the staircase, cracked from the ground floor to the very roof, appears like the inside of a broken shell. The staircase has two stories; the English, besieged on the staircase, and massed on its upper steps, had cut off the lower steps. These consisted of large slabs of blue stone, which form a heap among the nettles. Half a score of steps still cling to the wall; on the first is cut the figure of a trident. These inaccessible steps are solid in their niches. All the rest resembles a jaw that has been denuded of its teeth. There are two old trees there: one is dead; the other is wounded at its base, and is clothed with verdure in April. Since 1815 it has taken to growing through the staircase.

A massacre took place in the chapel. The interior, which has recovered its calm, is singular. The Mass has not been said there since the carnage Nevertheless, the altar has been left there—an altar of unpolished wood placed against a background of roughhewn stone. Four whitewashed walls a door opposite the altar, two small arched windows; over the door a large wooden crucifix, below the crucifix a square airhole stopped up with a bundle of hay; on the ground, in one corner, an old window frame with the glass all broken to pieces—such is the chapel. Near the altar there is nailed up wooden statue of Saint Anne, of the fifteenth century; the head of the infan Jesus has been carried off by a large ball. The French, who were masters of the chapel for a moment, and were then dislodged, set fire to it. The flame filled this building; it was a perfect furnace; the door was burned, the floor wa burned, the wooden Christ was not burned. The fire preyed upon his feet, o which only the blackened stumps are now to be seen; then it stopped, a miracle, according to the assertion of the people of the neighborhood. The infant Jesus, decapitated, was less fortunate than the Christ.

The walls are covered with inscriptions. Near the feet of Christ this name is to be read: Henquinez. Then these others: Conde de Rio Maior Marques y Marquesa de Almagro (Habana). There are French names with exclamation points, a sign of wrath. The wall was freshly whitewashed in 1849. The nations insulted each other there.

It was at the door of this chapel that the corpse was picked up, which held an ax in its hand; this corpse was Sub-Lieutenant Legros.

On emerging from the chapel, a well is visible on the left. There are two in this courtyard. One inquires, "Why is there no bucket and pulley to this? It is because water is no longer drawn there. Why is water not drawn there? Because it is full of skeletons."

The last person who drew water from the well was named Guillaume van Kylsom. He was a peasant who lived at Hougomont, and was gardener there. On the 18th of June, 1815, his family fled and concealed themselves in the woods.

The forest surrounding the Abbéy of Villiers sheltered these unfortunate people who had been scattered abroad, for many days and nights. There are at this day certain traces recognizable, such as old boles of burned trees, which mark the site of these poor bivouacs trembling in the depths of the thickets.

Guillaume van Kylsom remained at Hougomont, "to guard the chateau," and concealed himself in the cellar. The English discovered him there. They tore him from his hiding place, and the combatants forced this frightened man to serve them, by administering blows with the flats of their swords. They were thirsty; this Guillaume brought them water. It was from this well that he drew it. Many drank there their last draught. This well where drank so many of the dead was destined to die itself.

After the engagement, they were in haste to bury the dead bodies. Death has a fashion of harassing victory, and she causes the pest to follow glory. The typhus is a concomitant of triumph. This well was deep, and it was turned into a sepulchre. Three hundred dead bodies were cast into it. With too much haste perhaps. Were they all dead? Legend says they were not. It seems that on the night succeeding the interment, feeble voices were heard calling from the well.

This well is isolated in the middle of the courtyard. Three walls, part stone, part brick, and simulating a small, square tower, and folded like the leaves of a screen, surround it on all sides. The fourth side is open. It is there that the water was drawn. The wall at the bottom has a sort of shapeless loophole, possibly the hole made by a shell. This little tower had a platform, of which only the beams remain. The iron supports of the well on the right form cross. On leaning over, the eye is lost in a deep cylinder of brick that is fille with a heaped-up mass of shadows. The base of the walls all about the well i concealed in a growth of nettles.

This well has not in front of it that large blue slab, which forms the table fo all wells in Belgium. The slab has here been replaced by a crossbeam, agains which lean five or six shapeless fragments of knotty and petrified wood tha resemble huge bones. There is no longer either pail, chain, or pulley; but ther is still the stone basin that served the overflow. The rainwater collects there and from time to time a bird of the neighboring forests comes there to drink and then flies away. One house in this ruin, the farmhouse, is still inhabitec The door of this house opens on the courtyard. Upon this door, beside a prett Gothic lock plate, there is an iron handle with trefoils placed slanting. At th moment when the Hanoverian lieutenant, Wilda, grasped this handle in orde to take refuge in the farm, a French sapper hewed off his hand with an ax.

The family who occupy the house had for their grandfather Guillaume va Kylsom, the old gardener, dead long since. A woman with gray hair said t us, "I was there. I was three years old. My sister, who was older, was terrifie and wept. They carried us off to the woods. I went there in my mother's arms We glued our ears to the earth to hear. I imitated the cannon, and went Boom Boom!"

A door opening from the courtyard on the left led into the orchard, so w were told. The orchard is terrible.

It is in three parts; one might almost say, in three acts. The first part is garden, the second is an orchard, the third is a wood. These three parts hav a common enclosure: on the side of the entrance, the buildings of the chatea and the farm; on the left, a hedge; on the right, a wall; and at the end, a wal The wall on the right is of brick, the wall at the bottom is of stone. One enter the garden first. It slopes downward, is planted with gooseberry bushes, choke with a wild growth of vegetation, and terminated by a monumental terrace o cut stone, with balustrade with a double curve.

It was a master's garden in the first French style that preceded Le Notr today it is ruins and briars. The pilasters are surmounted by globes tha resemble cannonballs of stone. Forty-three balusters can still be counted o their sockets; the rest lie prostrate in the grass. Almost all bear scratches o bullets. One broken baluster is placed on the pediment like a fractured leg.

It was in this garden, further down than the orchard, that six light-infantr men of the 1st, having made their way there, and being unable to escape, hunted down and caught like bears in their dens, accepted the combat with two Hanoverian companies, one of which was armed with carbines. The Hanoverians lined this balustrade and fired from above. The infantry men, replying from below, six against two hundred, intrepid and with no shelter save the currant bushes, took a quarter of an hour to die.

One mounts a few steps and passes from the garden into the orchard, properly speaking. There, within the limits of those few square fathoms, fifteen hundred men fell in less than an hour. The wall seems ready to renew the combat. Thirty-eight loopholes, pierced by the English at irregular heights, are there still. In front of the sixth are placed two English tombs of granite. There are loopholes only in the south wall, as the principal attack came from that quarter. The wall is hidden on the outside by a tall hedge; the French came up, thinking that they had to deal only with a hedge, crossed it, and found the wall both an obstacle and an ambuscade, with the English guards behind it, the thirty-eight loopholes firing at once a shower of grapeshot and balls, and Soye's brigade was broken against it. Thus Waterloo began.

Nevertheless, the orchard was taken. As they had no ladders, the French scaled it with their nails. They fought hand to hand amid the trees. All this grass has been soaked in blood. A battalion of Nassau, seven hundred strong, was overwhelmed there. The outside of the wall, against which Kellermann's two batteries were trained, is gnawed by grapeshot.

This orchard is sentient, like others, in the month of May. It has its buttercups and its daisies; the grass is tall there; the cart horses browse there; cords of hair, on which linen is drying, traverse the spaces between the trees and force the passerby to bend his head; one walks over this uncultivated land, and one's foot dives into mole holes. In the middle of the grass one observes an uprooted tree trunk that lies there all verdant. Major Blackmann leaned against it to die. Beneath a great tree in the neighborhood fell the German general, Duplat, descended from a French family that fled on the revocation of the Edict of Nantes. An aged and falling apple tree leans far over to one side, its wound dressed with a bandage of straw and of clayey loam. Nearly all the apple trees are falling with age. There is not one which has not had its bullet or its biscayan. The skeletons of dead trees abound in this orchard. Crows fly through their branches, and at the end of it is a wood full of violets.

Bauduin, killed, Foy wounded, conflagration, massacre, carnage, a rivulet formed of English blood, French blood, German blood mingled in fury, a well crammed with corpses, the regiment of Nassau and the regiment of Brunswick destroyed, Duplat killed, Blackmann killed, the English Guards mutilated twenty French battalions, besides the forty from Reille's corps, decimated three thousand men in that hovel of Hougomont alone cut down, slashed to pieces, shot, burned, with their throats cut, and all this so that a peasant can say today to the traveler: Monsieur, give me three francs, and if you like, I will explain to you the affair of Waterloo!

CHAPTER III—THE EIGHTEENTH OF JUNE, 1815

L et us turn back, that is one of the storyteller's rights, and put ourselves once more in the year 1815, and even a little earlier than the epoch when the action narrated in the first part of this book took place.

If it had not rained in the night between the 17th and the 18th of June, 1815, the fate of Europe would have been different. A few drops of water, more or less, decided the downfall of Napoleon. All that Providence required in order to make Waterloo the end of Austerlitz was a little more rain, and a cloud traversing the sky out of season sufficed to make a world crumble.

The battle of Waterloo could not be begun until half-past eleven o'clock, and that gave Blucher time to come up. Why? Because the ground was wet. The artillery had to wait until it became a little firmer before they could maneuver.

Napoleon was an artillery officer, and felt the effects of this. The foundation of this wonderful captain was the man who, in the report to the Directory on Aboukir, said: Such a one of our balls killed six men. All his plans of battle were arranged for projectiles. The key to his victory was to make the artillery converge on one point. He treated the strategy of the hostile general like a citadel, and made a breach in it. He overwhelmed the weak point with grapeshot; he joined and dissolved battles with cannon. There was something of the sharpshooter in his genius. To beat in squares, to pulverize regiments, to break lines, to crush and disperse masses, for him everything lay in this, to strike, strike, strike incessantly, and he entrusted this task to the cannonball. A redoubtable method, and one which, united with genius, rendered this gloomy athlete of the pugilism of war invincible for the space of fifteen years.

On the 18th of June, 1815, he relied all the more on his artillery, because he had numbers on his side. Wellington had only one hundred and fifty-nine mouths of fire; Napoleon had two hundred and forty.

Suppose the soil dry, and the artillery capable of moving, the action would have begun at six o'clock in the morning. The battle would have been won and nded at two o'clock, three hours before the change of fortune in favor of the russians. What amount of blame attaches to Napoleon for the loss of this attle? Is the shipwreck due to the pilot?

Was it the evident physical decline of Napoleon that complicated this epoch y an inward diminution of force? Had the twenty years of war worn out the lade as it had worn the scabbard, the soul as well as the body? Did the veteran nake himself disastrously felt in the leader? In a word, was this genius, as many istorians of note have thought, suffering from an eclipse? Did he go into a renzy in order to disguise his weakened powers from himself? Did he begin o waver under the delusion of a breath of adventure? Had he become—a rave matter in a general—unconscious of peril? Is there an age, in this class f material great men, who may be called the giants of action, when genius rows shortsighted? Old age has no hold on the geniuses of the ideal; for the)antes and Michael Angelos to grow old is to grow in greatness; is it to grow ess for the Hannibals and the Bonapartes? Had Napoleon lost the direct sense f victory? Had he reached the point where he could no longer recognize the eef, could no longer divine the snare, no longer discern the crumbling brink f abysses? Had he lost his power of scenting out catastrophes? He who had 1 former days known all the roads to triumph, and who, from the summit of is chariot of lightning, pointed them out with a sovereign finger, had he now eached that state of sinister amazement when he could lead his tumultuous egions harnessed to it, to the precipice? Was he seized at the age of forty-ix with a supreme madness? Was that titanic charioteer of destiny no longer nything more than an immense daredevil?

We do not think so.

His plan of battle was, by the confession of all, a masterpiece. To go traight to the center of the Allies' line, to make a breach in the enemy, to cut hem in two, to drive the British half back on Hal, and the Prussian half on 'ongres, to make two shattered fragments of Wellington and Blucher, to carry Aont-Saint-Jean, to seize Brussels, to hurl the German into the Rhine, and he Englishman into the sea. All this was contained in that battle, according to Napoleon. Afterward people would see.

Of course, we do not here pretend to furnish a history of the battle of Waterloo; one of the scenes of the foundation of the story that we are relating s connected with this battle, but this history is not our subject; this history, noreover, has been finished, and finished in a masterly manner, from one point f view by Napoleon, and from another point of view by a whole group of lustrious historians.

As for us, we leave the historians at loggerheads; we are but a distant witness, a passerby on the plain, a seeker bending over that soil all made of human flesh, taking appearances for realities, perchance; we have no right to oppose, in the name of science, a collection of facts that contain illusions, no doubt; we possess neither military practice nor strategic ability that authorize a system; in our opinion, a chain of accidents dominated the two leaders at Waterloo; and when it becomes a question of destiny, that mysterious culprit, we judge like that ingenious judge, the populace.

CHAPTER IV—A

Those persons who wish to gain a clear idea of the battle of Waterloo have only to place, mentally, on the ground, a capital A. The left limb of the A is the road to Nivelles, the right limb is the road to Genappe, the tie of the A is the hollow road to Ohain from Braine-l'Alleud. The top of the A is Mont-Saint-Jean, where Wellington is; the lower left tip is Hougomont where Reille is stationed with Jerome Bonaparte; the right tip is the Belle-Alliance, where Napoleon was. At the center of this chord is the precise point where the final word of the battle was pronounced. It was there that the lion has been placed, the involuntary symbol of the supreme heroism of the Imperial Guard.

The triangle included in the top of the A, between the two limbs and the tie, is the plateau of Mont-Saint-Jean. The dispute over this plateau constituted the whole battle. The wings of the two armies extended to the right and left of the two roads to Genappe and Nivelles; d'Erlon facing Picton, Reille facing Hill.

Behind the tip of the A, behind the plateau of Mont-Saint-Jean, is the forest of Soignes.

As for the plain itself, let the reader picture to himself a vast undulating sweep of ground; each rise commands the next rise, and all the undulations mount toward Mont-Saint-Jean, and there end in the forest.

Two hostile troops on a field of battle are two wrestlers. It is a question of seizing the opponent around the waist. The one seeks to trip up the other. They clutch at everything: a bush is a point of support; an angle of the wall offers them a rest to the shoulder; for the lack of a hovel under whose cover they can draw up, a regiment yields its ground; an unevenness in the ground, a chance turn in the landscape, a cross-path encountered at the right moment, a grove, a ravine, can stay the heel of that colossus which is called an army, and prevent its retreat. He who quits the field is beaten; hence the necessity devolving on he responsible leader, of examining the most insignificant clump of trees, and of studying deeply the slightest relief in the ground.

The two generals had attentively studied the plain of Mont-Saint-Jean, now called the plain of Waterloo. In the preceding year, Wellington, with the sagacity of foresight, had examined it as the possible seat of a great battle. Upon this spot, and for this duel, on the 18th of June, Wellington had the good post, Napoleon the bad post. The English army was stationed above, the French army below.

It is almost superfluous here to sketch the appearance of Napoleon on horseback, glass in hand, upon the heights of Rossomme, at daybreak, on June 18, 1815. All the world has seen him before we can show him. That calm profile under the little three-cornered hat of the school of Brienne, that green uniform, the white revers concealing the star of the Legion of Honor, his great coat hiding his epaulets, the corner of red ribbon peeping from beneath his vest, his leather trousers, the white horse with the saddlecloth of purple velvet bearing on the corners crowned N's and eagles, Hessian boots over silk stockings, silver spurs, the sword of Marengo, that whole figure of the last of the Caesars is present to all imaginations, saluted with acclamations by some, severely regarded by others.

That figure stood for a long time wholly in the light; this arose from a certain legendary dimness evolved by the majority of heroes, and which always veils the truth for a longer or shorter time; but today history and daylight have arrived.

That light called history is pitiless; it possesses this peculiar and divine quality, that, pure light as it is, and precisely because it is wholly light, it often casts a shadow in places where people had hitherto beheld rays; from the same man it constructs two different phantoms, and the one attacks the other and executes justice on it, and the shadows of the despot contend with the brilliancy of the leader. Hence arises a truer measure in the definitive judgments of nations. Babylon violated lessens Alexander, Rome enchained lessens Caesar, Jerusalem murdered lessens Titus, tyranny follows the tyrant. It is a misfortune for a man to leave behind him the night which bears his form.

CHAPTER V—THE QUID
OBSCURUM OF BATTLES

Everyone is acquainted with the first phase of this battle; a beginning which was troubled, uncertain, hesitating, menacing to both armies, but still more so for the English than for the French.

It had rained all night, the earth had been cut up by the downpour, th water had accumulated here and there in the hollows of the plain as if in casks at some points the gear of the artillery carriages was buried up to the axles, th saddle bands of the horses were dripping with liquid mud. If the wheat and ry trampled down by this cohort of transports on the march had not filled in th ruts and strewn a litter beneath the wheels, all movement, particularly in th valleys, in the direction of Papelotte would have been impossible.

The affair began late. Napoleon, as we have already explained, was in th habit of keeping all his artillery well in hand, like a pistol, aiming it now a one point, now at another, of the battle; and it had been his wish to wait unt the horse batteries could move and gallop freely. In order to do that it wa necessary that the sun should come out and dry the soil. But the sun did no make its appearance. It was no longer the rendezvous of Austerlitz. When th first cannon was fired, the English general, Colville, looked at his watch, an noted that it was thirty-five minutes past eleven.

The action was begun furiously, with more fury, perhaps, than the Empero would have wished, by the left wing of the French resting on Hougomont. A the same time Napoleon attacked the center by hurling Quiot's brigade on L Haie-Sainte, and Ney pushed forward the right wing of the French against th left wing of the English, which rested on Papelotte.

The attack on Hougomont was something of a feint; the plan was to draw Wellington there, and to make him swerve to the left. This plan would hav succeeded if the four companies of the English guards and the brave Belgian of Perponcher's division had not held the position solidly, and Wellington instead of massing his troops there, could confine himself to dispatching there as reinforcements, only four more companies of guards and one battalion from Brunswick.

The attack of the right wing of the French on Papelotte was calculated in fact, to overthrow the English left, to cut off the road to Brussels, to ba the passage against possible Prussians, to force Mont-Saint-Jean, to turn Wellington back on Hougomont, thence on Braine-l'Alleud, thence on Hal nothing easier. With the exception of a few incidents this attack succeede Papelotte was taken; La Haie-Sainte was carried.

A detail to be noted. There was in the English infantry, particularly i Kempt's brigade, a great many raw recruits. These young soldiers were valian in the presence of our redoubtable infantry; their inexperience extricated then intrepidly from the dilemma; they performed particularly excellent service a skirmishers: the soldier skirmisher, left somewhat to himself, becomes, so t peak, his own general. These recruits displayed some of the French ingenuity and fury. This novice of an infantry had dash. This displeased Wellington.

After the taking of La Haie-Sainte the battle wavered.

There is in this day an obscure interval, from midday to four o'clock; the middle portion of this battle is almost indistinct, and participates in the somberness of the hand-to-hand conflict. Twilight reigns over it. We perceive vast fluctuations in that fog, a dizzy mirage, paraphernalia of war almost unknown today, pendant colbacks, floating sabretaches, cross-belts, cartridge boxes for grenades, hussar dolmans, red boots with a thousand wrinkles, heavy shakos garlanded with ribbons, the almost black infantry of Brunswick mingled with the scarlet infantry of England, the English soldiers with great, white circular pads on the slopes of their shoulders for epaulets, the Hanoverian light horse with their oblong helmets of leather, with brass hands and red horsetails, the Scotch with their bare knees and plaids, the great white gaiters of our grenadiers; pictures, not strategic lines—what Salvator Rosa requires, not what is suited to the needs of Gribeauval.

A certain amount of tempest is always mingled with a battle. *Quid obscurum, quid divinum.* Each historian traces, to some extent, the particular feature that pleases him amid this pell-mell. Whatever may be the combinations of the generals, the shock of armed masses has an incalculable ebb. During the action the plans of the two leaders enter into each other and become mutually thrown out of shape. Such a point of the field of battle devours more combatants than such another, just as more or less spongy soils soak up more or less quickly the water which is poured on them. It becomes necessary to pour out more soldiers than one would like; a series of expenditures which are the unforeseen. The line of battle waves and undulates like a thread, the trails of blood gush illogically, the fronts of the armies waver, the regiments form capes and gulfs as they enter and withdraw; all these reefs are continually moving in front of each other. Where the infantry stood the artillery arrives, the cavalry rushes in where the artillery was, the battalions are like smoke. There was something there; seek it. It has disappeared; the open spots change place, the somber folds advance and retreat, a sort of wind from the sepulchre pushes forward, hurls back, distends, and disperses these tragic multitudes. What is a fray? An oscillation? The immobility of a mathematical plan expresses a minute, not a day. In order to depict a battle, there is required one of those powerful painters who have chaos in their brushes. Rembrandt is better than Vandermeulen; Vandermeulen, exact at noon, lies at three o'clock. Geometry is deceptive; the hurricane alone is trustworthy. That is what confers on Folard the right to contradict Polybius.

Let us add, that there is a certain instant when the battle degenerates into combat, becomes specialized, and disperses into innumerable detailed feats which, to borrow the expression of Napoleon himself, "belong rather to the biography of the regiments than to the history of the army." The historian has, in this case, the evident right to sum up the whole. He cannot do more than seize the principal outlines of the struggle, and it is not given to anyone narrator, however conscientious he may be, to fix, absolutely, the form of that horrible cloud which is called a battle.

This, which is true of all great, armed encounters, is particularly applicable to Waterloo.

Nevertheless, at a certain moment in the afternoon the battle came to a point

CHAPTER VI—FOUR O'CLOCK
IN THE AFTERNOON

Toward four o'clock the condition of the English army was serious. The Prince of Orange was in command of the center, Hill of the right wing, Picton of the left wing. The Prince of Orange, desperate and intrepid, shouted to the Hollando-Belgians, "Nassau! Brunswick! Never retreat!" Hill, having been weakened, had come up to the support of Wellington; Picton was dead. At the very moment when the English had captured from the French the flag of the 105th of the line, the French had killed the English general, Picton, with a bullet through the head. The battle had, for Wellington, two bases of action, Hougomont and La Haie-Sainte; Hougomont still held out, but was on fire; La Haie-Sainte was taken. Of the German battalion that defended it, only forty two men survived; all the officers, except five, were either dead or captured. Three thousand combatants had been massacred in that barn. A sergeant of the English Guards, the foremost boxer in England, reputed invulnerable by his companions, had been killed there by a little French drummer boy. Baring had been dislodged, Alten put to the sword. Many flags had been lost, one from Alten's division, and one from the battalion of Lunenburg, carried by a prince of the house of Deux-Ponts. The Scotch Grays no longer existed; Ponsonby's great dragoons had been hacked to pieces. That valiant cavalry had bent beneath the lancers of Bro and beneath the cuirassiers of Travers; out of twelve hundred horses, six hundred remained; out of three Lieutenant colonels, two lay on the earth, Hamilton wounded, Mater slain. Ponsonby had fallen, riddled by seven lance-thrusts. Gordon was dead. Marsh was dead. Two divisions, the fifth and the sixth, had been annihilated.

Hougomont injured, La Haie-Sainte taken, there now existed but one rallying point, the center. That point still held firm. Wellington reinforced it. He summoned there Hill, who was at Merle-Braine; he summoned Chasse, who was at Braine-l'Alleud.

The center of the English army, rather concave, very dense, and very compact, was strongly posted. It occupied the plateau of Mont-Saint-Jean, having behind it the village, and in front of it the slope, which was tolerably steep then. It rested on that stout stone dwelling, which at that time belonged to the domain of Nivelles, and which marks the intersection of the roads—a pile of the sixteenth century, and so robust that the cannonballs rebounded from it without injuring it. All about the plateau the English had cut the hedges here and there, made embrasures in the hawthorn trees, thrust the throat of a cannon between two branches, embattled the shrubs. There artillery was ambushed in the brushwood. This punic labor, incontestably authorized by war, which permits traps, was so well done, that Haxo, who had been dispatched by the Emperor at nine o'clock in the morning to reconnoiter the enemy's batteries, had discovered nothing of it, and had returned and reported to Napoleon that there were no obstacles except the two barricades that barred the road to Nivelles and to Genappe. It was at the season when the grain is tall; on the edge of the plateau a battalion of Kempt's brigade, the 95th, armed with carbines, was concealed in the tall wheat.

Thus assured and buttressed, the center of the Anglo-Dutch army was well posted. The peril of this position lay in the forest of Soignes, then adjoining the field of battle, and intersected by the ponds of Groenendael and Boitsfort. An army could not retreat there without dissolving; the regiments would have broken up immediately there. The artillery would have been lost among the morasses. The retreat, according to many a man versed in the art, though it is disputed by others, would have been a disorganized flight.

To this center, Wellington added one of Chasse's brigades taken from the right wing, and one of Wincke's brigades taken from the left wing, plus Clinton's division. To his English, to the regiments of Halkett, to the brigades of Mitchell, to the guards of Maitland, he gave as reinforcements and aids, the infantry of Brunswick, Nassau's contingent, Kielmansegg's Hanoverians, and Ompteda's Germans. This placed twenty-six battalions under his hand. The right wing, as Charras says, was thrown back on the center. An enormous battery was masked by sacks of earth at the spot where there now stands what is called the "Museum of Waterloo." Besides this, Wellington had, behind a rise in the ground, Somerset's Dragoon Guards, fourteen-hundred horse strong.

It was the remaining half of the justly celebrated English cavalry. Ponsonby destroyed, Somerset remained.

The battery, which, if completed, would have been almost a redoubt, was ranged behind a very low garden wall, backed up with a coating of bags of sand and a large slope of earth. This work was not finished; there had been no time to make a palisade for it.

Wellington, uneasy but impassive, was on horseback, and there remained the whole day in the same attitude, a little in advance of the old mill of Mont-Saint-Jean, which is still in existence, beneath an elm, which an Englishman, an enthusiastic vandal, purchased later on for two hundred francs, cut down, and carried off. Wellington was coldly heroic. The bullets rained about him. His aide-de-camp, Gordon, fell at his side. Lord Hill, pointing to a shell that had burst, said to him, "My lord, what are your orders in case you are killed?"

"To do like me," replied Wellington. To Clinton he said laconically, "To hold this spot to the last man." The day was evidently turning out ill.

Wellington shouted to his old companions of Talavera, of Vittoria, of Salamanca, "Boys, can retreat be thought of? Think of old England!"

Toward four o'clock, the English line drew back. Suddenly nothing was visible on the crest of the plateau except the artillery and the sharpshooters; the rest had disappeared: the regiments, dislodged by the shells and the French bullets, retreated into the bottom, now intersected by the back road of the farm of Mont-Saint-Jean; a retrograde movement took place, the English front hid itself, Wellington drew back. "The beginning of retreat!" cried Napoleon.

CHAPTER VII—NAPOLEON
IN A GOOD HUMOR

The Emperor, though ill and discommoded on horseback by a local trouble, had never been in a better humor than on that day. His impenetrability had been smiling ever since the morning. On the 18th of June, that profound soul masked by marble beamed blindly. The man who had been gloomy at Austerlitz was gay at Waterloo. The greatest favorites of destiny make mistakes. Our joys are composed of shadow. The supreme smile is God's alone.

Ridet Caesar, Pompeius flebit, said the legionaries of the Fulminatrix Legion. Pompey was not destined to weep on that occasion, but it is certain that Caesar laughed. While exploring on horseback at one o'clock on the preceding night, in storm and rain, in company with Bertrand, the communes n the neighborhood of Rossomme, satisfied at the sight of the long line of the English campfires illuminating the whole horizon from Frischemont to Braine-'Alleud, it had seemed to him that fate, to whom he had assigned a day on the field of Waterloo, was exact to the appointment; he stopped his horse, and remained for some time motionless, gazing at the lightning and listening to the thunder; and this fatalist was heard to cast into the darkness this mysterious saying, "We are in accord." Napoleon was mistaken. They were no longer in accord.

He took not a moment for sleep; every instant of that night was marked by a joy for him. He traversed the line of the principal outposts, halting here and there to talk to the sentinels. At half-past two, near the wood of Hougomont, he heard the tread of a column on the march; he thought at the moment that it was a retreat on the part of Wellington. He said, "It is the rear-guard of the English getting under way for the purpose of decamping. I will take prisoners the six thousand English who have just arrived at Ostend." He conversed expansively; he regained the animation which he had shown at his landing on the first of March, when he pointed out to the Grand-Marshal the enthusiastic peasant of the Gulf Juan, and cried, "Well, Bertrand, here is a reinforcement already!" On the night of the 17th to the 18th of June he rallied Wellington. "That little Englishman needs a lesson," said Napoleon. The rain redoubled in violence; the thunder rolled while the Emperor was speaking.

At half-past three o'clock in the morning, he lost one illusion; officers who had been dispatched to reconnoiter announced to him that the enemy was not making any movement. Nothing was stirring; not a bivouac fire had been extinguished; the English army was asleep. The silence on earth was profound; the only noise was in the heavens. At four o'clock, a peasant was brought in to him by the scouts; this peasant had served as guide to a brigade of English cavalry, probably Vivian's brigade, which was on its way to take up a position in the village of Ohain, at the extreme left. At five o'clock, two Belgian deserters reported to him that they had just quitted their regiment, and that the English army was ready for battle. "So much the better!" exclaimed Napoleon. "I prefer to overthrow them rather than to drive them back."

In the morning he dismounted in the mud on the slope, which forms an angle with the Plancenoit road, had a kitchen table and a peasant's chair brought to him from the farm of Rossomme, seated himself, with a truss of straw for a carpet, and spread out on the table the chart of the battlefield, saying to Soult as he did so, "A pretty checkerboard."

In consequence of the rains during the night, the transports of provisions, embedded in the soft roads, had not been able to arrive by morning; the soldiers had had no sleep; they were wet and fasting. This did not prevent Napoleon from exclaiming cheerfully to Ney, "We have ninety chances out of a hundred." At eight o'clock the Emperor's breakfast was brought to him. He invited many generals to it. During breakfast, it was said that Wellington had been to a ball two nights before, in Brussels, at the Duchess of Richmond's; and Soult, a rough man of war, with a face of an archbishop, said, "The ball takes place today." The Emperor jested with Ney, who said, "Wellington will not be so simple as to wait for Your Majesty." That was his way, however. "He was fond of jesting," says Fleury de Chaboulon. "A merry humor was at the foundation of his character," says Gourgaud. "He abounded in pleasantries, which were more peculiar than witty," says Benjamin Constant. These gaieties of a giant are worthy of insistence. It was he who called his grenadiers "his grumblers"; he pinched their ears; he pulled their mustaches. "The Emperor did nothing but play pranks on us," is the remark of one of them. During the mysterious trip from the island of Elba to France, on the 27th of February, on the open sea, the French brig of war, Le Zephyr, having encountered the brig L'Inconstant, on which Napoleon was concealed, and having asked the news of Napoleon from L'Inconstant, the Emperor, who still wore in his hat the white and amaranthine cockade sown with bees, which he had adopted at the isle of Elba, laughingly seized the speaking trumpet, and answered for himself, "The Emperor is well." A man who laughs like that is on familiar terms with events. Napoleon indulged in many fits of this laughter during the breakfast at Waterloo. After breakfast he meditated for a quarter of an hour; then two generals seated themselves on the truss of straw, pen in hand and their paper on their knees, and the Emperor dictated to them the order of battle.

At nine o'clock, at the instant when the French army, ranged in echelons and set in motion in five columns, had deployed—the divisions in two lines, the artillery between the brigades, the music at their head; as they beat the march, with rolls on the drums and the blasts of trumpets, mighty, vast, joyous, a sea of helmets, of sabers, and of bayonets on the horizon, the Emperor was touched, and twice exclaimed, "Magnificent! Magnificent!"

Between nine o'clock and half-past ten the whole army, incredible as it may appear, had taken up its position and ranged itself in six lines, forming, to repeat the Emperor's expression, "the figure of six Vs." A few moments after the formation of the battle array, in the midst of that profound silence, like that which heralds the beginning of a storm, which precedes engagements, he Emperor tapped Haxo on the shoulder, as he beheld the three batteries of twelve-pounders, detached by his orders from the corps of Erlon, Reille, and Lobau, and destined to begin the action by taking Mont-Saint-Jean, which was situated at the intersection of the Nivelles and the Genappe roads, and said to him, "There are four and twenty handsome maids, General."

Sure of the issue, he encouraged with a smile, as they passed before him, the company of sappers of the first corps, which he had appointed to barricade Mont-Saint-Jean as soon as the village should be carried. All this serenity had been traversed by but a single word of haughty pity; perceiving on his left, at a spot where there now stands a large tomb, those admirable Scotch Grays, with their superb horses, massing themselves, he said, "It is a pity."

Then he mounted his horse, advanced beyond Rossomme, and selected for his post of observation a contracted elevation of turf to the right of the road from Genappe to Brussels, which was his second station during the battle. The third station, the one adopted at seven o'clock in the evening, between La Belle-Alliance and La Haie-Sainte, is formidable; it is a rather elevated knoll, which still exists, and behind which the guard was massed on a slope of the plain. Around this knoll the balls rebounded from the pavements of the road, up to Napoleon himself. As at Brienne, he had over his head the shriek of the bullets and of the heavy artillery. Moldy cannonballs, old sword blades, and shapeless projectiles, eaten up with rust, were picked up at the spot where his horse's feet stood. *Scabra rubigine.* A few years ago, a shell of sixty pounds, still charged, and with its fuse broken off level with the bomb, was unearthed. It was at this last post that the Emperor said to his guide, Lacoste, a hostile and terrified peasant, who was attached to the saddle of a hussar, and who turned around at every discharge of canister and tried to hide behind Napoleon, "Fool, it is shameful! You'll get yourself killed with a ball in the back." He who writes these lines has himself found, in the friable soil of this knoll, on turning over the sand, the remains of the neck of a bomb, disintegrated, by the oxidization of six and forty years, and old fragments of iron which parted like elder twigs between the fingers.

Everyone is aware that the variously inclined undulations of the plains, where the engagement between Napoleon and Wellington took place, are no longer what they were on June 18, 1815. By taking from this mournful field the wherewithal to make a monument to it, its real relief has been taken away, and history, disconcerted, no longer finds her bearings there. It has been disfigured for the sake of glorifying it. Wellington, when he beheld Waterloo once more, two years later, exclaimed, "They have altered my field of battle!" Where the great pyramid of earth, surmounted by the lion, rises today, there was a hillock which descended in an easy slope toward the Nivelles road, but which was almost an escarpment on the side of the highway to Genappe. The elevation of this escarpment can still be measured by the height of the two knolls of the two great sepulchres that enclose the road from Genappe to Brussels: one, the English tomb, is on the left; the other, the German tomb, is on the right. There is no French tomb. The whole of that plain is a sepulchre for France. Thanks to the thousands upon thousands of cartloads of earth employed in the hillock one hundred and fifty feet in height and half a mile in circumference, the plateau of Mont-Saint-Jean is now accessible by an easy slope. On the day of battle, particularly on the side of La Haie-Sainte, it was abrupt and difficult of approach. The slope there is so steep that the English cannon could not see the farm, situated in the bottom of the valley, which was the center of the combat. On the 18th of June, 1815, the rains had still farther increased this acclivity, the mud complicated the problem of the ascent, and the men not only slipped back, but stuck fast in the mire. Along the crest of the plateau ran a sort of trench whose presence it was impossible for the distant observer to divine.

What was this trench? Let us explain. Braine-l'Alleud is a Belgian village; Ohain is another. These villages, both of them concealed in curves of the landscape, are connected by a road about a league and a half in length, which traverses the plain along its undulating level, and often enters and buries itself in the hills like a furrow, which makes a ravine of this road in some places. In 1815, as at the present day, this road cut the crest of the plateau of Mont-Saint-Jean between the two highways from Genappe and Nivelles; only, it is now on a level with the plain; it was then a hollow way. Its two slopes have been appropriated for the monumental hillock. This road was, and still is, a trench throughout the greater portion of its course; a hollow trench, sometimes a dozen feet in depth, and whose banks, being too steep, crumbled away here and there, particularly in winter, under driving rains. Accidents happened here. The road was so narrow at the Braine-l'Alleud entrance that a passerby was crushed by a cart, as is proved by a stone cross which stands near the cemetery, and which gives the name of the dead, Monsieur Bernard Debrye, Merchant of Brussels, and the date of the accident, February, 1637. It was so deep on the tableland of Mont-Saint-Jean that a peasant, Mathieu Nicaise, was crushed there, in 1783, by a slide from the slope, as is stated on another stone cross, the top of which has disappeared in the process of clearing the ground, but whose overturned pedestal is still visible on the grassy slope to the left of the highway between La Haie-Sainte and the farm of Mont-Saint-Jean.

On the day of battle, this hollow road whose existence was in no way indicated, bordering the crest of Mont-Saint-Jean, a trench at the summit of the escarpment, a rut concealed in the soil, was invisible; that is to say, terrible.

CHAPTER VIII—THE EMPEROR PUTS A QUESTION TO THE GUIDE LACOSTE

So, on the morning of Waterloo, Napoleon was content.

He was right; the plan of battle conceived by him was, as we have seen, really admirable.

The battle once begun, its very various changes, the resistance of Hougomont; the tenacity of La Haie-Sainte; the killing of Bauduin; the disabling of Foy; the unexpected wall against which Soye's brigade was shattered; Guilleminot's fatal heedlessness when he had neither petard nor powder sacks; the miring of the batteries; the fifteen unescorted pieces overwhelmed in a hollow way by Uxbridge; the small effect of the bombs falling in the English lines, and there embedding themselves in the rain-soaked soil, and only succeeding in producing volcanoes of mud, so that the canister was turned into a splash; the uselessness of Pire's demonstration on Braine-l'Alleud; all that cavalry, fifteen squadrons, almost exterminated; the right wing of the English badly alarmed, the left wing badly cut into; Ney's strange mistake in massing, instead of echeloning the four divisions of the first corps; men delivered over to grapeshot, arranged in ranks twenty-seven deep and with a frontage of two hundred; the frightful holes made in these masses by the cannonballs; attacking columns disorganized; the side-battery suddenly unmasked on their flank; Bourgeois, Donzelot, and Durutte compromised; Quiot repulsed; Lieutenant Vieux, that Hercules graduated at the Polytechnic School, wounded at the moment when he was beating in with an ax the door of La Haie-Sainte under the downright fire of the English barricade, which barred the angle of the road from Genappe to Brussels; Marcognet's division caught between the infantry and the cavalry, shot down at the very muzzle of the guns amid the grain by Best and Pack, put to the sword by Ponsonby; his battery of seven pieces spiked; the Prince of Saxe-Weimar holding and guarding, in spite of the Comte d'Erlon, both Frischemont and Smohain; the flag of the 105th taken, the flag of the 45th captured; that black Prussian hussar stopped by runners of the flying column of three hundred light cavalry on the scout between Wavre and Plancenoit; the alarming things that had been said by prisoners; Grouchy's delay; fifteen hundred men killed in the orchard of Hougomont in less than an hour; eighteen hundred men overthrown in a still shorter time about La Haie-Sainte, all these stormy incidents passing like the clouds of battle before Napoleon, had hardly troubled his gaze and had not overshadowed that face of imperial certainty. Napoleon was accustomed to gaze steadily at war; he never added up the heart-rending details, cipher by cipher; ciphers mattered little to him, provided that they furnished the total, victory; he was not alarmed if the beginnings did go astray, since he thought himself the master and the possessor at the end; he knew how to wait, supposing himself to be out of the question, and he treated destiny as his equal: he seemed to say to fate, "Thou wilt not dare."

Composed half of light and half of shadow, Napoleon thought himself protected in good and tolerated in evil. He had, or thought that he had, a connivance, one might almost say a complicity, of events in his favor, which was equivalent to the invulnerability of antiquity.

Nevertheless, when one has Beresina, Leipzig, and Fontainebleau behind one, it seems as though one might distrust Waterloo. A mysterious frown becomes perceptible in the depths of the heavens.

At the moment when Wellington retreated, Napoleon shuddered. He suddenly beheld the tableland of Mont-Saint-Jean cleared, and the van of the English army disappear. It was rallying, but hiding itself. The Emperor half rose in his stirrups. The lightning of victory flashed from his eyes.

Wellington, driven into a corner at the forest of Soignes and destroyed—that was the definitive conquest of England by France; it was Crecy, Poitiers, Malplaquet, and Ramillies avenged. The man of Marengo was wiping out Agincourt.

So the Emperor, meditating on this terrible turn of fortune, swept his glass for the last time over all the points of the field of battle. His guard, standing behind him with grounded arms, watched him from below with a sort of religion. He pondered; he examined the slopes, noted the declivities, scrutinized the clumps of trees, the square of rye, the path; he seemed to be counting each bush. He gazed with some intentness at the English barricades of the two highways, two large abatis of trees, that on the road to Genappe above La Haie-Sainte, armed with two cannon, the only ones out of all the English artillery which commanded the extremity of the field of battle, and that on the road to Nivelles where gleamed the Dutch bayonets of Chasse's brigade. Near this barricade he observed the old chapel of Saint Nicholas, painted white, which stands at the angle of the crossroad near Braine-l'Alleud; he bent down and spoke in a low voice to the guide Lacoste. The guide made a negative sign with his head, which was probably perfidious.

The Emperor straightened himself up and fell to thinking.

Wellington had drawn back.

All that remained to do was to complete this retreat by crushing him.

Napoleon turning around abruptly, dispatched an express at full speed to Paris to announce that the battle was won.

Napoleon was one of those geniuses from whom thunder darts.

He had just found his clap of thunder.

He gave orders to Milhaud's cuirassiers to carry the tableland of Mont-Saint-Jean.

CHAPTER IX—THE UNEXPECTED

There were 3,500 of them. They formed a front a quarter of a league in extent. They were giant men, on colossal horses. There were six and twenty squadrons of them; and they had behind them to support them Lefebvre-Desnouettes's division, the one hundred and six picked gendarmes, the light cavalry of the Guard, eleven hundred and ninety-seven men, and the lancers of the guard of eight hundred and eighty lances. They wore helmets without horsetails, and cuirasses of beaten iron, with horse pistols in their holsters, and long saber swords. That morning the whole army had admired them, when, at nine o'clock, with braying of trumpets and all the music playing "Let us watch o'er the Safety of the Empire," they had come in a solid column, with one of their batteries on their flank, another in their center, and deployed in two ranks between the roads to Genappe and Frischemont, and taken up their position for battle in that powerful second line, so cleverly arranged by Napoleon, which, having on its extreme left Kellermann's cuirassiers and on its extreme right Milhaud's cuirassiers, had, so to speak, two wings of iron.

Aide-de-camp Bernard carried them the Emperor's orders. Ney drew his sword and placed himself at their head. The enormous squadrons were set in motion.

Then a formidable spectacle was seen.

All their cavalry, with upraised swords, standards and trumpets flung to the breeze, formed in columns by divisions, descended, by a simultaneous movement and like one man, with the precision of a brazen battering ram which is effecting a breach, the hill of La Belle Alliance, plunged into the terrible depths in which so many men had already fallen, disappeared there in the smoke, then emerging from that shadow, reappeared on the other side of the

valley, still compact and in close ranks, mounting at a full trot, through a storm
of grapeshot that burst upon them, the terrible muddy slope of the tableland
of Mont-Saint-Jean. They ascended, grave, threatening, imperturbable; in
the intervals between the musketry and the artillery, their colossal trampling
was audible. Being two divisions, there were two columns of them; Wathier's
division held the right, Delort's division was on the left. It seemed as though
two immense adders of steel were to be seen crawling toward the crest of the
tableland. It traversed the battle like a prodigy.

Nothing like it had been seen since the taking of the great redoubt of the
Muskowa by the heavy cavalry; Murat was lacking here, but Ney was again
present. It seemed as though that mass had become a monster and had but
one soul. Each column undulated and swelled like the ring of a polyp. They
could be seen through a vast cloud of smoke that was rent here and there. A
confusion of helmets, of cries, of sabers, a stormy heaving of the cruppers of
horses amid the cannons and the flourish of trumpets, a terrible and disciplined
tumult; over all, the cuirasses like the scales on the hydra.

These narrations seemed to belong to another age. Something parallel to
this vision appeared, no doubt, in the ancient Orphic epics, which told of the
centaurs, the old, those Titans with human heads and equestrian chests who
scaled Olympus at a gallop, horrible, invulnerable, sublime—gods and beasts.

Odd numerical coincidence, twenty-six battalions rode to meet twenty-
six battalions. Behind the crest of the plateau, in the shadow of the masked
battery, the English infantry, formed into thirteen squares, two battalions to
the square, in two lines, with seven in the first line, six in the second, the stocks
of their guns to their shoulders, taking aim at that which was on the point of
appearing, waited, calm, mute, motionless. They did not see the cuirassiers,
and the cuirassiers did not see them. They listened to the rise of this flood of
men. They heard the swelling noise of three thousand horse, the alternate and
symmetrical tramp of their hoofs at full trot, the jingling of the cuirasses, the
clang of the sabers and a sort of grand and savage breathing. There ensued a
most terrible silence; then, all at once, a long file of uplifted arms, brandishing
sabers, appeared above the crest, and helmets, trumpets, and standards, and
3,000 heads with gray mustaches, shouting, *"Vive l'Empèreur!"* All this cavalry
debouched on the plateau, and it was like the appearance of an earthquake.

All at once, a tragic incident; on the English left, on our right, the head of
the column of cuirassiers reared up with a frightful clamor. On arriving at the
culminating point of the crest, ungovernable, utterly given over to fury and
their course of extermination of the squares and cannon, the cuirassiers had

just caught sight of a trench, a trench between them and the English. It was the hollow road of Ohain.

It was a terrible moment. The ravine was there, unexpected, yawning, directly under the horses' feet, two fathoms deep between its double slopes; the second file pushed the first into it, and the third pushed on the second; the horses reared and fell backward, landed on their haunches, slid down, all four feet in the air, crushing and overwhelming the riders; and there being no means of retreat, the whole column being no longer anything more than a projectile, the force which had been acquired to crush the English crushed the French; the inexorable ravine could only yield when filled; horses and riders rolled there pell-mell, grinding each other, forming but one mass of flesh in this gulf: when this trench was full of living men, the rest marched over them and passed on. Almost a third of Dubois's brigade fell into that abyss.

This began the loss of the battle.

A local tradition, which evidently exaggerates matters, says that two thousand horses and fifteen hundred men were buried in the hollow road of Ohain. This figure probably comprises all the other corpses which were flung into this ravine the day after the combat.

Let us note in passing that it was Dubois's sorely tried brigade which, an hour previously, making a charge to one side, had captured the flag of the Lunenburg battalion.

Napoleon, before giving the order for this charge of Milhaud's cuirassiers, had scrutinized the ground, but had not been able to see that hollow road, which did not even form a wrinkle on the surface of the plateau. Warned, nevertheless, and put on the alert by the little white chapel which marks its angle of junction with the Nivelles highway, he had probably put a question as to the possibility of an obstacle, to the guide Lacoste. The guide had answered no. We might almost affirm that Napoleon's catastrophe originated in that sign of a peasant's head.

Other fatalities were destined to arise.

Was it possible that Napoleon should have won that battle? We answer no. Why? Because of Wellington? Because of Blucher? No. Because of God.

Bonaparte victor at Waterloo; that does not come within the law of the nineteenth century. Another series of facts was in preparation, in which there was no longer any room for Napoleon. The ill will of events had declared itself long before.

It was time that this vast man should fall.

The excessive weight of this man in human destiny disturbed the balance.

This individual alone counted for more than a universal group. This plethora of all human vitality concentrated in a single head; the world mounting to the brain of one man, this would be mortal to civilization were it to last. The moment had arrived for the incorruptible and supreme equity to alter its plan. Probably the principles and the elements, on which the regular gravitations of the moral, as of the material, world depend, had complained. Smoking blood, over-filled cemeteries, mothers in tears, these are formidable pleaders. When the earth is suffering from too heavy a burden, there are mysterious groanings of the shades, to which the abyss lends an ear.

Napoleon had been denounced in the infinite and his fall had been decided on. He embarrassed God.

Waterloo is not a battle; it is a change of front on the part of the Universe.

CHAPTER X—THE PLATEAU OF MONT-SAINT-JEAN

The battery was unmasked at the same moment with the ravine.

Sixty cannons and the thirteen squares darted lightning point-blank on the cuirassiers. The intrepid General Delort made the military salute to the English battery.

The whole of the flying artillery of the English had reentered the squares at a gallop. The cuirassiers had not had even the time for a halt. The disaster of the hollow road had decimated, but not discouraged them. They belonged to that class of men who, when diminished in number, increase in courage.

Wathier's column alone had suffered in the disaster; Delort's column, which Ney had deflected to the left, as though he had a presentiment of an ambush, had arrived whole.

The cuirassiers hurled themselves on the English squares.

At full speed, with bridles loose, swords in their teeth pistols in fist, such was the attack.

There are moments in battles in which the soul hardens the man until the soldier is changed into a statue, and when all this flesh turns into granite. The English battalions, desperately assaulted, did not stir.

Then it was terrible.

All the faces of the English squares were attacked at once. A frenzied whirl enveloped them. That cold infantry remained impassive. The first rank knelt and received the cuirassiers on their bayonets, the second ranks shot them down; behind the second rank the cannoneers charged their guns, the front of the square parted, permitted the passage of an eruption of grapeshot, and closed again. The cuirassiers replied by crushing them. Their great horses reared, strode across the ranks, leaped over the bayonets and fell, gigantic, in the midst of these four living wells. The cannonballs plowed furrows in these cuirassiers; the cuirassiers made breaches in the squares. Files of men disappeared, ground to dust under the horses. The bayonets plunged into the bellies of these centaurs; hence a hideousness of wounds that has probably never been seen anywhere else. The squares, wasted by this mad cavalry, closed up their ranks without flinching. Inexhaustible in the matter of grapeshot, they created explosions in their assailants' midst. The form of this combat was monstrous. These squares were no longer battalions, they were craters; those cuirassiers were no longer cavalry, they were a tempest. Each square was a volcano attacked by a cloud; lava contended with lightning.

The square on the extreme right, the most exposed of all, being in the air, was almost annihilated at the very first shock. It was formed of the 75th regiment of Highlanders. The bagpipe player in the center dropped his melancholy eyes, filled with the reflections of the forests and the lakes, in profound inattention, while men were being exterminated around him, and seated on a drum, with his bagpipe music under his arm, played the Highland airs. These Scotchmen died thinking of Ben Lothian, as did the Greeks recalling Argos. The sword of a cuirassier, which hewed down the bagpipes and the arm that bore it, put an end to the song by killing the singer.

The cuirassiers, relatively few in number, and still further diminished by the catastrophe of the ravine, had almost the whole English army against them, but they multiplied themselves so that each man of them was equal to ten. Nevertheless, some Hanoverian battalions yielded. Wellington perceived it, and thought of his cavalry. Had Napoleon at that same moment thought of his infantry, he would have won the battle. This forgetfulness was his great and fatal mistake.

All at once, the cuirassiers, who had been the assailants, found themselves assailed. The English cavalry was at their back. Before them two squares, behind them Somerset; Somerset meant fourteen hundred dragoons of the guard. On the right, Somerset had Dornberg with the German light-horse, and on his left, Trip with the Belgian carabineers; the cuirassiers attacked on the flank and in front, before and in the rear, by infantry and cavalry, had to face all sides. What mattered it to them? They were a whirlwind. Their valor was something indescribable.

In addition to this, they had behind them the battery, which was still thundering. It was necessary that it should be so, or they could never have been wounded in the back. One of their cuirasses, pierced on the shoulder by a ball from a biscayan, is in the collection of the Waterloo Museum.

For such Frenchmen nothing less than such Englishmen was needed. It was no longer a hand-to-hand conflict; it was a shadow, a fury, a dizzy transport of souls and courage, a hurricane of lightning swords. In an instant the fourteen hundred dragoon guards numbered only eight hundred. Fuller, their Lieutenant colonel, fell dead. Ney rushed up with the lancers and Lefebvre-Desnouettes's light horse. The plateau of Mont-Saint-Jean was captured, recaptured, captured again. The cuirassiers quitted the cavalry to return to the infantry; or, to put it more exactly, the whole of that formidable rout collared each other without releasing the other. The squares still held firm.

There were a dozen assaults. Ney had four horses killed under him. Half the cuirassiers remained on the plateau. This conflict lasted two hours.

The English army was profoundly shaken. There is no doubt that, had they not been enfeebled in their first shock by the disaster of the hollow road the cuirassiers would have overwhelmed the center and decided the victory. This extraordinary cavalry petrified Clinton, who had seen Talavera and Badajoz. Wellington, three-quarters vanquished, admired heroically. He said in an undertone, "Sublime!"

The cuirassiers annihilated seven squares out of thirteen, took or spiked sixty pieces of ordnance, and captured from the English regiments six flags, which three cuirassiers and three chasseurs of the Guard bore to the Emperor, in front of the farm of La Belle Alliance.

Wellington's situation had grown worse. This strange battle was like a duel between two raging, wounded men, each of whom, still fighting and still resisting, is expending all his blood.

Which of the two will be the first to fall?

The conflict on the plateau continued.

What had become of the cuirassiers? No one could have told. One thing is certain, that on the day after the battle, a cuirassier and his horse were found dead among the woodwork of the scales for vehicles at Mont-Saint-Jean, at the very point where the four roads from Nivelles, Genappe, La Hulpe, and Brussels meet and intersect each other. This horseman had pierced the English lines. One of the men who picked up the body still lives at Mont-Saint-Jean. His name is Dehaze. He was eighteen years old at that time.

Wellington felt that he was yielding. The crisis was at hand.

The cuirassiers had not succeeded, since the center was not broken through. As everyone was in possession of the plateau, no one held it, and in fact it remained, to a great extent, with the English. Wellington held the village and the culminating plain; Ney had only the crest and the slope. They seemed rooted in that fatal soil on both sides.

But the weakening of the English seemed irremediable. The bleeding of that army was horrible. Kempt, on the left wing, demanded reinforcements. "There are none," replied Wellington; "he must let himself be killed!" Almost at that same moment, a singular coincidence which paints the exhaustion of the two armies, Ney demanded infantry from Napoleon, and Napoleon exclaimed, "Infantry! Where does he expect me to get it? Does he think I can make it?"

Nevertheless, the English army was in the worse case of the two. The furious onsets of those great squadrons with cuirasses of iron and breasts of steel had ground the infantry to nothing. A few men clustered around a flag marked the post of a regiment; such and such a battalion was commanded only by a captain or a lieutenant; Alten's division, already so roughly handled at La Haie-Sainte, was almost destroyed; the intrepid Belgians of Van Kluze's brigade strewed the rye fields all along the Nivelles road; hardly anything was left of those Dutch grenadiers, who, intermingled with Spaniards in our ranks in 1811, fought against Wellington; and who, in 1815, rallied to the English standard, fought against Napoleon. The loss in officers was considerable. Lord Uxbridge, who had his leg buried on the following day, had his knee shattered. If, on the French side, in that tussle of the cuirassiers, Delort, l'Heritier, Colbert, Dnop, Travers, and Blancard were disabled, on the side of the English there was Alten wounded, Barne wounded, Delancey killed, Van Meeren killed, Ompteda killed, the whole of Wellington's staff decimated, and England had the worse of it in that bloody scale. The second regiment of foot guards had lost five lieutenant colonels, four captains, and three ensigns; the first battalion of the 30th infantry had lost 24 officers and 1,200 soldiers; the 79th Highlanders had lost 24 officers wounded, 18 officers killed, 450 soldiers killed. The Hanoverian hussars of Cumberland, a whole regiment, with Colonel Hacke at its head, who was destined to be tried later on and cashiered, had turned bridle in the presence of the fray, and had fled to the forest of Soignes, sowing defeat all the way to Brussels. The transports, ammunition wagons, the baggage wagons, the wagons filled with wounded, on perceiving that the French were gaining ground and approaching the forest, rushed headlong there. The Dutch, mowed down by the French cavalry, cried, "Alarm!" From Vert-Coucou to Groentendael, for a distance of nearly two leagues in the direction of Brussels, according to the testimony of eyewitnesses who are still alive, the roads were encumbered with fugitives. This panic was such that it attacked the Prince de Conde at Mechlin, and Louis XVIII at Ghent. With the exception of the feeble reserve echeloned behind the ambulance established at the farm of Mont-Saint-Jean, and of Vivian's and Vandeleur's brigades, which flanked the left wing, Wellington had no cavalry left. A number of batteries lay unhorsed. These facts are attested by Siborne; and Pringle, exaggerating the disaster, goes so far as to say that the Anglo-Dutch army was reduced to thirty-four thousand men. The Iron Duke remained calm, but his lips blanched. Vincent, the Austrian commissioner, Alava, the Spanish commissioner, who were present at the battle in the English staff, thought the Duke lost. At five o'clock Wellington drew out his watch, and he was heard to murmur these sinister words, "Blucher, or night!"

It was at about that moment that a distant line of bayonets gleamed on the heights in the direction of Frischemont.

Here comes the change of face in this giant drama.

CHAPTER XI—A BAD GUIDE TO NAPOLEON; A GOOD GUIDE TO BULOW

The painful surprise of Napoleon is well known. Grouchy hoped for, Blucher arriving. Death instead of life.

Fate has these turns; the throne of the world was expected; it was Saint Helena that was seen.

If the little shepherd who served as guide to Bulow, Blucher's lieutenant, had advised him to debouch from the forest above Frischemont, instead of below Plancenoit, the form of the nineteenth century might, perhaps, have been different. Napoleon would have won the battle of Waterloo. By any other route than that below Plancenoit, the Prussian army would have come out upon a ravine impassable for artillery, and Bulow would not have arrived.

Now the Prussian general, Muffling, declares that one-hour's delay, and Blucher would not have found Wellington on his feet. "The battle was lost."

It was time that Bulow should arrive, as will be seen. He had, moreover, been very much delayed. He had bivouacked at Dion-le-Mont, and had set out at daybreak; but the roads were impassable, and his divisions stuck fast in the mire. The ruts were up to the hubs of the cannons. Moreover, he had been obliged to pass the Dyle on the narrow bridge of Wavre; the street leading to the bridge had been fired by the French, so the caissons and ammunition wagons could not pass between two rows of burning houses, and had been obliged to wait until the conflagration was extinguished. It was midday before Bulow's vanguard had been able to reach Chapelle-Saint-Lambert.

Had the action been begun two hours earlier, it would have been over at four o'clock, and Blucher would have fallen on the battle won by Napoleon. Such are these immense risks proportioned to an infinite that we cannot comprehend.

The Emperor had been the first, as early as midday, to descry with his field glass, on the extreme horizon, something which had attracted his attention. He had said, "I see yonder a cloud, which seems to me to be troops." Then he asked the Duc de Dalmatie, "Soult, what do you see in the direction of Chapelle-Saint-Lambert?" The marshall, leveling his glass, answered, "Four or five thousand men, Sire; evidently Grouchy." But it remained motionless in the mist. All the glasses of the staff had studied "the cloud" pointed out by the Emperor. Some said, "It is trees." The truth is, that the cloud did not move. The Emperor detached Domon's division of light cavalry to reconnoiter in that quarter.

Bulow had not moved, in fact. His vanguard was very feeble, and could accomplish nothing. He was obliged to wait for the body of the army corps, and he had received orders to concentrate his forces before entering into line; but at five o'clock, perceiving Wellington's peril, Blucher ordered Bulow to attack, and uttered these remarkable words: "We must give air to the English army."

A little later, the divisions of Losthin, Hiller, Hacke, and Ryssel deployed before Lobau's corps, the cavalry of Prince William of Prussia debouched from the forest of Paris, Plancenoit was in flames, and the Prussian cannonballs began to rain even upon the ranks of the guard in reserve behind Napoleon.

CHAPTER XII—THE GUARD

Everyone knows the rest, the irruption of a third army; the battle broken to pieces; eighty-six mouths of fire thundering simultaneously; Pirch the first coming up with Bulow; Zieten's cavalry led by Blucher in person, the French driven back; Marcognet swept from the plateau of Ohain; Durutte dislodged from Papelotte; Donzelot and Quiot retreating; Lobau caught on the flank; a fresh battle precipitating itself on our dismantled regiments at nightfall; the whole English line resuming the offensive and thrust forward; the gigantic breach made in the French army; the English grapeshot and the Prussian grapeshot aiding each other; the extermination; disaster in front;

disaster on the flank; the Guard entering the line in the midst of this terrible crumbling of all things.

Conscious that they were about to die, they shouted, "Vive l'Empèreur!" History records nothing more touching than that agony bursting forth in acclamations.

The sky had been overcast all day long. All of a sudden, at that very moment, it was eight o'clock in the evening—the clouds on the horizon parted, and allowed the grand and sinister glow of the setting sun to pass through, athwart the elms on the Nivelles road. They had seen it rise at Austerlitz.

Each battalion of the Guard was commanded by a general for this final catastrophe. Friant, Michel, Roguet, Harlet, Mallet, Poret de Morvan, were there. When the tall caps of the grenadiers of the Guard, with their large plaques bearing the eagle appeared, symmetrical, in line, tranquil, in the midst of that combat, the enemy felt a respect for France; they thought they beheld twenty victories entering the field of battle, with wings outspread, and those who were the conquerors, believing themselves to be vanquished, retreated; but Wellington shouted, "Up, Guards, and aim straight!" The red regiment of English guards, lying flat behind the hedges, sprang up, a cloud of grapeshot riddled the tricolored flag and whistled around our eagles; all hurled themselves forward, and the final carnage began. In the darkness, the Imperial Guard felt the army losing ground around it, and in the vast shock of the rout it heard the desperate flight which had taken the place of the "Vive l'Empèreur!" and, with flight behind it, it continued to advance, more crushed, losing more men at every step that it took. There were none who hesitated, no timid men in its ranks. The soldier in that troop was as much of a hero as the general. Not a man was missing in that suicide.

Ney, bewildered, great with all the grandeur of accepted death, offered himself to all blows in that tempest. He had his fifth horse killed under him there. Perspiring, his eyes aflame, foaming at the mouth, with uniform unbuttoned, one of his epaulets half cut off by a sword stroke from a horse guard, his plaque with the great eagle dented by a bullet; bleeding, bemired, magnificent, a broken sword in his hand, he said, "Come and see how a Marshal of France dies on the field of battle!" But in vain; he did not die. He was haggard and angry. At Drouet d'Erlon he hurled this question, "Are you not going to get yourself killed?" In the midst of all that artillery engaged in crushing a handful of men, he shouted, "So there is nothing for me! Oh! I should like to have all these English bullets enter my bowels!" Unhappy man, thou wert reserved for French bullets!

CHAPTER XIII—THE CATASTROPHE

The rout behind the Guard was melancholy.

The army yielded suddenly on all sides at once, Hougomont, La Haie-Sainte, Papelotte, Plancenoit. The cry "Treachery!" was followed by a cry of "Save yourselves who can!" An army that is disbanding is like a thaw. All yields, splits, cracks, floats, rolls, falls, jostles, hastens, is precipitated. The disintegration is unprecedented. Ney borrows a horse, leaps upon it, and without hat, cravat, or sword, places himself across the Brussels road, stopping both English and French. He strives to detain the army, he recalls it to its duty, he insults it, he clings to the rout. He is overwhelmed. The soldiers fly from him, shouting, "Long live Marshal Ney!" Two of Durutte's regiments go and come in affright as though tossed back and forth between the swords of the Uhlans and the fusillade of the brigades of Kempt, Best, Pack, and Rylandt; the worst of hand-to-hand conflicts is the defeat; friends kill each other in order to escape; squadrons and battalions break and disperse against each other, like the tremendous foam of battle. Lobau at one extremity, and Reille at the other, are drawn into the tide. In vain does Napoleon erect walls from what is left to him of his Guard; in vain does he expend in a last effort his last serviceable squadrons. Quiot retreats before Vivian, Kellermann before Vandeleur, Lobau before Bulow, Morand before Pirch, Domon and Subervic before Prince William of Prussia; Guyot, who led the Emperor's squadrons to the charge, falls beneath the feet of the English dragoons. Napoleon gallops past the line of fugitives, harangues, urges, threatens, entreats them. All the mouths which in the morning had shouted, "Long live the Emperor!" remain gaping; they hardly recognize him. The Prussian cavalry, newly arrived, dashes forward, flies, hews, slashes, kills, exterminates. Horses lash out, the cannons flee; the soldiers of the artillery train unharness the caissons and use the horses to make their escape; transports overturned, with all four wheels in the air, clog the road and occasion massacres. Men are crushed, trampled down, others walk over the dead and the living. Arms are lost. A dizzy multitude fills the roads, the paths, the bridges, the plains, the hills, the valleys, the woods, encumbered by this invasion of forty thousand men. Shouts despair, knapsacks and guns flung among the rye, passages forced at the point of the sword, no more comrades, no more officers, no more generals, an inexpressible terror. Zieten putting France to the sword at its leisure. Lions converted into goats. Such was the flight.

At Genappe, an effort was made to wheel about, to present a battle front, to draw up in line. Lobau rallied three hundred men. The entrance to the village was barricaded, but at the first volley of Prussian canister, all took to flight again, and Lobau was taken. That volley of grapeshot can be seen today imprinted on the ancient gable of a brick building on the right of the road at a few minutes' distance before you enter Genappe. The Prussians threw themselves into Genappe, furious, no doubt, that they were not more entirely the conquerors. The pursuit was stupendous. Blucher ordered extermination. Roguet had set the lugubrious example of threatening with death any French grenadier who should bring him a Prussian prisoner. Blucher outdid Roguet. Duhesme, the general of the Young Guard, hemmed in at the doorway of an inn at Genappe, surrendered his sword to a huzzar of death, who took the sword and slew the prisoner. The victory was completed by the assassination of the vanquished. Let us inflict punishment, since we are history: old Blucher disgraced himself. This ferocity put the finishing touch to the disaster. The desperate route traversed Genappe, traversed Quatre-Bras, traversed Gosselies, traversed Frasnes, traversed Charleroi, traversed Thuin, and only halted at the frontier. Alas! And who, then, was fleeing in that manner? The Grand Army.

This vertigo, this terror, this downfall into ruin of the loftiest bravery that ever astounded history, is that causeless? No. The shadow of an enormous right is projected athwart Waterloo. It is the day of destiny. The force which is mightier than man produced that day. Hence the terrified wrinkle of those brows; hence all those great souls surrendering their swords. Those who had conquered Europe have fallen prone on the earth, with nothing left to say or to do, feeling the present shadow of a terrible presence. *Hoc erat in fatis.* That day the perspective of the human race underwent a change. Waterloo is the hinge of the nineteenth century. The disappearance of the great man was necessary to the advent of the great century. Someone, a person to whom one replies not, took the responsibility on himself. The panic of heroes can be explained. In the battle of Waterloo there is something more than a cloud, there is something of the meteor. God has passed by.

At nightfall, in a meadow near Genappe, Bernard and Bertrand seized by the skirt of his coat and detained a man, haggard, pensive, sinister, gloomy, who, dragged to that point by the current of the rout, had just dismounted, had passed the bridle of his horse over his arm, and with wild eye was returning alone to Waterloo. It was Napoleon, the immense somnambulist of this dream that had crumbled, essaying once more to advance.

CHAPTER XIV—THE LAST SQUARE

Several squares of the Guard, motionless amid this stream of the defeat, as rocks in running water, held their own until night. Night came, death also; they awaited that double shadow, and, invincible, allowed themselves to be enveloped therein. Each regiment, isolated from the rest, and having no bond with the army, now shattered in every part, died alone. They had taken up position for this final action, some on the heights of Rossomme, others on the plain of Mont-Saint-Jean. There, abandoned, vanquished, terrible, those gloomy squares endured their death throes in formidable fashion. Ulm, Wagram, Jena, Friedland, died with them.

At twilight, toward nine o'clock in the evening, one of them was left at the foot of the plateau of Mont-Saint-Jean. In that fatal valley, at the foot of that declivity which the cuirassiers had ascended, now inundated by the masses of the English, under the converging fires of the victorious hostile cavalry, under a frightful density of projectiles, this square fought on. It was commanded by an obscure officer named Cambronne. At each discharge, the square diminished and replied. It replied to the grapeshot with a fusillade, continually contracting its four walls. The fugitives pausing breathless for a moment in the distance, listened in the darkness to that gloomy and ever-decreasing thunder.

When this legion had been reduced to a handful, when nothing was left of their flag but a rag, when their guns, the bullets all gone, were no longer anything but clubs, when the heap of corpses was larger than the group of survivors, there reigned among the conquerors, around those men dying so sublimely, a sort of sacred terror, and the English artillery, taking breath, became silent. This furnished a sort of respite. These combatants had around them something in the nature of a swarm of specters, silhouettes of men on horseback, the black profiles of cannon, the white sky viewed through wheels and gun carriages, the colossal death's-head, which the heroes saw constantly through the smoke, in the depths of the battle, advanced upon them and gazed at them. Through the shades of twilight they could hear the pieces being loaded; the matches all lighted, like the eyes of tigers at night, formed a circle around their heads; all the linstocks of the English batteries approached the cannons, and then, with emotion, holding the supreme moment suspended above these men, an English general, Colville according to some, Maitland according to others, shouted to them, "Surrender, brave Frenchmen!"

Cambronne replied, "———."

CHAPTER XV — CAMBRONNE

If any French reader objected to having his susceptibilities offended, one would have to refrain from repeating in his presence what is perhaps the finest reply that a Frenchman ever made. This would enjoin us from consigning something sublime to history.

At our own risk and peril, let us violate this injunction.

Now, then, among those giants there was one Titan, Cambronne.

To make that reply and then perish, what could be grander? For being willing to die is the same as to die; and it was not this man's fault if he survived after he was shot.

The winner of the battle of Waterloo was not Napoleon, who was put to flight; nor Wellington, giving way at four o'clock, in despair at five; nor Blucher, who took no part in the engagement. The winner of Waterloo was Cambronne.

To thunder forth such a reply at the lightning flash that kills you is to conquer!

Thus to answer the Catastrophe, thus to speak to Fate, to give this pedestal to the future lion, to hurl such a challenge to the midnight rainstorm, to the treacherous wall of Hougomont, to the sunken road of Ohain, to Grouchy's delay, to Blucher's arrival, to be Irony itself in the tomb, to act so as to stand upright though fallen, to drown in two syllables the European coalition, to offer kings privies that the Caesars once knew, to make the lowest of words the most lofty by entwining with it the glory of France, insolently to end Waterloo with Mardigras, to finish Leonidas with Rabellais, to set the crown on this victory by a word impossible to speak, to lose the field and preserve history, to have the laugh on your side after such a carnage, this is immense!

It was an insult such as a thundercloud might hurl! It reaches the grandeur of Aeschylus!

Cambronne's reply produces the effect of a violent break. 'Tis like the breaking of a heart under a weight of scorn. 'Tis the overflow of agony bursting forth. Who conquered? Wellington? No! Had it not been for Blucher, he was lost. Was it Blucher? No! If Wellington had not begun, Blucher could not have finished. This Cambronne, this man spending his last hour, this unknown soldier, this infinitesimal of war, realizes that here is a falsehood, a falsehood in a catastrophe, and so doubly agonizing; and at the moment when his rage is bursting forth because of it, he is offered this mockery, life! How could he restrain himself? Yonder are all the kings of Europe, the generals flushed with victory, the Jupiter's darting thunderbolts; they have a hundred thousand victorious soldiers, and back of the hundred thousand a million; their cannon stand with yawning mouths, the match is lighted; they grind down under their heels the Imperial guards, and the grand army; they have just crushed Napoleon, and only Cambronne remains, only this earthworm is left to protest. He will protest. Then he seeks for the appropriate word as one seeks for a sword. His mouth froths, and the froth is the word. In face of this mean and mighty victory, in face of this victory that counts none victorious, this desperate soldier stands erect. He grants its overwhelming immensity, but he establishes its triviality; and he does more than spit upon it. Borne down by numbers, by superior force, by brute matter, he finds in his soul an expression, "Excrement!" We repeat it, to use that word, to do thus, to invent such an expression, is to be the conqueror!

The spirit of mighty days at that portentous moment made its descent on that unknown man. Cambronne invents the word for Waterloo as Rouget invents the "Marseillaise," under the visitation of a breath from on high. An emanation from the divine whirlwind leaps forth and comes sweeping over these men, and they shake, and one of them sings the song supreme, and the other utters the frightful cry.

This challenge of titanic scorn Cambronne hurls not only at Europe in the name of the Empire, which would be a trifle: he hurls it at the past in the name of the Revolution. It is heard, and Cambronne is recognized as possessed by the ancient spirit of the Titans. Danton seems to be speaking! Kleber seems to be bellowing!

At that word from Cambronne, the English voice responded, "Fire!" The batteries flamed, the hill trembled, from all those brazen mouths belched a last terrible gush of grapeshot; a vast volume of smoke, vaguely white in the light of the rising moon, rolled out, and when the smoke dispersed, there was no longer anything there. That formidable remnant had been annihilated; the guard was dead. The four walls of the living redoubt lay prone, and hardly was there discernible, here and there, even a quiver in the bodies; it was thus that the French legions, greater than the Roman legions, expired on Mont-Saint-Jean, on the soil watered with rain and blood, amid the gloomy grain, on the spot where nowadays Joseph, who drives the post-wagon from Nivelles, passes whistling, and cheerfully whipping up his horse at four o'clock in the morning.

CHAPTER XVI—QUOT LIBRAS IN DUCE?

The battle of Waterloo is an enigma. It is as obscure to those who won it as to those who lost it. For Napoleon it was a panic; Blucher sees nothing in it but fire; Wellington understands nothing in regard to it. Look at the reports. The bulletins are confused, the commentaries involved. Some stammer, others lisp. Jomini divides the battle of Waterloo into four moments; Muffling cuts it up into three changes; Charras alone, though we hold another judgment than his on some points, seized with his haughty glance the characteristic outlines of that catastrophe of human genius in conflict with divine chance. All the other historians suffer from being somewhat dazzled, and in this dazzled state they fumble about. It was a day of lightning brilliancy; in fact, a crumbling of the military monarchy which, to the vast stupefaction of kings, drew all the kingdoms after it—the fall of force, the defeat of war.

In this event, stamped with superhuman necessity, the part played by men amounts to nothing.

If we take Waterloo from Wellington and Blucher, do we thereby deprive England and Germany of anything? No. Neither that illustrious England nor that august Germany enter into the problem of Waterloo. Thank Heaven, nations are great, independently of the lugubrious feats of the sword. Neither England, nor Germany, nor France is contained in a scabbard. At this epoch when Waterloo is only a clashing of swords, above Blucher, Germany has Schiller; above Wellington, England has Byron. A vast dawn of ideas is the peculiarity of our century, and in that aurora England and Germany have a magnificent radiance. They are majestic because they think. The elevation of level that they contribute to civilization is intrinsic with them; it proceeds from themselves and not from an accident. The aggrandizement that they have brought to the nineteenth century has not Waterloo as its source. It is only barbarous peoples who undergo rapid growth after a victory. That is the temporary vanity of torrents swelled by a storm. Civilized people, especially in our day, are neither elevated nor abased by the good or bad fortune of a captain. Their specific gravity in the human species results from something more than a combat. Their honor, thank God! Their dignity, their intelligence, their genius, are not numbers that those gamblers, heroes, and conquerors, can put in the lottery of battles. Often a battle is lost and progress is conquered. There is less glory and more liberty. The drum holds its peace; reason takes the word. It is a game in which he who loses wins. Let us, therefore, speak of Waterloo coldly from both sides. Let us render to chance that which is due to chance, and to God that which is due to God. What is Waterloo? A victory? No. The winning number in the lottery.

The quine* won by Europe, paid by France.

It was not worthwhile to place a lion there.

Waterloo, moreover, is the strangest encounter in history. Napoleon and Wellington. They are not enemies; they are opposites. Never did God, who is fond of antitheses, make a more striking contrast, a more extraordinary comparison. On one side, precision, foresight, geometry, prudence, an assured retreat, reserves spared, with an obstinate coolness, an imperturbable method, strategy, which takes advantage of the ground, tactics, which preserve the equilibrium of battalions, carnage, executed according to rule, war regulated, watch in hand, nothing voluntarily left to chance, the ancient classic courage, absolute regularity; on the other, intuition, divination, military oddity, superhuman instinct, a flaming glance, an indescribable something, which gazes like an eagle, and which strikes like the lightning, a prodigious art in disdainful impetuosity, all the mysteries of a profound soul, associated with destiny; the stream, the plain, the forest, the hill, summoned, and in a manner, forced to obey, the despot going even so far as to tyrannize over the field of battle; faith in a star mingled with strategic science, elevating but perturbing it. Wellington was the Bareme of war; Napoleon was its Michelangelo; and on this occasion, genius was vanquished by calculation. On both sides someone was awaited. It was the exact calculator who succeeded. Napoleon was waiting for Grouchy; he did not come. Wellington expected Blucher; he came.

Wellington is classic war taking its revenge. Bonaparte, at his dawning, had encountered him in Italy, and beaten him superbly. The old owl had fled before the young vulture. The old tactics had been not only struck as by lightning, but disgraced. Who was that Corsican of six and twenty? What signified that splendid ignoramus, who, with everything against him, nothing in his favor, without provisions, without ammunition, without cannon, without shoes, almost without an army, with a mere handful of men against masses, hurled himself on Europe combined, and absurdly won victories in the impossible? Whence had issued that fulminating convict, who almost without taking breath, and with the same set of combatants in hand, pulverized, one after the other, the five armies of the emperor of Germany, upsetting Beaulieu on Alvinzi, Wurmser on Beaulieu, Melas on Wurmser, Mack on Melas? Who was this novice in war with the effrontery of a luminary? The academical military school excommunicated him, and as it lost its footing; hence, the implacable rancor of the old Caesarism against the new; of the regular sword against the flaming sword; and of the exchequer against genius. On the 18th of June, 1815,

---

* five winning lottery numbers

that rancor had the last word. And beneath Lodi, Montebello, Montenotte, Mantua, Arcola, it wrote: Waterloo. A triumph of the mediocre that is sweet to the majority. Destiny consented to this irony. In his decline, Napoleon found Wurmser, the younger, again in front of him.

In fact, to get Wurmser, it sufficed to blanch the hair of Wellington.

Waterloo is a battle of the first order, won by a captain of the second.

That which must be admired in the battle of Waterloo, is England; the English firmness, the English resolution, the English blood; the superb thing about England there, no offense to her, was herself. It was not her captain; it was her army.

Wellington, oddly ungrateful, declares in a letter to Lord Bathurst, that his army, the army which fought on the 18th of June, 1815, was a "detestable army." What does that somber intermingling of bones buried beneath the furrows of Waterloo think of that?

England has been too modest in the matter of Wellington. To make Wellington so great is to belittle England. Wellington is nothing but a hero like many another. Those Scotch Grays, those Horse Guards, those regiments of Maitland and of Mitchell, that infantry of Pack and Kempt, that cavalry of Ponsonby and Somerset, those Highlanders playing bagpipe music under the shower of grapeshot, those battalions of Rylandt, those utterly raw recruits, who hardly knew how to handle a musket holding their own against Essling's and Rivoli's old troops, that is what was grand. Wellington was tenacious; in that lay his merit, and we are not seeking to lessen it: but the least of his foot soldiers and of his cavalry would have been as solid as he. The iron soldier is worth as much as the Iron Duke. As for us, all our glorification goes to the English soldier, to the English army, to the English people. If trophy there be, it is to England that the trophy is due. The column of Waterloo would be more just, if, instead of the figure of a man, it bore on high the statue of a people.

But this great England will be angry at what we are saying here. She still cherishes, after her own 1688 and our 1789, the feudal illusion. She believes in heredity and hierarchy. These people, surpassed by none in power and glory, regards itself as a nation, and not as a people. And as a people, it willingly subordinates itself and takes a lord for its head. As a workman, it allows itself to be disdained; as a soldier, it allows itself to be flogged.

It will be remembered, that at the battle of Inkermann a sergeant who had, it appears, saved the army, could not be mentioned by Lord Paglan, as the English military hierarchy does not permit any hero below the grade of an officer to be mentioned in the reports.

That which we admire above all, in an encounter of the nature of Waterloo, is the marvelous cleverness of chance. A nocturnal rain, the wall of Hougomont, the hollow road of Ohain, Grouchy deaf to the cannon, Napoleon's guide deceiving him, Bulow's guide enlightening him, the whole of this cataclysm is wonderfully conducted.

On the whole, let us say it plainly, it was more of a massacre than of a battle at Waterloo.

Of all pitched battles, Waterloo is the one that has the smallest front for such a number of combatants. Napoleon three-quarters of a league; Wellington, half a league; seventy-two thousand combatants on each side. From this denseness the carnage arose.

The following calculation has been made, and the following proportion established: Loss of men: at Austerlitz, French, fourteen percent; Russians, thirty percent; Austrians, forty-four percent. At Wagram, French, thirteen percent; Austrians, fourteen. At the Moskowa, French, thirty-seven percent; Russians, forty-four. At Bautzen, French, thirteen percent; Russians and Prussians, fourteen. At Waterloo, French, fifty-six percent; the Allies, thirty-one. Total for Waterloo, forty-one percent; 144,000 combatants; 60,000 dead.

Today the field of Waterloo has the calm that belongs to the earth, the impassive support of man, and it resembles all plains.

At night, moreover, a sort of visionary mist arises from it; and if a traveler strolls there, if he listens, if he watches, if he dreams like Virgil in the fatal plains of Philippi, the hallucination of the catastrophe takes possession of him. The frightful 18th of June lives again; the false monumental hillock disappears, the lion vanishes in air, the battlefield resumes its reality, lines of infantry undulate over the plain, furious gallops traverse the horizon; the frightened dreamer beholds the flash of sabers, the gleam of bayonets, the flare of bombs, the tremendous interchange of thunders; he hears, as it were, the death rattle in the depths of a tomb, the vague clamor of the battle phantom; those shadows are grenadiers, those lights are cuirassiers; that skeleton Napoleon, that other skeleton is Wellington; all this no longer exists, and yet it clashes together and combats still; and the ravines are empurpled, and the trees quiver, and there is fury even in the clouds and in the shadows; all those terrible heights, Hougomont, Mont-Saint-Jean, Frischemont, Papelotte, Plancenoit, appear confusedly crowned with whirlwinds of specters engaged in exterminating each other.

CHAPTER XVII—IS WATERLOO TO BE CONSIDERED GOOD?

There exists a very respectable liberal school that does not hate Waterloo. We do not belong to it. To us, Waterloo is but the stupefied date of liberty. That such an eagle should emerge from such an egg is certainly unexpected.

If one places one's self at the culminating point of view of the question, Waterloo is intentionally a counter-revolutionary victory. It is Europe against France; it is Petersburg, Berlin, and Vienna against Paris; it is the status quo against the initiative; it is the 14th of July, 1789, attacked through the 20th of March, 1815; it is the monarchies clearing the decks in opposition to the indomitable French rioting. The final extinction of that vast people who had been in eruption for twenty-six years—such was the dream. The solidarity of the Brunswicks, the Nassaus, the Romanoffs, the Hohenzollerns, the Hapsburgs with the Bourbons. Waterloo bears divine right on its crupper. It is true, that the Empire having been despotic, the kingdom by the natural reaction of things, was forced to be liberal, and that a constitutional order was the unwilling result of Waterloo, to the great regret of the conquerors. It is because revolution cannot be really conquered, and that being providential and absolutely fatal, it is always cropping up afresh: before Waterloo, in Bonaparte overthrowing the old thrones; after Waterloo, in Louis XVIII, granting and conforming to the charter. Bonaparte places a postilion on the throne of Naples, and a sergeant on the throne of Sweden, employing inequality to demonstrate equality; Louis XVIII at Saint-Ouen countersigns the declaration of the rights of man. If you wish to gain an idea of what revolution is, call it progress; and if you wish to acquire an idea of the nature of progress, call it tomorrow. Tomorrow fulfils its work irresistibly, and it is already fulfilling it today. It always reaches its goal strangely. It employs Wellington to make of Foy, who was only a soldier, an orator. Foy falls at Hougomont and rises again in the tribune. Thus does progress proceed. There is no such thing as a bad tool for that workman. It does not become disconcerted, but adjusts to its divine work the man who has bestridden the Alps, and the good old tottering invalid of Father Elysee. It makes use of the gouty man as well as of the conqueror; of the conqueror without, of the gouty man within. Waterloo, by cutting short the demolition of European thrones by the sword, had no other effect than to cause the revolutionary work to be continued in another direction. The slashers have finished; it was the turn of the thinkers. The century that Waterloo was

ntended to arrest has pursued its march. That sinister victory was vanquished
y liberty.

In short, and incontestably, that which triumphed at Waterloo; that which
miled in Wellington's rear; that which brought him all the marshals' staffs
f Europe, including, it is said, the staff of a marshal of France; that which
oyously trundled the barrows full of bones to erect the knoll of the lion; that
vhich triumphantly inscribed on that pedestal the date "June 18, 1815"; that
vhich encouraged Blucher, as he put the flying army to the sword; that which,
rom the heights of the plateau of Mont-Saint-Jean, hovered over France as
)ver its prey, was the counter-revolution. It was the counter-revolution which
murmured that infamous word "dismemberment." On arriving in Paris, it
eheld the crater close at hand; it felt those ashes which scorched its feet, and it
hanged its mind; it returned to the stammer of a charter.

Let us behold in Waterloo only that which is in Waterloo. Of intentional
iberty there is none. The counter-revolution was involuntarily liberal, in the
ame manner as, by a corresponding phenomenon, Napoleon was involuntarily
evolutionary. On the 18th of June, 1815, the mounted Robespierre was hurled
rom his saddle.

CHAPTER XVIII—A RECRUDESCENCE
OF DIVINE RIGHT

End of the dictatorship. A whole European system crumbled away.
The Empire sank into a gloom that resembled that of the Roman world
as it expired. Again we behold the abyss, as in the days of the barbarians; only
he barbarism of 1815, which must be called by its pet name of the counter-
revolution, was not long breathed, soon fell to panting, and halted short. The
Empire wept, let us acknowledge the fact, and wept by heroic eyes. If glory lies
in the sword converted into a scepter, the Empire had been glory in person. It
had diffused over the earth all the light which tyranny can give a somber light.
We will say more; an obscure light. Compared to the true daylight, it is night.
This disappearance of night produces the effect of an eclipse.

Louis XVIII reentered Paris. The circling dances of the 8th of July effaced
the enthusiasms of the 20th of March. The Corsican became the antithesis
of the Bearnese. The flag on the dome of the Tuileries was white. The exile
reigned. Hartwell's pine table took its place in front of the fleur-de-lis-strewn
throne of Louis XIV Bouvines and Fontenoy were mentioned as though they
had taken place on the preceding day, Austerlitz having become antiquated.

The altar and the throne fraternized majestically. One of the most undisputed forms of the health of society in the nineteenth century was established over France, and over the continent. Europe adopted the white cockade. Trestaillon was celebrated. The device *nec pluribus impar** reappeared on the stone ray representing a sun upon the front of the barracks on the Quai d'Orsay. Where there had been an Imperial Guard, there was now a red house. The Arc de Carrousel, all laden with badly borne victories, thrown out of its element among these novelties, a little ashamed, it may be, of Marengo and Arcola extricated itself from its predicament with the statue of the Duc d'Angoulême The cemetery of the Madeleine, a terrible pauper's grave in 1793, was covered with jasper and marble, since the bones of Louis XVI and Marie Antoinette lay in that dust.

In the moat of Vincennes a sepulchral shaft sprang from the earth, recalling the fact that the Duc d'Enghien had perished in the very month when Napoleon was crowned. Pope Pius VII, who had performed the coronation very near this death, tranquilly bestowed his blessing on the fall as he had bestowed it on the elevation. At Schoenbrunn there was a little shadow, aged four, whom it was seditious to call the King of Rome. And these things took place, and the king resumed their thrones, and the master of Europe was put in a cage, and the old regime became the new regime, and all the shadows and all the light of the earth changed place, because, on the afternoon of a certain summer's day, a shepherd said to a Prussian in the forest, "Go this way, and not that!"

This 1815 was a sort of lugubrious April. Ancient unhealthy and poisonous realities were covered with new appearances. A lie wedded 1789; the right divine was masked under a charter; fictions became constitutional; prejudices superstitions and mental reservations, with Article 14 in the heart, were varnished over with liberalism. It was the serpent's change of skin.

Man had been rendered both greater and smaller by Napoleon. Under this reign of splendid matter, the ideal had received the strange name of ideology It is a grave imprudence in a great man to turn the future into derision. The populace, however, that food for cannon that is so fond of the cannoneer, sought him with its glance. Where is he? What is he doing? "Napoleon is dead," said a passerby to a veteran of Marengo and Waterloo. "He dead!" cried the soldier. "You don't know him." Imagination distrusted this man, even when overthrown. The depths of Europe were full of darkness after Waterloo. Something enormous remained long empty through Napoleon's disappearance

---

* not unequal to many

The kings placed themselves in this void. Ancient Europe profited by it to undertake reforms. There was a Holy Alliance; Belle-Alliance, Beautiful Alliance, the fatal field of Waterloo had said in advance.

In presence and in face of that antique Europe reconstructed, the features of a new France were sketched out. The future, which the Emperor had rallied, made its entry. On its brow it bore the star, Liberty. The glowing eyes of all young generations were turned on it. Singular fact! People were, at one and the same time, in love with the future, Liberty, and the past, Napoleon. Defeat had rendered the vanquished greater. Bonaparte fallen seemed more lofty than Napoleon erect. Those who had triumphed were alarmed. England had him guarded by Hudson Lowe, and France had him watched by Montchenu. His folded arms became a source of uneasiness to thrones. Alexander called him "my sleeplessness." This terror was the result of the quantity of revolution contained in him. That is what explains and excuses Bonapartist liberalism. This phantom caused the old world to tremble. The kings reigned, but ill at their ease, with the rock of Saint Helena on the horizon.

While Napoleon was passing through the death struggle at Longwood, the sixty thousand men who had fallen on the field of Waterloo were quietly rotting, and something of their peace was shed abroad over the world. The Congress of Vienna made the treaties in 1815, and Europe called this the Restoration.

This is what Waterloo was.

But what matters it to the Infinite? All that tempest, all that cloud, that war, then that peace? All that darkness did not trouble for a moment the light of that immense Eye before which a grub skipping from one blade of grass to another equals the eagle soaring from belfry to belfry on the towers of Notre Dame.

CHAPTER XIX—THE
BATTLEFIELD AT NIGHT

L et us return—it is a necessity in this book—to that fatal battlefield.

On the 18th of June the moon was full. Its light favored Blucher's ferocious pursuit, betrayed the traces of the fugitives, delivered up that disastrous mass to the eager Prussian cavalry, and aided the massacre. Such tragic favors of the night do occur sometimes during catastrophes.

After the last cannon shot had been fired, the plain of Mont-Saint-Jean remained deserted.

The English occupied the encampment of the French; it is the usual sign of

victory to sleep in the bed of the vanquished. They established their bivoua
beyond Rossomme. The Prussians, let loose on the retreating rout, pushe
forward. Wellington went to the village of Waterloo to draw up his report t
Lord Bathurst.

If ever the *sic vos non vobis*[*] was applicable, it certainly is to that villag
of Waterloo. Waterloo took no part, and lay half a league from the scene o
action. Mont-Saint-Jean was cannonaded, Hougomont was burned, La Haie
Sainte was taken by assault, Papelotte was burned, Plancenoit was burnec
La Belle-Alliance beheld the embrace of the two conquerors; these name
are hardly known, and Waterloo, which worked not in the battle, bears of
all the honor.

We are not of the number of those who flatter war; when the occasio
presents itself, we tell the truth about it. War has frightful beauties that we hav
not concealed; it has also, we acknowledge, some hideous features. One o
the most surprising is the prompt stripping of the bodies of the dead after th
victory. The dawn that follows a battle always rises on naked corpses.

Who does this? Who thus soils the triumph? What hideous, furtive han
is that which is slipped into the pocket of victory? What pickpockets are the
who ply their trade in the rear of glory? Some philosophers—Voltaire amon
the number—affirm that it is precisely those persons who have made the glor
It is the same men, they say; there is no relief corps; those who are erect pillag
those who are prone on the earth. The hero of the day is the vampire of th
night. One has assuredly the right, after all, to strip a corpse a bit when one i
the author of that corpse. For our own part, we do not think so; it seems to u
impossible that the same hand should pluck laurels and purloin the shoes fror
a dead man.

One thing is certain, which is, that generally after conquerors follo
thieves. But let us leave the soldier, especially the contemporary soldier, ou
of the question.

Every army has a rearguard, and it is that which must be blamed. Batlik
creatures, half brigands and lackeys; all the sorts of bats that that twilight calle
war engenders; wearers of uniforms, who take no part in the fighting; pretende
invalids; formidable limpers; interloping merchants, trotting along in littl
carts, sometimes accompanied by their wives, and stealing things which the
sell again; beggars offering themselves as guides to officers; soldiers' servants
marauders; armies on the march in days gone by—we are not speaking of th

---

[*] This you do not for yourselves

·resent—dragged all this behind them, so that in the special language they ·re called "stragglers." No army, no nation, was responsible for those beings; ·hey spoke Italian and followed the Germans, then spoke French and followed ·he English. It was by one of these wretches, a Spanish straggler who spoke ·rench, that the Marquis of Fervacques, deceived by his Picard jargon, and ·aking him for one of our own men, was traitorously slain and robbed on ·he battlefield itself, in the course of the night which followed the victory of ·erisoles. The rascal sprang from this marauding. The detestable maxim "Live ·n the enemy!" produced this leprosy, which a strict discipline alone could heal. ·here are reputations that are deceptive; one does not always know why certain ·enerals, great in other directions, have been so popular. Turenne was adored ·y his soldiers because he tolerated pillage; evil permitted constitutes part of ·oodness. Turenne was so good that he allowed the Palatinate to be delivered ·ver to fire and blood. The marauders in the train of an army were more or less ·n number, according as the chief was more or less severe. Hoche and Marceau ·ad no stragglers; Wellington had few, and we do him the justice to mention it.

Nevertheless, on the night from the 18th to the 19th of June, the dead were ·obbed. Wellington was rigid; he gave orders that anyone caught in the act ·hould be shot; but rapine is tenacious. The marauders stole in one corner of ·he battlefield while others were being shot in another.

The moon was sinister over this plain.

Toward midnight, a man was prowling about, or rather, climbing in the ·direction of the hollow road of Ohain. To all appearance he was one of those ·whom we have just described, neither English nor French, neither peasant nor ·oldier, less a man than a ghoul attracted by the scent of the dead bodies having ·heft for his victory, and come to rifle Waterloo. He was clad in a blouse that was ·omething like a great coat; he was uneasy and audacious; he walked forward ·and gazed behind him. Who was this man? The night probably knew more of ·him than the day. He had no sack, but evidently he had large pockets under his ·coat. From time to time he halted, scrutinized the plain around him as though ·to see whether he were observed, bent over abruptly, disturbed something ·silent and motionless on the ground, then rose and fled. His sliding motion, ·his attitudes, his mysterious and rapid gestures, caused him to resemble those ·twilight larvae which haunt ruins, and which ancient Norman legends call the ·Alleurs.

Certain nocturnal wading birds produce these silhouettes among the ·marshes.

A glance capable of piercing all that mist deeply would have perceived at some distance a sort of little sutler's wagon with a fluted wicker hood, harnesse to a famished nag that was cropping the grass across its bit as it halted, hidder as it were, behind the hovel that adjoins the highway to Nivelles, at the angl of the road from Mont-Saint-Jean to Braine l'Alleud; and in the wagon, a sor of woman seated on coffers and packages. Perhaps there was some connectio between that wagon and that prowler.

The darkness was serene. Not a cloud in the zenith. What matters it if th earth be red! The moon remains white; these are the indifferences of the sky In the fields, branches of trees broken by grapeshot, but not fallen, upheld b their bark, swayed gently in the breeze of night. A breath, almost a respiration moved the shrubbery. Quivers that resembled the departure of souls ra through the grass.

In the distance the coming and going of patrols and the general rounds o the English camp were audible.

Hougomont and La Haie-Sainte continued to burn, forming, one in th west, the other in the east, two great flames that were joined by the cordon o bivouac fires of the English, like a necklace of rubies with two carbuncles a the extremities, as they extended in an immense semicircle over the hills alon the horizon.

We have described the catastrophe of the road of Ohain. The heart i terrified at the thought of what that death must have been to so many brav men.

If there is anything terrible, if there exists a reality that surpasses dreams, i is this: to live, to see the sun; to be in full possession of virile force; to posses health and joy; to laugh valiantly; to rush toward a glory that one sees dazzling in front of one; to feel in one's breast lungs which breathe, a heart that beats, will that reasons; to speak, think, hope, love; to have a mother, to have a wife to have children; to have the light—and all at once, in the space of a shout, ir less than a minute, to sink into an abyss; to fall, to roll, to crush, to be crushed to see ears of wheat, flowers, leaves, branches; not to be able to catch hold of anything; to feel one's sword useless, men beneath one, horses on top of one to struggle in vain, since one's bones have been broken by some kick in th darkness; to feel a heel which makes one's eyes start from their sockets; to bit horses' shoes in one's rage; to stifle, to yell, to writhe; to be beneath, and to say to one's self, "But just a little while ago I was a living man!"

There, where that lamentable disaster had uttered its death rattle, all wa silence now. The edges of the hollow road were encumbered with horses and riders, inextricably heaped up. Terrible entanglement! There was no longe ny slope, for the corpses had leveled the road with the plain, and reached the rim like a well-filled bushel of barley. A heap of dead bodies in the upper part, a river of blood in the lower part—such was that road on the evening of the 18th of June, 1815. The blood ran even to the Nivelles highway, and there overflowed in a large pool in front of the abatis of trees that barred the way, at a spot that is still pointed out.

It will be remembered that it was at the opposite point, in the direction of the Genappe road, that the destruction of the cuirassiers had taken place. The thickness of the layer of bodies was proportioned to the depth of the hollow road. Toward the middle, at the point where it became level, where Delort's division had passed, the layer of corpses was thinner.

The nocturnal prowler whom we have just shown to the reader was going in that direction. He was searching that vast tomb. He gazed about. He passed the dead in some sort of hideous review. He walked with his feet in the blood.

All at once he paused.

A few paces in front of him, in the hollow road, at the point where the pile of dead came to an end, an open hand, illumined by the moon, projected from beneath that heap of men. That hand had on its finger something sparkling, which was a ring of gold.

The man bent over, remained in a crouching attitude for a moment, and when he rose there was no longer a ring on the hand.

He did not precisely rise; he remained in a stooping and frightened attitude, with his back turned to the heap of dead, scanning the horizon on his knees, with the whole upper portion of his body supported on his two forefingers, which rested on the earth, and his head peering above the edge of the hollow road. The jackal's four paws suit some actions.

Then coming to a decision, he rose to his feet.

At that moment, he gave a terrible start. He felt someone clutch him from behind.

He wheeled around; it was the open hand, which had closed, and had seized the skirt of his coat.

An honest man would have been terrified; this man burst into a laugh.

"Come," said he, "it's only a dead body. I prefer a spook to a gendarme."

But the hand weakened and released him. Effort is quickly exhausted in the grave.

"Well now," said the prowler, "is that dead fellow alive? Let's see."

He bent down again, fumbled among the heap, pushed aside everything that was in his way, seized the hand, grasped the arm, freed the head, pulled out

the body, and a few moments later he was dragging the lifeless, or at least th
unconscious, man, through the shadows of hollow road. He was a cuirassier, a
officer, and even an officer of considerable rank; a large gold epaulette peepe
from beneath the cuirass; this officer no longer possessed a helmet. A furiou
sword cut had scarred his face, where nothing was discernible but blood.

However, he did not appear to have any broken limbs, and, by some happy
chance, if that word is permissible here, the dead had been vaulted above him i
such a manner as to preserve him from being crushed. His eyes were still closed

On his cuirass he wore the silver cross of the Legion of Honor.

The prowler tore off this cross, which disappeared into one of the gulfs tha
he had beneath his great coat.

Then he felt of the officer's fob, discovered a watch there, and too
possession of it. Next he searched his waistcoat, found a purse and pocketed it

When he had arrived at this stage of succor that he was administering to
this dying man, the officer opened his eyes.

"Thanks," he said feebly.

The abruptness of the movements of the man who was manipulating him
the freshness of the night, the air, which he could inhale freely, had roused him
from his lethargy.

The prowler made no reply. He raised his head. A sound of footsteps was
audible in the plain; some patrol was probably approaching.

The officer murmured, for the death agony was still in his voice, "Who
won the battle?"

"The English," answered the prowler.

The officer went on, "Look in my pockets; you will find a watch and a
purse. Take them."

It was already done.

The prowler executed the required feint, and said, "There is nothing there."

"I have been robbed," said the officer; "I am sorry for that. You should
have had them."

The steps of the patrol became more and more distinct.

"Someone is coming," said the prowler, with the movement of a man who
is taking his departure.

The officer raised his arm feebly, and detained him.

"You have saved my life. Who are you?"

The prowler answered rapidly, and in a low voice, "Like yourself, I
belonged to the French army. I must leave you. If they were to catch me, they
would shoot me. I have saved your life. Now get out of the scrape yourself."

"What is your rank?"

"Sergeant."

"What is your name?"

"Thenardier."

"I shall not forget that name," said the officer; "and do you remember mine. My name is Pontmercy."

BOOK SECOND: THE SHIP ORION

CHAPTER I—NUMBER 24601 BECOMES NUMBER 9430

Jean Valjean had been recaptured.

The reader will be grateful to us if we pass rapidly over the sad details. We will confine ourselves to transcribing two paragraphs published by the journals of that day, a few months after the surprising events that had taken place at M. sur M.

These articles are rather summary. It must be remembered, that at that epoch the *Gazette des Tribunaux* was not yet in existence.

We borrow the first from the Drapeau Blanc. It bears the date of July 25, 1823.

An arrondissement of the Pas de Calais has just been the theater of an event quite out of the ordinary course. A man, who was a stranger in the Department, and who bore the name of M. Madeleine, had, thanks to the new methods, resuscitated some years ago an ancient local industry, the manufacture of jet and of black glass trinkets. He had made his fortune in the business, and that of the arrondissement as well, we will admit. He had been appointed mayor, in recognition of his services. The police discovered that M. Madeleine was no other than an ex-convict who had broken his ban, condemned in 1796 for theft, and named Jean Valjean. Jean Valjean has been recommitted to prison. It appears that previous to his arrest he had succeeded in withdrawing from the hands of M. Laffitte, a sum of over half a million which he had lodged there, and which he had, moreover, and by perfectly legitimate means, acquired in his business. No one has been able to discover where Jean Valjean has concealed this money since his return to prison at Toulon.

The second article, which enters a little more into detail, is an extract from the *Journal de Paris*, of the same date.

A former convict, who had been liberated, named Jean Valjean, has just appeared before the Court of Assizes of the Var, under circumstances calculated to attract attention. This wretch had succeeded in escaping the vigilance of the police, he had changed his name, and had succeeded in getting himself appointed mayor of one of our small northern towns; in this town he had established a considerable commerce. He has at last been unmasked and arrested, thanks to the indefatigable zeal of the public prosecutor. He had for his concubine a woman of the town, who died of a shock at the moment of his arrest. This scoundrel, who is endowed with Herculean strength, found means to escape; but three or four days after his flight the police laid their hands on him once more, in Paris itself, at the very moment when he was entering one of those little vehicles that run between the capital and the village of Montfermeil (Seine-et-Oise). He is said to have profited by this interval of three or four days of liberty, to withdraw a considerable sum deposited by him with one of our leading bankers. This sum has been estimated at six or seven hundred thousand francs. If the indictment is to be trusted, he has hidden it in some place known to himself alone, and it has not been possible to lay hands on it. However that may be, the said Jean Valjean has just been brought before the Assizes of the Department of the Var as accused of highway robbery accompanied with violence, about eight years ago, on the person of one of those honest children who, as the patriarch of Ferney has said, in immortal verse:

> ". . . Arrive from Savoy every year,
> And who, with gentle hands, do clear
> Those long canals choked up with soot."

This bandit refused to defend himself. It was proved by the skilful and eloquent representative of the public prosecutor that the theft was committed in complicity with others, and that Jean Valjean was a member of a band of robbers in the south. Jean Valjean was pronounced guilty and was condemned to the death penalty in consequence. This criminal refused to lodge an appeal. The king, in his inexhaustible clemency, has deigned to commute his penalty to that of penal servitude for life. Jean Valjean was immediately taken to the prison at Toulon.

The reader has not forgotten that Jean Valjean had religious habits at M. sur M. Some papers, among others the Constitutional, presented this commutation as a triumph of the priestly party.

Jean Valjean changed his number in the galleys. He was called 9430.

However, and we will mention it at once in order that we may not be obliged to recur to the subject, the prosperity of M. sur M. vanished with M. Madeleine; all that he had foreseen during his night of fever and hesitation was realized; lacking him, there actually was a soul lacking. After this fall, there took place at M. sur M. that egotistical division of great existences that have fallen, that fatal dismemberment of flourishing things, which is accomplished every day, obscurely, in the human community, and which history has noted only once, because it occurred after the death of Alexander. Lieutenants are crowned kings; superintendents improvise manufacturers out of themselves. Envious rivalries arose. M. Madeleine's vast workshops were shut; his buildings fell to ruin, his workmen were scattered. Some of them quitted the country, others abandoned the trade. Thenceforth, everything was done on a small scale, instead of on a grand scale; for lucre instead of the general good. There was no longer a center; everywhere there was competition and animosity. M. Madeleine had reigned over all and directed all. No sooner had he fallen, than each pulled things to himself; the spirit of combat succeeded to the spirit of organization, bitterness to cordiality, hatred of one another to the benevolence of the founder toward all; the threads that M. Madeleine had set were tangled and broken, the methods were adulterated, the products were debased, confidence was killed; the market diminished, for lack of orders; salaries were reduced, the workshops stood still, bankruptcy arrived. And then there was nothing more for the poor. All had vanished.

The state itself perceived that someone had been crushed somewhere. Less than four years after the judgment of the Court of Assizes establishing the identity of Jean Valjean and M. Madeleine, for the benefit of the galleys, the cost of collecting taxes had doubled in the arrondissement of M. sur M.; and M. de Villele called attention to the fact in the rostrum, in the month of February, 1827.

CHAPTER II—IN WHICH THE READER WILL PERUSE TWO VERSES, WHICH ARE OF THE DEVIL'S COMPOSITION, POSSIBLY

Before proceeding further, it will be to the purpose to narrate in some detail, a singular occurrence that took place at about the same epoch, in Montfermeil, and which is not lacking in coincidence with certain conjectures of the indictment.

There exists in the region of Montfermeil a very ancient superstition, which is all the more curious and all the more precious, because a popular superstition in the vicinity of Paris is like an aloe in Siberia. We are among those who respect everything that is in the nature of a rare plant. Here, then, is the superstition of Montfermeil: it is thought that the devil, from time immemorial, has selected the forest as a hiding place for his treasures. Goodwives affirm that it is no rarity to encounter at nightfall, in secluded nooks of the forest, a black man with the air of a carter or a wood chopper, wearing wooden shoes, clad in trousers and a blouse of linen, and recognizable by the fact, that, instead of a cap or hat, he has two immense horns on his head. This ought, in fact, to render him recognizable. This man is habitually engaged in digging a hole. There are three ways of profiting by such an encounter. The first is to approach the man and speak to him. Then it is seen that the man is simply a peasant, that he appears black because it is nightfall; that he is not digging any hole whatever, but is cutting grass for his cows, and that what had been taken for horns is nothing but a dung fork that he is carrying on his back, and whose teeth, thanks to the perspective of evening, seemed to spring from his head. The man returns home and dies within the week. The second way is to watch him, to wait until he has dug his hole, until he has filled it and has gone away; then to run with great speed to the trench, to open it once more and to seize the "treasure" that the black man has necessarily placed there. In this case one dies within the month. Finally, the last method is not to speak to the black man, not to look at him, and to flee at the best speed of one's legs. One then dies within the year.

As all three methods are attended with their special inconveniences, the second, which at all events, presents some advantages, among others that of possessing a treasure, if only for a month, is the one most generally adopted. So bold men, who are tempted by every chance, have quite frequently, as we are assured, opened the holes excavated by the black man, and tried to rob the devil. The success of the operation appears to be but moderate. At least, if the tradition is to be believed, and in particular the two enigmatical lines in barbarous Latin, which an evil Norman monk, a bit of a sorcerer, named Tryphon has left on this subject. This Tryphon is buried at the Abbéy of Saint-Georges de Bocherville, near Rouen, and toads spawn on his grave.

Accordingly, enormous efforts are made. Such trenches are ordinarily extremely deep; a man sweats, digs, toils all night—for it must be done at night; he wets his shirt, burns out his candle, breaks his mattock, and when he arrives at the bottom of the hole, when he lays his hand on the "treasure," what does he find? What is the devil's treasure? A sou, sometimes a crown-piece, a stone, a skeleton, a bleeding body, sometimes a specter folded in four like a sheet of paper in a portfolio, sometimes nothing. This is what Tryphon's verses seem to announce to the indiscreet and curious:

> *"Fodit, et in fossa thesauros condit opaca,*
> *As, nummas, lapides, cadaver, simulacra, nihilque."*

It seems that in our day there is sometimes found a powder horn with bullets, sometimes an old pack of cards greasy and worn, which has evidently served the devil. Tryphon does not record these two finds, since Tryphon lived in the twelfth century, and since the devil does not appear to have had the wit to invent powder before Roger Bacon's time, and cards before the time of Charles VI.

Moreover, if one plays at cards, one is sure to lose all that one possesses! And as for the powder in the horn, it possesses the property of making your gun burst in your face.

Now, a very short time after the epoch when it seemed to the prosecuting attorney that the liberated convict Jean Valjean during his flight of several days had been prowling around Montfermeil, it was remarked in that village that a certain old road laborer, named Boulatruelle, had "peculiar ways" in the forest. People thereabouts thought they knew that this Boulatruelle had been in the galleys. He was subjected to certain police supervision, and, as he could find work nowhere, the administration employed him at reduced rates as a road mender on the crossroad from Gagny to Lagny.

This Boulatruelle was a man who was viewed with disfavor by the inhabitants of the district as too respectful, too humble, too prompt in removing his cap to everyone, and trembling and smiling in the presence of the gendarmes, probably affiliated to robber bands, they said; suspected of lying in ambush at verge of copses at nightfall. The only thing in his favor was that he was a drunkard.

This is what people thought they had noticed:

Of late, Boulatruelle had taken to quitting his task of stone-breaking and care of the road at a very early hour, and to be taking himself to the forest with his pickax. He was encountered toward evening in the most deserted clearings, in the wildest thickets; and he had the appearance of being in search of something, and sometimes he was digging holes. The goodwives who passed took him at first for Beelzebub; then they recognized Boulatruelle, and were not in the least reassured thereby. These encounters seemed to cause Boulatruelle a lively displeasure. It was evident that he sought to hide, and that there was some mystery in what he was doing.

It was said in the village, "It is clear that the devil has appeared. Boulatruelle has seen him, and is on the search. In sooth, he is cunning enough to pocket Lucifer's hoard."

The Voltairians added, "Will Boulatruelle catch the devil, or will the devil catch Boulatruelle?" The old women made a great many signs of the cross.

In the meantime, Boulatruelle's maneuvers in the forest ceased; and he resumed his regular occupation of road mending; and people gossiped of something else.

Some persons, however, were still curious, surmising that in all this there was probably no fabulous treasure of the legends, but some fine windfall of a more serious and palpable sort than the devil's bank bills, and that the road mender had half discovered the secret. The most "puzzled" were the schoolmaster and Thenardier, the proprietor of the tavern, who was everybody's friend, and had not disdained to ally himself with Boulatruelle.

"He has been in the galleys," said Thenardier. "Eh! Good God! No one knows who has been there or will be there."

One evening the schoolmaster affirmed that in former times the law would have instituted an inquiry as to what Boulatruelle did in the forest, and that the latter would have been forced to speak, and that he would have been put to the torture in case of need, and that Boulatruelle would not have resisted the water test, for example. "Let us put him to the wine test," said Thenardier.

They made an effort, and got the old road mender to drinking. Boulatruelle drank an enormous amount, but said very little. He combined with admirable art, and in masterly proportions, the thirst of a gormandizer with the discretion of a judge. Nevertheless, by dint of returning to the charge and of comparing and putting together the few obscure words which he did allow to escape him, this is what Thenardier and the schoolmaster imagined that they had made out:

One morning, when Boulatruelle was on his way to his work, at daybreak, he had been surprised to see, at a nook of the forest in the underbrush, a shovel and a pickax, concealed, as one might say.

However, he might have supposed that they were probably the shovel and pick of Father Six-Fours, the water carrier, and would have thought no more about it. But, on the evening of that day, he saw, without being seen himself, as he was hidden by a large tree, "a person who did not belong in those parts, and whom he, Boulatruelle, knew well," directing his steps toward the densest part of the wood. Translation by Thenardier: A comrade of the galleys. Boulatruelle obstinately refused to reveal his name. This person carried a package—something square, like a large box or a small trunk. Surprise on the part of Boulatruelle. However, it was only after the expiration of seven or eight minutes that the idea of following that "person" had occurred to him. But it was too late; the person was already in the thicket, night had descended, and Boulatruelle had not been able to catch up with him. Then he had adopted the course of watching for him at the edge of the woods. "It was moonlight." Two or three hours later, Boulatruelle had seen this person emerge from the brushwood, carrying no longer the coffer, but a shovel and pick. Boulatruelle had allowed the person to pass, and had not dreamed of accosting him, because he said to himself that the other man was three times as strong as he was, and armed with a pickax, and that he would probably knock him over the head on recognizing him, and on perceiving that he was recognized. Touching effusion of two old comrades on meeting again. But the shovel and pick had served as a ray of light to Boulatruelle; he had hastened to the thicket in the morning, and had found neither shovel nor pick. From this he had drawn the inference that this person, once in the forest, had dug a hole with his pick, buried the coffer, and reclosed the hole with his shovel. Now, the coffer was too small to contain a body; therefore it contained money. Hence his researches. Boulatruelle had explored, sounded, searched the entire forest and the thicket, and had dug wherever the earth appeared to him to have been recently turned up. In vain.

He had "ferreted out" nothing. No one in Montfermeil thought any more about it. There were only a few brave gossips, who said, "You may be certain that the mender on the Gagny road did not take all that trouble for nothing; he was sure that the devil had come."

CHAPTER III—THE ANKLE-CHAIN MUST HAVE UNDERGONE A CERTAIN PREPARATORY MANIPULATION TO BE THUS BROKEN WITH A BLOW FROM A HAMMER

Toward the end of October, in that same year, 1823, the inhabitants of Toulon beheld the entry into their port, after heavy weather, and for the purpose of repairing some damages, of the ship *Orion*, which was employed later at Brest as a school ship, and which then formed a part of the Mediterranean squadron.

This vessel, battered as it was—for the sea had handled it roughly—produced a fine effect as it entered the roads. It flew some colors that procured for it the regulation salute of eleven guns, which it returned, shot for shot; total, twenty-two. It has been calculated that what with salvos, royal and military politeness, courteous exchanges of uproar, signals of etiquette, formalities of roadsteads and citadels, sunrises and sunsets, saluted every day by all fortresses and all ships of war, openings and closings of ports, etc., the civilized world, discharged all over the earth, in the course of four and twenty hours, one hundred and fifty thousand useless shots. At six francs per shot, that comes to nine hundred thousand francs a day, three hundred millions a year, which vanish in smoke. This is a mere detail. All this time the poor were dying of hunger.

The year 1823 was what the Restoration called "the epoch of the Spanish War."

This war contained many events in one, and a quantity of peculiarities. A grand family affair for the house of Bourbon; the branch of France succoring and protecting the branch of Madrid, that is to say, performing an act devolving on the elder; an apparent return to our national traditions, complicated by servitude and by subjection to the cabinets of the North; M. le Duc d'Angoulême, surnamed by the liberal sheets the hero of Andujar, compressing in a triumphal attitude that was somewhat contradicted by his peaceable air, the ancient and very powerful terrorism of the Holy Office at variance with the chimerical terrorism of the liberals; the sansculottes resuscitated, to the great terror of dowagers, under the name of descamisados; monarchy opposing an obstacle to progress described as anarchy; the theories of '89 roughly interrupted in the sap; a European halt, called to the French idea, which was making the tour of the world; beside the son of France as generalissimo, the Prince de Carignan, afterward Charles Albert, enrolling himself in that crusade of kings against people as a volunteer, with grenadier epaulets of red worsted; the soldiers of the Empire setting out on a fresh campaign, but aged, saddened, after eight years of repose, and under the white cockade; the tricolored standard waved abroad by a heroic handful of Frenchmen, as the white standard had been thirty years earlier at Coblentz; monks mingled with our troops; the spirit of liberty and of novelty brought to its senses by bayonets; principles slaughtered by cannonades; France undoing by her arms that which she had done by her mind; in addition to this, hostile leaders sold, soldiers hesitating, cities besieged by millions; no military perils, and yet possible explosions, as in every mine that is surprised and invaded; but little bloodshed, little honor won, shame for some, glory for no one. Such was this war, made by the princes descended from Louis XIV, and conducted by generals who had been under Napoleon. Its sad fate was to recall neither the grand war nor grand politics.

Some feats of arms were serious; the taking of the Trocadero, among others, was a fine military action; but after all, we repeat, the trumpets of this war give back a cracked sound, the whole effect was suspicious; history approves of France for making a difficulty about accepting this false triumph. It seemed evident that certain Spanish officers charged with resistance yielded too easily; the idea of corruption was connected with the victory; it appears as though generals and not battles had been won, and the conquering soldier returned humiliated. A debasing war, in short, in which the Bank of France could be read in the folds of the flag.

Soldiers of the war of 1808, on whom Saragossa had fallen in formidable ruin, frowned in 1823 at the easy surrender of citadels, and began to regret Palafox. It is the nature of France to prefer to have Rostopchine rather than Ballesteros in front of her.

From a still more serious point of view, and one which it is also proper to insist upon here, this war, which wounded the military spirit of France, enraged the democratic spirit. It was an enterprise of enthrallment. In that campaign, the object of the French soldier, the son of democracy, was the conquest of a yoke for others. A hideous contradiction. France is made to arouse the soul of nations, not to stifle it. All the revolutions of Europe since 1792 are the French Revolution: liberty darts rays from France. That is a solar fact. Blind is he who will not see! It was Bonaparte who said it.

The war of 1823, an outrage on the generous Spanish nation, was then, at the same time, an outrage on the French Revolution. It was France who committed this monstrous violence; by foul means, for, with the exception of wars of liberation, everything that armies do is by foul means. The words passive obedience indicate this. An army is a strange masterpiece of combination where force results from an enormous sum of impotence. Thus is war, made by humanity against humanity, despite humanity, explained.

As for the Bourbons, the war of 1823 was fatal to them. They took it for a success. They did not perceive the danger that lies in having an idea slain to order. They went astray, in their innocence, to such a degree that they introduced the immense enfeeblement of a crime into their establishment as an element of strength. The spirit of the ambush entered into their politics. 1830 had its germ in 1823. The Spanish campaign became in their counsels an argument for force and for adventures by right divine. France, having reestablished elrey netto in Spain, might well have re-established the absolute king at home. They fell into the alarming error of taking the obedience of the soldier for the consent of the nation. Such confidence is the ruin of thrones. It is not permitted to fall asleep, either in the shadow of a machineel tree, nor in the shadow of an army.

Let us return to the ship *Orion*.

During the operations of the army commanded by the prince generalissimo, a squadron had been cruising in the Mediterranean. We have just stated that the *Orion* belonged to this fleet, and that accidents of the sea had brought it into port at Toulon.

The presence of a vessel of war in a port has something about it that attracts and engages a crowd. It is because it is great, and the crowd loves what is great.

A ship of the line is one of the most magnificent combinations of the genius of man with the powers of nature.

A ship of the line is composed, at the same time, of the heaviest and the lightest of possible matter, for it deals at one and the same time with three forms of substance—solid, liquid, and fluid—and it must do battle with all three. It has eleven claws of iron with which to seize the granite on the bottom of the sea, and more wings and more antennae than winged insects, to catch the wind in the clouds. Its breath pours out through its hundred and twenty cannons as through enormous trumpets, and replies proudly to the thunder. The ocean seeks to lead it astray in the alarming sameness of its billows, but the vessel has its soul, its compass, which counsels it and always shows it the north. In the blackest nights, its lanterns supply the place of the stars. Thus, against the wind, it has its cordage and its canvas; against the water, wood; against the rocks, its iron, brass, and lead; against the shadows, its light; against immensity, a needle.

If one wishes to form an idea of all those gigantic proportions, which, taken as a whole, constitute the ship of the line, one has only to enter one of the six-story covered construction stocks, in the ports of Brest or Toulon. The vessels in process of construction are under a bell glass there, as it were. This colossal beam is a yard; that great column of wood that stretches out on the earth as far as the eye can reach is the mainmast. Taking it from its root in the stocks to its tip in the clouds, it is sixty fathoms long, and its diameter at its base is three feet. The English mainmast rises to a height of two hundred and seventeen feet above the waterline. The navy of our fathers employed cables, ours employs chains. The simple pile of chains on a ship of a hundred guns is four feet high, twenty feet in breadth, and eight feet in depth. And how much wood is required to make this ship? Three-thousand cubic meters. It is a floating forest.

And moreover, let this be borne in mind, it is only a question here of the military vessel of forty years ago, of the simple sailing vessel; steam, then in its infancy, has since added new miracles to that prodigy, which is called a war vessel. At the present time, for example, the mixed vessel with a screw is a surprising machine, propelled by three thousand square meters of canvas and by an engine of 2,500 horsepower.

Not to mention these new marvels, the ancient vessel of Christopher Columbus and of De Ruyter is one of the masterpieces of man. It is as inexhaustible in force as is the Infinite in gales; it stores up the wind in its sails, it is precise in the immense vagueness of the billows, it floats, and it reigns.

There comes an hour, nevertheless, when the gale breaks that sixty-foot yard like a straw, when the wind bends that mast four hundred feet tall, when that anchor, which weighs tens of thousands, is twisted in the jaws of the waves like a fisherman's hook in the jaws of a pike, when those monstrous cannons utter plaintive and futile roars, which the hurricane bears forth into the void and into night, when all that power and all that majesty are engulfed in a power and majesty, which are superior.

Every time that immense force is displayed to culminate in an immense feebleness it affords men food for thought. Hence in the ports curious people abound around these marvelous machines of war and of navigation, without being able to explain perfectly to themselves why. Every day, accordingly, from morning until night, the quays, sluices, and the jetties of the port of Toulon were covered with a multitude of idlers and loungers, as they say in Paris, whose business consisted in staring at the *Orion*.

The *Orion* was a ship that had been ailing for a long time; in the course of its previous cruises thick layers of barnacles had collected on its keel to such a degree as to deprive it of half its speed; it had gone into the dry dock the year before this, in order to have the barnacles scraped off, then it had put to sea again; but this cleaning had affected the bolts of the keel: in the neighborhood of the Balearic Isles the sides had been strained and had opened; and, as the plating in those days was not of sheet iron, the vessel had sprung a leak. A violent equinoctial gale had come up, which had first staved in a grating and a porthole on the larboard side, and damaged the foretop-gallant-shrouds; in consequence of these injuries, the *Orion* had run back to Toulon.

It anchored near the Arsenal; it was fully equipped, and repairs were begun. The hull had received no damage on the starboard, but some of the planks had been unnailed here and there, according to custom, to permit of air entering the hold.

One morning the crowd that was gazing at it witnessed an accident.

The crew was busy bending the sails; the topman, who had to take the upper corner of the main topsail on the starboard, lost his balance; he was seen to waver; the multitude thronging the Arsenal quay uttered a cry; the man's head overbalanced his body; the man fell around the yard, with his hands outstretched toward the abyss; on his way he seized the footrope, first with one hand, then with the other, and remained hanging from it: the sea lay below him at a dizzy depth; the shock of his fall had imparted to the footrope a violent swinging motion; the man swayed back and forth at the end of that rope, like a stone in a sling.

It was incurring a frightful risk to go to his assistance; not one of the sailors, all fishermen of the coast, recently levied for the service, dared to attempt it. In the meantime, the unfortunate topman was losing his strength; his anguish could not be discerned on his face, but his exhaustion was visible in every limb; his arms were contracted in horrible twitchings; every effort which he made to reascend served but to augment the oscillations of the footrope; he did not shout, for fear of exhausting his strength. All were awaiting the minute when he should release his hold on the rope, and, from instant to instant, heads were turned aside that his fall might not be seen. There are moments when a bit of rope, a pole, the branch of a tree, is life itself, and it is a terrible thing to see a living being detach himself from it and fall like a ripe fruit.

All at once a man was seen climbing into the rigging with the agility of a tiger; this man was dressed in red; he was a convict; he wore a green cap; he was a life convict. On arriving on a level with the top, a gust of wind carried away his cap, and allowed a perfectly white head to be seen: he was not a young man.

A convict employed on board with a detachment from the galleys had, in fact, at the very first instant, hastened to the officer of the watch, and, in the midst of the consternation and the hesitation of the crew, while all the sailors were trembling and drawing back, he had asked the officer's permission to risk his life to save the topman; at an affirmative sign from the officer he had broken the chain riveted to his ankle with one blow of a hammer, then he had caught up a rope, and had dashed into the rigging: no one noticed, at the instant, with what ease that chain had been broken; it was only later on that the incident was recalled.

In a twinkling he was on the yard; he paused for a few seconds and appeared to be measuring it with his eye; these seconds, during which the breeze swayed the topman at the extremity of a thread, seemed centuries to those who were looking on. At last, the convict raised his eyes to heaven and advanced a step: the crowd drew a long breath. He was seen to run out along the yard: on arriving at the point, he fastened the rope which he had brought to it, and allowed the other end to hang down, then he began to descend the rope, hand over hand, and then—and the anguish was indescribable—instead of one man suspended over the gulf, there were two.

One would have said it was a spider coming to seize a fly, only here the spider brought life, not death. Ten thousand glances were fastened on this group; not a cry, not a word; the same tremor contracted every brow; all mouths held their breath as though they feared to add the slightest puff to the wind which was swaying the two unfortunate men.

In the meantime, the convict had succeeded in lowering himself to a position near the sailor. It was high time; one minute more, and the exhausted and despairing man would have allowed himself to fall into the abyss. The convict had moored him securely with the cord to which he clung with one hand, while he was working with the other. At last, he was seen to climb back on the yard, and to drag the sailor up after him; he held him there a moment to allow him to recover his strength, then he grasped him in his arms and carried him, walking on the yard himself to the cap, and from there to the maintop, where he left him in the hands of his comrades.

At that moment the crowd broke into applause: old convict-sergeants among them wept, and women embraced each other on the quay, and all voices were heard to cry with a sort of tender rage, "Pardon for that man!"

He, in the meantime, had immediately begun to make his descent to rejoin his detachment. In order to reach them the more speedily, he dropped into the rigging, and ran along one of the lower yards; all eyes were following him. At a certain moment fear assailed them; whether it was that he was fatigued, or that his head turned, they thought they saw him hesitate and stagger. All at once the crowd uttered a loud shout: the convict had fallen into the sea.

The fall was perilous. The frigate Algesiras was anchored alongside the Orion, and the poor convict had fallen between the two vessels: it was to be feared that he would slip under one or the other of them. Four men flung themselves hastily into a boat; the crowd cheered them on; anxiety again took possession of all souls; the man had not risen to the surface; he had disappeared in the sea without leaving a ripple, as though he had fallen into a cask of oil: they sounded, they dived. In vain. The search was continued until the evening: they did not even find the body.

On the following day the Toulon newspaper printed these lines:

Nov. 17, 1823.
Yesterday, a convict belonging to the detachment on board of the Orion, on his return from rendering assistance to a sailor,

fell into the sea and was drowned. The body has not yet been found; it is supposed that it is entangled among the piles of the Arsenal point: this man was committed under the number 9430, and his name was Jean Valjean.

BOOK THIRD: ACCOMPLISHMENT OF THE PROMISE MADE TO THE DEAD WOMAN

CHAPTER I—THE WATER QUESTION AT MONTFERMEIL

Montfermeil is situated between Livry and Chelles, on the southern edge of that lofty tableland that separates the Ourcq from the Marne. At the present day it is a tolerably large town, ornamented all the year through with plaster villas, and on Sundays with beaming bourgeois. In 1823 there were at Montfermeil neither so many white houses nor so many well-satisfied citizens: it was only a village in the forest. Some pleasure-houses of the last century were to be met with there, to be sure, which were recognizable by their grand air, their balconies in twisted iron, and their long windows, whose tiny panes cast all sorts of varying shades of green on the white of the closed shutters; but Montfermeil was nonetheless a village. Retired cloth merchants and rusticating attorneys had not discovered it as yet; it was a peaceful and charming place, which was not on the road to anywhere: there people lived, and cheaply, that peasant rustic life which is so bounteous and so easy; only, water was rare there, on account of the elevation of the plateau.

It was necessary to fetch it from a considerable distance; the end of the village toward Gagny drew its water from the magnificent ponds that exist in the woods there. The other end, which surrounds the church and which lies in the direction of Chelles, found drinking water only at a little spring halfway down the slope, near the road to Chelles, about a quarter of an hour from Montfermeil.

Thus each household found it hard work to keep supplied with water. The large houses, the aristocracy, of which the Thenardier tavern formed a part, paid half a farthing a bucketful to a man who made a business of it, and who earned about eight sous a day in his enterprise of supplying Montfermeil with water; but this goodman only worked until seven o'clock in the evening in summer, and five in winter; and night once come and the shutters on the ground floor once closed, he who had no water to drink went to fetch it for himself or did without it.

This constituted the terror of the poor creature whom the reader has probably not forgotten, little Cosette. It will be remembered that Cosette was useful to the Thenardiers in two ways: they made the mother pay them, and they made the child serve them. So when the mother ceased to pay altogether, the reason for which we have read in preceding chapters, the Thenardiers kept Cosette. She took the place of a servant in their house. In this capacity it was she who ran to fetch water when it was required. So the child, who was greatly terrified at the idea of going to the spring at night, took great care that water should never be lacking in the house.

Christmas of the year 1823 was particularly brilliant at Montfermeil. The beginning of the winter had been mild; there had been neither snow nor frost up to that time. Some mountebanks from Paris had obtained permission of the mayor to erect their booths in the principal street of the village, and a band of itinerant merchants, under protection of the same tolerance, had constructed their stalls on the Church Square, and even extended them into Boulanger Alley, where, as the reader will perhaps remember, the Thenardiers' hostelry was situated. These people filled the inns and drinking shops, and communicated to that tranquil little district a noisy and joyous life. In order to play the part of a faithful historian, we ought even to add that, among the curiosities displayed in the square, there was a menagerie, in which frightful clowns, clad in rags and coming no one knew from where, exhibited to the peasants of Montfermeil in 1823 one of those horrible Brazilian vultures, such as our Royal Museum did not possess until 1845, and which have a tricolored cockade for an eye. I believe that naturalists call this bird *Caracara polyborus*; it belongs to the order of the Apicides, and to the family of the vultures. Some good old Bonapartist soldiers, who had retired to the village, went to see this creature with great devotion. The mountebanks gave out that the tricolored cockade was a unique phenomenon made by God expressly for their menagerie.

On Christmas eve itself, a number of men, carters, and peddlers, were seated at table, drinking and smoking around four or five candles in the public room of Thenardier's hostelry. This room resembled all drinking-shop rooms, tables, pewter jugs, bottles, drinkers, smokers; but little light and a great deal of noise. The date of the year 1823 was indicated, nevertheless, by two objects which were then fashionable in the bourgeois class: to wit, a kaleidoscope and a lamp of ribbed tin. The female Thenardier was attending to the supper, which was roasting in front of a clear fire; her husband was drinking with his customers and talking politics.

Besides political conversations which had for their principal subjects the Spanish war and M. le Duc d'Angoulême, strictly local parentheses, like the following, were audible amid the uproar, "About Nanterre and Suresnes the vines have flourished greatly. When ten pieces were reckoned on there have been twelve. They have yielded a great deal of juice under the press." "But the grapes cannot be ripe?" "In those parts the grapes should not be ripe; the wine turns oily as soon as spring comes." "Then it is very thin wine?" "There are wines poorer even than these. The grapes must be gathered while green." Etc.

Or a miller would call out, "Are we responsible for what is in the sacks? We find in them a quantity of small seed which we cannot sift out, and which we are obliged to send through the millstones; there are tares, fennel, vetches, hempseed, foxtail, and a host of other weeds, not to mention pebbles, which abound in certain wheat, especially in Breton wheat. I am not fond of grinding Breton wheat, any more than long-sawyers like to saw beams with nails in them. You can judge of the bad dust that makes in grinding. And then people complain of the flour. They are in the wrong. The flour is no fault of ours."

In a space between two windows a mower, who was seated at table with a landed proprietor who was fixing on a price for some meadow work to be performed in the spring, was saying, "It does no harm to have the grass wet. It cuts better. Dew is a good thing, Sir. It makes no difference with that grass. Your grass is young and very hard to cut still. It's terribly tender. It yields before the iron." Etc.

Cosette was in her usual place, seated on the crossbar of the kitchen table near the chimney. She was in rags; her bare feet were thrust into wooden shoes, and by the firelight she was engaged in knitting woolen stockings destined for the young Thenardiers. A very young kitten was playing about among the chairs. Laughter and chatter were audible in the adjoining room, from two fresh children's voices: it was Eponine and Azelma.

In the chimney corner a cat-o'-nine-tails was hanging on a nail.

At intervals the cry of a very young child, which was somewhere in the house, rang through the noise of the dramshop. It was a little boy who had been born to the Thenardiers during one of the preceding winters. She did not know why, she said, "the result of the cold"—and who was a little more than three years old. The mother had nursed him, but she did not love him.

When the persistent clamor of the brat became too annoying, "Your son is squalling," Thenardier would say; "do go and see what he wants."

"Bah!" the mother would reply. "He bothers me."

And the neglected child continued to shriek in the dark.

CHAPTER II—TWO COMPLETE PORTRAITS

So far in this book the Thenardiers have been viewed only in profile; the moment has arrived for making the circuit of this couple, and considering it under all its aspects.

Thenardier had just passed his fiftieth birthday; Madame Thenardier was approaching her forties, which is equivalent to fifty in a woman; so that there existed a balance of age between husband and wife.

Our readers have possibly preserved some recollection of this Thenardier woman, ever since her first appearance—tall, blonde, red, fat, angular, square, enormous, and agile—she belonged, as we have said, to the race of those colossal wild women, who contort themselves at fairs with paving stones hanging from their hair. She did everything about the house—made the beds, did the washing, the cooking, and everything else. Cosette was her only servant; a mouse in the service of an elephant. Everything trembled at the sound of her voice—window panes, furniture, and people. Her big face, dotted with red blotches, presented the appearance of a skimmer. She had a beard. She was an ideal market-porter dressed in woman's clothes. She swore splendidly; she boasted of being able to crack a nut with one blow of her fist. Except for the romances that she had read, and which made the affected lady peep through the ogress at times, in a very queer way, the idea would never have occurred to anyone to say of her, "That is a woman." This Thenardier female was like the product of a wench engrafted on a fishwife. When one heard her speak, one said, "That is a gendarme"; when one saw her drink, one said, "That is a carter"; when one saw her handle Cosette, one said, "That is the hangman." One of her teeth projected when her face was in repose.

Thenardier was a small, thin, pale, angular, bony, feeble man, who had a sickly air and who was wonderfully healthy. His cunning began here; he smiled habitually, by way of precaution, and was almost polite to everybody, even to the beggar to whom he refused half a farthing. He had the glance of a polecat and the bearing of a man of letters. He greatly resembled the portraits of the Abbé Delille. His coquetry consisted in drinking with the carters. No one had ever succeeded in rendering him drunk. He smoked a big pipe. He wore a blouse, and under his blouse an old black coat. He made pretensions to literature and to materialism. There were certain names that he often pronounced to support whatever things he might be saying—Voltaire, Raynal, Parny, and, singularly enough, Saint Augustine. He declared that he had "a system." In addition, he was a great swindler. A *filousophe*, a scientific thief. The species does exist. It will be remembered that he pretended to have served in the army; he was in the habit of relating with exuberance, how, being a sergeant in the 6th or the 9th light something or other, at Waterloo, he had alone, and in the presence of a squadron of death-dealing hussars, covered with his body and saved from death, in the midst of the grapeshot, "a general, who had been dangerously wounded." Thence arose for his wall the flaring sign, and for his inn the name which it bore in the neighborhood, of "the cabaret of the Sergeant of Waterloo." He was a liberal, a classic, and a Bonapartist. He had subscribed for the Champ d'Asile. It was said in the village that he had studied for the priesthood.

We believe that he had simply studied in Holland for an innkeeper. This rascal of composite order was, in all probability, some Fleming from Lille, in Flanders, a Frenchman in Paris, a Belgian at Brussels, being comfortably astride of both frontiers. As for his prowess at Waterloo, the reader is already acquainted with that. It will be perceived that he exaggerated it a trifle. Ebb and flow, wandering, adventure, was the leaven of his existence; a tattered conscience entails a fragmentary life, and, apparently at the stormy epoch of June 18, 1815, Thenardier belonged to that variety of marauding merchants of which we have spoken, beating about the country, selling to some, stealing from others, and traveling like a family man, with wife and children, in a rickety cart, in the rear of troops on the march, with an instinct for always attaching himself to the victorious army. This campaign ended, and having, as he said, "some quibus," he had come to Montfermeil and set up an inn there.

This quibus, composed of purses and watches, of gold rings and silver crosses, gathered in harvesttime in furrows sown with corpses, did not amount to a large total, and did not carry this merchant-turned-eating-housekeeper very far.

Thenardier had that peculiar rectilinear something about his gestures which, accompanied by an oath, recalls the barracks, and by a sign of the cross, the seminary. He was a fine talker. He allowed it to be thought that he was an educated man. Nevertheless, the schoolmaster had noticed that he pronounced improperly.

He composed the travelers' tariff card in a superior manner, but practiced eyes sometimes spied out orthographical errors in it. Thenardier was cunning, greedy, slothful, and clever. He did not disdain his servants, which caused his wife to dispense with them. This giantess was jealous. It seemed to her that that thin and yellow little man must be an object coveted by all.

Thenardier, who was, above all, an astute and well-balanced man, was a scamp of a temperate sort. This is the worst species; hypocrisy enters into it.

It is not that Thenardier was not, on occasion, capable of wrath to quite the same degree as his wife; but this was very rare, and at such times, since he was enraged with the human race in general, as he bore within him a deep furnace of hatred. And since he was one of those people who are continually avenging their wrongs, who accuse everything that passes before them of everything that has befallen them, and who are always ready to cast upon the first person who comes to hand, as a legitimate grievance, the sum total of the deceptions, the bankruptcies, and the calamities of their lives, when all this leaven was stirred up in him and boiled forth from his mouth and eyes, he was terrible. Woe to the person who came under his wrath at such a time!

In addition to his other qualities, Thenardier was attentive and penetrating, silent or talkative, according to circumstances, and always highly intelligent. He had something of the look of sailors, who are accustomed to screw up their eyes to gaze through marine glasses. Thenardier was a statesman.

Every newcomer who entered the tavern said, on catching sight of Madame Thenardier, "There is the master of the house." A mistake. She was not even the mistress. The husband was both master and mistress. She worked; he created. He directed everything by a sort of invisible and constant magnetic action. A word was sufficient for him, sometimes a sign; the mastodon obeyed. Thenardier was a sort of special and sovereign being in Madame Thenardier's eyes, though she did not thoroughly realize it. She was possessed of virtues after her own kind; if she had ever had a disagreement as to any detail with "Monsieur Thenardier"—which was an inadmissible hypothesis, by the way—she would not have blamed her husband in public on any subject whatever. She would never have committed "before strangers" that mistake so often committed by women, and which is called in parliamentary language, "exposing the crown." Although their concord had only evil as its result, there was contemplation in Madame Thenardier's submission to her husband. That mountain of noise and of flesh moved under the little finger of that frail despot. Viewed on its dwarfed and grotesque side, this was that grand and universal thing, the adoration of mind by matter; for certain ugly features have a cause in the very depths of eternal beauty. There was an unknown quantity about Thenardier; hence the absolute empire of the man over that woman. At certain moments she beheld him like a lighted candle; at others she felt him like a claw.

This woman was a formidable creature who loved no one except her children, and who did not fear anyone except her husband. She was a mother because she was mammiferous. But her maternity stopped short with her daughters, and, as we shall see, did not extend to boys. The man had but one thought: how to enrich himself.

He did not succeed in this. A theater worthy of this great talent was lacking. Thenardier was ruining himself at Montfermeil, if ruin is possible to zero; in Switzerland or in the Pyrenees this penniless scamp would have become a millionaire; but an innkeeper must browse where fate has hitched him.

It will be understood that the word "innkeeper" is here employed in a restricted sense, and does not extend to an entire class.

In this same year, 1823, Thenardier was burdened with about fifteen hundred francs' worth of petty debts, and this rendered him anxious.

Whatever may have been the obstinate injustice of destiny in this case, Thenardier was one of those men who understand best, with the most profundity and in the most modern fashion, that thing which is a virtue among barbarous peoples and an object of merchandise among civilized peoples, hospitality. Besides, he was an admirable poacher, and quoted for his skill in shooting. He had a certain cold and tranquil laugh, which was particularly dangerous.

His theories as a landlord sometimes burst forth in lightning flashes. He had professional aphorisms, which he inserted into his wife's mind. "The duty of the innkepper," he said to her one day, violently, and in a low voice, "is to sell to the first comer, stews, repose, light, fire, dirty sheets, a servant, lice, and a smile; to stop passersby, to empty small purses, and to honestly lighten heavy ones; to shelter traveling families respectfully: to shave the man, to pluck the woman, to pick the child clean; to quote the window open, the window shut, the chimney-corner, the armchair, the chair, the ottoman, the stool, the feather bed, the mattress and the truss of straw; to know how much the shadow uses up the mirror, and to put a price on it; and, by five hundred thousand devils, to make the traveler pay for everything, even for the flies that his dog eats!"

This man and this woman were ruse and rage wedded—a hideous and terrible team.

While the husband pondered and combined, Madame Thenardier thought not of absent creditors, took no heed of yesterday or of tomorrow, and lived in a fit of anger, all in a minute.

Such were these two beings. Cosette was between them, subjected to their double pressure, like a creature who is at the same time being ground up in a mill and pulled to pieces with pincers. The man and the woman each had a different method: Cosette was overwhelmed with blows—this was the woman's; she went barefooted in winter—that was the man's doing.

Cosette ran upstairs and down, washed, swept, rubbed, dusted, ran, fluttered about, panted, moved heavy articles, and weak as she was, did the coarse work. There was no mercy for her; a fierce mistress and venomous master. The Thenardier hostelry was like a spider's web, in which Cosette had been caught, and where she lay trembling. The ideal of oppression was realized by this sinister household. It was something like the fly serving the spiders.

The poor child passively held her peace.

What takes place within these souls when they have but just quitted God, find themselves thus, at the very dawn of life, very small and in the midst of men all naked!

CHAPTER III—MEN MUST HAVE WINE, AND HORSES MUST HAVE WATER

Four new travelers had arrived.

Cosette was meditating sadly; for, although she was only eight years old, she had already suffered so much that she reflected with the lugubrious air of an old woman. Her eye was black in consequence of a blow from Madame Thenardier's fist, which caused the latter to remark from time to time, "How ugly she is with her fist-blow on her eye!"

Cosette was thinking that it was dark, very dark, that the pitchers and carafes in the chambers of the travelers who had arrived must have been filled and that there was no more water in the cistern.

She was somewhat reassured because no one in the Thenardier establishment drank much water. Thirsty people were never lacking there; but their thirst was of the sort which applies to the jug rather than to the pitcher. Anyone who had asked for a glass of water among all those glasses of wine would have appeared a savage to all these men. But there came a moment when the child trembled; Madame Thenardier raised the cover of a stewpan that was boiling on the stove, then seized a glass and briskly approached the cistern. She turned the faucet; the child had raised her head and was following all the woman's movements. A thin stream of water trickled from the faucet, and half filled the glass. "Well," said she, "there is no more water!" A momentary silence ensued. The child did not breathe.

"Bah!" resumed Madame Thenardier, examining the half-filled glass. "This will be enough."

Cosette applied herself to her work once more, but for a quarter of an hour she felt her heart leaping in her bosom like a big snowflake.

She counted the minutes that passed in this manner, and wished it were the next morning.

From time to time one of the drinkers looked into the street, and exclaimed, "It's as black as an oven!" Or, "One must needs be a cat to go about the streets without a lantern at this hour!" And Cosette trembled.

All at once one of the peddlers who lodged in the hostelry entered, and said in a harsh voice, "My horse has not been watered."

"Yes, it has," said Madame Thenardier.

"I tell you that it has not," retorted the peddler.

Cosette had emerged from under the table.

"Oh, yes, Sir!" said she. "The horse has had a drink; he drank out of a bucket, a whole bucketful, and it was I who took the water to him, and I spoke to him."

It was not true; Cosette lied.

"There's a brat as big as my fist who tells lies as big as the house," exclaimed the peddler. "I tell you that he has not been watered, you little jade! He has a way of blowing when he has had no water, which I know well."

Cosette persisted, and added in a voice rendered hoarse with anguish, and which was hardly audible, "And he drank heartily."

"Come," said the peddler, in a rage, "this won't do at all, let my horse be watered, and let that be the end of it!"

Cosette crept under the table again.

"In truth, that is fair!" said Madame Thenardier. "If the beast has not been watered, it must be."

Then glancing about her, "Well, now! Where's that other beast?"

She bent down and discovered Cosette cowering at the other end of the table, almost under the drinkers' feet.

"Are you coming?" shrieked Madame Thenardier.

Cosette crawled out of the sort of hole in which she had hidden herself. The Thenardier resumed, "Mademoiselle Dog-lack-name, go and water that horse."

"But, Madame," said Cosette, feebly, "there is no water."

The Thenardier threw the street door wide open. "Well, go and get some, then!"

Cosette dropped her head, and went for an empty bucket which stood near the chimney-corner.

This bucket was bigger than she was, and the child could have set down in it at her ease.

The Thenardier returned to her stove, and tasted what was in the stewpan, with a wooden spoon, grumbling the while, "There's plenty in the spring. There never was such a malicious creature as that. I think I should have done better to strain my onions."

Then she rummaged in a drawer, which contained sous, pepper, and shallots.

"See here, Mam'selle Toad," she added, "on your way back, you will get a big loaf from the baker. Here's a fifteen-sou piece."

Cosette had a little pocket on one side of her apron; she took the coin without saying a word, and put it in that pocket.

Then she stood motionless, bucket in hand, the open door before her. She seemed to be waiting for someone to come to her rescue.

"Get along with you!" screamed the Thenardier.

Cosette went out. The door closed behind her.

CHAPTER IV—ENTRANCE ON THE SCENE OF A DOLL

The line of open-air booths starting at the church, extended, as the reader will remember, as far as the hostelry of the Thenardiers. These booths were all illuminated, because the citizens would soon pass on their way to the midnight mass, with candles burning in paper funnels, which, as the schoolmaster, then seated at the table at the Thenardiers' observed, produced "a magical effect." In compensation, not a star was visible in the sky.

The last of these stalls, established precisely opposite the Thenardiers' door, was a toy shop all glittering with tinsel, glass, and magnificent objects of tin. In the first row, and far forward, the merchant had placed on a background of white napkins, an immense doll, nearly two feet high, who was dressed in a robe of pink crepe, with gold wheat-ears on her head, which had real hair and enamel eyes. All that day, this marvel had been displayed to the wonderment of all passersby under ten years of age, without a mother being found in Montfermeil sufficiently rich or sufficiently extravagant to give it to her child.

Eponine and Azelma had passed hours in contemplating it, and Cosette herself had ventured to cast a glance at it, on the sly, it is true.

At the moment when Cosette emerged, bucket in hand, melancholy and overcome as she was, she could not refrain from lifting her eyes to that wonderful doll, toward the lady, as she called it. The poor child paused in amazement. She had not yet beheld that doll close to. The whole shop seemed a palace to her: the doll was not a doll; it was a vision. It was joy, splendor, riches, happiness, which appeared in a sort of chimerical halo to that unhappy little being so profoundly engulfed in gloomy and chilly misery. With the sad and innocent sagacity of childhood, Cosette measured the abyss that separated her from that doll. She said to herself that one must be a queen, or at least a princess, to have a "thing" like that. She gazed at that beautiful pink dress, that beautiful smooth hair, and she thought, "How happy that doll must be!" She could not take her eyes from that fantastic stall. The more she looked, the more dazzled she grew. She thought she was gazing at paradise. There were other dolls behind the large one, which seemed to her to be fairies and genie. The merchant, who was pacing back and forth in front of his shop, produced on her somewhat the effect of being the Eternal Father.

In this adoration she forgot everything, even the errand with which she was charged.

All at once the Thenardier's coarse voice recalled her to reality, "What, you silly jade! You have not gone? Wait! I'll give it to you! I want to know what you are doing there! Get along, you little monster!"

The Thenardier had cast a glance into the street, and had caught sight of Cosette in her ecstasy.

Cosette fled, dragging her pail, and taking the longest strides of which she was capable.

CHAPTER V—THE LITTLE ONE ALL ALONE

As the Thenardier hostelry was in that part of the village, which is near the church, it was to the spring in the forest in the direction of Chelles that Cosette was obliged to go for her water.

She did not glance at the display of a single other merchant. So long as she was in Boulanger Lane and in the neighborhood of the church, the lighted stalls illuminated the road; but soon the last light from the last stall vanished.

The poor child found herself in the dark. She plunged into it. Only, as a certain emotion overcame her, she made as much motion as possible with the handle of the bucket as she walked along. This made a noise which afforded her company.

The further she went, the denser the darkness became. There was no one in the streets. However, she did encounter a woman, who turned around on seeing her, and stood still, muttering between her teeth, "Where can that child be going? Is it a werewolf child?" Then the woman recognized Cosette. "Well," said she, "it's the Lark!"

In this manner Cosette traversed the labyrinth of tortuous and deserted streets, which terminate in the village of Montfermeil on the side of Chelles. So long as she had the houses or even the walls only on both sides of her path, she proceeded with tolerable boldness. From time to time she caught the flicker of a candle through the crack of a shutter—this was light and life; there were people there, and it reassured her. But in proportion as she advanced, her pace slackened mechanically, as it were. When she had passed the corner of the last house, Cosette paused. It had been hard to advance further than the last stall; it became impossible to proceed further than the last house. She set her bucket on the ground, thrust her hand into her hair, and began slowly to scratch her head, a gesture peculiar to children when terrified and undecided what to do. It was no longer Montfermeil; it was the open fields. Black and desert space was before her. She gazed in despair at that darkness, where there was no longer anyone, where there were beasts, where there were specters, possibly. She took a good look, and heard the beasts walking on the grass, and she distinctly saw specters moving in the trees. Then she seized her bucket again; fear had lent her audacity. "Bah!" said she; "I will tell him that there was no more water!" And she resolutely reentered Montfermeil.

Hardly had she gone a hundred paces when she paused and began to scratch her head again. Now it was the Thenardier who appeared to her, with her hideous, hyena mouth, and wrath flashing in her eyes. The child cast a melancholy glance before her and behind her. What was she to do? What was to become of her? Where was she to go? In front of her was the specter of the Thenardier; behind her all the phantoms of the night and of the forest. It was before the Thenardier that she recoiled. She resumed her path to the spring, and began to run. She emerged from the village, she entered the forest at a run, no longer looking at or listening to anything. She only paused in her course when her breath failed her; but she did not halt in her advance. She went straight before her in desperation.

As she ran she felt like crying.

The nocturnal quivering of the forest surrounded her completely.

She no longer thought, she no longer saw. The immensity of night wa facing this tiny creature. On the one hand, all shadow; on the other, an atom.

It was only seven or eight minutes' walk from the edge of the woods to the spring. Cosette knew the way, through having gone over it many time in daylight. Strange to say, she did not get lost. A remnant of instinct guide her vaguely. But she did not turn her eyes either to right or to left, for fear of seeing things in the branches and in the brushwood. In this manner she reached the spring.

It was a narrow, natural basin, hollowed out by the water in a clayey soil about two feet deep, surrounded with moss and with those tall, crimped grasse which are called Henry IV's frills, and paved with several large stones. A brook ran out of it, with a tranquil little noise.

Cosette did not take time to breathe. It was very dark, but she was in the habit of coming to this spring. She felt with her left hand in the dark for a young oak which leaned over the spring, and which usually served to suppor her, found one of its branches, clung to it, bent down, and plunged the bucke in the water. She was in a state of such violent excitement that her strength wa trebled. While thus bent over, she did not notice that the pocket of her apror had emptied itself into the spring. The fifteen-sou piece fell into the water Cosette neither saw nor heard it fall. She drew out the bucket nearly full, and set it on the grass.

That done, she perceived that she was worn out with fatigue. She would have liked to set out again at once, but the effort required to fill the bucket had been such that she found it impossible to take a step. She was forced to sit down She dropped on the grass, and remained crouching there.

She shut her eyes; then she opened them again, without knowing why, but because she could not do otherwise. The agitated water in the bucket beside her was describing circles which resembled tin serpents.

Overhead the sky was covered with vast black clouds, which were like masses of smoke. The tragic mask of shadow seemed to bend vaguely over the child.

Jupiter was setting in the depths.

The child stared with bewildered eyes at this great star, with which she was unfamiliar, and which terrified her. The planet was, in fact, very near the horizon and was traversing a dense layer of mist which imparted to it a horrible ruddy hue. The mist, gloomily empurpled, magnified the star. One would have called it a luminous wound.

A cold wind was blowing from the plain. The forest was dark, not a leaf was moving; there were none of the vague, fresh gleams of summertime. Great boughs uplifted themselves in frightful wise. Slender and misshapen bushes whistled in the clearings. The tall grasses undulated like eels under the north wind. The nettles seemed to twist long arms furnished with claws in search of prey. Some bits of dry heather, tossed by the breeze, flew rapidly by, and had the air of fleeing in terror before something which was coming after. On all sides there were lugubrious stretches.

The darkness was bewildering. Man requires light. Whoever buries himself in the opposite of day feels his heart contract. When the eye sees black, the heart sees trouble. In an eclipse in the night, in the sooty opacity, there is anxiety even for the stoutest of hearts. No one walks alone in the forest at night without trembling. Shadows and trees—two formidable densities. A chimerical reality appears in the indistinct depths. The inconceivable is outlined a few paces distant from you with a spectral clearness. One beholds floating, either in space or in one's own brain, one knows not what vague and intangible thing, like the dreams of sleeping flowers. There are fierce attitudes on the horizon. One inhales the effluvia of the great black void. One is afraid to glance behind him, yet desirous of doing so. The cavities of night, things grown haggard, taciturn profiles that vanish when one advances, obscure dishevelments, irritated tufts, livid pools, the lugubrious reflected in the funereal, the sepulchral immensity of silence, unknown but possible beings, bendings of mysterious branches, alarming torsos of trees, long handfuls of quivering plants, against all this one has no protection. There is no hardihood which does not shudder and which does not feel the vicinity of anguish. One is conscious of something hideous, as though one's soul were becoming amalgamated with the darkness. This penetration of the shadows is indescribably sinister in the case of a child.

Forests are apocalypses, and the beating of the wings of a tiny soul produces a sound of agony beneath their monstrous vault.

Without understanding her sensations, Cosette was conscious that she was seized upon by that black enormity of nature; it was no longer terror alone that was gaining possession of her; it was something more terrible even than terror; she shivered. There are no words to express the strangeness of that shiver, which chilled her to the very bottom of her heart; her eye grew wild; she thought she felt that she should not be able to refrain from returning there at the same hour on the morrow.

Then, by a sort of instinct, she began to count aloud—one, two, three, four, and so on up to ten—in order to escape from that singular state that she did not understand, but which terrified her, and, when she had finished, she began again; this restored her to a true perception of the things about her. Her hands which she had wet in drawing the water, felt cold; she rose; her terror, a natural and unconquerable terror, had returned: she had but one thought now, to flee at full speed through the forest, across the fields to the houses, to the windows, to the lighted candles. Her glance fell upon the water that stood before her; such was the fright that the Thenardier inspired in her, that she dared not flee without that bucket of water: she seized the handle with both hands; she could hardly lift the pail.

In this manner she advanced a dozen paces, but the bucket was full; it was heavy; she was forced to set it on the ground once more. She took breath for an instant, then lifted the handle of the bucket again, and resumed her march, proceeding a little further this time, but again she was obliged to pause. After some seconds of repose she set out again. She walked bent forward with drooping head, like an old woman; the weight of the bucket strained and stiffened her thin arms. The iron handle completed the benumbing and freezing of her wet and tiny hands; she was forced to halt from time to time, and each time that she did so, the cold water that splashed from the pail fell on her bare legs. This took place in the depths of a forest, at night, in winter, far from all human sight; she was a child of eight: no one but God saw that sad thing at the moment.

And her mother, no doubt, alas!

For there are things that make the dead open their eyes in their graves.

She panted with a sort of painful rattle; sobs contracted her throat, but she dared not weep, so afraid was she of the Thenardier, even at a distance: it was her custom to imagine the Thenardier always present.

However, she could not make much headway in that manner, and she went on very slowly. In spite of diminishing the length of her stops, and of walking as long as possible between them, she reflected with anguish that it would take her more than an hour to return to Montfermeil in this manner, and that the Thenardier would beat her. This anguish was mingled with her terror at being alone in the woods at night; she was worn out with fatigue, and had not yet emerged from the forest. On arriving near an old chestnut tree with which she was acquainted, made a last halt, longer than the rest, in order that she might get well rested; then she summoned up all her strength, picked up her bucket again, and courageously resumed her march, but the poor little desperate creature could not refrain from crying, "O my God! My God!"

At that moment she suddenly became conscious that her bucket no longer weighed anything at all: a hand, which seemed to her enormous, had just seized the handle, and lifted it vigorously. She raised her head. A large black form, straight and erect, was walking beside her through the darkness; it was a man who had come up behind her, and whose approach she had not heard. This man, without uttering a word, had seized the handle of the bucket she was carrying.

There are instincts for all the encounters of life.

The child was not afraid.

CHAPTER VI—WHICH POSSIBLY PROVES BOULATRUELLE'S INTELLIGENCE

On the afternoon of that same Christmas Day, 1823, a man had walked for rather a long time in the most deserted part of the Boulevard de l'Hopital in Paris. This man had the air of a person who is seeking lodgings, and he seemed to halt, by preference, at the most modest houses on that dilapidated border of the suburb of Saint-Marceau.

We shall see further on that this man had, in fact, hired a chamber in that isolated quarter.

This man, in his attire, as in all his person, realized the type of what may be called the well-bred mendicant, extreme wretchedness combined with extreme cleanliness. This is a very rare mixture, which inspires intelligent hearts with that double respect that one feels for the man who is very poor, and for the man who is very worthy. He wore a very old and very well brushed round hat; a coarse coat, worn perfectly threadbare, of an ochre yellow, a color that was not in the least eccentric at that epoch; a large waistcoat with pockets of a venerable cut; black breeches, worn gray at the knee, stockings of black worsted; and thick shoes with copper buckles. He would have been pronounced a preceptor in some good family, returned from the emigration. He would have been taken for more than sixty years of age, from his perfectly white hair, his wrinkled brow, his livid lips, and his countenance, where everything breathed depression and weariness of life. Judging from his firm tread, from the singular vigor which stamped all his movements, he would have hardly been thought fifty. The wrinkles on his brow were well placed, and would have disposed in his favor anyone who observed him attentively. His lip contracted with a strange fold, which seemed severe, and which was humble. There was in the depth of his glance an indescribable melancholy serenity. In his left hand he carried a little bundle tied up in a handkerchief; in his right he leaned on a sort of a cudgel, cut from some hedge. This stick had been carefully trimmed, and had an air that was not too threatening; the most had been made of its knots, and it had received a coral-like head, made from red wax: it was a cudgel, and it seemed to be a cane.

There are but few passersby on that boulevard, particularly in the winter. The man seemed to avoid them rather than to seek them, but this without any affectation.

At that epoch, King Louis XVIII went nearly every day to Choisy-le-Roi: it was one of his favorite excursions. Toward two o'clock, almost invariably, the royal carriage and cavalcade was seen to pass at full speed along the Boulevard de l'Hopital.

This served in lieu of a watch or clock to the poor women of the quarter who said, "It is two o'clock; there he is returning to the Tuileries."

And some rushed forward, and others drew up in line, for a passing king always creates a tumult; besides, the appearance and disappearance of Louis XVIII produced a certain effect in the streets of Paris. It was rapid but majestic. This impotent king had a taste for a fast gallop; as he was not able to walk, he wished to run: that cripple would gladly have had himself drawn by the lightning. He passed, pacific and severe, in the midst of naked swords. His massive couch, all covered with gilding, with great branches of lilies painted on the panels, thundered noisily along. There was hardly time to cast a glance upon it. In the rear angle on the right there was visible on tufted cushions of white satin a large, firm, and ruddy face, a brow freshly powdered, a *l'oiseau royal,* * a proud, hard, crafty eye, the smile of an educated man, two great epaulets with bullion fringe floating over a bourgeois coat, the Golden Fleece, the cross of Saint Louis, the cross of the Legion of Honor, the silver plaque of the Saint-Esprit, a huge belly, and a wide blue ribbon: it was the king. Outside of Paris, he held his hat decked with white ostrich plumes on his knees, enwrapped in high English gaiters; when he reentered the city, he put on his hat and saluted rarely; he stared coldly at the people, and they returned it in kind. When he appeared for the first time in the Saint-Marceau quarter, the whole success which he produced is contained in this remark of an inhabitant of the suburb to his comrade, "That big fellow yonder is the government."

This infallible passage of the king at the same hour was, therefore, the daily event of the Boulevard de l'Hopital.

The promenader in the yellow coat evidently did not belong in the quarter, and probably did not belong in Paris, for he was ignorant as to this detail.

---

* plumed, crested, feathered

When, at two o'clock, the royal carriage, surrounded by a squadron of the bodyguard all covered with silver lace, debouched on the boulevard, after having made the turn of the Salpetriere, he appeared surprised and almost alarmed. There was no one but himself in this cross-lane. He drew up hastily behind the corner of the wall of an enclosure, though this did not prevent M. le Duc de Havre from spying him out.

M. le Duc de Havre, as captain of the guard on duty that day, was seated in the carriage, opposite the king. He said to his Majesty, "Yonder is an evil-looking man." Members of the police, who were clearing the king's route, took equal note of him: one of them received an order to follow him. But the man plunged into the deserted little streets of the suburb, and as twilight was beginning to fall, the agent lost trace of him, as is stated in a report addressed that same evening to M. le Comte d'Angles, Minister of State, Prefect of Police.

When the man in the yellow coat had thrown the agent off his track, he redoubled his pace, not without turning around many a time to assure himself that he was not being followed. At a quarter-past four, that is to say, when night was fully come, he passed in front of the theater of the Porte Saint-Martin, where *The Two Convicts* was being played that day. This poster, illuminated by the theater lanterns, struck him; for, although he was walking rapidly, he halted to read it. An instant later he was in the blind alley of La Planchette, and he entered the Plat d'Etain, where the office of the coach for Lagny was then situated. This coach set out at half-past four. The horses were harnessed, and the travelers, summoned by the coachman, were hastily climbing the lofty iron ladder of the vehicle.

The man inquired, "Have you a place?"

"Only one—beside me on the box," said the coachman.

"I will take it."

"Climb up."

Nevertheless, before setting out, the coachman cast a glance at the traveler's shabby dress, at the diminutive size of his bundle, and made him pay his fare.

"Are you going as far as Lagny?" demanded the coachman.

"Yes," said the man.

The traveler paid to Lagny.

They started. When they had passed the barrier, the coachman tried to enter into conversation, but the traveler only replied in monosyllables. The coachman took to whistling and swearing at his horses.

The coachman wrapped himself up in his cloak. It was cold. The man did not appear to be thinking of that. Thus they passed Gournay and Neuilly-sur-Marne.

Toward six o'clock in the evening they reached Chelles. The coachman drew up in front of the carters' inn installed in the ancient buildings of the Royal Abbéy, to give his horses a breathing spell.

"I get down here," said the man.

He took his bundle and his cudgel and jumped down from the vehicle.

An instant later he had disappeared.

He did not enter the inn.

When the coach set out for Lagny a few minutes later, it did not encounter him in the principal street of Chelles.

The coachman turned to the inside travelers.

"There," said he, "is a man who does not belong here, for I do not know him. He had not the air of owning a sou, but he does not consider money; he pays to Lagny, and he goes only as far as Chelles. It is night; all the houses are shut; he does not enter the inn, and he is not to be found. So he has dived through the earth."

The man had not plunged into the earth, but he had gone with great strides through the dark, down the principal street of Chelles, then he had turned to the right before reaching the church, into the crossroad leading to Montfermeil, like a person who was acquainted with the country and had been there before.

He followed this road rapidly. At the spot where it is intersected by the ancient tree-bordered road, which runs from Gagny to Lagny, he heard people coming. He concealed himself precipitately in a ditch, and there waited until the passersby were at a distance. The precaution was nearly superfluous, however; for, as we have already said, it was a very dark December night. Not more than two or three stars were visible in the sky.

It is at this point that the ascent of the hill begins. The man did not return to the road to Montfermeil; he struck across the fields to the right, and entered the forest with long strides.

Once in the forest he slackened his pace, and began a careful examination of all the trees, advancing, step-by-step, as though seeking and following a mysterious road known to himself alone. There came a moment when he appeared to lose himself, and he paused in indecision. At last he arrived, by dint of feeling his way inch by inch, at a clearing where there was a great heap of whitish stones. He stepped up briskly to these stones, and examined them attentively through the mists of night, as though he were passing them in review. A large tree, covered with those excrescences which are the warts of vegetation, stood a few paces distant from the pile of stones. He went up to this tree and passed his hand over the bark of the trunk, as though seeking to recognize and count all the warts.

Opposite this tree, which was an ash, there was a chestnut tree, suffering from a peeling of the bark, to which a band of zinc had been nailed by way of dressing. He raised himself on tiptoe and touched this band of zinc.

Then he trod about for awhile on the ground comprised in the space between the tree and the heap of stones, like a person who is trying to assure himself that the soil has not recently been disturbed.

That done, he took his bearings, and resumed his march through the forest.

It was the man who had just met Cosette.

As he walked through the thicket in the direction of Montfermeil, he had espied that tiny shadow moving with a groan, depositing a burden on the ground, then taking it up and setting out again. He drew near, and perceived that it was a very young child, laden with an enormous bucket of water. Then he approached the child, and silently grasped the handle of the bucket.

CHAPTER VII—COSETTE SIDE BY SIDE WITH THE STRANGER IN THE DARK

Cosette, as we have said, was not frightened.

The man accosted her. He spoke in a voice that was grave and almost bass.

"My child, what you are carrying is very heavy for you."

Cosette raised her head and replied, "Yes, Sir."

"Give it to me," said the man; "I will carry it for you."

Cosette let go of the bucket handle. The man walked along beside her.

"It really is very heavy," he muttered between his teeth. Then he added, "How old are you, little one?"

"Eight, Sir."

"And have you come from far like this?"

"From the spring in the forest."

"Are you going far?"

"A good quarter of an hour's walk from here."

The man said nothing for a moment; then he remarked abruptly, "So you have no mother."

"I don't know," answered the child.

Before the man had time to speak again, she added, "I don't think so. Other people have mothers. I have none."

And after a silence she went on, "I think that I never had any."

The man halted; he set the bucket on the ground, bent down and placed both hands on the child's shoulders, making an effort to look at her and to see her face in the dark.

Cosette's thin and sickly face was vaguely outlined by the livid light in the sky.

"What is your name?" said the man.

"Cosette."

The man seemed to have received an electric shock. He looked at her once more; then he removed his hands from Cosette's shoulders, seized the bucket, and set out again.

After a moment he inquired, "Where do you live, little one?"

"At Montfermeil, if you know where that is."

"That is where we are going?"

"Yes, Sir."

He paused; then began again, "Who sent you at such an hour to get water in the forest?"

"It was Madame Thenardier."

The man resumed, in a voice that he strove to render indifferent, but in which there was, nevertheless, a singular tremor. "What does your Madame Thenardier do?"

"She is my mistress," said the child. "She keeps the inn."

"The inn?" said the man. "Well, I am going to lodge there tonight. Show me the way."

"We are on the way there," said the child.

The man walked tolerably fast. Cosette followed him without difficulty. She no longer felt any fatigue. From time to time she raised her eyes toward the man, with a sort of tranquillity and an indescribable confidence. She had never been taught to turn to Providence and to pray; nevertheless, she felt within her something that resembled hope and joy, and which mounted toward heaven.

Several minutes elapsed. The man resumed, "Is there no servant in Madame Thenardier's house?"

"No, Sir."

"Are you alone there?"

"Yes, Sir."

Another pause ensued. Cosette lifted up her voice, "That is to say, there are two little girls."

"What little girls?"

"Ponine and Zelma."

This was the way the child simplified the romantic names so dear to the female Thenardier.

"Who are Ponine and Zelma?"

"They are Madame Thenardier's young ladies; her daughters, as you would say."

"And what do those girls do?"

"Oh!" said the child. "They have beautiful dolls; things with gold in them, all full of affairs. They play; they amuse themselves."

"All day long?"

"Yes, Sir."

"And you?"

"I? I work."

"All day long?"

The child raised her great eyes, in which hung a tear, which was not visible because of the darkness, and replied gently, "Yes, Sir."

After an interval of silence she went on, "Sometimes, when I have finished my work and they let me, I amuse myself, too."

"How do you amuse yourself?"

"In the best way I can. They let me alone; but I have not many playthings. Ponine and Zelma will not let me play with their dolls. I have only a little lead sword, no longer than that."

The child held up her tiny finger.

"And it will not cut?"

"Yes, Sir," said the child; "it cuts salad and the heads of flies."

They reached the village. Cosette guided the stranger through the streets. They passed the bakeshop, but Cosette did not think of the bread that she had been ordered to fetch. The man had ceased to ply her with questions, and now preserved a gloomy silence.

When they had left the church behind them, the man, on perceiving all the open-air booths, asked Cosette, "So there is a fair going on here?"

"No, Sir; it is Christmas."

As they approached the tavern, Cosette timidly touched his arm. Monsieur?"

"What, my child?"

"We are quite near the house."

"Well?"

"Will you let me take my bucket now?"

"Why?"

"If Madame sees that someone has carried it for me, she will beat me."

The man handed her the bucket. An instant later they were at the tavern door.

CHAPTER VIII—THE UNPLEASANTNESS OF RECEIVING INTO ONE'S HOUSE A POOR MAN WHO MAY BE A RICH MAN

Cosette could not refrain from casting a sidelong glance at the big doll, which was still displayed at the toy merchant's; then she knocked. The door opened. The Thenardier appeared with a candle in her hand.

"Ah! So it's you, you little wretch! Good mercy, but you've taken your time! The hussy has been amusing herself!"

"Madame," said Cosette, trembling all over, "here's a gentleman who wants a lodging."

The Thenardier speedily replaced her gruff air by her amiable grimace, a change of aspect common to tavern-keepers, and eagerly sought the newcomer with her eyes.

"This is the gentleman?" said she.

"Yes, Madame," replied the man, raising his hand to his hat.

Wealthy travelers are not so polite. This gesture, and an inspection of the stranger's costume and baggage, which the Thenardier passed in review with one glance, caused the amiable grimace to vanish, and the gruff mien to reappear. She resumed dryly, "Enter, my good man."

The "good man" entered. The Thenardier cast a second glance at him, paid particular attention to his frock-coat, which was absolutely threadbare, and to his hat, which was a little battered, and, tossing her head, wrinkling her nose, and screwing up her eyes, she consulted her husband, who was still drinking with the carters. The husband replied by that imperceptible movement of the forefinger, which, backed up by an inflation of the lips, signifies in such cases: A regular beggar. Thereupon, the Thenardier exclaimed, "Ah! See here, my good man; I am very sorry, but I have no room left."

"Put me where you like," said the man; "in the attic, in the stable. I will pay as though I occupied a room."

"Forty sous."

"Forty sous; agreed."

"Very well, then!"

"Forty sous!" said a carter, in a low tone, to the Thenardier woman; "why, he charge is only twenty sous!"

"It is forty in his case," retorted the Thenardier, in the same tone. "I don't lodge poor folks for less."

"That's true," added her husband, gently; "it ruins a house to have such people in it."

In the meantime, the man, laying his bundle and his cudgel on a bench, had seated himself at a table, on which Cosette made haste to place a bottle of wine and a glass. The merchant who had demanded the bucket of water took it to his horse himself. Cosette resumed her place under the kitchen table, and her knitting.

The man, who had barely moistened his lips in the wine which he had poured out for himself, observed the child with peculiar attention.

Cosette was ugly. If she had been happy, she might have been pretty. We have already given a sketch of that somber little figure. Cosette was thin and pale; she was nearly eight years old, but she seemed to be hardly six. Her large eyes, sunken in a sort of shadow, were almost put out with weeping. The corners of her mouth had that curve of habitual anguish that is seen in condemned persons and desperately sick people. Her hands were, as her mother had divined, "ruined with chilblains." The fire that illuminated her at that moment brought into relief all the angles of her bones, and rendered her thinness frightfully apparent. As she was always shivering, she had acquired the habit of pressing her knees one against the other. Her entire clothing was but a rag which would have inspired pity in summer, and which inspired horror in winter. All she had on was hole-ridden linen, not a scrap of woolen. Her skin was visible here and there and everywhere black-and-blue spots could be descried, which marked the places where the Thenardier woman had touched her. Her naked legs were thin and red. The hollows in her neck were enough to make one weep. This child's whole person, her mien, her attitude, the sound of her voice, the intervals that she allowed to elapse between one word and the next, her glance, her silence, her slightest gesture, expressed and betrayed one sole idea: fear.

Fear was diffused all over her; she was covered with it, so to speak; fear drew her elbows close to her hips, withdrew her heels under her petticoat, made her occupy as little space as possible, allowed her only the breath that was absolutely necessary, and had become what might be called the habit of her body, admitting of no possible variation except an increase. In the depths of her eyes there was an astonished nook where terror lurked.

Her fear was such, that on her arrival, wet as she was, Cosette did not dare to approach the fire and dry herself, but sat silently down to her work again.

The expression in the glance of that child of eight years was habitually so gloomy, and at times so tragic, that it seemed at certain moments as though she were on the verge of becoming an idiot or a demon.

As we have stated, she had never known what it is to pray; she had never set foot in a church. "Have I the time?" said the Thenardier.

The man in the yellow coat never took his eyes from Cosette.

All at once, the Thenardier exclaimed, "By the way, where's that bread?"

Cosette, according to her custom whenever the Thenardier uplifted her voice, emerged with great haste from beneath the table.

She had completely forgotten the bread. She had recourse to the expedient of children who live in a constant state of fear. She lied.

"Madame, the baker's shop was shut."

"You should have knocked."

"I did knock, Madame."

"Well?"

"He did not open the door."

"I'll find out tomorrow whether that is true," said the Thenardier; "and if you are telling me a lie, I'll lead you a pretty dance. In the meantime, give me back my fifteen-sou piece."

Cosette plunged her hand into the pocket of her apron, and turned green. The fifteen-sou piece was not there.

"Ah, come now," said Madame Thenardier, "did you hear me?"

Cosette turned her pocket inside out; there was nothing in it. What could have become of that money? The unhappy little creature could not find a word to say. She was petrified.

"Have you lost that fifteen-sou piece?" screamed the Thenardier, hoarsely, "or do you want to rob me of it?"

At the same time, she stretched out her arm toward the cat-o'-nine-tails, which hung on a nail in the chimney corner.

This formidable gesture restored to Cosette sufficient strength to shriek, "Mercy, Madame, Madame! I will not do so anymore!"

The Thenardier took down the whip.

In the meantime, the man in the yellow coat had been fumbling in the fob of his waistcoat, without anyone having noticed his movements. Besides, the other travelers were drinking or playing cards, and were not paying attention to anything.

Cosette contracted herself into a ball, with anguish, within the angle of the chimney, endeavoring to gather up and conceal her poor half-nude limbs. The Thenardier raised her arm.

"Pardon me, Madame," said the man, "but just now I caught sight of something that had fallen from this little one's apron pocket, and rolled aside. Perhaps this is it."

At the same time he bent down and seemed to be searching on the floor for a moment.

"Exactly; here it is," he went on, straightening himself up.

And he held out a silver coin to the Thenardier.

"Yes, that's it," said she.

It was not it, for it was a twenty-sou piece; but the Thenardier found it to her advantage. She put the coin in her pocket, and confined herself to casting a fierce glance at the child, accompanied with the remark, "Don't let this ever happen again!"

Cosette returned to what the Thenardier called "her kennel," and her large eyes, which were riveted on the traveler, began to take on an expression such as they had never worn before. Thus far it was only an innocent amazement, but a sort of stupefied confidence was mingled with it.

"By the way, would you like some supper?" the Thenardier inquired of the traveler.

He made no reply. He appeared to be absorbed in thought.

"What sort of a man is that?" she muttered between her teeth. "He's some frightfully poor wretch. He hasn't a sou to pay for a supper. Will he even pay me for his lodging? It's very lucky, all the same, that it did not occur to him to steal the money that was on the floor."

In the meantime, a door had opened, and Eponine and Azelma entered.

They were two really pretty little girls, more bourgeois than peasant in looks, and very charming; the one with shining chestnut tresses, the other with long black braids hanging down her back, both vivacious, neat, plump, rosy, and healthy, and a delight to the eye. They were warmly clad, but with so much maternal art that the thickness of the stuffs did not detract from the coquetry of arrangement. There was a hint of winter, though the springtime was not wholly effaced. Light emanated from these two little beings. Besides this, they were on the throne. In their toilettes, in their gaiety, in the noise that they made, there was sovereignty. When they entered, the Thenardier said to them in a grumbling tone which was full of adoration, "Ah! There you are, you children!"

Then drawing them, one after the other to her knees, smoothing their hair, tying their ribbons afresh, and then releasing them with that gentle manner of shaking off which is peculiar to mothers, she exclaimed, "What frights they are!"

They went and seated themselves in the chimney corner. They had a doll, which they turned over and over on their knees with all sorts of joyous chatter. From time to time Cosette raised her eyes from her knitting, and watched their play with a melancholy air.

Eponine and Azelma did not look at Cosette. She was the same as a dog to them. These three little girls did not yet reckon up four and twenty years between them, but they already represented the whole society of man; envy on the one side, disdain on the other.

The doll of the Thenardier sisters was very much faded, very old, and much broken; but it seemed nonetheless admirable to Cosette, who had never had a doll in her life, a real doll, to make use of the expression that all children will understand.

All at once, the Thenardier, who had been going back and forth in the room, perceived that Cosette's mind was distracted, and that, instead of working, she was paying attention to the little ones at their play.

"Ah! I've caught you at it!" she cried. "So that's the way you work! I'll make you work to the tune of the whip; that I will."

The stranger turned to the Thenardier, without quitting his chair.

"Bah, Madame," he said, with an almost timid air, "let her play!"

Such a wish expressed by a traveler who had eaten a slice of mutton and had drunk a couple of bottles of wine with his supper, and who had not the air of being frightfully poor, would have been equivalent to an order. But that a man with such a hat should permit himself such a desire, and that a man with such a coat should permit himself to have a will, was something which Madame Thenardier did not intend to tolerate. She retorted with acrimony, "She must work, since she eats. I don't feed her to do nothing."

"What is she making?" went on the stranger, in a gentle voice that contrasted strangely with his beggarly garments and his porter's shoulders.

The Thenardier deigned to reply, "Stockings, if you please. Stockings for my little girls, who have none, so to speak, and who are absolutely barefoot just now."

The man looked at Cosette's poor little red feet, and continued, "When will she have finished this pair of stockings?"

"She has at least three or four good days' work on them still, the lazy creature!"

"And how much will that pair of stockings be worth when she has finished them?"

The Thenardier cast a glance of disdain on him.

"Thirty sous at least."

"Will you sell them for five francs?" went on the man.

"Good heavens!" exclaimed a carter who was listening, with a loud laugh; "five francs! The deuce, I should think so! Five balls!"

Thenardier thought it time to strike in.

"Yes, Sir; if such is your fancy, you will be allowed to have that pair of stockings for five francs. We can refuse nothing to travelers."

"You must pay on the spot," said the Thenardier, in her curt and peremptory fashion.

"I will buy that pair of stockings," replied the man, "and," he added, drawing a five-franc piece from his pocket, and laying it on the table, "I will pay for them."

Then he turned to Cosette.

"Now I own your work; play, my child."

The carter was so much touched by the five-franc piece, that he abandoned his glass and hastened up.

"But it's true!" he cried, examining it. "A real hind wheel! And not counterfeit!"

Thenardier approached and silently put the coin in his pocket.

The Thenardier had no reply to make. She bit her lips, and her face assumed an expression of hatred.

In the meantime, Cosette was trembling. She ventured to ask, "Is it true, Madame? May I play?"

"Play!" said the Thenardier, in a terrible voice.

"Thanks, Madame," said Cosette.

And while her mouth thanked the Thenardier, her whole little soul thanked the traveler.

Thenardier had resumed his drinking; his wife whispered in his ear, "Who can this yellow man be?"

"I have seen millionaires with coats like that," replied Thenardier, in a sovereign manner.

Cosette had dropped her knitting, but had not left her seat. Cosette always moved as little as possible. She picked up some old rags and her little lead sword from a box behind her.

Eponine and Azelma paid no attention to what was going on. They had just executed a very important operation; they had just got hold of the cat. They had thrown their doll on the ground, and Eponine, who was the elder, was swathing the little cat, in spite of its mewing and its contortions, in a quantity of clothes and red and blue scraps. While performing this serious and difficult work she was saying to her sister in that sweet and adorable language of children, whose grace, like the splendor of the butterfly's wing, vanishes when one essays to fix it fast.

"You see, sister, this doll is more amusing than the other. She twists, she cries, she is warm. See, sister, let us play with her. She shall be my little girl. I will be a lady. I will come to see you, and you shall look at her. Gradually, you will perceive her whiskers, and that will surprise you. And then you will see her ears, and then you will see her tail and it will amaze you. And you will say to me, 'Ah! *Mon Dieu!*' and I will say to you, 'Yes, Madame, it is my little girl. Little girls are made like that just at present.'"

Azelma listened admiringly to Eponine.

In the meantime, the drinkers had begun to sing an obscene song, and to laugh at it until the ceiling shook. Thenardier accompanied and encouraged them.

As birds make nests out of everything, so children make a doll out of anything that comes to hand. While Eponine and Azelma were bundling up the cat, Cosette, on her side, had dressed up her sword. That done, she laid it in her arms, and sang to it softly, to lull it to sleep.

The doll is one of the most imperious needs and, at the same time, one of the most charming instincts of feminine childhood. To care for, to clothe, to deck, to dress, to undress, to redress, to teach, scold a little, to rock, to dandle, to lull to sleep, to imagine that something is someone, therein lies the whole woman's future. While dreaming and chattering, making tiny outfits, and baby clothes, while sewing little gowns, and corsages and bodices, the child grows into a young girl, the young girl into a big girl, the big girl into a woman. The first child is the continuation of the last doll.

A little girl without a doll is almost as unhappy, and quite as impossible, as a woman without children.

So Cosette had made herself a doll out of the sword.

Madame Thenardier approached the yellow man; "My husband is right," she thought; "perhaps it is M. Laffitte; there are such queer rich men!"

She came and set her elbows on the table.

"Monsieur," said she. At this word, "Monsieur," the man turned; up to that time, the Thenardier had addressed him only as brave homme or bonhomme.

"You see, Sir," she pursued, assuming a sweetish air that was even more repulsive to behold than her fierce mien, "I am willing that the child should play; I do not oppose it, but it is good for once, because you are generous. You see, she has nothing; she must needs work."

"Then this child is not yours?" demanded the man.

"Oh! *Mon Dieu*! No, Sir! She is a little beggar whom we have taken in through charity; a sort of imbecile child. She must have water on the brain; she has a large head, as you see. We do what we can for her, for we are not rich; we have written in vain to her native place, and have received no reply these six months. It must be that her mother is dead."

"Ah!" said the man, and fell into his reverie once more.

"Her mother didn't amount to much," added the Thenardier; "she abandoned her child."

During the whole of this conversation Cosette, as though warned by some instinct that she was under discussion, had not taken her eyes from the Thenardier's face; she listened vaguely; she caught a few words here and there.

Meanwhile, the drinkers, all three-quarters intoxicated, were repeating their unclean refrain with redoubled gaiety; it was a highly spiced and wanton song, in which the Virgin and the infant Jesus were introduced. The Thenardier went off to take part in the shouts of laughter. Cosette, from her post under the table, gazed at the fire, which was reflected from her fixed eyes. She had begun to rock the sort of baby which she had made, and, as she rocked it, she sang in a low voice, "My mother is dead! My mother is dead! My mother is dead!"

On being urged afresh by the hostess, the yellow man, "the millionaire," consented at last to take supper.

"What does Monsieur wish?"

"Bread and cheese," said the man.

"Decidedly, he is a beggar" thought Madame Thenardier.

The drunken men were still singing their song, and the child under the table was singing hers.

All at once, Cosette paused; she had just turned around and caught sight of the little Thenardiers' doll, which they had abandoned for the cat and had left on the floor a few paces from the kitchen table.

Then she dropped the swaddled sword, which only half met her needs, and cast her eyes slowly around the room. Madame Thenardier was whispering to her husband and counting over some money; Ponine and Zelma were playing with the cat; the travelers were eating or drinking or singing; not a glance was fixed on her. She had not a moment to lose; she crept out from under the table on her hands and knees, made sure once more that no one was watching her; then she slipped quickly up to the doll and seized it. An instant later she was in her place again, seated motionless, and only turned so as to cast a shadow on the doll, which she held in her arms. The happiness of playing with a doll was so rare for her that it contained all the violence of voluptuousness.

No one had seen her, except the traveler, who was slowly devouring his meager supper.

This joy lasted about a quarter of an hour.

But with all the precautions that Cosette had taken she did not perceive that one of the doll's legs stuck out and that the fire on the hearth lighted it up very vividly. That pink and shining foot, projecting from the shadow, suddenly struck the eye of Azelma, who said to Eponine, "Look! Sister."

The two little girls paused in stupefaction; Cosette had dared to take their doll!

Eponine rose, and, without releasing the cat, she ran to her mother, and began to tug at her skirt.

"Let me alone!" said her mother;. "What do you want?"

"Mother," said the child, "look there!"

And she pointed to Cosette.

Cosette, absorbed in the ecstasies of possession, no longer saw or heard anything.

Madame Thenardier's countenance assumed that peculiar expression which is composed of the terrible mingled with the trifles of life, and which has caused this style of woman to be named meagerness.

On this occasion, wounded pride exasperated her wrath still further. Cosette had overstepped all bounds; Cosette had laid violent hands on the doll belonging to "these young ladies." A czarina who should see a muzhik trying on her imperial son's blue ribbon would wear no other face.

She shrieked in a voice rendered hoarse with indignation, "Cosette!"

Cosette started as though the earth had trembled beneath her; she turned around.

"Cosette!" repeated the Thenardier.

Cosette took the doll and laid it gently on the floor with a sort of veneration, mingled with despair; then, without taking her eyes from it, she clasped her hands, and, what is terrible to relate of a child of that age, she wrung them; then—not one of the emotions of the day, neither the trip to the forest, nor the weight of the bucket of water, nor the loss of the money, nor the sight of the whip, nor even the sad words that she had heard Madame Thenardier utter had been able to wring this from her—she wept; she burst out sobbing.

Meanwhile, the traveler had risen to his feet.

"What is the matter?" he said to the Thenardier.

"Don't you see?" said the Thenardier, pointing to the corpus delicti which lay at Cosette's feet.

"Well, what of it?" resumed the man.

"That beggar," replied the Thenardier, "has permitted herself to touch the children's doll!"

"All this noise for that!" said the man. "Well, what if she did play with that doll?"

"She touched it with her dirty hands!" pursued the Thenardier. "With her frightful hands!"

Here Cosette redoubled her sobs.

"Will you stop your noise?" screamed the Thenardier.

The man went straight to the street door, opened it, and stepped out.

As soon as he had gone, the Thenardier profited by his absence to give Cosette a hearty kick under the table, which made the child utter loud cries.

The door opened again, the man reappeared; he carried in both hands the fabulous doll that we have mentioned, and which all the village brats had been staring at ever since the morning, and he set it upright in front of Cosette, saying, "Here; this is for you."

It must be supposed that in the course of the hour and more that he had spent there he had taken confused notice through his reverie of that toy shop, lighted up by firepots and candles so splendidly that it was visible like an illumination through the window of the drinking shop.

Cosette raised her eyes; she gazed at the man approaching her with that doll as she might have gazed at the sun; she heard the unprecedented words, "It is for you"; she stared at him; she stared at the doll; then she slowly retreated, and hid herself at the extreme end, under the table in a corner of the wall.

She no longer cried; she no longer wept; she had the appearance of no longer daring to breathe.

The Thenardier, Eponine, and Azelma were like statues also; the very drinkers had paused; a solemn silence reigned through the whole room.

Madame Thenardier, petrified and mute, recommenced her conjectures. "Who is that old fellow? Is he a poor man? Is he a millionaire? Perhaps he is both; that is to say, a thief."

The face of the male Thenardier presented that expressive fold that accentuates the human countenance whenever the dominant instinct appears there in all its bestial force. The tavern-keeper stared alternately at the doll and at the traveler; he seemed to be scenting out the man, as he would have scented out a bag of money. This did not last longer than the space of a flash of lightning. He stepped up to his wife and said to her in a low voice, "That machine costs at least thirty francs. No nonsense. Down on your belly before that man!"

Gross natures have this in common with naive natures, that they possess no transition state.

"Well, Cosette," said the Thenardier, in a voice that strove to be sweet, and which was composed of the bitter honey of malicious women, "aren't you going to take your doll?"

Cosette ventured to emerge from her hole.

"The gentleman has given you a doll, my little Cosette," said Thenardier, with a caressing air. "Take it; it is yours."

Cosette gazed at the marvelous doll in a sort of terror. Her face was still flooded with tears, but her eyes began to fill, like the sky at daybreak, with strange beams of joy. What she felt at that moment was a little like what she would have felt if she had been abruptly told, "Little one, you are the Queen of France."

It seemed to her that if she touched that doll, lightning would dart from it.

This was true, up to a certain point, for she said to herself that the Thenardier would scold and beat her.

Nevertheless, the attraction carried the day. She ended by drawing near and murmuring timidly as she turned toward Madame Thenardier, "May I, Madame?"

No words can render that air, at once despairing, terrified, and ecstatic.

"Pardi!" cried the Thenardier. "It is yours. The gentleman has given it to you."

"Truly, Sir?" said Cosette. "Is it true? Is the 'lady' mine?"

The stranger's eyes seemed to be full of tears. He appeared to have reached that point of emotion where a man does not speak for fear lest he should weep. He nodded to Cosette, and placed the "lady's" hand in her tiny hand.

Cosette hastily withdrew her hand, as though that of the "lady" scorched her, and began to stare at the floor. We are forced to add that at that moment she stuck out her tongue immoderately. All at once she wheeled around and seized the doll in a transport.

"I shall call her Catherine," she said.

It was an odd moment when Cosette's rags met and clasped the ribbons and fresh pink muslins of the doll.

"Madame," she resumed, "may I put her on a chair?"

"Yes, my child," replied the Thenardier.

It was now the turn of Eponine and Azelma to gaze at Cosette with envy.

Cosette placed Catherine on a chair, then seated herself on the floor in front of her, and remained motionless, without uttering a word, in an attitude of contemplation.

"Play, Cosette," said the stranger.

"Oh! I am playing," returned the child.

This stranger, this unknown individual, who had the air of a visit which Providence was making on Cosette, was the person whom the Thenardier hated worse than anyone in the world at that moment. However, it was necessary to control herself. Habituated as she was to dissimulation through endeavoring to copy her husband in all his actions, these emotions were more than she could endure. She made haste to send her daughters to bed, then she asked the man's permission to send Cosette off also; "for she has worked hard all day," she added with a maternal air. Cosette went off to bed, carrying Catherine in her arms.

From time to time the Thenardier went to the other end of the room where her husband was, to relieve her soul, as she said. She exchanged with her husband words that were all the more furious because she dared not utter them aloud.

"Old beast! What has he got in his belly, to come and upset us in this manner! To want that little monster to play! To give away forty-franc dolls to a jade that I would sell for forty sous, so I would! A little more and he will be saying Your Majesty to her, as though to the Duchess de Berry! Is there any sense in it? Is he mad, then, that mysterious old fellow?"

"Why! It is perfectly simple," replied Thenardier, "if that amuses him! It amuses you to have the little one work; it amuses him to have her play. He's all right. A traveler can do what he pleases when he pays for it. If the old fellow is a philanthropist, what is that to you? If he is an imbecile, it does not concern you. What are you worrying for, so long as he has money?"

The language of a master, and the reasoning of an innkeeper, neither of which admitted of any reply.

The man had placed his elbows on the table, and resumed his thoughtful attitude. All the other travelers, both peddlers and carters, had withdrawn a little, and had ceased singing. They were staring at him from a distance, with a sort of respectful awe. This poorly dressed man, who drew "hind-wheels" from his pocket with so much ease, and who lavished gigantic dolls on dirty little brats in wooden shoes, was certainly a magnificent fellow, and one to be feared.

Many hours passed. The midnight Mass was over, the chimes had ceased, the drinkers had taken their departure, the drinking-shop was closed, the public room was deserted, the fire extinct, the stranger still remained in the same place and the same attitude. From time to time he changed the elbow on which he leaned. That was all; but he had not said a word since Cosette had left the room.

The Thenardiers alone, out of politeness and curiosity, had remained in the room.

"Is he going to pass the night in that fashion?" grumbled the Thenardier. When two o'clock in the morning struck, she declared herself vanquished, and said to her husband, "I'm going to bed. Do as you like." Her husband seated himself at a table in the corner, lighted a candle, and began to read the *Courrier Francais*.

A good hour passed thus. The worthy innkeeper had perused the *Courrier Francais* at least three times, from the date of the number to the printer's name. The stranger did not stir.

Thenardier fidgeted, coughed, spit, blew his nose, and creaked his chair. Not a movement on the man's part. "Is he asleep?" thought Thenardier. The man was not asleep, but nothing could arouse him.

At last Thenardier took off his cap, stepped gently up to him, and ventured to say, "Is not Monsieur going to his repose?"

Not going to bed would have seemed to him excessive and familiar. To repose smacked of luxury and respect. These words possess the mysterious and admirable property of swelling the bill on the following day. A chamber where one sleeps costs twenty sous; a chamber in which one reposes costs twenty francs.

"Well!" said the stranger. "You are right. Where is your stable?"

"Sir!" exclaimed Thenardier, with a smile, "I will conduct you, Sir."

He took the candle; the man picked up his bundle and cudgel, and Thenardier conducted him to a chamber on the first floor, which was of rare splendor, all furnished in mahogany, with a low bedstead, curtained with red calico.

"What is this?" said the traveler.

"It is really our bridal chamber," said the tavern-keeper. "My wife and I occupy another. This is only entered three or four times a year."

"I should have liked the stable quite as well," said the man, abruptly.

Thenardier pretended not to hear this unamiable remark.

He lighted two perfectly fresh wax candles that figured on the chimneypiece. A very good fire was flickering on the hearth.

On the chimneypiece, under a glass globe, stood a woman's headdress in silver wire and orange flowers.

"And what is this?" resumed the stranger.

"That, Sir," said Thenardier, "is my wife's wedding bonnet."

The traveler surveyed the object with a glance that seemed to say, "There really was a time, then, when that monster was a maiden?"

Thenardier lied, however. When he had leased this paltry building for the purpose of converting it into a tavern, he had found this chamber decorated in just this manner, and had purchased the furniture and obtained the orange flowers at second hand, with the idea that this would cast a graceful shadow on "his spouse," and would result in what the English call respectability for his house.

When the traveler turned around, the host had disappeared. Thenardier had withdrawn discreetly, without venturing to wish him a good night, as he did not wish to treat with disrespectful cordiality a man whom he proposed to fleece royally the following morning.

The innkeeper retired to his room. His wife was in bed, but she was not asleep. When she heard her husband's step she turned over and said to him, "Do you know, I'm going to turn Cosette out of doors tomorrow."

Thenardier replied coldly, "How you do go on!"

They exchanged no further words, and a few moments later their candle was extinguished.

As for the traveler, he had deposited his cudgel and his bundle in a corner. The landlord once gone, he threw himself into an armchair and remained for some time buried in thought. Then he removed his shoes, took one of the two candles, blew out the other, opened the door, and quitted the room, gazing about him like a person who is in search of something. He traversed a corridor and came upon a staircase. There he heard a very faint and gentle sound like the breathing of a child. He followed this sound, and came to a sort of triangular recess built under the staircase, or rather formed by the staircase itself. This recess was nothing else than the space under the steps. There, in the midst of all sorts of old papers and potsherds, among dust and spiders' webs, was a bed—if one can call by the name of bed a straw pallet so full of holes as to display the straw, and a coverlet so tattered as to show the pallet. No sheets. This was placed on the floor.

In this bed Cosette was sleeping.

The man approached and gazed down upon her.

Cosette was in a profound sleep; she was fully dressed. In the winter she did not undress, in order that she might not be so cold.

Against her breast was pressed the doll, whose large eyes, wide open, glittered in the dark. From time to time she gave vent to a deep sigh as though she were on the point of waking, and she strained the doll almost convulsively in her arms. Beside her bed there was only one of her wooden shoes.

A door, which stood open near Cosette's pallet, permitted a view of a rather large, dark room. The stranger stepped into it. At the further extremity, through a glass door, he saw two small, very white beds. They belonged to Eponine and Azelma. Behind these beds, and half hidden, stood an uncurtained wicker cradle, in which the little boy who had cried all the evening lay asleep.

The stranger conjectured that this chamber connected with that of the Thenardier pair. He was on the point of retreating when his eye fell upon the fireplace—one of those vast tavern chimneys where there is always so little fire when there is any fire at all, and which are so cold to look at. There was no fire in this one, there was not even ashes; but there was something that attracted the stranger's gaze, nevertheless. It was two tiny children's shoes, coquettish in shape and unequal in size. The traveler recalled the graceful and immemorial custom in accordance with which children place their shoes in the chimney on Christmas eve, there to await in the darkness some sparkling gift from their good fairy. Eponine and Azelma had taken care not to omit this, and each of them had set one of her shoes on the hearth.

The traveler bent over them.

The fairy, that is to say, their mother, had already paid her visit, and in each he saw a brand-new and shining ten-sou piece.

The man straightened himself up, and was on the point of withdrawing, when far in, in the darkest corner of the hearth, he caught sight of another object. He looked at it, and recognized a wooden shoe, a frightful shoe of the coarsest description, half dilapidated and all covered with ashes and dried mud. It was Cosette's sabot. Cosette, with that touching trust of childhood, which can always be deceived yet never discouraged, had placed her shoe on the hearth-stone also.

Hope in a child who has never known anything but despair is a sweet and touching thing.

There was nothing in this wooden shoe.

The stranger fumbled in his waistcoat, bent over and placed a *louis d'or** in Cosette's shoe.

Then he regained his own chamber with the stealthy tread of a wolf.

CHAPTER IX — THENARDIER AND HIS MANEUVERS

On the following morning, two hours at least before daybreak, Thenardier, seated beside a candle in the public room of the tavern, pen in hand, was making out the bill for the traveler with the yellow coat.

His wife, standing beside him, and half bent over him, was following him with her eyes. They exchanged not a word. On the one hand, there was profound meditation, on the other, the religious admiration with which one watches the birth and development of a marvel of the human mind. A noise was audible in the house; it was the Lark sweeping the stairs.

After the lapse of a good quarter of an hour, and some erasures, Thenardier produced the following masterpiece:

BILL OF THE GENTLEMAN IN No. 1.

Supper	3 francs
Chamber	10
Candle	5
Fire	4
Service	1
Total	23 francs

Service was written *servisse*.

"Twenty-three francs!" cried the woman, with an enthusiasm mingled with some hesitation.

Like all great artists, Thenardier was dissatisfied.

"Peuh!" he exclaimed.

It was the accent of Castlereagh auditing France's bill at the Congress of Vienna.

"Monsieur Thenardier, you are right; he certainly owes that," murmured the wife, who was thinking of the doll bestowed on Cosette in the presence of

---

* a French coin

her daughters. "It is just, but it is too much. He will not pay it."

Thenardier laughed coldly, as usual, and said, "He will pay."

This laugh was the supreme assertion of certainty and authority. Tha which was asserted in this manner must needs be so. His wife did not insist.

She set about arranging the table; her husband paced the room. A momen later he added, "I owe full fifteen hundred francs!"

He went and seated himself in the chimney corner, meditating, with his fee among the warm ashes.

"Ah! By the way," resumed his wife, "you don't forget that I'm going to turn Cosette out of doors today? The monster! She breaks my heart with tha doll of hers! I'd rather marry Louis XVIII than keep her another day in the house!"

Thenardier lighted his pipe, and replied between two puffs, "You will hand that bill to the man."

Then he went out.

Hardly had he left the room when the traveler entered.

Thenardier instantly reappeared behind him and remained motionless in the half-open door, visible only to his wife.

The yellow man carried his bundle and his cudgel in his hand.

"Up so early?" said Madame Thenardier. "Is Monsieur leaving us already?"

As she spoke thus, she was twisting the bill about in her hands with an embarrassed air, and making creases in it with her nails. Her hard face presented a shade which was not habitual with it, timidity and scruples.

To present such a bill to a man who had so completely the air "of a poor wretch" seemed difficult to her.

The traveler appeared to be preoccupied and absent-minded. He replied "Yes, Madame, I am going."

"So Monsieur has no business in Montfermeil?"

"No, I was passing through. That is all. What do I owe you, Madame," he added.

The Thenardier silently handed him the folded bill.

The man unfolded the paper and glanced at it; but his thoughts were evidently elsewhere.

"Madame," he resumed, "is business good here in Montfermeil?"

"So so, Monsieur," replied the Thenardier, stupefied at not witnessing another sort of explosion.

She continued, in a dreary and lamentable tone, "Oh! Monsieur, times are so hard! And then, we have so few bourgeois in the neighborhood! All the people are poor, you see. If we had not, now and then, some rich and generous travelers like Monsieur, we should not get along at all. We have so many expenses. Just see, that child is costing us our very eyes."

"What child?"

"Why, the little one, you know! Cosette—the Lark, as she is called hereabouts!"

"Ah!" said the man.

She went on, "How stupid these peasants are with their nicknames! She has more the air of a bat than of a lark. You see, Sir, we do not ask charity, and we cannot bestow it. We earn nothing and we have to pay out a great deal. The license, the imposts, the door and window tax, the hundredths! Monsieur is aware that the government demands a terrible deal of money. And then, I have my daughters. I have no need to bring up other people's children."

The man resumed, in that voice, which he strove to render indifferent, and in which there lingered a tremor, "What if one were to rid you of her?"

"Who? Cosette?"

"Yes."

The landlady's red and violent face brightened up hideously.

"Ah! Sir, my dear sir, take her, keep her, lead her off, carry her away, sugar her, stuff her with truffles, drink her, eat her, and the blessings of the good holy Virgin and of all the saints of paradise be upon you!"

"Agreed."

"Really! You will take her away?"

"I will take her away."

"Immediately?"

"Immediately. Call the child."

"Cosette!" screamed the Thenardier.

"In the meantime," pursued the man, "I will pay you what I owe you. How much is it?"

He cast a glance on the bill, and could not restrain a start of surprise, "Twenty-three francs!"

He looked at the landlady, and repeated, "Twenty-three francs?"

There was in the enunciation of these words, thus repeated, an accent between an exclamation and an interrogation point.

The Thenardier had had time to prepare herself for the shock. She replied, with assurance, "Good gracious, yes, Sir, it is twenty-three francs."

The stranger laid five five-franc pieces on the table.

"Go and get the child," said he.

At that moment Thenardier advanced to the middle of the room, and said, "Monsieur owes twenty-six sous."

"Twenty-six sous!" exclaimed his wife.

"Twenty sous for the chamber," resumed Thenardier, coldly, "and six sous for his supper. As for the child, I must discuss that matter a little with the gentleman. Leave us, wife."

Madame Thenardier was dazzled as with the shock caused by unexpected lightning flashes of talent. She was conscious that a great actor was making his entrance on the stage, uttered not a word in reply, and left the room.

As soon as they were alone, Thenardier offered the traveler a chair. The traveler seated himself; Thenardier remained standing, and his face assumed a singular expression of goodfellowship and simplicity.

"Sir," said he, "what I have to say to you is this, that I adore that child."

The stranger gazed intently at him.

"What child?"

Thenardier continued, "How strange it is, one grows attached. What money is that? Take back your hundred-sou piece. I adore the child."

"Whom do you mean?" demanded the stranger.

"Eh! Our little Cosette! Are you not intending to take her away from us? Well, I speak frankly; as true as you are an honest man, I will not consent to it. I shall miss that child. I saw her first when she was a tiny thing. It is true that she costs us money; it is true that she has her faults; it is true that we are not rich; it is true that I have paid out over four hundred francs for drugs for just one of her illnesses! But one must do something for the good God's sake. She has neither father nor mother. I have brought her up. I have bread enough for her and for myself. In truth, I think a great deal of that child. You understand, one conceives an affection for a person; I am a good sort of a beast, I am; I do not reason; I love that little girl; my wife is quick-tempered, but she loves her also. You see, she is just the same as our own child. I want to keep her to babble about the house."

The stranger kept his eye intently fixed on Thenardier. The latter continued, "Excuse me, Sir, but one does not give away one's child to a passerby, like that. I am right, am I not? Still, I don't say—you are rich; you have the air of a very good man, if it were for her happiness. But one must find out that. You understand: suppose that I were to let her go and to sacrifice myself, I should like to know what becomes of her; I should not wish to lose sight of her; I should like to know with whom she is living, so that I could go to see her from time to time; so that she may know that her good foster-father is alive, that he s watching over her. In short, there are things that are not possible. I do not even know your name. If you were to take her away, I should say, 'Well, and the Lark, what has become of her?' One must, at least, see some petty scrap of paper, some trifle in the way of a passport, you know!"

The stranger, still surveying him with that gaze, which penetrates, as the saying goes, to the very depths of the conscience, replied in a grave, firm voice, "Monsieur Thenardier, one does not require a passport to travel five leagues from Paris. If I take Cosette away, I shall take her away, and that is the end of the matter. You will not know my name, you will not know my residence, you will not know where she is; and my intention is that she shall never set eyes on you again so long as she lives. I break the thread which binds her foot, and she departs. Does that suit you? Yes or no?"

Since geniuses, like demons, recognize the presence of a superior God by certain signs, Thenardier comprehended that he had to deal with a very strong person. It was like an intuition; he comprehended it with his clear and sagacious promptitude. While drinking with the carters, smoking, and singing coarse songs on the preceding evening, he had devoted the whole of the time to observing the stranger, watching him like a cat, and studying him like a mathematician. He had watched him, both on his own account, for the pleasure of the thing, and through instinct, and had spied upon him as though he had been paid for so doing. Not a movement, not a gesture, on the part of the man in the yellow great-coat had escaped him. Even before the stranger had so clearly manifested his interest in Cosette, Thenardier had divined his purpose. He had caught the old man's deep glances returning constantly to the child. Who was this man? Why this interest? Why this hideous costume, when he had so much money in his purse? Questions, which he put to himself without being able to solve them, and which irritated him. He had pondered it all night long. He could not be Cosette's father. Was he her grandfather? Then why not make himself known at once? When one has a right, one asserts it. This man evidently had no right over Cosette. What was it, then? Thenardier lost himself in conjectures. He caught glimpses of everything, but he saw nothing. Be that as it may, on entering into conversation with the man, sure that there was some secret in the case, that the latter had some interest in remaining in the shadow, he felt himself strong; when he perceived from the stranger's clear and firm retort, that this mysterious personage was mysterious in so simple a way, he became conscious that he was weak. He had expected nothing of the sort. His conjectures were put to the rout. He rallied his ideas. He weighed everything in the space of a second. Thenardier was one of those men who

take in a situation at a glance. He decided that the moment had arrived for
proceeding straightforward, and quickly at that. He did as great leaders do at
the decisive moment, which they know that they alone recognize; he abruptly
unmasked his batteries.

"Sir," said he, "I am in need of fifteen hundred francs."

The stranger took from his side pocket an old pocketbook of black leather,
opened it, drew out three bank-bills, which he laid on the table. Then he placed
his large thumb on the notes and said to the innkepper, "Go and fetch Cosette."

While this was taking place, what had Cosette been doing?

On waking up, Cosette had run to get her shoe. In it she had found the
gold piece. It was not a Napoleon; it was one of those perfectly new twenty
franc pieces of the Restoration, on whose effigy the little Prussian queue
had replaced the laurel wreath. Cosette was dazzled. Her destiny began to
intoxicate her. She did not know what a gold piece was; she had never seen
one; she hid it quickly in her pocket, as though she had stolen it. Still, she
felt that it really was hers; she guessed from where her gift had come, but the
joy that she experienced was full of fear. She was happy; above all she was
stupefied. Such magnificent and beautiful things did not appear real. The doll
frightened her, the gold piece frightened her. She trembled vaguely in the
presence of this magnificence. The stranger alone did not frighten her. On
the contrary, he reassured her. Ever since the preceding evening, amid all her
amazement, even in her sleep, she had been thinking in her little childish mind
of that man who seemed to be so poor and so sad, and who was so rich and
so kind. Everything had changed for her since she had met that good man in
the forest. Cosette, less happy than the most insignificant swallow of heaven,
had never known what it was to take refuge under a mother's shadow and
under a wing. For the last five years, that is to say, as far back as her memory
ran, the poor child had shivered and trembled. She had always been exposed
completely naked to the sharp wind of adversity; now it seemed to her she
was clothed. Formerly her soul had seemed cold, now it was warm. Cosette
was no longer afraid of the Thenardier. She was no longer alone; there was
someone there.

She hastily set about her regular morning duties. That louis, which she had
about her, in the very apron pocket from which the fifteen-sou piece had fallen
on the night before, distracted her thoughts. She dared not touch it, but she
spent five minutes in gazing at it, with her tongue hanging out, if the truth
must be told. As she swept the staircase, she paused, remained standing there
motionless, forgetful of her broom and of the entire universe, occupied in

gazing at that star that was blazing at the bottom of her pocket.

It was during one of these periods of contemplation that the Thenardier joined her. She had gone in search of Cosette at her husband's orders. What was quite unprecedented, she neither struck her nor said an insulting word to her.

"Cosette," she said, almost gently, "come immediately."

An instant later Cosette entered the public room.

The stranger took up the bundle that he had brought and untied it. This bundle contained a little woolen gown, an apron, a fustian bodice, a kerchief, a petticoat, woolen stockings, shoes—a complete outfit for a girl of seven years. All was black.

"My child," said the man, "take these, and go and dress yourself quickly."

Daylight was appearing when those of the inhabitants of Montfermeil who had begun to open their doors beheld a poorly clad old man leading a little girl dressed in mourning, and carrying a pink doll in her arms, pass along the road to Paris. They were going in the direction of Livry.

It was our man and Cosette.

No one knew the man; as Cosette was no longer in rags, many did not recognize her. Cosette was going away. With whom? She did not know. Where? She knew not. All that she understood was that she was leaving the Thenardier tavern behind her. No one had thought of bidding her farewell, nor had she thought of taking leave of anyone. She was leaving that hated and hating house.

Poor, gentle creature, whose heart had been repressed up to that hour!

Cosette walked along gravely, with her large eyes wide open, and gazing at the sky. She had put her louis in the pocket of her new apron. From time to time, she bent down and glanced at it; then she looked at the good man. She felt something as though she were beside the good God.

CHAPTER X—HE WHO SEEKS TO BETTER HIMSELF MAY RENDER HIS SITUATION WORSE

Madame Thenardier had allowed her husband to have his own way, as was her wont. She had expected great results. When the man and Cosette had taken their departure, Thenardier allowed a full quarter of an hour to elapse; then he took her aside and showed her the fifteen hundred francs.

"Is that all?" said she.

It was the first time since they had set up housekeeping that she had dared to criticize one of the master's acts.

The blow told.

"You are right, in sooth," said he; "I am a fool. Give me my hat."

He folded up the three bank bills, thrust them into his pocket, and ran out in all haste; but he made a mistake and turned to the right first. Some neighbors of whom he made inquiries, put him on the track again; the Lark and the man had been seen going in the direction of Livry. He followed these hints, walking with great strides, and talking to himself the while, "That man is evidently a million dressed in yellow, and I am an animal. First he gave twenty sous, then five francs, then fifty francs, then fifteen hundred francs, all with equal readiness. He would have given fifteen thousand francs. But I shall overtake him."

And then, that bundle of clothes prepared beforehand for the child; all that was singular; many mysteries lay concealed under it. One does not let mysteries out of one's hand when one has once grasped them. The secrets of the wealthy are sponges of gold; one must know how to subject them to pressure. All these thoughts whirled through his brain. "I am an animal," said he.

When one leaves Montfermeil and reaches the turn which the road takes that runs to Livry, it can be seen stretching out before one to a great distance across the plateau. On arriving there, he calculated that he ought to be able to see the old man and the child. He looked as far as his vision reached, and saw nothing. He made fresh inquiries, but he had wasted time. Some passersby informed him that the man and child of whom he was in search had gone toward the forest in the direction of Gagny. He hastened in that direction.

They were far in advance of him; but a child walks slowly, and he walked fast; and then, he was well acquainted with the country.

All at once he paused and dealt himself a blow on his forehead like a man who has forgotten some essential point and who is ready to retrace his steps.

"I ought to have taken my gun," said he to himself.

Thenardier was one of those double natures, which sometimes pass through our midst without our being aware of the fact, and who disappear without our finding them out, because destiny has only exhibited one side of them. It is the fate of many men to live thus half submerged. In a calm and even situation Thenardier possessed all that is required to make—we will not say to be—what people have agreed to call an honest trader, a good bourgeois. At the same time certain circumstances being given, certain shocks arriving to bring his under-nature to the surface, he had all the requisites for a blackguard. He was shopkeeper in whom there was some taint of the monster. Satan must have occasionally crouched down in some corner of the hovel in which Thenardier welled, and have fallen a-dreaming in the presence of this hideous masterpiece.

After a momentary hesitation, "Bah!" he thought. "They will have time to 1ake their escape."

And he pursued his road, walking rapidly straight ahead, and with almost n air of certainty, with the sagacity of a fox scenting a covey of partridges.

In truth, when he had passed the ponds and had traversed in an oblique lirection the large clearing which lies on the right of the Avenue de Bellevue, 1d reached that turf alley which nearly makes the circuit of the hill, and overs the arch of the ancient aqueduct of the Abbéy of Chelles, he caught ight, over the top of the brushwood, of the hat on which he had already rected so many conjectures; it was that man's hat. The brushwood was not igh. Thenardier recognized the fact that the man and Cosette were sitting here. The child could not be seen on account of her small size, but the head f her doll was visible.

Thenardier was not mistaken. The man was sitting there, and letting osette get somewhat rested. The innkepper walked around the brushwood nd presented himself abruptly to the eyes of those whom he was in search of.

"Pardon, excuse me, Sir," he said, quite breathless, "but here are your fteen hundred francs."

So saying, he handed the stranger the three bank bills.

The man raised his eyes.

"What is the meaning of this?"

Thenardier replied respectfully, "It means, Sir, that I shall take back osette."

Cosette shuddered, and pressed close to the old man.

He replied, gazing to the very bottom of Thenardier's eyes the while, and nunciating every syllable distinctly, "You are go-ing to take back Co-sette?"

"Yes, Sir, I am. I will tell you; I have considered the matter. In fact, I have ot the right to give her to you. I am an honest man, you see; this child does not elong to me; she belongs to her mother. It was her mother who confided her o me; I can only resign her to her mother. You will say to me, 'But her mother s dead.' Good; in that case I can only give the child up to the person who shall ring me a writing, signed by her mother, to the effect that I am to hand the hild over to the person therein mentioned; that is clear."

The man, without making any reply, fumbled in his pocket, and Thenardier eheld the pocketbook of bank-bills make its appearance once more.

The tavern-keeper shivered with joy.

"Good!" thought he; "let us hold firm; he is going to bribe me!"

Before opening the pocketbook, the traveler cast a glance about him: th spot was absolutely deserted; there was not a soul either in the woods or in th valley. The man opened his pocketbook once more and drew from it, not th handful of bills which Thenardier expected, but a simple little paper, which h unfolded and presented fully open to the innkepper, saying, "You are righ read!"

Thenardier took the paper and read:

M. SUR M., March 25, 1823.
"MONSIEUR THENARDIER:
You will deliver Cosette to this person.
You will be paid for all the little things.
I have the honor to salute you with respect,
FANTINE."

"You know that signature?" resumed the man.

It certainly was Fantine's signature; Thenardier recognized it.

There was no reply to make; he experienced two violent vexations, th vexation of renouncing the bribery he had hoped for, and the vexation of bein beaten; the man added, "You may keep this paper as your receipt."

Thenardier retreated in tolerably good order.

"This signature is fairly well imitated," he growled between his teeth "however, let it go!"

Then he essayed a desperate effort.

"It is well, Sir," he said, "since you are the person, but I must be paid for a those little things. A great deal is owing to me."

The man rose to his feet, filliping the dust from his threadbare sleeve "Monsieur Thenardier, in January last, the mother reckoned that she owed yo one hundred and twenty francs. In February, you sent her a bill of five hundre francs; you received three hundred francs at the end of February, and thre hundred francs at the beginning of March. Since then nine months have elapse at fifteen francs a month, the price agreed upon, which makes one hundred an thirty-five francs. You had received one hundred francs too much; that make thirty-five still owing you. I have just given you fifteen hundred francs."

Thenardier's sensations were those of the wolf at the moment when h feels himself nipped and seized by the steel jaw of the trap.

"Who is this devil of a man?" he thought.

He did what the wolf does: he shook himself. Audacity had succeeded with him once.

"Monsieur-I-don't-know-your-name," he said resolutely, and this time casting aside all respectful ceremony, "I shall take back Cosette if you do not give me a thousand crowns."

The stranger said tranquilly, "Come, Cosette."

He took Cosette by his left hand, and with his right he picked up his cudgel, which was lying on the ground.

Thenardier noted the enormous size of the cudgel and the solitude of the spot.

The man plunged into the forest with the child, leaving the innkepper motionless and speechless.

While they were walking away, Thenardier scrutinized his huge shoulders, which were a little rounded, and his great fists.

Then, bringing his eyes back to his own person, they fell upon his feeble arms and his thin hands. "I really must have been exceedingly stupid not to have thought to bring my gun," he said to himself, "since I was going hunting!"

However, the innkepper did not give up.

"I want to know where he is going," said he, and he set out to follow them at a distance. Two things were left on his hands, an irony in the shape of the paper signed Fantine, and a consolation, the fifteen hundred francs.

The man led Cosette off in the direction of Livry and Bondy. He walked slowly, with drooping head, in an attitude of reflection and sadness. The winter had thinned out the forest, so that Thenardier did not lose them from sight, although he kept at a good distance. The man turned around from time to time, and looked to see if he was being followed. All at once he caught sight of Thenardier. He plunged suddenly into the brushwood with Cosette, where they could both hide themselves. "The deuce!" said Thenardier, and he redoubled his pace.

The thickness of the undergrowth forced him to draw nearer to them. When the man had reached the densest part of the thicket, he wheeled around. It was in vain that Thenardier sought to conceal himself in the branches; he could not prevent the man seeing him. The man cast upon him an uneasy glance, then elevated his head and continued his course. The innkepper set out again in pursuit. Thus they continued for two or three hundred paces. All at once the man turned around once more; he saw the innkepper. This time he gazed at him with so somber an air that Thenardier decided that it was "useless" to proceed further. Thenardier retraced his steps.

CHAPTER XI—NUMBER 9430 REAPPEARS, AND COSETTE WINS IT IN THE LOTTERY

Jean Valjean was not dead.

When he fell into the sea, or rather, when he threw himself into it, he was not ironed, as we have seen. He swam underwater until he reached a vessel at anchor, to which a boat was moored. He found means of hiding himself in this boat until night. At night he swam off again, and reached the shore a little way from Cape Brun. There, as he did not lack money, he procured clothing. A small country house in the neighborhood of Balaguier was at that time the dressing room of escaped convicts, a lucrative specialty. Then Jean Valjean, like all the sorry fugitives who are seeking to evade the vigilance of the law and social fatality, pursued an obscure and undulating itinerary. He found his first refuge at Pradeaux, near Beausset. Then he directed his course toward Grand Villard, near Briancon, in the Hautes-Alpes. It was a fumbling and uneasy flight, a mole's track, whose branchings are untraceable. Later on, some trace of his passage into Ain, in the territory of Civrieux, was discovered; in the Pyrenees, at Accons; at the spot called Grange-de-Doumec, near the market of Chavailles, and in the environs of Perigueux at Brunies, canton of La Chapelle-Gonaguet. He reached Paris. We have just seen him at Montfermeil.

His first care on arriving in Paris had been to buy mourning clothes for a little girl of from seven to eight years of age; then to procure a lodging. That done, he had betaken himself to Montfermeil. It will be remembered that already, during his preceding escape, he had made a mysterious trip there, or somewhere in that neighborhood, of which the law had gathered an inkling.

However, he was thought to be dead, and this still further increased the obscurity that had gathered about him. At Paris, one of the journals that chronicled the fact fell into his hands. He felt reassured and almost at peace, as though he had really been dead.

On the evening of the day when Jean Valjean rescued Cosette from the claws of the Thenardiers, he returned to Paris. He reentered it at nightfall, with the child, by way of the Barrier Monceaux. There he entered a cabriolet which took him to the esplanade of the Observatoire. There he got out, paid the coachman, took Cosette by the hand, and together they directed their steps through the darkness, through the deserted streets, which adjoin the Ourcine and the Glaciere, toward the Boulevard de l'Hopital.

The day had been strange and filled with emotions for Cosette. They had eaten some bread and cheese purchased in isolated taverns, behind hedges; they had changed carriages frequently; they had traveled short distances on foot. She made no complaint, but she was weary, and Jean Valjean perceived it by the way she dragged more and more on his hand as she walked. He took her on his back. Cosette, without letting go of Catherine, laid her head on Jean Valjean's shoulder, and there fell asleep.

BOOK FOURTH:
THE GORBEAU HOVEL

CHAPTER I—MASTER GORBEAU

Forty years ago, a rambler who had ventured into that unknown country of the Salpetriere, and who had mounted to the Barriere d'Italie by way of the boulevard, reached a point where it might be said that Paris disappeared. It was no longer solitude, for there were passersby; it was not the country, for there were houses and streets; it was not the city, for the streets had ruts like highways, and the grass grew in them; it was not a village, the houses were too lofty. What was it, then? It was an inhabited spot where there was no one; it was a desert place where there was someone; it was a boulevard of the great city, a street of Paris; more wild at night than the forest, more gloomy by day than a cemetery.

It was the old quarter of the Marche-aux-Chevaux.

The rambler, if he risked himself outside the four decrepit walls of this Marche-aux-Chevaux; if he consented even to pass beyond the Rue du Petit-Banquier, after leaving on his right a garden protected by high walls; then a field in which tanbark mills rose like gigantic beaver huts; then an enclosure encumbered with timber, with a heap of stumps, sawdust, and shavings, on which stood a large dog, barking; then a long, low, utterly dilapidated wall, with a little black door in mourning, laden with mosses, which were covered with flowers in the spring; then, in the most deserted spot, a frightful and decrepit building, on which ran the inscription in large letters: POST NO BILLS, this daring rambler would have reached little known latitudes at the corner of the Rue des Vignes-Saint-Marcel. There, near a factory, and between two garden walls, there could be seen, at that epoch, a mean building, which, at the first glance, seemed as small as a thatched hovel, and which was, in reality, as large as a cathedral. It presented its side and gable to the public road; hence its apparent diminutiveness. Nearly the whole of the house was hidden. Only the door and one window could be seen.

This hovel was only one story high.

The first detail that struck the observer was that the door could never have been anything but the door of a hovel, while the window, if it had been carved out of dressed stone instead of being in rough masonry, might have been the lattice of a lordly mansion.

The door was nothing but a collection of worm-eaten planks roughly bound together by crossbeams, which resembled roughly hewn logs. It opened directly on a steep staircase of lofty steps, muddy, chalky, plaster-stained, dusty steps, of the same width as itself, which could be seen from the street, running straight up like a ladder and disappearing in the darkness between two walls. The top of the shapeless bay into which this door shut was masked by a narrow scantling in the center of which a triangular hole had been sawed, which served both as wicket and airhole when the door was closed. On the inside of the door the figures 52 had been traced with a couple of strokes of a brush dipped in ink, and above the scantling the same hand had daubed the number 50, so that one hesitated. Where was one? Above the door it said, "Number 50"; the inside replied, "No, Number 52." No one knows what dust-colored figures were suspended like draperies from the triangular opening.

The window was large, sufficiently elevated, garnished with Venetian blinds, and with a frame in large square panes; only these large panes were suffering from various wounds, which were both concealed and betrayed by an ingenious paper bandage. And the blinds, dislocated and unpasted, threatened passersby rather than screened the occupants. The horizontal slats were missing here and there and had been naively replaced with boards nailed on perpendicularly; so that what began as a blind ended as a shutter. This door with an unclean, and this window with an honest though dilapidated air, thus beheld on the same house, produced the effect of two incomplete beggars walking side by side, with different miens beneath the same rags, the one having always been a mendicant, and the other having once been a gentleman.

The staircase led to a very vast edifice that resembled a shed, which had been converted into a house. This edifice had, for its intestinal tube, a long corridor, on which opened to right and left sorts of compartments of varied dimensions which were inhabitable under stress of circumstances, and rather more like stalls than cells. These chambers received their light from the vague waste grounds in the neighborhood.

All this was dark, disagreeable, wan, melancholy, coffinlike; traversed according as the crevices lay in the roof or in the door, by cold rays or by icy winds. An interesting and picturesque peculiarity of this sort of dwelling is the enormous size of the spiders.

To the left of the entrance door, on the boulevard side, at about the height of a man from the ground, a small window, which had been walled up formed a square niche full of stones that the children had thrown there as they passed by.

A portion of this building has recently been demolished. From what still remains of it one can form a judgment as to what it was in former days. As a whole, it was not over a hundred years old. A hundred years is youth in a church and age in a house. It seems as though man's lodging partook of his ephemeral character, and God's house of his eternity.

The postmen called the house Number 50-52; but it was known in the neighborhood as the Gorbeau house.

Let us explain frm where this appellation was derived.

Collectors of petty details, who become herbalists of anecdotes, and prick slippery dates into their memories with a pin, know that there was in Paris, during the last century, about 1770, two attorneys at the Chatelet named, one *Corbeau* (Raven), the other *Renard* (Fox). The two names had been forestalled by La Fontaine. The opportunity was too fine for the lawyers; they made the most of it. A parody was immediately put in circulation in the galleries of the courthouse, in verses that limped a little:

> "*Maître Corbeau, sur un dossier perché,*
> *Tenait dans son bec une saisie exécutoire;*
> *Maître Renard, par l'odeur alléché,*
> *Lui fit à peu près cette histoire:*
> *Hé! bonjour.' Etc.*"

The two honest practitioners, embarrassed by the jests, and finding the bearing of their heads interfered with by the shouts of laughter that followed them, resolved to get rid of their names, and hit upon the expedient of applying to the king.

Their petition was presented to Louis XV on the same day when the Papal Nuncio, on the one hand, and the Cardinal de la Roche-Aymon on the other, both devoutly kneeling, were each engaged in putting on, in his Majesty's presence, a slipper on the bare feet of Madame du Barry, who had just got out of bed. The king, who was laughing, continued to laugh, passed gaily from the two bishops to the two lawyers, and bestowed on these limbs of the law their former names, or nearly so. By the king's command, Maitre Corbeau was permitted to add a tail to his initial letter and to call himself Gorbeau. Maitre Renard was less lucky; all he obtained was leave to place a P in front of his R, and to call himself Prenard; so that the second name bore almost as much resemblance as the first.

Now, according to local tradition, this Maitre Gorbeau had been the proprietor of the building numbered 50-52 on the Boulevard de l'Hopital. He was even the author of the monumental window.

Hence the edifice bore the name of the Gorbeau house.

Opposite this house, among the trees of the boulevard, rose a great elm that was three-quarters dead; almost directly facing it opens the Rue de la Barrière des Gobelins, a street then without houses, unpaved, planted with unhealthy trees, which was green or muddy according to the season, and which ended squarely in the exterior wall of Paris. An odor of copperas issued in puffs from the roofs of the neighboring factory.

The barrier was close at hand. In 1823 the city wall was still in existence.

This barrier itself evoked gloomy fancies in the mind. It was the road to Bicêtre. It was through it that, under the Empire and the Restoration, prisoners condemned to death reentered Paris on the day of their execution. It was there, that, about 1829, was committed that mysterious assassination, called "The assassination of the Fontainebleau barrier," whose author's justice was never able to discover; a melancholy problem that has never been elucidated, a frightful enigma that has never been unriddled. Take a few steps, and you come upon that fatal Rue Croulebarbe, where Ulbach stabbed the goat girl of Ivry to the sound of thunder, as in the melodramas. A few paces more, and you arrive at the abominable pollarded elms of the Barriere Saint-Jacques, that expedient of the philanthropist to conceal the scaffold, that miserable and shameful Place de Grove of a shopkeeping and bourgeois society, which recoiled before the death penalty, neither daring to abolish it with grandeur, nor to uphold it with authority.

Leaving aside this Place Saint-Jacques, which was, as it were, predestined, and which has always been horrible, probably the most mournful spot on that mournful boulevard, seven and thirty years ago, was the spot which even today is so unattractive, where stood the building Number 50–52.

Bourgeois houses only began to spring up there twenty-five years later. The place was unpleasant. In addition to the gloomy thoughts that assailed one there, one was conscious of being between the Salpetriere, a glimpse of whose dome could be seen, and Bicêtre, whose outskirts one was fairly touching; that is to say, between the madness of women and the madness of men. As far as the eye could see, one could perceive nothing but the abattoirs, the city wall, and the fronts of a few factories, resembling barracks or monasteries; everywhere about stood hovels, rubbish, ancient walls blackened like cerecloths, new white walls like winding sheets; everywhere parallel rows of trees, buildings erected on a line, flat constructions, long, cold rows, and the melancholy sadness of right angles. Not an unevenness of the ground, not a caprice in the architecture, not a fold. The ensemble was glacial, regular, hideous. Nothing oppresses the heart like symmetry. It is because symmetry is ennui, and ennui is at the very foundation of grief. Despair yawns. Something more terrible than a hell where one suffers may be imagined, and that is a hell where one is bored. If such a hell existed, that bit of the Boulevard de l'Hopital might have formed the entrance to it.

Nevertheless, at nightfall, at the moment when the daylight is vanishing, especially in winter, at the hour when the twilight breeze tears from the elms their last russet leaves, when the darkness is deep and starless, or when the moon and the wind are making openings in the clouds and losing themselves in the shadows, this boulevard suddenly becomes frightful. The black lines sink inward and are lost in the shades, like morsels of the infinite. The passerby cannot refrain from recalling the innumerable traditions of the place ,which are connected with the gibbet. The solitude of this spot, where so many crimes have been committed, had something terrible about it. One almost had a presentiment of meeting with traps in that darkness; all the confused forms of the darkness seemed suspicious, and the long, hollow square, of which one caught a glimpse between each tree, seemed grave: by day it was ugly; in the evening melancholy; by night it was sinister.

In summer, at twilight, one saw, here and there, a few old women seated at the foot of the elm, on benches moldy with rain. These good old women were fond of begging.

However, this quarter, which had a superannuated rather than an antique air, was tending even then to transformation. Even at that time anyone who was desirous of seeing it had to make haste. Each day some detail of the whole effect was disappearing. For the last twenty years the station of the Orleans railway has stood beside the old suburb and distracted it, as it does today. Wherever it is placed on the borders of a capital, a railway station is the death of a suburb and the birth of a city. It seems as though, around these great centers of the movements of a people, the earth, full of germs, trembled and yawned, to engulf the ancient dwellings of men and to allow new ones to spring forth, at the rattle of these powerful machines, at the breath of these monstrous horses of civilization, which devour coal and vomit fire. The old houses crumble and new ones rise.

Since the Orleans railway has invaded the region of the Salpetriere, the ancient, narrow streets that adjoin the moats Saint-Victor and the Jardin des Plantes tremble, as they are violently traversed three or four times each day by those currents of coach fiacres and omnibuses, which, in a given time, crowd back the houses to the right and the left; for there are things that are odd when said rigorously exact; and just as it is true to say that in large cities the sun makes the southern fronts of houses to vegetate and grow, it is certain that the frequent passage of vehicles enlarges streets. The symptoms of a new life are evident. In this old provincial quarter, in the wildest nooks, the pavement shows itself, the sidewalks begin to crawl and to grow longer, even where there are as yet no pedestrians. One morning—a memorable morning in July, 1845—black pots of bitumen were seen smoking there; on that day it might be said that civilization had arrived in the Rue de l'Ourcine, and that Paris had entered the suburb of Saint-Marceau.

CHAPTER II—A NEST FOR OWL AND A WARBLER

It was in front of this Gorbeau house that Jean Valjean halted. Like wild birds, he had chosen this desert place to construct his nest.

He fumbled in his waistcoat pocket, drew out a sort of a passkey, opened the door, entered, closed it again carefully, and ascended the staircase, still carrying Cosette.

At the top of the stairs he drew from his pocket another key, with which he opened another door. The chamber that he entered, and which he closed again instantly, was a kind of moderately spacious attic, furnished with a mattress laid on the floor, a table, and several chairs; a stove in which a fire was burning, and whose embers were visible, stood in one corner. A lantern on the boulevard cast a vague light into this poor room. At the extreme end there was a dressing room with a folding bed; Jean Valjean carried the child to this bed and laid her down there without waking her.

He struck a match and lighted a candle. All this was prepared beforehand on the table, and, as he had done on the previous evening, he began to scrutinize Cosette's face with a gaze full of ecstasy, in which the expression of kindness and tenderness almost amounted to aberration. The little girl, with that tranquil confidence that belongs only to extreme strength and extreme weakness, had fallen asleep without knowing whom she was with, and continued to sleep without knowing where she was.

Jean Valjean bent down and kissed that child's hand.

Nine months before he had kissed the hand of the mother, who had also just fallen asleep.

The same sad, piercing, religious sentiment filled his heart.

He knelt beside Cosette's bed.

It was broad daylight, and the child still slept. A wan ray of the December sun penetrated the window of the attic and lay upon the ceiling in long threads of light and shade. All at once a heavily laden carrier's cart, which was passing along the boulevard, shook the frail bed, like a clap of thunder, and made it quiver from top to bottom.

"Yes, Madame!" cried Cosette, waking with a start. "Here I am! Here I am!"

And she sprang out of bed, her eyes still half shut with the heaviness of sleep, extending her arms toward the corner of the wall.

"Ah! *Mon Dieu*, my broom!" said she.

She opened her eyes wide now, and beheld the smiling countenance of Jean Valjean.

"Ah! So it is true!" said the child. "Good morning, Monsieur."

Children accept joy and happiness instantly and familiarly, being themselves by nature joy and happiness.

Cosette caught sight of Catherine at the foot of her bed, and took possession of her, and, as she played, she put a hundred questions to Jean Valjean. Where was she? Was Paris very large? Was Madame Thenardier very far away? Was she to go back? etc., etc. All at once she exclaimed, "How pretty it is here!"

It was a frightful hole, but she felt free.

"Must I sweep?" she resumed at last.

"Play!" said Jean Valjean.

The day passed thus. Cosette, without troubling herself to understand anything, was inexpressibly happy with that doll and that kind man.

CHAPTER III—TWO MISFORTUNES MAKE ONE PIECE OF GOOD FORTUNE

On the following morning, at daybreak, Jean Valjean was still by Cosette's bedside; he watched there motionless, waiting for her to wake.

Some new thing had come into his soul.

Jean Valjean had never loved anything; for twenty-five years he had been alone in the world. He had never been father, lover, husband, friend. In the prison he had been vicious, gloomy, chaste, ignorant, and shy. The heart of that ex-convict was full of virginity. His sister and his sister's children had left him only a vague and far-off memory, which had finally almost completely vanished; he had made every effort to find them, and not having been able to find them, he had forgotten them. Human nature is made thus; the other tender emotions of his youth, if he had ever had any, had fallen into an abyss.

When he saw Cosette, when he had taken possession of her, carried her off, and delivered her, he felt his heart moved within him.

All the passion and affection within him awoke, and rushed toward that child. He approached the bed, where she lay sleeping, and trembled with joy. He suffered all the pangs of a mother, and he knew not what it meant; for that great and singular movement of a heart that begins to love is a very obscure and a very sweet thing.

Poor old man, with a perfectly new heart!

Only, as he was five and fifty, and Cosette eight years of age, all that might have been love in the whole course of his life flowed together into a sort of ineffable light.

It was the second white apparition he had encountered. The Bishop had caused the dawn of virtue to rise on his horizon; Cosette caused the dawn of love to rise.

The early days passed in this dazzled state.

Cosette, on her side, had also, unknown to herself, become another being, poor little thing! She was so little when her mother left her, that she no longer remembered her. Like all children, who resemble young shoots of the vine, which cling to everything, she had tried to love; she had not succeeded. All had repulsed her, the Thenardiers, their children, other children. She had loved the dog, and he had died, after which nothing and nobody would have anything to do with her. It is a sad thing to say, and we have already intimated it, that, at eight years of age, her heart was cold. It was not her fault; it was not the faculty of loving that she lacked; alas! It was the possibility. Thus, from the very first day, all her sentient and thinking powers loved this kind man. She felt that which she had never felt before—a sensation of expansion.

The man no longer produced on her the effect of being old or poor; she thought Jean Valjean handsome, just as she thought the hovel pretty.

These are the effects of the dawn, of childhood, of joy. The novelty of the earth and of life counts for something here. Nothing is so charming as the coloring reflection of happiness on a garret. We all have in our past a delightful garret.

Nature, a difference of fifty years, had set a profound gulf between Jean Valjean and Cosette; destiny filled in this gulf. Destiny suddenly united and wedded with its irresistible power these two uprooted existences, differing in age, alike in sorrow. One, in fact, completed the other. Cosette's instinct sought a father, as Jean Valjean's instinct sought a child. To meet was to find each other. At the mysterious moment when their hands touched, they were welded together. When these two souls perceived each other, they recognized each other as necessary to each other, and embraced each other closely.

Taking the words in their most comprehensive and absolute sense, we may say that, separated from everyone by the walls of the tomb, Jean Valjean was the widower, and Cosette was the orphan: this situation caused Jean Valjean to become Cosette's father after a celestial fashion.

And in truth, the mysterious impression produced on Cosette in the depths of the forest of Chelles by the hand of Jean Valjean grasping hers in the dark was not an illusion, but a reality. The entrance of that man into the destiny of that child had been the advent of God.

Moreover, Jean Valjean had chosen his refuge well. There he seemed perfectly secure.

The chamber with a dressing room, which he occupied with Cosette, was the one whose window opened on the boulevard. This being the only window in the house, no neighbors' glances were to be feared from across the way or at the side.

The ground floor of Number 50-52, a sort of dilapidated penthouse, served as a wagon house for market gardeners, and no communication existed between it and the first story. It was separated by the flooring, which had neither traps nor stairs, and which formed the diaphragm of the building, as it were. The first story contained, as we have said, numerous chambers and several attics, only one of which was occupied by the old woman who took charge of Jean Valjean's housekeeping; all the rest was uninhabited.

It was this old woman, ornamented with the name of the principal lodger, and in reality entrusted with the functions of portress, who had let him the lodging on Christmas Eve. He had represented himself to her as a gentleman of means, who had been ruined by Spanish bonds, who was coming there to live with his little daughter. He had paid her six months in advance, and had commissioned the old woman to furnish the chamber and dressing room, as we have seen. It was this good woman who had lighted the fire in the stove, and prepared everything on the evening of their arrival.

Week followed week; these two beings led a happy life in that hovel.

Cosette laughed, chattered, and sang from daybreak. Children have their morning song as well as birds.

It sometimes happened that Jean Valjean clasped her tiny red hand, all cracked with chilblains, and kissed it. The poor child, who was used to being beaten, did not know the meaning of this, and ran away in confusion.

At times she became serious and stared at her little black gown. Cosette was no longer in rags; she was in mourning. She had emerged from misery, and she was entering into life.

Jean Valjean had undertaken to teach her to read. Sometimes, as he made the child spell, he remembered that it was with the idea of doing evil that he had learned to read in prison. This idea had ended in teaching a child to read. Then the ex-convict smiled with the pensive smile of the angels.

He felt in it a premeditation from on high, the will of someone who was not man, and he became absorbed in reverie. Good thoughts have their abysses as well as evil ones.

To teach Cosette to read, and to let her play, this constituted nearly the whole of Jean Valjean's existence. And then he talked of her mother, and he made her pray.

She called him father, and knew no other name for him.

He passed hours in watching her dressing and undressing her doll, and in listening to her prattle. Life, henceforth, appeared to him to be full of interest; men seemed to him good and just; he no longer reproached anyone in thought; he saw no reason why he should not live to be a very old man, now that this child loved him. He saw a whole future stretching out before him, illuminated by Cosette as by a charming light. The best of us are not exempt from egotistical thoughts. At times, he reflected with a sort of joy that she would be ugly.

This is only a personal opinion; but, to utter our whole thought, at the point where Jean Valjean had arrived when he began to love Cosette, it is by no means clear to us that he did not need this encouragement in order that he might persevere in well-doing. He had just viewed the malice of men and the misery of society under a new aspect—incomplete aspects, which unfortunately only exhibited one side of the truth, the fate of woman as summed up in Fantine, and public authority as personified in Javert. He had returned to prison, this time for having done right; he had quaffed fresh bitterness; disgust and lassitude were overpowering him; even the memory of the Bishop probably suffered a temporary eclipse, though sure to reappear later on luminous and triumphant; but, after all, that sacred memory was growing dim. Who knows whether Jean Valjean had not been on the eve of growing discouraged and of falling once more? He loved and grew strong again. Alas! He walked with no less indecision than Cosette. He protected her, and she strengthened him. Thanks to him, she could walk through life; thanks to her, he could continue in virtue. He was that child's stay, and she was his prop. Oh, unfathomable and divine mystery of the balances of destiny!

CHAPTER IV—THE REMARKS OF THE PRINCIPAL TENANT

Jean Valjean was prudent enough never to go out by day. Every evening, at twilight, he walked for an hour or two, sometimes alone, often with Cosette, seeking the most deserted side alleys of the boulevard, and entering churches at nightfall. He liked to go to Saint-Medard, which is the nearest church. When he did not take Cosette with him, she remained with the old woman; but the child's delight was to go out with the good man. She preferred an hour with him to all her rapturous tête-à-têtes with Catherine. He held her hand as they walked, and said sweet things to her.

It turned out that Cosette was a very gay little person.

The old woman attended to the housekeeping and cooking and went to market.

They lived soberly, always having a little fire, but like people in very moderate circumstances. Jean Valjean had made no alterations in the furniture as it was the first day; he had merely had the glass door leading to Cosette's dressing room replaced by a solid door.

He still wore his yellow coat, his black breeches, and his old hat. In the street, he was taken for a poor man. It sometimes happened that kind-hearted women turned back to bestow a sou on him. Jean Valjean accepted the sou with a deep bow. It also happened occasionally that he encountered some poor wretch asking alms; then he looked behind him to make sure that no one was observing him, stealthily approached the unfortunate man, put a piece of money into his hand, often a silver coin, and walked rapidly away. This had its disadvantages. He began to be known in the neighborhood under the name of the beggar who gives alms.

The old principal lodger, a cross-looking creature, who was thoroughly permeated, so far as her neighbors were concerned, with the inquisitiveness peculiar to envious persons, scrutinized Jean Valjean a great deal, without his suspecting the fact. She was a little deaf, which rendered her talkative. There remained to her from her past, two teeth, one above, the other below, which she was continually knocking against each other. She had questioned Cosette, who had not been able to tell her anything, since she knew nothing herself except that she had come from Montfermeil. One morning, this spy saw Jean Valjean, with an air that struck the old gossip as peculiar, entering one of the uninhabited compartments of the hovel. She followed him with the step of an old cat, and was able to observe him without being seen, through a crack in the door, which was directly opposite him. Jean Valjean had his back turned toward this door, by way of greater security, no doubt. The old woman saw him fumble in his pocket and draw from it a case, scissors, and thread; then he began to rip the lining of one of the skirts of his coat, and from the opening he took a bit of yellowish paper, which he unfolded. The old woman recognized, with terror, the fact that it was a bank bill for a thousand francs. It was the second or third only that she had seen in the course of her existence. She fled in alarm.

A moment later, Jean Valjean accosted her, and asked her to go and get this thousand-franc bill changed for him, adding that it was his quarterly income, which he had received the day before. "Where?" thought the old woman. "He did not go out until six o'clock in the evening, and the government bank certainly is not open at that hour." The old woman went to get the bill changed, and mentioned her surmises. That thousand-franc note, commented on and multiplied, produced a vast amount of terrified discussion among the gossips of the Rue des Vignes Saint-Marcel.

A few days later, it chanced that Jean Valjean was sawing some wood, in his shirtsleeves, in the corridor. The old woman was in the chamber, putting things in order. She was alone. Cosette was occupied in admiring the wood as it was sawed. The old woman caught sight of the coat hanging on a nail, and examined it. The lining had been sewed up again. The good woman felt of it carefully, and thought she observed in the skirts and revers thicknesses of paper. More thousand-franc bank bills, no doubt!

She also noticed that there were all sorts of things in the pockets. Not only the needles, thread, and scissors which she had seen, but a big pocketbook, a very large knife, and—a suspicious circumstance—several wigs of various colors. Each pocket of this coat had the air of being in a manner provided against unexpected accidents.

Thus the inhabitants of the house reached the last days of winter.

CHAPTER V—A FIVE-FRANC PIECE FALLS ON THE GROUND AND PRODUCES A TUMULT

Near Saint-Medard's church there was a poor man who was in the habit of crouching on the brink of a public well which had been condemned, and on whom Jean Valjean was fond of bestowing charity. He never passed this man without giving him a few sous. Sometimes he spoke to him. Those who envied this mendicant said that he belonged to the police. He was an ex-beadle of seventy-five, who was constantly mumbling his prayers.

One evening, as Jean Valjean was passing by, when he had not Cosette with him, he saw the beggar in his usual place, beneath the lantern, which had just been lighted. The man seemed engaged in prayer, according to his custom, and was much bent over. Jean Valjean stepped up to him and placed his customary alms in his hand. The mendicant raised his eyes suddenly, stared intently at Jean Valjean, then dropped his head quickly. This movement was like a flash of lightning. Jean Valjean was seized with a shudder. It seemed to him that he had just caught sight, by the light of the street lantern, not of the placid and beaming visage of the old beadle, but of a well-known and startling face. He experienced the same impression that one would have on finding one's self, all of a sudden, face-to-face, in the dark, with a tiger. He recoiled, terrified, petrified, daring neither to breathe, to speak, to remain, nor to flee, staring at the beggar who had dropped his head, which was enveloped in a rag, and no longer appeared to know that he was there. At this strange moment, an instinct—possibly the mysterious instinct of self-preservation, restrained Jean Valjean from uttering a word. The beggar had the same figure, the same rags, the same appearance as he had every day. "Bah!" said Jean Valjean, "I am mad! I am dreaming! Impossible!" And he returned profoundly troubled.

He hardly dared to confess, even to himself, that the face he thought he had seen was the face of Javert.

That night, on thinking the matter over, he regretted not having questioned the man, in order to force him to raise his head a second time.

On the following day, at nightfall, he went back. The beggar was at his post. "Good day, my good man," said Jean Valjean, resolutely, handing him a sou. The beggar raised his head, and replied in a whining voice, "Thanks, my good Sir." It was unmistakably the ex-beadle.

Jean Valjean felt completely reassured. He began to laugh. "How the deuce could I have thought that I saw Javert there?" he thought. "Am I going to lose my eyesight now?" And he thought no more about it.

A few days afterward, it might have been at eight o'clock in the evening, he was in his room, and engaged in making Cosette spell aloud, when he heard the house door open and then shut again. This struck him as singular. The old woman, who was the only inhabitant of the house except himself, always went to bed at nightfall, so that she might not burn out her candles. Jean Valjean made a sign to Cosette to be quiet. He heard someone ascending the stairs. It might possibly be the old woman, who might have fallen ill and have been out to the apothecary's. Jean Valjean listened.

The step was heavy, and sounded like that of a man; but the old woman wore stout shoes, and there is nothing that so strongly resembles the step of a man as that of an old woman. Nevertheless, Jean Valjean blew out his candle.

He had sent Cosette to bed, saying to her in a low voice, "Get into bed very softly"; and as he kissed her brow, the steps paused.

Jean Valjean remained silent, motionless, with his back toward the door, seated on the chair from which he had not stirred, and holding his breath in the dark.

After the expiration of a rather long interval, he turned around, as he heard nothing more, and, as he raised his eyes toward the door of his chamber, he saw a light through the keyhole. This light formed a sort of sinister star in the blackness of the door and the wall. There was evidently someone there, who was holding a candle in his hand and listening.

Several minutes elapsed thus, and the light retreated. But he heard no sound of footsteps, which seemed to indicate that the person who had been listening at the door had removed his shoes.

Jean Valjean threw himself, all dressed as he was, on his bed, and could not close his eyes all night.

At daybreak, just as he was falling into a doze through fatigue, he was awakened by the creaking of a door that opened on some attic at the end of the corridor, then he heard the same masculine footstep, which had ascended the stairs on the preceding evening. The step was approaching. He sprang off the bed and applied his eye to the keyhole, which was tolerably large, hoping to see the person who had made his way by night into the house and had listened at his door, as he passed. It was a man, in fact, who passed, this time without pausing, in front of Jean Valjean's chamber. The corridor was too dark to allow of the person's face being distinguished; but when the man reached the staircase, a ray of light from without made it stand out like a silhouette, and Jean Valjean had a complete view of his back. The man was of lofty stature, clad in a long frock coat, with a cudgel under his arm. The formidable neck and shoulders belonged to Javert.

Jean Valjean might have attempted to catch another glimpse of him through his window opening on the boulevard, but he would have been obliged to open the window; he dared not.

It was evident that this man had entered with a key, and like himself. Who had given him that key? What was the meaning of this?

When the old woman came to do the work, at seven o'clock in the morning, Jean Valjean cast a penetrating glance on her, but he did not question her. The good woman appeared as usual.

As she swept up she remarked to him, "Possibly Monsieur may have heard someone come in last night?"

At that age, and on that boulevard, eight o'clock in the evening was the dead of the night.

"That is true, by the way," he replied, in the most natural tone possible. "Who was it?"

"It was a new lodger who has come into the house," said the old woman.

"And what is his name?"

"I don't know exactly; Dumont, or Daumont, or some name of that sort."

"And who is this Monsieur Dumont?"

The old woman gazed at him with her little polecat eyes, and answered, "A gentleman of property, like yourself."

Perhaps she had no ulterior meaning. Jean Valjean thought he perceived one.

When the old woman had taken her departure, he did up a hundred francs that he had in a cupboard, into a roll, and put it in his pocket. In spite of all the precautions he took in this operation so that he might not be heard rattling silver, a hundred-sou piece escaped from his hands and rolled noisily on the floor.

When darkness came on, he descended and carefully scrutinized both sides of the boulevard. He saw no one. The boulevard appeared to be absolutely deserted. It is true that a person can conceal himself behind trees.

"He went upstairs again.

"Come," he said to Cosette.

He took her by the hand, and they both went out."

BOOK FIFTH: FOR A BLACK HUNT, A MUTE PACK

CHAPTER I—THE ZIGZAGS OF STRATEGY

An observation here becomes necessary, in view of the pages that the reader is about to peruse, and of others, which will be met with further on.

The author of this book, who regrets the necessity of mentioning himself, has been absent from Paris for many years. Paris has been transformed since he quitted it. A new city has arisen, which is, after a fashion, unknown to him. There is no need for him to say that he loves Paris: Paris is his mind's natal city. In consequence of demolitions and reconstructions, the Paris of his youth, that Paris which he bore away religiously in his memory, is now a Paris of days gone by. He must be permitted to speak of that Paris as though it still existed. It is possible that when the author conducts his readers to a spot and says, "In such a street there stands such and such a house," neither street nor house will any longer exist in that locality. Readers may verify the facts if they care to take the trouble. For his own part, he is unacquainted with the new Paris, and he writes with the old Paris before his eyes in an illusion that is precious to him. It is a delight to him to dream that there still lingers behind him something of that which he beheld when he was in his own country, and that all has not vanished. So long as you go and come in your native land, you imagine that those streets are a matter of indifference to you; that those windows, those roofs, and those doors are nothing to you; that those walls are strangers to you; that those trees are merely the first encountered haphazard; that those houses, which you do not enter, are useless to you; that the pavements, which you tread, are merely stones. Later on, when you are no longer there, you perceive that the streets are dear to you; that you miss those roofs, those doors; and that those walls are necessary to you, those trees are well-beloved by you; that you entered those houses, which you never entered, every day, and that you have left a part of your heart, of your blood, of your soul, in those pavements. All those places, which you no longer behold, which you may never behold again, perchance, and whose memory you have cherished, take on a melancholy charm, recur to your mind with the melancholy of an apparition, make the holy land visible to you, and are, so to speak, the very form of France, and you love them; and you call them up as they are, as they were, and you persist in this, and you will submit to no change: for you are attached to the figure of your fatherland as to the face of your mother.

May we, then, be permitted to speak of the past in the present? That said, we beg the reader to take note of it, and we continue.

Jean Valjean instantly quitted the boulevard and plunged into the streets, taking the most intricate lines thathe could devise, returning on his track at times, to make sure that he was not being followed.

This maneuver is peculiar to the hunted stag. On soil where an imprint of the track may be left, this maneuver possesses, among other advantages, that of deceiving the huntsmen and the dogs, by throwing them on the wrong scent. In venery, this is called a false reimbushment.

The moon was full that night. Jean Valjean was not sorry for this. The moon, still very close to the horizon, cast great masses of light and shadow in the streets. Jean Valjean could glide along close to the houses on the dark side, and yet keep watch on the light side. He did not, perhaps, take sufficiently into consideration the fact that the dark side escaped him. Still, in the deserted lanes that lie near the Rue Poliveau, he thought he felt certain that no one was following him.

Cosette walked on without asking any questions. The sufferings of the first six years of her life had instilled something passive into her nature. Moreover— and this is a remark to which we shall frequently have occasion to recur—she had grown used, without being herself aware of it, to the peculiarities of this good man and to the freaks of destiny. And then she was with him, and she felt safe.

Jean Valjean knew no more where he was going than did Cosette. He trusted in God, as she trusted in him. It seemed as though he also were clinging to the hand of someone greater than himself; he thought he felt a being leading him, though invisible. However, he had no settled idea, no plan, no project. He was not even absolutely sure that it was Javert, and then it might have been Javert, without Javert knowing that he was Jean Valjean. Was not he disguised? Was not he believed to be dead? Still, queer things had been going on for several days. He wanted no more of them. He was determined not to return to the Gorbeau house. Like the wild animal chased from its lair, he was seeking a hole in which he might hide until he could find one where he might dwell.

Jean Valjean described many and varied labyrinths in the Mouffetard quarter, which was already asleep, as though the discipline of the Middle Ages and the yoke of the curfew still existed; he combined in various manners, with cunning strategy, the Rue Censier and the Rue Copeau, the Rue du Battoir-Saint-Victor and the Rue du Puits l'Ermite. There are lodging houses in this locality, but he did not even enter one, finding nothing that suited him. He had no doubt that if anyone had chanced to be upon his track, they would have lost it.

As eleven o'clock struck from Saint-Etienne-du-Mont, he was traversing the Rue de Pontoise, in front of the office of the commissary of police, situated at No. 14. A few moments later, the instinct of which we have spoken above made him turn around. At that moment he saw distinctly, thanks to the commissary's lantern, which betrayed them, three men who were following him closely, pass, one after the other, under that lantern, on the dark side of the street. One of the three entered the alley leading to the commissary's house. The one who marched at their head struck him as decidedly suspicious.

"Come, child," he said to Cosette; and he made haste to quit the Rue Pontoise.

He took a circuit, turned into the Passage des Patriarches, which was closed on account of the hour, strode along the Rue de l'Epee-de-Bois and the Rue de l'Arbalete, and plunged into the Rue des Postes.

At that time there was a square formed by the intersection of streets, where the College Rollin stands today, and where the Rue Neuve-Sainte-Genevieve turns off.

It is understood, of course, that the Rue Neuve-Sainte-Genevieve is an old street, and that a posting-chaise does not pass through the Rue des Postes once in ten years. In the thirteenth century this Rue des Postes was inhabited by potters, and its real name is Rue des Pots.

The moon cast a livid light into this open space. Jean Valjean went into ambush in a doorway, calculating that if the men were still following him, he could not fail to get a good look at them, as they traversed this illuminated space.

In point of fact, three minutes had not elapsed when the men made their appearance. There were four of them now. All were tall, dressed in long, brown coats, with round hats, and huge cudgels in their hands. Their great stature and their vast fists rendered them no less alarming than did their sinister stride through the darkness. One would have pronounced them four specters disguised as bourgeois.

They halted in the middle of the space and formed a group, like men in consultation. They had an air of indecision. The one who appeared to be their eader turned around and pointed hastily with his right hand in the direction that Jean Valjean had taken; another seemed to indicate the contrary direction with considerable obstinacy. At the moment when the first man wheeled around, the moon fell full in his face. Jean Valjean recognized Javert perfectly.

CHAPTER II—IT IS LUCKY THAT THE PONT D'AUSTERLITZ BEARS CARRIAGES

Uncertainty was at an end for Jean Valjean: fortunately it still lasted for the men. He took advantage of their hesitation. It was time lost for them, but gained for him. He slipped from under the gate where he had concealed himself, and went down the Rue des Postes, toward the region of the Jardin des Plantes. Cosette was beginning to be tired. He took her in his arms and carried her. There were no passersby, and the street lanterns had not been lighted on account of there being a moon.

He redoubled his pace.

In a few strides he had reached the Goblet potteries, on the front of which the moonlight rendered distinctly legible the ancient inscription:

> *"This is the factory of goblet junior;*
> *Come choose your jugs and crocks,*
> *Flower pots, pipes, bricks.*
> *The Heart sells diamonds to everyone."*

He left behind him the Rue de la Clef, then the Fountain Saint-Victor, skirted the Jardin des Plantes by the lower streets, and reached the quay. There he turned around. The quay was deserted. The streets were deserted. There was no one behind him. He drew a long breath.

He gained the Pont d'Austerlitz.

Tolls were still collected there at that epoch.

He presented himself at the toll office and handed over a sou.

"It is two sous," said the old soldier in charge of the bridge. "You are carrying a child who can walk. Pay for two."

He paid, vexed that his passage should have aroused remark. Every flight should be an imperceptible slipping away.

A heavy cart was crossing the Seine at the same time as himself, and on its way, like him, to the right bank. This was of use to him. He could traverse the bridge in the shadow of the cart.

Toward the middle of the Bridge, Cosette, whose feet were benumbed wanted to walk. He set her on the ground and took her hand again.

The bridge once crossed, he perceived some timberyards on his right He directed his course there. In order to reach them, it was necessary to risk himself in a tolerably large unsheltered and illuminated space. He did no hesitate. Those who were on his track had evidently lost the scent, and Jean Valjean believed himself to be out of danger. Hunted, yes; followed, no.

A little street, the Rue du Chemin-Vert-Saint-Antoine, opened out between two timberyards enclosed in walls. This street was dark and narrow and seemed made expressly for him. Before entering it he cast a glance behind him.

From the point where he stood he could see the whole extent of the Pon d'Austerlitz.

Four shadows were just entering on the bridge.

These shadows had their backs turned to the Jardin des Plantes and were on their way to the right bank.

These four shadows were the four men.

Jean Valjean shuddered like the wild beast that is recaptured.

One hope remained to him; it was, that the men had not, perhaps, stepped on the bridge, and had not caught sight of him while he was crossing the large illuminated space, holding Cosette by the hand.

In that case, by plunging into the little street before him, he might escape if he could reach the timberyards, the marshes, the marketgardens, the uninhabited ground which was not built upon.

It seemed to him that he might commit himself to that silent little street He entered it.

CHAPTER III—TO WIT, THE PLAN
OF PARIS IN 1727

Three hundred paces farther on, he arrived at a point where the stree forked. It separated into two streets that ran in a slanting line, one to the right, and the other to the left.

Jean Valjean had before him what resembled the two branches of a Y Which should he choose? He did not hesitate, but took the one on the right.

Why?

Because that to the left ran toward a suburb, that is to say, toward inhabited regions, and the right branch toward the open country, that is to say, toward deserted regions.

However, they no longer walked very fast. Cosette's pace retarded Jean Valjean's.

He took her up and carried her again. Cosette laid her head on the shoulder of the good man and said not a word.

He turned around from time to time and looked behind him. He took care to keep always on the dark side of the street. The street was straight in his rear. The first two or three times that he turned around he saw nothing; the silence was profound, and he continued his march somewhat reassured. All at once, on turning around, he thought he perceived in the portion of the street he had just passed through, far off in the obscurity, something that was moving.

He rushed forward precipitately rather than walked, hoping to find some side street, to make his escape through it, and thus to break his scent once more.

He arrived at a wall.

This wall, however, did not absolutely prevent further progress; it was a wall that bordered a transverse street, in which the one he had taken ended.

Here again, he was obliged to come to a decision; should he go to the right or to the left.

He glanced to the right. The fragmentary lane was prolonged between buildings that were either sheds or barns, then ended at a blind alley. The extremity of the cul-de-sac was distinctly visible, a lofty white wall.

He glanced to the left. On that side the lane was open, and about two hundred paces further on, ran into a street of which it was the affluent. On that side lay safety.

At the moment when Jean Valjean was meditating a turn to the left, in an effort to reach the street he saw at the end of the lane, he perceived a sort of motionless, black statue at the corner of the lane and the street toward which he was on the point of directing his steps.

It was someone, a man, who had evidently just been posted there, and who was barring the passage and waiting.

Jean Valjean recoiled.

The point of Paris where Jean Valjean found himself, situated between the Faubourg Saint-Antoine and la Rapée, is one of those that recent improvements have transformed from top to bottom, resulting in disfigurement according to some, and in a transfiguration according to others. The market gardens, the timberyards, and the old buildings have been effaced. Today, there are brand-new, wide streets, arenas, circuses, hippodromes, railway stations, and a prison, Mazas, there; progress, as the reader sees, with its antidote.

Half a century ago, in that ordinary, popular tongue that is all compounded of traditions, which persists in calling the Institut les Quatre-Nations, and the Opera-Comique Feydeau, the precise spot where Jean Valjean had arrived was called le Petit Picpus. The Porte Saint-Jacques, the Porte Paris, the Barrière des Sergents, the Porcherons, la Galiote, les Celestins, les Capucins, le Mail, la Bourbe, l'Arbre de Cracovie, la Petite-Pologne—these are the names of old Paris which survive amid the new. The memory of the populace hovers over these relics of the past.

Le Petit-Picpus, which, moreover, hardly ever had any existence, and never was more than the outline of a quarter, had nearly the monkish aspect of a Spanish town. The roads were not much paved; the streets were not much built up. With the exception of the two or three streets, of which we shall presently speak, all was wall and solitude there. Not a shop, not a vehicle, hardly a candle lighted here and there in the windows; all lights extinguished after ten o'clock. Gardens, convents, timberyards, marshes; occasional lowly dwellings and great walls as high as the houses.

Such was this quarter in the last century. The Revolution snubbed it soundly. The republican government demolished and cut through it. Rubbish shoots were established there. Thirty years ago, this quarter was disappearing under the erasing process of new buildings. Today, it has been utterly blotted out. The Petit-Picpus, of which no existing plan has preserved a trace, is indicated with sufficient clearness in the plan of 1727, published at Paris by Denis Thierry, Rue Saint-Jacques, opposite the Rue du Platre; and at Lyons, by Jean Girin, Rue Merciere, at the sign of Prudence. Petit-Picpus had, as we have just mentioned, a Y of streets, formed by the Rue du Chemin-Vert-Saint-Antoine that spread out in two branches, taking on the left the name of Little Picpus Street, and on the right the name of the Rue Polonceau. The two limbs of the Y were connected at the apex as by a bar; this bar was called Rue Droit-Mur. The Rue Polonceau ended there; Rue Petit-Picpus passed on, and ascended toward the Lenoir market. A person coming from the Seine reached the extremity of the Rue Polonceau, and had on his right the Rue Droit-Mur turning abruptly at a right angle, in front of him the wall of that street, and on his right a truncated prolongation of the Rue Droit-Mur that had no issue and was called the Cul-de-Sac Genrot.

It was here that Jean Valjean stood.

As we have just said, on catching sight of that black silhouette standing on guard at the angle of the Rue Droit-Mur and the Rue Petit-Picpus, he recoiled. There could be no doubt of it. That phantom was lying in wait for him.

What was he to do?

The time for retreating was passed. That which he had perceived in movement an instant before, in the distant darkness, was Javert and his squad without a doubt. Javert was probably already at the commencement of the street at whose end Jean Valjean stood. Javert, to all appearances, was acquainted with this little labyrinth, and had taken his precautions by sending one of his men to guard the exit. These surmises that so closely resembled proofs, whirled suddenly, like a handful of dust caught up by an unexpected gust of wind, through Jean Valjean's mournful brain. He examined the Cul-de-Sac Genrot; there he was cut off. He examined the Rue Petit-Picpus; there stood a sentinel. He saw that black form standing out in relief against the white pavement, illuminated by the moon; to advance was to fall into this man's hands; to retreat was to fling himself into Javert's arms. Jean Valjean felt himself caught, as in a net that was slowly contracting; he gazed heavenward in despair.

CHAPTER IV — THE GROPINGS
OF FLIGHT

In order to understand what follows, it is requisite to form an exact idea of the Droit-Mur lane, and, in particular, of the angle that one leaves on the left when one emerges from the Rue Polonceau into this lane. Droit-Mur lane was almost entirely bordered on the right, as far as the Rue Petit-Picpus, by houses of mean aspect; on the left by a solitary building of severe outlines, composed of numerous parts, which grew gradually higher by a story or two as they approached the Rue Petit-Picpus side; so that this building, which was very lofty on the Rue Petit-Picpus side, was tolerably low on the side adjoining the Rue Polonceau. There, at the angle of which we have spoken, it descended to such a degree that it consisted of merely a wall. This wall did not abut directly on the street; it formed a deeply retreating niche, concealed by its two corners from two observers who might have been, one in the Rue Polonceau, the other in the Rue Droit-Mur.

Beginning with these angles of the niche, the wall extended along the Rue Polonceau as far as a house that bore the number 49, and along the Rue Droit-Mur, where the fragment was much shorter, as far as the gloomy building, which we have mentioned and whose gable it intersected, thus forming another retreating angle in the street. This gable was somber of aspect; only one window was visible, or, to speak more correctly, two shutters covered with a sheet of zinc and kept constantly closed.

The state of the places of which we are here giving a description is rigorously exact, and will certainly awaken a very precise memory in the mind of old inhabitants of the quarter.

The niche was entirely filled by a thing that resembled a colossal and wretched door; it was a vast, formless assemblage of perpendicular planks, the upper ones being broader than the lower, bound together by long transverse strips of iron. At one side there was a carriage gate of the ordinary dimensions, and which had evidently not been cut more than fifty years previously.

A linden tree showed its crest above the niche, and the wall was covered with ivy on the side of the Rue Polonceau.

In the imminent peril in which Jean Valjean found himself, this somber building had about it a solitary and uninhabited look that tempted him. He ran his eyes rapidly over it; he said to himself, that if he could contrive to get inside it, he might save himself. First he conceived an idea, then a hope.

In the central portion of the front of this building, on the Rue Droit-Mur side, there were at all the windows of the different stories ancient cistern pipes of lead. The various branches of the pipes that led from one central pipe to all these little basins sketched out a sort of tree on the front. These ramifications of pipes with their hundred elbows imitated those old leafless vine stocks that writhe over the fronts of old farmhouses.

This odd espalier, with its branches of lead and iron, was the first thing that struck Jean Valjean. He seated Cosette with her back against a stone post, with an injunction to be silent, and ran to the spot where the conduit touched the pavement. Perhaps there was some way of climbing up by it and entering the house. But the pipe was dilapidated and past service, and hardly hung to its fastenings. Moreover, all the windows of this silent dwelling were grated with heavy iron bars, even the attic windows in the roof. And then, the moon fell full upon that facade, and the man who was watching at the corner of the street would have seen Jean Valjean in the act of climbing. And finally, what was to be done with Cosette? How was she to be drawn up to the top of a three-story house?

He gave up all idea of climbing by means of the drainpipe, and crawled along the wall to get back into the Rue Polonceau.

When he reached the slant of the wall where he had left Cosette, he noticed that no one could see him there. As we have just explained, he was concealed from all eyes, no matter from which direction they were approaching; besides this, he was in the shadow. Finally, there were two doors; perhaps they might be forced. The wall above which he saw the linden tree and the ivy evidently abutted on a garden where he could, at least, hide himself, although there were s yet no leaves on the trees, and spend the remainder of the night.

Time was passing; he must act quickly.

He felt over the carriage door, and immediately recognized the fact that it vas impracticable outside and in.

He approached the other door with more hope; it was frightfully decrepit; s very immensity rendered it less solid; the planks were rotten; the iron ands—there were only three of them—were rusted. It seemed as though it night be possible to pierce this worm-eaten barrier.

On examining it he found that the door was not a door; it had neither hinges, rossbars, lock, nor fissure in the middle; the iron bands traversed it from side to ide without any break. Through the crevices in the planks he caught a view of nhewn slabs and blocks of stone roughly cemented together, which passersby night still have seen there ten years ago. He was forced to acknowledge with onsternation that this apparent door was simply the wooden decoration of a uilding against which it was placed. It was easy to tear off a plank; but then, ne found one's self face to face with a wall.

CHAPTER V—WHICH WOULD BE IMPOSSIBLE WITH GAS LANTERNS

At that moment a heavy and measured sound began to be audible at some distance. Jean Valjean risked a glance around the corner of the street. even or eight soldiers, drawn up in a platoon, had just debouched into the Rue Polonceau. He saw the gleam of their bayonets. They were advancing oward him; these soldiers, at whose head he distinguished Javert's tall figure, dvanced slowly and cautiously. They halted frequently; it was plain that they vere searching all the nooks of the walls and all the embrasures of the doors nd alleys.

This was some patrol that Javert had encountered—there could be no nistake as to this surmise—and whose aid he had demanded.

Javert's two acolytes were marching in their ranks.

At the rate at which they were marching, and in consideration of the halts hey were making, it would take them about a quarter of an hour to reach the pot where Jean Valjean stood. It was a frightful moment. A few minutes only eparated Jean Valjean from that terrible precipice that yawned before him for he third time. And the galleys now meant not only the galleys, but Cosette lost o him forever; that is to say, a life resembling the interior of a tomb.

There was but one thing that was possible.

Jean Valjean had this peculiarity, that he carried, as one might say, two beggar's pouches: in one he kept his saintly thoughts; in the other the redoubtable talents of a convict. He rummaged in the one or the other according to circumstances.

Among his other resources, thanks to his numerous escapes from the prison at Toulon, he was, as it will be remembered, a past master in the incredible art of crawling up without ladder or climbing irons, by sheer muscular force, by leaning on the nape of his neck, his shoulders, his hips and his knees, by helping himself on the rare projections of the stone, in the right angle of a wall, as high as the sixth story, if need be; an art that has rendered so celebrated and so alarming that corner of the wall of the Conciergerie of Paris by which Battemolle, condemned to death, made his escape twenty years ago.

Jean Valjean measured with his eyes the wall above which he espied the linden; it was about eighteen feet in height. The angle it formed with the gable of the large building was filled, at its lower extremity, by a mass of masonry of a triangular shape, probably intended to preserve that too convenient corner from the rubbish of those dirty creatures called the passersby. This practice of filling up corners of the wall is much in use in Paris.

This mass was about five feet in height; the space above the summit of this mass that it was necessary to climb was not more than fourteen feet.

The wall was surmounted by a flat stone without a coping.

Cosette was the difficulty, for she did not know how to climb a wall. Should he abandon her? Jean Valjean did not once think of that. It was impossible to carry her. A man's whole strength is required to successfully carry out these singular ascents. The least burden would disturb his center of gravity and pull him downward.

A rope would have been required; Jean Valjean had none. Where was he to get a rope at midnight, in the Rue Polonceau? Certainly, if Jean Valjean had had a kingdom, he would have given it for a rope at that moment.

All extreme situations have their lightning flashes that sometimes dazzle, sometimes illuminate us.

Jean Valjean's despairing glance fell on the street lantern–post of the blind alley Genrot.

At that epoch, there were no gas jets in the streets of Paris. At nightfall lanterns placed at regular distances were lighted; they were ascended and descended by means of a rope that traversed the street from side to side, and was adjusted in a groove of the post. The pulley over which this rope ran was astened underneath the lantern in a little iron box, the key to which was kept by the lamplighter, and the rope itself was protected by a metal case.

Jean Valjean, with the energy of a supreme struggle, crossed the street at one bound, entered the blind alley, broke the latch of the little box with the point of his knife, and an instant later he was beside Cosette once more. He had a rope. These gloomy inventors of expedients work rapidly when they are fighting against fatality.

We have already explained that the lanterns had not been lighted that night. The lantern in the Cul-de-Sac Genrot was thus naturally extinct, like the rest; and one could pass directly under it without even noticing that it was no longer in its place.

Nevertheless, the hour, the place, the darkness, Jean Valjean's absorption, his singular gestures, his goings and comings, all had begun to render Cosette uneasy. Any other child than she would have given vent to loud shrieks long before. She contented herself with plucking Jean Valjean by the skirt of his coat. They could hear the sound of the patrol's approach ever more and more distinctly.

"Father," said she, in a very low voice, "I am afraid. Who is coming yonder?"

"Hush!" replied the unhappy man. "It is Madame Thenardier."

Cosette shuddered. He added, "Say nothing. Don't interfere with me. If you cry out, if you weep, the Thenardier is lying in wait for you. She is coming to take you back."

Then, without haste, but without making a useless movement, with firm and curt precision, the more remarkable at a moment when the patrol and Javert might come upon him at any moment, he undid his cravat, passed it around Cosette's body under the armpits, taking care that it should not hurt the child, fastened this cravat to one end of the rope, by means of that knot which seafaring men call a "swallow knot," took the other end of the rope in his teeth, pulled off his shoes and stockings, which he threw over the wall, stepped upon the mass of masonry, and began to raise himself in the angle of the wall and the gable with as much solidity and certainty as though he had the rounds of a ladder under his feet and elbows. Half a minute had not elapsed when he was resting on his knees on the wall.

Cosette gazed at him in stupid amazement, without uttering a word. Jean Valjean's injunction, and the name of Madame Thenardier, had chilled her blood.

All at once she heard Jean Valjean's voice crying to her, though in a very low tone, "Put your back against the wall."

She obeyed.

"Don't say a word, and don't be alarmed," went on Jean Valjean.

And she felt herself lifted from the ground.

Before she had time to recover herself, she was on the top of the wall.

Jean Valjean grasped her, put her on his back, took her two tiny hands in his large left hand, lay down flat on his stomach and crawled along on top of the wall as far as the cant. As he had guessed, there stood a building whose roof started from the top of the wooden barricade and descended to within a very short distance of the ground, with a gentle slope that grazed the linden tree. A lucky circumstance, for the wall was much higher on this side than on the street side. Jean Valjean could only see the ground at a great depth below him.

He had just reached the slope of the roof, and had not yet left the crest of the wall, when a violent uproar announced the arrival of the patrol. The thundering voice of Javert was audible, "Search the blind alley! The Rue Droit-Mur is guarded! So is the Rue Petit-Picpus. I'll answer for it that he is in the blind alley."

The soldiers rushed into the Genrot alley.

Jean Valjean allowed himself to slide down the roof, still holding fast to Cosette, reached the linden tree, and leaped to the ground. Whether from terror or courage, Cosette had not breathed a sound, though her hands were a little abraded.

CHAPTER VI — THE BEGINNING OF AN ENIGMA

Jean Valjean found himself in a sort of garden that was very vast and of singular aspect; one of those melancholy gardens that seem made to be looked at in winter and at night. This garden was oblong in shape, with an alley of large poplars at the farther end, tolerably tall forest trees in the corners, and an unshaded space in the center, where could be seen a very large, solitary tree, then several fruit trees, gnarled and bristling like bushes, beds of vegetables, a melon patch, whose glass frames sparkled in the moonlight, and an old well. Here and there stood stone benches that seemed black with moss. The alleys were bordered with gloomy and very erect little shrubs. The grass had half taken possession of them, and a green mold covered the rest.

Jean Valjean had beside him the building whose roof had served him as a means of descent, a pile of fagots, and, behind the fagots, directly against the wall, a stone statue, whose mutilated face was no longer anything more than a hapeless mask which loomed vaguely through the gloom.

The building was a sort of ruin, where dismantled chambers were distinguishable, one of which, much encumbered, seemed to serve as a shed.

The large building of the Rue Droit-Mur, which had a wing on the Rue Petit-Picpus, turned two facades, at right angles, toward this garden. These interior facades were even more tragic than the exterior. All the windows were grated. Not a gleam of light was visible at anyone of them. The upper story had scuttles like prisons. One of those facades cast its shadow on the other, which fell over the garden like an immense black pall.

No other house was visible. The bottom of the garden was lost in mist and darkness. Nevertheless, walls could be confusedly made out that intersected as though there were more cultivated land beyond, and the low roofs of the Rue Polonceau.

Nothing more wild and solitary than this garden could be imagined. There was no one in it, which was quite natural in view of the hour; but it did not seem as though this spot were made for anyone to walk in, even in broad daylight.

Jean Valjean's first care had been to get hold of his shoes and put them on again, then to step under the shed with Cosette. A man who is fleeing never thinks himself sufficiently hidden. The child, whose thoughts were still on the Thenardier, shared his instinct for withdrawing from sight as much as possible.

Cosette trembled and pressed close to him. They heard the tumultuous noise of the patrol searching the blind alley and the streets; the blows of their gunstocks against the stones; Javert's appeals to the police spies whom he had posted, and his imprecations mingled with words which could not be distinguished.

At the expiration of a quarter of an hour it seemed as though that species of stormy roar were becoming more distant. Jean Valjean held his breath.

He had laid his hand lightly on Cosette's mouth.

However, the solitude in which he stood was so strangely calm, that this frightful uproar, close and furious as it was, did not disturb him by so much as the shadow of a misgiving. It seemed as though those walls had been built of the deaf stones of which the Scriptures speak.

All at once, in the midst of this profound calm, a fresh sound arose; a sound as celestial, divine, ineffable, ravishing, as the other had been horrible. It was a hymn that issued from the gloom, a dazzling burst of prayer and harmony in the obscure and alarming silence of the night; women's voices, but voices composed at one and the same time of the pure accents of virgins and the innocent accents of children, voices which are not of the earth, and which resemble those that the newborn infant still hears, and which the dying man hears already. This song proceeded from the gloomy edifice that towered above the garden. At the moment when the hubbub of demons retreated, one would have said that a choir of angels was approaching through the gloom.

Cosette and Jean Valjean fell on their knees.

They knew not what it was, they knew not where they were; but both of them, the man and the child, the penitent and the innocent, felt that they must kneel.

These voices had this strange characteristic, that they did not prevent the building from seeming to be deserted. It was a supernatural chant in an uninhabited house.

While these voices were singing, Jean Valjean thought of nothing. He no longer beheld the night; he beheld a blue sky. It seemed to him that he felt those wings that we all have within us, unfolding.

The song died away. It may have lasted a long time. Jean Valjean could not have told. Hours of ecstasy are never more than a moment.

All fell silent again. There was no longer anything in the street; there was nothing in the garden. That which had menaced, that which had reassured him— all had vanished. The breeze swayed a few dry weeds on the crest of the wall, and they gave out a faint, sweet, melancholy sound.

CHAPTER VII—CONTINUATION
OF THE ENIGMA

The night wind had risen, which indicated that it must be between one and two o'clock in the morning. Poor Cosette said nothing. As she had seated herself beside him and leaned her head against him, Jean Valjean had fancied that she was asleep. He bent down and looked at her. Cosette's eyes were wide open, and her thoughtful air pained Jean Valjean.

She was still trembling.

"Are you sleepy?" said Jean Valjean.

"I am very cold," she replied.

A moment later she resumed, "Is she still there?"

"Who?" said Jean Valjean.

"Madame Thenardier."

Jean Valjean had already forgotten the means he had employed to make Cosette keep silent.

"Ah!" said he. "She is gone. You need fear nothing further."

The child sighed as though a load had been lifted from her breast.

The ground was damp, the shed open on all sides, the breeze grew more keen every instant. The goodman took off his coat and wrapped it around Cosette.

"Are you less cold now?" said he.

"Oh, yes, Father."

"Well, wait for me a moment. I will soon be back."

He quitted the ruin and crept along the large building, seeking a better shelter. He came across doors, but they were closed. There were bars at all the windows of the ground floor.

Just after he had turned the inner angle of the edifice, he observed that he was coming to some arched windows, where he perceived a light. He stood on tiptoe and peeped through one of these windows. They all opened on a tolerably vast hall, paved with large flagstones, cut up by arcades and pillars, where only a tiny light and great shadows were visible. The light came from a taper burning in one corner. The apartment was deserted, and nothing was stirring in it. Nevertheless, by dint of gazing intently he thought he perceived on the ground something that appeared to be covered with a winding sheet, and which resembled a human form. This form was lying face down, flat on the pavement, with the arms extended in the form of a cross, in the immobility of death. One would have said, judging from a sort of serpent that undulated over the floor, that this sinister form had a rope around its neck.

The whole chamber was bathed in that mist of places sparely illuminated, which adds to horror.

Jean Valjean often said afterward, that, although many funereal specters had crossed his path in life, he had never beheld anything more blood-curdling and terrible than that enigmatical form accomplishing some inexplicable mystery in that gloomy place, and beheld thus at night. It was alarming to suppose that that thing was perhaps dead; and still more alarming to think that it was perhaps alive.

He had the courage to plaster his face to the glass, and to watch whether the thing would move. In spite of his remaining thus what seemed to him a very long time, the outstretched form made no movement. All at once he felt himself overpowered by an inexpressible terror, and he fled. He began to run toward the shed, not daring to look behind him. It seemed to him, that if he turned his head, he should see that form following him with great strides and waving its arms.

He reached the ruin all out of breath. His knees were giving way beneath him; the perspiration was pouring from him.

Where was he? Who could ever have imagined anything like that sort of sepulchre in the midst of Paris! What was this strange house? An edifice full of nocturnal mystery, calling to souls through the darkness with the voice of angels, and when they came, offering them abruptly that terrible vision, promising to open the radiant portals of heaven, and then opening the horrible gates of the tomb! And it actually was an edifice, a house that bore a number on the street! It was not a dream! He had to touch the stones to convince himself that such was the fact.

Cold, anxiety, uneasiness, the emotions of the night, had given him genuine fever, and all these ideas were clashing together in his brain.

He stepped up to Cosette. She was asleep.

CHAPTER VIII—THE ENIGMA BECOMES DOUBLY MYSTERIOUS

The child had laid her head on a stone and fallen asleep.

He sat down beside her and began to think. Little by little, as he gazed at her, he grew calm and regained possession of his freedom of mind.

He clearly perceived this truth, the foundation of his life henceforth, that so long as she was there, so long as he had her near him, he should need nothing except for her, he should fear nothing except for her. He was not even conscious that he was very cold, since he had taken off his coat to cover her.

Nevertheless, athwart this reverie into which he had fallen he had heard for some time a peculiar noise. It was like the tinkling of a bell. This sound proceeded from the garden. It could be heard distinctly though faintly. It resembled the faint, vague music produced by the bells of cattle at night in the pastures.

This noise made Valjean turn around.

He looked and saw that there was someone in the garden.

A being resembling a man was walking amid the bell-glasses of the melon beds, rising, stooping, halting, with regular movements, as though he were dragging or spreading out something on the ground. This person appeared to limp.

Jean Valjean shuddered with the continual tremor of the unhappy. For them everything is hostile and suspicious. They distrust the day because it enables people to see them, and the night because it aids in surprising them. A little while before, he had shivered because the garden was deserted, and now he shivered because there was someone there.

He fell back from chimerical terrors to real terrors. He said to himself that vert and the spies had, perhaps, not taken their departure; that they had, no oubt, left people on the watch in the street; that if this man should discover im in the garden, he would cry out for help against thieves and deliver him up. Ie took the sleeping Cosette gently in his arms and carried her behind a heap f old furniture that was out of use, in the most remote corner of the shed. osette did not stir.

From that point he scrutinized the appearance of the being in the melon atch. The strange thing about it was, that the sound of the bell followed each f this man's movements. When the man approached, the sound approached; hen the man retreated, the sound retreated; if he made any hasty gesture, a remolo accompanied the gesture; when he halted, the sound ceased. It appeared vident that the bell was attached to that man; but what could that signify? Who as this man who had a bell suspended about him like a ram or an ox?

As he put these questions to himself, he touched Cosette's hands. They ere icy cold.

"Ah! Good God!" he cried.

He spoke to her in a low voice, "Cosette!"

She did not open her eyes.

He shook her vigorously.

She did not wake.

"Is she dead?" he said to himself, and sprang to his feet, quivering from ead to foot.

The most frightful thoughts rushed pell-mell through his mind. There are noments when hideous surmises assail us like a cohort of furies, and violently orce the partitions of our brains. When those we love are in question, our rudence invents every sort of madness. He remembered that sleep in the open ir on a cold night may be fatal.

Cosette was pale, and had fallen at full length on the ground at his feet, vithout a movement.

He listened to her breathing: she still breathed, but with a respiration that eemed to him weak and on the point of extinction.

How was he to warm her back to life? How was he to rouse her? All that vas not connected with this vanished from his thoughts. He rushed wildly rom the ruin.

It was absolutely necessary that Cosette should be in bed and beside a fire n less than a quarter of an hour.

CHAPTER IX—THE MAN
WITH THE BELL

He walked straight up to the man whom he saw in the garden. He ha taken in his hand the roll of silver in the pocket of his waistcoat.

The man's head was bent down, and he did not see him approaching. In few strides Jean Valjean stood beside him.

Jean Valjean accosted him with the cry, "One hundred francs!"

The man gave a start and raised his eyes.

"You can earn a hundred francs," went on Jean Valjean, "if you will gran me shelter for this night."

The moon shone full upon Jean Valjean's terrified countenance.

"What! So it is you, Father Madeleine!" said the man.

That name, thus pronounced, at that obscure hour, in that unknown spot by that strange man, made Jean Valjean start back.

He had expected anything but that. The person who thus addressed him was a bent and lame old man, dressed almost like a peasant, who wore on hi left knee a leather kneecap, from which hung a moderately large bell. His face which was in the shadow, was not distinguishable.

However, the goodman had removed his cap, and exclaimed, trembling al over, "Ah, good God! How come you here, Father Madeleine? Where did you enter? Dieu-Jesus! Did you fall from heaven? There is no trouble about that if ever you do fall, it will be from there. And what a state you are in! You have no cravat; you have no hat; you have no coat! Do you know, you would have frightened anyone who did not know you? No coat! Lord God! Are the saint going mad nowadays? But how did you get in here?"

His words tumbled over each other. The goodman talked with a rustic volubility, in which there was nothing alarming. All this was uttered with a mixture of stupefaction and naive kindliness.

"Who are you? And what house is this?" demanded Jean Valjean.

"Ah! Pardieu, this is too much!" exclaimed the old man. "I am the person for whom you got the place here, and this house is the one where you had me placed. What! You don't recognize me?"

"No," said Jean Valjean, "and how happens it that you know me?"

"You saved my life," said the man.

He turned. A ray of moonlight outlined his profile, and Jean Valjean recognized old Fauchelevent.

"Ah!" said Jean Valjean. "So it is you? Yes, I recollect you."

"That is very lucky," said the old man, in a reproachful tone.

"And what are you doing here?" resumed Jean Valjean.

"Why, I am covering my melons, of course!"

In fact, at the moment when Jean Valjean accosted him, old Fauchelevent held in his hand the end of a straw mat, which he was occupied in spreading over the melon bed. During the hour or thereabouts that he had been in the garden he had already spread out a number of them. It was this operation that had caused him to execute the peculiar movements observed from the shed by Jean Valjean.

He continued, "I said to myself, 'The moon is bright; it is going to freeze. What if I were to put my melons into their greatcoats?' And," he added, looking at Jean Valjean with a broad smile, "Pardieu! You ought to have done the same! But how do you come here?"

Jean Valjean, finding himself known to this man, at least only under the name of Madeleine, thenceforth advanced only with caution. He multiplied his questions. Strange to say, their roles seemed to be reversed. It was he, the intruder, who interrogated.

"And what is this bell that you wear on your knee?"

"This," replied Fauchelevent, "is so that I may be avoided."

"What! So that you may be avoided?"

Old Fauchelevent winked with an indescribable air.

"Ah, goodness! There are only women in this house—many young girls. It appears that I should be a dangerous person to meet. The bell gives them warning. When I come, they go."

"What house is this?"

"Come, you know well enough."

"But I do not."

"Not when you got me the place here as gardener?"

"Answer me as though I knew nothing."

"Well, then, this is the Petit-Picpus convent."

Memories recurred to Jean Valjean. Chance, that is to say, Providence, had cast him into precisely that convent in the Quartier Saint-Antoine where old Fauchelevent, crippled by the fall from his cart, had been admitted on his recommendation two years previously. He repeated, as though talking to himself, "The Petit-Picpus convent."

"Exactly," returned old Fauchelevent. "But to come to the point, how the deuce did you manage to get in here, you, Father Madeleine? No matter if you are a saint; you are a man as well, and no man enters here."

"You certainly are here."

"There is no one but me."

"Still," said Jean Valjean, "I must stay here."

"Ah, good God!" cried Fauchelevent.

Jean Valjean drew near to the old man, and said to him in a grave voice, "Father Fauchelevent, I saved your life."

"I was the first to recall it," returned Fauchelevent.

"Well, you can do today for me that which I did for you in the olden days."

Fauchelevent took in his aged, trembling, and wrinkled hands Jean Valjean's two robust hands, and stood for several minutes as though incapable of speaking. At length he exclaimed, "Oh! That would be a blessing from the good God, if I could make you some little return for that! Save your life, Monsieur le Maire, dispose of the old man!"

A wonderful joy had transfigured this old man. His countenance seemed to emit a ray of light.

"What do you wish me to do?" he resumed.

"That I will explain to you. You have a chamber?"

"I have an isolated hovel yonder, behind the ruins of the old convent, in a corner, which no one ever looks into. There are three rooms in it."

The hut was, in fact, so well hidden behind the ruins, and so cleverly arranged to prevent it being seen, that Jean Valjean had not perceived it.

"Good," said Jean Valjean. "Now I am going to ask two things of you."

"What are they, Mr. Mayor?"

"In the first place, you are not to tell anyone what you know about me. In the second, you are not to try to find out anything more."

"As you please. I know that you can do nothing that is not honest, that you have always been a man after the good God's heart. And then, moreover, you it was who placed me here. That concerns you. I am at your service."

"That is settled then. Now, come with me. We will go and get the child."

"Ah!" said Fauchelevent. "So there is a child?"

He added not a word further, and followed Jean Valjean as a dog follows his master.

Less than half an hour afterward Cosette, who had grown rosy again before the flame of a good fire, was lying asleep in the old gardener's bed. Jean Valjean had put on his cravat and coat once more; his hat that he had flung over the wall, had been found and picked up. While Jean Valjean was putting on his coat, Fauchelevent had removed the bell and kneecap that now hung on a nail beside a vintage basket that adorned the wall. The two men were warming

hemselves with their elbows resting on a table upon which Fauchelevent had
placed a bit of cheese, black bread, a bottle of wine, and two glasses, and the
old man was saying to Jean Valjean, as he laid his hand on the latter's knee,
Ah! Father Madeleine! You did not recognize me immediately; you save
people's lives, and then you forget them! That is bad! But they remember you!
You are an ingrate!"

CHAPTER X—WHICH EXPLAINS HOW JAVERT GOT ON THE SCENT

The events of which we have just beheld the reverse side, so to speak, had
come about in the simplest possible manner.

When Jean Valjean, on the evening of the very day when Javert had
arrested him beside Fantine's deathbed, had escaped from the town jail of M.
sur M., the police had supposed that he had betaken himself to Paris. Paris is
a maelstrom where everything is lost, and everything disappears in this belly
of the world, as in the belly of the sea. No forest hides a man as does that
crowd. Fugitives of every sort know this. They go to Paris as to an abyss; there
are gulfs that save. The police know it also, and it is in Paris that they seek
what they have lost elsewhere. They sought the ex-mayor of M. sur M. Javert
was summoned to Paris to throw light on their researches. Javert had, in fact,
rendered powerful assistance in the recapture of Jean Valjean. Javert's zeal and
intelligence on that occasion had been remarked by M. Chabouillet, secretary
of the Prefecture under Comte Angles. M. Chabouillet, who had, moreover,
already been Javert's patron, had the inspector of M. sur M. attached to the
police force of Paris. There Javert rendered himself useful in diverse and,
though the word may seem strange for such services, honorable manners.

He no longer thought of Jean Valjean—the wolf of today causes these
dogs who are always on the chase to forget the wolf of yesterday—when,
in December, 1823, he read a newspaper, he who never read newspapers; but
Javert, a monarchical man, had a desire to know the particulars of the triumphal
entry of the "Prince Generalissimo" into Bayonne. Just as he was finishing the
article, which interested him; a name, the name of Jean Valjean, attracted his
attention at the bottom of a page. The paper announced that the convict Jean
Valjean was dead, and published the fact in such formal terms that Javert did
not doubt it. He confined himself to the remark, "That's a good entry." Then
he threw aside the paper, and thought no more about it.

Sometime afterward, it chanced that a police report was transmitted from the prefecture of the Seine-et-Oise to the prefecture of police in Paris, concerning the abduction of a child that had taken place, under peculiar circumstances, a it was said, in the commune of Montfermeil. A little girl of seven or eight year of age, the report said, who had been intrusted by her mother to an innkeeper of that neighborhood, had been stolen by a stranger; this child answered to the name of Cosette, and was the daughter of a girl named Fantine, who had died in the hospital, it was not known where or when.

This report came under Javert's eye and set him to thinking.

The name of Fantine was well known to him. He remembered that Jean Valjean had made him, Javert, burst into laughter, by asking him for a respite of three days, for the purpose of going to fetch that creature's child. He recalled the fact that Jean Valjean had been arrested in Paris at the very moment when he was stepping into the coach for Montfermeil. Some signs had made him suspect at the time that this was the second occasion of his entering that coach, and that he had already, on the previous day, made an excursion to the neighborhood of that village, for he had not been seen in the village itself. What had he been intending to do in that region of Montfermeil? It could not even be surmised. Javert understood it now. Fantine's daughter was there. Jean Valjean was going there in search of her. And now this child had been stolen by a stranger! Who could that stranger be? Could it be Jean Valjean? But Jean Valjean was dead. Javert, without saying anything to anybody, took the coach from the Pewter Platter, Cul-de-Sac de la Planchette, and made a trip to Montfermeil.

He expected to find a great deal of light on the subject there; he found a great deal of obscurity.

For the first few days the Thenardiers had chattered in their rage. The disappearance of the Lark had created a sensation in the village. He immediately obtained numerous versions of the story that ended in the abduction of a child. Hence the police report. But their first vexation having passed off, Thenardier, with his wonderful instinct, had very quickly comprehended that it is never advisable to stir up the prosecutor of the Crown, and that his complaints with regard to the abduction of Cosette would have as their first result to fix upon himself, and upon many dark affairs that he had on hand, the glittering eye of justice. The last thing that owls desire is to have a candle brought to them. And in the first place, how explain the 1,500 francs he had received? He turned squarely around, put a gag on his wife's mouth, and feigned astonishment when the stolen child was mentioned to him. He understood nothing about it; no doubt he had grumbled for awhile at having that dear little creature "taken from him" so hastily; he should have liked to keep her two or three days longer, out of tenderness; but her "grandfather" had come for her in the most natural way in the world. He added the "grandfather," which produced a good effect. This was the story that Javert hit upon when he arrived at Montfermeil. The grandfather caused Jean Valjean to vanish.

Nevertheless, Javert dropped a few questions, like plummets, into Thenardier's history. "Who was that grandfather? And what was his name?" Thenardier replied with simplicity, "He is a wealthy farmer. I saw his passport. I think his name was M. Guillaume Lambert."

Lambert is a respectable and extremely reassuring name. Thereupon Javert returned to Paris.

"Jean Valjean is certainly dead," said he, "and I am a ninny."

He had again begun to forget this history, when, in the course of March, 1824, he heard of a singular personage who dwelled in the parish of Saint-Medard and who had been surnamed "the mendicant who gives alms." This person, the story ran, was a man of means, whose name no one knew exactly, and who lived alone with a little girl of eight years, who knew nothing about herself, save that she had come from Montfermeil. Montfermeil! That name was always coming up, and it made Javert prick up his ears. An old beggar police spy, an ex-beadle, to whom this person had given alms, added a few more details. This gentleman of property was very shy, never coming out except in the evening, speaking to no one, except, occasionally to the poor, and never allowing anyone to approach him. He wore a horrible old yellow frock coat that was worth many millions, being all wadded with bank bills. This piqued Javert's curiosity in a decided manner. In order to get a close look at this fantastic gentleman without alarming him, he borrowed the beadle's outfit for a day, and the place where the old spy was in the habit of crouching every evening, whining orisons through his nose, and playing the spy under cover of prayer.

"The suspected individual" did indeed approach Javert thus disguised, and bestow alms on him. At that moment Javert raised his head, and the shock that Jean Valjean received on recognizing Javert was equal to the one received by Javert when he thought he recognized Jean Valjean.

However, the darkness might have misled him; Jean Valjean's death was official; Javert cherished very grave doubts; and when in doubt, Javert, the man of scruples, never laid a finger on anyone's collar.

He followed his man to the Gorbeau house, and got "the old woman" to talking, which was no difficult matter. The old woman confirmed the fact regarding the coat lined with millions, and narrated to him the episode of the thousand-franc bill. She had seen it! She had handled it! Javert hired a room; that evening he installed himself in it. He came and listened at the mysterious lodger's door, hoping to catch the sound of his voice, but Jean Valjean saw his candle through the keyhole, and foiled the spy by keeping silent.

On the following day Jean Valjean decamped; but the noise made by the fall of the five-franc piece was noticed by the old woman, who, hearing the rattling of coin, suspected that he might be intending to leave, and made haste to warn Javert. At night, when Jean Valjean came out, Javert was waiting for him behind the trees of the boulevard with two men.

Javert had demanded assistance at the Prefecture, but he had not mentioned the name of the individual whom he hoped to seize; that was his secret, and he had kept it for three reasons: in the first place, because the slightest indiscretion might put Jean Valjean on the alert; next, because, to lay hands on an ex-convict who had made his escape and was reputed dead, on a criminal whom justice had formerly classed forever as among malefactors of the most dangerous sort, was a magnificent success which the old members of the Parisian police would assuredly not leave to a newcomer like Javert, and he was afraid of being deprived of his convict; and lastly, because Javert, being an artist, had a taste for the unforeseen. He hated those well-heralded successes that are talked of long in advance and have had the bloom brushed off. He preferred to elaborate his masterpieces in the dark and to unveil them suddenly at the last.

Javert had followed Jean Valjean from tree to tree, then from corner to corner of the street, and had not lost sight of him for a single instant; even at the moments when Jean Valjean believed himself to be the most secure Javert's eye had been on him. Why had not Javert arrested Jean Valjean? Because he was still in doubt.

It must be remembered that at that epoch the police was not precisely at its ease; the free press embarrassed it; several arbitrary arrests denounced by the newspapers, had echoed even as far as the chambers, and had rendered the Prefecture timid. Interference with individual liberty was a grave matter. The police agents were afraid of making a mistake; the prefect laid the blame on them; a mistake meant dismissal. The reader can imagine the effect that this brief paragraph, reproduced by twenty newspapers, would have caused in Paris, "Yesterday, an aged grandfather, with white hair, a respectable and well-to-do gentleman, who was walking with his grandchild, aged eight, was arrested and conducted to the agency of the Prefecture as an escaped convict!"

Let us repeat in addition that Javert had scruples of his own; injunctions of his conscience were added to the injunctions of the prefect. He was really in doubt.

Jean Valjean turned his back on him and walked in the dark.

Sadness, uneasiness, anxiety, depression, this fresh misfortune of being forced to flee by night, to seek a chance refuge in Paris for Cosette and himself, the necessity of regulating his pace to the pace of the child—all this, without his being aware of it, had altered Jean Valjean's walk, and impressed on his bearing such senility, that the police themselves, incarnate in the person of Javert, might, and did in fact, make a mistake. The impossibility of approaching too close, his costume of an emigre preceptor, the declaration of Thenardier, which made a grandfather of him, and, finally, the belief in his death in prison, added still further to the uncertainty that gathered thick in Javert's mind.

For an instant it occurred to him to make an abrupt demand for his papers; but if the man was not Jean Valjean, and if this man was not a good, honest old fellow living on his income, he was probably some merry blade deeply and cunningly implicated in the obscure web of Parisian misdeeds, some chief of a dangerous band, who gave alms to conceal his other talents, which was an old dodge. He had trusty fellows, accomplices' retreats in case of emergencies, in which he would, no doubt, take refuge. All these turns that he was making through the streets seemed to indicate that he was not a simple and honest man. To arrest him too hastily would be "to kill the hen that laid the golden eggs." Where was the inconvenience in waiting? Javert was very sure that he would not escape.

Thus he proceeded in a tolerably perplexed state of mind, putting to himself a hundred questions about this enigmatical personage.

It was only quite late in the Rue de Pontoise, that, thanks to the brilliant light thrown from a dramshop, he decidedly recognized Jean Valjean.

There are in this world two beings who give a profound start—the mother who recovers her child and the tiger who recovers his prey. Javert gave that profound start.

As soon as he had positively recognized Jean Valjean, the formidable convict, he perceived that there were only three of them, and he asked for reinforcements at the police station of the Rue de Pontoise. One puts on gloves before grasping a thorn cudgel.

This delay and the halt at the Carrefour Rollin to consult with his agents came near causing him to lose the trail. He speedily divined, however, that Jean Valjean would want to put the river between his pursuers and himself. He bent his head and reflected like a bloodhound who puts his nose to the ground to make sure that he is on the right scent. Javert, with his powerful rectitude of instinct, went straight to the bridge of Austerlitz. A word with the toll-keeper furnished him with the information he required, "Have you seen a man with a little girl?"

"I made him pay two sous," replied the toll-keeper. Javert reached the bridge in season to see Jean Valjean traverse the small illuminated spot on the other side of the water, leading Cosette by the hand. He saw him enter the Rue du Chemin-Vert-Saint-Antoine; he remembered the Cul-de-Sac Genrot arranged there like a trap, and of the sole exit of the Rue Droit-Mur into the Rue Petit-Picpus. He made sure of his back burrows, as huntsmen say; he hastily dispatched one of his agents, by a roundabout way, to guard that issue. A patrol that was returning to the Arsenal post having passed him, he made a requisition on it, and caused it to accompany him. In such games soldiers are aces. Moreover, the principle is, that in order to get the best of a wild boar, one must employ the science of venery and plenty of dogs. These combinations having been affected, feeling that Jean Valjean was caught between the blind alley Genrot on the right, his agent on the left, and himself, Javert, in the rear, he took a pinch of snuff.

Then he began the game. He experienced one ecstatic and infernal moment; he allowed his man to go on ahead, knowing that he had him safe, but desirous of postponing the moment of arrest as long as possible, happy at the thought that he was taken and yet at seeing him free, gloating over him with his gaze, with that voluptuousness of the spider, which allows the fly to flutter, and of the cat, which lets the mouse run. Claws and talons possess a monstrous sensuality, the obscure movements of the creature imprisoned in their pincers. What a delight this strangling is!

Javert was enjoying himself. The meshes of his net were stoutly knotted. He was sure of success; all he had to do now was to close his hand.

Accompanied as he was, the very idea of resistance was impossible, however vigorous, energetic, and desperate Jean Valjean might be.

Javert advanced slowly, sounding, searching on his way all the nooks of the street like so many pockets of thieves.

When he reached the center of the web he found the fly no longer there.

His exasperation can be imagined.

He interrogated his sentinel of the Rues Droit-Mur and Petit-Picpus; that agent, who had remained imperturbably at his post, had not seen the man pass.

It sometimes happens that a stag is lost head and horns; that is to say, he escapes although he has the pack on his very heels, and then the oldest

untsmen know not what to say. Duvivier, Ligniville, and Desprez halt short.
In a discomfiture of this sort, Artonge exclaims, "It was not a stag, but a
sorcerer." Javert would have liked to utter the same cry.

His disappointment bordered for a moment on despair and rage.

It is certain that Napoleon made mistakes during the war with Russia, that
Alexander committed blunders in the war in India, that Caesar made mistakes
in the war in Africa, that Cyrus was at fault in the war in Scythia, and that Javert
blundered in this campaign against Jean Valjean. He was wrong, perhaps, in
hesitating in his recognition of the ex-convict. The first glance should have
sufficed him. He was wrong in not arresting him purely and simply in the old
building; he was wrong in not arresting him when he positively recognized him
in the Rue de Pontoise. He was wrong in taking counsel with his auxiliaries in
the full light of the moon in the Carrefour Rollin. Advice is certainly useful;
it is a good thing to know and to interrogate those of the dogs who deserve
confidence; but the hunter cannot be too cautious when he is chasing uneasy
animals like the wolf and the convict. Javert, by taking too much thought as to
how he should set the bloodhounds of the pack on the trail, alarmed the beast
by giving him wind of the dart, and so made him run. Above all, he was wrong
in that after he had picked up the scent again on the bridge of Austerlitz, he
played that formidable and puerile game of keeping such a man at the end of
a thread. He thought himself stronger than he was, and believed that he could
play at the game of the mouse and the lion. At the same time, he reckoned
himself as too weak, when he judged it necessary to obtain reinforcement. Fatal
precaution, waste of precious time! Javert committed all these blunders, and
nonetheless was one of the cleverest and most correct spies that ever existed.
He was, in the full force of the term, what is called in venery a knowing dog.
But what is there that is perfect?

Great strategists have their eclipses.

The greatest follies are often composed, like the largest ropes, of a multitude
of strands. Take the cable thread by thread, take all the petty determining
motives separately, and you can break them one after the other, and you
say, "That is all there is of it!" Braid them, twist them together; the result is
enormous: it is Attila hesitating between Marcian on the east and Valentinian
on the west; it is Hannibal tarrying at Capua; it is Danton falling asleep at
Arcis-sur-Aube.

However that may be, even at the moment when he saw that Jean Valjean
had escaped him, Javert did not lose his head. Sure that the convict who had
broken his ban could not be far off, he established sentinels, he organized traps

and ambuscades, and beat the quarter all that night. The first thing he saw wa
the disorder in the street lantern whose rope had been cut. A precious sign that
however, led him astray, since it caused him to turn all his researches in the
direction of the Cul-de-Sac Genrot. In this blind alley there were tolerably low
walls that abutted on gardens whose bounds adjoined the immense stretche
of wasteland. Jean Valjean evidently must have fled in that direction. The fac
is, that had he penetrated a little further in the Cul-de-Sac Genrot, he woul
probably have done so and have been lost. Javert explored these gardens an
these waste stretches as though he had been hunting for a needle.

At daybreak he left two intelligent men on the outlook, and returned to the
Prefecture of Police, as much ashamed as a police spy who had been captured
by a robber might have been.

BOOK SIXTH: LE PETIT-PICPUS

CHAPTER I—NUMBER 62 RUE PETIT-PICPUS

Nothing, half a century ago, more resembled every other carriage gate
than the carriage gate of Number 62 Rue Petit-Picpus. This entrance
which usually stood ajar in the most inviting fashion, permitted a view of two
things, neither of which have anything very funereal about them, a courtyard
surrounded by walls hung with vines, and the face of a lounging porter. Above
the wall, at the bottom of the court, tall trees were visible. When a ray of
sunlight enlivened the courtyard, when a glass of wine cheered up the porter
it was difficult to pass Number 62 Little Picpus Street without carrying away
a smiling impression of it. Nevertheless, it was a somber place of which one
had had a glimpse.

The threshold smiled; the house prayed and wept.

If one succeeded in passing the porter, which was not easy that was even
nearly impossible for everyone, for there was an open sesame! That it was
necessary to know, if, the porter once passed, one entered a little vestibule on
the right, on which opened a staircase shut in between two walls and so narrow
that only one person could ascend it at a time, if one did not allow one's self to
be alarmed by a daubing of canary yellow, with a dado of chocolate that clothed
this staircase, if one ventured to ascend it, one crossed a first landing, then a

econd, and arrived on the first story at a corridor where the yellow wash and he chocolate-hued plinth pursued one with a peaceable persistency. Staircase and corridor were lit by two beautiful windows. The corridor took a turn and became dark. If one doubled this cape, one arrived a few paces further on, in front of a door that was all the more mysterious because it was not fastened. If one opened it, one found one's self in a little chamber about six feet square, tiled, well scrubbed, clean, cold, and hung with cotton paper with green flowers, at fifteen sous the roll. A white, dull light fell from a large window, with tiny panes, on the left that usurped the whole width of the room. One gazed about, but saw no one; one listened, one heard neither a footstep nor a human murmur. The walls were bare, the chamber was not furnished; there was not even a chair.

One looked again, and beheld on the wall facing the door a quadrangular hole, about a foot square, with a grating of interlacing iron bars, black, knotted, solid, which formed squares—I had almost said meshes—of less than an inch and a half in diagonal length. The little green flowers of the cotton paper ran in a calm and orderly manner to those iron bars, without being startled or thrown into confusion by their funereal contact. Supposing that a living being had been so wonderfully thin as to essay an entrance or an exit through the square hole, this grating would have prevented it. It did not allow the passage of the body, but it did allow the passage of the eyes; that is to say, of the mind. This seems to have occurred to them, for it had been reenforced by a sheet of tin inserted in the wall a little in the rear, and pierced with a thousand holes more microscopic than the holes of a strainer. At the bottom of this plate, an aperture had been pierced exactly similar to the orifice of a letterbox. A bit of tape attached to a bellwire hung at the right of the grated opening.

If the tape was pulled, a bell rang, and one heard a voice very near at hand, which made one start.

"Who is there?" the voice demanded.

It was a woman's voice, a gentle voice, so gentle that it was mournful.

Here, again, there was a magical word that was necessary to know. If one did not know it, the voice ceased, the wall became silent once more, as though the terrified obscurity of the sepulchre had been on the other side of it.

If one knew the password, the voice resumed, "Enter on the right."

One then perceived on the right, facing the window, a glass door surmounted by a frame glazed and painted gray. On raising the latch and crossing the threshold, one experienced precisely the same impression as when one enters at the theater into a grated bathtub, before the grating is lowered and the chandelier is lighted. One was, in fact, in a sort of theater-box, narrow, furnished with two old chairs, and a much-frayed straw matting, sparely illuminated by the vague light from the glass door; a regular box, with its front just of a height to lean upon, bearing a tablet of black wood. This box was grated, only the grating of it was not of gilded wood, as at the opera; it was a monstrous lattice of iron bars, hideously interlaced and riveted to the wall by enormous fastenings that resembled clenched fists.

The first minutes passed; when one's eyes began to grow used to this cellarlike half-twilight, one tried to pass the grating, but got no further than six inches beyond it. There he encountered a barrier of black shutters, reenforced and fortified with transverse beams of wood painted a gingerbread-yellow. These shutters were divided into long, narrow slats, and they masked the entire length of the grating. They were always closed. At the expiration of a few moments one heard a voice proceeding from behind these shutters, and saying: "I am here. What do you wish with me?"

It was a beloved, sometimes an adored, voice. No one was visible. Hardly the sound of a breath was audible. It seemed as though it were a spirit that had been evoked, that was speaking to you across the walls of the tomb.

If one chanced to be within certain prescribed and very rare conditions, the slat of one of the shutters opened opposite you; the evoked spirit became an apparition. Behind the grating, behind the shutter, one perceived so far as the grating permitted sight, a head, of which only the mouth and the chin were visible; the rest was covered with a black veil. One caught a glimpse of a black blouse, and a form that was barely defined, covered with a black shroud. That head spoke with you, but did not look at you and never smiled at you.

The light that came from behind you was adjusted in such a manner that you saw her in the white, and she saw you in the black. This light was symbolical.

Nevertheless, your eyes plunged eagerly through that opening, which was made in that place shut off from all glances. A profound vagueness enveloped that form clad in mourning. Your eyes searched that vagueness, and sought to make out the surroundings of the apparition. At the expiration of a very short time you discovered that you could see nothing. What you beheld was night, emptiness, shadows, a wintry mist mingled with a vapor from the tomb, a sort of terrible peace, a silence from which you could gather nothing, not even sighs, a gloom in which you could distinguish nothing, not even phantoms.

What you beheld was the interior of a cloister.

It was the interior of that severe and gloomy edifice, which was called the Convent of the Bernardines of the Perpetual Adoration. The box in which you stood was the parlor. The first voice that had addressed you was that of the portress who always sat motionless and silent, on the other side of the wall, near the square opening, screened by the iron grating and the plate with its thousand holes, as by a double visor. The obscurity that bathed the grated box arose from the fact that the parlor, which had a window on the side of the world, had none on the side of the convent. Profane eyes must see nothing of that sacred place.

Nevertheless, there was something beyond that shadow; there was a light; there was life in the midst of that death. Although this was the most strictly walled of all convents, we shall endeavor to make our way into it, and to take the reader in, and to say, without transgressing the proper bounds, things which storytellers have never seen, and have, therefore, never described.

CHAPTER II—THE OBEDIENCE OF MARTIN VERGA

This convent, which in 1824 had already existed for many a long year in the Rue Petit-Picpus, was a community of Bernardines of the obedience of Martin Verga.

These Bernardines were attached, in consequence, not to Clairvaux, like the Bernardine monks, but to Citeaux, like the Benedictine monks. In other words, they were the subjects, not of Saint Bernard, but of Saint Benoit.

Anyone who has turned over old folios to any extent knows that Martin Verga founded in 1425 a congregation of Bernardines-Benedictines, with Salamanca for the head of the order, and Alcala as the branch establishment.

This congregation had sent out branches throughout all the Catholic countries of Europe.

There is nothing unusual in the Latin Church in these grafts of one order on another. To mention only a single order of Saint-Benoit, which is here in question: there are attached to this order, without counting the obedience of Martin Verga, four congregations, two in Italy, Mont-Cassin and Sainte-Justine of Padua; two in France, Cluny and Saint-Maur; and nine orders, Vallombrosa, Granmont, the Celestins, the Camaldules, the Carthusians, the Humilies, the Olivateurs, the Silvestrins, and lastly, Citeaux; for Citeaux itself, a trunk for other orders, is only an offshoot of Saint-Benoit. Citeaux dates from Saint Robert, Abbé de Molesme, in the diocese of Langres, in 1098. Now it was in 529 that the devil, having retired to the desert of Subiaco—he was old—had he turned hermit?—was chased from the ancient temple of Apollo, where he dwelled, by Saint-Benoit, then aged seventeen.

After the rule of the Carmelites, who go barefoot, wear a bit of willow on their throats, and never sit down, the harshest rule is that of the Bernardines-Benedictines of Martin Verga. They are clothed in black, with a guimpe which, in accordance with the express command of Saint-Benoit, mounts to the chin. A robe of serge with large sleeves, a large woolen veil, the guimpe, which mounts to the chin cut square on the breast, the band which descends over their brow to their eyes—this is their dress. All is black except the band, which is white. The novices wear the same habit, but all in white. The professed nuns also wear a rosary at their side.

The Bernardines-Benedictines of Martin Verga practice the Perpetual Adoration, like the Benedictines called Ladies of the Holy Sacrament, who, at the beginning of this century, had two houses in Paris, one at the Temple, the other in the Rue Neuve-Sainte-Genevieve. However, the Bernardines-Benedictines of the Petit-Picpus, of whom we are speaking, were a totally different order from the Ladies of the Holy Sacrament, cloistered in the Rue Neuve-Sainte-Genevieve and at the Temple. There were numerous differences in their rule; there were some in their costume. The Bernardines-Benedictines of the Petit-Picpus wore the black guimpe, and the Benedictines of the Holy Sacrament and of the Rue Neuve-Sainte-Genevieve wore a white one, and had, besides, on their breasts, a Holy Sacrament about three inches long, in silver gilt or gilded copper. The nuns of the Petit-Picpus did not wear this Holy Sacrament. The Perpetual Adoration, which was common to the house of the Petit-Picpus and to the house of the Temple, leaves those two orders perfectly distinct. Their only resemblance lies in this practice of the Ladies of the Holy Sacrament and the Bernardines of Martin Verga, just as there existed a similarity in the study and the glorification of all the mysteries relating to the infancy, the life, and death of Jesus Christ and the Virgin, between the two orders that were, nevertheless, widely separated, and on occasion even hostile. The Oratory of Italy, established at Florence by Philip de Neri, and the Oratory of France, established by Pierre de Berulle. The Oratory of France claimed the precedence, since Philip de Neri was only a saint, while Berulle was a cardinal.

Let us return to the harsh Spanish rule of Martin Verga.

The Bernardines-Benedictines of this obedience fast all the year-round, abstain from meat, fast in Lent and on many other days that are peculiar to them, rise from their first sleep, from one to three o'clock in the morning, to read their breviary and chant matins, sleep in all seasons between serge sheets and on straw, make no use of the bath, never light a fire, scourge themselves every Friday, observe the rule of silence, speak to each other only during the recreation hours that are very brief, and wear coarse, woolen chemises for six months in the year, from September 14th, which is the Exaltation of the Holy Cross, until Easter. These six months are a modification: the rule says all the year, but this woolen chemise, intolerable in the heat of summer, produced fevers and nervous spasms. The use of it had to be restricted. Even with this palliation, when the nuns put on this chemise on the 14th of September, they suffer from fever for three or four days. Obedience, poverty, chastity, perseverance in their seclusion, these are their vows that the rule greatly aggravates.

The prioress is elected for three years by the mothers, who are called *meres vocales* because they have a voice in the chapter. A prioress can only be reelected twice, which fixes the longest possible reign of a prioress at nine years.

They never see the officiating priest, who is always hidden from them by a serge curtain nine feet in height. During the sermon, when the preacher is in the chapel, they drop their veils over their faces. They must always speak low, walk with their eyes on the ground and their heads bowed. One man only is allowed to enter the convent, the archbishop of the diocese.

There is really one other, the gardener. But he is always an old man, and, in order that he may always be alone in the garden, and that the nuns may be warned to avoid him, a bell is attached to his knee.

Their submission to the prioress is absolute and passive. It is the canonical subjection in the full force of its abnegation. As at the voice of Christ, *ut voci Christi*, at a gesture, at the first sign, *ad nutum, ad primum signum*, immediately, with cheerfulness, with perseverance, with a certain blind obedience, *prompte, hilariter, perseveranter et caeca quadam obedientia, as the file in the hand of the workman, quasi limam in manibus fabri*, without power to read or to write without express permission, *legere vel scribere non addiscerit sine expressa superioris licentia.*

Each one of them in turn makes what they call reparation. The reparation is the prayer for all the sins, for all the faults, for all the dissensions, for all the violations, for all the iniquities, for all the crimes committed on earth. For the space of twelve consecutive hours, from four o'clock in the afternoon till four o'clock in the morning, or from four o'clock in the morning until four o'clock in the afternoon, the sister who is making reparation remains on her knees on the stone before the Holy Sacrament, with hands clasped, a rope around her neck. When her fatigue becomes unendurable, she prostrates herself flat on her face against the earth, with her arms outstretched in the form of a cross; this is her only relief. In this attitude she prays for all the guilty in the universe. This is great to sublimity.

As this act is performed in front of a post on which burns a candle, it is called without distinction, to make reparation or to be at the post. The nuns even prefer, out of humility, this last expression that contains an idea of torture and abasement.

To make reparation is a function in which the whole soul is absorbed. The sister at the post would not turn around were a thunderbolt to fall directly behind her.

Besides this, there is always a sister kneeling before the Holy Sacrament. This station lasts an hour. They relieve each other like soldiers on guard. This is the Perpetual Adoration.

The prioresses and the mothers almost always bear names stamped with peculiar solemnity, recalling, not the saints and martyrs, but moments in the life of Jesus Christ: as Mother Nativity, Mother Conception, Mother Presentation. Mother Passion. But the names of saints are not interdicted.

When one sees them, one never sees anything but their mouths.

All their teeth are yellow. No toothbrush ever entered that convent. Brushing one's teeth is at the top of a ladder at whose bottom is the loss of one's soul.

They never say "my." They possess nothing of their own, and they must not attach themselves to anything. They call everything "our"; thus: our veil, our chaplet; if they were speaking of their chemise, they would say our chemise. Sometimes they grow attached to some petty object, to a book of hours, a relic, a medal that has been blessed. As soon as they become aware that they are growing attached to this object, they must give it up. They recall the words of Saint Therese, to whom a great lady said, as she was on the point of entering her order, "Permit me, Mother, to send for a Bible to which I am greatly attached."

"Ah, you are attached to something! In that case, do not enter our order!"

Every person whatever is forbidden to shut herself up, to have a place of her own, a chamber. They live with their cells open. When they meet, one says, "Blessed and adored be the most Holy Sacrament of the altar!" The other responds, "Forever." The same ceremony when one taps at the other's door. Hardly has she touched the door when a soft voice on the other side is heard to say hastily, "Forever!" Like all practices, this becomes mechanical by force of habit; and one sometimes says forever before the other has had time to say the rather long sentence, "Praised and adored be the most Holy Sacrament of the altar."

Among the Visitandines the one who enters says, "Ave Maria," and the one whose cell is entered says, "Gratia plena." It is their way of saying "good day," which is, in fact, "full of grace. "

At each hour of the day three supplementary strokes sound from the church bell of the convent. At this signal prioress, vocal mothers, professed nuns, lay-sisters, novices, postulants, interrupt what they are saying, what they are doing, or what they are thinking, and all say in unison if it is five o'clock, for instance, "At five o'clock and at all hours praised and adored be the most Holy Sacrament of the altar!" If it is eight o'clock, "At eight o'clock and at all hours!" and so on, according to the hour.

This custom, the object of which is to break the thread of thought and to lead it back constantly to God, exists in many communities; the formula alone varies. Thus at the Infant Jesus they say, "At this hour and at every hour may the love of Jesus kindle my heart!" The Bernardines-Benedictines of Martin Verga, cloistered fifty years ago at Petit-Picpus, chant the offices to a solemn psalmody, a pure Gregorian chant, and always with full voice during the whole course of the office. Everywhere in the missal where an asterisk occurs they pause, and say in a low voice, "Jesus-Marie-Joseph." For the office of the dead they adopt a tone so low that the voices of women can hardly descend to such a depth. The effect produced is striking and tragic.

The nuns of the Petit-Picpus had made a vault under their grand altar for the burial of their community. The government, as they say, does not permit this vault to receive coffins so they leave the convent when they die. This is an affliction to them, and causes them consternation as an infraction of the rules.

They had obtained a mediocre consolation at best, permission to be interred at a special hour and in a special corner in the ancient Vaugirard cemetery, which was made of land that had formerly belonged to their community.

On Fridays the nuns hear High Mass, vespers, and all the offices, as on Sunday. They scrupulously observe in addition all the little festivals unknown to people of the world, of which the Church of France was so prodigal in the olden days, and of which it is still prodigal in Spain and Italy. Their stations in the chapel are interminable. As for the number and duration of their prayers we can convey no better idea of them than by quoting the ingenuous remark of one of them, "The prayers of the postulants are frightful, the prayers of the novices are still worse, and the prayers of the professed nuns are still worse."

Once a week the chapter assembles: the prioress presides; the vocal mothers assist. Each sister kneels in turn on the stones, and confesses aloud, in the presence of all, the faults and sins she has committed during the week. The vocal mothers consult after each confession and inflict the penance aloud.

Besides this confession in a loud tone, for which all faults in the least serious are reserved, they have for their venial offenses what they call the *coulpe*. To make one's coulpe means to prostrate one's self flat on one's face during the office in front of the prioress until the latter, who is never called anything but Our Mother, notifies the culprit by a slight tap of her foot against the wood of her stall that she can rise. The coulpe, or *peccavi*, is made for a very small matter—a broken glass, a torn veil, an involuntary delay of a few seconds at an office, a false note in church, etc.; this suffices, and the coulpe is made. The coulpe is entirely spontaneous; it is the culpable person herself (the word is etymologically in its place here) who judges herself and inflicts it on herself. On festival days and Sundays four mother presenters intone the offices before a large reading desk with four places. One day one of the mother presenters intoned a psalm beginning with *Ecce*, and instead of Ecce she uttered aloud the three notes do si sol; for this piece of absent-mindedness she underwent a coulpe, which lasted during the whole service: what rendered the fault enormous was the fact that the chapter had laughed.

When a nun is summoned to the parlor, even were it the prioress herself, she drops her veil, as will be remembered, so that only her mouth is visible.

The prioress alone can hold communication with strangers. The others can see only their immediate family, and that very rarely. If, by chance, an outsider presents herself to see a nun, or one whom she has known and loved in the outer world, a regular series of negotiations is required. If it is a woman, the authorization may sometimes be granted; the nun comes, and they talk to her through the shutters, which are opened only for a mother or sister. It is unnecessary to say that permission is always refused to men.

Such is the rule of Saint-Benoit, aggravated by Martin Verga.

These nuns are not gay, rosy, and fresh, as the daughters of other orders often are. They are pale and grave. Between 1825 and 1830 three of them went mad.

CHAPTER III—AUSTERITIES

One is a postulant for two years at least, often for four; a novice for four. It is rare that the definitive vows can be pronounced earlier than the age of twenty-three or twenty-four years. The Bernardines-Benedictines of Martin Verga do not admit widows to their order.

In their cells, they deliver themselves up to many unknown macerations, of which they must never speak.

On the day when a novice makes her profession, she is dressed in her handsomest attire, she is crowned with white roses, her hair is brushed until it shines, and curled. Then she prostrates herself; a great black veil is thrown over her, and the office for the dead is sung. Then the nuns separate into two files; one file passes close to her, saying in plaintive accents, "Our sister is dead"; and the other file responds in a voice of ecstasy, "Our sister is alive in Jesus Christ!"

At the epoch when this story takes place, a boarding school was attached to the convent—a boarding school for young girls of noble and mostly wealthy families, among whom could be remarked Mademoiselle de Saint-Aulaire and de Belissen, and an English girl bearing the illustrious Catholic name of Talbot. These young girls, reared by these nuns between four walls, grew up with a horror of the world and of the age. One of them said to us one day, "The sight of the street pavement made me shudder from head to foot." They were dressed in blue, with a white cap and a Holy Spirit of silver gilt or of copper on their breast. On certain grand festival days, particularly Saint Martha's day, they were permitted, as a high favor and a supreme happiness, to dress themselves as nuns and to carry out the offices and practice of Saint-Benoit for a whole day. In the early days the nuns were in the habit of lending them their black garments. This seemed profane, and the prioress forbade it. Only the novices were permitted to lend. It is remarkable that these performances, tolerated and encouraged, no doubt, in the convent out of a secret spirit of proselytism and in order to give these children a foretaste of the holy habit, were a genuine happiness and a real recreation for the scholars. They simply amused themselves with it. It was new; it gave them a change. Candid reasons of childhood that do not, however, succeed in making us worldlings comprehend the felicity of holding a holy water sprinkler in one's hand and standing for hours together singing hard enough for four in front of a reading desk.

The pupils conformed, with the exception of the austerities, to all the practices of the convent. There was a certain young woman who entered the world, and who after many years of married life had not succeeded in breaking herself of the habit of saying in great haste whenever anyone knocked at her door, "forever!" Like the nuns, the pupils saw their relatives only in the parlor. Their very mothers did not obtain permission to embrace them. The following illustrates to what a degree severity on that point was carried. One day a young girl received a visit from her mother, who was accompanied by a little sister three years of age. The young girl wept, for she wished greatly to embrace her sister. Impossible. She begged that, at least, the child might be permitted to pass her little hand through the bars so that she could kiss it. This was almost indignantly refused.

CHAPTER IV—GAYETIES

Nonetheless, these young girls filled this grave house with charming souvenirs.

At certain hours, childhood sparkled in that cloister. The recreation hour struck. A door swung on its hinges. The birds said, "Good; here come the children!" An irruption of youth inundated that garden intersected with a cross like a shroud. Radiant faces, white foreheads, innocent eyes, full of merry light, all sorts of auroras, were scattered about amid these shadows. After the psalmodies, the bells, the peals, and knells and offices, the sound of these little girls burst forth on a sudden more sweetly than the noise of bees. The hive of joy was opened, and each one brought her honey. They played, they called to each other, they formed into groups, they ran about; pretty little white teeth chattered in the corners; the veils superintended the laughs from a distance, shades kept watch of the sunbeams, but what mattered it? Still they beamed and laughed. Those four lugubrious walls had their moment of dazzling brilliancy. They looked on, vaguely blanched with the reflection of so much joy at this sweet swarming of the hives. It was like a shower of roses falling athwart this house of mourning. The young girls frolicked beneath the eyes of the nuns; the gaze of impeccability does not embarrass innocence. Thanks to these children, there was, among so many austere hours, one hour of ingenuousness. The little ones skipped about; the elder ones danced. In this cloister play was mingled with heaven. Nothing is so delightful and so august as all these fresh, expanding young souls. Homer would have come there to laugh with Perrault; and there was in that black garden, youth, health, noise, cries, giddiness, pleasure, happiness enough to smooth out the wrinkles of all their ancestries, those of the epic as well as those of the fairy tale, those of the throne as well as those of the thatched cottage from Hecuba to la Mère-Grand.

In that house more than anywhere else, perhaps, arise those children's sayings that are so graceful, and which evoke a smile that is full of thoughtfulness. It was between those four gloomy walls that a child of five years exclaimed one day, "Mother! One of the big girls has just told me that I have only nine years and ten months longer to remain here. What happiness!"

It was here, too, that this memorable dialogue took place:

A vocal mother. "Why are you weeping, my child?"

The child (aged six). "I told Alix that I knew my French history. She says that I do not know it, but I do."

Alix, the big girl (aged nine). "No; she does not know it. "

The Mother. "How is that, my child?"

Alix. "She told me to open the book at random and to ask her any question in the book, and she would answer it."

"Well?"

"She did not answer it."

"Let us see about it. What did you ask her?"

"I opened the book at random, as she proposed, and I put the first question that I came across."

"And what was the question?"

"It was, 'What happened after that?'"

It was there that that profound remark was made anent a rather greedy parrot that belonged to a lady boarder, "How well bred! It eats the top of the slice of bread and butter just like a person!"

It was on one of the flagstones of this cloister that there was once picked up a confession that had been written out in advance, in order that she might not forget it, by a sinner of seven years, "Father, I accuse myself of having been avaricious.

"Father, I accuse myself of having been an adulteress.

"Father, I accuse myself of having raised my eyes to the gentlemen."

It was on one of the turf benches of this garden that a rosy mouth six years of age improvised the following tale, which was listened to by blue eyes aged four and five years, "There were three little cocks who owned a country where there were a great many flowers. They plucked the flowers and put them in their pockets. After that they pluckd'aued the leaves and put them in their playthings. There was a wolf in that country; there was a great deal of forest; and the wolf was in the forest; and he ate the little cocks."

And this other poem,

> "There came a blow with a stick.
> It was Punchinello who bestowed it on the cat.
> It was not good for her; it hurt her.
> Then a lady put Punchinello in prison."

It was there that a little abandoned child, a foundling whom the convent was bringing up out of charity, uttered this sweet and heart-breaking saying.

She heard the others talking of their mothers, and she murmured in her corner, "As for me, my mother was not there when I was born!"

There was a stout portress who could always be seen hurrying through the corridors with her bunch of keys, and whose name was Sister Agatha. The big big girls—those over ten years of age—called her Agathocles.

The refectory, a large apartment of an oblong square form, which received no light except through a vaulted cloister on a level with the garden, was dark and damp, and, as the children say, full of beasts. All the places roundabout furnished their contingent of insects.

Each of its four corners had received, in the language of the pupils, a special and expressive name. There was Spider Corner, Caterpillar Corner, Wood louse Corner, and Cricket Corner.

Cricket corner was near the kitchen and was highly esteemed. It was not so cold there as elsewhere. From the refectory the names had passed to the boarding school, and there served as in the old College Mazarin to distinguish four nations. Every pupil belonged to one of these four nations according to the corner of the refectory in which she sat at meals. One day Monseigneur the Archbishop while making his pastoral visit saw a pretty little rosy girl with beautiful golden hair enter the classroom through which he was passing.

He inquired of another pupil, a charming brunette with rosy cheeks, who stood near him, "Who is that?"

"She is a spider, Monseigneur."

"Bah! And that one yonder?"

"She is a cricket."

"And that one?"

"She is a caterpillar."

"Really! And yourself?"

"I am a wood louse, Monseigneur."

Every house of this sort has its own peculiarities. At the beginning of this century Ecouen was one of those strict and graceful places where young girls pass their childhood in a shadow that is almost august. At Ecouen, in order to take rank in the procession of the Holy Sacrament, a distinction was made between virgins and florists. There were also the "dais" and the "censors"—the first who held the cords of the dais, and the others who carried incense before the Holy Sacrament. The flowers belonged by right to the florists. Four "virgins" walked in advance. On the morning of that great day it was no rare thing to hear the question put in the dormitory, "Who is a virgin?"

Madame Campan used to quote this saying of a "little one" of seven years

> a "big girl" of sixteen, who took the head of the procession, while she, the
ttle one, remained at the rear, "You are a virgin, but I am not."

CHAPTER V—DISTRACTIONS

Above the door of the refectory this prayer, which was called the white
Paternoster, and that possessed the property of bearing people straight
> paradise, was inscribed in large black letters,

> "Little white Paternoster, which God made, which God said,
> which God placed in paradise. In the evening, when I went to
> bed, I found three angels sitting on my bed, one at the foot,
> two at the head, the good Virgin Mary in the middle, who
> told me to lie down without hesitation. The good God is my
> father, the good Virgin is my mother, the three apostles are my
> brothers, the three virgins are my sisters. The shirt in which
> God was born envelopes my body; Saint Margaret's cross is
> written on my breast. Madame the Virgin was walking through
> the meadows, weeping for God, when she met M. Saint John.
> 'Monsieur Saint John, whence come you?' 'I come from Ave
> Salus.' 'You have not seen the good God; where is he?' 'He is
> on the tree of the Cross, his feet hanging, his hands nailed, a
> little cap of white thorns on his head.' Whoever shall say this
> thrice at eventide, thrice in the morning, shall win paradise at
> the last."

In 1827 this characteristic orison had disappeared from the wall under a
riple coating of daubing paint. At the present time it is finally disappearing
:om the memories of several who were young girls then, and who are old
vomen now.

A large crucifix fastened to the wall completed the decoration of this
efectory, whose only door, as we think we have mentioned, opened on the
arden. Two narrow tables, each flanked by two wooden benches, formed
wo long parallel lines from one end to the other of the refectory. The walls
vere white, the tables were black; these two mourning colors constitute the
nly variety in convents. The meals were plain, and the food of the children
hemselves severe. A single dish of meat and vegetables combined, or salt
sh—such was their luxury. This meager fare, which was reserved for the

pupils alone, was, nevertheless, an exception. The children ate in silence, unde
the eye of the mother whose turn it was, who, if a fly took a notion to fly or t
hum against the rule, opened and shut a wooden book from time to time. Th
silence was seasoned with the lives of the saints, read aloud from a little pulp
with a desk that was situated at the foot of the crucifix. The reader was one o
the big girls, in weekly turn. At regular distances, on the bare tables, there wer
large, varnished bowls in which the pupils washed their own silver cups an
knives and forks, and into which they sometimes threw some scrap of toug
meat or spoiled fish; this was punished. These bowls were called *ronds d'eau*
The child who broke the silence "made a cross with her tongue." Where
On the ground. She licked the pavement. The dust, that end of all joys, wa
charged with the chastisement of those poor little rose leaves that had bee
guilty of chirping.

There was in the convent a book which has never been printed except as
unique copy, and which it is forbidden to read. It is the rule of Saint-Benoit. A
arcanum which no profane eye must penetrate. *Nemo regulas, seu constitutione
nostras, externis communicabit.*

The pupils one day succeeded in getting possession of this book, and set t
reading it with avidity, a reading that was often interrupted by the fear of bein
caught, which caused them to close the volume precipitately.

From the great danger thus incurred they derived but a very moderat
amount of pleasure. The most "interesting thing" they found were som
unintelligible pages about the sins of young boys.

They played in an alley of the garden bordered with a few shabby fru
trees. In spite of the extreme surveillance and the severity of the punishment
administered, when the wind had shaken the trees, they sometimes succeede
in picking up a green apple or a spoiled apricot or an inhabited pear on the sl
I will now cede the privilege of speech to a letter that lies before me, a lette
written five and twenty years ago by an old pupil, now Madame la Duchess
de——one of the most elegant women in Paris. I quote literally, "One hide
one's pear or one's apple as best one may. When one goes upstairs to put th
veil on the bed before supper, one stuffs them under one's pillow and at nigh
one eats them in bed, and when one cannot do that, one eats them in the closet.
That was one of their greatest luxuries.

Once—it was at the epoch of the visit from the archbishop to the convent—
one of the young girls, Mademoiselle Bouchard, who was connected with th
Montmorency family, laid a wager that she would ask for a day's leave o
absence—an enormity in so austere a community. The wager was accepted

but not one of those who bet believed that she would do it. When the moment came, as the archbishop was passing in front of the pupils, Mademoiselle Bouchard, to the indescribable terror of her companions, stepped out of the ranks, and said, "Monseigneur, a day's leave of absence." Mademoiselle Bouchard was tall, blooming, with the prettiest little rosy face in the world. M. de Quelen smiled and said, "What, my dear child, a day's leave of absence! Three days if you like. I grant you three days." The prioress could do nothing; the archbishop had spoken. Horror of the convent, but joy of the pupil. The effect may be imagined.

This stern cloister was not so well walled off, however, but that the life of the passions of the outside world, drama, and even romance, did not make their way in. To prove this, we will confine ourselves to recording here and to briefly mentioning a real and incontestable fact, which, however, bears no reference in itself to, and is not connected by any thread whatever with the story which we are relating. We mention the fact for the sake of completing the physiognomy of the convent in the reader's mind.

About this time there was in the convent a mysterious person who was not a nun, who was treated with great respect, and who was addressed as Madame Albertine. Nothing was known about her, save that she was mad, and that in the world she passed for dead. Beneath this history it was said there lay the arrangements of fortune necessary for a great marriage.

This woman, hardly thirty years of age, of dark complexion and tolerably pretty, had a vague look in her large black eyes. Could she see? There was some doubt about this. She glided rather than walked, she never spoke; it was not quite known whether she breathed. Her nostrils were livid and pinched as after yielding up their last sigh. To touch her hand was like touching snow. She possessed a strange spectral grace. Wherever she entered, people felt cold. One day a sister, on seeing her pass, said to another sister, "She passes for a dead woman."

"Perhaps she is one," replied the other.

A hundred tales were told of Madame Albertine. This arose from the eternal curiosity of the pupils. In the chapel there was a gallery called L'Oeil de Boeuf. It was in this gallery that had only a circular bay, an *oeil de boeuf*, that Madame Albertine listened to the offices. She always occupied it alone because this gallery, being on the level of the first story, the preacher or the officiating priest could be seen, which was interdicted to the nuns. One day the pulpit was occupied by a young priest of high rank, M. Le Duc de Rohan, peer of France, officer of the Red Musketeers in 1815 when he was Prince de Leon, and who died afterward, in 1830, as cardinal and Archbishop of Besancon. It was the first time that M. de Rohan had preached at the Petit-Picpus convent. Madame Albertine usually preserved perfect calmness and complete immobility during the sermons and services. That day, as soon as she caught sight of M. de Rohan, she half rose, and said, in a loud voice, amid the silence of the chapel, "Ah! Auguste!" The whole community turned their heads in amazement, the preacher raised his eyes, but Madame Albertine had relapsed into her immobility. A breath from the outer world, a flash of life, had passed for an instant across that cold and lifeless face and had then vanished and the mad woman had become a corpse again.

Those two words, however, had set everyone in the convent who had the privilege of speech to chattering. How many things were contained in that "Ah! Auguste!" what revelations! M. de Rohan's name really was Auguste. It was evident that Madame Albertine belonged to the very highest society, since she knew M. de Rohan, and that her own rank there was of the highest, since she spoke thus familiarly of so great a lord, and that there existed between them some connection, of relationship, perhaps, but a very close one in any case, since she knew his "pet name."

Two very severe duchesses, Mesdames de Choiseul and de Serent, often visited the community, where they penetrated, no doubt, in virtue of the privileged oil magnets, and caused great consternation in the boarding school. When these two old ladies passed by, all the poor young girls trembled and dropped their eyes.

Moreover, M. de Rohan, quite unknown to himself, was an object of attention to the schoolgirls. At that epoch he had just been made, while waiting for the episcopate, vicar-general of the Archbishop of Paris. It was one of his habits to come tolerably often to celebrate the offices in the chapel of the nuns of the Petit-Picpus. Not one of the young recluses could see him, because of the serge curtain, but he had a sweet and rather shrill voice that they had come to know and to distinguish. He had been a musketeer, and then, he was said to be very coquettish, that his handsome brown hair was very well dressed in a roll around his head, and that he had a broad girdle of magnificent moire, and that his black cassock was of the most elegant cut in the world. He held a great place in all these imaginations of sixteen years.

Not a sound from without made its way into the convent. But there was one year when the sound of a flute penetrated there. This was an event, and the girls who were at school there at the time still recall it.

It was a flute that was played in the neighborhood. This flute always played he same air, an air that is very far away nowadays, "My Zetulbe, come reign ɔ'er my soul"——and it was heard two or three times a day. The young girls ɔassed hours in listening to it, the vocal mothers were upset by it, brains were ɔusy, punishments descended in showers. This lasted for several months. The girls were all more or less in love with the unknown musician. Each one dreamed hat she was Zetulbe. The sound of the flute proceeded from the direction ɔf the Rue Droit-Mur; and they would have given anything, compromised everything, attempted anything for the sake of seeing, of catching a glance, f only for a second, of the "young man" who played that flute so deliciously, and who, no doubt, played on all these souls at the same time. There were some who made their escape by a back door, and ascended to the third story on the Rue Droit-Mur side, in order to attempt to catch a glimpse through the gaps. mpossible! One even went so far as to thrust her arm through the grating, and :o wave her white handkerchief. Two were still bolder. They found means to :limb on a roof, and risked their lives there, and succeeded at last in seeing "the young man." He was an old exiled gentleman, blind and penniless, who was ɔlaying his flute in his attic, in order to pass the time.

CHAPTER VI—THE LITTLE CONVENT

In this enclosure of the Petit-Picpus there were three perfectly distinct buildings: the Great Convent, inhabited by the nuns, the boarding school, where the scholars were lodged; and lastly, what was called the Little Convent. It was a ɔuilding with a garden, in which lived all sorts of aged nuns of various orders, the relics of cloisters destroyed in the Revolution; a reunion of all the black, gray, and white medleys of all communities and all possible varieties; what might be called, if such a coupling of words is permissible, a sort of harlequin convent.

When the Empire was established, all these poor old dispersed and exiled women had been accorded permission to come and take shelter under the wings of the Bernardines-Benedictines. The government paid them a small ɔension, the ladies of the Petit-Picpus received them cordially. It was a singular ɔell-mell. Each followed her own rule, Sometimes the pupils of the boarding school were allowed, as a great recreation, to pay them a visit; the result is, that all those young memories have retained among other souvenirs that of Mother Sainte-Bazile, Mother Sainte-Scolastique, and Mother Jacob.

One of these refugees found herself almost at home. She was a nun of Sainte-Aure, the only one of her order who had survived. The ancient :onvent of the ladies of Sainte-Aure occupied, at the beginning of the eighteenth century, this very house of the Petit-Picpus, which belonged later to the Benedictines of Martin Verga. This holy woman, too poor to wear the magnificent habit of her order, which was a white robe with a scarlet scapulary, had piously put it on a little manikin, which she exhibited with complacency and which she bequeathed to the house at her death. In 1824, only one nun of this order remained; today, there remains only a doll.

In addition to these worthy mothers, some old society women had obtained permission of the prioress, like Madame Albertine, to retire into the Little Convent. Among the number were Madame Beaufort d'Hautpoul and Marquise Dufresne. Another was never known in the convent except by the formidable noise she made when she blew her nose. The pupils called her Madame Vacarmini.

About 1820 or 1821, Madame de Genlis, who was at that time editing a little periodical publication called *l'Intrepide*, asked to be allowed to enter the convent of the Petit-Picpus as lady resident. The Duc d'Orleans recommended her. Uproar in the hive; the vocal mothers were all in a flutter; Madame de Genlis had made romances. But she declared that she was the first to detest them, and then, she had reached her fierce stage of devotion. With the aid of God, and of the Prince, she entered. She departed at the end of six or eight months, alleging as a reason, that there was no shade in the garden. The nuns were delighted. Although very old, she still played the harp, and did it very well.

When she went away she left her mark in her cell. Madame de Genlis was superstitious and a Latinist. These two words furnish a tolerably good profile of her. A few years ago, there were still to be seen, pasted in the inside of a little cupboard in her cell in which she locked up her silverware and her jewels, these five lines in Latin, written with her own hand in red ink on yellow paper, and which, in her opinion, possessed the property of frightening away robbers:

> *"Imparibus meritis pendent tria corpora ramis:*
> *Dismas et Gesmas, media est divina potestas;*
> *Alta petit Dismas, infelix, infima, Gesmas;*
> *Nos et res nostras conservet summa potestas.*
> *Hos versus dicas, ne tu furto tua perdas."**

These verses in sixth-century Latin raise the question whether the two

---

* On the bough hang three bodies of unequal merits:/Dismas and Gesmas, between is the divine power;/Dismas seeks the heights, Gesmas, unhappy man,/the lowest regions;/the highest power will preserve us and our effects./If you repeat this verse, you will not lose your things by theft.

hieves of Calvary were named, as is commonly believed, Dismas and Gestas, or Dismas and Gesmas. This orthography might have confounded the pretensions put forward in the last century by the Vicomte de Gestas, of a descent from the wicked thief. However, the useful virtue attached to these verses forms an article of faith in the order of the Hospitallers.

The church of the house, constructed in such a manner as to separate the Great Convent from the Boarding School like a veritable entrenchment, was, of course, common to the Boarding School, the Great Convent, and the Little Convent. The public was even admitted by a sort of lazaretto entrance on the street. But all was so arranged, that none of the inhabitants of the cloister could see a face from the outside world. Suppose a church whose choir is grasped in a gigantic hand, and folded in such a manner as to form, not, as in ordinary churches, a prolongation behind the altar, but a sort of hall, or obscure cellar, to the right of the officiating priest; suppose this hall to be shut off by a curtain seven feet in height, of which we have already spoken; in the shadow of that curtain, pile up on wooden stalls the nuns in the choir on the left, the schoolgirls on the right, the lay sisters and the novices at the bottom, and you will have some idea of the nuns of the Petit-Picpus assisting at divine service. That cavern, which was called the choir, communicated with the cloister by a lobby. The church was lighted from the garden. When the nuns were present at services where their rule enjoined silence, the public was warned of their presence only by the folding seats of the stalls noisily rising and falling.

CHAPTER VII—SOME SILHOUETTES OF THIS DARKNESS

During the six years that separate 1819 from 1825, the prioress of the Petit-Picpus was Mademoiselle de Blemeur, whose name, in religion, was Mother Innocente. She came of the family of Marguerite de Blemeur, author of Lives of the Saints of the Order of Saint-Benoit. She had been reelected. She was a woman about sixty years of age, short, thick, "singing like a cracked pot," says the letter, which we have already quoted; an excellent woman, moreover, and the only merry one in the whole convent, and for that reason adored. She was learned, erudite, wise, competent, curiously proficient in history, crammed with Latin, stuffed with Greek, full of Hebrew, and more of a Benedictine monk than a Benedictine nun.

The subprioress was an old Spanish nun, Mother Cineres, who was almost blind.

The most esteemed among the vocal mothers were Mother Sainte-Honorine the treasurer, Mother Sainte-Gertrude, the chief mistress of the novices; Mother Saint-Ange, the assistant mistress; Mother Annonciation, the sacristan; Mothe Saint-Augustin, the nurse, the only one in the convent who was malicious then Mother Sainte-Mechtilde (Mademoiselle Gauvain), very young and witl a beautiful voice; Mother des Anges (Mademoiselle Drouet), who had been i the convent of the Filles-Dieu, and in the convent du Tresor, between Gisor and Magny; Mother Saint-Joseph (Mademoiselle de Cogolludo), Mother Sainte Adelaide (Mademoiselle d'Auverney), Mother Misericorde (Mademoiselle d Cifuentes, who could not resist austerities), Mother Compassion (Mademoisell de la Miltière, received at the age of sixty in defiance of the rule, and ver wealthy); Mother Providence (Mademoiselle de Laudiniere), Mothe Presentation (Mademoiselle de Siguenza), who was prioress in 1847; and finally Mother Sainte-Celigne (sister of the sculptor Ceracchi), who went mad; Mothe Sainte-Chantal (Mademoiselle de Suzon), who went mad.

There was also, among the prettiest of them, a charming girl of three an twenty, who was from the Isle de Bourbon, a descendant of the Chevalie Roze, whose name had been Mademoiselle Roze, and who was called Mothe Assumption.

Mother Sainte-Mechtilde, entrusted with the singing and the choir, wa fond of making use of the pupils in this quarter. She usually took a complet scale of them, that is to say, seven, from ten to sixteen years of age, inclusive of assorted voices and sizes, whom she made sing standing, drawn up in a line side by side, according to age, from the smallest to the largest. This presente to the eye, something in the nature of a reed pipe of young girls, a sort o living panpipe made of angels.

Those of the laysisters whom the scholars loved most were Sister Euphrasie Sister Sainte-Marguerite, Sister Sainte-Marthe, who was in her dotage, an Sister Sainte-Michel, whose long nose made them laugh.

All these women were gentle with the children. The nuns were severe only toward themselves. No fire was lighted except in the school, and the food wa choice compared to that in the convent. Moreover, they lavished a thousan cares on their scholars. Only, when a child passed near a nun and addresse her, the nun never replied.

This rule of silence had had this effect, that throughout the whole convent speech had been withdrawn from human creatures, and bestowed on inanimat objects. Now it was the church bell that spoke, now it was the gardener' bell. A very sonorous bell, placed beside the portress, and that was audibl hroughout the house, indicated by its varied peals, which formed a sort of coustic telegraph, all the actions of material life which were to be performed, nd summoned to the parlor, in case of need, such or such an inhabitant of the ouse. Each person and each thing had its own peal. The prioress had one and ne, the subprioress one and two. Six-five announced lessons, so that the pupils ever said "to go to lessons," but "to go to six-five." Four-four was Madame le Genlis's signal. It was very often heard. "*C'est le diable a quatre*"—it's the ery deuce—said the uncharitable. Ten-nine strokes announced a great event. t was the opening of the door of seclusion, a frightful sheet of iron bristling vith bolts that only turned on its hinges in the presence of the archbishop.

With the exception of the archbishop and the gardener, no man entered he convent, as we have already said. The schoolgirls saw two others: one, he chaplain, the Abbé Banes, old and ugly, whom they were permitted to ontemplate in the choir, through a grating; the other the drawing master, M. Ansiaux, whom the letter, of which we have perused a few lines, calls M. Anciot, and describes as a frightful old hunchback.

It will be seen that all these men were carefully chosen.

Such was this curious house.

CHAPTER VIII—POST CORDA LAPIDES

After having sketched its moral face, it will not prove unprofitable to point out, in a few words, its material configuration. The reader already has some idea of it.

The convent of the Petit-Picpus-Sainte-Antoine filled almost the whole of he vast trapezium, which resulted from the intersection of the Rue Polonceau, he Rue Droit-Mur, the Rue Petit-Picpus, and the unused lane, called Rue Aumarais on old plans. These four streets surrounded this trapezium like a moat. The convent was composed of several buildings and a garden. The principal building, taken in its entirety, was a juxtaposition of hybrid constructions which, viewed from a bird's-eye view, outlined, with considerable exactness, a gibbet laid flat on the ground. The main arm of the gibbet occupied the whole of the fragment of the Rue Droit-Mur comprised between the Rue Petit-Picpus and the Rue Polonceau; the lesser arm was a lofty, gray, severe grated facade that faced the Rue Petit-Picpus; the carriage entrance No. 62 marked its extremity. Toward the center of this facade was a low, arched door, whitened with dust and ashes, where the spiders wove their webs, and which was open only for an hour or two on Sundays, and on rare occasions, when the coffin of a nun left the convent. This was the public entrance of the church. The elbow of the gibbet was a square hall, which was used as the servants' hall, and which the nuns called the buttery. In the main arm were the cells of the mothers, the sisters, and the novices. In the lesser arm lay the kitchens, the refectory, backed up by the cloisters and the church. Between the door No. 62 and the corner of the closed lane Aumarais, was the school that was not visible from without. The remainder of the trapezium formed the garden that was much lower than the level of the Rue Polonceau, which caused the walls to be very much higher on the inside than on the outside. The garden, which was slightly arched, had in its center, on the summit of a hillock, a fine pointed and conical fir tree from which ran, as from the peaked boss of a shield, four grand alleys, and, ranged by twos in between the branchings of these, eight small ones, so that if the enclosure had been circular, the geometrical plan of the alleys would have resembled a cross superposed on a wheel. As the alleys all ended in the very irregular walls of the garden, they were of unequal length. They were bordered with currant bushes. At the bottom, an alley of tall poplars ran from the ruins of the old convent, which was at the angle of the Rue Droit-Mur to the house of the Little Convent, which was at the angle of the Aumarais lane. In front of the Little Convent was what was called the Little Garden. To this whole, let the reader add a courtyard, all sorts of varied angles formed by the interior buildings, prison walls, the long black line of roofs, which bordered the other side of the Rue Polonceau for its sole perspective and neighborhood, and he will be able to form for himself a complete image of what the house of the Bernardines of the Petit-Picpus was forty years ago. This holy house had been built on the precise site of a famous tennis ground of the fourteenth to the sixteenth century, which was called the "tennis-ground of the eleven thousand devils."

All these streets, moreover, were more ancient than Paris. These names, Droit-Mur and Aumarais, are very ancient; the streets that bear them are very much more ancient still. Aumarais Lane was called Maugout Lane; the Rue Droit-Mur was called the Rue des Eglantiers, for God opened flowers before man cut stones.

CHAPTER IX—A CENTURY UNDER A GUIMPE

Since we are engaged in giving details as to what the convent of the Petit-Picpus was in former times, and since we have ventured to open a window on that discreet retreat, the reader will permit us one other little digression, utterly foreign to this book, but characteristic and useful, since it shows that the cloister even has its original figures.

In the Little Convent there was a centenarian who came from the Abbéy of Fontevrault. She had even been in society before the Revolution. She talked a great deal of M. de Miromesnil, Keeper of the Seals under Louis XVI and of a Presidentes Duplat, with whom she had been very intimate. It was her pleasure and her vanity to drag in these names on every pretext. She told wonders of the Abbéy of Fontevrault, that it was like a city, and that there were streets in the monastery.

She talked with a Picard accent that amused the pupils. Every year, she solemnly renewed her vows, and at the moment of taking the oath, she said to the priest, "Monseigneur Saint-Francois gave it to Monseigneur Saint-Julien, Monseigneur Saint-Julien gave it to Monseigneur Saint-Eusebius, Monseigneur Saint-Eusebius gave it to Monseigneur Saint-Procopius, etc., etc.; and thus I give it to you, Father." And the school girls would begin to laugh, not in their sleeves, but under their veils; charming little stifled laughs that made the vocal mothers frown.

On another occasion, the centenarian was telling stories. She said that in her youth the Bernardine monks were every whit as good as the musketeers. It was a century that spoke through her, but it was the eighteenth century. She told about the custom of the four wines that existed before the Revolution in Champagne and Bourgogne. When a great personage, a marshal of France, a prince, a duke, and a peer, traversed a town in Burgundy or Champagne, the city fathers came out to harangue him and presented him with four silver gondolas into which they had poured four different sorts of wine. On the first goblet this inscription could be read, monkey wine; on the second, lion wine; on the third, sheep wine; on the fourth, hog wine. These four legends express the four stages descended by the drunkard; the first, intoxication, which enlivens; the second, that which irritates; the third, that which dulls; and the fourth, that which brutalizes.

In a cupboard, under lock and key, she kept a mysterious object of which she thought a great deal. The rule of Fontevrault did not forbid this. She would not show this object to anyone. She shut herself up, which her rule allowed her to do, and hid herself, every time that she desired to contemplate it. If she heard a footstep in the corridor, she closed the cupboard again as hastily as it was possible with her aged hands. As soon as it was mentioned to her, she became silent, she who was so fond of talking. The most curious were baffled by her silence and the most tenacious by her obstinacy. Thus it furnished a subject of comment for all those who were unoccupied or bored in the convent. What could that treasure of the centenarian be that was so precious and so secret? Some holy book, no doubt? Some unique chaplet? Some authentic relic? They lost themselves in conjectures. When the poor old woman died, they rushed to her cupboard more hastily than was fitting, perhaps, and opened it. They found the object beneath a triple linen cloth, like some consecrated paten. It was a Faenza platter representing little loves flitting away pursued by apothecary lads armed with enormous syringes. The chase abounds in grimaces and in comical postures. One of the charming little loves is already fairly spitted. He is resisting, fluttering his tiny wings, and still making an effort to fly, but the dancer is laughing with a satanic air. Moral: love conquered by the colic. This platter that is very curious, and which had, possibly, the honor of furnishing Moliere with an idea, was still in existence in September, 1845; it was for sale by a bric-a-brac merchant in the Boulevard Beaumarchais.

This good old woman would not receive any visits from outside because, said she, the parlor is too gloomy.

CHAPTER X—ORIGIN OF THE PERPETUAL ADORATION

However, this almost sepulchral parlor, of which we have sought to convey an idea, is a purely local trait that is not reproduced with the same severity in other convents. At the convent of the Rue du Temple, in particular, which belonged, in truth, to another order, the black shutters were replaced by brown curtains, and the parlor itself was a salon with a polished wood floor, whose windows were draped in white muslin curtains and whose walls admitted all sorts of frames, a portrait of a Benedictine nun with unveiled face, painted bouquets, and even the head of a Turk.

It is in that garden of the Temple convent, that stood that famous chestnut tree, which was renowned as the finest and the largest in France, and which bore the reputation among the good people of the eighteenth century of being the father of all the chestnut trees of the realm.

As we have said, this convent of the Temple was occupied by Benedictines of the Perpetual Adoration, Benedictines quite different from those who depended on Citeaux. This order of the Perpetual Adoration is not very ancient and does not go back more than two hundred years. In 1649 the holy sacrament was profaned on two occasions a few days apart, in two churches in Paris, at

Saint-Sulpice and at Saint-Jean en Greve, a rare and frightful sacrilege, which set the whole town in an uproar. M. the Prior and Vicar-General of Saint-Germain des Pres ordered a solemn procession of all his clergy, in which the Pope's Nuncio officiated. But this expiation did not satisfy two sainted women, Madame Courtin, Marquise de Boucs, and the Comtesse de Chateauvieux. This outrage committed on "the most holy sacrament of the altar," though but temporary, would not depart from these holy souls, and it seemed to them that it could only be extenuated by a "Perpetual Adoration" in some female monastery. Both of them—one in 1652, the other in 1653—made donations of notable sums to Mother Catherine de Bar, called of the Holy Sacrament, a Benedictine nun, for the purpose of founding, to this pious end, a monastery of the order of Saint-Benoit; the first permission for this foundation was given to Mother Catherine de Bar by M. de Metz, Abbé of Saint-Germain, "on condition that no woman could be received unless she contributed three hundred livres income, which amounts to six thousand livres, to the principal." After the Abbé of Saint-Germain, the king accorded letters patent; and all the rest, abbatial charter, and royal letters, was confirmed in 1654 by the Chamber of Accounts and the Parliament.

Such is the origin of the legal consecration of the establishment of the Benedictines of the Perpetual Adoration of the Holy Sacrament at Paris. Their first convent was "a new building" in the Rue Cassette, out of the contributions of Mesdames de Boucs and de Chateauvieux.

This order, as it will be seen, was not to be confounded with the Benedictine nuns of Citeaux. It mounted back to the Abbé of Saint-Germain des Pres, in the same manner that the ladies of the Sacred Heart go back to the general of the Jesuits, and the sisters of charity to the general of the Lazarists.

It was also totally different from the Bernardines of the Petit-Picpus, whose interior we have just shown. In 1657 Pope Alexander VII had authorized, by a special brief, the Bernardines of the Rue Petit-Picpus, to practice the Perpetual Adoration like the Benedictine nuns of the Holy Sacrament. But the two orders remained distinct nonetheless.

CHAPTER XI—END OF THE PETIT-PICPUS

At the beginning of the Restoration, the convent of the Petit-Picpus was in its decay; this forms a part of the general death of the order, which, after the eighteenth century, has been disappearing like all the religious orders.

Contemplation is, like prayer, one of humanity's needs; but, like everything the Revolution touched, it will be transformed, and from being hostile to social progress, it will become favorable to it.

The house of the Petit-Picpus was becoming rapidly depopulated. In 1840 the Little Convent had disappeared, the school had disappeared. There were no longer any old women, nor young girls; the first were dead, the latter had taken their departure. *Volaverunt.*

The rule of the Perpetual Adoration is so rigid in its nature that it alarms, vocations recoil before it, the order receives no recruits. In 1845 it still obtained lay sisters here and there. But of professed nuns, none at all. Forty years ago, the nuns numbered nearly a hundred; fifteen years ago there were not more than twenty-eight of them. How many are there today? In 1847 the prioress was young, a sign that the circle of choice was restricted. She was not forty years old. In proportion as the number diminishes, the fatigue increases, the service of each becomes more painful; the moment could then be seen drawing near when there would be but a dozen bent and aching shoulders to bear the heavy rule of Saint-Benoit. The burden is implacable, and remains the same for the few as for the many. It weighs down, it crushes. Thus they die. At the period when the author of this book still lived in Paris, two died. One was twenty-five years old, the other twenty-three. This latter can say, like Julia Alpinula, "*Hic jaceo. Vixi annos viginti et tres.*" It is in consequence of this decay that the convent gave up the education of girls.

We have not felt able to pass before this extraordinary house without entering it, and without introducing the minds that accompany us, and which are listening to our tale, to the profit of some, perchance, of the melancholy history of Jean Valjean. We have penetrated into this community, full of those old practices that seem so novel today. It is the closed garden, *hortus conclusus.* We have spoken of this singular place in detail, but with respect, insofar, at least, as detail and respect are compatible. We do not understand all, but we insult nothing. We are equally far removed from the hosanna of Joseph de Maistre, who wound up by anointing the executioner, and from the sneer of Voltaire, who even goes so far as to ridicule the cross.

An illogical act on Voltaire's part, we may remark, by the way; for Voltaire would have defended Jesus as he defended Calas; and even for those who deny superhuman incarnations, what does the crucifix represent? The assassinated sage.

In this nineteenth century, the religious idea is undergoing a crisis. People are unlearning certain things, and they do well, provided that, while unlearning them they learn this: There is no vacuum in the human heart.

Certain demolitions take place, and it is well that they do, but on condition that they are followed by reconstructions.

In the meantime, let us study things that are no more. It is necessary to know them, if only for the purpose of avoiding them. The counterfeits of the past assume false names, and gladly call themselves the future. This specter, this past, is given to falsifying its own passport. Let us inform ourselves of the trap. Let us be on our guard. The past has a visage, superstition, and a mask, hypocrisy. Let us denounce the visage and let us tear off the mask.

As for convents, they present a complex problem, a question of civilization, which condemns them; a question of liberty, which protects them.

BOOK SEVENTH: PARENTHESIS

CHAPTER I—THE CONVENT AS AN ABSTRACT IDEA

This book is a drama, whose leading personage is the Infinite. Man is the second.

Such being the case, and a convent having happened to be on our road, it has been our duty to enter it. Why? Because the convent, which is common to the Orient as well as to the Occident, to antiquity as well as to modern times, to paganism, to Buddhism, to Mahometanism, as well as to Christianity, is one of the optical apparatuses applied by man to the Infinite.

This is not the place for enlarging disproportionately on certain ideas; nevertheless, while absolutely maintaining our reserves, our restrictions, and even our indignations, we must say that every time we encounter man in the Infinite, either well or ill understood, we feel ourselves overpowered with respect. There is, in the synagogue, in the mosque, in the pagoda, in the wigwam, a hideous side that we execrate, and a sublime side that we adore. What a contemplation for the mind, and what endless food for thought, is the reverberation of God upon the human wall!

CHAPTER II—THE CONVENT AS
AN HISTORICAL FACT

From the point of view of history, of reason, and of truth, monasticism is condemned. Monasteries, when they abound in a nation, are clogs in its circulation, cumbrous establishments, centers of idleness where centers of labor should exist. Monastic communities are to the great social community what the mistletoe is to the oak, what the wart is to the human body. Their prosperity and their fatness mean the impoverishment of the country. The monastic regime, good at the beginning of civilization, useful in the reduction of the brutal by the spiritual, is bad when peoples have reached their manhood. Moreover, when it becomes relaxed, and when it enters into its period of disorder, it becomes bad for the very reasons which rendered it salutary in its period of purity, because it still continues to set the example.

Claustration has had its day. Cloisters, useful in the early education of modern civilization, have embarrassed its growth, and are injurious to its development. So far as institution and formation with relation to man are concerned, monasteries that were good in the tenth century, questionable in the fifteenth, are detestable in the nineteenth. The leprosy of monasticism has gnawed nearly to a skeleton two wonderful nations, Italy and Spain; the one the light, the other the splendor of Europe for centuries; and, at the present day, these two illustrious peoples are but just beginning to convalesce, thanks to the healthy and vigorous hygiene of 1789 alone.

The convent—the ancient female convent in particular, such as it still presents itself on the threshold of this century, in Italy, in Austria, in Spain—is one of the most somber concretions of the Middle Ages. The cloister, that cloister, is the point of intersection of horrors. The Catholic cloister, properly speaking, is wholly filled with the black radiance of death.

The Spanish convent is the most funereal of all. There rise, in obscurity, beneath vaults filled with gloom, beneath domes vague with shadow, massive altars of Babel, as high as cathedrals; there immense white crucifixes hang from chains in the dark; there are extended, all nude on the ebony, great Christs of ivory; more than bleeding, bloody; hideous and magnificent, with their elbows displaying the bones, their kneecaps showing their integuments, their wounds showing their flesh, crowned with silver thorns, nailed with nails of gold, with blood drops of rubies on their brows, and diamond tears in their eyes. The diamonds and rubies seem wet, and make veiled beings in the shadow below weep, their sides bruised with the hair shirt and their iron-tipped scourges, their breasts crushed with wicker hurdles, their knees excoriated with prayer; women who think themselves wives, specters who think themselves seraphim. Do these women think? No. Have they any will? No. Do they love? No. Do they live? No. Their nerves have turned to bone; their bones have turned to stone. Their veil is of woven night. Their breath under their veil resembles the indescribably tragic respiration of death. The abbess, a specter, sanctifies them and terrifies them. The immaculate one is there, and very fierce. Such are the ancient monasteries of Spain. Liars of terrible devotion, caverns of virgins, ferocious places.

Catholic Spain is more Roman than Rome herself. The Spanish convent was, above all others, the Catholic convent. There was a flavor of the Orient about it. The archbishop, the Kislar-Aga of heaven, locked up and kept watch over this seraglio of souls reserved for God. The nun was the odalisque, the priest was the eunuch. The fervent were chosen in dreams and possessed Christ. At night, the beautiful, nude young man descended from the cross and became the ecstasy of the cloistered one. Lofty walls guarded the mystic sultana, who had the crucified for her sultan, from all living distraction. A glance on the outer world was infidelity. The in pace replaced the leather sack. That which was cast into the sea in the East was thrown into the ground in the West. In both quarters, women wrung their hands; the waves for the first, the grave for the last; here the drowned, there the buried. Monstrous parallel.

Today the upholders of the past, unable to deny these things, have adopted the expedient of smiling at them. There has come into fashion a strange and easy manner of suppressing the revelations of history, of invalidating the commentaries of philosophy, of eliding all embarrassing facts and all gloomy questions. A matter for declamations, say the clever. Declamations, repeat the foolish. Jean-Jacques a declaimer; Diderot a declaimer; Voltaire on Calas, Labarre, and Sirven, declaimers. I know not who has recently discovered that Tacitus was a declaimer, that Nero was a victim, and that pity is decidedly due to "that poor Holofernes."

Facts, however, are awkward things to disconcert, and they are obstinate. The author of this book has seen, with his own eyes, eight leagues distant from Brussels, there are relics of the Middle Ages, there which are attainable for everybody, at the Abbéy of Villers, the hole of the oubliettes, in the middle of the field, which was formerly the courtyard of the cloister, and on the banks of the Thil, four stone dungeons, half under ground, half under the water. They were in pace. Each of these dungeons has the remains of an iron door, a vault, and a grated opening, which, on the outside, is two feet above the level of the river, and on the inside, six feet above the level of the ground. Four feet of river flow past along the outside wall. The ground is always soaked. The occupant of the in pace had this wet soil for his bed. In one of these dungeons, there is a fragment of an iron necklet riveted to the wall; in another, there can be seen a square box made of four slabs of granite, too short for a person to lie down in, too low for him to stand upright in. A human being was put inside, with a coverlid of stone on top. This exists. It can be seen. It can be touched. These in pace, these dungeons, these iron hinges, these necklets, that lofty peephole on a level with the river's current, that box of stone closed with a lid of granite like a tomb, with this difference, that the dead man here was a living being, that soil which is but mud, that vault hole, those oozing walls, what declaimers!

CHAPTER III—ON WHAT CONDITIONS ONE CAN RESPECT THE PAST

Monasticism, such as it existed in Spain, and such as it still exists in Thibet, is a sort of phthisis* for civilization. It stops life short. It simply depopulates. Claustration, castration. It has been the scourge of Europe. Add to this the violence so often done to the conscience, the forced vocations, feudalism bolstered up by the cloister, the right of the firstborn pouring the excess of the family into monasticism, the ferocities of which we have just spoken, the in pace, the closed mouths, the walled-up brains, so many unfortunate minds placed in the dungeon of eternal vows, the taking of the habit, the interment of living souls. Add individual tortures to national degradations, and, whoever you may be, you will shudder before the frock and the veil, those two winding sheets of human devising. Nevertheless, at certain points and in certain places, in spite of philosophy, in spite of progress, the spirit of the cloister persists in the midst of the nineteenth century, and a singular ascetic recrudescence is, at this moment, astonishing the civilized world. The obstinacy of antiquated institutions in perpetuating themselves resembles the stubbornness of the rancid perfume, which should claim our hair, the pretensions of the spoiled fish, which should persist in being eaten, the persecution of the child's garment, which should insist on clothing the man, the tenderness of corpses, which should return to embrace the living.

"Ingrates!" says the garment.

---

* a type of disease that causes the sufferer to waste away

"I protected you in inclement weather. Why will you have nothing to do with me?" "I have just come from the deep sea," says the fish.

"I have been a rose," says the perfume.

"I have loved you," says the corpse.

"I have civilized you," says the convent.

To this there is but one reply: "In former days."

To dream of the indefinite prolongation of defunct things, and of the government of men by embalming, to restore dogmas in a bad condition, to re-gild shrines, to patch up cloisters, to rebless reliquaries, to refurnish superstitions, to revictual fanaticisms, to put new handles on holy water brushes and militarism, to reconstitute monasticism and militarism, to believe in the salvation of society by the multiplication of parasites, to force the past on the present, this seems strange. Still, there are theorists who hold such theories. These theorists, who are in other respects people of intelligence, have a very simple process; they apply to the past a glazing, which they call social order, divine right, morality, family, the respect of elders, antique authority, sacred tradition, legitimacy, religion; and they go about shouting, "Look! Take this, honest people." This logic was known to the ancients. The soothsayers practice it. They rubbed a black heifer over with chalk, and said, "She is white, *bos cretatus*."

As for us, we respect the past here and there, and we spare it, above all, provided that it consents to be dead. If it insists on being alive, we attack it, and we try to kill it.

Superstitions, bigotries, affected devotion, prejudices, those forms all forms as they are, are tenacious of life; they have teeth and nails in their smoke, and they must be clasped close, body to body, and war must be made on them, and that without truce; for it is one of the fatalities of humanity to be condemned to eternal combat with phantoms. It is difficult to seize darkness by the throat, and to hurl it to the earth.

A convent in France, in the broad daylight of the nineteenth century, is a college of owls facing the light. A cloister, caught in the very act of asceticism, in the very heart of the city of '89 and of 1830 and of 1848, Rome blossoming out in Paris, is an anachronism. In ordinary times, in order to dissolve an anachronism and to cause it to vanish, one has only to make it spell out the date. But we are not in ordinary times.

Let us fight.

Let us fight, but let us make a distinction. The peculiar property of truth never to commit excesses. What need has it of exaggeration? There is that which it is necessary to destroy, and there is that which it is simply necessary t elucidate and examine. What a force is kindly and serious examination! Let u not apply a flame where only a light is required.

So, given the nineteenth century, we are opposed, as a general propositior and among all peoples, in Asia as well as in Europe, in India as well as i Turkey, to ascetic claustration. Whoever says cloister, says marsh. Thei putrescence is evident, their stagnation is unhealthy, their fermentation infect people with fever, and etiolates them; their multiplication becomes a plague o Egypt. We cannot think without affright of those lands where fakirs, bonze: santons, Greek monks, marabouts, talapoins, and dervishes multiply even lik swarms of vermin.

This said, the religious question remains. This question has certai mysterious, almost formidable sides; may we be permitted to look at it fixedl}

CHAPTER IV—THE CONVENT FROM THE POINT OF VIEW OF PRINCIPLES

Men unite themselves and dwell in communities. By virtue of what righ By virtue of the right of association.

They shut themselves up at home. By virtue of what right? By virtue of th right which every man has to open or shut his door.

They do not come forth. By virtue of what right? By virtue of the right t go and come, which implies the right to remain at home.

There, at home, what do they do?

They speak in low tones; they drop their eyes; they toil. They renounc the world, towns, sensualities, pleasures, vanities, pride, interests. They ai clothed in coarse woolen or coarse linen. Not one of them possesses in h own right anything whatever. On entering there, each one who was ric makes himself poor. What he has, he gives to all. He who was what is calle noble, a gentleman and a lord, is the equal of him who was a peasant. Th cell is identical for all. All undergo the same tonsure, wear the same froc eat the same black bread, sleep on the same straw, die on the same ashes. Th same sack on their backs, the same rope around their loins. If the decisio has been to go barefoot, all go barefoot. There may be a prince among then that prince is the same shadow as the rest. No titles. Even family names hav disappeared. They bear only first names. All are bowed beneath the equalit of baptismal names. They have dissolved the carnal family, and constituted i their community a spiritual family. They have no other relatives than all me

They succor the poor, they care for the sick. They elect those whom they obey. They call each other "my brother."

You stop me and exclaim, "But that is the ideal convent!"

It is sufficient that it may be the possible convent, that I should take notice of it.

Thence it results that, in the preceding book, I have spoken of a convent with respectful accents. The Middle Ages cast aside, Asia cast aside, the historical and political question held in reserve, from the purely philosophical point of view, outside the requirements of militant policy, on condition that the monastery shall be absolutely a voluntary matter and shall contain only consenting parties, I shall always consider a cloistered community with a certain attentive, and, in some respects, a deferential gravity.

Wherever there is a community, there is a commune; where there is a commune, there is right. The monastery is the product of the formula: Equality, Fraternity. Oh! How grand is liberty! And what a splendid transfiguration! Liberty suffices to transform the monastery into a republic.

Let us continue.

But these men, or these women who are behind these four walls. They dress themselves in coarse woolen, they are equals, they call each other brothers, that is well; but they do something else?

Yes.

What?

They gaze on the darkness, they kneel, and they clasp their hands.

What does this signify?

CHAPTER V — PRAYER

They pray.

To whom?

To God.

To pray to God, what is the meaning of these words?

Is there an infinite beyond us? Is that infinite there, inherent, permanent; necessarily substantial, since it is infinite; and because, if it lacked matter it would be bounded; necessarily intelligent, since it is infinite, and because, if it lacked intelligence, it would end there? Does this infinite awaken in us the idea of essence, while we can attribute to ourselves only the idea of existence? In other terms, is it not the absolute, of which we are only the relative?

At the same time that there is an infinite without us, is there not an infinite within us? Are not these two infinities (what an alarming plural!) superposed the one upon the other? Is not this second infinite, so to speak, subjacent to th first? Is it not the latter's mirror, reflection, echo, an abyss that is concentri with another abyss? Is this second infinity intelligent also? Does it think? Doe it love? Does it will? If these two infinities are intelligent, each of them has will principle, and there is an I in the upper infinity as there is an I in the lowe infinity. The I below is the soul; the I on high is God.

To place the infinity here below in contact, by the medium of thought, wit the infinity on high, is called praying.

Let us take nothing from the human mind; to suppress is bad. We mus reform and transform. Certain faculties in man are directed toward th unknown; thought, reverie, prayer. The unknown is an ocean. What i conscience? It is the compass of the unknown. Thought, reverie, praye these are great and mysterious radiations. Let us respect them. Where go thes majestic irradiations of the soul? Into the shadow; that is to say, to the light.

The grandeur of democracy is to disown nothing and to deny nothing o humanity. Close to the right of the man, beside it, at the least, there exists th right of the soul.

To crush fanaticism and to venerate the infinite, such is the law. Let u not confine ourselves to prostrating ourselves before the tree of creation, an to the contemplation of its branches full of stars. We have a duty to labe over the human soul, to defend the mystery against the miracle, to adore th incomprehensible and reject the absurd, to admit, as an inexplicable fact, on what is necessary, to purify belief, to remove superstitions from above religior to clear God of caterpillars.

CHAPTER VI—THE ABSOLUTE
GOODNESS OF PRAYER

With regard to the modes of prayer, all are good, provided that they ar sincere. Turn your book upside down and be in the infinite.

There is, as we know, a philosophy that denies the infinite. There is also philosophy, pathologically classified, which denies the sun; this philosophy called blindness.

To erect a sense that we lack into a source of truth, is a fine blind man self-sufficiency.

The curious thing is the haughty, superior, and compassionate airs, whic this groping philosophy assumes toward the philosophy that beholds Go

One fancies he hears a mole crying, "I pity them with their sun!"

There are, as we know, powerful and illustrious atheists. At bottom, led back to the truth by their very force, they are not absolutely sure that they are atheists; it is with them only a question of definition, and in any case, if they do not believe in God, being great minds, they prove God.

We salute them as philosophers, while inexorably denouncing their philosophy. Let us go on.

The remarkable thing about it is, also, their facility in paying themselves off with words. A metaphysical school of the North, impregnated to some extent with fog, has fancied that it has worked a revolution in human understanding by replacing the word force with the word "will."

To say, "The plant wills," instead of, "The plant grows": this would be fecund in results, indeed, if we were to add, "The universe wills." Why? Because it would come to this: the plant wills, therefore it has an I; the universe wills, therefore it has a God.

As for us, who, however, in contradistinction to this school, reject nothing a priori, a will in the plant, accepted by this school, appears to us more difficult to admit than a will in the universe denied by it.

To deny the will of the infinite, that is to say, God, is impossible on any other conditions than a denial of the infinite. We have demonstrated this.

The negation of the infinite leads straight to nihilism. Everything becomes "a mental conception."

With nihilism, no discussion is possible; for the nihilist logic doubts the existence of its interlocutor, and is not quite sure that it exists itself.

From its point of view, it is possible that it may be for itself, only "a mental conception."

Only, it does not perceive that all which it has denied it admits in the lump, simply by the utterance of the word, mind.

In short, no way is open to the thought by a philosophy that makes all end in the monosyllable, "No. "

To "No" there is only one reply, "Yes."

Nihilism has no point.

There is no such thing as nothingness. Zero does not exist. Everything is something. Nothing is nothing.

Man lives by affirmation even more than by bread.

Even to see and to show does not suffice. Philosophy should be an energy; it should have for effort and effect to ameliorate the condition of man. Socrates should enter into Adam and produce Marcus Aurelius; in other words, the man of wisdom should be made to emerge from the man of felicity. Eden should be changed into a Lyceum. Science should be a cordial. To enjoy, what a sad aim and what a paltry ambition! The brute enjoys. To offer thought to the thirst of men, to give them all as an elixir the notion of God, to make conscience and science fraternize in them, to render them just by this mysterious confrontation: such is the function of real philosophy. Morality is a blossoming out of truths Contemplation leads to action. The absolute should be practicable. It is necessary that the ideal should be breathable, drinkable, and eatable to the human mind It is the ideal that has the right to say, "Take, this!" It is on this condition that it ceases to be a sterile love of science and becomes the one and sovereign mode of human rallying, and that philosophy herself is promoted to religion.

Philosophy should not be a corbel erected on mystery to gaze upon it at its ease, without any other result than that of being convenient to curiosity.

For our part, adjourning the development of our thought to another occasion, we will confine ourselves to saying that we neither understand man as a point of departure nor progress as an end, without those two forces that are their two motors: faith and love.

Progress is the goal, the ideal is the type.

What is this ideal? It is God.

Ideal, absolute, perfection, infinity: identical words.

CHAPTER VII—PRECAUTIONS TO BE OBSERVED IN BLAME

History and philosophy have eternal duties, which are, at the same time simple duties; to combat Caiphas the High-Priest, Draco the Lawgiver Trimalcion the Legislator, Tiberius the Emperor; this is clear, direct, and limpid, and offers no obscurity.

But the right to live apart, even with its inconveniences and its abuses insists on being stated and taken into account. Cenobitism is a human problem

When one speaks of convents, those abodes of error, but of innocence, or aberration but of good will, of ignorance but of devotion, of torture but of martyrdom, it always becomes necessary to say either yes or no.

A convent is a contradiction. Its object, salvation; its means thereto, sacrifice The convent is supreme egoism having for its result supreme abnegation.

To abdicate with the object of reigning seems to be the device of monasticism.

In the cloister, one suffers in order to enjoy. One draws a bill of exchange n death. One discounts in terrestrial gloom celestial light. In the cloister, hell s accepted in advance as a post obit on paradise.

The taking of the veil or the frock is a suicide paid for with eternity.

It does not seem to us, that on such a subject mockery is permissible. All about it is serious, the good as well as the bad.

The just man frowns, but never smiles with a malicious sneer. We understand wrath, but not malice.

CHAPTER VIII—FAITH, LAW

A few words more.

We blame the church when she is saturated with intrigues, we despise the spiritual that is harsh toward the temporal; but we everywhere honor the thoughtful man.

We salute the man who kneels.

A faith; this is a necessity for man. Woe to him who believes nothing.

One is not unoccupied because one is absorbed. There is visible labor and invisible labor.

To contemplate is to labor, to think is to act.

Folded arms toil, clasped hands work. A gaze fixed on heaven is a work.

Thales remained motionless for four years. He founded philosophy.

In our opinion, cenobites are not lazy men, and recluses are not idlers.

To meditate on the Shadow is a serious thing.

Without invalidating anything that we have just said, we believe that a perpetual memory of the tomb is proper for the living. On this point, the priest and the philosopher agree. We must die. The Abbé de la Trappe replies to Horace.

To mingle with one's life a certain presence of the sepulchre, this is the law of the sage; and it is the law of the ascetic. In this respect, the ascetic and the sage converge. There is a material growth; we admit it. There is a moral grandeur; we hold to that. Thoughtless and vivacious spirits say, "What is the good of those motionless figures on the side of mystery? What purpose do they serve? What do they do?"

Alas! In the presence of the darkness that environs us, and which awaits us, in our ignorance of what the immense dispersion will make of us, we reply, There is probably no work more divine than that performed by these souls." And we add, "There is probably no work that is more useful."

There certainly must be some who pray constantly for those who never pray at all.

In our opinion the whole question lies in the amount of thought that is mingled with prayer.

Leibnitz praying is grand, Voltaire adoring is fine. *Deo erexit Voltaire.*

We are for religion as against religions.

We are of the number who believe in the wretchedness of orisons, and the sublimity of prayer.

Moreover, at this minute that we are now traversing, a minute that will not, fortunately, leave its impress on the nineteenth century, at this hour, when so many men have low brows and souls but little elevated, among so many mortals whose morality consists in enjoyment, and who are busied with the brief and misshapen things of matter, whoever exiles himself seems worthy of veneration to us.

The monastery is a renunciation. Sacrifice wrongly directed is still sacrifice. To mistake a grave error for a duty has a grandeur of its own.

Taken by itself, and ideally, and in order to examine the truth on all sides until all aspects have been impartially exhausted, the monastery, the female convent in particular, for in our century it is woman who suffers the most, and in this exile of the cloister there is something of protestation, the female convent has incontestably a certain majesty.

This cloistered existence which is so austere, so depressing, a few of whose features we have just traced, is not life, for it is not liberty; it is not the tomb, for it is not plenitude; it is the strange place from which one beholds, as from the crest of a lofty mountain, on one side the abyss where we are, on the other the abyss where we shall go; it is the narrow and misty frontier separating two worlds, illuminated and obscured by both at the same time, where the ray of life which has become enfeebled is mingled with the vague ray of death; it is the half obscurity of the tomb.

We, who do not believe what these women believe, but who, like them, live by faith, we have never been able to think without a sort of tender and religious terror, without a sort of pity, that is full of envy, of those devoted, trembling and trusting creatures, of these humble and august souls, who dare to dwell on the very brink of the mystery, waiting between the world, which is closed and heaven, which is not yet open, turned toward the light, which one cannot see, possessing the sole happiness of thinking that they know where it is, aspiring toward the gulf, and the unknown, their eyes fixed motionless on the darkness, kneeling, bewildered, stupefied, shuddering, half lifted, at times, by the deep breaths of eternity.

BOOK EIGHTH: CEMETERIES TAKE THAT WHICH IS COMMITTED THEM

CHAPTER I—WHICH TREATS OF THE MANNER OF ENTERING A CONVENT

It was into this house that Jean Valjean had, as Fauchelevent expressed it, "fallen from the sky."

He had scaled the wall of the garden that formed the angle of the Rue Polonceau. That hymn of the angels he had heard in the middle of the night, was the nuns chanting matins; that hall, of which he had caught a glimpse in the gloom, was the chapel. That phantom, which he had seen stretched on the ground, was the sister who was making reparation; that bell, the sound of which had so strangely surprised him, was the gardener's bell attached to the knee of Father Fauchelevent.

Cosette once put to bed, Jean Valjean and Fauchelevent had, as we have already seen, supped on a glass of wine and a bit of cheese before a good, crackling fire; then, the only bed in the hut being occupied by Cosette, each threw himself on a truss of straw.

Before he shut his eyes, Jean Valjean said, "I must remain here henceforth." This remark trotted through Fauchelevent's head all night long.

To tell the truth, neither of them slept.

Jean Valjean, feeling that he was discovered and that Javert was on his scent, understood that he and Cosette were lost if they returned to Paris. Then the new storm that had just burst upon him had stranded him in this cloister. Jean Valjean had, henceforth, but one thought, to remain there. Now, for an unfortunate man in his position, this convent was both the safest and the most dangerous of places; the most dangerous, because, as no men might enter there, if he were discovered, it was a flagrant offense, and Jean Valjean would find but one step intervening between the convent and prison; the safest, because, if he could manage to get himself accepted there and remain there, who would ever seek him in such a place? To dwell in an impossible place was safety.

On his side, Fauchelevent was cudgeling his brains. He began by declaring to himself that he understood nothing of the matter. How had M. Madeleine got here, when the walls were what they were? Cloister walls are not to be stepped over. How did he get there with a child? One cannot scale a perpendicular wall with a child in one's arms. Who was that child? Where did they both come from? Since Fauchelevent had lived in the convent, he had heard nothing of M sur M., and he knew nothing of what had taken place there. Father Madeleine had an air that discouraged questions; and besides, Fauchelevent said to himself, "One does not question a saint." M. Madeleine had preserved all his prestige in Fauchelevent's eyes. Only, from some words that Jean Valjean had let fall, the gardener thought he could draw the inference that M. Madeleine had probably become bankrupt through the hard times, and that he was pursued by his creditors; or that he had compromised himself in some political affair, and was in hiding; which last did not displease Fauchelevent, who, like many of our peasants of the North, had an old fund of Bonapartism about him. While in hiding, M. Madeleine had selected the convent as a refuge, and it was quite simple that he should wish to remain there. But the inexplicable point, to which Fauchelevent returned constantly and over which he wearied his brain was that M. Madeleine should be there, and that he should have that little girl with him. Fauchelevent saw them, touched them, spoke to them, and still did not believe it possible. The incomprehensible had just made its entrance into Fauchelevent's hut. Fauchelevent groped about amid conjectures, and could see nothing clearly but this, "M. Madeleine saved my life." This certainty alone was sufficient and decided his course. He said to himself, "It is my turn now." He added in his conscience, "M. Madeleine did not stop to deliberate when it was a question of thrusting himself under the cart for the purpose of dragging me out." He made up his mind to save M. Madeleine.

Nevertheless, he put many questions to himself and made himself divers replies, "After what he did for me, would I save him if he were a thief? Just the same. If he were an assassin, would I save him? Just the same. Since he is a saint, shall I save him? Just the same."

But what a problem it was to manage to have him remain in the convent Fauchelevent did not recoil in the face of this almost chimerical undertaking this poor peasant of Picardy without any other ladder than his self-devotion, his good will, and a little of that old rustic cunning, on this occasion enlisted in the service of a generous enterprise, undertook to scale the difficulties of the cloister and the steep escarpments of the rule of Saint-Benoit. Father Fauchelevent was an old man who had been an egoist all his life, and who, toward the end of his days, halt, infirm, with no interest left to him in the world, found it sweet to be grateful, and perceiving a generous action to be performed, flung himself upon it like a man, who at the moment when he is dying, should find close to his hand a glass of good wine, which he had never tasted, and should swallow it with avidity. We may add, that the air he had breathed for many years in this convent had destroyed all personality in him, and had ended by rendering a good action of some kind absolutely necessary to him.

So he took his resolve: to devote himself to M. Madeleine.

We have just called him a poor peasant of Picardy. That description is just, but incomplete. At the point of this story which we have now reached, a little of Father Fauchelevent's physiology becomes useful. He was a peasant, but he had been a notary, which added trickery to his cunning, and penetration to his ingenuousness. Having, through various causes, failed in his business, he had descended to the calling of a carter and a laborer. But, in spite of oaths and lashings, which horses seem to require, something of the notary had lingered in him. He had some natural wit; he talked good grammar; he conversed, which is a rare thing in a village; and the other peasants said of him, "He talks almost like a gentleman with a hat." Fauchelevent belonged, in fact, to that species, which the impertinent and flippant vocabulary of the last century qualified as demi-bourgeois, demi-lout, and which the metaphors showered by the chateau upon the thatched cottage ticketed in the pigeonhole of the plebeian: rather rustic, rather citified; pepper and salt. Fauchelevent, though sorely tried and harshly used by fate, worn out, a sort of poor, threadbare old soul, was, nevertheless, an impulsive man, and extremely spontaneous in his actions; a precious quality that prevents one from ever being wicked. His defects and his vices, for he had some, were all superficial; in short, his physiognomy was of the kind that succeeds with an observer. His aged face had none of those disagreeable wrinkles at the top of the forehead that signify malice or stupidity.

At daybreak, Father Fauchelevent opened his eyes, after having done an enormous deal of thinking, and beheld M. Madeleine seated on his truss of straw, and watching Cosette's slumbers. Fauchelevent sat up and said, "Now that you are here, how are you going to contrive to enter?"

This remark summed up the situation and aroused Jean Valjean from his reverie.

The two men took counsel together.

"In the first place," said Fauchelevent, "you will begin by not setting foot outside of this chamber, either you or the child. One step in the garden and we are done for."

"That is true."

"Monsieur Madeleine," resumed Fauchelevent, "you have arrived at a very auspicious moment, I mean to say a very inauspicious moment; one of the ladies is very ill. This will prevent them from looking much in our direction.

It seems that she is dying. The prayers of the forty hours are being said. The whole community is in confusion. That occupies them. The one who is on the point of departure is a saint. In fact, we are all saints here; all the difference between them and me is that they say 'our cell,' and that I say 'my cabin.' The prayers for the dying are to be said, and then the prayers for the dead. We shall be at peace here for today; but I will not answer for tomorrow."

"Still," observed Jean Valjean, "this cottage is in the niche of the wall, it is hidden by a sort of ruin, there are trees, it is not visible from the convent."

"And I add that the nuns never come near it."

"Well?" said Jean Valjean.

The interrogation mark that accentuated this "well" signified "it seems to me that one may remain concealed here?" It was to this interrogation point that Fauchelevent responded, "There are the little girls."

"What little girls?" asked Jean Valjean.

Just as Fauchelevent opened his mouth to explain the words that he had uttered, a bell emitted one stroke.

"The nun is dead," said he. "There is the knell."

And he made a sign to Jean Valjean to listen.

The bell struck a second time.

"It is the knell, Monsieur Madeleine. The bell will continue to strike once a minute for twenty-four hours, until the body is taken from the church. You see they play. At recreation hours it suffices to have a ball roll aside, to send them all hither, in spite of prohibitions, to hunt and rummage for it all about here. Those cherubs are devils."

"Who?" asked Jean Valjean.

"The little girls. You would be very quickly discovered. They would shriek: 'Oh! A man!' There is no danger today. There will be no recreation hour. The day will be entirely devoted to prayers. You hear the bell. As I told you, a stroke each minute. It is the death knell."

"I understand, Father Fauchelevent. There are pupils."

And Jean Valjean thought to himself, "Here is Cosette's education already provided."

Fauchelevent exclaimed, "Pardine! There are little girls indeed! And they would bawl around you! And they would rush off! To be a man here is to have the plague. You see how they fasten a bell to my paw as though I were a wild beast."

Jean Valjean fell into more and more profound thought. "This convent would be our salvation," he murmured.

Then he raised his voice, "Yes, the difficulty is to remain here."

"No," said Fauchelevent, "the difficulty is to get out."

Jean Valjean felt the blood rush back to his heart.

"To get out!"

"Yes, Monsieur Madeleine. In order to return here it is first necessary to get out."

And after waiting until another stroke of the knell had sounded, Fauchelevent went on, "You must not be found here in this fashion. From where do you come? For me, you fall from heaven, because I know you; but the nuns require one to enter by the door."

All at once they heard a rather complicated pealing from another bell.

"Ah!" said Fauchelevent, "they are ringing up the vocal mothers. They are going to the chapter. They always hold a chapter when anyone dies. She died at daybreak. People generally do die at daybreak. But cannot you get out by the way in which you entered? Come, I do not ask for the sake of questioning you, but how did you get in?"

Jean Valjean turned pale; the very thought of descending again into that terrible street made him shudder. You make your way out of a forest filled with tigers, and once out of it, imagine a friendly counsel that shall advise you to return there! Jean Valjean pictured to himself the whole police force still engaged in swarming in that quarter, agents on the watch, sentinels everywhere, frightful fists extended toward his collar, Javert at the corner of the intersection of the streets perhaps.

"Impossible!" said he. "Father Fauchelevent, say that I fell from the sky."

"But I believe it, I believe it," retorted Fauchelevent. "You have no need to tell me that. The good God must have taken you in his hand for the purpose of getting a good look at you close to, and then dropped you. Only, he meant to place you in a man's convent; he made a mistake. Come, there goes another peal, that is to order the porter to go and inform the municipality that the dead-doctor is to come here and view a corpse. All that is the ceremony of dying. These good ladies are not at all fond of that visit. A doctor is a man who does not believe in anything. He lifts the veil. Sometimes he lifts something else too. How quickly they have had the doctor summoned this time! What is the matter? Your little one is still asleep. What is her name?"

"Cosette."

"She is your daughter? You are her grandfather, that is?"

"Yes."

"It will be easy enough for her to get out of here. I have my service door

which opens on the courtyard. I knock. The porter opens; I have my vintag
basket on my back, the child is in it, I go out. Father Fauchelevent goes out wit
his basket—that is perfectly natural. You will tell the child to keep very quie
She will be under the cover. I will leave her for whatever time is required wit
a good old friend, a fruit seller whom I know in the Rue Chemin-Vert, who i
deaf, and who has a little bed. I will shout in the fruit seller's ear, that she is
niece of mine, and that she is to keep her for me until tomorrow. Then the litt
one will reenter with you; for I will contrive to have you reenter. It must b
done. But how will you manage to get out?"

Jean Valjean shook his head.

"No one must see me, the whole point lies there, Father Fauchelevent. Fin
some means of getting me out in a basket, under cover, like Cosette."

Fauchelevent scratched the lobe of his ear with the middle finger of his le
hand, a sign of serious embarrassment.

A third peal created a diversion.

"That is the dead-doctor taking his departure," said Fauchelevent. "H
has taken a look and said, 'She is dead, that is well.' When the doctor ha
signed the passport for paradise, the undertaker's company sends a coffin. I
it is a mother, the mothers lay her out; if she is a sister, the sisters lay he
out. After which, I nail her up. That forms a part of my gardener's duty. /
gardener is a bit of a grave digger. She is placed in a lower hall of the churc
that communicates with the street, and into which no man may enter save th
doctor of the dead. I don't count the undertaker's men and myself as men. I
is in that hall that I nail up the coffin. The undertaker's men come and get i
and whip up, coachman! that's the way one goes to heaven. They fetch a bo
with nothing in it, they take it away again with something in it. That's what
burial is like. *De profundis.*"

A horizontal ray of sunshine lightly touched the face of the sleepin
Cosette, who lay with her mouth vaguely open, and had the air of an ang
drinking in the light. Jean Valjean had fallen to gazing at her. He was no longe
listening to Fauchelevent.

That one is not listened to is no reason for preserving silence. The good ol
gardener went on tranquilly with his babble, "The grave is dug in the Vaugirar
cemetery. They declare that they are going to suppress that Vaugirard cemeter
It is an ancient cemetery that is outside the regulations, which has no uniform
and which is going to retire. It is a shame, for it is convenient. I have a frien
there, Father Mestienne, the grave digger. The nuns here possess one privileg
it is to be taken to that cemetery at nightfall. There is a special permissio

om the Prefecture on their behalf. But how many events have happened since esterday! Mother Crucifixion is dead, and Father Madeleine—"

"Is buried," said Jean Valjean, smiling sadly.

Fauchelevent caught the word.

"Goodness! If you were here for good, it would be a real burial."

A fourth peal burst out. Fauchelevent hastily detached the belled kneecap om its nail and buckled it on his knee again.

"This time it is for me. The Mother Prioress wants me. Good, now I am icking myself on the tongue of my buckle. Monsieur Madeleine, don't stir om here, and wait for me. Something new has come up. If you are hungry, ere is wine, bread, and cheese."

And he hastened out of the hut, crying, "Coming! Coming!"

Jean Valjean watched him hurrying across the garden as fast as his crooked g would permit, casting a sidelong glance by the way on his melon patch.

Less than ten minutes later, Father Fauchelevent, whose bell put the nuns in is road to flight, tapped gently at a door, and a gentle voice replied, "Forever! orever!" That is to say, "Enter."

The door was the one leading to the parlor reserved for seeing the gardener n business. This parlor adjoined the chapter hall. The prioress, seated on the nly chair in the parlor, was waiting for Fauchelevent.

CHAPTER II—FAUCHELEVENT IN THE PRESENCE OF A DIFFICULTY

It is the peculiarity of certain persons and certain professions, notably priests and nuns, to wear a grave and agitated air on critical occasions. At ie moment when Fauchelevent entered, this double form of preoccupation as imprinted on the countenance of the prioress, who was that wise and harming Mademoiselle de Blemeur, Mother Innocente, who was ordinarily heerful.

The gardener made a timid bow, and remained at the door of the cell. The rioress, who was telling her beads, raised her eyes and said, "Ah! It is you, ather Fauvent."

This abbreviation had been adopted in the convent.

Fauchelevent bowed again.

"Father Fauvent, I have sent for you."

"Here I am, reverend Mother."

"I have something to say to you."

"And so have I," said Fauchelevent with a boldness that caused him inwar
terror, "I have something to say to the very reverend Mother."

The prioress stared at him.

"Ah! You have a communication to make to me."

"A request."

"Very well, speak."

Goodman Fauchelevent, the ex-notary, belonged to the category of peasan
who have assurance. A certain clever ignorance constitutes a force; you do n
distrust it, and you are caught by it. Fauchelevent had been a success durin
the something more than two years that he had passed in the convent. Alway
solitary and busied about his gardening, he had nothing else to do than to indulg
his curiosity. As he was at a distance from all those veiled women passing to an
fro, he saw before him only an agitation of shadows. By dint of attention an
sharpness he had succeeded in clothing all those phantoms with flesh, and thos
corpses were alive for him. He was like a deaf man whose sight grows keene
and like a blind man whose hearing becomes more acute. He had applied himse
to riddling out the significance of the different peals, and he had succeede
so that this taciturn and enigmatical cloister possessed no secrets for him; th
sphinx babbled all her secrets in his ear. Fauchelevent knew all and concealed al
that constituted his art. The whole convent thought him stupid. A great mer
in religion. The vocal mothers made much of Fauchelevent. He was a curiou
mute. He inspired confidence. Moreover, he was regular, and never went ou
except for well-demonstrated requirements of the orchard and vegetable garder
This discretion of conduct had inured to his credit. Nonetheless, he had set tw
men to chattering: the porter, in the convent, and he knew the singularities o
their parlor; and the grave digger, at the cemetery, and he was acquainted wit
the peculiarities of their sepulture; in this way, he possessed a double light on th
subject of these nuns, one as to their life, the other as to their death. But he di
not abuse his knowledge. The congregation thought a great deal of him. Ol
lame, blind to everything, probably a little deaf into the bargain, what qualitie
They would have found it difficult to replace him.

The goodman, with the assurance of a person who feels that he i
appreciated, entered into a rather diffuse and very deep rustic harangue t
the reverend prioress. He talked a long time about his age, his infirmitie
the surcharge of years counting double for him henceforth, of the increasin
demands of his work, of the great size of the garden, of nights that must b
passed, like the last, for instance, when he had been obliged to put straw mat
over the melon beds, because of the moon, and he wound up as follows, "Tha

ne had a brother"—(the prioress made a movement), "a brother no longer young"—(a second movement on the part of the prioress, but one expressive of reassurance), "that, if he might be permitted, this brother would come and live with him and help him, that he was an excellent gardener, that the community would receive from him good service, better than his own; that, otherwise, if his brother were not admitted, as he, the elder, felt that his health was broken and that he was insufficient for the work, he should be obliged, greatly to his regret, to go away; and that his brother had a little daughter whom he would bring with him, who might be reared for God in the house, and who might, who knows, become a nun someday."

When he had finished speaking, the prioress stayed the slipping of her rosary between her fingers, and said to him, "Could you procure a stout iron bar between now and this evening?"

"For what purpose?"

"To serve as a lever."

"Yes, reverend Mother," replied Fauchelevent.

The prioress, without adding a word, rose and entered the adjoining room, which was the hall of the chapter, and where the vocal mothers were probably assembled. Fauchelevent was left alone.

CHAPTER III—MOTHER INNOCENTE

About a quarter of an hour elapsed. The prioress returned and seated herself once more on her chair.

The two interlocutors seemed preoccupied. We will present a stenographic report of the dialogue that then ensued, to the best of our ability.

"Father Fauvent!"

"Reverend Mother!"

"Do you know the chapel?"

"I have a little cage there, where I hear the Mass and the offices."

"And you have been in the choir in pursuance of your duties?"

"Two or three times."

"There is a stone to be raised."

"Heavy?"

"The slab of the pavement, which is at the side of the altar."

"The slab that closes the vault?"

"Yes."

"It would be a good thing to have two men for it."

"Mother Ascension, who is as strong as a man, will help you."

"A woman is never a man."

"We have only a woman here to help you. Each one does what he can. Because Dom Mabillon gives four hundred and seventeen epistles of Saint Bernard, while Merlonus Horstius only gives three hundred and sixty-seven, do not despise Merlonus Horstius."

"Neither do I."

"Merit consists in working according to one's strength. A cloister is not a dockyard."

"And a woman is not a man. But my brother is the strong one, though!"

"And can you get a lever?"

"That is the only sort of key that fits that sort of door."

"There is a ring in the stone."

"I will put the lever through it."

"And the stone is so arranged that it swings on a pivot."

"That is good, reverend Mother. I will open the vault."

"And the four Mother Precentors will help you."

"And when the vault is open?"

"It must be closed again."

"Will that be all?"

"No."

"Give me your orders, very reverend Mother."

"Fauvent, we have confidence in you."

"I am here to do anything you wish."

"And to hold your peace about everything!"

"Yes, reverend Mother."

"When the vault is open—"

"I will close it again."

"But before that—"

"What, reverend Mother?"

"Something must be lowered into it."

A silence ensued. The prioress, after a pout of the underlip, which resembled hesitation, broke it.

"Father Fauvent!"

"Reverend Mother!"

"You know that a Mother died this morning?"

"No."

"Did you not hear the bell?"

"Nothing can be heard at the bottom of the garden."

"Really?"

"I can hardly distinguish my own signal."

"She died at daybreak."

"And then, the wind is not blowing in my direction this morning."

"It was Mother Crucifixion. A blessed woman."

The prioress paused, moved her lips, as though in mental prayer, and resumed, "Three years ago, Madame de Bethune, a Jansenist, turned orthodox, merely from having seen Mother Crucifixion at prayer."

"Ah! Yes, now I hear the knell, reverend Mother."

"The mothers have taken her to the dead-room, which opens on the church."

"I know."

"No other man than you can or must enter that chamber. See to that. A fine sight it would be, to see a man enter the dead-room!"

"More often!"

"Hey?"

"More often!"

"What do you say?"

"I say more often."

"More often than what?"

"Reverend Mother, I did not say more often than what, I said more often."

"I don't understand you. Why do you say more often?"

"In order to speak like you, reverend Mother."

"But I did not say 'more often.'"

At that moment, nine o'clock struck.

"At nine o'clock in the morning and at all hours, praised and adored be the most Holy Sacrament of the altar," said the prioress.

"Amen," said Fauchelevent.

The clock struck opportunely. It cut "more often" short. It is probable, that had it not been for this, the prioress and Fauchelevent would never have unraveled that skein.

Fauchelevent mopped his forehead.

The prioress indulged in another little inward murmur, probably sacred, then raised her voice, "In her lifetime, Mother Crucifixion made converts; after her death, she will perform miracles."

"She will!" replied Father Fauchelevent, falling into step, and striving not to flinch again.

"Father Fauvent, the community has been blessed in Mother Crucifixion. No doubt, it is not granted to everyone to die, like Cardinal de Berulle, while saying the holy Mass, and to breathe forth their souls to God, while pronouncing these words: *Hanc igitur oblationem*. But without attaining to such happiness, Mother Crucifixion's death was very precious. She retained her consciousness to the very last moment. She spoke to us, then she spoke to the angels. She gave us her last commands. If you had a little more faith, and if you could have been in her cell, she would have cured your leg merely by touching it. She smiled. We felt that she was regaining her life in God. There was something of paradise in that death."

Fauchelevent thought that it was an orison which she was finishing.

"Amen," said he.

"Father Fauvent, what the dead wish must be done."

The prioress took off several beads of her chaplet. Fauchelevent held his peace.

She went on, "I have consulted upon this point many ecclesiastics laboring in Our Lord, who occupy themselves in the exercises of the clerical life, and who bear wonderful fruit."

"Reverend Mother, you can hear the knell much better here than in the garden."

"Besides, she is more than a dead woman, she is a saint."

"Like yourself, reverend Mother."

"She slept in her coffin for twenty years, by express permission of our Holy Father, Pius VII—"

"The one who crowned the Emp—Buonaparte."

For a clever man like Fauchelevent, this allusion was an awkward one. Fortunately, the prioress, completely absorbed in her own thoughts, did not hear it. She continued, "Father Fauvent?"

"Reverend Mother?"

"Saint Didorus, Archbishop of Cappadocia, desired that this single word might be inscribed on his tomb: Acarus, which signifies a worm of the earth, this was done. Is this true?"

"Yes, reverend Mother."

"The blessed Mezzocane, Abbot of Aquila, wished to be buried beneath the gallows; this was done."

"That is true."

"Saint Terentius, Bishop of Port, where the mouth of the Tiber empties into the sea, requested that on his tomb might be engraved the sign that was ᵻced on the graves of parricides, in the hope that passersby would spit on his ᵼᵻb. This was done. The dead must be obeyed."

"So be it."

"The body of Bernard Guidonis, born in France near Roche-Abeille, was, ᵼhe had ordered, and in spite of the king of Castile, borne to the church of ᵼ Dominicans in Limoges, although Bernard Guidonis was Bishop of Tuy in ᵼain. Can the contrary be affirmed?"

"For that matter, no, reverend Mother."

"The fact is attested by Plantavit de la Fosse."

Several beads of the chaplet were told off, still in silence. The prioress ᵼumed, "Father Fauvent, Mother Crucifixion will be interred in the coffin in ᵼich she has slept for the last twenty years."

"That is just."

"It is a continuation of her slumber."

"So I shall have to nail up that coffin?"

"Yes."

"And we are to reject the undertaker's coffin?"

"Precisely."

"I am at the orders of the very reverend community."

"The four Mother Precentors will assist you."

"In nailing up the coffin? I do not need them."

"No. In lowering the coffin."

"Where?"

"Into the vault."

"What vault?"

"Under the altar."

Fauchelevent started.

"The vault under the altar?"

"Under the altar."

"But—"

"You will have an iron bar."

"Yes, but—"

"You will raise the stone with the bar by means of the ring."

"But—"

"The dead must be obeyed. To be buried in the vault under the altar of the ᵼpel, not to go to profane earth; to remain there in death where she prayed ᵼle living; such was the last wish of Mother Crucifixion. She asked it of us; ᵼt is to say, commanded us."

"But it is forbidden."

"Forbidden by men, enjoined by God."

"What if it became known?"

"We have confidence in you."

"Oh! I am a stone in your walls."

"The chapter assembled. The vocal mothers, whom I have just consult again, and who are now deliberating, have decided that Mother Crucifixi shall be buried, according to her wish, in her own coffin, under our alt: Think, Father Fauvent, if she were to work miracles here! What a glory God for the community! And miracles issue from tombs."

"But, reverend Mother, if the agent of the sanitary commission—"

"Saint Benoit II, in the matter of sepulture, resisted Constanti Pogonatus."

"But the commissary of police—"

"Chonodemaire, one of the seven German kings who entered among t Gauls under the Empire of Constantius, expressly recognized the right of nu to be buried in religion, that is to say, beneath the altar."

"But the inspector from the Prefecture—"

"The world is nothing in the presence of the cross. Martin, the elever general of the Carthusians, gave to his order this device: *Stat crux dum volvi orbis.*"

"Amen," said Fauchelevent, who imperturbably extricated himself in t: manner from the dilemma, whenever he heard Latin.

Any audience suffices for a person who has held his peace too long. On t day when the rhetorician Gymnastoras left his prison, bearing in his body ma: dilemmas and numerous syllogisms that had struck in, he halted in front of t first tree that he came to, harangued it, and made very great efforts to convin it. The prioress, who was usually subjected to the barrier of silence, and whe reservoir was overfull, rose and exclaimed with the loquacity of a dam that I broken away, "I have on my right Benoit and on my left Bernard. Who v Bernard? The first abbot of Clairvaux. Fontaines in Burgundy is a coun that is blessed because it gave him birth. His father was named Tecelin, and mother Alethe. He began at Citeaux, to end in Clairvaux; he was ordained ab: by the bishop of Chalon-sur-Saone, Guillaume de Champeaux; he had sev hundred novices, and founded a hundred and sixty monasteries; he overthre Abeilard at the council of Sens in 1140, and Pierre de Bruys and Henry disciple, and another sort of erring spirits who were called the Apostoli he confounded Arnauld de Brescia, darted lightning at the monk Raoul, urderer of the Jews, dominated the council of Reims in 1148, caused the ondemnation of Gilbert de Porea, Bishop of Poitiers, caused the condemnation f Eon de l'Etoile, arranged the disputes of princes, enlightened King Louis the oung, advised Pope Eugene III, regulated the Temple, preached the crusade, erformed two hundred and fifty miracles during his lifetime, and as many s thirty-nine in one day. Who was Benoit? He was the patriarch of Mont-assin; he was the second founder of the Saintete Claustrale, he was the Basil f the West. His order has produced forty popes, two hundred cardinals, fifty atriarchs, sixteen hundred archbishops, four thousand six hundred bishops, four nperors, twelve empresses, forty-six kings, forty-one queens, 3,600 canonized ints, and has been in existence for 1,400 years. On one side Saint Bernard, n the other the agent of the sanitary department! On one side Saint Benoit, n the other the inspector of public ways! The state, the road commissioners, e public undertaker, regulations, the administration, what do we know of all at? There is not a chance passerby who would not be indignant to see how e are treated. We have not even the right to give our dust to Jesus Christ! our sanitary department is a revolutionary invention. God subordinated to the ommissary of police; such is the age. Silence, Fauchelevent!"

Fauchelevent was but ill at ease under this shower bath. The prioress ontinued, "No one doubts the right of the monastery to sepulture. Only natics and those in error deny it. We live in times of terrible confusion. We o not know that which is necessary to know, and we know that which we ould ignore. We are ignorant and impious. In this age there exist people ho do not distinguish between the very great Saint Bernard and the Saint ernard denominated of the poor Catholics, a certain good ecclesiastic who ved in the thirteenth century. Others are so blasphemous as to compare the affold of Louis XVI to the cross of Jesus Christ. Louis XVI was merely king. Let us beware of God! There is no longer just or unjust. The name f Voltaire is known, but not the name of Cesar de Bus. Nevertheless, Cesar e Bus is a man of blessed memory, and Voltaire one of unblessed memory. he last archbishop, the Cardinal de Perigord, did not even know that Charles e Gondren succeeded to Berulle, and Francois Bourgoin to Gondren, and an-Francois Senault to Bourgoin, and Father Sainte-Marthe to Jean-Francois enault. The name of Father Coton is known, not because he was one of the ree who urged the foundation of the Oratorie, but because he furnished enri IV, the Huguenot king, with the material for an oath. That which pleases eople of the world in Saint Francois de Sales, is that he cheated at play. And en, religion is attacked. Why? Because there have been bad priests, because

Sagittaire, Bishop of Gap, was the brother of Salone, Bishop of Embrun, a because both of them followed Mommol. What has that to do with the question Does that prevent Martin de Tours from being a saint, and giving half of h cloak to a beggar? They persecute the saints. They shut their eyes to the truth Darkness is the rule. The most ferocious beasts are beasts that are blind. N one thinks of hell as a reality. Oh! How wicked people are! By order of t king signifies today, by order of the revolution. One no longer knows wh is due to the living or to the dead. A holy death is prohibited. Burial is a civ matter. This is horrible. Saint Leo II wrote two special letters—one to Pier Notaire, the other to the king of the Visigoths—for the purpose of combatin and rejecting, in questions touching the dead, the authority of the exarch a the supremacy of the Emperor. Gauthier, Bishop of Chalons, held his own this matter against Otho, Duke of Burgundy. The ancient magistracy agree with him. In former times we had voices in the chapter, even on matters of t day. The Abbot of Citeaux, the general of the order, was counselor by right birth to the parliament of Burgundy. We do what we please with our dead. not the body of Saint Benoit himself in France, in the abbey of Fleury, call Saint Benoit-sur-Loire, although he died in Italy at Mont-Cassin, on Saturda the 21st of the month of March, of the year 543? All this is incontestable. abhor psalm singers, I hate priors, I execrate heretics, but I should detest y more anyone who should maintain the contrary. One has only to read Arno Wion, Gabriel Bucelin, Trithemus, Maurolics, and Dom Luc d'Achery."

The prioress took breath, then turned to Fauchelevent.

"Is it settled, Father Fauvent?"

"It is settled, reverend Mother."

"We may depend on you?"

"I will obey."

"That is well."

"I am entirely devoted to the convent."

"That is understood. You will close the coffin. The sisters will carry it the chapel. The office for the dead will then be said. Then we shall return to t cloister. Between eleven o'clock and midnight, you will come with your iro bar. All will be done in the most profound secrecy. There will be in the chap only the four Mother Precentors, Mother Ascension, and yourself."

"And the sister at the post?"

"She will not turn around."

"But she will hear."

"She will not listen. Besides, what the cloister knows the world learns not

A pause ensued. The prioress went on, "You will remove your bell. It is not necessary that the sister at the post should perceive your presence."

"Reverend Mother?"

"What, Father Fauvent?"

"Has the doctor for the dead paid his visit?"

"He will pay it at four o'clock today. The peal that orders the doctor for the dead to be summoned has already been rung. But you do not understand any of the peals?"

"I pay no attention to any but my own."

"That is well, Father Fauvent."

"Reverend Mother, a lever at least six feet long will be required."

"Where will you obtain it?"

"Where gratings are not lacking, iron bars are not lacking. I have my heap of old iron at the bottom of the garden."

"About three-quarters of an hour before midnight; do not forget."

"Reverend Mother?"

"What?"

"If you were ever to have any other jobs of this sort, my brother is the strong man for you. A perfect Turk!"

"You will do it as speedily as possible."

"I cannot work very fast. I am infirm; that is why I require an assistant. I limp."

"To limp is no sin, and perhaps it is a blessing. The Emperor Henry II, who combated Antipope Gregory and reestablished Benoit VIII, has two surnames: the Saint and the Lame."

"Two surtouts are a good thing," murmured Fauchelevent, who really was a little hard of hearing.

"Now that I think of it, Father Fauvent, let us give a whole hour to it. That is not too much. Be near the principal altar, with your iron bar, at eleven o'clock. The office begins at midnight. Everything must have been completed a good quarter of an hour before that."

"I will do anything to prove my zeal toward the community. These are my orders. I am to nail up the coffin. At eleven o'clock exactly, I am to be in the chapel. The Mother Precentors will be there. Mother Ascension will be there. Two men would be better. However, never mind! I shall have my lever. We will open the vault, we will lower the coffin, and we will close the vault again. After which, there will be no trace of anything. The government will have no suspicion. Thus all has been arranged, reverend Mother?"

"No!"

"What else remains?"

"The empty coffin remains."

This produced a pause. Fauchelevent meditated. The prioress meditated.

"What is to be done with that coffin, Father Fauvent?"

"It will be given to the earth."

"Empty?"

Another silence. Fauchelevent made, with his left hand, that sort of gesture that dismisses a troublesome subject.

"Reverend Mother, I am the one who is to nail up the coffin in the basement of the church, and no one can enter there but myself, and I will cover the coffin with the pall."

"Yes, but the bearers, when they place it in the hearse and lower it into the grave, will be sure to feel that there is nothing in it."

"Ah! The de—!" exclaimed Fauchelevent.

The prioress began to make the sign of the cross, and looked fixedly at the gardener. The "vil" stuck fast in his throat.

He made haste to improvise an expedient to make her forget the oath.

"I will put earth in the coffin, reverend Mother. That will produce the effect of a corpse."

"You are right. Earth, that is the same thing as man. So you will manage the empty coffin?"

"I will make that my special business."

The prioress's face, up to that moment troubled and clouded, grew serene once more. She made the sign of a superior dismissing an inferior to him. Fauchelevent went toward the door. As he was on the point of passing out, the prioress raised her voice gently, "I am pleased with you, Father Fauvent, bring your brother to me tomorrow, after the burial, and tell him to fetch his daughter."

CHAPTER IV—IN WHICH JEAN VALJEAN HAS QUITE THE AIR OF HAVING READ AUSTIN CASTILLEJO

The strides of a lame man are like the ogling glances of a one-eyed man; they do not reach their goal very promptly. Moreover, Fauchelevent was a dilemma. He took nearly a quarter of an hour to return to his cottage in the garden. Cosette had woken up. Jean Valjean had placed her near the fire. At the moment when Fauchelevent entered, Jean Valjean was pointing out to her the ntner's basket on the wall, and saying to her, "Listen attentively to me, my tle Cosette. We must go away from this house, but we shall return to it, and e shall be very happy here. The good man who lives here is going to carry ou off on his back in that. You will wait for me at a lady's house. I shall come fetch you. Obey, and say nothing, above all things, unless you want Madame henardier to get you again!"

Cosette nodded gravely.

Jean Valjean turned around at the noise made by Fauchelevent opening the oor.

"Well?"

"Everything is arranged, and nothing is," said Fauchelevent. "I have ermission to bring you in; but before bringing you in, you must be got out. hat's where the difficulty lies. It is easy enough with the child."

"You will carry her out?"

"And she will hold her tongue?"

"I answer for that."

"But you, Father Madeleine?"

And, after a silence, fraught with anxiety, Fauchelevent exclaimed, "Why, et out as you came in!"

Jean Valjean, as in the first instance, contented himself with saying, Impossible."

Fauchelevent grumbled, more to himself than to Jean Valjean, "There is nother thing which bothers me. I have said that I would put earth in it. When come to think it over, the earth instead of the corpse will not seem like the real ing, it won't do, it will get displaced, it will move about. The men will bear it. ou understand, Father Madeleine, the government will notice it."

Jean Valjean stared him straight in the eye and thought that he was raving.

Fauchelevent went on, "How the de—uce are you going to get out? It must ll be done by tomorrow morning. It is tomorrow that I am to bring you in. he prioress expects you."

Then he explained to Jean Valjean that this was his recompense for a service at he, Fauchelevent, was to render to the community. That it fell among his uties to take part in their burials, that he nailed up the coffins and helped the rave digger at the cemetery. That the nun who had died that morning had equested to be buried in the coffin that had served her for a bed, and interred

in the vault under the altar of the chapel. That the police regulations forba
this, but that she was one of those dead to whom nothing is refused. That th
prioress and the vocal mothers intended to fulfill the wish of the deceased. Th
it was so much the worse for the government. That he, Fauchelevent, was
nail up the coffin in the cell, raise the stone in the chapel, and lower the corp
into the vault. And that, by way of thanks, the prioress was to admit his broth
to the house as a gardener, and his niece as a pupil. That his brother was M
Madeleine, and that his niece was Cosette. That the prioress had told him
bring his brother on the following evening, after the counterfeit interment
the cemetery. But that he could not bring M. Madeleine in from the outside
M. Madeleine was not outside. That that was the first problem. And then, th
there was another: the empty coffin.

"What is that empty coffin?" asked Jean Valjean.

Fauchelevent replied, "The coffin of the administration."

"What coffin? What administration?"

"A nun dies. The municipal doctor comes and says, 'A nun has died.' Th
government sends a coffin. The next day it sends a hearse and undertaker's me
to get the coffin and carry it to the cemetery. The undertaker's men will com
and lift the coffin; there will be nothing in it."

"Put something in it."

"A corpse? I have none."

"No."

"What then?"

"A living person."

"What person?"

"Me!" said Jean Valjean.

Fauchelevent, who was seated, sprang up as though a bomb had burst und
his chair.

"You!"

"Why not?"

Jean Valjean gave way to one of those rare smiles which lighted up his fac
like a flash from heaven in the winter.

"You know, Fauchelevent, what you have said: 'Mother Crucifixion
dead.' And I add, 'And Father Madeleine is buried.'"

"Ah! Good, you can laugh; you are not speaking seriously."

"Very seriously, I must get out of this place."

"Certainly."

"I have told you to find a basket, and a cover for me also."

"Well?"

"The basket will be of pine, and the cover a black cloth."

"In the first place, it will be a white cloth. Nuns are buried in white."

"Let it be a white cloth, then."

"You are not like other men, Father Madeleine."

To behold such devices, which are nothing else than the savage and daring inventions of the galleys, spring forth from the peaceable things that surrounded him, and mingle with what he called the "petty course of life in the convent," caused Fauchelevent as much amazement as a gull fishing in the gutter of the Rue Saint-Denis would inspire in a passerby.

Jean Valjean went on, "The problem is to get out of here without being seen. This offers the means. But give me some information, in the first place. How is it managed? Where is this coffin?"

"The empty one?"

"Yes."

"Downstairs, in what is called the dead-room. It stands on two trestles, under the pall."

"How long is the coffin?"

"Six feet."

"What is this dead-room?"

"It is a chamber on the ground floor which has a grated window opening on the garden, which is closed on the outside by a shutter, and two doors; one leads into the convent, the other into the church."

"What church?"

"The church in the street, the church that anyone can enter."

"Have you the keys to those two doors?"

"No; I have the key to the door that communicates with the convent; the porter has the key to the door that communicates with the church."

"When does the porter open that door?"

"Only to allow the undertaker's men to enter, when they come to get the coffin. When the coffin has been taken out, the door is closed again."

"Who nails up the coffin?"

"I do."

"Who spreads the pall over it?"

"I do."

"Are you alone?"

"Not another man, except the police doctor, can enter the dead-room. That is even written on the wall."

"Could you hide me in that room tonight when everyone is asleep?"

"No. But I could hide you in a small, dark nook which opens on the dead-room, where I keep my tools to use for burials, and of which I have the key."

"At what time will the hearse come for the coffin tomorrow?"

"About three o'clock in the afternoon. The burial will take place at the Vaugirard cemetery a little before nightfall. It is not very near."

"I will remain concealed in your tool closet all night and all the morning. And how about food? I shall be hungry."

"I will bring you something."

"You can come and nail me up in the coffin at two o'clock."

Fauchelevent recoiled and cracked his finger joints.

"But that is impossible!"

"Bah! Impossible to take a hammer and drive some nails in a plank?"

What seemed unprecedented to Fauchelevent was, we repeat, a simple matter to Jean Valjean. Jean Valjean had been in worse straits than this. Any man who has been a prisoner understands how to contract himself to fit the diameter of the escape. The prisoner is subject to flight as the sick man is subject to a crisis that saves or kills him. An escape is a cure. What does not a man undergo for the sake of a cure? To have himself nailed up in a case and carried off like a bale of goods, to live for a long time in a box, to find air where there is none, to economize his breath for hours, to know how to stifle without dying—this was one of Jean Valjean's gloomy talents.

Moreover, a coffin containing a living being, that convict's expedient, is also an imperial expedient. If we are to credit the monk Austin Castillejo, this was the means employed by Charles the Fifth, desirous of seeing the Plombes for the last time after his abdication.

He had her brought into and carried out of the monastery of Saint-Yuste in this manner.

Fauchelevent, who had recovered himself a little, exclaimed, "But how will you manage to breathe?"

"I will breathe."

"In that box! The mere thought of it suffocates me."

"You surely must have a gimlet, you will make a few holes here and there, around my mouth, and you will nail the top plank on loosely."

"Good! And what if you should happen to cough or to sneeze?"

"A man who is making his escape does not cough or sneeze."

And Jean Valjean added, "Father Fauchelevent, we must come to a decision: I must either be caught here, or accept this escape through the hearse."

Everyone has noticed the taste that cats have for pausing and lounging between the two leaves of a half-shut door. Who is there who has not said to a cat, "Do come in!" There are men who, when an incident stands half-open before them, have the same tendency to halt in indecision between two resolutions, at the risk of getting crushed through the abrupt closing of the adventure by fate. The over-prudent, cats as they are, and because they are cats, sometimes incur more danger than the audacious. Fauchelevent was of this hesitating nature. But Jean Valjean's coolness prevailed over him in spite of himself. He grumbled, "Well, since there is no other means."

Jean Valjean resumed, "The only thing that troubles me is what will take place at the cemetery."

"That is the very point that is not troublesome," exclaimed Fauchelevent. "If you are sure of coming out of the coffin all right, I am sure of getting you out of the grave. The grave digger is a drunkard, and a friend of mine. He is Father Mestienne. An old fellow of the old school. The grave digger puts the corpses in the grave, and I put the grave digger in my pocket. I will tell you what will take place. They will arrive a little before dusk, three-quarters of an hour before the gates of the cemetery are closed. The hearse will drive directly up to the grave. I shall follow; that is my business. I shall have a hammer, a chisel, and some pincers in my pocket. The hearse halts, the undertaker's men knot a rope around your coffin and lower you down. The priest says the prayers, makes the sign of the cross, sprinkles the holy water, and takes his departure. I am left alone with Father Mestienne. He is my friend, I tell you. One of two things will happen, he will either be sober, or he will not be sober. If he is not drunk, I shall say to him, 'Come and drink a bout while the Bon Coing [the Good Quince] is open.' I carry him off, I get him drunk, it does not take long to make Father Mestienne drunk, he always has the beginning of it about him, lay him under the table, I take his card, so that I can get into the cemetery again, and I return without him. Then you have no longer anyone but me to deal with. If he is drunk, I shall say to him, 'Be off; I will do your work for you.' Off he goes, and I drag you out of the hole."

Jean Valjean held out his hand, and Fauchelevent precipitated himself upon it with the touching effusion of a peasant.

"That is settled, Father Fauchelevent. All will go well."

"Provided nothing goes wrong," thought Fauchelevent. "In that case, it would be terrible."

CHAPTER V—IT IS NOT NECESSARY TO BE DRUNK IN ORDER TO BE IMMORTAL

On the following day, as the sun was declining, the very rare passersby on the Boulevard du Maine pulled off their hats to an old-fashioned hearse, ornamented with skulls, crossbones, and tears. This hearse contained a coffin covered with a white cloth over which spread a large black cross, like a huge corpse with drooping arms. A mourning-coach, in which could be seen a priest in his surplice, and a choir boy in his red cap, followed. Two undertaker's men in gray uniforms trimmed with black walked on the right and the left of the hearse. Behind it came an old man in the garments of a laborer, who limped along. The procession was going in the direction of the Vaugirard cemetery.

The handle of a hammer, the blade of a cold chisel, and the antennae of a pair of pincers were visible, protruding from the man's pocket.

The Vaugirard cemetery formed an exception among the cemeteries of Paris. It had its peculiar usages, just as it had its carriage entrance and its house door, which old people in the quarter, who clung tenaciously to ancient words, still called the porte cavaliere and the porte pietonne. The Bernardines-Benedictines of the Rue Petit-Picpus had obtained permission, as we have already stated, to be buried there in a corner apart, and at night, the plot of land having formerly belonged to their community. The grave diggers being thus bound to service in the evening in summer and at night in winter, in this cemetery, they were subjected to a special discipline. The gates of the Paris cemeteries closed, at that epoch, at sundown, and this being a municipal regulation, the Vaugirard cemetery was bound by it like the rest. The carriage gate and the house door were two contiguous grated gates, adjoining a pavilion built by the architect Perronet, and inhabited by the door keeper of the cemetery. These gates, therefore, swung inexorably on their hinges at the instant when the sun disappeared behind the dome of the Invalides. If any grave digger were delayed after that moment in the cemetery, there was but one way for him to get out—his grave digger's card furnished by the department of public funerals. A sort of letterbox was constructed in the porter's window. The grave digger dropped his card into this box, the porter heard it fall, pulled the rope, and the small door opened. If the man had not his card, he mentioned his name, the porter—who was sometimes in bed and asleep—rose, came out, and identified the man, and opened the gate with his key; the grave digger stepped out, but had to pay a fine of fifteen francs.

This cemetery, with its peculiarities outside the regulations, embarrassed the symmetry of the administration. It was suppressed a little later than 1830. The cemetery of Mont-Parnasse, called the Eastern cemetery, succeeded to it, and inherited that famous dram shop next to the Vaugirard cemetery, which was surmounted by a quince painted on a board, and which formed an angle, one side on the drinkers' tables, and the other on the tombs, with this sign: *Au Bon Coing*.

The Vaugirard cemetery was what may be called a faded cemetery. It was falling into disuse. Dampness was invading it, the flowers were deserting it. The bourgeois did not care much about being buried in the Vaugirard; it hinted at poverty. Pere-Lachaise, if you please! To be buried in Pere-Lachaise is equivalent to having furniture of mahogany. It is recognized as elegant. The Vaugirard cemetery was a venerable enclosure, planted like an old-fashioned French garden. Straight alleys, box, thuya trees, holly, ancient tombs beneath aged cypress trees, and very tall grass. In the evening it was tragic there. There were very lugubrious lines about it.

The sun had not yet set when the hearse with the white pall and the black cross entered the avenue of the Vaugirard cemetery. The lame man who followed it was no other than Fauchelevent.

The interment of Mother Crucifixion in the vault under the altar, the exit of Cosette, the introduction of Jean Valjean to the dead-room—all had been executed without difficulty, and there had been no hitch.

Let us remark in passing, that the burial of Mother Crucifixion under the altar of the convent is a perfectly venial offense in our sight. It is one of the faults that resemble a duty. The nuns had committed it, not only without difficulty, but even with the applause of their own consciences. In the cloister, what is called the "government" is only an intermeddling with authority, an interference that is always questionable. In the first place, the rule; as for the code, we shall see. Make as many laws as you please, men; but keep them for yourselves. The tribute to Caesar is never anything but the remnants of the tribute to God. A prince is nothing in the presence of a principle.

Fauchelevent limped along behind the hearse in a very contented frame of mind. His twin plots, the one with the nuns, the one for the convent, the other against it, the other with M. Madeleine, had succeeded, to all appearance. Jean Valjean's composure was one of those powerful tranquilities that are contagious. Fauchelevent no longer felt doubtful as to his success.

What remained to be done was a mere nothing. Within the last two years, he had made good Father Mestienne, a chubby-cheeked person, drunk at least ten times. He played with Father Mestienne. He did what he liked with him. He made him dance according to his whim. Mestienne's head adjusted itself to the cap of Fauchelevent's will. Fauchelevent's confidence was perfect.

At the moment when the convoy entered the avenue leading to the cemetery, Fauchelevent glanced cheerfully at the hearse, and said half aloud, as he rubbed his big hands, "Here's a fine farce!"

All at once the hearse halted; it had reached the gate. The permission for interment must be exhibited. The undertaker's man addressed himself to the porter of the cemetery. During this colloquy, which always is productive of a delay of from one to two minutes, someone, a stranger, came and placed himself behind the hearse, beside Fauchelevent. He was a sort of laboring man, who wore a waistcoat with large pockets and carried a mattock under his arm.

Fauchelevent surveyed this stranger.

"Who are you?" he demanded.

The man replied, "The grave digger."

If a man could survive the blow of a cannonball full in the breast, he would make the same face that Fauchelevent made.

"The grave digger?"

"Yes."

"You?"

"I."

"Father Mestienne is the grave digger."

"He was."

"What! He was?"

"He is dead."

Fauchelevent had expected anything but this, that a grave digger could die. It is true, nevertheless, that grave diggers do die themselves. By dint of excavating graves for other people, one hollows out one's own.

Fauchelevent stood there with his mouth wide open. He had hardly the strength to stammer, "But it is not possible!"

"It is so."

"But," he persisted feebly, "Father Mestienne is the grave digger."

"After Napoleon, Louis XVIII. After Mestienne, Gribier. Peasant, my name is Gribier."

Fauchelevent, who was deadly pale, stared at this Gribier.

He was a tall, thin, livid, utterly funereal man. He had the air of an unsuccessful doctor who had turned grave digger.

Fauchelevent burst out laughing.

"Ah, said he, "what queer things do happen! Father Mestienne is dead, but long live little Father Lenoir! Do you know who little Father Lenoir is? He is a jug of red wine. It is a jug of Surene, morbigou! Of real Paris Surene? Ah! So old Mestienne is dead! I am sorry for it; he was a jolly fellow. But you are a jolly fellow, too. Are you not, comrade? We'll go and have a drink together presently."

The man replied, "I have been a student. I passed my fourth examination. I never drink."

The hearse had set out again, and was rolling up the grand alley of the cemetery.

Fauchelevent had slackened his pace. He limped more out of anxiety than from infirmity.

The grave digger walked on in front of him.

Fauchelevent passed the unexpected Gribier once more in review.

He was one of those men who, though very young, have the air of age, and who, though slender, are extremely strong.

"Comrade!" cried Fauchelevent.

The man turned around.

"I am the convent grave digger."

"My colleague," said the man.

Fauchelevent, who was illiterate but very sharp, understood that he had to deal with a formidable species of man, with a fine talker. He muttered, "So Father Mestienne is dead."

The man replied, "Completely. The good God consulted his notebook that shows when the time is up. It was Father Mestienne's turn. Father Mestienne died."

Fauchelevent repeated mechanically, "The good God—"

"The good God," said the man authoritatively. "According to the philosophers, the Eternal Father; according to the Jacobins, the Supreme Being."

"Shall we not make each other's acquaintance?" stammered Fauchelevent.

"It is made. You are a peasant, I am a Parisian."

"People do not know each other until they have drunk together. He who empties his glass empties his heart. You must come and have a drink with me. Such a thing cannot be refused."

"Business first."

Fauchelevent thought, "I am lost."

They were only a few turns of the wheel distant from the small alley leading to the nuns' corner.

The grave digger resumed, "Peasant, I have seven small children who must be fed. As they must eat, I cannot drink."

And he added, with the satisfaction of a serious man who is turning a phrase well, "Their hunger is the enemy of my thirst."

The hearse skirted a clump of cypress trees, quitted the grand alley, turned into a narrow one, entered the wasteland, and plunged into a thicket. This indicated the immediate proximity of the place of sepulture. Fauchelevent slackened his pace, but he could not detain the hearse. Fortunately, the soil which was light and wet with the winter rains, clogged the wheels and retarded its speed.

He approached the grave digger.

"They have such a nice little Argenteuil wine," murmured Fauchelevent.

"Villager," retorted the man, "I ought not be a grave digger. My father was a porter at the Prytaneum [Town Hall]. He destined me for literature. But he had reverses. He had losses on change. I was obliged to renounce the profession of author. But I am still a public writer."

"So you are not a grave digger, then?" returned Fauchelevent, clutching at this branch, feeble as it was.

"The one does not hinder the other. I cumulate."

Fauchelevent did not understand this last word.

"Come have a drink," said he.

Here a remark becomes necessary. Fauchelevent, whatever his anguish, offered a drink, but he did not explain himself on one point; who was to pay? Generally, Fauchelevent offered and Father Mestienne paid. An offer of a drink was the evident result of the novel situation created by the new grave digger, and it was necessary to make this offer, but the old gardener left the proverbial quarter of an hour named after Rabelais in the dark, and that not unintentionally. As for himself, Fauchelevent did not wish to pay, troubled as he was.

The grave digger went on with a superior smile, "One must eat. I have accepted Father Mestienne's reversion. One gets to be a philosopher when one has nearly completed his classes. To the labor of the hand I join the labor of the arm. I have my scrivener's stall in the market of the Rue de Sevres. You know! The Umbrella Market. All the cooks of the Red Cross apply to me. I scribble their declarations of love to the raw soldiers. In the morning I write love letters, in the evening I dig graves. Such is life, rustic."

The hearse was still advancing. Fauchelevent, uneasy to the last degree, was gazing about him on all sides. Great drops of perspiration trickled down from his brow.

"But," continued the grave digger, "a man cannot serve two mistresses. I must choose between the pen and the mattock. The mattock is ruining my hand."

The hearse halted.

The choir boy alighted from the mourning-coach, then the priest.

One of the small front wheels of the hearse had run up a little on a pile of earth, beyond which an open grave was visible.

"What a farce this is!" repeated Fauchelevent in consternation.

CHAPTER VI—BETWEEN FOUR PLANKS

Who was in the coffin? The reader knows. Jean Valjean.

Jean Valjean had arranged things so that he could exist there, and he could almost breathe.

It is a strange thing to what a degree security of conscience confers security of the rest. Every combination thought out by Jean Valjean had been progressing, and progressing favorably, since the preceding day. He, like Fauchelevent, counted on Father Mestienne. He had no doubt as to the end. Never was there a more critical situation, never more complete composure.

The four planks of the coffin breathe out a kind of terrible peace. It seemed as though something of the repose of the dead entered into Jean Valjean's tranquillity.

From the depths of that coffin he had been able to follow, and he had followed, all the phases of the terrible drama that he was playing with death.

Shortly after Fauchelevent had finished nailing on the upper plank, Jean Valjean had felt himself carried out, then driven off. He knew, from the diminution in the jolting, when they left the pavements and reached the earth road. He had divined, from a dull noise, that they were crossing the bridge of Austerlitz. At the first halt, he had understood that they were entering the cemetery; at the second halt, he said to himself, "Here is the grave."

Suddenly, he felt hands seize the coffin, then a harsh grating against the planks; he explained it to himself as the rope being fastened around the casket in order to lower it into the cavity.

Then he experienced a giddiness.

The undertaker's man and the grave digger had probably allowed the coffin to lose its balance, and had lowered the head before the foot. He recovered himself fully when he felt himself horizontal and motionless. He had just touched the bottom.

He had a certain sensation of cold.

A voice rose above him, glacial and solemn. He heard Latin words, which he did not understand, pass over him, so slowly that he was able to catch them one by one, "*Qui dormiunt in terrae pulvere, evigilabunt; alii in vitam aeternam, et alii in approbrium, ut videant semper.*"

A child's voice said, "*De profundis.*"

The grave voice began again, "*Requiem aeternam dona ei, Domine.*"

The child's voice responded, "*Et lux perpetua luceat ei.*"

He heard something like the gentle patter of several drops of rain on the plank that covered him. It was probably the holy water.

He thought, "This will be over soon now. Patience for a little while longer. The priest will take his departure. Fauchelevent will take Mestienne off to drink. I shall be left. Then Fauchelevent will return alone, and I shall get out. That will be the work of a good hour."

The grave voice resumed, "*Requiescat in pace.*"

And the child's voice said, "Amen."

Jean Valjean strained his ears, and heard something like retreating footsteps.

"There, they are going now," thought he. "I am alone."

All at once, he heard over his head a sound that seemed to him to be a clap of thunder.

It was a shovelful of earth falling on the coffin.

A second shovelful fell.

One of the holes through which he breathed had just been stopped up.

A third shovelful of earth fell.

Then a fourth.

There are things which are too strong for the strongest man. Jean Valjean lost consciousness.

CHAPTER VII—IN WHICH WILL BE FOUND THE ORIGIN OF THE SAYING: DON'T LOSE THE CARD

This is what had taken place above the coffin in which lay Jean Valjean.

When the hearse had driven off, when the priest and the choir boy had entered the carriage again and taken their departure, Fauchelevent, who had not taken his eyes from the grave digger, saw the latter bend over and grasp his shovel, which was sticking upright in the heap of dirt.

Then Fauchelevent took a supreme resolve.

He placed himself between the grave and the grave digger, crossed his arms and said, "I am the one to pay!"

The grave digger stared at him in amazement, and replied, "What's that, peasant?"

Fauchelevent repeated, "I am the one who pays!"

"What?"

"For the wine."

"What wine?"

"That Argenteuil wine."

"Where is the Argenteuil?"

"At the Bon Coing."

"Go to the devil!" said the grave digger.

And he flung a shovelful of earth on the coffin.

The coffin gave back a hollow sound. Fauchelevent felt himself stagger and on the point of falling headlong into the grave himself. He shouted in a voice in which the strangling sound of the death rattle began to mingle, "Comrade! Before the Bon Coing is shut!"

The grave digger took some more earth on his shovel. Fauchelevent continued.

"I will pay."

And he seized the man's arm.

"Listen to me, comrade. I am the convent grave digger, I have come to help you. It is a business that can be performed at night. Let us begin, then, by going for a drink."

And as he spoke, and clung to this desperate insistence, this melancholy reflection occurred to him, "And if he drinks, will he get drunk?"

"Provincial," said the man, "if you positively insist upon it, I consent. We will drink. After work, never before."

And he flourished his shovel briskly. Fauchelevent held him back.

"It is Argenteuil wine, at six."

"Oh, come," said the grave digger, "you are a bell-ringer. Ding-dong, ding-dong, that's all you know how to say. Go hang yourself."

And he threw in a second shovelful.

Fauchelevent had reached a point where he no longer knew what he was saying.

"Come along and drink," he cried, "since it is I who pays the bill."

"When we have put the child to bed," said the grave digger.

He flung in a third shovelful.

Then he thrust his shovel into the earth and added, "It's cold tonight, you see, and the corpse would shriek out after us if we were to plant her there without a coverlet."

At that moment, as he loaded his shovel, the grave digger bent over, and the pocket of his waistcoat gaped. Fauchelevent's wild gaze fell mechanically into that pocket, and there it stopped.

The sun was not yet hidden behind the horizon; there was still light enough to enable him to distinguish something white at the bottom of that yawning pocket.

The sum total of lightning that the eye of a Picard peasant can contain, traversed Fauchelevent's pupils. An idea had just occurred to him.

He thrust his hand into the pocket from behind, without the grave digger, who was wholly absorbed in his shovelful of earth, observing it, and pulled out the white object that lay at the bottom of it.

The man sent a fourth shovelful tumbling into the grave.

Just as he turned around to get the fifth, Fauchelevent looked calmly at him and said, "By the way, you new man, have you your card?"

The grave digger paused.

"What card?"

"The sun is on the point of setting."

"That's good, it is going to put on its nightcap."

"The gate of the cemetery will close immediately."

"Well, what then?"

"Have you your card?"

"Ah! My card?" said the grave digger.

And he fumbled in his pocket.

Having searched one pocket, he proceeded to search the other. He passed on to his fobs, explored the first, returned to the second.

"Why, no," said he, "I have not my card. I must have forgotten it."

"Fifteen francs fine," said Fauchelevent.

The grave digger turned green. Green is the pallor of livid people.

"Ah! *Jesus-mon-Dieu-bancroche-a-bas-la-lune!*"* he exclaimed. "Fifteen francs fine!"

---

* Jesus-my-God-bandy leg. Down with the moon!

"Three pieces of a hundred sous," said Fauchelevent.

The grave digger dropped his shovel.

Fauchelevent's turn had come.

"Ah, come now, conscript," said Fauchelevent, "none of this despair. There is no question of committing suicide and benefiting the grave. Fifteen francs is fifteen francs, and besides, you may not be able to pay it. I am an old hand, you are a new one. I know all the ropes and the devices. I will give you some friendly advice. One thing is clear, the sun is on the point of setting, it is touching the dome now, the cemetery will be closed in five minutes more."

"That is true," replied the man.

"Five minutes more and you will not have time to fill the grave, it is as hollow as the devil, this grave, and to reach the gate in season to pass it before it is shut."

"That is true."

"In that case, a fine of fifteen francs."

"Fifteen francs."

"But you have time. Where do you live?"

"A couple of steps from the barrier, a quarter of an hour from here. No. 87 Rue de Vaugirard."

"You have just time to get out by taking to your heels at your best speed."

"That is exactly so."

"Once outside the gate, you gallop home, you get your card, you return, the cemetery porter admits you. As you have your card, there will be nothing to pay. And you will bury your corpse. I'll watch it for you in the meantime, so that it shall not run away."

"I am indebted to you for my life, peasant."

"Decamp!" said Fauchelevent.

The grave digger, overwhelmed with gratitude, shook his hand and set off on a run.

When the man had disappeared in the thicket, Fauchelevent listened until he heard his footsteps die away in the distance, then he leaned over the grave, and said in a low tone, "Father Madeleine!"

There was no reply.

Fauchelevent was seized with a shudder. He tumbled rather than climbed into the grave, flung himself on the head of the coffin and cried, "Are you there?"

Silence in the coffin.

Fauchelevent, hardly able to draw his breath for trembling, seized his cold chisel and his hammer, and pried up the coffin lid.

Jean Valjean's face appeared in the twilight; it was pale and his eyes were closed.

Fauchelevent's hair rose upright on his head, he sprang to his feet, then fell back against the side of the grave, ready to swoon on the coffin. He stared at Jean Valjean.

Jean Valjean lay there pallid and motionless.

Fauchelevent murmured in a voice as faint as a sigh, "He is dead!"

And, drawing himself up, and folding his arms with such violence that his clenched fists came in contact with his shoulders, he cried, "And this is the way I save his life!"

Then the poor man fell to sobbing. He soliloquized the while, for it is an error to suppose that the soliloquy is unnatural. Powerful emotion often talks aloud.

"It is Father Mestienne's fault. Why did that fool die? What need was there for him to give up the ghost at the very moment when no one was expecting it? It is he who has killed M. Madeleine. Father Madeleine! He is in the coffin. It is quite handy. All is over. Now, is there any sense in these things? Ah! My God! He is dead! Well! And his little girl, what am I to do with her? What will the fruit seller say? The idea of its being possible for a man like that to die like this! When I think how he put himself under that cart! Father Madeleine! Father Madeleine! Pardine! He was suffocated, I said so. He wouldn't believe me. Well! Here's a pretty trick to play! He is dead, that good man, the very best man out of all the good God's good folks! And his little girl! Ah! In the first place, I won't go back there myself. I shall stay here. After having done such a thing as that! What's the use of being two old men, if we are two old fools! But, in the first place, how did he manage to enter the convent? That was the beginning of it all. One should not do such things. Father Madeleine! Father Madeleine! Father Madeleine! Madeleine! Monsieur Madeleine! Monsieur le Maire! He does not hear me. Now get out of this scrape if you can!"

And he tore his hair.

A grating sound became audible through the trees in the distance. It was the cemetery gate closing.

Fauchelevent bent over Jean Valjean, and all at once he bounded back and recoiled so far as the limits of a grave permit.

Jean Valjean's eyes were open and gazing at him.

To see a corpse is alarming, to behold a resurrection is almost as much so. Fauchelevent became like stone, pale, haggard, overwhelmed by all these excesses of emotion, not knowing whether he had to do with a living man or a dead one, and staring at Jean Valjean, who was gazing at him.

"I fell asleep," said Jean Valjean.

And he raised himself to a sitting posture.

Fauchelevent fell on his knees.

"Just, good Virgin! How you frightened me!"

Then he sprang to his feet and cried, "Thanks, Father Madeleine!"

Jean Valjean had merely fainted. The fresh air had revived him.

Joy is the ebb of terror. Fauchelevent found almost as much difficulty in recovering himself as Jean Valjean had.

"So you are not dead! Oh! How wise you are! I called you so much that you came back. When I saw your eyes shut, I said, 'Good! There he is, stifled,' I should have gone raving mad, mad enough for a straitjacket. They would have put me in Bicêtre. What do you suppose I should have done if you had been dead? And your little girl? There's that fruit seller, she would never have understood it! The child is thrust into your arms, and then—the grandfather is dead! What a story! Good saints of paradise, what a tale! Ah! You are alive, that's the best of it!"

"I am cold," said Jean Valjean.

This remark recalled Fauchelevent thoroughly to reality, and there was pressing need of it. The souls of these two men were troubled even when they had recovered themselves, although they did not realize it, and there was about them something uncanny, which was the sinister bewilderment inspired by the place.

"Let us get out of here quickly," exclaimed Fauchelevent.

He fumbled in his pocket, and pulled out a gourd with which he had provided himself.

"But first, take a drop," said he.

The flask finished what the fresh air had begun, Jean Valjean swallowed a mouthful of brandy, and regained full possession of his faculties.

He got out of the coffin, and helped Fauchelevent to nail on the lid again.

Three minutes later they were out of the grave.

Moreover, Fauchelevent was perfectly composed. He took his time. The cemetery was closed. The arrival of the grave digger Gribier was not to be apprehended. That "conscript" was at home busily engaged in looking for his card, and at some difficulty in finding it in his lodgings, since it was in Fauchelevent's pocket. Without a card, he could not get back into the cemetery.

Fauchelevent took the shovel, and Jean Valjean the pickax, and together they buried the empty coffin.

When the grave was full, Fauchelevent said to Jean Valjean, "Let us go. I will keep the shovel; do you carry off the mattock."

Night was falling.

Jean Valjean experienced some difficulty in moving and in walking. He had stiffened himself in that coffin, and had become a little like a corpse. The rigidity of death had seized upon him between those four planks. He had, in a manner, to thaw out, from the tomb.

"You are benumbed," said Fauchelevent. "It is a pity that I have a game leg, for otherwise we might step out briskly."

"Bah!" replied Jean Valjean, "Four paces will put life into my legs once more."

They set off by the alleys through which the hearse had passed. On arriving before the closed gate and the porter's pavilion Fauchelevent, who held the grave digger's card in his hand, dropped it into the box, the porter pulled the rope, the gate opened, and they went out.

"How well everything is going!" said Fauchelevent. "What a capital idea that was of yours, Father Madeleine!"

They passed the Vaugirard barrier in the simplest manner in the world. In the neighborhood of the cemetery, a shovel and pick are equal to two passports.

The Rue Vaugirard was deserted.

"Father Madeleine," said Fauchelevent as they went along, and raising his eyes to the houses, "Your eyes are better than mine. Show me No. 87."

"Here it is," said Jean Valjean.

"There is no one in the street," said Fauchelevent. "Give me your mattock and wait a couple of minutes for me."

Fauchelevent entered No. 87, ascended to the very top, guided by the instinct that always leads the poor man to the garret, and knocked in the dark, at the door of an attic.

A voice replied, "Come in."

It was Gribier's voice.

Fauchelevent opened the door. The grave digger's dwelling was, like all such wretched habitations, an unfurnished and encumbered garret. A packing case—a coffin, perhaps—took the place of a commode, a butterpot served for a drinking fountain, a straw mattress served for a bed, the floor served instead of tables and chairs. In a corner, on a tattered fragment that had been a piece of an old carpet, a thin woman and a number of children were piled in a heap. The hole of this poverty-stricken interior bore traces of having been overturned. One would have said that there had been an earthquake "for one." The covers were displaced, the rags scattered about, the jug broken, the mother had been crying, the children had probably been beaten; traces of a vigorous and ill-tempered search. It was plain that the grave digger had made a desperate search for his card, and had made everybody in the garret, from the jug to his wife, responsible for its loss. He wore an air of desperation.

But Fauchelevent was in too great a hurry to terminate this adventure to take any notice of this sad side of his success.

He entered and said, "I have brought you back your shovel and pick."

Gribier gazed at him in stupefaction.

"Is it you, peasant?"

"And tomorrow morning you will find your card with the porter of the cemetery."

And he laid the shovel and mattock on the floor.

"What is the meaning of this?" demanded Gribier.

"The meaning of it is, that you dropped your card out of your pocket, that I found it on the ground after you were gone, that I have buried the corpse, that I have filled the grave, that I have done your work, that the porter will return your card to you, and that you will not have to pay fifteen francs. There you have it, conscript."

"Thanks, villager!" exclaimed Gribier, radiant. "The next time I will pay for the drinks."

CHAPTER VIII—A SUCCESSFUL INTERROGATORY

An hour later, in the darkness of night, two men and a child presented themselves at No. 62 Rue Petit-Picpus. The elder of the men lifted the knocker and rapped.

They were Fauchelevent, Jean Valjean, and Cosette.

The two old men had gone to fetch Cosette from the fruiterer's in the Rue du Chemin-Vert, where Fauchelevent had deposited her on the preceding day. Cosette had passed these twenty-four hours trembling silently and understanding nothing. She trembled to such a degree that she wept. She had neither eaten nor slept. The worthy fruit seller had plied her with a hundred questions, without obtaining any other reply than a melancholy and unvarying gaze. Cosette had betrayed nothing of what she had seen and heard during the last two days. She divined that they were passing through a crisis. She wa deeply conscious that it was necessary to "be good." Who has not experience the sovereign power of those two words, pronounced with a certain accent i the ear of a terrified little being: Say nothing! Fear is mute. Moreover, no on guards a secret like a child.

But when, at the expiration of these lugubrious twenty-four hours, sh beheld Jean Valjean again, she gave vent to such a cry of joy that any thoughtfu person who had chanced to hear that cry, would have guessed that it issue from an abyss.

Fauchelevent belonged to the convent and knew the passwords. All th doors opened.

Thus was solved the double and alarming problem of how to get out an how to get in.

The porter, who had received his instructions, opened the little servant' door that connected the courtyard with the garden, and which could still b seen from the street twenty years ago, in the wall at the bottom of the court which faced the carriage entrance.

The porter admitted all three of them through this door, and from tha point they reached the inner, reserved parlor where Fauchelevent, on th preceding day, had received his orders from the prioress.

The prioress, rosary in hand, was waiting for them. A vocal mother, wit her veil lowered, stood beside her.

A discreet candle lighted, one might almost say, made a show of lightin the parlor.

The prioress passed Jean Valjean in review. There is nothing that examine like a downcast eye.

Then she questioned him, "You are the brother?"

"Yes, reverend Mother," replied Fauchelevent.

"What is your name?"

Fauchelevent replied, "Ultime Fauchelevent."

He really had had a brother named Ultime, who was dead.

"Where do you come from?"

Fauchelevent replied, "From Picquigny, near Amiens."

"What is your age?"

Fauchelevent replied, "Fifty."

"What is your profession?"

Fauchelevent replied, "Gardener."

"Are you a good Christian?"

Fauchelevent replied, "Everyone is in the family."

"Is this your little girl?"

Fauchelevent replied, "Yes, reverend Mother."

"You are her father?"

Fauchelevent replied, "Her grandfather."

The vocal mother said to the prioress in a low voice "He answers well."

Jean Valjean had not uttered a single word.

The prioress looked attentively at Cosette, and said half aloud to the vocal mother, "She will grow up ugly."

The two mothers consulted for a few moments in very low tones in the corner of the parlor, then the prioress turned around and said, "Father Fauvent, you will get another kneecap with a bell. Two will be required now."

On the following day, therefore, two bells were audible in the garden, and the nuns could not resist the temptation to raise the corner of their veils. At the extreme end of the garden, under the trees, two men, Fauvent and another man, were visible as they dug side by side. An enormous event. Their silence was broken to the extent of saying to each other, "He is an assistant gardener."

The vocal mothers added, "He is a brother of Father Fauvent."

Jean Valjean was, in fact, regularly installed; he had his belled kneecap; henceforth he was official. His name was Ultime Fauchelevent.

The most powerful determining cause of his admission had been the prioress's observation upon Cosette: "She will grow up ugly."

The prioress, that pronounced prognosticator, immediately took a fancy to Cosette and gave her a place in the school as a charity pupil.

There is nothing that is not strictly logical about this.

It is in vain that mirrors are banished from the convent, women are conscious of their faces; now, girls who are conscious of their beauty do not easily become nuns; the vocation being voluntary in inverse proportion to their good looks, more is to be hoped from the ugly than from the pretty. Hence a lively taste for plain girls.

The whole of this adventure increased the importance of good, old Fauchelevent; he won a triple success; in the eyes of Jean Valjean, whom he had saved and sheltered; in those of grave digger Gribier, who said to himself, "He spared me that fine"; with the convent, which, being enabled, thanks to him, to retain the coffin of Mother Crucifixion under the altar, eluded Caesar and satisfied God. There was a coffin containing a body in the Petit-Picpus, and a coffin without a body in the Vaugirard cemetery, public order had no doubt been deeply disturbed thereby, but no one was aware of it.

As for the convent, its gratitude to Fauchelevent was very great. Fauchelevent became the best of servitors and the most precious of gardeners. Upon the occasion of the archbishop's next visit, the prioress recounted the affair to his Grace, making something of a confession at the same time, and yet boasting of her deed. On leaving the convent, the archbishop mentioned it with approval, and in a whisper to M. de Latil, Monsieur's confessor, afterward Archbishop of Reims and Cardinal. This admiration for Fauchelevent became widespread, for it made its way to Rome. We have seen a note addressed by the then reigning Pope, Leo XII, to one of his relatives, a Monsignor in the Nuncio's establishment in Paris, and bearing, like himself, the name of Della Genga; it contained these lines: "It appears that there is in a convent in Paris an excellent gardener, who is also a holy man, named Fauvent." Nothing of this triumph reached Fauchelevent in his hut; he went on grafting, weeding, and covering up his melon beds, without in the least suspecting his excellencie and his sanctity. Neither did he suspect his glory, any more than a Durham or Surrey bull whose portrait is published in the *London Illustrated News*, with this inscription: "Bull that carried off the prize at the Cattle Show."

CHAPTER IX—CLOISTERED

Cosette continued to hold her tongue in the convent.

It was quite natural that Cosette should think herself Jean Valjean's daughter. Moreover, as she knew nothing, she could say nothing, and then, she would not have said anything in any case. As we have just observed, nothing trains children to silence like unhappiness. Cosette had suffered so much that she feared everything, even to speak or to breathe. A single word had so often brought down an avalanche upon her. She had hardly begun to regain her confidence since she had been with Jean Valjean. She speedily became accustomed to the convent. Only she regretted Catherine, but she dared not say so. Once, however, she did say to Jean Valjean, "Father, if I had known, I would have brought her away with me."

Cosette had been obliged, on becoming a scholar in the convent, to don the garb of the pupils of the house. Jean Valjean succeeded in getting them to restore to him the garments that she laid aside. This was the same mourning suit that he had made her put on when she had quitted the Thenardiers' inn. It was not very threadbare even now. Jean Valjean locked up these garments, plus the stockings and the shoes, with a quantity of camphor and all the aromatics n which convents abound, in a little valise which he found means of procuring. He set this valise on a chair near his bed, and he always carried the key about his person. "Father," Cosette asked him one day, "what is there in that box that smells so good?"

Father Fauchelevent received other recompense for his good action, in addition to the glory, which we just mentioned, and of which he knew nothing; in the first place it made him happy; next, he had much less work, since it was shared. Lastly, as he was very fond of snuff, he found the presence of M. Madeleine an advantage, in that he used three times as much as he had done previously, and that in an infinitely more luxurious manner, seeing that M. Madeleine paid for it.

The nuns did not adopt the name of Ultime; they called Jean Valjean the other Fauvent.

If these holy women had possessed anything of Javert's glance, they would eventually have noticed that when there was any errand to be done outside in the behalf of the garden, it was always the elder Fauchelevent, the old, the infirm, the lame man, who went, and never the other; but whether it is that eyes constantly fixed on God know not how to spy, or whether they were, by preference, occupied in keeping watch on each other, they paid no heed to this.

Moreover, it was well for Jean Valjean that he kept close and did not stir out. Javert watched the quarter for more than a month.

This convent was for Jean Valjean like an island surrounded by gulfs. Henceforth, those four walls constituted his world. He saw enough of the sky here to enable him to preserve his serenity, and Cosette enough to remain happy.

A very sweet life began for him.

He inhabited the old hut at the end of the garden, in company with Fauchelevent. This hovel, built of old rubbish, which was still in existence in 1845, was composed, as the reader already knows, of three chambers, all of which were utterly bare and had nothing beyond the walls. The principal one had been given up, by force, for Jean Valjean had opposed it in vain, to M. Madeleine, by Father Fauchelevent. The walls of this chamber had for ornament, in addition to the two nails whereon to hang the kneecap and the basket, a Royalist banknote of '93, applied to the wall over the mantel, and of which the following is an exact facsimile:

This specimen of Vendean paper money had been nailed to the wall by the preceding gardener, an old Chouan, who had died in the convent, and whose place Fauchelevent had taken.

Jean Valjean worked in the garden every day and made himself very useful. He had formerly been a pruner of trees, and he gladly found himself a gardener once more. It will be remembered that he knew all sorts of secrets and receipts for agriculture. He turned these to advantage. Almost all the trees in the orchard were ungrafted, and wild. He budded them and made them produce excellent fruit.

Cosette had permission to pass an hour with him every day. As the sisters were melancholy and he was kind, the child made comparisons and adored him. At the appointed hour she flew to the hut. When she entered the lowly cabin she filled it with paradise. Jean Valjean blossomed out and felt his happiness increase with the happiness that he afforded Cosette. The joy we inspire has this charming property, that, far from growing meager, like all reflections, it returns to us more radiant than ever. At recreation hours, Jean Valjean watched her running and playing in the distance, and he distinguished her laugh from that of the rest.

For Cosette laughed now.

Cosette's face had even undergone a change, to a certain extent. The gloom had disappeared from it. A smile is the same as sunshine; it banishes winter from the human countenance.

Recreation over, when Cosette went into the house again, Jean Valjean gazed at the windows of her classroom, and at night he rose to look at the windows of her dormitory.

God has his own ways, moreover; the convent contributed, like Cosette to uphold and complete the Bishop's work in Jean Valjean. It is certain that virtue adjoins pride on one side. A bridge built by the devil exists there. Jean Valjean had been, unconsciously, perhaps, tolerably near that side and that bridge, when Providence cast his lot in the convent of the Petit-Picpus; so long as he had compared himself only to the Bishop, he had regarded himself as unworthy and had remained humble; but for some time past he had been comparing himself to men in general, and pride was beginning to spring up. Who knows? He might have ended by returning very gradually to hatred.

The convent stopped him on that downward path.

This was the second place of captivity that he had seen. In his youth, in what had been for him the beginning of his life, and later on, quite recently again, he had beheld another, a frightful place, a terrible place, whose severities had always appeared to him the iniquity of justice, and the crime of the law. Now, after the galleys, he saw the cloister; and when he meditated how he had formed a part of the galleys, and that he now, so to speak, was a spectator of the cloister, he confronted the two in his own mind with anxiety.

Sometimes he crossed his arms and leaned on his hoe, and slowly descended the endless spirals of reverie.

He recalled his former companions: how wretched they were; they rose at dawn, and toiled until night; hardly were they permitted to sleep; they lay on camp beds, where nothing was tolerated but mattresses two inches thick, in rooms that were heated only in the very harshest months of the year; they were clothed in frightful red blouses; they were allowed, as a great favor, linen trousers in the hottest weather, and a woolen carter's blouse on their backs when it was very cold; they drank no wine, and ate no meat, except when they went on "fatigue duty." They lived nameless, designated only by numbers, and converted, after a manner, into ciphers themselves, with downcast eyes, with lowered voices, with shorn heads, beneath the cudgel, and in disgrace.

Then his mind reverted to the beings whom he had under his eyes.

These beings also lived with shorn heads, with downcast eyes, with lowered voices, not in disgrace, but amid the scoffs of the world, not with their backs bruised with the cudgel, but with their shoulders lacerated with their discipline. Their names, also, had vanished from among men; they no longer existed except under austere appellations. They never ate meat and they never drank wine; they often remained until evening without food; they were attired, not in a red blouse, but in a black shroud, of woolen, which was heavy in summer and thin in winter, without the power to add or subtract anything from it; without having even, according to the season, the resource of the linen garment or the woolen cloak; and for six months in the year they wore serge chemises, which gave them fever. They dwelled, not in rooms warmed only during rigorous cold, but in cells where no fire was ever lighted; they slept, not on mattresses two inches thick, but on straw. And finally, they were not even allowed their sleep; every night, after a day of toil, they were obliged, in the weariness of their first slumber, at the moment when they were falling sound asleep and beginning to get warm, to rouse themselves, to rise and to go and pray in an ice-cold and gloomy chapel, with their knees on the stones.

On certain days each of these beings in turn had to remain for twelve successive hours in a kneeling posture, or prostrate, with face upon the pavement, and arms outstretched in the form of a cross.

The others were men; these were women.

What had those men done? They had stolen, violated, pillaged, murdered, assassinated. They were bandits, counterfeiters, poisoners, incendiaries, murderers, parricides. What had these women done? They had done nothing whatever.

On the one hand, highway robbery, fraud, deceit, violence, sensuality, homicide, all sorts of sacrilege, every variety of crime; on the other, one thing only, innocence.

Perfect innocence, almost caught up into heaven in a mysterious assumption, attached to the earth by virtue, already possessing something of heaven through holiness.

On the one hand, confidences over crimes, which are exchanged in whispers; on the other, the confession of faults made aloud. And what crimes! And what faults!

On the one hand, miasma; on the other, an ineffable perfume. On the one hand, a moral pest, guarded from sight, penned up under the range of cannon, and literally devouring its plague-stricken victims; on the other, the chaste flame of all souls on the same hearth. There, darkness; here, the shadow; but a shadow filled with gleams of light, and of gleams full of radiance.

Two strongholds of slavery; but in the first, deliverance possible, a legal limit always in sight, and then, escape. In the second, perpetuity; the sole hope, at the distant extremity of the future, that faint light of liberty, which men call death.

In the first, men are bound only with chains; in the other, chained by faith.

What flowed from the first? An immense curse, the gnashing of teeth, hatred, desperate viciousness, a cry of rage against human society, a sarcasm against heaven.

What results flowed from the second? Blessings and love.

And in these two places, so similar yet so unlike, these two species of beings who were so very unlike, were undergoing the same work, expiation.

Jean Valjean understood thoroughly the expiation of the former; that personal expiation, the expiation for one's self. But he did not understand that of these last, that of creatures without reproach and without stain, and he trembled as he asked himself: The expiation of what? What expiation?

A voice within his conscience replied, "The most divine of human generosities, the expiation for others."

Here all personal theory is withheld; we are only the narrator; we place ourselves at Jean Valjean's point of view, and we translate his impressions.

Before his eyes he had the sublime summit of abnegation, the highest possible pitch of virtue; the innocence that pardons men their faults, and which expiates in their stead; servitude submitted to, torture accepted, punishment claimed by souls which have not sinned, for the sake of sparing it to souls which have fallen; the love of humanity swallowed up in the love of God, but even there preserving its distinct and mediatorial character; sweet and feeble beings possessing the misery of those who are punished and the smile of those who are recompensed.

And he remembered that he had dared to murmur!

Often, in the middle of the night, he rose to listen to the grateful song of those innocent creatures weighed down with severities, and the blood ran cold in his veins at the thought that those who were justly chastised raised their voices heavenward only in blasphemy, and that he, wretch that he was, had shaken his fist at God.

There was one striking thing that caused him to meditate deeply, like a warning whisper from Providence itself: the scaling of that wall, the passing of those barriers, the adventure accepted even at the risk of death, the painful and difficult ascent, all those efforts even, which he had made to escape from that other place of expiation, he had made in order to gain entrance into this one. Was this a symbol of his destiny? This house was a prison likewise and bore a melancholy resemblance to that other one from which he had fled, and yet he had never conceived an idea of anything similar.

Again he beheld gratings, bolts, iron bars—to guard whom? Angels.

These lofty walls that he had seen around tigers, he now beheld once more around lambs.

This was a place of expiation, and not of punishment; and yet, it was still more austere, more gloomy, and more pitiless than the other.

These virgins were even more heavily burdened than the convicts. A cold, harsh wind, that wind which had chilled his youth, traversed the barred and padlocked grating of the vultures; a still harsher and more biting breeze blew in the cage of these doves.

Why?

When he thought on these things, all that was within him was lost in amazement before this mystery of sublimity.

In these meditations, his pride vanished. He scrutinized his own heart in all manner of ways; he felt his pettiness, and many a time he wept. All that had entered into his life for the last six months had led him back toward the Bishop's holy injunctions; Cosette through love, the convent through humility.

Sometimes at eventide, in the twilight, at an hour when the garden was deserted, he could be seen on his knees in the middle of the walk, which skirted the chapel, in front of the window through which he had gazed on the night of his arrival, and turned toward the spot where, as he knew, the sister was making reparation, prostrated in prayer. Thus he prayed as he knelt before the sister.

It seemed as though he dared not kneel directly before God.

Everything that surrounded him, that peaceful garden, those fragrant flowers, those children who uttered joyous cries, those grave and simple women, that silent cloister, slowly permeated him, and little by little, his soul became compounded of silence like the cloister, of perfume like the flowers, of simplicity like the women, of joy like the children. And then he reflected that these had been two houses of God that had received him in succession at two critical moments in his life: the first, when all doors were closed and when human society rejected him; the second, at a moment when human society had again set out in pursuit of him, and when the galleys were again yawning; and that, had it not been for the first, he should have relapsed into crime, and had it not been for the second, into torment.

His whole heart melted in gratitude, and he loved more and more.

Many years passed in this manner; Cosette was growing up.

VOLUME III: MARIUS

BOOK FIRST: PARIS STUDIED IN ITS ATOM

CHAPTER I—PARVULUS

Paris has a child, and the forest has a bird; the bird is called the sparrow; the child is called the gamin.

Couple these two ideas, which contain the one all the furnace, the other all the dawn; strike these two sparks together, Paris, childhood; there leaps out from them a little being. *Homuncio*,* Plautus would say.

This little being is joyous. He has not food every day, and he goes to the play every evening, if he sees good. He has no shirt on his body, no shoes on his feet, no roof over his head; he is like the flies of heaven, who have none of these things. He is from seven to thirteen years of age, he lives in bands, roams the streets, lodges in the open air, wears an old pair of trousers of his father's, which descend below his heels, an old hat of some other father, which descends below his ears, a single suspender of yellow listing; he runs, lies in wait, rummages about, wastes time, blackens pipes, swears like a convict, haunts the wine shop, knows thieves, calls gay women "thou," talks slang, sings obscene songs, and has no evil in his heart. This is because he has in his heart a pearl, innocence; and pearls are not to be dissolved in mud. So long as man is in his childhood, God wills that he shall be innocent.

If one were to ask that enormous city, "What is this?" she would reply, "It is my little one."

---

* a small man

CHAPTER II—SOME OF HIS PARTICULAR CHARACTERISTICS

The gamin—the street Arab—of Paris is the dwarf of the giant.

Let us not exaggerate, this cherub of the gutter sometimes has a shirt, but, in that case, he owns but one; he sometimes has shoes, but then they have no soles; he sometimes has a lodging, and he loves it, for he finds his mother there; but he prefers the street, because there he finds liberty. He has his own games, his own bits of mischief, whose foundation consists of hatred for the bourgeois; his peculiar metaphors: to be dead is to eat dandelions by the root; his own occupations, calling hackney coaches, letting down carriage steps, establishing means of transit between the two sides of a street in heavy rains, which he calls making the bridge of arts, crying discourses pronounced by the authorities in favor of the French people, cleaning out the cracks in the pavement; he has his own coinage, which is composed of all the little morsels of worked copper that are found on the public streets. This curious money, called *loques* (rags, or scraps) has an invariable and well-regulated currency in this little Bohemia of children.

Lastly, he has his own fauna, which he observes attentively in the corners; the lady bird, the death's head plant louse, the daddy longlegs, "the devil," a black insect, which menaces by twisting about its tail armed with two horns. He has his fabulous monster, which has scales under its belly, but is not a lizard, which has pustules on its back, but is not a toad, which inhabits the nooks of old lime kilns and wells that have run dry, which is black, hairy, sticky, which crawls sometimes slowly, sometimes rapidly, which has no cry, but which has a look, and is so terrible that no one has ever beheld it; he calls this monster "the deaf thing." The search for these "deaf things" among the stones is a joy of formidable nature. Another pleasure consists in suddenly prying up a paving stone, and taking a look at the wood lice. Each region of Paris is celebrated for the interesting treasures found there. There are earwigs in the timberyards of the Ursulines, there are millipedes in the Pantheon, there are tadpoles in the ditches of the Champs-de-Mars.

As far as sayings are concerned, this child has as many of them as Talleyrand. He is no less cynical, but he is more honest. He is endowed with a certain indescribable, unexpected joviality; he upsets the composure of the shopkeeper with his wild laughter. He ranges boldly from high comedy to farce.

A funeral passes by. Among those who accompany the dead there is a doctor. "Hey there!" shouts some street Arab, "how long has it been customary for doctors to carry home their own work?"

Another is in a crowd. A grave man, adorned with spectacles and trinkets, turns around indignantly. "You good-for-nothing, you have seized my wife's waist!"

"I, sir? Search me!"

CHAPTER III—HE IS AGREEABLE

In the evening, thanks to a few sous, which he always finds means to procure, the homuncio enters a theater. On crossing that magic threshold, he becomes transfigured; he was the street Arab, he becomes the *titi.** Theaters are a sort of ship turned upside down with the keel in the air. It is in that keel that the titi huddle together. The titi is to the gamin what the moth is to the larva; the same being endowed with wings and soaring. It suffices for him to be there, with his radiance of happiness, with his power of enthusiasm and joy, with his hand-clapping, which resembles a clapping of wings, to confer on that narrow, dark, fetid, sordid, unhealthy, hideous, abominable keel, the name of Paradise.

Bestow on an individual the useless and deprive him of the necessary, and you have the gamin.

The gamin is not devoid of literary intuition. His tendency, and we say it with the proper amount of regret, would not constitute classic taste. He is not very academic by nature. Thus, to give an example, the popularity of Mademoiselle Mars among that little audience of stormy children was seasoned with a touch of irony. The gamin called her Mademoiselle Muche—"hide yourself."

This being bawls and scoffs and ridicules and fights, has rags like a baby and tatters like a philosopher, fishes in the sewer, hunts in the cesspool, extracts mirth from foulness, whips up the squares with his wit, grins and bites, whistles and sings, shouts and shrieks, tempers Alleluia with Matantur-lurette, chants every rhythm from the De Profundis to the Jack-pudding, finds without seeking, knows what he is ignorant of, is a Spartan to the point of thieving, is mad to wisdom, is lyrical to filth, would crouch down on Olympus, wallows

---

* A slang phrase that refers to children in Paris.

in the dunghill and emerges from it covered with stars. The gamin of Paris is Rabelais in this youth.

He is not content with his trousers unless they have a watch pocket.

He is not easily astonished, he is still less easily terrified, he makes songs on superstitions, he takes the wind out of exaggerations, he twits mysteries, he thrusts out his tongue at ghosts, he takes the poetry out of stilted things, he introduces caricature into epic extravaganzas. It is not that he is prosaic; far from that; but he replaces the solemn vision by the farcical phantasmagoria. If Adamastor were to appear to him, the street Arab would say, "Hi there! The bugaboo!"

CHAPTER IV—HE MAY BE OF USE

Paris begins with the lounger and ends with the street Arab, two beings of which no other city is capable; the passive acceptance, which contents itself with gazing, and the inexhaustible initiative; Prudhomme and Fouillou. Paris alone has this in its natural history. The whole of the monarchy is contained in the lounger; the whole of anarchy in the gamin.

This pale child of the Parisian foubourgs' lives and develops, makes connections, "grows supple" in suffering, in the presence of social realities and of human things, a thoughtful witness. He thinks himself heedless; and he is not. He looks and is on the verge of laughter; he is on the verge of something else also. Whoever you may be, if your name is Prejudice, Abuse, Ignorance, Oppression, Iniquity, Despotism, Injustice, Fanaticism, Tyranny, beware of the gaping gamin.

The little fellow will grow up.

Of what clay is he made? Of the first mud that comes to hand. A handful of dirt, a breath, and behold Adam. It suffices for a God to pass by. A God has always passed over the street Arab. Fortune labors at this tiny being. By the word "fortune" we mean chance, to some extent. That pygmy kneaded out of common earth, ignorant, unlettered, giddy, vulgar, low. Will that become an Ionian or a Boeotian? Wait, *currit rota*, the Spirit of Paris, that demon that creates the children of chance and the men of destiny, reversing the process of the Latin potter, makes of a jug an amphora.

---

* suburbs

CHAPTER V—HIS FRONTIERS

The gamin loves the city, he also loves solitude, since he has something of the sage in him. *Urbis amator*, like Fuscus; *ruris amator*, like Flaccus.

To roam thoughtfully about, that is to say, to lounge, is a fine employment of time in the eyes of the philosopher; particularly in that rather illegitimate species of campaign, which is tolerably ugly but odd and composed of two natures, which surrounds certain great cities, notably Paris. To study the foubourgs is to study the amphibious animal. End of the trees, beginning of the roofs; end of the grass, beginning of the pavements; end of the furrows, beginning of the shops, end of the wheel-ruts, beginning of the passions; end of the divine murmur, beginning of the human uproar; hence an extraordinary interest.

Hence, in these not very attractive places, indelibly stamped by the passing stroller with the epithet: melancholy, the apparently objectless promenades of the dreamer.

He who writes these lines has long been a prowler about the barriers of Paris, and it is for him a source of profound souvenirs. That close-shaven turf, those pebbly paths, that chalk, those pools, those harsh monotonies of waste and fallow lands, the plants of early market-garden suddenly springing into sight in a bottom, that mixture of the savage and the citizen, those vast desert nooks where the garrison drums practice noisily, and produce a sort of lisping of battle, those hermits by day and cutthroats by night, that clumsy mill that turns in the wind, the hoisting-wheels of the quarries, the tea gardens at the corners of the cemeteries; the mysterious charm of great, somber walls squarely intersecting immense, vague stretches of land inundated with sunshine and full of butterflies—all this attracted him.

There is hardly anyone on earth who is not acquainted with those singular spots, the Glaciere, the Cunette, the hideous wall of Grenelle all speckled with balls, Mont-Parnasse, the Fosse-aux-Loups, Aubiers on the bank of the Marne, Mont-Souris, the Tombe-Issoire, the Pierre-Plate de Chatillon, where there is an old, exhausted quarry that no longer serves any purpose except to raise mushrooms, and that is closed, on a level with the ground, by a trapdoor of rotten planks. The campagna of Rome is one idea, the banlieue of Paris is another; to behold nothing but fields, houses, or trees in what a stretch of country offers us, is to remain on the surface; all aspects of things are thoughts of God. The spot where a plain affects its junction with a city is always stamped with a certain piercing melancholy. Nature and humanity both appeal to you at the same time there. Local originalities there make their appearance.

Anyone who, like ourselves, has wandered about in these solitudes contiguous to our faubourgs, which may be designated as the limbos of Paris, has seen here and there, in the most desert spot, at the most unexpected moment, behind a meager hedge, or in the corner of a lugubrious wall, children grouped tumultuously, fetid, muddy, dusty, ragged, disheveled, playing hide-and-seek, and crowned with cornflowers. All of them are little ones who have made their escape from poor families. The outer boulevard is their breathing space; the suburbs belong to them. There they are eternally playing truant. There they innocently sing their repertory of dirty songs. There they are, or rather, there they exist, far from every eye, in the sweet light of May or June, kneeling around a hole in the ground, snapping marbles with their thumbs, quarrelling over half-farthings, irresponsible, volatile, free, and happy; and, no sooner do they catch sight of you than they recollect that they have an industry, and that they must earn their living, and they offer to sell you an old woolen stocking filled with cockchafers, or a bunch of lilacs. These encounters with strange children are one of the charming and at the same time poignant graces of the environs of Paris.

Sometimes there are little girls among the throng of boys—are they their sisters?—who are almost young maidens, thin, feverish, with sunburnt hands, covered with freckles, crowned with poppies and ears of rye, gay, haggard, barefooted. They can be seen devouring cherries among the wheat. In the evening they can be heard laughing. These groups, warmly illuminated by the full glow of midday, or indistinctly seen in the twilight, occupy the thoughtful man for a very long time, and these visions mingle with his dreams.

Paris, center, banlieue, circumference; this constitutes all the earth to those children. They never venture beyond this. They can no more escape from the Parisian atmosphere than fish can escape from the water. For them, nothing exists two leagues beyond the barriers: Ivry, Gentilly, Arcueil, Belleville, Aubervilliers, Menilmontant, Choisy-le-Roi, Billancourt, Mendon, Issy, Vanvre, Sevres, Puteaux, Neuilly, Gennevilliers, Colombes, Romainville, Chatou, Asnieres, Bougival, Nanterre, Enghien, Noisy-le-Sec, Nogent, Gournay, Drancy, Gonesse; the universe ends there.

CHAPTER VI—A BIT OF HISTORY

At the epoch, nearly contemporary by the way, when the action of this book takes place, there was not, as there is today, a policeman at the corner of every street (a benefit that there is no time to discuss here); stray children abounded in Paris. The statistics give an average of two hundred and sixty homeless children picked up annually at that period, by the police patrols, in unenclosed lands, in houses in process of construction, and under the arches of the bridges. One of these nests, which has become famous, produced "the swallows of the bridge of Arcola." This is, moreover, the most disastrous of social symptoms. All crimes of the man begin in the vagabondage of the child.

Let us make an exception in favor of Paris, nevertheless. In a relative measure, and in spite of the souvenir that we have just recalled, the exception is just. While in any other great city the vagabond child is a lost man, while nearly everywhere the child left to itself is, in some sort, sacrificed and abandoned to a kind of fatal immersion in the public vices that devour in him honesty and conscience, the street boy of Paris, we insist on this point, however defaced and injured on the surface, is almost intact on the interior. It is a magnificent thing to put on record, and one that shines forth in the splendid probity of our popular revolutions, that a certain incorruptibility results from the idea that exists in the air of Paris, as salt exists in the water of the ocean. To breathe Paris preserves the soul.

What we have just said takes away nothing of the anguish of heart that one experiences every time one meets one of these children around whom one fancies that he beholds floating the threads of a broken family. In the civilization of the present day, incomplete as it still is, it is not a very abnormal thing to behold these fractured families pouring themselves out into the darkness, not knowing clearly what has become of their children, and allowing their own entrails to fall on the public highway. Hence these obscure destinies. This is called, for this sad thing has given rise to an expression, "to be cast on the pavements of Paris."

Let it be said by the way, that this abandonment of children was not discouraged by the ancient monarchy. A little of Egypt and Bohemia in the lower regions suited the upper spheres, and compassed the aims of the powerful. The hatred of instruction for the children of the people was a dogma. What is the use of "half-lights"? Such was the countersign. Now, the erring child is the corollary of the ignorant child.

Besides this, the monarchy sometimes was in need of children, and in that case it skimmed the streets.

Under Louis XIV, not to go any further back, the king rightly desired to create a fleet. The idea was a good one. But let us consider the means. There can be no fleet, if, beside the sailing ship, that plaything of the winds, and for the purpose of towing it, in case of necessity, there is not the vessel that goes where it pleases, either by means of oars or of steam; the galleys were then to the marine what steamers are today. Therefore, galleys were necessary; but the galley is moved only by the galley slave; hence, galley slaves were required. Colbert had the commissioners of provinces and the parliaments make as many convicts as possible. The magistracy showed a great deal of complaisance in the matter. A man kept his hat on in the presence of a procession—it was a Huguenot attitude; he was sent to the galleys. A child was encountered in the streets; provided that he was fifteen years of age and did not know where he was to sleep, he was sent to the galleys. Grand reign; grand century.

Under Louis XV, children disappeared in Paris; the police carried them off, for what mysterious purpose no one knew. People whispered with terror monstrous conjectures as to the king's baths of purple. Barbier speaks ingenuously of these things. It sometimes happened that the exempts of the guard, when they ran short of children, took those who had fathers. The fathers, in despair, attacked the exempts. In that case, the parliament intervened and had someone hung. Who? The exempts? No, the fathers.

CHAPTER VII—THE GAMIN SHOULD HAVE HIS PLACE IN THE CLASSIFICATIONS OF INDIA

The body of street Arabs in Paris almost constitutes a caste. One might almost say: not everyone who wishes to belong to it can do so.

This word "gamin" was printed for the first time, and reached popular speech through the literary tongue, in 1834. It is in a little work entitled *Claude Gueux* that this word made its appearance. The horror was lively. The word passed into circulation.

The elements that constitute the consideration of the gamins for each other are very various. We have known and associated with one who was greatly respected and vastly admired because he had seen a man fall from the top of the tower of Notre-Dame; another, because he had succeeded in making his way into the rear courtyard where the statues of the dome of the Invalides had been temporarily deposited, and had "prigged" some lead from them; a third, because he had seen a diligence tip over; still another, because he "knew" a soldier who came near putting out the eye of a citizen.

This explains that famous exclamation of a Parisian gamin, a profound epiphonema, which the vulgar herd laughs at without comprehending, *Dieu de Dieu!* What ill luck I do have! To think that I have never yet seen anybody tumble from a fifth-story window! ("I have" pronounced "I'ave" and "fifth" pronounced "fift.")

Surely, this saying of a peasant is a fine one: "Father So-and-So, your wife has died of her malady; why did you not send for the doctor?" "What would you have, Sir, we poor folks die of ourselves." But if the peasant's whole passivity lies in this saying, the whole of the free thinking anarchy of the brat of the faubourgs is, assuredly, contained in this other saying. A man condemned to death is listening to his confessor in the tumbrel. The child of Paris exclaims, "He is talking to his black cap! Oh, the sneak!"

A certain audacity on matters of religion sets off the gamin. To be strong-minded is an important item.

To be present at executions constitutes a duty. He shows himself at the guillotine, and he laughs. He calls it by all sorts of pet names: the End of the Soup, the Growler, the Mother in the Blue (the sky), the Last Mouthful, etc., etc. In order not to lose anything of the affair, he scales the walls, he hoists himself to balconies, he ascends trees, he suspends himself to gratings, he clings fast to chimneys. The gamin is born a tiler as he is born a mariner. A roof inspires him with no more fear than a mast. There is no festival that comes up to an execution on the Place de Greve. Samson and the Abbé Montes are the truly popular names. They hoot at the victim in order to encourage him. They sometimes admire him. Lacenaire, when a gamin, on seeing the hideous Dautin die bravely, uttered these words that contain a future: "I was jealous of him." In the brotherhood of gamins Voltaire is not known, but Papavoine is. "Politicians" are confused with assassins in the same legend. They have a tradition as to everybody's last garment. It is known that Tolleron had a fireman's cap, Avril an otter cap, Losvel a round hat, that old Delaporte was bald and bare-headed, that Castaing was all ruddy and very handsome, that Bories had a romantic small beard, that Jean Martin kept on his suspenders, that Lecouffe and his mother quarreled. "Don't reproach each other for your basket," shouted a gamin to them. Another, in order to get a look at Debacker as he passed, and being too small in the crowd, caught sight of the lantern on the quay and climbed it. A gendarme stationed opposite frowned. "Let me climb up, m'sieu le gendarme," said the gamin. And, to soften the heart of the authorities he added, "I will not fall."

"I don't care if you do," retorted the gendarme.

In the brotherhood of gamins, a memorable accident counts for a great deal. One reaches the height of consideration if one chances to cut one's self very deeply, "to the very bone."

The fist is no mediocre element of respect. One of the things that the gamin is fondest of saying is, "I am fine and strong, come now!" To be left-handed renders you very enviable. A squint is highly esteemed.

CHAPTER VIII—IN WHICH THE READER WILL FIND A CHARMING SAYING OF THE LAST KING

In summer, he metamorphoses himself into a frog; and in the evening, when night is falling, in front of the bridges of Austerlitz and Jena, from the tops of coal wagons, and the washerwomen's boats, he hurls himself headlong into the Seine, and into all possible infractions of the laws of modesty and of the police. Nevertheless the police keep an eye on him, and the result is a highly dramatic situation that once gave rise to a fraternal and memorable cry; that cry that was celebrated about 1830, is a strategic warning from gamin to gamin; it scans like a verse from Homer, with a notation as inexpressible as the eleusiac chant of the Panathenaea, and in it one encounters again the ancient Evohe. Here it is: "Ohe, Titi, oheee! Here comes the bobby, here comes the p'lice, pick up your duds and be off, through the sewer with you!"

Sometimes this gnat—that is what he calls himself—knows how to read; sometimes he knows how to write; he always knows how to daub. He does not hesitate to acquire, but no one knows what mysterious mutual instruction, all the talents that can be of use to the public; from 1815 to 1830, he imitated the cry of the turkey; from 1830 to 1848, he scrawled pears on the walls. One summer evening, when Louis Philippe was returning home on foot, he saw a little fellow, no higher than his knee, perspiring and climbing up to draw a gigantic pear in charcoal on one of the pillars of the gate of Neuilly; the King, with that good nature that came to him from Henry IV, helped the gamin,

finished the pear, and gave the child a louis, saying, "The pear is on that also."*
The gamin loves uproar. A certain state of violence pleases him. He execrates
"the Curés." One day, in the Rue de l'Universite, one of these scamps was
putting his thumb to his nose at the carriage gate of No. 69. "Why are you
doing that at the gate?" a passerby asked.

The boy replied: "There is a Curé there." It was there, in fact, that the
Papal Nuncio lived.

Nevertheless, whatever may be the Voltairianism of the small gamin, if the
occasion to become a chorister presents itself, it is quite possible that he will
accept, and in that case he serves the mass civilly. There are two things to which
he plays Tantalus, and that he always desires without ever attaining them: to
overthrow the government, and to get his trousers sewed up again.

The gamin in his perfect state possesses all the policemen of Paris, and can
always put the name to the face of anyone that he chances to meet. He can tell
them off on the tips of his fingers. He studies their habits, and he has special
notes on each one of them. He reads the souls of the police like an open book.
He will tell you fluently and without flinching, "Such a one is a traitor; such
another is very malicious; such another is great; such another is ridiculous."
(All these words: traitor, malicious, great, ridiculous, have a particular meaning
in his mouth.) That one imagines that he owns the Pont-Neuf, and he prevents
people from walking on the cornice outside the parapet; that other has a mania
for pulling person's ears; etc., etc.

CHAPTER IX—THE OLD SOUL OF GAUL

There was something of that boy in Poquelin, the son of the fish market;
Beaumarchais had something of it. Gaminerie is a shade of the Gallic
spirit. Mingled with good sense, it sometimes adds force to the latter, as alcohol
does to wine. Sometimes it is a defect. Homer repeats himself eternally,
granted; one may say that Voltaire plays the gamin. Camille Desmoulins was
a native of the faubourgs. Championnet, who treated miracles brutally, rose
from the pavements of Paris; he had, when a small lad, inundated the porticos
of Saint-Jean de Beauvais, and of Saint-Etienne du Mont; he had addressed
the shrine of Sainte-Genevieve familiarly to give orders to the phial of Saint
Januarius.

---

* In comics of the period, King Louis XVIII was often portrayed as having a pear-shaped head.

The gamin of Paris is respectful, ironical, and insolent. He has villainous teeth, because he is badly fed and his stomach suffers, and handsome eyes because he has wit. If Jehovah himself were present, he would go hopping up the steps of paradise on one foot. He is strong on boxing. All beliefs are possible to him. He plays in the gutter, and straightens himself up with a revolt, his effrontery persists even in the presence of grapeshot; he was a scapegrace, he is a hero; like the little Theban, he shakes the skin from the lion; Barra the drummer boy was a gamin of Paris; he shouts: "Forward!" as the horse of scripture says, "Vah!" and in a moment he has passed from the small brat to the giant.

This child of the puddle is also the child of the ideal. Measure that spread of wings that reaches from Moliere to Barra.

To sum up the whole, and in one word, the gamin is a being who amuses himself, because he is unhappy.

CHAPTER X—ECCE PARIS, ECCE HOMO

To sum it all up once more, the Paris gamin of today, like the graeculus of Rome in days gone by, is the infant populace with the wrinkle of the old world on his brow.

The gamin is a grace to the nation, and at the same time a disease; a disease that must be cured, how? By light.

Light renders healthy.

Light kindles.

All generous social irradiations spring from science, letters, arts, education. Make men, make men. Give them light that they may warm you. Sooner or later the splendid question of universal education will present itself with the irresistible authority of the absolute truth; and then, those who govern under the superintendence of the French idea will have to make this choice; the children of France or the gamins of Paris; flames in the light or will-o'-the-wisps in the gloom.

The gamin expresses Paris, and Paris expresses the world.

For Paris is a total. Paris is the ceiling of the human race. The whole of this prodigious city is a foreshortening of dead manners and living manners. He who sees Paris thinks he sees the bottom of all history with heaven and constellations in the intervals. Paris has a capital, the Town Hall, a Parthenon, Notre-Dame, a Mount Aventine, the Faubourg Saint-Antoine, an Asinarium, he Sorbonne, a Pantheon, the Pantheon, a Via Sacra, the Boulevard des Italiens, temple of the winds, opinion; and it replaces the Gemoniae by ridicule. Its *1ajo* is called "faraud," its Transteverin is the man of the faubourgs, its *hammal* s the market porter, its *la\:\:arone* is the pegre, its cockney is the native of Ghent. :verything that exists elsewhere exists at Paris. The fishwoman of Dumarsais an retort on the herb seller of Euripides, the discobols Vejanus lives again n the Forioso, the tightrope dancer. Therapontigonus Miles could walk arm n arm with Vadeboncœur the grenadier, Damasippus the secondhand dealer vould be happy among bric-a-brac merchants, Vincennes could grasp Socrates n its fist as just as Agora could imprison Diderot, Grimod de la Reynière liscovered larded roast beef, as Curtillus invented roast hedgehog, we see the rapeze, which figures in Plautus reappear under the vault of the Arc of l'Etoile, he sword eater of Poecilus encountered by Apuleius is a sword swallower on he Pont Neuf, the nephew of Rameau and Curculio the parasite make a pair, .rgasilus could get himself presented to Cambaceres by d'Aigrefeuille; the our dandies of Rome: Alcesimarchus, Phoedromus, Diabolus, and Argyrippus lescend from Courtille in Labatut's posting-chaise; Aulus Gellius would alt no longer in front of Congrio than would Charles Nodier in front of 'unchinello; Marto is not a tigress, but Pardalisca was not a dragon; Pantolabus he wag jeers in the Café Anglais at Nomentanus the fast liver, Hermogenus s a tenor in the Champs-Elysees, and around him, Thracius the beggar, clad ke Bobeche, takes up a collection; the bore who stops you by the button of our coat in the Tuileries makes you repeat after a lapse of two thousand years Thesprion's apostrophe: *Quis properantem me prehendit pallio?* The wine on urene is a parody of the wine of Alba, the red border of Desaugiers forms a alance to the great cutting of Balatro, Pere Lachaise exhales beneath nocturnal ains same gleams as the Esquiliae, and the grave of the poor bought for five ears, is certainly the equivalent of the slave's hived coffin.

Seek something that Paris has not. The vat of Trophonius contains nothing hat is not in Mesmer's tub; Ergaphilas lives again in Cagliostro; the Brahmin Vasaphanta become incarnate in the Comte de Saint-Germain; the cemetery of Saint-Medard works quite as good miracles as the Mosque of Oumoumie t Damascus.

Paris has an AEsop-Mayeux, and a Canidia, Mademoiselle Lenormand. t is terrified, like Delphos at the fulgurating realities of the vision; it makes ables turn as Dodona did tripods. It places the *grisette** on the throne, as Rome

a working-class woman

placed the courtesan there; and, taking it altogether, if Louis XV is worse than Claudian, Madame Dubarry is better than Messalina. Paris combines in an unprecedented type, which has existed and that we have elbowed, Grecian nudity, the Hebraic ulcer, and the Gascon pun. It mingles Diogenes, Job, and Jack-pudding, dresses up a specter in old numbers of the Constitutional, and makes Chodruc Duclos.

Although Plutarch says, "The tyrant never grows old," Rome, under Sylla as under Domitian, resigned itself and willingly put water in its wine. The Tiber was a Lethe, if the rather doctrinary eulogium made of it by Varus Vibiscus is to be credited: *Contra Gracchos Tiberim habemus, Bibere Tiberim id est seditionem oblivisci.* Paris drinks a million liters of water a day, but that does not prevent it from occasionally beating the general alarm and ringing the tocsin.

With that exception, Paris is amiable. It accepts everything royally; it is not too particular about its Venus; its Callipyge is Hottentot; provided that it is made to laugh, it condones; ugliness cheers it, deformity provokes it to laughter, vice diverts it; be eccentric and you may be an eccentric; even hypocrisy, that supreme cynicism, does not disgust it; it is so literary that it does not hold its nose before Basile, and is no more scandalized by the prayer of Tartuffe than Horace was repelled by the "hiccup" of Priapus. No trait of the universal face is lacking in the profile of Paris. The bal Mabile is not the polymnia dance of the Janiculum, but the dealer in ladies' wearing apparel there devours the lorette with her eyes, exactly as the procuress Staphyla lay in wait for the virgin Planesium. The Barriere du Combat is not the Coliseum, but people are as ferocious there as though Caesar were looking on. The Syrian hostess has more grace than Mother Saguet, but, if Virgil haunted the Roman wine shop, David d'Angers, Balzac and Charlet have sat at the tables of Parisian taverns. Paris reigns. Geniuses flash forth there, the red tails prosper there. Adonai passes on his chariot with its twelve wheels of thunder and lightning; Silenus makes his entry there on his ass. For Silenus read Ramponneau.

Paris is the synonym of Cosmos, Paris is Athens, Sybaris, Jerusalem, Pantin. All civilizations are there in an abridged form, all barbarisms also. Paris would greatly regret it if it had not a guillotine.

A little of the Place de Greve is a good thing. What would all that eternal festival be without this seasoning? Our laws are wisely provided, and thanks to them, this blade drips on this Shrove Tuesday.

CHAPTER XI—TO SCOFF, TO REIGN

There is no limit to Paris. No city has had that domination that sometimes derides those whom it subjugates. "To please you, O Athenians!" exclaimed Alexander. Paris makes more than the law, it makes the fashion; Paris sets more than the fashion, it sets the routine. Paris may be stupid, if it sees fit; it sometimes allows itself this luxury; then the universe is stupid in company with it; then Paris awakes, rubs its eyes, says, "How stupid I am!" and bursts out laughing in the face of the human race. What a marvel is such a city! It is a strange thing that this grandioseness and this burlesque should be amicable neighbors, that all this majesty should not be thrown into disorder by all this parody, and that the same mouth can today blow into the trump of the Judgment Day, and tomorrow into the reed flute! Paris has a sovereign joviality. Its gaiety is of the thunder and its farce holds a scepter.

Its tempest sometimes proceeds from a grimace. Its explosions, its days, its masterpieces, its prodigies, its epics, go forth to the bounds of the universe, and so also do its cock-and-bull stories. Its laugh is the mouth of a volcano that spatters the whole earth. Its jests are sparks. It imposes its caricatures as well as its ideal on people; the highest monuments of human civilization accept its ironies and lend their eternity to its mischievous pranks. It is superb; it has a prodigious 14th of July, which delivers the globe; it forces all nations to take the oath of tennis; its night of the 4th of August dissolves in three hours a thousand years of feudalism; it makes of its logic the muscle of unanimous will; it multiplies itself under all sorts of forms of the sublime; it fills with its light Washington, Kosciusko, Bolivar, Bozzaris, Riego, Bem, Manin, Lopez, John Brown, Garibaldi; it is everywhere where the future is being lighted up, at Boston in 1779, at the Isle de Leon in 1820, at Pesth in 1848, at Palermo in 1860, it whispers the mighty countersign: Liberty, in the ear of the American abolitionists grouped about the boat at Harper's Ferry, and in the ear of the patriots of Ancona assembled in the shadow, to the Archi before the Gozzi inn on the seashore; it creates Canaris; it creates Quiroga; it creates Pisacane; it irradiates the great on earth; it was while proceeding where its breath urge them, that Byron perished at Missolonghi, and that Mazet died at Barcelona; it is the tribune under the feet of Mirabeau, and a crater under the feet of Robespierre; its books, its theater, its art, its science, its literature, its philosophy, are the manuals of the human race; it has Pascal, Regnier, Corneille, Descartes, Jean-Jacques: Voltaire for all moments, Moliere for all centuries; it makes its language to be talked by the universal mouth, and tha language becomes the word; it constructs in all minds the idea of progress, th liberating dogmas that it forges are for the generations trusty friends, and i is with the soul of its thinkers and its poets that all heroes of all nations hav been made since 1789; this does not prevent vagabondism, and that enormou genius that is called Paris, while transfiguring the world by its light, sketche in charcoal Bouginier's nose on the wall of the temple of Theseus and write Credeville the thief on the Pyramids.

Paris is always showing its teeth; when it is not scolding, it is laughing.

Such is Paris. The smoke of its roofs forms the ideas of the universe. A heap of mud and stone, if you will, but, above all, a moral being. It is mor than great, it is immense. Why? Because it is daring.

To dare; that is the price of progress.

All sublime conquests are, more or less, the prizes of daring. In order tha the Revolution should take place, it does not suffice that Montesquieu shoul foresee it, that Diderot should preach it, that Beaumarchais should announce it that Condorcet should calculate it, that Arouet should prepare it, that Roussea should premeditate it; it is necessary that Danton should dare it.

The cry: "Audacity!" is a fiat lux. It is necessary, for the sake of the forwar march of the human race, that there should be proud lessons of courag permanently on the heights. Daring deeds dazzle history and are one of man' great sources of light. The dawn dares when it rises. To attempt, to brave to persist, to persevere, to be faithful to one's self, to grasp fate bodily, t astound catastrophe by the small amount of fear that it occasions us, now t affront unjust power, again to insult drunken victory, to hold one's position, t stand one's ground; that is the example that nations need, that is the light tha electrifies them. The same formidable lightning proceeds from the torch o Prometheus to Cambronne's short pipe.

CHAPTER XII—THE FUTURE
LATENT IN THE PEOPLE

As for the Parisian populace, even when a man grown, it is always th street Arab; to paint the child is to paint the city; and it is for that reaso that we have studied this eagle in this arrant sparrow. It is in the faubourg above all, we maintain, that the Parisian race appears; there is the pure blood there is the true physiognomy; there this people toils and suffers, and sufferin

nd toil are the two faces of man. There exist there immense numbers of
nknown beings, among whom swarm types of the strangest, from the porter
f la Rapée to the knacker of Montfaucon. *"Fex urbis,"* exclaims Cicero; mob,
dds Burke, indignantly; rabble, multitude, populace. These are words and
uickly uttered. But so be it. What does it matter? What is it to me if they
o go barefoot! They do not know how to read; so much the worse. Would
ou abandon them for that? Would you turn their distress into a malediction?
annot the light penetrate these masses? Let us return to that cry: Light! And
t us obstinately persist therein! Light! Light! Who knows whether these
pacities will not become transparent? Are not revolutions transfigurations?
ome, philosophers, teach, enlighten, light up, think aloud, speak aloud, hasten
oyously to the great sun, fraternize with the public place, announce the good
ews, spend your alphabets lavishly, proclaim rights, sing the Marseillaises,
ow enthusiasms, tear green boughs from the oaks. Make a whirlwind of the
lea. This crowd may be rendered sublime. Let us learn how to make use of
nat vast conflagration of principles and virtues, which sparkles, bursts forth,
nd quivers at certain hours. These bare feet, these bare arms, these rags,
nese ignorances, these abjectnesses, these darknesses, may be employed in the
onquest of the ideal. Gaze past the people, and you will perceive truth. Let
nat vile sand that you trample under foot be cast into the furnace, let it melt
nd seethe there, it will become a splendid crystal, and it is thanks to it that
alileo and Newton will discover stars.

CHAPTER XIII—LITTLE GAVROCHE

Eight or nine years after the events narrated in the second part of this story,
people noticed on the Boulevard du Temple, and in the regions of the
hateau-d'Eau, a little boy eleven or twelve years of age, who would have
ealized with tolerable accuracy that ideal of the gamin sketched out above, if,
vith the laugh of his age on his lips, he had not had a heart absolutely somber
nd empty. This child was well muffled up in a pair of man's trousers, but he
id not get them from his father, and a woman's chemise, but he did not get it
rom his mother. Some people or other had clothed him in rags out of charity.
till, he had a father and a mother. But his father did not think of him, and his
nother did not love him.

He was one of those children most deserving of pity, among all, one of
nose who have father and mother, and who are orphans nevertheless.

This child never felt so well as when he was in the street. The pavement were less hard to him than his mother's heart.

His parents had dispatched him into life with a kick.

He simply took flight.

He was a boisterous, pallid, nimble, wide-awake, jeering lad, with vivacious but sickly air. He went and came, sang, played at hopscotch, scrape the gutters, stole a little, but, like cats and sparrows, gaily laughed when he wa called a rogue, and got angry when called a thief. He had no shelter, no brea no fire, no love; but he was merry because he was free.

When these poor creatures grow to be men, the millstones of the soci order meet them and crush them, but so long as they are children, they escap because of their smallness. The tiniest hole saves them.

Nevertheless, abandoned as this child was, it sometimes happened, ever two or three months, that he said, "Come, I'll go and see mama!" Then h quitted the boulevard, the Cirque, the Porte Saint-Martin, descended to th quays, crossed the bridges, reached the suburbs, arrived at the Salpetriere, an came to a halt, where? Precisely at that double number 50–52 with which th reader is acquainted—at the Gorbeau hovel.

At that epoch, the hovel 50–52 generally deserted and eternally decorate with the placard, "Chambers to let," chanced to be, a rare thing, inhabite by numerous individuals who, however, as is always the case in Paris, had n connection with each other. All belonged to that indigent class that begins t separate from the lowest of petty bourgeoisie in straitened circumstances, an that extends from misery to misery into the lowest depths of society down t those two beings in whom all the material things of civilization end, the sewe man who sweeps up the mud, and the ragpicker who collects scraps.

The "principal lodger" of Jean Valjean's day was dead and had bee replaced by another exactly like her. I know not what philosopher has sai "Old women are never lacking."

This new old woman was named Madame Bourgon, and had nothin remarkable about her life except a dynasty of three paroquets, who had reigne in succession over her soul.

The most miserable of those who inhabited the hovel were a family of fou persons, consisting of father, mother, and two daughters, already well grow all four of whom were lodged in the same attic, one of the cells that we hav already mentioned.

At first sight, this family presented no very special feature except i extreme destitution; the father, when he hired the chamber, had stated that h

ame was Jondrette. Some time after his moving in, which had borne a singular
esemblance to the entrance of nothing at all, to borrow the memorable
xpression of the principal tenant, this Jondrette had said to the woman, who,
ke her predecessor, was at the same time portress and stair sweeper, "Mother
o-and-So, if anyone should chance to come and inquire for a Pole or an
alian, or even a Spaniard, perchance, it is I."

This family was that of the merry barefoot boy. He arrived there and found
istress, and, what is still sadder, no smile; a cold hearth and cold hearts. When
e entered, he was asked, "From where come you?"

He replied: "From the street."

When he went away, they asked him, "Where are you going?"

He replied, "Into the streets."

His mother said to him, "What did you come here for?"

This child lived, in this absence of affection, like the pale plants that spring
p in cellars. It did not cause him suffering, and he blamed no one. He did not
now exactly how a father and mother should be.

Nevertheless, his mother loved his sisters.

We have forgotten to mention, that on the Boulevard du Temple this child
as called Little Gavroche. Why was he called Little Gavroche?

Probably because his father's name was Jondrette.

It seems to be the instinct of certain wretched families to break the thread.

The chamber that the Jondrettes inhabited in the Gorbeau hovel was the
st at the end of the corridor. The cell next to it was occupied by a very poor
oung man who was called M. Marius.

Let us explain who this M. Marius was.

BOOK SECOND: THE GREAT BOURGEOIS

CHAPTER I—NINETY YEARS AND THIRTY-TWO TEETH

In the Rue Boucherat, Rue de Normandie and the Rue de Saintonge there sti exist a few ancient inhabitants who have preserved the memory of a worth man named M. Gillenormand, and who mention him with complaisance. Th goodman was old when they were young. This silhouette has not yet entirel disappeared—for those who regard with melancholy that vague swarm c shadows that is called the past—from the labyrinth of streets in the vicinit of the Temple to which, under Louis XIV, the names of all the province of France were appended exactly as in our day, the streets of the new Tivo quarter have received the names of all the capitals of Europe; a progression, b the way, in which progress is visible.

M. Gillenormand, who was as much alive as possible in 1831, was one o those men who had become curiosities to be viewed, simply because the have lived a long time, and who are strange because they formerly resemble everybody, and now resemble nobody. He was a peculiar old man, and in ver truth, a man of another age, the real, complete and rather haughty bourgeo of the eighteenth century, who wore his good, old bourgeoisie with the a with which marquises wear their marquisates. He was over ninety years c age, his walk was erect, he talked loudly, saw clearly, drank neat, ate, slep and snored. He had all thirty-two of his teeth. He only wore spectacles whe he read. He was of an amorous disposition, but declared that, for the last te years, he had wholly and decidedly renounced women. He could no long please, he said; he did not add, "I am too old," but, "I am too poor." He sai "If I were not ruined—Heee!" All he had left, in fact, was an income c about fifteen thousand francs. His dream was to come into an inheritance ar to have a hundred-thousand livres income for mistresses. He did not belon as the reader will perceive, to that puny variety of octogenaries who, like N de Voltaire, have been dying all their life; his was no longevity of a cracke pot; this jovial old man had always had good health. He was superficial, rapi easily angered. He flew into a passion at everything, generally quite contrai o all reason. When contradicted, he raised his cane; he beat people as he had done in the great century. He had a daughter over fifty years of age, and unmarried, whom he chastised severely with his tongue, when in a rage, and whom he would have liked to whip. She seemed to him to be eight years old. He boxed his servants' ears soundly, and said, "Ah! Carogne!" One of his oaths was, "By the pantoufloche of the pantouflochade!" He had singular freaks of tranquillity; he had himself shaved every day by a barber who had been mad and who detested him, being jealous of M. Gillenormand on account of his wife, a pretty and coquettish barberess. M. Gillenormand admired his own discernment in all things, and declared that he was extremely sagacious; here is one of his sayings: "I have, in truth, some penetration; I am able to say when a flea bites me, from what woman it came."

The words he uttered the most frequently were: the sensible man, and nature. He did not give to this last word the grand acceptation that our epoch has accorded to it, but he made it enter, after his own fashion, into his little chimney-corner satires. "Nature," he said, "in order that civilization may have a little of everything, gives it even specimens of its amusing barbarism. Europe possesses specimens of Asia and Africa on a small scale. The cat is a drawing room tiger, the lizard is a pocket crocodile. The dancers at the opera are pink female savages. They do not eat men, they crunch them; or, magicians that they are, they transform them into oysters and swallow them. The Caribbeans leave only the bones, they leave only the shell. Such are our morals. We do not devour, we gnaw; we do not exterminate, we claw."

CHAPTER II—LIKE MASTER, LIKE HOUSE

He lived in the Marais, Rue des Filles-du-Calvaire, No. 6. He owned the house. This house has since been demolished and rebuilt, and the number has probably been changed in those revolutions of numeration that the streets of Paris undergo. He occupied an ancient and vast apartment on the first floor, between street and gardens, furnished to the very ceilings with great Gobelins and Beauvais tapestries representing pastoral scenes; the subjects of the ceilings and the panels were repeated in miniature on the armchairs. He enveloped his bed in a vast, nine-leaved screen of Coromandel lacquer. Long, full curtains hung from the windows, and formed great, broken folds that were very magnificent. The garden situated immediately under his windows was attached to that one of them that formed the angle, by means of a staircase

twelve or fifteen steps long, which the old gentleman ascended and descende
with great agility. In addition to a library adjoining his chamber, he had
boudoir of which he thought a great deal, a gallant and elegant retreat, wit
magnificent hangings of straw, with a pattern of flowers and fleurs-de-lis mad
on the galleys of Louis XIV and ordered of his convicts by M. de Vivonne fc
his mistress. M. Gillenormand had inherited it from a grim maternal grea
aunt, who had died a centenarian. He had had two wives. His manners wei
something between those of the courtier, which he had never been, and th
lawyer, which he might have been. He was gay, and caressing when he had
mind. In his youth he had been one of those men who are always deceived b
their wives and never by their mistresses, because they are, at the same time
the most sullen of husbands and the most charming of lovers in existence. H
was a connoisseur of painting. He had in his chamber a marvelous portra
of no one knows whom, painted by Jordaens, executed with great dashes o
the brush, with millions of details, in a confused and haphazard manner. M
Gillenormand's attire was not the habit of Louis XIV nor yet that of Lou
XVI; it was that of the Incroyables of the Directory. He had thought himse
young up to that period and had followed the fashions. His coat was o
lightweight cloth with voluminous revers, a long swallowtail and large stee
buttons. With this he wore knee breeches and buckle shoes. He always thru
his hands into his fobs. He said authoritatively, "The French Revolution is
heap of blackguards."

CHAPTER III—LUC-ESPRIT

At the age of sixteen, one evening at the opera, he had had the honor to b
stared at through opera glasses by two beauties at the same time—rip
and celebrated beauties then, and sung by Voltaire, the Camargo and the Salle
Caught between two fires, he had beaten a heroic retreat toward a little dancer
a young girl named Nahenry, who was sixteen like himself, obscure as a ca
and with whom he was in love. He abounded in memories. He was accustome
to exclaim, "How pretty she was—that Guimard-Guimardini-Guimardinette
the last time I saw her at Longchamps, her hair curled in sustained sentiments
with her come-and-see of turquoises, her gown of the color of persons newl
arrived, and her little agitation muff!" He had worn in his young manhoo
a waistcoat of Nain-Londrin, which he was fond of talking about effusively
"I was dressed like a Turk of the Levant Levantin," said he. Madame d

oufflers, having seen him by chance when he was twenty, had described him s "a charming fool." He was horrified by all the names that he saw in politics nd in power, regarding them as vulgar and bourgeois. He read the journals, ne newspapers, the gazettes as he said, stifling outbursts of laughter the while. Oh!" he said. "What people these are! Corbiere! Humann! Casimir Perier! 'here's a minister for you! I can imagine this in a journal: 'M. Gillenorman, inister!' That would be a farce. Well! They are so stupid that it would pass." le merrily called everything by its name, whether decent or indecent, and id not restrain himself in the least before ladies. He uttered coarse speeches, bscenities, and filth with a certain tranquility and lack of astonishment that as elegant. It was in keeping with the unceremoniousness of his century. It is) be noted that the age of periphrase in verse was the age of crudities in prose. lis godfather had predicted that he would turn out a man of genius, and had estowed on him these two significant names: Luc-Esprit.

CHAPTER IV—A CENTENARIAN ASPIRANT

He had taken prizes in his boyhood at the College of Moulins, where he was born, and he had been crowned by the hand of the Duc de ivernais, whom he called the Duc de Nevers. Neither the Convention, nor he death of Louis XVI, nor the Napoleon, nor the return of the Bourbons, nor nything else had been able to efface the memory of this crowning. The Duc e Nevers was, in his eyes, the great figure of the century. "What a charming rand seigneur," he said, "and what a fine air he had with his blue ribbon!"

In the eyes of M. Gillenormand, Catherine the Second had made reparation or the crime of the partition of Poland by purchasing, for three thousand oubles, the secret of the elixir of gold, from Bestucheff. He grew animated on his subject: "The elixir of gold," he exclaimed, "the yellow dye of Bestucheff, general Lamotte's drops, in the eighteenth century, this was the great remedy or the catastrophes of love, the panacea against Venus, at one Louis the half-ounce phial. Louis XV sent two hundred phials of it to the Pope." He would ave been greatly irritated and thrown off his balance, had anyone told him hat the elixir of gold is nothing but the perchloride of iron. M. Gillenormand dored the Bourbons, and had a horror of 1789; he was forever narrating in vhat manner he had saved himself during the Terror, and how he had been bliged to display a vast deal of gaiety and cleverness in order to escape having

his head cut off. If any young man ventured to pronounce an eulogium on th
Republic in his presence, he turned purple and grew so angry that he was o
the point of swooning. He sometimes alluded to his ninety years, and said, "
hope that I shall not see ninety-three twice." On these occasions, he hinted t
people that he meant to live to be a hundred.

CHAPTER V—BASQUE AND NICOLETTE

He had theories. Here is one of them: "When a man is passionately fon
of women, and when he has himself a wife for whom he cares bu
little, who is homely, cross, legitimate, with plenty of rights, perched on th
code, and jealous at need, there is but one way of extricating himself fror
the quandary and of procuring peace, and that is to let his wife control th
purse strings. This abdication sets him free. Then his wife busies herself, grow
passionately fond of handling coin, gets her fingers covered with verdigris i
the process, undertakes the education of half-share tenants and the training o
farmers, convokes lawyers, presides over notaries, harangues scriveners, visit
limbs of the law, follows lawsuits, draws up leases, dictates contracts, fee
herself the sovereign, sells, buys, regulates, promises and compromises, binc
fast and annuls, yields, concedes and retrocedes, arranges, disarranges, hoard
lavishes; she commits follies, a supreme and personal delight, and that console
her. While her husband disdains her, she has the satisfaction of ruining he
husband." This theory M. Gillenormand had himself applied, and it ha
become his history. His wife—the second one—had administered his fortun
in such a manner that, one fine day, when M. Gillenormand found himself
widower, there remained to him just sufficient to live on, by sinking nearly th
whole of it in an annuity of fifteen thousand francs, three-quarters of whic
would expire with him. He had not hesitated on this point, not being anxiou
to leave a property behind him. Besides, he had noticed that patrimonies ar
subject to adventures, and, for instance, become national property; he ha
been present at the avatars of consolidated three percents, and he had no grea
faith in the Great Book of the Public Debt. "All that's the Rue Quincampois!
he said. His house in the Rue Filles-du-Clavaire belonged to him, as we hav
already stated. He had two servants, "a male and a female." When a servar
entered his establishment, M. Gillenormand rebaptized him. He bestowed o
the men the name of their province: Nimois, Comtois, Poitevin, Picard. Hi
last valet was a big, foundered, short-winded fellow of fifty-five, who wa

capable of running twenty paces; but, as he had been born at Bayonne, M. Gillenormand called him Basque. All the female servants in his house were called Nicolette (even the Magnon, of whom we shall hear more further on). One day, a haughty cook, a cordon bleu, of the lofty race of porters, presented herself. "How much wages do you want a month?" asked M. Gillenormand.

"Thirty francs."

"What is your name?"

"Olympie."

"You shall have fifty francs, and you shall be called Nicolette."

CHAPTER VI—IN WHICH MAGNON AND HER TWO CHILDREN ARE SEEN

With M. Gillenormand, sorrow was converted into wrath; he was furious at being in despair. He had all sorts of prejudices and took all sorts of liberties. One of the facts of which his exterior relief and his internal satisfaction was composed, was, as we have just hinted, that he had remained a brisk spark, and that he passed energetically for such. This he called having "royal renown." This royal renown sometimes drew down upon him singular windfalls. One day, there was brought to him in a basket, as though it had been a basket of oysters, a stout, newly born boy, who was yelling like the deuce, and duly wrapped in swaddling clothes, which a servant-maid, dismissed six months previously, attributed to him. M. Gillenormand had, at that time, fully completed his eighty-fourth year. Indignation and uproar in the establishment. And whom did that bold hussy think she could persuade to believe that? What audacity! What an abominable calumny! M. Gillenormand himself was not at all enraged. He gazed at the brat with the amiable smile of a goodman who is flattered by the calumny, and said in an aside, "Well, what now? What's the matter? You are finely taken aback, and really, you are excessively ignorant. M. le Duc d'Angoulême, the bastard of his Majesty Charles IX, married a silly jade of fifteen when he was eighty-five; M. Virginal, Marquis d'Alluye, brother to the Cardinal de Sourdis, Archbishop of Bordeaux, had, at the age of eighty-three, by the maid of Madame la Presidente Jacquin, a son, a real child of love, who became a Chevalier of Malta and a counselor of state; one of the great men of this century, the Abbé Tabaraud, is the son of a man of eighty-seven. There is nothing out of the ordinary in these things. And then, the Bible! Upon that I declare that this little gentleman is none of mine. Let him be taken care of. It is not his fault." This manner of procedure was good-tempered. The woman, whose name was Magnon, sent him another parcel in the following year. It was a boy again. Thereupon, M. Gillenormand capitulated. He sent the two brats back to their mother, promising to pay eighty francs a month for their maintenance, on the condition that the said mother would not do so any more. He added, "I insist upon it that the mother shall treat them well. I shall go to see them from time to time." And this he did. He had had a brother who was a priest, and who had been rector of the Academy of Poitiers for three and thirty years, and had died at seventy-nine. "I lost him young," said he. This brother, of whom but little memory remains, was a peaceable miser, who, being a priest, thought himself bound to bestow alms on the poor whom he met, but he never gave them anything except bad or demonetized sous, thereby discovering a means of going to hell by way of paradise. As for M. Gillenormand the elder, he never haggled over his alms-giving, but gave gladly and nobly. He was kindly, abrupt, charitable, and if he had been rich, his turn of mind would have been magnificent. He desired that all that concerned him should be done in a grand manner, even his rogueries. One day, having been cheated by a businessman in a matter of inheritance, in a gross and apparent manner, he uttered this solemn exclamation: "That was indecently done! I am really ashamed of this pilfering. Everything has degenerated in this century, even the rascals. *Morbleu!* This is not the way to rob a man of my standing. I am robbed as though in a forest, but badly robbed. *Silva, sint consule dignae!*" He had had two wives, as we have already mentioned; by the first he had had a daughter, who had remained unmarried, and by the second another daughter, who had died at about the age of thirty, who had wedded, through love, or chance, or otherwise, a soldier of fortune who had served in the armies of the Republic and of the Empire, who had won the cross at Austerlitz and had been made colonel at Waterloo. "He is the disgrace of my family," said the old bourgeois. He took an immense amount of snuff, and had a particularly graceful manner of plucking at his lace ruffle with the back of one hand. He believed very little in God.

CHAPTER VII—RULE: RECEIVE NO ONE EXCEPT IN THE EVENING

Such was M. Luc-Esprit Gillenormand, who had not lost his hair, which was gray rather than white, and which was always dressed in "dog's ears." To sum up, he was venerable in spite of all this.

He had something of the eighteenth century about him—frivolous and great.

In 1814 and during the early years of the Restoration, M. Gillenormand, who was still young—he was only seventy-four—lived in the Faubourg Saint Germain, Rue Servandoni, near Saint-Sulpice. He had only retired to the Marais when he quitted society, long after attaining the age of eighty.

And, on abandoning society, he had immured himself in his habits. The principal one, and that which was invariable, was to keep his door absolutely closed during the day, and never to receive anyone whatever, except in the evening. He dined at five o'clock, and after that his door was open. That had been the fashion of his century, and he would not swerve from it. "The day is vulgar," said he, "and deserves only a closed shutter. Fashionable people only light up their minds when the zenith lights up its stars." And he barricaded himself against everyone, even had it been the king himself. This was the antiquated elegance of his day.

CHAPTER VIII—TWO DO NOT MAKE A PAIR

We have just spoken of M. Gillenormand's two daughters. They had come into the world ten years apart. In their youth they had borne very little resemblance to each other, either in character or countenance, and had also been as little like sisters to each other as possible. The youngest had a charming soul, which turned toward all that belongs to the light, was occupied with flowers, with verses, with music, which fluttered away into glorious space, enthusiastic, ethereal, and was wedded from her very youth, in ideal, to a vague and heroic figure. The elder had also her chimera; she espied in the future some very wealthy purveyor, a contractor, a splendidly stupid husband, a million made man, or even a prefect; the receptions of the Prefecture, an usher in the antechamber with a chain on his neck, official balls, the harangues of the town hall, to be "Madame la Préfète"—all this had created a whirlwind in her imagination. Thus the two sisters strayed, each in her own dream, at the epoch when they were young girls. Both had wings, the one like an angel, the other like a goose.

No ambition is ever fully realized, here below at least. No paradise becomes terrestrial in our day. The younger wedded the man of her dreams, but she died. The elder did not marry at all.

At the moment when she makes her entrance into this history that we are relating, she was an antique virtue, an incombustible prude, with one of the sharpest noses, and one of the most obtuse minds that it is possible to see. A characteristic detail; outside of her immediate family, no one had ever known her first name. She was called Mademoiselle Gillenormand, the elder.

In the matter of cant, Mademoiselle Gillenormand could have given point to a miss. Her modesty was carried to the other extreme of blackness. She cherished a frightful memory of her life; one day, a man had beheld her garter.

Age had only served to accentuate this pitiless modesty. Her guimpe was never sufficiently opaque, and never ascended sufficiently high. She multiplied clasps and pins where no one would have dreamed of looking. The peculiarity of prudery is to place all the more sentinels in proportion as the fortress is the less menaced.

Nevertheless, let him who can explain these antique mysteries of innocence, she allowed an officer of the Lancers, her grand nephew, named Theodule, to embrace her without displeasure.

In spite of this favored Lancer, the label: Prude, under which we have classed her, suited her to absolute perfection. Mademoiselle Gillenormand was a sort of twilight soul. Prudery is a demi-virtue and a demi-vice.

To prudery she added bigotry, a well-assorted lining. She belonged to the society of the Virgin, wore a white veil on certain festivals, mumbled special orisons, revered "the holy blood," venerated "the sacred heart," remained for hours in contemplation before a rococo-Jesuit altar in a chapel, which was inaccessible to the rank and file of the faithful, and there allowed her soul to soar among little clouds of marble, and through great rays of gilded wood.

She had a chapel friend, an ancient virgin like herself, named Mademoiselle Vaubois, who was a positive blockhead, and beside whom Mademoiselle Gillenormand had the pleasure of being an eagle. Beyond the Agnus Dei and Ave Maria, Mademoiselle Vaubois had no knowledge of anything except of the different ways of making preserves. Mademoiselle Vaubois, perfect in her style, was the ermine of stupidity without a single spot of intelligence.

Let us say it plainly, Mademoiselle Gillenormand had gained rather than lost as she grew older. This is the case with passive natures. She had never been malicious, which is relative kindness; and then, years wear away the angles, and the softening that comes with time had come to her. She was melancholy with an obscure sadness of which she did not herself know the secret. There breathed from her whole person the stupor of a life that was finished, and that had never had a beginning.

She kept house for her father. M. Gillenormand had his daughter near him, as we have seen that Monseigneur Bienvenu had his sister with him. These households comprised of an old man and an old spinster are not rare, and always have the touching aspect of two weaknesses leaning on each other for support.

There was also in this house, between this elderly spinster and this old man, a child, a little boy, who was always trembling and mute in the presence of M. Gillenormand. M. Gillenormand never addressed this child except in a severe voice, and sometimes, with uplifted cane. "Here, Sir! Rascal, scoundrel, come here! Answer me, you scamp! Just let me see you, you good-for-nothing!" etc., etc. He idolized him.

This was his grandson. We shall meet with this child again later on.

BOOK THIRD: THE GRANDFATHER AND THE GRANDSON

CHAPTER I—AN ANCIENT SALON

When M. Gillenormand lived in the Rue Servandoni, he had frequented many very good and very aristocratic salons. Although a bourgeois, M. Gillenormand was received in society. As he had a double measure of wit, in the first place, that which was born with him, and secondly, that which was attributed to him, he was even sought out and made much of. He never went anywhere except on condition of being the chief person there. There are people who will have influence at any price, and who will have other people busy themselves over them; when they cannot be oracles, they turn wags. M. Gillenormand was not of this nature; his domination in the Royalist salons that he frequented cost his self-respect nothing. He was an oracle everywhere. It had happened to him to hold his own against M. de Bonald, and even against M. Bengy-Puy-Vallee.

About 1817, he invariably passed two afternoons a week in a house in his own neighborhood, in the Rue Ferou, with Madame la Baronne de T., a worthy and respectable person, whose husband had been Ambassador of France to Berlin under Louis XVI Baron de T., who, during his lifetime, had gone very passionately into ecstasies and magnetic visions, had died bankrupt, during the emigration, leaving, as his entire fortune, some very curious Memoirs about Mesmer and his tub, in ten manuscript volumes, bound in red morocco and gilded on the edges. Madame de T. had not published the memoirs, out of pride, and maintained herself on a meager income that had survived no one knew how.

Madame de T. lived far from the Court; "a very mixed society," as she said, in a noble isolation, proud and poor. A few friends assembled twice a week about her widowed hearth, and these constituted a purely Royalist salon They sipped tea there, and uttered groans or cries of horror at the century, the charter, the Bonapartists, the prostitution of the blue ribbon, or the Jacobinism of Louis XVIII, according as the wind veered toward elegy or dithyrambs; and they spoke in low tones of the hopes that were presented by Monsieur, afterward Charles X.

The songs of the fishwomen, in which Napoleon was called Nicolas, were received there with transports of joy. Duchesses, the most delicate and charming women in the world, went into ecstasies over couplets like the following, addressed to "the federates":

> "Refoncez dans vos culottes
> Le bout d' chemis' qui vous pend.
> Qu'on n' dis' pas qu' les patriotes
> Ont arboré l' drapeau blanc?"*

There they amused themselves with puns that were considered terrible with innocent plays upon words that they supposed to be venomous, with quatrains, with distiches even; thus, upon the Dessolles ministry, a moderate cabinet, of which MM. Decazes and Deserre were members:

> "To reestablish the shaken throne firmly on its base,
> Soil, greenhouse, and house must be changed."

---

* Tuck into your trousers/the shirttail that is hanging out./Let it not be said that patriots/ have hoisted the white flag.

Or they drew up a list of the chamber of peers, "an abominably Jacobin chamber," and from this list they combined alliances of names, in such a manner as to form, for example, phrases like the following: Damas. Sabran. Gouvion-Saint-Cyr. All this was done merrily. In that society, they parodied the Revolution. They used I know not what desires to give point to the same wrath in inverse sense. They sang their little *Ça Ira*:

> *"Ah! ça ira ça ira ça ira*!
> *Les Bonapartistes à la lanterne*!"

Songs are like the guillotine; they chop away indifferently, today this head, tomorrow that. It is only a variation.

In the Fualdes affair, which belongs to this epoch, 1816, they took part for Bastide and Jausion, because Fualdes was "a Buonapartist." They designated the liberals as friends and brothers; this constituted the most deadly insult.

Like certain church towers, Madame de T.'s salon had two cocks. One of them was M. Gillenormand, the other was Comte de Lamothe-Valois, of whom it was whispered about, with a sort of respect, "Do you know? That is the Lamothe of the affair of the necklace." These singular amnesties do occur in parties.

Let us add the following: in the bourgeoisie, honored situations decay through too easy relations; one must beware whom one admits; in the same way that there is a loss of caloric in the vicinity of those who are cold, there is a diminution of consideration in the approach of despised persons. The ancient society of the upper classes held themselves above this law, as above every other. Marigny, the brother of the Pompadour, had his entry with M. le Prince de Soubise. In spite of? No, because. Du Barry, the godfather of the Vaubernier, was very welcome at the house of M. le Marechal de Richelieu. This society is Olympus. Mercury and the Prince de Guemenee are at home there. A thief is admitted there, provided he be a god.

The Comte de Lamothe, who, in 1815, was an old man seventy-five years of age, had nothing remarkable about him except his silent and sententious air, his cold and angular face, his perfectly polished manners, his coat buttoned up to his cravat, and his long legs always crossed in long, flabby trousers of the hue of burnt sienna. His face was the same color as his trousers.

This M. de Lamothe was "held in consideration" in this salon on account of his "celebrity" and, strange to say, though true, because of his name of Valois.

As for M. Gillenormand, his consideration was of absolutely first-rate quality. He had, in spite of his levity, and without its interfering in any way with his dignity, a certain manner about him that was imposing, dignified, honest, and lofty, in a bourgeois fashion; and his great age added to it. One is not a century with impunity. The years finally produce around a head a venerable dishevelment.

In addition to this, he said things that had the genuine sparkle of the old rock. Thus, when the King of Prussia, after having restored Louis XVIII, came to pay the latter a visit under the name of the Count de Ruppin, he was received by the descendant of Louis XIV somewhat as though he had been the Marquis de Brandebourg, and with the most delicate impertinence. M. Gillenormand approved. "All kings who are not the King of France," said he, "are provincial kings." One day, the following question was put and the following answer returned in his presence: "To what was the editor of the Courrier Francais condemned?" "To be hanged." "Sus is superfluous," observed M. Gillenormand. Remarks of this nature found a situation.

At the Te Deum on the anniversary of the return of the Bourbons, he said, on seeing M. de Talleyrand pass by, "There goes his Excellency the Evil One."

M. Gillenormand was always accompanied by his daughter, that tall mademoiselle, who was over forty and looked fifty, and by a handsome little boy of seven years, white, rosy, fresh, with happy and trusting eyes, who never appeared in that salon without hearing voices murmur around him, "How handsome he is! What a pity! Poor child!" This child was the one of whom we dropped a word a while ago. He was called "poor child," because he had for father "a brigand of the Loire."

This brigand of the Loire was M. Gillenormand's son-in-law, who has already been mentioned, and whom M. Gillenormand called "the disgrace of his family."

CHAPTER II—ONE OF THE RED SPECTRES OF THAT EPOCH

Anyone who had chanced to pass through the little town of Vernon at this epoch, and who had happened to walk across that fine monumental bridge, which will soon be succeeded, let us hope, by some hideous iron cable bridge, might have observed, had he dropped his eyes over the parapet, a man about fifty years of age wearing a leather cap, and trousers and a waistcoat of coarse gray cloth, to which something yellow that had been a red ribbon, was sewn, shod with wooden sabots, tanned by the sun, his face nearly black and his hair nearly white, a large scar on his forehead that ran down upon his cheek, bowed, bent, prematurely aged, who walked nearly every day, hoe and sickle in hand, in one of those compartments surrounded by walls that abut on the bridge, and border the left bank of the Seine like a chain of terraces, charming enclosures full of flowers of which one could say, were they much larger, "These are gardens," and were they a little smaller, "These are bouquets." All these enclosures abut upon the river at one end, and on a house at the other. The man in the waistcoat and the wooden shoes of whom we have just spoken, inhabited the smallest of these enclosures and the most humble of these houses about 1817. He lived there alone and solitary, silently and poorly, with a woman who was neither young nor old, neither homely nor pretty, neither a peasant nor a bourgeoisie, who served him. The plot of earth that he called his garden was celebrated in the town for the beauty of the flowers he cultivated there. These flowers were his occupation.

By dint of labor, of perseverance, of attention, and of buckets of water, he had succeeded in creating after the Creator, and he had invented certain tulips and certain dahlias that seemed to have been forgotten by nature. He was ingenious; he had forestalled Soulange Bodin in the formation of little clumps of earth of heath mold, for the cultivation of rare and precious shrubs from America and China. He was in his alleys from the break of day, in summer, planting, cutting, hoeing, watering, walking amid his flowers with an air of kindness, sadness, and sweetness, sometimes standing motionless and thoughtful for hours, listening to the song of a bird in the trees, the babble of a child in a house, or with his eyes fixed on a drop of dew at the tip of a spear of grass, of which the sun made a carbuncle. His table was very plain, and he drank more milk than wine. A child could make him give way, and his servant scolded him. He was so timid that he seemed shy, he rarely went out, and he saw no one but the poor people who tapped at his pane and his cure, the Abbé Mabeuf, a good old man. Nevertheless, if the inhabitants of the town, or strangers, or any chance comers, curious to see his tulips, rang at his little cottage, he opened his door with a smile. He was the "brigand of the Loire."

Anyone who had, at the same time, read military memoirs, biographies, the Moniteur, and the bulletins of the grand army, would have been struck by a name that occurs there with tolerable frequency, the name of Georges Pontmercy. When very young, this Georges Pontmercy had been a soldier in Saintonge's regiment. The revolution broke out. Saintonge's regiment formed a part of the army of the Rhine; for the old regiments of the monarchy preserved their names of provinces even after the fall of the monarchy, and were only divided into brigades in 1794. Pontmercy fought at Spire, at Worms, at Neustadt, at Turkheim, at Alzey, at Mayence, where he was one of the two hundred who formed Houchard's rearguard. It was the twelfth to hold its ground against the corps of the Prince of Hesse, behind the old rampart of Andernach, and only rejoined the main body of the army when the enemy's cannon had opened a breach from the cord of the parapet to the foot of the glacis. He was under Kleber at Marchiennes and at the battle of Mont-Palissel, where a ball from a biscaien broke his arm. Then he passed to the frontier of Italy, and was one of the thirty grenadiers who defended the Col de Tende with Joubert. Joubert was appointed its adjutant-general, and Pontmercy sub-lieutenant. Pontmercy was by Berthier's side in the midst of the grapeshot of that day at Lodi that caused Bonaparte to say, "Berthier has been cannoneer, cavalier, and grenadier." He beheld his old general, Joubert, fall at Novi, at the moment when, with uplifted saber, he was shouting, "Forward!" Having been embarked with his company in the exigencies of the campaign, on board a pinnace that was proceeding from Genoa to some obscure port on the coast, he fell into a wasps' nest of seven or eight English vessels. The Genoese commander wanted to throw his cannon into the sea, to hide the soldiers between decks, and to slip along in the dark as a merchant vessel. Pontmercy had the colors hoisted to the peak, and sailed proudly past under the guns of the British frigates. Twenty leagues further on, his audacity having increased, he attacked with his pinnace, and captured a large English transport that was carrying troops to Sicily, and that was so loaded down with men and horses that the vessel was sunk to the level of the sea. In 1805 he was in that Malher division that took Gunzberg from the Archduke Ferdinand. At Weltingen he received into his arms, beneath a storm of bullets, Colonel Maupetit, mortally wounded at the head of the 9th Dragoons. He distinguished himself at Austerlitz in that admirable march in echelons effected under the enemy's fire. When the cavalry of the Imperial Russian Guard crushed a battalion of the 4th of the line, Pontmercy was one of those who took their revenge and overthrew the Guard. The Emperor gave him the cross. Pontmercy saw Wurmser at Mantua, Melas, and Alexandria, Mack at Ulm, made prisoners in succession. He formed a part of the eighth corps of the grand army that Mortier commanded, and that captured Hamburg. Then he was transferred to the 55th of the line, which was the old regiment of Flanders. At Eylau he was in the cemetery where, for the space of two hours, the heroic Captain Louis

Hugo, the uncle of the author of this book, sustained alone with his company of eighty-three men every effort of the hostile army. Pontmercy was one of the three who emerged alive from that cemetery. He was at Friedland. Then he saw Moscow. Then La Beresina, then Lutzen, Bautzen, Dresden, Wachau, Leipzig, and the defiles of Gelenhausen; then Montmirail, Chateau-Thierry, Craon, the banks of the Marne, the banks of the Aisne, and the redoubtable position of Laon. At Arnay-Le-Duc, being then a captain, he put ten Cossacks to the sword, and saved, not his general, but his corporal. He was well slashed up on this occasion, and twenty-seven splinters were extracted from his left arm alone. Eight days before the capitulation of Paris he had just exchanged with a comrade and entered the cavalry. He had what was called under the old regime, the double hand, that is to say, an equal aptitude for handling the saber or the musket as a soldier, or a squadron or a battalion as an officer. It is from this aptitude, perfected by a military education, which certain special branches of the service arise, the dragoons, for example, who are both cavalrymen and infantry at one and the same time. He accompanied Napoleon to the Island of Elba. At Waterloo, he was chief of a squadron of cuirassiers, in Dubois's brigade. It was he who captured the standard of the Lunenburg battalion. He came and cast the flag at the Emperor's feet. He was covered with blood. While tearing down the banner he had received a sword-cut across his face. The Emperor, greatly pleased, shouted to him, "You are a colonel, you are a baron, you are an officer of the Legion of Honor!"

Pontmercy replied, "Sire, I thank you for my widow." An hour later, he fell in the ravine of Ohain. Now, who was this Georges Pontmercy? He was this same "brigand of the Loire."

We have already seen something of his history. After Waterloo, Pontmercy, who had been pulled out of the hollow road of Ohain, as it will be remembered, had succeeded in joining the army, and had dragged himself from ambulance to ambulance as far as the cantonments of the Loire.

The Restoration had placed him on half-pay, then had sent him into residence, that is to say, under surveillance, at Vernon. King Louis XVIII, regarding all that which had taken place during the Hundred Days as not having occurred at all, did not recognize his quality as an officer of the Legion of Honor, nor his grade of colonel, nor his title of baron. He, on his side, neglected no occasion of signing himself "Colonel Baron Pontmercy." He had only an old blue coat, and he never went out without fastening to it his rosette as an officer of the Legion of Honor. The Attorney for the Crown had him warned that the authorities would prosecute him for "illegal" wearing of this decoration. When this notice was conveyed to him through an officious intermediary, Pontmercy retorted with a bitter smile, "I do not know whether I no longer understand French, or whether you no longer speak it; but the fact is that I do not understand." Then he went out for eight successive days with his rosette. They dared not interfere with him. Two or three times the Minister of War and the general in command of the department wrote to him with the following address: "A Monsieur le Commandant Pontmercy." He sent back the letters with the seals unbroken. At the same moment, Napoleon at Saint Helena was treating in the same fashion the missives of Sir Hudson Lowe addressed to General Bonaparte. Pontmercy had ended, may we be pardoned the expression, by having in his mouth the same saliva as his Emperor.

In the same way, there were at Rome Carthaginian prisoners who refused to salute Flaminius, and who had a little of Hannibal's spirit.

One day he encountered the district attorney in one of the streets of Vernon, stepped up to him, and said, "Mr. Crown Attorney, am I permitted to wear my scar?"

He had nothing save his meager half-pay as chief of squadron. He had hired the smallest house that he could find at Vernon. He lived there alone, we have just seen how. Under the Empire, between two wars, he had found time to marry Mademoiselle Gillenormand. The old bourgeois, thoroughly indignant at bottom, had given his consent with a sigh, saying, "The greatest families are forced into it." In 1815 Madame Pontmercy, an admirable woman in every sense, by the way, lofty in sentiment and rare, and worthy of her husband, died, leaving a child. This child had been the colonel's joy in his solitude; but the grandfather had imperatively claimed his grandson, declaring that if the child were not given to him he would disinherit him. The father had yielded in the little one's interest, and had transferred his love to flowers.

Moreover, he had renounced everything, and neither stirred up mischief nor conspired. He shared his thoughts between the innocent things he was then doing and the great things he had done. He passed his time in expecting a pink or in recalling Austerlitz.

M. Gillenormand kept up no relations with his son-in-law. The colonel was "a bandit" to him. M. Gillenormand never mentioned the colonel, except when he occasionally made mocking allusions to "his Baronship." It had been expressly agreed that Pontmercy should never attempt to see his son nor to speak to him, under penalty of having the latter handed over to him disowned and disinherited. For the Gillenormands, Pontmercy was a man afflicted with the plague. They intended to bring up the child in their own way. Perhaps he colonel was wrong to accept these conditions, but he submitted to them, thinking that he was doing right and sacrificing no one but himself.

The inheritance of Father Gillenormand did not amount to much; but the inheritance of Mademoiselle Gillenormand the elder was considerable. This aunt, who had remained unmarried, was very rich on the maternal side, and her sister's son was her natural heir. The boy, whose name was Marius, knew that he had a father, but nothing more. No one opened his mouth to him about it. Nevertheless, in the society into which his grandfather took him, whispers, innuendoes, and winks, had eventually enlightened the little boy's mind; he had finally understood something of the case, and as he naturally took in the ideas and opinions that were, so to speak, the air he breathed, by a sort of infiltration and slow penetration, he gradually came to think of his father only with shame and with a pain at his heart.

While he was growing up in this fashion, the colonel slipped away every two or three months, came to Paris on the sly, like a criminal breaking his ban, and went and posted himself at Saint-Sulpice, at the hour when Aunt Gillenormand led Marius to the Mass. There, trembling lest the aunt should turn around, concealed behind a pillar, motionless, not daring to breathe, he gazed at his child. The scarred veteran was afraid of that old spinster.

From this had arisen his connection with the Curé of Vernon, M. l' Abbé Mabeuf.

That worthy priest was the brother of a warden of Saint-Sulpice, who had often observed this man gazing at his child, and the scar on his cheek, and the large tears in his eyes. That man, who had so manly an air, yet who was weeping like a woman, had struck the warden. That face had clung to his mind. One day, having gone to Vernon to see his brother, he had encountered Colonel Pontmercy on the bridge, and had recognized the man of Saint-Sulpice. The warden had mentioned the circumstance to the Curé, and both had paid the colonel a visit, on some pretext or other. This visit led to others. The colonel, who had been extremely reserved at first, ended by opening his heart, and the Curé and the warden finally came to know the whole history, and how Pontmercy was sacrificing his happiness to his child's future. This caused the Curé to regard him with veneration and tenderness, and the colonel, on his side, became fond of the Curé. And moreover, when both are sincere and good, no men so penetrate each other, and so amalgamate with each other, as an old priest and an old soldier. At bottom, the man is the same. The one has devoted his life to his country here below, the other to his country on high; that is the only difference.

Twice a year, on the first of January and on St. George's day, Mariu
wrote duty letters to his father, which were dictated by his aunt, and that on
would have pronounced to be copied from some formula; this was all that M
Gillenormand tolerated; and the father answered them with very tender letter
that the grandfather thrust into his pocket unread.

CHAPTER III—REQUIESCANT

Madame de T.'s salon was all that Marius Pontmercy knew of the world. I
was the only opening through which he could get a glimpse of life. Thi
opening was somber, and more cold than warmth, more night than day, came to
him through this skylight. This child, who had been all joy and light on entering
this strange world, soon became melancholy, and, what is still more contrary
to his age, grave. Surrounded by all those singular and imposing personages
he gazed about him with serious amazement. Everything conspired to increase
this astonishment in him. There were in Madame de T.'s salon some very
noble ladies named Mathan, Noe, Levis, which was pronounced Levi, Cambis
pronounced Cambyse. These antique visages and these Biblical names mingle
in the child's mind with the Old Testament, which he was learning by heart
and when they were all there, seated in a circle around a dying fire, sparely
lighted by a lamp shaded with green, with their severe profiles, their gray or
white hair, their long gowns of another age, whose lugubrious colors could no
be distinguished, dropping, at rare intervals, words that were both majestic and
severe, little Marius stared at them with frightened eyes, in the conviction tha
he beheld not women, but patriarchs and magi, not real beings, but phantoms.

With these phantoms, priests were sometimes mingled, frequenters of thi
ancient salon, and some gentlemen; the Marquis de Sass———, private secretary
to Madame de Berry, the Vicomte de Val———, who published, under the
pseudonym of Charles-Antoine, monorhymed odes, the Prince de Beauff———
who, though very young, had a gray head and a pretty and witty wife, whose
very low-necked toilettes of scarlet velvet with gold torsades alarmed these
shadows, the Marquis de C——— d'E———, the man in all France who bes
understood "proportioned politeness," the Comte d'Am———, the kindly mar
with the amiable chin, and the Chevalier de Port-de-Guy, a pillar of the library
of the Louvre, called the King's cabinet, M. de Port-de-Guy, bald, and rathei
aged than old, was wont to relate that in 1793, at the age of sixteen, he had beer
put in the galleys as refractory and chained with an octogenarian, the Bishop

of Mirepoix, also refractory, but as a priest, while he was so in the capacity of a soldier. This was at Toulon. Their business was to go at night and gather up on the scaffold the heads and bodies of the persons who had been guillotined during the day; they bore away on their backs these dripping corpses, and their red galley-slave blouses had a clot of blood at the back of the neck, which was dry in the morning and wet at night. These tragic tales abounded in Madame de T.'s salon, and by dint of cursing Marat, they applauded Trestaillon. Some deputies of the undiscoverable variety played their whist there; M. Thibord du Chalard, M. Lemarchant de Gomicourt, and the celebrated scoffer of the right, M. Cornet-Dincourt. The bailiff de Ferrette, with his short breeches and his thin legs, sometimes traversed this salon on his way to M. de Talleyrand. He had been M. le Comte d'Artois's companion in pleasures and, unlike Aristotle crouching under Campaspe, he had made the Guimard crawl on all fours, and in that way he had exhibited to the ages a philosopher avenged by a bailiff. As for the priests, there was the Abbé Halma, the same to whom M. Larose, his collaborator on la Foudre, said, "Bah! Who is there who is not fifty years old? a few greenhorns perhaps?" The Abbé Letourneur, preacher to the King, the Abbé Frayssinous, who was not, as yet, either count, or bishop, or minister, or peer, and who wore an old cassock whose buttons were missing, and the Abbé Keravenant, Curé of Saint-Germain-des-Pres; also the Pope's Nuncio, then Monsignor Macchi, Archbishop of Nisibi, later on Cardinal, remarkable for his long, pensive nose, and another Monsignor, entitled thus: Abbate Palmieri, domestic prelate, one of the seven participant prothonotaries of the Holy See, Canon of the illustrious Liberian basilica, Advocate of the saints, Postulatore dei Santi, which refers to matters of canonization, and signifies very nearly: Master of Requests of the section of Paradise. Lastly, two cardinals, M. de la Luzerne, and M. de Cl——— T———. The Cardinal of Luzerne was a writer and was destined to have, a few years later, the honor of signing in the Conservateur articles side by side with Chateaubriand; M. de Cl——— T——— was Archbishop of Toul———, and often made trips to Paris, to his nephew, the Marquis de T———, who was Minister of Marine and War. The Cardinal of Cl——— T——— was a merry little man, who displayed his red stockings beneath his tucked-up cassock; his specialty was a hatred of the Encyclopaedia, and his desperate play at billiards, and persons who, at that epoch, passed through the Rue M——— on summer evenings, where the hotel de Cl——— T——— then stood, halted to listen to the shock of the balls and the piercing voice of the Cardinal shouting to his conclavist, Monseigneur Cotiret, Bishop in partibus of Caryste, "Mark, Abbé, I make a cannon." The Cardinal de Cl—— T—— had been brought to Madame de T.'s by his most intimate friend, M. de Roquelaure, former Bishop of Senlis, and one of the Forty. M. de Roquelaure was notable for his lofty figure and his assiduity at the Academy; through the glass door of the neighboring hall of the library where the French Academy then held its meetings, the curious could, on every Tuesday, contemplate the Ex-Bishop of Senlis, usually standing erect, freshly powdered, in violet hose, with his back turned to the door, apparently for the purpose of allowing a better view of his little collar. All these ecclesiastics, though for the most part as much courtiers as churchmen, added to the gravity of the T. salon, whose seigniorial aspect was accentuated by five peers of France, the Marquis de Vib——, the Marquis de Tal——, the Marquis de Herb——, the Vicomte Damb——, and the Duc de Val——. This Duc de Val——, although Prince de Mon——, that is to say a reigning prince abroad, had so high an idea of France and its peerage, that he viewed everything through their medium. It was he who said, "The Cardinals are the peers of France of Rome; the lords are the peers of France of England." Moreover, as it is indispensable that the Revolution should be everywhere in this century, this feudal salon was, as we have said, dominated by a bourgeois. M. Gillenormand reigned there.

There lay the essence and quintessence of the Parisian white society. There reputations, even Royalist reputations, were held in quarantine. There is always a trace of anarchy in renown. Chateaubriand, had he entered there, would have produced the effect of Pere Duchene. Some of the scoffed at did, nevertheless, penetrate there on sufferance. Comte Beug—— was received there, subject to correction.

The "noble" salons of the present day no longer resemble those salons. The Faubourg Saint-Germain reeks of the fagot even now. The Royalists of today are demagogues, let us record it to their credit.

At Madame de T.'s the society was superior, taste was exquisite and haughty, under the cover of a great show of politeness. Manners there admitted of all sorts of involuntary refinements that were the old regime itself, buried but still alive. Some of these habits, especially in the matter of language, seem eccentric. Persons but superficially acquainted with them would have taken for provincial that which was only antique. A woman was called Madame la Générale. Madame la Colonelle was not entirely disused. The charming Madame de Leon, in memory, no doubt, of the Duchesses de Longueville and de Chevreuse, preferred this appellation to her title of Princess. The Marquise de Crequy was also called Madame la Colonelle.

It was this little high society that invented at the Tuileries the refinement of speaking to the King in private as the King, in the third person, and never as Your Majesty, the designation of Your Majesty having been "soiled by the usurper."

Men and deeds were brought to judgment there. They jeered at the age, which released them from the necessity of understanding it. They abetted each other in amazement. They communicated to each other that modicum of light that they possessed. Methuselah bestowed information on Epimenides. The deaf man made the blind man acquainted with the course of things. They declared that the time that had elapsed since Coblentz had not existed. In the same manner that Louis XVIII was by the grace of God, in the five and twentieth year of his reign, the emigrants were, by rights, in the five and twentieth year of their adolescence.

All was harmonious; nothing was too much alive; speech hardly amounted to a breath; the newspapers, agreeing with the salons, seemed a papyrus. There were some young people, but they were rather dead. The liveries in the antechamber were antiquated. These utterly obsolete personages were served by domestics of the same stamp.

They all had the air of having lived a long time ago, and of obstinately resisting the sepulchre. Nearly the whole dictionary consisted of Conserver, Conservation, Conservateur; to be in good odor, that was the point. There are, in fact, aromatics in the opinions of these venerable groups, and their ideas smelled of it. It was a mummified society. The masters were embalmed, the servants were stuffed with straw.

A worthy old marquise, an emigree and ruined, who had but a solitary maid, continued to say, "My people."

What did they do in Madame de T.'s salon? They were ultra.

To be ultra; this word, although what it represents may not have disappeared, has no longer any meaning at the present day. Let us explain it.

To be ultra is to go beyond. It is to attack the scepter in the name of the throne, and the miter in the name of the attar; it is to ill treat the thing that one is dragging, it is to kick over the traces; it is to cavil at the fagot on the score of the amount of cooking received by heretics; it is to reproach the idol with its small amount of idolatry; it is to insult through excess of respect; it is to discover that the Pope is not sufficiently papish, that the King is not sufficiently royal, and that the night has too much light; it is to be discontented with alabaster, with snow, with the swan and the lily in the name of whiteness; it is to be a partisan of things to the point of becoming their enemy; it is to be so strongly for, as to be against.

The ultra spirit especially characterizes the first phase of the Restoration.

Nothing in history resembles that quarter of an hour that begins in 1814 and terminates about 1820, with the advent of M. de Villele, the practical man of the Right. These six years were an extraordinary moment; at one and the same time brilliant and gloomy, smiling and somber, illuminated as by the radiance of dawn and entirely covered, at the same time, with the shadows of the great catastrophes that still filled the horizon and were slowly sinking into the past. There existed in that light and that shadow, a complete little new and old world, comic and sad, juvenile and senile, which was rubbing its eyes; nothing resembles an awakening like a return; a group that regarded France with ill-temper, and that France regarded with irony; good old owls of marquises by the streetful, who had returned, and of ghosts, the "former" subjects of amazement at everything, brave and noble gentlemen who smiled at being in France but wept also, delighted to behold their country once more, in despair at not finding their monarchy; the nobility of the Crusades treating the nobility of the Empire, that is to say, the nobility of the sword, with scorn; historic races who had lost the sense of history; the sons of the companions of Charlemagne disdaining the companions of Napoleon. The swords, as we have just remarked, returned the insult; the sword of Fontenoy was laughable and nothing but a scrap of rusty iron; the sword of Marengo was odious and was only a saber. Former days did not recognize Yesterday. People no longer had the feeling for what was grand. There was someone who called Bonaparte Scapin. This Society no longer exists. Nothing of it, we repeat, exists today. When we select from it someone figure at random, and attempt to make it live again in thought, it seems as strange to us as the world before the Deluge. It is because it, too, as a matter of fact, has been engulfed in a deluge. It has disappeared beneath two Revolutions. What billows are ideas! How quickly they cover all that it is their mission to destroy and to bury, and how promptly they create frightful gulfs!

Such was the physiognomy of the salons of those distant and candid times when M. Martainville had more wit than Voltaire.

These salons had a literature and politics of their own. They believed in Fievee. M. Agier laid down the law in them. They commentated M. Colnet, the old bookseller and publicist of the Quay Malaquais. Napoleon was to them thoroughly the Corsican Ogre. Later on the introduction into history of M. le Marquis de Bonaparte, Lieutenant General of the King's armies, was a concession to the spirit of the age.

These salons did not long preserve their purity. Beginning with 1818, doctrinarians began to spring up in them, a disturbing shade. Their way was to e Royalists and to excuse themselves for being so. Where the ultras were very proud, the doctrinarians were rather ashamed. They had wit; they had silence; their political dogma was suitably impregnated with arrogance; they should have succeeded. They indulged, and usefully too, in excesses in the matter of white neckties and tightly buttoned coats. The mistake or the misfortune of the doctrinarian party was to create aged youth. They assumed the poses of wise men. They dreamed of engrafting a temperate power on the absolute and excessive principle. They opposed, and sometimes with rare intelligence, conservative liberalism to the liberalism that demolishes. They were heard to say, "Thanks for Royalism! It has rendered more than one service. It has brought back tradition, worship, religion, respect. It is faithful, brave, chivalric, loving, devoted. It has mingled, though with regret, the secular grandeurs of the monarchy with the new grandeurs of the nation. Its mistake is not to understand the Revolution, the Empire, glory, liberty, young ideas, young generations, the age. But this mistake it makes with regard to us, have we not sometimes been guilty of it toward them? The Revolution, whose heirs we are, ought to be intelligent on all points. To attack Royalism is a misconstruction of liberalism. What an error! And what blindness! Revolutionary France is wanting in respect toward historic France, that is to say, toward its mother, that is to say, toward itself. After the 5th of September, the nobility of the monarchy is treated as the nobility of the Empire was treated after the 5th of July. They were unjust to the eagle, we are unjust to the fleur-de-lis. It seems that we must always have something to proscribe! Does it serve any purpose to ungild the crown of Louis XIV, to scrape the coat of arms of Henry IV? We scoff at M. de Vaublanc for erasing the N's from the bridge of Jena! What was it that he did? What are we doing? Bouvines belongs to us as well as Marengo. The fleurs-de-lis are ours as well as the N's. That is our patrimony. To what purpose shall we diminish it? We must not deny our country in the past any more than in the present. Why not accept the whole of history? Why not love the whole of France?"

It is thus that doctrinarians criticized and protected Royalism, which was displeased at criticism and furious at protection.

The ultras marked the first epoch of Royalism, congregation characterized the second. Skill follows ardor. Let us confine ourselves here to this sketch.

In the course of this narrative, the author of this book has encountered in his path this curious moment of contemporary history; he has been forced to cast a passing glance upon it, and to trace once more some of the singular features of this society that is unknown today. But he does it rapidly and without any bitter or derisive idea. Souvenirs both respectful and affectionate, for they touch his mother, attach him to this past. Moreover, let us remark, this same petty world had a grandeur of its own. One may smile at it, but one can neither despise nor hate it. It was the France of former days.

Marius Pontmercy pursued some studies, as all children do. When he emerged from the hands of Aunt Gillenormand, his grandfather confided him to a worthy professor of the most purely classic innocence. This young soul that was expanding passed from a prude to a vulgar pedant.

Marius went through his years of college, then he entered the law school. He was a Royalist, fanatical and severe. He did not love his grandfather much, as the latter's gaiety and cynicism repelled him, and his feelings toward his father were gloomy.

He was, on the whole, a cold and ardent, noble, generous, proud, religious, enthusiastic lad; dignified to harshness, pure to shyness.

CHAPTER IV—END OF THE BRIGAND

The conclusion of Marius's classical studies coincided with M. Gillenormand's departure from society. The old man bade farewell to the Faubourg Saint-Germain and to Madame de T.'s salon, and established himself in the Mardis, in his house of the Rue des Filles-du-Calvaire. There he had for servants, in addition to the porter, that chambermaid, Nicolette, who had succeeded to Magnon, and that short-breathed and pursy Basque, who have been mentioned above.

In 1827 Marius had just attained his seventeenth year. One evening, on his return home, he saw his grandfather holding a letter in his hand.

"Marius," said M. Gillenormand, "you will set out for Vernon tomorrow."

"Why?" said Marius.

"To see your father."

Marius was seized with a trembling fit. He had thought of everything except this—that he should one day be called upon to see his father. Nothing could be more unexpected, more surprising, and, let us admit it, more disagreeable to him. It was forcing estrangement into reconciliation. It was not an affliction, but it was an unpleasant duty.

Marius, in addition to his motives of political antipathy, was convinced that his father, the slasher, as M. Gillenormand called him on his amiable days, did not love him; this was evident, since he had abandoned him to others. Feeling

1at he was not beloved, he did not love. "Nothing is more simple," he said to imself.

He was so astounded that he did not question M. Gillenormand. The randfather resumed:

"It appears that he is ill. He demands your presence." And after a pause, 1e added, "Set out tomorrow morning. I think there is a coach that leaves the Cour des Fontaines at six o'clock, and that arrives in the evening. Take it. He ays that here is haste."

Then he crushed the letter in his hand and thrust it into his pocket. Marius night have set out that very evening and have been with his father on the ollowing morning. A diligence from the Rue du Bouloi took the trip to Rouen »y night at that date, and passed through Vernon. Neither Marius nor M. Gillenormand thought of making inquiries about it.

The next day, at twilight, Marius reached Vernon. People were just »eginning to light their candles. He asked the first person whom he met for M. Pontmercy's house." For in his own mind, he agreed with the Restoration, nd like it, did not recognize his father's claim to the title of either colonel or »aron.

The house was pointed out to him. He rang; a woman with a little lamp in 1er hand opened the door.

"M. Pontmercy?" said Marius.

The woman remained motionless.

"Is this his house?" demanded Marius.

The woman nodded affirmatively.

"Can I speak with him?"

The woman shook her head.

"But I am his son!" persisted Marius. "He is expecting me."

"He no longer expects you," said the woman.

Then he perceived that she was weeping.

She pointed to the door of a room on the ground floor; he entered.

In that room, which was lighted by a tallow candle standing on the :himneypiece, there were three men, one standing erect, another kneeling, and one lying at full length, on the floor in his shirt. The one on the floor was the :olonel.

The other two were the doctor, and the priest, who was engaged in prayer.

The colonel had been attacked by brain fever three days previously. As he 1ad a foreboding of evil at the very beginning of his illness, he had written to M. Gillenormand to demand his son. The malady had grown worse. On the

very evening of Marius's arrival at Vernon, the colonel had had an attack o
delirium; he had risen from his bed, in spite of the servant's efforts to preven
him, crying, "My son is not coming! I shall go to meet him!" Then he ran ou
of his room and fell prostrate on the floor of the antechamber. He had jus
expired.

The doctor had been summoned, and the Curé. The doctor had arrived too
late. The son had also arrived too late.

By the dim light of the candle, a large tear could be distinguished on the pal
and prostrate colonel's cheek, where it had trickled from his dead eye. The ey
was extinguished, but the tear was not yet dry. That tear was his son's delay.

Marius gazed upon that man whom he beheld for the first time, on tha
venerable and manly face, on those open eyes that saw not, on those whit
locks, those robust limbs, on which, here and there, brown lines, markin
sword thrusts, and a sort of red stars, which indicated bullet holes, were visible
He contemplated that gigantic sear that stamped heroism on that countenanc
upon which God had imprinted goodness. He reflected that this man was hi
father, and that this man was dead, and a chill ran over him.

The sorrow he felt was the sorrow he would have felt in the presence of an
other man whom he had chanced to behold stretched out in death.

Anguish, poignant anguish, was in that chamber. The servant-woman wa
lamenting in a corner, the Curé was praying, and his sobs were audible, th
doctor was wiping his eyes; the corpse itself was weeping.

The doctor, the priest, and the woman gazed at Marius in the midst of thei
affliction without uttering a word; he was the stranger there. Marius, who wa
far too little affected, felt ashamed and embarrassed at his own attitude; h
held his hat in his hand; and he dropped it on the floor, in order to produce th
impression that grief had deprived him of the strength to hold it.

At the same time, he experienced remorse, and he despised himself fo
behaving in this manner. But was it his fault? He did not love his father? Wh
should he!

The colonel had left nothing. The sale of big furniture barely paid th
expenses of his burial.

The servant found a scrap of paper, which she handed to Marius. I
contained the following, in the colonel's handwriting:

> "For my son.
> The Emperor made me a Baron on the battlefield of Waterloo.
> Since the Restoration disputes my right to this title which I

purchased with my blood, my son shall take it and bear it.
That he will be worthy of it is a matter of course." Below,
the colonel had added: "At that same battle of Waterloo, a
sergeant saved my life. The man's name was Thenardier. I
think that he has recently been keeping a little inn, in a village
in the neighborhood of Paris, at Chelles or Montfermeil. If my
son meets him, he will do all the good he can to Thenardier."

Marius took this paper and preserved it, not out of duty to his father, but
because of that vague respect for death that is always imperious in the heart
of man.

Nothing remained of the colonel. M. Gillenormand had his sword and
uniform sold to an old-clothes dealer. The neighbors devastated the garden
and pillaged the rare flowers. The other plants turned to nettles and weeds,
and died.

Marius remained only forty-eight hours at Vernon. After the interment he
returned to Paris, and applied himself again to his law studies, with no more
thought of his father than if the latter had never lived. In two days the colonel
was buried, and in three forgotten.

Marius wore crape on his hat. That was all.

CHAPTER V—THE UTILITY OF GOING TO MASS, IN ORDER TO BECOME A REVOLUTIONIST

Marius had preserved the religious habits of his childhood. One Sunday,
when he went to hear Mass at Saint-Sulpice, at that same chapel of the
Virgin where his aunt had led him when a small lad, he placed himself behind
a pillar, being more absent-minded and thoughtful than usual on that occasion,
and knelt down, without paying any special heed, upon a chair of Utrecht
velvet, on the back of that was inscribed this name: Monsieur Mabeuf, warden.
Mass had hardly begun when an old man presented himself and said to Marius,
"This is my place, Sir."

Marius stepped aside promptly, and the old man took possession of his chair.

The Mass concluded, Marius still stood thoughtfully a few paces distant;
the old man approached him again and said, "I beg your pardon, sir, for having
disturbed you a while ago, and for again disturbing you at this moment; you

must have thought me intrusive, and I will explain myself."

"There is no need of that, Sir," said Marius.

"Yes!" went on the old man. "I do not wish you to have a bad opinion of me. You see, I am attached to this place. It seems to me that the Mass is better from here. Why? I will tell you. It is from this place, that I have watched a poor, brave father come regularly, every two or three months, for the last ten years, since he had no other opportunity and no other way of seeing his child, because he was prevented by family arrangements. He came at the hour when he knew that his son would be brought to Mass. The little one never suspected that his father was there. Perhaps he did not even know that he had a father, poor innocent! The father kept behind a pillar, so that he might not be seen. He gazed at his child and he wept. He adored that little fellow, poor man! I could see that. This spot has become sanctified in my sight, and I have contracted a habit of coming here to listen to the Mass. I prefer it to the stall to which I have a right, in my capacity of warden. I knew that unhappy gentleman a little, too. He had a father-in-law, a wealthy aunt, relatives, I don't know exactly what all, who threatened to disinherit the child if he, the father, saw him. He sacrificed himself in order that his son might be rich and happy some day. He was separated from him because of political opinions. Certainly, I approve of political opinions, but there are people who do not know where to stop. Mon Dieu! A man is not a monster because he was at Waterloo; a father is not separated from his child for such a reason as that. He was one of Bonaparte's colonels. He is dead, I believe. He lived at Vernon, where I have a brother who is a Curé, and his name was something like Pontmarie or Montpercy. He had a fine sword cut, on my honor."

"Pontmercy," suggested Marius, turning pale.

"Precisely, Pontmercy. Did you know him?"

"Sir," said Marius, "he was my father."

The old warden clasped his hands and exclaimed, "Ah! You are the child! Yes, that's true, he must be a man by this time. Well! Poor child, you may say that you had a father who loved you dearly!"

Marius offered his arm to the old man and conducted him to his lodgings.

On the following day, he said to M. Gillenormand, "I have arranged a hunting party with some friends. Will you permit me to be absent for three days?"

"Four!" replied his grandfather. "Go and amuse yourself."

And he said to his daughter in a low tone, and with a wink, "Some love affair!"

CHAPTER VI—THE CONSEQUENCES OF HAVING MET A WARDEN

Where it was that Marius went will be disclosed a little further on.

Marius was absent for three days, then he returned to Paris, went straight to the library of the law school and asked for the files of the Moniteur.

He read the Moniteur, he read all the histories of the Republic and the Empire, the Memorial de Sainte-Helene, all the memoirs, all the newspapers, the bulletins, the proclamations; he devoured everything. The first time that he came across his father's name in the bulletins of the grand army, he had a fever for a week. He went to see the generals under whom Georges Pontmercy had served, among others, Comte H. Church-warden Mabeuf, whom he went to see again, told him about the life at Vernon, the colonel's retreat, his flowers, his solitude. Marius came to a full knowledge of that rare, sweet, and sublime man, that species of lion-lamb who had been his father.

In the meanwhile, occupied as he was with this study that absorbed all his moments as well as his thoughts, he hardly saw the Gillenormands at all. He made his appearance at meals; then they searched for him, and he was not to be found. Father Gillenormand smiled. "Bah! Bah! He is just of the age for the girls!" Sometimes the old man added, "The deuce! I thought it was only an affair of gallantry; it seems that it is an affair of passion!"

It was a passion, in fact. Marius was on the high road to adoring his father.

At the same time, his ideas underwent an extraordinary change. The phases of this change were numerous and successive. As this is the history of many minds of our day, we think it will prove useful to follow these phases step by step and to indicate them all.

That history upon which he had just cast his eyes appalled him.

The first effect was to dazzle him.

Up to that time, the Republic, the Empire, had been to him only monstrous words. The Republic, a guillotine in the twilight; the Empire, a sword in the night. He had just taken a look at it, and where he had expected to find only a chaos of shadows, he had beheld, with a sort of unprecedented surprise, mingled with fear and joy, stars sparkling, Mirabeau, Vergniaud, Saint-Just, Robespierre, Camille, Desmoulins, Danton, and a sun arise, Napoleon. He did not know where he stood. He recoiled, blinded by the brilliant lights. Little by little, when his astonishment had passed off, he grew accustomed to this radiance, he contemplated these deeds without dizziness, he examined these personages without terror; the Revolution and the Empire presented themselves luminously, in perspective, before his mind's eye; he beheld each of these groups of events and of men summed up in two tremendous facts the Republic in the sovereignty of civil right restored to the masses, the Empire in the sovereignty of the French idea imposed on Europe; he beheld the grand figure of the people emerge from the Revolution, and the grand figure of France spring forth from the Empire. He asserted in his conscience, that all this had been good. What his dazzled state neglected in this, his first far too synthetic estimation, we do not think it necessary to point out here. It is the state of a mind on the march that we are recording. Progress is not accomplished in one stage. That stated, once for all, in connection with what precedes as well as with what is to follow, we continue.

He then perceived that, up to that moment, he had comprehended his country no more than he had comprehended his father. He had not known either the one or the other, and a sort of voluntary night had obscured his eyes. Now he saw, and on the one hand he admired, while on the other he adored.

He was filled with regret and remorse, and he reflected in despair that all he had in his soul could now be said only to the tomb. Oh! If his father had still been in existence, if he had still had him, if God, in his compassion and his goodness, had permitted his father to be still among the living, how he would have run, how he would have precipitated himself, how he would have cried to his father, "Father! Here I am! It is I! I have the same heart as thou! I am thy son!" How he would have embraced that white head, bathed his hair in tears, gazed upon his scar, pressed his hands, adored his garment, kissed his feet! Oh! Why had his father died so early, before his time, before the justice, the love of his son had come to him? Marius had a continual sob in his heart, which said to him every moment, "Alas!" At the same time, he became more truly serious, more truly grave, more sure of his thought and his faith. At each instant, gleams of the true came to complete his reason. An inward growth seemed to be in progress within him. He was conscious of a sort of natural enlargement, which gave him two things that were new to him—his father and his country.

As everything opens when one has a key, so he explained to himself that which he had hated, he penetrated that which he had abhorred; henceforth he plainly perceived the providential, divine and human sense of the great things he had been taught to detest, and of the great men whom he had been instructed to curse. When he reflected on his former opinions, which were but those of yesterday, and which, nevertheless, seemed to him already so very ancient, he grew indignant, yet he smiled.

From the rehabilitation of his father, he naturally passed to the rehabilitation of Napoleon.

But the latter, we will confess, was not effected without labor.

From his infancy, he had been imbued with the judgments of the party of 814, on Bonaparte. Now, all the prejudices of the Restoration, all its interests, all its instincts tended to disfigure Napoleon. It execrated him even more than it did Robespierre. It had very cleverly turned to sufficiently good account the fatigue of the nation, and the hatred of mothers. Bonaparte had become an almost fabulous monster, and in order to paint him to the imagination of the people, which, as we lately pointed out, resembles the imagination of children, the party of 1814 made him appear under all sorts of terrifying masks in succession, from that which is terrible though it remains grandiose to that which is terrible and becomes grotesque, from Tiberius to the bugaboo. Thus, in speaking of Bonaparte, one was free to sob or to puff up with laughter, provided that hatred lay at the bottom. Marius had never entertained—about that man, as he was called—any other ideas in his mind. They had combined with the tenacity that existed in his nature. There was in him a headstrong little man who hated Napoleon.

On reading history, on studying him, especially in the documents and materials for history, the veil that concealed Napoleon from the eyes of Marius was gradually rent. He caught a glimpse of something immense, and he suspected that he had been deceived up to that moment, on the score of Bonaparte as about all the rest; each day he saw more distinctly; and he set about mounting, slowly, step by step, almost regretfully in the beginning, then with intoxication and as though attracted by an irresistible fascination, first the somber steps, then the vaguely illuminated steps, at last the luminous and splendid steps of enthusiasm.

One night, he was alone in his little chamber near the roof. His candle was burning; he was reading, with his elbows resting on his table close to the open window. All sorts of reveries reached him from space, and mingled with his thoughts. What a spectacle is the night! One hears dull sounds, without knowing from where they proceed; one beholds Jupiter, which is twelve hundred times larger than the earth, glowing like a firebrand, the azure is black, the stars shine; it is formidable.

He was perusing the bulletins of the grand army, those heroic strophes penned on the field of battle; there, at intervals, he beheld his father's name, always the name of the Emperor; the whole of that great Empire presented itself to him; he felt a flood swelling and rising within him; it seemed to him at moments that his father passed close to him like a breath, and whispered in his ear; he gradually got into a singular state; he thought that he heard drums, cannon, trumpets, the measured tread of battalions, the dull and distant gallop of the cavalry; from time to time, his eyes were raised heavenward, and gazed upon the colossal constellations as they gleamed in the measureless depths of space, then they fell upon his book once more, and there they beheld other colossal things moving confusedly. His heart contracted within him. He was in a transport, trembling, panting. All at once, without himself knowing what was in him, and what impulse he was obeying, he sprang to his feet, stretched both arms out of the window, gazed intently into the gloom, the silence, the infinite darkness, the eternal immensity, and exclaimed, "Long live the Emperor!"

From that moment forth, all was over; the Ogre of Corsica, the usurper, the tyrant, the monster who was the lover of his own sisters, the actor who took lessons of Talma, the poisoner of Jaffa, the tiger, Buonaparte, all this vanished and gave place in his mind to a vague and brilliant radiance in which shone at an inaccessible height, the pale marble phantom of Caesar. The Emperor had been for his father only the well-beloved captain whom one admires, for whom one sacrifices one's self; he was something more to Marius. He was the predestined constructor of the French group, succeeding the Roman group in the domination of the universe. He was a prodigious architect, of a destruction, the continuer of Charlemagne, of Louis XI, of Henry IV, of Richelieu, of Louis XIV, and of the Committee of Public Safety, having his spots, no doubt, his faults, his crimes even, being a man, that is to say; but august in his faults, brilliant in his spots, powerful in his crime.

He was the predestined man, who had forced all nations to say, "The great nation!" He was better than that, he was the very incarnation of France conquering Europe by the sword that he grasped, and the world by the light that he shed. Marius saw in Bonaparte the dazzling specter that will always rise upon the frontier, and that will guard the future. Despot but dictator; a despot resulting from a republic and summing up a revolution. Napoleon became for him the man-people as Jesus Christ is the man-God.

It will be perceived, that like all new converts to a religion, his conversion intoxicated him, he hurled himself headlong into adhesion and he went too far. His nature was so constructed; once on the downward slope, it was almost impossible for him to put on the drag. Fanaticism for the sword took possession of him, and complicated in his mind his enthusiasm for the idea. He did not perceive that, along with genius, and pell-mell, he was admitting force, that is to say, that he was installing in two compartments of his idolatry, on the one hand that which is divine, on the other that which is brutal. In many respects, he had set about deceiving himself otherwise. He admitted everything. There is a way of encountering error while on one's way to the truth. He had a violent sort of good faith that took everything in the lump. In the new path that he had entered on, in judging the mistakes of the old regime, as in measuring the glory of Napoleon, he neglected the attenuating circumstances.

At all events, a tremendous step had been taken. Where he had formerly beheld the fall of the monarchy, he now saw the advent of France. His orientation had changed. What had been his East became the West. He had turned squarely around.

All these revolutions were accomplished within him, without his family obtaining an inkling of the case.

When, during this mysterious labor, he had entirely shed his old Bourbon and ultra skin, when he had cast off the aristocrat, the Jacobite and the Royalist, when he had become thoroughly a revolutionist, profoundly democratic and republican, he went to an engraver on the Quai des Orfevres and ordered a hundred cards bearing this name: Le Baron Marius Pontmercy.

This was only the strictly logical consequence of the change that had taken place in him, a change in which everything gravitated around his father.

Only, as he did not know anyone and could not sow his cards with any porter, he put them in his pocket.

By another natural consequence, in proportion as he drew nearer to his father, to the latter's memory, and to the things for which the colonel had fought five and twenty years before, he receded from his grandfather. We have long ago said, that M. Gillenormand's temper did not please him. There already existed between them all the dissonances of the grave young man and the frivolous old man. The gaiety of Geronte shocks and exasperates the melancholy of Werther. So long as the same political opinions and the same ideas had been common to them both, Marius had met M. Gillenormand there as on a bridge. When the bridge fell, an abyss was formed. And then, over and above all, Marius experienced unutterable impulses to revolt, when he reflected that it was M. Gillenormand who had, from stupid motives, torn him ruthlessly from the colonel, thus depriving the father of the child, and the child of the father.

By dint of pity for his father, Marius had nearly arrived at aversion for his grandfather.

Nothing of this sort, however, was betrayed on the exterior, as we have already said. Only he grew colder and colder; laconic at meals, and rare in the house. When his aunt scolded him for it, he was very gentle and alleged his studies, his lectures, the examinations, etc., as a pretext. His grandfather never departed from his infallible diagnosis: "In love! I know all about it."

From time to time Marius absented himself.

"Where is it that he goes off like this?" said his aunt.

On one of these trips, which were always very brief, he went to Montfermeil, in order to obey the injunction that his father had left him, and he sought the old sergeant to Waterloo, the innkeeper Thenardier. Thenardier had failed, the inn was closed, and no one knew what had become of him. Marius was away from the house for four days on this quest.

"He is getting decidedly wild," said his grandfather.

They thought they had noticed that he wore something on his breast, under his shirt, which was attached to his neck by a black ribbon.

CHAPTER VII—SOME PETTICOAT

We have mentioned a lancer.

He was a great-grand-nephew of M. Gillenormand, on the paternal side, who led a garrison life, outside the family and far from the domestic hearth. Lieutenant Theodule Gillenormand fulfilled all the conditions required to make what is called a fine officer. He had "a lady's waist," a victorious manner of trailing his sword and of twirling his mustache in a hook. He visited Paris very rarely, and so rarely that Marius had never seen him. The cousins knew each other only by name. We think we have said that Theodule was the favorite of Aunt Gillenormand, who preferred him because she did not see him. Not seeing people permits one to attribute to them all possible perfections.

One morning, Mademoiselle Gillenormand the elder returned to her apartment as much disturbed as her placidity was capable of allowing. Marius had just asked his grandfather's permission to take a little trip, adding that he meant to set out that very evening. "Go!" had been his grandfather's reply, and M. Gillenormand had added in an aside, as he raised his eyebrows to the top of his forehead, "Here he is passing the night out again." Mademoiselle Gillenormand had ascended to her chamber greatly puzzled, and on the staircase had dropped this exclamation: "This is too much!" And this interrogation: "But where is it that he goes?" She espied some adventure of the heart, more or less illicit, a woman in the shadow, a rendezvous, a mystery, and she would not have been sorry to thrust her spectacles into the affair. Tasting a mystery

sembles getting the first flavor of a scandal; sainted souls do not detest this.
There is some curiosity about scandal in the secret compartments of bigotry.

So she was the prey of a vague appetite for learning a history.

In order to get rid of this curiosity that agitated her a little beyond her wont,
he took refuge in her talents, and set about scalloping, with one layer of cotton
after another, one of those embroideries of the Empire and the Restoration,
in which there are numerous cartwheels. The work was clumsy, the worker
cross. She had been seated at this for several hours when the door opened.
Mademoiselle Gillenormand raised her nose. Lieutenant Theodule stood
before her, making the regulation salute. She uttered a cry of delight. One may
be old, one may be a prude, one may be pious, one may be an aunt, but it is
always agreeable to see a lancer enter one's chamber.

"You here, Theodule!" she exclaimed.

"On my way through town, Aunt."

"Embrace me."

"Here goes!" said Theodule.

And he kissed her. Aunt Gillenormand went to her writing desk and opened it.

"You will remain with us a week at least?"

"I leave this very evening, Aunt."

"It is not possible!"

"Mathematically!"

"Remain, my little Theodule, I beseech you."

"My heart says 'yes,' but my orders say 'no.' The matter is simple. They
are changing our garrison; we have been at Melun, we are being transferred to
Gaillon. It is necessary to pass through Paris in order to get from the old post
to the new one. I said, 'I am going to see my aunt.'"

"Here is something for your trouble."

And she put ten Louis into his hand.

"For my pleasure, you mean to say, my dear aunt."

Theodule kissed her again, and she experienced the joy of having some of
the skin scratched from her neck by the braidings on his uniform.

"Are you making the journey on horseback, with your regiment?" she
asked him.

"No, Aunt. I wanted to see you. I have special permission. My servant is
taking my horse; I am traveling by diligence. And, by the way, I want to ask
you something."

"What is it?"

"Is my cousin Marius Pontmercy traveling so, too?"

565

"How do you know that?" said his aunt, suddenly pricked to the quick with a lively curiosity.

"On my arrival, I went to the diligence to engage my seat in the coupe."

"Well?"

"A traveler had already come to engage a seat in the imperial. I saw his name on the card."

"What name?"

"Marius Pontmercy."

"The wicked fellow!" exclaimed his aunt. "Ah! Your cousin is not a steady lad like yourself. To think that he is to pass the night in a diligence!"

"Just as I am going to do."

"But you—it is your duty; in his case, it is wildness."

"Bosh!" said Theodule.

Here an event occurred to Mademoiselle Gillenormand the elder, an idea struck her. If she had been a man, she would have slapped her brow. She apostrophized Theodule, "Are you aware whether your cousin knows you?"

"No. I have seen him; but he has never deigned to notice me."

"So you are going to travel together?"

"He in the imperial, I in the coupe."

"Where does this diligence run?"

"To Andelys."

"Then that is where Marius is going?"

"Unless, like myself, he should stop on the way. I get down at Vernon, in order to take the branch coach for Gaillon. I know nothing of Marius's plan of travel."

"Marius! what an ugly name! What possessed them to name him Marius. While you, at least, are called Theodule."

"I would rather be called Alfred," said the officer.

"Listen, Theodule."

"I am listening, Aunt."

"Pay attention."

"I am paying attention."

"You understand?"

"Yes."

"Well, Marius absents himself!"

"Eh! Eh!"

"He travels."

"Ah! Ah!"

"He spends the night out."

"Oh! Oh!"

"We should like to know what there is behind all this."

Theodule replied with the composure of a man of bronze, "Some petticoat or other." And with that inward laugh that denotes certainty, he added, "A lass."

"That is evident," exclaimed his aunt, who thought she heard M. Gillenormand speaking, and who felt her conviction become irresistible at that word fillette, accentuated in almost the very same fashion by the granduncle and the grandnephew. She resumed, "Do us a favor. Follow Marius a little. He does not know you, it will be easy. Since a lass there is, try to get a sight of her. You must write us the tale. It will amuse his grandfather."

Theodule had no excessive taste for this sort of spying; but he was much touched by the ten Louis, and he thought he saw a chance for a possible sequel. He accepted the commission and said, "As you please, Aunt."

And he added in an aside, to himself, "Here I am a duenna."

Mademoiselle Gillenormand embraced him.

"You are not the man to play such pranks, Theodule. You obey discipline, you are the slave of orders, you are a man of scruples and duty, and you would not quit your family to go and see a creature."

The lancer made the pleased grimace of Cartouche when praised for his probity.

Marius, on the evening following this dialogue, mounted the diligence without suspecting that he was watched. As for the watcher, the first thing he did was to fall asleep. His slumber was complete and conscientious. Argus snored all night long.

At daybreak, the conductor of the diligence shouted, "Vernon! Relay of Vernon! Travelers for Vernon!" And Lieutenant Theodule woke.

"Good," he growled, still half asleep, "this is where I get out."

Then, as his memory cleared by degrees, the effect of waking, he recalled his aunt, the ten Louis, and the account that he had undertaken to render of the deeds and proceedings of Marius. This set him to laughing.

"Perhaps he is no longer in the coach," he thought, as he rebuttoned the waistcoat of his undress uniform. "He may have stopped at Poissy; he may have stopped at Triel; if he did not get out at Meulan, he may have got out at Mantes, unless he got out at Rolleboise, or if he did not go on as far as Pacy, with the choice of turning to the left at Evreus, or to the right at Laroche-Guyon. Run after him, Auntie. What the devil am I to write to that good old soul?"

At that moment a pair of black trousers descending from the imperial made its appearance at the window of the coupe.

"Can that be Marius?" said the lieutenant.

It was Marius.

A little peasant girl, all entangled with the horses and the postilions at the end of the vehicle, was offering flowers to the travelers. "Give your ladies flowers!" she cried.

Marius approached her and purchased the finest flowers in her flat basket.

"Come now," said Theodule, leaping down from the coupe, "this piques my curiosity. Who the deuce is he going to carry those flowers to? She must be a splendidly handsome woman for so fine a bouquet. I want to see her."

And no longer in pursuance of orders, but from personal curiosity, like dogs who hunt on their own account, he set out to follow Marius.

Marius paid no attention to Theodule. Elegant women descended from the diligence; he did not glance at them. He seemed to see nothing around him.

"He is pretty deeply in love!" thought Theodule.

Marius directed his steps toward the church.

"Capital," said Theodule to himself. "Rendezvous seasoned with a bit of Mass are the best sort. Nothing is so exquisite as an ogle that passes over the good God's head."

On arriving at the church, Marius did not enter it, but skirted the apse. He disappeared behind one of the angles of the apse.

"The rendezvous is appointed outside," said Theodule. "Let's have a look at the lass."

And he advanced on the tips of his boots toward the corner that Marius had turned.

On arriving there, he halted in amazement.

Marius, with his forehead clasped in his hands, was kneeling upon the grass on a grave. He had strewn his bouquet there. At the extremity of the grave, on a little swelling that marked the head, there stood a cross of black wood with this name in white letters: COLONEL BARON PONTMERCY. Marius's sobs were audible.

The "lass" was a grave.

CHAPTER VIII—MARBLE
AGAINST GRANITE

It was here that Marius had come on the first occasion of his absenting himself from Paris. It was here that he had come every time that M. Gillenormand had said, "He is sleeping out."

Lieutenant Theodule was absolutely put out of countenance by this unexpected encounter with a sepulchre; he experienced a singular and disagreeable sensation that he was incapable of analyzing, and that was composed of respect for the tomb, mingled with respect for the colonel. He retreated, leaving Marius alone in the cemetery, and there was discipline in his retreat. Death appeared to him with large epaulets, and he almost made the military salute to him. Not knowing what to write to his aunt, he decided not to write at all; and it is probable that nothing would have resulted from the discovery made by Theodule as to the love affairs of Marius, if, by one of those mysterious arrangements that are so frequent in chance, the scene at Vernon had not had an almost immediate counter-shock at Paris.

Marius returned from Vernon on the third day, in the middle of the morning, descended at his grandfather's door, and, wearied by the two nights spent in the diligence, and feeling the need of repairing his loss of sleep by an hour at the swimming school, he mounted rapidly to his chamber, took merely time enough to throw off his traveling coat, and the black ribbon that he wore around his neck, and went off to the bath.

M. Gillenormand, who had risen betimes like all old men in good health, had heard his entrance, and had made haste to climb, as quickly as his old legs permitted, the stairs to the upper story where Marius lived, in order to embrace him, and to question him while so doing, and to find out where he had been.

But the youth had taken less time to descend than the old man had to ascend, and when Father Gillenormand entered the attic, Marius was no longer there.

The bed had not been disturbed, and on the bed lay, outspread, but not defiantly the greatcoat and the black ribbon.

"I like this better," said M. Gillenormand.

And a moment later, he made his entrance into the salon, where Mademoiselle Gillenormand was already seated, busily embroidering her cartwheels.

The entrance was a triumphant one.

M. Gillenormand held in one hand the great-coat, and in the other the neck-ribbon, and exclaimed, "Victory! We are about to penetrate the mystery! We are going to learn the most minute details; we are going to lay our finger on the debaucheries of our sly friend! Here we have the romance itself. I have the portrait!"

In fact, a case of black shagreen, resembling a medallion portrait, was suspended from the ribbon.

The old man took this case and gazed at it for some time without opening it, with that air of enjoyment, rapture, and wrath, with which a poor hungry fellow beholds an admirable dinner that is not for him, pass under his very nose.

"For this evidently is a portrait. I know all about such things. That is worn tenderly on the heart. How stupid they are! Some abominable fright that will make us shudder, probably! Young men have such bad taste nowadays!"

"Let us see, Father," said the old spinster.

The case opened by the pressure of a spring. They found in it nothing but a carefully folded paper.

"From the same to the same," said M. Gillenormand, bursting with laughter. "I know what it is. A billet-doux."

"Ah! Let us read it!" said the aunt.

And she put on her spectacles. They unfolded the paper and read as follows:
"For my son.

The Emperor made me a Baron on the battlefield of Waterloo. Since the Restoration disputes my right to this title that I purchased with my blood, my son shall take it and bear it. That he will be worthy of it is a matter of course.'

The feelings of father and daughter cannot be described. They felt chilled as by the breath of a death's-head. They did not exchange a word.

Only, M. Gillenormand said in a low voice and as though speaking to himself, "It is the slasher's handwriting."

The aunt examined the paper, turned it about in all directions, then put it back in its case.

At the same moment a little oblong packet, enveloped in blue paper, fell from one of the pockets of the greatcoat. Mademoiselle Gillenormand picked it up and unfolded the blue paper.

It contained Marius's hundred cards. She handed one of them to M. Gillenormand, who read: "Le Baron Marius Pontmercy."

The old man rang the bell. Nicolette came. M. Gillenormand took the ribbon, the case, and the coat, flung them all on the floor in the middle of the room, and said, "Carry those duds away."

A full hour passed in the most profound silence. The old man and the ld spinster had seated themselves with their backs to each other, and were thinking, each on his own account, the same things, in all probability.

At the expiration of this hour, Aunt Gillenormand said, "A pretty state of things!"

A few moments later, Marius made his appearance. He entered. Even before he had crossed the threshold, he saw his grandfather holding one of his own cards in his hand, and on catching sight of him, the latter exclaimed with his air of bourgeois and grinning superiority that was something crushing, "Well! Well! Well! Well! Well! So you are a baron now. I present you my compliments. What is the meaning of this?"

Marius reddened slightly and replied, "It means that I am the son of my father."

M. Gillenormand ceased to laugh, and said harshly, "I am your father."

"My father," retorted Marius, with downcast eyes and a severe air, "was a humble and heroic man, who served the Republic and France gloriously, who was great in the greatest history that men have ever made, who lived in the bivouac for a quarter of a century, beneath grapeshot and bullets, in snow and mud by day, beneath rain at night, who captured two flags, who received twenty wounds, who died forgotten and abandoned, and who never committed but one mistake, which was to love too fondly two ingrates, his country and myself."

This was more than M. Gillenormand could bear to hear. At the word "republic," he rose, or, to speak more correctly, he sprang to his feet. Every word that Marius had just uttered produced on the visage of the old Royalist the effect of the puffs of air from a forge upon a blazing brand. From a dull hue he had turned red, from red, purple, and from purple, flame-colored.

"Marius!" he cried. "Abominable child! I do not know what your father was! I do not wish to know! I know nothing about that, and I do not know him! But what I do know is, that there never was anything but scoundrels among those men! They were all rascals, assassins, redcaps, thieves! I say all! I say all! I know not one! I say all! Do you hear me, Marius! See here, you are no more a baron than my slipper is! They were all bandits in the service of Robespierre! All who served B-u-o-naparte were brigands! They were all traitors who betrayed, betrayed, betrayed their legitimate king! All cowards who fled before the Prussians and the English at Waterloo! That is what I do know! Whether Monsieur your father comes in that category, I do not know! I am sorry for it, so much the worse, your humble servant!"

In his turn, it was Marius who was the firebrand and M. Gillenormand who was the bellows. Marius quivered in every limb, he did not know what would

happen next, his brain was on fire. He was the priest who beholds all his sacre
wafers cast to the winds, the fakir who beholds a passerby spit upon his idc
It could not be that such things had been uttered in his presence. What was h
to do? His father had just been trampled under foot and stamped upon in h
presence, but by whom? By his grandfather. How was he to avenge the on
without outraging the other? It was impossible for him to insult his grandfathe
and it was equally impossible for him to leave his father unavenged. On the on
hand was a sacred grave, on the other hoary locks.

He stood there for several moments, staggering as though intoxicated, wit
all this whirlwind dashing through his head; then he raised his eyes, gaze
fixedly at his grandfather, and cried in a voice of thunder, "Down with th
Bourbons, and that great hog of a Louis XVIII!"

Louis XVIII had been dead for four years; but it was all the same to him.

The old man, who had been crimson, turned whiter than his hair. H
wheeled around toward a bust of M. le Duc de Berry, which stood on th
mantel, and made a profound bow, with a sort of peculiar majesty. Then h
paced twice, slowly and in silence, from the fireplace to the window and fro
the window to the fireplace, traversing the whole length of the room, an
making the polished floor creak as though he had been a stone statue walking

On his second turn, he bent over his daughter, who was watching th
encounter with the stupefied air of an antiquated lamb, and said to her with
smile that was almost calm, "A baron like this gentleman, and a bourgeois lik
myself cannot remain under the same roof."

And drawing himself up, all at once, pallid, trembling, terrible, with h
brow rendered more lofty by the terrible radiance of wrath, he extended h
arm toward Marius and shouted to him, "Be off!"

Marius left the house.

On the following day, M. Gillenormand said to his daughter, "You wi
send sixty pistoles every six months to that blood drinker, and you will neve
mention his name to me."

Having an immense reserve fund of wrath to get rid of, and not knowing
what to do with it, he continued to address his daughter as "you" instead o
"thou" for the next three months.

Marius, on his side, had gone forth in indignation. There was on
circumstance that, it must be admitted, aggravated his exasperation. Ther
are always petty fatalities of the sort that complicate domestic dramas. The
augment the grievances in such cases, although, in reality, the wrongs are nc
increased by them. While carrying Marius's "duds" precipitately to his chambe

his grandfather's command, Nicolette had, inadvertently, let fall, probably, on the attic staircase, which was dark, that medallion of black shagreen that contained the paper penned by the colonel. Neither paper nor case could afterward be found. Marius was convinced that "Monsieur Gillenormand"— from that day forth he never alluded to him otherwise—had flung "his father's testament" in the fire. He knew by heart the few lines that the colonel had written, and, consequently, nothing was lost. But the paper, the writing, that sacred relic, all that was his very heart. What had been done with it?

Marius had taken his departure without saying where he was going, and without knowing where, with thirty francs, his watch, and a few clothes in a handbag. He had entered a hackney-coach, had engaged it by the hour, and had directed his course at haphazard toward the Latin quarter.

What was to become of Marius?

BOOK FOURTH: THE FRIENDS
OF THE A B C

CHAPTER I—A GROUP THAT BARELY
MISSED BECOMING HISTORIC

At that epoch, which was, to all appearances indifferent, a certain revolutionary quiver was vaguely current. Breaths that had started forth from the depths of '89 and '93 were in the air. Youth was on the point, may the reader pardon us the word, of molting. People were undergoing a transformation, almost without being conscious of it, through the movement of the age. The needle that moves around the compass also moves in souls. Each person was taking that step in advance that he was bound to take. The Royalists were becoming liberals, liberals were turning democrats. It was a flood tide complicated with a thousand ebb movements; the peculiarity of ebbs is to create intermixtures; hence the combination of very singular ideas; people adored both Napoleon and liberty. We are making history here. These were the mirages of that period. Opinions traverse phases. Voltairian royalism, a quaint variety, had a no less singular sequel, Bonapartist liberalism.

Other groups of minds were more serious. In that direction, they sounded principles, they attached themselves to the right. They grew enthusiastic for the absolute, they caught glimpses of infinite realizations; the absolute, by it very rigidity, urges spirits toward the sky and causes them to float in illimitabl space. There is nothing like dogma for bringing forth dreams. And there i nothing like dreams for engendering the future. Utopia today, flesh and bloo tomorrow.

These advanced opinions had a double foundation. A beginning o mystery menaced "the established order of things," which was suspicious an underhand. A sign that was revolutionary to the highest degree. The secon thoughts of power meet the second thoughts of the populace in the min The incubation of insurrections gives the retort to the premeditation of coup d'etat.

There did not, as yet, exist in France any of those vast underlyin organizations, like the German Tugendbund and Italian Carbonarism; bu here and there were dark underminings, which were in process of throwin off shoots. The Cougourde was being outlined at Aix; there existed at Paris among other affiliations of that nature, the society of the Friends of the A B C

What were these Friends of the A B C? A society that had for its objec apparently the education of children, in reality the elevation of man.

They declared themselves the Friends of the A B C—the Abaisse—th debased—that is to say, the people. They wished to elevate the people. It wa a pun that we should do wrong to smile at. Puns are sometimes serious factor in politics; witness the *Castratus ad castra*, which made a general of the army o Narses; witness: Barbari et Barberini; witness: *Tu es Petrus et super hanc petram* etc., etc.

The Friends of the A B C were not numerous, it was a secret society in th state of embryo, we might almost say a coterie, if coteries ended in heroes They assembled in Paris in two localities, near the fish market, in a wine sho called Corinthe, of which more will be heard later on, and near the Pantheo in a little café in the Rue Saint-Michel called the Café Musain, now torn down the first of these meeting places was close to the workingman, the second t the students.

The assemblies of the Friends of the A B C were usually held in a bac room of the Café Musain.

This hall, which was tolerably remote from the café, with which it wa connected by an extremely long corridor, had two windows and an exit witl a private stairway on the little Rue des Gres. There they smoked and drank and gambled and laughed. There they conversed in very loud tones abou everything, and in whispers of other things. An old map of France under th

Republic was nailed to the wall, a sign quite sufficient to excite the suspicion of a police agent.

The greater part of the Friends of the A B C were students, who were on cordial terms with the working classes. Here are the names of the principal ones. They belong, in a certain measure, to history: Enjolras, Combeferre, Jean Prouvaire, Feuilly, Courfeyrac, Bahorel, Lesgle or Laigle, Joly, Grantaire.

These young men formed a sort of family, through the bond of friendship. All, with the exception of Laigle, were from the South.

This was a remarkable group. It vanished in the invisible depths that lie behind us. At the point of this drama that we have now reached, it will not perhaps be superfluous to throw a ray of light upon these youthful heads, before the reader beholds them plunging into the shadow of a tragic adventure.

Enjolras, whose name we have mentioned first of all, the reader shall see why later on, was an only son and wealthy.

Enjolras was a charming young man, who was capable of being terrible. He was angelically handsome. He was a savage Antinous. One would have said, to see the pensive thoughtfulness of his glance, that he had already, in some previous state of existence, traversed the revolutionary apocalypse. He possessed the tradition of it as though he had been a witness. He was acquainted with all the minute details of the great affair. A pontifical and warlike nature, a singular thing in a youth. He was an officiating priest and a man of war; from the immediate point of view, a soldier of the democracy; above the contemporary movement, the priest of the ideal. His eyes were deep, his lids a little red, his lower lip was thick and easily became disdainful, his brow was lofty. A great deal of brow in a face is like a great deal of horizon in a view. Like certain young men at the beginning of this century and the end of the last, who became illustrious at an early age, he was endowed with excessive youth, and was as rosy as a young girl, although subject to hours of pallor. Already a man, he still seemed a child. His two and twenty years appeared to be but seventeen; he was serious, it did not seem as though he were aware there was on earth a thing called woman. He had but one passion—the right; but one thought—to overthrow the obstacle. On Mount Aventine, he would have been Gracchus; in the Convention, he would have been Saint-Just. He hardly saw the roses, he ignored spring, he did not hear the caroling of the birds; the bare throat of Evadne would have moved him no more than it would have moved Aristogeiton; he, like Harmodius, thought flowers good for nothing except to conceal the sword. He was severe in his enjoyments. He chastely dropped his eyes before everything that was not the Republic. He was the marble lover of

VICTOR HUGO

liberty. His speech was harshly inspired, and had the thrill of a hymn. He wa
subject to unexpected outbursts of soul. Woe to the love affair that should hav
risked itself beside him! If any grisette of the Place Cambrai or the Rue Saint
Jean-de-Beauvais, seeing that face of a youth escaped from college, that page'
mien, those long, golden lashes, those blue eyes, that hair billowing in the
wind, those rosy cheeks, those fresh lips, those exquisite teeth, had conceived
an appetite for that complete aurora, and had tried her beauty on Enjolras, ai
astounding and terrible glance would have promptly shown her the abyss, and
would have taught her not to confound the mighty cherub of Ezekiel with the
gallant Cherubino of Beaumarchais.

By the side of Enjolras, who represented the logic of the Revolution
Combeferre represented its philosophy. Between the logic of the Revolution
and its philosophy there exists this difference—that its logic may end in war
whereas its philosophy can end only in peace. Combeferre complemented and
rectified Enjolras. He was less lofty, but broader. He desired to pour into al
minds the extensive principles of general ideas. He said, "Revolution, bu
civilization"; and around the mountain peak he opened out a vast view of the
blue sky. The Revolution was more adapted for breathing with Combeferre
than with Enjolras. Enjolras expressed its divine right, and Combeferre its
natural right. The first attached himself to Robespierre; the second confinec
himself to Condorcet. Combeferre lived the life of all the rest of the world
more than did Enjolras. If it had been granted to these two young men to attair
to history, the one would have been the just, the other the wise man. Enjolra
was the more virile, Combeferre the more humane. Homo and vir, that was the
exact effect of their different shades. Combeferre was as gentle as Enjolras was
severe, through natural whiteness. He loved the word "citizen," but he preferred
the word "man." He would gladly have said, "hombre," like the Spanish. He
read everything, went to the theaters, attended the courses of public lecturers,
learned the polarization of light from Arago, grew enthusiastic over a lesson
in which Geoffrey Sainte-Hilaire explained the double function of the external
carotid artery, and the internal, the one that makes the face, and the one that
makes the brain; he kept up with what was going on, followed science step by
step, compared Saint-Simon with Fourier, deciphered hieroglyphics, broke the
pebble that he found and reasoned on geology, drew from memory a silkworm
moth, pointed out the faulty French in the *Dictionary of the Academy*, studied
Puysegur and Deleuze, affirmed nothing, not even miracles; denied nothing,
not even ghosts; turned over the files of the Moniteur, reflected. He declared
that the future lies in the hand of the schoolmaster, and busied himself with

ducational questions. He desired that society should labor without relaxation
t the elevation of the moral and intellectual level, at coining science, at
utting ideas into circulation, at increasing the mind in youthful persons, and
e feared lest the present poverty of method, the paltriness from a literary
oint of view confined to two or three centuries called classic, the tyrannical
ogmatism of official pedants, scholastic prejudices and routines should end
y converting our colleges into artificial oyster beds. He was learned, a purist,
xact, a graduate of the Polytechnic, a close student, and at the same time,
houghtful "even to chimeras," so his friends said. He believed in all dreams,
ailroads, the suppression of suffering in chirurgical operations, the fixing of
mages in the dark chamber, the electric telegraph, the steering of balloons.
Moreover, he was not much alarmed by the citadels erected against the human
mind in every direction, by superstition, despotism, and prejudice. He was
one of those who think that science will eventually turn the position. Enjolras
was a chief, Combeferre was a guide. One would have liked to fight under the
one and to march behind the other. It is not that Combeferre was not capable
of fighting, he did not refuse a hand-to-hand combat with the obstacle, and
to attack it by main force and explosively; but it suited him better to bring
the human race into accord with its destiny gradually, by means of education,
the inculcation of axioms, the promulgation of positive laws; and, between
two lights, his preference was rather for illumination than for conflagration.
A conflagration can create an aurora, no doubt, but why not await the dawn?
A volcano illuminates, but daybreak furnishes a still better illumination.
Possibly, Combeferre preferred the whiteness of the beautiful to the blaze of
the sublime. A light troubled by smoke, progress purchased at the expense
of violence, only half satisfied this tender and serious spirit. The headlong
precipitation of a people into the truth, a '93, terrified him; nevertheless,
stagnation was still more repulsive to him, in it he detected putrefaction and
death; on the whole, he preferred scum to miasma, and he preferred the torrent
to the cesspool, and the falls of Niagara to the lake of Montfaucon. In short, he
desired neither halt nor haste. While his tumultuous friends, captivated by the
absolute, adored and invoked splendid revolutionary adventures, Combeferre
was inclined to let progress, good progress, take its own course; he may have
been cold, but he was pure; methodical, but irreproachable; phlegmatic, but
imperturbable. Combeferre would have knelt and clasped his hands to enable
the future to arrive in all its candor, and that nothing might disturb the immense
and virtuous evolution of the races. The good must be innocent, he repeated
incessantly. And in fact, if the grandeur of the Revolution consists in keeping

the dazzling ideal fixedly in view, and of soaring there athwart the lightnings with fire and blood in its talons, the beauty of progress lies in being spotless and there exists between Washington, who represents the one, and Danton who incarnates the other, that difference that separates the swan from the angel with the wings of an eagle.

Jean Prouvaire was a still softer shade than Combeferre. His name was Jehan, owing to that petty momentary freak that mingled with the powerful and profound movement from which sprang the very essential study of the Middle Ages. Jean Prouvaire was in love; he cultivated a pot of flowers, played on the flute, made verses, loved the people, pitied woman, wept over the child, confounded God and the future in the same confidence, and blamed the Revolution for having caused the fall of a royal head, that of Andre Chenier. His voice was ordinarily delicate, but suddenly grew manly. He was learned even to erudition, and almost an Orientalist. Above all, he was good; and, a very simple thing to those who know how nearly goodness borders on grandeur, in the matter of poetry, he preferred the immense. He knew Italian, Latin, Greek, and Hebrew; and these served him only for the perusal of four poets: Dante, Juvenal, AEschylus, and Isaiah. In French, he preferred Corneille to Racine, and Agrippa d'Aubigne to Corneille. He loved to saunter through fields of wild oats and cornflowers, and busied himself with clouds nearly as much as with events. His mind had two attitudes, one on the side toward man, the other on that toward God; he studied or he contemplated. All day long, he buried himself in social questions, salary, capital, credit, marriage, religion, liberty of thought, education, penal servitude, poverty, association, property, production and sharing, the enigma of this lower world that covers the human anthill with darkness; and at night, he gazed upon the planets, those enormous beings. Like Enjolras, he was wealthy and an only son. He spoke softly, bowed his head, lowered his eyes, smiled with embarrassment, dressed badly, had an awkward air, blushed at a mere nothing, and was very timid. Yet he was intrepid.

Feuilly was a workingman, a fan maker, orphaned both of father and mother, who earned with difficulty three francs a day, and had but one thought: to deliver the world. He had one other preoccupation, to educate himself; he called this also, delivering himself. He had taught himself to read and write; everything that he knew, he had learned by himself. Feuilly had a generous heart. The range of his embrace was immense. This orphan had adopted the peoples. As his mother had failed him, he meditated on his country. He brooded with the profound divination of the man of the people, over what we now call the idea of the nationality, had learned history with the express object f raging with full knowledge of the case. In this club of young Utopians, occupied chiefly with France, he represented the outside world. He had for his specialty Greece, Poland, Hungary, Roumania, Italy. He uttered these names incessantly, appropriately and inappropriately, with the tenacity of right. The violations of Turkey on Greece and Thessaly, of Russia on Warsaw, of Austria on Venice, enraged him. Above all things, the great violence of 1772 aroused him. There is no more sovereign eloquence than the true in indignation; he was eloquent with that eloquence. He was inexhaustible on that infamous date of 1772, on the subject of that noble and valiant race suppressed by treason, and that three-sided crime, on that monstrous ambush, the prototype and pattern of all those horrible suppressions of states, which, since that time, have struck many a noble nation, and have annulled their certificate of birth, so to speak. All contemporary social crimes have their origin in the partition of Poland. The partition of Poland is a theorem of which all present political outrages are the corollaries. There has not been a despot, nor a traitor, for nearly a century back, who has not signed, approved, countersigned, and copied, *ne variatur*, the partition of Poland. When the record of modern treasons was examined, that was the first thing that made its appearance. The congress of Vienna consulted that crime before consummating its own. 1772 sounded the onset; 1815 was the death of the game. Such was Feuilly's habitual text. This poor workingman had constituted himself the tutor of Justice, and she recompensed him by rendering him great. The fact is, that there is eternity in right. Warsaw can no more be Tartar than Venice can be Teuton. Kings lose their pains and their honor in the attempt to make them so. Sooner or later, the submerged part floats to the surface and reappears. Greece becomes Greece again, Italy is once more Italy. The protest of right against the deed persists forever. The theft of a nation cannot be allowed by prescription. These lofty deeds of rascality have no future. A nation cannot have its mark extracted like a pocket handkerchief.

Courfeyrac had a father who was called M. de Courfeyrac. One of the false ideas of the bourgeoisie under the Restoration as regards aristocracy and the nobility was to believe in the particle. The particle, as everyone knows, possesses no significance. But the bourgeois of the epoch of la Minerve estimated so highly that they thought themselves bound to abdicate it. M. de Chauvelin had himself called M. Chauvelin; M. de Caumartin, M. Caumartin; M. de Constant de Robecque, Benjamin Constant; M. de Lafayette, M. Lafayette. Courfeyrac had not wished to remain behind the rest, and called himself plain Courfeyrac.

We might almost, so far as Courfeyrac is concerned, stop here, and confine ourselves to saying with regard to what remains: "For Courfeyrac, see Tholomyes."

Courfeyrac had, in fact, that animation of youth that may be called the *beaute du diable* of the mind. Later on, this disappears like the playfulness of the kitten, and all this grace ends, with the bourgeois, on two legs, and with the tomcat, on four paws.

This sort of wit is transmitted from generation to generation of the successive levies of youth who traverse the schools, who pass it from hand to hand, *quasi cursores*, and is almost always exactly the same; so that, as we have just pointed out, anyone who had listened to Courfeyrac in 1828 would have thought he heard Tholomyes in 1817. Only, Courfeyrac was an honorable fellow. Beneath the apparent similarities of the exterior mind, the difference between him and Tholomyes was very great. The latent man who existed in the two was totally different in the first from what it was in the second. There was in Tholomyes a district attorney, and in Courfeyrac a paladin.

Enjolras was the chief, Combeferre was the guide, Courfeyrac was the center. The others gave more light, he shed more warmth; the truth is, that he possessed all the qualities of a center, roundness and radiance.

Bahorel had figured in the bloody tumult of June 1822, on the occasion of the burial of young Lallemand.

Bahorel was a good-natured mortal, who kept bad company, brave, a spendthrift, prodigal, and to the verge of generosity, talkative, and at times eloquent, bold to the verge of effrontery; the best fellow possible; he had daring waistcoats, and scarlet opinions; a wholesale blusterer, that is to say, loving nothing so much as a quarrel, unless it were an uprising; and nothing so much as an uprising, unless it were a revolution; always ready to smash a windowpane, then to tear up the pavement, then to demolish a government, just to see the effect of it; a student in his eleventh year. He had nosed about the law, but did not practice it. He had taken for his device: "Never a lawyer," and for his armorial bearings a nightstand in which was visible a square cap. Every time that he passed the law school, which rarely happened, he buttoned up his frock coat, the paletot had not yet been invented, and took hygienic precautions. Of the school porter he said, "What a fine old man!" and of the dean, M. Delvincourt, "What a monument!" In his lectures he espied subjects for ballads, and in his professors occasions for caricature. He wasted a tolerably large allowance, something like three thousand francs a year, in doing nothing.

He had peasant parents whom he had contrived to imbue with respect for their son.

He said of them, "They are peasants and not bourgeois; that is the reason they are intelligent."

Bahorel, a man of caprice, was scattered over numerous cafes; the others had habits, he had none. He sauntered. To stray is human. To saunter is Parisian. In reality, he had a penetrating mind and was more of a thinker than appeared to view.

He served as a connecting link between the Friends of the A B C and other still unorganized groups, which were destined to take form later on.

In this conclave of young heads, there was one bald member.

The Marquis d'Avaray, whom Louis XVIII made a duke for having assisted him to enter a hackney coach on the day when he emigrated, was wont to relate, that in 1814, on his return to France, as the King was disembarking at Calais, a man handed him a petition.

"What is your request?" said the King.

"Sire, a post office."

"What is your name?"

"L'Aigle."

The King frowned, glanced at the signature of the petition and beheld the name written thus: LESGLE. This non-Bonaparte orthography touched the King and he began to smile. "Sire," resumed the man with the petition, "I had for ancestor a keeper of the hounds surnamed Lesgueules. This surname furnished my name. I am called Lesgueules, by contraction Lesgle, and by corruption l'Aigle." This caused the King to smile broadly. Later on he gave the man the posting office of Meaux, either intentionally or accidentally.

The bald member of the group was the son of this Lesgle, or Legle, and he signed himself, Legle [de Meaux]. As an abbreviation, his companions called him Bossuet.

Bossuet was a gay but unlucky fellow. His specialty was not to succeed in anything. As an offset, he laughed at everything. At five and twenty he was bald. His father had ended by owning a house and a field; but he, the son, had made haste to lose that house and field in a bad speculation. He had nothing left. He possessed knowledge and wit, but all he did miscarried. Everything failed him and everybody deceived him; what he was building tumbled down on top of him. If he were splitting wood, he cut off a finger. If he had a mistress, he speedily discovered that he had a friend also. Some misfortune happened to him every moment, hence his joviality. He said, "I live under falling tiles." He was not easily astonished, because, for him, an accident was what he had foreseen, he took his bad luck serenely, and smiled at the teasing of fate, like a person who is listening to pleasantries. He was poor, but his fund of good humor was inexhaustible. He soon reached his last sou, never his last burst of laughter. When adversity entered his doors, he saluted this old acquaintance cordially; he tapped all catastrophes on the stomach; he was familiar with fatality to the point of calling it by its nickname. "Good day, Guignon," he said to it.

These persecutions of fate had rendered him inventive. He was full of resources. He had no money, but he found means, when it seemed good to him, to indulge in "unbridled extravagance." One night, he went so far as to eat a "hundred francs" in a supper with a wench, which inspired him to make this memorable remark in the midst of the orgy: "Pull off my boots, you five-Louis jade."

Bossuet was slowly directing his steps toward the profession of a lawyer; he was pursuing his law studies after the manner of Bahorel. Bossuet had not much domicile, sometimes none at all. He lodged now with one, now with another, most often with Joly. Joly was studying medicine. He was two years younger than Bossuet.

Joly was the "*malade imaginaire*" junior. What he had won in medicine was to be more of an invalid than a doctor. At three and twenty he thought himself a valetudinarian, and passed his life in inspecting his tongue in the mirror. He affirmed that man becomes magnetic like a needle, and in his chamber he placed his bed with its head to the south, and the foot to the north, so that, at night, the circulation of his blood might not be interfered with by the great electric current of the globe. During thunderstorms, he felt his pulse. Otherwise, he was the gayest of them all. All these young, maniacal, puny, merry incoherences lived in harmony together, and the result was an eccentric and agreeable being whom his comrades, who were prodigal of winged consonants, called Jolllly. "You may fly away on the four Ls,"* Jean Prouvaire said to him.

Joly had a trick of touching his nose with the tip of his cane, which is an indication of a sagacious mind.

All these young men who differed so greatly, and who, on the whole, can only be discussed seriously, held the same religion: Progress.

All were the direct sons of the French Revolution. The most giddy of them became solemn when they pronounced that date: '89. Their fathers in the flesh had been, either royalists, doctrinaires, it matters not what; this confusion anterior to themselves, who were young, did not concern them at all; the pure blood of principle ran in their veins. They attached themselves, without

---

* ailes, "wings" in French

intermediate shades, to incorruptible right and absolute duty.

Affiliated and initiated, they sketched out the ideal underground.

Among all these glowing hearts and thoroughly convinced minds, there was one skeptic. How came he there? By juxtaposition. This skeptic's name was Grantaire, and he was in the habit of signing himself with this rebus: R. Grantaire was a man who took good care not to believe in anything. Moreover, he was one of the students who had learned the most during their course at Paris; he knew that the best coffee was to be had at the Cafe Lemblin, and the best billiards at the Café Voltaire, that good cakes and lasses were to be found at the Ermitage, on the Boulevard du Maine, spatchcocked chickens at Mother Sauget's, excellent matelotes at the Barriere de la Cunette, and a certain thin white wine at the Barriere du Com pat. He knew the best place for everything; in addition, boxing and foot-fencing and some dances; and he was a thorough single-stick player. He was a tremendous drinker to boot. He was inordinately homely: the prettiest boot stitcher of that day, Irma Boissy, enraged with his homeliness, pronounced sentence on him as follows: "Grantaire is impossible"; but Grantaire's fatuity was not to be disconcerted. He stared tenderly and fixedly at all women, with the air of saying to them all, "If I only chose!" And of trying to make his comrades believe that he was in general demand.

All those words: rights of the people, rights of man, the social contract, the French Revolution, the Republic, democracy, humanity, civilization, religion, progress, came very near to signifying nothing whatever to Grantaire. He smiled at them. Skepticism, that caries of the intelligence, had not left him a single whole idea. He lived with irony. This was his axiom: "There is but one certainty, my full glass." He sneered at all devotion in all parties, the father as well as the brother, Robespierre junior as well as Loizerolles. "They are greatly in advance to be dead," he exclaimed. He said of the crucifix, "There is a gibbet that has been a success." A rover, a gambler, a libertine, often drunk, he displeased these young dreamers by humming incessantly, "*J'aimons les filles, et j'aimons le bon vin.*" Air: Vive Henri IV.

However, this skeptic had one fanaticism. This fanaticism was neither a dogma, nor an idea, nor an art, nor a science; it was a man: Enjolras. Grantaire admired, loved, and venerated Enjolras. To whom did this anarchical scoffer unite himself in this phalanx of absolute minds? To the most absolute. In what manner had Enjolras subjugated him? By his ideas? No. By his character. A phenomenon that is often observable. A skeptic who adheres to a believer is as simple as the law of complementary colors. That which we lack attracts us. No one loves the light like the blind man. The dwarf adores the drum major.

The toad always has his eyes fixed on heaven. Why? In order to watch the bird in its flight. Grantaire, in whom writhed doubt, loved to watch faith soar in Enjolras. He had need of Enjolras. That chaste, healthy, firm, upright, hard, candid nature charmed him, without his being clearly aware of it, and without the idea of explaining it to himself having occurred to him. He admired his opposite by instinct. His soft, yielding, dislocated, sickly, shapeless ideas attached themselves to Enjolras as to a spinal column. His moral backbone leaned on that firmness. Grantaire in the presence of Enjolras became someone once more. He was, himself, moreover, composed of two elements, which were, to all appearance, incompatible. He was ironical and cordial. His indifference loved. His mind could get along without belief, but his heart could not get along without friendship. A profound contradiction; for an affection is a conviction. His nature was thus constituted. There are men who seem to be born to be the reverse, the obverse, the wrong side. They are Pollux, Patrocles, Nisus, Eudamidas, Ephestion, Pechmeja. They only exist on condition that they are backed up with another man; their name is a sequel, and is only written preceded by the conjunction and; and their existence is not their own; it is the other side of an existence that is not theirs. Grantaire was one of these men. He was the obverse of Enjolras.

One might almost say that affinities begin with the letters of the alphabet. In the series, O and P are inseparable. You can, at will, pronounce O and P or Orestes and Pylades.

Grantaire, Enjolras's true satellite, inhabited this circle of young men; he lived there, he took no pleasure anywhere but there; he followed them everywhere. His joy was to see these forms go and come through the fumes of wine. They tolerated him on account of his good humor.

Enjolras, the believer, disdained this skeptic; and, a sober man himself, scorned this drunkard. He accorded him a little lofty pity. Grantaire was an unaccepted Pylades. Always harshly treated by Enjolras, roughly repulsed, rejected yet ever returning to the charge, he said of Enjolras, "What fine marble!"

CHAPTER II—BLONDEAU'S FUNERAL ORATION BY BOSSUET

On a certain afternoon, which had, as will be seen hereafter, some coincidence with the events heretofore related, Laigle de Meaux was to be seen leaning in a sensual manner against the doorpost of the Café Musain.

He had the air of a caryatid on a vacation; he carried nothing but his reverie, however. He was staring at the Place Saint-Michel. To lean one's back against a thing is equivalent to lying down while standing erect, which attitude is not hated by thinkers. Laigle de Meaux was pondering without melancholy, over a little misadventure that had befallen him two days previously at the law school, and that had modified his personal plans for the future, plans that were rather indistinct in any case.

Reverie does not prevent a cab from passing by, nor the dreamer from taking note of that cab. Laigle de Meaux, whose eyes were straying about in a sort of diffuse lounging, perceived, athwart his somnambulism, a two-wheeled vehicle proceeding through the place, at a foot pace and apparently in indecision. For whom was this cabriolet? Why was it driving at a walk? Laigle took a survey. In it, beside the coachman, sat a young man, and in front of the young man lay a rather bulky handbag. The bag displayed to passersby the following name inscribed in large black letters on a card that was sewn to the stuff: MARIUS PONTMERCY.

This name caused Laigle to change his attitude. He drew himself up and hurled this apostrophe at the young man in the cabriolet, "Monsieur Marius Pontmercy!"

The cabriolet thus addressed came to a halt.

The young man, who also seemed deeply buried in thought, raised his eyes. "Hey?" said he.

"You are M. Marius Pontmercy?"

"Certainly."

"I was looking for you," resumed Laigle de Meaux.

"How so?" demanded Marius; for it was he. In fact, he had just quitted his grandfather's, and had before him a face that he now beheld for the first time. "I do not know you."

"Neither do I know you," responded Laigle.

Marius thought he had encountered a wag, the beginning of a mystification in the open street. He was not in a very good humor at the moment. He frowned. Laigle de Meaux went on imperturbably, "You were not at the school day before yesterday."

"That is possible."

"That is certain."

"You are a student?" demanded Marius.

"Yes, Sir. Like yourself. Day before yesterday, I entered the school, by chance. You know, one does have such freaks sometimes. The professor was just calling the roll. You are not unaware that they are very ridiculous on such occasions. At the third call, unanswered, your name is erased from the list. Sixty francs in the gulf."

Marius began to listen.

"It was Blondeau who was making the call. You know Blondeau, he has a very pointed and very malicious nose, and he delights to scent out the absent. He slyly began with the letter P. I was not listening, not being compromised by that letter. The call was not going badly. No erasures; the universe was present. Blondeau was grieved. I said to myself, 'Blondeau, my love, you will not get the very smallest sort of an execution today.' All at once Blondeau calls, 'Marius Pontmercy!' No one answers. Blondeau, filled with hope, repeats more loudly, 'Marius Pontmercy!' And he takes his pen. Monsieur, I have bowels of compassion. I said to myself hastily, 'Here's a brave fellow who is going to get scratched out. Attention. Here is a veritable mortal who is not exact. He's not a good student. Here is none of your heavy-sides, a student who studies, a greenhorn pedant, strong on letters, theology, science, and sapience, one of those dull wits cut by the square; a pin by profession. He is an honorable idler who lounges, who practices country jaunts, who cultivates the grisette, who pays court to the fair sex, who is at this very moment, perhaps, with my mistress. Let us save him. Death to Blondeau!' At that moment, Blondeau dipped his pen in, all black with erasures in the ink, cast his yellow eyes around the audience room, and repeated for the third time, 'Marius Pontmercy!' I replied, 'Present!' This is why you were not crossed off."

"Monsieur—" said Marius.

"And why I was," added Laigle de Meaux.

"I do not understand you," said Marius.

Laigle resumed, "Nothing is more simple. I was close to the desk to reply, and close to the door for the purpose of flight. The professor gazed at me with a certain intensity. All of a sudden, Blondeau, who must be the malicious nose alluded to by Boileau, skipped to the letter L. L is my letter. I am from Meaux, and my name is Lesgle."

"L'Aigle!" interrupted Marius. "What a fine name!"

"Monsieur, Blondeau came to this fine name, and called, 'Laigle!' I reply, 'Present!' Then Blondeau gazes at me, with the gentleness of a tiger, and says to me, 'If you are Pontmercy, you are not Laigle.' A phrase that has a disobliging air for you, but that was lugubrious only for me. That said, he crossed me off."

Marius exclaimed, "I am mortified, sir—"

"First of all," interposed Laigle, "I demand permission to embalm

Blondeau in a few phrases of deeply felt eulogies. I will assume that he is dead. There will be no great change required in his gauntness, in his pallor, in his coldness, and in his smell. And I say, '*Erudimini qui judicatis terram*. Here lies Blondeau, Blondeau the Nose, Blondeau Nasica, the ox of discipline, *bos disciplinae*, the bloodhound of the password, the angel of the roll call, who was upright, square exact, rigid, honest, and hideous. God crossed him off as he crossed me off.'"

Marius resumed, "I am very sorry—"

"Young man," said Laigle de Meaux, "let this serve you as a lesson. In future, be exact."

"I really beg you a thousand pardons."

"Do not expose your neighbor to the danger of having his name erased again."

"I am extremely sorry—"

Laigle burst out laughing.

"And I am delighted. I was on the brink of becoming a lawyer. This erasure saves me. I renounce the triumphs of the bar. I shall not defend the widow, and I shall not attack the orphan. No more toga, no more stage. Here is my erasure all ready for me. It is to you that I am indebted for it, Monsieur Pontmercy. I intend to pay a solemn call of thanks upon you. Where do you live?"

"In this cab," said Marius.

"A sign of opulence," retorted Laigle calmly. "I congratulate you. You have there a rent of nine thousand francs per annum."

At that moment, Courfeyrac emerged from the café.

Marius smiled sadly.

"I have paid this rent for the last two hours, and I aspire to get rid of it; but there is a sort of history attached to it, and I don't know where to go."

"Come to my place, Sir," said Courfeyrac.

"I have the priority," observed Laigle, "but I have no home."

"Hold your tongue, Bossuet," said Courfeyrac.

"Bossuet," said Marius, "but I thought that your name was Laigle."

"De Meaux," replied Laigle; "by metaphor, Bossuet."

Courfeyrac entered the cab.

"Coachman," said he, "hotel de la Porte-Saint-Jacques."

And that very evening, Marius found himself installed in a chamber of the hotel de la Porte-Saint-Jacques side by side with Courfeyrac.

CHAPTER III—MARIUS'S ASTONISHMENTS

In a few days, Marius had become Courfeyrac's friend. Youth is the season for prompt welding and the rapid healing of scars. Marius breathed freely in Courfeyrac's society, a decidedly new thing for him. Courfeyrac put no questions to him. He did not even think of such a thing. At that age, faces disclose everything on the spot. Words are superfluous. There are young men of whom it can be said that their countenances chatter. One looks at them and one knows them.

One morning, however, Courfeyrac abruptly addressed this interrogation to him: "By the way, have you any political opinions?"

"The idea!" said Marius, almost affronted by the question.

"What are you?"

"A democrat-Bonapartist."

"The gray hue of a reassured rat," said Courfeyrac.

On the following day, Courfeyrac introduced Marius at the Cafe Musain. Then he whispered in his ear, with a smile, "I must give you your entry to the revolution." And he led him to the hall of the Friends of the A B C. He presented him to the other comrades, saying this simple word that Marius did not understand: "A pupil."

Marius had fallen into a wasps' nest of wits. However, although he was silent and grave, he was, nonetheless, both winged and armed.

Marius, up to that time solitary and inclined to soliloquy, and to asides, both by habit and by taste, was a little fluttered by this covey of young men around him. All these various initiatives solicited his attention at once, and pulled him about. The tumultuous movements of these minds at liberty and at work set his ideas in a whirl. Sometimes, in his trouble, they fled so far from him, that he had difficulty in recovering them. He heard them talk of philosophy, of literature, of art, of history, of religion, in unexpected fashion. He caught glimpses of strange aspects; and, as he did not place them in proper perspective, he was not altogether sure that it was not chaos that he grasped. On abandoning his grandfather's opinions for the opinions of his father, he had supposed himself fixed; he now suspected, with uneasiness, and without daring to avow it to himself, that he was not. The angle at which he saw everything began to be displaced anew. A certain oscillation set all the horizons of his brains in motion. An odd internal upsetting. He almost suffered from it.

It seemed as though there were no "consecrated things" for those young men. Marius heard singular propositions on every sort of subject, which embarrassed his still timid mind.

A theater poster presented itself, adorned with the title of a tragedy from the ancient repertory called classic. "Down with tragedy dear to the bourgeois!" cried Bahorel.

And Marius heard Combeferre reply, "You are wrong, Bahorel. The bourgeoisie loves tragedy, and the bourgeoisie must be left at peace on that score. Bewigged tragedy has a reason for its existence, and I am not one of those who, by order of AEschylus, contest its right to existence. There are rough outlines in nature; there are, in creation, ready-made parodies; a beak that is not a beak, wings that are not wings, gills that are not gills, paws that are not paws, a cry of pain that arouses a desire to laugh, there is the duck. Now, since poultry exists by the side of the bird, I do not see why classic tragedy should not exist in the face of antique tragedy."

Or chance decreed that Marius should traverse Rue Jean-Jacques Rousseau between Enjolras and Courfeyrac.

Courfeyrac took his arm. "Pay attention. This is the Rue Platriere, now called Rue Jean-Jacques Rousseau, on account of a singular household that lived in it sixty years ago. This consisted of Jean-Jacques and Therese. From time to time, little beings were born there. Therese gave birth to them, Jean-Jacques represented them as foundlings."

And Enjolras addressed Courfeyrac roughly, "Silence in the presence of Jean-Jacques! I admire that man. He denied his own children, that may be; but he adopted the people."

Not one of these young men articulated the word: the Emperor. Jean Prouvaire alone sometimes said Napoleon; all the others said "Bonaparte." Enjolras pronounced it "Buonaparte."

Marius was vaguely surprised. *Initium sapientiae.**

---

* Latin, "the beginning of wisdom"

CHAPTER IV—THE BACK ROOM
OF THE CAFÉ MUSAIN

One of the conversations among the young men, at which Marius was present and in which he sometimes joined, was a veritable shock to his mind.

This took place in the back room of the Café Musain. Nearly all the Friends of the A B C had convened that evening. The argand lamp was solemnly lighted. They talked of one thing and another, without passion and with noise. With the exception of Enjolras and Marius, who held their peace, all were haranguing rather at haphazard. Conversations between comrades sometimes are subject to these peaceable tumults. It was a game and an uproar as much as a conversation. They tossed words to each other and caught them up in turn. They were chattering in all quarters.

No woman was admitted to this back room, except Louison, the dishwasher of the café, who passed through it from time to time, to go to her washing in the "lavatory."

Grantaire, thoroughly drunk, was deafening the corner of which he had taken possession, reasoning and contradicting at the top of his lungs, and shouting, "I am thirsty. Mortals, I am dreaming: that the tun of Heidelberg has an attack of apoplexy, and that I am one of the dozen leeches that will be applied to it. I want a drink. I desire to forget life. Life is a hideous invention of I know not whom. It lasts no time at all, and is worth nothing. One breaks one's neck in living. Life is a theater set in which there are but few practicable entrances. Happiness is an antique reliquary painted on one side only. Ecclesiastes says, 'All is vanity.' I agree with that good man, who never existed, perhaps. Zero not wishing to go stark naked, clothed himself in vanity. O vanity! The patching up of everything with big words! A kitchen is a laboratory, a dancer is a professor, an acrobat is a gymnast, a boxer is a pugilist, an apothecary is a chemist, a wigmaker is an artist, a hodman is an architect, a jockey is a sportsman, a woodlouse is a pterigybranche. Vanity has a right and a wrong side; the right side is stupid, it is the Negro with his glass beads; the wrong side is foolish, it is the philosopher with his rags. I weep over the one and I laugh over the other. What are called honors and dignities, and even dignity and honor, are generally of pinchbeck. Kings make playthings of human pride. Caligula made a horse a consul; Charles II made a knight of a sirloin. Wrap yourself up now, then, between Consul Incitatus and Baronet Roastbeef. As for the intrinsic value of people, it is no longer respectable in the least. Listen to the panegyric that neighbor makes of neighbor. White on white is ferocious; if the lily could speak, what a setting down it would give the dove! A bigoted woman prating of a devout woman is more venomous than the asp and the cobra. It is a shame that I am ignorant, otherwise I would quote to you a mass of things; but I know nothing. For instance, I have always been witty; when I was a pupil of Gros, instead of daubing wretched little pictures, I passed my time in pilfering apples; *rapin* is the masculine of *rapine*.* So much for myself; as for the rest of you, you are worth no more than I am. I scoff at your perfections, excellencies, and qualities. Every good quality tends toward a defect; economy borders on avarice, the generous man is next door to the prodigal, the brave man rubs elbows with the braggart; he who says very pious says a trifle bigoted; there are just as many vices in virtue as there are holes in Diogenes' cloak. Whom do you admire, the slain or the slayer, Caesar or Brutus? Generally men are in favor of the slayer. Long live Brutus, he has slain! There lies the virtue. Virtue, granted, but madness also. There are queer spots on those great men. The Brutus who killed Caesar was in love with the statue of a little boy. This statue was from the hand of the Greek sculptor Strongylion, who also carved that figure of an Amazon known as the *Beautiful Leg*, Eucnemos, which Nero carried with him in his travels. This Strongylion left but two statues that placed Nero and Brutus in accord. Brutus was in love with the one, Nero with the other. All history is nothing but wearisome repetition. One century is the plagiarist of the other. The battle of Marengo copies the battle of Pydna; the Tolbiac of Clovis and the Austerlitz of Napoleon are as like each other as two drops of water. I don't attach much importance to victory. Nothing is so stupid as to conquer; true glory lies in convincing. But try to prove something! If you are content with success, what mediocrity, and with conquering, what wretchedness! Alas, vanity and cowardice everywhere. Everything obeys success, even grammar. '*Si volet usus*,' says Horace. Therefore I disdain the human race. Shall we descend to the party at all? Do you wish me to begin admiring the peoples? What people, if you please? Shall it be Greece? The Athenians, those Parisians of days gone by, slew Phocion, as we might say Coligny, and fawned upon tyrants to such an extent that Anacephorus said of Pisistratus, "His urine attracts the bees." The most prominent man in Greece for fifty years was that grammarian Philetas, who was so small and so thin that he was obliged to load his shoes with lead in order not to be blown away

---

* a painter's assistant, slang

by the wind. There stood on the great square in Corinth a statue carved by Silanion and catalogued by Pliny; this statue represented Episthates. What did Episthates do? He invented a trip. That sums up Greece and glory. Let us pass on to others. Shall I admire England? Shall I admire France? France? Why? Because of Paris? I have just told you my opinion of Athens. England? Why? Because of London? I hate Carthage. And then, London, the metropolis of luxury, is the headquarters of wretchedness. There are a hundred deaths a year of hunger in the parish of Charing Cross alone. Such is Albion. I add, as the climax, that I have seen an Englishwoman dancing in a wreath of roses and blue spectacles. A fig then for England! If I do not admire John Bull, shall I admire Brother Jonathan? I have but little taste for that slave-holding brother. Take away "Time is money," what remains of England? Take away "Cotton is king," what remains of America? Germany is the lymph, Italy is the bile. Shall we go into ecstasies over Russia? Voltaire admired it. He also admired China. I admit that Russia has its beauties, among others, a stout despotism; but I pity the despots. Their health is delicate. A decapitated Alexis, a poignarded Peter, a strangled Paul, another Paul crushed flat with kicks, divers Ivans strangled, with their throats cut, numerous Nicholases and Basils poisoned, all this indicates that the palace of the Emperors of Russia is in a condition of flagrant insalubrity. All civilized peoples offer this detail to the admiration of the thinker; war; now, war, civilized war, exhausts and sums up all the forms of ruffianism, from the brigandage of the Trabuceros in the gorges of Mont Jaxa to the marauding of the Comanche Indians in the Doubtful Pass. 'Bah!' you will say to me, 'but Europe is certainly better than Asia?' I admit that Asia is a farce; but I do not precisely see what you find to laugh at in the Grand Lama, you peoples of the west, who have mingled with your fashions and your elegances all the complicated filth of majesty, from the dirty chemise of Queen Isabella to the chamber-chair of the Dauphin. Gentlemen of the human race, I tell you, not a bit of it! It is at Brussels that the most beer is consumed, at Stockholm the most brandy, at Madrid the most chocolate, at Amsterdam the most gin, at London the most wine, at Constantinople the most coffee, at Paris the most absinthe; there are all the useful notions. Paris carries the day, in short. In Paris, even the rag pickers are sybarites; Diogenes would have loved to be a rag picker of the Place Maubert better than to be a philosopher at the Piraeus. Learn this in addition; the wine shops of the rag pickers are called *bibines*; the most celebrated are the Saucepan and the Slaughter-House Hence, tea gardens, goguettes, caboulots, bouibuis, mastroquets, bastringues, manezingues, bibines of the rag pickers, caravanseries of the caliphs, I certify to you, I am a voluptuary, I eat at Richard's at forty sous a head, I must have Persian carpets to roll naked Cleopatra in! Where is Cleopatra? Ah! So it is you, Louison. Good day."

Thus did Grantaire, more than intoxicated, launch into speech, catching at the dishwasher in her passage, from his corner in the back room of the Café Musain.

Bossuet, extending his hand toward him, tried to impose silence on him, and Grantaire began again worse than ever, "Aigle de Meaux, down with your paws. You produce on me no effect with your gesture of Hippocrates refusing Artaxerxes' bric-a-brac. I excuse you from the task of soothing me. Moreover, I am sad. What do you wish me to say to you? Man is evil, man is deformed; the butterfly is a success, man is a failure. God made a mistake with that animal. A crowd offers a choice of ugliness. The first comer is a wretch. Femme— woman—rhymes with *infame*, infamous. Yes, I have the spleen, complicated with melancholy, with homesickness, plus hypochondria, and I am vexed and I rage, and I yawn, and I am bored, and I am tired to death, and I am stupid! Let God go to the devil!"

"Silence then, capital R!" resumed Bossuet, who was discussing a point of law behind the scenes, and who was plunged more than waist high in a phrase of judicial slang, of which this is the conclusion: "And as for me, although I am hardly a legist, and at the most, an amateur attorney, I maintain this: that, in accordance with the terms of the customs of Normandy, at Saint-Michel, and for each year, an equivalent must be paid to the profit of the lord of the manor, saving the rights of others, and by all and several, the proprietors as well as those seized with inheritance, and that, for all emphyteuses, leases, freeholds, contracts of domain, mortgages—"

"Echo, plaintive nymph," hummed Grantaire.

Near Grantaire, an almost silent table, a sheet of paper, an inkstand and a pen between two glasses of brandy, announced that a vaudeville was being sketched out.

This great affair was being discussed in a low voice, and the two heads at work touched each other. "Let us begin by finding names. When one has the names, one finds the subject."

"That is true. Dictate. I will write."

"Monsieur Dorimon."

"An independent gentleman?"

"Of course."

"His daughter, Celestine."

"—tine. What next?"

"Colonel Sainval."

"Sainval is stale. I should say Valsin."

Beside the vaudeville aspirants, another group, which was also taking advantage of the uproar to talk low, was discussing a duel. An old fellow of thirty was counseling a young one of eighteen, and explaining to him what sort of an adversary he had to deal with.

"The deuce! Look out for yourself. He is a fine swordsman. His play is neat. He has the attack, no wasted feints, wrist, dash, lightning, a just parade, mathematical parries, bigre! And he is left-handed."

In the angle opposite Grantaire, Joly and Bahorel were playing dominoes, and talking of love.

"You are in luck, that you are," Joly was saying. "You have a mistress who is always laughing."

"That is a fault of hers," returned Bahorel. "One's mistress does wrong to laugh. That encourages one to deceive her. To see her gay removes your remorse; if you see her sad, your conscience pricks you."

"Ingrate! A woman who laughs is such a good thing! And you never quarrel!"

"That is because of the treaty that we have made. On forming our little Holy Alliance we assigned ourselves each our frontier, which we never cross. What is situated on the side of winter belongs to Vaud, on the side of the wind to Gex. Hence the peace."

"Peace is happiness digesting."

"And you, Jolllly, where do you stand in your entanglement with Mamselle—you know whom I mean?"

"She sulks at me with cruel patience."

"Yet you are a lover to soften the heart with gauntness."

"Alas!"

"In your place, I would let her alone."

"That is easy enough to say."

"And to do. Is not her name Musichetta?"

"Yes. Ah! My poor Bahorel, she is a superb girl, very literary, with tiny feet, little hands, she dresses well, and is white and dimpled, with the eyes of a fortune-teller. I am wild over her."

"My dear fellow, then in order to please her, you must be elegant, and produce effects with your knees. Buy a good pair of trousers of double-milled cloth at Staub's. That will assist."

"At what price?" shouted Grantaire.

The third corner was delivered up to a poetical discussion. Pagan mythology was giving battle to Christian mythology. The question was about Olympus, whose part was taken by Jean Prouvaire, out of pure romanticism.

Jean Prouvaire was timid only in repose. Once excited, he burst forth, a sort of mirth accentuated his enthusiasm, and he was at once both laughing and lyric.

"Let us not insult the gods," said he. "The gods may not have taken their departure. Jupiter does not impress me as dead. The gods are dreams, you say. Well, even in nature, such as it is today, after the flight of these dreams, we still find all the grand old pagan myths. Such and such a mountain with the profile of a citadel, like the Vignemale, for example, is still to me the headdress of Cybele; it has not been proved to me that Pan does not come at night to breathe into the hollow trunks of the willows, stopping up the holes in turn with his fingers, and I have always believed that I had something to do with the cascade of Pissevache."

In the last corner, they were talking politics. The charter that had been granted was getting roughly handled. Combeferre was upholding it weakly. Courfeyrac was energetically making a breach in it. On the table lay an unfortunate copy of the famous Touquet Charter. Courfeyrac had seized it, and was brandishing it, mingling with his arguments the rattling of this sheet of paper.

"In the first place, I won't have any kings; if it were only from an economical point of view, I don't want any; a king is a parasite. One does not have kings gratis. Listen to this: the dearness of kings. At the death of Francois I, the national debt of France amounted to an income of thirty-thousand livres; at the death of Louis XIV it was two milliards, six hundred millions, at twenty-eight livres the mark, which was equivalent in 1760, according to Desmarets, to four milliards, five hundred millions, which would today be equivalent to twelve milliards. In the second place, and no offense to Combeferre, a charter granted is but a poor expedient of civilization. To save the transition, to soften the passage, to deaden the shock, to cause the nation to pass insensibly from the monarchy to democracy by the practice of constitutional fictions, what detestable reasons all those are! No! no! Let us never enlighten the people with false daylight. Principles dwindle and pale in your constitutional cellar. No illegitimacy, no compromise, no grant from the king to the people. In all such grants there is an Article 14. By the side of the hand that gives there is the claw that snatches back. I refuse your charter point-blank. A charter is a mask; the lie lurks beneath it. A people that accepts a charter abdicates. The law is only the law when entire. No! No charter!"

It was winter; a couple of fagots were crackling in the fireplace. This was tempting, and Courfeyrac could not resist. He crumpled the poor Touquet Charter in his fist, and flung it in the fire. The paper flashed up. Combeferre watched the masterpiece of Louis XVIII burn philosophically, and contented himself with saying, "The charter metamorphosed into flame."

And sarcasms, sallies, jests, that French thing that is called entrain, and that English thing that is called humor, good and bad taste, good and bad reasons, all the wild pyrotechnics of dialogue, mounting together and crossing from all points of the room, produced a sort of merry bombardment over their heads.

CHAPTER V—ENLARGEMENT OF HORIZON

The shocks of youthful minds among themselves have this admirable property, that one can never foresee the spark, nor divine the lightning flash. What will dart out presently? No one knows. The burst of laughter starts from a tender feeling.

At the moment of jest, the serious makes its entry. Impulses depend on the first chance word. The spirit of each is sovereign, jest suffices to open the field to the unexpected. These are conversations with abrupt turns, in which the perspective changes suddenly. Chance is the stage manager of such conversations.

A severe thought, starting oddly from a clash of words, suddenly traversed the conflict of quips in which Grantaire, Bahorel, Prouvaire, Bossuet, Combeferre, and Courfeyrac were confusedly fencing.

How does a phrase crop up in a dialogue? From where comes it that it suddenly impresses itself on the attention of those who hear it? We have just said, that no one knows anything about it. In the midst of the uproar, Bossuet all at once terminated some apostrophe to Combeferre, with this date: "June 18th, 1815, Waterloo."

At this name of Waterloo, Marius, who was leaning his elbows on a table, beside a glass of water, removed his wrist from beneath his chin, and began to gaze fixedly at the audience.

"Pardieu!" exclaimed Courfeyrac ("Parbleu" was falling into disuse at this period), "that number 18 is strange and strikes me. It is Bonaparte's fatal number. Place Louis in front and Brumaire behind, you have the whole destiny of the man, with this significant peculiarity, that the end treads close on the heels of the commencement."

Enjolras, who had remained mute up to that point, broke the silence and addressed this remark to Combeferre: "You mean to say, the crime and the expiation."

This word crime overpassed the measure of what Marius, who was already greatly agitated by the abrupt evocation of Waterloo, could accept.

He rose, walked slowly to the map of France spread out on the wall, and at whose base an island was visible in a separate compartment, laid his finger on this compartment and said, "Corsica, a little island that has rendered France very great."

This was like a breath of icy air. All ceased talking. They felt that something was on the point of occurring.

Bahorel, replying to Bossuet, was just assuming an attitude of the torso to which he was addicted. He gave it up to listen.

Enjolras, whose blue eye was not fixed on anyone, and who seemed to be gazing at space, replied, without glancing at Marius, "France needs no Corsica to be great. France is great because she is France. *Quia nomina leo.*"*

Marius felt no desire to retreat; he turned toward Enjolras, and his voice burst forth with a vibration that came from a quiver of his very being. "God forbid that I should diminish France! But amalgamating Napoleon with her is not diminishing her. Come! Let us argue the question. I am a newcomer among you, but I will confess that you amaze me. Where do we stand? Who are we? Who are you? Who am I? Let us come to an explanation about the Emperor. I hear you say Buonaparte, accenting the "u" like the Royalists. I warn you that my grandfather does better still; he says, 'Buonaparte.' I thought you were young men. Where, then, is your enthusiasm? And what are you doing with it? Whom do you admire, if you do not admire the Emperor? And what more do you want? If you will have none of that great man, what great men would you like? He had everything. He was complete. He had in his brain the sum of human faculties. He made codes like Justinian, he dictated like Caesar, his conversation was mingled with the lightning flash of Pascal, with the thunderclap of Tacitus, he made history and he wrote it, his bulletins are Iliads, he combined the cipher of Newton with the metaphor of Mahomet, he left behind him in the East words as great as the pyramids,

---

* A proverb, "because my name is lion," that comes from a well-known fable.

at Tilsit he taught Emperors majesty, at the Academy of Sciences he replied to Laplace, in the Council of State be held his own against Merlin, he gave a soul to the geometry of the first, and to the chicanery of the last, he was a legist with the attorneys and sidereal with the astronomers; like Cromwell blowing out one of two candles, he went to the Temple to bargain for a curtain tassel; he saw everything; he knew everything; which did not prevent him from laughing good-naturedly beside the cradle of his little child; and all at once, frightened Europe lent an ear, armies put themselves in motion, parks of artillery rumbled, pontoons stretched over the rivers, clouds of cavalry galloped in the storm, cries, trumpets, a trembling of thrones in every direction, the frontiers of kingdoms oscillated on the map, the sound of a superhuman sword was heard, as it was drawn from its sheath; they beheld him, him, rise erect on the horizon with a blazing brand in his hand, and a glow in his eyes, unfolding amid the thunder, his two wings, the grand army and the old guard, and he was the archangel of war!"

All held their peace, and Enjolras bowed his head. Silence always produces somewhat the effect of acquiescence, of the enemy being driven to the wall. Marius continued with increased enthusiasm, and almost without pausing for breath, "Let us be just, my friends! What a splendid destiny for a nation to be the Empire of such an Emperor, when that nation is France and when it adds its own genius to the genius of that man! To appear and to reign, to march and to triumph, to have for halting-places all capitals, to take his grenadiers and to make kings of them, to decree the falls of dynasties, and to transfigure Europe at the pace of a charge; to make you feel that when you threaten you lay your hand on the hilt of the sword of God; to follow in a single man, Hannibal, Caesar, Charlemagne; to be the people of someone who mingles with your dawns the startling announcement of a battle won, to have the cannon of the Invalides to rouse you in the morning, to hurl into abysses of light prodigious words that flame forever, Marengo, Arcola, Austerlitz, Jena, Wagram! To cause constellations of victories to flash forth at each instant from the zenith of the centuries, to make the French Empire a pendant to the Roman Empire, to be the great nation and to give birth to the grand army, to make its legions fly forth over all the earth, as a mountain sends out its eagles on all sides to conquer, to dominate, to strike with lightning, to be in Europe a sort of nation gilded through glory, to sound athwart the centuries a trumpet-blast of Titans, to conquer the world twice, by conquest and by dazzling, that is sublime; and what greater thing is there?"

"To be free," said Combeferre.

Marius lowered his head in his turn; that cold and simple word had traversed his epic effusion like a blade of steel, and he felt it vanishing within him. When he raised his eyes, Combeferre was no longer there. Probably satisfied with his reply to the apotheosis, he had just taken his departure, and all, with the exception of Enjolras, had followed him. The room had been emptied. Enjolras, left alone with Marius, was gazing gravely at him. Marius, however, having rallied his ideas to some extent, did not consider himself beaten; there lingered in him a trace of inward fermentation, which was on the point, no doubt, of translating itself into syllogisms arrayed against Enjolras, when all of a sudden, they heard someone singing on the stairs as he went. It was Combeferre, and this is what he was singing:

> "If Caesar had given me
> Glory and war,
> And I had to abandon
> The love of my mother,
> I would say to great Caesar:
> Take your scepter and car,
> I prefer my mother, ah me!
> I prefer my mother!"

The wild and tender accents with which Combeferre sang communicated to his couplet a sort of strange grandeur. Marius, thoughtfully, and with his eyes fixed on the ceiling, repeated almost mechanically: "My mother?"

At that moment, he felt Enjolras's hand on his shoulder.

"Citizen," said Enjolras to him, "my mother is the Republic."

CHAPTER VI—RES ANGUSTA

That evening left Marius profoundly shaken, and with a melancholy shadow in his soul. He felt what the earth may possibly feel, at the moment when it is torn open with the iron, in order that grain may be deposited within it; it feels only the wound; the quiver of the germ and the joy of the fruit only arrive later.

Marius was gloomy. He had but just acquired a faith; must he then reject it already? He affirmed to himself that he would not. He declared to himself that he would not doubt, and he began to doubt in spite of himself. To stand between two religions, from one of which you have not as yet emerged, and another into which you have not yet entered, is intolerable; and twilight is pleasing only to batlike souls. Marius was clear-eyed, and he required the true light. The half-lights of doubt pained him. Whatever may have been his desire to remain where he was, he could not halt there, he was irresistibly constrained to continue, to advance, to examine, to think, to march farther. Where would this lead him? He feared, after having taken so many steps that had brought him nearer to his father, to now take a step that should estrange him from that father. His discomfort was augmented by all the reflections that occurred to him. An escarpment rose around him. He was in accord neither with his grandfather nor with his friends; daring in the eyes of the one, he was behind the times in the eyes of the others, and he recognized the fact that he was doubly isolated, on the side of age and on the side of youth. He ceased to go to the Café Musain.

In the troubled state of his conscience, he no longer thought of certain serious sides of existence. The realities of life do not allow themselves to be forgotten. They soon elbowed him abruptly.

One morning, the proprietor of the hotel entered Marius's room and said to him, "Monsieur Courfeyrac answered for you."

"Yes."

"But I must have my money."

"Request Courfeyrac to come and talk with me," said Marius.

Courfeyrac having made his appearance, the host left them. Marius then told him what it had not before occurred to him to relate, that he was the same as alone in the world, and had no relatives.

"What is to become of you?" said Courfeyrac.

"I do not know in the least," replied Marius.

"What are you going to do?"

"I do not know."

"Have you any money?"

"Fifteen francs."

"Do you want me to lend you some?"

"Never."

"Have you clothes?"

"Here is what I have."

"Have you trinkets?"

"A watch."

"Silver?"

"Gold; here it is."

"I know a clothes-dealer who will take your frock coat and a pair of trousers."

"That is good."

"You will then have only a pair of trousers, a waistcoat, a hat, and a coat."

"And my boots."

"What! You will not go barefoot? What opulence!"

"That will be enough."

"I know a watchmaker who will buy your watch."

"That is good."

"No; it is not good. What will you do after that?"

"Whatever is necessary. Anything honest, that is to say."

"Do you know English?"

"No."

"Do you know German?"

"No."

"So much the worse."

"Why?"

"Because one of my friends, a publisher, is getting up a sort of an encyclopedia, for which you might have translated English or German articles. It is badly paid work, but one can live by it."

"I will learn English and German."

"And in the meanwhile?"

"In the meanwhile I will live on my clothes and my watch."

The clothes-dealer was sent for. He paid twenty francs for the castoff garments. They went to the watchmaker's. He bought the watch for forty-five francs.

"That is not bad," said Marius to Courfeyrac, on their return to the hotel, "with my fifteen francs, that makes eighty."

"And the hotel bill?" observed Courfeyrac.

"Hello, I had forgotten that," said Marius.

The landlord presented his bill, which had to be paid on the spot. It amounted to seventy francs.

"I have ten francs left," said Marius.

"The deuce," exclaimed Courfeyrac, "you will eat up five francs while you are learning English, and five while learning German. That will be swallowing tongue very fast, or a hundred sous very slowly."

In the meantime Aunt Gillenormand, a rather good-hearted person at bottom in difficulties, had finally hunted up Marius's abode.

One morning, on his return from the law school, Marius found a letter from his aunt, and the sixty pistoles, that is to say, six hundred francs in gold, in sealed box.

Marius sent back the thirty Louis to his aunt, with a respectful letter, in which he stated that he had sufficient means of subsistence and that he should be able thenceforth to supply all his needs. At that moment, he had three francs left.

His aunt did not inform his grandfather of this refusal for fear of exasperating him. Besides, had he not said, "Let me never hear the name of that blood drinker again!"

Marius left the hotel de la Porte Saint-Jacques, as he did not wish to run in debt there.

BOOK FIFTH: THE EXCELLENCE OF MISFORTUNE

CHAPTER I—MARIUS INDIGENT

Life became hard for Marius. It was nothing to eat his clothes and his watch. He ate of that terrible, inexpressible thing that is called *de la vache enragé* that is to say, he endured great hardships and privations. A terrible thing it is, containing days without bread, nights without sleep, evenings without candle, a hearth without a fire, weeks without work, a future without hope, a coat out at the elbows, an old hat that evokes the laughter of young girls, a door that one finds locked on one at night because one's rent is not paid, the insolence of the porter and the cookshop man, the sneers of neighbors, humiliations, dignity trampled on, work of whatever nature accepted, disgusts, bitterness, despondency. Marius learned how all this is eaten, and how such are often the only things that one has to devour. At that moment of his existence, when a man needs his pride, because he needs love, he felt that he was jeered at because he was badly dressed, and ridiculous because he was poor. At the age when youth swells the heart with imperial pride, he dropped his eyes more than once on his dilapidated boots, and he knew the unjust shame and the poignant lushes of wretchedness. Admirable and terrible trial from which the feeble merge base, from which the strong emerge sublime. A crucible into which estiny casts a man, whenever it desires a scoundrel or a demigod.

For many great deeds are performed in petty combats. There are instances f bravery ignored and obstinate, which defend themselves step by step in that atal onslaught of necessities and turpitudes. Noble and mysterious triumphs hat no eye beholds, that are requited with no renown, that are saluted with no rumpet blast. Life, misfortune, isolation, abandonment, poverty, are the fields f battle that have their heroes; obscure heroes, who are, sometimes, grander han the heroes who win renown.

Firm and rare natures are thus created; misery, almost always a stepmother, s sometimes a mother; destitution gives birth to might of soul and spirit; istress is the nurse of pride; unhappiness is a good milk for the magnanimous.

There came a moment in Marius's life when he swept his own landing, when e bought his sou's worth of Brie cheese at the fruiter's, when he waited until wilight had fallen to slip into the baker's and purchase a loaf, which he carried ff furtively to his attic as though he had stolen it. Sometimes there could be een gliding into the butcher's shop on the corner, in the midst of the bantering ooks who elbowed him, an awkward young man, carrying big books under is arm, who had a timid yet angry air, who, on entering, removed his hat rom a brow whereon stood drops of perspiration, made a profound bow to he butcher's astonished wife, asked for a mutton cutlet, paid six or seven sous or it, wrapped it up in a paper, put it under his arm, between two books, and vent away. It was Marius. On this cutlet, which he cooked for himself, he lived or three days.

On the first day he ate the meat, on the second he ate the fat, on the third e gnawed the bone. Aunt Gillenormand made repeated attempts, and sent im the sixty pistoles several times. Marius returned them on every occasion, aying that he needed nothing.

He was still in mourning for his father when the revolution we have just escribed was affected within him. From that time forth, he had not put off is black garments. But his garments were quitting him. The day came when e had no longer a coat. The trousers would go next. What was to be done? ourfeyrac, to whom he had, on his side, done some good turns, gave him an ld coat. For thirty sous, Marius got it turned by some porter or other, and it vas a new coat. But this coat was green. Then Marius ceased to go out until fter nightfall. This made his coat black. As he wished always to appear in nourning, he clothed himself with the night.

In spite of all this, he got admitted to practice as a lawyer. He was suppose to live in Courfeyrac's room, which was decent, and where a certain numbe of law books backed up and completed by several dilapidated volumes o romance, passed as the library required by the regulations. He had his lettei addressed to Courfeyrac's quarters.

When Marius became a lawyer, he informed his grandfather of the fa in a letter that was cold but full of submission and respect. M. Gillenorman trembled as he took the letter, read it, tore it in four pieces, and threw it into th wastebasket. Two or three days later, Mademoiselle Gillenormand heard he father, who was alone in his room, talking aloud to himself. He always did th whenever he was greatly agitated. She listened, and the old man was sayin $ "If you were not a fool, you would know that one cannot be a baron and lawyer at the same time."

CHAPTER II—MARIUS POOR

It is the same with wretchedness as with everything else. It ends by becomin bearable. It finally assumes a form, and adjusts itself. One vegetates, tha is to say, one develops in a certain meager fashion that is, however, sufficiei for life. This is the mode in which the existence of Marius Pontmercy wa arranged: He had passed the worst straits; the narrow pass was opening ou a little in front of him. By dint of toil, perseverance, courage, and will, h had managed to draw from his work about seven hundred francs a year. H had learned German and English; thanks to Courfeyrac, who had put him i communication with his friend the publisher, Marius filled the modest post c utility man in the literature of the publishing house. He drew up prospectuse translated newspapers, annotated editions, compiled biographies, etc.; ne product, year in and year out, seven hundred francs. He lived on it. How? Nc so badly. We will explain.

Marius occupied in the Gorbeau house, for an annual sum of thirty franc a den minus a fireplace, called a cabinet, which contained only the mos indispensable articles of furniture. This furniture belonged to him. He gav three francs a month to the old principal tenant to come and sweep his hol and to bring him a little hot water every morning, a fresh egg, and a penny rol He breakfasted on this egg and roll. His breakfast varied in cost from two t four sous, according as eggs were dear or cheap. At six o'clock in the evenin he descended the Rue Saint-Jacques to dine at Rousseau's, opposite Basset' the stamp dealer's, on the corner of the Rue des Mathurins. He ate no soup. He took a six-sou plate of meat, a half-portion of vegetables for three sous, and a three-sou dessert. For three sous he got as much bread as he wished. As for wine, he drank water. When he paid at the desk where Madam Rousseau, at that period still plump and rosy majestically presided, he gave a sou to the waiter, and Madam Rousseau gave him a smile. Then he went away. For sixteen sous he had a smile and a dinner.

This Restaurant Rousseau, where so few bottles and so many water carafes were emptied, was a calming potion rather than a restaurant. It no longer exists. The proprietor had a fine nickname: he was called Rousseau the Aquatic.

Thus, breakfast four sous, dinner sixteen sous; his food cost him twenty sous a day; which made three hundred and sixty-five francs a year. Add the thirty francs for rent, and the thirty-six francs to the old woman, plus a few trifling expenses; for four hundred and fifty francs, Marius was fed, lodged, and waited on. His clothing cost him a hundred francs, his linen fifty francs, his washing fifty francs; the whole did not exceed six hundred and fifty francs. He was rich. He sometimes lent ten francs to a friend. Courfeyrac had once been able to borrow sixty francs of him. As far as fire was concerned, as Marius had no fireplace, he had "simplified matters."

Marius always had two complete suits of clothes, the one old, "for every day;" the other, brand new for special occasions. Both were black. He had but three shirts, one on his person, the second in the commode, and the third in the washerwoman's hands. He renewed them as they wore out. They were always ragged, which caused him to button his coat to the chin.

It had required years for Marius to attain to this flourishing condition. Hard years; difficult, some of them, to traverse, others to climb. Marius had not failed for a single day. He had endured everything in the way of destitution; he had done everything except contract debts. He did himself the justice to say that he had never owed anyone a sou. A debt was, to him, the beginning of slavery. He even said to himself, that a creditor is worse than a master; for the master possesses only your person, a creditor possesses your dignity and can administer to it a box on the ear. Rather than borrow, he went without food. He had passed many a day fasting. Feeling that all extremes meet, and that, if one is not on one's guard, lowered fortunes may lead to baseness of soul, he kept a jealous watch on his pride. Such and such a formality or action, which, in any other situation would have appeared merely a deference to him, now seemed insipidity, and he nerved himself against it. His face wore a sort of severe flush. He was timid even to rudeness.

During all these trials he had felt himself encouraged and even uplifted, at times, by a secret force that he possessed within himself. The soul aids the body, and at certain moments, raises it. It is the only bird that bears up its own cage.

Besides his father's name, another name was graven in Marius's heart, the name of Thenardier. Marius, with his grave and enthusiastic nature, surrounded with a sort of aureole the man to whom, in his thoughts, he owed his father's life, that intrepid sergeant who had saved the colonel amid the bullets and the cannonballs of Waterloo. He never separated the memory of this man from the memory of his father, and he associated them in his veneration. It was a sort of worship in two steps, with the grand altar for the colonel and the lesser one for Thenardier. What redoubled the tenderness of his gratitude toward Thenardier, was the idea of the distress into which he knew that Thenardier had fallen, and that had engulfed the latter. Marius had learned at Montfermeil of the ruin and bankruptcy of the unfortunate innkeeper. Since that time, he had made unheard-of efforts to find traces of him and to reach him in that dark abyss of misery in which Thenardier had disappeared. Marius had beaten the whole country; he had gone to Chelles, to Bondy, to Gourney, to Nogent, to Lagny. He had persisted for three years, expending in these explorations the little money that he had laid by. No one had been able to give him any news of Thenardier: he was supposed to have gone abroad. His creditors had also sought him, with less love than Marius, but with as much assiduity, and had not been able to lay their hands on him. Marius blamed himself, and was almost angry with himself for his lack of success in his researches. It was the only debt left him by the colonel, and Marius made it a matter of honor to pay it. "What," he thought, "when my father lay dying on the field of battle, did Thenardier contrive to find him amid the smoke and the grapeshot, and bear him off on his shoulders, and yet he owed him nothing, and I, who owe so much to Thenardier, cannot join him in this shadow where he is lying in the pangs of death, and in my turn bring him back from death to life! Oh! I will find him!" To find Thenardier, in fact, Marius would have given one of his arms, to rescue him from his misery, he would have sacrificed all his blood. To see Thenardier, to render Thenardier some service, to say to him, "You do not know me; well, I do know you! Here I am. Dispose of me!" This was Marius's sweetest and most magnificent dream.

CHAPTER III—MARIUS GROWN UP

At this epoch, Marius was twenty years of age. It was three years since he had left his grandfather. Both parties had remained on the same terms, without attempting to approach each other, and without seeking to see each other. Besides, what was the use of seeing each other? Marius was the brass vase, while Father Gillenormand was the iron pot.

We admit that Marius was mistaken as to his grandfather's heart. He had imagined that M. Gillenormand had never loved him, and that that crusty, harsh, and smiling old fellow who cursed, shouted, and stormed and brandished his cane, cherished for him, at the most, only that affection, which is at once slight and severe, of the dotards of comedy. Marius was in error. There are fathers who do not love their children; there exists no grandfather who does not adore his grandson. At bottom, as we have said, M. Gillenormand idolized Marius. He idolized him after his own fashion, with an accompaniment of snappishness and boxes on the ear; but, this child once gone, he felt a black void in his heart; he would allow no one to mention the child to him, and all the while secretly regretted that he was so well obeyed. At first, he hoped that this Buonapartist, this Jacobin, this terrorist, this Septembrist, would return. But the weeks passed by, years passed; to M. Gillenormand's great despair, the "blood drinker" did not make his appearance. "I could not do otherwise than turn him out," said the grandfather to himself, and he asked himself, "If the thing were to do over again, would I do it?" His pride instantly answered "yes," but his aged head, which he shook in silence, replied sadly "no." He had his hours of depression. He missed Marius. Old men need affection as they need the sun. It is warmth. Strong as his nature was, the absence of Marius had wrought some change in him. Nothing in the world could have induced him to take a step toward "that rogue;" but he suffered. He never inquired about him, but he thought of him incessantly. He lived in the Marais in a more and more retired manner; he was still merry and violent as of old, but his merriment had a convulsive harshness, and his violences always terminated in a sort of gentle and gloomy dejection. He sometimes said, "Oh! If he only would return, what a good box on the ear I would give him!"

As for his aunt, she thought too little to love much; Marius was no longer for her much more than a vague black form; and she eventually came to occupy herself with him much less than with the cat or the paroquet that she probably had. What augmented Father Gillenormand's secret suffering was that he locked it all up within his breast, and did not allow its existence to be divined. His sorrow was like those recently invented furnaces that consume their own smoke. It sometimes happened that officious busybodies spoke to him of Marius, and asked him, "What is your grandson doing?" "What has become of him?" The old bourgeois replied with a sigh, that he was a sad case, and giving a fillip to his cuff, if he wished to appear gay, "Monsieur le Baron de Pontmercy is practicing pettifogging in some corner or other."

While the old man regretted, Marius applauded himself. As is the case with all good-hearted people, misfortune had eradicated his bitterness. He only thought of M. Gillenormand in an amiable light, but he had set his mind on not receiving anything more from the man who had been unkind to his father. This was the mitigated translation of his first indignation. Moreover, he was happy at having suffered, and at suffering still. It was for his father's sake. The hardness of his life satisfied and pleased him. He said to himself with a sort of joy that—it was certainly the least he could do; that it was an atonement— that, had it not been for that, he would have been punished in some other way and later on for his impious indifference toward his father, and such a father! That it would not have been just that his father should have all the suffering, and he none of it; and that, in any case, what were his toils and his destitution compared with the colonel's heroic life? That, in short, the only way for him to approach his father and resemble him, was to be brave in the face of indigence, as the other had been valiant before the enemy; and that that was, no doubt, what the colonel had meant to imply by the words: "He will be worthy of it." Words that Marius continued to wear, not on his breast, since the colonel's writing had disappeared, but in his heart.

And then, on the day when his grandfather had turned him out of doors, he had been only a child, now he was a man. He felt it. Misery, we repeat, had been good for him. Poverty in youth, when it succeeds, has this magnificent property about it, that it turns the whole will toward effort, and the whole soul toward aspiration. Poverty instantly lays material life bare and renders it hideous; hence inexpressible bounds toward the ideal life. The wealthy young man has a hundred coarse and brilliant distractions, horse races, hunting, dogs, tobacco, gaming, good repasts, and all the rest of it; occupations for the baser side of the soul, at the expense of the loftier and more delicate sides. The poor young man wins his bread with difficulty; he eats; when he has eaten, he has nothing more but meditation. He goes to the spectacles that God furnishes gratis; he gazes at the sky, space, the stars, flowers, children, the humanity among which he is suffering, the creation amid which he beams. He gazes so much on humanity that he perceives its soul, he gazes upon creation to such an extent that he beholds God. He dreams, he feels himself great; he dreams on, and feels himself tender. From the egotism of the man who suffers he passes to the compassion of the man who meditates. An admirable sentiment breaks forth in him, forgetfulness of self and pity for all. As he thinks of the innumerable enjoyments that nature offers, gives, and lavishes to souls that stand open, and refuses to souls that are closed, he comes to pity, he the millionaire of the mind, the millionaire of money. All hatred departs from his heart, in proportion as light penetrates his spirit. And is he unhappy? No. The misery of a young man is never miserable. The first young lad who comes to hand, however poor he may be, with his strength, his health, his rapid walk, his brilliant eyes, his warmly circulating blood, his black hair, his red lips, his white teeth, his pure breath, will always arouse the envy of an aged emperor. And then, every morning, he sets himself afresh to the task of earning his bread; and while his hands earn his bread, his dorsal column gains pride, his brain gathers ideas. His task finished, he returns to ineffable ecstasies, to contemplation, to joys; he beholds his feet set in afflictions, in obstacles, on the pavement, in the nettles, sometimes in the mire; his head in the light. He is firm, serene, gentle, peaceful, attentive, serious, content with little, kindly; and he thanks God for having bestowed on him those two forms of riches that many a rich man lacks: work, which makes him free; and thought, which makes him dignified.

This is what had happened with Marius. To tell the truth, he inclined a little too much to the side of contemplation. From the day when he had succeeded in earning his living with some approach to certainty, he had stopped, thinking it good to be poor, and retrenching time from his work to give to thought; that is to say, he sometimes passed entire days in meditation, absorbed, engulfed, like a visionary, in the mute voluptuousness of ecstasy and inward radiance. He had thus propounded the problem of his life: to toil as little as possible at material labor, in order to toil as much as possible at the labor that is impalpable; in other words, to bestow a few hours on real life, and to cast the rest to the infinite. As he believed that he lacked nothing, he did not perceive that contemplation, thus understood, ends by becoming one of the forms of idleness; that he was contenting himself with conquering the first necessities of life, and that he was resting from his labors too soon.

It was evident that, for this energetic and enthusiastic nature, this could only be a transitory state, and that, at the first shock against the inevitable complications of destiny, Marius would awaken.

In the meantime, although he was a lawyer, and whatever Father

Gillenormand thought about the matter, he was not practicing, he was not even pettifogging. Meditation had turned him aside from pleading. To haunt attorneys, to follow the court, to hunt up cases—what a bore! Why should he do it? He saw no reason for changing the manner of gaining his livelihood! The obscure and ill-paid publishing establishment had come to mean for him a sure source of work that did not involve too much labor, as we have explained, and that sufficed for his wants.

One of the publishers for whom he worked, M. Magimel, I think, offered to take him into his own house, to lodge him well, to furnish him with regular occupation, and to give him fifteen hundred francs a year. To be well lodged! Fifteen hundred francs! No doubt. But renounce his liberty! Be on fixed wages! A sort of hired man of letters! According to Marius's opinion, if he accepted, his position would become both better and worse at the same time—he acquired comfort, and lost his dignity; it was a fine and complete unhappiness converted into a repulsive and ridiculous state of torture: something like the case of a blind man who should recover the sight of one eye. He refused.

Marius dwelled in solitude. Owing to his taste for remaining outside of everything, and through having been too much alarmed, he had not entered decidedly into the group presided over by Enjolras. They had remained good friends; they were ready to assist each other on occasion in every possible way; but nothing more. Marius had two friends: one young, Courfeyrac; and one old, M. Mabeuf. He inclined more to the old man. In the first place, he owed to him the revolution that had taken place within him; to him he was indebted for having known and loved his father. "He operated on me for a cataract," he said.

The churchwarden had certainly played a decisive part.

It was not, however, that M. Mabeuf had been anything but the calm and impassive agent of Providence in this connection. He had enlightened Marius by chance and without being aware of the fact, as does a candle that someone brings; he had been the candle and not the someone.

As for Marius's inward political revolution, M. Mabeuf was totally incapable of comprehending it, of willing or of directing it.

As we shall see M. Mabeuf again, later on, a few words will not be superfluous.

CHAPTER IV—M. MABEUF

On the day when M. Mabeuf said to Marius, "Certainly I approve of political opinions," he expressed the real state of his mind. All political opinions were matters of indifference to him, and he approved them all, without distinction, provided they left him in peace, as the Greeks called the Furies "the beautiful, the good, the charming," the Eumenides. M. Mabeuf's political opinion consisted in a passionate love for plants, and, above all, for books. Like all the rest of the world, he possessed the termination in -ist, without which no one could exist at that time, but he was neither a Royalist, a Bonapartist, a Chartist, an Orleanist, nor an Anarchist; he was a bouquinist, a collector of old books. He did not understand how men could busy themselves with hating each other because of silly stuff like the charter, democracy, legitimacy, monarchy, the republic, etc., when there were in the world all sorts of mosses, grasses, and shrubs that they might be looking at, and heaps of folios, and even of 32mos,* which they might turn over. He took good care not to become useless; having books did not prevent his reading, being a botanist did not prevent his being a gardener. When he made Pontmercy's acquaintance, this sympathy had existed between the colonel and himself—that what the colonel did for flowers, he did for fruits. M. Mabeuf had succeeded in producing seedling pears as savory as the pears of St. Germain; it is from one of his combinations, apparently, that the October Mirabelle, now celebrated and no less perfumed than the summer Mirabelle, owes its origin. He went to Mass rather from gentleness than from piety, and because, as he loved the faces of men, but hated their noise, he found them assembled and silent only in church. Feeling that he must be something in the State, he had chosen the career of warden. However, he had never succeeded in loving any woman as much as a tulip bulb, nor any man as much as an Elzevir. He had long passed sixty, when, one day, someone asked him, "Have you never been married?"

"I have forgotten," said he. When it sometimes happened to him—and to whom does it not happen?—to say, "Oh! If I were only rich!" it was not when ogling a pretty girl, as was the case with Father Gillenormand, but when contemplating an old book. He lived alone with an old housekeeper. He was somewhat gouty, and when he was asleep, his aged fingers, stiffened with rheumatism, lay crooked up in the folds of his sheets. He had composed

---

* A type of paper, about the size of a modern paperback book, cut from standard sheets and folded into 32 leaves

and published a *Flora of the Environs of Cauterez*, with colored plates, a work that enjoyed a tolerable measure of esteem and that sold well. People rang his bell, in the Rue Mesieres, two or three times a day, to ask for it. He drew as much as two thousand francs a year from it; this constituted nearly the whole of his fortune. Although poor, he had had the talent to form for himself, by dint of patience, privations, and time, a precious collection of rare copies of every sort. He never went out without a book under his arm, and he often returned with two. The sole decoration of the four rooms on the ground floor, which composed his lodgings, consisted of framed herbariums, and engravings of the old masters. The sight of a sword or a gun chilled his blood. He had never approached a cannon in his life, even at the Invalides. He had a passable stomach, a brother who was a Curé, perfectly white hair, no teeth, either in his mouth or in his mind, a trembling in every limb, a Picard accent, an infantile laugh, the air of an old sheep, and he was easily frightened. Add to this, that he had no other friendship, no other acquaintance among the living, than an old bookseller of the Porte-Saint-Jacques, named Royal. His dream was to naturalize indigo in France.

His servant was also a sort of innocent. The poor good old woman was a spinster. Sultan, her cat, which might have mewed Allegri's miserere in the Sixtine Chapel, had filled her heart and sufficed for the quantity of passion that existed in her. None of her dreams had ever proceeded as far as man. She had never been able to get further than her cat. Like him, she had a mustache. Her glory consisted in her caps, which were always white. She passed her time, on Sundays, after Mass, in counting over the linen in her chest, and in spreading out on her bed the dresses in the piece that she bought and never had made up. She knew how to read. M. Mabeuf had nicknamed her Mother Plutarque.

M. Mabeuf had taken a fancy to Marius, because Marius, being young and gentle, warmed his age without startling his timidity. Youth combined with gentleness produces on old people the effect of the sun without wind. When Marius was saturated with military glory, with gunpowder, with marches and countermarches, and with all those prodigious battles in which his father had given and received such tremendous blows of the sword, he went to see M. Mabeuf, and M. Mabeuf talked to him of his hero from the point of view of flowers.

His brother the Curé died about 1830, and almost immediately, as when the night is drawing on, the whole horizon grew dark for M. Mabeuf. A notary's failure deprived him of the sum of ten thousand francs, which was all that he possessed in his brother's right and his own. The Revolution of July brought a crisis to publishing. In a period of embarrassment, the first thing that does not sell is a Flora. The Flora of the Environs of Cauteretz stopped short. Weeks passed by without a single purchaser. Sometimes M. Mabeuf started at the sound of the bell. "Monsieur," said Mother Plutarque sadly, "it is the water-carrier." In short, one day, M. Mabeuf quitted the Rue Mesieres, abdicated the functions of warden, gave up Saint-Sulpice, sold not a part of his books, but of his prints—that to which he was the least attached—and installed himself in a little house on the Rue Montparnasse, where, however, he remained but one quarter for two reasons: in the first place, the ground floor and the garden cost three hundred francs, and he dared not spend more than two hundred francs on his rent; in the second, being near Faton's shooting gallery, he could hear the pistol shots, which was intolerable to him.

He carried off his Flora, his copperplates, his herbariums, his portfolios, and his books, and established himself near the Salpetriere, in a sort of thatched cottage of the village of Austerlitz, where, for fifty crowns a year, he got three rooms and a garden enclosed by a hedge, and containing a well. He took advantage of this removal to sell off nearly all his furniture. On the day of his entrance into his new quarters, he was very gay, and drove the nails on which his engravings and herbariums were to hang, with his own hands, dug in his garden the rest of the day, and at night, perceiving that Mother Plutarque had a melancholy air, and was very thoughtful, he tapped her on the shoulder and said to her with a smile, "We have the indigo!"

Only two visitors, the bookseller of the Porte-Saint-Jacques and Marius, were admitted to view the thatched cottage at Austerlitz, a brawling name that was, to tell the truth, extremely disagreeable to him.

However, as we have just pointed out, brains that are absorbed in some bit of wisdom, or folly, or, as it often happens, in both at once, are but slowly accessible to the things of actual life. Their own destiny is a far-off thing to them. There results from such concentration a passivity, which, if it were the outcome of reasoning, would resemble philosophy. One declines, descends, trickles away, even crumbles away, and yet is hardly conscious of it one's self. It always ends, it is true, in an awakening, but the awakening is tardy. In the meantime, it seems as though we held ourselves neutral in the game that is going on between our happiness and our unhappiness. We are the stake, and we look on at the game with indifference.

It is thus that, athwart the cloud that formed about him, when all his hopes were extinguished one after the other, M. Mabeuf remained rather puerilely, but profoundly serene. His habits of mind had the regular swing of a pendulum. Once mounted on an illusion, he went for a very long time, even after the illusion had disappeared. A clock does not stop short at the precise moment when the key is lost.

M. Mabeuf had his innocent pleasures. These pleasures were inexpensive and unexpected; the merest chance furnished them. One day, Mother Plutarque was reading a romance in one corner of the room. She was reading aloud, finding that she understood better thus. To read aloud is to assure one's self of what one is reading. There are people who read very loud, and who have the appearance of giving themselves their word of honor as to what they are perusing.

It was with this sort of energy that Mother Plutarque was reading the romance that she had in hand. M. Mabeuf heard her without listening to her.

In the course of her reading, Mother Plutarque came to this phrase. It was a question of an officer of dragoons and a beauty: "The beauty pouted, and the dragoon—"

Here she interrupted herself to wipe her glasses.

"Bouddha and the Dragon," struck in M. Mabeuf in a low voice. "Yes, it is true that there was a dragon, which, from the depths of its cave, spouted flame through his maw and set the heavens on fire. Many stars had already been consumed by this monster, which, besides, had the claws of a tiger. Bouddha went into its den and succeeded in converting the dragon. That is a good book that you are reading, Mother Plutarque. There is no more beautiful legend in existence."

And M. Mabeuf fell into a delicious reverie.

CHAPTER V—POVERTY A GOOD NEIGHBOR FOR MISERY

Marius liked this candid old man who saw himself gradually falling into the clutches of indigence, and who came to feel astonishment, little by little, without, however, being made melancholy by it. Marius met Courfeyrac and sought out M. Mabeuf. Very rarely, however; twice a month at most.

Marius's pleasure consisted in taking long walks alone on the outer boulevards, or in the Champs-de-Mars, or in the least frequented alleys of the Luxembourg. He often spent half a day in gazing at a market garden, the beds of lettuce, the chickens on the dung-heap, the horse turning the water-wheel. The passersby stared at him in surprise, and some of them thought his attire suspicious and his mien sinister. He was only a poor young man dreaming in an objectless way.

It was during one of his strolls that he had hit upon the Gorbeau house, and, tempted by its isolation and its cheapness, had taken up his abode there. He was known there only under the name of M. Marius.

Some of his father's old generals or old comrades had invited him to go and see them, when they learned about him. Marius had not refused their invitations. They afforded opportunities of talking about his father. Thus he went from time to time, to Comte Pajol, to General Bellavesne, to General Fririon, to the Invalides. There was music and dancing there. On such evenings, Marius put on his new coat. But he never went to these evening parties or balls except on days when it was freezing cold, because he could not afford a carriage, and he did not wish to arrive with boots otherwise than like mirrors.

He said sometimes, but without bitterness, "Men are so made that in a drawing room you may be soiled everywhere except on your shoes. In order to ensure a good reception there, only one irreproachable thing is asked of you; your conscience? No, your boots."

All passions except those of the heart are dissipated by reverie. Marius's political fevers vanished thus. The Revolution of 1830 assisted in the process, by satisfying and calming him. He remained the same, setting aside his fits of wrath. He still held the same opinions. Only, they had been tempered. To speak accurately, he had no longer any opinions, he had sympathies. To what party did he belong? To the party of humanity. Out of humanity he chose France; out of the Nation he chose the people; out of the people he chose the woman. It was to that point above all, that his pity was directed. Now he preferred an idea to a deed, a poet to a hero, and he admired a book like Job more than an event like Marengo. And then, when, after a day spent in meditation, he returned in the evening through the boulevards, and caught a glimpse through the branches of the trees of the fathomless space beyond, the nameless gleams, the abyss, the shadow, the mystery, all that which is only human seemed very pretty indeed to him.

He thought that he had, and he really had, in fact, arrived at the truth of life and of human philosophy, and he had ended by gazing at nothing but heaven, the only thing that Truth can perceive from the bottom of her well.

This did not prevent him from multiplying his plans, his combinations, his scaffoldings, his projects for the future. In this state of reverie, an eye that could have cast a glance into Marius's interior would have been dazzled with the purity of that soul. In fact, had it been given to our eyes of the flesh to gaze into the consciences of others, we should be able to judge a man much more surely according to what he dreams, than according to what he thinks. There is will in thought, there is none in dreams. Reverie, which is utterly spontaneous, takes and keeps, even in the gigantic and the ideal, the form of our spirit. Nothing proceeds more directly and more sincerely from the very depth of our soul, than our unpremeditated and boundless aspirations toward the splendors of destiny. In these aspirations, much more than in deliberate, rational coordinated ideas, is the real character of a man to be found. Our chimeras are the things that the most resemble us. Each one of us dreams of the unknown and the impossible in accordance with his nature.

Toward the middle of this year 1831, the old woman who waited on Marius told him that his neighbors, the wretched Jondrette family, had been turned out of doors. Marius, who passed nearly the whole of his days out of the house, hardly knew that he had any neighbors.

"Why are they turned out?" he asked.

"Because they do not pay their rent; they owe for two quarters."

"How much is it?"

"Twenty francs," said the old woman.

Marius had thirty francs saved up in a drawer.

"Here," he said to the old woman, "take these twenty-five francs. Pay for the poor people and give them five francs, and do not tell them that it was I."

CHAPTER VI—THE SUBSTITUTE

It chanced that the regiment to which Lieutenant Theodule belonged came to perform garrison duty in Paris. This inspired Aunt Gillenormand with a second idea. She had, on the first occasion, hit upon the plan of having Marius spied upon by Theodule; now she plotted to have Theodule take Marius's place.

At all events and in case the grandfather should feel the vague need of a young face in the house, these rays of dawn are sometimes sweet to ruin, it was expedient to find another Marius. "Take it as a simple erratum," she thought, "such as one sees in books. For Marius, read Theodule."

A grandnephew is almost the same as a grandson; in default of a lawyer one takes a lancer.

One morning, when M. Gillenormand was about to read something in the Quotidienne, his daughter entered and said to him in her sweetest voice, for the question concerned her favorite, "Father, Theodule is coming to present his respects to you this morning."

"Who's Theodule?"

"Your grandnephew."

"Ah!" said the grandfather.

Then he went back to his reading, thought no more of his grandnephew, who was merely some Theodule or other, and soon flew into a rage, which almost always happened when he read. The "sheet" that he held, although Royalist, of course, announced for the following day, without any softening phrases, one of these little events that were of daily occurrence at that date in Paris: "That the students of the schools of law and medicine were to assemble on the Place du Pantheon, at midday, to deliberate." The discussion concerned one of the questions of the moment, the artillery of the National Guard, and a conflict between the Minister of War and "the citizen's militia," on the subject of the cannon parked in the courtyard of the Louvre. The students were to "deliberate" over this. It did not take much more than this to swell M. Gillenormand's rage.

He thought of Marius, who was a student, and who would probably go with the rest, to "deliberate, at midday, on the Place du Pantheon."

As he was indulging in this painful dream, Lieutenant Theodule entered clad in plain clothes as a bourgeois, which was clever of him, and was discreetly introduced by Mademoiselle Gillenormand. The lancer had reasoned as follows: "The old druid has not sunk all his money in a life pension. It is well to disguise one's self as a civilian from time to time."

Mademoiselle Gillenormand said aloud to her father, "Theodule, your grandnephew."

And in a low voice to the lieutenant, "Approve of everything."

And she withdrew.

The lieutenant, who was but little accustomed to such venerable encounters, stammered with some timidity, "Good day, uncle,"—and made a salute composed of the involuntary and mechanical outline of the military salute finished off as a bourgeois salute.

"Ah! So it's you; that is well, sit down," said the old gentleman.

That said, he totally forgot the lancer.

Theodule seated himself, and M. Gillenormand rose.

M. Gillenormand began to pace back and forth, his hands in his pockets, talking aloud, and twitching, with his irritated old fingers, at the two watches he wore in his two fobs.

"That pack of brats! They convene on the Place du Pantheon! By my life! Urchins who were with their nurses but yesterday! If one were to squeeze their noses, milk would burst out. And they deliberate tomorrow, at midday. What are we coming to? What are we coming to? It is clear that we are making for the abyss. That is what the *descamisados* (shirtless) have brought us to! To deliberate on the citizen artillery! To go and jabber in the open air over the jibes of the National Guard! And with whom are they to meet there? Just see where Jacobinism leads. I will bet anything you like, a million against a counter, that there will be no one there but returned convicts and released galley slaves. The Republicans and the galley slaves, they form but one nose and one handkerchief. Carnot used to say, 'Where would you have me go, traitor?' Fouche replied, 'Wherever you please, imbecile!' That's what the Republicans are like."

"That is true," said Theodule.

M. Gillenormand half turned his head, saw Theodule, and went on, "When one reflects that that scoundrel was so vile as to turn carbonaro! Why did you leave my house? To go and become a Republican! Pssst! In the first place, the people want none of your republic, they have common sense, they know well that there always have been kings, and that there always will be; they know well that the people are only the people, after all, they make sport of it, of your republic—do you understand, idiot? Is it not a horrible caprice? To fall in love with Pere Duchesne, to make sheep's-eyes at the guillotine, to sing romances, and play on the guitar under the balcony of '93—it's enough to make one spit on all these young fellows, such fools are they! They are all alike. Not one escapes. It suffices for them to breathe the air that blows through the street to lose their senses. The nineteenth century is poison. The first scamp that happens along lets his beard grow like a goat's, thinks himself a real scoundrel, and abandons his old relatives. He's a Republican, he's a romantic. What does that mean, romantic? Do me the favor to tell me what it is. All possible follies. A year ago, they ran to Hernani. Now, I just ask you, Hernani! Antitheses! Abominations that are not even written in French! And then, they have cannons in the courtyard of the Louvre. Such are the rascalities of this age!"

"You are right, Uncle," said Theodule.

M. Gillenormand resumed, "Cannons in the courtyard of the Museum! For what purpose? Do you want to fire grapeshot at the Apollo Belvedere? What have those cartridges to do with the Venus de Medici? Oh! The young men of the present day are all blackguards! What a pretty creature is their Benjamin Constant! And those who are not rascals are simpletons! They do all they can to make themselves ugly, they are badly dressed, they are afraid of women, in the presence of petticoats they have a mendicant air that sets the girls into fits of laughter; on my word of honor, one would say the poor creatures were ashamed of love. They are deformed, and they complete themselves by being stupid; they repeat the puns of Tiercelin and Potier, they have sack coats, stablemen's waistcoats, shirts of coarse linen, trousers of coarse cloth, boots of coarse leather, and their rigmarole resembles their plumage. One might make use of their jargon to put new soles on their old shoes. And all this awkward batch of brats has political opinions, if you please. Political opinions should be strictly forbidden. They fabricate systems, they recast society, they demolish the monarchy, they fling all laws to the earth, they put the attic in the cellar's place and my porter in the place of the King, they turn Europe topsy-turvy, they reconstruct the world, and all their love affairs consist in staring slyly at the ankles of the laundresses as these women climb into their carts. Ah! Marius! Ah! You blackguard! To go and vociferate on the public place! To discuss, to debate, to take measures! They call that measures, just God! Disorder humbles itself and becomes silly. I have seen chaos, I now see a mess. Students deliberating on the National Guard, such a thing could not be seen among the Ogibewas nor the Cadodaches! Savages who go naked, with their noddles dressed like a shuttlecock, with a club in their paws, are less of brutes than those bachelors of arts! The four-penny monkeys! And they set up for judges! Those creatures deliberate and ratiocinate! The end of the world is come! This is plainly the end of this miserable terraqueous globe! A final hiccup was required, and France has emitted it. Deliberate, my rascals! Such things will happen so long as they go and read the newspapers under the arcades of the Odeon. That costs them a sou, and their good sense, and their intelligence, and their heart and their soul, and their wits. They emerge thence, and decamp from their families. All newspapers are pests; all, even the Drapeau Blanc! At bottom, Martainville was a Jacobin. Ah! Just Heaven! You may boast of having driven your grandfather to despair, that you may!"

"That is evident," said Theodule.

And profiting by the fact that M. Gillenormand was taking breath, the lancer added in a magisterial manner, "There should be no other newspaper than the Moniteur, and no other book than the Annuaire Militaire."

M. Gillenormand continued, "It is like their Sieyes! A regicide ending in a senator; for that is the way they always end. They give themselves a scar with the address of thou as citizens, in order to get themselves called, eventually, Monsieur le Comte. Monsieur le Comte as big as my arm, assassins of

September. The philosopher Sieyes! I will do myself the justice to say, that I have never had any better opinion of the philosophies of all those philosophers, than of the spectacles of the grimacer of Tivoli! One day I saw the Senators cross the Quai Malplaquet in mantles of violet velvet sown with bees, with hats a la Henri IV. They were hideous. One would have pronounced them monkeys from the tiger's court. Citizens, I declare to you, that your progress is madness, that your humanity is a dream, that your revolution is a crime, that your republic is a monster, that your young and virgin France comes from the brothel, and I maintain it against all, whoever you may be, whether journalists, economists, legists, or even were you better judges of liberty, of equality, and fraternity than the knife of the guillotine! And that I announce to you, my fine fellows!"

"Parbleu!" cried the lieutenant. "That is wonderfully true."

M. Gillenormand paused in a gesture that he had begun, wheeled around, stared Lancer Theodule intently in the eyes, and said to him, "You are a fool."

BOOK SIXTH: THE CONJUNCTION OF TWO STARS

CHAPTER I—THE SOBRIQUET: MODE OF FORMATION OF FAMILY NAMES

Marius was, at this epoch, a handsome young man, of medium stature, with thick and intensely black hair, a lofty and intelligent brow, well-opened and passionate nostrils, an air of calmness and sincerity, and with something indescribably proud, thoughtful, and innocent over his whole countenance. His profile, all of whose lines were rounded, without thereby losing their firmness, had a certain Germanic sweetness, which has made its way into the French physiognomy by way of Alsace and Lorraine, and that complete absence of angles that rendered the Sicambres so easily recognizable among the Romans, and that distinguishes the leonine from the aquiline race. He was at that period of life when the mind of men who think is composed, in nearly equal parts, of depth and ingenuousness. A grave situation being given, he had all that is required to be stupid: one more turn of the key, and he might be sublime. His manners were reserved, cold, polished, not very genial. As his mouth was charming, his lips the reddest, and his teeth the whitest in the world,

is smile corrected the severity of his face, as a whole. At certain moments, that
pure brow and that voluptuous smile presented a singular contrast. His eyes
were small, but his glance was large.

At the period of his most abject misery, he had observed that young girls
turned around when he passed by, and he fled or hid, with death in his soul. He
thought that they were staring at him because of his old clothes, and that they
were laughing at them; the fact is, that they stared at him because of his grace,
and that they dreamed of him.

This mute misunderstanding between him and the pretty passersby had
made him shy. He chose none of them for the excellent reason that he fled from
all of them. He lived thus indefinitely, stupidly, as Courfeyrac said.

Courfeyrac also said to him, "Do not aspire to be venerable." Let me give
you a piece of advice, my dear fellow. Don't read so many books, and look
a little more at the lasses. The jades have some good points about them, O
Marius! By dint of fleeing and blushing, you will become brutalized."

On other occasions, Courfeyrac encountered him and said, "Good
morning, Monsieur l' Abbé!"

When Courfeyrac had addressed to him some remark of this nature, Marius
avoided women, both young and old, more than ever for a week to come, and
he avoided Courfeyrac to boot.

Nevertheless, there existed in all the immensity of creation, two women
whom Marius did not flee, and to whom he paid no attention whatever. In
truth, he would have been very much amazed if he had been informed that they
were women. One was the bearded old woman who swept out his chamber,
and caused Courfeyrac to say, "Seeing that his servant woman wears his beard,
Marius does not wear his own beard." The other was a sort of little girl whom
he saw very often, and whom he never looked at.

For more than a year, Marius had noticed in one of the walks of the
Luxembourg, the one that skirts the parapet of the Pepiniere, a man and a very
young girl, who were almost always seated side by side on the same bench, at the
most solitary end of the alley, on the Rue de l'Ouest side. Every time that that
chance that meddles with the strolls of persons whose gaze is turned inwards,
led Marius to that walk, and it was nearly every day, he found this couple there.
The man appeared to be about sixty years of age; he seemed sad and serious;
his whole person presented the robust and weary aspect peculiar to military
men who have retired from the service. If he had worn a decoration, Marius
would have said, "He is an ex-officer." He had a kindly but unapproachable air,
and he never let his glance linger on the eyes of anyone. He wore blue trousers,

a blue frock coat and a broad-brimmed hat, which always appeared to be new, a black cravat, a Quaker shirt, that is to say, it was dazzlingly white, but of coarse linen. A grisette who passed near him one day, said, "Here's a very tidy widower." His hair was very white.

The first time that the young girl who accompanied him came and seated herself on the bench that they seemed to have adopted, she was a sort of child thirteen or fourteen years of age, so thin as to be almost homely, awkward, insignificant, and with a possible promise of handsome eyes. Only, they were always raised with a sort of displeasing assurance. Her dress was both aged and childish, like the dress of the scholars in a convent; it consisted of a badly cut gown of black merino. They had the air of being father and daughter.

Marius scanned this old man, who was not yet aged, and this little girl, who was not yet a person, for a few days, and thereafter paid no attention to them. They, on their side, did not appear even to see him. They conversed together with a peaceful and indifferent air. The girl chattered incessantly and merrily. The old man talked but little, and, at times, he fixed on her eyes overflowing with an ineffable paternity.

Marius had acquired the mechanical habit of strolling in that walk. He invariably found them there.

This is the way things went:

Marius liked to arrive by the end of the alley that was farthest from their bench; he walked the whole length of the alley, passed in front of them, then returned to the extremity from which he had come, and began again. This he did five or six times in the course of his promenade, and the promenade was taken five or six times a week, without its having occurred to him or to these people to exchange a greeting. That personage, and that young girl, although they appeared, and perhaps because they appeared, to shun all glances, had naturally, caused some attention on the part of the five or six students who strolled along the Pepiniere from time to time; the studious after their lectures, the others after their game of billiards. Courfeyrac, who was among the last, had observed them several times, but, finding the girl homely, he had speedily and carefully kept out of the way. He had fled, discharging at them a sobriquet like a Parthian dart. Impressed solely with the child's gown and the old man's hair, he had dubbed the daughter Mademoiselle Lanoire, and the father Monsieur Leblanc, so that as no one knew them under any other title, this nickname became a law in the default of any other name. The students said, "Ah! Monsieur Leblanc is on his bench." And Marius, like the rest, had found it convenient to call this unknown gentleman Monsieur Leblanc.

We shall follow their example, and we shall say M. Leblanc, in order to facilitate this tale.

So Marius saw them nearly every day, at the same hour, during the first year. He found the man to his taste, but the girl insipid.

CHAPTER II—LUX FACTA EST

During the second year, precisely at the point in this history that the reader has now reached, it chanced that this habit of the Luxembourg was interrupted, without Marius himself being quite aware why, and nearly six months elapsed, during which he did not set foot in the alley. One day, at last, he returned there once more; it was a serene summer morning, and Marius was in joyous mood, as one is when the weather is fine. It seemed to him that he had in his heart all the songs of the birds that he was listening to, and all the bits of blue sky of which he caught glimpses through the leaves of the trees.

He went straight to "his alley," and when he reached the end of it he perceived, still on the same bench, that well-known couple. Only, when he approached, it certainly was the same man; but it seemed to him that it was no longer the same girl. The person whom he now beheld was a tall and beautiful creature, possessed of all the most charming lines of a woman at the precise moment when they are still combined with all the most ingenuous graces of the child; a pure and fugitive moment, which can be expressed only by these two words, "fifteen years." She had wonderful brown hair, shaded with threads of gold, a brow that seemed made of marble, cheeks that seemed made of rose leaf, a pale flush, an agitated whiteness, an exquisite mouth, from which smiles darted like sunbeams, and words like music, a head such as Raphael would have given to Mary, set upon a neck that Jean Goujon would have attributed to a Venus. And, in order that nothing might be lacking to this bewitching face, her nose was not handsome—it was pretty; neither straight nor curved, neither Italian nor Greek; it was the Parisian nose, that is to say, spiritual, delicate, irregular, pure, which drives painters to despair, and charms poets.

When Marius passed near her, he could not see her eyes, which were constantly lowered. He saw only her long chestnut lashes, permeated with shadow and modesty.

This did not prevent the beautiful child from smiling as she listened to what the white-haired old man was saying to her, and nothing could be more fascinating than that fresh smile, combined with those drooping eyes.

For a moment, Marius thought that she was another daughter of the same man, a sister of the former, no doubt. But when the invariable habit of his stroll brought him, for the second time, near the bench, and he had examined her attentively, he recognized her as the same. In six months the little girl had become a young maiden; that was all. Nothing is more frequent than this phenomenon. There is a moment when girls blossom out in the twinkling of an eye, and become roses all at once. One left them children but yesterday; today, one finds them disquieting to the feelings.

This child had not only grown, she had become idealized. As three days in April suffice to cover certain trees with flowers, six months had sufficed to clothe her with beauty. Her April had arrived.

One sometimes sees people, who, poor and mean, seem to wake up, pass suddenly from indigence to luxury, indulge in expenditures of all sorts, and become dazzling, prodigal, magnificent, all of a sudden. That is the result of having pocketed an income; a note fell due yesterday. The young girl had received her quarterly income.

And then, she was no longer the school girl with her felt hat, her merino gown, her scholar's shoes, and red hands; taste had come to her with beauty; she was a well-dressed person, clad with a sort of rich and simple elegance, and without affectation. She wore a dress of black damask, a cape of the same material, and a bonnet of white crape. Her white gloves displayed the delicacy of the hand that toyed with the carved, Chinese ivory handle of a parasol, and her silken shoe outlined the smallness of her foot. When one passed near her, her whole toilette exhaled a youthful and penetrating perfume.

As for the man, he was the same as usual.

The second time that Marius approached her, the young girl raised her eyelids; her eyes were of a deep, celestial blue, but in that veiled azure, there was, as yet, nothing but the glance of a child. She looked at Marius indifferently, as she would have stared at the brat running beneath the sycamores, or the marble vase that cast a shadow on the bench, and Marius, on his side, continued his promenade, and thought about something else.

He passed near the bench where the young girl sat, five or six times, but without even turning his eyes in her direction.

On the following days, he returned, as was his wont, to the Luxembourg; as usual, he found there "the father and daughter;" but he paid no further attention to them. He thought no more about the girl now that she was beautiful than he had when she was homely. He passed very near the bench where she sat because such was his habit.

CHAPTER III—EFFECT OF THE SPRING

One day, the air was warm, the Luxembourg was inundated with light and shade, the sky was as pure as though the angels had washed it that morning, the sparrows were giving vent to little twitters in the depths of the chestnut trees. Marius had thrown open his whole soul to nature, he was not thinking of anything, he simply lived and breathed, he passed near the bench, the young girl raised her eyes to him, the two glances met.

What was there in the young girl's glance on this occasion? Marius could not have told. There was nothing and there was everything. It was a strange flash.

She dropped her eyes, and he pursued his way.

What he had just seen was no longer the ingenuous and simple eye of a child; it was a mysterious gulf that had half opened, then abruptly closed again.

There comes a day when the young girl glances in this manner. Woe to him who chances to be there!

That first gaze of a soul that does not, as yet, know itself, is like the dawn in the sky. It is the awakening of something radiant and strange. Nothing can give any idea of the dangerous charm of that unexpected gleam, which flashes suddenly and vaguely forth from adorable shadows, and which is composed of all the innocence of the present, and of all the passion of the future. It is a sort of undecided tenderness that reveals itself by chance, and that waits. It is a snare that the innocent maiden sets unknown to herself, and in which she captures hearts without either wishing or knowing it. It is a virgin looking like a woman.

It is rare that a profound reverie does not spring from that glance, where it falls. All purities and all candors meet in that celestial and fatal gleam that, more than all the best-planned tender glances of coquettes, possesses the magic power of causing the sudden blossoming, in the depths of the soul, of that somber flower, impregnated with perfume and with poison, which is called love.

That evening, on his return to his garret, Marius cast his eyes over his garments, and perceived, for the first time, that he had been so slovenly, indecorous, and inconceivably stupid as to go for his walk in the Luxembourg with his "everyday clothes," that is to say, with a hat battered near the band, coarse carter's boots, black trousers that showed white at the knees, and a black coat that was pale at the elbows.

CHAPTER IV—BEGINNING OF A GREAT MALADY

On the following day, at the accustomed hour, Marius drew from hi wardrobe his new coat, his new trousers, his new hat, and his new boots he clothed himself in this complete panoply, put on his gloves, a tremendou luxury, and set off for the Luxembourg.

On the way there, he encountered Courfeyrac, and pretended not to se him. Courfeyrac, on his return home, said to his friends, "I have just me Marius's new hat and new coat, with Marius inside them. He was going to pas an examination, no doubt. He looked utterly stupid."

On arriving at the Luxembourg, Marius made the tour of the fountain basin and stared at the swans; then he remained for a long time in contemplatio before a statue whose head was perfectly black with mold, and one of whos hips was missing. Near the basin there was a bourgeois forty years of age, witl a prominent stomach, who was holding by the hand a little urchin of five, an saying to him, "Shun excess, my son, keep at an equal distance from despotisn and from anarchy." Marius listened to this bourgeois. Then he made the circui of the basin once more. At last he directed his course toward "his alley," slowly and as if with regret. One would have said that he was both forced to go ther and withheld from doing so. He did not perceive it himself, and thought that h was doing as he always did.

On turning into the walk, he saw M. Leblanc and the young girl at th other end, "on their bench." He buttoned his coat up to the very top, pulled i down on his body so that there might be no wrinkles, examined, with a certai complaisance, the lustrous gleams of his trousers, and marched on the bench This march savored of an attack, and certainly of a desire for conquest. So I sa that he marched on the bench, as I should say, "Hannibal marched on Rome."

However, all his movements were purely mechanical, and he had interrupte none of the habitual preoccupations of his mind and labors. At that moment he was thinking that the Manuel du Baccalaureat was a stupid book, and that i must have been drawn up by rare idiots, to allow of three tragedies of Racin and only one comedy of Moliere being analyzed therein as masterpieces o the human mind. There was a piercing whistling going on in his ears. As h approached the bench, he held fast to the folds in his coat, and fixed his eyes o the young girl. It seemed to him that she filled the entire extremity of the alle with a vague blue light.

In proportion as he drew near, his pace slackened more and more. On arriving at some little distance from the bench, and long before he had reached the end of the walk, he halted, and could not explain to himself why he retraced his steps. He did not even say to himself that he would not go as far as the end. It was only with difficulty that the young girl could have perceived him in the distance and noted his fine appearance in his new clothes. Nevertheless, he held himself very erect, in case anyone should be looking at him from behind.

He attained the opposite end, then came back, and this time he approached a little nearer to the bench. He even got to within three intervals of trees, but there he felt an indescribable impossibility of proceeding further, and he hesitated. He thought he saw the young girl's face bending toward him. But he exerted a manly and violent effort, subdued his hesitation, and walked straight ahead. A few seconds later, he rushed in front of the bench, erect and firm, reddening to the very ears, without daring to cast a glance either to the right or to the left, with his hand thrust into his coat like a statesman. At the moment when he passed, under the cannon of the place, he felt his heart beat wildly. As on the preceding day, she wore her damask gown and her crape bonnet. He heard an ineffable voice, which must have been "her voice." She was talking tranquilly. She was very pretty. He felt it, although he made no attempt to see her. "She could not, however," he thought, "help feeling esteem and consideration for me, if she only knew that I am the veritable author of the dissertation on Marcos Obregon de la Ronde, which M. Francois de Neufchateau put, as though it were his own, at the head of his edition of Gil Blas." He went beyond the bench as far as the extremity of the walk, which was very near, then turned on his heel and passed once more in front of the lovely girl. This time, he was very pale. Moreover, all his emotions were disagreeable. As he went further from the bench and the young girl, and while his back was turned to her, he fancied that she was gazing after him, and that made him stumble.

He did not attempt to approach the bench again; he halted near the middle of the walk, and there, a thing that he never did, he sat down, and reflecting in the most profoundly indistinct depths of his spirit, that after all, it was hard that persons whose white bonnet and black gown he admired should be absolutely insensible to his splendid trousers and his new coat.

At the expiration of a quarter of an hour, he rose, as though he were on the point of again beginning his march toward that bench, which was surrounded by an aureole. But he remained standing there, motionless. For the first time in fifteen months, he said to himself that that gentleman who sat there every day with his daughter had, on his side, noticed him, and probably considered hi assiduity singular.

For the first time, also, he was conscious of some irreverence in designatin that stranger, even in his secret thoughts, by the sobriquet of M. le Blanc.

He stood thus for several minutes, with drooping head, tracing figures i the sand, with the cane that he held in his hand.

Then he turned abruptly in the direction opposite to the bench, to M Leblanc and his daughter, and went home.

That day he forgot to dine. At eight o'clock in the evening he perceived thi fact, and as it was too late to go down to the Rue Saint-Jacques, he said, "Neve mind!" and ate a bit of bread.

He did not go to bed until he had brushed his coat and folded it up wit great care.

CHAPTER V—DIVRS CLAPS OF THUNDEF FALL ON MA'AM BOUGON

On the following day, Ma'am Bougon, as Courfeyrac styled the ol portress-principal-tenant, housekeeper of the Gorbeau hovel, Ma'ar Bougon, whose name was, in reality, Madame Burgon, as we have found ou but this iconoclast, Courfeyrac, respected nothing—Ma'am Bougon observed with stupefaction, that M. Marius was going out again in his new coat.

He went to the Luxembourg again, but he did not proceed further than hi bench midway of the alley. He seated himself there, as on the preceding day surveying from a distance, and clearly making out, the white bonnet, the blacl dress, and above all, that blue light. He did not stir from it, and only went hom when the gates of the Luxembourg closed. He did not see M. Leblanc and hi daughter retire. He concluded that they had quitted the garden by the gate o the Rue de l'Ouest. Later on, several weeks afterward, when he came to thin it over, he could never recall where he had dined that evening.

On the following day, which was the third, Ma'am Bougon wa thunderstruck. Marius went out in his new coat. "Three days in succession!" she exclaimed.

She tried to follow him, but Marius walked briskly, and with immens strides; it was a hippopotamus undertaking the pursuit of a chamois. She los sight of him in two minutes, and returned breathless, three-quarters choke with asthma, and furious. "If there is any sense," she growled, "in putting o one's best clothes every day, and making people run like this!"

Marius betook himself to the Luxembourg.

The young girl was there with M. Leblanc. Marius approached as near as he could, pretending to be busy reading a book, but he halted afar off, then returned and seated himself on his bench, where he spent four hours in watching the house-sparrows who were skipping about the walk, and who produced on him the impression that they were making sport of him.

A fortnight passed thus. Marius went to the Luxembourg no longer for the sake of strolling there, but to seat himself always in the same spot, and that without knowing why. Once arrived there, he did not stir. He put on his new coat every morning, for the purpose of not showing himself, and he began all over again on the morrow.

She was decidedly a marvelous beauty. The only remark approaching a criticism that could be made was that the contradiction between her gaze, which was melancholy, and her smile, which was merry, gave a rather wild effect to her face, which sometimes caused this sweet countenance to become strange without ceasing to be charming.

CHAPTER VI—TAKEN PRISONER

On one of the last days of the second week, Marius was seated on his bench, as usual, holding in his hand an open book, of which he had not turned a page for the last two hours. All at once he started. An event was taking place at the other extremity of the walk. Leblanc and his daughter had just left their seat, and the daughter had taken her father's arm, and both were advancing slowly, toward the middle of the alley where Marius was. Marius closed his book, then opened it again, then forced himself to read; he trembled; the aureole was coming straight toward him. "Ah! Good Heavens!" thought he, "I shall not have time to strike an attitude." Still the white-haired man and the girl advanced. It seemed to him that this lasted for a century, and that it was but a second. "What are they coming in this direction for?" he asked himself. "What! She will pass here? Her feet will tread this sand, this walk, two paces from me?" He was utterly upset, he would have liked to be very handsome, he would have liked to own the cross. He heard the soft and measured sound of their approaching footsteps. He imagined that M. Leblanc was darting angry glances at him. "Is that gentleman going to address me?" he thought to himself. He dropped his head; when he raised it again, they were very near him. The young girl passed, and as she passed, she glanced at him. She gazed steadily at him, with a pensive sweetness that thrilled Marius from head to foot. It seemed to him that she was reproaching him for having allowed so long a time to elapse without coming as far as her, and that she was saying to him, "I am coming myself." Marius was dazzled by those eyes fraught with rays and abysses.

He felt his brain on fire. She had come to him, what joy! And then, how she had looked at him! She appeared to him more beautiful than he had ever seen her yet. Beautiful with a beauty that was wholly feminine and angelic, with a complete beauty that would have made Petrarch sing and Dante kneel. It seemed to him that he was floating free in the azure heavens. At the same time, he was horribly vexed because there was dust on his boots.

He thought he felt sure that she had looked at his boots too.

He followed her with his eyes until she disappeared. Then he started up and walked about the Luxembourg garden like a madman. It is possible that, at times, he laughed to himself and talked aloud. He was so dreamy when he came near the children's nurses, that each one of them thought him in love with her.

He quitted the Luxembourg, hoping to find her again in the street.

He encountered Courfeyrac under the arcades of the Odeon, and said to him, "Come and dine with me." They went off to Rousseau's and spent six francs. Marius ate like an ogre. He gave the waiter six sous. At dessert, he said to Courfeyrac, "Have you read the paper? What a fine discourse Audry de Puyraveau delivered!"

He was desperately in love.

After dinner, he said to Courfeyrac, "I will treat you to the play." They went to the Porte-Sainte-Martin to see Frederick in l'Auberge des Adrets. Marius was enormously amused.

At the same time, he had a redoubled attack of shyness. On emerging from the theater, he refused to look at the garter of a modiste who was stepping across a gutter, and Courfeyrac, who said, "I should like to put that woman in my collection," almost horrified him.

Courfeyrac invited him to breakfast at the Café Voltaire on the following morning. Marius went there, and ate even more than on the preceding evening. He was very thoughtful and very merry. One would have said that he was taking advantage of every occasion to laugh uproariously. He tenderly embraced some man or other from the provinces, who was presented to him. A circle of students formed around the table, and they spoke of the nonsense paid for by the State that was uttered from the rostrum in the Sorbonne, then the conversation fell upon the faults and omissions in Guicherat's dictionaries and grammars. Marius interrupted the discussion to exclaim, "But it is very agreeable, all the same to have the cross!"

"That's queer!" whispered Courfeyrac to Jean Prouvaire.

"No," responded Prouvaire, "that's serious."

It was serious; in fact, Marius had reached that first violent and charming hour with which grand passions begin.

A glance had wrought all this.

When the mine is charged, when the conflagration is ready, nothing is more simple. A glance is a spark.

It was all over with him. Marius loved a woman. His fate was entering the unknown.

The glance of women resembles certain combinations of wheels, which are tranquil in appearance yet formidable. You pass close to them every day, peaceably and with impunity, and without a suspicion of anything. A moment arrives when you forget that the thing is there. You go and come, dream, speak, laugh. All at once you feel yourself clutched; all is over. The wheels hold you fast, the glance has ensnared you. It has caught you, no matter where or how, by some portion of your thought that was fluttering loose, by some distraction that had attacked you. You are lost. The whole of you passes into it. A chain of mysterious forces takes possession of you. You struggle in vain; no more human succor is possible. You go on falling from gearing to gearing, from agony to agony, from torture to torture, you, your mind, your fortune, your future, your soul; and, according to whether you are in the power of a wicked creature, or of a noble heart, you will not escape from this terrifying machine otherwise than disfigured with shame, or transfigured by passion.

CHAPTER VII—ADVENTURES OF
THE LETTER U DELIVERED OVER TO
CONJECTURES

Isolation, detachment from everything, pride, independence, the taste of nature, the absence of daily and material activity, the life within himself, the secret conflicts of chastity, a benevolent ecstasy toward all creation, had prepared Marius for this possession that is called passion. His worship of his father had gradually become a religion, and, like all religions, it had retreated to the depths of his soul. Something was required in the foreground. Love came.

A full month elapsed, during which Marius went every day to the Luxembourg. When the hour arrived, nothing could hold him back. "He is on duty," said Courfeyrac. Marius lived in a state of delight. It is certain that the young girl did look at him.

He had finally grown bold, and approached the bench. Still, he did not pass in front of it anymore, in obedience to the instinct of timidity and to the instinct of prudence common to lovers. He considered it better not to attract "the attention of the father." He combined his stations behind the trees and the pedestals of the statues with a profound diplomacy, so that he might be seen as much as possible by the young girl and as little as possible by the old gentleman. Sometimes, he remained motionless by the half-hour together in the shade of a Leonidas or a Spartacus, holding in his hand a book, above which his eyes, gently raised, sought the beautiful girl, and she, on her side, turned her charming profile toward him with a vague smile. While conversing in the most natural and tranquil manner in the world with the white-haired man, she bent upon Marius all the reveries of a virginal and passionate eye. Ancient and time-honored maneuver, which Eve understood from the very first day of the world, and which every woman understands from the very first day of her life! Her mouth replied to one, and her glance replied to another.

It must be supposed, that M. Leblanc finally noticed something, for often, when Marius arrived, he rose and began to walk about. He had abandoned their accustomed place and had adopted the bench by the Gladiator, near the other end of the walk, as though with the object of seeing whether Marius would pursue them there. Marius did not understand, and committed this error. "The father" began to grow inexact, and no longer brought "his daughter" every day. Sometimes, he came alone. Then Marius did not stay. Another blunder.

Marius paid no heed to these symptoms. From the phase of timidity, he had passed, by a natural and fatal progress, to the phase of blindness. His love increased. He dreamed of it every night. And then, an unexpected bliss had happened to him, oil on the fire, a redoubling of the shadows over his eyes. One evening, at dusk, he had found, on the bench that "M. Leblanc and his daughter" had just quitted, a handkerchief, a very simple handkerchief without embroidery, but white, and fine, and that seemed to him to exhale ineffable perfume. He seized it with rapture. This handkerchief was marked with the letters U. F. Marius knew nothing about this beautiful child, neither her family name, her Christian name nor her abode; these two letters were

e first thing of her that he had gained possession of, adorable initials, upon
hich he immediately began to construct his scaffolding. U was evidently the
hristian name. "Ursule!" he thought. "What a delicious name!" He kissed the
andkerchief, drank it in, placed it on his heart, on his flesh, during the day, and
 night, laid it beneath his lips that he might fall asleep on it.

"I feel that her whole soul lies within it!" he exclaimed.

This handkerchief belonged to the old gentleman, who had simply let it fall
om his pocket.

In the days that followed the finding of this treasure, he only displayed
mself at the Luxembourg in the act of kissing the handkerchief and laying it
n his heart. The beautiful child understood nothing of all this, and signified it
 him by imperceptible signs.

"O modesty!" said Marius.

CHAPTER VIII—THE VETERANS THEMSELVES CAN BE HAPPY

Since we have pronounced the word modesty, and since we conceal nothing,
we ought to say that once, nevertheless, in spite of his ecstasies, "his
Ursule" caused him very serious grief. It was on one of the days when she
ersuaded M. Leblanc to leave the bench and stroll along the walk. A brisk May
reeze was blowing, which swayed the crests of the plantain trees. The father
nd daughter, arm in arm, had just passed Marius's bench. Marius had risen to
is feet behind them, and was following them with his eyes, as was fitting in the
esperate situation of his soul.

All at once, a gust of wind, more merry than the rest, and probably charged
ith performing the affairs of Springtime, swept down from the nursery, flung
self on the alley, enveloped the young girl in a delicious shiver, worthy of
irgil's nymphs, and the fawns of Theocritus, and lifted her dress, the robe
ore sacred than that of Isis, almost to the height of her garter. A leg of
xquisite shape appeared. Marius saw it. He was exasperated and furious.

The young girl had hastily thrust down her dress, with a divinely troubled
otion, but he was nonetheless angry for all that. He was alone in the alley,
 is true. But there might have been someone there. And what if there had
een someone there! Can anyone comprehend such a thing? What she had just
one is horrible! Alas, the poor child had done nothing; there had been but
ne culprit, the wind; but Marius, in whom quivered the Bartholo who exists

in Cherubin, was determined to be vexed, and was jealous of his own shado
It is thus, in fact, that the harsh and capricious jealousy of the flesh awakens
the human heart, and takes possession of it, even without any right. Moreove
setting aside even that jealousy, the sight of that charming leg had contain
nothing agreeable for him; the white stocking of the first woman he chanced
meet would have afforded him more pleasure.

When "his Ursule," after having reached the end of the walk, retrac
her steps with M. Leblanc, and passed in front of the bench on which Mari
had seated himself once more, Marius darted a sullen and ferocious glance
her. The young girl gave way to that slight straightening up with a backwai
movement, accompanied by a raising of the eyelids, that signifies, "Well, wh
is the matter?"

This was "their first quarrel."

Marius had hardly made this scene at her with his eyes, when someor
crossed the walk. It was a veteran, very much bent, extremely wrinkled, ar
pale, in a uniform of the Louis XV pattern, bearing on his breast the litt
oval plaque of red cloth, with the crossed swords, the soldier's cross of Sain
Louis, and adorned, in addition, with a coat sleeve, which had no arm with
it, with a silver chin and a wooden leg. Marius thought he perceived that th
man had an extremely well satisfied air. It even struck him that the aged cyni
as he hobbled along past him, addressed to him a very fraternal and very mer
wink, as though some chance had created an understanding between ther
and as though they had shared some piece of good luck together. What d
that relic of Mars mean by being so contented? What had passed between th
wooden leg and the other? Marius reached a paroxysm of jealousy. "Perha
he was there!" he said to himself; "perhaps he saw!" And he felt a desire
exterminate the veteran.

With the aid of time, all points grow dull. Marius's wrath against "Ursule
just and legitimate as it was, passed off. He finally pardoned her; but this co
him a great effort; he sulked for three days.

Nevertheless, in spite of all this, and because of all this, his passic
augmented and grew to madness.

CHAPTER IX—ECLIPSE

The reader has just seen how Marius discovered, or thought that h
discovered, that she was named Ursule.

Appetite grows with loving. To know that her name was Ursule was a great deal; it was very little. In three or four weeks, Marius had devoured this bliss. He wanted another. He wanted to know where she lived.

He had committed his first blunder, by falling into the ambush of the bench by the Gladiator. He had committed a second, by not remaining at the Luxembourg when M. Leblanc came there alone. He now committed a third, and an immense one. He followed "Ursule."

She lived in the Rue de l'Ouest, in the most unfrequented spot, in a new, three-story house, of modest appearance.

From that moment forth, Marius added to his happiness of seeing her at the Luxembourg the happiness of following her home.

His hunger was increasing. He knew her first name, at least, a charming name, a genuine woman's name; he knew where she lived; he wanted to know who she was.

One evening, after he had followed them to their dwelling, and had seen them disappear through the carriage gate, he entered in their train and said boldly to the porter, "Is that the gentleman who lives on the first floor, who has just come in?"

"No," replied the porter. "He is the gentleman on the third floor."

Another step gained. This success emboldened Marius.

"On the front?" he asked.

"Parbleu!" said the porter. "The house is only built on the street."

"And what is that gentleman's business?" began Marius again.

"He is a gentleman of property, Sir. A very kind man who does good to the unfortunate, though not rich himself."

"What is his name?" resumed Marius.

The porter raised his head and said, "Are you a police spy, Sir?"

Marius went off quite abashed, but delighted. He was getting on.

"Good," thought he, "I know that her name is Ursule, that she is the daughter of a gentleman who lives on his income, and that she lives there, on the third floor, in the Rue de l'Ouest."

On the following day, M. Leblanc and his daughter made only a very brief stay in the Luxembourg; they went away while it was still broad daylight. Marius followed them to the Rue de l'Ouest, as he had taken up the habit of doing. On arriving at the carriage entrance M. Leblanc made his daughter pass in first, then paused, before crossing the threshold, and stared intently at Marius.

On the next day they did not come to the Luxembourg. Marius waited for them all day in vain.

At nightfall, he went to the Rue de l'Ouest, and saw a light in the window of the third story.

He walked about beneath the windows until the light was extinguished.

The next day, no one at the Luxembourg. Marius waited all day, then we and did sentinel duty under their windows. This carried him on to ten o'clo in the evening.

His dinner took care of itself. Fever nourishes the sick man, and love t lover.

He spent a week in this manner. M. Leblanc no longer appeared at t. Luxembourg.

Marius indulged in melancholy conjectures; he dared not watch the por cochere during the day; he contented himself with going at night to gaze up the red light of the windows. At times he saw shadows flit across them, and h heart began to beat.

On the eighth day, when he arrived under the windows, there was no lig in them.

"Hello!" he said, "the lamp is not lighted yet. But it is dark. Can th have gone out?" He waited until ten o'clock. Until midnight. Until one in t morning. Not a light appeared in the windows of the third story, and no o entered the house.

He went away in a very gloomy frame of mind.

On the morrow—for he only existed from morrow to morrow, the was, so to speak, no today for him—on the morrow, he found no one at t Luxembourg; he had expected this. At dusk, he went to the house.

No light in the windows; the shades were drawn; the third floor was total dark.

Marius rapped at the *porte cochere*, entered, and said to the porter, "T gentleman on the third floor?"

"Has moved away," replied the porter.

Marius reeled and said feebly, "How long ago?"

"Yesterday."

"Where is he living now?"

"I don't know anything about it."

"So he has not left his new address?"

"No."

And the porter, raising his eyes, recognized Marius.

"Come! So it's you!" said he. "But you are decidedly a spy then?"

BOOK SEVENTH: PATRON MINETTE

CHAPTER I—MINES AND MINERS

Human societies all have what is called in theatrical parlance, a third lower floor. The social soil is everywhere undermined, sometimes for good, sometimes for evil. These works are superposed one upon the other. There are superior mines and inferior mines. There is a top and a bottom in this obscure subsoil, which sometimes gives way beneath civilization, and which our indifference and heedlessness trample under foot. The encyclopedia, in the last century, was a mine that was almost open to the sky. The shades, those somber hatchers of primitive Christianity, only awaited an opportunity to bring about an explosion under the Caesars and to inundate the human race with light. For in the sacred shadows there lies latent light. Volcanoes are full of a shadow that is capable of flashing forth. Every form begins by being night. The catacombs, in which the first mass was said, were not alone the cellar of Rome, they were the vaults of the world.

Beneath the social construction, that complicated marvel of a structure, there are excavations of all sorts. There is the religious mine, the philosophical mine, the economic mine, the revolutionary mine. Such and such a pickax with the idea, such a pick with ciphers. Such another with wrath. People hail and answer each other from one catacomb to another. Utopias travel about underground, in the pipes. There they branch out in every direction. They sometimes meet, and fraternize there. Jean-Jacques lends his pick to Diogenes, who lends him his lantern. Sometimes they enter into combat there. Calvin seizes Socinius by the hair. But nothing arrests nor interrupts the tension of all these energies toward the goal, and the vast, simultaneous activity, which goes and comes, mounts, descends, and mounts again in these obscurities, and which immense unknown swarming slowly transforms the top and the bottom and the inside and the outside. Society hardly even suspects this digging, which leaves its surface intact and changes its bowels. There are as many different subterranean stages as there are varying works, as there are extractions. What emerges from these deep excavations? The future.

The deeper one goes, the more mysterious are the toilers. The work is good, up to a degree, which the social philosophies are able to recognize; beyond that degree it is doubtful and mixed; lower down, it becomes terrible.

At a certain depth, the excavations are no longer penetrable by the spirit of civilization, the limit breathable by man has been passed; a beginning of monsters is possible.

The descending scale is a strange one; and each one of the rungs of this ladder corresponds to a stage where philosophy can find foothold, and where one encounters one of these workmen, sometimes divine, sometimes misshapen. Below John Huss, there is Luther; below Luther, there is Descartes, below Descartes, there is Voltaire; below Voltaire, there is Condorcet; below Condorcet, there is Robespierre; below Robespierre, there is Marat; below Marat there is Babeuf. And so it goes on. Lower down, confusedly, at the limit that separates the indistinct from the invisible, one perceives other gloomy men, who perhaps do not exist as yet. The men of yesterday are specters; those of tomorrow are forms. The eye of the spirit distinguishes them but obscurely. The embryonic work of the future is one of the visions of philosophy.

A world in limbo, in the state of fetus, what an unheard-of specter!

Saint-Simon, Owen, Fourier, are there also, in lateral galleries.

Surely, although a divine and invisible chain unknown to themselves, binds together all these subterranean pioneers who, almost always, think themselves isolated, and who are not so, their works vary greatly, and the light of some contrasts with the blaze of others. The first are paradisiacal, the last are tragic. Nevertheless, whatever may be the contrast, all these toilers, from the highest to the most nocturnal, from the wisest to the most foolish, possess one likeness, and this is it: disinterestedness. Marat forgets himself like Jesus. They throw themselves on one side, they omit themselves, they think not of themselves. They have a glance, and that glance seeks the absolute. The first has the whole heavens in his eyes; the last, enigmatical though he may be, has still, beneath his eyelids, the pale beam of the infinite. Venerate the man, whoever he may be, who has this sign—the starry eye.

The shadowy eye is the other sign.

With it, evil commences. Reflect and tremble in the presence of anyone who has no glance at all. The social order has its black miners.

There is a point where depth is tantamount to burial, and where light becomes extinct.

Below all these mines that we have just mentioned, below all these galleries, below this whole immense, subterranean, venous system of progress and utopia, much further on in the earth, much lower than Marat, lower than Babeuf, lower, much lower, and without any connection with the upper levels, there lies the last mine. A formidable spot. This is what we have designated as

he *le troisième dessous.* It is the grave of shadows. It is the cellar of the blind.
nferi.

This communicates with the abyss.

CHAPTER II—THE LOWEST DEPTHS

There disinterestedness vanishes. The demon is vaguely outlined; each one is for himself. The I in the eyes howls, seeks, fumbles, and gnaws. The social Ugolino is in this gulf.

The wild specters who roam in this grave, almost beasts, almost phantoms, are not occupied with universal progress; they are ignorant both of the idea and of the word; they take no thought for anything but the satisfaction of their individual desires. They are almost unconscious, and there exists within them a sort of terrible obliteration. They have two mothers, both stepmothers, ignorance and misery. They have a guide, necessity; and for all forms of satisfaction, appetite. They are brutally voracious, that is to say, ferocious, not after the fashion of the tyrant, but after the fashion of the tiger. From suffering these specters pass to crime; fatal affiliation, dizzy creation, logic of darkness. That which crawls in the social third lower level is no longer complaint stifled by the absolute; it is the protest of matter. Man there becomes a dragon. To be hungry, to be thirsty—that is the point of departure; to be Satan—that is the point reached. From that vault Lacenaire emerges.

We have just seen, in Book Fourth, one of the compartments of the upper mine, of the great political, revolutionary, and philosophical excavation. There, as we have just said, all is pure, noble, dignified, honest. There, assuredly, one might be misled; but error is worthy of veneration there, so thoroughly does it imply heroism. The work there effected, taken as a whole has a name: Progress.

The moment has now come when we must take a look at other depths, hideous depths. There exists beneath society, we insist upon this point, and there will exist, until that day when ignorance shall be dissipated, the great cavern of evil.

This cavern is below all, and is the foe of all. It is hatred, without exception. This cavern knows no philosophers; its dagger has never cut a pen. Its blackness has no connection with the sublime blackness of the inkstand. Never have the fingers of night, which contract beneath this stifling ceiling, turned the leaves of a book nor unfolded a newspaper. Babeuf is a speculator to Cartouche; Marat is an aristocrat to Schinderhannes. This cavern has for its object the destruction of everything.

Of everything. Including the upper superior mines, which it execrates. It not only undermines, in its hideous swarming, the actual social order: it undermines philosophy, it undermines human thought, it undermine civilization, it undermines revolution, it undermines progress. Its name i simply theft, prostitution, murder, assassination. It is darkness, and it desire: chaos. Its vault is formed of ignorance.

All the others, those above it, have but one object—to suppress it. It is to this point that philosophy and progress tend, with all their organs simultaneously by their amelioration of the real, as well as by their contemplation of the absolute. Destroy the cavern Ignorance and you destroy the lair Crime.

Let us condense, in a few words, a part of what we have just written. The only social peril is darkness.

Humanity is identity. All men are made of the same clay. There is no difference, here below, at least, in predestination. The same shadow in front, the same flesh in the present, the same ashes afterward. But ignorance, mingled with the human paste, blackens it. This incurable blackness takes possession of the interior of a man and is there converted into evil.

CHAPTER III—BABET, GUEULEMER, CLAQUESOUS, AND MONTPARNASSE

A quartette of ruffians, Claquesous, Gueulemer, Babet, and Montparnasse governed the third lower floor of Paris, from 1830 to 1835.

Gueulemer was a Hercules of no defined position. For his lair he had the sewer of the Arche-Marion. He was six feet high, his pectoral muscles were of marble, his biceps of brass, his breath was that of a cavern, his torso that of a colossus, his head that of a bird. One thought one beheld the Farnese Hercules clad in duck trousers and a cotton velvet waistcoat. Gueulemer, built after this sculptural fashion, might have subdued monsters; he had found it more expeditious to be one. A low brow, large temples, less than forty years of age, but with crow's-feet, harsh, short hair, cheeks like a brush, a beard like that of a wild boar; the reader can see the man before him. His muscles called for work, his stupidity would have none of it. He was a great, idle force. He was an assassin through coolness. He was thought to be a Creole. He had, probably, somewhat to do with Marshal Brune, having been a porter at Avignon in 1815. After this stage, he had turned ruffian.

The diaphaneity of Babet contrasted with the grossness of Gueulemer. Babet was thin and learned. He was transparent but impenetrable. Daylight was visible through his bones, but nothing through his eyes. He declared that he was a chemist. He had been a jack-of-all-trades. He had played in vaudeville at Saint-Mihiel. He was a man of purpose, a fine talker, who underlined his smiles and accentuated his gestures. His occupation consisted in selling, in the open air, plaster busts and portraits of "the head of the State." In addition to this, he extracted teeth. He had exhibited phenomena at fairs, and he had owned a booth with a trumpet and this poster: "Babet, Dental Artist, Member of the Academies, makes physical experiments on metals and metalloids, extracts teeth, undertakes stumps abandoned by his brother practitioners. Price: one tooth, one franc, fifty centimes; two teeth, two francs; three teeth, two francs, fifty. Take advantage of this opportunity." This "Take advantage of this opportunity" meant: Have as many teeth extracted as possible. He had been married and had had children. He did not know what had become of his wife and children. He had lost them as one loses his handkerchief. Babet read the papers, a striking exception in the world to which he belonged. One day, at the period when he had his family with him in his booth on wheels, he had read in the *Messager*, that a woman had just given birth to a child, who was doing well, and had a calf's muzzle, and he exclaimed, "There's a fortune! My wife has not the wit to present me with a child like that!"

Later on he had abandoned everything, in order to "undertake Paris." This was his expression.

Who was Claquesous? He was night. He waited until the sky was daubed with black, before he showed himself. At nightfall he emerged from the hole where he returned before daylight. Where was this hole? No one knew. He only addressed his accomplices in the most absolute darkness, and with his back turned to them. Was his name Claquesous? Certainly not. If a candle was brought, he put on a mask. He was a ventriloquist. Babet said, "Claquesous is a nocturne for two voices." Claquesous was vague, terrible, and a roamer. No one was sure whether he had a name, Claquesous being a sobriquet; none was sure that he had a voice, as his stomach spoke more frequently than his voice; no one was sure that he had a face, as he was never seen without his mask. He disappeared as though he had vanished into thin air; when he appeared, it was as though he sprang from the earth.

A lugubrious being was Montparnasse. Montparnasse was a child; less than twenty years of age, with a handsome face, lips like cherries, charming black hair, the brilliant light of springtime in his eyes; he had all vices and aspired to all crimes.

The digestion of evil aroused in him an appetite for worse. It was the street boy turned pickpocket, and a pickpocket turned *garroter*. He was genteel, effeminate, graceful, robust, sluggish, ferocious. The rim of his hat was curled up on the left side, in order to make room for a tuft of hair, after the style of 1829. He lived by robbery with violence. His coat was of the best cut, but threadbare. Montparnasse was a fashion plate in misery and given to the commission of murders. The cause of all this youth's crimes was the desire to be well dressed. The first grisette who had said to him, "You are handsome!" had cast the stain of darkness into his heart, and had made a Cain of this Abel. Finding that he was handsome, he desired to be elegant: now, the height of elegance is idleness; idleness in a poor man means crime. Few prowlers were so dreaded as Montparnasse. At eighteen, he had already numerous corpses in his past. More than one passerby lay with outstretched arms in the presence of this wretch, with his face in a pool of blood. Curled, pomaded, with laced waist, the hips of a woman, the bust of a Prussian officer, the murmur of admiration from the boulevard wenches surrounding him, his cravat knowingly tied, a bludgeon in his pocket, a flower in his buttonhole; such was this dandy of the sepulchre.

CHAPTER IV—COMPOSITION OF THE TROUPE

These four ruffians formed a sort of Proteus, winding like a serpent among the police, and striving to escape Vidocq's indiscreet glances "under divers forms, tree, flame, fountain," lending each other their names and their traps, hiding in their own shadows, boxes with secret compartments and refuges for each other, stripping off their personalities, as one removes his false nose at a masked ball, sometimes simplifying matters to the point of consisting of but one individual, sometimes multiplying themselves to such a point that Coco-Latour himself took them for a whole throng.

These four men were not four men; they were a sort of mysterious robber with four heads, operating on a grand scale on Paris; they were that monstrous polyp of evil that inhabits the crypt of society.

Thanks to their ramifications, and to the network underlying their relations, Babet, Gueulemer, Claquesous, and Montparnasse were charged with the general enterprise of the ambushes of the department of the Seine. The inventors of ideas of that nature, men with nocturnal imaginations, applied to them to have their ideas executed. They furnished the canvas to the four rascals, and the latter undertook the preparation of the scenery. They labored at the stage setting. They were always in a condition to lend a force proportioned and suitable to all crimes that demanded a lift of the shoulder, and that were sufficiently lucrative. When a crime was in quest of arms, they under-let their accomplices. They kept a troupe of actors of the shadows at the disposition of all underground tragedies.

They were in the habit of assembling at nightfall, the hour when they woke up, on the plains that adjoin the Salpetriere. There they held their conferences. They had twelve black hours before them; they regulated their employment accordingly.

Patron-Minette, such was the name bestowed in the subterranean circulation on the association of these four men. In the fantastic, ancient, popular parlance, which is vanishing day by day, Patron-Minette signifies the morning, the same as *entre chien et loup*—between dog and wolf—signifies the evening. This appellation, Patron-Minette, was probably derived from the hour at which their work ended, the dawn being the vanishing moment for phantoms and for the separation of ruffians. These four men were known under this title. When the President of the Assizes visited Lacenaire in his prison, and questioned him concerning a misdeed that Lacenaire denied, "Who did it?" demanded the President. Lacenaire made this response, enigmatical so far as the magistrate was concerned, but clear to the police: "Perhaps it was Patron-Minette."

A piece can sometimes be divined on the enunciation of the personages; in the same manner a band can almost be judged from the list of ruffians composing it. Here are the appellations to which the principal members of Patron-Minette answered, for the names have survived in special memoirs.

Panchaud, alias Printanier, alias Bigrenaille.
Brujon.
Boulatruelle, the road mender already introduced.
Laveuve.
Finistere.
Homere-Hogu, a Negro.
Mardisoir. (Tuesday evening.)
Depeche. (Make haste.)
Fauntleroy, alias Bouquetiere (the flower girl).
Glorieux, a discharged convict.
Barrecarrosse (stop-carriage), called Monsieur Dupont.
L'Esplanade-du-Sud.

Poussagrive.

Carmagnolet.

Kruideniers, called Bizarro.

Mangedentelle. (Lace-eater.)

Les-pieds-en-l'Air. (Feet in the air.)

Demi-Liard, called Deux-Milliards.

Etc., etc.

We pass over some, and not the worst of them. These names have faces attached. They do not express merely beings, but species. Each one of these names corresponds to a variety of those misshapen fungi from the under side of civilization.

Those beings, who were not very lavish with their countenances, were not among the men whom one sees passing along the streets. Fatigued by the wild nights they passed, they went off by day to sleep, sometimes in the lime kilns, sometimes in the abandoned quarries of Montmatre or Montrouge, sometimes in the sewers. They ran to earth.

What became of these men? They still exist. They have always existed. Horace speaks of them: *Ambubaiarum collegia, pharmacopolae, mendici, mimae*; and so long as society remains what it is, they will remain what they are. Beneath the obscure roof of their cavern, they are continually born again from the social ooze. They return, specters, but always identical; only, they no longer bear the same names and they are no longer in the same skins. The individuals extirpated, the tribe subsists.

They always have the same faculties. From the vagrant to the tramp, the race is maintained in its purity. They divine purses in pockets, they scent out watches in fobs. Gold and silver possess an odor for them. There exist ingenuous bourgeois, of whom it might be said, that they have a "stealable" air. These men patiently pursue these bourgeois. They experience the quivers of a spider at the passage of a stranger or of a man from the country.

These men are terrible, when one encounters them, or catches a glimpse of them, toward midnight, on a deserted boulevard. They do not seem to be men but forms composed of living mists; one would say that they habitually constitute one mass with the shadows, that they are in no wise distinct from them, that they possess no other soul than the darkness, and that it is only momentarily and for the purpose of living for a few minutes a monstrous life, that they have separated from the night.

What is necessary to cause these specters to vanish? Light. Light in floods. Not a single bat can resist the dawn. Light up society from below.

BOOK EIGHTH: THE WICKED POOR MAN

CHAPTER I—MARIUS, WHILE SEEKING A GIRL IN A BONNET, ENCOUNTERS A MAN IN A CAP

Summer passed, then the autumn; winter came. Neither M. Leblanc nor the young girl had again set foot in the Luxembourg garden. Thenceforth, Marius had but one thought, to gaze once more on that sweet and adorable face. He sought constantly, he sought everywhere; he found nothing. He was no longer Marius, the enthusiastic dreamer, the firm, resolute, ardent man, the bold defier of fate, the brain that erected future on future, the young spirit encumbered with plans, with projects, with pride, with ideas and wishes; he was a lost dog. He fell into a black melancholy. All was over. Work disgusted him, walking tired him. Vast nature, formerly so filled with forms, lights, voices, counsels, perspectives, horizons, teachings, now lay empty before him. It seemed to him that everything had disappeared.

He thought incessantly, for he could not do otherwise; but he no longer took pleasure in his thoughts. To everything that they proposed to him in a whisper, he replied in his darkness, "What is the use?"

He heaped a hundred reproaches on himself. "Why did I follow her? I was so happy at the mere sight of her! She looked at me; was not that immense? She had the air of loving me. Was not that everything? I wished to have, what? There was nothing after that. I have been absurd. It is my own fault," etc., etc. Courfeyrac, to whom he confided nothing, it was his nature, but who made some little guess at everything, that was his nature, had begun by congratulating him on being in love, though he was amazed at it; then, seeing Marius fall into this melancholy state, he ended by saying to him, "I see that you have been simply an animal. Here, come to the Chaumiere."

Once, having confidence in a fine September sun, Marius had allowed himself to be taken to the ball at Sceaux by Courfeyrac, Bossuet, and Grantaire, hoping—what a dream!—that he might, perhaps, find her there. Of course he did not see the one he sought. "But this is the place, all the same, where all lost women are found," grumbled Grantaire in an aside. Marius left his friends at the ball and returned home on foot, alone, through the night, weary, feverish, with sad and troubled eyes, stunned by the noise and dust of the merry wagons filled with singing creatures on their way home from the feast, which passed close to him, as he, in his discouragement, breathed in the acrid scent of the walnut trees, along the road, in order to refresh his head.

He took to living more and more alone, utterly overwhelmed, wholly given up to his inward anguish, going and coming in his pain like the wolf in the trap, seeking the absent one everywhere, stupefied by love.

On another occasion, he had an encounter that produced on him a singular effect. He met, in the narrow streets in the vicinity of the Boulevard des Invalides, a man dressed like a workingman and wearing a cap with a long visor, which allowed a glimpse of locks of very white hair. Marius was struck with the beauty of this white hair, and scrutinized the man, who was walking slowly and as though absorbed in painful meditation. Strange to say, he thought that he recognized M. Leblanc. The hair was the same, also the profile, so far as the cap permitted a view of it, the mien identical, only more depressed. But why these workingman's clothes? What was the meaning of this? What signified that disguise? Marius was greatly astonished. When he recovered himself, his first impulse was to follow the man; who knows whether he did not hold at last the clue he was seeking? In any case, he must see the man near at hand, and clear up the mystery. But the idea occurred to him too late, the man was no longer there. He had turned into some little side street, and Marius could not find him. This encounter occupied his mind for three days and then was effaced. "After all," he said to himself, "it was probably only a resemblance."

CHAPTER II—TREASURE TROVE

Marius had not left the Gorbeau house. He paid no attention to anyone there.

At that epoch, to tell the truth, there were no other inhabitants in the house, except himself and those Jondrettes whose rent he had once paid without, moreover, ever having spoken to either father, mother, or daughters. The other lodgers had moved away or had died, or had been turned out in default of payment.

One day during that winter, the sun had shown itself a little in the afternoon but it was the 2nd of February, that ancient Candlemas day whose treacherou sun, the precursor of a six weeks' cold spell, inspired Mathieu Laensberg with these two lines, which have with justice remained classic:

"Whether the sun shines brightly or dim,
The bear returns to his cave."

Marius had just emerged from his: night was falling. It was the hour for his dinner; for he had been obliged to take to dining again, alas! Oh, infirmities of ideal passions!

He had just crossed his threshold, where Ma'am Bougon was sweeping at the moment, as she uttered this memorable monologue, "What is there that is cheap now? Everything is dear. There is nothing in the world that is cheap except trouble; you can get that for nothing, the trouble of the world!"

Marius slowly ascended the boulevard toward the barrier, in order to reach the Rue Saint-Jacques. He was walking along with drooping head.

All at once, he felt someone elbow him in the dusk; he wheeled around, and saw two young girls clad in rags, the one tall and slim, the other a little shorter, who were passing rapidly, all out of breath, in terror, and with the appearance of fleeing; they had been coming to meet him, had not seen him, and had jostled him as they passed. Through the twilight, Marius could distinguish their livid faces, their wild heads, their disheveled hair, their hideous bonnets, their ragged petticoats, and their bare feet. They were talking as they ran. The taller said in a very low voice, "The bobbies have come. They came near nabbing me at the half-circle."

The other answered, "I saw them. I bolted, bolted, bolted!"

Through this repulsive slang, Marius understood that gendarmes or the police had come near apprehending these two children, and that the latter had escaped.

They plunged among the trees of the boulevard behind him, and there created, for a few minutes, in the gloom, a sort of vague white spot, then disappeared.

Marius had halted for a moment.

He was about to pursue his way, when his eye lighted on a little grayish package lying on the ground at his feet. He stooped and picked it up. It was a sort of envelope that appeared to contain papers.

"Good," he said to himself, "those unhappy girls dropped it."

He retraced his steps, he called, he did not find them; he reflected that they must already be far away, put the package in his pocket, and went off to dine.

On the way, he saw in an alley of the Rue Mouffetard, a child's coffin, covered with a black cloth resting on three chairs, and illuminated by a candle. The two girls of the twilight recurred to his mind.

"Poor mothers!" he thought. "There is one thing sadder than to see one's children die; it is to see them leading an evil life."

Then those shadows that had varied his melancholy vanished from his thoughts, and he fell back once more into his habitual preoccupations. He fell to thinking once more of his six months of love and happiness in the open air and the broad daylight, beneath the beautiful trees of Luxembourg.

"How gloomy my life has become!" he said to himself. "Young girls are always appearing to me, only formerly they were angels and now they are ghouls."

CHAPTER III—QUADRIFRONS

That evening, as he was undressing, preparing to going to bed, his hand came in contact, in the pocket of his coat, with the packet that he had picked up on the boulevard. He had forgotten it. He thought that it would be well to open it, and that this package might possibly contain the address of the young girls, if it really belonged to them, and, in any case, the information necessary to a restitution to the person who had lost it.

He opened the envelope.

It was not sealed and contained four letters, also unsealed.

They bore addresses.

All four exhaled a horrible odor of tobacco.

The first was addressed: "To Madame, Madame la Marquise de Grucheray, the place opposite the Chamber of Deputies, No.—"

Marius said to himself, that he should probably find in it the information he sought, and that, moreover, the letter being open, it was probable that it could be read without impropriety.

It was conceived as follows:

> Madame la Marquise: The virtue of clemency and piety is
> that which most closely unites society. Turn your Christian
> spirit and cast a look of compassion on this unfortunate
> Spanish victim of loyalty and attachment to the sacred cause
> of legitimacy, who has given with his blood, consecrated
> his fortune, everything, to defend that cause, and today

finds himself in the greatest misery. He doubts not that your honorable person will grant succor to preserve an existence extremely painful for a military man of education and honor full of wounds, counts in advance on the humanity that animates you and on the interest that Madame la Marquise bears to a nation so unfortunate. Their prayer will not be in vain, and their gratitude will preserve theirs charming souvenir.

My respectful sentiments, with which I have the honor to be Madame, Don Alvares, Spanish Captain of Cavalry, a royalist who has take refuge in France, who finds himself on travels for his country, and the resources are lacking him to continue his travels.

No address was joined to the signature. Marius hoped to find the address in the second letter, whose superscription read: "A Madame, Madame la Comtesse de Montvernet, Rue Cassette, No. 9." This is what Marius read in it:

Madame la Comtesse:
It is an unhappy mother of a family of six children the last of which is only eight months old. I sick since my last confinement, abandoned by my husband five months ago, haveing no resources in the world the most frightful indigance.

In the hope of Madame la Comtesse, she has the honor to be, Madame, with profound respect, Mistress Balizard.

Marius turned to the third letter, which was a petition like the preceding; he read:

Monsieur Pabourgeot, Elector, wholesale stocking merchant, Rue Saint-Denis on the corner of the Rue aux Fers.

I permit myself to address you this letter to beg you to grant me the pretious favor of your simpaties and to interest yourself in a man of letters who has just sent a drama to the Theater-Francais. The subject is historical, and the action takes place in Auvergne in the time of the Empire; the style, I think, is natural, laconic, and may have some merit. There are couplets to be sung in four places. The comic, the serious, the unexpected, are mingled in a variety of characters, and a tinge of romanticism lightly spread through all the intrigue that proceeds misteriously, and ends, after striking altarations, in the midst of many beautiful strokes of brilliant scenes.

My principal object is to satisfi the desire that progressively animates the man of our century, that is to say, the fashion, that capritious and bizarre weathervane, which changes at almost every new wind.

In spite of these qualities I have reason to fear that jealousy, the egotism of priviliged authors, may obtaine my exclusion from the theater, for I am not ignorant of the mortifications with which newcomers are treated.

Monsiuer Pabourgeot, your just reputation as an enlightened protector of men of litters emboldens me to send you my daughter who will explain our indigant situation to you, lacking bread and fire in this wynter season. When I say to you that I beg you to accept the dedication of my drama, which I desire to make to you and of all those that I shall make, is to prove to you how great is my ambition to have the honor of sheltering myself under your protection, and of adorning my writings with your name. If you deign to honor me with the most modest offering, I shall immediately occupy myself in making a piesse of verse to pay you my tribute of gratitude. Which I shall endeavor to render this piesse as perfect as possible, will be sent to you before it is inserted at the beginning of the drama and delivered on the stage.

To Monsieur and Madame Pabourgeot,
My most respectful complements, Genflot, man of letters.
P. S. Even if it is only forty sous.
Excuse me for sending my daughter and not presenting myself, but sad motives connected with the toilette do not permit me, alas! To go out.

Finally, Marius opened the fourth letter. The address ran: To the benevolent Gentleman of the church of Saint-Jacquesdu-haut-Pas. It contained the following lines:

Benevolent Man: If you deign to accompany my daughter, you will behold a misserable calamity, and I will show you my certificates.

At the aspect of these writings your generous soul will be moved with a sentiment of obvious benevolence, for true philosophers always feel lively emotions.

Admit, compassionate man, that it is necessary to suffer the most cruel need, and that it is very painful, for the sake of obtaining a little relief, to get oneself attested by the authorities as though one were not free to suffer and to die of inanition while waiting to have our misery relieved. Destinies are very fatal for several and too prodigal or too protecting for others.

I await your presence or your offering, if you deign to make one, and I beseech you to accept the respectful sentiments with which I have the honor to be, truly magnanimous man, your very humble and very obedient servant, P. Fabantou, dramatic artist.

After perusing these four letters, Marius did not find himself much further advanced than before.

In the first place, not one of the signers gave his address.

Then, they seemed to come from four different individuals, Don Alveras, Mistress Balizard, the poet Genflot, and dramatic artist Fabantou; but the singular thing about these letters was that all four were written by the same hand.

What conclusion was to be drawn from this, except that they all come from the same person?

Moreover, and this rendered the conjecture all the more probable, the coarse and yellow paper was the same in all four, the odor of tobacco was the same, and, although an attempt had been made to vary the style, the same orthographical faults were reproduced with the greatest tranquility, and the man of letters Genflot was no more exempt from them than the Spanish captain.

It was waste of trouble to try to solve this petty mystery. Had it not been a chance find, it would have borne the air of a mystification. Marius was too melancholy to take even a chance pleasantry well, and to lend himself to a game that the pavement of the street seemed desirous of playing with him. It seemed to him that he was playing the part of the blind man in blind man's buff between the four letters, and that they were making sport of him.

Nothing, however, indicated that these letters belonged to the two young girls whom Marius had met on the boulevard. After all, they were evidently papers of no value. Marius replaced them in their envelope, flung the whole into a corner and went to bed. About seven o'clock in the morning, he had just risen and breakfasted, and was trying to settle down to work, when there came a soft knock at his door.

As he owned nothing, he never locked his door, unless occasionally, though very rarely, when he was engaged in some pressing work. Even when absent, he left his key in the lock. "You will be robbed," said Ma'am Bougon.

"Of what?" said Marius. The truth is, however, that he had, one day, been robbed of an old pair of boots, to the great triumph of Ma'am Bougon.

There came a second knock, as gentle as the first.

"Come in," said Marius.

The door opened.

"What do you want, Ma'am Bougon?" asked Marius, without raising his eyes from the books and manuscripts on his table.

A voice that did not belong to Ma'am Bougon replied, "Excuse me, Sir—"

It was a dull, broken, hoarse, strangled voice, the voice of an old man, roughened with brandy and liquor.

Marius turned around hastily, and beheld a young girl.

CHAPTER IV — A ROSE IN MISERY

A very young girl was standing in the half-open door. The dormer window of the garret, through which the light fell, was precisely opposite the door, and illuminated the figure with a wan light. She was a frail, emaciated, slender creature; there was nothing but a chemise and a petticoat upon that chilled and shivering nakedness. Her girdle was a string, her head ribbon a string, her pointed shoulders emerged from her chemise, a blond and lymphatic pallor, earth-colored collarbones, red hands, a half-open and degraded mouth, missing teeth, dull, bold, base eyes; she had the form of a young girl who has missed her youth, and the look of a corrupt old woman; fifty years mingled with fifteen; one of those beings that are both feeble and horrible, and that cause those to shudder whom they do not cause to weep.

Marius had risen, and was staring in a sort of stupor at this being, who was almost like the forms of the shadows that traverse dreams.

The most heartbreaking thing of all was that this young girl had not come into the world to be homely. In her early childhood she must even have been pretty. The grace of her age was still struggling against the hideous, premature decrepitude of debauchery and poverty. The remains of beauty were dying away in that face of sixteen, like the pale sunlight that is extinguished under hideous clouds at dawn on a winter's day.

That face was not wholly unknown to Marius. He thought he remembered having seen it somewhere.

"What do you wish, Mademoiselle?" he asked.

The young girl replied in her voice of a drunken convict, "Here is a letter for you, Monsieur Marius."

She called Marius by his name; he could not doubt that he was the person whom she wanted; but who was this girl? How did she know his name?

Without waiting for him to tell her to advance, she entered. She entered resolutely, staring, with a sort of assurance that made the heart bleed, at the whole room and the unmade bed. Her feet were bare. Large holes in her petticoat permitted glimpses of her long legs and her thin knees. She was shivering.

She held a letter in her hand, which she presented to Marius.

Marius, as he opened the letter, noticed that the enormous wafer that sealed it was still moist. The message could not have come from a distance. He read:

> My amiable neighbor, young man:
> I have learned of your goodness to me, that you paid my rent
> six months ago. I bless you, young man. My eldest daughter
> will tell you that we have been without a morsel of bread for
> two days, four persons and my spouse ill. If I am not deseaved
> in my opinion, I think I may hope that your generous heart
> will melt at this statement and the desire will subjugate you to
> be propitious to me by daigning to lavish on me a slight favor.
>
> I am with the distinguished consideration that is due to the
> benefactors of humanity,
>
> > Jondrette
> P.S. My eldest daughter will await your orders, dear Monsieur
> Marius.

This letter, coming in the very midst of the mysterious adventure that had occupied Marius's thoughts ever since the preceding evening, was like a candle in a cellar. All was suddenly illuminated.

This letter came from the same place as the other four. There was the same writing, the same style, the same orthography, the same paper, the same odor of tobacco.

There were five missives, five histories, five signatures, and a single signer. The Spanish Captain Don Alvares, the unhappy Mistress Balizard, the dramatic poet Genflot, the old comedian Fabantou, were all four named Jondrette, if, indeed, Jondrette himself were named Jondrette.

Marius had lived in the house for a tolerably long time, and he had had, as we have said, but very rare occasion to see, to even catch a glimpse of, his extremely mean neighbors. His mind was elsewhere, and where the mind is, there the eyes are also. He had been obliged more than once to pass the Jondrettes in the corridor or on the stairs; but they were mere forms to him; he had paid so little heed to them, that, on the preceding evening, he had jostled the Jondrette girls on the boulevard, without recognizing them, for it had evidently been they, and it was with great difficulty that the one who had just entered his room had awakened in him, in spite of disgust and pity, a vague recollection of having met her elsewhere.

Now he saw everything clearly. He understood that his neighbor Jondrette, in his distress, exercised the industry of speculating on the charity of benevolent persons, that he procured addresses, and that he wrote under feigned names to people whom he judged to be wealthy and compassionate, letters that his daughters delivered at their risk and peril, for this father had come to such a pass, that he risked his daughters; he was playing a game with fate, and he used them as the stake. Marius understood that probably, judging from their flight on the evening before, from their breathless condition, from their terror and from the words of slang that he had overheard, these unfortunate creatures were plying some inexplicably sad profession, and that the result of the whole was, in the midst of human society, as it is now constituted, two miserable beings who were neither girls nor women, a species of impure and innocent monsters produced by misery.

Sad creatures, without name, or sex, or age, to whom neither good nor evil were any longer possible, and who, on emerging from childhood, have already nothing in this world, neither liberty, nor virtue, nor responsibility. Souls that blossomed out yesterday, and are faded today, like those flowers let fall in the streets, that are soiled with every sort of mire, while waiting for some wheel to crush them. Nevertheless, while Marius bent a pained and astonished gaze

n her, the young girl was wandering back and forth in the garret with the
udacity of a specter. She kicked about, without troubling herself as to her
akedness. Occasionally her chemise, which was untied and torn, fell almost
o her waist. She moved the chairs about, she disarranged the toilette articles
hath stood on the commode, she handled Marius's clothes, she rummaged
bout to see what there was in the corners.

"Hullo!" said she. "You have a mirror!"

And she hummed scraps of vaudevilles, as though she had been alone,
rolicsome refrains, which her hoarse and guttural voice rendered lugubrious.

An indescribable constraint, weariness, and humiliation were perceptible
beneath this hardihood. Effrontery is a disgrace.

Nothing could be more melancholy than to see her sport about the room, and,
o to speak, flit with the movements of a bird that is frightened by the daylight,
or that has broken its wing. One felt that under other conditions of education
and destiny, the gay and over-free mien of this young girl might have turned out
weet and charming. Never, even among animals, does the creature born to be a
love change into an osprey. That is only to be seen among men.

Marius reflected, and allowed her to have her way.

She approached the table.

"Ah!" said she. "Books!"

A flash pierced her glassy eye. She resumed, and her accent expressed the
happiness she felt in boasting of something, to which no human creature is
nsensible, "I know how to read, I do!"

She eagerly seized a book that lay open on the table, and read with tolerable
fluency: "General Bauduin received orders to take the chateau of Hougomont
that stands in the middle of the plain of Waterloo, with five battalions of his
brigade."

She paused.

"Ah! Waterloo! I know about that. It was a battle long ago. My father was
there. My father has served in the armies. We are fine Bonapartists in our
house, that we are! Waterloo was against the English."

She laid down the book, caught up a pen, and exclaimed, "And I know how
to write, too!"

She dipped her pen in the ink, and turning to Marius: "Do you want to see?
Look here, I'm going to write a word to show you."

And before he had time to answer, she wrote on a sheet of white paper that
lay in the middle of the table: "The bobbies are here."

Then throwing down the pen: "There are no faults of orthography. You

can look. We have received an education, my sister and I. We have not alway
been as we are now. We were not made—"

Here she paused, fixed her dull eyes on Marius, and burst out laughing
saying, with an intonation that contained every form of anguish, stifled b
every form of cynicism, "Bah!"

And she began to hum these words to a gay air: "I am hungry, Father. I hav
no food. I am cold, Mother. I have no clothes. Lolotte! Shiver, sob, Jacquot!

She had hardly finished this couplet, when she exclaimed, "Do you ever g
to the play, Monsieur Marius? I do. I have a little brother who is a friend of th
artists, and who gives me tickets sometimes. But I don't like the benches in th
galleries. One is cramped and uncomfortable there. There are rough peop
there sometimes; and people who smell bad."

Then she scrutinized Marius, assumed a singular air and said, "Do yo
know, Mr. Marius, that you are a very handsome fellow?"

And at the same moment the same idea occurred to them both, and made he
smile and him blush. She stepped up to him, and laid her hand on his shoulde
"You pay no heed to me, but I know you, Mr. Marius. I meet you here on th
staircase, and then I often see you going to a person named Father Mabeuf wh
lives in the direction of Austerlitz, sometimes when I have been strolling in tha
quarter. It is very becoming to you to have your hair tumbled thus."

She tried to render her voice soft, but only succeeded in making it ver
deep. A portion of her words was lost in the transit from her larynx to her lips
as though on a piano where some notes are missing.

Marius had retreated gently.

"Mademoiselle," said he, with his cool gravity, "I have here a package tha
belongs to you, I think. Permit me to return it to you."

And he held out the envelope containing the four letters.

She clapped her hands and exclaimed, "We have been looking everywher
for that!"

Then she eagerly seized the package and opened the envelope, saying as sh
did so, "*Dieu de Dieu*! How my sister and I have hunted! And it was you wh
found it! On the boulevard, was it not? It must have been on the boulevard.
You see, we let it fall when we were running. It was that brat of a sister of min
who was so stupid. When we got home, we could not find it anywhere. As w
did not wish to be beaten, as that is useless, as that is entirely useless, as that i
absolutely useless, we said that we had carried the letters to the proper persons
and that they had said to us, 'Nix.' So here they are, those poor letters! An
how did you find out that they belonged to me? Ah! Yes, the writing. So it wa

ou that we jostled as we passed last night. We couldn't see. I said to my sister, 'Is it a gentleman?' My sister said to me, 'I think it is a gentleman.'"

In the meanwhile she had unfolded the petition addressed to "the benevolent gentleman of the church of Saint-Jacquesdu-Haut-Pas."

"Here!" said she. "This is for that old fellow who goes to Mass. By the way, this is his hour. I'll go and carry it to him. Perhaps he will give us something to breakfast on."

Then she began to laugh again, and added, "Do you know what it will mean if we get a breakfast today? It will mean that we shall have had our breakfast of the day before yesterday, our breakfast of yesterday, our dinner of today, and all that at once, and this morning. Come! Parbleu! If you are not satisfied, dogs, burst!"

This reminded Marius of the wretched girl's errand to himself. He fumbled in his waistcoat pocket, and found nothing there.

The young girl went on, and seemed to have no consciousness of Marius's presence.

"I often go off in the evening. Sometimes I don't come home again. Last winter, before we came here, we lived under the arches of the bridges. We huddled together to keep from freezing. My little sister cried. How melancholy the water is! When I thought of drowning myself, I said to myself, 'No, it's too cold.' I go out alone, whenever I choose, I sometimes sleep in the ditches. Do you know, at night, when I walk along the boulevard, I see the trees like forks, I see houses, all black and as big as Notre Dame, I fancy that the white walls are the river, I say to myself, 'Why, there's water there!' The stars are like the lamps in illuminations, one would say that they smoked and that the wind blew them out, I am bewildered, as though horses were breathing in my ears; although it is night, I hear hand organs and spinning machines, and I don't know what all. I think people are flinging stones at me, I flee without knowing where, everything whirls and whirls. You feel very queer when you have had no food."

And then she stared at him with a bewildered air.

By dint of searching and ransacking his pockets, Marius had finally collected five francs sixteen sous. This was all he owned in the world for the moment. "At all events," he thought, "there is my dinner for today, and tomorrow we will see." He kept the sixteen sous, and handed the five francs to the young girl.

She seized the coin.

"Good!" said she. "The sun is shining!"

And, as though the sun had possessed the property of melting the avalanches

of slang in her brain, she went on, "Five francs! The shiner! A monarch! In th
hole! Ain't this fine! You're a jolly thief! I'm your humble servant! Bravo f
the good fellows! Two days' wine! And meat! And stew! We'll have a roy
feast! And a good fill!"

She pulled her chemise up on her shoulders, made a low bow to Mariu
then a familiar sign with her hand, and went toward the door, saying, "Goo
morning, Sir. It's all right. I'll go and find my old man."

As she passed, she caught sight of a dry crust of bread on the commod
which was molding there amid the dust; she flung herself upon it and bit int
it, muttering, "That's good! It's hard! It breaks my teeth!"

Then she departed.

CHAPTER V—A PROVIDENTIAL
PEEPHOLE

Marius had lived for five years in poverty, in destitution, even in distres
but he now perceived that he had not known real misery. True miser
he had but just had a view of. It was its specter that had just passed before h
eyes. In fact, he who has only beheld the misery of man has seen nothing; th
misery of woman is what he must see; he who has seen only the misery c
woman has seen nothing; he must see the misery of the child.

When a man has reached his last extremity, he has reached his last resourc
at the same time. Woe to the defenseless beings who surround him! Wor
wages, bread, fire, courage, good will, all fail him simultaneously. The lig
of day seems extinguished without, the moral light within; in these shadow
man encounters the feebleness of the woman and the child, and bends the
violently to ignominy.

Then all horrors become possible. Despair is surrounded with fragi
partitions, which all open on either vice or crime.

Health, youth, honor, all the shy delicacies of the young body, the hea
virginity, modesty, that epidermis of the soul, are manipulated in sinister wi
by that fumbling that seeks resources, that encounters opprobrium, and th
accommodates itself to it. Fathers, mothers, children, brothers, sisters, me
women, daughters, adhere and become incorporated, almost like a miner
formation, in that dusky promiscuousness of sexes, relationships, ag
infamies, and innocences. They crouch, back to back, in a sort of hut of fat
They exchange woebegone glances. Oh, the unfortunate wretches! How p

hey are! How cold they are! It seems as though they dwelled in a planet much urther from the sun than ours.

This young girl was to Marius a sort of messenger from the realm of sad hadows. She revealed to him a hideous side of the night.

Marius almost reproached himself for the preoccupations of reverie and assion that had prevented his bestowing a glance on his neighbors up to hat day. The payment of their rent had been a mechanical movement, which nyone would have yielded to; but he, Marius, should have done better than hat. What! Only a wall separated him from those abandoned beings who ved gropingly in the dark outside the pale of the rest of the world, he was lbow-to-elbow with them, he was, in some sort, the last link of the human ace that they touched, he heard them live, or rather, rattle in the death agony eside him, and he paid no heed to them! Every day, every instant, he heard hem walking on the other side of the wall, he heard them go, and come, and peak, and he did not even lend an ear! And groans lay in those words, and he id not even listen to them, his thoughts were elsewhere, given up to dreams,) impossible radiances, to loves in the air, to follies; and all the while, human reatures, his brothers in Jesus Christ, his brothers in the people, were gonizing in vain beside him! He even formed a part of their misfortune, nd he aggravated it. For if they had had another neighbor who was less himerical and more attentive, any ordinary and charitable man, evidently heir indigence would have been noticed, their signals of distress would have een perceived, and they would have been taken hold of and rescued! They ppeared very corrupt and very depraved, no doubt, very vile, very odious ven; but those who fall without becoming degraded are rare; besides, there ; a point where the unfortunate and the infamous unite and are confounded 1 a single word, a fatal word, the miserable; whose fault is this? And then hould not the charity be all the more profound, in proportion as the fall is reat?

While reading himself this moral lesson, for there were occasions on which 1arius, like all truly honest hearts, was his own pedagogue and scolded himself iore than he deserved, he stared at the wall that separated him from the ondrettes, as though he were able to make his gaze, full of pity, penetrate that artition and warm these wretched people. The wall was a thin layer of plaster pheld by lathes and beams, and, as the reader had just learned, it allowed the ound of voices and words to be clearly distinguished. Only a man as dreamy ; Marius could have failed to perceive this long before. There was no paper asted on the wall, either on the side of the Jondrettes or on that of Marius; the coarse construction was visible in its nakedness. Marius examined the partition almost unconsciously; sometimes reverie examines, observes, and scrutinizes as thought would. All at once he sprang up; he had just perceived, near the top close to the ceiling, a triangular hole, which resulted from the space between three lathes. The plaster that should have filled this cavity was missing, and by mounting on the commode, a view could be had through this aperture into the Jondrettes' attic. Commiseration has, and should have, its curiosity. The aperture formed a sort of peephole. It is permissible to gaze at misfortune like a traitor in order to succor it.

"Let us get some little idea of what these people are like," thought Marius, "and in what condition they are."

He climbed upon the commode, put his eye to the crevice, and looked.

CHAPTER VI—THE WILD MAN IN HIS LAIR

Cities, like forests, have their caverns in which all the most wicked and formidable creatures that they contain conceal themselves. Only, in cities that which thus conceals itself is ferocious, unclean, and petty, that is to say, ugly; in forests, that which conceals itself is ferocious, savage, and grand, that is to say, beautiful. Taking one lair with another, the beast's is preferable to the man's. Caverns are better than hovels.

What Marius now beheld was a hovel.

Marius was poor, and his chamber was poverty-stricken, but as his poverty was noble, his garret was neat. The den upon which his eye now rested was abject, dirty, fetid, pestiferous, mean, sordid. The only furniture consisted of a straw chair, an infirm table, some old bits of crockery, and in two of the corners, two indescribable pallets; all the light was furnished by a dormer window of four panes, draped with spiders' webs. Through this aperture there penetrated just enough light to make the face of a man appear like the face of a phantom. The walls had a leprous aspect, and were covered with seams and scars, like a visage disfigured by some horrible malady; a repulsive moisture exuded from them. Obscene sketches roughly sketched with charcoal could be distinguished upon them.

The chamber Marius occupied had a dilapidated brick pavement; this one was neither tiled nor planked; its inhabitants stepped directly on the antique plaster of the hovel, which had grown black under the long-continued pressure of feet. Upon this uneven floor, where the dirt seemed to be fairly encrusted, and that possessed but one virginity, that of the broom, were capriciously grouped constellations of old shoes, socks, and repulsive rags; however, this room had a fireplace, so it was let for forty francs a year. There was every sort of thing in that fireplace, a brazier, a pot, broken boards, rags suspended from nails, a birdcage, ashes, and even a little fire. Two brands were smoldering there in a melancholy way.

One thing that added still more to the horrors of this garret was that it was large. It had projections and angles and black holes, the lower sides of roofs, bays, and promontories. Hence horrible, unfathomable nooks where it seemed as though spiders as big as one's fist, wood lice as large as one's foot, and perhaps even—who knows?—some monstrous human beings, must be hiding.

One of the pallets was near the door, the other near the window. One end of each touched the fireplace and faced Marius. In a corner near the aperture through which Marius was gazing, a colored engraving in a black frame was suspended to a nail on the wall, and at its bottom, in large letters, was the inscription: THE DREAM. This represented a sleeping woman, and a child, also asleep, the child on the woman's lap, an eagle in a cloud, with a crown in his beak, and the woman thrusting the crown away from the child's head, without awaking the latter; in the background, Napoleon in a glory, leaning on a very blue column with a yellow capital ornamented with this inscription:

MARINGO
AUSTERLITS
IENA
WAGRAMME
ELOT

Beneath this frame, a sort of wooden panel, which was no longer than it was broad, stood on the ground and rested in a sloping attitude against the wall. It had the appearance of a picture with its face turned to the wall, of a frame probably showing a daub on the other side, of some pier glass detached from a wall and lying forgotten there while waiting to be rehung.

Near the table, upon which Marius descried a pen, ink, and paper, sat a man about sixty years of age, small, thin, livid, haggard, with a cunning, cruel, and uneasy air—a hideous scoundrel.

If Lavater had studied this visage, he would have found the vulture mingled with the attorney there, the bird of prey and the pettifogger rendering each other mutually hideous and complementing each other; the pettifogger making the bird of prey ignoble, the bird of prey making the pettifogger horrible.

This man had a long gray beard. He was clad in a woman's chemise, which allowed his hairy breast and his bare arms, bristling with gray hair, to be seen. Beneath this chemise, muddy trousers and boots through which his toes projected were visible.

He had a pipe in his mouth and was smoking. There was no bread in the hovel, but there was still tobacco.

He was writing probably some more letters like those that Marius had read.

On the corner of the table lay an ancient, dilapidated, reddish volume, and the size, which was the antique 12mo* of reading-rooms, betrayed a romance. On the cover sprawled the following title, printed in large capitals: GOD; THE KING; HONOR AND THE LADIES; BY DUCRAY DUMINIL, 1814.

As the man wrote, he talked aloud, and Marius heard his words, "The idea that there is no equality, even when you are dead! Just look at Pere Lachaise! The great, those who are rich, are up above, in the acacia alley, which is paved. They can reach it in a carriage. The little people, the poor, the unhappy, well, what of them? They are put down below, where the mud is up to your knees, in the damp places. They are put there so that they will decay the sooner! You cannot go to see them without sinking into the earth."

He paused, smote the table with his fist, and added, as he ground his teeth, "Oh! I could eat the whole world!"

A big woman, who might be forty years of age, or a hundred, was crouching near the fireplace on her bare heels.

She, too, was clad only in a chemise and a knitted petticoat patched with bits of old cloth. A coarse linen apron concealed the half of her petticoat. Although this woman was doubled up and bent together, it could be seen that she was of very lofty stature. She was a sort of giant, beside her husband. She had hideous hair, of a reddish blond that was turning gray, and that she thrust back from time to time, with her enormous shining hands, with their flat nails.

Beside her, on the floor, wide open, lay a book of the same form as the other, and probably a volume of the same romance.

On one of the pallets, Marius caught a glimpse of a sort of tall pale young girl, who sat there half naked and with pendant feet, and who did not seem to be listening or seeing or living.

---

* A book size

No doubt the younger sister of the one who had come to his room.

She seemed to be eleven or twelve years of age. On closer scrutiny it was evident that she really was fourteen. She was the child who had said, on the boulevard the evening before, "I bolted, bolted, bolted!"

She was of that puny sort that remains backward for a long time, then suddenly starts up rapidly. It is indigence that produces these melancholy human plants. These creatures have neither childhood nor youth. At fifteen years of age they appear to be twelve, at sixteen they seem twenty. Today a little girl, tomorrow a woman. One might say that they stride through life, in order to get through with it the more speedily.

At this moment, this being had the air of a child.

Moreover, no trace of work was revealed in that dwelling; no handicraft, no spinning wheel, not a tool. In one corner lay some ironmongery of dubious aspect. It was the dull listlessness that follows despair and precedes the death agony.

Marius gazed for a while at this gloomy interior, more terrifying than the interior of a tomb, for the human soul could be felt fluttering there, and life was palpitating there. The garret, the cellar, the lowly ditch where certain indigent wretches crawl at the very bottom of the social edifice, is not exactly the sepulchre, but only its antechamber; but, as the wealthy display their greatest magnificence at the entrance of their palaces, it seems that death, which stands directly side by side with them, places its greatest miseries in that vestibule.

The man held his peace, the woman spoke no word, the young girl did not even seem to breathe. The scratching of the pen on the paper was audible.

The man grumbled, without pausing in his writing. "Canaille! Canaille! Everybody is canaille!"

This variation to Solomon's exclamation elicited a sigh from the woman.

"Calm yourself, my little friend," she said. "Don't hurt yourself, my dear. You are too good to write to all those people, husband."

Bodies press close to each other in misery, as in cold, but hearts draw apart. This woman must have loved this man, to all appearance, judging from the amount of love within her; but probably, in the daily and reciprocal reproaches of the horrible distress that weighed on the whole group, this had become extinct. There no longer existed in her anything more than the ashes of affection for her husband. Nevertheless, caressing appellations had survived, as is often the case. She called him: My dear, my little friend, my good man, etc., with her mouth while her heart was silent.

The man resumed his writing.

CHAPTER VII—STRATEGY AND TACTICS

Marius, with a load upon his breast, was on the point of descending from the species of observatory he had improvised, when a sound attracted his attention and caused him to remain at his post.

The door of the attic had just burst open abruptly. The eldest girl made her appearance on the threshold. On her feet, she had large, coarse, men's shoes bespattered with mud, which had splashed even to her red ankles, and she was wrapped in an old mantle that hung in tatters. Marius had not seen it on her an hour previously, but she had probably deposited it at his door, in order that she might inspire the more pity, and had picked it up again on emerging. She entered, pushed the door to behind her, paused to take breath, for she was completely breathless, then exclaimed with an expression of triumph and joy: "He is coming!"

The father turned his eyes toward her, the woman turned her head, the little sister did not stir.

"Who?" demanded her father.

"The gentleman!"

"The philanthropist?"

"Yes."

"From the church of Saint-Jacques?"

"Yes."

"That old fellow?"

"Yes."

"And he is coming?"

"He is following me."

"You are sure?"

"I am sure."

"There, truly, he is coming?"

"He is coming in a fiacre."

"In a fiacre. He is Rothschild."

The father rose.

"How are you sure? If he is coming in a fiacre, how is it that you arrive before him? You gave him our address at least? Did you tell him that it was the last door at the end of the corridor, on the right? If he only does not make a mistake! So you found him at the church? Did he read my letter? What did he say to you?"

"Ta, ta, ta," said the girl, "how you do gallop on, my good man! See here: entered the church, he was in his usual place, I made him a reverence, and handed him the letter; he read it and said to me, 'Where do you live, my hild?' I said, 'Monsieur, I will show you.' He said to me, 'No, give me your ddress, my daughter has some purchases to make, I will take a carriage and each your house at the same time that you do.' I gave him the address. When mentioned the house, he seemed surprised and hesitated for an instant, then ¹e said, 'Never mind, I will come.' When the Mass was finished, I watched him eave the church with his daughter, and I saw them enter a carriage. I certainly ¹id tell him the last door in the corridor, on the right."

"And what makes you think that he will come?"

"I have just seen the fiacre turn into the Rue Petit-Banquier. That is what ¹ade me run so."

"How do you know that it was the same fiacre?"

"Because I took notice of the number, so there!"

"What was the number?"

"440."

"Good, you are a clever girl."

The girl stared boldly at her father, and showing the shoes that she had on ¹er feet: "A clever girl, possibly; but I tell you I won't put these shoes on again, nd that I won't, for the sake of my health, in the first place, and for the sake of leanliness, in the next. I don't know anything more irritating than shoes that quelch, and go *ghi, ghi, ghi* the whole time. I prefer to go barefoot."

"You are right," said her father, in a sweet tone that contrasted with the oung girl's rudeness, "but then, you will not be allowed to enter churches, for ¹oor people must have shoes to do that. One cannot go barefoot to the good ¹od," he added bitterly.

Then, returning to the subject, which absorbed him:

"So you are sure that he will come?"

"He is following on my heels," said she.

The man started up. A sort of illumination appeared on his countenance.

"Wife!" he exclaimed. "You hear. Here is the philanthropist. Extinguish ¹he fire."

The stupefied mother did not stir.

The father, with the agility of an acrobat, seized a broken-nosed jug that ¹tood on the chimney, and flung the water on the brands.

Then, addressing his eldest daughter, "Here you! Pull the straw off that hair!"

His daughter did not understand.

He seized the chair, and with one kick he rendered it seatless. His leg passe through it.

As he withdrew his leg, he asked his daughter, "Is it cold?"

"Very cold. It is snowing."

The father turned toward the younger girl who sat on the bed near th window, and shouted to her in a thundering voice, "Quick! Get off that bec you lazy thing! Will you never do anything? Break a pane of glass!"

The little girl jumped off the bed with a shiver.

"Break a pane!" he repeated.

The child stood still in bewilderment.

"Do you hear me?" repeated her father. "I tell you to break a pane!"

The child, with a sort of terrified obedience, rose on tiptoe, and struck pane with her fist. The glass broke and fell with a loud clatter.

"Good," said the father.

He was grave and abrupt. His glance swept rapidly over all the crannie of the garret. One would have said that he was a general making the fina preparation at the moment when the battle is on the point of beginning.

The mother, who had not said a word so far, now rose and demande in a dull, slow, languid voice, from which her words seemed to emerge in congealed state. "What do you mean to do, my dear?"

"Get into bed," replied the man.

His intonation admitted of no deliberation. The mother obeyed, and threv herself heavily on one of the pallets.

In the meantime, a sob became audible in one corner.

"What's that?" cried the father.

The younger daughter exhibited her bleeding fist, without quitting th corner in which she was cowering. She had wounded herself while breakin, the window; she went off, near her mother's pallet and wept silently.

It was now the mother's turn to start up and exclaim, "Just see there! Wha follies you commit! She has cut herself breaking that pane for you!"

"So much the better!" said the man. "I foresaw that."

"What? So much the better?" retorted his wife.

"Peace!" replied the father. "I suppress the liberty of the press."

Then tearing the woman's chemise that he was wearing, he made a strip o cloth with which he hastily swathed the little girl's bleeding wrist.

That done, his eye fell with a satisfied expression on his torn chemise.

"And the chemise too," said he, "this has a good appearance."

An icy breeze whistled through the window and entered the room. The outer mist penetrated there and diffused itself like a whitish sheet of wadding vaguely spread by invisible fingers. Through the broken pane the snow could be seen falling. The snow promised by the Candlemas sun of the preceding day had actually come.

The father cast a glance about him as though to make sure that he had forgotten nothing. He seized an old shovel and spread ashes over the wet brands in such a manner as to entirely conceal them.

Then drawing himself up and leaning against the chimneypiece:

"Now," said he, "we can receive the philanthropist."

CHAPTER VIII—THE RAY OF LIGHT IN THE HOVEL

The big girl approached and laid her hand in her father's.

"Feel how cold I am," said she.

"Bah!" replied the father, "I am much colder than that."

The mother exclaimed impetuously, "You always have something better than anyone else, so you do! Even bad things."

"Down with you!" said the man.

The mother, being eyed after a certain fashion, held her tongue.

Silence reigned for a moment in the hovel. The elder girl was removing the mud from the bottom of her mantle, with a careless air; her younger sister continued to sob; the mother had taken the latter's head between her hands, and was covering it with kisses, whispering to her the while, "My treasure, I entreat you, it is nothing of consequence, don't cry, you will anger your father."

"No!" exclaimed the father. "Quite the contrary! Sob! Sob! That's right."

Then turning to the elder: "There now! He is not coming! What if he were not to come! I shall have extinguished my fire, wrecked my chair, torn my shirt, and broken my pane all for nothing."

"And wounded the child!" murmured the mother.

"Do you know," went on the father, "that it's beastly cold in this devil's garret! What if that man should not come! Oh! See there, you! He makes us wait! He says to himself: 'Well! They will wait for me! That's what they're there for.' Oh! How I hate them, and with what joy, jubilation, enthusiasm, and satisfaction I could strangle all those rich folks! All those rich folks! These men who pretend to be charitable, who put on airs, who go to Mass, who make

presents to the priesthood, preachy, preachy, in their skullcaps, and who think
themselves above us, and who come for the purpose of humiliating us, and
to bring us 'clothes,' as they say! Old duds that are not worth four sous! And
bread! That's not what I want, pack of rascals that they are, it's money! Ah!
Money! Never! Because they say that we would go off and drink it up, and
that we are drunkards and idlers! And they! What are they, then, and what
have they been in their time! Thieves! They never could have become rich
otherwise! Oh! Society ought to be grasped by the four corners of the cloth
and tossed into the air, all of it! It would all be smashed, very likely, but at least
no one would have anything, and there would be that much gained! But what
is that blockhead of a benevolent gentleman doing? Will he come? Perhaps the
animal has forgotten the address! I'll bet that that old beast—"

At that moment there came a light tap at the door, the man rushed to it and
opened it, exclaiming, amid profound bows and smiles of adoration, "Enter
Sir! Deign to enter, most respected benefactor, and your charming young lady
also."

A man of ripe age and a young girl made their appearance on the threshold
of the attic.

Marius had not quitted his post. His feelings for the moment surpassed the
powers of the human tongue.

It was she!

Whoever has loved knows all the radiant meanings contained in those three
letters of that word: she.

It was certainly she. Marius could hardly distinguish her through the
luminous vapor that had suddenly spread before his eyes. It was that sweet
absent being, that star that had beamed upon him for six months; it was those
eyes, that brow, that mouth, that lovely vanished face that had created night by
its departure. The vision had been eclipsed, now it reappeared.

It reappeared in that gloom, in that garret, in that misshapen attic, in all
that horror.

Marius shuddered in dismay. What! It was she! The palpitations of his heart
troubled his sight. He felt that he was on the brink of bursting into tears! What!
He beheld her again at last, after having sought her so long! It seemed to him
that he had lost his soul, and that he had just found it again.

She was the same as ever, only a little pale; her delicate face was framed in
a bonnet of violet velvet, her figure was concealed beneath a pelisse of black
satin. Beneath her long dress, a glimpse could be caught of her tiny foot shod
in a silken boot.

She was still accompanied by M. Leblanc.

She had taken a few steps into the room, and had deposited a tolerably bulky parcel on the table.

The eldest Jondrette girl had retired behind the door, and was staring with somber eyes at that velvet bonnet, that silk mantle, and that charming, happy face.

CHAPTER IX—JONDRETTE COMES NEAR WEEPING

The hovel was so dark, that people coming from without felt on entering it the effect produced on entering a cellar. The two newcomers advanced, therefore, with a certain hesitation, being hardly able to distinguish the vague forms surrounding them, while they could be clearly seen and scrutinized by the eyes of the inhabitants of the garret, who were accustomed to this twilight.

M. Leblanc approached, with his sad but kindly look, and said to Jondrette the father, "Monsieur, in this package you will find some new clothes and some woolen stockings and blankets."

"Our angelic benefactor overwhelms us," said Jondrette, bowing to the very earth.

Then, bending down to the ear of his eldest daughter, while the two visitors were engaged in examining this lamentable interior, he added in a low and rapid voice, "Hey? What did I say? Duds! No money! They are all alike! By the way, how was the letter to that old blockhead signed?"

"Fabantou," replied the girl.

"The dramatic artist, good!"

It was lucky for Jondrette, that this had occurred to him, for at the very moment, M. Leblanc turned to him, and said to him with the air of a person who is seeking to recall a name, "I see that you are greatly to be pitied, Monsieur—"

"Fabantou," replied Jondrette quickly.

"Monsieur Fabantou, yes, that is it. I remember."

"Dramatic artist, Sir, and one who has had some success."

Here Jondrette evidently judged the moment propitious for capturing the "philanthropist." He exclaimed with an accent that smacked at the same time of the vainglory of the mountebank at fairs, and the humility of the mendicant on the highway, "A pupil of Talma! Sir! I am a pupil of Talma! Fortune formerly smiled on me—Alas! Now it is misfortune's turn. You see, my benefactor, no bread, no fire. My poor babes have no fire! My only chair has no seat! A broken pane! And in such weather! My spouse in bed! Ill!"

"Poor woman!" said M. Leblanc.

"My child wounded!" added Jondrette.

The child, diverted by the arrival of the strangers, had fallen to contemplating "the young lady," and had ceased to sob.

"Cry! Bawl!" said Jondrette to her in a low voice.

At the same time he pinched her sore hand. All this was done with the talent of a juggler.

The little girl gave vent to loud shrieks.

The adorable young girl, whom Marius, in his heart, called "his Ursule," approached her hastily.

"Poor, dear child!" said she.

"You see, my beautiful young lady," pursued Jondrette "her bleeding wrist. It came through an accident while working at a machine to earn six sous a day. It may be necessary to cut off her arm."

"Really?" said the old gentleman, in alarm.

The little girl, taking this seriously, fell to sobbing more violently than ever.

"Alas! Yes, my benefactor!" replied the father.

For several minutes, Jondrette had been scrutinizing "the benefactor" in a singular fashion. As he spoke, he seemed to be examining the other attentively, as though seeking to summon up his recollections. All at once, profiting by a moment when the newcomers were questioning the child with interest as to her injured hand, he passed near his wife, who lay in her bed with a stupid and dejected air, and said to her in a rapid but very low tone, "Take a look at that man!"

Then, turning to M. Leblanc, and continuing his lamentations, "You see, Sir! All the clothing that I have is my wife's chemise! And all torn at that! In the depths of winter! I can't go out for lack of a coat. If I had a coat of any sort, I would go and see Mademoiselle Mars, who knows me and is very fond of me. Does she not still reside in the Rue de la Tour-des-Dames? Do you know, Sir? We played together in the provinces. I shared her laurels. Célimène would come to my succor, Sir! Elmire would bestow alms on Belisaire! But no, nothing! And not a sou in the house! My wife ill, and not a sou! My daughter dangerously injured, not a sou! My wife suffers from fits of suffocation. It comes from her age, and besides, her nervous system is affected. She ought to have assistance, and my daughter also! But the doctor! But the apothecary! How am I to pay them? I would kneel to a penny, sir! Such is the condition to which the arts are reduced. And do you know, my charming young lady, and you, my generous protector, do you know, you who breathe forth virtue and goodness, and who perfume that church where my daughter sees you every day when she says her prayers?——For I have brought up my children religiously, Sir. I did not want them to take to the theater. Ah! The hussies! If I catch them tripping! I do not jest, that I don't! I read them lessons on honor, on morality, on virtue! Ask them! They have got to walk straight. They are none of your unhappy wretches who begin by having no family, and end by espousing the public. One is Mamselle Nobody, and one becomes Madame Everybody. Deuce take it! None of that in the Fabantou family! I mean to bring them up virtuously, and they shall be honest, and nice, and believe in God, by the sacred name! Well, Sir, my worthy sir, do you know what is going to happen tomorrow? Tomorrow is the fourth day of February, the fatal day, the last day of grace allowed me by my landlord; if by this evening I have not paid my rent, tomorrow my oldest daughter, my spouse with her fever, my child with her wound, we shall all four be turned out of here and thrown into the street, on the boulevard, without shelter, in the rain, in the snow. There, Sir. I owe for four quarters—a whole year! That is to say, sixty francs."

Jondrette lied. Four quarters would have amounted to only forty francs, and he could not owe four, because six months had not elapsed since Marius had paid for two.

M. Leblanc drew five francs from his pocket and threw them on the table.

Jondrette found time to mutter in the ear of his eldest daughter, "The scoundrel! What does he think I can do with his five francs? That won't pay me for my chair and pane of glass! That's what comes of incurring expenses!"

In the meanwhile, M. Leblanc had removed the large brown greatcoat, which he wore over his blue coat, and had thrown it over the back of the chair.

"Monsieur Fabantou," he said, "these five francs are all that I have about me, but I shall now take my daughter home, and I will return this evening, it is this evening that you must pay, is it not?"

Jondrette's face lighted up with a strange expression. He replied vivaciously, "Yes, respected sir. At eight o'clock, I must be at my landlord's."

"I will be here at six, and I will fetch you the sixty francs."

"My benefactor!" exclaimed Jondrette, overwhelmed. And he added, in a low tone, "Take a good look at him, wife!"

M. Leblanc had taken the arm of the young girl, once more, and had turned toward the door.

"Farewell until this evening, my friends!" said he.

"Six o'clock?" said Jondrette.

"Six o'clock precisely."

At that moment, the overcoat lying on the chair caught the eye of the elder Jondrette girl.

"You are forgetting your coat, Sir," said she.

Jondrette darted an annihilating look at his daughter, accompanied by a formidable shrug of the shoulders.

M. Leblanc turned back and said, with a smile, "I have not forgotten it, I am leaving it."

"O my protector!" said Jondrette. "My august benefactor, I melt into tears. Permit me to accompany you to your carriage."

"If you come out," answered M. Leblanc, "put on this coat. It really is very cold."

Jondrette did not need to be told twice. He hastily donned the brown greatcoat. And all three went out, Jondrette preceding the two strangers.

CHAPTER X—TARIFF OF LICENSED CABS: TWO FRANCS AN HOUR

Marius had lost nothing of this entire scene, and yet, in reality, had seen nothing. His eyes had remained fixed on the young girl, his heart had, so to speak, seized her and wholly enveloped her from the moment of her very first step in that garret. During her entire stay there, he had lived that life of ecstasy that suspends material perceptions and precipitates the whole soul on a single point. He contemplated, not that girl, but that light that wore a satin pelisse and a velvet bonnet. The star Sirius might have entered the room, and he would not have been any more dazzled.

While the young girl was engaged in opening the package, unfolding the clothing and the blankets, questioning the sick mother kindly, and the little injured girl tenderly, he watched her every movement, he sought to catch her words. He knew her eyes, her brow, her beauty, her form, her walk, he did not know the sound of her voice. He had once fancied that he had caught a few words at the Luxembourg, but he was not absolutely sure of the fact. He would have given ten years of his life to hear it, in order that he might bear away in his soul a little of that music. But everything was drowned in the lamentable exclamations and trumpet bursts of Jondrette. This added a touch of genuine wrath to Marius's ecstasy. He devoured her with his eyes. He could not believe that it really was that divine creature whom he saw in the midst of those vile

creatures in that monstrous lair. It seemed to him that he beheld a hummingbird
in the midst of toads.

When she took her departure, he had but one thought, to follow her, to
cling to her trace, not to quit her until he learned where she lived, not to lose
her again, at least, after having so miraculously rediscovered her. He leaped
down from the commode and seized his hat. As he laid his hand on the lock of
the door, and was on the point of opening it, a sudden reflection caused him
to pause. The corridor was long, the staircase steep, Jondrette was talkative,
M. Leblanc had, no doubt, not yet regained his carriage; if, on turning around
in the corridor, or on the staircase, he were to catch sight of him, Marius, in
that house, he would, evidently, take the alarm, and find means to escape from
him again, and this time it would be final. What was he to do? Should he wait
a little? But while he was waiting, the carriage might drive off. Marius was
perplexed. At last he accepted the risk and quitted his room.

There was no one in the corridor. He hastened to the stairs. There was no
one on the staircase. He descended in all haste, and reached the boulevard in
time to see a fiacre turning the corner of the Rue du Petit-Banquier, on its way
back to Paris.

Marius rushed headlong in that direction. On arriving at the angle of the
boulevard, he caught sight of the fiacre again, rapidly descending the Rue
Mouffetard; the carriage was already a long way off, and there was no means
of overtaking it; what! Run after it? Impossible; and besides, the people in the
carriage would assuredly notice an individual running at full speed in pursuit
of a fiacre, and the father would recognize him. At that moment, wonderful
and unprecedented good luck, Marius perceived an empty cab passing along
the boulevard. There was but one thing to be done, to jump into this cab and
follow the fiacre. That was sure, efficacious, and free from danger.

Marius made the driver a sign to halt, and called to him, "By the hour?"

Marius wore no cravat, he had on his working coat, which was destitute of
buttons, his shirt was torn along one of the plaits on the bosom.

The driver halted, winked, and held out his left hand to Marius, rubbing his
forefinger gently with his thumb.

"What is it?" said Marius.

"Pay in advance," said the coachman.

Marius recollected that he had but sixteen sous about him.

"How much?" he demanded.

"Forty sous."

"I will pay on my return."

The driver's only reply was to whistle the air of La Palisse and to whip up his horse.

Marius stared at the retreating cabriolet with a bewildered air. For the lack of four and twenty sous, he was losing his joy, his happiness, his love! He had seen, and he was becoming blind again. He reflected bitterly, and it must be confessed, with profound regret, on the five francs he had bestowed, that very morning, on that miserable girl. If he had had those five francs, he would have been saved, he would have been born again, he would have emerged from the limbo and darkness, he would have made his escape from isolation and spleen, from his widowed state; he might have reknotted the black thread of his destiny to that beautiful golden thread, which had just floated before his eyes and had broken at the same instant, once more! He returned to his hovel in despair.

He might have told himself that M. Leblanc had promised to return in the evening, and that all he had to do was to set about the matter more skillfully so that he might follow him on that occasion; but, in his contemplation, it is doubtful whether he had heard this.

As he was on the point of mounting the staircase, he perceived, on the other side of the boulevard, near the deserted wall skirting the Rue De la Barriere-des-Gobelins, Jondrette, wrapped in the "philanthropist's" great-coat, engaged in conversation with one of those men of disquieting aspect who have been dubbed by common consent, prowlers of the barriers; people of equivocal face, of suspicious monologues, who present the air of having evil minds, and who generally sleep in the daytime, which suggests the supposition that they work by night.

These two men, standing there motionless and in conversation, in the snow that was falling in whirlwinds, formed a group that a policeman would surely have observed, but that Marius hardly noticed.

Still, in spite of his mournful preoccupation, he could not refrain from saying to himself that this prowler of the barriers with whom Jondrette was talking resembled a certain Panchaud, alias Printanier, alias Bigrenaille, whom Courfeyrac had once pointed out to him as a very dangerous nocturnal roamer. This man's name the reader has learned in the preceding book. This Panchaud, alias Printanier, alias Bigrenaille, figured later on in many criminal trials, and became a notorious rascal. He was at that time only a famous rascal. Today he exists in the state of tradition among ruffians and assassins. He was at the head of a school toward the end of the last reign. And in the evening, at nightfall, at the hour when groups form and talk in whispers, he was discussed at La Force in the Fosse-aux-Lions. One might even, in that prison, precisely at the spot where the sewer that served the unprecedented escape in broad daylight, of thirty prisoners, in 1843, passes under the culvert, read his name, PANCHAUD, audaciously carved by his own hand on the wall of the sewer, during one of his attempts at flight. In 1832 the police already had their eye on him, but he had not as yet made a serious beginning.

CHAPTER XI—OFFERS OF SERVICE FROM MISERY TO WRETCHEDNESS

Marius ascended the stairs of the hovel with slow steps; at the moment when he was about to reenter his cell, he caught sight of the elder Jondrette girl following him through the corridor. The very sight of this girl was odious to him; it was she who had his five francs, it was too late to demand them back, the cab was no longer there, the fiacre was far away. Moreover, she would not have given them back. As for questioning her about the residence of the persons who had just been there, that was useless; it was evident that she did not know, since the letter signed Fabantou had been addressed "to the benevolent gentleman of the church of Saint-Jacquesdu-Haut-Pas."

Marius entered his room and pushed the door to after him.

It did not close; he turned around and beheld a hand that held the door half open.

"What is it?" he asked. "Who is there?"

It was the Jondrette girl.

"Is it you?" resumed Marius almost harshly. "Still you! What do you want with me?"

She appeared to be thoughtful and did not look at him. She no longer had the air of assurance that had characterized her that morning. She did not enter, but held back in the darkness of the corridor, where Marius could see her through the half-open door.

"Come now, will you answer?" cried Marius. "What do you want with me?"

She raised her dull eyes, in which a sort of gleam seemed to flicker vaguely, and said, "Monsieur Marius, you look sad. What is the matter with you?"

"With me!" said Marius.

"Yes, you."

"There is nothing the matter with me."

"Yes, there is!"

"No."

"I tell you there is!"

"Let me alone!"

Marius gave the door another push, but she retained her hold on it.

"Stop," said she, "you are in the wrong. Although you are not rich, you were kind this morning. Be so again now. You gave me something to eat, now tell me what ails you. You are grieved, that is plain. I do not want you to be grieved. What can be done for it? Can I be of any service? Employ me. I do not ask for your secrets, you need not tell them to me, but I may be of use, nevertheless. I may be able to help you, since I help my father. When it is necessary to carry letters, to go to houses, to inquire from door to door, to find out an address, to follow anyone, I am of service. Well, you may assuredly tell me what is the matter with you, and I will go and speak to the persons; sometimes it is enough if someone speaks to the persons, that suffices to let them understand matters, and everything comes right. Make use of me."

An idea flashed across Marius's mind. What branch does one disdain when one feels that one is falling?

He drew near to the Jondrette girl.

"Listen—" he said to her.

She interrupted him with a gleam of joy in her eyes.

"Oh yes, do call me thou! I like that better."

"Well," he resumed, "thou hast brought here that old gentleman and his daughter!"

"Yes."

"Dost thou know their address?"

"No."

"Find it for me."

The Jondrette's dull eyes had grown joyous, and they now became gloomy.

"Is that what you want?" she demanded.

"Yes."

"Do you know them?"

"No."

"That is to say," she resumed quickly, "you do not know her, but you wish to know her."

This "them" that had turned into "her" had something indescribably significant and bitter about it.

"Well, can you do it?" said Marius.

"You shall have the beautiful lady's address."

There was still a shade in the words "the beautiful lady" that troubled Marius. He resumed, "Never mind, after all, the address of the father and daughter. Their address, indeed!"

She gazed fixedly at him.

"What will you give me?"

"Anything you like."

"Anything I like?"

"Yes."

"You shall have the address."

She dropped her head; then, with a brusque movement, she pulled to the door, which closed behind her.

Marius found himself alone.

He dropped into a chair, with his head and both elbows on his bed, absorbed in thoughts that he could not grasp, and as though a prey to vertigo. All that had taken place since the morning, the appearance of the angel, her disappearance, what that creature had just said to him, a gleam of hope floating in an immense despair, this was what filled his brain confusedly.

All at once he was violently aroused from his reverie.

He heard the shrill, hard voice of Jondrette utter these words, which were fraught with a strange interest for him, "I tell you that I am sure of it, and that I recognized him."

Of whom was Jondrette speaking? Whom had he recognized? M. Leblanc? The father of "his Ursule"? What! Did Jondrette know him? Was Marius about to obtain in this abrupt and unexpected fashion all the information without which his life was so dark to him? Was he about to learn at last who it was that he loved, who that young girl was? Who her father was? Was the dense shadow that enwrapped them on the point of being dispelled? Was the veil about to be rent? Ah! Heavens!

He bounded rather than climbed upon his commode, and resumed his post near the little peephole in the partition wall.

Again he beheld the interior of Jondrette's hovel.

CHAPTER XII—THE USE MADE OF M. LEBLANC'S FIVE-FRANC PIECE

Nothing in the aspect of the family was altered, except that the wife and daughters had levied on the package and put on woolen stockings and jackets. Two new blankets were thrown across the two beds.

Jondrette had evidently just returned. He still had the breathlessness of out of doors. His daughters were seated on the floor near the fireplace, the elder engaged in dressing the younger's wounded hand. His wife had sunk back on the bed near the fireplace, with a face indicative of astonishment. Jondrette was pacing up and down the garret with long strides. His eyes were extraordinary.

The woman, who seemed timid and overwhelmed with stupor in the presence of her husband, turned to say, "What, really? You are sure?"

"Sure! Eight years have passed! But I recognize him! Ah! I recognize him. I knew him at once! What! Didn't it force itself on you?"

"No."

"But I told you: 'Pay attention!' Why, it is his figure, it is his face, only older, there are people who do not grow old, I don't know how they manage it, it is the very sound of his voice. He is better dressed, that is all! Ah! You mysterious old devil, I've got you, that I have!"

He paused, and said to his daughters, "Get out of here, you!—It's queer that it didn't strike you!"

They arose to obey.

The mother stammered, "With her injured hand."

"The air will do it good," said Jondrette. "Be off."

It was plain that this man was of the sort to whom no one offers to reply. The two girls departed.

At the moment when they were about to pass through the door, the father detained the elder by the arm, and said to her with a peculiar accent, "You will be here at five o'clock precisely. Both of you. I shall need you."

Marius redoubled his attention.

On being left alone with his wife, Jondrette began to pace the room again, and made the tour of it two or three times in silence. Then he spent several minutes in tucking the lower part of the woman's chemise that he wore into his trousers.

All at once, he turned to the female Jondrette, folded his arms and exclaimed,

"And would you like to have me tell you something? The young lady—"

"Well, what?" retorted his wife. "The young lady?"

Marius could not doubt that it was really she of whom they were speaking. He listened with ardent anxiety. His whole life was in his ears.

But Jondrette had bent over and spoke to his wife in a whisper. Then he straightened himself up and concluded aloud, "It is she!"

"That one?" said his wife.

"That very one," said the husband.

No expression can reproduce the significance of the mother's words. Surprise, rage, hate, wrath, were mingled and combined in one monstrous intonation. The pronunciation of a few words, the name, no doubt, which her husband had whispered in her ear, had sufficed to rouse this huge, somnolent woman, and from being repulsive she became terrible.

"It is not possible!" she cried. "When I think that my daughters are going barefoot, and have not a gown to their backs! What! A satin pelisse, a velvet bonnet, boots, and everything; more than two hundred francs' worth of clothes! So that one would think she was a lady! No, you are mistaken! Why, in the first place, the other was hideous, and this one is not so bad looking! She really is not bad looking! It can't be she!"

"I tell you that it is she. You will see."

At this absolute assertion, the Jondrette woman raised her large, red, blonde face and stared at the ceiling with a horrible expression. At that moment, she seemed to Marius even more to be feared than her husband. She was a sow with the look of a tigress.

"What!" she resumed, "that horrible, beautiful young lady, who gazed at my daughters with an air of pity, she is that beggar brat! Oh! I should like to kick her stomach in for her!"

She sprang off of the bed, and remained standing for a moment, her hair in disorder, her nostrils dilating, her mouth half open, her fists clenched and drawn back. Then she fell back on the bed once more. The man paced to and fro and paid no attention to his female.

After a silence lasting several minutes, he approached the female Jondrette, and halted in front of her, with folded arms, as he had done a moment before. "And shall I tell you another thing?"

"What is it?" she asked.

He answered in a low, curt voice, "My fortune is made."

The woman stared at him with the look that signifies: "Is the person who is addressing me on the point of going mad?"

He went on, "Thunder! It was not so very long ago that I was a parishioner of the parish of die-of-hunger-if-you-have-a-fire-die-of-cold-if-you-have-bread! I have had enough of misery! My share and other people's share! I am not joking any longer, I don't find it comic any more, I've had enough of puns, good God! No more farces, Eternal Father! I want to eat till I am full, I want to drink my fill! To gormandize! To sleep! To do nothing! I want to have my turn, so I do, come now! Before I die! I want to be a bit of a millionaire!"

He took a turn around the hovel, and added, "Like other people."

"What do you mean by that?" asked the woman.

He shook his head, winked, screwed up one eye, and raised his voice like a medical professor who is about to make a demonstration: "What do I mean by that? Listen!"

"Hush!" muttered the woman. "Not so loud! These are matters that must not be overheard."

"Bah! Who's here? Our neighbor? I saw him go out a little while ago. Besides, he doesn't listen, the big booby. And I tell you that I saw him go out."

Nevertheless, by a sort of instinct, Jondrette lowered his voice, although not sufficiently to prevent Marius hearing his words. One favorable circumstance that enabled Marius not to lose a word of this conversation was the falling snow, which deadened the sound of vehicles on the boulevard.

This is what Marius heard:

"Listen carefully. The Croesus is caught, or as good as caught! That's all settled already. Everything is arranged. I have seen some people. He will come here this evening at six o'clock. To bring sixty francs, the rascal! Did you notice how I played that game on him, my sixty francs, my landlord, my fourth of February? I don't even owe for one quarter! Isn't he a fool! So he will come at six o'clock! That's the hour when our neighbor goes to his dinner. Mother Bougon is off washing dishes in the city. There's not a soul in the house. The neighbor never comes home until eleven o'clock. The children shall stand on watch. You shall help us. He will give in."

"And what if he does not give in?" demanded his wife.

Jondrette made a sinister gesture, and said, "We'll fix him."

And he burst out laughing.

This was the first time Marius had seen him laugh. The laugh was cold and sweet, and provoked a shudder.

Jondrette opened a cupboard near the fireplace, and drew from it an old cap, which he placed on his head, after brushing it with his sleeve.

"Now," said he, "I'm going out. I have some more people that I must see.

Good ones. You'll see how well the whole thing will work. I shall be away as short a time as possible, it's a fine stroke of business, do you look after the house."

And with both fists thrust into the pockets of his trousers, he stood for a moment in thought, then exclaimed, "Do you know, it's mighty lucky, by the way, that he didn't recognize me! If he had recognized me on his side, he would not have come back again. He would have slipped through our fingers! It was my beard that saved us! My romantic beard! My pretty little romantic beard!"

And again he broke into a laugh.

He stepped to the window. The snow was still falling, and streaking the gray of the sky.

"What beastly weather!" said he.

Then lapping his overcoat across his breast: "This rind is too large for me. Never mind," he added, "he did a devilish good thing in leaving it for me, the old scoundrel! If it hadn't been for that, I couldn't have gone out, and everything would have gone wrong! What small points things hang on, anyway!"

And pulling his cap down over his eyes, he quitted the room.

He had barely had time to take half a dozen steps from the door, when the door opened again, and his savage but intelligent face made its appearance once more in the opening.

"I came near forgetting," said he. "You are to have a brazier of charcoal ready."

And he flung into his wife's apron the five-franc piece that the "philanthropist" had left with him.

"A brazier of charcoal?" asked his wife.

"Yes."

"How many bushels?"

"Two good ones."

"That will come to thirty sous. With the rest I will buy something for dinner."

"The devil, no."

"Why?"

"Don't go and spend the hundred-sou piece."

"Why?"

"Because I shall have to buy something, too."

"What?"

"Something."

"How much shall you need?"

"Whereabouts in the neighborhood is there an ironmonger's shop?"

"Rue Mouffetard."

"Ah! Yes, at the corner of a street; I can see the shop."

"But tell me how much you will need for what you have to purchase?"

"Fifty sous—three francs."

"There won't be much left for dinner."

"Eating is not the point today. There's something better to be done."

"That's enough, my jewel."

At this word from his wife, Jondrette closed the door again, and this time, Marius heard his step die away in the corridor of the hovel, and descend the staircase rapidly.

At that moment, one o'clock struck from the church of Saint-Medard.

CHAPTER XIII—SOLUS CUM SOLO, IN LOCO REMOTO, NON COGITABUNTUR ORARE PATER NOSTER

Marius, dreamer as he was, was, as we have said, firm and energetic by nature. His habits of solitary meditation, while they had developed in him sympathy and compassion, had, perhaps, diminished the faculty for irritation, but had left intact the power of waxing indignant; he had the kindliness of a Brahmin, and the severity of a judge; he took pity upon a toad, but he crushed a viper. Now, it was into a hole of vipers that his glance had just been directed, it was a nest of monsters that he had beneath his eyes.

"These wretches must be stamped upon," said he.

Not one of the enigmas that he had hoped to see solved had been elucidated; on the contrary, all of them had been rendered more dense, if anything; he knew nothing more about the beautiful maiden of the Luxembourg and the man whom he called M. Leblanc, except that Jondrette was acquainted with them. Athwart the mysterious words that had been uttered, the only thing of which he caught a distinct glimpse was the fact that an ambush was in course of preparation, a dark but terrible trap; that both of them were incurring great danger, she probably, her father certainly; that they must be saved; that the hideous plots of the Jondrettes must be thwarted, and the web of these spiders broken.

He scanned the female Jondrette for a moment. She had pulled an old sheet-iron stove from a corner, and she was rummaging among the old heap of iron.

He descended from the commode as softly as possible, taking care not to make the least noise. Amid his terror as to what was in preparation, and in the horror with which the Jondrettes had inspired him, he experienced a sort of joy at the idea that it might be granted to him perhaps to render a service to the one whom he loved.

But how was it to be done? How warn the persons threatened? He did not know their address. They had reappeared for an instant before his eyes, and had then plunged back again into the immense depths of Paris. Should he wait for M. Leblanc at the door that evening at six o'clock, at the moment of his arrival, and warn him of the trap? But Jondrette and his men would see him on the watch, the spot was lonely, they were stronger than he, they would devise means to seize him or to get him away, and the man whom Marius was anxious to save would be lost. One o'clock had just struck, the trap was to be sprung at six. Marius had five hours before him.

There was but one thing to be done.

He put on his decent coat, knotted a silk handkerchief around his neck, took his hat, and went out, without making any more noise than if he had been treading on moss with bare feet.

Moreover, the Jondrette woman continued to rummage among her old iron.

Once outside of the house, he made for the Rue du Petit-Banquier.

He had almost reached the middle of this street, near a very low wall that a man can easily step over at certain points, and that abuts on a waste space, and was walking slowly, in consequence of his preoccupied condition, and the snow deadened the sound of his steps; all at once he heard voices talking very close by. He turned his head, the street was deserted, there was not a soul in it, it was broad daylight, and yet he distinctly heard voices.

It occurred to him to glance over the wall that he was skirting.

There, in fact, sat two men, flat on the snow, with their backs against the wall, talking together in subdued tones.

These two persons were strangers to him; one was a bearded man in a blouse, and the other a long-haired individual in rags. The bearded man had on a fez, the other's head was bare, and the snow had lodged in his hair.

By thrusting his head over the wall, Marius could hear their remarks.

The hairy one jogged the other man's elbow and said, "—With the assistance of Patron-Minette, it can't fail."

"Do you think so?" said the bearded man.

And the long-haired one began again, "It's as good as a warrant for each one, of five hundred balls, and the worst that can happen is five years, six years, ten years at the most!"

The other replied with some hesitation, and shivering beneath his fez, "That's a real thing. You can't go against such things."

"I tell you that the affair can't go wrong," resumed the long-haired man. "Father What's-his-name's team will be already harnessed."

Then they began to discuss a melodrama that they had seen on the preceding evening at the Gaite Theater.

Marius went his way.

It seemed to him that the mysterious words of these men, so strangely hidden behind that wall, and crouching in the snow, could not but bear some relation to Jondrette's abominable projects. That must be the affair.

He directed his course toward the Faubourg Saint-Marceau and asked at the first shop he came to where he could find a commissary of police.

He was directed to Rue de Pontoise, No. 14.

There Marius betook himself.

As he passed a baker's shop, he bought a two-penny roll, and ate it, foreseeing that he should not dine.

On the way, he rendered justice to Providence. He reflected that had he not given his five francs to the Jondrette girl in the morning, he would have followed M. Leblanc's fiacre, and consequently have remained ignorant of everything, and that there would have been no obstacle to the trap of the Jondrettes and that M. Leblanc would have been lost, and his daughter with him, no doubt.

CHAPTER XIV—IN WHICH A POLICE AGENT BESTOWS TWO FISTFULS ON A LAWYER

On arriving at No. 14, Rue de Pontoise, he ascended to the first floor and inquired for the commissary of police.

"The commissary of police is not here," said a clerk; "but there is an inspector who takes his place. Would you like to speak to him? Are you in haste?"

"Yes," said Marius.

The clerk introduced him into the commissary's office. There stood a tall man behind a grating, leaning against a stove, and holding up with both hands the tails of a vast topcoat, with three collars. His face was square, with a thin, firm mouth, thick, gray, and very ferocious whiskers, and a look that was enough to turn your pockets inside out. Of that glance it might have been well said, not that it penetrated, but that it searched.

This man's air was not much less ferocious nor less terrible than Jondrette's; the dog is, at times, no less terrible to meet than the wolf.

"What do you want?" he said to Marius, without adding "monsieur."

"Is this Monsieur le Commissaire de Police?"

"He is absent. I am here in his stead."

"The matter is very private."

"Then speak."

"And great haste is required."

"Then speak quick."

This calm, abrupt man was both terrifying and reassuring at one and the same time. He inspired fear and confidence. Marius related the adventure to him: that a person with whom he was not acquainted otherwise than by sight, was to be inveigled into a trap that very evening; that, as he occupied the room adjoining the den, he, Marius Pontmercy, a lawyer, had heard the whole plot through the partition; that the wretch who had planned the trap was a certain Jondrette; that there would be accomplices, probably some prowlers of the barriers, among others a certain Panchaud, alias Printanier, alias Bigrenaille; that Jondrette's daughters were to lie in wait; that there was no way of warning the threatened man, since he did not even know his name; and that, finally, all this was to be carried out at six o'clock that evening, at the most deserted point of the Boulevard de l'Hopital, in house No. 50–52.

At the sound of this number, the inspector raised his head, and said coldly, "So it is in the room at the end of the corridor?"

"Precisely," answered Marius, and he added, "Are you acquainted with that house?"

The inspector remained silent for a moment, then replied, as he warmed the heel of his boot at the door of the stove, "Apparently."

He went on, muttering between his teeth, and not addressing Marius so much as his cravat, "Patron-Minette must have had a hand in this."

This word struck Marius.

"Patron-Minette," said he, "I did hear that word pronounced, in fact."

And he repeated to the inspector the dialogue between the long-haired man and the bearded man in the snow behind the wall of the Rue du Petit-Banquier.

The inspector muttered, "The long-haired man must be Brujon, and the bearded one Demi-Liard, alias Deux-Milliards."

He had dropped his eyelids again, and became absorbed in thought.

"As for Father What's-his-name, I think I recognize him. Here, I've burned my coat. They always have too much fire in these cursed stoves. Number 50–52. Former property of Gorbeau."

Then he glanced at Marius.

"You saw only that bearded and that long-haired man?"

"And Panchaud."

"You didn't see a little imp of a dandy prowling about the premises?"

"No."

"Nor a big lump of matter, resembling an elephant in the Jardin des Plantes?"

"No."

"Nor a scamp with the air of an old red tail?"

"No."

"As for the fourth, no one sees him, not even his adjutants, clerks, and employees. It is not surprising that you did not see him."

"No. Who are all those persons?" asked Marius.

The inspector answered, "Besides, this is not the time for them."

He relapsed into silence, then resumed, "50-52. I know that barrack. Impossible to conceal ourselves inside it without the artists seeing us, and then they will get off simply by countermanding the vaudeville. They are so modest! An audience embarrasses them. None of that, none of that. I want to hear them sing and make them dance."

This monologue concluded, he turned to Marius, and demanded, gazing at him intently the while, "Are you afraid?"

"Of what?" said Marius.

"Of these men?"

"No more than yourself!" retorted Marius rudely, who had begun to notice that this police agent had not yet said "monsieur" to him.

The inspector stared still more intently at Marius, and continued with sententious solemnity, "There, you speak like a brave man, and like an honest man. Courage does not fear crime, and honesty does not fear authority."

Marius interrupted him, "That is well, but what do you intend to do?"

The inspector contented himself with the remark, "The lodgers have passkeys with which to get in at night. You must have one."

"Yes," said Marius.

"Have you it about you?"

"Yes."

"Give it to me," said the inspector.

Marius took his key from his waistcoat pocket, handed it to the inspector and added, "If you will take my advice, you will come in force."

The inspector cast on Marius such a glance as Voltaire might have bestowed on a provincial academician who had suggested a rhyme to him; with one movement he plunged his hands, which were enormous, into the two immense pockets of his topcoat, and pulled out two small steel pistols, of the sort called "knock-me-downs." Then he presented them to Marius, saying rapidly, in a curt tone, "Take these. Go home. Hide in your chamber, so that you may be supposed to have gone out. They are loaded. Each one carries two balls. You will keep watch; there is a hole in the wall, as you have informed me. These men will come. Leave them to their own devices for a time. When you think matters have reached a crisis, and that it is time to put a stop to them, fire a shot. Not too soon. The rest concerns me. A shot into the ceiling, the air, no matter where. Above all things, not too soon. Wait until they begin to put their project into execution; you are a lawyer; you know the proper point." Marius took the pistols and put them in the side pocket of his coat.

"That makes a lump that can be seen," said the inspector. "Put them in your trousers pocket."

Marius hid the pistols in his trousers pockets.

"Now," pursued the inspector, "there is not a minute more to be lost by anyone. What time is it? Half-past two. Seven o'clock is the hour?"

"Six o'clock," answered Marius.

"I have plenty of time," said the inspector, "but no more than enough. Don't forget anything that I have said to you. Bang. A pistol shot."

"Rest easy," said Marius.

And as Marius laid his hand on the handle of the door on his way out, the inspector called to him, "By the way, if you have occasion for my services between now and then, come or send here. You will ask for Inspector Javert."

CHAPTER XV—JONDRETTE MAKES HIS PURCHASES

A few moments later, about three o'clock, Courfeyrac chanced to be passing along the Rue Mouffetard in company with Bossuet. The snow had redoubled in violence, and filled the air. Bossuet was just saying to Courfeyrac, "One would say, to see all these snowflakes fall, that there was a plague of white butterflies in heaven." All at once, Bossuet caught sight of Marius coming up the street toward the barrier with a peculiar air.

"Hold!" said Bossuet. "There's Marius."

"I saw him," said Courfeyrac. "Don't let's speak to him."

"Why?"

"He is busy."

"With what?"

"Don't you see his air?"

"What air?"

"He has the air of a man who is following someone."

"That's true," said Bossuet.

"Just see the eyes he is making!" said Courfeyrac.

"But who the deuce is he following?"

"Some fine, flowery bonneted wench! He's in love."

"But," observed Bossuet, "I don't see any wench nor any flowery bonnet in the street. There's not a woman around."

Courfeyrac took a survey, and exclaimed, "He's following a man!"

A man, in fact, wearing a gray cap, and whose gray beard could be distinguished, although they only saw his back, was walking along about twenty paces in advance of Marius.

This man was dressed in a greatcoat that was perfectly new and too large for him, and in a frightful pair of trousers all hanging in rags and black with mud.

Bossuet burst out laughing.

"Who is that man?"

"He?" retorted Courfeyrac. "He's a poet. Poets are very fond of wearing the trousers of dealers in rabbit skins and the overcoats of peers of France."

"Let's see where Marius will go," said Bossuet; "let's see where the man is going, let's follow them, hey?"

"Bossuet!" exclaimed Courfeyrac. "Eagle of Meaux! You are a prodigious brute. Follow a man who is following another man, indeed!"

They retraced their steps.

Marius had, in fact, seen Jondrette passing along the Rue Mouffetard, and was spying on his proceedings.

Jondrette walked straight ahead, without a suspicion that he was already held by a glance.

He quitted the Rue Mouffetard, and Marius saw him enter one of the most terrible hovels in the Rue Gracieuse; he remained there about a quarter of an hour, then returned to the Rue Mouffetard. He halted at an ironmonger's shop, which then stood at the corner of the Rue Pierre-Lombard, and a few minutes later Marius saw him emerge from the shop, holding in his hand a huge cold chisel with a white wood handle, which he concealed beneath his greatcoat. At the top of the Rue Petit-Gentilly he turned to the left and proceeded rapidly to the Rue du Petit-Banquier. The day was declining; the snow, which had ceased for a moment, had just begun again. Marius posted himself on the watch at the very corner of the Rue du Petit-Banquier, which was deserted, as usual, and did not follow Jondrette into it. It was lucky that he did so, for, on arriving in the vicinity of the wall where Marius had heard the long-haired man and the bearded man conversing, Jondrette turned around, made sure that no one was following him, did not see him, then sprang across the wall and disappeared.

The wasteland bordered by this wall communicated with the back yard of an ex-livery stable-keeper of bad repute, who had failed and who still kept a few old single-seated berlins under his sheds.

Marius thought that it would be wise to profit by Jondrette's absence to return home; moreover, it was growing late; every evening, Ma'am Bougon when she set out for her dishwashing in town, had a habit of locking the door, which was always closed at dusk. Marius had given his key to the inspector of police; it was important, therefore, that he should make haste.

Evening had arrived, night had almost closed in; on the horizon and in the immensity of space, there remained but one spot illuminated by the sun, and that was the moon.

It was rising in a ruddy glow behind the low dome of Salpetriere.

Marius returned to No. 50-52 with great strides. The door was still open when he arrived. He mounted the stairs on tiptoe and glided along the wall of the corridor to his chamber. This corridor, as the reader will remember, was bordered on both sides by attics, all of which were, for the moment, empty and to let. Ma'am Bougon was in the habit of leaving all the doors open. As he passed one of these attics, Marius thought he perceived in the uninhabited cell the motionless heads of four men, vaguely lighted up by a remnant of daylight, falling through a dormer window.

Marius made no attempt to see, not wishing to be seen himself. He succeeded in reaching his chamber without being seen and without making any noise. It was high time. A moment later he heard Ma'am Bougon take her departure, locking the door of the house behind her.

CHAPTER XVI—IN WHICH WILL BE FOUND THE WORDS TO AN ENGLISH AIR THAT WAS IN FASHION IN 1832

Marius seated himself on his bed. It might have been half-past five o'clock. Only half an hour separated him from what was about to happen. He heard the beating of his arteries as one hears the ticking of a watch in the dark. He thought of the double march that was going on at that moment in the dark, crime advancing on one side, justice coming up on the other. He was not afraid, but he could not think without a shudder of what was about to take place. As is the case with all those who are suddenly assailed by an unforeseen adventure, the entire day produced upon him the effect of a dream, and in order to persuade himself that he was not the prey of a nightmare, he had to feel the cold barrels of the steel pistols in his trousers pockets.

It was no longer snowing; the moon disengaged itself more and more clearly from the mist, and its light, mingled with the white reflection of the snow that had fallen, communicated to the chamber a sort of twilight aspect.

There was a light in the Jondrette den. Marius saw the hole in the wall shining with a reddish glow that seemed bloody to him.

It was true that the light could not be produced by a candle. However, there was not a sound in the Jondrette quarters, not a soul was moving there, not a soul speaking, not a breath; the silence was glacial and profound, and had it not been for that light, he might have thought himself next door to a sepulchre.

Marius softly removed his boots and pushed them under his bed.

Several minutes elapsed. Marius heard the lower door turn on its hinges; a heavy step mounted the staircase, and hastened along the corridor; the latch of the hovel was noisily lifted; it was Jondrette returning.

Instantly, several voices arose. The whole family was in the garret. Only, it had been silent in the master's absence, like wolf whelps in the absence of the wolf.

"It's I," said he.

"Good evening, daddy," yelped the girls.

"Well?" said the mother.

"All's going first rate," responded Jondrette, "but my feet are beastly cold. Good! You have dressed up. You have done well! You must inspire confidence."

"All ready to go out."

"Don't forget what I told you. You will do everything sure?"

"Rest easy."

"Because——" said Jondrette. And he left the phrase unfinished.

Marius heard him lay something heavy on the table, probably the chisel he had purchased.

"By the way," said Jondrette, "have you been eating here?"

"Yes," said the mother. "I got three large potatoes and some salt. I took advantage of the fire to cook them."

"Good," returned Jondrette. "Tomorrow I will take you out to dine with me. We will have a duck and fixings. You shall dine like Charles the Tenth; all is going well!"

Then he added, "The mousetrap is open. The cats are there."

He lowered his voice still further, and said, "Put this in the fire."

Marius heard a sound of charcoal being knocked with the tongs or some iron utensil, and Jondrette continued, "Have you greased the hinges of the door so that they will not squeak?"

"Yes," replied the mother.

"What time is it?"

"Nearly six. The half-hour struck from Saint-Medard a while ago."

"The devil!" ejaculated Jondrette; "the children must go and watch. Come you, do you listen here."

A whispering ensued.

Jondrette's voice became audible again, "Has old Bougon left?"

"Yes," said the mother.

"Are you sure that there is no one in our neighbor's room?"

"He has not been in all day, and you know very well that this is his dinner hour."

"You are sure?"

"Sure."

"All the same," said Jondrette, "there's no harm in going to see whether he is there. Here, my girl, take the candle and go there."

Marius fell on his hands and knees and crawled silently under his bed.

Hardly had he concealed himself, when he perceived a light through the crack of his door.

"P'pa," cried a voice, "he is not in here."

He recognized the voice of the eldest daughter.

"Did you go in?" demanded her father.

"No," replied the girl, "but as his key is in the door, he must be out."

The father exclaimed, "Go in, nevertheless."

The door opened, and Marius saw the tall Jondrette come in with a candle in her hand. She was as she had been in the morning, only still more repulsive in this light.

She walked straight up to the bed. Marius endured an indescribable moment of anxiety; but near the bed there was a mirror nailed to the wall, and it was there that she was directing her steps. She raised herself on tiptoe and looked at herself in it. In the neighboring room, the sound of iron articles being moved was audible.

She smoothed her hair with the palm of her hand, and smiled into the mirror, humming with her cracked and sepulchral voice:

> "Our love has lasted a whole week,
> But how short are the instants of happiness!
> To adore each other for eight days was hardly worth the while!
> The time of love should last forever."

In the meantime, Marius trembled. It seemed impossible to him that she should not hear his breathing.

She stepped to the window and looked out with the half-foolish way she had.

"How ugly Paris is when it has put on a white chemise!" said she.

She returned to the mirror and began again to put on airs before it, scrutinizing herself full-face and three-quarters face in turn.

"Well!" cried her father. "What are you about there?"

"I am looking under the bed and the furniture," she replied, continuing to arrange her hair; "there's no one here."

"Booby!" yelled her father. "Come here this minute! And don't waste any time about it!"

"Coming! Coming!" said she. "One has no time for anything in this hovel!"

She hummed, "*Vous me quittez pour aller à la gloire; mon triste cœur suivra partout.*"*

She cast a parting glance in the mirror and went out, shutting the door behind her.

A moment more, and Marius heard the sound of the two young girls' bare feet in the corridor, and Jondrette's voice shouting to them, "Pay strict heed! One on the side of the barrier, the other at the corner of the Rue du Petit-Banquier. Don't lose sight for a moment of the door of this house, and the moment you see anything, rush here on the instant! As hard as you can go!

---

* "You leave me to go to glory; my sad heart will follow you everywhere."

You have a key to get in."

The eldest girl grumbled, "The idea of standing watch in the snow barefoot!"

"Tomorrow you shall have some dainty little green silk boots!" said the father.

They ran downstairs, and a few seconds later the shock of the outer door as it banged to announced that they were outside.

There now remained in the house only Marius, the Jondrettes and probably, also, the mysterious persons of whom Marius had caught a glimpse in the twilight, behind the door of the unused attic.

CHAPTER XVII—THE USE MADE OF MARIUS'S FIVE-FRANC PIECE

Marius decided that the moment had now arrived when he must resume his post at his observatory. In a twinkling, and with the agility of his age, he had reached the hole in the partition.

He looked.

The interior of the Jondrette apartment presented a curious aspect, and Marius found an explanation of the singular light that he had noticed. A candle was burning in a candlestick covered with verdigris, but that was not what really lighted the chamber. The hovel was completely illuminated, as it were, by the reflection from a rather large sheet-iron brazier standing in the fireplace, and filled with burning charcoal, the brazier prepared by the Jondrette woman that morning. The charcoal was glowing hot and the brazier was red; a blue flame flickered over it, and helped him to make out the form of the chisel purchased by Jondrette in the Rue Pierre-Lombard, where it had been thrust into the brazier to heat. In one corner, near the door, and as though prepared for some definite use, two heaps were visible, which appeared to be, the one a heap of old iron, the other a heap of ropes. All this would have caused the mind of a person who knew nothing of what was in preparation, to waver between a very sinister and a very simple idea. The lair thus lighted up more resembled a forge than a mouth of hell, but Jondrette, in this light, had rather the air of a demon than of a smith.

The heat of the brazier was so great, that the candle on the table was melting on the side next the chafing dish, and was drooping over. An old dark lantern of copper, worthy of Diogenes turned Cartouche, stood on the mantel.

The brazier, placed in the fireplace itself, beside the nearly extinct brands, sent its vapors up the chimney, and gave out no odor.

The moon, entering through the four panes of the window, cast its whiteness into the crimson and flaming garret; and to the poetic spirit of Marius, who was dreamy even in the moment of action, it was like a thought of heaven mingled with the misshapen reveries of earth.

A breath of air that made its way in through the open pane, helped to dissipate the smell of the charcoal and to conceal the presence of the brazier.

The Jondrette lair was, if the reader recalls what we have said of the Gorbeau building, admirably chosen to serve as the theater of a violent and somber deed, and as the envelope for a crime. It was the most retired chamber in the most isolated house on the most deserted boulevard in Paris. If the system of ambush and traps had not already existed, they would have been invented there.

The whole thickness of a house and a multitude of uninhabited rooms separated this den from the boulevard, and the only window that existed opened on wastelands enclosed with walls and palisades.

Jondrette had lighted his pipe, seated himself on the seatless chair, and was engaged in smoking. His wife was talking to him in a low tone.

If Marius had been Courfeyrac, that is to say, one of those men who laugh on every occasion in life, he would have burst with laughter when his gaze fell on the Jondrette woman. She had on a black bonnet with plumes not unlike the hats of the heralds-at-arms at the coronation of Charles X, an immense tartan shawl over her knitted petticoat, and the man's shoes that her daughter had scorned in the morning. It was this toilette that had extracted from Jondrette the exclamation: "Good! You have dressed up. You have done well. You must inspire confidence!"

As for Jondrette, he had not taken off the new surtout, which was too large for him, and which M. Leblanc had given him, and his costume continued to present that contrast of coat and trousers that constituted the ideal of a poet in Courfeyrac's eyes.

All at once, Jondrette lifted up his voice, "By the way! Now that I think of it. In this weather, he will come in a carriage. Light the lantern, take it and go downstairs. You will stand behind the lower door. The very moment that you hear the carriage stop, you will open the door, instantly, he will come up, you will light the staircase and the corridor, and when he enters here, you will go downstairs again as speedily as possible, you will pay the coachman, and dismiss the fiacre."

"And the money?" inquired the woman.

Jondrette fumbled in his trousers pocket and handed her five francs.

"What's this?" she exclaimed.

Jondrette replied with dignity, "That is the monarch that our neighbor gave us this morning."

And he added, "Do you know what? Two chairs will be needed here."

"What for?"

"To sit on."

Marius felt a cold chill pass through his limbs at hearing this mild answer from Jondrette.

"Pardieu! I'll go and get one of our neighbor's."

And with a rapid movement, she opened the door of the den, and went out into the corridor.

Marius absolutely had not the time to descend from the commode, reach his bed, and conceal himself beneath it.

"Take the candle," cried Jondrette.

"No," said she, "it would embarrass me, I have the two chairs to carry. There is moonlight."

Marius heard Mother Jondrette's heavy hand fumbling at his lock in the dark. The door opened. He remained nailed to the spot with the shock and with horror.

The Jondrette entered.

The dormer window permitted the entrance of a ray of moonlight between two blocks of shadow. One of these blocks of shadow entirely covered the wall against which Marius was leaning, so that he disappeared within it.

Mother Jondrette raised her eyes, did not see Marius, took the two chairs, the only ones that Marius possessed, and went away, letting the door fall heavily to behind her.

She reentered the lair.

"Here are the two chairs."

"And here is the lantern. Go down as quick as you can."

She hastily obeyed, and Jondrette was left alone.

He placed the two chairs on opposite sides of the table, turned the chisel in the brazier, set in front of the fireplace an old screen that masked the chafing dish, then went to the corner where lay the pile of rope, and bent down as though to examine something. Marius then recognized the fact, that what he had taken for a shapeless mass was a very well-made rope ladder, with wooden rungs and two hooks with which to attach it.

This ladder, and some large tools, veritable masses of iron, which were mingled with the old iron piled up behind the door, had not been in the Jondrette hovel in the morning, and had evidently been brought there in the afternoon, during Marius's absence.

"Those are the utensils of an edge-tool maker," thought Marius.

Had Marius been a little more learned in this line, he would have recognized in what he took for the engines of an edge-tool maker, certain instruments that will force a lock or pick a lock, and others that will cut or slice, the two families of tools that burglars call cadets and *fauchants*.

The fireplace and the two chairs were exactly opposite Marius. The brazier being concealed, the only light in the room was now furnished by the candle; the smallest bit of crockery on the table or on the chimneypiece cast a large shadow. There was something indescribably calm, threatening, and hideous about this chamber. One felt that there existed in it the anticipation of something terrible.

Jondrette had allowed his pipe to go out, a serious sign of preoccupation, and had again seated himself. The candle brought out the fierce and the fine angles of his countenance. He indulged in scowls and in abrupt unfoldings of the right hand, as though he were responding to the last counsels of a somber inward monologue. In the course of one of these dark replies that he was making to himself, he pulled the table drawer rapidly toward him, took out a long kitchen knife that was concealed there, and tried the edge of its blade on his nail. That done, he put the knife back in the drawer and shut it.

Marius, on his side, grasped the pistol in his right pocket, drew it out and cocked it.

The pistol emitted a sharp, clear click, as he cocked it.

Jondrette started, half rose, listened a moment, then began to laugh and said, "What a fool I am! It's the partition cracking!"

Marius kept the pistol in his hand.

CHAPTER XVIII—MARIUS'S TWO CHAIRS FORM A VIS-A-VIS

Suddenly, the distant and melancholy vibration of a clock shook the panes. Six o'clock was striking from Saint-Medard.

Jondrette marked off each stroke with a toss of his head. When the sixth had struck, he snuffed the candle with his fingers.

Then he began to pace up and down the room, listened at the corridor, walked on again, then listened once more.

"Provided only that he comes!" he muttered, then he returned to his chair.

He had hardly reseated himself when the door opened.

Mother Jondrette had opened it, and now remained in the corridor making a horrible, amiable grimace, which one of the holes of the dark lantern illuminated from below.

"Enter, Sir," she said.

"Enter, my benefactor," repeated Jondrette, rising hastily.

M. Leblanc made his appearance.

He wore an air of serenity that rendered him singularly venerable.

He laid four Louis on the table.

"Monsieur Fabantou," said he, "this is for your rent and your most pressing necessities. We will attend to the rest hereafter."

"May God requite it to you, my generous benefactor!" said Jondrette.

And rapidly approaching his wife: "Dismiss the carriage!"

She slipped out while her husband was lavishing salutes and offering M. Leblanc a chair. An instant later she returned and whispered in his ear, "'Tis done."

The snow, which had not ceased falling since the morning, was so deep that the arrival of the fiacre had not been audible, and they did not now hear its departure.

Meanwhile, M. Leblanc had seated himself.

Jondrette had taken possession of the other chair, facing M. Leblanc.

Now, in order to form an idea of the scene that is to follow, let the reader picture to himself in his own mind, a cold night, the solitudes of the Salpetriere covered with snow and white as winding-sheets in the moonlight, the taperlike lights of the street lanterns that shone redly here and there along those tragic boulevards, and the long rows of black elms, not a passerby for perhaps a quarter of a league around, the Gorbeau hovel, at its highest pitch of silence, of horror, and of darkness; in that building, in the midst of those solitudes, in the midst of that darkness, the vast Jondrette garret lighted by a single candle, and in that den two men seated at a table, M. Leblanc tranquil, Jondrette smiling and alarming, the Jondrette woman, the female wolf, in one corner, and, behind the partition, Marius, invisible, erect, not losing a word, not missing a single movement, his eye on the watch, and pistol in hand.

However, Marius experienced only an emotion of horror, but no fear. He clasped the stock of the pistol firmly and felt reassured. "I shall be able to stop that wretch whenever I please," he thought.

He felt that the police were there somewhere in ambuscade, waiting for the signal agreed upon and ready to stretch out their arm.

Moreover, he was in hopes, that this violent encounter between Jondrette and M. Leblanc would cast some light on all the things he was interested in learning.

CHAPTER XIX—OCCUPYING ONE'S SELF WITH OBSCURE DEPTHS

Hardly was M. Leblanc seated, when he turned his eyes toward the pallets, which were empty.

"How is the poor little wounded girl?" he inquired.

"Bad," replied Jondrette with a heartbroken and grateful smile, "very bad, my worthy sir. Her elder sister has taken her to the Bourbe to have her hurt dressed. You will see them presently; they will be back immediately."

"Madame Fabantou seems to me to be better," went on M. Leblanc, casting his eyes on the eccentric costume of the Jondrette woman, as she stood between him and the door, as though already guarding the exit, and gazed at him in an attitude of menace and almost of combat.

"She is dying," said Jondrette. "But what do you expect, Sir! She has so much courage, that woman has! She's not a woman, she's an ox."

The Jondrette, touched by his compliment, deprecated it with the affected airs of a flattered monster.

"You are always too good to me, Monsieur Jondrette!"

"Jondrette!" said M. Leblanc, "I thought your name was Fabantou?"

"Fabantou, alias Jondrette!" replied the husband hurriedly. "An artistic sobriquet!"

And launching at his wife a shrug of the shoulders that M. Leblanc did not catch, he continued with an emphatic and caressing inflection of voice, "Ah! We have had a happy life together, this poor darling and I! What would there be left for us if we had not that? We are so wretched, my respectable sir! We have arms, but there is no work! We have the will, no work! I don't know how the government arranges that, but, on my word of honor, Sir, I am not Jacobin, Sir, I am not a *bousingot*.* I don't wish them any evil, but if I were

---

* a democrat

the ministers, on my most sacred word, things would be different. Here, for instance, I wanted to have my girls taught the trade of paper-box makers. You will say to me, 'What! A trade?' Yes! A trade! A simple trade! A breadwinner! What a fall, my benefactor! What a degradation, when one has been what we have been! Alas! There is nothing left to us of our days of prosperity! One thing only, a picture, of which I think a great deal, but that I am willing to part with, for I must live! Item, one must live!"

While Jondrette thus talked, with an apparent incoherence that detracted nothing from the thoughtful and sagacious expression of his physiognomy, Marius raised his eyes, and perceived at the other end of the room a person whom he had not seen before. A man had just entered, so softly that the door had not been heard to turn on its hinges. This man wore a violet knitted vest, which was old, worn, spotted, cut and gaping at every fold, wide trousers of cotton velvet, wooden shoes on his feet, no shirt, had his neck bare, his bare arms tattooed, and his face smeared with black. He had seated himself in silence on the nearest bed, and, as he was behind Jondrette, he could only be indistinctly seen.

That sort of magnetic instinct that turns aside the gaze, caused M. Leblanc to turn around almost at the same moment as Marius. He could not refrain from a gesture of surprise that did not escape Jondrette.

"Ah! I see!" exclaimed Jondrette, buttoning up his coat with an air of complaisance. "You are looking at your overcoat? It fits me! My faith, but it fits me!"

"Who is that man?" said M. Leblanc.

"Him?" ejaculated Jondrette. "He's a neighbor of mine. Don't pay any attention to him."

The neighbor was a singular-looking individual. However, manufactories of chemical products abound in the Faubourg Saint-Marceau. Many of the workmen might have black faces. Besides this, M. Leblanc's whole person was expressive of candid and intrepid confidence.

He went on, "Excuse me; what were you saying, M. Fabantou?"

"I was telling you, Sir, and dear protector," replied Jondrette placing his elbows on the table and contemplating M. Leblanc with steady and tender eyes, not unlike the eyes of the boa constrictor, "I was telling you, that I have a picture to sell."

A slight sound came from the door. A second man had just entered and seated himself on the bed, behind Jondrette.

Like the first, his arms were bare, and he had a mask of ink or lampblack.

Although this man had, literally, glided into the room, he had not been able to prevent M. Leblanc catching sight of him.

"Don't mind them," said Jondrette, "they are people who belong in the house. So I was saying, that there remains in my possession a valuable picture. But stop, Sir, take a look at it."

He rose, went to the wall at the foot of which stood the panel that we have already mentioned, and turned it around, still leaving it supported against the wall. It really was something that resembled a picture, and that the candle illuminated, somewhat. Marius could make nothing out of it, as Jondrette stood between the picture and him; he only saw a coarse daub, and a sort of principal personage colored with the harsh crudity of foreign canvasses and screen paintings.

"What is that?" asked M. Leblanc.

Jondrette exclaimed, "A painting by a master, a picture of great value, my benefactor! I am as much attached to it as I am to my two daughters; it recalls souvenirs to me! But I have told you, and I will not take it back, that I am so wretched that I will part with it."

Either by chance, or because he had begun to feel a dawning uneasiness, M. Leblanc's glance returned to the bottom of the room as he examined the picture.

There were now four men, three seated on the bed, one standing near the doorpost, all four with bare arms and motionless, with faces smeared with black. One of those on the bed was leaning against the wall, with closed eyes, and it might have been supposed that he was asleep. He was old; his white hair contrasting with his blackened face produced a horrible effect. The other two seemed to be young; one wore a beard, the other wore his hair long. None of them had on shoes; those who did not wear socks were barefooted.

Jondrette noticed that M. Leblanc's eye was fixed on these men.

"They are friends. They are neighbors," said he. "Their faces are black because they work in charcoal. They are chimney builders. Don't trouble yourself about them, my benefactor, but buy my picture. Have pity on my misery. I will not ask you much for it. How much do you think it is worth?"

"Well," said M. Leblanc, looking Jondrette full in the eye, and with the manner of a man who is on his guard, "it is some signboard for a tavern, and is worth about three francs."

Jondrette replied sweetly, "Have you your pocketbook with you? I should be satisfied with a thousand crowns."

M. Leblanc sprang up, placed his back against the wall, and cast a rapid glance around the room. He had Jondrette on his left, on the side next the window, and the Jondrette woman and the four men on his right, on the side next the door. The four men did not stir, and did not even seem to be looking on.

Jondrette had again begun to speak in a plaintive tone, with so vague an eye, and so lamentable an intonation, that M. Leblanc might have supposed that what he had before him was a man who had simply gone mad with misery.

"If you do not buy my picture, my dear benefactor," said Jondrette, "I shall be left without resources; there will be nothing left for me but to throw myself into the river. When I think that I wanted to have my two girls taught the middle-class paper-box trade, the making of boxes for New Year's gifts! Well! A table with a board at the end to keep the glasses from falling off is required, then a special stove is needed, a pot with three compartments for the different degrees of strength of the paste, according as it is to be used for wood, paper, or stuff, a paring knife to cut the cardboard, a mold to adjust it, a hammer to nail the steels, pincers, how the devil do I know what all? And all that in order to earn four sous a day! And you have to work fourteen hours a day! And each box passes through the workwoman's hands thirteen times! And you can't wet the paper! And you mustn't spot anything! And you must keep the paste hot. The devil, I tell you! Four sous a day! How do you suppose a man is to live?"

As he spoke, Jondrette did not look at M. Leblanc, who was observing him. M. Leblanc's eye was fixed on Jondrette, and Jondrette's eye was fixed on the door. Marius's eager attention was transferred from one to the other. M. Leblanc seemed to be asking himself, "Is this man an idiot?" Jondrette repeated two or three distinct times, with all manner of varying inflections of the whining and supplicating order, "There is nothing left for me but to throw myself into the river! I went down three steps at the side of the bridge of Austerlitz the other day for that purpose."

All at once his dull eyes lighted up with a hideous flash; the little man drew himself up and became terrible, took a step toward M. Leblanc and cried in a voice of thunder, "That has nothing to do with the question! Do you know me?"

CHAPTER XX—THE TRAP

The door of the garret had just opened abruptly, and allowed a view of three men clad in blue linen blouses, and masked with masks of black paper. The first was thin, and had a long, iron-tipped cudgel; the second, who was a sort of colossus, carried, by the middle of the handle, with the blade downward, a butcher's poleax for slaughtering cattle. The third, a man with thick-set shoulders, not so slender as the first, held in his hand an enormous key stolen from the door of some prison.

It appeared that the arrival of these men was what Jondrette had been waiting for. A rapid dialogue ensued between him and the man with the cudgel, the thin one.

"Is everything ready?" said Jondrette.

"Yes," replied the thin man.

"Where is Montparnasse?"

"The young principal actor stopped to chat with your girl."

"Which?"

"The eldest."

"Is there a carriage at the door?"

"Yes."

"Is the team harnessed?"

"Yes."

"With two good horses?"

"Excellent."

"Is it waiting where I ordered?"

"Yes."

"Good," said Jondrette.

M. Leblanc was very pale. He was scrutinizing everything around him in the den, like a man who understands what he has fallen into, and his head, directed in turn toward all the heads that surrounded him, moved on his neck with an astonished and attentive slowness, but there was nothing in his air that resembled fear. He had improvised an entrenchment out of the table; and the man, who but an instant previously, had borne merely the appearance of a kindly old man, had suddenly become a sort of athlete, and placed his robust fist on the back of his chair, with a formidable and surprising gesture.

This old man, who was so firm and so brave in the presence of such a danger, seemed to possess one of those natures that are as courageous as they are kind, both easily and simply. The father of a woman whom we love is never a stranger to us. Marius felt proud of that unknown man.

Three of the men, of whom Jondrette had said, "They are chimney builders," had armed themselves from the pile of old iron, one with a heavy pair of shears, the second with weighing-tongs, the third with a hammer, and had placed themselves across the entrance without uttering a syllable. The old man had remained on the bed, and had merely opened his eyes. The Jondrette woman had seated herself beside him.

Marius decided that in a few seconds more the moment for intervention would arrive, and he raised his right hand toward the ceiling, in the direction of the corridor, in readiness to discharge his pistol.

Jondrette having terminated his colloquy with the man with the cudgel, turned once more to M. Leblanc, and repeated his question, accompanying it with that low, repressed, and terrible laugh that was peculiar to him, "So you do not recognize me?"

M. Leblanc looked him full in the face, and replied, "No."

Then Jondrette advanced to the table. He leaned across the candle, crossing his arms, putting his angular and ferocious jaw close to M. Leblanc's calm face, and advancing as far as possible without forcing M. Leblanc to retreat, and, in this posture of a wild beast who is about to bite, he exclaimed, "My name is not Fabantou, my name is not Jondrette, my name is Thenardier. I am the innkeeper of Montfermeil! Do you understand? Thenardier! Now do you know me?"

An almost imperceptible flush crossed M. Leblanc's brow, and he replied with a voice that neither trembled nor rose above its ordinary level, with his accustomed placidity, "No more than before."

Marius did not hear this reply. Anyone who had seen him at that moment through the darkness would have perceived that he was haggard, stupid, thunder-struck. At the moment when Jondrette said, "My name is Thenardier," Marius had trembled in every limb, and had leaned against the wall, as though he felt the cold of a steel blade through his heart. Then his right arm, all ready to discharge the signal shot, dropped slowly, and at the moment when Jondrette repeated, "Thenardier, do you understand?" Marius's faltering fingers had come near letting the pistol fall. Jondrette, by revealing his identity, had not moved M. Leblanc, but he had quite upset Marius. That name of Thenardier, with which M. Leblanc did not seem to be acquainted, Marius knew well. Let the reader recall what that name meant to him! That name he had worn on his heart, inscribed in his father's testament! He bore it at the bottom of his mind, in the depths of his memory, in that sacred injunction, "A certain Thenardier saved my life. If my son encounters him, he will do him all the good that lies in his power." That name, it will be remembered, was one of the pieties of his soul; he mingled it with the name of his father in his worship. What! This man was that Thenardier, that innkeeper of Montfermeil whom he had so long and so vainly sought! He had found him at last, and how? His father's savior was a ruffian! That man, to whose service Marius was burning to devote himself, was a monster! That liberator of Colonel Pontmercy was on the point of committing a crime whose scope Marius did not, as yet, clearly comprehend, but that resembled an assassination! And against whom, great God! What a fatality! What a bitter mockery of fate! His father had commanded him from the depths of his coffin to do all the good in his power to this Thenardier, and for four years Marius had cherished no other thought than to acquit this debt of his father's, and at the moment when he was on the eve of having a brigand seized in the very act of crime by justice, destiny cried to him, "This is Thenardier!" He could at last repay this man for his father's life, saved amid a hailstorm of grapeshot on the heroic field of Waterloo, and repay it with the scaffold! He had sworn to himself that if ever he found that Thenardier, he would address him only by throwing himself at his feet; and now he actually had found him, but it was only to deliver him over to the executioner! His father said to him, "Succor Thenardier!" And he replied to that adored and sainted voice by crushing Thenardier! He was about to offer to his father in his grave the spectacle of that man who had torn him from death at the peril of his own life, executed on the Place Saint-Jacques through the means of his son, of that Marius to whom he had entrusted that man by his will! And what a mockery to have so long worn on his breast his father's last commands, written in his own hand, only to act in so horribly contrary a sense! But, on the other hand, now look on that trap and not prevent it! Condemn the victim and to spare the assassin! Could one be held to any gratitude toward so miserable a wretch? All the ideas that Marius had cherished for the last four years were pierced through and through, as it were, by this unforeseen blow.

He shuddered. Everything depended on him. Unknown to themselves, he held in his hand all those beings who were moving about there before his eyes. If he fired his pistol, M. Leblanc was saved, and Thenardier lost; if he did not fire, M. Leblanc would be sacrificed, and, who knows? Thenardier would escape. Should he dash down the one or allow the other to fall? Remorse awaited him in either case.

What was he to do? What should he choose? Be false to the most imperious souvenirs, to all those solemn vows to himself, to the most sacred duty, to the most venerated text! Should he ignore his father's testament, or allow the perpetration of a crime! On the one hand, it seemed to him that he heard "his Ursule" supplicating for her father and on the other, the colonel commending Thenardier to his care. He felt that he was going mad. His knees gave way beneath him. And he had not even the time for deliberation, so great was the fury with which the scene before his eyes was hastening to its catastrophe. It was like a whirlwind of which he had thought himself the master, and that was now sweeping him away. He was on the verge of swooning.

In the meantime, Thenardier, whom we shall henceforth call by no other name, was pacing up and down in front of the table in a sort of frenzy and wild triumph.

He seized the candle in his fist, and set it on the mantel with so violent a bang that the wick came near being extinguished, and the tallow bespattered the wall.

Then he turned to M. Leblanc with a horrible look, and spit out these words, "Done for! Smoked brown! Cooked! Spatchcocked!"

And again he began to march back and forth, in full eruption.

"Ah!" he cried. "So I've found you again at last, Mister philanthropist! Mister threadbare millionaire! Mister giver of dolls! You old ninny! Ah! So you don't recognize me! No, it wasn't you who came to Montfermeil, to my inn, eight years ago, on Christmas Eve, 1823! It wasn't you who carried off that Fantine's child from me! The Lark! It wasn't you who had a yellow greatcoat! No! Nor a package of duds in your hand, as you had this morning here! Say, wife, it seems to be his mania to carry packets of woolen stockings into houses! Old charity monger, get out with you! Are you a hosier, Mister millionaire? You give away your stock in trade to the poor, holy man! What bosh! Merry Andrew! Ah! And you don't recognize me? Well, I recognize you, that I do! I recognized you the very moment you poked your snout in here. Ah! You'll find out presently, that it isn't all roses to thrust yourself in that fashion into people's houses, under the pretext that they are taverns, in wretched clothes, with the air of a poor man, to whom one would give a sou, to deceive persons, to play the generous, to take away their means of livelihood, and to make threats in the woods, and you can't call things quits because afterward, when people are ruined, you bring a coat that is too large, and two miserable hospital blankets, you old blackguard, you child-stealer!"

He paused, and seemed to be talking to himself for a moment. One would have said that his wrath had fallen into some hole, like the Rhone; then, as though he were concluding aloud the things that he had been saying to himself in a whisper, he smote the table with his fist, and shouted, "And with his goody-goody air!"

And, apostrophizing M. Leblanc, "Parbleu! You made game of me in the past! You are the cause of all my misfortunes! For fifteen hundred francs you got a girl whom I had, and who certainly belonged to rich people, and who had already brought in a great deal of money, and from whom I might have extracted enough to live on all my life! A girl who would have made up to me for everything that I lost in that vile cookshop, where there was nothing but one continual row, and where, like a fool, I ate up my last farthing! Oh! I wish all the wine folks drank in my house had been poison to those who drank it! Well, never mind! Say, now! You must have thought me ridiculous when you went off with the Lark! You had your cudgel in the forest. You were the stronger. Revenge. I'm the one to hold the trumps today! You're in a sorry case, my good fellow! Oh, but I can laugh! Really, I laugh! Didn't he fall into the trap! I told him that I was an actor, that my name was Fabantou, that I had played comedy with Mamselle Mars, with Mamselle Muche, that my landlord insisted on being paid tomorrow, the 4th of February, and he didn't even notice that the 8th of January, and not the 4th of February is the time when the quarter runs out! Absurd idiot! And the four miserable Philippes that he has brought me! Scoundrel! He hadn't the heart even to go as high as a hundred francs! And how he swallowed my platitudes! That did amuse me. I said to myself, 'Blockhead! Come, I've got you! I lick your paws this morning, but I'll gnaw your heart this evening!'"

Thenardier paused. He was out of breath. His little, narrow chest panted like a forge bellows. His eyes were full of the ignoble happiness of a feeble, cruel, and cowardly creature that finds that it can, at last, harass what it has feared, and insult what it has flattered, the joy of a dwarf who should be able to set his heel on the head of Goliath, the joy of a jackal that is beginning to rend a sick bull, so nearly dead that he can no longer defend himself, but sufficiently alive to suffer still.

M. Leblanc did not interrupt him, but said to him when he paused, "I do not know what you mean to say. You are mistaken in me. I am a very poor man, and anything but a millionaire. I do not know you. You are mistaking me for some other person."

"Ah!" roared Thenardier hoarsely. "A pretty lie! You stick to that pleasantry, do you! You're floundering, my old buck! Ah! You don't remember! You don't see who I am?"

"Excuse me, Sir," said M. Leblanc with a politeness of accent, which at that moment seemed peculiarly strange and powerful, "I see that you are a villain!"

Who has not remarked the fact that odious creatures possess a susceptibility of their own, that monsters are ticklish! At this word "villain," the female Thenardier sprang from the bed, Thenardier grasped his chair as though he were about to crush it in his hands. "Don't you stir!" he shouted to his wife;

and, turning to M. Leblanc, "Villain! Yes, I know that you call us that, you rich gentlemen! Stop! It's true that I became bankrupt, that I am in hiding, that I have no bread, that I have not a single sou, that I am a villain! It's three days since I have had anything to eat, so I'm a villain! Ah! You folks warm your feet, you have Sakoski boots, you have wadded great-coats, like archbishops, you lodge on the first floor in houses that have porters, you eat truffles, you eat asparagus at forty francs the bunch in the month of January, and green peas, you gorge yourselves, and when you want to know whether it is cold, you look in the papers to see what the engineer Chevalier's thermometer says about it. We, it is we who are thermometers. We don't need to go out and look on the quay at the corner of the Tour de l'Horologe, to find out the number of degrees of cold; we feel our blood congealing in our veins, and the ice forming around our hearts, and we say, 'There is no God!' And you come to our caverns, yes our caverns, for the purpose of calling us villains! But we'll devour you! But we'll devour you, poor little things! Just see here, Mister millionaire: I have been a solid man, I have held a license, I have been an elector, I am a bourgeois, that I am! And it's quite possible that you are not!"

Here Thenardier took a step toward the men who stood near the door, and added with a shudder, "When I think that he has dared to come here and talk to me like a cobbler!"

Then addressing M. Leblanc with a fresh outburst of frenzy, "And listen to this also, Mister philanthropist! I'm not a suspicious character, not a bit of it! I'm not a man whose name nobody knows, and who comes and abducts children from houses! I'm an old French soldier, I ought to have been decorated! I was at Waterloo, so I was! And in the battle I saved a general called the Comte of I don't know what. He told me his name, but his beastly voice was so weak that I didn't hear. All I caught was 'Merci' [thanks]. I'd rather have had his name than his thanks. That would have helped me to find him again. The picture that you see here, which was painted by David at Bruqueselles, do you know what it represents? It represents me. David wished to immortalize that feat of prowess. I have that general on my back, and I am carrying him through the grapeshot. There's the history of it! That general never did a single thing for me; he was no better than the rest! But nonetheless, I saved his life at the risk of my own, and I have the certificate of the fact in my pocket! I am a soldier of Waterloo, by all the furies! And now that I have had the goodness to tell you all this, let's have an end of it. I want money, I want a deal of money, I must have an enormous lot of money, or I'll exterminate you, by the thunder of the good God!"

Marius had regained some measure of control over his anguish, and was listening. The last possibility of doubt had just vanished. It certainly was the Thenardier of the will. Marius shuddered at that reproach of ingratitude directed against his father, and that he was on the point of so fatally justifying. His perplexity was redoubled.

Moreover, there was in all these words of Thenardier, in his accent, in his gesture, in his glance that darted flames at every word, there was, in this explosion of an evil nature disclosing everything, in that mixture of braggadocio and abjectness, of pride and pettiness, of rage and folly, in that chaos of real griefs and false sentiments, in that immodesty of a malicious man tasting the voluptuous delights of violence, in that shameless nudity of a repulsive soul, in that conflagration of all sufferings combined with all hatreds, something that was as hideous as evil, and as heart-rending as the truth.

The picture of the master, the painting by David that he had proposed that M. Leblanc should purchase, was nothing else, as the reader has divined, than the sign of his tavern painted, as it will be remembered, by himself, the only relic that he had preserved from his shipwreck at Montfermeil.

As he had ceased to intercept Marius's visual ray, Marius could examine this thing, and in the daub, he actually did recognize a battle, a background of smoke, and a man carrying another man. It was the group composed of Pontmercy and Thenardier; the sergeant the rescuer, the colonel rescued. Marius was like a drunken man; this picture restored his father to life in some sort; it was no longer the signboard of the wine shop at Montfermeil, it was a resurrection; a tomb had yawned, a phantom had risen there. Marius heard his heart beating in his temples, he had the cannon of Waterloo in his ears, his bleeding father, vaguely depicted on that sinister panel terrified him, and it seemed to him that the misshapen specter was gazing intently at him.

When Thenardier had recovered his breath, he turned his bloodshot eyes on M. Leblanc, and said to him in a low, curt voice, "What have you to say before we put the handcuffs on you?"

M. Leblanc held his peace.

In the midst of this silence, a cracked voice launched this lugubrious sarcasm from the corridor, "If there's any wood to be split, I'm there!"

It was the man with the ax, who was growing merry.

At the same moment, an enormous, bristling, and clayey face made its appearance at the door, with a hideous laugh that exhibited not teeth, but fangs.

It was the face of the man with the butcher's ax.

"Why have you taken off your mask?" cried Thenardier in a rage.

"For fun," retorted the man.

For the last few minutes M. Leblanc had appeared to be watching and following all the movements of Thenardier, who, blinded and dazzled by his own rage, was stalking to and fro in the den with full confidence that the door was guarded, and of holding an unarmed man fast, he being armed himself, of being nine against one, supposing that the female Thenardier counted for but one man.

During his address to the man with the poleax, he had turned his back to M. Leblanc.

M. Leblanc seized this moment, overturned the chair with his foot and the table with his fist, and with one bound, with prodigious agility, before Thenardier had time to turn around, he had reached the window. To open it, to scale the frame, to bestride it, was the work of a second only. He was half out when six robust fists seized him and dragged him back energetically into the hovel. These were the three "chimney builders," who had flung themselves upon him. At the same time the Thenardier woman had wound her hands in his hair.

At the trampling that ensued, the other ruffians rushed up from the corridor. The old man on the bed, who seemed under the influence of wine, descended from the pallet and came reeling up, with a stone-breaker's hammer in his hand.

One of the "chimney builders," whose smirched face was lighted up by the candle, and in whom Marius recognized, in spite of his daubing, Panchaud, alias Printanier, alias Bigrenaille, lifted above M. Leblanc's head a sort of bludgeon made of two balls of lead, at the two ends of a bar of iron.

Marius could not resist this sight. "My father," he thought, "forgive me!"

And his finger sought the trigger of his pistol.

The shot was on the point of being discharged when Thenardier's voice shouted, "Don't harm him!"

This desperate attempt of the victim, far from exasperating Thenardier, had calmed him. There existed in him two men, the ferocious man and the adroit man. Up to that moment, in the excess of his triumph in the presence of the prey, which had been brought down, and which did not stir, the ferocious man had prevailed; when the victim struggled and tried to resist, the adroit man reappeared and took the upper hand.

"Don't hurt him!" he repeated, and without suspecting it, his first success was to arrest the pistol in the act of being discharged, and to paralyze Marius, in whose opinion the urgency of the case disappeared, and who, in the face of this new phase, saw no inconvenience in waiting a while longer.

Who knows whether some chance would not arise that would deliver him from the horrible alternative of allowing Ursule's father to perish, or of destroying the colonel's savior?

A Herculean struggle had begun. With one blow full in the chest, M. Leblanc had sent the old man tumbling, rolling in the middle of the room, then with two backward sweeps of his hand he had overthrown two more assailants, and he held one under each of his knees; the wretches were rattling in the throat beneath this pressure as under a granite millstone; but the other four had seized the formidable old man by both arms and the back of his neck, and were holding him doubled up over the two "chimney builders" on the floor.

Thus, the master of some and mastered by the rest, crushing those beneath him and stifling under those on top of him, endeavoring in vain to shake off all the efforts that were heaped upon him, M. Leblanc disappeared under the horrible group of ruffians like the wild boar beneath a howling pile of dogs and hounds.

They succeeded in overthrowing him upon the bed nearest the window, and there they held him in awe. The Thenardier woman had not released her clutch on his hair.

"Don't you mix yourself up in this affair," said Thenardier. "You'll tear your shawl."

The Thenardier obeyed, as the female wolf obeys the male wolf, with a growl.

"Now," said Thenardier, "search him, you other fellows!"

M. Leblanc seemed to have renounced the idea of resistance.

They searched him.

He had nothing on his person except a leather purse containing six francs, and his handkerchief.

Thenardier put the handkerchief into his own pocket.

"What! No pocketbook?" he demanded.

"No, nor watch," replied one of the "chimney builders."

"Never mind," murmured the masked man who carried the big key, in the voice of a ventriloquist, "he's a tough old fellow."

Thenardier went to the corner near the door, picked up a bundle of ropes, and threw them at the men.

"Tie him to the leg of the bed," said he.

And, catching sight of the old man who had been stretched across the room by the blow from M. Leblanc's fist, and who made no movement, he added, "Is Boulatruelle dead?"

"No," replied Bigrenaille, "he's drunk."

"Sweep him into a corner," said Thenardier.

Two of the "chimney builders" pushed the drunken man into the corner near the heap of old iron with their feet.

"Babet," said Thenardier in a low tone to the man with the cudgel, "why did you bring so many; they were not needed."

"What can you do?" replied the man with the cudgel. "They all wanted to be in it. This is a bad season. There's no business going on."

The pallet on which M. Leblanc had been thrown was a sort of hospital bed, elevated on four coarse wooden legs, roughly hewn.

M. Leblanc let them take their own course.

The ruffians bound him securely, in an upright attitude, with his feet on the ground at the head of the bed, the end that was most remote from the window, and nearest to the fireplace.

When the last knot had been tied, Thenardier took a chair and seated himself almost facing M. Leblanc.

Thenardier no longer looked like himself; in the course of a few moments his face had passed from unbridled violence to tranquil and cunning sweetness.

Marius found it difficult to recognize in that polished smile of a man in official life the almost bestial mouth that had been foaming but a moment before; he gazed with amazement on that fantastic and alarming metamorphosis, and he felt as a man might feel who should behold a tiger converted into a lawyer.

"Monsieur—" said Thenardier.

And dismissing with a gesture the ruffians who still kept their hands on M. Leblanc, "Stand off a little, and let me have a talk with the gentleman."

All retired toward the door.

He went on, "Monsieur, you did wrong to try to jump out of the window. You might have broken your leg. Now, if you will permit me, we will converse quietly. In the first place, I must communicate to you an observation that I have made, which is, that you have not uttered the faintest cry."

Thenardier was right, this detail was correct, although it had escaped Marius in his agitation. M. Leblanc had barely pronounced a few words, without raising his voice, and even during his struggle with the six ruffians near the window he had preserved the most profound and singular silence.

Thenardier continued, "*Mon Dieu!* You might have shouted 'stop thief' a bit, and I should not have thought it improper. 'Murder!' That, too, is said occasionally, and, so far as I am concerned, I should not have taken it in bad part. It is very natural that you should make a little row when you find yourself with persons who don't inspire you with sufficient confidence. You might have done that, and no one would have troubled you on that account. You would not even have been gagged. And I will tell you why. This room is very private. That's its only recommendation, but it has that in its favor. You might fire off a mortar and it would produce about as much noise at the nearest police station as the snores of a drunken man. Here a cannon would make a boom, and the thunder would make a poof. It's a handy lodging. But, in short, you did not shout, and it is better so. I present you my compliments, and I will tell you the conclusion that I draw from that fact: My dear sir, when a man shouts, who comes? The police. And after the police? Justice. Well! You have not made an outcry; that is because you don't care to have the police and the courts come in any more than we do. It is because, I have long suspected it, you have some interest in hiding something. On our side we have the same interest. So we can come to an understanding."

As he spoke thus, it seemed as though Thenardier, who kept his eyes fixed on M. Leblanc, were trying to plunge the sharp points that darted from the pupils into the very conscience of his prisoner. Moreover, his language, which was stamped with a sort of moderated, subdued insolence and crafty insolence, was reserved and almost choice, and in that rascal, who had been nothing but a robber a short time previously, one now felt "the man who had studied for the priesthood."

The silence preserved by the prisoner, that precaution that had been carried to the point of forgetting all anxiety for his own life, that resistance opposed to the first impulse of nature, which is to utter a cry, all this, it must be confessed, now that his attention had been called to it, troubled Marius, and affected him with painful astonishment.

Thenardier's well-grounded observation still further obscured for Marius the dense mystery that enveloped that grave and singular person on whom Courfeyrac had bestowed the sobriquet of Monsieur Leblanc.

But whoever he was, bound with ropes, surrounded with executioners, half plunged, so to speak, in a grave that was closing in upon him to the extent of a degree with every moment that passed, in the presence of Thenardier's wrath, as in the presence of his sweetness, this man remained impassive; and Marius could not refrain from admiring at such a moment the superbly melancholy visage.

Here, evidently, was a soul that was inaccessible to terror, and that did not know the meaning of despair. Here was one of those men who command amazement in desperate circumstances. Extreme as was the crisis, inevitable as was the catastrophe, there was nothing here of the agony of the drowning man, who opens his horror-filled eyes under the water.

Thenardier rose in an unpretending manner, went to the fireplace, shoved aside the screen, which he leaned against the neighboring pallet, and thus unmasked the brazier full of glowing coals, in which the prisoner could plainly see the chisel white-hot and spotted here and there with tiny scarlet stars.

Then Thenardier returned to his seat beside M. Leblanc.

"I continue," said he. "We can come to an understanding. Let us arrange this matter in an amicable way. I was wrong to lose my temper just now, I don't know what I was thinking of, I went a great deal too far, I said extravagant things. For example, because you are a millionaire, I told you that I exacted money, a lot of money, a deal of money. That would not be reasonable. Mon Dieu, in spite of your riches, you have expenses of your own—who has not? I don't want to ruin you, I am not a greedy fellow, after all. I am not one of those people who, because they have the advantage of the position, profit by the fact to make themselves ridiculous. Why, I'm taking things into consideration and making a sacrifice on my side. I only want two hundred thousand francs."

M. Leblanc uttered not a word.

Thenardier went on, "You see that I put not a little water in my wine; I'm very moderate. I don't know the state of your fortune, but I do know that you don't stick at money, and a benevolent man like yourself can certainly give two hundred thousand francs to the father of a family who is out of luck. Certainly, you are reasonable, too; you haven't imagined that I should take all the trouble I have today and organized this affair this evening, which has been labor well bestowed, in the opinion of these gentlemen, merely to wind up by asking you for enough to go and drink red wine at fifteen sous and eat veal at Desnoyer's. Two hundred thousand francs—it's surely worth all that. This trifle once out of your pocket, I guarantee you that that's the end of the matter, and that you have no further demands to fear. You will say to me, 'But I haven't two hundred thousand francs about me.' Oh! I'm not extortionate. I don't demand that. I only ask one thing of you. Have the goodness to write what I am about to dictate to you."

Here Thenardier paused; then he added, emphasizing his words, and casting a smile in the direction of the brazier, "I warn you that I shall not admit that you don't know how to write."

A grand inquisitor might have envied that smile.

Thenardier pushed the table close to M. Leblanc, and took an inkstand, a pen, and a sheet of paper from the drawer that he left half open, and in which gleamed the long blade of the knife.

He placed the sheet of paper before M. Leblanc.

"Write," said he.

The prisoner spoke at last.

"How do you expect me to write? I am bound."

"That's true, excuse me!" ejaculated Thenardier. "You are quite right."

And turning to Bigrenaille, "Untie the gentleman's right arm."

Panchaud, alias Printanier, alias Bigrenaille, executed Thenardier's order.

When the prisoner's right arm was free, Thenardier dipped the pen in the ink and presented it to him.

"Understand thoroughly, Sir, that you are in our power, at our discretion, that no human power can get you out of this, and that we shall be really grieved if we are forced to proceed to disagreeable extremities. I know neither your name, nor your address, but I warn you, that you will remain bound until the person charged with carrying the letter that you are about to write shall have returned. Now, be so good as to write."

"What?" demanded the prisoner.

"I will dictate."

M. Leblanc took the pen.

Thenardier began to dictate:

"My daughter—"

The prisoner shuddered, and raised his eyes to Thenardier.

"Put down 'My dear daughter—'" said Thenardier.

M. Leblanc obeyed.

Thenardier continued, "Come instantly—" He paused. "You address her as thou, do you not?"

"Who?" asked M. Leblanc.

"Parbleu!" cried Thenardier. "The little one, the Lark."

M. Leblanc replied without the slightest apparent emotion, "I do not know what you mean."

"Go on, nevertheless," ejaculated Thenardier, and he continued to dictate: "Come immediately, I am in absolute need of thee. The person who will deliver this note to thee is instructed to conduct thee to me. I am waiting for thee. Come with confidence."

M. Leblanc had written the whole of this.

Thenardier resumed, "Ah! erase 'come with confidence;' that might lead her to suppose that everything was not as it should be, and that distrust is possible."

M. Leblanc erased the three words.

"Now," pursued Thenardier, "sign it. What's your name?"

The prisoner laid down the pen and demanded, "For whom is this letter?"

"You know well," retorted Thenardier, "for the little one I just told you so."

It was evident that Thenardier avoided naming the young girl in question. He said "the Lark," he said "the little one," but he did not pronounce her name—the precaution of a clever man guarding his secret from his accomplices. To mention the name was to deliver the whole "affair" into their hands, and to tell them more about it than there was any need of their knowing.

He went on, "Sign. What is your name?"

"Urbain Fabre," said the prisoner.

Thenardier, with the movement of a cat, dashed his hand into his pocket and drew out the handkerchief that had been seized on M. Leblanc. He looked for the mark on it, and held it close to the candle.

"U. F. That's it. Urbain Fabre. Well, sign it U. F."

The prisoner signed.

"As two hands are required to fold the letter, give it to me, I will fold it."

That done, Thenardier resumed, "Address it, 'Mademoiselle Fabre,' at your house. I know that you live a long distance from here, near Saint-Jacquesdu-Haut-Pas, because you go to Mass there every day, but I don't know in what street. I see that you understand your situation. As you have not lied about your name, you will not lie about your address. Write it yourself."

The prisoner paused thoughtfully for a moment, then he took the pen and wrote, "Mademoiselle Fabre, at M. Urbain Fabre's, Rue Saint-Dominique-D'Enfer, No. 17."

Thenardier seized the letter with a sort of feverish convulsion.

"Wife!" he cried.

The Thenardier woman hastened to him.

"Here's the letter. You know what you have to do. There is a carriage at the door. Set out at once, and return ditto."

And addressing the man with the meat-ax, "Since you have taken off your nose-screen, accompany the mistress. You will get up behind the fiacre. You know where you left the team?"

"Yes," said the man.

And depositing his ax in a corner, he followed Madame Thenardier.

As they set off, Thenardier thrust his head through the half-open door, and shouted into the corridor, "Above all things, don't lose the letter! Remember that you carry 200,000 francs with you!"

The Thenardier's hoarse voice replied, "Be easy. I have it in my bosom."

A minute had not elapsed, when the sound of the cracking of a whip was heard, which rapidly retreated and died away.

"Good!" growled Thenardier. "They're going at a fine pace. At such a gallop, the bourgeoise will be back inside three-quarters of an hour."

He drew a chair close to the fireplace, folding his arms, and presenting his muddy boots to the brazier.

"My feet are cold!" said he.

Only five ruffians now remained in the den with Thenardier and the prisoner.

These men, through the black masks or paste that covered their faces, and made of them, at fear's pleasure, charcoal-burners, Negroes, or demons, had a stupid and gloomy air, and it could be felt that they perpetrated a crime like a bit of work, tranquilly, without either wrath or mercy, with a sort of ennui. They were crowded together in one corner like brutes, and remained silent.

Thenardier warmed his feet.

The prisoner had relapsed into his taciturnity. A somber calm had succeeded to the wild uproar that had filled the garret but a few moments before.

The candle, on which a large "stranger" had formed, cast but a dim light in the immense hovel, the brazier had grown dull, and all those monstrous heads cast misshapen shadows on the walls and ceiling.

No sound was audible except the quiet breathing of the old drunken man, who was fast asleep.

Marius waited in a state of anxiety that was augmented by every trifle. The enigma was more impenetrable than ever.

Who was this "little one" whom Thenardier had called the Lark? Was she his "Ursule"? The prisoner had not seemed to be affected by that word, "the Lark," and had replied in the most natural manner in the world, "I do not know what you mean." On the other hand, the two letters U. F. were explained; they meant Urbain Fabre; and Ursule was no longer named Ursule. This was what Marius perceived most clearly of all.

A sort of horrible fascination held him nailed to his post, from which he was observing and commanding this whole scene. There he stood, almost incapable of movement or reflection, as though annihilated by the abominable things viewed at such close quarters. He waited, in the hope of some incident, no matter of what nature, since he could not collect his thoughts and did not know upon what course to decide.

"In any case," he said, "if she is the Lark, I shall see her, for the Thenardier woman is to bring her here. That will be the end, and then I will give my life and my blood if necessary, but I will deliver her! Nothing shall stop me."

Nearly half an hour passed in this manner. Thenardier seemed to be absorbed in gloomy reflections, the prisoner did not stir. Still, Marius fancied that at intervals, and for the last few moments, he had heard a faint, dull noise in the direction of the prisoner.

All at once, Thenardier addressed the prisoner, "By the way, Monsieur Fabre, I might as well say it to you at once."

These few words appeared to be the beginning of an explanation. Marius strained his ears.

"My wife will be back shortly, don't get impatient. I think that the Lark really is your daughter, and it seems to me quite natural that you should keep her. Only, listen to me a bit. My wife will go and hunt her up with your letter. I told my wife to dress herself in the way she did, so that your young lady might make no difficulty about following her. They will both enter the carriage with my comrade behind. Somewhere, outside the barrier, there is a trap harnessed to two very good horses. Your young lady will be taken to it. She will alight from the fiacre. My comrade will enter the other vehicle with her, and my wife will come back here to tell us, 'It's done.' As for the young lady, no harm will be done to her; the trap will conduct her to a place where she will be quiet, and just as soon as you have handed over to me those little two hundred thousand francs, she will be returned to you. If you have me arrested, my comrade will give a turn of his thumb to the Lark, that's all."

The prisoner uttered not a syllable. After a pause, Thenardier continued, "It's very simple, as you see. There'll be no harm done unless you wish that there should be harm done. I'm telling you how things stand. I warn you so that you may be prepared."

He paused; the prisoner did not break the silence, and Thenardier resumed, "As soon as my wife returns and says to me, 'The Lark is on the way,' we will release you, and you will be free to go and sleep at home. You see that our intentions are not evil."

Terrible images passed through Marius's mind. What! That young girl whom they were abducting was not to be brought back? One of those monsters was to bear her off into the darkness? Where? And what if it were she!

It was clear that it was she. Marius felt his heart stop beating.

What was he to do? Discharge the pistol? Place all those scoundrels in the hands of justice? But the horrible man with the meat-ax would, nonetheless, be out of reach with the young girl, and Marius reflected on Thenardier's words, of which he perceived the bloody significance. "If you have me arrested, my comrade will give a turn of his thumb to the Lark."

Now, it was not alone by the colonel's testament, it was by his own love, it was by the peril of the one he loved, that he felt himself restrained.

This frightful situation, which had already lasted above half an hour, was changing its aspect every moment.

Marius had sufficient strength of mind to review in succession all the most heartbreaking conjectures, seeking hope and finding none.

The tumult of his thoughts contrasted with the funereal silence of the den.

In the midst of this silence, the door at the bottom of the staircase was heard to open and shut again.

The prisoner made a movement in his bonds.

"Here's the bourgeoise," said Thenardier.

He had hardly uttered the words, when the Thenardier woman did in fact rush hastily into the room, red, panting, breathless, with flaming eyes, and cried, as she smote her huge hands on her thighs simultaneously, "False address!"

The ruffian who had gone with her made his appearance behind her and picked up his ax again.

She resumed, "Nobody there! Rue Saint-Dominique, No. 17, no Monsieur Urbain Fabre! They know not what it means!"

She paused, choking, then went on, "Monsieur Thenardier! That old fellow has duped you! You are too good, you see! If it had been me, I'd have chopped the beast in four quarters to begin with! And if he had acted ugly, I'd have boiled him alive! He would have been obliged to speak, and say where the girl is, and where he keeps his shiners! That's the way I should have managed matters! People are perfectly right when they say that men are a deal stupider than women! Nobody at No. 17. It's nothing but a big carriage gate! No Monsieur Fabre in the Rue Saint-Dominique! And after all that racing and fee to the coachman and all! I spoke to both the porter and the portress, a fine, stout woman, and they know nothing about him!"

Marius breathed freely once more.

She, Ursule or the Lark, he no longer knew what to call her, was safe.

While his exasperated wife vociferated, Thenardier had seated himself on the table.

For several minutes he uttered not a word, but swung his right foot, which hung down, and stared at the brazier with an air of savage reverie.

Finally, he said to the prisoner, with a slow and singularly ferocious tone:

"A false address? What did you expect to gain by that?"

"To gain time!" cried the prisoner in a thundering voice, and at the same instant he shook off his bonds; they were cut. The prisoner was only attached to the bed now by one leg.

Before the seven men had time to collect their senses and dash forward, he had bent down into the fireplace, had stretched out his hand to the brazier, and had then straightened himself up again, and now Thenardier, the female Thenardier, and the ruffians, huddled in amazement at the extremity of the hovel, stared at him in stupefaction, as almost free and in a formidable attitude, he brandished above his head the red-hot chisel, which emitted a threatening glow.

The judicial examination to which the ambush in the Gorbeau house eventually gave rise, established the fact that a large sou piece, cut and worked in a peculiar fashion, was found in the garret, when the police made their descent on it. This sou piece was one of those marvels of industry that are engendered by the patience of the galleys in the shadows and for the shadows, marvels that are nothing else than instruments of escape. These hideous and delicate products of wonderful art are to jewelers' work what the metaphors of slang are to poetry. There are Benvenuto Cellinis in the galleys, just as there are Villons in language. The unhappy wretch who aspires to deliverance finds means sometimes without tools, sometimes with a common wooden-handled knife, to saw a sou into two thin plates, to hollow out these plates without affecting the coinage stamp, and to make a furrow on the edge of the sou in such a manner that the plates will adhere again. This can be screwed together and unscrewed at will; it is a box. In this box he hides a watch-spring, and this watch-spring, properly handled, cuts good-sized chains and bars of iron. The unfortunate convict is supposed to possess merely a sou; not at all, he possesses liberty. It was a large sou of this sort that, during the subsequent search of the police, was found under the bed near the window. They also found a tiny saw of blue steel that would fit the sou.

It is probable that the prisoner had this sou piece on his person at the moment when the ruffians searched him, that he contrived to conceal it in his hand, and that afterward, having his right hand free, he unscrewed it, and used it as a saw to cut the cords that fastened him, which would explain the faint noise and almost imperceptible movements that Marius had observed.

As he had not been able to bend down, for fear of betraying himself, he had not cut the bonds of his left leg.

The ruffians had recovered from their first surprise.

"Be easy," said Bigrenaille to Thenardier. "He still holds by one leg, and he can't get away. I'll answer for that. I tied that paw for him."

In the meanwhile, the prisoner had begun to speak, "You are wretches, but my life is not worth the trouble of defending it. When you think that you can make me speak, that you can make me write what I do not choose to write, that you can make me say what I do not choose to say—"

He stripped up his left sleeve, and added, "See here."

At the same moment he extended his arm, and laid the glowing chisel that he held in his left hand by its wooden handle on his bare flesh.

The crackling of the burning flesh became audible, and the odor peculiar to chambers of torture filled the hovel.

Marius reeled in utter horror, the very ruffians shuddered, hardly a muscle of the old man's face contracted, and while the red-hot iron sank into the smoking wound, impassive and almost august, he fixed on Thenardier his beautiful glance, in which there was no hatred, and where suffering vanished in serene majesty.

With grand and lofty natures, the revolts of the flesh and the senses when subjected to physical suffering cause the soul to spring forth, and make it appear on the brow, just as rebellions among the soldiery force the captain to show himself.

"Wretches!" said he. "Have no more fear of me than I have for you!"

And, tearing the chisel from the wound, he hurled it through the window, which had been left open; the horrible, glowing tool disappeared into the night, whirling as it flew, and fell far away on the snow.

The prisoner resumed, "Do what you please with me." He was disarmed.

"Seize him!" said Thenardier.

Two of the ruffians laid their hands on his shoulder, and the masked man with the ventriloquist's voice took up his station in front of him, ready to smash his skull at the slightest movement.

At the same time, Marius heard below him, at the base of the partition, but so near that he could not see who was speaking, this colloquy conducted in a low tone, "There is only one thing left to do."

"Cut his throat."

"That's it."

It was the husband and wife taking counsel together.

Thenardier walked slowly toward the table, opened the drawer, and took out the knife. Marius fretted with the handle of his pistol. Unprecedented perplexity! For the last hour he had had two voices in his conscience, the one enjoining him to respect his father's testament, the other crying to him to rescue the prisoner. These two voices continued uninterruptedly that struggle, which tormented him to agony. Up to that moment he had cherished a vague hope that he should find some means of reconciling these two duties, but nothing within the limits of possibility had presented itself.

However, the peril was urgent, the last bounds of delay had been reached; Thenardier was standing thoughtfully a few paces distant from the prisoner.

Marius cast a wild glance about him, the last mechanical resource of despair. All at once a shudder ran through him.

At his feet, on the table, a bright ray of light from the full moon illuminated and seemed to point out to him a sheet of paper. On this paper he read the following line written that very morning, in large letters, by the eldest of the Thenardier girls: "THE BOBBIES ARE HERE."

An idea, a flash, crossed Marius's mind; this was the expedient of which he was in search, the solution of that frightful problem that was torturing him, of sparing the assassin and saving the victim.

He knelt down on his commode, stretched out his arm, seized the sheet of paper, softly detached a bit of plaster from the wall, wrapped the paper around it, and tossed the whole through the crevice into the middle of the den.

It was high time. Thenardier had conquered his last fears or his last scruples, and was advancing on the prisoner.

"Something is falling!" cried the Thenardier woman.

"What is it?" asked her husband.

The woman darted forward and picked up the bit of plaster. She handed it to her husband.

"Where did this come from?" demanded Thenardier.

"Pardie!" ejaculated his wife. "Where do you suppose it came from? Through the window, of course."

"I saw it pass," said Bigrenaille.

Thenardier rapidly unfolded the paper and held it close to the candle.

"It's in Eponine's handwriting. The devil!"

He made a sign to his wife, who hastily drew near, and showed her the line written on the sheet of paper, then he added in a subdued voice, "Quick! The ladder! Let's leave the bacon in the mousetrap and decamp!"

"Without cutting that man's throat?" asked, the Thenardier woman.

"We haven't the time."

"Through what?" resumed Bigrenaille.

"Through the window," replied Thenardier. "Since Ponine has thrown the stone through the window, it indicates that the house is not watched on that side."

The mask with the ventriloquist's voice deposited his huge key on the floor, raised both arms in the air, and opened and clenched his fists, three times rapidly without uttering a word.

This was the signal like the signal for clearing the decks for action on board ship.

The ruffians who were holding the prisoner released him; in the twinkling of an eye the rope ladder was unrolled outside the window, and solidly fastened to the sill by the two iron hooks.

The prisoner paid no attention to what was going on around him. He seemed to be dreaming or praying.

As soon as the ladder was arranged, Thenardier cried, "Come! The bourgeoise first!"

And he rushed headlong to the window.

But just as he was about to throw his leg over, Bigrenaille seized him roughly by the collar.

"Not much, come now, you old dog, after us!"

"After us!" yelled the ruffians.

"You are children," said Thenardier, "we are losing time. The police are on our heels."

"Well," said the ruffians, "let's draw lots to see who shall go down first."

Thenardier exclaimed, "Are you mad! Are you crazy! What a pack of boobies! You want to waste time, do you? Draw lots, do you? By a wet finger, by a short straw! With written names! Thrown into a hat!"

"Would you like my hat?" cried a voice on the threshold.

All wheeled around. It was Javert.

He had his hat in his hand, and was holding it out to them with a smile.

CHAPTER XXI—ONE SHOULD ALWAYS BEGIN BY ARRESTING THE VICTIMS

At nightfall, Javert had posted his men and had gone into ambush himself between the trees of the Rue de la Barrière-des-Gobelins that faced the Gorbeau house, on the other side of the boulevard. He had begun operations by opening "his pockets," and dropping into it the two young girls who were charged with keeping a watch on the approaches to the den. But he had only "caged" Azelma. As for Eponine, she was not at her post, she had disappeared, and he had not been able to seize her. Then Javert had made a point and had bent his ear to waiting for the signal agreed upon. The comings and goings of the fiacres had greatly agitated him. At last, he had grown impatient, and, sure that there was a nest there, sure of being in "luck," having recognized many of the ruffians who had entered, he had finally decided to go upstairs without waiting for the pistol-shot.

It will be remembered that he had Marius's passkey.

He had arrived just in the nick of time.

The terrified ruffians flung themselves on the arms that they had abandoned in all the corners at the moment of flight. In less than a second, these seven men, horrible to behold, had grouped themselves in an attitude of defense, one with his meat-ax, another with his key, another with his bludgeon, the rest with shears, pincers, and hammers. Thenardier had his knife in his fist. The Thenardier woman snatched up an enormous paving stone that lay in the angle of the window and served her daughters as an ottoman.

Javert put on his hat again, and advanced a couple of paces into the room, with arms folded, his cane under one arm, his sword in its sheath.

"Halt there," said he. "You shall not go out by the window, you shall go through the door. It's less unhealthy. There are seven of you, there are fifteen of us. Don't let's fall to collaring each other like men of Auvergne."

Bigrenaille drew out a pistol that he had kept concealed under his blouse, and put it in Thenardier's hand, whispering in the latter's ear, "It's Javert. I don't dare fire at that man. Do you dare?"

"Parbleu!" replied Thenardier.

"Well, then, fire."

Thenardier took the pistol and aimed at Javert.

Javert, who was only three paces from him, stared intently at him and contented himself with saying, "Come now, don't fire. You'll miss fire."

Thenardier pulled the trigger. The pistol missed fire.

"Didn't I tell you so!" ejaculated Javert.

Bigrenaille flung his bludgeon at Javert's feet.

"You're the emperor of the fiends! I surrender."

"And you?" Javert asked the rest of the ruffians.

They replied, "So do we."

Javert began again calmly, "That's right, that's good, I said so, you are nice fellows."

"I only ask one thing," said Bigrenaille, "and that is, that I may not be denied tobacco while I am in confinement."

"Granted," said Javert.

And turning around and calling behind him, "Come in now!"

A squad of policemen, sword in hand, and agents armed with bludgeons and cudgels, rushed in at Javert's summons. They pinioned the ruffians.

This throng of men, sparely lighted by the single candle, filled the den with shadows.

"Handcuff them all!" shouted Javert.

"Come on!" cried a voice that was not the voice of a man, but of which no one would ever have said, "It is a woman's voice."

The Thenardier woman had entrenched herself in one of the angles of the window, and it was she who had just given vent to this roar.

The policemen and agents recoiled.

She had thrown off her shawl, but retained her bonnet; her husband, who was crouching behind her, was almost hidden under the discarded shawl, and she was shielding him with her body, as she elevated the paving stone above her head with the gesture of a giantess on the point of hurling a rock.

"Beware!" she shouted.

All crowded back toward the corridor. A broad open space was cleared in the middle of the garret.

The Thenardier woman cast a glance at the ruffians who had allowed themselves to be pinioned, and muttered in hoarse and guttural accents, "The cowards!"

Javert smiled, and advanced across the open space that the Thenardier was devouring with her eyes.

"Don't come near me," she cried, "or I'll crush you."

"What a grenadier!" ejaculated Javert. "You've got a beard like a man, mother, but I have claws like a woman."

And he continued to advance.

The Thenardier, disheveled and terrible, set her feet far apart, threw herself backward, and hurled the paving stone at Javert's head. Javert ducked, the stone passed over him, struck the wall behind, knocked off a huge piece of plastering, and, rebounding from angle to angle across the hovel, now luckily almost empty, rested at Javert's feet.

At the same moment, Javert reached the Thenardier couple. One of his big hands descended on the woman's shoulder; the other on the husband's head.

"The handcuffs!" he shouted.

The policemen trooped in in force, and in a few seconds Javert's order had been executed.

The Thenardier female, overwhelmed, stared at her pinioned hands, and at those of her husband, who had dropped to the floor, and exclaimed, weeping, "My daughters!"

"They are in the jug," said Javert.

In the meanwhile, the agents had caught sight of the drunken man asleep behind the door, and were shaking him.

He awoke, stammering, "Is it all over, Jondrette?"

"Yes," replied Javert.

The six pinioned ruffians were standing, and still preserved their spectral mien; all three besmeared with black, all three masked.

"Keep on your masks," said Javert.

And passing them in review with a glance of a Frederick II at a Potsdam parade, he said to the three "chimney builders," "Good day, Bigrenaille! Good day, Brujon! Good day, Deuxmilliards!"

Then turning to the three masked men, he said to the man with the meat-ax, "Good day, Gueulemer!"

And to the man with the cudgel, "Good day, Babet!"

And to the ventriloquist, "Your health, Claquesous."

At that moment, he caught sight of the ruffians' prisoner, who, ever since the entrance of the police, had not uttered a word, and had held his head down.

"Untie the gentleman!" said Javert. "And let no one go out!"

That said, he seated himself with sovereign dignity before the table, where the candle and the writing materials still remained, drew a stamped paper from his pocket, and began to prepare his report.

When he had written the first lines, which are formulas that never vary, he raised his eyes, "Let the gentleman whom these gentlemen bound step forward."

The policemen glanced around them.

"Well," said Javert, "where is he?"

The prisoner of the ruffians, M. Leblanc, M. Urbain Fabre, the father of Ursule or the Lark, had disappeared.

The door was guarded, but the window was not. As soon as he had found himself released from his bonds, and while Javert was drawing up his report, he had taken advantage of confusion, the crowd, the darkness, and of a moment when the general attention was diverted from him, to dash out of the window.

An agent sprang to the opening and looked out. He saw no one outside.

The rope ladder was still shaking.

"The devil!" ejaculated Javert between his teeth. "He must have been the most valuable of the lot."

CHAPTER XXII—THE LITTLE ONE WHO WAS CRYING IN VOLUME TWO

On the day following that on which these events took place in the house on the Boulevard de l'Hopital, a child, who seemed to be coming from the direction of the bridge of Austerlitz, was ascending the side alley on the right in the direction of the Barriere de Fontainebleau. Night had fully come.

This lad was pale, thin, clad in rags, with linen trousers in the month of February, and was singing at the top of his voice.

At the corner of the Rue du Petit-Banquier, a bent old woman was rummaging in a heap of refuse by the light of a street lantern; the child jostled her as he passed, then recoiled, exclaiming, "Hello! And I took it for an enormous, enormous dog!"

He pronounced the word enormous the second time with a jeering swell of the voice that might be tolerably well represented by capitals: "an enormous, ENORMOUS dog."

The old woman straightened herself up in a fury.

"Nasty brat!" she grumbled. "If I hadn't been bending over, I know well where I would have planted my foot on you."

The boy was already far away.

"Kisss! Kisss!" he cried. "After that, I don't think I was mistaken!"

The old woman, choking with indignation, now rose completely upright, and the red gleam of the lantern fully lighted up her livid face, all hollowed into angles and wrinkles, with crow's-feet meeting the corners of her mouth.

Her body was lost in the darkness, and only her head was visible. One would have pronounced her a mask of Decrepitude carved out by a light from the night.

The boy surveyed her.

"Madame," said he, "does not possess that style of beauty that pleases me."

He then pursued his road, and resumed his song:

> *Le roi Coupdesabot*
> *S'en allait à la chasse,*
> *A la chasse aux corbeaux—*

At the end of these three lines he paused. He had arrived in front of No. 50–52, and finding the door fastened, he began to assault it with resounding and heroic kicks, which betrayed rather the man's shoes that he was wearing than the child's feet, which he owned.

In the meanwhile, the very old woman whom he had encountered at the corner of the Rue du Petit-Banquier hastened up behind him, uttering clamorous cries and indulging in lavish and exaggerated gestures.

"What's this? What's this? Lord God! He's battering the door down! He's knocking the house down."

The kicks continued.

The old woman strained her lungs.

"Is that the way buildings are treated nowadays?"

All at once she paused.

She had recognized the gamin.

"What! So it's that imp!"

"Why, it's the old lady," said the lad. "Good day, Bougonmuche. I have come to see my ancestors."

The old woman retorted with a composite grimace, and a wonderful improvisation of hatred taking advantage of feebleness and ugliness, which was, unfortunately, wasted in the dark, "There's no one here."

"Bah!" retorted the boy. "Where's my father?"

"At La Force."

"Come, now! And my mother?"

"At Saint-Lazare."

"Well! And my sisters?"

"At the Madelonettes."

The lad scratched his head behind his ear, stared at Ma'am Bougon, and said, "Ah!"

Then he executed a pirouette on his heel; a moment later, the old woman, who had remained on the door step, heard him singing in his clear, young voice, as he plunged under the black elm trees, in the wintry wind:

"King Bootkick
Went a-hunting,
A-hunting after crows,
Mounted on two stilts.
When one passed beneath them,
One paid him two sous."

VOLUME IV: SAINT-DENIS. THE IDYL IN THE RUE PLUMET AND THE EPIC IN THE RUE SAINT-DENIS

BOOK FIRST: A FEW PAGES OF HISTORY

CHAPTER I—WELL CUT

1831 and 1832, the two years that are immediately connected with the Revolution of July, form one of the most peculiar and striking moments of history. These two years rise like two mountains midway between those that precede and those that follow them. They have a revolutionary grandeur. Precipices are to be distinguished there. The social masses, the very assizes of civilization, the solid group of superposed and adhering interests, the century-old profiles of the ancient French formation, appear and disappear in them every instant, athwart the storm clouds of systems, of passions, and of theories. These appearances and disappearances have been designated as movement and resistance. At intervals, truth, that daylight of the human soul, can be descried shining there.

This remarkable epoch is decidedly circumscribed and is beginning to be sufficiently distant from us to allow of our grasping the principal lines even at the present day.

We shall make the attempt.

The Restoration had been one of those intermediate phases, hard to define, in which there is fatigue, buzzing, murmurs, sleep, tumult, and which are nothing else than the arrival of a great nation at a halting place.

These epochs are peculiar and mislead the politicians who desire to convert them to profit. In the beginning, the nation asks nothing but repose; it thirsts for but one thing, peace; it has but one ambition, to be small. Which is the translation of remaining tranquil. Of great events, great hazards, great adventures, great men, thank God, we have seen enough, we have them heaped higher than our heads. We would exchange Caesar for Prusias, and Napoleon for the King of Yvetot. "What a good little king was he!" We have marched since daybreak, we have reached the evening of a long and toilsome day; we have made our first change with Mirabeau, the second with Robespierre, the third with Bonaparte; we are worn out. Each one demands a bed.

Devotion, which is weary; heroism, which has grown old; ambitions, which are sated; fortunes, which are made; seek, demand, implore, solicit, what? A shelter. They have it. They take possession of peace, of tranquility, of leisure; behold, they are content. But, at the same time certain facts arise, compel recognition, and knock at the door in their turn. These facts are the products of revolutions and wars, they are, they exist, they have the right to install themselves in society, and they do install themselves therein; and most of the time, facts are the stewards of the household and *fouriers** who do nothing but prepare lodgings for principles.

This, then, is what appears to philosophical politicians:

At the same time that weary men demand repose, accomplished facts demand guarantees. Guarantees are the same to facts that repose is to men.

This is what England demanded of the Stuarts after the Protector; this is what France demanded of the Bourbons after the Empire.

These guarantees are a necessity of the times. They must be accorded. Princes "grant" them, but in reality, it is the force of things that gives them. A profound truth, and one useful to know, which the Stuarts did not suspect in 1662 and which the Bourbons did not even obtain a glimpse of in 1814.

The predestined family, which returned to France when Napoleon fell, had the fatal simplicity to believe that it was itself, which bestowed, and that what it had bestowed it could take back again; that the House of Bourbon possessed the right divine, that France possessed nothing, and that the political right conceded in the charter of Louis XVIII was merely a branch of the right divine, was detached by the House of Bourbon and graciously given to the people until such day as it should please the King to reassume it. Still, the House of Bourbon should have felt, from the displeasure created by the gift, that it did not come from it.

This house was churlish to the nineteenth century. It put on an ill-tempered look at every development of the nation. To make use of a trivial word, that is to say, of a popular and a true word, it looked glum. The people saw this.

It thought it possessed strength because the Empire had been carried away before it like a theatrical stage-setting. It did not perceive that it had, itself, been brought in in the same fashion. It did not perceive that it also lay in that hand which had removed Napoleon.

It thought that it had roots, because it was the past. It was mistaken; it formed a part of the past, but the whole past was France. The roots of French

*the officials who arrived before members
of the Court and set up accommodations

society were not fixed in the Bourbons, but in the nations. These obscure and lively roots constituted, not the right of a family, but the history of a people. They were everywhere, except under the throne.

The House of Bourbon was to France the illustrious and bleeding knot in her history, but was no longer the principal element of her destiny, and the necessary base of her politics. She could get along without the Bourbons; she had done without them for two and twenty years; there had been a break of continuity; they did not suspect the fact. And how should they have suspected it, they who fancied that Louis XVII reigned on the 9th of Thermidor, and that Louis XVIII was reigning at the battle of Marengo? Never, since the origin of history, had princes been so blind in the presence of facts and the portion of divine authority that facts contain and promulgate. Never had that pretension here below which is called the right of kings denied to such a point the right from on high.

A capital error that led this family to lay its hand once more on the guarantees "granted" in 1814, on the concessions, as it termed them. Sad. A sad thing! What it termed its concessions were our conquests; what it termed our encroachments were our rights.

When the hour seemed to it to have come, the Restoration, supposing itself victorious over Bonaparte and well-rooted in the country, that is to say, believing itself to be strong and deep, abruptly decided on its plan of action, and risked its stroke. One morning it drew itself up before the face of France, and, elevating its voice, it contested the collective title and the individual right of the nation to sovereignty, of the citizen to liberty. In other words, it denied to the nation that which made it a nation, and to the citizen that which made him a citizen.

This is the foundation of those famous acts that are called the ordinances of July. The Restoration fell.

It fell justly. But, we admit, it had not been absolutely hostile to all forms of progress. Great things had been accomplished, with it alongside.

Under the Restoration, the nation had grown accustomed to calm discussion, which had been lacking under the Republic, and to grandeur in peace, which had been wanting under the Empire. France free and strong had offered an encouraging spectacle to the other peoples of Europe. The Revolution had had the word under Robespierre; the cannon had had the word under Bonaparte; it was under Louis XVIII and Charles X that it was the turn of intelligence to have the word. The wind ceased, the torch was lighted once more. On the lofty heights, the pure light of mind could be seen flickering. A magnificent, useful, and charming spectacle. For a space of fifteen years, those great principles which are so old for the thinker, so new for the statesman, could be seen at work in perfect peace, on the public square; equality before the law, liberty of conscience, liberty of speech, liberty of the press, the accessibility of all aptitudes to all functions. Thus it proceeded until 1830. The Bourbons were an instrument of civilization that broke in the hands of Providence.

The fall of the Bourbons was full of grandeur, not on their side, but on the side of the nation. They quitted the throne with gravity, but without authority; their descent into the night was not one of those solemn disappearances that leave a somber emotion in history; it was neither the spectral calm of Charles I, nor the eagle scream of Napoleon. They departed, that is all. They laid down the crown, and retained no aureole. They were worthy, but they were not august. They lacked, in a certain measure, the majesty of their misfortune. Charles X during the voyage from Cherbourg, causing a round table to be cut over into a square table, appeared to be more anxious about imperiled etiquette than about the crumbling monarchy. This diminution saddened devoted men who loved their persons, and serious men who honored their race. The populace was admirable. The nation, attacked one morning with weapons, by a sort of royal insurrection, felt itself in the possession of so much force that it did not go into a rage. It defended itself, restrained itself, restored things to their places, the government to law, the Bourbons to exile, alas! And then halted! It took the old king Charles X from beneath that dais, which had sheltered Louis XIV and set him gently on the ground. It touched the royal personages only with sadness and precaution. It was not one man, it was not a few men, it was France, France entire, France victorious and intoxicated with her victory, who seemed to be coming to herself, and who put into practice, before the eyes of the whole world, these grave words of Guillaume du Vair after the day of the Barricades:

"It is easy for those who are accustomed to skim the favors of the great, and to spring, like a bird from bough to bough, from an afflicted fortune to a flourishing one, to show themselves harsh toward their Prince in his adversity; but as for me, the fortune of my Kings and especially of my afflicted Kings, will always be venerable to me."

The Bourbons carried away with them respect, but not regret. As we have just stated, their misfortune was greater than they were. They faded out in the horizon.

The Revolution of July instantly had friends and enemies throughout the entire world. The first rushed toward her with joy and enthusiasm, the others turned away, each according to his nature. At the first blush, the princes of Europe, the owls of this dawn, shut their eyes, wounded and stupefied, and only opened them to threaten. A fright that can be comprehended, a wrath that can be pardoned. This strange revolution had hardly produced a shock; it had not even paid to vanquished royalty the honor of treating it as an enemy, and of shedding its blood. In the eyes of despotic governments, who are always interested in having liberty calumniate itself, the Revolution of July committed the fault of being formidable and of remaining gentle. Nothing, however, was attempted or plotted against it. The most discontented, the most irritated, the most trembling, saluted it; whatever our egotism and our rancor may be, a mysterious respect springs from events in which we are sensible of the collaboration of someone who is working above man.

The Revolution of July is the triumph of right overthrowing the fact. A thing that is full of splendor.

Right overthrowing the fact. Hence the brilliancy of the Revolution of 1830, hence, also, its mildness. Right triumphant has no need of being violent.

Right is the just and the true.

The property of right is to remain eternally beautiful and pure. The fact, even when most necessary to all appearances, even when most thoroughly accepted by contemporaries, if it exist only as a fact, and if it contain only too little of right, or none at all, is infallibly destined to become, in the course of time, deformed, impure, perhaps, even monstrous. If one desires to learn at one blow, to what degree of hideousness the fact can attain, viewed at the distance of centuries, let him look at Machiavelli. Machiavelli is not an evil genius, nor a demon, nor a miserable and cowardly writer; he is nothing but the fact. And he is not only the Italian fact; he is the European fact, the fact of the sixteenth century. He seems hideous, and so he is, in the presence of the moral idea of the nineteenth.

This conflict of right and fact has been going on ever since the origin of society. To terminate this duel, to amalgamate the pure idea with the humane reality, to cause right to penetrate pacifically into the fact and the fact into right, that is the task of sages.

CHAPTER II—BADLY SEWED

But the task of sages is one thing, the task of clever men is another. The Revolution of 1830 came to a sudden halt.

As soon as a revolution has made the coast, the skillful make haste to prepare the shipwreck.

The skillful in our century have conferred on themselves the title of Statesmen; so that this word, "statesmen," has ended by becoming somewhat of a slang word. It must be borne in mind, in fact, that wherever there is nothing but skill, there is necessarily pettiness. To say "the skillful" amounts to saying "the mediocre."

In the same way, to say "statesmen" is sometimes equivalent to saying "traitors." If, then, we are to believe the skillful, revolutions like the Revolution of July are severed arteries; a prompt ligature is indispensable. The right, too grandly proclaimed, is shaken. Also, right once firmly fixed, the state must be strengthened. Liberty once assured, attention must be directed to power.

Here the sages are not, as yet, separated from the skillful, but they begin to be distrustful. Power, very good. But, in the first place, what is power? In the second, from where does comes it? The skillful do not seem to hear the murmured objection, and they continue their maneuvers.

According to the politicians, who are ingenious in putting the mask of necessity on profitable fictions, the first requirement of a people after a revolution, when this people forms part of a monarchical continent, is to procure for itself a dynasty. In this way, say they, peace, that is to say, time to dress our wounds, and to repair the house, can be had after a revolution. The dynasty conceals the scaffolding and covers the ambulance. Now, it is not always easy to procure a dynasty.

If it is absolutely necessary, the first man of genius or even the first man of fortune who comes to hand suffices for the manufacturing of a king. You have, in the first case, Napoleon; in the second, Iturbide.

But the first family that comes to hand does not suffice to make a dynasty. There is necessarily required a certain modicum of antiquity in a race, and the wrinkle of the centuries cannot be improvised.

If we place ourselves at the point of view of the "statesmen," after making all allowances, of course, after a revolution, what are the qualities of the king that result from it? He may be and it is useful for him to be a revolutionary; that is to say, a participant in his own person in that revolution, that he should have lent a hand to it, that he should have either compromised or distinguished himself therein, that he should have touched the ax or wielded the sword in it.

What are the qualities of a dynasty? It should be national; that is to say, revolutionary at a distance, not through acts committed, but by reason of ideas accepted. It should be composed of past and be historic; be composed of future and be sympathetic.

All this explains why the early revolutions contented themselves with finding a man, Cromwell or Napoleon; and why the second absolutely insisted on finding a family, the House of Brunswick or the House of Orleans.

Royal houses resemble those Indian fig trees, each branch of which, bending over to the earth, takes root and becomes a fig tree itself. Each branch may become a dynasty. On the sole condition that it shall bend down to the people.

Such is the theory of the skillful.

Here, then, lies the great art: to make a little render to success the sound of a catastrophe in order that those who profit by it may tremble from it also, to season with fear every step that is taken, to augment the curve of the transition to the point of retarding progress, to dull that aurora, to denounce and retrench the harshness of enthusiasm, to cut all angles and nails, to wad triumph, to muffle up right, to envelop the giant people in flannel, and to put it to bed very speedily, to impose a diet on that excess of health, to put Hercules on the treatment of a convalescent, to dilute the event with the expedient, to offer to spirits thirsting for the ideal that nectar thinned out with a potion, to take one's precautions against too much success, to garnish the revolution with a shade.

1830 practiced this theory, already applied to England by 1688.

1830 is a revolution arrested midway. Half of progress, quasi-right. Now, logic knows not the "almost," absolutely as the sun knows not the candle.

Who arrests revolutions halfway? The bourgeoisie?

Why?

Because the bourgeoisie is interest that has reached satisfaction. Yesterday it was appetite, today it is plenitude, tomorrow it will be satiety.

The phenomenon of 1814 after Napoleon was reproduced in 1830 after Charles X.

The attempt has been made, and wrongly, to make a class of the bourgeoisie. The bourgeoisie is simply the contented portion of the people. The bourgeois is the man who now has time to sit down. A chair is not a caste.

But through a desire to sit down too soon, one may arrest the very march of the human race. This has often been the fault of the bourgeoisie.

One is not a class because one has committed a fault. Selfishness is not one of the divisions of the social order.

Moreover, we must be just to selfishness. The state to which that part of the nation that is called the bourgeoisie aspired after the shock of 1830 was not the inertia that is complicated with indifference and laziness, and which contains a little shame; it was not the slumber that presupposes a momentary forgetfulness accessible to dreams; it was the halt.

The halt is a word formed of a singular double and almost contradictory sense: a troop on the march, that is to say, movement; a stand, that is to say, repose.

The halt is the restoration of forces; it is repose armed and on the alert; it is the accomplished fact that posts sentinels and holds itself on its guard.

The halt presupposes the combat of yesterday and the combat of tomorrow.

It is the partition between 1830 and 1848.

What we here call combat may also be designated as progress.

The bourgeoisie then, as well as the statesmen, required a man who should express this word "halt." An although-because. A composite individuality, signifying revolution and signifying stability, in other terms, strengthening the present by the evident compatibility of the past with the future.

This man was "already found." His name was Louis Philippe d'Orleans.

The 221 made Louis Philippe King. Lafayette undertook the coronation.

He called it the best of republics. The town hall of Paris took the place of the Cathedral of Rheims.

This substitution of a half-throne for a whole throne was "the work of 1830."

When the skillful had finished, the immense vice of their solution became apparent. All this had been accomplished outside the bounds of absolute right. Absolute right cried; "I protest!" Then, terrible to say, it retired into the darkness.

CHAPTER III—LOUIS PHILIPPE

Revolutions have a terrible arm and a happy hand, they strike firmly and choose well. Even incomplete, even debased and abused and reduced to the state of a junior revolution like the Revolution of 1830, they nearly always retain sufficient providential lucidity to prevent them from falling amiss. Their eclipse is never an abdication.

Nevertheless, let us not boast too loudly; revolutions also may be deceived, and grave errors have been seen.

Let us return to 1830. 1830, in its deviation, had good luck. In the establishment, which entitled itself order after the revolution had been cut short, the King amounted to more than royalty. Louis Philippe was a rare man.

The son of a father to whom history will accord certain attenuating circumstances, but also as worthy of esteem as that father had been of blame; possessing all private virtues and many public virtues; careful of his health, of his fortune, of his person, of his affairs, knowing the value of a minute and not always the value of a year; sober, serene, peaceable, patient; a good man and a good prince; sleeping with his wife, and having in his palace lackeys charged with the duty of showing the conjugal bed to the bourgeois, an ostentation of the regular sleeping apartment, which had become useful after the former illegitimate displays of the elder branch; knowing all the languages of Europe, and, what is more rare, all the languages of all interests, and speaking them; an admirable representative of the "middle class," but outstripping it, and in every way greater than it; possessing excellent sense, while appreciating the blood from which he had sprung, counting most of all on his intrinsic worth, and, on the question of his race, very particular, declaring himself Orleans and not Bourbon; thoroughly the first Prince of the Blood Royal while he was still only a Serene Highness, but a frank bourgeois from the day he became king; diffuse in public, concise in private; reputed, but not proved to be a miser; at bottom, one of those economists who are readily prodigal at their own fancy or duty; lettered, but not very sensitive to letters; a gentleman, but not a chevalier; simple, calm, and strong; adored by his family and his household; a fascinating talker, an undeceived statesman, inwardly cold, dominated by immediate interest, always governing at the shortest range, incapable of rancor and of gratitude, making use without mercy of superiority on mediocrity, clever in getting parliamentary majorities to put in the wrong those mysterious unanimities, which mutter dully under thrones; unreserved, sometimes imprudent in his lack of reserve, but with marvelous address in that imprudence; fertile in expedients, in countenances, in masks; making France fear Europe and Europe France! Incontestably fond of his country, but preferring his family; assuming more domination than authority and more authority than dignity, a disposition, which has this unfortunate property, that as it turns everything to success, it admits of ruse and does not absolutely repudiate baseness, but which has this valuable side, that it preserves politics from violent shocks, the state from fractures, and society from catastrophes; minute, correct, vigilant, attentive, sagacious, indefatigable; contradicting himself at times and giving himself the lie; bold against Austria at Ancona, obstinate against England in Spain, bombarding Antwerp, and paying off Pritchard; singing the Marseillaise with conviction, inaccessible to despondency, to lassitude, to the taste for the beautiful and the ideal, to daring generosity, to Utopia, to chimeras, to wrath, to vanity, to fear; possessing all the forms of personal intrepidity; a general at Valmy; a soldier at Jemappes; attacked eight times by regicides and always smiling. Brave as a grenadier, courageous as a thinker; uneasy only in the face of the chances of a European shaking up, and unfitted for great political adventures; always ready to risk his life, never his work; disguising his will in influence, in order that he might be obeyed as an intelligence rather than as a king; endowed with observation and not with divination; not very attentive to minds, but knowing men, that is to say requiring to see in order to judge; prompt and penetrating good sense, practical wisdom, easy speech, prodigious memory; drawing incessantly on this memory, his only point of resemblance with Caesar, Alexander, and Napoleon; knowing deeds, facts, details, dates, proper names, ignorant of tendencies, passions, the diverse geniuses of the crowd, the interior aspirations, the hidden and obscure uprisings of souls, in a word, all that can be designated as the invisible currents of consciences; accepted by the surface, but little in accord with France lower down; extricating himself by dint of tact; governing too much and not enough; his own first minister; excellent at creating out of the pettiness of realities an obstacle to the immensity of ideas; mingling a genuine creative faculty of civilization, of order and organization, an indescribable spirit of proceedings and chicanery, the founder and lawyer of a dynasty; having something of Charlemagne and something of an attorney; in short, a lofty and original figure, a prince who understood how to create authority in spite of the uneasiness of France, and power in spite of the jealousy of Europe. Louis Philippe will be classed among the eminent men of his century, and would be ranked among the most illustrious governors of history had he loved glory but a little, and if he had had the sentiment of what is great to the same degree as the feeling for what is useful.

Louis Philippe had been handsome, and in his old age he remained graceful; not always approved by the nation, he always was so by the masses; he pleased.

He had that gift of charming. He lacked majesty; he wore no crown, although a king, and no white hair, although an old man; his manners belonged to the old regime and his habits to the new; a mixture of the noble and the bourgeois which suited 1830; Louis Philippe was transition reigning; he had preserved the ancient pronunciation and the ancient orthography, which he placed at the service of opinions modern; he loved Poland and Hungary, but he wrote les Polonois, and he pronounced les Hongrais. He wore the uniform of the National Guard, like Charles X, and the ribbon of the Legion of Honor, like Napoleon.

He went a little to chapel, not at all to the chase, never to the opera. Incorruptible by sacristans, by whippers-in, by ballet dancers; this made a part of his bourgeois popularity. He had no heart. He went out with his umbrella under his arm, and this umbrella long formed a part of his aureole. He was a bit of a mason, a bit of a gardener, something of a doctor; he bled a postilion who had tumbled from his horse; Louis Philippe no more went about without his lancet, than did Henri IV without his poniard. The Royalists jeered at this ridiculous king, the first who had ever shed blood with the object of healing.

For the grievances against Louis Philippe, there is one deduction to be made; there is that which accuses royalty, that which accuses the reign, that which accuses the King; three columns, which all give different totals. Democratic right confiscated, progress becomes a matter of secondary interest, the protests of the street violently repressed, military execution of insurrections, the rising passed over by arms, the Rue Transnonain, the counsels of war, the absorption of the real country by the legal country, on half shares with three hundred thousand privileged persons, these are the deeds of royalty; Belgium refused, Algeria too harshly conquered, and, as in the case of India by the English, with more barbarism than civilization, the breach of faith, to Abd-el-Kader, Blaye, Deutz bought, Pritchard paid, these are the doings of the reign; the policy, which was more domestic than national, was the doing of the King.

As will be seen, the proper deduction having been made, the King's charge is decreased.

This is his great fault; he was modest in the name of France.

From where arises this fault?

We will state it.

Louis Philippe was rather too much of a paternal king; that incubation of a family with the object of founding a dynasty is afraid of everything and does not like to be disturbed; hence excessive timidity, which is displeasing to the people, who have the 14th of July in their civil and Austerlitz in their military tradition.

Moreover, if we deduct the public duties that require to be fulfilled first of all, that deep tenderness of Louis Philippe toward his family was deserved by the family. That domestic group was worthy of admiration. Virtues there dwelled side by side with talents. One of Louis Philippe's daughters, Marie d'Orleans, placed the name of her race among artists, as Charles d'Orleans had placed it among poets. She made of her soul a marble that she named Jeanne d'Arc. Two of Louis Philippe's daughters elicited from Metternich this eulogy: "They are young people such as are rarely seen, and princes such as are never seen."

This, without any dissimulation, and also without any exaggeration, is the truth about Louis Philippe.

To be Prince Equality, to bear in his own person the contradiction of the Restoration and the Revolution, to have that disquieting side of the revolutionary which becomes reassuring in governing power, therein lay the fortune of Louis Philippe in 1830; never was there a more complete adaptation of a man to an event; the one entered into the other, and the incarnation took place. Louis Philippe is 1830 made man. Moreover, he had in his favor that great recommendation to the throne, exile. He had been proscribed, a wanderer, poor. He had lived by his own labor. In Switzerland, this heir to the richest princely domains in France had sold an old horse in order to obtain bread. At Reichenau, he gave lessons in mathematics, while his sister Adelaide did wool work and sewed. These souvenirs connected with a king rendered the bourgeoisie enthusiastic. He had, with his own hands, demolished the iron cage of Mont-Saint-Michel, built by Louis XI, and used by Louis XV. He was the companion of Dumouriez, he was the friend of Lafayette; he had belonged to the Jacobins' club; Mirabeau had slapped him on the shoulder; Danton had said to him, "Young man!" At the age of four and twenty, in '93, being then M. de Chartres, he had witnessed, from the depth of a box, the trial of Louis XVI, so well named that poor tyrant. The blind clairvoyance of the Revolution, breaking royalty in the King and the King with royalty, did so almost without noticing the man in the fierce crushing of the idea, the vast storm of the Assembly-Tribunal, the public wrath interrogating, Capet not knowing what to reply, the alarming, stupefied vacillation by that royal head beneath that somber breath, the relative innocence of all in that catastrophe, of those who condemned as well as of the man condemned, he had looked on those things, he had contemplated that giddiness; he had seen the centuries appear before the bar of the Assembly-Convention; he had beheld, behind Louis XVI, that unfortunate passerby who was made responsible, the terrible culprit, the monarchy, rise through the shadows; and there had lingered in his soul the respectful fear of these immense justices of the populace, which are almost as impersonal as the justice of God.

The trace left in him by the Revolution was prodigious. Its memory was like a living imprint of those great years, minute by minute. One day, in the presence of a witness whom we are not permitted to doubt, he rectified from memory the whole of the letter A in the alphabetical list of the Constituent Assembly.

Louis Philippe was a king of the broad daylight. While he reigned the press was free, the tribune was free, conscience and speech were free. The laws of September are open to sight. Although fully aware of the gnawing power of light on privileges, he left his throne exposed to the light. History will do justice to him for this loyalty.

Louis Philippe, like all historical men who have passed from the scene, is today put on his trial by the human conscience. His case is, as yet, only in the lower court.

The hour when history speaks with its free and venerable accent, has not yet sounded for him; the moment has not come to pronounce a definite judgment on this king; the austere and illustrious historian Louis Blanc has himself recently softened his first verdict; Louis Philippe was elected by those two almosts which are called the 221 and 1830, that is to say, by a half-Parliament, and a half-Revolution; and in any case, from the superior point of view where philosophy must place itself, we cannot judge him here, as the reader has seen above, except with certain reservations in the name of the absolute democratic principle; in the eyes of the absolute, outside these two rights, the right of man in the first place, the right of the people in the second, all is usurpation; but what we can say, even at the present day, that after making these reserves is, that to sum up the whole, and in whatever manner he is considered, Louis Philippe, taken in himself, and from the point of view of human goodness, will remain, to use the antique language of ancient history, one of the best princes who ever sat on a throne.

What is there against him? That throne. Take away Louis Philippe the king, there remains the man. And the man is good. He is good at times even to the point of being admirable. Often, in the midst of his gravest souvenirs, after a day of conflict with the whole diplomacy of the continent, he returned at night to his apartments, and there, exhausted with fatigue, overwhelmed with sleep, what did he do? He took a death sentence and passed the night in revising a criminal suit, considering it something to hold his own against Europe, but that it was a still greater matter to rescue a man from the executioner. He obstinately maintained his opinion against his keeper of the seals; he disputed the ground with the guillotine foot by foot against the crown attorneys, those chatterers of the law, as he called them. Sometimes the pile of sentences covered his table; he examined them all; it was anguish to him to abandon these miserable, condemned heads. One day, he said to the same witness to whom we have recently referred, "I won seven last night." During the early years of his reign, the death penalty was as good as abolished, and the erection of a scaffold was a violence committed against the King. The Greve having disappeared with the elder branch, a bourgeois place of execution was instituted under the name of the Barriere-Saint-Jacques; "practical men" felt the necessity of a quasi-legitimate guillotine; and this was one of the victories of Casimir Perier, who represented the narrow sides of the bourgeoisie, over Louis Philippe, who represented its liberal sides. Louis Philippe annotated Beccaria with his own hand. After the Fieschi machine, he exclaimed, "What a pity that I was not wounded! Then I might have pardoned!" On another occasion, alluding to the resistance offered by his ministry, he wrote in connection with a political criminal, who is one of the most generous figures of our day, "His pardon is granted; it only remains for me to obtain it." Louis Philippe was as gentle as Louis IX and as kindly as Henri IV.

Now, to our mind, in history, where kindness is the rarest of pearls, the man who is kindly almost takes precedence of the man who is great.

Louis Philippe having been severely judged by some, harshly, perhaps, by others, it is quite natural that a man, himself a phantom at the present day, who knew that king, should come and testify in his favor before history; this deposition, whatever else it may be, is evidently and above all things, entirely disinterested; an epitaph penned by a dead man is sincere; one shade may console another shade; the sharing of the same shadows confers the right to praise it; it is not greatly to be feared that it will ever be said of two tombs in exile: "This one flattered the other."

CHAPTER IV—CRACKS BENEATH THE FOUNDATION

At the moment when the drama which we are narrating is on the point of penetrating into the depths of one of the tragic clouds which envelop the beginning of Louis Philippe's reign, it was necessary that there should be no equivoque, and it became requisite that this book should offer some explanation with regard to this king.

Louis Philippe had entered into possession of his royal authority without violence, without any direct action on his part, by virtue of a revolutionary change, evidently quite distinct from the real aim of the Revolution, but in which he, the Duc d'Orleans, exercised no personal initiative. He had been born a Prince, and he believed himself to have been elected King. He had not served this mandate on himself; he had not taken it; it had been offered to him, and he had accepted it; convinced, wrongly, to be sure, but convinced nevertheless, that the offer was in accordance with right and that the acceptance of it was in accordance with duty. Hence his possession was in good faith. Now, we say it in good conscience, Louis Philippe being in possession in perfect good faith, and the democracy being in good faith in its attack, the amount of terror discharged by the social conflicts weighs neither on the King nor on the democracy. A clash of principles resembles a clash of elements. The ocean defends the water, the hurricane defends the air, the King defends Royalty, the democracy defends the people; the relative, which is the monarchy, resists the absolute, which is the republic; society bleeds in this conflict, but that which constitutes its suffering today will constitute its safety later on; and, in any case, those who combat are not to be blamed; one of the two parties is evidently mistaken; the right is not, like the Colossus of Rhodes, on two shores at once, with one foot on the republic, and one in Royalty; it is indivisible, and all on one side; but those who are in error are so sincerely; a blind man is no more a criminal than a Vendean is a ruffian. Let us, then, impute to the fatality of things alone these formidable collisions. Whatever the nature of these tempests may be, human irresponsibility is mingled with them.

Let us complete this exposition.

The government of 1840 led a hard life immediately. Born yesterday, it was obliged to fight today.

Hardly installed, it was already everywhere conscious of vague movements of traction on the apparatus of July so recently laid, and so lacking in solidity.

Resistance was born on the morrow; perhaps even, it was born on the preceding evening. From month to month the hostility increased, and from being concealed it became patent.

The Revolution of July, which gained but little acceptance outside of France by kings, had been diversely interpreted in France, as we have said.

God delivers over to men his visible will in events, an obscure text written in a mysterious tongue. Men immediately make translations of it; translations hasty, incorrect, full of errors, of gaps, and of nonsense. Very few minds comprehend the divine language. The most sagacious, the calmest, the most profound, decipher slowly, and when they arrive with their text, the task has long been completed; there are already twenty translations on the public place. From each remaining springs a party, and from each misinterpretation a faction; and each party thinks that it alone has the true text, and each faction thinks that it possesses the light.

Power itself is often a faction.

There are, in revolutions, swimmers who go against the current; they are the old parties.

For the old parties who clung to heredity by the grace of God, think that revolutions, having sprung from the right to revolt, one has the right to revolt against them. Error. For in these revolutions, the one who revolts is not the people; it is the king. Revolution is precisely the contrary of revolt. Every revolution, being a normal outcome, contains within itself its legitimacy, which false revolutionists sometimes dishonor, but which remains even when soiled, which survives even when stained with blood.

Revolutions spring not from an accident, but from necessity. A revolution is a return from the fictitious to the real. It is because it must be that it is.

Nonetheless did the old legitimist parties assail the Revolution of 1830 with all the vehemence that arises from false reasoning. Errors make excellent projectiles. They strike it cleverly in its vulnerable spot, in default of a cuirass, in its lack of logic; they attacked this revolution in its royalty. They shouted to it, "Revolution, why this king?" Factions are blind men who aim correctly.

This cry was uttered equally by the republicans. But coming from them, this cry was logical. What was blindness in the legitimists was clearness of vision in the democrats. 1830 had bankrupted the people. The enraged democracy reproached it with this.

Between the attack of the past and the attack of the future, the establishment of July struggled. It represented the minute at loggerheads on the one hand with the monarchical centuries, on the other hand with eternal right.

In addition, and beside all this, as it was no longer revolution and had become a monarchy, 1830 was obliged to take precedence of all Europe. To keep the peace was an increase of complication. A harmony established contrary to sense is often more onerous than a war. From this secret conflict, always muzzled, but always growling, was born armed peace, that ruinous expedient of civilization that in the harness of the European cabinets is suspicious in itself. The Royalty of July reared up, in spite of the fact that it caught it in the harness of European cabinets. Metternich would gladly have put it in kicking-straps. Pushed on in France by progress, it pushed on the monarchies, those loiterers in Europe. After having been towed, it undertook to tow.

Meanwhile, within her, pauperism, the proletariat, salary, education, penal servitude, prostitution, the fate of the woman, wealth, misery, production, consumption, division, exchange, coin, credit, the rights of capital, the rights of labor, all these questions were multiplied above society, a terrible slope.

Outside of political parties properly so-called, another movement became manifest. Philosophical fermentation replied to democratic fermentation. The elect felt troubled as well as the masses; in another manner, but quite as much.

Thinkers meditated, while the soil, that is to say, the people, traversed by revolutionary currents, trembled under them with indescribably vague epileptic shocks. These dreamers, some isolated, others united in families and almost in communion, turned over social questions in a pacific but profound manner; impassive miners, who tranquilly pushed their galleries into the depths of a volcano, hardly disturbed by the dull commotion and the furnaces of which they caught glimpses.

This tranquility was not the least beautiful spectacle of this agitated epoch.

These men left to political parties the question of rights, they occupied themselves with the question of happiness.

The well being of man, that was what they wanted to extract from society.

They raised material questions, questions of agriculture, of industry, of commerce, almost to the dignity of a religion. In civilization, such as it has formed itself, a little by the command of God, a great deal by the agency of man, interests combine, unite, and amalgamate in a manner to form a veritable hard rock, in accordance with a dynamic law, patiently studied by economists, those geologists of politics. These men who grouped themselves under different appellations, but who may all be designated by the generic title of socialists, endeavored to pierce that rock and to cause it to spout forth the living waters of human felicity.

From the question of the scaffold to the question of war, their works embraced everything. To the rights of man, as proclaimed by the French Revolution, they added the rights of woman and the rights of the child.

The reader will not be surprised if, for various reasons, we do not here treat in a thorough manner, from the theoretical point of view, the questions raised by Socialism. We confine ourselves to indicating them.

All the problems that the socialists proposed to themselves, cosmogonic visions, reverie and mysticism being cast aside, can be reduced to two principal problems.

First problem: to produce wealth.

Second problem: to share it.

The first problem contains the question of work.

The second contains the question of salary.

In the first problem the employment of forces is in question.

In the second, the distribution of enjoyment.

From the proper employment of forces results public power.

From a good distribution of enjoyments results individual happiness.

By a good distribution, not an equal but an equitable distribution must be understood.

From these two things combined, the public power without, individual happiness within, results social prosperity.

Social prosperity means the man happy, the citizen free, the nation great.

England solves the first of these two problems. She creates wealth admirably, she divides it badly. This solution, which is complete on one side, only leads her fatally to two extremes: monstrous opulence, monstrous wretchedness. All enjoyments for some, all privations for the rest, that is to say, for the people; privilege, exception, monopoly, feudalism, born from toil itself. A false and dangerous situation, which sates public power or private misery, which sets the roots of the State in the sufferings of the individual. A badly constituted grandeur in which are combined all the material elements and into which no moral element enters.

Communism and agrarian law think that they solve the second problem. They are mistaken. Their division kills production. Equal partition abolishes emulation; and consequently labor. It is a partition made by the butcher, which kills that which it divides. It is therefore impossible to pause over these pretended solutions. Slaying wealth is not the same thing as dividing it.

The two problems require to be solved together, to be well solved. The two problems must be combined and made but one.

Solve only the first of the two problems; you will be Venice, you will be England. You will have, like Venice, an artificial power, or, like England, a material power; you will be the wicked rich man. You will die by an act of violence, as Venice died, or by bankruptcy, as England will fall. And the world will allow to die and fall all that is merely selfishness, all that does not represent for the human race either a virtue or an idea.

It is well understood here, that by the words Venice, England, we designate not the peoples, but social structures; the oligarchies superposed on nations, and not the nations themselves. The nations always have our respect and our sympathy. Venice, as a people, will live again; England, the aristocracy, will fall, but England, the nation, is immortal. That said, we continue.

Solve the two problems, encourage the wealthy, and protect the poor, suppress misery, put an end to the unjust farming out of the feeble by the strong, put a bridle on the iniquitous jealousy of the man who is making his way against the man who has reached the goal, adjust, mathematically and fraternally, salary to labor, mingle gratuitous and compulsory education with the growth of childhood, and make of science the base of manliness, develop minds while keeping arms busy, be at one and the same time a powerful people and a family of happy men, render property democratic, not by abolishing it, but by making it universal, so that every citizen, without exception, may be a proprietor, an easier matter than is generally supposed; in two words, learn how to produce wealth and how to distribute it, and you will have at once moral and material greatness; and you will be worthy to call yourself France.

This is what socialism said outside and above a few sects, which have gone astray; that is what it sought in facts, that is what it sketched out in minds.

Efforts worthy of admiration! Sacred attempts!

These doctrines, these theories, these resistances, the unforeseen necessity for the statesman to take philosophers into account, confused evidences of which we catch a glimpse, a new system of politics to be created, which shall be in accord with the old world without too much disaccord with the new revolutionary ideal, a situation in which it became necessary to use Lafayette to defend Polignac, the intuition of progress transparent beneath the revolt, the chambers and streets, the competitions to be brought into equilibrium around him, his faith in the Revolution, perhaps an eventual indefinable resignation born of the vague acceptance of a superior definitive right, his desire to remain of his race, his domestic spirit, his sincere respect for the people, his own honesty, preoccupied Louis Philippe almost painfully, and there were moments when strong and courageous as he was, he was overwhelmed by the difficulties of being a king.

He felt under his feet a formidable disaggregation, which was not, nevertheless, a reduction to dust, France being more France than ever.

Piles of shadows covered the horizon. A strange shade, gradually drawing nearer, extended little by little over men, over things, over ideas; a shade that came from wraths and systems. Everything that had been hastily stifled was moving and fermenting. At times the conscience of the honest man resumed its breathing, so great was the discomfort of that air in which sophisms were intermingled with truths. Spirits trembled in the social anxiety like leaves at the approach of a storm. The electric tension was such that at certain instants, the first comer, a stranger, brought light. Then the twilight obscurity closed in again. At intervals, deep and dull mutterings allowed a judgment to be formed as to the quantity of thunder contained by the cloud.

Twenty months had barely elapsed since the Revolution of July, the year 1832 had opened with an aspect of something impending and threatening.

The distress of the people, the laborers without bread, the last Prince de Conde engulfed in the shadows, Brussels expelling the Nassaus as Paris did the Bourbons, Belgium offering herself to a French Prince and giving herself to an English Prince, the Russian hatred of Nicolas, behind us the demons of the South, Ferdinand in Spain, Miguel in Portugal, the earth quaking in Italy, Metternich extending his hand over Bologna, France treating Austria sharply at Ancona, at the North no one knew what sinister sound of the hammer nailing up Poland in her coffin, irritated glances watching France narrowly all over Europe, England, a suspected ally, ready to give a push to that which was tottering and to hurl herself on that which should fall, the peerage sheltering itself behind Beccaria to refuse four heads to the law, the fleurs-de-lis erased from the King's carriage, the cross torn from Notre Dame, Lafayette lessened, Laffitte ruined, Benjamin Constant dead in indigence, Casimir Perier dead in the exhaustion of his power; political and social malady breaking out simultaneously in the two capitals of the kingdom, the one in the city of thought, the other in the city of toil; at Paris civil war, at Lyons servile war; in the two cities, the same glare of the furnace; a craterlike crimson on the brow of the people; the South rendered fanatic, the West troubled, the Duchesse de Berry in la Vendee, plots, conspiracies, risings, cholera, added the somber roar of tumult of events to the somber roar of ideas.

CHAPTER V—FACTS FROM WHICH HISTORY SPRINGS AND WHICH HISTORY IGNORES

Toward the end of April, everything had become aggravated. The fermentation entered the boiling state. Ever since 1830, petty partial revolts had been going on here and there, which were quickly suppressed, but ever bursting forth afresh, the sign of a vast underlying conflagration. Something terrible was in preparation. Glimpses could be caught of the features still indistinct and imperfectly lighted, of a possible revolution. France kept an eye on Paris; Paris kept an eye on the Faubourg Saint-Antoine.

The Faubourg Saint-Antoine, which was in a dull glow, was beginning its ebullition.

The wine shops of the Rue de Charonne were, although the union of the two epithets seems singular when applied to wine shops, grave and stormy.

The government was there purely and simply called in question. There people publicly discussed the question of fighting or of keeping quiet. There were back shops where workingmen were made to swear that they would hasten into the street at the first cry of alarm, and "that they would fight without counting the number of the enemy." This engagement once entered into, a man seated in the corner of the wine shop "assumed a sonorous tone," and said, "You understand! You have sworn!"

Sometimes they went upstairs, to a private room on the first floor, and there scenes that were almost Masonic were enacted. They made the initiated take oaths to render service to himself as well as to the fathers of families. That was the formula.

In the taprooms, "subversive" pamphlets were read. They treated the government with contempt, says a secret report of that time.

Words like the following could be heard there:

"I don't know the names of the leaders. We folks shall not know the day until two hours beforehand."

One workman said, "There are three hundred of us, let each contribute ten sous, that will make one hundred and fifty francs with which to procure powder and shot."

Another said, "I don't ask for six months, I don't ask for even two. In less than a fortnight we shall be parallel with the government. With twenty-five thousand men we can face them."

Another said, "I don't sleep at night, because I make cartridges all night." From time to time, men "of bourgeois appearance, and in good coats" came and "caused embarrassment," and with the air of "command," shook hands with the most important, and then went away. They never stayed more than ten minutes. Significant remarks were exchanged in a low tone, "The plot is ripe, the matter is arranged." "It was murmured by all who were there," to borrow the very expression of one of those who were present. The exaltation was such that one day, a workingman exclaimed, before the whole wine shop, "We have no arms!"

One of his comrades replied, "The soldiers have!" thus parodying without being aware of the fact, Bonaparte's proclamation to the army in Italy, "When they had anything of a more secret nature on hand," adds one report, "they did not communicate it to each other." It is not easy to understand what they could conceal after what they said.

These reunions were sometimes periodical. At certain ones of them, there were never more than eight or ten persons present, and they were always the same. In others, anyone entered who wished, and the room was so full that they were forced to stand. Some went there through enthusiasm and passion; others because it was on their way to their work. As during the Revolution, there were patriotic women in some of these wine shops who embraced newcomers.

Other expressive facts came to light.

A man would enter a shop, drink, and go his way with the remark, "Wine merchant, the revolution will pay what is due to you."

Revolutionary agents were appointed in a wine shop facing the Rue de Charonne. The balloting was carried on in their caps.

Workingmen met at the house of a fencing master who gave lessons in the Rue de Cotte. There was a trophy of arms formed of wooden broadswords, canes, clubs, and foils. One day, the buttons were removed from the foils.

A workman said, "There are twenty-five of us, but they don't count on me, because I am looked upon as a machine." Later on, that machine became Quenisset.

The indefinite things that were brewing gradually acquired a strange and indescribable notoriety. A woman sweeping off her doorsteps said to another woman, "For a long time, there has been a strong force busy making cartridges." In the open street, proclamation could be seen addressed to the National Guard in the departments. One of these proclamations was signed: Burtot, wine merchant.

One day a man with his beard worn like a collar and with an Italian accent mounted a stone post at the door of a liquor seller in the Marche Lenoir, and read aloud a singular document, which seemed to emanate from an occult power. Groups formed around him, and applauded.

The passages that touched the crowd most deeply were collected and noted down. "—Our doctrines are trammeled, our proclamations torn, our bill-stickers are spied upon and thrown into prison."—"The breakdown, which has recently taken place in cottons, has converted to us many mediums."—"The future of nations is being worked out in our obscure ranks."—"Here are the fixed terms: action or reaction, revolution or counter-revolution. For, at our epoch, we no longer believe either in inertia or in immobility. For the people against the people, that is the question. There is no other."—"On the day when we cease to suit you, break us, but up to that day, help us to march on." All this in broad daylight.

Other deeds, more audacious still, were suspicious in the eyes of the people by reason of their very audacity. On the 4th of April, 1832, a passerby mounted the post on the corner that forms the angle of the Rue Sainte-Marguerite and shouted, "I am a Babouvist!" But beneath Babeuf, the people scented Gisquet.

Among other things, this man said, "Down with property! The opposition of the left is cowardly and treacherous. When it wants to be on the right side, it preaches revolution, it is democratic in order to escape being beaten, and royalist so that it may not have to fight. The republicans are beasts with feathers. Distrust the republicans, citizens of the laboring classes."

"Silence, citizen spy!" cried an artisan.

This shout put an end to the discourse.

Mysterious incidents occurred.

At nightfall, a workingman encountered near the canal a "very well dressed man," who said to him, "Where are you bound, citizen?"

"Sir," replied the workingman, "I have not the honor of your acquaintance."

"I know you very well, however."

And the man added, "Don't be alarmed, I am an agent of the committee. You are suspected of not being quite faithful. You know that if you reveal anything, there is an eye fixed on you." Then he shook hands with the workingman and went away, saying, "We shall meet again soon."

The police, who were on the alert, collected singular dialogues, not only in the wine shops, but in the street.

"Get yourself received very soon," said a weaver to a cabinet maker.

"Why?"

"There is going to be a shot to fire."

Two ragged pedestrians exchanged these remarkable replies, fraught with evident Jacquerie, "Who governs us?"

"M. Philippe."

"No, it is the bourgeoisie."

The reader is mistaken if he thinks that we take the word Jacquerie in a bad sense. The Jacques were the poor.

On another occasion two men were heard to say to each other as they passed by, "We have a good plan of attack."

Only the following was caught of a private conversation between four men who were crouching in a ditch of the circle of the Barrière du Trône, "Everything possible will be done to prevent his walking about Paris any more."

Who was the "he?" Menacing obscurity.

"The principal leaders," as they said in the Faubourg, held themselves apart. It was supposed that they met for consultation in a wine shop near the point Saint-Eustache. A certain Aug——, chief of the Society aid for tailors, Rue Mondetour, had the reputation of serving as intermediary central between the leaders and the Faubourg Saint-Antoine.

Nevertheless, there was always a great deal of mystery about these leaders, and no certain fact can invalidate the singular arrogance of this reply made later on by a man accused before the Court of Peers, "Who was your leader?"

"I knew of none and I recognized none."

There was nothing but words, transparent but vague; sometimes idle reports, rumors, hearsay. Other indications cropped up.

A carpenter, occupied in nailing boards to a fence around the ground on which a house was in process of construction, in the Rue de Reuilly found on that plot the torn fragment of a letter on which were still legible the following lines:

The committee must take measures to prevent recruiting in the sections for the different societies.

And, as a postscript:

We have learned that there are guns in the Rue du Faubourg-Poissonniere, No. 5 [bis], to the number of five or six thousand, in the house of a gunsmith in that court. The section owns no arms.

What excited the carpenter and caused him to show this thing to his neighbors was the fact, that a few paces further on he picked up another paper, torn like the first, and still more significant, of which we reproduce a facsimile, because of the historical interest attaching to these strange documents:

+————————————————————————
————————————————+ | Q | C | D | E | Learn this list by heart.' After so doing | | | | | | you will tear it up.' The men admitted | | | | | | will do the same when you have transmitted | | | | | | their orders to them. | | | | | | Health and Fraternity, | | | | | | u og a fe L. | +————————

—+

It was only later on that the persons who were in the secret of this find at the time, learned the significance of those four capital letters: quinturions, centurions, decurions, eclaireurs [scouts], and the sense of the letters: u og a fe, which was a date, and meant April 15th, 1832. Under each capital letter were inscribed names followed by very characteristic notes. Thus: Q. Bannerel. 8 guns, 83 cartridges. A safe man.—C. Boubiere. 1 pistol, 40 cartridges.—D. Rollet. 1 foil, 1 pistol, 1 pound of powder.—E. Tessier. 1 sword, 1 cartridge-box. Exact.—Terreur. 8 guns. Brave, etc.

Finally, this carpenter found, still in the same enclosure, a third paper on which was written in pencil, but very legibly, this sort of enigmatical list:

Unite: Blanchard: Arbre-Sec. 6. Barra.' Soize.' Salle-au-Comte. Kosciusko. Aubry the Butcher? J. J. R. Caius Gracchus. Right of revision. Dufond. Four. Fall of the Girondists. Derbac. Maubuee. Washington. Pinson. 1 pistol, 86 cartridges. Marseillaise. Sovereignty of the people. Michel. Quincampoix. Sword. Hoche. Marceau. Plato. Arbre-Sec. Warsaw. Tilly, crier of the Populaire.

The honest bourgeois into whose hands this list fell knew its significance. It appears that this list was the complete nomenclature of the sections of the fourth arondissement of the Society of the Rights of Man, with the names and dwellings of the chiefs of sections. Today, when all these facts, which were obscure, are nothing more than history, we may publish them. It should be added, that the foundation of the Society of the Rights of Man seems to have been posterior to the date when this paper was found. Perhaps this was only a rough draft.

Still, according to all the remarks and the words, according to written notes, material facts begin to make their appearance.

In the Rue Popincourt, in the house of a dealer in bric-a-brac, there were seized seven sheets of gray paper, all folded alike lengthwise and in four; these sheets enclosed twenty-six squares of this same gray paper folded in the form of a cartridge, and a card, on which was written the following:

Saltpetre .... 12 ounces.
Sulfur .... 2 ounces.
Charcoal.. 2 ounces and a half.
Water .... 2 ounces.

The report of the seizure stated that the drawer exhaled a strong smell of powder.

A mason returning from his day's work, left behind him a little package on a bench near the bridge of Austerlitz. This package was taken to the police station. It was opened, and in it were found two printed dialogues, signed Lahautiere, a song entitled, "Workmen, band together," and a tin box full of cartridges.

One artisan drinking with a comrade made the latter feel him to see how warm he was; the other man felt a pistol under his waistcoat.

In a ditch on the boulevard, between Pere-Lachaise and the Barriere du Trone, at the most deserted spot, some children, while playing, discovered beneath a mass of shavings and refuse bits of wood, a bag containing a bullet-mould, a wooden punch for the preparation of cartridges, a wooden bowl, in which there were grains of hunting powder, and a little cast-iron pot whose interior presented evident traces of melted lead.

Police agents, making their way suddenly and unexpectedly at five o'clock in the morning, into the dwelling of a certain Pardon, who was afterward a member of the Barricade-Merry section and got himself killed in the insurrection of April, 1834, found him standing near his bed, and holding in his hand some cartridges which he was in the act of preparing.

Toward the hour when workingmen repose, two men were seen to meet between the Barriere Picpus and the Barriere Charenton in a little lane between two walls, near a wine shop, in front of which there was a "Jeu de Siam." One drew a pistol from beneath his blouse and handed it to the other. As he was handing it to him, he noticed that the perspiration of his chest had made the powder damp. He primed the pistol and added more powder to what was already in the pan. Then the two men parted.

A certain Gallais, afterward killed in the Rue Beaubourg in the affair of April, boasted of having in his house seven hundred cartridges and twenty-four flints.

The government one day received a warning that arms and two hundred thousand cartridges had just been distributed in the Faubourg. On the following week thirty thousand cartridges were distributed. The remarkable point about it was, that the police were not able to seize a single one.

An intercepted letter read, "The day is not far distant when, within four hours by the clock, eighty thousand patriots will be under arms."

All this fermentation was public, one might almost say tranquil. The approaching insurrection was preparing its storm calmly in the face of the government. No singularity was lacking to this still subterranean crisis, which was already perceptible. The bourgeois talked peaceably to the working classes of what was in preparation. They said, "How is the rising coming along?" in the same tone in which they would have said, "How is your wife?"

A furniture dealer, of the Rue Moreau, inquired, "Well, when are you going to make the attack?"

Another shopkeeper said, "The attack will be made soon."

"I know it. A month ago, there were fifteen thousand of you, now there are twenty-five thousand." He offered his gun, and a neighbor offered a small pistol that he was willing to sell for seven francs.

Moreover, the revolutionary fever was growing. Not a point in Paris or in France was exempt from it. The artery was beating everywhere. Like those membranes that arise from certain inflammations and form in the human body, the network of secret societies began to spread all over the country. From the associations of the Friends of the People, which was at the same time public and secret, sprang the Society of the Rights of Man, which also dated from one of the orders of the day: Pluviose, Year 40 of the republican era, which was destined to survive even the mandate of the Court of Assizes, which pronounced its dissolution, and which did not hesitate to bestow on its sections significant names like the following: Pikes. Tocsin. Signal cannon. Phrygian cap. January 21. The beggars. The vagabonds. Forward march. Robespierre. Level. *Ca Ira*.

The Society of the Rights of Man engendered the Society of Action.

These were impatient individuals who broke away and hastened ahead. Other associations sought to recruit themselves from the great mother societies. The members of sections complained that they were torn asunder. Thus, the Gallic Society, and the committee of organization of the Municipalities. Thus the associations for the liberty of the press, for individual liberty, for the instruction of the people against indirect taxes. Then the Society of Equal Workingmen that was divided into three fractions, the levelers, the communists, the reformers. Then the Army of the Bastilles, a sort of cohort organized on a military footing, four men commanded by a corporal, ten by a sergeant, twenty by a sub-lieutenant, forty by a lieutenant; there were never more than five men who knew each other. Creation where precaution is combined with audacity and which seemed stamped with the genius of Venice.

The central committee, which was at the head, had two arms: the Society of Action, and the Army of the Bastilles.

A legitimist association, the Chevaliers of Fidelity, stirred about among these the republican affiliations. It was denounced and repudiated there.

The Parisian societies had ramifications in the principal cities, Lyons, Nantes, Lille, Marseilles, and each had its Society of the Rights of Man, the Charbonniere, and the Free Men. All had a revolutionary society that was called the Cougourde. We have already mentioned this word.

In Paris, the Faubourg Saint-Marceau kept up an equal buzzing with the Faubourg Saint-Antoine, and the schools were no less moved than the faubourgs. A café in the Rue Saint-Hyacinthe and the wine shop of the Seven Billiards, Rue des Mathurins-Saint-Jacques, served as rallying points for the students. The Society of the Friends of the A B C affiliated to the Mutualists of Angers, and to the Cougourde of Aix, met, as we have seen, in the Café Musain. These same young men assembled also, as we have stated already, in a restaurant wine shop of the Rue Mondetour that was called Corinthe. These meetings were secret. Others were as public as possible, and the reader can judge of their boldness from these fragments of an interrogatory undergone in one of the ulterior prosecutions, "Where was this meeting held?"

"In the Rue de la Paix."

"At whose house?"

"In the street."

"What sections were there?"

"Only one."

"Which?"

"The Manuel section."

"Who was its leader?"

"I."

"You are too young to have decided alone upon the bold course of attacking the government. Where did your instructions come from?"

"From the central committee."

The army was mined at the same time as the population, as was proved subsequently by the operations of Beford, Luneville, and Epinard. They counted on the fifty-second regiment, on the fifth, on the eighth, on the thirty-seventh, and on the twentieth light cavalry. In Burgundy and in the southern towns they planted the liberty tree; that is to say, a pole surmounted by a red cap.

Such was the situation.

The Faubourg Saint-Antoine, more than any other group of the population, as we stated in the beginning, accentuated this situation and made it felt. That was the sore point. This old Faubourg, peopled like an anthill, laborious, courageous, and angry as a hive of bees, was quivering with expectation and with the desire for a tumult. Everything was in a state of agitation there, without any interruption, however, of the regular work. It is impossible to convey an idea of this lively yet somber physiognomy. In this Faubourg exists poignant distress hidden under attic roofs; there also exist rare and ardent minds. It is particularly in the matter of distress and intelligence that it is dangerous to have extremes meet.

The Faubourg Saint-Antoine had also other causes to tremble; for it received the countershock of commercial crises, of failures, strikes, slack seasons, all inherent to great political disturbances. In times of revolution misery is both cause and effect. The blow it deals rebounds upon it. This population full of proud virtue, capable to the highest degree of latent heat, always ready to fly to arms, prompt to explode, irritated, deep, undermined, seemed to be only awaiting the fall of a spark. Whenever certain sparks float on the horizon chased by the wind of events, it is impossible not to think of the Faubourg Saint-Antoine and of the formidable chance, which has placed at the very gates of Paris that powder house of suffering and ideas.

The wine shops of the Faubourg Antoine, which have been more than once drawn in the sketches that the reader has just perused, possess historical notoriety. In troublous times people grow intoxicated there more on words than on wine. A sort of prophetic spirit and an afflatus of the future circulates there, swelling hearts and enlarging souls. The cabarets of the Faubourg Saint-Antoine resemble those taverns of Mont Aventine erected on the cave of the Sibyl and communicating with the profound and sacred breath; taverns where the tables were almost tripods, and where was drunk what Ennius calls the sibylline wine.

The Faubourg Saint-Antoine is a reservoir of people. Revolutionary agitations create fissures there, through which trickles the popular sovereignty. This sovereignty may do evil; it can be mistaken like any other; but, even when led astray, it remains great. We may say of it as of the blind Cyclops, Ingens.

In '93, according as the idea that was floating about was good or evil, according as it was the day of fanaticism or of enthusiasm, there leaped forth from the Faubourg Saint-Antoine now savage legions, now heroic bands.

Savage. Let us explain this word. When these bristling men, who in the early days of the revolutionary chaos, tattered, howling, wild, with uplifted bludgeon, pike on high, hurled themselves upon ancient Paris in an uproar, what did they want? They wanted an end to oppression, an end to tyranny, an end to the sword, work for men, instruction for the child, social sweetness for the woman, liberty, equality, fraternity, bread for all, the idea for all, the Edenizing of the world. Progress—and that holy, sweet, and good thing, progress, they claimed in terrible wise, driven to extremities as they were, half naked, club in fist, a roar in their mouths. They were savages, yes; but the savages of civilization.

They proclaimed right furiously; they were desirous, if only with fear and trembling, to force the human race to paradise. They seemed barbarians, and they were saviors. They demanded light with the mask of night.

Facing these men, who were ferocious, we admit, and terrifying, but ferocious and terrifying for good ends, there are other men, smiling, embroidered, gilded, beribboned, starred, in silk stockings, in white plumes, in yellow gloves, in varnished shoes, who, with their elbows on a velvet table, beside a marble chimneypiece, insist gently on demeanor and the preservation of the past, of the Middle Ages, of divine right, of fanaticism, of innocence, of slavery, of the death penalty, of war, glorifying in low tones and with politeness, the sword, the stake, and the scaffold. For our part, if we were forced to make a choice between the barbarians of civilization and the civilized men of barbarism, we should choose the barbarians.

But, thank Heaven, still another choice is possible. No perpendicular fall is necessary, in front any more than in the rear.

Neither despotism nor terrorism. We desire progress with a gentle slope.

God takes care of that. God's whole policy consists in rendering slopes less steep.

CHAPTER VI—ENJOLRAS AND HIS LIEUTENANTS

It was about this epoch that Enjolras, in view of a possible catastrophe, instituted a kind of mysterious census.

All were present at a secret meeting at the Café Musain.

Enjolras said, mixing his words with a few half-enigmatical but significant metaphors:

"It is proper that we should know where we stand and on whom we may count. If combatants are required, they must be provided. It can do no harm to have something with which to strike. Passersby always have more chance of being gored when there are bulls on the road than when there are none. Let us, therefore, reckon a little on the herd. How many of us are there? There is no question of postponing this task until tomorrow. Revolutionists should always be hurried; progress has no time to lose. Let us mistrust the unexpected. Let us not be caught unprepared. We must go over all the seams that we have made and see whether they hold fast. This business ought to be concluded today. Courfeyrac, you will see the polytechnic students. It is their day to go out. Today is Wednesday. Feuilly, you will see those of the Glaciere, will you not? Combeferre has promised me to go to Picpus. There is a perfect swarm and an excellent one there. Bahorel will visit the Estrapade. Prouvaire, the masons are growing lukewarm; you will bring us news from the lodge of the Rue de Grenelle-Saint-Honore. Joly will go to Dupuytren's clinical lecture, and feel the pulse of the medical school. Bossuet will take a little turn in the court and talk with the young law licentiates. I will take charge of the Cougourde myself."

"That arranges everything," said Courfeyrac.

"No."

"What else is there?"

"A very important thing."

"What is that?" asked Courfeyrac.

"The Barriere du Maine," replied Enjolras.

Enjolras remained for a moment as though absorbed in reflection, then he resumed:

"At the Barriere du Maine there are marble workers, painters, and journeymen in the studios of sculptors. They are an enthusiastic family, but liable to cool off. I don't know what has been the matter with them for some time past. They are thinking of something else. They are becoming extinguished. They pass their time playing dominoes. There is urgent need that someone should go and talk with them a little, but with firmness. They meet at Richefeu's. They are to be found there between twelve and one o'clock. Those ashes must be fanned into a glow. For that errand I had counted on that abstracted Marius, who is a good fellow on the whole, but he no longer comes to us. I need someone for the Barriere du Maine. I have no one."

"What about me?" said Grantaire. "Here am I."

"You?"

"I."

"You indoctrinate republicans! You warm up hearts that have grown cold in the name of principle!"

"Why not?"

"Are you good for anything?"

"I have a vague ambition in that direction," said Grantaire.

"You do not believe in everything."

"I believe in you."

"Grantaire will you do me a service?"

"Anything. I'll black your boots."

"Well, don't meddle with our affairs. Sleep yourself sober from your absinthe."

"You are an ingrate, Enjolras."

"You the man to go to the Barriere du Maine! You capable of it!"

"I am capable of descending the Rue de Gres, of crossing the Place Saint-Michel, of sloping through the Rue Monsieur-le-Prince, of taking the Rue de Vaugirard, of passing the Carmelites, of turning into the Rue d'Assas, of reaching the Rue du Cherche-Midi, of leaving behind me the Conseil de Guerre, of pacing the Rue des Vielles Tuileries, of striding across the boulevard, of following the Chaussée du Maine, of passing the barrier, and entering Richefeu's. I am capable of that. My shoes are capable of that."

"Do you know anything of those comrades who meet at Richefeu's?"

"Not much. We only address each other as thou."

"What will you say to them?"

"I will speak to them of Robespierre, pardi! Of Danton. Of principles."

"You?"

"I. But I don't receive justice. When I set about it, I am terrible. I have read Prudhomme, I know the Social Contract, I know my constitution of the year two by heart. 'The liberty of one citizen ends where the liberty of another citizen begins.' Do you take me for a brute? I have an old bankbill of the Republic in my drawer. The Rights of Man, the sovereignty of the people, sapristi! I am even a bit of a Hebertist. I can talk the most superb twaddle for six hours by the clock, watch in hand."

"Be serious," said Enjolras.

"I am wild," replied Grantaire.

Enjolras meditated for a few moments, and made the gesture of a man who has taken a resolution.

"Grantaire," he said gravely, "I consent to try you. You shall go to the Barriere du Maine."

Grantaire lived in furnished lodgings very near the Café Musain. He went out, and five minutes later he returned. He had gone home to put on a Robespierre waistcoat.

"Red," said he as he entered, and he looked intently at Enjolras. Then, with the palm of his energetic hand, he laid the two scarlet points of the waistcoat across his breast.

And stepping up to Enjolras, he whispered in his ear, "Be easy."

He jammed his hat on resolutely and departed.

A quarter of an hour later, the back room of the Café Musain was deserted. All the friends of the A B C were gone, each in his own direction, each to his own task. Enjolras, who had reserved the Cougourde of Aix for himself, was the last to leave.

Those members of the Cougourde of Aix who were in Paris then met on the plain of Issy, in one of the abandoned quarries which are so numerous in that side of Paris.

As Enjolras walked toward this place, he passed the whole situation in review in his own mind. The gravity of events was self-evident. When facts, the premonitory symptoms of latent social malady, move heavily, the slightest complication stops and entangles them. A phenomenon from which arises ruin and new births. Enjolras descried a luminous uplifting beneath the gloomy skirts of the future. Who knows? Perhaps the moment was at hand. The people were again taking possession of right, and what a fine spectacle! The revolution was again majestically taking possession of France and saying to the world: "The sequel tomorrow!" Enjolras was content. The furnace was being heated. He had at that moment a powder train of friends scattered all over Paris. He composed, in his own mind, with Combeferre's philosophical and penetrating eloquence, Feuilly's cosmopolitan enthusiasm, Courfeyrac's dash, Bahorel's smile, Jean Prouvaire's melancholy, Joly's science, Bossuet's sarcasms, a sort of electric spark that took fire nearly everywhere at once. All hands to work. Surely, the result would answer to the effort. This was well. This made him think of Grantaire.

"Hold," said he to himself, "the Barriere du Maine will not take me far out of my way. What if I were to go on as far as Richefeu's? Let us have a look at what Grantaire is about, and see how he is getting on."

One o'clock was striking from the Vaugirard steeple when Enjolras reached the Richefeu smoking room.

He pushed open the door, entered, folded his arms, letting the door fall to and strike his shoulders, and gazed at that room filled with tables, men, and smoke.

A voice broke forth from the mist of smoke, interrupted by another voice. It was Grantaire holding a dialogue with an adversary.

Grantaire was sitting opposite another figure, at a marble Saint-Anne table, strewn with grains of bran and dotted with dominos. He was hammering the table with his fist, and this is what Enjolras heard:

"Double-six."

"Fours."

"The pig! I have no more."

"You are dead. A two."

"Six."

"Three."

"One."

"It's my move."

"Four points."

"Not much."

"It's your turn."

"I have made an enormous mistake."

"You are doing well."

"Fifteen."

"Seven more."

"That makes me twenty-two."

"You weren't expecting that double-six. If I had placed it at the beginning, the whole play would have been changed."

"A two again."

"One."

"One! Well, five."

"I haven't any."

"It was your play, I believe?"

"Yes."

"Blank."

"What luck he has! Ah! You are lucky! [Long reverie.] Two."

"One."

"Neither five nor one. That's bad for you."

"Domino."

"Plague take it!"

BOOK SECOND: EPONINE

CHAPTER I—THE LARK'S MEADOW

Marius had witnessed the unexpected termination of the ambush upon whose track he had set Javert; but Javert had no sooner quitted the building, bearing off his prisoners in three hackney coaches, than Marius also glided out of the house. It was only nine o'clock in the evening. Marius betook himself to Courfeyrac. Courfeyrac was no longer the imperturbable inhabitant of the Latin Quarter, he had gone to live in the Rue de la Verrerie "for political reasons"; this quarter was one where, at that epoch, insurrection liked to install itself. Marius said to Courfeyrac, "I have come to sleep with you." Courfeyrac dragged a mattress off his bed, which was furnished with two, spread it out on the floor, and said, "There."

At seven o'clock on the following morning, Marius returned to the hovel, paid the quarter's rent which he owed to Ma'am Bougon, had his books, his bed, his table, his commode, and his two chairs loaded on a handcart and went off without leaving his address, so that when Javert returned in the course of the morning, for the purpose of questioning Marius as to the events of the preceding evening, he found only Ma'am Bougon, who answered, "Moved away!"

Ma'am Bougon was convinced that Marius was to some extent an accomplice of the robbers who had been seized the night before. "Who would ever have said it?" she exclaimed to the portresses of the quarter, "a young man like that, who had the air of a girl!"

Marius had two reasons for this prompt change of residence. The first was, that he now had a horror of that house, where he had beheld, so close at hand, and in its most repulsive and most ferocious development, a social deformity which is, perhaps, even more terrible than the wicked rich man, the wicked poor man. The second was, that he did not wish to figure in the lawsuit that would ensue in all probability, and be brought in to testify against Thenardier.

Javert thought that the young man, whose name he had forgotten, was afraid, and had fled, or perhaps, had not even returned home at the time of the ambush; he made some efforts to find him, however, but without success.

A month passed, then another. Marius was still with Courfeyrac. He had learned from a young licentiate in law, an habitual frequenter of the courts, that Thenardier was in close confinement. Every Monday, Marius had five francs handed in to the clerk's office of La Force for Thenardier.

As Marius had no longer any money, he borrowed the five francs from Courfeyrac. It was the first time in his life that he had ever borrowed money. These periodical five francs were a double riddle to Courfeyrac who lent and to Thenardier who received them. "To whom can they go?" thought Courfeyrac. "From where can this come to me?" Thenardier asked himself.

Moreover, Marius was heartbroken. Everything had plunged through a trapdoor once more. He no longer saw anything before him; his life was again buried in mystery where he wandered fumblingly. He had for a moment beheld very close at hand, in that obscurity, the young girl whom he loved, the old man who seemed to be her father, those unknown beings, who were his only interest and his only hope in this world; and, at the very moment when he thought himself on the point of grasping them, a gust had swept all these shadows away. Not a spark of certainty and truth had been emitted even in the most terrible of collisions. No conjecture was possible. He no longer knew even the name that he thought he knew. It certainly was not Ursule. And the Lark was a nickname. And what was he to think of the old man? Was he actually in hiding from the police? The white-haired workman whom Marius had encountered in the vicinity of the Invalides recurred to his mind. It now seemed probable that that workingman and M. Leblanc were one and the same person. So he disguised himself? That man had his heroic and his equivocal sides. Why had he not called for help? Why had he fled? Was he, or was he not, the father of the young girl? Was he, in short, the man whom Thenardier thought that he recognized?

Thenardier might have been mistaken. These formed so many insoluble problems. All this, it is true, detracted nothing from the angelic charms of the young girl of the Luxembourg. Heart-rending distress; Marius bore a passion in his heart, and night over his eyes. He was thrust onward, he was drawn, and he could not stir. All had vanished, save love. Of love itself he had lost the instincts and the sudden illuminations. Ordinarily, this flame that burns us lights us also a little, and casts some useful gleams without. But Marius no longer even heard these mute counsels of passion. He never said to himself: "What if I were to go to such a place? What if I were to try such and such a thing?" The girl whom he could no longer call Ursule was evidently somewhere; nothing warned Marius in what direction he should seek her. His whole life was now summed up in two words; absolute uncertainty within an impenetrable fog. To see her once again; he still aspired to this, but he no longer expected it.

To crown all, his poverty had returned. He felt that icy breath close to him, on his heels. In the midst of his torments, and long before this, he had discontinued his work, and nothing is more dangerous than discontinued work; it is a habit that vanishes. A habit that is easy to get rid of, and difficult to take up again.

A certain amount of dreaming is good, like a narcotic in discreet doses. It lulls to sleep the fevers of the mind at labor, which are sometimes severe, and produces in the spirit a soft and fresh vapor which corrects the over-harsh contours of pure thought, fills in gaps here and there, binds together and rounds off the angles of the ideas. But too much dreaming sinks and drowns. Woe to the brain worker who allows himself to fall entirely from thought into reverie! He thinks that he can reascend with equal ease, and he tells himself that, after all, it is the same thing. Error!

Thought is the toil of the intelligence, reverie its voluptuousness. To replace thought with reverie is to confound a poison with a food.

Marius had begun in that way, as the reader will remember. Passion had supervened and had finished the work of precipitating him into chimeras without object or bottom. One no longer emerges from one's self except for the purpose of going off to dream. Idle production. Tumultuous and stagnant gulf. And, in proportion as labor diminishes, needs increase. This is a law. Man, in a state of reverie, is generally prodigal and slack; the unstrung mind cannot hold life within close bounds.

There is, in that mode of life, good mingled with evil, for if enervation is baleful, generosity is good and healthful. But the poor man who is generous and noble, and who does not work, is lost. Resources are exhausted, needs crop up.

Fatal declivity down which the most honest and the firmest as well as the most feeble and most vicious are drawn, and which ends in one of two holds—suicide or crime.

By dint of going outdoors to think, the day comes when one goes out to throw one's self in the water.

Excess of reverie breeds men like Escousse and Lebras.

Marius was descending this declivity at a slow pace, with his eyes fixed on the girl whom he no longer saw. What we have just written seems strange, and yet it is true. The memory of an absent being kindles in the darkness of the heart; the more it has disappeared, the more it beams; the gloomy and despairing soul sees this light on its horizon; the star of the inner night. She—that was Marius's whole thought. He meditated of nothing else; he was confusedly conscious that his old coat was becoming an impossible coat, and that his new coat was growing old, that his shirts were wearing out, that his hat was wearing out, that his boots were giving out, and he said to himself, "If I could but see her once again before I die!"

One sweet idea alone was left to him, that she had loved him, that her glance had told him so, that she did not know his name, but that she did know his soul, and that, wherever she was, however mysterious the place, she still loved him perhaps. Who knows whether she were not thinking of him as he was thinking of her? Sometimes, in those inexplicable hours such as are experienced by every heart that loves, though he had no reasons for anything but sadness and yet felt an obscure quiver of joy, he said to himself, "It is her thoughts that are coming to me!" Then he added, "Perhaps my thoughts reach her also."

This illusion, at which he shook his head a moment later, was sufficient, nevertheless, to throw beams, which at times resembled hope, into his soul. From time to time, especially at that evening hour, which is the most depressing to even the dreamy, he allowed the purest, the most impersonal, the most ideal of the reveries that filled his brain, to fall upon a notebook, which contained nothing else. He called this "writing to her."

It must not be supposed that his reason was deranged. Quite the contrary. He had lost the faculty of working and of moving firmly toward any fixed goal, but he was endowed with more clear-sightedness and rectitude than ever. Marius surveyed by a calm and real, although peculiar light, what passed before his eyes, even the most indifferent deeds and men; he pronounced a just criticism on everything with a sort of honest dejection and candid disinterestedness. His judgment, which was almost wholly disassociated from hope, held itself aloof and soared on high.

In this state of mind nothing escaped him, nothing deceived him, and every moment he was discovering the foundation of life, of humanity, and of destiny. Happy, even in the midst of anguish, is he to whom God has given a soul worthy of love and of unhappiness! He who has not viewed the things of this world and the heart of man under this double light has seen nothing and knows nothing of the true.

The soul that loves and suffers is in a state of sublimity.

However, day followed day, and nothing new presented itself. It merely seemed to him, that the somber space that still remained to be traversed by him was growing shorter with every instant. He thought that he already distinctly perceived the brink of the bottomless abyss.

"What!" he repeated to himself. "Shall I not see her again before then!"

When you have ascended the Rue Saint-Jacques, left the barrier on one side and followed the old inner boulevard for some distance, you reach the Rue de la Santé, then the Glaciere, and, a little while before arriving at the little river of the Gobelins, you come to a sort of field, which is the only spot in the long and monotonous chain of the boulevards of Paris, where Ruysdeel would be tempted to sit down.

There is something indescribable there that exhales grace, a green meadow traversed by tightly stretched lines, from which flutter rags drying in the wind, and an old market-gardener's house, built in the time of Louis XIII, with its great roof oddly pierced with dormer windows, dilapidated palisades, a little water amid poplar-trees, women, voices, laughter; on the horizon the Pantheon, the pole of the Deaf-Mutes, the Val-de-Grace, black, squat, fantastic, amusing, magnificent, and in the background, the severe square crests of the towers of Notre Dame.

As the place is worth looking at, no one goes there. Hardly one cart or wagoner passes in a quarter of an hour.

It chanced that Marius's solitary strolls led him to this plot of ground, near the water. That day, there was a rarity on the boulevard, a passerby. Marius, vaguely impressed with the almost savage beauty of the place, asked this passerby, "What is the name of this spot?"

The person replied, "It is the Lark's meadow."

And he added, "It was here that Ulbach killed the shepherdess of Ivry."

But after the word "Lark" Marius heard nothing more. These sudden congealments in the state of reverie, which a single word suffices to evoke, do occur. The entire thought is abruptly condensed around an idea, and it is no longer capable of perceiving anything else.

The Lark was the appellation that had replaced Ursule in the depths of Marius's melancholy. "Stop," said he with a sort of unreasoning stupor peculiar to these mysterious asides, "this is her meadow. I shall know where she lives now."

It was absurd, but irresistible.

And every day he returned to that meadow of the Lark.

CHAPTER II—EMBRYONIC FORMATION OF CRIMES IN THE INCUBATION OF PRISONS

Javert's triumph in the Gorbeau hovel seemed complete, but had not been so. In the first place, and this constituted the principal anxiety, Javert had not taken the prisoner prisoner. The assassinated man who flees is more suspicious than the assassin, and it is probable that this personage, who had been so precious a capture for the ruffians, would be no less fine a prize for the authorities.

And then, Montparnasse had escaped Javert.

Another opportunity of laying hands on that "devil's dandy" must be waited for. Montparnasse had, in fact, encountered Eponine as she stood on the watch under the trees of the boulevard, and had led her off, preferring to play Nemorin with the daughter rather than Schinderhannes with the father. It was well that he did so. He was free. As for Eponine, Javert had caused her to be seized; a mediocre consolation. Eponine had joined Azelma at Les Madelonettes.

And finally, on the way from the Gorbeau house to La Force, one of the principal prisoners, Claquesous, had been lost. It was not known how this had been affected, the police agents and the sergeants "could not understand it at all." He had converted himself into vapor, he had slipped through the handcuffs, he had trickled through the crevices of the carriage, the fiacre was cracked, and he had fled; all that they were able to say was, that on arriving at the prison, there was no Claquesous. Either the fairies or the police had had a hand in it. Had Claquesous melted into the shadows like a snowflake in water? Had there been unavowed connivance of the police agents? Did this man belong to the double enigma of order and disorder? Was he concentric with infraction and repression? Had this sphinx his fore paws in crime and his hind paws in authority? Javert did not accept such comminations, and would have bristled up against such compromises; but his squad included other inspectors besides himself, who were more initiated than he, perhaps, although they were his subordinates in the secrets of the Prefecture, and Claquesous had been such a villain that he might make a very good agent. It is an excellent thing for ruffianism and an admirable thing for the police to be on such intimate juggling terms with the night. These double-edged rascals do exist. However that may be, Claquesous had gone astray and was not found again. Javert appeared to be more irritated than amazed at this.

As for Marius, "that booby of a lawyer," who had probably become frightened, and whose name Javert had forgotten, Javert attached very little importance to him. Moreover, a lawyer can be hunted up at any time. But was he a lawyer after all?

The investigation had begun.

The magistrate had thought it advisable not to put one of these men of the band of Patron Minette in close confinement, in the hope that he would chatter. This man was Brujon, the long-haired man of the Rue du Petit-Banquier. He had been let loose in the Charlemagne courtyard, and the eyes of the watchers were fixed on him.

This name of Brujon is one of the souvenirs of La Force. In that hideous courtyard, called the court of the Batiment-Neuf (New Building), which the administration called the court Saint-Bernard, and which the robbers called the Fosseaux-Lions (the Lion's Ditch), on that wall covered with scales and leprosy, which rose on the left to a level with the roofs, near an old door of rusty iron which led to the ancient chapel of the ducal residence of La Force, then turned in a dormitory for ruffians, there could still be seen, twelve years ago, a sort of fortress roughly carved in the stone with a nail, and beneath it this signature: BRUJON, 1811.

The Brujon of 1811 was the father of the Brujon of 1832.

The latter, of whom the reader caught but a glimpse at the Gorbeau house, was a very cunning and very adroit young spark, with a bewildered and plaintive air. It was in consequence of this plaintive air that the magistrate had released him, thinking him more useful in the Charlemagne yard than in close confinement.

Robbers do not interrupt their profession because they are in the hands of justice. They do not let themselves be put out by such a trifle as that. To be in prison for one crime is no reason for not beginning on another crime. They are artists, who have one picture in the salon, and who toil, nonetheless, on a new work in their studios.

Brujon seemed to be stupefied by prison. He could sometimes be seen standing by the hour together in front of the sutler's window in the Charlemagne yard, staring like an idiot at the sordid list of prices that began with: garlic, 62 centimes, and ended with: cigar, 5 centimes. Or he passed his time in trembling, chattering his teeth, saying that he had a fever, and inquiring whether one of the eight and twenty beds in the fever ward was vacant.

All at once, toward the end of February, 1832, it was discovered that Brujon, that somnolent fellow, had had three different commissions executed by the errand-men of the establishment, not under his own name, but in the name of three of his comrades; and they had cost him in all fifty sous, an exorbitant outlay, which attracted the attention of the prison corporal.

Inquiries were instituted, and on consulting the tariff of commissions posted in the convict's parlor, it was learned that the fifty sous could be analyzed as follows: three commissions; one to the Pantheon, ten sous; one to Val-de-Grace, fifteen sous; and one to the Barriere de Grenelle, twenty-five sous. This last was the dearest of the whole tariff. Now, at the Pantheon, at the Val-de-Grace, and at the Barriere de Grenelle were situated the domiciles of the three very redoubtable prowlers of the barriers, Kruideniers, alias Bizarre, Glorieux, an ex-convict, and Barre-Carosse, upon whom the attention of the police was directed by this incident. It was thought that these men were members of Patron Minette; two of those leaders, Babet and Gueulemer, had been captured. It was supposed that the messages, which had been addressed, not to houses, but to people who were waiting for them in the street, must have contained information with regard to some crime that had been plotted. They were in possession of other indications; they laid hand on the three prowlers, and supposed that they had circumvented some one or other of Brujon's machinations.

About a week after these measures had been taken, one night, as the superintendent of the watch who had been inspecting the lower dormitory in the Batiment-Neuf, was about to drop his chestnut in the box—this was the means adopted to make sure that the watchmen performed their duties punctually; every hour a chestnut must be dropped into all the boxes nailed to the doors of the dormitories—a watchman looked through the peephole of the dormitory and beheld Brujon sitting on his bed and writing something by the light of the hall lamp. The guardian entered, Brujon was put in a solitary cell for a month, but they were not able to seize what he had written. The police learned nothing further about it.

What is certain is, that on the following morning, a "postilion" was flung from the Charlemagne yard into the Lions' Ditch, over the five-story building that separated the two courtyards.

What prisoners call a "postilion" is a pallet of bread artistically molded, which is sent into Ireland, that is to say, over the roofs of a prison, from one courtyard to another. Etymology: over England; from one land to another; into Ireland. This little pellet falls in the yard. The man who picks it up opens it and finds in it a note addressed to some prisoner in that yard. If it is a prisoner who finds the treasure, he forwards the note to its destination; if it is a keeper, or one of the prisoners secretly sold who are called sheep in prisons and foxes in the galleys, the note is taken to the office and handed over to the police.

On this occasion, the postilion reached its address, although the person to whom it was addressed was, at that moment, in solitary confinement. This person was no other than Babet, one of the four heads of Patron Minette.

The postilion contained a roll of paper on which only these two lines were written:

"Babet. There is an affair in the Rue Plumet. A gate on a garden."

This is what Brujon had written the night before.

In spite of male and female searchers, Babet managed to pass the note on from La Force to the Salpetriere, to a "good friend" whom he had and who was shut up there. This woman, in turn, transmitted the note to another woman of her acquaintance, a certain Magnon, who was strongly suspected by the police, though not yet arrested. This Magnon, whose name the reader has already seen, had relations with the Thenardier, which will be described in detail later on, and she could, by going to see Eponine, serve as a bridge between the Salpetriere and Les Madelonettes.

It happened, that at precisely that moment, as proofs were wanting in the investigation directed against Thenardier in the matter of his daughters, Eponine and Azelma were released. When Eponine came out, Magnon, who was watching the gate of the Madelonettes, handed her Brujon's note to Babet, charging her to look into the matter.

Eponine went to the Rue Plumet, recognized the gate and the garden, observed the house, spied, lurked, and, a few days later, brought to Magnon, who delivers in the Rue Clocheperce, a biscuit, which Magnon transmitted to Babet's mistress in the Salpetriere. A biscuit, in the shady symbolism of prisons, signifies: nothing to be done.

So that in less than a week from that time, as Brujon and Babet met in the circle of La Force, the one on his way to the examination, the other on his way from it:

"Well?" asked Brujon, "the Rue P.?"

"Biscuit," replied Babet. Thus did the fetus of crime engendered by Brujon in La Force miscarry.

This miscarriage had its consequences, however, which were perfectly distinct from Brujon's program. The reader will see what they were.

Often when we think we are knotting one thread, we are tying quite another.

CHAPTER III—APPARITION TO FATHER MABEUF

Marius no longer went to see anyone, but he sometimes encountered Father Mabeuf by chance.

While Marius was slowly descending those melancholy steps, which may be called the cellar stairs, and which lead to places without light, where the happy can be heard walking overhead, M. Mabeuf was descending on his side.

The Flora of Cauteretz no longer sold at all. The experiments on indigo had not been successful in the little garden of Austerlitz, which had a bad exposure. M. Mabeuf could cultivate there only a few plants that love shade and dampness. Nevertheless, he did not become discouraged. He had obtained a corner in the Jardin des Plantes, with a good exposure, to make his trials with indigo "at his own expense." For this purpose he had pawned his copperplates of the Flora. He had reduced his breakfast to two eggs, and he left one of these for his old servant, to whom he had paid no wages for the last fifteen months. And often his breakfast was his only meal. He no longer smiled with his infantile smile, he had grown morose and no longer received visitors. Marius did well not to dream of going there. Sometimes, at the hour when M. Mabeuf was on his way to the Jardin des Plantes, the old man and the young man passed each other on the Boulevard de l'Hopital. They did not speak, and only exchanged a melancholy sign of the head. A heartbreaking thing it is that there comes a moment when misery looses bonds! Two men who have been friends become two chance passersby.

Royal the bookseller was dead. M. Mabeuf no longer knew his books, his garden, or his indigo; these were the three forms which happiness, pleasure, and hope had assumed for him. This sufficed him for his living. He said to himself, "When I shall have made my balls of bluing, I shall be rich, I will withdraw my copperplates from the pawn shop, I will put my flora in vogue again with trickery, plenty of money and advertisements in the newspapers and I will buy, I know well where, a copy of Pierre de Medine's *Art de Naviguer*, with wood-cuts, edition of 1655." In the meantime, he toiled all day over his plot of indigo, and at night he returned home to water his garden, and to read his books. At that epoch, M. Mabeuf was nearly eighty years of age.

One evening he had a singular apparition.

He had returned home while it was still broad daylight. Mother Plutarque, whose health was declining, was ill and in bed. He had dined on a bone, on which a little meat lingered, and a bit of bread that he had found on the kitchen table, and had seated himself on an overturned stone post, which took the place of a bench in his garden.

Near this bench there rose, after the fashion in orchard gardens, a sort of large chest, of beams and planks, much dilapidated, a rabbit hutch on the ground floor, a fruit closet on the first. There was nothing in the hutch, but there were a few apples in the fruit closet, the remains of the winter's provision.

M. Mabeuf had set himself to turning over and reading, with the aid of his glasses, two books of which he was passionately fond and in which, a serious thing at his age, he was interested. His natural timidity rendered him accessible to the acceptance of superstitions in a certain degree. The first of these books was the famous treatise of President Delancre, De l'inconstance des Demons; the other was a quarto by Mutor de la Rubaudière, Sur les Diables de Vauvert et les Gobelins de la Bievre. This last-mentioned old volume interested him all the more, because his garden had been one of the spots haunted by goblins in former times. The twilight had begun to whiten what was on high and to blacken all below. As he read, over the top of the book, which he held in his hand, Father Mabeuf was surveying his plants, and among others a magnificent rhododendron which was one of his consolations; four days of heat, wind, and sun without a drop of rain, had passed; the stalks were bending, the buds drooping, the leaves falling; all this needed water, the rhododendron was particularly sad. Father Mabeuf was one of those persons for whom plants have souls. The old man had toiled all day over his indigo plot, he was worn out with fatigue, but he rose, laid his books on the bench, and walked, all bent over and with tottering footsteps, to the well, but when he had grasped the chain, he could not even draw it sufficiently to unhook it. Then he turned around and cast a glance of anguish toward heaven that was becoming studded with stars.

The evening had that serenity which overwhelms the troubles of man beneath an indescribably mournful and eternal joy. The night promised to be as arid as the day had been.

"Stars everywhere!" thought the old man; "not the tiniest cloud! Not a drop of water!"

And his head, which had been upraised for a moment, fell back upon his breast.

He raised it again, and once more looked at the sky, murmuring, "A tear of dew! A little pity!"

He tried again to unhook the chain of the well, and could not.

At that moment, he heard a voice saying, "Father Mabeuf, would you like to have me water your garden for you?"

At the same time, a noise as of a wild animal passing became audible in the hedge, and he beheld emerging from the shrubbery a sort of tall, slender girl, who drew herself up in front of him and stared boldly at him. She had less the air of a human being than of a form that had just blossomed forth from the twilight.

Before Father Mabeuf, who was easily terrified, and who was, as we have said, quick to take alarm, was able to reply by a single syllable, this being, whose movements had a sort of odd abruptness in the darkness, had unhooked the chain, plunged in, and withdrawn the bucket, and filled the watering pot, and the goodman beheld this apparition, which had bare feet and a tattered petticoat, running about among the flower beds distributing life around her. The sound of the watering pot on the leaves filled Father Mabeuf's soul with ecstasy. It seemed to him that the rhododendron was happy now.

The first bucketful emptied, the girl drew a second, then a third. She watered the whole garden.

There was something about her, as she thus ran about among paths, where her outline appeared perfectly black, waving her angular arms, and with her fichu all in rags, that resembled a bat.

When she had finished, Father Mabeuf approached her with tears in his eyes, and laid his hand on her brow.

"God will bless you," said he, "you are an angel since you take care of the flowers."

"No," she replied. "I am the devil, but that's all the same to me."

The old man exclaimed, without either waiting for or hearing her response, "What a pity that I am so unhappy and so poor, and that I can do nothing for you!"

"You can do something," said she.

"What?"

"Tell me where M. Marius lives."

The old man did not understand. "What Monsieur Marius?"

He raised his glassy eyes and seemed to be seeking something that had vanished.

"A young man who used to come here."

In the meantime, M. Mabeuf had searched his memory.

"Ah! Yes——" he exclaimed. "I know what you mean. Wait! Monsieur Marius—the Baron Marius Pontmercy, *parbleu*! He lives, or rather, he no longer lives, ah well, I don't know."

As he spoke, he had bent over to train a branch of rhododendron, and he continued, "Hold, I know now. He very often passes along the boulevard, and goes in the direction of the Glaciere, Rue Croulebarbe. The meadow of the Lark. Go there. It is not hard to meet him."

When M. Mabeuf straightened himself up, there was no longer anyone there; the girl had disappeared.

He was decidedly terrified.

"Really," he thought, "if my garden had not been watered, I should think that she was a spirit."

An hour later, when he was in bed, it came back to him, and as he fell asleep, at that confused moment when thought, like that fabulous bird which changes itself into a fish in order to cross the sea, little by little assumes the form of a dream in order to traverse slumber, he said to himself in a bewildered way, "In sooth, that greatly resembles what Rubaudière narrates of the goblins. Could it have been a goblin?"

CHAPTER IV—AN APPARITION
TO MARIUS

Some days after this visit of a "spirit" to Farmer Mabeuf, one morning, it was on a Monday, the day when Marius borrowed the hundred-sou piece from Courfeyrac for Thenardier—Marius had put this coin in his pocket, and before carrying it to the clerk's office, he had gone "to take a little stroll," in the hope that this would make him work on his return. It was always thus, however. As soon as he rose, he seated himself before a book and a sheet of paper in order to scribble some translation; his task at that epoch consisted in turning into French a celebrated quarrel between Germans, the Gans and Savigny controversy; he took Savigny, he took Gans, read four lines, tried to write one, could not, saw a star between him and his paper, and rose from his chair, saying, "I shall go out. That will put me in spirits."

And off he went to the Lark's meadow.

There he beheld more than ever the star, and less than ever Savigny and Gans.

He returned home, tried to take up his work again, and did not succeed; there was no means of reknotting a single one of the threads that was broken in his brain; then he said to himself, "I will not go out tomorrow. It prevents my working." And he went out every day.

He lived in the Lark's meadow more than in Courfeyrac's lodgings. That was his real address: Boulevard de la Santé, at the seventh tree from the Rue Croulebarbe.

That morning he had quitted the seventh tree and had seated himself on the parapet of the River des Gobelins. A cheerful sunlight penetrated the freshly unfolded and luminous leaves.

He was dreaming of "Her." And his meditation turning to a reproach, fell back upon himself; he reflected dolefully on his idleness, his paralysis of soul, which was gaining on him, and of that night which was growing more dense every moment before him, to such a point that he no longer even saw the sun.

Nevertheless, athwart this painful extrication of indistinct ideas that was not even a monologue, so feeble had action become in him, and he had no longer the force to care to despair, athwart this melancholy absorption, sensations from without did reach him. He heard behind him, beneath him, on both banks of the river, the laundresses of the Gobelins beating their linen, and above his head, the birds chattering and singing in the elm trees. On the one hand, the sound of liberty, the careless happiness of the leisure, which has wings; on the other, the sound of toil. What caused him to meditate deeply, and almost reflect, were two cheerful sounds.

All at once, in the midst of his dejected ecstasy, he heard a familiar voice saying, "Come! Here he is!"

He raised his eyes, and recognized that wretched child who had come to him one morning, the elder of the Thenardier daughters, Eponine; he knew her name now. Strange to say, she had grown poorer and prettier, two steps, which it had not seemed within her power to take. She had accomplished a double progress, toward the light and toward distress. She was barefooted and in rags, as on the day when she had so resolutely entered his chamber, only her rags were two months older now, the holes were larger, the tatters more sordid. It was the same harsh voice, the same brow dimmed and wrinkled with tan, the same free, wild, and vacillating glance. She had besides, more than formerly, in her face that indescribably terrified and lamentable something that a sojourn in a prison adds to wretchedness.

She had bits of straw and hay in her hair, not like Ophelia through having gone mad from the contagion of Hamlet's madness, but because she had slept in the loft of some stable.

And in spite of it all, she was beautiful. What a star art thou, O youth!

In the meantime, she had halted in front of Marius with a trace of joy in her livid countenance, and something that resembled a smile.

She stood for several moments as though incapable of speech.

"So I have met you at last!" she said at length. "Father Mabeuf was right, it was on this boulevard! How I have hunted for you! If you only knew! Do you know? I have been in the jug. A fortnight! They let me out! Seeing that there was nothing against me, and that, moreover, I had not reached years of discretion. I lack two months of it. Oh! How I have hunted for you! These six weeks! So you don't live down there any more?"

"No," said Marius.

"Ah! I understand. Because of that affair. Those takedowns are disagreeable. You cleared out. Come now! Why do you wear old hats like this! A young man like you ought to have fine clothes. Do you know, Monsieur Marius, Father Mabeuf calls you Baron Marius, I don't know what. It isn't true that you are a baron? Barons are old fellows, they go to the Luxembourg, in front of the château, where there is the most sun, and they read the Quotidienne for a sou. I once carried a letter to a baron of that sort. He was over a hundred years old. Say, where do you live now?"

Marius made no reply.

"Ah!" she went on. "You have a hole in your shirt. I must sew it up for you."

She resumed with an expression that gradually clouded over, "You don't seem glad to see me."

Marius held his peace; she remained silent for a moment, then exclaimed, "But if I choose, nevertheless, I could force you to look glad!"

"What?" demanded Marius. "What do you mean?"

"Ah! You used to call me thou," she retorted.

"Well, then, what dost thou mean?"

She bit her lips; she seemed to hesitate, as though a prey to some sort of inward conflict. At last she appeared to come to a decision.

"So much the worse, I don't care. You have a melancholy air, I want you to be pleased. Only promise me that you will smile. I want to see you smile and hear you say, 'Ah, well, that's good.' Poor Mr. Marius! You know? You promised me that you would give me anything I like—"

"Yes! Only speak!"

She looked Marius full in the eye, and said, "I have the address."

Marius turned pale. All the blood flowed back to his heart.

"What address?"

"The address that you asked me to get!"

She added, as though with an effort, "The address—you know very well!"

"Yes!" stammered Marius.

"Of that young lady."

This word uttered, she sighed deeply.

Marius sprang from the parapet on which he had been sitting and seized her hand distractedly.

"Oh! Well! Lead me there! Tell me! Ask of me anything you wish! Where is it?"

"Come with me," she responded. "I don't know the street or number very well; it is in quite the other direction from here, but I know the house well, I will take you to it."

She withdrew her hand and went on, in a tone which could have rent the heart of an observer, but which did not even graze Marius in his intoxicated and ecstatic state, "Oh! How glad you are!"

A cloud swept across Marius' brow. He seized Eponine by the arm, "Swear one thing to me!"

"Swear!" said she. "What does that mean? Come! You want me to swear?"

And she laughed.

"Your father! Promise me, Eponine! Swear to me that you will not give this address to your father!"

She turned to him with a stupefied air.

"Eponine! How do you know that my name is Eponine?"

"Promise what I tell you!"

But she did not seem to hear him.

"That's nice! You have called me Eponine!"

Marius grasped both her arms at once.

"But answer me, in the name of Heaven! Pay attention to what I am saying to you, swear to me that you will not tell your father this address that you know!"

"My father!" said she. "Ah yes, my father! Be at ease. He's in close confinement. Besides, what do I care for my father!"

"But you do not promise me!" exclaimed Marius.

"Let go of me!" she said, bursting into a laugh. "How you do shake me! Yes! Yes! I promise that! I swear that to you! What is that to me? I will not tell my father the address. There! Is that right? Is that it?"

"Nor to anyone?" said Marius.

"Nor to anyone."

"Now," resumed Marius, "take me there."

"Immediately?"

"Immediately."

"Come along. Ah! How pleased he is!" said she.

After a few steps she halted.

"You are following me too closely, Monsieur Marius. Let me go on ahead, and follow me so, without seeming to do it. A nice young man like you must not be seen with a woman like me."

No tongue can express all that lay in that word, woman, thus pronounced by that child.

She proceeded a dozen paces and then halted once more; Marius joined her. She addressed him sideways, and without turning toward him, "By the way, you know that you promised me something?"

Marius fumbled in his pocket. All that he owned in the world was the five francs intended for Thenardier the father. He took them and laid them in Eponine's hand.

She opened her fingers and let the coin fall to the ground, and gazed at him with a gloomy air.

"I don't want your money," said she.

BOOK THIRD: THE HOUSE IN THE RUE PLUMET

CHAPTER I—THE HOUSE WITH A SECRET

About the middle of the last century, a chief justice in the Parliament of Paris having a mistress and concealing the fact—for at that period the grand seignors displayed their mistresses, and the bourgeois concealed them— had "a little house" built in the Faubourg Saint-Germain, in the deserted Rue Blomet, which is now called Rue Plumet, not far from the spot that was then designated as Combat des Animaux.

This house was composed of a single-storied pavilion; two rooms on the ground floor, two chambers on the first floor, a kitchen downstairs, a boudoir upstairs, an attic under the roof, the whole preceded by a garden with a large gate opening on the street. This garden was about an acre and a half in extent. This was all that could be seen by passersby; but behind the pavilion there was a narrow courtyard, and at the end of the courtyard a low building consisting of two rooms and a cellar, a sort of preparation destined to conceal a child and nurse in case of need. This building communicated in the rear by a masked door that opened by a secret spring, with a long, narrow, paved winding corridor, open to the sky, hemmed in with two lofty walls, which, hidden with wonderful art, and lost as it were between garden enclosures and cultivated land, all of whose angles and detours it followed, ended in another door, also with a secret lock, which opened a quarter of a league away, almost in another quarter, at the solitary extremity of the Rue du Babylone.

Through this the chief justice entered, so that even those who were spying on him and following him would merely have observed that the justice betook himself every day in a mysterious way somewhere, and would never have suspected that to go to the Rue de Babylone was to go to the Rue Blomet. Thanks to clever purchasers of land, the magistrate had been able to make a secret, sewerlike passage on his own property, and consequently, without interference. Later on, he had sold in little parcels, for gardens and market gardens, the lots of ground adjoining the corridor, and the proprietors of these lots on both sides thought they had a party wall before their eyes, and did not even suspect the long, paved ribbon winding between two walls amid their flowerbeds and their orchards. Only the birds beheld this curiosity. It is probable that the linnets and tomtits of the last century gossiped a great deal about the chief justice.

The pavilion, built of stone in the taste of Mansard, wainscoted and furnished in the Watteau style, rocaille on the inside, old-fashioned on the outside, walled-in with a triple hedge of flowers, had something discreet, coquettish, and solemn about it, as befits a caprice of love and magistracy.

This house and corridor, which have now disappeared, were in existence fifteen years ago. In '93 a coppersmith had purchased the house with the idea of demolishing it, but had not been able to pay the price; the nation made him bankrupt. So that it was the house that demolished the coppersmith. After that, the house remained uninhabited, and fell slowly to ruin, as does every dwelling to which the presence of man does not communicate life. It had remained fitted with its old furniture, was always for sale or to let, and the ten or a dozen people who passed through the Rue Plumet were warned of the fact by a yellow and illegible bit of writing which had hung on the garden wall since 1819.

Toward the end of the Restoration, these same passersby might have noticed that the bill had disappeared, and even that the shutters on the first floor were open. The house was occupied, in fact. The windows had short curtains, a sign that there was a woman about.

In the month of October, 1829, a man of a certain age had presented himself and had hired the house just as it stood, including, of course, the back building and the lane which ended in the Rue de Babylone. He had had the secret openings of the two doors to this passage repaired. The house, as we have just mentioned, was still very nearly furnished with the justice's old fitting; the new tenant had ordered some repairs, had added what was lacking here and there, had replaced the paving-stones in the yard, bricks in the floors, steps in the stairs, missing bits in the inlaid floors and the glass in the lattice windows, and had finally installed himself there with a young girl and an elderly maid servant, without commotion, rather like a person who is slipping in than like a man who is entering his own house. The neighbors did not gossip about him, for the reason that there were no neighbors.

This unobtrusive tenant was Jean Valjean, the young girl was Cosette. The servant was a woman named Toussaint, whom Jean Valjean had saved from the hospital and from wretchedness, and who was elderly, a stammerer, and from the provinces, three qualities which had decided Jean Valjean to take her with him. He had hired the house under the name of M. Fauchelevent, independent gentleman. In all that has been related heretofore, the reader has, doubtless, been no less prompt than Thenardier to recognize Jean Valjean.

Why had Jean Valjean quitted the convent of the Petit-Picpus? What had happened?

Nothing had happened.

It will be remembered that Jean Valjean was happy in the convent, so happy that his conscience finally took the alarm. He saw Cosette every day, he felt paternity spring up and develop within him more and more, he brooded over the soul of that child, he said to himself that she was his, that nothing could take her from him, that this would last indefinitely, that she would certainly become a nun, being thereto gently incited every day, that thus the convent was henceforth the universe for her as it was for him, that he should grow old there, and that she would grow up there, that she would grow old there, and that he should die there; that, in short, delightful hope, no separation was possible. On reflecting upon this, he fell into perplexity. He interrogated himself. He asked himself if all that happiness were really his, if it were not composed of the happiness of another, of the happiness of that child which he, an old man, was confiscating and stealing; if that were not theft? He said to himself, that this child had a right to know life before renouncing it, that to deprive her in advance, and in some sort without consulting her, of all joys, under the pretext of saving her from all trials, to take advantage of her ignorance of her isolation, in order to make an artificial vocation germinate in her, was to rob a human creature of its nature and to lie to God. And who knows if, when she came to be aware of all this someday, and found herself a nun to her sorrow, Cosette would not come to hate him? A last, almost selfish thought, and less heroic than the rest, but that was intolerable to him. He resolved to quit the convent.

He resolved on this; he recognized with anguish, the fact that it was necessary. As for objections, there were none. Five years' sojourn between these four walls and of disappearance had necessarily destroyed or dispersed the elements of fear. He could return tranquilly among men. He had grown old, and all had undergone a change. Who would recognize him now? And then, to face the worst, there was danger only for himself, and he had no right to condemn Cosette to the cloister for the reason that he had been condemned to the galleys. Besides, what is danger in comparison with the right? Finally, nothing prevented his being prudent and taking his precautions.

As for Cosette's education, it was almost finished and complete.

His determination once taken, he awaited an opportunity. It was not long in presenting itself. Old Fauchelevent died.

Jean Valjean demanded an audience with the revered prioress and told her that, having come into a little inheritance at the death of his brother, which permitted him henceforth to live without working, he should leave the service of the convent and take his daughter with him; but that, as it was not just that Cosette, since she had not taken the vows, should have received her education gratuitously, he humbly begged the Reverend Prioress to see fit that he should offer to the community, as indemnity, for the five years which Cosette had spent there, the sum of five thousand francs.

It was thus that Jean Valjean quitted the convent of the Perpetual Adoration.

On leaving the convent, he took in his own arms the little valise the key to which he still wore on his person, and would permit no porter to touch it. This puzzled Cosette, because of the odor of embalming that proceeded from it.

Let us state at once, that this trunk never quitted him more. He always had it in his chamber. It was the first and only thing sometimes, that he carried off in his moving when he moved about. Cosette laughed at it, and called this valise his inseparable, saying, "I am jealous of it."

Nevertheless, Jean Valjean did not reappear in the open air without profound anxiety.

He discovered the house in the Rue Plumet, and hid himself from sight there. Henceforth he was in the possession of the name: Ultime Fauchelevent.

At the same time he hired two other apartments in Paris, in order that he might attract less attention than if he were to remain always in the same quarter, and so that he could, at need, take himself off at the slightest disquietude which should assail him, and in short, so that he might not again be caught unprovided as on the night when he had so miraculously escaped from Javert. These two apartments were very pitiable, poor in appearance, and in two quarters that were far remote from each other, the one in the Rue de l'Ouest, the other in the Rue de l'Homme Arme.

He went from time to time, now to the Rue de l'Homme Arme, now to the Rue de l'Ouest, to pass a month or six weeks, without taking Toussaint. He had himself served by the porters, and gave himself out as a gentleman from the suburbs, living on his funds, and having a little temporary resting place in town. This lofty virtue had three domiciles in Paris for the sake of escaping from the police.

CHAPTER II—JEAN VALJEAN AS
A NATIONAL GUARD

However, properly speaking, he lived in the Rue Plumet, and he had arranged his existence there in the following fashion:

Cosette and the servant occupied the pavilion; she had the big sleeping room with the painted pier glasses, the boudoir with the gilded fillets, the justice's drawing room furnished with tapestries and vast arm chairs; she had the garden. Jean Valjean had a canopied bed of antique damask in three colors and a beautiful Persian rug purchased in the Rue du Figuier-Saint-Paul at Mother Gaucher's, put into Cosette's chamber, and, in order to redeem the severity of these magnificent old things, he had amalgamated with this bric-a-brac all the gay and graceful little pieces of furniture suitable to young girls, an étagère, a bookcase filled with gilt-edged books, an inkstand, a blotting book, paper, a work table encrusted with mother of pearl, a silver-gilt dressing case, a toilette service in Japanese porcelain. Long damask curtains with a red foundation and three colors, like those on the bed, hung at the windows of the first floor. On the ground floor, the curtains were of tapestry. All winter long, Cosette's little house was heated from top to bottom. Jean Valjean inhabited the sort of porter's lodge, which was situated at the end of the back courtyard, with a mattress on a folding bed, a white wood table, two straw chairs, an earthenware water jug, a few old volumes on a shelf, his beloved valise in one corner, and never any fire. He dined with Cosette, and he had a loaf of black bread on the table for his own use.

When Toussaint came, he had said to her, "It is the young lady who is the mistress of this house."

"And you, Monsieur?"

Toussaint replied in amazement, "I am a much better thing than the master; I am the father."

Cosette had been taught housekeeping in the convent, and she regulated their expenditure, which was very modest. Every day, Jean Valjean put his arm through Cosette's and took her for a walk. He led her to the Luxembourg, to the least-frequented walk, and every Sunday he took her to Mass at Saint-Jacques-du-Haut-Pas, because that was a long way off. As it was a very poor quarter, he bestowed alms largely there, and the poor people surrounded him in church, which had drawn down upon him Thenardier's epistle: "To the benevolent gentleman of the church of Saint-Jacques-du-Haut-Pas." He was fond of taking Cosette to visit the poor and the sick. No stranger ever entered the house in the Rue Plumet. Toussaint brought their provisions, and Jean Valjean went himself for water to a fountain near by on the boulevard. Their wood and wine were put into a half-subterranean hollow lined with rock-work, which lay near the Rue de Babylone and which had formerly served the chief-justice as a grotto; for at the epoch of follies and "Little Houses" no love was without a grotto.

In the door opening on the Rue de Babylone, there was a box destined for the reception of letters and papers; only, as the three inhabitants of the pavilion in the Rue Plumet received neither papers nor letters, the entire usefulness of that box, formerly the go-between of a love affair, and the confidant of a lovelorn lawyer, was now limited to the tax collector's notices, and the summons of the guard. For M. Fauchelevent, independent gentleman, belonged to the national guard; he had not been able to escape through the fine meshes of the census of 1831. The municipal information collected at that time had even reached the convent of the Petit-Picpus, a sort of impenetrable and holy cloud, from which Jean Valjean had emerged in venerable guise, and, consequently, worthy of mounting guard in the eyes of the town hall.

Three or four times a year, Jean Valjean donned his uniform and mounted guard; he did this willingly, however; it was a correct disguise that mixed him with everyone, and yet left him solitary. Jean Valjean had just attained his sixtieth birthday, the age of legal exemption; but he did not appear to be over fifty; moreover, he had no desire to escape his sergeant-major nor to quibble with Comte de Lobau; he possessed no civil status, he was concealing his name, he was concealing his identity, so he concealed his age, he concealed everything; and, as we have just said, he willingly did his duty as a national guard; the sum of his ambition lay in resembling any other man who paid his taxes. This man had for his ideal, within, the angel, without, the bourgeois.

Let us note one detail, however; when Jean Valjean went out with Cosette, he dressed as the reader has already seen, and had the air of a retired officer. When he went out alone, which was generally at night, he was always dressed in a workingman's trousers and blouse, and wore a cap that concealed his face. Was this precaution or humility? Both. Cosette was accustomed to the enigmatical side of her destiny, and hardly noticed her father's peculiarities. As for Toussaint, she venerated Jean Valjean, and thought everything he did right.

One day, her butcher, who had caught a glimpse of Jean Valjean, said to her, "That's a queer fish."

She replied, "He's a saint."

Neither Jean Valjean nor Cosette nor Toussaint ever entered or emerged except by the door on the Rue de Babylone. Unless seen through the garden gate it would have been difficult to guess that they lived in the Rue Plumet. That gate was always closed. Jean Valjean had left the garden uncultivated, in order not to attract attention.

In this, possibly, he made a mistake.

CHAPTER III—FOLIIS AC FRONDIBUS

The garden thus left to itself for more than half a century had become extraordinary and charming. The passersby of forty years ago halted to gaze at it, without a suspicion of the secrets it hid in its fresh and verdant depths. More than one dreamer of that epoch often allowed his thoughts and his eyes to penetrate indiscreetly between the bars of that ancient, padlocked gate, twisted, tottering, fastened to two green and moss-covered pillars, and oddly crowned with a pediment of undecipherable arabesque.

There was a stone bench in one corner, one or two moldy statues, several lattices which had lost their nails with time, were rotting on the wall, and there were no walks or turf; but there was enough grass everywhere. Gardening had taken its departure, and nature had returned. Weeds abounded, which was a great piece of luck for a poor corner of land. The festival of gillyflowers was something splendid. Nothing in this garden obstructed the sacred effort of things toward life; venerable growth reigned there among them. The trees had bent over toward the nettles, the plant had sprung upward, the branch had inclined, that which crawls on the earth had gone in search of that which expands in the air, that which floats on the wind had bent over toward that which trails in the moss; trunks, boughs, leaves, fibers, clusters, tendrils, shoots, spines, thorns, had mingled, crossed, married, confounded themselves in each other; vegetation in a deep and close embrace, had celebrated and accomplished there, under the well-pleased eye of the Creator, in that enclosure three hundred feet square, the holy mystery of fraternity, symbol of the human fraternity. This garden was no longer a garden, it was a colossal thicket, that is to say, something as impenetrable as a forest, as peopled as a city, quivering like a nest, somber like a cathedral, fragrant like a bouquet, solitary as a tomb, living as a throng.

In Floreal this enormous thicket, free behind its gate and within its four walls, entered upon the secret labor of germination, quivered in the rising sun, almost like an animal which drinks in the breaths of cosmic love, and which feels the sap of April rising and boiling in its veins, and shakes to the wind its enormous wonderful green locks, sprinkled on the damp earth, on the defaced statues, on the crumbling steps of the pavilion, and even on the pavement of the deserted street, flowers like stars, dew like pearls, fecundity, beauty, life, joy, perfumes. At midday, a thousand white butterflies took refuge there, and it was a divine spectacle to see that living summer snow whirling about there in flakes amid the shade. There, in those gay shadows of verdure, a throng of innocent voices spoke sweetly to the soul, and what the twittering forgot to say the humming completed. In the evening, a dreamy vapor exhaled from the garden and enveloped it; a shroud of mist, a calm and celestial sadness covered it; the intoxicating perfume of the honeysuckles and convolvulus poured out from every part of it, like an exquisite and subtle poison; the last appeals of the woodpeckers and the wagtails were audible as they dozed among the branches; one felt the sacred intimacy of the birds and the trees; by day the wings rejoice the leaves, by night the leaves protect the wings.

In winter the thicket was black, dripping, bristling, shivering, and allowed some glimpse of the house. Instead of flowers on the branches and dew in the flowers, the long silvery tracks of the snails were visible on the cold, thick carpet of yellow leaves; but in any fashion, under any aspect, at all seasons, spring, winter, summer, autumn, this tiny enclosure breathed forth melancholy, contemplation, solitude, liberty, the absence of man, the presence of God; and the rusty old gate had the air of saying, "This garden belongs to me."

It was of no avail that the pavements of Paris were there on every side, the classic and splendid hotels of the Rue de Varennes a couple of paces away, the dome of the Invalides close at hand, the Chamber of Deputies not far off; the carriages of the Rue de Bourgogne and of the Rue Saint-Dominique rumbled luxuriously, in vain, in the vicinity, in vain did the yellow, brown, white, and red omnibuses cross each other's course at the neighboring crossroads; the Rue Plumet was the desert; and the death of the former proprietors, the revolution, which had passed over it, the crumbling away of ancient fortunes, absence, forgetfulness, forty years of abandonment and widowhood, had sufficed to restore to this privileged spot ferns, mulleins, hemlock, yarrow, tall weeds, great crimped plants, with large leaves of pale green cloth, lizards, beetles, uneasy and rapid insects; to cause to spring forth from the depths of the earth and to reappear between those four walls a certain indescribable and savage grandeur; and for nature, which disconcerts the petty arrangements of man, and which sheds herself always thoroughly where she diffuses herself at all, in the ant as well as in the eagle, to blossom out in a petty little Parisian garden with as much rude force and majesty as in a virgin forest of the New World.

Nothing is small, in fact; anyone who is subject to the profound and penetrating influence of nature knows this. Although no absolute satisfaction is given to philosophy, either to circumscribe the cause or to limit the effect, the contemplator falls into those unfathomable ecstasies caused by these decompositions of force terminating in unity. Everything toils at everything.

Algebra is applied to the clouds; the radiation of the star profits the rose; no thinker would venture to affirm that the perfume of the hawthorn is useless to the constellations. Who, then, can calculate the course of a molecule? How do we know that the creation of worlds is not determined by the fall of grains of sand? Who knows the reciprocal ebb and flow of the infinitely great and the infinitely little, the reverberations of causes in the precipices of being, and the avalanches of creation? The tiniest worm is of importance; the great is little, the little is great; everything is balanced in necessity; alarming vision for the mind. There are marvelous relations between beings and things; in that inexhaustible whole, from the sun to the grub, nothing despises the other; all have need of each other. The light does not bear away terrestrial perfumes into the azure depths, without knowing what it is doing; the night distributes stellar essences to the sleeping flowers. All birds that fly have around their leg the thread of the infinite. Germination is complicated with the bursting forth of a meteor and with the peck of a swallow cracking its egg, and it places on one level the birth of an earthworm and the advent of Socrates. Where the telescope ends, the microscope begins. Which of the two possesses the larger field of vision? Choose. A bit of mould is a pleiad of flowers; a nebula is an anthill of stars. The same promiscuousness, and yet more unprecedented, exists between the things of the intelligence and the facts of substance. Elements and principles mingle, combine, wed, multiply with each other, to such a point that the material and the moral world are brought eventually to the same clearness. The phenomenon is perpetually returning upon itself. In the vast cosmic exchanges the universal life goes and comes in unknown quantities, rolling entirely in the invisible mystery of effluvia, employing everything, not losing a single dream, not a single slumber, sowing an animalcule here, crumbling to bits a planet there, oscillating and winding, making of light a force and of thought an element, disseminated and invisible, dissolving all, except that geometrical point, the I; bringing everything back to the soul-atom; expanding everything in God, entangling all activity, from summit to base, in the obscurity of a dizzy mechanism, attaching the flight of an insect to the movement of the earth, subordinating, who knows? Were it only by the identity of the law, the evolution of the comet in the firmament to the whirling of the infusoria in the drop of water. A machine made of mind. Enormous gearing, the prime motor of which is the gnat, and whose final wheel is the zodiac.

CHAPTER IV—CHANGE OF GATE

It seemed that this garden, created in olden days to conceal wanton mysteries, had been transformed and become fitted to shelter chaste mysteries. There were no longer either arbors, or bowling greens, or tunnels, or grottos; there was a magnificent, disheveled obscurity falling like a veil over all. Paphos had been made over into Eden. It is impossible to say what element of repentance had rendered this retreat wholesome. This flowergirl now offered her blossom to the soul. This coquettish garden, formerly decidedly compromised, had returned to virginity and modesty. A justice assisted by a gardener, a goodman who thought that he was a continuation of Lamoignon, and another goodman who thought that he was a continuation of Lenotre, had turned it about, cut, ruffled, decked, molded it to gallantry; nature had taken possession of it once more, had filled it with shade, and had arranged it for love.

There was, also, in this solitude, a heart that was quite ready. Love had only to show himself; he had here a temple composed of verdure, grass, moss, the sight of birds, tender shadows, agitated branches, and a soul made of sweetness, of faith, of candor, of hope, of aspiration, and of illusion.

Cosette had left the convent when she was still almost a child; she was a little more than fourteen, and she was at the "ungrateful age;" we have already said, that with the exception of her eyes, she was homely rather than pretty; she had no ungraceful feature, but she was awkward, thin, timid and bold at once, a grown-up little girl, in short.

Her education was finished, that is to say, she has been taught religion, and even and above all, devotion; then "history," that is to say the thing that bears that name in convents, geography, grammar, the participles, the kings of France, a little music, a little drawing, etc.; but in all other respects she was utterly ignorant, which is a great charm and a great peril. The soul of a young girl should not be left in the dark; later on, mirages that are too abrupt and too lively are formed there, as in a dark chamber. She should be gently and discreetly enlightened, rather with the reflection of realities than with their harsh and direct light. A useful and graciously austere half-light that dissipates puerile fears and obviates falls. There is nothing but the maternal instinct, that admirable intuition composed of the memories of the virgin and the experience of the woman, which knows how this half-light is to be created and of what it should consist.

Nothing supplies the place of this instinct. All the nuns in the world are not worth as much as one mother in the formation of a young girl's soul.

Cosette had had no mother. She had only had many mothers, in the plural.

As for Jean Valjean, he was, indeed, all tenderness, all solicitude; but he was only an old man and he knew nothing at all.

Now, in this work of education, in this grave matter of preparing a woman for life, what science is required to combat that vast ignorance which is called innocence!

Nothing prepares a young girl for passions like the convent. The convent turns the thoughts in the direction of the unknown. The heart, thus thrown back upon itself, works downward within itself, since it cannot overflow, and grows deep, since it cannot expand. Hence visions, suppositions, conjectures, outlines of romances, a desire for adventures, fantastic constructions, edifices built wholly in the inner obscurity of the mind, somber and secret abodes where the passions immediately find a lodgment as soon as the open gate permits them to enter. The convent is a compression, which, in order to triumph over the human heart, should last during the whole life.

On quitting the convent, Cosette could have found nothing more sweet and more dangerous than the house in the Rue Plumet. It was the continuation of solitude with the beginning of liberty; a garden that was closed, but a nature that was acrid, rich, voluptuous, and fragrant; the same dreams as in the convent, but with glimpses of young men; a grating, but one that opened on the street.

Still, when she arrived there, we repeat, she was only a child. Jean Valjean gave this neglected garden over to her. "Do what you like with it," he said to her. This amused Cosette; she turned over all the clumps and all the stones, she hunted for "beasts;" she played in it, while awaiting the time when she would dream in it; she loved this garden for the insects that she found beneath her feet amid the grass, while awaiting the day when she would love it for the stars that she would see through the boughs above her head.

And then, she loved her father, that is to say, Jean Valjean, with all her soul, with an innocent filial passion that made the goodman a beloved and charming companion to her. It will be remembered that M. Madeleine had been in the habit of reading a great deal. Jean Valjean had continued this practice; he had come to converse well; he possessed the secret riches and the eloquence of a true and humble mind that has spontaneously cultivated itself. He retained just enough sharpness to season his kindness; his mind was rough and his heart was soft. During their conversations in the Luxembourg, he gave her explanations of everything, drawing on what he had read, and also on what he had suffered. As she listened to him, Cosette's eyes wandered vaguely about.

This simple man sufficed for Cosette's thought, the same as the wild garden sufficed for her eyes. When she had had a good chase after the butterflies, she came panting up to him and said: "Ah! How I have run!" He kissed her brow.

Cosette adored the goodman. She was always at his heels. Where Jean Valjean was, there happiness was. Jean Valjean lived neither in the pavilion nor the garden; she took greater pleasure in the paved back courtyard, than in the enclosure filled with flowers, and in his little lodge furnished with straw-seated chairs than in the great drawing room hung with tapestry, against which stood tufted easy chairs. Jean Valjean sometimes said to her, smiling at his happiness in being importuned, "Do go to your own quarters! Leave me alone a little!"

She gave him those charming and tender scoldings that are so graceful when they come from a daughter to her father.

"Father, I am very cold in your rooms; why don't you have a carpet here and a stove?"

"Dear child, there are so many people who are better than I and who have not even a roof over their heads."

"Then why is there a fire in my rooms, and everything that is needed?"

"Because you are a woman and a child."

"Bah! Must men be cold and feel uncomfortable?"

"Certain men."

"That is good, I shall come here so often that you will be obliged to have a fire."

And again she said to him, "Father, why do you eat horrible bread like that?"

"Because, my daughter."

"Well, if you eat it, I will eat it too."

Then, in order to prevent Cosette eating black bread, Jean Valjean ate white bread.

Cosette had but a confused recollection of her childhood. She prayed morning and evening for her mother whom she had never known. The Thenardiers had remained with her as two hideous figures in a dream. She remembered that she had gone "one day, at night," to fetch water in a forest. She thought that it had been very far from Paris. It seemed to her that she had begun to live in an abyss, and that it was Jean Valjean who had rescued her from it. Her childhood produced upon her the effect of a time when there had been nothing around her but millipedes, spiders, and serpents. When she meditated in the evening, before falling asleep, as she had not a very clear idea that she was Jean Valjean's daughter, and that he was her father, she fancied that the soul of her mother had passed into that good man and had come to dwell near her.

When he was seated, she leaned her cheek against his white hair, and dropped a silent tear, saying to herself, "Perhaps this man is my mother."

Cosette—although this is a strange statement to make, in the profound ignorance of a girl brought up in a convent, maternity being also absolutely unintelligible to virginity—had ended by fancying that she had had as little mother as possible. She did not even know her mother's name. Whenever she asked Jean Valjean, Jean Valjean remained silent. If she repeated her question, he responded with a smile. Once she insisted; the smile ended in a tear.

This silence on the part of Jean Valjean covered Fantine with darkness.

Was it prudence? Was it respect? Was it a fear that he should deliver this name to the hazards of another memory than his own?

So long as Cosette had been small, Jean Valjean had been willing to talk to her of her mother; when she became a young girl, it was impossible for him to do so. It seemed to him that he no longer dared. Was it because of Cosette? Was it because of Fantine? He felt a certain religious horror at letting that shadow enter Cosette's thought; and of placing a third in their destiny. The more sacred this shade was to him, the more did it seem that it was to be feared. He thought of Fantine, and felt himself overwhelmed with silence.

Through the darkness, he vaguely perceived something that appeared to have its finger on its lips. Had all the modesty which had been in Fantine, and which had violently quitted her during her lifetime, returned to rest upon her after her death, to watch in indignation over the peace of that dead woman, and in its shyness, to keep her in her grave? Was Jean Valjean unconsciously submitting to the pressure? We who believe in death are not among the number who will reject this mysterious explanation.

Hence the impossibility of uttering, even for Cosette, that name of Fantine.

One day Cosette said to him, "Father, I saw my mother in a dream last night. She had two big wings. My mother must have been almost a saint during her life."

"Through martyrdom," replied Jean Valjean.

However, Jean Valjean was happy.

When Cosette went out with him, she leaned on his arm, proud and happy, in the plenitude of her heart. Jean Valjean felt his heart melt within him with delight, at all these sparks of a tenderness so exclusive, so wholly satisfied with himself alone. The poor man trembled, inundated with angelic joy; he declared to himself ecstatically that this would last all their lives; he told himself that he really had not suffered sufficiently to merit so radiant a bliss, and he thanked God, in the depths of his soul, for having permitted him to be loved thus, he, a wretch, by that innocent being.

CHAPTER V—THE ROSE PERCEIVES THAT IT IS AN ENGINE OF WAR

One day, Cosette chanced to look at herself in her mirror, and she said to herself, "Really!" It seemed to her almost that she was pretty. This threw her in a singularly troubled state of mind. Up to that moment she had never thought of her face. She saw herself in her mirror, but she did not look at herself. And then, she had so often been told that she was homely; Jean Valjean alone said gently, "No indeed! No indeed!" At all events, Cosette had always thought herself homely, and had grown up in that belief with the easy resignation of childhood. And here, all at once, was her mirror saying to her, as Jean Valjean had said, "No indeed!" That night, she did not sleep. "What if I were pretty!" she thought. "How odd it would be if I were pretty!" And she recalled those of her companions whose beauty had produced a sensation in the convent, and she said to herself, "What! Am I to be like Mademoiselle So-and-So?"

The next morning she looked at herself again, not by accident this time, and she was assailed with doubts, "Where did I get such an idea?" said she, "No, I am ugly." She had not slept well, that was all, her eyes were sunken and she was pale. She had not felt very joyous on the preceding evening in the belief that she was beautiful, but it made her very sad not to be able to believe in it any longer. She did not look at herself again, and for more than a fortnight she tried to dress her hair with her back turned to the mirror.

In the evening, after dinner, she generally embroidered in wool or did some convent needlework in the drawing room, and Jean Valjean read beside her. Once she raised her eyes from her work, and was rendered quite uneasy by the manner in which her father was gazing at her.

On another occasion, she was passing along the street, and it seemed to her that someone behind her, whom she did not see, said, "A pretty woman! But badly dressed."

"Bah!" she thought. "He does not mean me. I am well dressed and ugly." She was then wearing a plush hat and her merino gown.

At last, one day when she was in the garden, she heard poor old Toussaint saying, "Do you notice how pretty Cosette is growing, Sir?" Cosette did not hear her father's reply, but Toussaint's words caused a sort of commotion within her. She fled from the garden, ran up to her room, flew to the looking-glass, it was three months since she had looked at herself, and gave vent to a cry. She had just dazzled herself.

She was beautiful and lovely; she could not help agreeing with Toussaint and her mirror. Her figure was formed, her skin had grown white, her hair was lustrous, an unaccustomed splendor had been lighted in her blue eyes. The consciousness of her beauty burst upon her in an instant, like the sudden advent of daylight; other people noticed it also, Toussaint had said so, it was evidently she of whom the passerby had spoken, there could no longer be any doubt of that; she descended to the garden again, thinking herself a queen, imagining that she heard the birds singing, though it was winter, seeing the sky gilded, the sun among the trees, flowers in the thickets, distracted, wild, in inexpressible delight.

Jean Valjean, on his side, experienced a deep and undefinable oppression at heart.

In fact, he had, for some time past, been contemplating with terror that beauty, which seemed to grow more radiant every day on Cosette's sweet face. The dawn that was smiling for all was gloomy for him.

Cosette had been beautiful for a tolerably long time before she became aware of it herself. But, from the very first day, that unexpected light, which was rising slowly and enveloping the whole of the young girl's person, wounded Jean Valjean's somber eye. He felt that it was a change in a happy life, a life so happy that he did not dare to move for fear of disarranging something. This man, who had passed through all manner of distresses, who was still all bleeding from the bruises of fate, who had been almost wicked and who had become almost a saint, who, after having dragged the chain of the galleys, was now dragging the invisible but heavy chain of indefinite misery, this man whom the law had not released from its grasp and who could be seized at any moment and brought back from the obscurity of his virtue to the broad daylight of public opprobrium, this man accepted all, excused all, pardoned all, and merely asked of Providence, of man, of the law, of society, of nature, of the world, one thing—that Cosette might love him!

That Cosette might continue to love him! That God would not prevent the heart of the child from coming to him, and from remaining with him! Beloved by Cosette, he felt that he was healed, rested, appeased, loaded with benefits, recompensed, crowned. Beloved by Cosette, it was well with him! He asked nothing more! Had anyone said to him, "Do you want anything better?" he would have answered, "No." God might have said to him, "Do you desire heaven?" and he would have replied, "I should lose by it."

Everything that could affect this situation, if only on the surface, made him shudder like the beginning of something new. He had never known very distinctly himself what the beauty of a woman means; but he understood instinctively, that it was something terrible.

He gazed with terror on this beauty, which was blossoming out ever more triumphant and superb beside him, beneath his very eyes, on the innocent and formidable brow of that child, from the depths of her homeliness, of his old age, of his misery, of his reprobation.

He said to himself, "How beautiful she is! What is to become of me?"

There, moreover, lay the difference between his tenderness and the tenderness of a mother. What he beheld with anguish, a mother would have gazed upon with joy.

The first symptoms were not long in making their appearance.

On the very morrow of the day on which she had said to herself, "Decidedly I am beautiful!" Cosette began to pay attention to her toilette. She recalled the remark of that passerby: "Pretty, but badly dressed," the breath of an oracle which had passed beside her and had vanished, after depositing in her heart one of the two germs which are destined, later on, to fill the whole life of woman, coquetry. Love is the other.

With faith in her beauty, the whole feminine soul expanded within her. She conceived a horror for her merinos, and shame for her plush hat. Her father had never refused her anything. She at once acquired the whole science of the bonnet, the gown, the mantle, the boot, the cuff, the stuff that is in fashion, the color which is becoming, that science that makes of the Parisian woman something so charming, so deep, and so dangerous. The words heady woman were invented for the Parisienne.

In less than a month, little Cosette, in that Thebaid of the Rue de Babylone, was not only one of the prettiest, but one of the "best dressed" women in Paris, which means a great deal more.

She would have liked to encounter her "passerby," to see what he would say, and to "teach him a lesson!" The truth is, that she was ravishing in every respect, and that she distinguished the difference between a bonnet from Gerard and one from Herbaut in the most marvelous way.

Jean Valjean watched these ravages with anxiety. He who felt that he could never do anything but crawl, walk at the most, beheld wings sprouting on Cosette.

Moreover, from the mere inspection of Cosette's toilette, a woman would have recognized the fact that she had no mother. Certain little proprieties, certain special conventionalities, were not observed by Cosette. A mother, for instance, would have told her that a young girl does not dress in damask.

The first day that Cosette went out in her black damask gown and mantle, and her white crape bonnet, she took Jean Valjean's arm, gay, radiant, rosy, proud, dazzling. "Father," she said, "how do you like me in this guise?" Jean Valjean replied in a voice that resembled the bitter voice of an envious man, "Charming!" He was the same as usual during their walk. On their return home, he asked Cosette, "Won't you put on that other gown and bonnet again, you know the ones I mean?"

This took place in Cosette's chamber. Cosette turned toward the wardrobe where her cast-off schoolgirl's clothes were hanging.

"That disguise!" said she. "Father, what do you want me to do with it? Oh no, the idea! I shall never put on those horrors again. With that machine on my head, I have the air of Madame Mad-dog."

Jean Valjean heaved a deep sigh.

From that moment forth, he noticed that Cosette, who had always heretofore asked to remain at home, saying, "Father, I enjoy myself more here with you," now was always asking to go out. In fact, what is the use of having a handsome face and a delicious costume if one does not display them?

He also noticed that Cosette had no longer the same taste for the back garden. Now she preferred the garden, and did not dislike to promenade back and forth in front of the railed fence. Jean Valjean, who was shy, never set foot in the garden. He kept to his back yard, like a dog.

Cosette, in gaining the knowledge that she was beautiful, lost the grace of ignoring it. An exquisite grace, for beauty enhanced by ingenuousness is ineffable, and nothing is so adorable as a dazzling and innocent creature who walks along, holding in her hand the key to paradise without being conscious of it. But what she had lost in ingenuous grace, she gained in pensive and serious charm. Her whole person, permeated with the joy of youth, of innocence, and of beauty, breathed forth a splendid melancholy.

It was at this epoch that Marius, after the lapse of six months, saw her once more at the Luxembourg.

CHAPTER VI—THE BATTLE BEGUN

Cosette in her shadow, like Marius in his, was all ready to take fire. Destiny, with its mysterious and fatal patience, slowly drew together these two beings, all charged and all languishing with the stormy electricity of passion, these two souls which were laden with love as two clouds are laden with lightning, and which were bound to overflow and mingle in a look, like the clouds in a flash of fire.

The glance has been so much abused in love romances that it has finally fallen into disrepute. One hardly dares to say, nowadays, that two beings fell in love because they looked at each other. That is the way people do fall in love, nevertheless, and the only way. The rest is nothing, but the rest comes afterward. Nothing is more real than these great shocks that two souls convey to each other by the exchange of that spark.

At that particular hour when Cosette unconsciously darted that glance which troubled Marius, Marius had no suspicion that he had also launched a look that disturbed Cosette.

He caused her the same good and the same evil.

She had been in the habit of seeing him for a long time, and she had scrutinized him as girls scrutinize and see, while looking elsewhere. Marius still considered Cosette ugly, when she had already begun to think Marius handsome. But as he paid no attention to her, the young man was nothing to her.

Still, she could not refrain from saying to herself that he had beautiful hair, beautiful eyes, handsome teeth, a charming tone of voice when she heard him conversing with his comrades, that he held himself badly when he walked, if you like, but with a grace that was all his own, that he did not appear to be at all stupid, that his whole person was noble, gentle, simple, proud, and that, in short, though he seemed to be poor, yet his air was fine.

On the day when their eyes met at last, and said to each other those first, obscure, and ineffable things that the glance lisps, Cosette did not immediately understand. She returned thoughtfully to the house in the Rue de l'Ouest, where Jean Valjean, according to his custom, had come to spend six weeks. The next morning, on waking, she thought of that strange young man, so long indifferent and icy, who now seemed to pay attention to her, and it did not appear to her that this attention was the least in the world agreeable to her. She was, on the contrary, somewhat incensed at this handsome and disdainful individual. A substratum of war stirred within her. It struck her, and the idea caused her a wholly childish joy, that she was going to take her revenge at last.

Knowing that she was beautiful, she was thoroughly conscious, though in an indistinct fashion, that she possessed a weapon. Women play with their beauty as children do with a knife. They wound themselves.

The reader will recall Marius's hesitations, his palpitations, his terrors. He remained on his bench and did not approach. This vexed Cosette. One day, she said to Jean Valjean, "Father, let us stroll about a little in that direction." Seeing that Marius did not come to her, she went to him. In such cases, all women resemble Mahomet. And then, strange to say, the first symptom of true love in a young man is timidity; in a young girl it is boldness. This is surprising, and yet nothing is more simple. It is the two sexes tending to approach each other and assuming, each the other's qualities.

That day, Cosette's glance drove Marius beside himself, and Marius's glance set Cosette to trembling. Marius went away confident, and Cosette uneasy. From that day forth, they adored each other.

The first thing that Cosette felt was a confused and profound melancholy. It seemed to her that her soul had become black since the day before. She no longer recognized it. The whiteness of soul in young girls, which is composed of coldness and gaiety, resembles snow. It melts in love, which is its sun.

Cosette did not know what love was. She had never heard the word uttered in its terrestrial sense. On the books of profane music that entered the convent, amour (love) was replaced by tambour (drum) or pandour. This created enigmas that exercised the imaginations of the big girls, such as: Ah, how delightful is the drum! Or, Pity is not a pandour. But Cosette had left the convent too early to have occupied herself much with the "drum." Therefore, she did not know what name to give to what she now felt. Is anyone the less ill because one does not know the name of one's malady?

She loved with all the more passion because she loved ignorantly. She did not know whether it was a good thing or a bad thing, useful or dangerous, eternal or temporary, allowable or prohibited; she loved. She would have been greatly astonished, had anyone said to her, "You do not sleep? But that is forbidden! You do not eat? Why, that is very bad! You have oppressions and palpitations of the heart? That must not be! You blush and turn pale, when a certain being clad in black appears at the end of a certain green walk? But that is abominable!" She would not have understood, and she would have replied,"What fault is there of mine in a matter in which I have no power and of which I know nothing?"

It turned out that the love that presented itself was exactly suited to the state of her soul. It was a sort of admiration at a distance, a mute contemplation, the deification of a stranger. It was the apparition of youth to youth, the dream of nights become a reality yet remaining a dream, the longed-for phantom realized and made flesh at last, but having as yet, neither name, nor fault, nor spot, nor exigency, nor defect; in a word, the distant lover who lingered in the ideal, a chimera with a form. Any nearer and more palpable meeting would have alarmed Cosette at this first stage, when she was still half immersed in the exaggerated mists of the cloister. She had all the fears of children and all the fears of nuns combined. The spirit of the convent, with which she had been permeated for the space of five years, was still in the process of slow evaporation from her person, and made everything tremble around her. In this situation he was not a lover, he was not even an admirer; he was a vision. She set herself to adoring Marius as something charming, luminous, and impossible.

As extreme innocence borders on extreme coquetry, she smiled at him with all frankness.

Every day, she looked forward to the hour for their walk with impatience, she found Marius there, she felt herself unspeakably happy, and thought in all sincerity that she was expressing her whole thought when she said to Jean Valjean, "What a delicious garden that Luxembourg is!"

Marius and Cosette were in the dark as to one another. They did not address each other, they did not salute each other, they did not know each other; they saw each other; and like stars of heaven that are separated by millions of leagues, they lived by gazing at each other.

It was thus that Cosette gradually became a woman and developed, beautiful and loving, with a consciousness of her beauty, and in ignorance of her love. She was a coquette to boot through her ignorance.

CHAPTER VII—TO ONE SADNESS
OPPOSE A SADNESS AND A HALF

All situations have their instincts. Old and eternal Mother Nature warned Jean Valjean in a dim way of the presence of Marius. Jean Valjean shuddered to the very bottom of his soul. Jean Valjean saw nothing, knew nothing, and yet he scanned with obstinate attention, the darkness in which he walked, as though he felt on one side of him something in process of construction, and on the other, something that was crumbling away. Marius—also warned, and, in accordance with the deep law of God, by that same Mother Nature—did all he could to keep out of sight of "the father." Nevertheless, it came to pass that Jean Valjean sometimes espied him. Marius's manners were no longer in the least natural. He exhibited ambiguous prudence and awkward daring. He no longer came quite close to them as formerly. He seated himself at a distance and pretended to be reading; why did he pretend that? Formerly he had come in his old coat, now he wore his new one every day; Jean Valjean was not sure that he did not have his hair curled, his eyes were very queer, he wore gloves; in short, Jean Valjean cordially detested this young man.

Cosette allowed nothing to be divined. Without knowing just what was the matter with her she was convinced that there was something in it, and that it must be concealed.

There was a coincidence between the taste for the toilette that had recently come to Cosette, and the habit of new clothes developed by that stranger, which was very repugnant to Jean Valjean. It might be accidental, no doubt, certainly, but it was a menacing accident.

He never opened his mouth to Cosette about this stranger. One day, however, he could not refrain from so doing, and, with that vague despair which suddenly casts the lead into the depths of its despair, he said to her, "What a very pedantic air that young man has!"

Cosette, but a year before only an indifferent little girl, would have replied, "Why, no, he is charming." Ten years later, with the love of Marius in her heart, she would have answered, "A pedant, and insufferable to the sight! You are right!" At the moment in life and the heart that she had then attained, she contented herself with replying, with supreme calmness, "That young man!"

As though she now beheld him for the first time in her life.

"How stupid I am!" thought Jean Valjean. "She had not noticed him. It is I who have pointed him out to her."

Oh, simplicity of the old! Oh, the depth of children!

It is one of the laws of those fresh years of suffering and trouble, of those vivacious conflicts between a first love and the first obstacles, that the young girl does not allow herself to be caught in any trap whatever, and that the young man falls into everyone. Jean Valjean had instituted an undeclared war against Marius, which Marius, with the sublime stupidity of his passion and his age, did not divine. Jean Valjean laid a host of ambushes for him; he changed his hour, he changed his bench, he forgot his handkerchief, he came alone to the Luxembourg; Marius dashed headlong into all these snares; and to all the interrogation marks planted by Jean Valjean in his pathway, he ingenuously answered "yes." But Cosette remained immured in her apparent unconcern and in her imperturbable tranquility, so that Jean Valjean arrived at the following conclusion, "That ninny is madly in love with Cosette, but Cosette does not even know that he exists."

Nonetheless did he bear in his heart a mournful tremor. The minute when Cosette would love might strike at any moment. Does not everything begin with indifference?

Only once did Cosette make a mistake and alarm him. He rose from his seat to depart, after a stay of three hours, and she said, "What, already?"

Jean Valjean had not discontinued his trips to the Luxembourg, as he did not wish to do anything out of the way, and as, above all things, he feared to arouse Cosette; but during the hours that were so sweet to the lovers, while Cosette was sending her smile to the intoxicated Marius, who perceived nothing else now, and who now saw nothing in all the world but an adored and radiant face, Jean Valjean was fixing on Marius flashing and terrible eyes. He, who had finally come to believe himself incapable of a malevolent feeling, experienced moments when Marius was present, in which he thought he was becoming savage and ferocious once more, and he felt the old depths of his soul, which had formerly contained so much wrath, opening once more and rising up against that young man. It almost seemed to him that unknown craters were forming in his bosom.

What! He was there, that creature! What was he there for? He came creeping about, smelling out, examining, trying! He came, saying, "Hey! Why not?" He came to prowl about his—Jean Valjean's—life! To prowl about his happiness, with the purpose of seizing it and bearing it away!

Jean Valjean added: "Yes, that's it! What is he in search of? An adventure! What does he want? A love affair! A love affair! And I? What! I have been first, the most wretched of men, and then the most unhappy, and I have traversed sixty years of life on my knees, I have suffered everything that man can suffer, I have grown old without having been young, I have lived without a family, without relatives, without friends, without life, without children, I have left my blood on every stone, on every bramble, on every mile post, along every wall, I have been gentle, though others have been hard to me, and kind, although others have been malicious, I have become an honest man once more, in spite of everything, I have repented of the evil that I have done and have forgiven the evil that has been done to me, and at the moment when I receive my recompense, at the moment when it is all over, at the moment when I am just touching the goal, at the moment when I have what I desire, it is well, it is good, I have paid, I have earned it, all this is to take flight, all this will vanish, and I shall lose Cosette, and I shall lose my life, my joy, my soul, because it has pleased a great booby to come and lounge at the Luxembourg."

Then his eyes were filled with a sad and extraordinary gleam.

It was no longer a man gazing at a man; it was no longer an enemy surveying an enemy. It was a dog scanning a thief.

The reader knows the rest. Marius pursued his senseless course. One day he followed Cosette to the Rue de l'Ouest. Another day he spoke to the porter. The porter, on his side, spoke, and said to Jean Valjean, "Monsieur, who is that curious young man who is asking for you?" On the morrow Jean Valjean bestowed on Marius that glance which Marius at last perceived. A week later, Jean Valjean had taken his departure. He swore to himself that he would never again set foot either in the Luxembourg or in the Rue de l'Ouest. He returned to the Rue Plumet.

Cosette did not complain, she said nothing, she asked no questions, she did not seek to learn his reasons; she had already reached the point where she was afraid of being divined, and of betraying herself. Jean Valjean had no experience of these miseries, the only miseries that are charming and the only ones with which he was not acquainted; the consequence was that he did not understand the grave significance of Cosette's silence.

He merely noticed that she had grown sad, and he grew gloomy. On his side and on hers, inexperience had joined issue.

Once he made a trial. He asked Cosette, "Would you like to come to the Luxembourg?"

A ray illuminated Cosette's pale face.

"Yes," said she.

They went there. Three months had elapsed. Marius no longer went there. Marius was not there.

On the following day, Jean Valjean asked Cosette again, "Would you like to come to the Luxembourg?"

She replied, sadly and gently, "No."

Jean Valjean was hurt by this sadness, and heartbroken at this gentleness.

What was going on in that mind, which was so young and yet already so impenetrable? What was on its way there within? What was taking place in Cosette's soul? Sometimes, instead of going to bed, Jean Valjean remained seated on his pallet, with his head in his hands, and he passed whole nights asking himself, "What has Cosette in her mind?" and in thinking of the things that she might be thinking about.

Oh! At such moments, what mournful glances did he cast toward that cloister, that chaste peak, that abode of angels, that inaccessible glacier of virtue! How he contemplated, with despairing ecstasy, that convent garden, full of ignored flowers and cloistered virgins, where all perfumes and all souls mount straight to heaven! How he adored that Eden forever closed against him, from which he had voluntarily and madly emerged! How he regretted his abnegation and his folly in having brought Cosette back into the world, poor hero of sacrifice, seized and hurled to the earth by his very self-devotion! How he said to himself, "What have I done?"

However, nothing of all this was perceptible to Cosette. No ill temper, no harshness. His face was always serene and kind. Jean Valjean's manners were more tender and more paternal than ever. If anything could have betrayed his lack of joy, it was his increased suavity.

On her side, Cosette languished. She suffered from the absence of Marius as she had rejoiced in his presence, peculiarly, without exactly being conscious of it. When Jean Valjean ceased to take her on their customary strolls, a feminine instinct murmured confusedly, at the bottom of her heart, that she must not seem to set store on the Luxembourg garden, and that if this proved to be a matter of indifference to her, her father would take her there once more. But days, weeks, months, elapsed. Jean Valjean had tacitly accepted Cosette's tacit consent. She regretted it. It was too late. So Marius had disappeared; all was over. The day on which she returned to the Luxembourg, Marius was no longer there. What was to be done? Should she ever find him again? She felt an anguish at her heart, which nothing relieved, and which augmented every day; she no longer knew whether it was winter or summer, whether it was raining or shining, whether the birds were singing, whether it was the season for dahlias or daisies, whether the Luxembourg was more charming than the Tuileries, whether the linen which the laundress brought home was starched too much or not enough, whether Toussaint had done "her marketing" well or ill; and she remained dejected, absorbed, attentive to but a single thought, her eyes vague and staring as when one gazes by night at a black and fathomless spot where an apparition has vanished.

However, she did not allow Jean Valjean to perceive anything of this, except her pallor.

She still wore her sweet face for him.

This pallor sufficed but too thoroughly to trouble Jean Valjean. Sometimes he asked her, "What is the matter with you?"

She replied, "There is nothing the matter with me."

And after a silence, when she divined that he was sad also, she would add, "And you, father—is there anything wrong with you?"

"With me? Nothing," said he.

These two beings who had loved each other so exclusively, and with so touching an affection, and who had lived so long for each other now suffered side by side, each on the other's account; without acknowledging it to each other, without anger toward each other, and with a smile.

CHAPTER VIII—THE CHAIN GANG

Jean Valjean was the more unhappy of the two. Youth, even in its sorrows, always possesses its own peculiar radiance.

At times, Jean Valjean suffered so greatly that he became puerile. It is the property of grief to cause the childish side of man to reappear. He had an unconquerable conviction that Cosette was escaping from him. He would have liked to resist, to retain her, to arouse her enthusiasm by some external and brilliant matter. These ideas, puerile, as we have just said, and at the same time senile, conveyed to him, by their very childishness, a tolerably just notion of the influence of gold lace on the imaginations of young girls. He once chanced to see a general on horseback, in full uniform, pass along the street, Comte Coutard, the commandant of Paris. He envied that gilded man; what happiness it would be, he said to himself, if he could put on that suit, which was an incontestable thing; and if Cosette could behold him thus, she would be dazzled, and when he had Cosette on his arm and passed the gates of the Tuileries, the guard would present arms to him, and that would suffice for Cosette, and would dispel her idea of looking at young men.

An unforeseen shock was added to these sad reflections.

In the isolated life they led, and since they had come to dwell in the Rue Plumet, they had contracted one habit. They sometimes took a pleasure trip to see the sunrise, a mild species of enjoyment that befits those who are entering life and those who are quitting it.

For those who love solitude, a walk in the early morning is equivalent to a stroll by night, with the cheerfulness of nature added. The streets are deserted and the birds are singing. Cosette, a bird herself, liked to rise early. These matutinal excursions were planned on the preceding evening. He proposed, and she agreed. It was arranged like a plot, they set out before daybreak, and these trips were so many small delights for Cosette. These innocent eccentricities please young people.

Jean Valjean's inclination led him, as we have seen, to the least frequented spots, to solitary nooks, to forgotten places. There then existed, in the vicinity of the barriers of Paris, a sort of poor meadows, which were almost confounded with the city, where grew in summer sickly grain, and which, in autumn, after the harvest had been gathered, presented the appearance, not of having been reaped, but peeled. Jean Valjean loved to haunt these fields. Cosette was not bored there. It meant solitude to him and liberty to her. There, she became a little girl once more, she could run and almost play; she took off her hat, laid it on Jean Valjean's knees, and gathered bunches of flowers. She gazed at the butterflies on the flowers, but did not catch them; gentleness and tenderness are born with love, and the young girl who cherishes within her breast a trembling and fragile ideal has mercy on the wing of a butterfly. She wove garlands of poppies, which she placed on her head, and which, crossed and penetrated with sunlight, glowing until they flamed, formed for her rosy face a crown of burning embers.

Even after their life had grown sad, they kept up their custom of early strolls.

One morning in October, therefore, tempted by the serene perfection of the autumn of 1831, they set out, and found themselves at break of day near the Barriere du Maine. It was not dawn, it was daybreak; a delightful and stern moment. A few constellations here and there in the deep, pale azure, the earth all black, the heavens all white, a quiver amid the blades of grass, everywhere the mysterious chill of twilight. A lark, which seemed mingled with the stars, was caroling at a prodigious height, and one would have declared that that hymn of pettiness calmed immensity. In the East, the Valde-Grace projected its dark mass on the clear horizon with the sharpness of steel; Venus dazzlingly brilliant was rising behind that dome and had the air of a soul making its escape from a gloomy edifice.

All was peace and silence; there was no one on the road; a few stray laborers, of whom they caught barely a glimpse, were on their way to their work along the side paths.

Jean Valjean was sitting in a crosswalk on some planks deposited at the gate of a timberyard. His face was turned toward the highway, his back toward the light; he had forgotten the sun, which was on the point of rising; he had sunk into one of those profound absorptions in which the mind becomes concentrated, which imprison even the eye, and which are equivalent to four walls. There are meditations that may be called vertical; when one is at the bottom of them, time is required to return to earth. Jean Valjean had plunged into one of these reveries. He was thinking of Cosette, of the happiness that was possible if nothing came between him and her, of the light with which she filled his life, a light that was but the emanation of her soul. He was almost happy in his reverie. Cosette, who was standing beside him, was gazing at the clouds as they turned rosy.

All at once Cosette exclaimed, "Father, I should think someone was coming yonder." Jean Valjean raised his eyes.

Cosette was right. The causeway that leads to the ancient Barriere du Maine is a prolongation, as the reader knows, of the Rue de Sevres, and is cut at right angles by the inner boulevard. At the elbow of the causeway and the boulevard, at the spot where it branches, they heard a noise that it was difficult to account for at that hour, and a sort of confused pile made its appearance. Some shapeless thing that was coming from the boulevard was turning into the road.

It grew larger, it seemed to move in an orderly manner, though it was bristling and quivering; it seemed to be a vehicle, but its load could not be distinctly made out. There were horses, wheels, shouts; whips were cracking. By degrees the outlines became fixed, although bathed in shadows. It was a vehicle, in fact, that had just turned from the boulevard into the highway, and that was directing its course toward the barrier near which sat Jean Valjean; a second, of the same aspect, followed, then a third, then a fourth; seven chariots made their appearance in succession, the heads of the horses touching the rear of the wagon in front. Figures were moving on these vehicles, flashes were visible through the dusk as though there were naked swords there, a clanking became audible that resembled the rattling of chains, and as this something advanced, the sound of voices waxed louder, and it turned into a terrible thing such as emerges from the cave of dreams.

As it drew nearer, it assumed a form, and was outlined behind the trees with the pallid hue of an apparition; the mass grew white; the day, which was slowly dawning, cast a wan light on this swarming heap, which was at once both sepulchral and living, the heads of the figures turned into the faces of corpses, and this is what it proved to be:

Seven wagons were driving in a file along the road. The first six were singularly constructed. They resembled coopers' drays; they consisted of long ladders placed on two wheels and forming barrows at their rear extremities. Each dray, or rather let us say, each ladder, was attached to four horses harnessed tandem. On these ladders strange clusters of men were being drawn. In the faint light, these men were to be divined rather than seen. Twenty-four on each vehicle, twelve on a side, back-to-back, facing the passersby, their legs dangling in the air, this was the manner in which these men were traveling, and behind their backs they had something that clanked, and which was a chain, and on their necks something that shone, and which was an iron collar. Each man had his collar, but the chain was for all; so that if these four and twenty men had occasion to alight from the dray and walk, they were seized with a sort of inexorable unity, and were obliged to wind over the ground with the chain for a backbone, somewhat after the fashion of millipedes. In the back and front of each vehicle, two men armed with muskets stood erect, each holding one end of the chain under his foot. The iron necklets were square. The seventh vehicle, a huge rack-sided baggage wagon, without a hood, had four wheels and six horses, and carried a sonorous pile of iron boilers, cast-iron pots, braziers, and chains, among which were mingled several men who were pinioned and stretched at full length, and who seemed to be ill. This wagon, all latticework, was garnished with dilapidated hurdles that appeared to have served for former punishments. These vehicles kept to the middle of the road. On each side marched a double hedge of guards of infamous aspect, wearing three-cornered hats, like the soldiers under the Directory, shabby, covered with spots and holes, muffled in uniforms of veterans and the trousers of undertakers' men, half gray, half blue, which were almost hanging in rags, with red epaulets, yellow shoulder belts, short sabers, muskets, and cudgels; they were a species of soldier-blackguards. These myrmidons seemed composed of the abjectness of the beggar and the authority of the executioner. The one who appeared to be their chief held a postilion's whip in his hand. All these details, blurred by the dimness of dawn, became more and more clearly outlined as the light increased. At the head and in the rear of the convoy rode mounted gendarmes, serious and with sword in fist.

This procession was so long that when the first vehicle reached the barrier, the last was barely debauching from the boulevard. A throng, sprung, it is impossible to say from where, and formed in a twinkling—as is frequently the case in Paris—pressed forward from both sides of the road and looked on. In the neighboring lanes the shouts of people calling to each other and the wooden shoes of market gardeners hastening up to gaze were audible.

The men massed upon the drays allowed themselves to be jolted along in silence. They were livid with the chill of morning. They all wore linen trousers, and their bare feet were thrust into wooden shoes. The rest of their costume was a fantasy of wretchedness. Their accoutrements were horribly incongruous; nothing is more funereal than the harlequin in rags. Battered felt hats, tarpaulin caps, hideous woolen nightcaps, and, side by side with a short blouse, a black coat broken at the elbow; many wore women's headgear, others had baskets on their heads; hairy breasts were visible, and through the rent in their garments tattooed designs could be descried; temples of Love, flaming hearts, Cupids; eruptions and unhealthy red blotches could also be seen. Two or three had a straw rope attached to the crossbar of the dray, and suspended under them like a stirrup, which supported their feet. One of them held in his hand and raised to his mouth something that had the appearance of a black stone, which he seemed to be gnawing; it was bread that he was eating. There were no eyes there that were not either dry, dulled, or flaming with an evil light. The escort troop cursed, the men in chains did not utter a syllable; from time to time the sound of a blow became audible as the cudgels descended on shoulder blades or skulls; some of these men were yawning; their rags were terrible; their feet hung down, their shoulders oscillated, their heads clashed together, their fetters clanked, their eyes glared ferociously, their fists clenched or fell open inertly like the hands of corpses; in the rear of the convoy ran a band of children screaming with laughter.

This file of vehicles, whatever its nature was, was mournful. It was evident that tomorrow, that an hour hence, a pouring rain might descend, that it might be followed by another and another, and that their dilapidated garments would be drenched, that once soaked, these men would not get dry again, that once chilled, they would not again get warm, that their linen trousers would be glued to their bones by the downpour, that the water would fill their shoes, that no lashes from the whips would be able to prevent their jaws from chattering, that the chain would continue to bind them by the neck, that their legs would continue to dangle, and it was impossible not to shudder at the sight of these human beings thus bound and passive beneath the cold clouds of autumn, and delivered over to the rain, to the blast, to all the furies of the air, like trees and stones.

Blows from the cudgel were not omitted even in the case of the sick men, who lay there knotted with ropes and motionless on the seventh wagon, and who appeared to have been tossed there like sacks filled with misery.

Suddenly, the sun made its appearance; the immense light of the Orient burst forth, and one would have said that it had set fire to all those ferocious heads. Their tongues were unloosed; a conflagration of grins, oaths, and songs exploded. The broad horizontal sheet of light severed the file in two parts, illuminating heads and bodies, leaving feet and wheels in the obscurity. Thoughts made their appearance on these faces; it was a terrible moment; visible demons with their masks removed, fierce souls laid bare. Though lighted up, this wild throng remained in gloom. Some, who were gay, had in their mouths quills through which they blew vermin over the crowd, picking out the women; the dawn accentuated these lamentable profiles with the blackness of its shadows; there was not one of these creatures who was not deformed by reason of wretchedness; and the whole was so monstrous that one would have said that the sun's brilliancy had been changed into the glare of the lightning. The wagon load that headed the line had struck up a song, and were shouting at the top of their voices with a haggard joviality, a potpourri by Desaugiers, then famous, called the Vestal; the trees shivered mournfully; in the cross-lanes, countenances of bourgeois listened in an idiotic delight to these coarse strains droned by specters.

All sorts of distress met in this procession as in chaos; here were to be found the facial angles of every sort of beast, old men, youths, bald heads, gray beards, cynical monstrosities, sour resignation, savage grins, senseless attitudes, snouts surmounted by caps, heads like those of young girls with corkscrew curls on the temples, infantile visages, and by reason of that, horrible thin skeleton faces, to which death alone was lacking. On the first cart was a Negro, who had been a slave, in all probability, and who could make a comparison of his chains. The frightful leveler from below, shame, had passed over these brows; at that degree of abasement, the last transformations were suffered by all in their extremest depths, and ignorance, converted into dullness, was the equal of intelligence converted into despair. There was no choice possible between these men who appeared to the eye as the flower of the mud. It was evident that the person who had had the ordering of that unclean procession had not classified them. These beings had been fettered and coupled pell-mell, in alphabetical disorder, probably, and loaded haphazard on those carts. Nevertheless, horrors, when grouped together, always end by evolving a result; all additions of wretched men give a sum total, each chain exhaled a common soul, and each dray-load had its own physiognomy. By the side of the one where they were singing, there was one where they were howling; a third where they were begging; one could be seen in which they were gnashing their teeth; another load menaced the spectators, another blasphemed God; the last was as silent as the tomb. Dante would have thought that he beheld his seven circles of hell on the march. The march of the damned to their tortures, performed in sinister wise, not on the formidable and flaming chariot of the Apocalypse, but, what was more mournful than that, on the gibbet cart.

One of the guards, who had a hook on the end of his cudgel, made a pretense from time to time, of stirring up this mass of human filth. An old woman in the crowd pointed them out to her little boy five years old, and said to him, "Rascal, let that be a warning to you!"

As the songs and blasphemies increased, the man who appeared to be the captain of the escort cracked his whip, and at that signal a fearful dull and blind flogging, which produced the sound of hail, fell upon the seven dray-loads; many roared and foamed at the mouth; which redoubled the delight of the street urchins who had hastened up, a swarm of flies on these wounds.

Jean Valjean's eyes had assumed a frightful expression. They were no longer eyes; they were those deep and glassy objects that replace the glance in the case of certain wretched men, which seem unconscious of reality, and in which flames the reflection of terrors and of catastrophes. He was not looking at a spectacle, he was seeing a vision. He tried to rise, to flee, to make his escape; he could not move his feet. Sometimes, the things that you see seize upon you and hold you fast. He remained nailed to the spot, petrified, stupid, asking himself, athwart confused and inexpressible anguish, what this sepulchral persecution signified, and from where had come that pandemonium, which was pursuing him. All at once, he raised his hand to his brow, a gesture habitual to those whose memory suddenly returns; he remembered that this was, in fact, the usual itinerary, that it was customary to make this detour in order to avoid all possibility of encountering royalty on the road to Fontainebleau, and that, five and thirty years before, he had himself passed through that barrier.

Cosette was no less terrified, but in a different way. She did not understand; what she beheld did not seem to her to be possible; at length she cried, "Father! What are those men in those carts?"

Jean Valjean replied, "Convicts."

"Where are they going?"

"To the galleys."

At that moment, the cudgeling, multiplied by a hundred hands, became zealous, blows with the flat of the sword were mingled with it, it was a perfect storm of whips and clubs; the convicts bent before it, a hideous obedience was evoked by the torture, and all held their peace, darting glances like chained wolves.

Cosette trembled in every limb; she resumed, "Father, are they still men?"

"Sometimes," answered the unhappy man.

It was the chain gang, in fact, which had set out before daybreak from Bicêtre, and had taken the road to Mans in order to avoid Fontainebleau, where the King then was. This caused the horrible journey to last three or four days longer; but torture may surely be prolonged with the object of sparing the royal personage a sight of it.

Jean Valjean returned home utterly overwhelmed. Such encounters are shocks, and the memory that they leave behind them resembles a thorough shaking up.

Nevertheless, Jean Valjean did not observe that, on his way back to the Rue de Babylone with Cosette, the latter was plying him with other questions on the subject of what they had just seen; perhaps he was too much absorbed in his own dejection to notice her words and reply to them. But when Cosette was leaving him in the evening, to betake herself to bed, he heard her say in a low voice, and as though talking to herself, "It seems to me, that if I were to find one of those men in my pathway, oh, my God, I should die merely from the sight of him close at hand."

Fortunately, chance ordained that on the morrow of that tragic day, there was some official solemnity apropos of I know not what, fetes in Paris, a review in the Champ de Mars, jousts on the Seine, theatrical performances in the Champs-Elysees, fireworks at the Arc de l'Etoile, illuminations everywhere. Jean Valjean did violence to his habits, and took Cosette to see these rejoicings, for the purpose of diverting her from the memory of the day before, and of effacing, beneath the smiling tumult of all Paris, the abominable thing that had passed before her. The review with which the festival was spiced made the presence of uniforms perfectly natural; Jean Valjean donned his uniform of a national guard with the vague inward feeling of a man who is betaking himself to shelter. However, this trip seemed to attain its object. Cosette, who made it her law to please her father, and to whom, moreover, all spectacles were a novelty, accepted this diversion with the light and easy good grace of youth, and did not pout too disdainfully at that flutter of enjoyment called a public fete; so that Jean Valjean was able to believe that he had succeeded, and that no trace of that hideous vision remained.

Some days later, one morning, when the sun was shining brightly, and they were both on the steps leading to the garden, another infraction of the rules, which Jean Valjean seemed to have imposed upon himself, and to the custom of remaining in her chamber, which melancholy had caused Cosette to adopt, Cosette, in a wrapper, was standing erect in that negligent attire of early morning, which envelops young girls in an adorable way and which produces the effect of a cloud drawn over a star; and, with her head bathed in light, rosy after a good sleep, submitting to the gentle glances of the tender old man, she was picking a daisy to pieces. Cosette did not know the delightful legend, I love a little, passionately, etc.—who was there who could have taught her? She was handling the flower instinctively, innocently, without a suspicion that to pluck a daisy apart is to do the same by a heart. If there were a fourth, and smiling Grace called Melancholy, she would have worn the air of that Grace. Jean Valjean was fascinated by the contemplation of those tiny fingers on that flower, and forgetful of everything in the radiance emitted by that child. A redbreast was warbling in the thicket, on one side. White cloudlets floated across the sky, so gaily, that one would have said that they had just been set at liberty. Cosette went on attentively tearing the leaves from her flower; she seemed to be thinking about something; but whatever it was, it must be something charming; all at once she turned her head over her shoulder with the delicate languor of a swan, and said to Jean Valjean, "Father, what are the galleys like?"

BOOK FOURTH: SUCCOR FROM BELOW MAY TURN OUT TO BE SUCCOR FROM ON HIGH

CHAPTER I—A WOUND WITHOUT, HEALING WITHIN

Thus their life clouded over by degrees.

But one diversion, which had formerly been a happiness, remained to them, which was to carry bread to those who were hungry, and clothing to those who were cold. Cosette often accompanied Jean Valjean on these visits to the poor, on which they recovered some remnants of their former free intercourse; and sometimes, when the day had been a good one, and they had assisted many in distress, and cheered and warmed many little children, Cosette was rather merry in the evening. It was at this epoch that they paid their visit to the Jondrette den.

On the day following that visit, Jean Valjean made his appearance in the pavilion in the morning, calm as was his wont, but with a large wound on his left arm, which was much inflamed, and very angry, which resembled a burn, and which he explained in some way or other. This wound resulted in his being detained in the house for a month with fever. He would not call in a doctor. When Cosette urged him, "Call the dog doctor," said he.

Cosette dressed the wound morning and evening with so divine an air and such angelic happiness at being of use to him, that Jean Valjean felt all his former joy returning, his fears and anxieties dissipating, and he gazed at Cosette, saying, "Oh! What a kindly wound! Oh! What a good misfortune!"

Cosette on perceiving that her father was ill, had deserted the pavilion and again taken a fancy to the little lodging and the back courtyard. She passed nearly all her days beside Jean Valjean and read to him the books he desired. Generally they were books of travel. Jean Valjean was undergoing a new birth; his happiness was reviving in these ineffable rays; the Luxembourg, the prowling young stranger, Cosette's coldness, all these clouds upon his soul were growing dim. He had reached the point where he said to himself, "I imagined all that. I am an old fool."

His happiness was so great that the horrible discovery of the Thenardiers made in the Jondrette hovel, unexpected as it was, had, after a fashion, glided over him unnoticed. He had succeeded in making his escape; all trace of him was lost—what more did he care for! He only thought of those wretched beings to pity them. "Here they are in prison, and henceforth they will be incapacitated for doing any harm," he thought, "but what a lamentable family in distress!"

As for the hideous vision of the Barriere du Maine, Cosette had not referred to it again.

Sister Sainte-Mechtilde had taught Cosette music in the convent; Cosette had the voice of a linnet with a soul, and sometimes, in the evening, in the wounded man's humble abode, she warbled melancholy songs that delighted Jean Valjean.

Spring came; the garden was so delightful at that season of the year, that Jean Valjean said to Cosette, "You never go there; I want you to stroll in it."

"As you like, father," said Cosette.

And for the sake of obeying her father, she resumed her walks in the garden, generally alone, for, as we have mentioned, Jean Valjean, who was probably afraid of being seen through the fence, hardly ever went there.

Jean Valjean's wound had created a diversion.

When Cosette saw that her father was suffering less, that he was convalescing, and that he appeared to be happy, she experienced a contentment she did not even perceive, so gently and naturally had it come. Then, it was in the month of March, the days were growing longer, the winter was departing, the winter always bears away with it a portion of our sadness; then came April, that daybreak of summer, fresh as dawn always is, gay like every childhood; a little inclined to weep at times like the newborn being that it is. In that month, nature has charming gleams that pass from the sky, from the trees, from the meadows and the flowers into the heart of man.

Cosette was still too young to escape the penetrating influence of that April joy, which bore so strong a resemblance to herself. Insensibly, and without her suspecting the fact, the blackness departed from her spirit. In spring, sad souls grow light, as light falls into cellars at midday. Cosette was no longer sad. However, though this was so, she did not account for it to herself. In the morning, about ten o'clock, after breakfast, when she had succeeded in enticing her father into the garden for a quarter of an hour, and when she was pacing up and down in the sunlight in front of the steps, supporting his left arm for him, she did not perceive that she laughed every moment and that she was happy.

Jean Valjean, intoxicated, beheld her growing fresh and rosy once more.

"Oh! What a good wound!" he repeated in a whisper.

And he felt grateful to the Thenardiers.

His wound once healed, he resumed his solitary twilight strolls.

It is a mistake to suppose that a person can stroll alone in that fashion in the uninhabited regions of Paris without meeting with some adventure.

CHAPTER II—MOTHER PLUTARQUE FINDS NO DIFFICULTY IN EXPLAINING A PHENOMENON

One evening, little Gavroche had had nothing to eat; he remembered that he had not dined on the preceding day either; this was becoming tiresome. He resolved to make an effort to secure some supper. He strolled out beyond the Salpetriere into deserted regions; that is where windfalls are to be found; where there is no one, one always finds something. He reached a settlement that appeared to him to be the village of Austerlitz.

In one of his preceding lounges he had noticed there an old garden haunted by an old man and an old woman, and in that garden, a passable apple tree. Beside the apple tree stood a sort of fruit house, which was not securely fastened, and where one might contrive to get an apple. One apple is a supper; one apple is life. That which was Adam's ruin might prove Gavroche's salvation. The garden abutted on a solitary, unpaved lane, bordered with brushwood while awaiting the arrival of houses; the garden was separated from it by a hedge.

Gavroche directed his steps toward this garden; he found the lane, he recognized the apple tree, he verified the fruit house, he examined the hedge; a hedge means merely one stride. The day was declining, there was not even a cat in the lane, the hour was propitious. Gavroche began the operation of scaling the hedge, then suddenly paused. Someone was talking in the garden. Gavroche peeped through one of the breaks in the hedge.

A couple of paces distant, at the foot of the hedge on the other side, exactly at the point where the gap that he was meditating would have been made, there was a sort of recumbent stone that formed a bench, and on this bench was seated the old man of the garden, while the old woman was standing in front of him. The old woman was grumbling. Gavroche, who was not very discreet, listened.

"Monsieur Mabeuf!" said the old woman.

"Mabeuf!" thought Gavroche. "That name is a perfect farce."

The old man who was thus addressed, did not stir. The old woman repeated, "Monsieur Mabeuf!"

The old man, without raising his eyes from the ground, made up his mind to answer, "What is it, Mother Plutarque?"

"Mother Plutarque!" thought Gavroche. "Another farcical name."

Mother Plutarque began again, and the old man was forced to accept the conversation, "The landlord is not pleased."

"Why?"

"We owe three quarters rent."

"In three months, we shall owe him for four quarters."

"He says that he will turn you out to sleep."

"I will go."

"The green grocer insists on being paid. She will no longer leave her fagots. What will you warm yourself with this winter? We shall have no wood."

"There is the sun."

"The butcher refuses to give credit; he will not let us have any more meat."

"That is quite right. I do not digest meat well. It is too heavy."

"What shall we have for dinner?"

"Bread."

"The baker demands a settlement, and says, 'no money, no bread.'"

"That is well."

"What will you eat?"

"We have apples in the apple room."

"But, Monsieur, we can't live like that without money."

"I have none."

The old woman went away, the old man remained alone. He fell into thought. Gavroche became thoughtful also. It was almost dark.

The first result of Gavroche's meditation was, that instead of scaling the hedge, he crouched down under it. The branches stood apart a little at the foot of the thicket.

"Come," exclaimed Gavroche mentally, "here's a nook!" and he curled up in it. His back was almost in contact with Father Mabeuf's bench. He could hear the octogenarian breathe.

Then, by way of dinner, he tried to sleep.

It was a catnap, with one eye open. While he dozed, Gavroche kept on the watch.

The twilight pallor of the sky blanched the earth, and the lane formed a livid line between two rows of dark bushes.

All at once, in this whitish band, two figures made their appearance. One was in front, the other some distance in the rear.

"There come two creatures," muttered Gavroche.

The first form seemed to be some elderly bourgeois, who was bent and thoughtful, dressed more than plainly, and who was walking slowly because of his age, and strolling about in the open evening air.

The second was straight, firm, slender. It regulated its pace by that of the first; but in the voluntary slowness of its gait, suppleness and agility were discernible. This figure had also something fierce and disquieting about it, the whole shape was that of what was then called an elegant; the hat was of good shape, the coat black, well cut, probably of fine cloth, and well fitted in at the waist. The head was held erect with a sort of robust grace, and beneath the hat the pale profile of a young man could be made out in the dim light. The profile had a rose in its mouth. This second form was well known to Gavroche; it was Montparnasse.

He could have told nothing about the other, except that he was a respectable old man.

Gavroche immediately began to take observations.

One of these two pedestrians evidently had a project connected with the other. Gavroche was well placed to watch the course of events. The bedroom had turned into a hiding place at a very opportune moment.

Montparnasse on the hunt at such an hour, in such a place, betokened something threatening. Gavroche felt his gamin's heart moved with compassion for the old man.

What was he to do? Interfere? One weakness coming to the aid of another! It would be merely a laughing matter for Montparnasse. Gavroche did not shut his eyes to the fact that the old man, in the first place, and the child in the second, would make but two mouthfuls for that redoubtable ruffian eighteen years of age.

While Gavroche was deliberating, the attack took place, abruptly and hideously. The attack of the tiger on the wild ass, the attack of the spider on the fly. Montparnasse suddenly tossed away his rose, bounded upon the old man, seized him by the collar, grasped and clung to him, and Gavroche with difficulty restrained a scream. A moment later one of these men was underneath the other, groaning, struggling, with a knee of marble upon his breast. Only, it was not just what Gavroche had expected. The one who lay on the earth was Montparnasse; the one who was on top was the old man. All this took place a few paces distant from Gavroche.

The old man had received the shock, had returned it, and that in such a terrible fashion, that in a twinkling, the assailant and the assailed had exchanged roles.

"Here's a hearty veteran!" thought Gavroche.

He could not refrain from clapping his hands. But it was applause wasted. It did not reach the combatants, absorbed and deafened as they were, each by the other, as their breath mingled in the struggle.

Silence ensued. Montparnasse ceased his struggles. Gavroche indulged in this aside, "Can he be dead!"

The goodman had not uttered a word, nor given vent to a cry. He rose to his feet, and Gavroche heard him say to Montparnasse, "Get up."

Montparnasse rose, but the goodman held him fast. Montparnasse's attitude was the humiliated and furious attitude of the wolf who has been caught by a sheep.

Gavroche looked on and listened, making an effort to reinforce his eyes with his ears. He was enjoying himself immensely.

He was repaid for his conscientious anxiety in the character of a spectator. He was able to catch on the wing a dialogue that borrowed from the darkness an indescribably tragic accent. The goodman questioned, Montparnasse replied.

"How old are you?"

"Nineteen."

"You are strong and healthy. Why do you not work?"

"It bores me."

"What is your trade?"

"An idler."

"Speak seriously. Can anything be done for you? What would you like to be?"

"A thief."

A pause ensued. The old man seemed absorbed in profound thought. He stood motionless, and did not relax his hold on Montparnasse.

Every moment the vigorous and agile young ruffian indulged in the twitchings of a wild beast caught in a snare. He gave a jerk, tried a crook of the knee, twisted his limbs desperately, and made efforts to escape.

The old man did not appear to notice it, and held both his arms with one hand, with the sovereign indifference of absolute force.

The old man's reverie lasted for some time, then, looking steadily at Montparnasse, he addressed to him in a gentle voice, in the midst of the darkness where they stood, a solemn harangue, of which Gavroche did not lose a single syllable, "My child, you are entering, through indolence, on one of the most laborious of lives. Ah! You declare yourself to be an idler! Prepare to toil. There is a certain formidable machine, have you seen it? It is the rolling-mill. You must be on your guard against it, it is crafty and ferocious; if it catches hold of the skirt of your coat, you will be drawn in bodily. That machine is laziness. Stop while there is yet time, and save yourself! Otherwise, it is all over with you; in a short time you will be among the gearing. Once entangled, hope for nothing more. Toil, lazybones! There is no more repose for you! The iron hand of implacable toil has seized you. You do not wish to earn your living, to have a task, to fulfill a duty! It bores you to be like other men? Well! You will be different. Labor is the law; he who rejects it will find ennui his torment. You do not wish to be a workingman, you will be a slave. Toil lets go of you on one side only to grasp you again on the other. You do not desire to be its friend, you shall be its Negro slave. Ah! You would have none of the honest weariness of men, you shall have the sweat of the damned. Where others sing, you will rattle in your throat. You will see afar off, from below, other men at work; it will seem to you that they are resting. The laborer, the harvester, the sailor, the blacksmith, will appear to you in glory like the blessed spirits in paradise. What radiance surrounds the forge! To guide the plough, to bind the sheaves, is joy. The bark at liberty in the wind, what delight! Do you, lazy idler, delve, drag on, roll, march! Drag your halter. You are a beast of burden in the team of hell! Ah! To do nothing is your object. Well, not a week, not a day, not an hour shall you have free from oppression. You will be able to lift nothing without anguish. Every minute that passes will make your muscles crack. What is a feather to others will be a rock to you. The simplest things will become steep acclivities. Life will become monstrous all about you. To go, to come, to breathe, will be just so many terrible labors. Your lungs will produce on you the effect of weighing a hundred pounds. Whether you shall walk here rather than there, will become a problem that must be solved. Anyone who wants to go out simply gives his door a push, and there he is in the open air. If you wish to go out, you will be obliged to pierce your wall. What does everyone who wants to step into the street do? He goes downstairs; you will tear up your sheets, little by little you will make of them a rope, then you will climb out of your window, and you will suspend yourself by that thread over an abyss, and it will be night, amid storm, rain, and the hurricane, and if the rope is too short, but one way of descending will remain to you, to fall. To drop haphazard into the gulf, from an unknown height, on what? On what is beneath, on the unknown. Or you will crawl up a chimney-flue, at the risk of burning; or you will creep through a sewer-pipe, at the risk of drowning; I do not speak of the holes that you will be obliged to mask, of the stones which you will have to take up and replace twenty times a day, of the plaster that you will have to hide in your straw pallet. A lock presents itself; the bourgeois has in his pocket a key made by a locksmith. If you wish to pass out, you will be condemned to execute a terrible work of art; you will take a large sou, you will cut it in two plates; with what tools? You will have to invent them. That is your business. Then you will hollow out the interior of these plates, taking great care of the outside, and you will make on the edges a thread, so that they can be adjusted one upon the other like a box and its cover. The top and bottom thus screwed together, nothing will be suspected. To the overseers it will be only a sou; to you it will be a box. What will you put in this box? A small bit of steel. A watch spring, in which you will have cut teeth, and which will form a saw. With this saw, as long as a pin, and concealed in a sou, you will cut the bolt of the lock, you will sever bolts, the padlock of your chain, and the bar at your window, and the fetter on your leg. This masterpiece finished, this prodigy accomplished, all these miracles of art, address, skill, and patience executed, what will be your recompense if it becomes known that you are the author? The dungeon. There is your future. What precipices are idleness and pleasure! Do you know that to do nothing is a melancholy resolution? To live in idleness on the property of society! To be useless, that is to say, pernicious! This leads straight to the depth of wretchedness. Woe to the man who desires to be a parasite! He will become vermin! Ah! So it does not please you to work? Ah! You have but one thought, to drink well, to eat well, to sleep well. You will drink water, you will eat black bread, you will sleep on a plank with a fetter whose cold touch you will feel on your flesh all night long, riveted to your limbs. You will break those fetters, you will flee. That is well. You will crawl on your belly through the brushwood, and you will eat grass like the beasts of the forest. And you will be recaptured. And then you will pass years in a dungeon, riveted to a wall, groping for your jug that you may drink, gnawing at a horrible loaf of darkness that dogs would not touch, eating beans that the worms have eaten before you. You will be a woodlouse in a cellar. Ah! Have pity on yourself, you miserable young child, who were sucking at nurse less than twenty years ago, and who have, no doubt, a mother still alive! I conjure you, listen to me, I entreat you. You desire fine black cloth, varnished shoes, to have your hair curled and sweet-smelling oils on your locks, to please low women, to be handsome. You will be shaven clean, and you will wear a red blouse and wooden shoes. You want rings on your fingers, you will have an iron necklet on your neck. If you glance at a woman, you will receive a blow. And you will enter there at the age of twenty. And you will come out at fifty! You will enter young, rosy, fresh, with brilliant eyes, and all your white teeth, and your handsome, youthful hair; you will come out broken, bent, wrinkled, toothless, horrible, with white locks! Ah! My poor child, you are on the wrong road; idleness is counseling you badly; the hardest of all work is thieving. Believe me, do not undertake that painful profession of an idle man. It is not comfortable to become a rascal. It is less disagreeable to be an honest man. Now go, and ponder on what I have said to you. By the way, what did you want of me? My purse? Here it is."

And the old man, releasing Montparnasse, put his purse in the latter's hand; Montparnasse weighed it for a moment, after which he allowed it to slide gently into the back pocket of his coat, with the same mechanical precaution as though he had stolen it.

All this having been said and done, the goodman turned his back and tranquilly resumed his stroll.

"The blockhead!" muttered Montparnasse.

Who was this goodman? The reader has, no doubt, already divined.

Montparnasse watched him with amazement, as he disappeared in the dusk. This contemplation was fatal to him.

While the old man was walking away, Gavroche drew near.

Gavroche had assured himself, with a sidelong glance, that Father Mabeuf was still sitting on his bench, probably sound asleep. Then the gamin emerged from his thicket, and began to crawl after Montparnasse in the dark, as the latter stood there motionless. In this manner he came up to Montparnasse without being seen or heard, gently insinuated his hand into the back pocket of that frock-coat of fine black cloth, seized the purse, withdrew his hand, and having recourse once more to his crawling, he slipped away like an adder through the shadows. Montparnasse, who had no reason to be on his guard, and who was engaged in thought for the first time in his life, perceived nothing. When Gavroche had once more attained the point where Father Mabeuf was, he flung the purse over the hedge, and fled as fast as his legs would carry him.

The purse fell on Father Mabeuf's foot. This commotion roused him.

He bent over and picked up the purse.

He did not understand in the least, and opened it.

The purse had two compartments; in one of them there was some small change; in the other lay six napoleons.

M. Mabeuf, in great alarm, referred the matter to his housekeeper.

"That has fallen from heaven," said Mother Plutarque.

BOOK FIFTH: THE END OF WHICH DOES NOT RESEMBLE THE BEGINNING

CHAPTER I—SOLITUDE AND THE BARRACKS COMBINED

Cosette's grief, which had been so poignant and lively four or five months previously, had, without her being conscious of the fact, entered upon its convalescence. Nature, spring, youth, love for her father, the gaiety of the birds and flowers, caused something almost resembling forgetfulness to filter gradually, drop by drop, into that soul, which was so virgin and so young. Was the fire wholly extinct there? Or was it merely that layers of ashes had formed? The truth is, that she hardly felt the painful and burning spot any longer.

One day she suddenly thought of Marius, "Why!" said she. "I no longer think of him."

That same week, she noticed a very handsome officer of lancers, with a wasplike waist, a delicious uniform, the cheeks of a young girl, a sword under his arm, waxed mustaches, and a glazed schapka, passing the gate. Moreover, he had light hair, prominent blue eyes, a round face, was vain, insolent, and goodlooking; quite the reverse of Marius. He had a cigar in his mouth. Cosette thought that this officer doubtless belonged to the regiment in barracks in the Rue de Babylone.

On the following day, she saw him pass again. She took note of the hour.

From that time forth, was it chance? She saw him pass nearly every day.

The officer's comrades perceived that there was, in that "badly kept" garden, behind that malicious rococo fence, a very pretty creature, who was almost always there when the handsome lieutenant, who is not unknown to the reader, and whose name was Theodule Gillenormand, passed by.

"See here!" they said to him. "There's a little creature there who is making eyes at you, look."

"Have I the time," replied the lancer, "to look at all the girls who look at me?"

This was at the precise moment when Marius was descending heavily toward agony, and was saying, "If I could but see her before I die!" Had his wish been realized, had he beheld Cosette at that moment gazing at the lancer, he would not have been able to utter a word, and he would have expired with grief.

Whose fault was it? No one's.

Marius possessed one of those temperaments that bury themselves in sorrow and there abide; Cosette was one of those persons who plunge into sorrow and emerge from it again.

Cosette was, moreover, passing through that dangerous period, the fatal phase of feminine reverie abandoned to itself, in which the isolated heart of a young girl resembles the tendrils of the vine that cling, as chance directs, to the capital of a marble column or to the post of a wine shop: a rapid and decisive moment, critical for every orphan, be she rich or poor, for wealth does not prevent a bad choice; misalliances are made in very high circles, real misalliance is that of souls; and as many an unknown young man, without name, without birth, without fortune, is a marble column that bears up a temple of grand sentiments and grand ideas, so such and such a man of the world satisfied and opulent, who has polished boots and varnished words, if looked at not outside, but inside, a thing that is reserved for his wife, is nothing more than a block obscurely haunted by violent, unclean, and vinous passions; the post of a drinking shop.

What did Cosette's soul contain? Passion calmed or lulled to sleep; something limpid, brilliant, troubled to a certain depth, and gloomy lower down. The image of the handsome officer was reflected in the surface. Did a souvenir linger in the depths? Quite at the bottom? Possibly. Cosette did not know.

A singular incident supervened.

CHAPTER II—COSETTE'S APPREHENSIONS

During the first fortnight in April, Jean Valjean took a journey. This, as the reader knows, happened from time to time, at very long intervals. He remained absent a day or two days at the utmost. Where did he go? No one knew, not even Cosette. Once only, on the occasion of one of these departures, she had accompanied him in a hackney-coach as far as a little blind alley at the corner of which she read: Impasse de la Planchette. There he alighted, and the coach took Cosette back to the Rue de Babylone. It was usually when money was lacking in the house that Jean Valjean took these little trips.

So Jean Valjean was absent. He had said, "I shall return in three days."

That evening, Cosette was alone in the drawing room. In order to get rid of her ennui, she had opened her piano-organ, and had begun to sing, accompanying herself the while, the chorus from Euryanthe, "Hunters astray in the wood!" which is probably the most beautiful thing in all the sphere of music. When she had finished, she remained wrapped in thought.

All at once, it seemed to her that she heard the sound of footsteps in the garden.

It could not be her father, he was absent; it could not be Toussaint, she was in bed, and it was ten o'clock at night.

She stepped to the shutter of the drawing room, which was closed, and laid her ear against it.

It seemed to her that it was the tread of a man, and that he was walking very softly.

She mounted rapidly to the first floor, to her own chamber, opened a small wicket in her shutter, and peeped into the garden. The moon was at the full. Everything could be seen as plainly as by day.

There was no one there.

She opened the window. The garden was absolutely calm, and all that was visible was that the street was deserted as usual.

Cosette thought that she had been mistaken. She thought that she had heard a noise. It was a hallucination produced by the melancholy and magnificent chorus of Weber, which lays open before the mind terrified depths, which trembles before the gaze like a dizzy forest, and in which one hears the crackling of dead branches beneath the uneasy tread of the huntsmen of whom one catches a glimpse through the twilight.

She thought no more about it.

Moreover, Cosette was not very timid by nature. There flowed in her veins some of the blood of the bohemian and the adventuress who runs barefoot. It will be remembered that she was more of a lark than a dove. There was a foundation of wildness and bravery in her.

On the following day, at an earlier hour, toward nightfall, she was strolling in the garden. In the midst of the confused thoughts which occupied her, she fancied that she caught for an instant a sound similar to that of the preceding evening, as though someone were walking beneath the trees in the dusk, and not very far from her; but she told herself that nothing so closely resembles a step on the grass as the friction of two branches which have moved from side to side, and she paid no heed to it. Besides, she could see nothing.

She emerged from "the thicket;" she had still to cross a small lawn to regain the steps.

The moon, which had just risen behind her, cast Cosette's shadow in front of her upon this lawn, as she came out from the shrubbery.

Cosette halted in alarm.

Beside her shadow, the moon outlined distinctly upon the turf another shadow, which was particularly startling and terrible, a shadow that had a round hat.

It was the shadow of a man, who must have been standing on the border of the clump of shrubbery, a few paces in the rear of Cosette.

She stood for a moment without the power to speak, or cry, or call, or stir, or turn her head.

Then she summoned up all her courage, and turned around resolutely.

There was no one there.

She glanced on the ground. The figure had disappeared.

She reentered the thicket, searched the corners boldly, went as far as the gate, and found nothing.

She felt herself absolutely chilled with terror. Was this another hallucination? What! Two days in succession! One hallucination might pass, but two hallucinations? The disquieting point about it was, that the shadow had assuredly not been a phantom. Phantoms do not wear round hats.

On the following day Jean Valjean returned. Cosette told him what she thought she had heard and seen. She wanted to be reassured and to see her father shrug his shoulders and say to her, "You are a little goose."

Jean Valjean grew anxious.

"It cannot be anything," said he.

He left her under some pretext, and went into the garden, and she saw him examining the gate with great attention.

During the night she woke up; this time she was sure, and she distinctly heard someone walking close to the flight of steps beneath her window. She ran to her little wicket and opened it. In point of fact, there was a man in the garden, with a large club in his hand. Just as she was about to scream, the moon lighted up the man's profile. It was her father. She returned to her bed, saying to herself, "He is very uneasy!"

Jean Valjean passed that night and the two succeeding nights in the garden. Cosette saw him through the hole in her shutter.

On the third night, the moon was on the wane, and had begun to rise later; at one o'clock in the morning, possibly, she heard a loud burst of laughter and her father's voice calling her, "Cosette!"

She jumped out of bed, threw on her dressing gown, and opened her window.

Her father was standing on the grass plot below.

"I have waked you for the purpose of reassuring you," said he; "look, there is your shadow with the round hat."

And he pointed out to her on the turf a shadow cast by the moon, and which did indeed, bear considerable resemblance to the specter of a man wearing a round hat. It was the shadow produced by a chimney-pipe of sheet iron, with a hood, which rose above a neighboring roof.

Cosette joined in his laughter, all her lugubrious suppositions were allayed, and the next morning, as she was at breakfast with her father, she made merry over the sinister garden haunted by the shadows of iron chimney pots.

Jean Valjean became quite tranquil once more; as for Cosette, she did not pay much attention to the question whether the chimney pot was really in the direction of the shadow she had seen, or thought she had seen, and whether the moon had been in the same spot in the sky.

She did not question herself as to the peculiarity of a chimney pot that is afraid of being caught in the act, and that retires when someone looks at its shadow, for the shadow had taken the alarm when Cosette had turned around, and Cosette had thought herself very sure of this. Cosette's serenity was fully restored. The proof appeared to her to be complete, and it quite vanished from her mind, whether there could possibly be anyone walking in the garden during the evening or at night.

A few days later, however, a fresh incident occurred.

CHAPTER III—ENRICHED WITH COMMENTARIES BY TOUSSAINT

In the garden, near the railing on the street, there was a stone bench, screened from the eyes of the curious by a plantation of yoke elms, but which could, in case of necessity, be reached by an arm from the outside, past the trees and the gate.

One evening during that same month of April, Jean Valjean had gone out; Cosette had seated herself on this bench after sundown. The breeze was blowing briskly in the trees, Cosette was meditating; an objectless sadness was taking possession of her little by little, that invincible sadness evoked by the evening, and which arises, perhaps, who knows, from the mystery of the tomb which is ajar at that hour.

Perhaps Fantine was within that shadow.

Cosette rose, slowly made the tour of the garden, walking on the grass drenched in dew, and saying to herself, through the species of melancholy somnambulism in which she was plunged, "Really, one needs wooden shoes for the garden at this hour. One takes cold."

She returned to the bench.

As she was about to resume her seat there, she observed on the spot she had quitted, a tolerably large stone that had, evidently, not been there a moment before.

Cosette gazed at the stone, asking herself what it meant. All at once the idea occurred to her that the stone had not reached the bench all by itself, that someone had placed it there, that an arm had been thrust through the railing, and this idea appeared to alarm her. This time, the fear was genuine; the stone was there. No doubt was possible; she did not touch it, fled without glancing behind her, took refuge in the house, and immediately closed with shutter, bolt, and bar the doorlike window opening on the flight of steps. She inquired of Toussaint, "Has my father returned yet?"

"Not yet, Mademoiselle."

Jean Valjean, a thoughtful man, and given to nocturnal strolls, often returned quite late at night.

"Toussaint," went on Cosette, "are you careful to thoroughly barricade the shutters opening on the garden, at least with bars, in the evening, and to put the little iron things in the little rings that close them?"

"Oh! Be easy on that score, Miss."

Toussaint did not fail in her duty, and Cosette was well aware of the fact, but she could not refrain from adding, "It is so solitary here."

"So far as that is concerned," said Toussaint, "it is true. We might be assassinated before we had time to say ouf! And Monsieur does not sleep in the house, to boot. But fear nothing, Miss, I fasten the shutters up like prisons. Lone women! That is enough to make one shudder, I believe you! Just imagine, what if you were to see men enter your chamber at night and say, 'Hold your tongue!' and begin to cut your throat. It's not the dying so much; you die, for one must die, and that's all right; it's the abomination of feeling those people touch you. And then, their knives; they can't be able to cut well with them! Ah, good gracious!"

"Be quiet," said Cosette. "Fasten everything thoroughly."

Cosette, terrified by the melodrama improvised by Toussaint, and possibly, also, by the recollection of the apparitions of the past week, which recurred to her memory, dared not even say to her, "Go and look at the stone that has been placed on the bench!" for fear of opening the garden gate and allowing "the men" to enter. She saw that all the doors and windows were carefully fastened, made Toussaint go all over the house from garret to cellar, locked herself up in her own chamber, bolted her door, looked under her couch, went to bed and slept badly. All night long she saw that big stone, as large as a mountain and full of caverns.

At sunrise, the property of the rising sun is to make us laugh at all our terrors of the past night, and our laughter is in direct proportion to our terror which they have caused, at sunrise Cosette, when she woke, viewed her fright as a nightmare, and said to herself, "What have I been thinking of? It is like the footsteps that I thought I heard a week or two ago in the garden at night! It is like the shadow of the chimney pot! Am I becoming a coward?" The sun, which was glowing through the crevices in her shutters, and turning the damask curtains crimson, reassured her to such an extent that everything vanished from her thoughts, even the stone.

"There was no more a stone on the bench than there was a man in a round hat in the garden; I dreamed about the stone, as I did all the rest."

She dressed herself, descended to the garden, ran to the bench, and broke out in a cold perspiration. The stone was there.

But this lasted only for a moment. That which is terror by night is curiosity by day.

"Bah!" said she. "Come, let us see what it is."

She lifted the stone, which was tolerably large. Beneath it was something that resembled a letter. It was a white envelope. Cosette seized it. There was no address on one side, no seal on the other. Yet the envelope, though unsealed, was not empty. Papers could be seen inside.

Cosette examined it. It was no longer alarm, it was no longer curiosity; it was a beginning of anxiety.

Cosette drew from the envelope its contents, a little notebook of paper, each page of which was numbered and bore a few lines in a very fine and rather pretty handwriting, as Cosette thought.

Cosette looked for a name; there was none. To whom was this addressed? To her, probably, since a hand had deposited the packet on her bench. From whom did it come? An irresistible fascination took possession of her; she tried to turn away her eyes from the leaflets which were trembling in her hand, she gazed at the sky, the street, the acacias all bathed in light, the pigeons fluttering over a neighboring roof, and then her glance suddenly fell upon the manuscript, and she said to herself that she must know what it contained.

This is what she read.

CHAPTER IV—A HEART BENEATH A STONE

The reduction of the universe to a single being, the expansion of a single being even to God, that is love.

Love is the salutation of the angels to the stars.

How sad is the soul, when it is sad through love!

What a void in the absence of the being who, by herself alone fills the world! Oh! How true it is that the beloved being becomes God. One could comprehend that God might be jealous of this had not God the Father of all evidently made creation for the soul, and the soul for love.

The glimpse of a smile beneath a white crape bonnet with a lilac curtain is sufficient to cause the soul to enter into the palace of dreams.

God is behind everything, but everything hides God. Things are black, creatures are opaque. To love a being is to render that being transparent.

Certain thoughts are prayers. There are moments when, whatever the attitude of the body may be, the soul is on its knees.

Parted lovers beguile absence by a thousand chimerical devices, which possess, however, a reality of their own. They are prevented from seeing each other, they cannot write to each other; they discover a multitude of mysterious means to correspond. They send each other the song of the birds, the perfume of the flowers, the smiles of children, the light of the sun, the sighings of the breeze, the rays of stars, all creation. And why not? All the works of God are made to serve love. Love is sufficiently potent to charge all nature with its messages.

Oh Spring! Thou art a letter that I write to her.

The future belongs to hearts even more than it does to minds. Love, that is the only thing that can occupy and fill eternity. In the infinite, the inexhaustible is requisite.

Love participates of the soul itself. It is of the same nature. Like it, it is the divine spark; like it, it is incorruptible, indivisible, imperishable. It is a point of fire that exists within us, which is immortal and infinite, which nothing can confine, and which nothing can extinguish. We feel it burning even to the very marrow of our bones, and we see it beaming in the very depths of heaven.

Oh Love! Adorations! Voluptuousness of two minds that understand each other, of two hearts that exchange with each other, of two glances that penetrate each other! You will come to me, will you not, bliss! Strolls by twos in the solitudes! Blessed and radiant days! I have sometimes dreamed that from time to time hours detached themselves from the lives of the angels and came here below to traverse the destinies of men.

God can add nothing to the happiness of those who love, except to give them endless duration. After a life of love, an eternity of love is, in fact, an augmentation; but to increase in intensity even the ineffable felicity, which love bestows on the soul even in this world, is impossible, even to God. God is the plenitude of heaven; love is the plenitude of man.

You look at a star for two reasons, because it is luminous, and because it is impenetrable. You have beside you a sweeter radiance and a greater mystery, woman.

All of us, whoever we may be, have our respirable beings. We lack air and we stifle. Then we die. To die for lack of love is horrible. Suffocation of the soul.

When love has fused and mingled two beings in a sacred and angelic unity, the secret of life has been discovered so far as they are concerned; they are no longer anything more than the two boundaries of the same destiny; they are no longer anything but the two wings of the same spirit. Love, soar.

On the day when a woman as she passes before you emits light as she walks, you are lost, you love. But one thing remains for you to do: to think of her so intently that she is constrained to think of you.

What love commences can be finished by God alone.

True love is in despair and is enchanted over a glove lost or a handkerchief found, and eternity is required for its devotion and its hopes. It is composed both of the infinitely great and the infinitely little.

If you are a stone, be adamant; if you are a plant, be the sensitive plant; if you are a man, be love.

Nothing suffices for love. We have happiness, we desire paradise; we possess paradise, we desire heaven.

Oh ye who love each other, all this is contained in love. Understand how to find it there. Love has contemplation as well as heaven, and more than heaven, it has voluptuousness.

"Does she still come to the Luxembourg?"

"No, sir."

"This is the church where she attends mass, is it not?"

"She no longer comes here."

"Does she still live in this house?"

"She has moved away."

"Where has she gone to dwell?"

"She did not say."

What a melancholy thing not to know the address of one's soul!

Love has its childishness, other passions have their pettinesses. Shame on the passions that belittle man! Honor to the one that makes a child of him!

There is one strange thing, do you know it? I dwell in the night. There is a being who carried off my sky when she went away.

Oh! Would that we were lying side by side in the same grave, hand in hand, and from time to time, in the darkness, gently caressing a finger, that would suffice for my eternity!

Ye who suffer because ye love, love yet more. To die of love, is to live in it.

Love. A somber and starry transfiguration is mingled with this torture. There is ecstasy in agony.

Oh joy of the birds! It is because they have nests that they sing.

Love is a celestial respiration of the air of paradise.

Deep hearts, sage minds, take life as God has made it; it is a long trial, an incomprehensible preparation for an unknown destiny. This destiny, the true one, begins for a man with the first step inside the tomb. Then something appears to him, and he begins to distinguish the definitive. The definitive, meditate upon that word. The living perceive the infinite; the definitive permits itself to be seen only by the dead. In the meanwhile, love and suffer, hope and contemplate. Woe, alas! To him who shall have loved only bodies, forms, appearances! Death will deprive him of all. Try to love souls, you will find them again.

I encountered in the street, a very poor young man who was in love. His hat was old, his coat was worn, his elbows were in holes; water trickled through his shoes, and the stars through his soul.

What a grand thing it is to be loved! What a far grander thing it is to love! The heart becomes heroic, by dint of passion. It is no longer composed of anything but what is pure; it no longer rests on anything that is not elevated and great. An unworthy thought can no more germinate in it, than a nettle on a glacier. The serene and lofty soul, inaccessible to vulgar passions and emotions, dominating the clouds and the shades of this world, its follies, its lies, its hatreds, its vanities, its miseries, inhabits the blue of heaven, and no longer feels anything but profound and subterranean shocks of destiny, as the crests of mountains feel the shocks of earthquake.

If there did not exist someone who loved, the sun would become extinct.

CHAPTER V—COSETTE
AFTER THE LETTER

As Cosette read, she gradually fell into thought. At the very moment when she raised her eyes from the last line of the notebook, the handsome officer passed triumphantly in front of the gate, it was his hour; Cosette thought him hideous.

She resumed her contemplation of the book. It was written in the most charming of chirography, thought Cosette; in the same hand, but with divers' inks, sometimes very black, again whitish, as when ink has been added to the inkstand, and consequently on different days. It was, then, a mind that had unfolded itself there, sigh by sigh, irregularly, without order, without choice, without object, haphazard. Cosette had never read anything like it. This manuscript, in which she already perceived more light than obscurity, produced upon her the effect of a half-open sanctuary. Each one of these mysterious lines shone before her eyes and inundated her heart with a strange radiance. The education she had received had always talked to her of the soul, and never of love, very much as one might talk of the firebrand and not of the flame. This manuscript of fifteen pages suddenly and sweetly revealed to her all of love, sorrow, destiny, life, eternity, the beginning, the end. It was as if a hand had opened and suddenly flung upon her a handful of rays of light. In these few lines she felt a passionate, ardent, generous, honest nature, a sacred will, an immense sorrow, and an immense despair, a suffering heart, an ecstasy fully expanded. What was this manuscript? A letter. A letter without name, without address, without date, without signature, pressing and disinterested, an enigma composed of truths, a message of love made to be brought by an angel and read by a virgin, an appointment made beyond the bounds of earth, the love letter of a phantom to a shade. It was an absent one, tranquil and dejected, who seemed ready to take refuge in death and who sent to the absent love, his lady, the secret of fate, the key of life, love. This had been written with one foot in the grave and one finger in heaven. These lines, which had fallen one by one on the paper, were what might be called drops of soul.

Now, from whom could these pages come? Who could have penned them? Cosette did not hesitate a moment. One man only.

He!

Day had dawned once more in her spirit; all had reappeared. She felt an unheard-of joy, and a profound anguish. It was he! He who had written! He was there! It was he whose arm had been thrust through that railing! While she was forgetful of him, he had found her again! But had she forgotten him? No, never! She was foolish to have thought so for a single moment. She had always loved him, always adored him. The fire had been smothered, and had smoldered for a time, but she saw all plainly now; it had but made headway, and now it had burst forth afresh, and had inflamed her whole being. This notebook was like a spark which had fallen from that other soul into hers. She felt the conflagration starting up once more.

She imbued herself thoroughly with every word of the manuscript, "Oh yes!" said she. "How perfectly I recognize all that! That is what I had already read in his eyes." As she was finishing it for the third time, Lieutenant Theodule passed the gate once more, and rattled his spurs upon the pavement. Cosette was forced to raise her eyes. She thought him insipid, silly, stupid, useless, foppish, displeasing, impertinent, and extremely ugly. The officer thought it his duty to smile at her.

She turned away as in shame and indignation. She would gladly have thrown something at his head.

She fled, reentered the house, and shut herself up in her chamber to peruse the manuscript once more, to learn it by heart, and to dream. When she had thoroughly mastered it she kissed it and put it in her bosom.

All was over, Cosette had fallen back into deep, seraphic love. The abyss of Eden had yawned once more.

All day long, Cosette remained in a sort of bewilderment. She scarcely thought, her ideas were in the state of a tangled skein in her brain, she could not manage to conjecture anything, she hoped through a tremor, what? Vague things. She dared make herself no promises, and she did not wish to refuse herself anything. Flashes of pallor passed over her countenance, and shivers ran through her frame. It seemed to her, at intervals, that she was entering the land of chimeras; she said to herself, "Is this reality?" Then she felt of the dear paper within her bosom under her gown, she pressed it to her heart, she felt its angles against her flesh; and if Jean Valjean had seen her at the moment, he would have shuddered in the presence of that luminous and unknown joy, which overflowed from beneath her eyelids. "Oh yes!" she thought. "It is certainly he! This comes from him, and is for me!"

And she told herself that an intervention of the angels, a celestial chance, had given him back to her.

Oh transfiguration of love! Oh dreams! That celestial chance, that intervention of the angels, was a pellet of bread tossed by one thief to another thief, from the Charlemagne Courtyard to the Lion's Ditch, over the roofs of La Force.

CHAPTER VI—OLD PEOPLE ARE MADE TO GO OUT OPPORTUNELY

When evening came, Jean Valjean went out; Cosette dressed herself. She arranged her hair in the most becoming manner, and she put on a dress whose bodice had received one snip of the scissors too much, and which, through this slope, permitted a view of the beginning of her throat, and was, as young girls say, "a trifle indecent." It was not in the least indecent, but it was prettier than usual. She made her toilette thus without knowing why she did so.

Did she mean to go out? No.

Was she expecting a visitor? No.

At dusk, she went down to the garden. Toussaint was busy in her kitchen, which opened on the backyard.

She began to stroll about under the trees, thrusting aside the branches from time to time with her hand, because there were some that hung very low.

In this manner she reached the bench.

The stone was still there.

She sat down, and gently laid her white hand on this stone as though she wished to caress and thank it.

All at once, she experienced that indefinable impression which one undergoes when there is someone standing behind one, even when she does not see the person.

She turned her head and rose to her feet.

It was he.

His head was bare. He appeared to have grown thin and pale. His black clothes were hardly discernible. The twilight threw a wan light on his fine brow, and covered his eyes in shadows. Beneath a veil of incomparable sweetness, he had something about him that suggested death and night. His face was illuminated by the light of the dying day, and by the thought of a soul that is taking flight.

He seemed to be not yet a ghost, and he was no longer a man.

He had flung away his hat in the thicket, a few paces distant.

Cosette, though ready to swoon, uttered no cry. She retreated slowly, for she felt herself attracted. He did not stir. By virtue of something ineffable and melancholy, which enveloped him, she felt the look in his eyes that she could not see.

Cosette, in her retreat, encountered a tree and leaned against it. Had it not been for this tree, she would have fallen.

Then she heard his voice—that voice which she had really never heard—barely rising above the rustle of the leaves, and murmuring, "Pardon me, here I am. My heart is full. I could not live on as I was living, and I have come. Have you read what I placed there on the bench? Do you recognize me at all? Have no fear of me. It is a long time, you remember the day, since you looked at me at the Luxembourg, near the Gladiator. And the day when you passed before me? It was on the 16th of June and the 2nd of July. It is nearly a year ago. I have not seen you for a long time. I inquired of the woman who let the chairs, and she told me that she no longer saw you. You lived in the Rue de l'Ouest, on the third floor, in the front apartments of a new house, you see that I know! I followed you. What else was there for me to do? And then you disappeared. I thought I saw you pass once, while I was reading the newspapers under the arcade of the Odeon. I ran after you. But no. It was a person who had a bonnet like yours. At night I came here. Do not be afraid, no one sees me. I come to gaze upon your windows near at hand. I walk very softly, so that you may not hear, for you might be alarmed. The other evening I was behind you, you turned around, I fled. Once, I heard you singing. I was happy. Did it affect you because I heard you singing through the shutters? That could not hurt you. No, it is not so? You see, you are my angel! Let me come sometimes; I think that I am going to die. If you only knew! I adore you. Forgive me, I speak to you, but I do not know what I am saying; I may have displeased you; have I displeased you?"

"Oh! My mother!" said she.

And she sank down as though on the point of death.

He grasped her, she fell, he took her in his arms, he pressed her close, without knowing what he was doing. He supported her, though he was tottering himself. It was as though his brain were full of smoke; lightnings darted between his lips; his ideas vanished; it seemed to him that he was accomplishing some religious act, and that he was committing a profanation. Moreover, he had not the least passion for this lovely woman whose force he felt against his breast. He was beside himself with love.

She took his hand and laid it on her heart. He felt the paper there, he stammered, "You love me, then?"

She replied in a voice so low that it was no longer anything more than a barely audible breath, "Hush! Thou knowest it!"

And she hid her blushing face on the breast of the superb and intoxicated young man.

He fell upon the bench, and she beside him. They had no words more. The stars were beginning to gleam. How did it come to pass that their lips met? How comes it to pass that the birds sing, that snow melts, that the rose unfolds, that May expands, that the dawn grows white behind the black trees on the shivering crest of the hills?

A kiss, and that was all.

Both started, and gazed into the darkness with sparkling eyes.

They felt neither the cool night, nor the cold stone, nor the damp earth, nor the wet grass; they looked at each other, and their hearts were full of thoughts. They had clasped hands unconsciously.

She did not ask him, she did not even wonder, how he had entered there, and how he had made his way into the garden. It seemed so simple to her that he should be there!

From time to time, Marius's knee touched Cosette's knee, and both shivered.

At intervals, Cosette stammered a word. Her soul fluttered on her lips like a drop of dew on a flower.

Little by little they began to talk to each other. Effusion followed silence, which is fullness. The night was serene and splendid overhead. These two beings, pure as spirits, told each other everything, their dreams, their intoxications, their ecstasies, their chimeras, their weaknesses, how they had adored each other from afar, how they had longed for each other, their despair when they had ceased to see each other. They confided to each other in an ideal intimacy, which nothing could augment, their most secret and most mysterious thoughts. They related to each other, with candid faith in their illusions, all that love, youth, and the remains of childhood that still lingered about them, suggested to their minds. Their two hearts poured themselves out into each other in such wise, that at the expiration of a quarter of an hour, it was the young man who had the young girl's soul, and the young girl who had the young man's soul. Each became permeated with the other, were enchanted with each other, they dazzled each other.

When they had finished, when they had told each other everything, she laid her head on his shoulder and asked him, "What is your name?"

"My name is Marius," said he. "And yours?"

"My name is Cosette."

BOOK SIXTH: LITTLE GAVROCHE

CHAPTER I—THE MALICIOUS PLAYFULNESS OF THE WIND

Since 1823, when the tavern of Montfermeil was on the way to shipwreck and was being gradually engulfed, not in the abyss of a bankruptcy, but in the cesspool of petty debts, the Thenardier pair had had two other children; both males. That made five; two girls and three boys.

Madame Thenardier had got rid of the last two, while they were still young and very small, with remarkable luck.

Got rid of is the word. There was but a mere fragment of nature in that woman. A phenomenon, by the way, of which there is more than one example extant. Like the Marechale de La Mothe-Houdancourt, the Thenardier was a mother to her daughters only. There her maternity ended. Her hatred of the human race began with her own sons. In the direction of her sons her evil disposition was uncompromising, and her heart had a lugubrious wall in that quarter. As the reader has seen, she detested the eldest; she cursed the other two. Why? Because. The most terrible of motives, the most unanswerable of retorts—because. "I have no need of a litter of squalling brats," said this mother.

Let us explain how the Thenardiers had succeeded in getting rid of their last two children; and even in drawing profit from the operation.

The woman Magnon, who was mentioned a few pages further back, was the same one who had succeeded in making old Gillenormand support the two children she had had. She lived on the Quai des Celestins, at the corner of this ancient street of the Petit-Musc that afforded her the opportunity of changing her evil repute into good odor. The reader will remember the great epidemic of croup that ravaged the river districts of the Seine in Paris thirty-five years ago, and of which science took advantage to make experiments on a grand scale as to the efficacy of inhalations of alum, so beneficially replaced at the present day by the external tincture of iodine. During this epidemic, the Magnon lost both her boys, who were still very young, one in the morning, the other in the evening of the same day. This was a blow. These children were precious to their mother; they represented eighty francs a month. These eighty francs were punctually paid in the name of M. Gillenormand, by collector of his rents, M. Barge, a retired tipstaff, in the Rue du Roi-de-Sicile. The children dead, the income was at an end. The Magnon sought an expedient. In that dark free masonry of evil of which she formed a part, everything is known, all secrets are kept, and all lend mutual aid. Magnon needed two children; the Thenardiers had two. The same sex, the same age. A good arrangement for the one, a good investment for the other. The little Thenardiers became little Magnons. Magnon quitted the Quai des Celestins and went to live in the Rue Clocheperce. In Paris, the identity that binds an individual to himself is broken between one street and another.

The registry office being in no way warned, raised no objections, and the substitution was effected in the most simple manner in the world. Only, the Thenardier exacted for this loan of her children, ten francs a month, which Magnon promised to pay, and which she actually did pay. It is unnecessary to add that M. Gillenormand continued to perform his compact. He came to see the children every six months. He did not perceive the change. "Monsieur," Magnon said to him, "how much they resemble you!"

Thenardier, to whom avatars were easy, seized this occasion to become Jondrette. His two daughters and Gavroche had hardly had time to discover that they had two little brothers. When a certain degree of misery is reached, one is overpowered with a sort of spectral indifference, and one regards human beings as though they were specters. Your nearest relations are often no more for you than vague shadowy forms, barely outlined against a nebulous background of life and easily confounded again with the invisible.

On the evening of the day when she had handed over her two little ones to Magnon, with express intention of renouncing them forever, the Thenardier had felt, or had appeared to feel, a scruple. She said to her husband: "But this is abandoning our children!"

Thenardier, masterful and phlegmatic, cauterized the scruple with this saying, "Jean Jacques Rousseau did even better!" From scruples, the mother proceeded to uneasiness, "But what if the police were to annoy us? Tell me, Monsieur Thenardier, is what we have done permissible?"

Thenardier replied, "Everything is permissible. No one will see anything but true blue in it. Besides, no one has any interest in looking closely after children who have not a sou."

Magnon was a sort of fashionable woman in the sphere of crime. She was careful about her toilette. She shared her lodgings, which were furnished in an affected and wretched style, with a clever gallicized English thief. This English woman, who had become a naturalized Parisienne, recommended by very wealthy relations, intimately connected with the medals in the Library and Mademoiselle Mar's diamonds, became celebrated later on in judicial accounts. She was called Mamselle Miss.

The two little creatures who had fallen to Magnon had no reason to complain of their lot. Recommended by the eighty francs, they were well cared for, as is everything from which profit is derived; they were neither badly clothed, nor badly fed; they were treated almost like "little gentlemen"—better by their false mother than by their real one. Magnon played the lady, and talked no thieves' slang in their presence.

Thus passed several years. Thenardier augured well from the fact. One day, he chanced to say to Magnon as she handed him his monthly stipend of ten francs, "The father must give them some education."

All at once, these two poor children, who had up to that time been protected tolerably well, even by their evil fate, were abruptly hurled into life and forced to begin it for themselves.

A wholesale arrest of malefactors, like that in the Jondrette garret, necessarily complicated by investigations and subsequent incarcerations, is a veritable disaster for that hideous and occult counter-society, which pursues its existence beneath public society; an adventure of this description entails all sorts of catastrophes in that somber world. The Thenardier catastrophe involved the catastrophe of Magnon.

One day, a short time after Magnon had handed to Eponine the note relating to the Rue Plumet, a sudden raid was made by the police in the Rue Clocheperce; Magnon was seized, as was also Mamselle Miss; and all the inhabitants of the house, which was of a suspicious character, were gathered into the net. While this was going on, the two little boys were playing in the backyard, and saw nothing of the raid. When they tried to enter the house again, they found the door fastened and the house empty. A cobbler opposite called them to him, and delivered to them a paper that "their mother" had left for them. On this paper there was an address: M. Barge, collector of rents, Rue du Roi-de-Sicile, No. 8. The proprietor of the stall said to them, "You cannot live here any longer. Go there. It is nearby. The first street on the left. Ask your way from this paper."

The children set out, the elder leading the younger, and holding in his hand the paper that was to guide them. It was cold, and his benumbed little fingers could not close very firmly, and they did not keep a very good hold on the paper. At the corner of the Rue Clocheperce, a gust of wind tore it from him, and as night was falling, the child was not able to find it again.

They began to wander aimlessly through the streets.

CHAPTER II—IN WHICH LITTLE GAVROCHE EXTRACTS PROFIT FROM NAPOLEON THE GREAT

Spring in Paris is often traversed by harsh and piercing breezes that do not precisely chill but freeze one; these north winds, which sadden the most beautiful days produce exactly the effect of those puffs of cold air that enter a warm room through the cracks of a badly fitting door or window. It seems as though the gloomy door of winter had remained ajar, and as though the wind were pouring through it. In the spring of 1832, the epoch when the first great epidemic of this century broke out in Europe, these north gales were more harsh and piercing than ever. It was a door even more glacial than that of winter that was ajar. It was the door of the sepulchre. In these winds one felt the breath of the cholera.

From a meteorological point of view, these cold winds possessed this peculiarity, that they did not preclude a strong electric tension. Frequent storms, accompanied by thunder and lightning, burst forth at this epoch.

One evening, when these gales were blowing rudely, to such a degree that January seemed to have returned and that the bourgeois had resumed their cloaks, Little Gavroche, who was always shivering gaily under his rags, was standing as though in ecstasy before a wigmaker's shop in the vicinity of the Orme-Saint-Gervais. He was adorned with a woman's woolen shawl, picked up no one knows where, and which he had converted into a neck comforter. Little Gavroche appeared to be engaged in intent admiration of a wax bride, in a low-necked dress, and crowned with orange flowers, who was revolving in the window, and displaying her smile to passersby, between two argand lamps; but in reality, he was taking an observation of the shop, in order to discover whether he could not "prig" from the shop front a cake of soap, which he would then proceed to sell for a sou to a hairdresser in the suburbs. He had often managed to breakfast off of such a roll. He called his species of work, for which he possessed special aptitude, "shaving barbers."

While contemplating the bride, and eyeing the cake of soap, he muttered between his teeth, "Tuesday. It was not Tuesday. Was it Tuesday? Perhaps it was Tuesday. Yes, it was Tuesday."

No one has ever discovered to what this monologue referred.

Yes, perchance, this monologue had some connection with the last occasion on which he had dined, three days before, for it was now Friday.

The barber in his shop, which was warmed by a good stove, was shaving a customer and casting a glance from time to time at the enemy, that freezing and impudent street urchin both of whose hands were in his pockets, but whose mind was evidently unsheathed.

While Gavroche was scrutinizing the shop window and the cakes of Windsor soap, two children of unequal stature, very neatly dressed, and still smaller than himself, one apparently about seven years of age, the other five, timidly turned the handle and entered the shop, with a request for something or other, alms possibly, in a plaintive murmur that resembled a groan rather than a prayer. They both spoke at once, and their words were unintelligible because sobs broke the voice of the younger, and the teeth of the elder were chattering with cold. The barber wheeled around with a furious look, and, without abandoning his razor, thrust back the elder with his left hand and the younger with his knee, and slammed his door, saying, "The idea of coming in and freezing everybody for nothing!"

The two children resumed their march in tears. In the meantime, a cloud had risen; it had begun to rain.

Little Gavroche ran after them and accosted them, "What's the matter with you, brats?"

"We don't know where we are to sleep," replied the elder.

"Is that all?" said Gavroche. "A great matter, truly. The idea of bawling about that. They must be greenies!"

And adopting, in addition to his superiority, which was rather bantering, an accent of tender authority and gentle patronage:

"Come along with me, young 'uns!"

"Yes, Sir," said the elder.

And the two children followed him as they would have followed an archbishop. They had stopped crying.

Gavroche led them up the Rue Saint-Antoine in the direction of the Bastille.

As Gavroche walked along, he cast an indignant backward glance at the barber's shop.

"That fellow has no heart, the whiting," he muttered. "He's an Englishman."

A woman who caught sight of these three marching in a file, with Gavroche at their head, burst into noisy laughter. This laugh was wanting in respect toward the group.

"Good day, Mamselle Omnibus," said Gavroche to her.

An instant later, the wig maker occurred to his mind once more, and he added, "I am making a mistake in the beast; he's not a whiting, he's a serpent. Barber, I'll go and fetch a locksmith, and I'll have a bell hung to your tail."

This wig maker had rendered him aggressive. As he strode over a gutter, he apostrophized a bearded portress who was worthy to meet Faust on the Brocken, and who had a broom in her hand.

"Madam," said he, "so you are going out with your horse?"

And thereupon, he spattered the polished boots of a pedestrian.

"You scamp!" shouted the furious pedestrian.

Gavroche elevated his nose above his shawl.

"Is Monsieur complaining?"

"Of you!" ejaculated the man.

"The office is closed," said Gavroche, "I do not receive any more complaints."

In the meanwhile, as he went on up the street, he perceived a beggar girl, thirteen or fourteen years old, and clad in so short a gown that her knees were visible, lying thoroughly chilled under a porte cochère. The little girl was getting to be too old for such a thing. Growth does play these tricks. The petticoat becomes short at the moment when nudity becomes indecent.

"Poor girl!" said Gavroche. "She hasn't even trousers. Hold on, take this."

And unwinding all the comfortable woolen that he had around his neck, he flung it on the thin and purple shoulders of the beggar girl, where the scarf became a shawl once more.

The child stared at him in astonishment, and received the shawl in silence. When a certain stage of distress has been reached in his misery, the poor man no longer groans over evil, no longer returns thanks for good.

That done, "Brrr!" said Gavroche, who was shivering more than Saint Martin, for the latter retained one-half of his cloak.

At this "brrr!" the downpour of rain, redoubled in its spite, became furious. The wicked skies punish good deeds.

"Ah, come now!" exclaimed Gavroche. "What's the meaning of this? It's re-raining! Good Heavens, if it goes on like this, I shall stop my subscription."

And he set out on the march once more.

"It's all right," he resumed, casting a glance at the beggar girl, as she coiled up under the shawl, "she's got a famous peel."

And looking up at the clouds he exclaimed, "Caught!"

The two children followed close on his heels.

As they were passing one of these heavy grated lattices, which indicate a baker's shop, for bread is put behind bars like gold, Gavroche turned around, "Ah, by the way, brats, have we dined?"

"Monsieur," replied the elder, "we have had nothing to eat since this morning."

"So you have neither father nor mother?" resumed Gavroche majestically.

"Excuse us, Sir, we have a papa and a mama, but we don't know where they are."

"Sometimes that's better than knowing where they are," said Gavroche, who was a thinker.

"We have been wandering about these two hours," continued the elder, "we have hunted for things at the corners of the streets, but we have found nothing."

"I know," ejaculated Gavroche, "it's the dogs who eat everything." He went on, after a pause, "Ah! We have lost our authors. We don't know what we have done with them. This should not be, gamins. It's stupid to let old people stray off like that. Come now! We must have a snooze all the same."

However, he asked them no questions. What was more simple than that they should have no dwelling place!

The elder of the two children, who had almost entirely recovered the prompt heedlessness of childhood, uttered this exclamation, "It's queer, all the same. Mama told us that she would take us to get a blessed spray on Palm Sunday."

"Bosh," said Gavroche.

"Mama," resumed the elder, "is a lady who lives with Mamselle Miss."

"Tanflute!" retorted Gavroche.

Meanwhile he had halted, and for the last two minutes he had been feeling and fumbling in all sorts of nooks that his rags contained.

At last he tossed his head with an air intended to be merely satisfied, but which was triumphant, in reality.

"Let us be calm, young 'uns. Here's supper for three."

And from one of his pockets he drew forth a sou.

Without allowing the two urchins time for amazement, he pushed both of them before him into the baker's shop, and flung his sou on the counter, crying, "Boy! Five centimes' worth of bread."

The baker, who was the proprietor in person, took up a loaf and a knife.

"In three pieces, my boy!" went on Gavroche.

And he added with dignity, "There are three of us."

And seeing that the baker, after scrutinizing the three customers, had taken down a black loaf, he thrust his finger far up his nose with an inhalation as imperious as though he had had a pinch of the great Frederick's snuff on the tip of his thumb, and hurled this indignant apostrophe full in the baker's face, "*Keksekca?*"

Those of our readers who might be tempted to espy in this interpellation of Gavroche's to the baker a Russian or a Polish word, or one of those savage cries which the Yoways and the Botocudos hurl at each other from bank to bank of a river, athwart the solitudes, are warned that it is a word which they [our readers] utter every day, and which takes the place of the phrase: "*Qu'est-ce que c'est que cela?*" The baker understood perfectly, and replied, "Well! It's bread, and very good bread of the second quality."

"You mean *larton brutal* [black bread]!" retorted Gavroche, calmly and coldly disdainful. "White bread, boy! White bread! I'm standing treat."

The baker could not repress a smile, and as he cut the white bread he surveyed them in a compassionate way that shocked Gavroche.

"Come, now, baker's boy!" said he. "What are you taking our measure like that for?"

All three of them placed end to end would have hardly made a measure.

When the bread was cut, the baker threw the sou into his drawer, and Gavroche said to the two children, "Grub away."

The little boys stared at him in surprise.

Gavroche began to laugh.

"Ah! Hullo, that's so! They don't understand yet, they're too small."

And he repeated, "Eat away."

At the same time, he held out a piece of bread to each of them.

And thinking that the elder, who seemed to him the more worthy of his conversation, deserved some special encouragement and ought to be relieved from all hesitation to satisfy his appetite, he added, as he handed him the largest share, "Ram that into your muzzle."

One piece was smaller than the others; he kept this for himself.

The poor children, including Gavroche, were famished. As they tore their bread apart in big mouthfuls, they blocked up the shop of the baker, who, now that they had paid their money, looked angrily at them.

"Let's go into the street again," said Gavroche.

They set off once more in the direction of the Bastille.

From time to time, as they passed the lighted shop windows, the smallest halted to look at the time on a leaden watch suspended from his neck by a cord.

"Well, he is a very green 'un," said Gavroche.

Then, becoming thoughtful, he muttered between his teeth, "All the same, if I had charge of the babes I'd lock 'em up better than that."

Just as they were finishing their morsel of bread, and had reached the angle of that gloomy Rue des Ballets, at the other end of which the low and threatening wicket of La Force was visible, "Hullo, is that you, Gavroche?" said someone.

"Hullo, is that you, Montparnasse?" said Gavroche.

A man had just accosted the street urchin, and the man was no other than Montparnasse in disguise, with blue spectacles, but recognizable to Gavroche.

"The bow-wows!" went on Gavroche. "You've got a hide the color of a linseed plaster, and blue specs like a doctor. You're putting on style, 'pon my word!"

"Hush!" ejaculated Montparnasse. "Not so loud."

And he drew Gavroche hastily out of range of the lighted shops.

The two little ones followed mechanically, holding each other by the hand.

When they were ensconced under the arch of a porte cochère, sheltered from the rain and from all eyes, "Do you know where I'm going?" demanded Montparnasse.

"To the Abbéy of Ascend-with-Regret," replied Gavroche.

"Joker!"

And Montparnasse went on, "I'm going to find Babet."

"Ah!" exclaimed Gavroche, "so her name is Babet."

Montparnasse lowered his voice, "Not she, he."

"Ah! Babet."

"Yes, Babet."

"I thought he was buckled."

"He has undone the buckle," replied Montparnasse.

And he rapidly related to the gamin how, on the morning of that very day, Babet, having been transferred to La Conciergerie, had made his escape, by turning to the left instead of to the right in "the police office."

Gavroche expressed his admiration for this skill.

"What a dentist!" he cried.

Montparnasse added a few details as to Babet's flight, and ended with, "Oh! That's not all."

Gavroche, as he listened, had seized a cane that Montparnasse held in his hand, and mechanically pulled at the upper part, and the blade of a dagger made its appearance.

"Ah!" he exclaimed, pushing the dagger back in haste. "You have brought along your gendarme disguised as a bourgeois."

Montparnasse winked.

"The deuce!" resumed Gavroche. "So you're going to have a bout with the bobbies?"

"You can't tell," replied Montparnasse with an indifferent air. "It's always a good thing to have a pin about one."

Gavroche persisted, "What are you up to tonight?"

Again Montparnasse took a grave tone, and said, mouthing every syllable, "Things."

And abruptly changing the conversation, "By the way!"

"What?"

"Something happened t'other day. Fancy. I meet a bourgeois. He makes me a present of a sermon and his purse. I put it in my pocket. A minute later, I feel in my pocket. There's nothing there."

"Except the sermon," said Gavroche.

"But you," went on Montparnasse, "where are you bound for now?"

Gavroche pointed to his two proteges, and said, "I'm going to put these infants to bed."

"Whereabouts is the bed?"

"At my house."

"Where's your house?"

"At my house."

"So you have a lodging?"

"Yes, I have."

"And where is your lodging?"

"In the elephant," said Gavroche.

Montparnasse, though not naturally inclined to astonishment, could not restrain an exclamation.

"In the elephant!"

"Well, yes, in the elephant!" retorted Gavroche. "*Kekcaa?*"

This is another word of the language which no one writes, and which everyone speaks.

Kekcaa signifies: *Quest que c'est que cela a?*[*]

The urchin's profound remark recalled Montparnasse to calmness and good

---

[*] What's the matter with that?

sense. He appeared to return to better sentiments with regard to Gavroche's lodging.

"Of course," said he, "yes, the elephant. Is it comfortable there?"

"Very," said Gavroche. "It's really bully there. There ain't any draughts, as there are under the bridges."

"How do you get in?"

"Oh, I get in."

"So there is a hole?" demanded Montparnasse.

"*Parbleu*! I should say so. But you mustn't tell. It's between the forelegs. The bobbies haven't seen it."

"And you climb up? Yes, I understand."

"A turn of the hand, crick, crack, and it's all over, no one there."

After a pause, Gavroche added, "I shall have a ladder for these children."

Montparnasse burst out laughing, "Where the devil did you pick up those young 'uns?"

Gavroche replied with great simplicity, "They are some brats that a wig maker made me a present of."

Meanwhile, Montparnasse had fallen to thinking, "You recognized me very readily," he muttered.

He took from his pocket two small objects that were nothing more than two quills wrapped in cotton, and thrust one up each of his nostrils. This gave him a different nose.

"That changes you," remarked Gavroche. "You are less homely so, you ought to keep them on all the time."

Montparnasse was a handsome fellow, but Gavroche was a tease.

"Seriously," demanded Montparnasse, "how do you like me so?"

The sound of his voice was different also. In a twinkling, Montparnasse had become unrecognizable.

"Oh! Do play Porrichinelle for us!" exclaimed Gavroche.

The two children, who had not been listening up to this point, being occupied themselves in thrusting their fingers up their noses, drew near at this name, and stared at Montparnasse with dawning joy and admiration.

Unfortunately, Montparnasse was troubled.

He laid his hand on Gavroche's shoulder, and said to him, emphasizing his words, "Listen to what I tell you, boy! If I were on the square with my dog, my knife, and my wife, and if you were to squander ten sous on me, I wouldn't refuse to work, but this isn't Shrove Tuesday."

This odd phrase produced a singular effect on the gamin. He wheeled around hastily, darted his little sparkling eyes about him with profound attention, and perceived a police sergeant standing with his back to them a few paces off. Gavroche allowed an "Ah! Good!" to escape him, but immediately suppressed it, and shaking Montparnasse's hand, "Well, good evening," said he, "I'm going off to my elephant with my brats. Supposing that you should need me some night, you can come and hunt me up there. I lodge on the entresol. There is no porter. You will inquire for Monsieur Gavroche."

"Very good," said Montparnasse.

And they parted, Montparnasse betaking himself in the direction of the Greve, and Gavroche toward the Bastille. The little one of five, dragged along by his brother who was dragged by Gavroche, turned his head back several times to watch "Porrichinelle" as he went.

The ambiguous phrase by means of which Montparnasse had warned Gavroche of the presence of the policeman, contained no other talisman than the assonance dig repeated five or six times in different forms. This syllable, dig, uttered alone or artistically mingled with the words of a phrase, means: "Take care, we can no longer talk freely." There was besides, in Montparnasse's sentence, a literary beauty which was lost upon Gavroche, that is *mon dogue*, *ma dague, et ma digue*, a slang expression of the Temple, which signifies my dog, my knife, and my wife, greatly in vogue among clowns and the red tails in the great century when Moliere wrote and Callot drew.

Twenty years ago, there was still to be seen in the southwest corner of the Place de la Bastille, near the basin of the canal, excavated in the ancient ditch of the fortress-prison, a singular monument, which has already been effaced from the memories of Parisians, and which deserved to leave some trace, for it was the idea of a "member of the Institute, the General-in-Chief of the army of Egypt."

We say monument, although it was only a rough model. But this model itself, a marvelous sketch, the grandiose skeleton of an idea of Napoleon's, which successive gusts of wind have carried away and thrown, on each occasion, still further from us, had become historical and had acquired a certain definiteness, which contrasted with its provisional aspect. It was an elephant forty feet high, constructed of timber and masonry, bearing on its back a tower that resembled a house, formerly painted green by some dauber, and now painted black by heaven, the wind, and time. In this deserted and unprotected corner of the place, the broad brow of the colossus, his trunk, his tusks, his tower, his enormous crupper, his four feet, like columns produced, at night, under the starry heavens, a surprising and terrible form. It was a sort of symbol of popular force. It was somber, mysterious, and immense. It was some mighty, visible phantom, one knew not what, standing erect beside the invisible specter of the Bastille.

Few strangers visited this edifice, no passerby looked at it. It was falling into ruins; every season the plaster that detached itself from its sides formed hideous wounds upon it. "The aediles," as the expression ran in elegant dialect, had forgotten it ever since 1814. There it stood in its corner, melancholy, sick, crumbling, surrounded by a rotten palisade, soiled continually by drunken coachmen; cracks meandered athwart its belly, a lath projected from its tail, tall grass flourished between its legs; and, as the level of the place had been rising all around it for a space of thirty years, by that slow and continuous movement which insensibly elevates the soil of large towns, it stood in a hollow, and it looked as though the ground were giving way beneath it. It was unclean, despised, repulsive, and superb, ugly in the eyes of the bourgeois, melancholy in the eyes of the thinker. There was something about it of the dirt that is on the point of being swept out, and something of the majesty that is on the point of being decapitated. As we have said, at night, its aspect changed. Night is the real element of everything that is dark. As soon as twilight descended, the old elephant became transfigured; he assumed a tranquil and redoubtable appearance in the formidable serenity of the shadows. Being of the past, he belonged to night; and obscurity was in keeping with his grandeur.

This rough, squat, heavy, hard, austere, almost misshapen, but assuredly majestic monument, stamped with a sort of magnificent and savage gravity, has disappeared, and left to reign in peace, a sort of gigantic stove, ornamented with its pipe, which has replaced the somber fortress with its nine towers, very much as the bourgeoisie replaces the feudal classes. It is quite natural that a stove should be the symbol of an epoch in which a pot contains power. This epoch will pass away, people have already begun to understand that, if there can be force in a boiler, there can be no force except in the brain; in other words, that which leads and drags on the world, is not locomotives, but ideas. Harness locomotives to ideas, that is well done; but do not mistake the horse for the rider.

At all events, to return to the Place de la Bastille, the architect of this elephant succeeded in making a grand thing out of plaster; the architect of the stove has succeeded in making a pretty thing out of bronze.

This stove-pipe, which has been baptized by a sonorous name, and called the column of July, this monument of a revolution that miscarried, was still enveloped in 1832, in an immense shirt of woodwork, which we regret, for our part, and by a vast plank enclosure, which completed the task of isolating the elephant.

It was toward this corner of the place, dimly lighted by the reflection of a distant street lamp, that the gamin guided his two "brats."

The reader must permit us to interrupt ourselves here and to remind him that we are dealing with simple reality, and that twenty years ago, the tribunals were called upon to judge, under the charge of vagabondage, and mutilation of a public monument, a child who had been caught asleep in this very elephant of the Bastille. This fact noted, we proceed.

On arriving in the vicinity of the colossus, Gavroche comprehended the effect which the infinitely great might produce on the infinitely small, and said, "Don't be scared, infants."

Then he entered through a gap in the fence into the elephant's enclosure and helped the young ones to clamber through the breach. The two children, somewhat frightened, followed Gavroche without uttering a word, and confided themselves to this little Providence in rags which had given them bread and had promised them a shelter.

There, extended along the fence, lay a ladder that by day served the laborers in the neighboring timberyard. Gavroche raised it with remarkable vigor, and placed it against one of the elephant's forelegs. Near the point where the ladder ended, a sort of black hole in the belly of the colossus could be distinguished.

Gavroche pointed out the ladder and the hole to his guests, and said to them, "Climb up and go in."

The two little boys exchanged terrified glances.

"You're afraid, brats!" exclaimed Gavroche.

And he added, "You shall see!"

He clasped the rough leg of the elephant, and in a twinkling, without deigning to make use of the ladder, he had reached the aperture. He entered it as an adder slips through a crevice, and disappeared within, and an instant later, the two children saw his head, which looked pale, appear vaguely, on the edge of the shadowy hole, like a wan and whitish specter.

"Well!" he exclaimed. "Climb up, young 'uns! You'll see how snug it is here! Come up, you!" he said to the elder, "I'll lend you a hand."

The little fellows nudged each other, the gamin frightened and inspired them with confidence at one and the same time, and then, it was raining very hard. The elder one undertook the risk. The younger, on seeing his brother climbing up, and himself left alone between the paws of this huge beast, felt greatly inclined to cry, but he did not dare.

The elder lad climbed, with uncertain steps, up the rungs of the ladder; Gavroche, in the meanwhile, encouraging him with exclamations like a fencing master to his pupils, or a muleteer to his mules.

"Don't be afraid!—That's it!—Come on!—Put your feet there!—Give us your hand here!—Boldly!"

And when the child was within reach, he seized him suddenly and vigorously by the arm, and pulled him toward him.

"Nabbed!" said he.

The brat had passed through the crack.

"Now," said Gavroche, "wait for me. Be so good as to take a seat, Monsieur."

And making his way out of the hole as he had entered it, he slipped down the elephant's leg with the agility of a monkey, landed on his feet in the grass, grasped the child of five around the body, and planted him fairly in the middle of the ladder, then he began to climb up behind him, shouting to the elder, "I'm going to boost him, do you tug."

And in another instant, the small lad was pushed, dragged, pulled, thrust, stuffed into the hole, before he had time to recover himself, and Gavroche, entering behind him, and repulsing the ladder with a kick which sent it flat on the grass, began to clap his hands and to cry, "Here we are! Long live General Lafayette!"

This explosion over, he added, "Now, young 'uns, you are in my house."

Gavroche was at home, in fact.

Oh, unforeseen utility of the useless! Charity of great things! Goodness of giants! This huge monument, which had embodied an idea of the Emperor's, had become the box of a street urchin. The brat had been accepted and sheltered by the colossus. The bourgeois decked out in their Sunday finery who passed the elephant of the Bastille, were fond of saying as they scanned it disdainfully with their prominent eyes, "What's the good of that?" It served to save from the cold, the frost, the hail, and rain, to shelter from the winds of winter, to preserve from slumber in the mud, which produces fever, and from slumber in the snow, which produces death, a little being who had no father, no mother, no bread, no clothes, no refuge. It served to receive the innocent whom society repulsed. It served to diminish public crime. It was a lair open to one against whom all doors were shut. It seemed as though the miserable old mastodon, invaded by vermin and oblivion, covered with warts, with mold, and ulcers, tottering, worm-eaten, abandoned, condemned, a sort of mendicant colossus, asking alms in vain with a benevolent look in the midst of the crossroads, had taken pity on that other mendicant, the poor pygmy, who roamed without shoes to his feet, without a roof over his head, blowing on his fingers, clad in rags, fed on rejected scraps. That was what the elephant of the Bastille was good for. This idea of Napoleon, disdained by men, had been taken back by God. That which had been merely illustrious, had become august. In order to realize his thought, the Emperor should have had porphyry, brass, iron, gold, marble; the old collection of planks, beams and plaster sufficed for God. The Emperor had had the dream of a genius; in that Titanic elephant, armed, prodigious, with trunk uplifted, bearing its tower and scattering on all sides its merry and vivifying waters, he wished to incarnate the people. God had done a grander thing with it, he had lodged a child there.

The hole through which Gavroche had entered was a breach, which was hardly visible from the outside, being concealed, as we have stated, beneath the elephant's belly, and so narrow that it was only cats and homeless children who could pass through it.

"Let's begin," said Gavroche, "by telling the porter that we are not at home."

And plunging into the darkness with the assurance of a person who is well acquainted with his apartments, he took a plank and stopped up the aperture.

Again Gavroche plunged into the obscurity. The children heard the crackling of the match thrust into the phosphoric bottle. The chemical match was not yet in existence; at that epoch the Fumade steel represented progress.

A sudden light made them blink; Gavroche had just managed to ignite one of those bits of cord dipped in resin that are called cellar rats. The cellar rat, which emitted more smoke than light, rendered the interior of the elephant confusedly visible.

Gavroche's two guests glanced about them, and the sensation that they experienced was something like that which one would feel if shut up in the great tun of Heidelberg, or, better still, like what Jonah must have felt in the biblical belly of the whale. An entire and gigantic skeleton appeared enveloping them. Above, a long brown beam, from which started at regular distances, massive, arching ribs, represented the vertebral column with its sides, stalactites of plaster depended from them like entrails, and vast spiders' webs stretching from side to side, formed dirty diaphragms. Here and there, in the corners, were visible large blackish spots that had the appearance of being alive, and which changed places rapidly with an abrupt and frightened movement.

Fragments that had fallen from the elephant's back into his belly had filled up the cavity, so that it was possible to walk upon it as on a floor.

The smaller child nestled up against his brother, and whispered to him, "It's black."

This remark drew an exclamation from Gavroche. The petrified air of the two brats rendered some shock necessary.

"What's that you are gabbling about there?" he exclaimed. "Are you scoffing at me? Are you turning up your noses? Do you want the Tuileries? Are you brutes? Come, say! I warn you that I don't belong to the regiment of simpletons. Ah, come now, are you brats from the Pope's establishment?"

A little roughness is good in cases of fear. It is reassuring. The two children drew close to Gavroche.

Gavroche, paternally touched by this confidence, passed from grave to gentle, and addressing the smaller, "Stupid," said he, accenting the insulting word, with a caressing intonation, "it's outside that it is black. Outside it's raining, here it does not rain; outside it's cold, here there's not an atom of wind; outside there are heaps of people, here there's no one; outside there ain't even the moon, here there's my candle, confound it!"

The two children began to look upon the apartment with less terror; but Gavroche allowed them no more time for contemplation.

"Quick," said he.

And he pushed them toward what we are very glad to be able to call the end of the room.

There stood his bed.

Gavroche's bed was complete; that is to say, it had a mattress, a blanket, and an alcove with curtains.

The mattress was a straw mat, the blanket a rather large strip of gray woolen stuff, very warm and almost new. This is what the alcove consisted of:

Three rather long poles, thrust into and consolidated, with the rubbish which formed the floor, that is to say, the belly of the elephant, two in front and one behind, and united by a rope at their summits, so as to form a pyramidal bundle. This cluster supported a trelliswork of brass wire that was simply placed upon it, but artistically applied, and held by fastenings of iron wire, so that it enveloped all three holes. A row of very heavy stones kept this network down to the floor so that nothing could pass under it. This grating was nothing else than a piece of the brass screens with which aviaries are covered in menageries. Gavroche's bed stood as in a cage, behind this net. The whole resembled an Esquimaux tent.

This trelliswork took the place of curtains.

Gavroche moved aside the stones that fastened the net down in front, and the two folds of the net that lapped over each other fell apart.

"Down on all fours, brats!" said Gavroche.

He made his guests enter the cage with great precaution, then he crawled in after them, pulled the stones together, and closed the opening hermetically again.

All three had stretched out on the mat. Gavroche still had the cellar rat in his hand.

"Now," said he, "go to sleep! I'm going to suppress the candelabra."

"Monsieur," the elder of the brothers asked Gavroche, pointing to the netting, "what's that for?"

"That," answered Gavroche gravely, "is for the rats. Go to sleep!"

Nevertheless, he felt obliged to add a few words of instruction for the benefit of these young creatures, and he continued, "It's a thing from the Jardin des Plantes. It's used for fierce animals. There's a whole shopful of them there. All you've got to do is to climb over a wall, crawl through a window, and pass through a door. You can get as much as you want."

As he spoke, he wrapped the younger one up bodily in a fold of the blanket, and the little one murmured, "Oh! How good that is! It's warm!"

Gavroche cast a pleased eye on the blanket.

"That's from the Jardin des Plantes, too," said he. "I took that from the monkeys."

And, pointing out to the eldest the mat on which he was lying, a very thick and admirably made mat, he added, "That belonged to the giraffe."

After a pause he went on, "The beasts had all these things. I took them away from them. It didn't trouble them. I told them, 'It's for the elephant.'"

He paused, and then resumed, "You crawl over the walls and you don't care a straw for the government. So there now!"

The two children gazed with timid and stupefied respect on this intrepid and ingenious being, a vagabond like themselves, isolated like themselves, frail like themselves, who had something admirable and all-powerful about him, who seemed supernatural to them, and whose physiognomy was composed of all the grimaces of an old mountebank, mingled with the most ingenuous and charming smiles.

"Monsieur," ventured the elder timidly, "you are not afraid of the police, then?"

Gavroche contented himself with replying, "Brat! Nobody says 'police,' they say 'bobbies.'"

The smaller had his eyes wide open, but he said nothing. As he was on the edge of the mat, the elder being in the middle, Gavroche tucked the blanket around him as a mother might have done, and heightened the mat under his head with old rags, in such a way as to form a pillow for the child. Then he turned to the elder, "Hey! We're jolly comfortable here, ain't we?"

"Ah, yes!" replied the elder, gazing at Gavroche with the expression of a saved angel.

The two poor little children who had been soaked through, began to grow warm once more.

"Ah, by the way," continued Gavroche, "what were you bawling about?"

And pointing out the little one to his brother, "A mite like that, I've nothing to say about, but the idea of a big fellow like you crying! It's idiotic; you looked like a calf."

"Gracious," replied the child, "we have no lodging."

"Bother!" retorted Gavroche. "You don't say 'lodgings,' you say 'crib.'"

"And then, we were afraid of being alone like that at night."

"You don't say 'night,' you say 'darkmans.'"

"Thank you, Sir," said the child.

"Listen," went on Gavroche, "you must never bawl again over anything. I'll take care of you. You shall see what fun we'll have. In summer, we'll go to the Glaciere with Navet, one of my pals, we'll bathe in the Gare, we'll run stark naked in front of the rafts on the bridge at Austerlitz, that makes the laundresses raging. They scream, they get mad, and if you only knew how ridiculous they are! We'll go and see the man-skeleton. And then I'll take you to the play. I'll take you to see Frederick Lemaitre. I have tickets, I know some of the actors, I even played in a piece once. There were a lot of us fellers, and we ran under a cloth, and that made the sea. I'll get you an engagement at my theater. We'll go to see the savages. They ain't real, those savages ain't. They wear pink tights that go all in wrinkles, and you can see where their elbows have been darned with white. Then, we'll go to the opera. We'll get in with the hired applauders. The opera claque is well managed. I wouldn't associate with the claque on the boulevard. At the opera, just fancy! Some of them pay twenty sous, but they're ninnies. They're called dishclouts. And then we'll go to see the guillotine work. I'll show you the executioner. He lives in the Rue des Marais. Monsieur Sanson. He has a letterbox at his door. Ah! We'll have famous fun!"

At that moment a drop of wax fell on Gavroche's finger, and recalled him to the realities of life.

"The deuce!" said he. "There's the wick giving out. Attention! I can't spend more than a sou a month on my lighting. When a body goes to bed, he must sleep. We haven't the time to read M. Paul de Kock's romances. And besides, the light might pass through the cracks of the porte-cochère, and all the bobbies need to do is to see it."

"And then," remarked the elder timidly, he alone dared talk to Gavroche, and reply to him, "a spark might fall in the straw, and we must look out and not burn the house down."

"People don't say 'burn the house down,'" remarked Gavroche, "they say 'blaze the crib.'"

The storm increased in violence, and the heavy downpour beat upon the back of the colossus amid claps of thunder. "You're taken in, rain!" said Gavroche. "It amuses me to hear the decanter run down the legs of the house. Winter is stupid; it wastes its merchandise, it loses its labor, it can't wet us, and that makes it kick up a row, old water carrier that it is."

This allusion to the thunder, all the consequences of which Gavroche, in his character of a philosopher of the nineteenth century, accepted, was followed by a broad flash of lightning, so dazzling that a hint of it entered the belly of the elephant through the crack. Almost at the same instant, the thunder rumbled with great fury. The two little creatures uttered a shriek, and started up so eagerly that the network came near being displaced, but Gavroche turned his bold face to them, and took advantage of the clap of thunder to burst into a laugh.

"Calm down, children. Don't topple over the edifice. That's fine, first-class thunder; all right. That's no slouch of a streak of lightning. Bravo for the good God! Deuce take it! It's almost as good as it is at the Ambigu."

That said, he restored order in the netting, pushed the two children gently down on the bed, pressed their knees, in order to stretch them out at full length, and exclaimed, "Since the good God is lighting his candle, I can blow out mine. Now, babes, now, my young humans, you must shut your peepers. It's very bad not to sleep. It'll make you swallow the strainer, or, as they say, in fashionable society, stink in the gullet. Wrap yourself up well in the hide! I'm going to put out the light. Are you ready?"

"Yes," murmured the elder, "I'm all right. I seem to have feathers under my head."

"People don't say 'head,'" cried Gavroche, "they say 'nut.'"

The two children nestled close to each other, Gavroche finished arranging them on the mat, drew the blanket up to their very ears, then repeated, for the third time, his injunction in the hieratical tongue, "Shut your peepers!"

And he snuffed out his tiny light.

Hardly had the light been extinguished, when a peculiar trembling began to affect the netting under which the three children lay.

It consisted of a multitude of dull scratches that produced a metallic sound, as if claws and teeth were gnawing at the copper wire. This was accompanied by all sorts of little piercing cries.

The little five-year-old boy, on hearing this hubbub overhead, and chilled with terror, jogged his brother's elbow; but the elder brother had already shut his peepers, as Gavroche had ordered. Then the little one, who could no longer control his terror, questioned Gavroche, but in a very low tone, and with bated breath, "Sir?"

"Hey?" said Gavroche, who had just closed his eyes.

"What is that?"

"It's the rats," replied Gavroche.

And he laid his head down on the mat again.

The rats, in fact, who swarmed by thousands in the carcass of the elephant, and who were the living black spots which we have already mentioned, had been held in awe by the flame of the candle, so long as it had been lighted; but as soon as the cavern, which was the same as their city, had returned to darkness, scenting what the good storyteller Perrault calls "fresh meat," they had hurled themselves in throngs on Gavroche's tent, had climbed to the top of it, and had begun to bite the meshes as though seeking to pierce this newfangled trap.

Still the little one could not sleep.

"Sir?" he began again.

"Hey?" said Gavroche.

"What are rats?"

"They are mice."

This explanation reassured the child a little. He had seen white mice in the course of his life, and he was not afraid of them. Nevertheless, he lifted up his voice once more.

"Sir?"

"Hey?" said Gavroche again.

"Why don't you have a cat?"

"I did have one," replied Gavroche, "I brought one here, but they ate her."

This second explanation undid the work of the first, and the little fellow began to tremble again.

The dialogue between him and Gavroche began again for the fourth time, "Monsieur?"

"Hey?"

"Who was it that was eaten?"

"The cat."

"And who ate the cat?"

"The rats."

"The mice?"

"Yes, the rats."

The child, in consternation, dismayed at the thought of mice which ate cats, pursued, "Sir, would those mice eat us?"

"Wouldn't they just!" ejaculated Gavroche.

The child's terror had reached its climax. But Gavroche added, "Don't be afraid. They can't get in. And besides, I'm here! Here, catch hold of my hand. Hold your tongue and shut your peepers!"

At the same time Gavroche grasped the little fellow's hand across his brother. The child pressed the hand close to him, and felt reassured. Courage and strength have these mysterious ways of communicating themselves. Silence reigned around them once more, the sound of their voices had frightened off the rats; at the expiration of a few minutes, they came raging back, but in vain, the three little fellows were fast asleep and heard nothing more.

The hours of the night fled away. Darkness covered the vast Place de la Bastille. A wintry gale, which mingled with the rain, blew in gusts, the patrol searched all the doorways, alleys, enclosures, and obscure nooks, and in their search for nocturnal vagabonds they passed in silence before the elephant; the monster, erect, motionless, staring open-eyed into the shadows, had the appearance of dreaming happily over his good deed; and sheltered from heaven and from men the three poor sleeping children.

In order to understand what is about to follow, the reader must remember, that, at that epoch, the Bastille guard house was situated at the other end of the square, and that what took place in the vicinity of the elephant could neither be seen nor heard by the sentinel.

Toward the end of that hour, which immediately precedes the dawn, a man turned from the Rue Saint-Antoine at a run, made the circuit of the enclosure of the column of July, and glided between the palings until he was underneath the belly of the elephant. If any light had illuminated that man, it might have been divined from the thorough manner in which he was soaked that he had passed the night in the rain. Arrived beneath the elephant, he uttered a peculiar cry, which did not belong to any human tongue, and which a paroquet alone could have imitated. Twice he repeated this cry, of whose orthography the following barely conveys an idea, "*Kirikikiou!*"

At the second cry, a clear, young, merry voice responded from the belly of the elephant, "Yes!"

Almost immediately, the plank that closed the hole was drawn aside, and gave passage to a child who descended the elephant's leg, and fell briskly near the man. It was Gavroche. The man was Montparnasse.

As for his cry of "*Kirikikiou*," that was, doubtless, what the child had meant, when he said, "You will ask for Monsieur Gavroche."

On hearing it, he had waked with a start, had crawled out of his "alcove," pushing apart the netting a little, and carefully drawing it together again, then he had opened the trap, and descended.

The man and the child recognized each other silently amid the gloom; Montparnasse confined himself to the remark, "We need you. Come, lend us a hand."

The lad asked for no further enlightenment.

"I'm with you," said he.

And both took their way toward the Rue Saint-Antoine, from which Montparnasse had emerged, winding rapidly through the long file of market-gardeners' carts which descend toward the markets at that hour.

The market-gardeners, crouching, half-asleep, in their wagons, amid the salads and vegetables, enveloped to their very eyes in their mufflers on account of the beating rain, did not even glance at these strange pedestrians.

CHAPTER III—THE VICISSITUDES OF FLIGHT

This is what had taken place that same night at the La Force:

An escape had been planned between Babet, Brujon, Guelemer, and Thenardier, although Thenardier was in close confinement. Babet had arranged the matter for his own benefit, on the same day, as the reader has seen from Montparnasse's account to Gavroche. Montparnasse was to help them from outside.

Brujon, after having passed a month in the punishment cell, had had time, in the first place, to weave a rope, in the second, to mature a plan. In former times, those severe places where the discipline of the prison delivers the convict into his own hands, were composed of four stone walls, a stone ceiling, a flagged pavement, a camp bed, a grated window, and a door lined with iron, and were called dungeons; but the dungeon was judged to be too terrible; nowadays they are composed of an iron door, a grated window, a camp bed, a flagged pavement, four stone walls, and a stone ceiling, and are called chambers of punishment. A little light penetrates toward midday. The inconvenient point about these chambers that, as the reader sees, are not dungeons, is that they allow the persons who should be at work to think.

So Brujon meditated, and he emerged from the chamber of punishment with a rope. As he had the name of being very dangerous in the Charlemagne courtyard, he was placed in the New Building. The first thing he found in the New Building was Guelemer, the second was a nail; Guelemer, that is to say, crime; a nail, that is to say, liberty. Brujon, of whom it is high time that the reader should have a complete idea, was, with an appearance of delicate health and a profoundly premeditated languor, a polished, intelligent sprig, and a thief, who had a caressing glance, and an atrocious smile. His glance resulted from his will, and his smile from his nature. His first studies in his art had been directed to roofs. He had made great progress in the industry of the men who tear off lead, who plunder the roofs and despoil the gutters by the process called double pickings.

The circumstance that put the finishing touch on the moment peculiarly favorable for an attempt at escape, was that the roofers were relaying and rejointing, at that very moment, a portion of the slates on the prison. The Saint-Bernard courtyard was no longer absolutely isolated from the Charlemagne and the Saint-Louis courts. Up above there were scaffoldings and ladders; in other words, bridges and stairs in the direction of liberty.

The New Building, which was the most cracked and decrepit thing to be seen anywhere in the world, was the weak point in the prison. The walls were eaten by saltpeter to such an extent that the authorities had been obliged to line the vaults of the dormitories with a sheathing of wood, because stones were in the habit of becoming detached and falling on the prisoners in their beds. In spite of this antiquity, the authorities committed the error of confining in the New Building the most troublesome prisoners, of placing there "the hard cases," as they say in prison parlance.

The New Building contained four dormitories, one above the other, and a top story that was called the Bel-Air. A large chimney flue, probably from some ancient kitchen of the Dukes de la Force, started from the ground floor, traversed all four stories, cut the dormitories, where it figured as a flattened pillar, into two portions, and finally pierced the roof.

Guelemer and Brujon were in the same dormitory. They had been placed, by way of precaution, on the lower story. Chance ordained that the heads of their beds should rest against the chimney.

Thenardier was directly over their heads in the top story known as Fine-Air. The pedestrian who halts on the Rue Culture-Sainte-Catherine, after passing the barracks of the firemen, in front of the porte-cochère of the bathing establishment, beholds a yard full of flowers and shrubs in wooden boxes, at the extremity of which spreads out a little white rotunda with two wings, brightened up with green shutters, the bucolic dream of Jean Jacques.

Not more than ten years ago, there rose above that rotunda an enormous black, hideous, bare wall by which it was backed up.

This was the outer wall of La Force.

This wall, beside that rotunda, was Milton viewed through Berquin.

Lofty as it was, this wall was overtopped by a still blacker roof, which could be seen beyond. This was the roof of the New Building. There one could descry four dormer windows, guarded with bars; they were the windows of the Fine-Air.

A chimney pierced the roof; this was the chimney that traversed the dormitories.

The Bel-Air (Fine Air), that top story of the New Building, was a sort of large hall, with a Mansard roof, guarded with triple gratings and double doors of sheet iron, which were studded with enormous bolts. When one entered from the north end, one had on one's left the four dormer windows, on one's right, facing the windows, at regular intervals, four square, tolerably vast cages, separated by narrow passages, built of masonry to about the height of the elbow, and the rest, up to the roof, of iron bars.

Thenardier had been in solitary confinement in one of these cages since the night of the 3rd of February. No one was ever able to discover how, and by what connivance, he succeeded in procuring, and secreting a bottle of wine, invented, so it is said, by Desrues, with which a narcotic is mixed, and which the band of the Endormeurs, or Sleep-compellers, rendered famous.

There are, in many prisons, treacherous employees, half-jailers, half-thieves, who assist in escapes, who sell to the police an unfaithful service, and who turn a penny whenever they can.

On that same night, then, when Little Gavroche picked up the two lost children, Brujon and Guelemer, who knew that Babet, who had escaped that morning, was waiting for them in the street as well as Montparnasse, rose softly, and with the nail which Brujon had found, began to pierce the chimney against which their beds stood. The rubbish fell on Brujon's bed, so that they were not heard. Showers mingled with thunder shook the doors on their hinges, and created in the prison a terrible and opportune uproar. Those of the prisoners who woke, pretended to fall asleep again, and left Guelemer and Brujon to their own devices. Brujon was adroit; Guelemer was vigorous. Before any sound had reached the watcher, who was sleeping in the grated cell, which opened into the dormitory, the wall had been pierced, the chimney scaled, the iron grating which barred the upper orifice of the flue forced, and the two redoubtable ruffians were on the roof. The wind and rain redoubled, the roof was slippery.

"What a good night to leg it!" said Brujon.

An abyss six feet broad and eighty feet deep separated them from the surrounding wall. At the bottom of this abyss, they could see the musket of a sentinel gleaming through the gloom. They fastened one end of the rope that Brujon had spun in his dungeon to the stumps of the iron bars, which they had just wrenched off, flung the other over the outer wall, crossed the abyss at one bound, clung to the coping of the wall, got astride of it, let themselves slip, one after the other, along the rope, upon a little roof, which touches the bathhouse, pulled their rope after them, jumped down into the courtyard of the bathhouse, traversed it, pushed open the porter's wicket, beside which hung his rope, pulled this, opened the porte-cochère, and found themselves in the street.

Three-quarters of an hour had not elapsed since they had risen in bed in the dark, nail in hand, and their project in their heads.

A few moments later they had joined Babet and Montparnasse, who were prowling about the neighborhood.

They had broken their rope in pulling it after them, and a bit of it remained attached to the chimney on the roof. They had sustained no other damage, however, than that of scratching nearly all the skin off their hands.

That night, Thenardier was warned, without anyone being able to explain how, and was not asleep.

Toward one o'clock in the morning, the night being very dark, he saw two shadows pass along the roof, in the rain and squalls, in front of the dormer window opposite his cage. One halted at the window, long enough to dart in a glance. This was Brujon.

Thenardier recognized him, and understood. This was enough.

Thenardier, rated as a burglar, and detained as a measure of precaution under the charge of organizing a nocturnal ambush, with armed force, was kept in sight. The sentry, who was relieved every two hours, marched up and down in front of his cage with loaded musket. The Fine-Air was lighted by a skylight. The prisoner had on his feet fetters weighing fifty pounds. Every day, at four o'clock in the afternoon, a jailer, escorted by two dogs, this was still in vogue at that time, entered his cage, deposited beside his bed a loaf of black bread weighing two pounds, a jug of water, a bowl filled with rather thin bouillon, in which swam a few Mayagan beans, inspected his irons and tapped the bars. This man and his dogs made two visits during the night.

Thenardier had obtained permission to keep a sort of iron bolt, which he used to spike his bread into a crack in the wall, "in order to preserve it from the rats," as he said. As Thenardier was kept in sight, no objection had been made to this spike. Still, it was remembered afterward, that one of the jailers had said, "It would be better to let him have only a wooden spike."

At two o'clock in the morning, the sentinel, who was an old soldier, was relieved, and replaced by a conscript. A few moments later, the man with the dogs paid his visit, and went off without noticing anything, except, possibly, the excessive youth and "the rustic air" of the "raw recruit." Two hours afterward, at four o'clock, when they came to relieve the conscript, he was found asleep on the floor, lying like a log near Thenardier's cage. As for Thenardier, he was no longer there. There was a hole in the ceiling of his cage, and, above it, another hole in the roof. One of the planks of his bed had been wrenched off, and probably carried away with him, as it was not found. They also seized in his cell a half-empty bottle that contained the remains of the stupefying wine with which the soldier had been drugged. The soldier's bayonet had disappeared.

At the moment when this discovery was made, it was assumed that Thenardier was out of reach. The truth is, that he was no longer in the New Building, but that he was still in great danger.

Thenardier, on reaching the roof of the New Building, had found the remains of Brujon's rope hanging to the bars of the upper trap of the chimney, but, as this broken fragment was much too short, he had not been able to escape by the outer wall, as Brujon and Guelemer had done.

When one turns from the Rue des Ballets into the Rue du Roi-de-Sicile, one almost immediately encounters a repulsive ruin. There stood on that spot, in the last century, a house of which only the back wall now remains, a regular wall of masonry, which rises to the height of the third story between the adjoining buildings. This ruin can be recognized by two large square windows still to be seen there; the middle one, that nearest the right gable, is barred with a worm-eaten beam adjusted like a prop. Through these windows there was formerly visible a lofty and lugubrious wall, which was a fragment of the outer wall of La Force.

The empty space on the street left by the demolished house is half-filled by a fence of rotten boards, shored up by five stone posts. In this recess lies concealed a little shanty that leans against the portion of the ruin, which has remained standing. The fence has a gate, which, a few years ago, was fastened only by a latch.

It was the crest of this ruin that Thenardier had succeeded in reaching, a little after one o'clock in the morning.

How had he got there? That is what no one has ever been able to explain or understand. The lightning must, at the same time, have hindered and helped him. Had he made use of the ladders and scaffoldings of the slaters to get from roof to roof, from enclosure to enclosure, from compartment to compartment, to the buildings of the Charlemagne court, then to the buildings of the Saint-Louis court, to the outer wall, and there to the hut on the Rue du Roi-de-Sicile? But in that itinerary there existed breaks that seemed to render it an impossibility. Had he placed the plank from his bed like a bridge from the roof of the Fine-Air to the outer wall, and crawled flat, on his belly on the coping of the outer wall the whole distance around the prison as far as the hut? But the outer wall of La Force formed a crenellated and unequal line; it mounted and descended, it dropped at the firemen's barracks, it rose toward the bathhouse, it was cut in twain by buildings, it was not even of the same height on the Hotel Lamoignon as on the Rue Pavee; everywhere occurred falls and right angles; and then, the sentinels must have espied the dark form of the fugitive; hence, the route taken by Thenardier still remains rather inexplicable. In two manners, flight was impossible. Had Thenardier, spurred on by that thirst for liberty, which changes precipices into ditches, iron bars into wattles of osier, a legless man into an athlete, a gouty man into a bird, stupidity into instinct,

instinct into intelligence, and intelligence into genius, had Thenardier invented a third mode? No one has ever found out.

The marvels of escape cannot always be accounted for. The man who makes his escape, we repeat, is inspired; there is something of the star and of the lightning in the mysterious gleam of flight; the effort toward deliverance is no less surprising than the flight toward the sublime, and one says of the escaped thief, "How did he contrive to scale that wall?" in the same way that one says of Corneille, "Where did he find the means of dying?"

At all events, dripping with perspiration, drenched with rain, with his clothes hanging in ribbons, his hands flayed, his elbows bleeding, his knees torn, Thenardier had reached what children, in their figurative language, call the edge of the wall of the ruin, there he had stretched himself out at full length, and there his strength had failed him. A steep escarpment three stories high separated him from the pavement of the street.

The rope he had was too short.

There he waited, pale, exhausted, desperate with all the despair that he had undergone, still hidden by the night, but telling himself that the day was on the point of dawning, alarmed at the idea of hearing the neighboring clock of Saint-Paul strike four within a few minutes, an hour when the sentinel was relieved and when the latter would be found asleep under the pierced roof, staring in horror at a terrible depth, at the light of the street lanterns, the wet, black pavement, that pavement longed for yet frightful, which meant death, and which meant liberty.

He asked himself whether his three accomplices in flight had succeeded, if they had heard him, and if they would come to his assistance. He listened. With the exception of the patrol, no one had passed through the street since he had been there. Nearly the whole of the descent of the market-gardeners from Montreuil, from Charonne, from Vincennes, and from Bercy to the markets was accomplished through the Rue Saint-Antoine.

Four o'clock struck. Thenardier shuddered. A few moments later, that terrified and confused uproar that follows the discovery of an escape broke forth in the prison. The sound of doors opening and shutting, the creaking of gratings on their hinges, a tumult in the guard-house, the hoarse shouts of the turnkeys, the shock of musket-butts on the pavement of the courts, reached his ears. Lights ascended and descended past the grated windows of the dormitories, a torch ran along the ridge-pole of the top story of the New Building, the firemen belonging in the barracks on the right had been summoned. Their helmets, which the torch lighted up in the rain, went and came along the roofs. At the same time, Thenardier perceived in the direction of the Bastille a wan whiteness lighting up the edge of the sky in doleful wise.

He was on top of a wall ten inches wide, stretched out under the heavy rains, with two gulfs to right and left, unable to stir, subject to the giddiness of a possible fall, and to the horror of a certain arrest, and his thoughts, like the pendulum of a clock, swung from one of these ideas to the other: "Dead if I fall, caught if I stay." In the midst of this anguish, he suddenly saw, the street being still dark, a man who was gliding along the walls and coming from the Rue Pavee, halt in the recess above which Thenardier was, as it were, suspended. Here this man was joined by a second, who walked with the same caution, then by a third, then by a fourth. When these men were reunited, one of them lifted the latch of the gate in the fence, and all four entered the enclosure in which the shanty stood. They halted directly under Thenardier. These men had evidently chosen this vacant space in order that they might consult without being seen by the passersby or by the sentinel who guards the wicket of La Force a few paces distant. It must be added, that the rain kept this sentinel blocked in his box. Thenardier, not being able to distinguish their visages, lent an ear to their words with the desperate attention of a wretch who feels himself lost.

Thenardier saw something resembling a gleam of hope flash before his eyes, these men conversed in slang.

The first said in a low but distinct voice, "Let's cut. What are we up to here?"

The second replied, "It's raining hard enough to put out the very devil's fire. And the bobbies will be along instanter. There's a soldier on guard yonder. We shall get nabbed here."

These two words, *icigo* and *icicaille*, both of which mean "here," and which belong, the first to the slang of the barriers, the second to the slang of the Temple, were flashes of light for Thenardier. By the *icigo* he recognized Brujon, who was a prowler of the barriers, by the *icicaille* he knew Babet, who, among his other trades, had been an old-clothes broker at the Temple.

The antique slang of the great century is no longer spoken except in the Temple, and Babet was really the only person who spoke it in all its purity. Had it not been for the *icicaille*, Thenardier would not have recognized him, for he had entirely changed his voice.

In the meanwhile, the third man had intervened.

"There's no hurry yet, let's wait a bit. How do we know that he doesn't stand in need of us?"

By this, which was nothing but French, Thenardier recognized Montparnasse, who made it a point in his elegance to understand all slangs and to speak none of them.

As for the fourth, he held his peace, but his huge shoulders betrayed him. Thenardier did not hesitate. It was Guelemer.

Brujon replied almost impetuously but still in a low tone, "What are you jabbering about? The tavern keeper hasn't managed to cut his stick. He don't tumble to the racket, that he don't! You have to be a pretty knowing cove to tear up your shirt, cut up your sheet to make a rope, punch holes in doors, get up false papers, make false keys, file your irons, hang out your cord, hide yourself, and disguise yourself! The old fellow hasn't managed to play it, he doesn't understand how to work the business."

Babet added, still in that classical slang which was spoken by Poulailler and Cartouche, and which is to the bold, new, highly colored and risky argot used by Brujon what the language of Racine is to the language of Andre Chenier, "Your tavern keeper must have been nabbed in the act. You have to be knowing. He's only a greenhorn. He must have let himself be taken in by a bobby, perhaps even by a sheep who played it on him as his pal. Listen, Montparnasse, do you hear those shouts in the prison? You have seen all those lights. He's recaptured, there! He'll get off with twenty years. I ain't afraid, I ain't a coward, but there ain't anything more to do, or otherwise they'd lead us a dance. Don't get mad, come with us, let's go drink a bottle of old wine together."

"One doesn't desert one's friends in a scrape," grumbled Montparnasse.

"I tell you he's nabbed!" retorted Brujon. "At the present moment, the innkeeper ain't worth a ha'penny. We can't do nothing for him. Let's be off. Every minute I think a bobby has got me in his fist."

Montparnasse no longer offered more than a feeble resistance; the fact is, that these four men, with the fidelity of ruffians who never abandon each other, had prowled all night long about La Force, great as was their peril, in the hope of seeing Thenardier make his appearance on the top of some wall. But the night, which was really growing too fine, for the downpour was such as to render all the streets deserted, the cold that was overpowering them, their soaked garments, their hole-ridden shoes, the alarming noise that had just burst forth in the prison, the hours that had elapsed, the patrol that they had encountered, the hope that was vanishing, all urged them to beat a retreat. Montparnasse himself, who was, perhaps, almost Thenardier's son-in-law, yielded. A moment more, and they would be gone. Thenardier was panting on his wall like the shipwrecked sufferers of the Meduse on their raft when they beheld the vessel that had appeared in sight vanish on the horizon.

He dared not call to them; a cry might be heard and ruin everything. An idea occurred to him, a last idea, a flash of inspiration; he drew from his pocket the end of Brujon's rope, which he had detached from the chimney of the New Building, and flung it into the space enclosed by the fence.

This rope fell at their feet.

"A widow," said Babet.

"My rope!" said Brujon.

"The tavern keeper is there," said Montparnasse.

They raised their eyes. Thenardier thrust out his head a very little.

"Quick!" said Montparnasse. "Have you the other end of the rope, Brujon?"

"Yes."

"Knot the two pieces together, we'll fling him the rope, he can fasten it to the wall, and he'll have enough of it to get down with."

Thenardier ran the risk, and spoke, "I am paralyzed with cold."

"We'll warm you up."

"I can't budge."

"Let yourself slide, we'll catch you."

"My hands are benumbed."

"Only fasten the rope to the wall."

"I can't."

"Then one of us must climb up," said Montparnasse.

"Three stories!" ejaculated Brujon.

An ancient plaster flue, which had served for a stove that had been used in the shanty in former times, ran along the wall and mounted almost to the very spot where they could see Thenardier. This flue, then much damaged and full of cracks, has since fallen, but the marks of it are still visible.

It was very narrow.

"One might get up by the help of that," said Montparnasse.

"By that flue?" exclaimed Babet. "A grown-up cove, never! It would take a brat."

"A brat must be got," resumed Brujon.

"Where are we to find a young 'un?" said Guelemer.

"Wait," said Montparnasse. "I've got the very article."

He opened the gate of the fence very softly, made sure that no one was passing along the street, stepped out cautiously, shut the gate behind him, and set off at a run in the direction of the Bastille.

Seven or eight minutes elapsed, eight thousand centuries to Thenardier; Babet, Brujon, and Guelemer did not open their lips; at last the gate opened once more, and Montparnasse appeared, breathless, and followed by Gavroche. The rain still rendered the street completely deserted.

Little Gavroche entered the enclosure and gazed at the forms of these ruffians with a tranquil air. The water was dripping from his hair. Guelemer addressed him, "Are you a man, young 'un?"

Gavroche shrugged his shoulders, and replied, "A young 'un like me's a man, and men like you are babes."

"The brat's tongue's well hung!" exclaimed Babet.

"The Paris brat ain't made of straw," added Brujon.

"What do you want?" asked Gavroche.

Montparnasse answered, "Climb up that flue."

"With this rope," said Babet.

"And fasten it," continued Brujon.

"To the top of the wall," went on Babet.

"To the crossbar of the window," added Brujon.

"And then?" said Gavroche.

"There!" said Guelemer.

The gamin examined the rope, the flue, the wall, the windows, and made that indescribable and disdainful noise with his lips which signifies, "Is that all!"

"There's a man up there whom you are to save," resumed Montparnasse.

"Will you?" began Brujon again.

"Greenhorn!" replied the lad, as though the question appeared a most unprecedented one to him.

And he took off his shoes.

Guelemer seized Gavroche by one arm, set him on the roof of the shanty, whose worm-eaten planks bent beneath the urchin's weight, and handed him the rope that Brujon had knotted together during Montparnasse's absence. The gamin directed his steps toward the flue, which it was easy to enter, thanks to a large crack which touched the roof. At the moment when he was on the point of ascending, Thenardier, who saw life and safety approaching, bent over the edge of the wall; the first light of dawn struck white upon his brow dripping with sweat, upon his livid cheekbones, his sharp and savage nose, his bristling gray beard, and Gavroche recognized him.

"Hullo! It's my father! Oh, that won't hinder."

And taking the rope in his teeth, he resolutely began the ascent.

He reached the summit of the hut, bestrode the old wall as though it had been a horse, and knotted the rope firmly to the upper crossbar of the window.

A moment later, Thenardier was in the street.

As soon as he touched the pavement, as soon as he found himself out of danger, he was no longer either weary, or chilled or trembling; the terrible things from which he had escaped vanished like smoke, all that strange and ferocious mind awoke once more, and stood erect and free, ready to march onward.

These were this man's first words, "Now, whom are we to eat?"

It is useless to explain the sense of this frightfully transparent remark, which signifies both to kill, to assassinate, and to plunder. To eat, true sense: to devour.

"Let's get well into a corner," said Brujon. "Let's settle it in three words, and part at once. There was an affair that promised well in the Rue Plumet, a deserted street, an isolated house, an old rotten gate on a garden, and lone women."

"Well! Why not?" demanded Thenardier.

"Your girl, Eponine, went to see about the matter," replied Babet.

"And she brought a biscuit to Magnon," added Guelemer. "Nothing to be made there."

"The girl's no fool," said Thenardier. "Still, it must be seen to."

"Yes, yes," said Brujon. "It must be looked up."

In the meanwhile, none of the men seemed to see Gavroche, who, during this colloquy, had seated himself on one of the fence posts; he waited a few moments, thinking that perhaps his father would turn toward him, then he put on his shoes again, and said, "Is that all? You don't want any more, my men? Now you're out of your scrape. I'm off. I must go and get my brats out of bed."

And off he went.

The five men emerged, one after another, from the enclosure.

When Gavroche had disappeared at the corner of the Rue des Ballets, Babet took Thenardier aside.

"Did you take a good look at that young 'un?" he asked.

"What young 'un?"

"The one who climbed the wall and carried you the rope."

"Not particularly."

"Well, I don't know, but it strikes me that it was your son."

"Bah!" said Thenardier, "do you think so?"

BOOK SEVENTH: SLANG

CHAPTER I—ORIGIN

*P*igritia is a terrible word.

It engenders a whole world, *la pègre*, for which read theft, and a hell, *la pègrenne*, for which read hunger.

Thus, idleness is the mother.

She has a son, theft, and a daughter, hunger.

Where are we at this moment? In the land of slang.

What is slang? It is at one and the same time, a nation and a dialect; it is theft in its two kinds; people and language.

When, four and thirty years ago, the narrator of this grave and somber history introduced into a work written with the same aim as this a thief who talked argot, there arose amazement and clamor. "What! How! Argot! Why, argot is horrible! It is the language of prisons, galleys, convicts, of everything that is most abominable in society!" etc., etc.

We have never understood this sort of objection.

Since that time, two powerful romancers, one of whom is a profound observer of the human heart, the other an intrepid friend of the people, Balzac and Eugene Sue, having represented their ruffians as talking their natural language, as the author of *The Last Day of a Condemned Man* did in 1828, the same objections have been raised. People repeated, "What do authors mean by that revolting dialect? Slang is odious! Slang makes one shudder!"

Who denies that? Of course it does.

When it is a question of probing a wound, a gulf, a society, since when has it been considered wrong to go too far? To go to the bottom? We have always thought that it was sometimes a courageous act, and, at least, a simple and useful deed, worthy of the sympathetic attention, which duty accepted and fulfilled merits. Why should one not explore everything, and study everything? Why should one halt on the way? The halt is a matter depending on the sounding line, and not on the leadsman.

Certainly, too, it is neither an attractive nor an easy task to undertake an investigation into the lowest depths of the social order, where terra firma comes to an end and where mud begins, to rummage in those vague, murky waves, to follow up, to seize and to fling, still quivering, upon the pavement that abject dialect, which is dripping with filth when thus brought to the light, that pustulous vocabulary each word of which seems an unclean ring from a monster of the mire and the shadows. Nothing is more lugubrious than the contemplation thus in its nudity, in the broad light of thought, of the horrible swarming of slang. It seems, in fact, to be a sort of horrible beast made for the night that has just been torn from its cesspool. One thinks one beholds a frightful, living, and bristling thicket that quivers, rustles, wavers, returns to shadow, threatens, and glares. One word resembles a claw, another an extinguished and bleeding eye, such and such a phrase seems to move like the claw of a crab. All this is alive with the hideous vitality of things that have been organized out of disorganization.

Now, when has horror ever excluded study? Since when has malady banished medicine? Can one imagine a naturalist refusing to study the viper, the bat, the scorpion, the centipede, the tarantula, and one who would cast them back into their darkness, saying, "Oh! How ugly that is!" The thinker who should turn aside from slang would resemble a surgeon who should avert his face from an ulcer or a wart. He would be like a philologist refusing to examine a fact in language, a philosopher hesitating to scrutinize a fact in humanity. For, it must be stated to those who are ignorant of the case, that argot is both a literary phenomenon and a social result. What is slang, properly speaking? It is the language of wretchedness.

We may be stopped; the fact may be put to us in general terms, which is one way of attenuating it; we may be told, that all trades, professions, it may be added, all the accidents of the social hierarchy and all forms of intelligence, have their own slang. The merchant who says, "Montpellier not active, Marseilles fine quality," the broker on change who says, "Assets at end of current month," the gambler who says, "*Tiers et tout, refait de pique,*" the sheriff of the Norman Isles who says, "The holder in fee reverting to his landed estate cannot claim the fruits of that estate during the hereditary seizure of the real estate by the mortgagor," the playwright who says, "The piece was hissed," the comedian who says, "I've made a hit," the philosopher who says, "Phenomenal triplicity," the huntsman who says, "*Voileci allais, Voileci fuyant,*" the phrenologist who says, "Amativeness, combativeness, secretiveness," the infantry soldier who says, "My shooting-iron," the cavalryman who says, "My turkey-cock," the fencing master who says, "Tierce, quarte, break," the printer who says, "My shooting-stick and galley,"—all, printer, fencing master, cavalry dragoon, infantry man, phrenologist, huntsman, philosopher, comedian, playwright, sheriff, gambler, stockbroker, and merchant, speak slang. The painter who says, "My grinder," the notary who says, "My Skip-the-Gutter," the hairdresser who says, "My mealyback," the cobbler who says, "My cub," talks slang. Strictly speaking, if one absolutely insists on the point, all the different fashions of saying the right and the left, the sailor's port and starboard, the scene shifter's courtside, and gardenside, the beadle's Gospel-side and Epistle-side, are slang. There is the slang of the affected lady as well as of the precieuses. The Hotel Rambouillet nearly adjoins the Cour des Miracles. There is a slang of duchesses, witness this phrase contained in a love letter from a very great lady and a very pretty woman of the Restoration: "You will find in this gossip a fultitude of reasons why I should libertize." Diplomatic ciphers are slang; the pontifical chancellery by using for Rome, grkztntgzyal for despatch, and abfxustgrnogrkzu tu XI for the Due de Modena, speaks slang. The physicians of the Middle Ages who, for carrot, radish, and turnip, said Opoponach, perfroschinum, reptitalmus, dracatholicum, angelorum, postmegorum, talked slang. The sugar manufacturer who says, "Loaf, clarified, lumps, bastard, common, burnt"—this honest manufacturer talks slang. A certain school of criticism twenty years ago, which used to say, "Half of the works of Shakespeare consists of plays upon words and puns"—talked slang. The poet, and the artist who, with profound understanding, would designate M. de Montmorency as "a bourgeois," if he were not a judge of verses and statues, speaks slang. The classic Academician who calls flowers "Flora," fruits, "Pomona," the sea, "Neptune," love, "fires," beauty, "charms," a horse, "a courser," the white or tricolored cockade, "the rose of Bellona," the three-cornered hat, "Mars' triangle,"—that classical Academician talks slang. Algebra, medicine, botany, have each their slang. The tongue that is employed on board ship, that wonderful language of the sea, which is so complete and so picturesque, which was spoken by Jean Bart, Duquesne, Suffren, and Duperre, which mingles with the whistling of the rigging, the sound of the speaking trumpets, the shock of the boarding irons, the roll of the sea, the wind, the gale, the cannon, is wholly a heroic and dazzling slang, which is to the fierce slang of the thieves what the lion is to the jackal.

No doubt. But say what we will, this manner of understanding the word slang is an extension that everyone will not admit. For our part, we reserve to the word its ancient and precise, circumscribed and determined significance, and we restrict slang to slang. The veritable slang and the slang that is preeminently slang, if the two words can be coupled thus, the slang immemorial which was a kingdom, is nothing else, we repeat, than the homely, uneasy, crafty, treacherous, venomous, cruel, equivocal, vile, profound, fatal tongue of wretchedness. There exists, at the extremity of all abasement and all misfortunes, a last misery that revolts and makes up its mind to enter into conflict with the whole mass of fortunate facts and reigning rights; a fearful conflict, where, now cunning, now violent, unhealthy and ferocious at one and the same time, it attacks the social order with pin pricks through vice, and with club blows through crime. To meet the needs of this conflict, wretchedness has invented a language of combat, which is slang.

To keep afloat and to rescue from oblivion, to hold above the gulf, were it but a fragment of some language that man has spoken and that would, otherwise be lost—that is to say, one of the elements, good or bad, of which civilization is composed, or by which it is complicated, to extend the records of social observation—is to serve civilization itself. This service Plautus rendered, consciously or unconsciously, by making two Carthaginian soldiers talk Phoenician; that service Moliere rendered, by making so many of his characters talk Levantine and all sorts of dialects. Here objections spring up afresh. Phoenician, very good! Levantine, quite right! Even dialect, let that pass! They are tongues that have belonged to nations or provinces; but slang! What is the use of preserving slang? What is the good of assisting slang "to survive"?

To this we reply in one word, only. Assuredly, if the tongue that a nation or a province has spoken is worthy of interest, the language that has been spoken by a misery is still more worthy of attention and study.

It is the language that has been spoken, in France, for example, for more than four centuries, not only by a misery, but by every possible human misery.

And then, we insist upon it, the study of social deformities and infirmities, and the task of pointing them out with a view to remedy, is not a business in which choice is permitted. The historian of manners and ideas has no less austere a mission than the historian of events. The latter has the surface of civilization, the conflicts of crowns, the births of princes, the marriages of kings, battles, assemblages, great public men, revolutions in the daylight, everything on the exterior; the other historian has the interior, the depths, the people who toil, suffer, wait, the oppressed woman, the agonizing child, the secret war between man and man, obscure ferocities, prejudices, plotted iniquities, the subterranean, the indistinct tremors of multitudes, the die-of-hunger, the counter-blows of the law, the secret evolution of souls, the go-barefoot, the bare-armed, the disinherited, the orphans, the unhappy, and the infamous, all the forms that roam through the darkness. He must descend with his heart full of charity, and severity at the same time, as a brother and as a judge, to those impenetrable casemates where crawl, pell-mell, those who bleed and those who deal the blow, those who weep and those who curse, those who fast and those who devour, those who endure evil and those who inflict it. Have these historians of hearts and souls duties at all inferior to the historians of external facts? Does anyone think that Alighieri has any fewer things to say than Machiavelli? Is the under side of civilization any less important than the upper side merely because it is deeper and more somber? Do we really know the mountain well when we are not acquainted with the cavern?

Let us say, moreover, parenthetically, that from a few words of what precedes a marked separation might be inferred between the two classes of historians that does not exist in our mind. No one is a good historian of the patent, visible, striking, and public life of peoples, if he is not, at the same time, in a certain measure, the historian of their deep and hidden life; and no one is a good historian of the interior unless he understands how, at need, to be the historian of the exterior also. The history of manners and ideas permeates the history of events, and this is true reciprocally. They constitute two different orders of facts that correspond to each other, which are always interlaced, and which often bring forth results. All the lineaments that providence traces on the surface of a nation have their parallels, somber but distinct, in their depths, and all convulsions of the depths produce ebullitions on the surface. True history being a mixture of all things, the true historian mingles in everything.

Man is not a circle with a single center; he is an ellipse with a double focus. Facts form one of these, and ideas the other.

Slang is nothing but a dressing room where the tongue having some bad action to perform, disguises itself. There it clothes itself in word-masks, in metaphor-rags. In this guise it becomes horrible.

One finds it difficult to recognize. Is it really the French tongue, the great human tongue? Behold it ready to step upon the stage and to retort upon crime, and prepared for all the employments of the repertory of evil. It no longer walks, it hobbles; it limps on the crutch of the Court of Miracles, a crutch metamorphosable into a club; it is called vagrancy; every sort of specter, its dressers, have painted its face, it crawls and rears, the double gait of the reptile. Henceforth, it is apt at all roles, it is made suspicious by the counterfeiter, covered with verdigris by the forger, blacked by the soot of the incendiary; and the murderer applies its rouge.

When one listens, by the side of honest men, at the portals of society, one overhears the dialogues of those who are on the outside. One distinguishes questions and replies. One perceives, without understanding it, a hideous murmur, sounding almost like human accents, but more nearly resembling a howl than an articulate word. It is slang. The words are misshapen and stamped with an indescribable and fantastic bestiality. One thinks one hears hydras talking.

It is unintelligible in the dark. It gnashes and whispers, completing the gloom with mystery. It is black in misfortune, it is blacker still in crime; these two blacknesses amalgamated, compose slang. Obscurity in the atmosphere, obscurity in acts, obscurity in voices. Terrible, toadlike tongue, which goes and comes, leaps, crawls, slobbers, and stirs about in monstrous wise in that immense gray fog composed of rain and night, of hunger, of vice, of falsehood, of injustice, of nudity, of suffocation, and of winter, the high noonday of the miserable.

Let us have compassion on the chastised. Alas! Who are we ourselves? Who am I who now address you? Who are you who are listening to me? And are you very sure that we have done nothing before we were born? The earth is not devoid of resemblance to a jail. Who knows whether man is not a recaptured offender against divine justice? Look closely at life. It is so made, that everywhere we feel the sense of punishment.

Are you what is called a happy man? Well! You are sad every day. Each day has its own great grief or its little care. Yesterday you were trembling for a health that is dear to you, today you fear for your own; tomorrow it will be anxiety about money, the day after tomorrow the diatribe of a slanderer, the day after that, the misfortune of some friend; then the prevailing weather, then something that has been broken or lost, then a pleasure with which your conscience and your vertebral column reproach you; again, the course of public affairs. This without reckoning in the pains of the heart. And so it goes on. One cloud is dispelled, another forms. There is hardly one day out of a hundred which is wholly joyous and sunny. And you belong to that small class who are happy! As for the rest of mankind, stagnating night rests upon them.

Thoughtful minds make but little use of the phrase: the fortunate and the unfortunate. In this world, evidently the vestibule of another, there are no fortunate.

The real human division is this: the luminous and the shady. To diminish the number of the shady, to augment the number of the luminous, that is the object. That is why we cry: Education! Science! To teach reading, means to light the fire; every syllable spelled out sparkles.

However, he who says light does not, necessarily, say joy. People suffer in the light; excess burns. The flame is the enemy of the wing. To burn without ceasing to fly, therein lies the marvel of genius.

When you shall have learned to know, and to love, you will still suffer. The day is born in tears. The luminous weep, if only over those in darkness.

CHAPTER II—ROOTS

Slang is the tongue of those who sit in darkness.

Thought is moved in its most somber depths, social philosophy is bidden to its most poignant meditations, in the presence of that enigmatic dialect at once so blighted and rebellious. Therein lies chastisement made visible. Every syllable has an air of being marked. The words of the vulgar tongue appear therein wrinkled and shriveled, as it were, beneath the hot iron of the executioner. Some seem to be still smoking. Such and such a phrase produces upon you the effect of the shoulder of a thief branded with the fleur-de-lis, which has suddenly been laid bare. Ideas almost refuse to be expressed in these substantives that are fugitives from justice. Metaphor is sometimes so shameless, that one feels that it has worn the iron neck-fetter.

Moreover, in spite of all this, and because of all this, this strange dialect has by rights, its own compartment in that great impartial case of pigeonholes where there is room for the rusty farthing as well as for the gold medal, and which is called literature. Slang, whether the public admit the fact or not has its syntax and its poetry. It is a language. Yes, by the deformity of certain terms, we recognize the fact that it was chewed by Mandrin, and by the splendor of certain metonymies, we feel that Villon spoke it.

That exquisite and celebrated verse—*Mais où sont les neiges d'antan?* (But where are the snows of years gone by?)—is a verse of slang. Antam—*ante annum*—is a word of Thunes slang, which signified the past year, and by extension, formerly. Thirty-five years ago, at the epoch of the departure of the great chain gang, there could be read in one of the cells at Bicêtre, this maxim engraved with a nail on the wall by a king of Thunes condemned to the galleys: *Les dabs d'antan trimaient siempre pour la pierre du Coesre.* This means "Kings in days gone by always went and had themselves anointed." In the opinion of that king, anointment meant the galleys.

The word *decarade*, which expresses the departure of heavy vehicles at a gallop, is attributed to Villon, and it is worthy of him. This word, which strikes fire with all four of its feet, sums up in a masterly onomatopoeia the whole of La Fontaine's admirable verse: *Six forts chevaux tiraient un coche.* (Six stout horses drew a coach.)

From a purely literary point of view, few studies would prove more curious and fruitful than the study of slang. It is a whole language within a language, a sort of sickly excrescence, an unhealthy graft that has produced a vegetation, a parasite that has its roots in the old Gallic trunk, and whose sinister foliage crawls all over one side of the language. This is what may be called the first, the vulgar aspect of slang. But, for those who study the tongue as it should be studied, that is to say, as geologists study the earth, slang appears like a veritable alluvial deposit. According as one digs a longer or shorter distance into it, one finds in slang, below the old popular French, Provencal, Spanish, Italian, Levantine, that language of the Mediterranean ports, English and German, the Romance language in its three varieties, French, Italian, and Romance, Latin, and finally Basque and Celtic. A profound and unique formation. A subterranean edifice erected in common by all the miserable. Each accursed race has deposited its layer, each suffering has dropped its stone there, each heart has contributed its pebble. A throng of evil, base, or irritated souls, who have traversed life and have vanished into eternity, linger there almost entirely visible still beneath the form of some monstrous word.

Do you want Spanish? The old Gothic slang abounded in it. Here is *boffete*, a box on the ear, which is derived from *bofeton*; *vantane*, window (later on *vanterne*), which comes from *vantana*; gat, cat, which comes from *gato*; *acite*, oil, which comes from *aceyte*. Do you want Italian? Here is spade, sword, which comes from *spada*; carvel, boat, which comes from *caravella*. Do you want English? Here is *bichot*, which comes from bishop; *raille*, spy, which comes from rascal, *rascalion*; *pilche*, a case, which comes from *pilcher*, a sheath. Do you want German? Here is the *caleur*, the waiter, *kellner*; the hers, the master, *herʒog* (duke). Do you want Latin? Here is *frangir*, to break, *frangere*; *affurer*, to steal, fur; *cadene*, chain, *catena*. There is one word that crops up in every language of the continent, with a sort of mysterious power and authority. It is the word magnus; the Scotchman makes of it his mac, which designates the chief of the clan; Mac-Farlane, Mac-Callumore, the great Farlane, the great Callumore; slang turns it into meck and later *le meg*, that is to say, God. Would you like Basque? Here is *gahisto*, the devil, which comes from *gaiʒtoa*, evil; *sorgabon*, good night, which comes from *gabon*, good evening. Do you want Celtic? Here is *blavin*, a handkerchief, which comes from *blavet*, gushing water; *menesse*, a woman (in a bad sense), which comes from *meinec*, full of stones; *barant*, brook, from *baranton*, fountain; *goffeur*, locksmith, from *goff*, blacksmith; *guedouʒe*, death, which comes from *guenn-du*, black-white. Finally, would you like history? Slang calls crowns *les malteses*, a souvenir of the coin in circulation on the galleys of Malta.

In addition to the philological origins just indicated, slang possesses other and still more natural roots, which spring, so to speak, from the mind of man itself.

In the first place, the direct creation of words. Therein lies the mystery of tongues. To paint with words, which contains figures one knows not how or why, is the primitive foundation of all human languages, what may be called their granite.

Slang abounds in words of this description, immediate words, words created instantaneously no one knows either where or by whom, without etymology, without analogies, without derivatives, solitary, barbarous, sometimes hideous words, which at times possess a singular power of expression and which live. The executioner, *le taule*; the forest, *le sabri*; fear, flight, *taf*; the lackey, *le larbin*; the mineral, the prefect, the minister, pharos; the devil, *le rabouin*. Nothing is stranger than these words that both mask and reveal. Some, *le rabouin*, for example, are at the same time grotesque and terrible, and produce on you the effect of a cyclopean grimace.

In the second place, metaphor. The peculiarity of a language that is desirous of saying all yet concealing all is that it is rich in figures. Metaphor is an enigma, wherein the thief who is plotting a stroke, the prisoner who is arranging an escape, take refuge. No idiom is more metaphorical than slang: *devisser le coco* (to unscrew the nut), to twist the neck; *tortiller* (to wriggle), to eat; *etre gerbe*, to be tried; a rat, a bread thief; *il lansquine*, it rains, a striking, ancient figure that partly bears its date about it, which assimilates long oblique lines of rain, with the dense and slanting pikes of the lancers, and which compresses into a single word the popular expression: it rains halberds. Sometimes, in proportion as slang progresses from the first epoch to the second, words pass from the primitive and savage sense to the metaphorical sense. The devil ceases to be *le rabouin*, and becomes *le boulanger* (the baker), who puts the bread into the oven. This is more witty, but less grand, something like Racine after Corneille, like Euripides after Aeschylus. Certain slang phrases that participate in the two epochs and have at once the barbaric character and the metaphorical character resemble phantasmagories. *Les sorgueurs vont solliciter des gails à la lune*—the prowlers are going to steal horses by night, this passes before the mind like a group of specters. One knows not what one sees.

In the third place, the expedient. Slang lives on the language. It uses it in accordance with its fancy, it dips into it haphazard, and it often confines itself, when occasion arises, to alter it in a gross and summary fashion. Occasionally, with the ordinary words thus deformed and complicated with words of pure slang, picturesque phrases are formed, in which there can be felt the mixture of the two preceding elements, the direct creation and the metaphor: *le cab jaspine, je marronne que la roulotte de Pantin trime dans le sabri*, the dog is barking, I suspect that the diligence for Paris is passing through the woods. *Le dab est sinve, la dabuge est merloussiere, la fée est bative*, the bourgeois is stupid, the bourgeoise is cunning, the daughter is pretty. Generally, to throw listeners off the track, slang confines itself to adding to all the words of the language without distinction, an ignoble tail, a termination in *aille*, in *orgue*, in *iergue*, or in *uche*. Thus: *Vousiergue trouvaille bonorgue ce gigotmuche?* Do you think that leg of mutton good? A phrase addressed by Cartouche to a turnkey in order to find out whether the sum offered for his escape suited him.

The termination in mar has been added recently.

Slang, being the dialect of corruption, quickly becomes corrupted itself.

Besides this, as it is always seeking concealment, as soon as it feels that it is understood, it changes its form. Contrary to what happens with every other vegetation, every ray of light that falls upon it kills whatever it touches. Thus slang is in constant process of decomposition and recomposition; an obscure and rapid work that never pauses. It passes over more ground in ten years than a language in ten centuries. Thus *le larton* (bread) becomes *le lartif*; *le gail* (horse) becomes *le gaye*; *la fertanche* (straw) becomes *la fertille*; *le momignard* (brat), *le momacque*; *les fiques* (duds), *frusques*; *la chique* (the church), *l'egrugeoir*; *le colabre* (neck), *le colas*. The devil is at first, *gahisto*, then *le rabouin*, then the baker; the priest is a *ratichon*, then the boar (*le sanglier*); the dagger is *le vingt-deux* (twenty-two), then *le surin*, then *le lingre*; the police are *railles*, then *roussins*, then *rousses*, then *marchands de lacets* (dealers in stay-laces), then *coquers*, then *cognes*; the executioner is *le taule*, then *Charlot*, *l'atigeur*, then *le becquillard*. In the seventeenth century, to fight was "to give each other snuff;" in the nineteenth it is "to chew each other's throats." There have been twenty different phrases between these two extremes. Cartouche's talk would have been Hebrew to Lacenaire. All the words of this language are perpetually engaged in flight like the men who utter them.

Still, from time to time, and in consequence of this very movement, the ancient slang crops up again and becomes new once more. It has its headquarters where it maintains its sway. The Temple preserved the slang of the seventeenth century; Bicêtre, when it was a prison, preserved the slang of Thunes. There one could hear the termination in anche of the old Thuneurs. Boyanches-tu (bois-tu), do you drink? But perpetual movement remains its law, nevertheless.

If the philosopher succeeds in fixing, for a moment, for purposes of observation, this language, which is incessantly evaporating, he falls into doleful and useful meditation. No study is more efficacious and more fecund in instruction. There is not a metaphor, not an analogy, in slang, which does not contain a lesson. Among these men, to beat means to feign; one beats a malady; ruse is their strength.

For them, the idea of the man is not separated from the idea of darkness. The night is called *la sorgue*; man, *l'orgue*. Man is a derivative of the night.

They have taken up the practice of considering society in the light of an atmosphere that kills them, of a fatal force, and they speak of their liberty as one would speak of his health. A man under arrest is a sick man; one who is condemned is a dead man.

The most terrible thing for the prisoner within the four walls in which he is buried, is a sort of glacial chastity, and he calls the dungeon the castus. In that funereal place, life outside always presents itself under its most smiling aspect. The prisoner has irons on his feet; you think, perhaps, that his thought is that it is with the feet that one walks? No; he is thinking that it is with the feet that one dances; so, when he has succeeded in severing his fetters, his first idea is that now he can dance, and he calls the saw the *bastringue* (public house ball). A name is a center; profound assimilation. The ruffian has two heads, one of which reasons out his actions and leads him all his life long, and the other, which he has upon his shoulders on the day of his death; he calls the head which counsels him in crime *la sorbonne*, and the head that expiates it *la tronche*.—When a man has no longer anything but rags upon his body and vices in his heart, when he has arrived at that double moral and material degradation that the word blackguard characterizes in its two acceptations, he is ripe for crime; he is like a well-whetted knife; he has two cutting edges, his distress and his malice; so slang does not say a blackguard, it says *un reguise*. What are the galleys? A brazier of damnation, a hell. The convict calls himself a fagot. And finally, what name do malefactors give to their prison? The college. A whole penitentiary system can be evolved from that word.

Does the reader wish to know where the majority of the songs of the galleys, those refrains called in the special vocabulary *lirlonfa*, have had their birth?

Let him listen to what follows:

There existed at the Chatelet in Paris a large and long cellar. This cellar was eight feet below the level of the Seine. It had neither windows nor air holes, its only aperture was the door; men could enter there, air could not. This vault had for ceiling a vault of stone, and for floor ten inches of mud. It was flagged; but the pavement had rotted and cracked under the oozing of the water. Eight feet above the floor, a long and massive beam traversed this subterranean excavation from side to side; from this beam hung, at short distances apart, chains three feet long, and at the end of these chains there were rings for the neck. In this vault, men who had been condemned to the galleys were incarcerated until the day of their departure for Toulon. They were thrust under this beam, where each one found his fetters swinging in the darkness and waiting for him.

The chains, those pendant arms, and the necklets, those open hands, caught the unhappy wretches by the throat. They were riveted and left there. As the chain was too short, they could not lie down. They remained motionless in that cavern, in that night, beneath that beam, almost hanging, forced to unheard-of efforts to reach their bread, jug, or their vault overhead, mud even to mid-leg, filth flowing to their very calves, broken asunder with fatigue, with thighs and knees giving way, clinging fast to the chain with their hands in order to obtain some rest, unable to sleep except when standing erect, and awakened every moment by the strangling of the collar; some woke no more. In order to eat, they pushed the bread, which was flung to them in the mud, along their leg with their heel until it reached their hand.

How long did they remain thus? One month, two months, six months sometimes; one stayed a year. It was the antechamber of the galleys. Men were put there for stealing a hare from the king. In this sepulcher hell, what did they do? What man can do in a sepulchre, they went through the agonies of death, and what can man do in hell, they sang; for song lingers where there is no longer any hope. In the waters of Malta, when a galley was approaching, the song could be heard before the sound of the oars. Poor Survincent, the poacher, who had gone through the prison-cellar of the Chatelet, said, "It was the rhymes that kept me up." Uselessness of poetry. What is the good of rhyme?

It is in this cellar that nearly all the slang songs had their birth. It is from the dungeon of the Grand-Chatelet of Paris that comes the melancholy refrain of the Montgomery galley, "Timaloumisaine, timaloumison." The majority of these:

Icicaille est la theatre. (Here is the theater.)
Du petit dardant. (Of the little archer—Cupid).

Do what you will, you cannot annihilate that eternal relic in the heart of man, love.

In this world of dismal deeds, people keep their secrets. The secret is the thing above all others. The secret, in the eyes of these wretches, is unity that serves as a base of union. To betray a secret is to tear from each member of this fierce community something of his own personality. To inform against, in the energetic slang dialect, is called "to eat the bit." As though the informer drew to himself a little of the substance of all and nourished himself on a bit of each one's flesh.

What does it signify to receive a box on the ear? Commonplace metaphor replies, "It is to see thirty-six candles."

Here slang intervenes and takes it up: Candle, *camoufle*. Thereupon, the ordinary tongue gives *camouflet* as the synonym for *soufflet*. Thus, by a sort of infiltration from below upwards, with the aid of metaphor, that incalculable, trajectory slang mounts from the cavern to the Academy; and Poulailler saying, "I light my *camoufle*," causes Voltaire to write, "Langleviel La Beaumelle deserves a hundred *camouflets*."

Researches in slang mean discoveries at every step. Study and investigation of this strange idiom lead to the mysterious point of intersection of regular society with society that is accursed.

The thief also has his food for cannon, stealable matter, you, I, whoever passes by; *le pantre*. (Pan, everybody.)

Slang is language turned convict.

That the thinking principle of man be thrust down ever so low, that it can be dragged and pinioned there by obscure tyrannies of fatality, that it can be bound by no one knows what fetters in that abyss, is sufficient to create consternation.

Oh, poor thought of miserable wretches!

Alas! Will no one come to the succor of the human soul in that darkness? Is it her destiny there to await forever the mind, the liberator, the immense rider of Pegasi and hippogriffs, the combatant of heroes of the dawn who shall descend from the azure between two wings, the radiant knight of the future? Will she forever summon in vain to her assistance the lance of light of the ideal? Is she condemned to hear the fearful approach of Evil through the density of the gulf, and to catch glimpses, nearer and nearer at hand, beneath the hideous water of that dragon's head, that maw streaked with foam, and that writhing undulation of claws, swellings, and rings? Must it remain there, without a gleam of light, without hope, given over to that terrible approach, vaguely scented out by the monster, shuddering, disheveled, wringing its arms, forever chained to the rock of night, a somber Andromeda white and naked amid the shadows!

CHAPTER III—SLANG THAT WEEPS AND SLANG THAT LAUGHS

As the reader perceives, slang in its entirety, slang of four hundred years ago, like the slang of today, is permeated with that somber, symbolical spirit which gives to all words a mien that is now mournful, now menacing. One feels in it the wild and ancient sadness of those vagrants of the Court of Miracles who played at cards with packs of their own, some of which have come down to us. The eight of clubs, for instance, represented a huge tree bearing eight enormous trefoil leaves, a sort of fantastic personification of the forest. At the foot of this tree a fire was burning, over which three hares were roasting a huntsman on a spit, and behind him, on another fire, hung a steaming pot, from which emerged the head of a dog. Nothing can be more melancholy than these reprisals in painting, by a pack of cards, in the presence of stakes for the roasting of smugglers and of the cauldron for the boiling of counterfeiters. The diverse forms assumed by thought in the realm of slang, even song, even raillery, even menace, all partook of this powerless and dejected character. All the songs, the melodies of some of which have been collected were humble and lamentable to the point of evoking tears. The *pegre* is always the poor *pegre*, and he is always the hare in hiding, the fugitive mouse, the flying bird. He hardly complains, he contents himself with sighing; one of his moans has come down to us: "I do not understand how God, the father of men, can torture his children and his grandchildren and hear them cry, without himself suffering torture." The wretch, whenever he has time to think, makes himself small before the low, and frail in the presence of society; he lies down flat on his face, he entreats, he appeals to the side of compassion; we feel that he is conscious of his guilt.

Toward the middle of the last century a change took place, prison songs and thieves' *ritournelles* assumed, so to speak, an insolent and jovial mien. The plaintive *malure* was replaced by the *larifla*. We find in the eighteenth century, in nearly all the songs of the galleys and prisons, a diabolical and enigmatical gaiety. We hear this strident and lilting refrain, which we should say had been lighted up by a phosphorescent gleam, and which seems to have been flung into the forest by a will-o'-the-wisp playing the fife:

> *"Miralabi suslababo*
> *Mirliton ribonribette*
> *Surlababi mirlababo*
> *Mirliton ribonribo."*

This was sung in a cellar or in a nook of the forest while cutting a man's throat.

A serious symptom. In the eighteenth century, the ancient melancholy of the dejected classes vanishes. They began to laugh. They rally the grand meg and the grand dab. Given Louis XV, they call the King of France "le Marquis de Pantin." And behold, they are almost gay. A sort of gleam proceeds from these miserable wretches, as though their consciences were not heavy within them anymore. These lamentable tribes of darkness have no longer merely the desperate audacity of actions, they possess the heedless audacity of mind. A sign that they are losing the sense of their criminality, and that they feel, even among thinkers and dreamers, some indefinable support, which the latter themselves know not of. A sign that theft and pillage are beginning to filter into doctrines and sophisms, in such a way as to lose somewhat of their ugliness, while communicating much of it to sophisms and doctrines. A sign, in short, of some outbreak which is prodigious and near unless some diversion shall arise.

Let us pause a moment. Whom are we accusing here? Is it the eighteenth century? Is it philosophy? Certainly not. The work of the eighteenth century is healthy and good and wholesome. The encyclopedists, Diderot at their head; the physiocrates, Turgot at their head; the philosophers, Voltaire at their head; the Utopians, Rousseau at their head, these are four sacred legions. Humanity's immense advance toward the light is due to them. They are the four vanguards of the human race, marching toward the four cardinal points of progress. Diderot toward the beautiful, Turgot toward the useful, Voltaire toward the true, Rousseau toward the just. But by the side of and above the philosophers, there were the sophists, a venomous vegetation mingled with a healthy growth, hemlock in the virgin forest. While the executioner was burning the great books of the liberators of the century on the grand staircase of the courthouse, writers now forgotten were publishing, with the King's sanction, no one knows what strangely disorganizing writings, which were eagerly read by the unfortunate. Some of these publications, odd to say, which were patronized by a prince, are to be found in the Secret Library. These facts, significant but unknown, were imperceptible on the surface. Sometimes, in the very obscurity of a fact lurks its danger. It is obscure because it is underhand. Of all these writers, the one who probably then excavated in the masses the most unhealthy gallery was Restif de La Bretonne.

This work, peculiar to the whole of Europe, affected more ravages in Germany than anywhere else. In Germany, during a given period, summed up by Schiller in his famous drama *The Robbers*, theft and pillage rose up in protest against property and labor, assimilated certain specious and false elementary ideas, which, though just in appearance, were absurd in reality, enveloped themselves in these ideas, disappeared within them, after a fashion, assumed an abstract name, passed into the state of theory, and in that shape circulated among the laborious, suffering, and honest masses, unknown even to the imprudent chemists who had prepared the mixture, unknown even to the masses who accepted it. Whenever a fact of this sort presents itself, the case is grave. Suffering engenders wrath; and while the prosperous classes blind themselves or fall asleep, which is the same thing as shutting one's eyes, the hatred of the unfortunate classes lights its torch at some aggrieved or ill-made spirit, which dreams in a corner, and sets itself to the scrutiny of society. The scrutiny of hatred is a terrible thing.

Hence, if the ill-fortune of the times so wills it, those fearful commotions which were formerly called *jacqueries*, beside which purely political agitations are the merest child's play, which are no longer the conflict of the oppressed and the oppressor, but the revolt of discomfort against comfort. Then everything crumbles.

Jacqueries are earthquakes of the people.

It is this peril, possibly imminent toward the close of the eighteenth century, which the French Revolution, that immense act of probity, cut short.

The French Revolution, which is nothing else than the idea armed with the sword, rose erect, and, with the same abrupt movement, closed the door of ill and opened the door of good.

It put a stop to torture, promulgated the truth, expelled miasma, rendered the century healthy, crowned the populace.

It may be said of it that it created man a second time, by giving him a second soul, the right.

The nineteenth century has inherited and profited by its work, and today, the social catastrophe to which we lately alluded is simply impossible. Blind is he who announces it! Foolish is he who fears it! Revolution is the vaccine of Jacquerie.

Thanks to the Revolution, social conditions have changed. Feudal and monarchical maladies no longer run in our blood. There is no more of the Middle Ages in our constitution. We no longer live in the days when terrible swarms within made irruptions, when one heard beneath his feet the obscure course of a dull rumble, when indescribable elevations from molelike tunnels appeared on the surface of civilization, where the soil cracked open, where the roofs of caverns yawned, and where one suddenly beheld monstrous heads emerging from the earth.

The revolutionary sense is a moral sense. The sentiment of right, once developed, develops the sentiment of duty. The law of all is liberty, which ends where the liberty of others begins, according to Robespierre's admirable definition. Since '89, the whole people has been dilating into a sublime individual; there is not a poor man, who, possessing his right, has not his ray of sun; the die-of-hunger feels within him the honesty of France; the dignity of the citizen is an internal armor; he who is free is scrupulous; he who votes reigns. Hence incorruptibility; hence the miscarriage of unhealthy lusts; hence eyes heroically lowered before temptations. The revolutionary wholesomeness is such, that on a day of deliverance, a 14th of July, a 10th of August, there is no longer any populace. The first cry of the enlightened and increasing throngs is: death to thieves! Progress is an honest man; the ideal and the absolute do not filch pocket-handkerchiefs. By whom were the wagons containing the wealth of the Tuileries escorted in 1848? By the rag pickers of the Faubourg Saint-Antoine. Rags mounted guard over the treasure. Virtue rendered these tatterdemalions resplendent. In those wagons in chests, hardly closed, and some, even, half-open, amid a hundred dazzling caskets, was that ancient crown of France, studded with diamonds, surmounted by the carbuncle of royalty, by the Regent diamond, which was worth thirty millions. Barefooted, they guarded that crown.

Hence, no more Jacquerie. I regret it for the sake of the skillful. The old fear has produced its last effects in that quarter; and henceforth it can no longer be employed in politics. The principal spring of the red specter is broken. Everyone knows it now. The scarecrow scares no longer. The birds take liberties with the mannequin, foul creatures alight upon it, the bourgeois laugh at it.

CHAPTER IV—THE TWO DUTIES: TO WATCH AND TO HOPE

This being the case, is all social danger dispelled? Certainly not. There is no Jacquerie; society may rest assured on that point; blood will no longer rush to its head. But let society take heed to the manner in which it breathes.

Apoplexy is no longer to be feared, but phthisis is there. Social phthisis is called misery.

One can perish from being undermined as well as from being struck by lightning.

Let us not weary of repeating, and sympathetic souls must not forget that this is the first of fraternal obligations, and selfish hearts must understand that the first of political necessities consists in thinking first of all of the disinherited and sorrowing throngs, in solacing, airing, enlightening, loving them, in enlarging their horizon to a magnificent extent, in lavishing upon them education in every form, in offering them the example of labor, never the example of idleness, in diminishing the individual burden by enlarging the notion of the universal aim, in setting a limit to poverty without setting a limit to wealth, in creating vast fields of public and popular activity, in having, like Briareus, a hundred hands to extend in all directions to the oppressed and the feeble, in employing the collective power for that grand duty of opening workshops for all arms, schools for all aptitudes, and laboratories for all degrees of intelligence, in augmenting salaries, diminishing trouble, balancing what should be and what is, that is to say, in proportioning enjoyment to effort and a glut to need; in a word, in evolving from the social apparatus more light and more comfort for the benefit of those who suffer and those who are ignorant.

And, let us say it, all this is but the beginning. The true question is this: labor cannot be a law without being a right.

We will not insist upon this point; this is not the proper place for that.

If nature calls itself Providence, society should call itself Foresight.

Intellectual and moral growth is no less indispensable than material improvement. To know is a sacrament, to think is the prime necessity, truth is nourishment as well as grain. A reason that fasts from science and wisdom grows thin. Let us enter equal complaint against stomachs and minds that do not eat. If there is anything more heartbreaking than a body perishing for lack of bread, it is a soul that is dying from hunger for the light.

The whole of progress tends in the direction of solution. Some day we shall be amazed. As the human race mounts upward, the deep layers emerge naturally from the zone of distress. The obliteration of misery will be accomplished by a simple elevation of level.

We should do wrong were we to doubt this blessed consummation.

The past is very strong, it is true, at the present moment. It censures. This rejuvenation of a corpse is surprising. Behold, it is walking and advancing. It seems a victor; this dead body is a conqueror. He arrives with his legions, superstitions; with his sword, despotism; with his banner, ignorance; a while ago, he won ten battles. He advances, he threatens, he laughs, he is at our doors. Let us not despair, on our side. Let us sell the field on which Hannibal is encamped.

What have we to fear, we who believe?

No such thing as a backflow of ideas exists any more than there exists a return of a river on its course.

But let those who do not desire a future reflect on this matter. When they say "no" to progress, it is not the future but themselves that they are condemning. They are giving themselves a sad malady; they are inoculating themselves with the past. There is but one way of rejecting tomorrow, and that is to die.

Now, no death, that of the body as late as possible, that of the soul never, this is what we desire.

Yes, the enigma will utter its word, the sphinx will speak, the problem will be solved.

Yes, the people, sketched out by the eighteenth century, will be finished by the nineteenth. He who doubts this is an idiot! The future blossoming, the near blossoming forth of universal well-being, is a divinely fatal phenomenon.

Immense combined propulsions direct human affairs and conduct them within a given time to a logical state, that is to say, to a state of equilibrium; that is to say, to equity. A force composed of earth and heaven results from humanity and governs it; this force is a worker of miracles; marvelous issues are no more difficult to it than extraordinary vicissitudes. Aided by science, which comes from one man, and by the event, which comes from another, it is not greatly alarmed by these contradictions in the attitude of problems, which seem impossibilities to the vulgar herd. It is no less skillful at causing a solution to spring forth from the reconciliation of ideas, than a lesson from the reconciliation of facts, and we may expect anything from that mysterious power of progress, which brought the Orient and the Occident face-to-face one fine day, in the depths of a sepulchre, and made the imaums converse with Bonaparte in the interior of the Great Pyramid.

In the meantime, let there be no halt, no hesitation, no pause in the grandiose onward march of minds. Social philosophy consists essentially in science and peace. Its object is, and its result must be, to dissolve wrath by the study of antagonisms. It examines, it scrutinizes, it analyzes; then it puts together once more, it proceeds by means of reduction, discarding all hatred.

More than once, a society has been seen to give way before the wind, which is let loose upon mankind; history is full of the shipwrecks of nations and empires; manners, customs, laws, religions, and some fine day that unknown force, the hurricane, passes by and bears them all away. The civilizations of India, of Chaldea, of Persia, of Syria, of Egypt, have disappeared one after the other. Why? We know not. What are the causes of these disasters? We do not know. Could these societies have been saved? Was it their fault? Did they persist in the fatal vice that destroyed them? What is the amount of suicide in these terrible deaths of a nation and a race? Questions to which there exists no reply. Darkness enwraps condemned civilizations. They sprung a leak, then they sank. We have nothing more to say; and it is with a sort of terror that we look on, at the bottom of that sea, which is called the past, behind those colossal waves, at the shipwreck of those immense vessels, Babylon, Nineveh, Tarsus, Thebes, Rome, beneath the fearful gusts that emerge from all the mouths of the shadows. But shadows are there, and light is here. We are not acquainted with the maladies of these ancient civilizations, we do not know the infirmities of our own. Everywhere upon it we have the right of light, we contemplate its beauties, we lay bare its defects. Where it is ill, we probe; and the sickness once diagnosed, the study of the cause leads to the discovery of the remedy. Our civilization, the work of twenty centuries, is its law and its prodigy; it is worth the trouble of saving. It will be saved. It is already much to have solaced it; its enlightenment is yet another point. All the labors of modern social philosophies must converge toward this point. The thinker of today has a great duty—to auscultate civilization.

We repeat, that this auscultation brings encouragement; it is by this persistence in encouragement that we wish to conclude these pages, an austere interlude in a mournful drama. Beneath the social mortality, we feel human imperishableness. The globe does not perish, because it has these wounds, craters, eruptions, sulfur pits, here and there, nor because of a volcano that ejects its pus. The maladies of the people do not kill man.

And yet, anyone who follows the course of social clinics shakes his head at times. The strongest, the tenderest, the most logical have their hours of weakness.

Will the future arrive? It seems as though we might almost put this question, when we behold so much terrible darkness. Melancholy face-to-face encounter of selfish and wretched. On the part of the selfish, the prejudices, shadows of costly education, appetite increasing through intoxication, a giddiness of prosperity that dulls, a fear of suffering that, in some, goes as far as an aversion for the suffering, an implacable satisfaction, the I so swollen that it bars the soul; on the side of the wretched covetousness, envy, hatred of seeing others enjoy, the profound impulses of the human beast toward assuaging its desires, hearts full of mist, sadness, need, fatality, impure and simple ignorance.

Shall we continue to raise our eyes to heaven? Is the luminous point, which we distinguish there, one of those that vanish? The ideal is frightful to behold, thus lost in the depths, small, isolated, imperceptible, brilliant, but surrounded by those great, black menaces, monstrously heaped around it; yet no more in danger than a star in the maw of the clouds.

BOOK EIGHTH: ENCHANTMENTS AND DESOLATIONS

CHAPTER I—FULL LIGHT

The reader has probably understood that Eponine, having recognized through the gate, the inhabitant of that Rue Plumet where Magnon had sent her, had begun by keeping the ruffians away from the Rue Plumet, and had then conducted Marius there, and that, after many days spent in ecstasy before that gate, Marius, drawn on by that force, which draws the iron to the magnet and a lover toward the stones of which is built the house of her whom he loves, had finally entered Cosette's garden as Romeo entered the garden of Juliet. This had even proved easier for him than for Romeo; Romeo was obliged to scale a wall, Marius had only to use a little force on one of the bars of the decrepit gate, which vacillated in its rusty recess, after the fashion of old people's teeth. Marius was slender and readily passed through.

As there was never anyone in the street, and as Marius never entered the garden except at night, he ran no risk of being seen.

Beginning with that blessed and holy hour when a kiss betrothed these two souls, Marius was there every evening. If, at that period of her existence, Cosette had fallen in love with a man in the least unscrupulous or debauched, she would have been lost; for there are generous natures that yield themselves, and Cosette was one of them. One of woman's magnanimities is to yield. Love, at the height where it is absolute, is complicated with some indescribably celestial blindness of modesty. But what dangers you run, O noble souls! Often you give the heart, and we take the body. Your heart remains with you, you gaze upon it in the gloom with a shudder. Love has no middle course; it either ruins or it saves. All human destiny lies in this dilemma. This dilemma, ruin, or safety, is set forth no more inexorably by any fatality than by love. Love is life, if it is not death. Cradle; also coffin. The same sentiment says "yes" and "no" in the human heart. Of all the things that God has made, the human heart is the one that sheds the most light, alas! And the most darkness.

God willed that Cosette's love should encounter one of the loves that save.

Throughout the whole of the month of May of that year 1832, there were there, in every night, in that poor, neglected garden, beneath that thicket, which grew thicker and more fragrant day by day, two beings composed of all chastity, all innocence, overflowing with all the felicity of heaven, nearer to the archangels than to mankind, pure, honest, intoxicated, radiant, who shone for each other amid the shadows. It seemed to Cosette that Marius had a crown, and to Marius that Cosette had a nimbus. They touched each other, they gazed at each other, they clasped each other's hands, they pressed close to each other; but there was a distance that they did not pass. Not that they respected it; they did not know of its existence. Marius was conscious of a barrier, Cosette's innocence; and Cosette of a support, Marius's loyalty. The first kiss had also been the last. Marius, since that time, had not gone further than to touch Cosette's hand, or her kerchief, or a lock of her hair, with his lips. For him, Cosette was a perfume and not a woman. He inhaled her. She refused nothing, and he asked nothing. Cosette was happy, and Marius was satisfied. They lived in this ecstatic state that can be described as the dazzling of one soul by another soul. It was the ineffable first embrace of two maiden souls in the ideal. Two swans meeting on the Jungfrau.

At that hour of love, an hour when voluptuousness is absolutely mute, beneath the omnipotence of ecstasy, Marius, the pure and seraphic Marius, would rather have gone to a woman of the town than have raised Cosette's robe to the height of her ankle. Once, in the moonlight, Cosette stooped to pick up something on the ground, her bodice fell apart and permitted a glimpse of the beginning of her throat. Marius turned away his eyes.

What took place between these two beings? Nothing. They adored each other.

At night, when they were there, that garden seemed a living and a sacred spot. All flowers unfolded around them and sent them incense; and they opened their souls and scattered them over the flowers. The wanton and vigorous vegetation quivered, full of strength and intoxication, around these two innocents, and they uttered words of love that set the trees to trembling.

What words were these? Breaths. Nothing more. These breaths sufficed to trouble and to touch all nature roundabout. Magic power, which we should find it difficult to understand were we to read in a book, these conversations that are made to be borne away and dispersed like smoke wreaths by the breeze beneath the leaves. Take from those murmurs of two lovers that melody, which proceeds from the soul and which accompanies them like a lyre, and what remains is nothing more than a shade; you say, "What! Is that all!" Eh! Yes, childish prattle, repetitions, laughter at nothing, nonsense, everything that is deepest and most sublime in the world! The only things that are worth the trouble of saying and hearing!

The man who has never heard, the man who has never uttered these absurdities, these paltry remarks, is an imbecile and a malicious fellow. Cosette said to Marius, "Dost thou know—?"

"Dost thou know? My name is Euphrasie."

"Euphrasie? Why, no, thy name is Cosette."

"Oh! Cosette is a very ugly name that was given to me when I was a little thing. But my real name is Euphrasie. Dost thou like that name—Euphrasie?"

"Yes. But Cosette is not ugly."

"Do you like it better than Euphrasie?"

"Why, yes."

"Then I like it better too. Truly, it is pretty, Cosette. Call me Cosette."

And the smile that she added made of this dialogue an idyll worthy of a grove situated in heaven. On another occasion she gazed intently at him and exclaimed, "Monsieur, you are handsome, you are goodlooking, you are witty, you are not at all stupid, you are much more learned than I am, but I bid you defiance with this word: I love you!"

And Marius, in the very heavens, thought he heard a strain sung by a star.

Or she bestowed on him a gentle tap because he coughed, and she said to him:

"Don't cough, Sir; I will not have people cough on my domain without my permission. It's very naughty to cough and to disturb me. I want you to be well, because, in the first place, if you were not well, I should be very unhappy. What should I do then?"

And this was simply divine.

Once Marius said to Cosette, "Just imagine, I thought at one time that your name was Ursule."

This made both of them laugh the whole evening.

In the middle of another conversation, he chanced to exclaim, "Oh! One day, at the Luxembourg, I had a good mind to finish breaking up a veteran!" But he stopped short, and went no further. He would have been obliged to speak to Cosette of her garter, and that was impossible. This bordered on a strange theme, the flesh, before which that immense and innocent love recoiled with a sort of sacred fright.

Marius pictured life with Cosette to himself like this, without anything else; to come every evening to the Rue Plumet, to displace the old and accommodating bar of the chief-justice's gate, to sit elbow to elbow on that bench, to gaze through the trees at the scintillation of the oncoming night, to fit a fold of the knee of his trousers into the ample fall of Cosette's gown, to caress her thumbnail, to call her thou, to smell of the same flower, one after the other, forever, indefinitely. During this time, clouds passed above their heads. Every time that the wind blows, it bears with it more of the dreams of men than of the clouds of heaven.

This chaste, almost shy love was not devoid of gallantry, by any means. To pay compliments to the woman whom a man loves is the first method of bestowing caresses, and he is half audacious who tries it. A compliment is something like a kiss through a veil. Voluptuousness mingles there with its sweet tiny point, while it hides itself. The heart draws back before voluptuousness only to love the more. Marius's blandishments, all saturated with fancy, were, so to speak, of azure hue. The birds when they fly up yonder, in the direction of the angels, must hear such words. There were mingled with them, nevertheless, life, humanity, all the positiveness of which Marius was capable. It was what is said in the bower, a prelude to what will be said in the chamber; a lyrical effusion, strophe and sonnet intermingled, pleasing hyperboles of cooing, all the refinements of adoration arranged in a bouquet and exhaling a celestial perfume, an ineffable twitter of heart to heart.

"Oh!" murmured Marius. "How beautiful you are! I dare not look at you. It is all over with me when I contemplate you. You are a grace. I know not what is the matter with me. The hem of your gown, when the tip of your shoe peeps from beneath, upsets me. And then, what an enchanted gleam when you open your thought even but a little! You talk astonishingly good sense. It seems to me at times that you are a dream. Speak, I listen, I admire. Oh Cosette! How strange it is and how charming! I am really beside myself. You are adorable, Mademoiselle. I study your feet with the microscope and your soul with the telescope."

And Cosette answered, "I have been loving a little more all the time that has passed since this morning."

Questions and replies took care of themselves in this dialogue, which always turned with mutual consent upon love, as the little pith figures always turn on their peg.

Cosette's whole person was ingenuousness, ingenuity, transparency, whiteness, candor, radiance. It might have been said of Cosette that she was clear. She produced on those who saw her the sensation of April and dawn. There was dew in her eyes. Cosette was a condensation of the auroral light in the form of a woman.

It was quite simple that Marius should admire her, since he adored her. But the truth is, that this little schoolgirl, fresh from the convent, talked with exquisite penetration and uttered, at times, all sorts of true and delicate sayings. Her prattle was conversation. She never made a mistake about anything, and she saw things justly. The woman feels and speaks with the tender instinct of the heart, which is infallible.

No one understands so well as a woman, how to say things that are, at once, both sweet and deep. Sweetness and depth, they are the whole of woman; in them lies the whole of heaven.

In this full felicity, tears welled up to their eyes every instant. A crushed ladybug, a feather fallen from a nest, a branch of hawthorn broken, aroused their pity, and their ecstasy, sweetly mingled with melancholy, seemed to ask nothing better than to weep. The most sovereign symptom of love is a tenderness that is, at times, almost unbearable.

And, in addition to this, all these contradictions are the lightning play of love, they were fond of laughing, they laughed readily and with a delicious freedom, and so familiarly that they sometimes presented the air of two boys.

Still, though unknown to hearts intoxicated with purity, nature is always present and will not be forgotten. She is there with her brutal and sublime object; and however great may be the innocence of souls, one feels in the most modest private interview, the adorable and mysterious shade that separates a couple of lovers from a pair of friends.

They idolized each other.

The permanent and the immutable are persistent. People live, they smile, they laugh, they make little grimaces with the tips of their lips, they interlace their fingers, they call each other thou, and that does not prevent eternity.

Two lovers hide themselves in the evening, in the twilight, in the invisible, with the birds, with the roses; they fascinate each other in the darkness with their hearts, which they throw into their eyes, they murmur, they whisper, and in the meantime, immense librations of the planets fill the infinite universe.

CHAPTER II—THE BEWILDERMENT
OF PERFECT HAPPINESS

They existed vaguely, frightened at their happiness. They did not notice the cholera that decimated Paris precisely during that very month. They had confided in each other as far as possible, but this had not extended much further than their names. Marius had told Cosette that he was an orphan, that his name was Marius Pontmercy, that he was a lawyer, that he lived by writing things for publishers, that his father had been a colonel, that the latter had been a hero, and that he, Marius, was on bad terms with his grandfather who was rich. He had also hinted at being a baron, but this had produced no effect on Cosette. She did not know the meaning of the word. Marius was Marius. On her side, she had confided to him that she had been brought up at the Petit-Picpus convent, that her mother, like his own, was dead, that her father's name was M. Fauchelevent, that he was very good, that he gave a great deal to the poor, but that he was poor himself, and that he denied himself everything though he denied her nothing.

Strange to say, in the sort of symphony that Marius had lived since he had been in the habit of seeing Cosette, the past, even the most recent past, had become so confused and distant to him, that what Cosette told him satisfied him completely. It did not even occur to him to tell her about the nocturnal adventure in the hovel, about Thenardier, about the burn, and about the strange attitude and singular flight of her father. Marius had momentarily forgotten all this; in the evening he did not even know that there had been a morning, what he had done, where he had breakfasted, nor who had spoken to him; he had songs in his ears that rendered him deaf to every other thought; he only existed at the hours when he saw Cosette. Then, as he was in heaven, it was quite natural that he should forget earth. Both bore languidly the indefinable burden of immaterial pleasures. Thus lived these somnambulists who are called lovers.

Alas! Who is there who has not felt all these things? Why does there come an hour when one emerges from this azure, and why does life go on afterward?

Loving almost takes the place of thinking. Love is an ardent forgetfulness of all the rest. Then ask logic of passion if you will. There is no more absolute logical sequence in the human heart than there is a perfect geometrical figure in the celestial mechanism. For Cosette and Marius, nothing existed except Marius and Cosette. The universe around them had fallen into a hole. They lived in a golden minute. There was nothing before them, nothing behind. It hardly occurred to Marius that Cosette had a father. His brain was dazzled and obliterated. Of what did these lovers talk then? We have seen, of the flowers, and the swallows, the setting sun and the rising moon, and all sorts of important things. They had told each other everything except everything. The everything of lovers is nothing. But the father, the realities, that lair, the ruffians, that adventure, to what purpose? And was he very sure that this nightmare had actually existed? They were two, and they adored each other, and beyond that there was nothing. Nothing else existed. It is probable that this vanishing of hell in our rear is inherent to the arrival of paradise. Have we beheld demons? Are there any? Have we trembled? Have we suffered? We no longer know. A rosy cloud hangs over it.

So these two beings lived in this manner, high aloft, with all that improbability, which is in nature; neither at the nadir nor at the zenith, between man and seraphim, above the mire, below the ether, in the clouds; hardly flesh and blood, soul and ecstasy from head to foot; already too sublime to walk the earth, still too heavily charged with humanity to disappear in the blue, suspended like atoms that are waiting to be precipitated; apparently beyond the bounds of destiny; ignorant of that rut; yesterday, today, tomorrow; amazed, rapturous, floating, soaring; at times so light that they could take their flight out into the infinite; almost prepared to soar away to all eternity. They slept wide awake, thus sweetly lulled. Oh! Splendid lethargy of the real overwhelmed by the ideal.

Sometimes, beautiful as Cosette was, Marius shut his eyes in her presence. The best way to look at the soul is through closed eyes.

Marius and Cosette never asked themselves where this was to lead them. They considered that they had already arrived. It is a strange claim on man's part to wish that love should lead to something.

CHAPTER III—THE BEGINNING
OF SHADOW

Jean Valjean suspected nothing.

Cosette, who was rather less dreamy than Marius, was gay, and that sufficed for Jean Valjean's happiness. The thoughts that Cosette cherished, her tender preoccupations, Marius's image, which filled her heart, took away nothing from the incomparable purity of her beautiful, chaste, and smiling brow. She was at the age when the virgin bears her love as the angel his lily. So Jean Valjean was at ease. And then, when two lovers have come to an understanding, things always go well; the third party who might disturb their love is kept in a state of perfect blindness by a restricted number of precautions that are always the same in the case of all lovers. Thus, Cosette never objected to any of Jean Valjean's proposals. Did she want to take a walk? "Yes, dear little father." Did she want to stay at home? Very good. Did he wish to pass the evening with Cosette? She was delighted. As he always went to bed at ten o'clock, Marius did not come to the garden on such occasions until after that hour, when, from the street, he heard Cosette open the long glass door on the veranda. Of course, no one ever met Marius in the daytime. Jean Valjean never even dreamed any longer that Marius was in existence. Only once, one morning, he chanced to say to Cosette, "Why, you have whitewash on your back!" On the previous evening, Marius, in a transport, had pushed Cosette against the wall.

Old Toussaint, who retired early, thought of nothing but her sleep, and was as ignorant of the whole matter as Jean Valjean.

Marius never set foot in the house. When he was with Cosette, they hid themselves in a recess near the steps, in order that they might neither be seen nor heard from the street, and there they sat, frequently contenting themselves, by way of conversation, with pressing each other's hands twenty times a minute as they gazed at the branches of the trees. At such times, a thunderbolt might have fallen thirty paces from them, and they would not have noticed it, so deeply was the reverie of the one absorbed and sunk in the reverie of the other.

Limpid purity. Hours wholly white; almost all alike. This sort of love is a recollection of lily petals and the plumage of the dove.

The whole extent of the garden lay between them and the street. Every time that Marius entered and left, he carefully adjusted the bar of the gate in such a manner that no displacement was visible.

He usually went away about midnight, and returned to Courfeyrac's lodgings. Courfeyrac said to Bahorel, "Would you believe it? Marius comes home nowadays at one o'clock in the morning."

Bahorel replied, "What do you expect? There's always a petard in a seminary fellow."

At times, Courfeyrac folded his arms, assumed a serious air, and said to Marius, "You are getting irregular in your habits, young man."

Courfeyrac, being a practical man, did not take in good part this reflection of an invisible paradise upon Marius; he was not much in the habit of concealed passions; it made him impatient, and now and then he called upon Marius to come back to reality.

One morning, he threw him this admonition, "My dear fellow, you produce upon me the effect of being located in the moon, the realm of dreams, the province of illusions, capital, soap bubble. Come, be a good boy, what's her name?"

But nothing could induce Marius "to talk." They might have torn out his nails before one of the two sacred syllables of which that ineffable name, Cosette, was composed. True love is as luminous as the dawn and as silent as the tomb. Only, Courfeyrac saw this change in Marius, that his taciturnity was of the beaming order.

During this sweet month of May, Marius and Cosette learned to know these immense delights. To dispute and to say you for thou, simply that they might say thou the better afterward. To talk at great length with very minute details, of persons in whom they took not the slightest interest in the world; another proof that in that ravishing opera called love, the libretto counts for almost nothing.

For Marius, to listen to Cosette discussing finery.

For Cosette, to listen to Marius talk in politics.

To listen, knee pressed to knee, to the carriages rolling along the Rue de Babylone.

To gaze upon the same planet in space, or at the same glowworm gleaming in the grass.

To hold their peace together; a still greater delight than conversation.

Etc., etc.

In the meantime, diverse complications were approaching.

One evening, Marius was on his way to the rendezvous, by way of the Boulevard des Invalides. He habitually walked with drooping head. As he was on the point of turning the corner of the Rue Plumet, he heard someone quite close to him say, "Good evening, Monsieur Marius."

He raised his head and recognized Eponine.

This produced a singular effect upon him. He had not thought of that girl a single time since the day when she had conducted him to the Rue Plumet, he had not seen her again, and she had gone completely out of his mind. He had no reasons for anything but gratitude toward her, he owed her his happiness, and yet, it was embarrassing to him to meet her.

It is an error to think that passion, when it is pure and happy, leads man to a state of perfection; it simply leads him, as we have noted, to a state of oblivion. In this situation, man forgets to be bad, but he also forgets to be good. Gratitude, duty, matters essential and important to be remembered, vanish. At any other time, Marius would have behaved quite differently to Eponine. Absorbed in Cosette, he had not even clearly put it to himself that this Eponine was named Eponine Thenardier, and that she bore the name inscribed in his father's will, that name, for which, but a few months before, he would have so ardently sacrificed himself. We show Marius as he was. His father himself was fading out of his soul to some extent, under the splendor of his love.

He replied with some embarrassment, "Ah! So it's you, Eponine?"

"Why do you call me you? Have I done anything to you?"

"No," he answered.

Certainly, he had nothing against her. Far from it. Only, he felt that he could not do otherwise, now that he used thou to Cosette, than say you to Eponine.

As he remained silent, she exclaimed, "Say—"

Then she paused. It seemed as though words failed that creature formerly so heedless and so bold. She tried to smile and could not. Then she resumed, "Well?"

Then she paused again, and remained with downcast eyes.

"Good evening, Mr. Marius," said she suddenly and abruptly; and away she went.

CHAPTER IV—A CAB RUNS IN ENGLISH AND BARKS IN SLANG

The following day was the 3rd of June, 1832, a date that is necessary to indicate on account of the grave events that, at that epoch, hung on the horizon of Paris in the state of lightning-charged clouds. Marius, at nightfall, was pursuing the same road as on the preceding evening, with the same thoughts of delight in his heart, when he caught sight of Eponine approaching, through the trees of the boulevard. Two days in succession—this was too much. He turned hastily aside, quitted the boulevard, changed his course and went to the Rue Plumet through the Rue Monsieur.

This caused Eponine to follow him to the Rue Plumet, a thing that she had not yet done. Up to that time, she had contented herself with watching him on his passage along the boulevard without ever seeking to encounter him. It was only on the evening before that she had attempted to address him.

So Eponine followed him, without his suspecting the fact. She saw him displace the bar and slip into the garden.

She approached the railing, felt of the bars one after the other, and readily recognized the one that Marius had moved.

She murmured in a low voice and in gloomy accents, "None of that, Lisette!"

She seated herself on the underpinning of the railing, close beside the bar, as though she were guarding it. It was precisely at the point where the railing touched the neighboring wall. There was a dim nook there, in which Eponine was entirely concealed.

She remained thus for more than an hour, without stirring and without breathing, a prey to her thoughts.

Toward ten o'clock in the evening, one of the two or three persons who passed through the Rue Plumet, an old, belated bourgeois who was making haste to escape from this deserted spot of evil repute, as he skirted the garden railings and reached the angle which it made with the wall, heard a dull and threatening voice saying, "I'm no longer surprised that he comes here every evening."

The passerby cast a glance around him, saw no one, dared not peer into the black niche, and was greatly alarmed. He redoubled his pace.

This passerby had reason to make haste, for a very few instants later, six men, who were marching separately and at some distance from each other, along the wall, and who might have been taken for a gray patrol, entered the Rue Plumet.

The first to arrive at the garden railing halted, and waited for the others; a second later, all six were reunited.

These men began to talk in a low voice.

"This is the place," said one of them.

"Is there a cab [dog] in the garden?" asked another.

"I don't know. In any case, I have fetched a ball that we'll make him eat."

"Have you some putty to break the pane with?"

"Yes."

"The railing is old," interpolated a fifth, who had the voice of a ventriloquist.

"So much the better," said the second who had spoken. "It won't screech under the saw, and it won't be hard to cut."

The sixth, who had not yet opened his lips, now began to inspect the gate, as Eponine had done an hour earlier, grasping each bar in succession, and shaking them cautiously.

Thus he came to the bar that Marius had loosened. As he was on the point of grasping this bar, a hand emerged abruptly from the darkness, fell upon his arm; he felt himself vigorously thrust aside by a push in the middle of his breast, and a hoarse voice said to him, but not loudly, "There's a dog."

At the same moment, he perceived a pale girl standing before him.

The man underwent that shock which the unexpected always brings. He bristled up in hideous wise; nothing is so formidable to behold as ferocious beasts who are uneasy; their terrified air evokes terror.

He recoiled and stammered, "What jade is this?"

"Your daughter."

It was, in fact, Eponine, who had addressed Thenardier.

At the apparition of Eponine, the other five, that is to say, Claquesous, Guelemer, Babet, Brujon, and Montparnasse had noiselessly drawn near, without precipitation, without uttering a word, with the sinister slowness peculiar to these men of the night.

Some indescribable but hideous tools were visible in their hands. Guelemer held one of those pairs of curved pincers which prowlers call *fanchons*.

"Ah, see here, what are you about there? What do you want with us? Are you crazy?" exclaimed Thenardier, as loudly as one can exclaim and still speak low; "what have you come here to hinder our work for?"

Eponine burst out laughing, and threw herself on his neck.

"I am here, little father, because I am here. Isn't a person allowed to sit on the stones nowadays? It's you who ought not to be here. What have you come here for, since it's a biscuit? I told Magnon so. There's nothing to be done here. But embrace me, my good little father! It's a long time since I've seen you! So you're out?"

Thenardier tried to disentangle himself from Eponine's arms, and grumbled, "That's good. You've embraced me. Yes, I'm out. I'm not in. Now, get away with you."

But Eponine did not release her hold, and redoubled her caresses.

"But how did you manage it, little pa? You must have been very clever to get out of that. Tell me about it! And my mother? Where is mother? Tell me about mama."

Thenardier replied, "She's well. I don't know, let me alone, and be off, I tell you."

"I won't go, so there now," pouted Eponine like a spoiled child; "you send me off, and it's four months since I saw you, and I've hardly had time to kiss you."

And she caught her father around the neck again.

"Come, now, this is stupid!" said Babet.

"Make haste!" said Guelemer. "The cops may pass."

The ventriloquist's voice repeated his distich:

> *Nous n' sommes pas le jour de l'an,*
> This isn't New Year's day
> *A bécoter papa, maman."*
> To peck at pa and ma.

Eponine turned to the five ruffians.

"Why, it's Monsieur Brujon. Good day, Monsieur Babet. Good day, Monsieur Claquesous. Don't you know me, Monsieur Guelemer? How goes it, Montparnasse?"

"Yes, they know you!" ejaculated Thenardier. "But good day, good evening, sheer off! Leave us alone!"

"It's the hour for foxes, not for chickens," said Montparnasse.

"You see the job we have on hand here," added Babet.

Eponine caught Montparnasse's hand.

"Take care," said he, "you'll cut yourself, I've a knife open."

"My little Montparnasse," responded Eponine very gently, "you must have confidence in people. I am the daughter of my father, perhaps. Monsieur Babet, Monsieur Guelemer, I'm the person who was charged to investigate this matter."

It is remarkable that Eponine did not talk slang. That frightful tongue had become impossible to her since she had known Marius.

She pressed in her hand, small, bony, and feeble as that of a skeleton, Guelemer's huge, coarse fingers, and continued, "You know well that I'm no fool. Ordinarily, I am believed. I have rendered your service on various occasions. Well, I have made inquiries; you will expose yourselves to no purpose, you see. I swear to you that there is nothing in this house."

"There are lone women," said Guelemer.

"No, the persons have moved away."

"The candles haven't, anyway!" ejaculated Babet.

And he pointed out to Eponine, across the tops of the trees, a light that was wandering about in the mansard roof of the pavilion. It was Toussaint, who had stayed up to spread out some linen to dry.

Eponine made a final effort.

"Well," said she, "they're very poor folks, and it's a hovel where there isn't a sou."

"Go to the devil!" cried Thenardier. "When we've turned the house upside down and put the cellar at the top and the attic below, we'll tell you what there is inside, and whether it's francs or sous or half-farthings."

And he pushed her aside with the intention of entering.

"My good friend, Mr. Montparnasse," said Eponine, "I entreat you, you are a good fellow, don't enter."

"Take care, you'll cut yourself," replied Montparnasse.

Thenardier resumed in his decided tone, "Decamp, my girl, and leave men to their own affairs!"

Eponine released Montparnasse's hand, which she had grasped again, and said, "So you mean to enter this house?"

"Rather!" grinned the ventriloquist.

Then she set her back against the gate, faced the six ruffians who were armed to the teeth, and to whom the night lent the visages of demons, and said in a firm, low voice, "Well, I don't mean that you shall."

They halted in amazement. The ventriloquist, however, finished his grin. She went on:

"Friends! Listen well. This is not what you want. Now I'm talking. In the first place, if you enter this garden, if you lay a hand on this gate, I'll scream, I'll beat on the door, I'll rouse everybody, I'll have the whole six of you seized, I'll call the police."

"She'd do it, too," said Thenardier in a low tone to Brujon and the ventriloquist.

She shook her head and added, "Beginning with my father!"

Thenardier stepped nearer.

"Not so close, my good man!" said she.

He retreated, growling between his teeth, "Why, what's the matter with her?"

And he added, "Bitch!"

She began to laugh in a terrible way, "As you like, but you shall not enter here. I'm not the daughter of a dog, since I'm the daughter of a wolf. There are six of you, what matters that to me? You are men. Well, I'm a woman. You don't frighten me. I tell you that you shan't enter this house, because it doesn't suit me. If you approach, I'll bark. I told you, I'm the dog, and I don't care a straw for you. Go your way, you bore me! Go where you please, but don't come here, I forbid it! You can use your knives. I'll use kicks; it's all the same to me, come on!"

She advanced a pace nearer the ruffians, she was terrible, she burst out laughing.

"Pardine! I'm not afraid. I shall be hungry this summer, and I shall be cold this winter. Aren't they ridiculous, these ninnies of men, to think they can scare a girl! What! Scare? Oh, yes, much! Because you have finical poppets of mistresses who hide under the bed when you put on a big voice, forsooth! I ain't afraid of anything, that I ain't!"

She fastened her intent gaze upon Thenardier and said, "Not even of you, father!"

Then she continued, as she cast her bloodshot, specterlike eyes upon the ruffians in turn, "What do I care if I'm picked up tomorrow morning on the pavement of the Rue Plumet, killed by the blows of my father's club, or whether I'm found a year from now in the nets at Saint-Cloud or the Isle of Swans in the midst of rotten old corks and drowned dogs?"

She was forced to pause; she was seized by a dry cough, her breath came from her weak and narrow chest like the death rattle.

She resumed, "I have only to cry out, and people will come, and then slap, bang! There are six of you; I represent the whole world."

Thenardier made a movement toward her.

"Don't approach!" she cried.

He halted, and said gently, "Well, no; I won't approach, but don't speak so loud. So you intend to hinder us in our work, my daughter? But we must earn our living all the same. Have you no longer any kind feeling for your father?"

"You bother me," said Eponine.

"But we must live, we must eat—"

"Burst!"

So saying, she seated herself on the underpinning of the fence and hummed,

> *Mon bras si dodu,*
> *Ma jambe bien faite*
> *Et le temps perdu.**

She had set her elbow on her knee and her chin in her hand, and she swung her foot with an air of indifference. Her tattered gown permitted a view of her thin shoulder blades. The neighboring street lantern illuminated her profile and her attitude. Nothing more resolute and more surprising could be seen.

The six rascals, speechless and gloomy at being held in check by a girl, retreated beneath the shadow cast by the lantern, and held counsel with furious and humiliated shrugs.

In the meantime she stared at them with a stern but peaceful air.

"There's something the matter with her," said Babet. "A reason. Is she in love with the dog? It's a shame to miss this, anyway. Two women, an old fellow who lodges in the backyard, and curtains that ain't so bad at the windows. The old cove must be a Jew. I think the job's a good one."

"Well, go in, then, the rest of you," exclaimed Montparnasse. "Do the job. I'll stay here with the girl, and if she fails us—"

He flashed the knife, which he held open in his hand, in the light of the lantern.

Thenardier said not a word, and seemed ready for whatever the rest pleased.

Brujon, who was somewhat of an oracle, and who had, as the reader knows, "put up the job," had not as yet spoken. He seemed thoughtful. He had the reputation of not sticking at anything, and it was known that he had plundered a police post simply out of bravado. Besides this he made verses and songs, which gave him great authority.

Babet interrogated him, "You say nothing, Brujon?"

Brujon remained silent an instant longer, then he shook his head in various ways, and finally concluded to speak, "See here; this morning I came across

---

* My arm so plump/My leg well formed,/And time wasted.

two sparrows fighting, this evening I jostled a woman who was quarrelling. All that's bad. Let's quit."

They went away.

As they went, Montparnasse muttered, "Never mind! If they had wanted, I'd have cut her throat."

Babet responded, "I wouldn't. I don't hit a lady."

At the corner of the street they halted and exchanged the following enigmatical dialogue in a low tone, "Where shall we go to sleep tonight?"

"Under Pantin [Paris]."

"Have you the key to the gate, Thenardier?"

"*Pardi*."

Eponine, who never took her eyes off of them, saw them retreat by the road by which they had come. She rose and began to creep after them along the walls and the houses. She followed them thus as far as the boulevard.

There they parted, and she saw these six men plunge into the gloom, where they appeared to melt away.

CHAPTER V—THINGS OF THE NIGHT

After the departure of the ruffians, the Rue Plumet resumed its tranquil, nocturnal aspect. That which had just taken place in this street would not have astonished a forest. The lofty trees, the copses, the heaths, the branches rudely interlaced, the tall grass, exist in a somber manner; the savage swarming there catches glimpses of sudden apparitions of the invisible; that which is below man distinguishes, through the mists, that which is beyond man; and the things of which we living beings are ignorant there meet face-to-face in the night. Nature, bristling and wild, takes alarm at certain approaches in which she fancies that she feels the supernatural. The forces of the gloom know each other, and are strangely balanced by each other. Teeth and claws fear what they cannot grasp. Blood-drinking bestiality, voracious appetites, hunger in search of prey, the armed instincts of nails and jaws that have for source and aim the belly, glare and smell out uneasily the impassive spectral forms straying beneath a shroud, erect in its vague and shuddering robe, and which seem to them to live with a dead and terrible life. These brutalities, which are only matter, entertain a confused fear of having to deal with the immense obscurity condensed into an unknown being. A black figure barring the way stops the wild beast short. That which emerges from the cemetery intimidates and disconcerts that which emerges from the cave; the ferocious fear the sinister; wolves recoil when they encounter a ghoul.

CHAPTER VI—MARIUS BECOMES PRACTICAL ONCE MORE TO THE EXTENT OF GIVING COSETTE HIS ADDRESS

While this sort of a dog with a human face was mounting guard over the gate, and while the six ruffians were yielding to a girl, Marius was by Cosette's side.

Never had the sky been more studded with stars and more charming, the trees more trembling, the odor of the grass more penetrating; never had the birds fallen asleep among the leaves with a sweeter noise; never had all the harmonies of universal serenity responded more thoroughly to the inward music of love; never had Marius been more captivated, more happy, more ecstatic.

But he had found Cosette sad; Cosette had been weeping. Her eyes were red. This was the first cloud in that wonderful dream.

Marius' first word had been, "What is the matter?"

And she had replied, "This."

Then she had seated herself on the bench near the steps, and while he tremblingly took his place beside her, she had continued, "My father told me this morning to hold myself in readiness, because he has business, and we may go away from here."

Marius shivered from head to foot.

When one is at the end of one's life, to die means to go away; when one is at the beginning of it, to go away means to die.

For the last six weeks, Marius had little by little, slowly, by degrees, taken possession of Cosette each day. As we have already explained, in the case of first love, the soul is taken long before the body; later on, one takes the body long before the soul; sometimes one does not take the soul at all; the Faublas and the Prudhommes add, "Because there is none;" but the sarcasm is, fortunately, a blasphemy. So Marius possessed Cosette, as spirits possess, but he enveloped her with all his soul, and seized her jealously with incredible conviction. He possessed her smile, her breath, her perfume, the profound radiance of her blue eyes, the sweetness of her skin when he touched her hand, the charming mark that she had on her neck, all her thoughts. Therefore, he possessed all Cosette's dreams.

He incessantly gazed at, and he sometimes touched lightly with his breath, the short locks on the nape of her neck, and he declared to himself that there was not one of those short hairs that did not belong to him, Marius. He gazed upon and adored the things that she wore, her knot of ribbon, her gloves, her sleeves, her shoes, her cuffs, as sacred objects of which he was the master. He dreamed that he was the lord of those pretty shell combs that she wore in her hair, and he even said to himself, in confused and suppressed stammerings of voluptuousness, which did not make their way to the light, that there was not a ribbon of her gown, not a mesh in her stockings, not a fold in her bodice, which was not his. Beside Cosette he felt himself beside his own property, his own thing, his own despot and his slave. It seemed as though they had so intermingled their souls, that it would have been impossible to tell them apart had they wished to take them back again. "This is mine."

"No, it is mine."

"I assure you that you are mistaken. This is my property."

"What you are taking as your own is myself."

Marius was something that made a part of Cosette, and Cosette was something that made a part of Marius. Marius felt Cosette within him. To have Cosette, to possess Cosette, this, to him, was not to be distinguished from breathing. It was in the midst of this faith, of this intoxication, of this virgin possession, unprecedented and absolute, of this sovereignty, that these words, "We are going away," fell suddenly, at a blow, and that the harsh voice of reality cried to him, "Cosette is not yours!"

Marius awoke. For six weeks Marius had been living, as we have said, outside of life; those words, "going away!" caused him to reenter it harshly.

He found not a word to say. Cosette merely felt that his hand was very cold. She said to him in her turn, "What is the matter?"

He replied in so low a tone that Cosette hardly heard him, "I did not understand what you said."

She began again, "This morning my father told me to settle all my little affairs and to hold myself in readiness, that he would give me his linen to put in a trunk, that he was obliged to go on a journey, that we were to go away, that it is necessary to have a large trunk for me and a small one for him, and that all is to be ready in a week from now, and that we might go to England."

"But this is outrageous!" exclaimed Marius.

It is certain, that, at that moment, no abuse of power, no violence, not one of the abominations of the worst tyrants, no action of Busiris, of Tiberius, or of Henry VIII, could have equaled this in atrocity, in the opinion of Marius; M. Fauchelevent taking his daughter off to England because he had business there.

He demanded in a weak voice, "And when do you start?"

"He did not say when."

"And when shall you return?"

"He did not say when."

Marius rose and said coldly, "Cosette, shall you go?"

Cosette turned toward him her beautiful eyes, all filled with anguish, and replied in a sort of bewilderment, "Where?"

"To England. Shall you go?"

"Why do you say you to me?"

"I ask you whether you will go?"

"What do you expect me to do?" she said, clasping her hands.

"So, you will go?"

"If my father goes."

"So, you will go?"

Cosette took Marius' hand, and pressed it without replying.

"Very well," said Marius, "then I will go elsewhere."

Cosette felt rather than understood the meaning of these words. She turned so pale that her face shone white through the gloom. She stammered, "What do you mean?"

Marius looked at her, then raised his eyes to heaven, and answered, "Nothing."

When his eyes fell again, he saw Cosette smiling at him. The smile of a woman whom one loves possesses a visible radiance, even at night.

"How silly we are! Marius, I have an idea."

"What is it?"

"If we go away, do you go too! I will tell you where! Come and join me wherever I am."

Marius was now a thoroughly roused man. He had fallen back into reality. He cried to Cosette, "Go away with you! Are you mad? Why, I should have to have money, and I have none! Go to England? But I am in debt now, I owe, I don't know how much, more than ten Louis to Courfeyrac, one of my friends with whom you are not acquainted! I have an old hat that is not worth three francs, I have a coat that lacks buttons in front, my shirt is all ragged, my elbows are torn, my boots let in the water; for the last six weeks I have not thought about it, and I have not told you about it. You only see me at night, and you give me your love; if you were to see me in the daytime, you would give me a sou! Go to England! Eh! I haven't enough to pay for a passport!"

He threw himself against a tree that was close at hand, erect, his brow pressed close to the bark, feeling neither the wood that flayed his skin, nor the fever that was throbbing in his temples, and there he stood motionless, on the point of falling, like the statue of despair.

He remained a long time thus. One could remain for eternity in such abysses. At last he turned around. He heard behind him a faint stifled noise, which was sweet yet sad.

It was Cosette sobbing.

She had been weeping for more than two hours beside Marius as he meditated.

He came to her, fell at her knees, and slowly prostrating himself, he took the tip of her foot, which peeped out from beneath her robe, and kissed it.

She let him have his way in silence. There are moments when a woman accepts, like a somber and resigned goddess, the religion of love.

"Do not weep," he said.

She murmured, "Not when I may be going away, and you cannot come!"

He went on, "Do you love me?"

She replied, sobbing, by that word from paradise that is never more charming than amid tears, "I adore you!"

He continued in a tone that was an indescribable caress, "Do not weep. Tell me, will you do this for me, and cease to weep?"

"Do you love me?" said she.

He took her hand.

"Cosette, I have never given my word of honor to anyone, because my word of honor terrifies me. I feel that my father is by my side. Well, I give you my most sacred word of honor, that if you go away I shall die."

In the tone with which he uttered these words there lay a melancholy so solemn and so tranquil, that Cosette trembled. She felt that chill which is produced by a true and gloomy thing as it passes by. The shock made her cease weeping.

"Now, listen," said he, "do not expect me tomorrow."

"Why?"

"Do not expect me until the day after tomorrow."

"Oh! Why?"

"You will see."

"A day without seeing you! But that is impossible!"

"Let us sacrifice one day in order to gain our whole lives, perhaps."

And Marius added in a low tone and in an aside, "He is a man who never changes his habits, and he has never received anyone except in the evening."

"Of what man are you speaking?" asked Cosette.

"I? I said nothing."

"What do you hope, then?"

"Wait until the day after tomorrow."

"You wish it?"

"Yes, Cosette."

She took his head in both her hands, raising herself on tiptoe in order to be on a level with him, and tried to read his hope in his eyes.

Marius resumed, "Now that I think of it, you ought to know my address: something might happen, one never knows; I live with that friend named Courfeyrac, Rue de la Verrerie, No. 16."

He searched in his pocket, pulled out his penknife, and with the blade he wrote on the plaster of the wall, "16 Rue de la Verrerie."

In the meantime, Cosette had begun to gaze into his eyes once more.

"Tell me your thought, Marius; you have some idea. Tell it to me. Oh! Tell me, so that I may pass a pleasant night."

"This is my idea: that it is impossible that God should mean to part us. Wait; expect me the day after tomorrow."

"What shall I do until then?" said Cosette. "You are outside, you go, and come! How happy men are! I shall remain entirely alone! Oh! How sad I shall be! What is it that you are going to do tomorrow evening? Tell me."

"I am going to try something."

"Then I will pray to God and I will think of you here, so that you may be successful. I will question you no further, since you do not wish it. You are my master. I shall pass the evening tomorrow in singing that music from Euryanthe that you love, and that you came one evening to listen to, outside my shutters. But day after tomorrow you will come early. I shall expect you at dusk, at nine o'clock precisely, I warn you. *Mon Dieu*! How sad it is that the days are so long! On the stroke of nine, do you understand, I shall be in the garden."

"And I also."

And without having uttered it, moved by the same thought, impelled by those electric currents that place lovers in continual communication, both being intoxicated with delight even in their sorrow, they fell into each other's arms, without perceiving that their lips met while their uplifted eyes, overflowing with rapture and full of tears, gazed upon the stars.

When Marius went forth, the street was deserted. This was the moment when Eponine was following the ruffians to the boulevard.

While Marius had been dreaming with his head pressed to the tree, an idea had crossed his mind; an idea, alas! That he himself judged to be senseless and impossible. He had come to a desperate decision.

CHAPTER VII—THE OLD HEART AND THE YOUNG HEART IN THE PRESENCE OF EACH OTHER

At that epoch, Father Gillenormand was well past his ninety-first birthday. He still lived with Mademoiselle Gillenormand in the Rue des Filles-du-Calvaire, No. 6, in the old house he owned. He was, as the reader will remember, one of those antique old men who await death perfectly erect, whom age bears down without bending, and whom even sorrow cannot curve.

Still, his daughter had been saying for some time, "My father is sinking." He no longer boxed the maids' ears; he no longer thumped the landing place so vigorously with his cane when Basque was slow in opening the door. The Revolution of July had exasperated him for the space of barely six months. He had viewed, almost tranquilly, that coupling of words, in the Moniteur:

M. Humblot-Conte, peer of France. The fact is, that the old man was deeply dejected. He did not bend, he did not yield; this was no more a characteristic of his physical than of his moral nature, but he felt himself giving way internally. For four years he had been waiting for Marius, with his foot firmly planted, that is the exact word, in the conviction that that good-for-nothing young scamp would ring at his door some day or other; now he had reached the point, where, at certain gloomy hours, he said to himself, that if Marius made him wait much longer—it was not death that was insupportable to him; it was the idea that perhaps he should never see Marius again. The idea of never seeing Marius again had never entered his brain until that day; now the thought began to recur to him, and it chilled him. Absence, as is always the case in genuine and natural sentiments, had only served to augment the grandfather's love for the ungrateful child, who had gone off like a flash. It is during December nights, when the cold stands at ten degrees, that one thinks oftenest of the son.

M. Gillenormand was, or thought himself, above all things, incapable of taking a single step, he—the grandfather, toward his grandson, "I would die rather," he said to himself. He did not consider himself as the least to blame; but he thought of Marius only with profound tenderness, and the mute despair of an elderly, kindly old man who is about to vanish in the dark.

He began to lose his teeth, which added to his sadness.

M. Gillenormand, without however acknowledging it to himself, for it would have rendered him furious and ashamed, had never loved a mistress as he loved Marius.

He had had placed in his chamber, opposite the head of his bed, so that it should be the first thing on which his eyes fell on waking, an old portrait of his other daughter, who was dead, Madame Pontmercy, a portrait which had been taken when she was eighteen. He gazed incessantly at that portrait. One day, he happened to say, as he gazed upon it, "I think the likeness is strong."

"To my sister?" inquired Mademoiselle Gillenormand. "Yes, certainly."

The old man added, "And to him also."

Once as he sat with his knees pressed together, and his eyes almost closed, in a despondent attitude, his daughter ventured to say to him, "Father, are you as angry with him as ever?"

She paused, not daring to proceed further.

"With whom?" he demanded.

"With that poor Marius."

He raised his aged head, laid his withered and emaciated fist on the table, and exclaimed in his most irritated and vibrating tone, "Poor Marius, do you say! That gentleman is a knave, a wretched scoundrel, a vain little ingrate, a heartless, soulless, haughty, and wicked man!"

And he turned away so that his daughter might not see the tear that stood in his eye.

Three days later he broke a silence that had lasted four hours, to say to his daughter point-blank, "I had the honor to ask Mademoiselle Gillenormand never to mention him to me."

Aunt Gillenormand renounced every effort, and pronounced this acute diagnosis, "My father never cared very much for my sister after her folly. It is clear that he detests Marius."

"After her folly" meant "after she had married the colonel."

However, as the reader has been able to conjecture, Mademoiselle Gillenormand had failed in her attempt to substitute her favorite, the officer of lancers, for Marius. The substitute, Theodule, had not been a success. M. Gillenormand had not accepted the quid pro quo. A vacancy in the heart does not accommodate itself to a stopgap. Theodule, on his side, though he scented the inheritance, was disgusted at the task of pleasing. The goodman bored the lancer; and the lancer shocked the goodman. Lieutenant Theodule was gay, no doubt, but a chatterbox, frivolous, but vulgar; a high liver, but a frequenter of bad company; he had mistresses, it is true, and he had a great deal to say about them, it is true also; but he talked badly. All his good qualities had a defect. M. Gillenormand was worn out with hearing him tell about the love affairs that he had in the vicinity of the barracks in the Rue de Babylone. And then, Lieutenant Gillenormand sometimes came in his uniform, with the tricolored cockade. This rendered him downright intolerable. Finally, Father Gillenormand had said to his daughter, "I've had enough of that Theodule. I haven't much taste for warriors in time of peace. Receive him if you choose. I don't know but I prefer slashers to fellows that drag their swords. The clash of blades in battle is less dismal, after all, than the clank of the scabbard on the pavement. And then, throwing out your chest like a bully and lacing yourself like a girl, with stays under your cuirass, is doubly ridiculous. When one is a veritable man, one holds equally aloof from swagger and from affected airs. He is neither a blusterer nor a finnicky-hearted man. Keep your Theodule for yourself."

It was in vain that his daughter said to him, "But he is your grandnephew, nevertheless." It turned out that M. Gillenormand, who was a grandfather to the very fingertips, was not in the least a grand-uncle.

In fact, as he had good sense, and as he had compared the two, Theodule had only served to make him regret Marius all the more.

One evening, it was the 24th of June, which did not prevent Father Gillenormand having a rousing fire on the hearth, he had dismissed his daughter, who was sewing in a neighboring apartment. He was alone in his chamber, amid its pastoral scenes, with his feet propped on the andirons, half enveloped in his huge screen of coromandel lacquer, with its nine leaves, with his elbow resting on a table where burned two candles under a green shade, engulfed in his tapestry armchair, and in his hand a book, which he was not reading. He was dressed, according to his wont, like an *incroyable*, and resembled an antique portrait by Garat. This would have made people run after him in the street, had not his daughter covered him up, whenever he went out, in a vast bishop's wadded cloak, which concealed his attire. At home, he never wore a dressing gown, except when he rose and retired. "It gives one a look of age," said he.

Father Gillenormand was thinking of Marius lovingly and bitterly; and, as usual, bitterness predominated. His tenderness once soured always ended by boiling and turning to indignation. He had reached the point where a man tries to make up his mind and to accept that which rends his heart. He was explaining to himself that there was no longer any reason why Marius should return, that if he intended to return, he should have done it long ago, that he must renounce the idea. He was trying to accustom himself to the thought that all was over, and that he should die without having beheld "that gentleman" again. But his whole nature revolted; his aged paternity would not consent to this. "Well!" said he, this was his doleful refrain, "he will not return!" His bald head had fallen upon his breast, and he fixed a melancholy and irritated gaze upon the ashes on his hearth.

In the very midst of his reverie, his old servant Basque entered, and inquired, "Can Monsieur receive M. Marius?"

The old man sat up erect, pallid, and like a corpse that rises under the influence of a galvanic shock. All his blood had retreated to his heart. He stammered, "M. Marius what?"

"I don't know," replied Basque, intimidated and put out of countenance by his master's air; "I have not seen him. Nicolette came in and said to me, 'There's a young man here; say that it is M. Marius.'"

Father Gillenormand stammered in a low voice, "Show him in."

And he remained in the same attitude, with shaking head, and his eyes fixed on the door. It opened once more. A young man entered. It was Marius.

Marius halted at the door, as though waiting to be bidden to enter.

His almost squalid attire was not perceptible in the obscurity caused by the shade. Nothing could be seen but his calm, grave, but strangely sad face.

It was several minutes before Father Gillenormand, dulled with amazement and joy, could see anything except a brightness as when one is in the presence of an apparition. He was on the point of swooning; he saw Marius through a dazzling light. It certainly was he, it certainly was Marius.

At last! After the lapse of four years! He grasped him entire, so to speak, in a single glance. He found him noble, handsome, distinguished, well-grown, a complete man, with a suitable mien and a charming air. He felt a desire to open his arms, to call him, to fling himself forward; his heart melted with rapture, affectionate words swelled and overflowed his breast; at length all his tenderness came to the light and reached his lips, and, by a contrast which constituted the very foundation of his nature, what came forth was harshness. He said abruptly, "What have you come here for?"

Marius replied with embarrassment, "Monsieur—"

M. Gillenormand would have liked to have Marius throw himself into his arms. He was displeased with Marius and with himself. He was conscious that he was brusque, and that Marius was cold. It caused the goodman unendurable and irritating anxiety to feel so tender and forlorn within, and only to be able to be hard outside. Bitterness returned. He interrupted Marius in a peevish tone, "Then why did you come?"

That "then" signified: If you do not come to embrace me. Marius looked at his grandfather, whose pallor gave him a face of marble.

"Monsieur—"

"Have you come to beg my pardon? Do you acknowledge your faults?"

He thought he was putting Marius on the right road, and that "the child" would yield. Marius shivered; it was the denial of his father that was required of him; he dropped his eyes and replied, "No, Sir."

"Then," exclaimed the old man impetuously, with a grief that was poignant and full of wrath, "what do you want of me?"

Marius clasped his hands, advanced a step, and said in a feeble and trembling voice, "Sir, have pity on me."

These words touched M. Gillenormand; uttered a little sooner, they would have rendered him tender, but they came too late. The grandfather rose; he supported himself with both hands on his cane; his lips were white, his brow wavered, but his lofty form towered above Marius as he bowed.

"Pity on you, Sir! It is youth demanding pity of the old man of ninety-one! You are entering into life, I am leaving it; you go to the play, to balls, to the café, to the billiard hall; you have wit, you please the women, you are a handsome fellow; as for me, I spit on my brands in the heart of summer; you are rich with the only riches that are really such, I possess all the poverty of age; infirmity, isolation! You have your thirty-two teeth, a good digestion, bright eyes, strength, appetite, health, gaiety, a forest of black hair; I have no longer even white hair, I have lost my teeth, I am losing my legs, I am losing my memory; there are three names of streets that I confound incessantly, the Rue Charlot, the Rue du Chaume, and the Rue Saint-Claude, that is what I have come to; you have before you the whole future, full of sunshine, and I am beginning to lose my sight, so far am I advancing into the night; you are in love, that is a matter of course, I am beloved by no one in all the world; and you ask pity of me! *Parbleu*! Moliere forgot that. If that is the way you jest at the courthouse, Messieurs the lawyers, I sincerely compliment you. You are droll."

And the octogenarian went on in a grave and angry voice, "Come, now, what do you want of me?"

"Sir," said Marius, "I know that my presence is displeasing to you, but I have come merely to ask one thing of you, and then I shall go away immediately."

"You are a fool!" said the old man. "Who said that you were to go away?"

This was the translation of the tender words that lay at the bottom of his heart, "Ask my pardon! Throw yourself on my neck!"

M. Gillenormand felt that Marius would leave him in a few moments, that his harsh reception had repelled the lad, that his hardness was driving him away; he said all this to himself, and it augmented his grief; and as his grief was straightway converted into wrath, it increased his harshness. He would have liked to have Marius understand, and Marius did not understand, which made the goodman furious.

He began again, "What! You deserted me, your grandfather, you left my house to go no one knows where, you drove your aunt to despair, you went off, it is easily guessed, to lead a bachelor life; it's more convenient, to play the dandy, to come in at all hours, to amuse yourself; you have given me no signs of life, you have contracted debts without even telling me to pay them, you have become a smasher of windows and a blusterer, and, at the end of four years, you come to me, and that is all you have to say to me!"

This violent fashion of driving a grandson to tenderness was productive only of silence on the part of Marius. M. Gillenormand folded his arms; a gesture which with him was peculiarly imperious, and apostrophized Marius bitterly, "Let us make an end of this. You have come to ask something of me, you say? Well, what? What is it? Speak!"

"Sir," said Marius, with the look of a man who feels that he is falling over a precipice, "I have come to ask your permission to marry."

M. Gillenormand rang the bell. Basque opened the door halfway.

"Call my daughter."

A second later, the door was opened once more, Mademoiselle Gillenormand did not enter, but showed herself; Marius was standing, mute, with pendant arms and the face of a criminal; M. Gillenormand was pacing back and forth in the room. He turned to his daughter and said to her, "Nothing. It is Monsieur Marius. Say good day to him. Monsieur wishes to marry. That's all. Go away."

The curt, hoarse sound of the old man's voice announced a strange degree of excitement. The aunt gazed at Marius with a frightened air, hardly appeared to recognize him, did not allow a gesture or a syllable to escape her, and disappeared at her father's breath more swiftly than a straw before the hurricane.

In the meantime, Father Gillenormand had returned and placed his back against the mantle once more.

"You marry! At one and twenty! You have arranged that! You have only a permission to ask! A formality. Sit down, Sir. Well, you have had a revolution since I had the honor to see you last. The Jacobins got the upper hand. You must have been delighted. Are you not a Republican since you are a Baron?

You can make that agree. The Republic makes a good sauce for the barony. Are you one of those decorated by July? Have you taken the Louvre at all, Sir? Quite near here, in the Rue Saint-Antoine, opposite the Rue des Nonamdieres, there is a cannonball encrusted in the wall of the third story of a house with this inscription: 'July 28th, 1830.' Go take a look at that. It produces a good effect. Ah! Those friends of yours do pretty things. By the way, aren't they erecting a fountain in the place of the monument of M. le Duc de Berry? So you want to marry? Whom? Can one inquire without indiscretion?"

He paused, and, before Marius had time to answer, he added violently, "Come now, you have a profession? A fortune made? How much do you earn at your trade of lawyer?"

"Nothing," said Marius, with a sort of firmness and resolution that was almost fierce.

"Nothing? Then all that you have to live upon is the twelve hundred livres that I allow you?"

Marius did not reply. M. Gillenormand continued, "Then I understand the girl is rich?"

"As rich as I am."

"What! No dowry?"

"No."

"Expectations?"

"I think not."

"Utterly naked! What's the father?"

"I don't know."

"And what's her name?"

"Mademoiselle Fauchelevent."

"Fauchewhat?"

"Fauchelevent."

"Pttt!" ejaculated the old gentleman.

"Sir!" exclaimed Marius.

M. Gillenormand interrupted him with the tone of a man who is speaking to himself, "That's right, one and twenty years of age, no profession, twelve hundred livres a year, Madame la Baronne de Pontmercy will go and purchase a couple of sous' worth of parsley from the fruiterer."

"Sir," repeated Marius, in the despair at the last hope, which was vanishing, "I entreat you! I conjure you in the name of Heaven, with clasped hands, Sir, I throw myself at your feet, permit me to marry her!"

The old man burst into a shout of strident and mournful laughter, coughing and laughing at the same time.

"Ah! Ah! Ah! You said to yourself, 'Pardine! I'll go hunt up that old blockhead, that absurd numskull! What a shame that I'm not twenty-five! How I'd treat him to a nice respectful summons! How nicely I'd get along without him! It's nothing to me. I'd say to him: You're only too happy to see me, you old idiot, I want to marry, I desire to wed Mamselle No-matter-whom, daughter of Monsieur No-matter-what, I have no shoes, she has no chemise, that just suits; I want to throw my career, my future, my youth, my life to the dogs; I wish to take a plunge into wretchedness with a woman around my neck, that's an idea, and you must consent to it!—and the old fossil will consent.' Go, my lad, do as you like, attach your paving-stone, marry your Pousselevent, your Coupelevent—Never, Sir, never!"

"Father—"

"Never!"

At the tone in which that "never" was uttered, Marius lost all hope. He traversed the chamber with slow steps, with bowed head, tottering and more like a dying man than like one merely taking his departure. M. Gillenormand followed him with his eyes, and at the moment when the door opened, and Marius was on the point of going out, he advanced four paces, with the senile vivacity of impetuous and spoiled old gentlemen, seized Marius by the collar, brought him back energetically into the room, flung him into an armchair and said to him, "Tell me all about it!"

It was that single word—"father"—which had affected this revolution.

Marius stared at him in bewilderment. M. Gillenormand's mobile face was no longer expressive of anything but rough and ineffable good nature. The grandsire had given way before the grandfather.

"Come, see here, speak, tell me about your love affairs, jabber, tell me everything! *Sapristi*! How stupid young folks are!"

"Father—" repeated Marius.

The old man's entire countenance lighted up with indescribable radiance.

"Yes, that's right, call me father, and you'll see!"

There was now something so kind, so gentle, so openhearted, and so paternal in this brusqueness, that Marius, in the sudden transition from discouragement to hope, was stunned and intoxicated by it, as it were. He was seated near the table, the light from the candles brought out the dilapidation of his costume, which Father Gillenormand regarded with amazement.

"Well, father—" said Marius.

"Ah, by the way," interrupted M. Gillenormand, "you really have not a penny then? You are dressed like a pickpocket."

He rummaged in a drawer, drew forth a purse, which he laid on the table, "Here are a hundred Louis, buy yourself a hat."

"Father," pursued Marius, "my good father, if you only knew! I love her. You cannot imagine it; the first time I saw her was at the Luxembourg, she came there; in the beginning, I did not pay much heed to her, and then, I don't know how it came about, I fell in love with her. Oh! How unhappy that made me! Now, at last, I see her every day, at her own home, her father does not know it, just fancy, they are going away, it is in the garden that we meet, in the evening, her father means to take her to England, then I said to myself, 'I'll go and see my grandfather and tell him all about the affair. I should go mad first, I should die, I should fall ill, I should throw myself into the water. I absolutely must marry her, since I should go mad otherwise.' This is the whole truth, and I do not think that I have omitted anything. She lives in a garden with an iron fence, in the Rue Plumet. It is in the neighborhood of the Invalides."

Father Gillenormand had seated himself, with a beaming countenance, beside Marius. As he listened to him and drank in the sound of his voice, he enjoyed at the same time a protracted pinch of snuff. At the words "Rue Plumet" he interrupted his inhalation and allowed the remainder of his snuff to fall upon his knees.

"The Rue Plumet, the Rue Plumet, did you say?—Let us see!—Are there not barracks in that vicinity?—Why, yes, that's it. Your cousin Theodule has spoken to me about it. The lancer, the officer. A gay girl, my good friend, a gay girl!—Pardieu, yes, the Rue Plumet. It is what used to be called the Rue Blomet.—It all comes back to me now. I have heard of that little girl of the iron railing in the Rue Plumet. In a garden, a Pamela. Your taste is not bad. She is said to be a very tidy creature. Between ourselves, I think that simpleton of a lancer has been courting her a bit. I don't know where he did it. However, that's not to the purpose. Besides, he is not to be believed. He brags, Marius! I think it quite proper that a young man like you should be in love. It's the right thing at your age. I like you better as a lover than as a Jacobin. I like you better in love with a petticoat, sapristi! With twenty petticoats, than with M. de Robespierre. For my part, I will do myself the justice to say, that in the line of sans-culottes, I have never loved anyone but women. Pretty girls are pretty girls, the deuce! There's no objection to that. As for the little one, she receives you without her father's knowledge. That's in the established order of things. I have had adventures of that same sort myself. More than one. Do you know what is done then? One does not take the matter ferociously; one does not precipitate himself into the tragic; one does not make one's mind to marriage and M. le Maire with his scarf. One simply behaves like a fellow of spirit. One shows good sense. Slip along, mortals; don't marry. You come and look up your grandfather, who is a good-natured fellow at bottom, and who always has a few rolls of Louis in an old drawer; you say to him, 'See here, Grandfather.' And the grandfather says, 'That's a simple matter. Youth must amuse itself, and old age must wear out. I have been young, you will be old. Come, my boy, you shall pass it on to your grandson. Here are two hundred pistoles. Amuse yourself, deuce take it!' Nothing better! That's the way the affair should be treated. You don't marry, but that does no harm. You understand me?"

Marius, petrified and incapable of uttering a syllable, made a sign with his head that he did not.

The old man burst out laughing, winked his aged eye, gave him a slap on the knee, stared him full in the face with a mysterious and beaming air, and said to him, with the tenderest of shrugs of the shoulder, "Booby! Make her your mistress."

Marius turned pale. He had understood nothing of what his grandfather had just said. This twaddle about the Rue Blomet, Pamela, the barracks, the lancer, had passed before Marius like a dissolving view. Nothing of all that could bear any reference to Cosette, who was a lily. The good man was wandering in his mind. But this wandering terminated in words that Marius did understand, and which were a mortal insult to Cosette. Those words, "make her your mistress," entered the heart of the strict young man like a sword.

He rose, picked up his hat that lay on the floor, and walked to the door with a firm, assured step. There he turned around, bowed deeply to his grandfather, raised his head erect again, and said, "Five years ago you insulted my father; today you have insulted my wife. I ask nothing more of you, Sir. Farewell."

Father Gillenormand, utterly confounded, opened his mouth, extended his arms, tried to rise, and before he could utter a word, the door closed once more, and Marius had disappeared.

The old man remained for several minutes motionless and as though struck by lightning, without the power to speak or breathe, as though a clenched fist grasped his throat. At last he tore himself from his armchair, ran, so far as a man can run at ninety-one, to the door, opened it, and cried, "Help! Help!"

His daughter made her appearance, then the domestics. He began again, with a pitiful rattle, "Run after him! Bring him back! What have I done to him? He is mad! He is going away! Ah! My God! Ah! My God! This time he will not come back!"

He went to the window, which looked out on the street, threw it open with his aged and palsied hands, leaned out more than halfway, while Basque and Nicolette held him behind, and shouted, "Marius! Marius! Marius! Marius!"

But Marius could no longer hear him, for at that moment he was turning the corner of the Rue Saint-Louis.

The octogenarian raised his hands to his temples two or three times with an expression of anguish, recoiled tottering, and fell back into an armchair, pulseless, voiceless, tearless, with quivering head and lips which moved with a stupid air, with nothing in his eyes and nothing any longer in his heart except a gloomy and profound something that resembled night.

BOOK NINTH: WHERE ARE THEY GOING?

CHAPTER I—JEAN VALJEAN

That same day, toward four o'clock in the afternoon, Jean Valjean was sitting alone on the backside of one of the most solitary slopes in the Champ-de-Mars. Either from prudence, or from a desire to meditate, or simply in consequence of one of those insensible changes of habit that gradually introduce themselves into the existence of everyone, he now rarely went out with Cosette. He had on his workman's waistcoat, and trousers of gray linen; and his long-visored cap concealed his countenance.

He was calm and happy now beside Cosette; that which had, for a time, alarmed and troubled him had been dissipated; but for the last week or two, anxieties of another nature had come up. One day, while walking on the boulevard, he had caught sight of Thenardier; thanks to his disguise, Thenardier had not recognized him; but since that day, Jean Valjean had seen him repeatedly, and he was now certain that Thenardier was prowling about in their neighborhood.

This had been sufficient to make him come to a decision.

Moreover, Paris was not tranquil; political troubles presented this inconvenient feature, for anyone who had anything to conceal in his life, that the police had grown very uneasy and very suspicious, and that while seeking to ferret out a man like Pepin or Morey, they might very readily discover a man like Jean Valjean.

Jean Valjean had made up his mind to quit Paris, and even France, and go over to England.

He had warned Cosette. He wished to set out before the end of the week.

He had seated himself on the slope in the Champ-de-Mars, turning over all sorts of thoughts in his mind, Thenardier, the police, the journey, and the difficulty of procuring a passport.

He was troubled from all these points of view.

Last of all, an inexplicable circumstance that had just attracted his attention, and from which he had not yet recovered, had added to his state of alarm.

On the morning of that very day, when he alone of the household was stirring, while strolling in the garden before Cosette's shutters were open, he had suddenly perceived on the wall, the following line, engraved, probably with a nail: 16 Rue de la Verrerie.

This was perfectly fresh, the grooves in the ancient black mortar were white, a tuft of nettles at the foot of the wall was powdered with the fine, fresh plaster.

This had probably been written on the preceding night.

What was this? A signal for others? A warning for himself?

In any case, it was evident that the garden had been violated, and that strangers had made their way into it.

He recalled the odd incidents that had already alarmed the household.

His mind was now filling in this canvas.

He took good care not to speak to Cosette of the line written on the wall, for fear of alarming her.

In the midst of his preoccupations, he perceived, from a shadow cast by the sun, that someone had halted on the crest of the slope immediately behind him.

He was on the point of turning around, when a paper folded in four fell upon his knees as though a hand had dropped it over his head.

He took the paper, unfolded it, and read these words written in large characters, with a pencil: "MOVE AWAY FROM YOUR HOUSE."

Jean Valjean sprang hastily to his feet; there was no one on the slope; he gazed all around him and perceived a creature larger than a child, not so large as a man, clad in a gray blouse and trousers of dust-colored cotton velvet, who was jumping over the parapet and who slipped into the moat of the Champ de-Mars.

Jean Valjean returned home at once, in a very thoughtful mood.

CHAPTER II—MARIUS

Marius had left M. Gillenormand in despair. He had entered the house with very little hope, and quitted it with immense despair.

However, and those who have observed the depths of the human heart will understand this, the officer, the lancer, the ninny, Cousin Theodule, had left no trace in his mind. Not the slightest. The dramatic poet might, apparently, expect some complications from this revelation made point-blank by the grandfather to the grandson. But what the drama would gain thereby, truth would lose. Marius was at an age when one believes nothing in the line of evil; later on comes the age when one believes everything. Suspicions are nothing else than wrinkles. Early youth has none of them. That which overwhelmed Othello glides innocuous over Candide. Suspect Cosette! There are hosts of crimes that Marius could sooner have committed.

He began to wander about the streets, the resource of those who suffer. He thought of nothing, so far as he could afterward remember. At two o'clock in the morning he returned to Courfeyrac's quarters and flung himself, without undressing, on his mattress. The sun was shining brightly when he sank into that frightful leaden slumber which permits ideas to go and come in the brain. When he awoke, he saw Courfeyrac, Enjolras, Feuilly, and Combeferre standing in the room with their hats on and all ready to go out.

Courfeyrac said to him, "Are you coming to General Lamarque's funeral?"

It seemed to him that Courfeyrac was speaking Chinese.

He went out some time after them. He put in his pocket the pistols that Javert had given him at the time of the adventure on the 3rd of February, and which had remained in his hands. These pistols were still loaded. It would be difficult to say what vague thought he had in his mind when he took them with him.

All day long he prowled about, without knowing where he was going; it rained at times, he did not perceive it; for his dinner, he purchased a penny roll at a baker's, put it in his pocket and forgot it. It appears that he took a bath in the Seine without being aware of it. There are moments when a man has a furnace within his skull. Marius was passing through one of those moments. He no longer hoped for anything; this step he had taken since the preceding evening. He waited for night with feverish impatience, he had but one idea clearly before his mind—this was, that at nine o'clock he should see Cosette. This last happiness now constituted his whole future; after that, gloom. At intervals, as he roamed through the most deserted boulevards, it seemed to him that he heard strange noises in Paris. He thrust his head out of his reverie and said, "Is there fighting on hand?"

At nightfall, at nine o'clock precisely, as he had promised Cosette, he was in the Rue Plumet. When he approached the grating he forgot everything. It was forty-eight hours since he had seen Cosette; he was about to behold her once more; every other thought was effaced, and he felt only a profound and unheard-of joy. Those minutes in which one lives centuries always have this sovereign and wonderful property, that at the moment when they are passing they fill the heart completely.

Marius displaced the bar, and rushed headlong into the garden. Cosette was not at the spot where she ordinarily waited for him. He traversed the thicket, and approached the recess near the flight of steps, "She is waiting for me there," said he. Cosette was not there. He raised his eyes, and saw that the shutters of the house were closed. He made the tour of the garden, the garden was deserted. Then he returned to the house, and, rendered senseless by love, intoxicated, terrified, exasperated with grief and uneasiness, like a master who returns home at an evil hour, he tapped on the shutters. He knocked and knocked again, at the risk of seeing the window open, and her father's gloomy face make its appearance, and demand, "What do you want?" This was nothing in comparison with what he dimly caught a glimpse of. When he had rapped, he lifted up his voice and called Cosette. "Cosette!" he cried.

"Cosette!" he repeated imperiously. There was no reply. All was over. No one in the garden; no one in the house.

Marius fixed his despairing eyes on that dismal house, which was as black and as silent as a tomb and far more empty. He gazed at the stone seat on which he had passed so many adorable hours with Cosette. Then he seated himself on the flight of steps, his heart filled with sweetness and resolution, he blessed his love in the depths of his thought, and he said to himself that, since Cosette was gone, all that there was left for him was to die.

All at once he heard a voice which seemed to proceed from the street, and which was calling to him through the trees, "Mr. Marius!"

He started to his feet.

"Hey?" said he.

"Mr. Marius, are you there?"

"Yes."

"Mr. Marius," went on the voice, "your friends are waiting for you at the barricade of the Rue de la Chanvrerie."

This voice was not wholly unfamiliar to him. It resembled the hoarse, rough voice of Eponine. Marius hastened to the gate, thrust aside the movable bar, passed his head through the aperture, and saw someone who appeared to him to be a young man, disappearing at a run into the gloom.

CHAPTER III—M. MABEUF

Jean Valjean's purse was of no use to M. Mabeuf. M. Mabeuf, in his venerable, infantile austerity, had not accepted the gift of the stars; he had not admitted that a star could coin itself into Louis d'or. He had not divined that what had fallen from heaven had come from Gavroche. He had taken the purse to the police commissioner of the quarter, as a lost article placed by the finder at the disposal of claimants. The purse was actually lost. It is unnecessary to say that no one claimed it, and that it did not succor M. Mabeuf.

Moreover, M. Mabeuf had continued his downward course.

His experiments on indigo had been no more successful in the Jardin des Plantes than in his garden at Austerlitz. The year before he had owed his housekeeper's wages; now, as we have seen, he owed three quarters of his rent. The pawnshop had sold the plates of his Flora after the expiration of thirteen months. Some coppersmith had made stewpans of them. His copper plates gone, and being unable to complete even the incomplete copies of his Flora which were in his possession, he had disposed of the text, at a miserable price, as waste paper, to a secondhand bookseller. Nothing now remained to him of his life's work. He set to work to eat up the money for these copies. When he saw that this wretched resource was becoming exhausted, he gave up his garden and allowed it to run to waste. Before this, a long time before, he had given up his two eggs and the morsel of beef that he ate from time to time. He dined on bread and potatoes. He had sold the last of his furniture, then all duplicates of his bedding, his clothing and his blankets, then his herbariums and prints; but he still retained his most precious books, many of which were of the greatest rarity, among others, Les Quadrins Historiques de la Bible, edition of 1560; La Concordance des Bibles, by Pierre de Besse; Les Marguerites de la Marguerite, of Jean de La Haye, with a dedication to the Queen of Navarre; the book de la Charge et Dignite de l'Ambassadeur, by the Sieur de Villiers Hotman; a Florilegium Rabbinicum of 1644; a Tibullus of 1567, with this magnificent inscription: Venetiis, in aedibus Manutianis; and lastly, a Diogenes Laertius, printed at Lyons in 1644, which contained the famous variant of the manuscript 411, thirteenth century, of the Vatican, and those of the two manuscripts of Venice, 393 and 394, consulted with such fruitful results by Henri Estienne, and all the passages in Doric dialect, which are only found in the celebrated manuscript of the twelfth century belonging to the Naples Library. M. Mabeuf never had any fire in his chamber, and went to bed at sundown, in order not to consume any candles. It seemed as though he had no longer any neighbors: people avoided him when he went out; he perceived the fact. The wretchedness of a child interests a mother, the wretchedness of a young man interests a young girl, the wretchedness of an old man interests no one. It is, of all distresses, the coldest. Still, Father Mabeuf had not entirely lost his childlike serenity. His eyes acquired some vivacity when they rested on his books, and he smiled when he gazed at the Diogenes Laertius, which was a unique copy. His bookcase with glass doors was the only piece of furniture he had kept beyond what was strictly indispensable.

One day, Mother Plutarque said to him, "I have no money to buy any dinner."

What she called dinner was a loaf of bread and four or five potatoes.

"On credit?" suggested M. Mabeuf.

"You know well that people refuse me."

M. Mabeuf opened his bookcase, took a long look at all his books, one after another, as a father obliged to decimate his children would gaze upon them before making a choice, then seized one hastily, put it in under his arm and went out. He returned two hours later, without anything under his arm, laid thirty sous on the table, and said, "You will get something for dinner."

From that moment forth, Mother Plutarque saw a somber veil, which was never more lifted, descend over the old man's candid face.

On the following day, on the day after, and on the day after that, it had to be done again.

M. Mabeuf went out with a book and returned with a coin. As the secondhand dealers perceived that he was forced to sell, they purchased of him for twenty sous that for which he had paid twenty francs, sometimes at those very shops. Volume by volume, the whole library went the same road. He said at times, "But I am eighty," as though he cherished some secret hope that he should arrive at the end of his days before reaching the end of his books. His melancholy increased. Once, however, he had a pleasure. He had gone out with a Robert Estienne, which he had sold for thirty-five sous under the Quai Malaquais, and he returned with an Aldus which he had bought for forty sous in the Rue des Grès. "I owe five sous," he said, beaming on Mother Plutarque. That day he had no dinner.

He belonged to the Horticultural Society. His destitution became known there. The president of the society came to see him, promised to speak to the Minister of Agriculture and Commerce about him, and did so. "Why, what!" exclaimed the Minister, "I should think so! An old savant! A botanist! An inoffensive man! Something must be done for him!" On the following day, M. Mabeuf received an invitation to dine with the Minister. Trembling with joy, he showed the letter to Mother Plutarque. "We are saved!" said he. On the day appointed, he went to the Minister's house. He perceived that his ragged cravat, his long, square coat, and his waxed shoes astonished the ushers. No one spoke to him, not even the Minister. About ten o'clock in the evening, while he was still waiting for a word, he heard the Minister's wife, a beautiful woman in a low-necked gown whom he had not ventured to approach, inquire, "Who is that old gentleman?" He returned home on foot at midnight, in a driving rainstorm. He had sold an Elzevir to pay for a carriage in which to go there.

He had acquired the habit of reading a few pages in his Diogenes Laertius every night, before he went to bed. He knew enough Greek to enjoy the peculiarities of the text that he owned. He had now no other enjoyment. Several weeks passed. All at once, Mother Plutarque fell ill. There is one thing sadder than having no money with which to buy bread at the baker's and that is having no money to purchase drugs at the apothecary's. One evening, the doctor had ordered a very expensive potion. And the malady was growing worse; a nurse was required. M. Mabeuf opened his bookcase; there was nothing there. The last volume had taken its departure. All that was left to him was Diogenes Laertius. He put this unique copy under his arm, and went out. It was the 4th of June, 1832; he went to the Porte Saint-Jacques, to Royal's successor, and returned with one hundred francs. He laid the pile of five-franc pieces on the old serving-woman's nightstand, and returned to his chamber without saying a word.

On the following morning, at dawn, he seated himself on the overturned post in his garden, and he could be seen over the top of the hedge, sitting the whole morning motionless, with drooping head, his eyes vaguely fixed on the withered flowerbeds. It rained at intervals; the old man did not seem to perceive the fact.

In the afternoon, extraordinary noises broke out in Paris. They resembled shots and the clamors of a multitude.

Father Mabeuf raised his head. He saw a gardener passing, and inquired, "What is it?"

The gardener, spade on back, replied in the most unconcerned tone:

"It is the riots."

"What riots?"

"Yes, they are fighting."

"Why are they fighting?"

"Ah, good Heavens!" ejaculated the gardener.

"In what direction?" went on M. Mabeuf.

"In the neighborhood of the Arsenal."

Father Mabeuf went to his room, took his hat, mechanically sought for a book to place under his arm, found none, said, "Ah! Truly!" and went off with a bewildered air.

BOOK TENTH:
THE 5TH OF JUNE, 1832

CHAPTER I—THE SURFACE OF THE QUESTION

Of what is revolt composed? Of nothing and of everything. Of an electricity disengaged, little by little, of a flame suddenly darting forth, of a wandering force, of a passing breath. This breath encounters heads that speak, brains that dream, souls that suffer, passions that burn, wretchedness which howls, and bears them away.

Where?

At random. Athwart the state, the laws, athwart prosperity and the insolence of others.

Irritated convictions, embittered enthusiasms, agitated indignations, instincts of war that have been repressed, youthful courage that has been exalted, generous blindness; curiosity, the taste for change, the thirst for the unexpected, the sentiment that causes one to take pleasure in reading the posters for the new play, and love, the prompter's whistle, at the theater; the vague hatreds, rancors, disappointments, every vanity that thinks that destiny has bankrupted it; discomfort, empty dreams, ambitious that are hedged about, whoever hopes for a downfall, some outcome, in short, at the very bottom, the rabble, that mud which catches fire, such are the elements of revolt. That which is grandest and that which is basest; the beings who prowl outside of all bounds, awaiting an occasion, bohemians, vagrants, vagabonds of the crossroads, those who sleep at night in a desert of houses with no other roof than the cold clouds of heaven, those who, each day, demand their bread from chance and not from toil, the unknown of poverty and nothingness, the bare-armed, the bare-footed, belong to revolt. Whoever cherishes in his soul a secret revolt against any deed whatever on the part of the state, of life or of fate, is ripe for riot, and, as soon as it makes its appearance, he begins to quiver, and to feel himself borne away with the whirlwind.

Revolt is a sort of waterspout in the social atmosphere, which forms suddenly in certain conditions of temperature, and which, as it eddies about, mounts, descends, thunders, tears, razes, crushes, demolishes, uproots, bearing with it great natures and small, the strong man and the feeble mind, the tree trunk and the stalk of straw. Woe to him whom it bears away as well as to him whom it strikes! It breaks the one against the other.

It communicates to those whom it seizes an indescribable and extraordinary power. It fills the firstcomer with the force of events; it converts everything into projectiles. It makes a cannonball of a rough stone, and a general of a porter.

If we are to believe certain oracles of crafty political views, a little revolt is desirable from the point of view of power. System: revolt strengthens those governments that it does not overthrow. It puts the army to the test; it consecrates the bourgeoisie, it draws out the muscles of the police; it demonstrates the force of the social framework. It is an exercise in gymnastics; it is almost hygiene. Power is in better health after a revolt, as a man is after a good rubbing down.

Revolt, thirty years ago, was regarded from still other points of view.

There is for everything a theory, which proclaims itself "good sense;" Philintus against Alcestis; mediation offered between the false and the true; explanation, admonition, rather haughty extenuation, which, because it is mingled with blame and excuse, thinks itself wisdom, and is often only pedantry. A whole political school called "the golden mean" has been the outcome of this. As between cold water and hot water, it is the lukewarm water party. This school with its false depth, all on the surface, which dissects effects without going back to first causes, chides from its height of a demi-science, the agitation of the public square.

If we listen to this school, "The riots, which complicated the affair of 1830, deprived that great event of a portion of its purity. The Revolution of July had been a fine popular gale, abruptly followed by blue sky. They made the cloudy sky reappear. They caused that revolution, at first so remarkable for its unanimity, to degenerate into a quarrel. In the Revolution of July, as in all progress accomplished by fits and starts, there had been secret fractures; these riots rendered them perceptible. It might have been said, 'Ah! This is broken.' After the Revolution of July, one was sensible only of deliverance; after the riots, one was conscious of a catastrophe.

"All revolt closes the shops, depresses the funds, throws the Exchange into consternation, suspends commerce, clogs business, precipitates failures; no more money, private fortunes rendered uneasy, public credit shaken, industry disconcerted, capital withdrawing, work at a discount, fear everywhere; countershocks in every town. Hence gulfs. It has been calculated that the first day of a riot costs France twenty millions, the second day forty, the third sixty, a three days' uprising costs one hundred and twenty millions, that is to say, if only the financial result be taken into consideration, it is equivalent to a disaster, a shipwreck or a lost battle, which should annihilate a fleet of sixty ships of the line.

"No doubt, historically, uprisings have their beauty; the war of the pavements is no less grandiose, and no less pathetic, than the war of thickets: in the one there is the soul of forests, in the other the heart of cities; the one has Jean Chouan, the other has a Jeanne. Revolts have illuminated with a red glare all the most original points of the Parisian character, generosity, devotion, stormy gaiety, students proving that bravery forms part of intelligence, the National Guard invincible, bivouacs of shopkeepers, fortresses of street urchins, contempt of death on the part of passersby. Schools and legions clashed together. After all, between the combatants, there was only a difference of age; the race is the same; it is the same stoical men who died at the age of twenty for their ideas, at forty for their families. The army, always a sad thing in civil wars, opposed prudence to audacity. Uprisings, while proving popular intrepidity, also educated the courage of the bourgeois.

"This is well. But is all this worth the bloodshed? And to the bloodshed add the future darkness, progress compromised, uneasiness among the best men, honest liberals in despair, foreign absolutism happy in these wounds dealt to revolution by its own hand, the vanquished of 1830 triumphing and saying, 'We told you so!' Add Paris enlarged, possibly, but France most assuredly diminished. Add, for all must needs be told, the massacres that have too often dishonored the victory of order grown ferocious over liberty gone mad. To sum up all, uprisings have been disastrous."

Thus speaks that approximation to wisdom with which the bourgeoisie, that approximation to the people, so willingly contents itself.

For our parts, we reject this word uprisings as too large, and consequently as too convenient. We make a distinction between one popular movement and another popular movement. We do not inquire whether an uprising costs as much as a battle. Why a battle, in the first place? Here the question of war comes up. Is war less of a scourge than an uprising is of a calamity? And then, are all uprisings calamities? And what if the revolt of July did cost a hundred and twenty millions? The establishment of Philip V in Spain cost France two milliards. Even at the same price, we should prefer the 14th of July. However, we reject these figures, which appear to be reasons and which are only words. An uprising being given, we examine it by itself. In all that is said by the doctrinarian objection above presented, there is no question of anything but effect, we seek the cause.

We will be explicit.

CHAPTER II—THE ROOT OF THE MATTER

There is such a thing as an uprising, and there is such a thing as insurrection; these are two separate phases of wrath; one is in the wrong, the other is in the right. In democratic states, the only ones founded on justice, it sometimes happens that the fraction usurps; then the whole rises and the necessary claim of its rights may proceed as far as resort to arms. In all questions that result from collective sovereignty, the war of the whole against the fraction is insurrection; the attack of the fraction against the whole is revolt; according as the Tuileries contain a king or the Convention, they are justly or unjustly attacked. The same cannon, pointed against the populace, is wrong on the 10th of August, and right on the 14th of Vendemiaire. Alike in appearance, fundamentally different in reality; the Swiss defend the false, Bonaparte defends the true. That which universal suffrage has effected in its liberty and in its sovereignty cannot be undone by the street. It is the same in things pertaining purely to civilization; the instinct of the masses, clear-sighted today, may be troubled tomorrow. The same fury legitimate when directed against Terray and absurd when directed against Turgot. The destruction of machines, the pillage of warehouses, the breaking of rails, the demolition of docks, the false routes of multitudes, the refusal by the people of justice to progress, Ramus assassinated by students, Rousseau driven out of Switzerland and stoned, that is revolt. Israel against Moses, Athens against Phocian, Rome against Cicero, that is an uprising; Paris against the Bastille, that is insurrection. The soldiers against Alexander, the sailors against Christopher Columbus, this is the same revolt; impious revolt; why? Because Alexander is doing for Asia with the sword that which Christopher Columbus is doing for America with the compass; Alexander like Columbus, is finding a world. These gifts of a world to civilization are such augmentations of light, that all resistance in that case is culpable. Sometimes the populace counterfeits fidelity to itself. The masses are traitors to the people. Is there, for example, anything stranger than that long and bloody protest of dealers in contraband salt, a legitimate chronic revolt, which, at the decisive moment, on the day of salvation, at the very hour of popular victory, espouses the throne, turns into *chouannerie*, and, from having been an insurrection against, becomes an uprising for, somber masterpieces of ignorance! The contraband salt dealer escapes the royal gibbets, and with a rope's end around his neck, mounts the white cockade. "Death to the salt duties," brings forth, "Long live the King!" The assassins of Saint-Barthelemy, the cutthroats of September, the manslaughterers of Avignon, the assassins of Coligny, the assassins of Madam Lamballe, the assassins of Brune, Miquelets, Verdets, Cadenettes, the companions of Jehu, the chevaliers of Brassard, behold an uprising. La Vendee is a grand, catholic uprising. The sound of right in movement is recognizable, it does not always proceed from the trembling of excited masses; there are mad rages, there are cracked bells, all tocsins do not give out the sound of bronze. The brawl of passions and ignorances is quite another thing from the shock of progress. Show me in what direction you are going. Rise, if you will, but let it be that you may grow great. There is no insurrection except in a forward direction. Any other sort of rising is bad; every violent step toward the rear is a revolt; to retreat is to commit a deed of violence against the human race. Insurrection is a fit of rage on the part of truth; the pavements that the uprising disturbs give forth the spark of right. These pavements bequeath to the uprising only their mud. Danton against Louis XIV is insurrection; Hebert against Danton is revolt.

Hence it results that if insurrection in given cases may be, as Lafayette says, the most holy of duties, an uprising may be the most fatal of crimes.

There is also a difference in the intensity of heat; insurrection is often a volcano, revolt is often only a fire of straw.

Revolt, as we have said, is sometimes found among those in power. Polignac is a rioter; Camille Desmoulins is one of the governing powers.

Insurrection is sometimes resurrection.

The solution of everything by universal suffrage being an absolutely modern fact, and all history anterior to this fact being, for the space of four thousand years, filled with violated right, and the suffering of peoples, each epoch of history brings with it that protest of which it is capable. Under the Caesars, there was no insurrection, but there was Juvenal.

The facit indignatio replaces the Gracchi.

Under the Caesars, there is the exile to Syene; there is also the man of the Annales. We do not speak of the immense exile of Patmos who, on his part also, overwhelms the real world with a protest in the name of the ideal world, who makes of his vision an enormous satire and casts on Rome-Nineveh, on Rome-Babylon, on Rome-Sodom, the flaming reflection of the Apocalypse. John on his rock is the sphinx on its pedestal; we may understand him, he is a Jew, and it is Hebrew; but the man who writes the Annales is of the Latin race, let us rather say he is a Roman.

As the Neros reign in a black way, they should be painted to match. The work of the graving tool alone would be too pale; there must be poured into the channel a concentrated prose that bites.

Despots count for something in the question of philosophers. A word that is chained is a terrible word. The writer doubles and trebles his style when silence is imposed on a nation by its master. From this silence there arises a certain mysterious plenitude that filters into thought and there congeals into bronze. The compression of history produces conciseness in the historian. The granite solidity of such and such a celebrated prose is nothing but the accumulation effected by the tyrant.

Tyranny constrains the writer to conditions of diameter that are augmentations of force. The Ciceronian period, which hardly sufficed for Verres, would be blunted on Caligula. The less spread of sail in the phrase, the more intensity in the blow. Tacitus thinks with all his might.

The honesty of a great heart, condensed in justice and truth, overwhelms as with lightning.

Be it remarked, in passing, that Tacitus is not historically superposed upon Caesar. The Tiberii were reserved for him. Caesar and Tacitus are two successive phenomena, a meeting between whom seems to be mysteriously avoided, by the One who, when He sets the centuries on the stage, regulates the entrances and the exits. Caesar is great, Tacitus is great; God spares these two greatnesses by not allowing them to clash with one another. The guardian of justice, in striking Caesar, might strike too hard and be unjust. God does not will it. The great wars of Africa and Spain, the pirates of Sicily destroyed, civilization introduced into Gaul, into Britanny, into Germany, all this glory covers the Rubicon. There is here a sort of delicacy of the divine justice, hesitating to let loose upon the illustrious usurper the formidable historian, sparing Caesar Tacitus, and according extenuating circumstances to genius.

Certainly, despotism remains despotism, even under the despot of genius. There is corruption under all illustrious tyrants, but the moral pest is still more hideous under infamous tyrants. In such reigns, nothing veils the shame; and those who make examples, Tacitus as well as Juvenal, slap this ignominy, which cannot reply, in the face, more usefully in the presence of all humanity.

Rome smells worse under Vitellius than under Sylla. Under Claudius and under Domitian, there is a deformity of baseness corresponding to the repulsiveness of the tyrant. The villainy of slaves is a direct product of the despot; a miasma exhales from these cowering consciences wherein the master is reflected; public powers are unclean; hearts are small; consciences are dull, souls are like vermin; thus it is under Caracalla, thus it is under Commodus, thus it is under Heliogabalus, while, from the Roman Senate, under Caesar, there comes nothing but the odor of the dung which is peculiar to the aeries of the eagles.

Hence the advent, apparently tardy, of the Tacituses and the Juvenals; it is in the hour for evidence, that the demonstrator makes his appearance.

But Juvenal and Tacitus, like Isaiah in Biblical times, like Dante in the Middle Ages, is man; riot and insurrection are the multitude, which is sometimes right and sometimes wrong.

In the majority of cases, riot proceeds from a material fact; insurrection is always a moral phenomenon. Riot is Masaniello; insurrection, Spartacus. Insurrection borders on mind, riot on the stomach; Gaster grows irritated; but Gaster, assuredly, is not always in the wrong. In questions of famine, riot, Buzancais, for example, holds a true, pathetic, and just point of departure. Nevertheless, it remains a riot. Why? It is because, right at bottom, it was wrong in form. Shy although in the right, violent although strong, it struck at random; it walked like a blind elephant; it left behind it the corpses of old men, of women, and of children; it wished the blood of inoffensive and innocent persons without knowing why. The nourishment of the people is a good object; to massacre them is a bad means.

All armed protests, even the most legitimate, even that of the 10th of August, even that of July 14th, begin with the same troubles. Before the right gets set free, there is foam and tumult. In the beginning, the insurrection is a riot, just as a river is a torrent. Ordinarily it ends in that ocean: revolution. Sometimes, however, coming from those lofty mountains which dominate the moral horizon, justice, wisdom, reason, right, formed of the pure snow of the ideal, after a long fall from rock to rock, after having reflected the sky in its transparency and increased by a hundred affluents in the majestic mien of triumph, insurrection is suddenly lost in some quagmire, as the Rhine is in a swamp.

All this is of the past, the future is another thing. Universal suffrage has this admirable property, that it dissolves riot in its inception, and, by giving the vote to insurrection, it deprives it of its arms. The disappearance of wars, of street wars as well as of wars on the frontiers, such is the inevitable progression. Whatever today may be, tomorrow will be peace.

However, insurrection, riot, and points of difference between the former and the latter, the bourgeois, properly speaking, knows nothing of such shades. In his mind, all is sedition, rebellion pure and simple, the revolt of the dog against his master, an attempt to bite whom must be punished by the chain and the kennel, barking, snapping, until such day as the head of the dog, suddenly enlarged, is outlined vaguely in the gloom face to face with the lion.

Then the bourgeois shouts, "Long live the people!"

This explanation given, what does the movement of June, 1832, signify, so far as history is concerned? Is it a revolt? Is it an insurrection?

It may happen to us, in placing this formidable event on the stage, to say revolt now and then, but merely to distinguish superficial facts, and always preserving the distinction between revolt, the form, and insurrection, the foundation.

This movement of 1832 had, in its rapid outbreak and in its melancholy extinction, so much grandeur, that even those who see in it only an uprising, never refer to it otherwise than with respect. For them, it is like a relic of 1830. Excited imaginations, say they, are not to be calmed in a day. A revolution cannot be cut off short. It must need undergo some undulations before it returns to a state of rest, like a mountain sinking into the plain. There are no Alps without their Jura, nor Pyrenees without the Asturias.

This pathetic crisis of contemporary history that the memory of Parisians calls "the epoch of the riots," is certainly a characteristic hour amid the stormy hours of this century. A last word, before we enter on the recital.

The facts that we are about to relate belong to that dramatic and living reality, which the historian sometimes neglects for lack of time and space. There, nevertheless, we insist upon it, is life, palpitation, human tremor. Petty details, as we think we have already said, are, so to speak, the foliage of great events, and are lost in the distance of history. The epoch, surnamed "of the riots," abounds in details of this nature. Judicial inquiries have not revealed, and perhaps have not sounded the depths, for another reason than history. We shall therefore bring to light, among the known and published peculiarities, things that have not heretofore been known, about facts over which have passed the forgetfulness of some, and the death of others. The majority of the actors in these gigantic scenes have disappeared; beginning with the very next day they held their peace; but of what we shall relate, we shall be able to say, "We have seen this." We alter a few names, for history relates and does not inform against, but the deed we shall paint will be genuine. In accordance with the conditions of the book which we are now writing, we shall show only one side and one episode, and certainly, the least known at that, of the two days, the 5th and the 6th of June, 1832, but we shall do it in such wise that the reader may catch a glimpse, beneath the gloomy veil, which we are about to lift, of the real form of this frightful public adventure.

CHAPTER III—A BURIAL;
AN OCCASION TO BE BORN AGAIN

In the spring of 1832, although the cholera had been chilling all minds for the last three months and had cast over their agitation an indescribable and gloomy pacification, Paris had already long been ripe for commotion. As we have said, the great city resembles a piece of artillery; when it is loaded, it suffices for a spark to fall, and the shot is discharged. In June, 1832, the spark was the death of General Lamarque.

Lamarque was a man of renown and of action. He had had in succession, under the Empire and under the Restoration, the sorts of bravery requisite for the two epochs, the bravery of the battlefield and the bravery of the tribune. He was as eloquent as he had been valiant; a sword was discernible in his speech. Like Foy, his predecessor, after upholding the command, he upheld liberty; he sat between the left and the extreme left, beloved of the people because he accepted the chances of the future, beloved of the populace because he had served the Emperor well; he was, in company with Comtes Gerard and Drouet, one of Napoleon's marshals in petto. The treaties of 1815 removed him as a personal offense. He hated Wellington with a downright hatred that pleased the multitude; and, for seventeen years, he majestically preserved the sadness of Waterloo, paying hardly any attention to intervening events. In his death agony, at his last hour, he clasped to his breast a sword that had been presented to him by the officers of the Hundred Days. Napoleon had died uttering the word army, Lamarque uttering the word country.

His death, which was expected, was dreaded by the people as a loss, and by the government as an occasion. This death was an affliction. Like everything that is bitter, affliction may turn to revolt. This is what took place.

On the preceding evening, and on the morning of the 5th of June, the day appointed for Lamarque's burial, the Faubourg Saint-Antoine, which the procession was to touch at, assumed a formidable aspect. This tumultuous network of streets was filled with rumors. They armed themselves as best they might. Joiners carried off door weights of their establishment "to break down doors." One of them had made himself a dagger of a stocking weaver's hook by breaking off the hook and sharpening the stump. Another, who was in a fever "to attack," slept wholly dressed for three days. A carpenter named Lombier met a comrade, who asked him: "Where are you going?"

"Eh! Well, I have no weapons."

"What then?"

"I'm going to my timberyard to get my compasses."

"What for?"

"I don't know," said Lombier.

A certain Jacqueline, an expeditious man, accosted some passing artisans, "Come here, you!"

He treated them to ten sous' worth of wine and said, "Have you work?"

"No."

"Go to Filspierre, between the Barriere Charonne and the Barriere Montreuil, and you will find work."

At Filspierre's they found cartridges and arms. Certain well-known leaders were going the rounds, that is to say, running from one house to another, to collect their men. At Barthelemy's, near the Barriere du Trone, at Capel's, near the Petit-Chapeau, the drinkers accosted each other with a grave air. They were heard to say, "Have you your pistol?"

"Under my blouse."

"And you?"

"Under my shirt."

In the Rue Traversiere, in front of the Bland workshop, and in the yard of the Maison-Brulee, in front of toolmaker Bernier's, groups whispered together. Among them was observed a certain Mavot, who never remained more than a week in one shop, as the masters always discharged him "because they were obliged to dispute with him every day." Mavot was killed on the following day at the barricade of the Rue Menilmontant. Pretot, who was destined to perish also in the struggle, seconded Mavot, and to the question, "What is your object?"

He replied, "Insurrection."

Workmen assembled at the corner of the Rue de Bercy, waited for a certain Lemarin, the revolutionary agent for the Faubourg Saint-Marceau. Watchwords were exchanged almost publicly.

On the 5th of June, accordingly, a day of mingled rain and sun, General Lamarque's funeral procession traversed Paris with official military pomp, somewhat augmented through precaution. Two battalions, with draped drums and reversed arms, ten thousand National Guards, with their swords at their sides, escorted the coffin. The hearse was drawn by young men. The officers of the Invalides came immediately behind it, bearing laurel branches. Then came an innumerable, strange, agitated multitude, the sectionaries of the Friends of the People, the Law School, the Medical School, refugees of all nationalities, and Spanish, Italian, German, and Polish flags, tricolored horizontal banners, every possible sort of banner, children waving green boughs, stonecutters and carpenters who were on strike at the moment, printers who were recognizable by their paper caps, marching two by two, three by three, uttering cries, nearly all of them brandishing sticks, some brandishing sabers, without order and yet with a single soul, now a tumultuous rout, again a column. Squads chose themselves leaders; a man armed with a pair of pistols in full view, seemed to pass the host in review, and the files separated before him. On the side alleys of the boulevards, in the branches of the trees, on balconies, in windows, on the roofs, swarmed the heads of men, women, and children; all eyes were filled with anxiety. An armed throng was passing, and a terrified throng looked on.

The Government, on its side, was taking observations. It observed with its hand on its sword. Four squadrons of carabineers could be seen in the Place Louis XV in their saddles, with their trumpets at their head, cartridge boxes filled and muskets loaded, all in readiness to march; in the Latin country and at the Jardin des Plantes, the Municipal Guard echeloned from street to street; at the Halle-aux-Vins, a squadron of dragoons; at the Greve half of the 12th Light Infantry, the other half being at the Bastille; the 6th Dragoons at the Celestins; and the courtyard of the Louvre full of artillery. The remainder of the troops were confined to their barracks, without reckoning the regiments of the environs of Paris. Power being uneasy, held suspended over the menacing multitude twenty-four thousand soldiers in the city and thirty thousand in the banlieue.

Divers reports were in circulation in the cortege. Legitimist tricks were hinted at; they spoke of the Duc de Reichstadt, whom God had marked out for death at that very moment when the populace were designating him for the Empire. One personage, whose name has remained unknown, announced that at a given hour two overseers who had been won over, would throw open the doors of a factory of arms to the people. That which predominated on the uncovered brows of the majority of those present was enthusiasm mingled with dejection. Here and there, also, in that multitude given over to such violent but noble emotions, there were visible genuine visages of criminals and ignoble mouths that said, "Let us plunder!" There are certain agitations that stir up the bottoms of marshes and make clouds of mud rise through the water. A phenomenon to which "well drilled" policemen are no strangers.

The procession proceeded, with feverish slowness, from the house of the deceased, by way of the boulevards as far as the Bastille. It rained from time to time; the rain mattered nothing to that throng. Many incidents, the coffin borne around the Vendome column, stones thrown at the Duc de Fitz-James, who was seen on a balcony with his hat on his head, the Gallic cock torn from a popular flag and dragged in the mire, a policeman wounded with a blow from a sword at the Porte Saint-Martin, an officer of the 12th Light Infantry saying aloud, "I am a Republican," the Polytechnic School coming up unexpectedly against orders to remain at home, the shouts of, "Long live the Polytechnique! Long live the Republic!" marked the passage of the funeral train. At the Bastille, long files of curious and formidable people who descended from the Faubourg Saint-Antoine, effected a junction with the procession, and a certain terrible seething began to agitate the throng.

One man was heard to say to another, "Do you see that fellow with a red beard, he's the one who will give the word when we are to fire." It appears that this red beard was present, at another riot, the Quenisset affair, entrusted with this same function.

The hearse passed the Bastille, traversed the small bridge, and reached the esplanade of the bridge of Austerlitz. There it halted. The crowd, surveyed at that moment with a bird's-eye view, would have presented the aspect of a comet whose head was on the esplanade and whose tail spread out over the Quai Bourdon, covered the Bastille, and was prolonged on the boulevard as far as the Porte Saint-Martin. A circle was traced around the hearse. The vast rout held their peace. Lafayette spoke and bade Lamarque farewell. This was a touching and august instant, all heads uncovered, all hearts beat high.

All at once, a man on horseback, clad in black, made his appearance in the middle of the group with a red flag, others say, with a pike surmounted with a red liberty cap. Lafayette turned aside his head. Exelmans quitted the procession.

This red flag raised a storm, and disappeared in the midst of it. From the Boulevard Bourdon to the bridge of Austerlitz one of those clamors that resemble billows stirred the multitude. Two prodigious shouts went up, "Lamarque to the Pantheon!—Lafayette to the town hall!" Some young men, amid the declamations of the throng, harnessed themselves and began to drag Lamarque in the hearse across the bridge of Austerlitz and Lafayette in a hackney-coach along the Quai Morland.

In the crowd that surrounded and cheered Lafayette, it was noticed that a German showed himself named Ludwig Snyder, who died a centenarian afterward, who had also been in the war of 1776, and who had fought at Trenton under Washington, and at Brandywine under Lafayette.

In the meantime, the municipal cavalry on the left bank had been set in motion, and came to bar the bridge, on the right bank the dragoons emerged from the Celestins and deployed along the Quai Morland. The men who were dragging Lafayette suddenly caught sight of them at the corner of the quay and shouted, "The dragoons!" The dragoons advanced at a walk, in silence, with their pistols in their holsters, their swords in their scabbards, their guns slung in their leather sockets, with an air of gloomy expectation.

They halted two hundred paces from the little bridge. The carriage in which sat Lafayette advanced to them, their ranks opened and allowed it to pass, and then closed behind it. At that moment the dragoons and the crowd touched. The women fled in terror. What took place during that fatal minute? No one can say. It is the dark moment when two clouds come together. Some declare that a blast of trumpets sounding the charge was heard in the direction of the Arsenal others that a blow from a dagger was given by a child to a dragoon. The fact is, that three shots were suddenly discharged: the first killed Cholet, chief of the squadron; the second killed an old deaf woman who was in the act of closing her window; the third singed the shoulder of an officer. A woman screamed, "They are beginning too soon!" and all at once, a squadron of dragoons, which had remained in the barracks up to this time, was seen to debouch at a gallop with bared swords, through the Rue Bassompierre and the Boulevard Bourdon, sweeping all before them.

Then all is said, the tempest is loosed, stones rain down, a fusillade breaks forth, many precipitate themselves to the bottom of the bank, and pass the small arm of the Seine, now filled in, the timberyards of the Isle Louviers, that vast citadel ready to hand, bristle with combatants, stakes are torn up, pistol shots fired, a barricade begun, the young men who are thrust back pass the Austerlitz bridge with the hearse at a run, and the municipal guard, the carabineers rush up, the dragoons ply their swords, the crowd disperses in all directions, a rumor of war flies to all four quarters of Paris, men shout, "To arms!" they run, tumble down, flee, resist. Wrath spreads abroad the riot as wind spreads a fire.

CHAPTER IV—THE EBULLITIONS OF FORMER DAYS

Nothing is more extraordinary than the first breaking out of a riot. Everything bursts forth everywhere at once. Was it foreseen? Yes. Was it prepared? No. From where comes it? From the pavements. From where falls it? From the clouds. Here insurrection assumes the character of a plot; there of an improvisation. The first comer seizes a current of the throng and leads it where he wills. A beginning full of terror, in which is mingled a sort of formidable gaiety. First come clamors, the shops are closed, the displays of the merchants disappear; then come isolated shots; people flee; blows from gun stocks beat against porte cochères, servants can be heard laughing in the courtyards of houses and saying, "There's going to be a row!"

A quarter of an hour had not elapsed when this is what was taking place at twenty different spots in Paris at once.

In the Rue Sainte-Croix-de-la-Bretonnerie, twenty young men, bearded and with long hair, entered a dram shop and emerged a moment later, carrying a horizontal tricolored flag covered with crape, and having at their head three men armed, one with a sword, one with a gun, and the third with a pike.

In the Rue des Nonaindieres, a very well-dressed bourgeois, who had a prominent belly, a sonorous voice, a bald head, a lofty brow, a black beard, and one of these stiff mustaches which will not lie flat, offered cartridges publicly to passersby.

In the Rue Saint-Pierre-Montmartre, men with bare arms carried about a black flag, on which could be read in white letters this inscription: "Republic or Death!" In the Rue des Jeuneurs, Rue du Cadran, Rue Montorgueil, Rue Mandar, groups appeared waving flags on which could be distinguished in gold letters, the word section with a number. One of these flags was red and blue with an almost imperceptible stripe of white between.

They pillaged a factory of small arms on the Boulevard Saint-Martin, and three armorers' shops, the first in the Rue Beaubourg, the second in the Rue Michel-le-Comte, the other in the Rue du Temple. In a few minutes, the thousand hands of the crowd had seized and carried off two hundred and thirty guns, nearly all double-barreled, sixty-four swords, and eighty-three pistols. In order to provide more arms, one man took the gun, the other the bayonet.

Opposite the Quai de la Grève, young men armed with muskets installed themselves in the houses of some women for the purpose of firing. One of them had a flintlock. They rang, entered, and set about making cartridges.

One of these women relates, "I did not know what cartridges were; it was my husband who told me."

One cluster broke into a curiosity shop in the Rue des Vielles Haudriettes, and seized yataghans and Turkish arms.

The body of a mason who had been killed by a gunshot lay in the Rue de la Perle.

And then on the right bank, the left bank, on the quays, on the boulevards, in the Latin country, in the quarter of the Halles, panting men, artisans, students, members of sections read proclamations and shouted, "To arms!" broke street lanterns, unharnessed carriages, unpaved the streets, broke in the doors of houses, uprooted trees, rummaged cellars, rolled out hogsheads, heaped up paving stones, rough slabs, furniture and planks, and made barricades.

They forced the bourgeois to assist them in this. They entered the dwellings of women, they forced them to hand over the swords and guns of their absent husbands, and they wrote on the door, with whiting, "The arms have been delivered;" some signed "their names" to receipts for the guns and swords and said, "Send for them tomorrow at the Mayor's office." They disarmed isolated sentinels and National Guardsmen in the streets on their way to the town hall. They tore the epaulets from officers. In the Rue du Cimitiere-Saint-Nicholas, an officer of the National Guard, on being pursued by a crowd armed with clubs and foils, took refuge with difficulty in a house, from which he was only able to emerge at nightfall and in disguise.

In the Quartier Saint-Jacques, the students swarmed out of their hotels and ascended the Rue Saint-Hyacinthe to the Café du Progress, or descended to the Café des Sept-Billards, in the Rue des Mathurins. There, in front of the door, young men mounted on the stone corner posts, distributed arms. They plundered the timberyard in the Rue Transnonain in order to obtain material for barricades. On a single point the inhabitants resisted, at the corner of the Rue Sainte-Avoye and the Rue Simon-Le-Franc, where they destroyed the barricade with their own hands. At a single point the insurgents yielded; they abandoned a barricade begun in the Rue de Temple after having fired on a detachment of the National Guard, and fled through the Rue de la Corderie. The detachment picked up in the barricade a red flag, a package of cartridges, and three hundred pistol balls. The National Guardsmen tore up the flag, and carried off its tattered remains on the points of their bayonets.

All that we are here relating slowly and successively took place simultaneously at all points of the city in the midst of a vast tumult, like a mass of tongues of lightning in one clap of thunder. In less than an hour, twenty-seven barricades sprang out of the earth in the quarter of the Halles alone. In the center was that famous house No. 50, which was the fortress of Jeanne and her six hundred companions, and which, flanked on the one hand by a barricade at Saint-Merry, and on the other by a barricade of the Rue Maubuee, commanded three streets, the Rue des Arcis, the Rue Saint-Martin, and the Rue Aubry-le-Boucher, which it faced. The barricades at right angles fell back, the one of the Rue Montorgueil on the Grande-Truanderie, the other of the Rue Geoffroy-Langevin on the Rue Sainte-Avoye. Without reckoning innumerable barricades in twenty other quarters of Paris, in the Marais, at Mont-Sainte-Genevieve; one in the Rue Menilmontant, where was visible a porte cochère torn from its hinges; another near the little bridge of the Hotel-Dieu made with an "ecossais," which had been unharnessed and overthrown, three hundred paces from the Prefecture of Police.

At the barricade of the Rue des Menetriers, a well-dressed man distributed money to the workmen. At the barricade of the Rue Grenetat, a horseman made his appearance and handed to the one who seemed to be the commander of the barricade what had the appearance of a roll of silver. "Here," said he, "this is to pay expenses, wine, et cetera." A light-haired young man, without a cravat, went from barricade to barricade, carrying passwords. Another, with a naked sword, a blue police cap on his head, placed sentinels. In the interior, beyond the barricades, the wine shops and porters' lodges were converted into guardhouses. Otherwise the riot was conducted after the most scientific military tactics. The narrow, uneven, sinuous streets, full of angles and turns, were admirably chosen; the neighborhood of the Halles, in particular, a network of streets more intricate than a forest. The Society of the Friends of the People had, it was said, undertaken to direct the insurrection in the Quartier Sainte-Avoye. A man killed in the Rue du Ponceau who was searched had on his person a plan of Paris.

That which had really undertaken the direction of the uprising was a sort of strange impetuosity that was in the air. The insurrection had abruptly built barricades with one hand, and with the other seized nearly all the posts of the garrison. In less than three hours, like a train of powder catching fire, the insurgents had invaded and occupied, on the right bank, the Arsenal, the Mayoralty of the Place Royale, the whole of the Marais, the Popincourt arms manufactory, la Galiote, the Chateau-d'Eau, and all the streets near the Halles; on the left bank, the barracks of the Veterans, Sainte-Pelagie, the Place Maubert, the powder magazine of the Deux-Moulins, and all the barriers. At five o'clock in the evening, they were masters of the Bastille, of the Lingerie, of the Blancs-Manteaux; their scouts had reached the Place des Victoires, and menaced the bank, the Petits-Peres barracks, and the post office. A third of Paris was in the hands of the rioters.

The conflict had been begun on a gigantic scale at all points; and, as a result of the disarming domiciliary visits, and armorers' shops hastily invaded, was, that the combat which had begun with the throwing of stones was continued with gunshots.

About six o'clock in the evening, the Passage du Saumon became the field of battle. The uprising was at one end, the troops were at the other. They fired from one gate to the other. An observer, a dreamer, the author of this book, who had gone to get a near view of this volcano, found himself in the passage between the two fires. All that he had to protect him from the bullets was the swell of the two half-columns which separate the shops; he remained in this delicate situation for nearly half an hour.

Meanwhile the call to arms was beaten, the National Guard armed in haste, the legions emerged from the Mayoralities, the regiments from their barracks. Opposite the passage de l'Ancre a drummer received a blow from a dagger. Another, in the Rue du Cygne, was assailed by thirty young men who broke his instrument, and took away his sword. Another was killed in the Rue Grenier-Saint-Lazare. In the Rue-Michelle-Comte, three officers fell dead one after the other. Many of the Municipal Guards, on being wounded, in the Rue des Lombards, retreated.

In front of the Cour-Batave, a detachment of National Guards found a red flag bearing the following inscription: Republican revolution, No. 127. Was this a revolution, in fact?

The insurrection had made of the center of Paris a sort of inextricable, tortuous, colossal citadel.

There was the hearth; there, evidently, was the question. All the rest was nothing but skirmishes. The proof that all would be decided there lay in the fact that there was no fighting going on there as yet.

In some regiments, the soldiers were uncertain, which added to the fearful uncertainty of the crisis. They recalled the popular ovation that had greeted the neutrality of the 53rd of the Line in July, 1830. Two intrepid men, tried in great wars, the Marshal Lobau and General Bugeaud, were in command, Bugeaud under Lobau. Enormous patrols, composed of battalions of the Line, enclosed in entire companies of the National Guard, and preceded by a commissary of police wearing his scarf of office, went to reconnoiter the streets in rebellion. The insurgents, on their side, placed *vedettes** at the corners of all open spaces, and audaciously sent their patrols outside the barricades. Each side was watching the other. The Government, with an army in its hand, hesitated; the night was almost upon them, and the Saint-Merry tocsin began to make itself heard. The Minister of War at that time, Marshal Soult, who had seen Austerlitz, regarded this with a gloomy air.

These old sailors, accustomed to correct maneuvers and having as resource and guide only tactics, that compass of battles, are utterly disconcerted in the presence of that immense foam which is called public wrath.

The National Guards of the suburbs rushed up in haste and disorder. A battalion of the 12th Light came at a run from Saint-Denis, the 14th of the

---

* a mounted sentry who relayed warnings or messages to troops

Line arrived from Courbevoie, the batteries of the Military School had taken up their position on the Carrousel; cannons were descending from Vincennes.

Solitude was formed around the Tuileries. Louis Philippe was perfectly serene.

CHAPTER V—ORIGINALITY OF PARIS

During the last two years, as we have said, Paris had witnessed more than one insurrection. Nothing is, generally, more singularly calm than the physiognomy of Paris during an uprising beyond the bounds of the rebellious quarters. Paris very speedily accustoms herself to anything, it is only a riot, and Paris has so many affairs on hand, that she does not put herself out for so small a matter. These colossal cities alone can offer such spectacles. These immense enclosures alone can contain at the same time civil war and an odd and indescribable tranquility. Ordinarily, when an insurrection commences, when the shopkeeper hears the drum, the call to arms, the general alarm, he contents himself with the remark, "There appears to be a squabble in the Rue Saint-Martin." Or, "In the Faubourg Saint-Antoine."

Often he adds carelessly, "Or somewhere in that direction."

Later on, when the heart-rending and mournful hubbub of musketry and firing by platoons becomes audible, the shopkeeper says, "It's getting hot! Hullo, it's getting hot!"

A moment later, the riot approaches and gains in force, he shuts up his shop precipitately, hastily dons his uniform, that is to say, he places his merchandise in safety and risks his own person.

Men fire in a square, in a passage, in a blind alley; they take and retake the barricade; blood flows, the grapeshot riddles the fronts of the houses, the balls kill people in their beds, corpses encumber the streets. A few streets away, the shock of billiard balls can be heard in the cafés.

The theaters open their doors and present vaudevilles; the curious laugh and chat a couple of paces distant from these streets filled with war. Hackney carriages go their way; passersby are going to a dinner somewhere in town. Sometimes in the very quarter where the fighting is going on.

In 1831, a fusillade was stopped to allow a wedding party to pass.

At the time of the insurrection of 1839, in the Rue Saint-Martin a little, infirm old man, pushing a handcart surmounted by a tricolored rag, in which he had carafes filled with some sort of liquid, went and came from barricade to troops and from troops to the barricade, offering his glasses of cocoa impartially, now to the Government, now to anarchy.

Nothing can be stranger; and this is the peculiar character of uprisings in Paris, which cannot be found in any other capital. To this end, two things are requisite, the size of Paris and its gaiety. The city of Voltaire and Napoleon is necessary.

On this occasion, however, in the resort to arms of June 25th, 1832, the great city felt something that was, perhaps, stronger than itself. It was afraid.

Closed doors, windows, and shutters were to be seen everywhere, in the most distant and most "disinterested" quarters. The courageous took to arms, the poltroons hid. The busy and heedless passerby disappeared. Many streets were empty at four o'clock in the morning.

Alarming details were hawked about, fatal news was disseminated, that they were masters of the bank—that there were six hundred of them in the Cloister of Saint-Merry alone, entrenched and embattled in the church; that the line was not to be depended on; that Armand Carrel had been to see Marshal Clausel and that the Marshal had said: "Get a regiment first;" that Lafayette was ill, but that he had said to them, nevertheless, "I am with you. I will follow you wherever there is room for a chair;" that one must be on one's guard; that at night there would be people pillaging isolated dwellings in the deserted corners of Paris (there the imagination of the police, that Anne Radcliffe mixed up with the Government was recognizable); that a battery had been established in the Rue Aubry le Boucher; that Lobau and Bugeaud were putting their heads together, and that, at midnight, or at daybreak at latest, four columns would march simultaneously on the center of the uprising, the first coming from the Bastille, the second from the Porte Saint-Martin, the third from the Greve, the fourth from the Halles; that perhaps, also, the troops would evacuate Paris and withdraw to the Champ-de-Mars; that no one knew what would happen, but that this time, it certainly was serious.

People busied themselves over Marshal Soult's hesitations. Why did not he attack at once? It is certain that he was profoundly absorbed. The old lion seemed to scent an unknown monster in that gloom.

Evening came, the theaters did not open; the patrols circulated with an air of irritation; passersby were searched; suspicious persons were arrested. By nine o'clock, more than eight hundred persons had been arrested, the Prefecture of Police was encumbered with them, so was the Conciergerie, so was La Force.

At the Conciergerie in particular, the long vault called the Rue de Paris was littered with trusses of straw upon which lay a heap of prisoners, whom the man of Lyons, Lagrange, harangued valiantly. All that straw rustled by all these men, produced the sound of a heavy shower. Elsewhere prisoners slept in the open air in the meadows, piled on top of each other.

Anxiety reigned everywhere, and a certain tremor, which was not habitual with Paris.

People barricaded themselves in their houses; wives and mothers were uneasy; nothing was to be heard but this, "Ah! My God! He has not come home!" There was hardly even the distant rumble of a vehicle to be heard.

People listened on their thresholds, to the rumors, the shouts, the tumult, the dull and indistinct sounds, to the things that were said, "It is cavalry," or, "Those are the caissons galloping," to the trumpets, the drums, the firing, and, above all, to that lamentable alarm peal from Saint-Merry.

They waited for the first cannon shot. Men sprang up at the corners of the streets and disappeared, shouting, "Go home!" And people made haste to bolt their doors. They said, "How will all this end?" From moment to moment, in proportion as the darkness descended, Paris seemed to take on a more mournful hue from the formidable flaming of the revolt.

BOOK ELEVENTH: THE ATOM FRATERNIZES WITH THE HURRICANE

CHAPTER I—SOME EXPLANATIONS WITH REGARD TO THE ORIGIN OF GAVROCHE'S POETRY. THE INFLUENCE OF AN ACADEMICIAN ON THIS POETRY

At the instant when the insurrection, arising from the shock of the populace and the military in front of the Arsenal, started a movement in advance and toward the rear in the multitude that was following the hearse and which, through the whole length of the boulevards, weighed, so to speak, on the head of the procession, there arose a frightful ebb. The rout was shaken, their ranks were broken, all ran, fled, made their escape, some with shouts of attack, others with the pallor of flight. The great river that covered the boulevards divided in a twinkling, overflowed to right and left, and spread in torrents over two hundred streets at once with the roar of a sewer that has broken loose.

At that moment, a ragged child who was coming down through the Rue Menilmontant, holding in his hand a branch of blossoming laburnum, which he had just plucked on the heights of Belleville, caught sight of an old holster pistol in the show window of a bric-a-brac merchant's shop.

"Mother What's-your-name, I'm going to borrow your machine."

And off he ran with the pistol.

Two minutes later, a flood of frightened bourgeois who were fleeing through the Rue Amelot and the Rue Basse, encountered the lad brandishing his pistol and singing:

"At night, one sees nothing,
By day, one sees very well,
The bourgeois gets flurried over
An apocryphal scrawl,
Practice virtue,
Tutu, pointed hat!"

It was little Gavroche on his way to the wars. On the boulevard he noticed that the pistol had no trigger.

Who was the author of that couplet, which served to punctuate his march, and of all the other songs that he was fond of singing on occasion? We know not. Who does know? Himself, perhaps. However, Gavroche was well up in all the popular tunes in circulation, and he mingled with them his own chirpings. An observing urchin and a rogue, he made a potpourri of the voices of nature and the voices of Paris. He combined the repertory of the birds with the repertory of the workshops. He was acquainted with thieves, a tribe contiguous to his own. He had, it appears, been for three months apprenticed to a printer. He had one day executed a commission for M. Baour-Lormian, one of the Forty. Gavroche was a gamin of letters.

Moreover, Gavroche had no suspicion of the fact that when he had offered the hospitality of his elephant to two brats on that villainously rainy night, it was to his own brothers that he had played the part of Providence. His brothers in the evening, his father in the morning; that is what his night had been like. On quitting the Rue des Ballets at daybreak, he had returned in haste to the elephant, had artistically extracted from it the two brats, had shared with them some sort of breakfast that he had invented, and had then gone away, confiding them to that good mother, the street, who had brought him up, almost entirely. On leaving them, he had appointed to meet them at the same spot in the evening, and had left them this discourse by way of a farewell, "I break a cane, otherwise expressed, I cut my stick, or, as they say at the court, I file off. If you don't find papa and mama, young 'uns, come back here this evening. I'll scramble you up some supper, and I'll give you a shakedown." The two children, picked up by some policeman and placed in the refuge, or stolen by some mountebank, or having simply strayed off in that immense Chinese puzzle of a Paris, did not return. The lowest depths of the actual social world are full of these lost traces. Gavroche did not see them again. Ten or twelve weeks had elapsed since that night. More than once he had scratched the back of his head and said, "Where the devil are my two children?"

In the meantime, he had arrived, pistol in hand, in the Rue du Pont-aux-Choux. He noticed that there was but one shop open in that street, and, a matter worthy of reflection, that was a pastry cook's shop. This presented a providential occasion to eat another apple turnover before entering the unknown. Gavroche halted, fumbled in his fob, turned his pocket inside out, found nothing, not even a sou, and began to shout, "Help!"

It is hard to miss the last cake.

Nevertheless, Gavroche pursued his way.

Two minutes later he was in the Rue Saint-Louis. While traversing the Rue du Parc-Royal, he felt called upon to make good the loss of the apple turnover, which had been impossible, and he indulged himself in the immense delight of tearing down the theater posters in broad daylight.

A little further on, on catching sight of a group of comfortable-looking persons, who seemed to be landed proprietors, he shrugged his shoulders and spit out at random before him this mouthful of philosophical bile as they passed, "How fat those moneyed men are! They're drunk! They just wallow in good dinners. Ask 'em what they do with their money. They don't know. They eat it, that's what they do! As much as their bellies will hold."

CHAPTER II—GAVROCHE ON THE MARCH

The brandishing of a triggerless pistol, grasped in one's hand in the open street, is so much of a public function that Gavroche felt his fervor increasing with every moment. Amid the scraps of the Marseillaise that he was singing, he shouted, "All goes well. I suffer a great deal in my left paw, I'm all broken up with rheumatism, but I'm satisfied, citizens. All that the bourgeois have to do is to bear themselves well, I'll sneeze them out subversive couplets. What are the police spies? Dogs. And I'd just like to have one of them at the end of my pistol. I'm just from the boulevard, my friends. It's getting hot there, it's getting into a little boil, it's simmering. It's time to skim the pot. Forward march, men! Let an impure blood inundate the furrows! I give my days to my country, I shall never see my concubine more, Nini, finished, yes, Nini? But never mind! Long live joy! Let's fight, *crebleu*! I've had enough of despotism."

At that moment, the horse of a lancer of the National Guard having fallen, Gavroche laid his pistol on the pavement, and picked up the man, then he assisted in raising the horse. After which he picked up his pistol and resumed his way. In the Rue de Thorigny, all was peace and silence. This apathy, peculiar to the Marais, presented a contrast with the vast surrounding uproar. Four gossips were chatting in a doorway.

Scotland has trios of witches, Paris has quartettes of old gossiping hags; and the "Thou shalt be King" could be quite as mournfully hurled at Bonaparte in the Carrefour Baudoyer as at Macbeth on the heath of Armuyr. The croak would be almost identical.

The gossips of the Rue de Thorigny busied themselves only with their own concerns. Three of them were portresses, and the fourth was a rag picker with her basket on her back.

All four of them seemed to be standing at the four corners of old age, which are decrepitude, decay, ruin, and sadness.

The rag picker was humble. In this open-air society, it is the rag picker who salutes and the portress who patronizes. This is caused by the corner for refuse, which is fat or lean, according to the will of the portresses, and after the fancy of the one who makes the heap. There may be kindness in the broom.

This rag picker was a grateful creature, and she smiled, with what a smile! On the three portresses. Things of this nature were said, "Ah, by the way, is your cat still cross?"

"Good gracious, cats are naturally the enemies of dogs, you know. It's the dogs who complain."

"And people also."

"But the fleas from a cat don't go after people."

"That's not the trouble, dogs are dangerous. I remember one year when there were so many dogs that it was necessary to put it in the newspapers. That was at the time when there were at the Tuileries great sheep that drew the little carriage of the King of Rome. Do you remember the King of Rome?"

"I liked the Duc de Bordeau better."

"I knew Louis XVIII. I prefer Louis XVIII."

"Meat is awfully dear, isn't it, Mother Patagon?"

"Ah! Don't mention it, the butcher's shop is a horror. A horrible horror— one can't afford anything but the poor cuts nowadays."

Here the rag picker interposed, "Ladies, business is dull. The refuse heaps are miserable. No one throws anything away any more. They eat everything."

"There are poorer people than you, la Vargouleme."

"Ah, that's true," replied the rag picker, with deference, "I have a profession."

A pause succeeded, and the rag picker, yielding to that necessity for boasting which lies at the bottom of man, added, "In the morning, on my return home, I pick over my basket, I sort my things. This makes heaps in my room. I put the rags in a basket, the cores and stalks in a bucket, the linen in my cupboard, the woolen stuff in my commode, the old papers in the corner of the window, the things that are good to eat in my bowl, the bits of glass in my fireplace, the old shoes behind my door, and the bones under my bed."

Gavroche had stopped behind her and was listening.

"Old ladies," said he, "what do you mean by talking politics?"

He was assailed by a broadside, composed of a quadruple howl.

"Here's another rascal."

"What's that he's got in his paddle? A pistol?"

"Well, I'd like to know what sort of a beggar's brat this is?"

"That sort of animal is never easy unless he's overturning the authorities."

Gavroche disdainfully contented himself, by way of reprisal, with elevating the tip of his nose with his thumb and opening his hand wide.

The rag picker cried, "You malicious, bare-pawed little wretch!"

The one who answered to the name of Patagon clapped her hands together in horror.

"There's going to be evil doings, that's certain. The errand boy next door has a little pointed beard, I have seen him pass every day with a young person in a pink bonnet on his arm; today I saw him pass, and he had a gun on his arm. Mame Bacheux says, that last week there was a revolution at—at—at—where's the calf!—at Pontoise. And then, there you see him, that horrid scamp, with his pistol! It seems that the Celestins are full of pistols. What do you suppose the Government can do with good-for-nothings who don't know how to do anything but contrive ways of upsetting the world, when we had just begun to get a little quiet after all the misfortunes that have happened, good Lord! To that poor queen whom I saw pass in the tumbril! And all this is going to make tobacco dearer. It's infamous! And I shall certainly go to see him beheaded on the guillotine, the wretch!"

"You've got the sniffles, old lady," said Gavroche. "Blow your promontory."

And he passed on. When he was in the Rue Pavee, the rag picker occurred to his mind, and he indulged in this soliloquy, "You're in the wrong to insult the revolutionists, Mother Dust-Heap-Corner. This pistol is in your interests. It's so that you may have more good things to eat in your basket."

All at once, he heard a shout behind him; it was the portress Patagon who had followed him, and who was shaking her fist at him in the distance and crying, "You're nothing but a bastard."

"Oh! Come now," said Gavroche, "I don't care a brass farthing for that!"

Shortly afterward, he passed the Hotel Lamoignon. There he uttered this appeal, "Forward march to the battle!"

And he was seized with a fit of melancholy. He gazed at his pistol with an air of reproach that seemed an attempt to appease it, "I'm going off," said he, "but you won't go off!"

One dog may distract the attention from another dog. A very gaunt poodle came along at the moment. Gavroche felt compassion for him.

"My poor doggy," said he, "you must have gone and swallowed a cask, for all the hoops are visible."

Then he directed his course toward l'Orme-Saint-Gervais.

CHAPTER III—JUST INDIGNATION
OF A HAIRDRESSER

The worthy hairdresser who had chased from his shop the two little fellows to whom Gavroche had opened the paternal interior of the elephant was at that moment in his shop engaged in shaving an old soldier of the legion, who had served under the Empire. They were talking. The hairdresser had, naturally, spoken to the veteran of the riot, then of General Lamarque, and from Lamarque they had passed to the Emperor. Thence sprang up a conversation between barber and soldier which Prudhomme, had he been present, would have enriched with arabesques, and which he would have entitled, "Dialogue between the razor and the sword."

"How did the Emperor ride, Sir?" said the barber.

"Badly. He did not know how to fall—so he never fell."

"Did he have fine horses? He must have had fine horses!"

"On the day when he gave me my cross, I noticed his beast. It was a racing mare, perfectly white. Her ears were very wide apart, her saddle deep, a fine head marked with a black star, a very long neck, strongly articulated knees, prominent ribs, oblique shoulders and a powerful crupper. A little more than fifteen hands in height."

"A pretty horse," remarked the hairdresser.

"It was His Majesty's beast."

The hairdresser felt, that after this observation, a short silence would be fitting, so he conformed himself to it, and then went on, "The Emperor was never wounded but once, was he, Sir?"

The old soldier replied with the calm and sovereign tone of a man who had been there. "In the heel. At Ratisbon. I never saw him so well dressed as on that day. He was as neat as a new sou."

"And you, Mr. Veteran, you must have been often wounded?"

"I?" said the soldier. "Ah! Not to amount to anything. At Marengo, I received two saber blows on the back of my neck, a bullet in the right arm at Austerlitz, another in the left hip at Jena. At Friedland, a thrust from a bayonet, there, at the Moskowa seven or eight lance thrusts, no matter where, at Lutzen a splinter of a shell crushed one of my fingers. Ah! And then at Waterloo, a ball from a biscaien in the thigh, that's all."

"How fine that is!" exclaimed the hairdresser, in Pindaric accents, "to die on the field of battle! On my word of honor, rather than die in bed, of an illness, slowly, a bit by bit each day, with drugs, cataplasms, syringes, medicines; I should prefer to receive a cannonball in my belly!"

"You're not over fastidious," said the soldier.

He had hardly spoken when a fearful crash shook the shop. The show window had suddenly been fractured.

The wig maker turned pale.

"Ah, good God!" he exclaimed. "It's one of them!"

"What?"

"A cannonball."

"Here it is," said the soldier.

And he picked up something that was rolling about the floor. It was a pebble.

The hairdresser ran to the broken window and beheld Gavroche fleeing at the full speed, toward the Marche Saint-Jean. As he passed the hairdresser's shop, Gavroche, who had the two brats still in his mind, had not been able to resist the impulse to say good day to him, and had flung a stone through his panes.

"You see!" shrieked the hairdresser, who from white had turned blue, "that fellow returns and does mischief for the pure pleasure of it. What has anyone done to that gamin?"

CHAPTER IV—THE CHILD IS AMAZED AT THE OLD MAN

In the meantime, in the Marche Saint-Jean, where the post had already been disarmed, Gavroche had just "effected a junction" with a band led by Enjolras, Courfeyrac, Combeferre, and Feuilly. They were armed after a fashion. Bahorel and Jean Prouvaire had found them and swelled the group. Enjolras had a double-barreled hunting gun, Combeferre the gun of a National Guard bearing the number of his legion, and in his belt, two pistols, which his unbuttoned coat allowed to be seen, Jean Prouvaire an old cavalry musket, Bahorel a rifle; Courfeyrac was brandishing an unsheathed sword cane. Feuilly, with a naked sword in his hand, marched at their head shouting, "Long live Poland!"

They reached the Quai Morland. Cravatless, hatless, breathless, soaked by the rain, with lightning in their eyes. Gavroche accosted them calmly, "Where are we going?"

"Come along," said Courfeyrac.

Behind Feuilly marched, or rather bounded, Bahorel, who was like a fish in water in a riot. He wore a scarlet waistcoat, and indulged in the sort of words that break everything. His waistcoat astounded a passerby, who cried in bewilderment, "Here are the reds!"

"The reds, the reds!" retorted Bahorel. "A queer kind of fear, bourgeois. For my part I don't tremble before a poppy, the little red hat inspires me with no alarm. Take my advice, bourgeois, let's leave fear of the red to horned cattle."

He caught sight of a corner of the wall on which was placarded the most peaceable sheet of paper in the world, a permission to eat eggs, a Lenten admonition addressed by the Archbishop of Paris to his "flock."

Bahorel exclaimed, "'Flock'—a polite way of saying 'geese.'"

And he tore the charge from the nail. This conquered Gavroche. From that instant Gavroche set himself to study Bahorel.

"Bahorel," observed Enjolras, "you are wrong. You should have let that charge alone, he is not the person with whom we have to deal, you are wasting your wrath to no purpose. Take care of your supply. One does not fire out of the ranks with the soul any more than with a gun."

"Each one in his own fashion, Enjolras," retorted Bahorel. "This bishop's prose shocks me; I want to eat eggs without being permitted. Your style is the hot and cold; I am amusing myself. Besides, I'm not wasting myself, I'm getting a start; and if I tore down that charge, *Hercle!* 'Twas only to whet my appetite."

This word, "Hercle," struck Gavroche. He sought all occasions for learning, and that tearer-down of posters possessed his esteem. He inquired of him, "What does Hercle mean?"

Bahorel answered, "It means cursed name of a dog, in Latin."

Here Bahorel recognized at a window a pale young man with a black beard who was watching them as they passed, probably a Friend of the A B C. He shouted to him, "Quick, cartridges, *para bellum.*"

"A fine man! That's true," said Gavroche, who now understood Latin.

A tumultuous retinue accompanied them, students, artists, young men affiliated to the Cougourde of Aix, artisans, longshoremen, armed with clubs and bayonets; some, like Combeferre, with pistols thrust into their trousers.

An old man, who appeared to be extremely aged, was walking in the band.

He had no arms, and he made great haste, so that he might not be left behind, although he had a thoughtful air.

Gavroche caught sight of him, *"Keksekca?"* said he to Courfeyrac.

"He's an old duffer."

It was M. Mabeuf.

CHAPTER V—THE OLD MAN

Let us recount what had taken place.

Enjolras and his friends had been on the Boulevard Bourdon, near the public storehouses, at the moment when the dragoons had made their charge. Enjolras, Courfeyrac, and Combeferre were among those who had taken to the Rue Bassompierre, shouting, "To the barricades!" In the Rue Lesdiguieres they had met an old man walking along. What had attracted their attention was that the goodman was walking in a zig-zag, as though he were intoxicated. Moreover, he had his hat in his hand, although it had been raining all the morning, and was raining pretty briskly at the very time. Courfeyrac had recognized Father Mabeuf. He knew him through having many times accompanied Marius as far as his door. As he was acquainted with the peaceful and more than timid habits of the old beadle-book collector, and was amazed at the sight of him in the midst of that uproar, a couple of paces from the cavalry charges, almost in the midst of a fusillade, hatless in the rain, and strolling about among the bullets, he had accosted him, and the following dialogue had been exchanged between the rioter of fire and the octogenarian:

"M. Mabeuf, go to your home."

"Why?"

"There's going to be a row."

"That's well."

"Thrusts with the sword and firing, M. Mabeuf."

"That is well."

"Firing from cannon."

"That is good. Where are the rest of you going?"

"We are going to fling the government to the earth."

"That is good."

And he had set out to follow them. From that moment forth he had not uttered a word. His step had suddenly become firm; artisans had offered him their arms; he had refused with a sign of the head. He advanced nearly to the front rank of the column, with the movement of a man who is marching and the countenance of a man who is sleeping.

"What a fierce old fellow!" muttered the students. The rumor spread through the troop that he was a former member of the Convention, an old regicide. The mob had turned in through the Rue de la Verrerie.

Little Gavroche marched in front with that deafening song which made of him a sort of trumpet.

He sang:

> "Here is the morn appearing. When shall we go to the forest?
> Charlot asked Charlotte. Tou, tou, tou, for Chatou, I have
> but one God, one King, one half-farthing, and one boot. And
> these two poor little wolves were as tipsy as sparrows from
> having drunk dew and thyme very early in the morning. And
> these two poor little things were as drunk as thrushes in a
> vineyard; a tiger laughed at them in his cave. The one cursed,
> the other swore. When shall we go to the forest? Charlot asked
> Charlotte."

They directed their course toward Saint-Merry.

CHAPTER VI—RECRUITS

The band augmented every moment. Near the Rue des Billettes, a man of lofty stature, whose hair was turning gray, and whose bold and daring mien was remarked by Courfeyrac, Enjolras, and Combeferre, but whom none of them knew, joined them. Gavroche, who was occupied in singing, whistling, humming, running on ahead and pounding on the shutters of the shops with the butt of his triggerless pistol; paid no attention to this man.

It chanced that in the Rue de la Verrerie, they passed in front of Courfeyrac's door.

"This happens just right," said Courfeyrac, "I have forgotten my purse, and I have lost my hat."

He quitted the mob and ran up to his quarters at full speed. He seized an old hat and his purse.

He also seized a large square coffer, of the dimensions of a large valise, which was concealed under his soiled linen.

As he descended again at a run, the portress hailed him, "Monsieur de Courfeyrac!"

"What's your name, portress?"

The portress stood bewildered.

"Why, you know perfectly well, I'm the concierge; my name is Mother Veuvain."

"Well, if you call me Monsieur de Courfeyrac again, I shall call you Mother de Veuvain. Now speak, what's the matter? What do you want?"

"There is someone who wants to speak with you."

"Who is it?"

"I don't know."

"Where is he?"

"In my lodge."

"The devil!" ejaculated Courfeyrac.

"But the person has been waiting your return for over an hour," said the portress.

At the same time, a sort of pale, thin, small, freckled, and youthful artisan, clad in a tattered blouse and patched trousers of ribbed velvet, and who had rather the air of a girl accoutered as a man than of a man, emerged from the lodge and said to Courfeyrac in a voice which was not the least in the world like a woman's voice, "Monsieur Marius, if you please."

"He is not here."

"Will he return this evening?"

"I know nothing about it."

And Courfeyrac added, "For my part, I shall not return."

The young man gazed steadily at him and said, "Why not?"

"Because."

"Where are you going, then?"

"What business is that of yours?"

"Would you like to have me carry your coffer for you?"

"I am going to the barricades."

"Would you like to have me go with you?"

"If you like!" replied Courfeyrac. "The street is free, the pavements belong to everyone."

And he made his escape at a run to join his friends. When he had rejoined them, he gave the coffer to one of them to carry. It was only a quarter of an hour after this that he saw the young man, who had actually followed them.

A mob does not go precisely where it intends. We have explained that a gust of wind carries it away. They overshot Saint-Merry and found themselves, without precisely knowing how, in the Rue Saint-Denis.

BOOK TWELFTH: CORINTHE

CHAPTER I—HISTORY OF CORINTHE FROM ITS FOUNDATION

The Parisians who nowadays on entering on the Rue Rambuteau at the end near the Halles, notice on their right, opposite the Rue Mondetour, a basket maker's shop having for its sign a basket in the form of Napoleon the Great with this inscription: NAPOLEON IS MADE WHOLLY OF WILLOW, have no suspicion of the terrible scenes which this very spot witnessed hardly thirty years ago.

It was there that lay the Rue de la Chanvrerie, which ancient deeds spell Chanverrerie, and the celebrated public house called Corinthe.

The reader will remember all that has been said about the barricade effected at this point, and eclipsed, by the way, by the barricade Saint-Merry. It was on this famous barricade of the Rue de la Chanvrerie, now fallen into profound obscurity, that we are about to shed a little light.

May we be permitted to recur, for the sake of clearness in the recital, to the simple means that we have already employed in the case of Waterloo. Persons who wish to picture to themselves in a tolerably exact manner the constitution of the houses which stood at that epoch near the Pointe Saint-Eustache, at the northeast angle of the Halles of Paris, where today lies the embouchure of the Rue Rambuteau, have only to imagine an N touching the Rue Saint-Denis with its summit and the Halles with its base, and whose two vertical bars should form the Rue de la Grande-Truanderie, and the Rue de la Chanvrerie, and whose transverse bar should be formed by the Rue de la Petite-Truanderie. The old Rue Mondetour cut the three strokes of the N at the most crooked angles. So that the labyrinthine confusion of these four streets sufficed to form, on a space three fathoms square, between the Halles and the Rue Saint-Denis on the one hand, and between the Rue du Cygne and the Rue des Prêcheurs on the other, seven islands of houses, oddly cut up, of varying sizes, placed crosswise and haphazard, and barely separated, like the blocks of stone in a dock, by narrow crannies.

We say narrow crannies, and we can give no more just idea of those dark, contracted, many-angled alleys, lined with eight-story buildings. These buildings were so decrepit that, in the Rue de la Chanvrerie and the Rue de la Petite-Truanderie, the fronts were shored up with beams running from one house to another. The street was narrow and the gutter broad, the pedestrian there walked on a pavement that was always wet, skirting little stalls resembling cellars, big posts encircled with iron hoops, excessive heaps of refuse, and gates armed with enormous, century-old gratings. The Rue Rambuteau has devastated all that.

The name of Mondetour paints marvelously well the sinuosities of that whole set of streets. A little further on, they are found still better expressed by the Rue Pirouette, which ran into the Rue Mondetour.

The passerby who got entangled from the Rue Saint-Denis in the Rue de la Chanvrerie beheld it gradually close in before him as though he had entered an elongated funnel. At the end of this street, which was very short, he found further passage barred in the direction of the Halles by a tall row of houses, and he would have thought himself in a blind alley, had he not perceived on the right and left two dark cuts through which he could make his escape. This was the Rue Mondetour, which on one side ran into the Rue de Prêcheurs, and on the other into the Rue du Cygne and the Petite-Truanderie. At the bottom of this sort of cul-de-sac, at the angle of the cutting on the right, there was to be seen a house that was not so tall as the rest, and that formed a sort of cape in the street. It is in this house, of two stories only, that an illustrious wine shop had been merrily installed three hundred years before. This tavern created a joyous noise in the very spot which old Theophilus described in the following couplet:

> "There swings the horrible skeleton
> of a poor lover who hung himself."

The situation was good, and tavern keepers succeeded each other there, from father to son.

In the time of Mathurin Regnier, this cabaret was called the Pot-aux-Roses, and as the rebus was then in fashion, it had for its signboard, a post painted rose color. In the last century, the worthy Natoire, one of the fantastic masters nowadays despised by the stiff school, having got drunk many times in this wine shop at the very table where Regnier had drunk his fill, had painted, by way of gratitude, a bunch of Corinth grapes on the pink post. The keeper of the cabaret, in his joy, had changed his device and had caused to be placed in gilt letters beneath the bunch these words: "At the Bunch of Corinth Grapes" ("Au Raisin de Corinthe"). Hence the name of Corinthe. Nothing is more natural to drunken men than ellipses. The ellipsis is the zig-zag of the phrase. Corinthe gradually dethroned the Pot-aux-Roses. The last proprietor of the dynasty, Father Hucheloup, no longer acquainted even with the tradition, had the post painted blue.

A room on the ground floor, where the bar was situated, one on the first floor containing a billiard table, a wooden spiral staircase piercing the ceiling, wine on the tables, smoke on the walls, candles in broad daylight, this was the style of this cabaret. A staircase with a trapdoor in the lower room led to the cellar. On the second floor were the lodgings of the Hucheloup family. They were reached by a staircase that was a ladder rather than a staircase, and had for their entrance only a private door in the large room on the first floor. Under the roof, in two mansard attics, were the nests for the servants. The kitchen shared the ground floor with the taproom.

Father Hucheloup had, possibly, been born a chemist, but the fact is that he was a cook; people did not confine themselves to drinking alone in his wine shop, they also ate there. Hucheloup had invented a capital thing that could be eaten nowhere but in his house, stuffed carps, which he called *carpes au gras*. These were eaten by the light of a tallow candle or of a lamp of the time of Louis XVI, on tables to which were nailed waxed cloths in lieu of tablecloths. People came there from a distance. Hucheloup, one fine morning, had seen fit to notify passersby of this "specialty"; he had dipped a brush in a pot of black paint, and as he was an orthographer on his own account, as well as a cook after his own fashion, he had improvised on his wall this remarkable inscription: CARPES HO GRAS.

One winter, the rainstorms and the showers had taken a fancy to obliterate the S that terminated the first word, and the G which began the third; this is what remained: CARPE HO RAS.

Time and rain assisting, a humble gastronomical announcement had become a profound piece of advice.

In this way it came about, that though he knew no French, Father Hucheloup understood Latin, that he had evoked philosophy from his kitchen, and that, desirous simply of effacing Lent, he had equaled Horace. And the striking thing about it was, that that also meant, "Enter my wine shop."

Nothing of all this is in existence now. The Mondetour labyrinth was disemboweled and widely opened in 1847, and probably no longer exists at the present moment. The Rue de la Chanvrerie and Corinthe have disappeared beneath the pavement of the Rue Rambuteau.

As we have already said, Corinthe was the meeting place, if not the rallying point, of Courfeyrac and his friends. It was Grantaire who had discovered Corinthe. He had entered it on account of the Carpe horas, and had returned there on account of the Carpes au gras. There they drank, there they ate, there they shouted; they did not pay much, they paid badly, they did not pay at all, but they were always welcome. Father Hucheloup was a jovial host.

Hucheloup, that amiable man, as was just said, was a wine shop keeper with a mustache; an amusing variety. He always had an ill-tempered air, seemed to wish to intimidate his customers, grumbled at the people who entered his establishment, and had rather the mien of seeking a quarrel with them than of serving them with soup. And yet, we insist upon the word, people were always welcome there. This oddity had attracted customers to his shop, and brought him young men, who said to each other, "Come hear Father Hucheloup growl." He had been a fencing master. All of a sudden, he would burst out laughing. A big voice, a good fellow. He had a comic foundation under a tragic exterior, he asked nothing better than to frighten you, very much like those snuff boxes which are in the shape of a pistol. The detonation makes one sneeze.

Mother Hucheloup, his wife, was a bearded and a very homely creature.

About 1830, Father Hucheloup died. With him disappeared the secret of stuffed carps. His inconsolable widow continued to keep the wine shop. But the cooking deteriorated, and became execrable; the wine, which had always been bad, became fearfully bad. Nevertheless, Courfeyrac and his friends continued to go to Corinthe, out of pity, as Bossuet said.

The Widow Hucheloup was breathless and misshapen and given to rustic recollections. She deprived them of their flatness by her pronunciation. She had a way of her own of saying things, which spiced her reminiscences of the village and of her springtime. It had formerly been her delight, so she affirmed, to hear the redbreasts sing in the hawthorn trees.

The hall on the first floor, where "the restaurant" was situated, was a large and long apartment encumbered with stools, chairs, benches, and tables, and with a crippled, lame, old billiard table. It was reached by a spiral staircase that terminated in the corner of the room at a square hole like the hatchway of a ship.

This room, lighted by a single narrow window, and by a lamp that was always burning, had the air of a garret. All the four-footed furniture comported itself as though it had but three legs—the whitewashed walls had for their only ornament the following quatrain in honor of Mame Hucheloup:

"She astounds at ten paces,
She frightens at two,
A wart inhabits her hazardous nose;
You tremble every instant lest she should blow it at you,
And lest, some find day, her nose should tumble into her mouth."

This was scrawled in charcoal on the wall.

Mame Hucheloup, a good likeness, went and came from morning till night before this quatrain with the most perfect tranquility. Two serving-maids, named Matelote and Gibelotte* and who had never been known by any other names, helped Mame Hucheloup to set on the tables the jugs of poor wine, and the various broths, which were served to the hungry patrons in earthenware bowls. Matelote, large, plump, redhaired, and noisy, the favorite ex-sultana of the defunct Hucheloup, was homelier than any mythological monster, be it what it may; still, as it becomes the servant to always keep in the rear of the mistress, she was less homely than Mame Hucheloup. Gibelotte, tall, delicate, white with a lymphatic pallor, with circles around her eyes, and drooping lids, always languid and weary, afflicted with what may be called chronic lassitude, the first up in the house and the last in bed, waited on everyone, even the other maid, silently and gently, smiling through her fatigue with a vague and sleepy smile.

Before entering the restaurant room, the visitor read on the door the following line written there in chalk by Courfeyrac: Treat if you can; eat if you dare.

CHAPTER II—PRELIMINARY GAIETIES

Laigle de Meaux, as the reader knows, lived more with Joly than elsewhere. He had a lodging, as a bird has one on a branch. The two friends lived together, ate together, slept together. They had everything in common, even Musichetta, to some extent. They were, what the subordinate monks who accompany monks are called, *bini*. On the morning of the 5th of June, they went to Corinthe to breakfast. Joly, who was all stuffed up, had a catarrh that Laigle was beginning to share. Laigle's coat was threadbare, but Joly was well dressed.

It was about nine o'clock in the morning, when they opened the door of Corinthe.

They ascended to the first floor.

Matelote and Gibelotte received them.

"Oysters, cheese, and ham," said Laigle.

---

* Matelote was a culinary dish made with various types of fish.
Geibelotte was stewed rabbits.

And they seated themselves at a table.

The wine shop was empty; there was no one there but themselves.

Gibelotte, knowing Joly and Laigle, set a bottle of wine on the table.

While they were busy with their first oysters, a head appeared at the hatchway of the staircase, and a voice said, "I am passing by. I smell from the street a delicious odor of Brie cheese. I enter." It was Grantaire.

Grantaire took a stool and drew up to the table.

At the sight of Grantaire, Gibelotte placed two bottles of wine on the table. That made three.

"Are you going to drink those two bottles?" Laigle inquired of Grantaire.

Grantaire replied, "All are ingenious, thou alone art ingenuous. Two bottles never yet astonished a man."

The others had begun by eating, Grantaire began by drinking. Half a bottle was rapidly gulped down.

"So you have a hole in your stomach?" began Laigle again.

"You have one in your elbow," said Grantaire.

And after having emptied his glass, he added, "Ah, by the way, Laigle of the funeral oration, your coat is old."

"I should hope so," retorted Laigle. "That's why we get on well together, my coat and I. It has acquired all my folds, it does not bind me anywhere, it is molded on my deformities, it falls in with all my movements, I am only conscious of it because it keeps me warm. Old coats are just like old friends."

"That's true," ejaculated Joly, striking into the dialogue, "an old goat is an old friend."

"Especially in the mouth of a man whose head is stuffed up," said Grantaire.

"Grantaire," demanded Laigle, "have you just come from the boulevard?"

"No."

"We have just seen the head of the procession pass, Joly and I."

"It's a marvelous sight," said Joly.

"How quiet this street is!" exclaimed Laigle. "Who would suspect that Paris was turned upside down? How plainly it is to be seen that in former days there were nothing but convents here! In this neighborhood! Du Breul and Sauval give a list of them, and so does the Abbé Lebeuf. They were all around here, they fairly swarmed, booted and barefooted, shaven, bearded, gray, black, white, Franciscans, Minims, Capuchins, Carmelites, Little Augustines, Great Augustines, old Augustines—there was no end of them."

"Don't let's talk of monks," interrupted Grantaire, "it makes one want to scratch one's self."

Then he exclaimed, "Bouh! I've just swallowed a bad oyster. Now hypochondria is taking possession of me again. The oysters are spoiled, the servants are ugly. I hate the human race. I just passed through the Rue Richelieu, in front of the big public library. That pile of oyster shells that is called a library is disgusting even to think of. What paper! What ink! What scrawling! And all that has been written! What rascal was it who said that man was a featherless biped? And then, I met a pretty girl of my acquaintance, who is as beautiful as the spring, worthy to be called Floreal, and who is delighted, enraptured, as happy as the angels, because a wretch yesterday, a frightful banker all spotted with small pox, deigned to take a fancy to her! Alas! Woman keeps on the watch for a protector as much as for a lover; cats chase mice as well as birds. Two months ago that young woman was virtuous in an attic, she adjusted little brass rings in the eyelet-holes of corsets, what do you call it? She sewed, she had a camp bed, she dwelled beside a pot of flowers, she was contented. Now here she is a bankeress. This transformation took place last night. I met the victim this morning in high spirits. The hideous point about it is, that the jade is as pretty today as she was yesterday. Her financier did not show in her face. Roses have this advantage or disadvantage over women, that the traces left upon them by caterpillars are visible. Ah! There is no morality on earth. I call to witness the myrtle, the symbol of love, the laurel, the symbol of air, the olive, that ninny, the symbol of peace, the apple tree which came nearest rangling Adam with its pips, and the fig tree, the grandfather of petticoats. As for right, do you know what right is? The Gauls covet Clusium, Rome protects Clusium, and demands what wrong Clusium has done to them. Brennus answers, 'The wrong that Alba did to you, the wrong that Fidenae did to you, the wrong that the Eques, the Volsci, and the Sabines have done to you. They were your neighbors. The Clusians are ours. We understand neighborliness just as you do. You have stolen Alba, we shall take Clusium.' Rome said, 'You shall not take Clusium.' Brennus took Rome. Then he cried, 'Vae victis!' That is what right is. Ah! What beasts of prey there are in this world! What eagles! It makes my flesh creep."

He held out his glass to Joly, who filled it, then he drank and went on, having hardly been interrupted by this glass of wine, of which no one, not even himself, had taken any notice, "Brennus, who takes Rome, is an eagle; the banker who takes the grisette is an eagle. There is no more modesty in the one case than in the other. So we believe in nothing. There is but one reality: drink. Whatever your opinion may be in favor of the lean cock, like the Canton of Uri, or in favor of the fat cock, like the Canton of Glaris, it matters little, drink. You talk to me of the boulevard, of that procession, et cetera, et cetera. Come now, is there going to be another revolution? This poverty of means on the part of the good God astounds me. He has to keep greasing the groove of events every moment. There is a hitch, it won't work. Quick, a revolution! The good God has his hands perpetually black with that cart grease. If I were in his place, I'd be perfectly simple about it, I would not wind up my mechanism every minute, I'd lead the human race in a straightforward way, I'd weave matters mesh by mesh, without breaking the thread, I would have no provisional arrangements, I would have no extraordinary repertory. What the rest of you call progress advances by means of two motors, men and events. But, sad to say, from time to time, the exceptional becomes necessary. The ordinary troupe suffices neither for event nor for men: among men geniuses are required, among events revolutions. Great accidents are the law; the order of things cannot do without them; and, judging from the apparition of comets, one would be tempted to think that Heaven itself finds actors needed for its performance. At the moment when one expects it the least, God placards a meteor on the wall of the firmament. Some queer star turns up, underlined by an enormous tail. And that causes the death of Caesar. Brutus deals him a blow with a knife, and God a blow with a comet. Crack, and behold an aurora borealis, behold a revolution, behold a great man; '93 in big letters, Napoleon on guard, the comet of 1811 at the head of the poster. Ah! What a beautiful blue theater all studded with unexpected flashes! Boom! Boom! Extraordinary show! Raise your eyes, boobies. Everything is in disorder, the star as well as the drama. Good God, it is too much and not enough. These resources, gathered from exception, seem magnificence and poverty. My friends, Providence has come down to expedients. What does a revolution prove? That God is in a quandary. He effects a coup d'etat because he, God, has not been able to make both ends meet. In fact, this confirms me in my conjectures as to Jehovah's fortune; and when I see so much distress in heaven and on earth, from the bird who has not a grain of millet to myself without a hundred thousand livres of income, when I see human destiny, which is very badly worn, and even royal destiny, which is threadbare, witness the Prince de Conde hung, when I see winter, which is nothing but a rent in the zenith through which the wind blows, when I see so many rags even in the perfectly new purple of the morning on the crests of hills, when I see the drops of dew, those mock pearls, when I see the frost, that paste, when I see humanity ripped apart and events patched up, and so many spots on the sun and so many holes in the moon, when I see so much misery everywhere, I suspect that God is not rich. The appearance exists, it is true, but I feel that he is hard up. He gives a revolution as a tradesman whose moneybox is empty gives a ball. God must not be judged from appearances. Beneath the gilding of heaven I perceive a poverty-stricken universe. Creation is bankrupt. That is why I am discontented. Here it is the 4th of June, it is almost night; ever since this morning I have been waiting for daylight to come; it has not come, and I bet that it won't come all day. This is the inexactness of an ill-paid clerk. Yes, everything is badly arranged, nothing fits anything else, this old world is all warped, I take my stand on the opposition, everything goes awry; the universe is a tease. It's like children, those who want them have none, and those who don't want them have them. Total: I'm vexed. Besides, Laigle de Meaux, that bald head, offends my sight. It humiliates me to think that I am of the same age as that baldy. However, I criticize, but I do not insult. The universe is what it is. I speak here without evil intent and to ease my conscience. Receive, Eternal Father, the assurance of my distinguished consideration. Ah! By all the saints of Olympus and by all the gods of paradise, I was not intended to be a Parisian, that is to say, to rebound forever, like a shuttlecock between two battledores, from the group of the loungers to the group of the roysterers. I was made to be a Turk, watching oriental houris all day long, executing those exquisite Egyptian dances, as sensuous as the dream of a chaste man, or a Beauceron peasant, or a Venetian gentleman surrounded by gentlewoman, or a petty German prince, furnishing the half of a foot soldier to the Germanic confederation, and occupying his leisure with drying his breeches on his hedge, that is to say, his frontier. Those are the positions for which I was born! Yes, I have said a Turk, and I will not retract. I do not understand how people can habitually take Turks in bad part; Mohammed had his good points; respect for the inventor of seraglios with houris and paradises with odalisques! Let us not insult Mohammedanism, the only religion that is ornamented with a hen roost! Now, I insist on a drink. The earth is a great piece of stupidity. And it appears that they are going to fight, all those imbeciles, and to break each other's profiles and to massacre each other in the heart of summer, in the month of June, when they might go off with a creature on their arm, to breathe the immense heaps of new-mown hay in the meadows! Really, people do commit altogether too many follies. An old broken lantern I have just seen at a bric-a-brac merchant's suggests a reflection to my mind; it is time to enlighten the human race. Yes, behold me sad again. That's what comes of swallowing an oyster and a revolution the wrong way! I am growing melancholy once more. Oh! Frightful old world. People strive, turn each other out, prostitute themselves, kill each other, and get used to it!"

And Grantaire, after this fit of eloquence, had a fit of coughing, which was well earned.

"A propos of revolution," said Joly, "it is decidedly abberent that Barius is in lub."

"Does anyone know with whom?" demanded Laigle.

"Do."

"No?"

"Do! I tell you."

"Marius's love affairs!" exclaimed Grantaire. "I can imagine it. Marius is a fog, and he must have found a vapor. Marius is of the race of poets. He who says poet, says fool, madman, Tymbraeus Apollo. Marius and his Marie, or his Marion, or his Maria, or his Mariette. They must make a queer pair of lovers. I know just what it is like. Ecstasies in which they forget to kiss. Pure on earth, but joined in heaven. They are souls possessed of senses. They lie among the stars."

Grantaire was attacking his second bottle and, possibly, his second harangue, when a new personage emerged from the square aperture of the stairs. It was a boy less than ten years of age, ragged, very small, yellow, with an odd phiz, a vivacious eye, an enormous amount of hair drenched with rain, and wearing a contented air.

The child unhesitatingly making his choice among the three, addressed himself to Laigle de Meaux.

"Are you Monsieur Bossuet?"

"That is my nickname," replied Laigle. "What do you want with me?"

"This. A tall blond fellow on the boulevard said to me, 'Do you know Mother Hucheloup?' I said, 'Yes, Rue Chanvrerie, the old man's widow;' he said to me, 'Go there. There you will find M. Bossuet. Tell him from me, "A B C".' It's a joke that they're playing on you, isn't it. He gave me ten sous."

"Joly, lend me ten sous," said Laigle; and, turning to Grantaire, "Grantaire, lend me ten sous."

This made twenty sous, which Laigle handed to the lad.

"Thank you, Sir," said the urchin.

"What is your name?" inquired Laigle.

"Navet, Gavroche's friend."

"Stay with us," said Laigle.

"Breakfast with us," said Grantaire.

The child replied, "I can't, I belong in the procession, I'm the one to shout 'Down with Polignac!'"

And executing a prolonged scrape of his foot behind him, which is the most respectful of all possible salutes, he took his departure.

The child gone, Grantaire took the word, "That is the pure-bred gamin. There are a great many varieties of the gamin species. The notary's gamin is called Skip-the-Gutter, the cook's gamin is called a scullion, the baker's gamin is called a mitron, the lackey's gamin is called a groom, the marine gamin is called the cabin boy, the soldier's gamin is called the drummer boy, the painter's gamin is called paint grinder, the tradesman's gamin is called an errand boy, the courtesan gamin is called the minion, the kingly gamin is called the dauphin, the god gamin is called the bambino."

In the meantime, Laigle was engaged in reflection; he said half aloud, "A B C, that is to say: the burial of Lamarque."

"The tall blond," remarked Grantaire, "is Enjolras, who is sending you a warning."

"Shall we go?" ejaculated Bossuet.

"It's raining," said Joly. "I have sworn to go through fire, but not through water. I don't wand to ged a gold."

"I shall stay here," said Grantaire. "I prefer a breakfast to a hearse."

"Conclusion: we remain," said Laigle. "Well, then, let us drink. Besides, we might miss the funeral without missing the riot."

"Ah! The riot, I am with you!" cried Joly.

Laigle rubbed his hands.

"Now we're going to touch up the revolution of 1830. As a matter of fact, it does hurt the people along the seams."

"I don't think much of your revolution," said Grantaire. "I don't execrate this Government. It is the crown tempered by the cotton nightcap. It is a scepter ending in an umbrella. In fact, I think that today, with the present weather, Louis Philippe might utilize his royalty in two directions, he might extend the tip of the scepter end against the people, and open the umbrella end against heaven."

The room was dark, large clouds had just finished the extinction of daylight. There was no one in the wine shop, or in the street, everyone having gone off "to watch events."

"Is it midday or midnight?" cried Bossuet. "You can't see your hand before your face. Gibelotte, fetch a light."

Grantaire was drinking in a melancholy way.

"Enjolras disdains me," he muttered. "Enjolras said, 'Joly is ill, Grantaire is drunk.' It was to Bossuet that he sent Navet. If he had come for me, I would have followed him. So much the worse for Enjolras! I won't go to his funeral."

This resolution once arrived at, Bossuet, Joly, and Grantaire did not stir from the wine shop. By two o'clock in the afternoon, the table at which they sat was covered with empty bottles. Two candles were burning on it, one in a flat copper candlestick that was perfectly green, the other in the neck of a cracked carafe. Grantaire had seduced Joly and Bossuet to wine; Bossuet and Joly had conducted Grantaire back toward cheerfulness.

As for Grantaire, he had got beyond wine, that merely moderate inspirer of dreams, ever since midday. Wine enjoys only a conventional popularity with serious drinkers. There is, in fact, in the matter of inebriety, white magic and black magic; wine is only white magic. Grantaire was a daring drinker of dreams. The blackness of a terrible fit of drunkenness yawning before him, far from arresting him, attracted him. He had abandoned the bottle and taken to the beer glass. The beer glass is the abyss. Having neither opium nor hashish on hand, and being desirous of filling his brain with twilight, he had had recourse to that fearful mixture of brandy, stout, absinthe, which produces the most terrible of lethargies. It is of these three vapors, beer, brandy, and absinthe, that the lead of the soul is composed. They are three grooms; the celestial butterfly is drowned in them; and there are formed there in a membranous smoke, vaguely condensed into the wing of the bat, three mute furies, Nightmare, Night, and Death, which hover about the slumbering Psyche.

Grantaire had not yet reached that lamentable phase; far from it. He was tremendously gay, and Bossuet and Joly retorted. They clinked glasses. Grantaire added to the eccentric accentuation of words and ideas, a peculiarity of gesture; he rested his left fist on his knee with dignity, his arm forming a right angle, and, with cravat untied, seated astride a stool, his full glass in his right hand, he hurled solemn words at the big maidservant Matelote, "Let the doors of the palace be thrown open! Let everyone be a member of the French Academy and have the right to embrace Madame Hucheloup. Let us drink."

And turning to Madame Hucheloup, he added, "Woman ancient and consecrated by use, draw near that I may contemplate thee!"

And Joly exclaimed, "Matelote and Gibelotte, dod't gib Grantaire anything more to drink. He has already devoured, since this bording, in wild prodigality, two francs and ninety-five centibes."

And Grantaire began again, "Who has been unhooking the stars without my permission, and putting them on the table in the guise of candles?"

Bossuet, though very drunk, preserved his equanimity.

He was seated on the sill of the open window, wetting his back in the falling rain, and gazing at his two friends.

All at once, he heard a tumult behind him, hurried footsteps, cries of "To arms!" He turned around and saw in the Rue Saint-Denis, at the end of the Rue de la Chanvrerie, Enjolras passing, gun in hand, and Gavroche with his pistol, Feuilly with his sword, Courfeyrac with his sword, and Jean Prouvaire with his blunderbuss, Combeferre with his gun, Bahorel with his gun, and the whole armed and stormy rabble which was following them.

The Rue de la Chanvrerie was not more than a gunshot long. Bossuet improvised a speaking-trumpet from his two hands placed around his mouth, and shouted, "Courfeyrac! Courfeyrac! Hohee!"

Courfeyrac heard the shout, caught sight of Bossuet, and advanced a few paces into the Rue de la Chanvrerie, shouting, "What do you want?" which crossed a "Where are you going?"

"To make a barricade," replied Courfeyrac.

"Well, here! This is a good place! Make it here!"

"That's true, Aigle," said Courfeyrac.

And at a signal from Courfeyrac, the mob flung themselves into the Rue de la Chanvrerie.

CHAPTER III—NIGHT BEGINS TO DESCEND UPON GRANTAIRE

The spot was, in fact, admirably adapted, the entrance to the street widened out, the other extremity narrowed together into a pocket without exit. Corinthe created an obstacle, the Rue Mondetour was easily barricaded on the right and the left, no attack was possible except from the Rue Saint-Denis, that is to say, in front, and in full sight. Bossuet had the comprehensive glance of a fasting Hannibal.

Terror had seized on the whole street at the irruption of the mob. There was not a passerby who did not get out of sight. In the space of a flash of lightning, in the rear, to right and left, shops, stables, area doors, windows, blinds, attic skylights, shutters of every description were closed, from the ground floor to the roof. A terrified old woman fixed a mattress in front of her window on two clothes poles for drying linen, in order to deaden the effect of musketry. The wine shop alone remained open; and that for a very good reason, that the mob had rushed into it. "Ah my God! Ah my God!" sighed Mame Hucheloup.

Bossuet had gone down to meet Courfeyrac.

Joly, who had placed himself at the window, exclaimed, "Courfeyrac, you ought to have brought an umbrella. You will catch cold."

In the meantime, in the space of a few minutes, twenty iron bars had been wrenched from the grated front of the wine shop, ten fathoms of street had been unpaved; Gavroche and Bahorel had seized in its passage, and overturned, the dray of a lime dealer named Anceau; this dray contained three barrels of lime, which they placed beneath the piles of paving stones: Enjolras raised the cellar trap, and all the widow Hucheloup's empty casks were used to flank the barrels of lime; Feuilly, with his fingers skilled in painting the delicate sticks of fans, had backed up the barrels and the dray with two massive heaps of blocks of rough stone. Blocks that were improvised like the rest and procured no one knows where. The beams that served as props were torn from the neighboring house fronts and laid on the casks. When Bossuet and Courfeyrac turned around, half the street was already barred with a rampart higher than a man. There is nothing like the hand of the populace for building everything that is built by demolishing.

Matelote and Gibelotte had mingled with the workers. Gibelotte went and came loaded with rubbish. Her lassitude helped on the barricade. She served the barricade as she would have served wine, with a sleepy air.

An omnibus with two white horses passed the end of the street.

Bossuet strode over the paving stones, ran to it, stopped the driver, made the passengers alight, offered his hand to "the ladies," dismissed the conductor, and returned, leading the vehicle and the horses by the bridle.

"Omnibuses," said he, "do not pass the Corinthe. *Non licet omnibus adire Corinthum.*"

An instant later, the horses were unharnessed and went off at their will, through the Rue Mondetour, and the omnibus lying on its side completed the bar across the street.

Mame Hucheloup, quite upset, had taken refuge in the first story.

Her eyes were vague, and stared without seeing anything, and she cried in a low tone. Her terrified shrieks did not dare to emerge from her throat.

"The end of the world has come," she muttered.

Joly deposited a kiss on Mame Hucheloup's fat, red, wrinkled neck, and said to Grantaire, "My dear fellow, I have always regarded a woman's neck as an infinitely delicate thing."

But Grantaire attained to the highest regions of dithyramb. Matelote had mounted to the first floor once more, Grantaire seized her around her waist, and gave vent to long bursts of laughter at the window.

"Matelote is homely!" he cried, "Matelote is of a dream of ugliness! Matelote is a chimera. This is the secret of her birth: a Gothic Pygmalion, who was making gargoyles for cathedrals, fell in love with one of them, the most horrible, one fine morning. He besought Love to give it life, and this produced Matelote. Look at her, citizens! She has chromate-of-lead-colored hair, like Titian's mistress, and she is a good girl. I guarantee that she will fight well. Every good girl contains a hero. As for Mother Hucheloup, she's an old warrior. Look at her moustaches! She inherited them from her husband. A hussar indeed! She will fight too. These two alone will strike terror to the heart of the banlieue. Comrades, we shall overthrow the government as true as there are fifteen intermediary acids between margaric acid and formic acid; however, that is a matter of perfect indifference to me. Gentlemen, my father always detested me because I could not understand mathematics. I understand only love and liberty. I am Grantaire, the good fellow. Having never had any money, I never acquired the habit of it, and the result is that I have never lacked it; but, if I had been rich, there would have been no more poor people! You would have seen! Oh, if the kind hearts only had fat purses, how much better things would go! I picture myself Jesus Christ with Rothschild's fortune! How much good he would do! Matelote, embrace me! You are voluptuous and timid! You have cheeks which invite the kiss of a sister, and lips which claim the kiss of a lover."

"Hold your tongue, you cask!" said Courfeyrac.

Grantaire retorted, "I am the capitoul* and the master of the floral games!"

Enjolras, who was standing on the crest of the barricade, gun in hand, raised his beautiful, austere face. Enjolras, as the reader knows, had something of the Spartan and of the Puritan in his composition. He would have perished at Thermopylae with Leonidas, and burned at Drogheda with Cromwell.

"Grantaire," he shouted, "go get rid of the fumes of your wine somewhere else than here. This is the place for enthusiasm, not for drunkenness. Don't disgrace the barricade!"

This angry speech produced a singular effect on Grantaire. One would have said that he had had a glass of cold water flung in his face. He seemed to be rendered suddenly sober.

He sat down, put his elbows on a table near the window, looked at Enjolras with indescribable gentleness, and said to him, "Let me sleep here."

* a municipal officer in Tolouse

"Go and sleep somewhere else," cried Enjolras.

But Grantaire, still keeping his tender and troubled eyes fixed on him, replied, "Let me sleep here, until I die."

Enjolras regarded him with disdainful eyes, "Grantaire, you are incapable of believing, of thinking, of willing, of living, and of dying."

Grantaire replied in a grave tone, "You will see."

He stammered a few more unintelligible words, then his head fell heavily on the table, and, as is the usual effect of the second period of inebriety, into which Enjolras had roughly and abruptly thrust him, an instant later he had fallen asleep.

CHAPTER IV—AN ATTEMPT TO CONSOLE THE WIDOW HUCHELOUP

Bahorel, in ecstasies over the barricade, shouted, "Here's the street in its low-necked dress! How well it looks!"

Courfeyrac, as he demolished the wine shop to some extent, sought to console the widowed proprietress.

"Mother Hucheloup, weren't you complaining the other day because you had had a notice served on you for infringing the law, because Gibelotte shook a counterpane out of your window?"

"Yes, my good Monsieur Courfeyrac. Ah! Good Heavens, are you going to put that table of mine in your horror, too? And it was for the counterpane, and also for a pot of flowers that fell from the attic window into the street, that the government collected a fine of a hundred francs. If that isn't an abomination, what is?"

"Well, Mother Hucheloup, we are avenging you."

Mother Hucheloup did not appear to understand very clearly the benefit she was to derive from these reprisals made on her account. She was satisfied after the manner of that Arab woman, who, having received a box on the ear from her husband, went to complain to her father, and cried for vengeance, saying, "Father, you owe my husband affront for affront."

The father asked, "On which cheek did you receive the blow?"

"On the left cheek."

The father slapped her right cheek and said, "Now you are satisfied. Go tell your husband that he boxed my daughter's ears, and that I have accordingly boxed his wife's."

The rain had ceased. Recruits had arrived. Workmen had brought under their blouses a barrel of powder, a basket containing bottles of vitriol, two or three carnival torches, and a basket filled with firepots, "left over from the King's festival." This festival was very recent, having taken place on the 1st of May. It was said that these munitions came from a grocer in the Faubourg Saint-Antoine named Pepin. They smashed the only street lantern in the Rue de la Chanvrerie, the lantern corresponding to one in the Rue Saint-Denis, and all the lanterns in the surrounding streets, de Mondetour, du Cygne, des Prêcheurs, and de la Grande and de la Petite-Truanderie.

Enjolras, Combeferre, and Courfeyrac directed everything. Two barricades were now in process of construction at once, both of them resting on the Corinthe house and forming a right angle; the larger shut off the Rue de la Chanvrerie, the other closed the Rue Mondetour, on the side of the Rue de Cygne. This last barricade, which was very narrow, was constructed only of casks and paving stones. There were about fifty workers on it; thirty were armed with guns; for, on their way, they had affected a wholesale loan from an armorer's shop.

Nothing could be more bizarre and at the same time more motley than this troop. One had a round jacket, a cavalry saber, and two holster pistols, another was in his shirtsleeves, with a round hat, and a powderhorn slung at his side, a third wore a plastron of nine sheets of gray paper and was armed with a saddler's awl. There was one who was shouting, "Let us exterminate them to the last man and die at the point of our bayonet." This man had no bayonet. Another spread out over his coat the crossbelt and cartridge box of a National Guardsman, the cover of the cartridge-box being ornamented with this inscription in red worsted: Public Order. There were a great many guns bearing the numbers of the legions, few hats, no cravats, many bare arms, some pikes. Add to this, all ages, all sorts of faces, small, pale young men, and bronzed longshoremen. All were in haste; and as they helped each other, they discussed the possible chances. That they would receive succor about three o'clock in the morning—that they were sure of one regiment, that Paris would rise. Terrible sayings with which was mingled a sort of cordial joviality. One would have pronounced them brothers, but they did not know each other's names. Great perils have this fine characteristic, that they bring to light the fraternity of strangers. A fire had been lighted in the kitchen, and there they were engaged in molding into bullets, pewter mugs, spoons, forks, and all the brass tableware of the establishment. In the midst of it all, they drank. Caps and buckshot were mixed pell-mell on the tables with glasses of wine. In the billiard hall, Mame Hucheloup, Matelote, and Gibelotte, variously modified by terror, which had stupefied one, rendered another breathless, and roused the third, were tearing up old dish cloths and making lint; three insurgents were assisting them, three bushy-haired, jolly blades with beards and moustaches, who plucked away at the linen with the fingers of seamstresses and who made them tremble.

The man of lofty stature whom Courfeyrac, Combeferre, and Enjolras had observed at the moment when he joined the mob at the corner of the Rue des Billettes, was at work on the smaller barricade and was making himself useful there. Gavroche was working on the larger one. As for the young man who had been waiting for Courfeyrac at his lodgings, and who had inquired for M. Marius, he had disappeared at about the time when the omnibus had been overturned.

Gavroche, completely carried away and radiant, had undertaken to get everything in readiness. He went, came, mounted, descended, remounted, whistled, and sparkled. He seemed to be there for the encouragement of all. Had he any incentive? Yes, certainly, his poverty; had he wings? Yes, certainly, his joy. Gavroche was a whirlwind. He was constantly visible, he was incessantly audible. He filled the air, as he was everywhere at once. He was a sort of almost irritating ubiquity; no halt was possible with him. The enormous barricade felt him on its haunches. He troubled the loungers, he excited the idle, he reanimated the weary, he grew impatient over the thoughtful, he inspired gaiety in some, and breath in others, wrath in others, movement in all, now pricking a student, now biting an artisan; he alighted, paused, flew off again, hovered over the tumult, and the effort, sprang from one party to another, murmuring and humming, and harassed the whole company; a fly on the immense revolutionary coach.

Perpetual motion was in his little arms and perpetual clamor in his little lungs.

"Courage! More paving stones! More casks! More machines! Where are you now? A hod of plaster for me to stop this hole with! Your barricade is very small. It must be carried up. Put everything on it, fling everything there, stick it all in. Break down the house. A barricade is Mother Gibou's tea. Hullo, here's a glass door."

This elicited an exclamation from the workers.

"A glass door? What do you expect us to do with a glass door, tubercle?"

"Hercules yourselves!" retorted Gavroche. "A glass door is an excellent thing in a barricade. It does not prevent an attack, but it prevents the enemy taking it. So you've never prigged apples over a wall where there were broken bottles? A glass door cuts the corns of the National Guard when they try to mount on the barricade. *Pardi!* Glass is a treacherous thing. Well, you haven't a very wildly lively imagination, comrades."

However, he was furious over his triggerless pistol. He went from one to another, demanding, "A gun, I want a gun! Why don't you give me a gun?"

"Give you a gun!" said Combeferre.

"Come now!" said Gavroche, "why not? I had one in 1830 when we had a dispute with Charles X."

Enjolras shrugged his shoulders.

"When there are enough for the men, we will give some to the children."

Gavroche wheeled around haughtily, and answered, "If you are killed before me, I shall take yours."

"Gamin!" said Enjolras.

"Greenhorn!" said Gavroche.

A dandy who had lost his way and who lounged past the end of the street created a diversion. Gavroche shouted to him, "Come with us, young fellow! Well now, don't we do anything for this old country of ours?"

The dandy fled.

CHAPTER V—PREPARATIONS

The journals of the day that said that that nearly impregnable structure, of the barricade of the Rue de la Chanvrerie, as they call it, reached to the level of the first floor, were mistaken. The fact is, that it did not exceed an average height of six or seven feet. It was built in such a manner that the combatants could, at their will, either disappear behind it or dominate the barrier and even scale its crest by means of a quadruple row of paving stones placed on top of each other and arranged as steps in the interior. On the outside, the front of the barricade, composed of piles of paving stones and casks bound together by beams and planks, which were entangled in the wheels of Anceau's dray and of the overturned omnibus, had a bristling and inextricable aspect.

An aperture large enough to allow a man to pass through had been made between the wall of the houses and the extremity of the barricade that was furthest from the wine shop, so that an exit was possible at this point. The pole of the omnibus was placed upright and held up with ropes, and a red flag, fastened to this pole, floated over the barricade.

The little Mondetour barricade, hidden behind the wine shop building, was not visible. The two barricades united formed a veritable redoubt. Enjolras and Courfeyrac had not thought fit to barricade the other fragment of the Rue Mondetour which opens through the Rue des Prêcheurs an issue into the Halles, wishing, no doubt, to preserve a possible communication with the outside, and not entertaining much fear of an attack through the dangerous and difficult street of the Rue des Prêcheurs.

With the exception of this issue which was left free, and which constituted what Folard in his strategical style would have termed a branch and taking into account, also, the narrow cutting arranged on the Rue de la Chanvrerie, the interior of the barricade, where the wine shop formed a salient angle, presented an irregular square, closed on all sides. There existed an interval of twenty paces between the grand barrier and the lofty houses that formed the background of the street, so that one might say that the barricade rested on these houses, all inhabited, but closed from top to bottom.

All this work was performed without any hindrance, in less than an hour, and without this handful of bold men seeing a single bearskin cap or a single bayonet make their appearance. The very bourgeois who still ventured at this hour of riot to enter the Rue Saint-Denis cast a glance at the Rue de la Chanvrerie, caught sight of the barricade, and redoubled their pace.

The two barricades being finished, and the flag run up, a table was dragged out of the wine shop; and Courfeyrac mounted on the table. Enjolras brought the square coffer, and Courfeyrac opened it. This coffer was filled with cartridges. When the mob saw the cartridges, a tremor ran through the bravest, and a momentary silence ensued.

Courfeyrac distributed them with a smile.

Each one received thirty cartridges. Many had powder, and set about making others with the bullets that they had run. As for the barrel of powder, it stood on a table on one side, near the door, and was held in reserve.

The alarm beat that ran through all Paris, did not cease, but it had finally come to be nothing more than a monotonous noise to which they no longer paid any attention. This noise retreated at times, and again drew near, with melancholy undulations.

They loaded the guns and carbines, all together, without haste, with solemn gravity. Enjolras went and stationed three sentinels outside the barricades, one in the Rue de la Chanvrerie, the second in the Rue des Prêcheurs, the third at the corner of the Rue de la Petite Truanderie.

Then, the barricades having been built, the posts assigned, the guns loaded, the sentinels stationed, they waited, alone in those redoubtable streets through which no one passed any longer, surrounded by those dumb houses, which seemed dead and in which no human movement palpitated, enveloped in the deepening shades of twilight that was drawing on, in the midst of that silence through which something could be felt advancing, and which had about it something tragic and terrifying, isolated, armed, determined, and tranquil.

CHAPTER VI—WAITING

During those hours of waiting, what did they do? We need to tell, since this is a matter of history.

While the men made bullets and the women lint, while a large saucepan of melted brass and lead, destined to the bullet mold smoked over a glowing brazier, while the sentinels watched, weapon in hand, on the barricade, while Enjolras, whom it was impossible to divert, kept an eye on the sentinels, Combeferre, Courfeyrac, Jean Prouvaire, Feuilly, Bossuet, Joly, Bahorel, and some others, sought each other out and united as in the most peaceful days of their conversations in their student life, and, in one corner of this wine shop which had been converted into a casement, a couple of paces distant from the redoubt which they had built, with their carbines loaded and primed resting against the backs of their chairs, these fine young fellows, so close to a supreme hour, began to recite love verses. What verses? These:

"Do you remember our sweet life, when we were both so young, and when we had no other desire in our hearts than to be well dressed and in love? When, by adding your age to my age, we could not count forty years between us, and when, in our humble and tiny household, everything was spring to us even in winter. Fair days! Manuel was proud and wise, Paris sat at sacred banquets, Foy launched thunderbolts, and your corsage had a pin on which I pricked myself. Everything gazed upon you. A briefless lawyer, when I took you to the Prado to dine, you were so beautiful that the roses seemed to me to turn around, and I heard them say, 'Is she not beautiful! How good she smells! What billowing hair! Beneath her mantle she hides a wing. Her charming bonnet is hardly unfolded.' I wandered with thee, pressing thy supple arm. The passersby thought that love bewitched had wedded, in our happy couple, the gentle month of April to the fair month of May. We lived concealed, content, with closed doors, devouring love, that sweet forbidden fruit. My mouth had not uttered a thing when thy heart had already responded. The Sorbonne was the bucolic spot where I adored thee from eve till morn. 'Tis thus that an amorous soul applies the chart of the Tender to the Latin country. O Place Maubert! O Place Dauphine! When in the fresh springlike hut thou didst draw thy stocking on thy delicate leg, I saw a star in the depths of the garret. I have read a great deal of Plato, but nothing of it remains by me; better than Malebranche and then Lamennais thou didst demonstrate to me celestial goodness with a flower, which thou gavest to me, I obeyed thee, thou didst submit to me; oh gilded garret! To lace thee! To behold thee going and coming from dawn in thy chemise, gazing at thy young brow in thine ancient mirror! And who, then, would forego the memory of those days of aurora and the firmament, of flowers, of gauze and of moire, when love stammers a charming slang? Our gardens consisted of a pot of tulips; thou didst mask the window with thy petticoat; I took the earthenware bowl and I gave thee the Japanese cup. And those great misfortunes that made us laugh! Thy cuff scorched, thy boa lost! And that dear portrait of the divine Shakespeare that we sold one evening that we might sup! I was a beggar and thou wert charitable. I kissed thy fresh round arms in haste. A folio Dante served us as a table on which to eat merrily a centime's worth of chestnuts. The first time that, in my joyous den, I snatched a kiss from thy fiery lip, when thou wentest forth, disheveled and blushing, I turned deathly pale and I believed in God. Dost thou recall our innumerable joys, and all those fichus changed to rags? Oh! What sighs from our hearts full of gloom fluttered forth to the heavenly depths! The hour, the spot, these souvenirs of youth recalled, a few stars, which began to twinkle in the sky, the funeral repose of those deserted streets, the imminence of the inexorable adventure, which was in preparation, gave a pathetic charm to these verses murmured in a low tone in the dusk by Jean Prouvaire, who, as we have said, was a gentle poet."

In the meantime, a lamp had been lighted in the small barricade, and in the large one, one of those wax torches such as are to be met with on Shrove Tuesday in front of vehicles loaded with masks, on their way to la Courtille. These torches, as the reader has seen, came from the Faubourg Saint-Antoine.

The torch had been placed in a sort of cage of paving stones closed on three sides to shelter it from the wind, and disposed in such a fashion that all the light fell on the flag. The street and the barricade remained sunk in gloom, and nothing was to be seen except the red flag formidably illuminated as by an enormous dark lantern.

This light enhanced the scarlet of the flag, with an indescribable and terrible purple.

CHAPTER VII—THE MAN RECRUITED
IN THE RUE DES BILLETTES

Night was fully come, nothing made its appearance. All that they heard was confused noises, and at intervals, fusillades; but these were rare, badly sustained and distant. This respite, which was thus prolonged, was a sign that the Government was taking its time, and collecting its forces. These fifty men were waiting for sixty thousand.

Enjolras felt attacked by that impatience which seizes on strong souls on the threshold of redoubtable events. He went in search of Gavroche, who had set to making cartridges in the taproom, by the dubious light of two candles placed on the counter by way of precaution, on account of the powder that was scattered on the tables. These two candles cast no gleam outside. The insurgents had, moreover, taken pains not to have any light in the upper stories.

Gavroche was deeply preoccupied at that moment, but not precisely with his cartridges. The man of the Rue des Billettes had just entered the taproom and had seated himself at the table that was the least lighted. A musket of large model had fallen to his share, and he held it between his legs. Gavroche, who had been, up to that moment, distracted by a hundred "amusing" things, had not even seen this man.

When he entered, Gavroche followed him mechanically with his eyes, admiring his gun; then, all at once, when the man was seated, the street urchin sprang to his feet. Anyone who had spied upon that man up to that moment, would have seen that he was observing everything in the barricade and in the band of insurgents, with singular attention; but, from the moment when he had entered this room, he had fallen into a sort of brown study, and no longer seemed to see anything that was going on. The gamin approached this pensive personage, and began to step around him on tiptoe, as one walks in the vicinity of a person whom one is afraid of waking. At the same time, over his childish countenance which was, at once so impudent and so serious, so giddy and so profound, so gay and so heartbreaking, passed all those grimaces of an old man which signify: Ah bah! Impossible! My sight is bad! I am dreaming! Can this be? No, it is not! But yes! Why, no! Etc. Gavroche balanced on his heels, clenched both fists in his pockets, moved his neck around like a bird, expended in a gigantic pout all the sagacity of his lower lip. He was astounded, uncertain, incredulous, convinced, dazzled. He had the mien of the chief of the eunuchs in the slave mart, discovering a Venus among the blowsy females, and the air of an amateur recognizing a Raphael in a heap of daubs. His whole being was at work, the instinct that scents out, and the intelligence that combines. It was evident that a great event had happened in Gavroche's life.

It was at the most intense point of this preoccupation that Enjolras accosted him.

"You are small," said Enjolras, "you will not be seen. Go out of the barricade, slip along close to the houses, skirmish about a bit in the streets, and come back and tell me what is going on."

Gavroche raised himself on his haunches.

"So the little chaps are good for something! That's very lucky! I'll go! In the meanwhile, trust to the little fellows, and distrust the big ones." And Gavroche, raising his head and lowering his voice, added, as he indicated the man of the Rue des Billettes, "Do you see that big fellow there?"

"Well?"

"He's a police spy."

"Are you sure of it?"

"It isn't two weeks since he pulled me off the cornice of the Port Royal, where I was taking the air, by my ear."

Enjolras hastily quitted the urchin and murmured a few words in a very low tone to a longshoreman from the winedocks who chanced to be at hand. The man left the room, and returned almost immediately, accompanied by three others. The four men, four porters with broad shoulders, went and placed themselves without doing anything to attract his attention, behind the table on which the man of the Rue des Billettes was leaning with his elbows. They were evidently ready to hurl themselves upon him.

Then Enjolras approached the man and demanded of him, "Who are you?"

At this abrupt query, the man started. He plunged his gaze deep into Enjolras' clear eyes and appeared to grasp the latter's meaning. He smiled with a smile than which nothing more disdainful, more energetic, and more resolute could be seen in the world, and replied with haughty gravity, "I see what it is. Well, yes!"

"You are a police spy?"

"I am an agent of the authorities."

"And your name?"

"Javert."

Enjolras made a sign to the four men. In the twinkling of an eye, before Javert had time to turn around, he was collared, thrown down, pinioned and searched.

They found on him a little round card pasted between two pieces of glass, and bearing on one side the arms of France, engraved, and with this motto: Supervision and vigilance, and on the other this note: "JAVERT, inspector of police, aged fifty-two," and the signature of the Prefect of Police of that day, M. Gisquet.

Besides this, he had his watch and his purse, which contained several gold pieces. They left him his purse and his watch. Under the watch, at the bottom of his fob, they felt and seized a paper in an envelope, which Enjolras unfolded, and on which he read these five lines, written in the very hand of the Prefect of Police, "As soon as his political mission is accomplished, Inspector Javert will make sure, by special supervision, whether it is true that the malefactors have instituted intrigues on the right bank of the Seine, near the Jena bridge."

The search ended, they lifted Javert to his feet, bound his arms behind his back, and fastened him to that celebrated post in the middle of the room that had formerly given the wine shop its name.

Gavroche, who had looked on at the whole of this scene and had approved of everything with a silent toss of his head, stepped up to Javert and said to him, "It's the mouse who has caught the cat."

All this was so rapidly executed, that it was all over when those about the wine shop noticed it.

Javert had not uttered a single cry.

At the sight of Javert bound to the post, Courfeyrac, Bossuet, Joly, Combeferre, and the men scattered over the two barricades came running up.

Javert, with his back to the post, and so surrounded with ropes that he could not make a movement, raised his head with the intrepid serenity of the man who has never lied.

"He is a police spy," said Enjolras.

And turning to Javert, "You will be shot ten minutes before the barricade is taken."

Javert replied in his most imperious tone, "Why not at once?"

"We are saving our powder."

"Then finish the business with a blow from a knife."

"Spy," said the handsome Enjolras, "we are judges and not assassins."

Then he called Gavroche, "Here you! Go about your business! Do what I told you!"

"I'm going!" cried Gavroche.

And halting as he was on the point of setting out, "By the way, you will give me his gun!" and he added, "I leave you the musician, but I want the clarinet."

The gamin made the military salute and passed gaily through the opening in the large barricade.

CHAPTER VIII—MANY INTERROGATION POINTS WITH REGARD TO A CERTAIN LE CABUC WHOSE NAME MAY NOT HAVE BEEN LE CABUC

The tragic picture which we have undertaken would not be complete, the reader would not see those grand moments of social birth-pangs in a revolutionary birth, which contain convulsion mingled with effort, in their exact and real relief, were we to omit, in the sketch here outlined, an incident full of epic and savage horror, which occurred almost immediately after Gavroche's departure.

Mobs, as the reader knows, are like a snowball, and collect as they roll along, a throng of tumultuous men. These men do not ask each other from where they come. Among the passersby who had joined the rabble led by Enjolras, Combeferre, and Courfeyrac, there had been a person wearing the jacket of a street porter, which was very threadbare on the shoulders, who gesticulated and vociferated, and who had the look of a drunken savage. This man, whose name or nickname was Le Cabuc, and who was, moreover, an utter stranger to those who pretended to know him, was very drunk, or assumed the appearance of being so, and had seated himself with several others at a table, which they had dragged outside of the wine shop. This Cabuc, while making those who vied with him drunk seemed to be examining with a thoughtful air the large house at the extremity of the barricade, whose five stories commanded the whole street and faced the Rue Saint-Denis. All at once he exclaimed, "Do you know, comrades, it is from that house yonder that we must fire. When we are at the windows, the deuce is in it if anyone can advance into the street!"

"Yes, but the house is closed," said one of the drinkers.

"Let us knock!"

"They will not open."

"Let us break in the door!"

Le Cabuc runs to the door, which had a very massive knocker, and knocks. The door opens not. He strikes a second blow. No one answers. A third stroke. The same silence.

"Is there anyone here?" shouts Cabuc.

Nothing stirs.

Then he seizes a gun and begins to batter the door with the butt end.

It was an ancient alley door, low, vaulted, narrow, solid, entirely of oak, lined on the inside with a sheet of iron and iron stays, a genuine prison postern. The blows from the butt end of the gun made the house tremble, but did not shake the door.

Nevertheless, it is probable that the inhabitants were disturbed, for a tiny, square window was finally seen to open on the third story, and at this aperture appeared the reverend and terrified face of a gray-haired old man, who was the porter, and who held a candle.

The man who was knocking paused.

"Gentlemen," said the porter, "what do you want?"

"Open!" said Cabuc.

"That cannot be, gentlemen."

"Open, nevertheless."

"Impossible, gentlemen."

Le Cabuc took his gun and aimed at the porter; but as he was below, and as it was very dark, the porter did not see him.

"Will you open, yes or no?"

"No, gentlemen."

"Do you say no?"

"I say no, my goo—"

The porter did not finish. The shot was fired; the ball entered under his chin and came out at the nape of his neck, after traversing the jugular vein.

The old man fell back without a sigh. The candle fell and was extinguished, and nothing more was to be seen except a motionless head lying on the sill of the small window, and a little whitish smoke, which floated off toward the roof.

"There!" said Le Cabuc, dropping the butt end of his gun to the pavement.

He had hardly uttered this word, when he felt a hand laid on his shoulder with the weight of an eagle's talon, and he heard a voice saying to him, "On your knees."

The murderer turned around and saw before him Enjolras' cold, white face. Enjolras held a pistol in his hand.

He had hastened up at the sound of the discharge.

He had seized Cabuc's collar, blouse, shirt, and suspender with his left hand.

"On your knees!" he repeated.

And, with an imperious motion, the frail young man of twenty years bent the thickset and sturdy porter like a reed, and brought him to his knees in the mire.

Le Cabuc attempted to resist, but he seemed to have been seized by a superhuman hand.

Enjolras, pale, with bare neck and disheveled hair, and his woman's face, had about him at that moment something of the antique Themis. His dilated nostrils, his downcast eyes, gave to his implacable Greek profile that expression of wrath and that expression of Chastity that, as the ancient world viewed the matter, befit Justice.

The whole barricade hastened up, then all ranged themselves in a circle at a distance, feeling that it was impossible to utter a word in the presence of the thing which they were about to behold.

Le Cabuc, vanquished, no longer tried to struggle, and trembled in every limb.

Enjolras released him and drew out his watch.

"Collect yourself," said he. "Think or pray. You have one minute."

"Mercy!" murmured the murderer; then he dropped his head and stammered a few inarticulate oaths.

Enjolras never took his eyes off of him; he allowed a minute to pass, then he replaced his watch in his fob. That done, he grasped Le Cabuc by the hair, as the latter coiled himself into a ball at his knees and shrieked, and placed the muzzle of the pistol to his ear. Many of those intrepid men, who had so tranquilly entered upon the most terrible of adventures, turned aside their heads.

An explosion was heard, the assassin fell to the pavement face downward.

Enjolras straightened himself up, and cast a convinced and severe glance around him. Then he spurned the corpse with his foot and said, "Throw that outside."

Three men raised the body of the unhappy wretch, which was still agitated by the last mechanical convulsions of the life that had fled, and flung it over the little barricade into the Rue Mondetour.

Enjolras was thoughtful. It is impossible to say what grandiose shadows slowly spread over his redoubtable serenity. All at once he raised his voice.

A silence fell upon them.

"Citizens," said Enjolras, "what that man did is frightful, what I have done is horrible. He killed, therefore I killed him. I had to do it, because insurrection must have its discipline. Assassination is even more of a crime here than elsewhere; we are under the eyes of the Revolution, we are the priests of the Republic, we are the victims of duty, and must not be possible to slander our combat. I have, therefore, tried that man, and condemned him to death. As for myself, constrained as I am to do what I have done, and yet abhorring it, I have judged myself also, and you shall soon see to what I have condemned myself."

Those who listened to him shuddered.

"We will share thy fate," cried Combeferre.

"So be it," replied Enjolras. "One word more. In executing this man, I have obeyed necessity; but necessity is a monster of the old world, necessity's name is Fatality. Now, the law of progress is, that monsters shall disappear before the angels, and that Fatality shall vanish before Fraternity. It is a bad moment to pronounce the word love. No matter, I do pronounce it. And I glorify it.

Love, the future is thine. Death, I make use of thee, but I hate thee. Citizens, in the future there will be neither darkness nor thunderbolts; neither ferocious ignorance, nor bloody retaliation. As there will be no more Satan, there will be no more Michael. In the future no one will kill anyone else, the earth will beam with radiance, the human race will love. The day will come, citizens, when all will be concord, harmony, light, joy and life; it will come, and it is in order that it may come that we are about to die."

Enjolras ceased. His virgin lips closed; and he remained for some time standing on the spot where he had shed blood, in marble immobility. His staring eye caused those about him to speak in low tones.

Jean Prouvaire and Combeferre pressed each other's hands silently, and, leaning against each other in an angle of the barricade, they watched with an admiration in which there was some compassion, that grave young man, executioner and priest, composed of light, like crystal, and also of rock.

Let us say at once that later on, after the action, when the bodies were taken to the morgue and searched, a police agent's card was found on Le Cabuc. The author of this book had in his hands, in 1848, the special report on this subject made to the Prefect of Police in 1832.

We will add, that if we are to believe a tradition of the police, which is strange but probably well founded, Le Cabuc was Claquesous. The fact is, that dating from the death of Le Cabuc, there was no longer any question of Claquesous. Claquesous had nowhere left any trace of his disappearance; he would seem to have amalgamated himself with the invisible. His life had been all shadows, his end was night.

The whole insurgent group was still under the influence of the emotion of that tragic case that had been so quickly tried and so quickly terminated, when Courfeyrac again beheld on the barricade, the small young man who had inquired of him that morning for Marius.

This lad, who had a bold and reckless air, had come by night to join the insurgents.

BOOK THIRTEENTH: MARIUS ENTERS THE SHADOW

CHAPTER I—FROM THE RUE PLUMET TO THE QUARTIER SAINT-DENIS

The voice that had summoned Marius through the twilight to the barricade of the Rue de la Chanvrerie, had produced on him the effect of the voice of destiny. He wished to die; the opportunity presented itself; he knocked at the door of the tomb, a hand in the darkness offered him the key. These melancholy openings that take place in the gloom before despair, are tempting. Marius thrust aside the bar that had so often allowed him to pass, emerged from the garden, and said, "I will go."

Mad with grief, no longer conscious of anything fixed or solid in his brain, incapable of accepting anything thenceforth of fate after those two months passed in the intoxication of youth and love, overwhelmed at once by all the reveries of despair, he had but one desire remaining, to make a speedy end of all.

He set out at rapid pace. He found himself most opportunely armed, as he had Javert's pistols with him.

The young man of whom he thought that he had caught a glimpse, had vanished from his sight in the street.

Marius, who had emerged from the Rue Plumet by the boulevard, traversed the Esplanade and the bridge of the Invalides, the Champs Elysees, the Place Louis XV, and reached the Rue de Rivoli. The shops were open there, the gas was burning under the arcades, women were making their purchases in the stalls, people were eating ices in the Cafe Laiter, and nibbling small cakes at the English pastry cook's shop. Only a few posting chaises were setting out at a gallop from the Hotel des Princes and the Hotel Meurice.

Marius entered the Rue Saint-Honore through the Passage Delorme. There the shops were closed, the merchants were chatting in front of their half-open doors, people were walking about, the street lanterns were lighted, beginning with the first floor, all the windows were lighted as usual. There was cavalry on the Place du Palais-Royal.

Marius followed the Rue Saint-Honore. In proportion as he left the Palais-Royal behind him, there were fewer lighted windows, the shops were fast shut, no one was chatting on the thresholds, the street grew somber, and, at the same time, the crowd increased in density. For the passersby now amounted to a crowd. No one could be seen to speak in this throng, and yet there arose from it a dull, deep murmur.

Near the fountain of the Arbre-Sec, there were "assemblages," motionless and gloomy groups which were to those who went and came as stones in the midst of running water.

At the entrance to the Rue des Prouvaires, the crowd no longer walked. It formed a resisting, massive, solid, compact, almost impenetrable block of people who were huddled together, and conversing in low tones. There were hardly any black coats or round hats now, but smock frocks, blouses, caps, and bristling and cadaverous heads. This multitude undulated confusedly in the nocturnal gloom. Its whisperings had the hoarse accent of a vibration. Although not one of them was walking, a dull trampling was audible in the mire. Beyond this dense portion of the throng, in the Rue du Roule, in the Rue des Prouvaires, and in the extension of the Rue Saint-Honore, there was no longer a single window in which a candle was burning. Only the solitary and diminishing rows of lanterns could be seen vanishing into the street in the distance. The lanterns of that date resembled large red stars, hanging to ropes, and shed upon the pavement a shadow that had the form of a huge spider. These streets were not deserted. There could be descried piles of guns, moving bayonets, and troops bivouacking. No curious observer passed that limit. There circulation ceased. There the rabble ended and the army began.

Marius willed with the will of a man who hopes no more. He had been summoned, he must go. He found a means to traverse the throng and to pass the bivouac of the troops, he shunned the patrols, he avoided the sentinels. He made a circuit, reached the Rue de Bethisy, and directed his course toward the Halles. At the corner of the Rue des Bourdonnais, there were no longer any lanterns.

After having passed the zone of the crowd, he had passed the limits of the troops; he found himself in something startling. There was no longer a passerby, no longer a soldier, no longer a light, there was no one; solitude, silence, night, I know not what chill that seized hold upon one. Entering a street was like entering a cellar.

He continued to advance.

He took a few steps. Someone passed close to him at a run. Was it a man? Or a woman? Were there many of them? he could not have told. It had passed and vanished.

Proceeding from circuit to circuit, he reached a lane that he judged to be the Rue de la Poterie; near the middle of this street, he came in contact with an obstacle. He extended his hands. It was an overturned wagon; his foot recognized pools of water, gullies, and paving stones scattered and piled up. A barricade had been begun there and abandoned. He climbed over the stones and found himself on the other side of the barrier. He walked very near the street-posts, and guided himself along the walls of the houses. A little beyond the barricade, it seemed to him that he could make out something white in front of him. He approached, it took on a form. It was two white horses; the horses of the omnibus harnessed by Bossuet in the morning, who had been straying at random all day from street to street, and had finally halted there, with the weary patience of brutes who no more understand the actions of men, than man understands the actions of Providence.

Marius left the horses behind him. As he was approaching a street, which seemed to him to be the Rue du Contrat-Social, a shot coming no one knows from where, and traversing the darkness at random, whistled close by him, and the bullet pierced a brass shaving-dish suspended above his head over a hairdresser's shop. This pierced shaving-dish was still to be seen in 1848, in the Rue du Contrat-Social, at the corner of the pillars of the market.

This shot still betokened life. From that instant forth he encountered nothing more.

The whole of this itinerary resembled a descent of black steps.

Nevertheless, Marius pressed forward.

CHAPTER II—AN OWL'S VIEW OF PARIS

A being who could have hovered over Paris that night with the wing of the bat or the owl would have had beneath his eyes a gloomy spectacle.

All that old quarter of the Halles, which is like a city within a city, through which run the Rues Saint-Denis and Saint-Martin, where a thousand lanes cross, and of which the insurgents had made their redoubt and their stronghold, would have appeared to him like a dark and enormous cavity hollowed out in the center of Paris. There the glance fell into an abyss. Thanks to the broken lanterns, thanks to the closed windows, there all radiance, all life, all sound, all movement ceased. The invisible police of the insurrection were on the watch everywhere, and maintained order, that is to say, night. The necessary tactics of insurrection are to drown small numbers in a vast obscurity, to multiply every combatant by the possibilities that obscurity contains. At dusk, every window where a candle was burning received a shot. The light was extinguished, sometimes the inhabitant was killed. Hence nothing was stirring. There was nothing but fright, mourning, stupor in the houses; and in the streets, a sort of sacred horror. Not even the long rows of windows and stores, the indentations of the chimneys, and the roofs, and the vague reflections cast back by the wet and muddy pavements, were visible. An eye cast upward at that mass of shadows might, perhaps, have caught a glimpse here and there, at intervals, of indistinct gleams which brought out broken and eccentric lines, and profiles of singular buildings, something like the lights which go and come in ruins; it was at such points that the barricades were situated. The rest was a lake of obscurity, foggy, heavy, and funereal, above which, in motionless and melancholy outlines, rose the tower of Saint-Jacques, the church of Saint-Merry, and two or three more of those grand edifices of which man makes giants and the night makes phantoms.

All around this deserted and disquieting labyrinth, in the quarters where the Parisian circulation had not been annihilated, and where a few street lanterns still burned, the aerial observer might have distinguished the metallic gleam of swords and bayonets, the dull rumble of artillery, and the swarming of silent battalions whose ranks were swelling from minute to minute; a formidable girdle which was slowly drawing in and around the insurrection.

The invested quarter was no longer anything more than a monstrous cavern; everything there appeared to be asleep or motionless, and, as we have just seen, any street which one might come to offered nothing but darkness.

A wild darkness, full of traps, full of unseen and formidable shocks, into which it was alarming to penetrate, and in which it was terrible to remain, where those who entered shivered before those whom they awaited, where those who waited shuddered before those who were coming. Invisible combatants were entrenched at every corner of the street; snares of the sepulchre concealed in the density of night. All was over. No more light was to be hoped for, henceforth, except the lightning of guns, no further encounter except the abrupt and rapid apparition of death. Where? How? When? No one knew, but it was certain and inevitable. In this place that had been marked out for the struggle, the Government and the insurrection, the National Guard, and popular societies, the bourgeois and the uprising, groping their way, were about to come into contact. The necessity was the same for both. The only possible issue thenceforth was to emerge thence killed or conquerors. A situation so extreme, an obscurity so powerful, that the most timid felt themselves seized with resolution, and the most daring with terror.

Moreover, on both sides, the fury, the rage, and the determination were equal. For the one party, to advance meant death, and no one dreamed of retreating; for the other, to remain meant death, and no one dreamed of flight.

It was indispensable that all should be ended on the following day, that triumph should rest either here or there, that the insurrection should prove itself a revolution or a skirmish. The Government understood this as well as the parties; the most insignificant bourgeois felt it. Hence a thought of anguish which mingled with the impenetrable gloom of this quarter where all was at the point of being decided; hence a redoubled anxiety around that silence from which a catastrophe was on the point of emerging. Here only one sound was audible, a sound as heart-rending as the death rattle, as menacing as a malediction, the tocsin of Saint-Merry. Nothing could be more blood curdling than the clamor of that wild and desperate bell, wailing amid the shadows.

As it often happens, nature seemed to have fallen into accord with what men were about to do. Nothing disturbed the harmony of the whole effect. The stars had disappeared, heavy clouds filled the horizon with their melancholy folds. A black sky rested on these dead streets, as though an immense winding-sheet were being outspread over this immense tomb.

While a battle that was still wholly political was in preparation in the same locality, which had already witnessed so many revolutionary events, while youth, the secret associations, the schools, in the name of principles, and the middle classes, in the name of interests, were approaching preparatory to dashing themselves together, clasping and throwing each other, while each one hastened and invited the last and decisive hour of the crisis, far away and quite outside of this fatal quarter, in the most profound depths of the unfathomable cavities of that wretched old Paris which disappears under the splendor of happy and opulent Paris, the somber voice of the people could be heard giving utterance to a dull roar.

A fearful and sacred voice which is composed of the roar of the brute and of the word of God, which terrifies the weak and which warns the wise, which comes both from below like the voice of the lion, and from on high like the voice of the thunder.

CHAPTER III—THE EXTREME EDGE

Marius had reached the Halles.

There everything was still calmer, more obscure and more motionless than in the neighboring streets. One would have said that the glacial peace of the sepulchre had sprung forth from the earth and had spread over the heavens.

Nevertheless, a red glow brought out against this black background the lofty roofs of the houses that barred the Rue de la Chanvrerie on the Saint-Eustache side. It was the reflection of the torch that was burning in the Corinthe barricade. Marius directed his steps toward that red light. It had drawn him to the Marche-aux-Poirees, and he caught a glimpse of the dark mouth of the Rue des Prêcheurs. He entered it. The insurgents' sentinel, who was guarding the other end, did not see him. He felt that he was very close to that which he had come in search of, and he walked on tiptoe. In this manner he reached the elbow of that short section of the Rue Mondetour which was, as the reader will remember, the only communication which Enjolras had preserved with the outside world. At the corner of the last house, on his left, he thrust his head forward, and looked into the fragment of the Rue Mondetour.

A little beyond the angle of the lane and the Rue de la Chanvrerie, which cast a broad curtain of shadow, in which he was himself engulfed, he perceived some light on the pavement, a bit of the wine shop, and beyond, a flickering lamp within a sort of shapeless wall, and men crouching down with guns on their knees. All this was ten fathoms distant from him. It was the interior of the barricade.

The houses that bordered the lane on the right concealed the rest of the wine shop, the large barricade, and the flag from him.

Marius had but a step more to take.

Then the unhappy young man seated himself on a post, folded his arms, and fell to thinking about his father.

He thought of that heroic Colonel Pontmercy, who had been so proud a soldier, who had guarded the frontier of France under the Republic, and had touched the frontier of Asia under Napoleon, who had beheld Genoa, Alexandria, Milan, Turin, Madrid, Vienna, Dresden, Berlin, Moscow, who had left on all the victorious battlefields of Europe drops of that same blood, which he, Marius, had in his veins, who had grown gray before his time in discipline and command, who had lived with his sword-belt buckled, his epaulets falling on his breast, his cockade blackened with powder, his brow furrowed with his helmet, in barracks, in camp, in the bivouac, in ambulances, and who, at the expiration of twenty years, had returned from the great wars with a scarred cheek, a smiling countenance, tranquil, admirable, pure as a child, having done everything for France and nothing against her.

He said to himself that his day had also come now, that his hour had struck, that following his father, he too was about to show himself brave, intrepid, bold, to run to meet the bullets, to offer his breast to bayonets, to shed his blood, to seek the enemy, to seek death, that he was about to wage war in his turn and descend to the field of battle, and that the field of battle upon which he was to descend was the street, and that the war in which he was about to engage was civil war!

He beheld civil war laid open like a gulf before him, and into this he was about to fall. Then he shuddered.

He thought of his father's sword, which his grandfather had sold to a secondhand dealer, and which he had so mournfully regretted. He said to himself that that chaste and valiant sword had done well to escape from him, and to depart in wrath into the gloom; that if it had thus fled, it was because it was intelligent and because it had foreseen the future; that it had had a presentiment of this rebellion, the war of the gutters, the war of the pavements, fusillades through cellar windows, blows given and received in the rear; it was because, coming from Marengo and Friedland, it did not wish to go to the Rue de la Chanvrerie; it was because, after what it had done with the father, it did not wish to do this for the son! He told himself that if that sword were there, if after taking possession of it at his father's pillow, he had dared to take it and carry it off for this combat of darkness between Frenchmen in the streets, it would assuredly have scorched his hands and burst out aflame before his eyes, like the sword of the angel! He told himself that it was fortunate that it was not there and that it had disappeared, that that was well, that that was just, that his grandfather had been the true guardian of his father's glory, and that it was far better that the colonel's sword should be sold at auction, sold to the old-clothes man, thrown among the old junk, than that it should, today, wound the side of his country.

And then he fell to weeping bitterly.

This was horrible. But what was he to do? Live without Cosette he could not. Since she was gone, he must needs die. Had he not given her his word of honor that he would die? She had gone knowing that; this meant that it pleased her that Marius should die. And then, it was clear that she no longer loved him, since she had departed thus without warning, without a word, without a letter, although she knew his address! What was the good of living, and why should he live now? And then, what! Should he retreat after going so far? Should he flee from danger after having approached it? Should he slip away after having come and peeped into the barricade? Slip away, all in a tremble, saying, "After all, I have had enough of it as it is. I have seen it, that suffices, this is civil war, and I shall take my leave!" Should he abandon his friends who were expecting him? Who were in need of him possibly! Who were a mere handful against an army! Should he be untrue at once to his love, to country, to his word? Should he give to his cowardice the pretext of patriotism? But this was impossible, and if the phantom of his father was there in the gloom, and beheld him retreating, he would beat him on the loins with the flat of his sword, and shout to him, "March on, you poltroon!"

Thus a prey to the conflicting movements of his thoughts, he dropped his head.

All at once he raised it. A sort of splendid rectification had just been affected in his mind. There is a widening of the sphere of thought that is peculiar to the vicinity of the grave; it makes one see clearly to be near death. The vision of the action into which he felt that he was, perhaps, on the point of entering, appeared to him no more as lamentable, but as superb. The war of the street was suddenly transfigured by some unfathomable inward working of his soul, before the eye of his thought. All the tumultuous interrogation points of reverie recurred to him in throngs, but without troubling him. He left none of them unanswered.

Let us see, why should his father be indignant? Are there not cases where insurrection rises to the dignity of duty? What was there that was degrading for the son of Colonel Pontmercy in the combat that was about to begin? It is no longer Montmirail or Champaubert; it is something quite different. The question is no longer one of sacred territory, but of a holy idea. The country wails, that may be, but humanity applauds. But is it true that the country does wail? France bleeds, but liberty smiles; and in the presence of liberty's smile, France forgets her wound. And then if we look at things from a still more lofty point of view, why do we speak of civil war?

Civil war—what does that mean? Is there a foreign war? Is not all war between men, war between brothers? War is qualified only by its object. There is no such thing as foreign or civil war; there is only just and unjust war. Until that day when the grand human agreement is concluded, war, that at least which is the effort of the future, which is hastening on against the past, which is lagging in the rear, may be necessary. What have we to reproach that war with? War does not become a disgrace, the sword does not become a disgrace, except when it is used for assassinating the right, progress, reason, civilization, truth. Then war, whether foreign or civil, is iniquitous; it is called crime. Outside the pale of that holy thing, justice, by what right does one form of man despise another? By what right should the sword of Washington disown the pike of Camille Desmoulins? Leonidas against the stranger, Timoleon against the tyrant, which is the greater? The one is the defender, the other the liberator. Shall we brand every appeal to arms within a city's limits without taking the object into a consideration? Then note the infamy of Brutus, Marcel, Arnould von Blankenheim, Coligny, Hedgerow war? War of the streets? Why not? That was the war of Ambiorix, of Artevelde, of Marnix, of Pelagius. But Ambiorix fought against Rome, Artevelde against France, Marnix against Spain, Pelagius against the Moors; all against the foreigner. Well, the monarchy is a foreigner; oppression is a stranger; the right divine is a stranger. Despotism violates the moral frontier, an invasion violates the geographical frontier. Driving out the tyrant or driving out the English, in both cases, regaining possession of one's own territory. There comes an hour when protestation no longer suffices; after philosophy, action is required; live force finishes what the idea has sketched out; Prometheus chained begins, Arostogeiton ends; the encyclopedia enlightens souls, the 10th of August electrifies them. After Æschylus, Thrasybulus; after Diderot, Danton. Multitudes have a tendency to accept the master. Their mass bears witness to apathy. A crowd is easily led as a whole to obedience. Men must be stirred up, pushed on, treated roughly by the very benefit of their deliverance, their eyes must be wounded by the true, light must be hurled at them in terrible handfuls. They must be a little thunderstruck themselves at their own well-being; this dazzling awakens them. Hence the necessity of tocsins and wars. Great combatants must rise, must enlighten nations with audacity, and shake up that sad humanity, which is covered with gloom by the right divine, Caesarian glory, force, fanaticism, irresponsible power, and absolute majesty; a rabble stupidly occupied in the contemplation, in their twilight splendor, of these somber triumphs of the night. Down with the tyrant! Of whom are you speaking? Do you call Louis Philippe the tyrant? No; no more than Louis XVI Both of them are what history is in the habit of calling good kings; but principles are not to be parceled out, the logic of the true is rectilinear, the peculiarity of truth is that it lacks complaisance; no concessions, then; all encroachments on man should be repressed. There is a divine right in Louis XVI, there is because a Bourbon in Louis Philippe; both represent in a certain measure the confiscation of right, and, in order to clear away universal insurrection, they must be combated; it must be done, France being always the one to begin. When the master falls in France, he falls everywhere. In short, what cause is more just, and consequently, what war is greater, than that which reestablishes social truth, restores her throne to liberty, restores the people to the people, restores sovereignty to man, replaces the purple on the head of France, restores equity and reason in their plenitude, suppresses every germ of antagonism by restoring each one to himself, annihilates the obstacle, which royalty presents to the whole immense universal concord, and places the human race once more on a level with the right? These wars build up peace. An enormous fortress of prejudices, privileges, superstitions, lies, exactions, abuses, violences, iniquities, and darkness still stands erect in this world, with its towers of hatred. It must be cast down. This monstrous mass must be made to crumble. To conquer at Austerlitz is grand; to take the Bastille is immense.

There is no one who has not noticed it in his own case—the soul, and therein lies the marvel of its unity complicated with ubiquity, has a strange aptitude for reasoning almost coldly in the most violent extremities, and it often happens that heartbroken passion and profound despair in the very agony of their blackest monologues, treat subjects and discuss theses. Logic is mingled with convulsion, and the thread of the syllogism floats, without breaking, in the mournful storm of thought. This was the situation of Marius's mind.

As he meditated thus, dejected but resolute, hesitating in every direction, and, in short, shuddering at what he was about to do, his glance strayed to the interior of the barricade. The insurgents were here conversing in a low voice, without moving, and there was perceptible that quasi-silence, which marks the last stage of expectation. Overhead, at the small window in the third story Marius descried a sort of spectator who appeared to him to be singularly attentive. This was the porter who had been killed by Le Cabuc. Below, by the lights of the torch, which was thrust between the paving stones, this head could be vaguely distinguished. Nothing could be stranger, in that somber and uncertain gleam, than that livid, motionless, astonished face, with its bristling hair, its eyes fixed and staring, and its yawning mouth, bent over the street in an attitude of curiosity. One would have said that the man who was dead was surveying those who were about to die. A long trail of blood which had flowed from that head, descended in reddish threads from the window to the height of the first floor, where it stopped.

BOOK FOURTEENTH:
THE GRANDEURS OF DESPAIR

CHAPTER I—THE FLAG: ACT FIRST

As yet, nothing had come. Ten o'clock had sounded from Saint-Merry. Enjolras and Combeferre had gone and seated themselves, carbines in hand, near the outlet of the grand barricade. They no longer addressed each other, they listened, seeking to catch even the faintest and most distant sound of marching.

Suddenly, in the midst of the dismal calm, a clear, gay, young voice, which seemed to come from the Rue Saint-Denis, rose and began to sing distinctly, to the old popular air of "By the Light of the Moon," this bit of poetry, terminated by a cry like the crow of a cock: "My nose is in tears, my friend Bugeaud, lend me thy gendarmes that I may say a word to them. With a blue capote and a chicken in his shako, here's the *banlieue*, co-cocorico."

They pressed each other's hands.

"That is Gavroche," said Enjolras.

"He is warning us," said Combeferre.

A hasty rush troubled the deserted street; they beheld a being more agile than a clown climb over the omnibus, and Gavroche bounded into the barricade, all breathless, saying, "My gun! Here they are!"

An electric quiver shot through the whole barricade, and the sound of hands seeking their guns became audible.

"Would you like my carbine?" said Enjolras to the lad.

"I want a big gun," replied Gavroche.

And he seized Javert's gun.

Two sentinels had fallen back, and had come in almost at the same moment as Gavroche. They were the sentinels from the end of the street, and the vidette of the Rue de la Petite-Truanderie. The vidette of the Lane des Prêcheurs had remained at his post, which indicated that nothing was approaching from the direction of the bridges and Halles.

The Rue de la Chanvrerie, of which a few paving stones alone were dimly visible in the reflection of the light projected on the flag, offered to the insurgents the aspect of a vast black door vaguely opened into a smoke.

Each man had taken up his position for the conflict.

Forty-three insurgents, among whom were Enjolras, Combeferre, Courfeyrac, Bossuet, Joly, Bahorel, and Gavroche, were kneeling inside the large barricade, with their heads on a level with the crest of the barrier, the barrels of their guns and carbines aimed on the stones as though at loopholes, attentive, mute, ready to fire. Six, commanded by Feuilly, had installed themselves, with their guns leveled at their shoulders, at the windows of the two stories of Corinthe.

Several minutes passed thus, then a sound of footsteps, measured, heavy, and numerous, became distinctly audible in the direction of Saint-Leu. This sound, faint at first, then precise, then heavy and sonorous, approached slowly, without halt, without intermission, with a tranquil and terrible continuity. Nothing was to be heard but this. It was that combined silence and sound, of the statue of the commander, but this stony step had something indescribably enormous and multiple about it, which awakened the idea of a throng, and, at the same time, the idea of a specter. One thought one heard the terrible statue Legion marching onward. This tread drew near; it drew still nearer, and stopped. It seemed as though the breathing of many men could be heard at the end of the street. Nothing was to be seen, however, but at the bottom of that dense obscurity there could be distinguished a multitude of metallic threads, as fine as needles and almost imperceptible, which moved about like those indescribable phosphoric networks which one sees beneath one's closed eyelids, in the first mists of slumber at the moment when one is dropping off to sleep. These were bayonets and gun barrels confusedly illuminated by the distant reflection of the torch.

A pause ensued, as though both sides were waiting. All at once, from the depths of this darkness, a voice, which was all the more sinister, since no one was visible, and which appeared to be the gloom itself speaking, shouted, "Who goes there?"

At the same time, the click of guns, as they were lowered into position, was heard.

Enjolras replied in a haughty and vibrating tone, "The French Revolution!"

"Fire!" shouted the voice.

A flash empurpled all the facades in the street as though the door of a furnace had been flung open, and hastily closed again.

A fearful detonation burst forth on the barricade. The red flag fell. The discharge had been so violent and so dense that it had cut the staff, that is to say, the very tip of the omnibus pole.

Bullets which had rebounded from the cornices of the houses penetrated the barricade and wounded several men.

The impression produced by this first discharge was freezing. The attack had been rough, and of a nature to inspire reflection in the boldest. It was evident that they had to deal with an entire regiment at the very least.

"Comrades!" shouted Courfeyrac. "Let us not waste our powder. Let us wait until they are in the street before replying."

"And, above all," said Enjolras, "let us raise the flag again."

He picked up the flag, which had fallen precisely at his feet.

Outside, the clatter of the ramrods in the guns could be heard; the troops were reloading their arms.

Enjolras went on, "Who is there here with a bold heart? Who will plant the flag on the barricade again?"

Not a man responded. To mount on the barricade at the very moment when, without any doubt, it was again the object of their aim, was simply death. The bravest hesitated to pronounce his own condemnation. Enjolras himself felt a thrill. He repeated, "Does no one volunteer?"

CHAPTER II—THE FLAG: ACT SECOND

Since they had arrived at Corinthe, and had begun the construction of the barricade, no attention had been paid to Father Mabeuf. M. Mabeuf had not quitted the mob, however; he had entered the ground floor of the wine shop and had seated himself behind the counter. There he had, so to speak, retreated into himself. He no longer seemed to look or to think. Courfeyrac and others had accosted him two or three times, warning him of his peril, beseeching him to withdraw, but he did not hear them. When they were not speaking to him, his mouth moved as though he were replying to someone, and as soon as he was addressed, his lips became motionless and his eyes no longer had the appearance of being alive.

Several hours before the barricade was attacked, he had assumed an attitude that he did not afterward abandon, with both fists planted on his knees and his head thrust forward as though he were gazing over a precipice. Nothing had been able to move him from this attitude; it did not seem as though his mind were in the barricade. When each had gone to take up his position for the combat, there remained in the taproom where Javert was bound to the post, only a single insurgent with a naked sword, watching over Javert, and himself, Mabeuf. At the moment of the attack, at the detonation, the physical shock had reached him and had, as it were, awakened him; he started up abruptly, crossed the room, and at the instant when Enjolras repeated his appeal, "Does no one volunteer?"

The old man was seen to make his appearance on the threshold of the wine shop. His presence produced a sort of commotion in the different groups. A shout went up, "It is the voter! It is the member of the Convention! It is the representative of the people!"

It is probable that he did not hear them.

He strode straight up to Enjolras, the insurgents withdrawing before him with a religious fear; he tore the flag from Enjolras, who recoiled in amazement and then, since no one dared to stop or to assist him, this old man of eighty, with shaking head but firm foot, began slowly to ascend the staircase of paving stones arranged in the barricade. This was so melancholy and so grand that all around him cried, "Off with your hats!" At every step that he mounted, it was a frightful spectacle; his white locks, his decrepit face, his lofty, bald, and wrinkled brow, his amazed and open mouth, his aged arm upholding the red banner, rose through the gloom and were enlarged in the bloody light of the torch, and the bystanders thought that they beheld the specter of '93 emerging from the earth, with the flag of terror in his hand.

When he had reached the last step, when this trembling and terrible phantom, erect on that pile of rubbish in the presence of twelve hundred invisible guns, drew himself up in the face of death and as though he were more powerful than it, the whole barricade assumed amid the darkness, a supernatural and colossal form.

There ensued one of those silences that occur only in the presence of prodigies. In the midst of this silence, the old man waved the red flag and shouted, "Long live the Revolution! Long live the Republic! Fraternity! Equality! And Death!"

Those in the barricade heard a low and rapid whisper, like the murmur of a priest who is dispatching a prayer in haste. It was probably the commissary of police who was making the legal summons at the other end of the street.

Then the same piercing voice which had shouted, "Who goes there?" shouted, "Retire!"

M. Mabeuf, pale, haggard, his eyes lighted up with the mournful flame of aberration, raised the flag above his head and repeated, "Long live the Republic!"

"Fire!" said the voice.

A second discharge, similar to the first, rained down upon the barricade.

The old man fell on his knees, then rose again, dropped the flag and fell backward on the pavement, like a log, at full length, with outstretched arms.

Rivulets of blood flowed beneath him. His aged head, pale and sad, seemed to be gazing at the sky.

One of those emotions that are superior to man, which make him forget even to defend himself, seized upon the insurgents, and they approached the body with respectful awe.

"What men these regicides were!" said Enjolras.

Courfeyrac bent down to Enjolras' ear, "This is for yourself alone, I do not wish to dampen the enthusiasm. But this man was anything rather than a regicide. I knew him. His name was Father Mabeuf. I do not know what was the matter with him today. But he was a brave blockhead. Just look at his head."

"The head of a blockhead and the heart of a Brutus," replied Enjolras.

Then he raised his voice, "Citizens! This is the example that the old give to the young. We hesitated, he came! We were drawing back, he advanced! This is what those who are trembling with age teach to those who tremble with fear! This aged man is august in the eyes of his country. He has had a long life and a magnificent death! Now, let us place the body undercover, that each one of us may defend this old man dead as he would his father living, and may his presence in our midst render the barricade impregnable!"

A murmur of gloomy and energetic assent followed these words.

Enjolras bent down, raised the old man's head, and fierce as he was, he kissed him on the brow, then, throwing wide his arms, and handling this dead man with tender precaution, as though he feared to hurt it, he removed his coat, showed the bloody holes in it to all, and said, "This is our flag now."

CHAPTER III—GAVROCHE WOULD HAVE DONE BETTER TO ACCEPT ENJOLRAS' CARBINE

They threw a long black shawl of Widow Hucheloup's over Father Mabeuf. Six men made a litter of their guns; on this they laid the body, and bore it, with bared heads, with solemn slowness, to the large table in the taproom.

These men, wholly absorbed in the grave and sacred task in which they were engaged, thought no more of the perilous situation in which they stood.

When the corpse passed near Javert, who was still impassive, Enjolras said to the spy, "It will be your turn presently!"

During all this time, Little Gavroche, who alone had not quitted his post, but had remained on guard, thought he espied some men stealthily approaching the barricade. All at once he shouted, "Look out!"

Courfeyrac, Enjolras, Jean Prouvaire, Combeferre, Joly, Bahorel, Bossuet, and all the rest ran tumultuously from the wine shop. It was almost too late. They saw a glistening density of bayonets undulating above the barricade. Municipal guards of lofty stature were making their way in, some striding over the omnibus, others through the cut, thrusting before them the urchin, who retreated, but did not flee.

The moment was critical. It was that first, redoubtable moment of inundation, when the stream rises to the level of the levee and when the water begins to filter through the fissures of dike. A second more and the barricade would have been taken.

Bahorel dashed upon the first municipal guard who was entering, and killed him on the spot with a blow from his gun; the second killed Bahorel with a blow from his bayonet. Another had already overthrown Courfeyrac, who was shouting, "Follow me!" The largest of all, a sort of colossus, marched on

Gavroche with his bayonet fixed. The urchin took in his arms Javert's immense gun, leveled it resolutely at the giant, and fired. No discharge followed. Javert's gun was not loaded. The municipal guard burst into a laugh and raised his bayonet at the child.

Before the bayonet had touched Gavroche, the gun slipped from the soldier's grasp, a bullet had struck the municipal guardsman in the center of the forehead, and he fell over on his back. A second bullet struck the other guard, who had assaulted Courfeyrac in the breast, and laid him low on the pavement.

This was the work of Marius, who had just entered the barricade.

CHAPTER IV—THE BARREL OF POWDER

Marius, still concealed in the turn of the Rue Mondetour, had witnessed, shuddering and irresolute, the first phase of the combat. But he had not long been able to resist that mysterious and sovereign vertigo, which may be designated as the call of the abyss. In the presence of the imminence of the peril, in the presence of the death of M. Mabeuf, that melancholy enigma, in the presence of Bahorel killed, and Courfeyrac shouting, "Follow me!" of that child threatened, of his friends to succor or to avenge, all hesitation had vanished, and he had flung himself into the conflict, his two pistols in hand. With his first shot he had saved Gavroche, and with the second delivered Courfeyrac.

Amid the sound of the shots, amid the cries of the assaulted guards, the assailants had climbed the entrenchment, on whose summit Municipal Guards, soldiers of the line and National Guards from the suburbs could now be seen, gun in hand, rearing themselves to more than half the height of their bodies.

They already covered more than two-thirds of the barrier, but they did not leap into the enclosure, as though wavering in the fear of some trap. They gazed into the dark barricade as one would gaze into a lion's den. The light of the torch illuminated only their bayonets, their bearskin caps, and the upper part of their uneasy and angry faces.

Marius had no longer any weapons; he had flung away his discharged pistols after firing them; but he had caught sight of the barrel of powder in the taproom, near the door.

As he turned half around, gazing in that direction, a soldier took aim at him. At the moment when the soldier was sighting Marius, a hand was laid on the muzzle of the gun and obstructed it. This was done by someone who had darted forward, the young workman in velvet trousers. The shot sped, traversed the hand and possibly, also, the workman, since he fell, but the ball did not strike Marius. All this, which was rather to be apprehended than seen through the smoke, Marius, who was entering the taproom, hardly noticed. Still, he had, in a confused way, perceived that gun barrel aimed at him, and the hand that had blocked it, and he had heard the discharge. But in moments like this, the things which one sees vacillate and are precipitated, and one pauses for nothing. One feels obscurely impelled toward more darkness still, and all is cloud.

The insurgents, surprised but not terrified, had rallied. Enjolras had shouted, "Wait! Don't fire at random!" In the first confusion, they might, in fact, wound each other. The majority of them had ascended to the window on the first story and to the attic windows, from which they commanded the assailants.

The most determined, with Enjolras, Courfeyrac, Jean Prouvaire, and Combeferre, had proudly placed themselves with their backs against the houses at the rear, unsheltered and facing the ranks of soldiers and guards who crowned the barricade.

All this was accomplished without haste, with that strange and threatening gravity that precedes engagements. They took aim, point blank, on both sides, they were so close that they could talk together without raising their voices.

When they had reached this point where the spark is on the brink of darting forth, an officer in a gorget extended his sword and said, "Lay down your arms!"

"Fire!" replied Enjolras.

The two discharges took place at the same moment, and all disappeared in smoke.

An acrid and stifling smoke in which dying and wounded lay with weak, dull groans. When the smoke cleared away, the combatants on both sides could be seen to be thinned out, but still in the same positions, reloading in silence. All at once, a thundering voice was heard, shouting, "Be off with you, or I'll blow up the barricade!"

All turned in the direction from which the voice proceeded.

Marius had entered the taproom, and had seized the barrel of powder, then he had taken advantage of the smoke, and the sort of obscure mist, which filled the entrenched enclosure, to glide along the barricade as far as that cage of paving stones where the torch was fixed. To tear it from the torch, to replace it by the barrel of powder, to thrust the pile of stones under the barrel, which was instantly staved in, with a sort of horrible obedience, all this had cost Marius but the time necessary to stoop and rise again; and now all, National Guards, Municipal Guards, officers, soldiers, huddled at the other extremity of the barricade, gazed stupidly at him, as he stood with his foot on the stones, his torch in his hand, his haughty face illuminated by a fatal resolution, drooping the flame of the torch toward that redoubtable pile where they could make out the broken barrel of powder, and giving vent to that startling cry, "Be off with you, or I'll blow up the barricade!"

Marius on that barricade after the octogenarian was the vision of the young revolution after the apparition of the old.

"Blow up the barricade!" said a sergeant. "And yourself with it!"

Marius retorted, "And myself also."

And he dropped the torch toward the barrel of powder.

But there was no longer anyone on the barrier. The assailants, abandoning their dead and wounded, flowed back pell-mell and in disorder toward the extremity of the street, and there were again lost in the night. It was a headlong flight.

The barricade was free.

CHAPTER V—END OF THE VERSES OF JEAN PROUVAIRE

All flocked around Marius. Courfeyrac flung himself on his neck.

"Here you are!"

"What luck!" said Combeferre.

"You came in opportunely!" ejaculated Bossuet.

"If it had not been for you, I should have been dead!" began Courfeyrac again.

"If it had not been for you, I should have been gobbled up!" added Gavroche.

Marius asked, "Where is the chief?"

"You are he!" said Enjolras.

Marius had had a furnace in his brain all day long; now it was a whirlwind. This whirlwind that was within him, produced on him the effect of being outside of him and of bearing him away. It seemed to him that he was already at an immense distance from life. His two luminous months of joy and love, ending abruptly at that frightful precipice, Cosette lost to him, that barricade, M. Mabeuf getting himself killed for the Republic, himself the leader of the insurgents, all these things appeared to him like a tremendous nightmare. He was obliged to make a mental effort to recall the fact that all that surrounded him was real. Marius had already seen too much of life not to know that nothing is more imminent than the impossible, and that what it is always necessary to foresee is the unforeseen. He had looked on at his own drama as a piece that one does not understand.

In the mists that enveloped his thoughts, he did not recognize Javert, who, bound to his post, had not so much as moved his head during the whole of the attack on the barricade, and who had gazed on the revolt seething around him with the resignation of a martyr and the majesty of a judge. Marius had not even seen him.

In the meanwhile, the assailants did not stir, they could be heard marching and swarming through at the end of the street but they did not venture into it, either because they were awaiting orders or because they were awaiting reinforcements before hurling themselves afresh on this impregnable redoubt. The insurgents had posted sentinels, and some of them, who were medical students, set about caring for the wounded.

They had thrown the tables out of the wine shop, with the exception of the two tables reserved for lint and cartridges, and of the one on which lay Father Mabeuf; they had added them to the barricade, and had replaced them in the taproom with mattresses from the bed of the widow Hucheloup and her servants. On these mattresses they had laid the wounded. As for the three poor creatures who inhabited Corinthe, no one knew what had become of them. They were finally found, however, hidden in the cellar.

A poignant emotion clouded the joy of the disencumbered barricade.

The roll was called. One of the insurgents was missing. And who was it? One of the dearest. One of the most valiant. Jean Prouvaire. He was sought among the wounded, he was not there. He was sought among the dead, he was not there. He was evidently a prisoner. Combeferre said to Enjolras, "They have our friend; we have their agent. Are you set on the death of that spy?"

"Yes," replied Enjolras; "but less so than on the life of Jean Prouvaire."

This took place in the taproom near Javert's post.

"Well," resumed Combeferre, "I am going to fasten my handkerchief to my cane, and go as a flag of truce, to offer to exchange our man for theirs."

"Listen," said Enjolras, laying his hand on Combeferre's arm.

At the end of the street there was a significant clash of arms.

They heard a manly voice shout, "Vive la France! Long live France! Long live the future!"

They recognized the voice of Prouvaire.

A flash passed, a report rang out.

Silence fell again.

"They have killed him," exclaimed Combeferre.

Enjolras glanced at Javert, and said to him, "Your friends have just shot you."

CHAPTER VI—THE AGONY OF DEATH AFTER THE AGONY OF LIFE

A peculiarity of this species of war is, that the attack of the barricades is almost always made from the front, and that the assailants generally abstain from turning the position, either because they fear ambushes, or because they are afraid of getting entangled in the tortuous streets. The insurgents' whole attention had been directed, therefore, to the grand barricade, which was, evidently, the spot always menaced, and there the struggle would infallibly recommence. But Marius thought of the little barricade, and went there. It was deserted and guarded only by the firepot that trembled between the paving stones. Moreover, the Mondetour alley, and the branches of the Rue de la Petite Truanderie and the Rue du Cygne were profoundly calm.

As Marius was withdrawing, after concluding his inspection, he heard his name pronounced feebly in the darkness.

"Monsieur Marius!"

He started, for he recognized the voice that had called to him two hours before through the gate in the Rue Plumet.

Only, the voice now seemed to be nothing more than a breath.

He looked about him, but saw no one.

Marius thought he had been mistaken, that it was an illusion added by his mind to the extraordinary realities clashing around him. He advanced a step, in order to quit the distant recess where the barricade lay.

"Monsieur Marius!" repeated the voice.

This time he could not doubt that he had heard it distinctly; he looked and saw nothing.

"At your feet," said the voice.

He bent down, and saw in the darkness a form that was dragging itself toward him.

It was crawling along the pavement. It was this that had spoken to him.

The firepot allowed him to distinguish a blouse, torn trousers of coarse velvet, bare feet, and something that resembled a pool of blood. Marius indistinctly made out a pale head, which was lifted toward him and which was saying to him, "You do not recognize me?"

"No."

"Eponine."

Marius bent hastily down. It was, in fact, that unhappy child. She was dressed in men's clothes.

"How come you here? What are you doing here?"

"I am dying," said she.

There are words and incidents that arouse dejected beings. Marius cried out with a start, "You are wounded! Wait, I will carry you into the room! They will attend to you there. Is it serious? How must I take hold of you in order not to hurt you? Where do you suffer? Help! My God! But why did you come here?"

And he tried to pass his arm under her, in order to raise her.

She uttered a feeble cry.

"Have I hurt you?" asked Marius.

"A little."

"But I only touched your hand."

She raised her hand to Marius, and in the middle of that hand Marius saw a black hole.

"What is the matter with your hand?" said he.

"It is pierced."

"Pierced?"

"Yes."

"What with?"

"A bullet."

"How?"

"Did you see a gun aimed at you?"

"Yes, and a hand stopping it."

"It was mine."

Marius was seized with a shudder.

"What madness! Poor child! But so much the better, if that is all, it is nothing, let me carry you to a bed. They will dress your wound; one does not die of a pierced hand."

She murmured, "The bullet traversed my hand, but it came out through my back. It is useless to remove me from this spot. I will tell you how you can care for me better than any surgeon. Sit down near me on this stone."

He obeyed; she laid her head on Marius' knees, and, without looking at him, she said, "Oh! How good this is! How comfortable this is! There; I no longer suffer."

She remained silent for a moment, then she turned her face with an effort, and looked at Marius.

"Do you know what, Monsieur Marius? It puzzled me because you entered that garden; it was stupid, because it was I who showed you that house; and then, I ought to have said to myself that a young man like you—"

She paused, and overstepping the somber transitions that undoubtedly existed in her mind, she resumed with a heartrending smile, "You thought me ugly, didn't you?"

She continued, "You see, you are lost! Now, no one can get out of the barricade. It was I who led you here, by the way! You are going to die, I count upon that. And yet, when I saw them taking aim at you, I put my hand on the muzzle of the gun. How queer it is! But it was because I wanted to die before you. When I received that bullet, I dragged myself here, no one saw me, no one picked me up, I was waiting for you, I said, 'So he is not coming!' Oh, if you only knew. I bit my blouse, I suffered so! Now I am well. Do you remember the day I entered your chamber and when I looked at myself in your mirror, and the day when I came to you on the boulevard near the washerwomen? How the birds sang! That was a long time ago. You gave me a hundred sous, and I said to you, 'I don't want your money.' I hope you picked up your coin? You are not rich. I did not think to tell you to pick it up. The sun was shining bright, and it was not cold. Do you remember, Monsieur Marius? Oh! How happy I am! Everyone is going to die."

She had a mad, grave, and heartbreaking air. Her torn blouse disclosed her bare throat.

As she talked, she pressed her pierced hand to her breast, where there was another hole, and from which there spurted from moment to moment a stream of blood, like a jet of wine from an open bunghole.

Marius gazed at this unfortunate creature with profound compassion.

"Oh!" she resumed. "It is coming again, I am stifling!"

She caught up her blouse and bit it, and her limbs stiffened on the pavement.

At that moment the young cock's crow executed by little Gavroche resounded through the barricade.

The child had mounted a table to load his gun, and was singing gaily the song then so popular:

"On beholding Lafayette, the gendarme repeats: Let us flee! Let us flee! Let us flee!"

Eponine raised herself and listened; then she murmured, "It is he."

And turning to Marius, "My brother is here. He must not see me. He would scold me."

"Your brother?" inquired Marius, who was meditating in the most bitter and sorrowful depths of his heart on the duties to the Thenardiers that his father had bequeathed to him. "Who is your brother?"

"That little fellow."

"The one who is singing?"

"Yes."

Marius made a movement.

"Oh! Don't go away," said she, "it will not be long now."

She was sitting almost upright, but her voice was very low and broken by hiccoughs.

At intervals, the death rattle interrupted her. She put her face as near that of Marius as possible. She added with a strange expression, "Listen, I do not wish to play you a trick. I have a letter in my pocket for you. I was told to put it in the post. I kept it. I did not want to have it reach you. But perhaps you will be angry with me for it when we meet again presently? Take your letter."

She grasped Marius's hand convulsively with her pierced hand, but she no longer seemed to feel her sufferings. She put Marius's hand in the pocket of her blouse. There, in fact, Marius felt a paper.

"Take it," said she.

Marius took the letter.

She made a sign of satisfaction and contentment.

"Now, for my trouble, promise me—"

And she stopped.

"What?" asked Marius.

"Promise me!"

"I promise."

"Promise to give me a kiss on my brow when I am dead. I shall feel it."

She dropped her head again on Marius's knees, and her eyelids closed. He thought the poor soul had departed. Eponine remained motionless. All at once, at the very moment when Marius fancied her asleep forever, she slowly opened her eyes in which appeared the somber profundity of death, and said to him in a tone whose sweetness seemed already to proceed from another world, "And by the way, Monsieur Marius, I believe that I was a little bit in love with you."

She tried to smile once more and expired.

CHAPTER VII—GAVROCHE AS A PROFOUND CALCULATOR OF DISTANCES

Marius kept his promise. He dropped a kiss on that livid brow, where the icy perspiration stood in beads.

This was no infidelity to Cosette; it was a gentle and pensive farewell to an unhappy soul.

It was not without a tremor that he had taken the letter that Eponine had given him. He had immediately felt that it was an event of weight. He was impatient to read it. The heart of man is so constituted that the unhappy child had hardly closed her eyes when Marius began to think of unfolding this paper.

He laid her gently on the ground, and went away. Something told him that he could not peruse that letter in the presence of that body.

He drew near to a candle in the taproom. It was a small note, folded and sealed with a woman's elegant care. The address was in a woman's hand and ran:

"To Monsieur, Monsieur Marius Pontmercy, at M. Courfeyrac's, Rue de la Verrerie, No. 16."

He broke the seal and read: "My dearest, alas! My father insists on our setting out immediately. We shall be this evening in the Rue de l'Homme Arme, No. 7. In a week we shall be in England. COSETTE. June 4th."

Such was the innocence of their love that Marius was not even acquainted with Cosette's handwriting.

What had taken place may be related in a few words. Eponine had been the cause of everything. After the evening of the 3rd of June she had cherished a double idea, to defeat the projects of her father and the ruffians on the house of the Rue Plumet, and to separate Marius and Cosette. She had exchanged rags with the first young scamp she came across who had thought it amusing to dress like a woman, while Eponine disguised herself like a man. It was she who had conveyed to Jean Valjean in the Champ de Mars the expressive warning, "Leave your house."

Jean Valjean had, in fact, returned home, and had said to Cosette, "We set out this evening and we go to the Rue de l'Homme Arme with Toussaint. Next week, we shall be in London." Cosette, utterly overwhelmed by this unexpected blow, had hastily penned a couple of lines to Marius. But how was she to get the letter to the post? She never went out alone, and Toussaint, surprised at such a commission, would certainly show the letter to M. Fauchelevent. In this dilemma, Cosette had caught sight through the fence of Eponine in man's clothes, who now prowled incessantly around the garden. Cosette had called to "this young workman" and had handed him five francs and the letter, saying, "Carry this letter immediately to its address." Eponine had put the letter in her pocket. The next day, on the 5th of June, she went to Courfeyrac's quarters to inquire for Marius, not for the purpose of delivering the letter, but, a thing that every jealous and loving soul will comprehend "to see." There she had waited for Marius, or at least for Courfeyrac, still for the purpose of seeing. When Courfeyrac had told her, "We are going to the barricades," an idea flashed through her mind, to fling herself into that death, as she would have done into any other, and to thrust Marius into it also. She had followed Courfeyrac, had made sure of the locality where the barricade was in process of construction; and, quite certain, since Marius had received no warning, and since she had intercepted the letter, that he would go at dusk to his trysting place for every evening, she had betaken herself to the Rue Plumet, had there awaited Marius, and had sent him, in the name of his friends, the appeal which would, she thought, lead him to the barricade. She reckoned on Marius's despair when he should fail to find Cosette; she was not mistaken. She had returned to the Rue de la Chanvrerie herself. What she did there the reader has just seen. She died with the tragic joy of jealous hearts who drag the beloved being into their own death, and who say, "No one shall have him!"

Marius covered Cosette's letter with kisses. So she loved him! For one moment the idea occurred to him that he ought not to die now. Then he said to himself, "She is going away. Her father is taking her to England, and my grandfather refuses his consent to the marriage. Nothing is changed in our fates." Dreamers like Marius are subject to supreme attacks of dejection, and desperate resolves are the result. The fatigue of living is insupportable; death is sooner over with. Then he reflected that he had still two duties to fulfill: to inform Cosette of his death and send her a final farewell, and to save from the impending catastrophe which was in preparation, that poor child, Eponine's brother and Thenardier's son.

He had a pocketbook about him; the same one that had contained the notebook in which he had inscribed so many thoughts of love for Cosette. He tore out a leaf and wrote on it a few lines in pencil:

"Our marriage was impossible. I asked my grandfather, he refused; I have no fortune, neither hast thou. I hastened to thee, thou wert no longer there. Thou knowest the promise that I gave thee, I shall keep it. I die. I love thee. When thou readest this, my soul will be near thee, and thou wilt smile."

Having nothing wherewith to seal this letter, he contented himself with folding the paper in four, and added the address:

"To Mademoiselle Cosette Fauchelevent, at M. Fauchelevent's, Rue de l'Homme Arme, No. 7."

Having folded the letter, he stood in thought for a moment, drew out his pocketbook again, opened it, and wrote, with the same pencil, these four lines on the first page:

"My name is Marius Pontmercy. Carry my body to my grandfather, M. Gillenormand, Rue des Filles-du-Calvaire, No. 6, in the Marais."

He put his pocketbook back in his pocket, then he called Gavroche.

The gamin, at the sound of Marius's voice, ran up to him with his merry and devoted air.

"Will you do something for me?"

"Anything," said Gavroche. "Good God! If it had not been for you, I should have been done for."

"Do you see this letter?"

"Yes."

"Take it. Leave the barricade instantly" (Gavroche began to scratch his ear uneasily) "and tomorrow morning, you will deliver it at its address to Mademoiselle Cosette, at M. Fauchelevent's, Rue de l'Homme Arme, No. 7."

The heroic child replied, "Well, but! In the meanwhile the barricade will be taken, and I shall not be there."

"The barricade will not be attacked until daybreak, according to all appearances, and will not be taken before tomorrow noon."

The fresh respite that the assailants were granting to the barricade had, in fact, been prolonged. It was one of those intermissions that frequently occur in nocturnal combats, which are always followed by an increase of rage.

"Well," said Gavroche, "what if I were to go and carry your letter tomorrow?"

"It will be too late. The barricade will probably be blockaded, all the streets will be guarded, and you will not be able to get out. Go at once."

Gavroche could think of no reply to this, and stood there in indecision, scratching his ear sadly.

All at once, he took the letter with one of those birdlike movements that were common with him.

"All right," said he.

And he started off at a run through Mondetour lane.

An idea had occurred to Gavroche that had brought him to a decision, but he had not mentioned it for fear that Marius might offer some objection to it.

This was the idea, "It is barely midnight, the Rue de l'Homme Arme is not far off; I will go and deliver the letter at once, and I shall get back in time."

BOOK FIFTEENTH: THE RUE DE L'HOMME ARME

CHAPTER I—A DRINKER IS A BABBLER

What are the convulsions of a city in comparison with the insurrections of the soul? Man is a depth still greater than the people. Jean Valjean at that very moment was the prey of a terrible upheaval. Every sort of gulf had opened again within him. He also was trembling, like Paris, on the brink of an obscure and formidable revolution. A few hours had sufficed to bring this about. His destiny and his conscience had suddenly been covered with gloom. Of him also, as well as of Paris, it might have been said, "Two principles are face to face. The white angel and the black angel are about to seize each other on the bridge of the abyss. Which of the two will hurl the other over? Who will carry the day?"

On the evening preceding this same 5th of June, Jean Valjean, accompanied by Cosette and Toussaint had installed himself in the Rue de l'Homme Arme. A change awaited him there.

Cosette had not quitted the Rue Plumet without making an effort at resistance. For the first time since they had lived side by side, Cosette's will and the will of Jean Valjean had proved to be distinct, and had been in opposition, at least, if they had not clashed. There had been objections on one side and inflexibility on the other. The abrupt advice, "Leave your house," hurled at Jean Valjean by a stranger, had alarmed him to the extent of rendering him peremptory. He thought that he had been traced and followed. Cosette had been obliged to give way.

Both had arrived in the Rue de l'Homme Arme without opening their lips, and without uttering a word, each being absorbed in his own personal preoccupation; Jean Valjean so uneasy that he did not notice Cosette's sadness, Cosette so sad that she did not notice Jean Valjean's uneasiness.

Jean Valjean had taken Toussaint with him, a thing that he had never done in his previous absences. He perceived the possibility of not returning to the Rue Plumet, and he could neither leave Toussaint behind nor confide his secret to her. Besides, he felt that she was devoted and trustworthy. Treachery between master and servant begins in curiosity. Now Toussaint, as though she had been destined to be Jean Valjean's servant, was not curious. She stammered in her peasant dialect of Barneville, "I am made so; I do my work; the rest is no affair of mine."

In this departure from the Rue Plumet, which had been almost a flight, Jean Valjean had carried away nothing but the little embalmed valise, baptized by Cosette "the inseparable." Full trunks would have required porters, and porters are witnesses. A fiacre had been summoned to the door on the Rue de Babylone, and they had taken their departure.

It was with difficulty that Toussaint had obtained permission to pack up a little linen and clothes and a few toilette articles. Cosette had taken only her portfolio and her blotting book.

Jean Valjean, with a view to augmenting the solitude and the mystery of this departure, had arranged to quit the pavilion of the Rue Plumet only at dusk, which had allowed Cosette time to write her note to Marius. They had arrived in the Rue de l'Homme Arme after night had fully fallen.

They had gone to bed in silence.

The lodgings in the Rue de l'Homme Arme were situated on a back court, on the second floor, and were composed of two sleeping rooms, a dining room and a kitchen adjoining the dining room, with a garret where there was a folding bed, and which fell to Toussaint's share. The dining room was an antechamber as well, and separated the two bedrooms. The apartment was provided with all necessary utensils.

People reacquire confidence as foolishly as they lose it; human nature is so constituted. Hardly had Jean Valjean reached the Rue de l'Homme Arme when his anxiety was lightened and by degrees dissipated. There are soothing spots that act in some sort mechanically on the mind. An obscure street, peaceable inhabitants. Jean Valjean experienced an indescribable contagion of tranquility in that alley of ancient Paris, which is so narrow that it is barred against carriages by a transverse beam placed on two posts, which is deaf and dumb in the midst of the clamorous city, dimly lighted at midday, and is, so to speak, incapable of emotions between two rows of lofty houses centuries old, which hold their peace like ancients as they are. There was a touch of stagnant oblivion in that street. Jean Valjean drew his breath once more there. How could he be found there?

His first care was to place the inseparable beside him.

He slept well. Night brings wisdom; we may add, night soothes. On the following morning he awoke in a mood that was almost gay. He thought the dining room charming, though it was hideous, furnished with an old round table, a long sideboard surmounted by a slanting mirror, a dilapidated armchair, and several plain chairs that were encumbered with Toussaint's packages. In one of these packages Jean Valjean's uniform of a National Guard was visible through a rent.

As for Cosette, she had had Toussaint take some broth to her room, and did not make her appearance until evening.

About five o'clock, Toussaint, who was going and coming and busying herself with the tiny establishment, set on the table a cold chicken, which Cosette, out of deference to her father, consented to glance at.

That done, Cosette, under the pretext of an obstinate sick headache, had bade Jean Valjean good night and had shut herself up in her chamber. Jean Valjean had eaten a wing of the chicken with a good appetite, and with his elbows on the table, having gradually recovered his serenity, had regained possession of his sense of security.

While he was discussing this modest dinner, he had, twice or thrice, noticed in a confused way, Toussaint's stammering words as she said to him, "Monsieur, there is something going on, they are fighting in Paris." But absorbed in a throng of inward calculations, he had paid no heed to it. To tell the truth, he had not heard her. He rose and began to pace from the door to the window and from the window to the door, growing ever more serene.

With this calm, Cosette, his sole anxiety, recurred to his thoughts. Not that he was troubled by this headache, a little nervous crisis, a young girl's fit of sulks, the cloud of a moment, there would be nothing left of it in a day or two; but he meditated on the future, and, as was his habit, he thought of it with pleasure. After all, he saw no obstacle to their happy life resuming its course. At certain hours, everything seems impossible, at others everything appears easy; Jean Valjean was in the midst of one of these good hours. They generally succeed the bad ones, as day follows night, by virtue of that law of succession and of contrast, which lies at the very foundation of nature, and which superficial minds call antithesis. In this peaceful street where he had taken refuge, Jean Valjean got rid of all that had been troubling him for some time past. This very fact, that he had seen many shadows, made him begin to perceive a little azure. To have quitted the Rue Plumet without complications or incidents was one good step already accomplished. Perhaps it would be wise to go abroad, if only for a few months, and to set out for London. Well, they would go. What difference did it make to him whether he was in France or in England, provided he had Cosette beside him? Cosette was his nation. Cosette sufficed for his happiness; the idea that he, perhaps, did not suffice for Cosette's happiness, that idea which had formerly been the cause of his fever and sleeplessness, did not even present itself to his mind. He was in a state of collapse from all his past sufferings, and he was fully entered on optimism. Cosette was by his side, she seemed to be his; an optical illusion which everyone has experienced. He arranged in his own mind, with all sorts of felicitous devices, his departure for England with Cosette, and he beheld his felicity reconstituted wherever he pleased, in the perspective of his reverie.

As he paced to and fro with long strides, his glance suddenly encountered something strange.

In the inclined mirror facing him that surmounted the sideboard, he saw the four lines that follow: My dearest, alas! My father insists on our setting out immediately. We shall be this evening in the Rue de l'Homme Armé, No. 7. In a week we shall be in England. COSETTE. June 4th."

Jean Valjean halted, perfectly haggard.

Cosette on her arrival had placed her blotting book on the sideboard in front of the mirror, and, utterly absorbed in her agony of grief, had forgotten it and left it there, without even observing that she had left it wide open, and open at precisely the page on which she had laid to dry the four lines, which she had penned, and which she had given in charge of the young workman in the Rue Plumet. The writing had been printed off on the blotter.

The mirror reflected the writing.

The result was, what is called in geometry, the symmetrical image; so that the writing, reversed on the blotter, was righted in the mirror and presented its natural appearance; and Jean Valjean had beneath his eyes the letter written by Cosette to Marius on the preceding evening.

It was simple and withering.

Jean Valjean stepped up to the mirror. He read the four lines again, but he did not believe them. They produced on him the effect of appearing in a flash of lightning. It was a hallucination, it was impossible. It was not so.

Little by little, his perceptions became more precise; he looked at Cosette's blotting book, and the consciousness of the reality returned to him. He caught up the blotter and said, "It comes from there." He feverishly examined the four lines imprinted on the blotter, the reversal of the letters converted into an odd scrawl, and he saw no sense in it. Then he said to himself, "But this signifies nothing; there is nothing written here." And he drew a long breath with inexpressible relief. Who has not experienced those foolish joys in horrible instants? The soul does not surrender to despair until it has exhausted all illusions.

He held the blotter in his hand and contemplated it in stupid delight, almost ready to laugh at the hallucination of which he had been the dupe. All at once his eyes fell upon the mirror again, and again he beheld the vision. There were the four lines outlined with inexorable clearness. This time it was no mirage. The recurrence of a vision is a reality; it was palpable, it was the writing restored in the mirror. He understood.

Jean Valjean tottered, dropped the blotter, and fell into the old armchair beside the buffet, with drooping head, and glassy eyes, in utter bewilderment. He told himself that it was plain, that the light of the world had been eclipsed forever, and that Cosette had written that to someone. Then he heard his soul, which had become terrible once more, give vent to a dull roar in the gloom. Try then the effect of taking from the lion the dog that he has in his cage!

Strange and sad to say, at that very moment, Marius had not yet received Cosette's letter; chance had treacherously carried it to Jean Valjean before delivering it to Marius. Up to that day, Jean Valjean had not been vanquished by trial. He had been subjected to fearful proofs; no violence of bad fortune had been spared him; the ferocity of fate, armed with all vindictiveness and all social scorn, had taken him for her prey and had raged against him. He had accepted every extremity when it had been necessary; he had sacrificed his inviolability as a reformed man, had yielded up his liberty, risked his head, lost everything, suffered everything, and he had remained disinterested and stoical to such a point that he might have been thought to be absent from himself like a martyr. His conscience inured to every assault of destiny, might have appeared to be forever impregnable. Well, anyone who had beheld his spiritual self would have been obliged to concede that it weakened at that moment. It was because, of all the tortures that he had undergone in the course of this long inquisition to which destiny had doomed him, this was the most terrible. Never had such pincers seized him hitherto. He felt the mysterious stirring of all his latent sensibilities. He felt the plucking at the strange chord. Alas! The supreme trial, let us say rather, the only trial, is the loss of the beloved being.

Poor old Jean Valjean certainly did not love Cosette otherwise than as a father; but we have already remarked, above, that into this paternity the widowhood of his life had introduced all the shades of love; he loved Cosette as his daughter, and he loved her as his mother, and he loved her as his sister; and, as he had never had either a woman to love or a wife, as nature is a creditor who accepts no protest, that sentiment also, the most impossible to lose, was mingled with the rest, vague, ignorant, pure with the purity of blindness, unconscious, celestial, angelic, divine; less like a sentiment than like an instinct, less like an instinct than like an imperceptible and invisible but real attraction; and love, properly speaking, was, in his immense tenderness for Cosette, like the thread of gold in the mountain, concealed and virgin.

Let the reader recall the situation of heart that we have already indicated. No marriage was possible between them; not even that of souls; and yet, it is certain that their destinies were wedded. With the exception of Cosette, that is to say, with the exception of a childhood, Jean Valjean had never, in the whole of his long life, known anything of that which may be loved. The passions and loves that succeed each other had not produced in him those successive green growths, tender green or dark green, which can be seen in foliage which passes through the winter and in men who pass fifty. In short, and we have insisted on it more than once, all this interior fusion, all this whole, of which the sum total was a lofty virtue, ended in rendering Jean Valjean a father to Cosette. A strange father, forged from the grandfather, the son, the brother, and the husband, that existed in Jean Valjean; a father in whom there was included even a mother; a father who loved Cosette and adored her, and who held that child as his light, his home, his family, his country, his paradise.

Thus when he saw that the end had absolutely come, that she was escaping from him, that she was slipping from his hands, that she was gliding from him, like a cloud, like water, when he had before his eyes this crushing proof: "another is the goal of her heart, another is the wish of her life; there is a dearest one, I am no longer anything but her father, I no longer exist;" when he could no longer doubt, when he said to himself, "She is going away from me!" the grief that he felt surpassed the bounds of possibility. To have done all that he had done for the purpose of ending like this! And the very idea of being nothing! Then, as we have just said, a quiver of revolt ran through him from head to foot. He felt, even in the very roots of his hair, the immense reawakening of egotism, and the "I" in this man's abyss howled.

There is such a thing as the sudden giving way of the inward subsoil. A despairing certainty does not make its way into a man without thrusting aside and breaking certain profound elements that, in some cases, are the very man himself. Grief, when it attains this shape, is a headlong flight of all the forces of the conscience. These are fatal crises. Few among us emerge from them still like ourselves and firm in duty. When the limit of endurance is overstepped, the most imperturbable virtue is disconcerted. Jean Valjean took the blotter again, and convinced himself afresh; he remained bowed and as though petrified and with staring eyes, over those four unobjectionable lines; and there arose within him such a cloud that one might have thought that everything in this soul was crumbling away.

He examined this revelation, athwart the exaggerations of reverie, with an apparent and terrifying calmness, for it is a fearful thing when a man's calmness reaches the coldness of the statue.

He measured the terrible step which his destiny had taken without his having a suspicion of the fact; he recalled his fears of the preceding summer, so foolishly dissipated; he recognized the precipice, it was still the same; only, Jean Valjean was no longer on the brink, he was at the bottom of it.

The unprecedented and heart-rending thing about it was that he had fallen without perceiving it. All the light of his life had departed, while he still fancied that he beheld the sun.

His instinct did not hesitate. He put together certain circumstances, certain dates, certain blushes and certain pallors on Cosette's part, and he said to himself, "It is he."

The divination of despair is a sort of mysterious bow that never misses its aim. He struck Marius with his first conjecture. He did not know the name, but he found the man instantly. He distinctly perceived, in the background of the implacable conjuration of his memories, the unknown prowler of the Luxembourg, that wretched seeker of love adventures, that idler of romance, that idiot, that coward, for it is cowardly to come and make eyes at young girls who have beside them a father who loves them.

After he had thoroughly verified the fact that this young man was at the bottom of this situation, and that everything proceeded from that quarter, he, Jean Valjean, the regenerated man, the man who had so labored over his soul, the man who had made so many efforts to resolve all life, all misery, and all unhappiness into love, looked into his own breast and there beheld a specter—Hate.

Great griefs contain something of dejection. They discourage one with existence. The man into whom they enter feels something within him withdraw from him. In his youth, their visits are lugubrious; later on they are sinister. Alas, if despair is a fearful thing when the blood is hot, when the hair is black, when the head is erect on the body like the flame on the torch, when the roll of destiny still retains its full thickness, when the heart, full of desirable love, still possesses beats which can be returned to it, when one has time for redress, when all women and all smiles and all the future and all the horizon are before one, when the force of life is complete, what is it in old age, when the years hasten on, growing ever paler, to that twilight hour when one begins to behold the stars of the tomb?

While he was meditating, Toussaint entered. Jean Valjean rose and asked her, "In what quarter is it? Do you know?"

Toussaint was struck dumb, and could only answer him, "What is it, sir?"

Jean Valjean began again, "Did you not tell me that just now that there is fighting going on?"

"Ah! Yes, Sir," replied Toussaint. "It is in the direction of Saint-Merry."

There is a mechanical movement that comes to us, unconsciously, from the most profound depths of our thought. It was, no doubt, under the impulse of a movement of this sort, and of which he was hardly conscious, that Jean Valjean, five minutes later, found himself in the street.

Bareheaded, he sat upon the stone post at the door of his house. He seemed to be listening.

Night had come.

CHAPTER II—THE STREET URCHIN AN ENEMY OF LIGHT

How long did he remain thus? What was the ebb and flow of this tragic meditation? Did he straighten up? Did he remain bowed? Had he been bent to breaking? Could he still rise and regain his footing in his conscience upon something solid? He probably would not have been able to tell himself.

The street was deserted. A few uneasy bourgeois, who were rapidly returning home, hardly saw him. Each one for himself in times of peril. The lamplighter came as usual to light the lantern that was situated precisely opposite the door of No. 7, and then went away. Jean Valjean would not have appeared like a living man to anyone who had examined him in that shadow. He sat there on the post of his door, motionless as a form of ice. There is congealment in despair. The alarm bells and a vague and stormy uproar were audible. In the midst of all these convulsions of the bell mingled with the revolt, the clock of Saint-Paul struck eleven, gravely and without haste; for the tocsin is man; the hour is God. The passage of the hour produced no effect on Jean Valjean; Jean Valjean did not stir. Still, at about that moment, a brusque report burst forth in the direction of the Halles, a second yet more violent followed; it was probably that attack on the barricade in the Rue de la Chanvrerie ,which we have just seen repulsed by Marius. At this double discharge, whose fury seemed augmented by the stupor of the night, Jean Valjean started; he rose, turning toward the quarter from which the noise proceeded; then he fell back upon the post again, folded his arms, and his head slowly sank on his bosom again.

He resumed his gloomy dialogue with himself.

All at once, he raised his eyes; someone was walking in the street, he heard steps near him. He looked, and by the light of the lanterns, in the direction of the street that ran into the Rue-aux-Archives, he perceived a young, livid, and beaming face.

Gavroche had just arrived in the Rue l'Homme Arme.

Gavroche was staring into the air, apparently in search of something. He saw Jean Valjean perfectly well but he took no notice of him.

Gavroche after staring into the air, stared below; he raised himself on tiptoe, and felt of the doors and windows of the ground floor; they were all shut, bolted, and padlocked. After having authenticated the fronts of five or six barricaded houses in this manner, the urchin shrugged his shoulders, and took himself to task in these terms, "*Pardi!*"

Then he began to stare into the air again.

Jean Valjean, who, an instant previously, in his then state of mind, would not have spoken to or even answered anyone, felt irresistibly impelled to accost that child.

"What is the matter with you, my little fellow?" he said.

"The matter with me is that I am hungry," replied Gavroche frankly. And he added, "Little fellow, yourself."

Jean Valjean fumbled in his fob and pulled out a five-franc piece.

But Gavroche, who was of the wagtail species, and who skipped vivaciously from one gesture to another, had just picked up a stone. He had caught sight of the lantern.

"See here," said he, "you still have your lanterns here. You are disobeying the regulations, my friend. This is disorderly. Smash that for me."

And he flung the stone at the lantern, whose broken glass fell with such a clatter that the bourgeois in hiding behind their curtains in the opposite house cried, "There is 'Ninety-three' come again."

The lantern oscillated violently, and went out. The street had suddenly become black.

"That's right, old street," ejaculated Gavroche, "put on your nightcap."

And turning to Jean Valjean, "What do you call that gigantic monument that you have there at the end of the street? It's the Archives, isn't it? I must crumble up those big stupids of pillars a bit and make a nice barricade out of them."

Jean Valjean stepped up to Gavroche.

"Poor creature," he said in a low tone, and speaking to himself, "he is hungry."

And he laid the hundred-sou piece in his hand.

Gavroche raised his face, astonished at the size of this sou; he stared at it in the darkness, and the whiteness of the big sou dazzled him. He knew five-franc pieces by hearsay; their reputation was agreeable to him; he was delighted to see one close to. He said, "Let us contemplate the tiger."

He gazed at it for several minutes in ecstasy; then, turning to Jean Valjean, he held out the coin to him, and said majestically to him, "Bourgeois, I prefer to smash lanterns. Take back your ferocious beast. You can't bribe me. That has got five claws; but it doesn't scratch me."

"Have you a mother?" asked Jean Valjean.

Gavroche replied, "More than you have, perhaps."

"Well," returned Jean Valjean, "keep the money for your mother!"

Gavroche was touched. Moreover, he had just noticed that the man who was addressing him had no hat, and this inspired him with confidence.

"Truly," said he, "so it wasn't to keep me from breaking the lanterns?"

"Break whatever you please."

"You're a fine man," said Gavroche.

And he put the five-franc piece into one of his pockets.

His confidence having increased, he added, "Do you belong in this street?"

"Yes, why?"

"Can you tell me where No. 7 is?"

"What do you want with No. 7?"

Here the child paused, he feared that he had said too much; he thrust his nails energetically into his hair and contented himself with replying, "Ah! Here it is."

An idea flashed through Jean Valjean's mind. Anguish does have these gleams. He said to the lad, "Are you the person who is bringing a letter that I am expecting?"

"You?" said Gavroche. "You are not a woman."

"The letter is for Mademoiselle Cosette, is it not?"

"Cosette," muttered Gavroche. "Yes, I believe that is the queer name."

"Well," resumed Jean Valjean, "I am the person to whom you are to deliver the letter. Give it here."

"In that case, you must know that I was sent from the barricade."

"Of course," said Jean Valjean.

Gavroche engulfed his hand in another of his pockets and drew out a paper folded in four.

Then he made the military salute.

"Respect for dispatches," said he. "It comes from the Provisional Government."

"Give it to me," said Jean Valjean.

Gavroche held the paper elevated above his head.

"Don't go and fancy it's a love letter. It is for a woman, but it's for the people. We men fight and we respect the fair sex. We are not as they are in fine society, where there are lions who send chickens to camels."

"Give it to me."

"After all," continued Gavroche, "you have the air of an honest man."

"Give it to me quick."

"Catch hold of it."

And he handed the paper to Jean Valjean.

"And make haste, Monsieur What's-your-name, for Mamselle Cosette is waiting."

Gavroche was satisfied with himself for having produced this remark.

Jean Valjean began again, "Is it to Saint-Merry that the answer is to be sent?"

"There you are making some of those bits of pastry vulgarly called *brioches.* This letter comes from the barricade of the Rue de la Chanvrerie, and I'm going back there. Good evening, citizen."

That said, Gavroche took himself off, or, to describe it more exactly, fluttered away in the direction from which he had come with a flight like that of an escaped bird. He plunged back into the gloom as though he made a hole in it, with the rigid rapidity of a projectile; the alley of l'Homme Armé became silent and solitary once more; in a twinkling, that strange child, who had about him something of the shadow and of the dream, had buried himself in the mists of the rows of black houses, and was lost there, like smoke in the dark; and one might have thought that he had dissipated and vanished, had there not taken place, a few minutes after his disappearance, a startling shiver of glass, and had not the magnificent crash of a lantern rattling down on the pavement once more abruptly awakened the indignant bourgeois. It was Gavroche upon his way through the Rue du Chaume.

* blunders

CHAPTER III—WHILE COSETTE
AND TOUSSAINT ARE ASLEEP

Jean Valjean went into the house with Marius's letter.

He groped his way up the stairs, as pleased with the darkness as an owl who grips his prey, opened and shut his door softly, listened to see whether he could hear any noise, made sure that, to all appearances, Cosette and Toussaint were asleep, and plunged three or four matches into the bottle of the Fumade lighter before he could evoke a spark, so greatly did his hand tremble. What he had just done smacked of theft. At last the candle was lighted; he leaned his elbows on the table, unfolded the paper, and read.

In violent emotions, one does not read, one flings to the earth, so to speak, the paper which one holds, one clutches it like a victim, one crushes it, one digs into it the nails of one's wrath, or of one's joy; one hastens to the end, one leaps to the beginning; attention is at fever heat; it takes up in the gross, as it were, the essential points; it seizes on one point, and the rest disappears. In Marius's note to Cosette, Jean Valjean saw only these words: "I die. When thou readest this, my soul will be near thee."

In the presence of these two lines, he was horribly dazzled; he remained for a moment, crushed, as it were, by the change of emotion that was taking place within him, he stared at Marius's note with a sort of intoxicated amazement, he had before his eyes that splendor, the death of a hated individual.

He uttered a frightful cry of inward joy. So it was all over. The catastrophe had arrived sooner than he had dared to hope. The being who obstructed his destiny was disappearing. That man had taken himself off of his own accord, freely, willingly. This man was going to his death, and he, Jean Valjean, had had no hand in the matter, and it was through no fault of his. Perhaps, even, he is already dead. Here his fever entered into calculations. No, he is not dead yet. The letter had evidently been intended for Cosette to read on the following morning; after the two discharges that were heard between eleven o'clock and midnight, nothing more has taken place; the barricade will not be attacked seriously until daybreak; but that makes no difference, from the moment when "that man" is concerned in this war, he is lost; he is caught in the gearing. Jean Valjean felt himself delivered. So he was about to find himself alone with Cosette once more. The rivalry would cease; the future was beginning again. He had but to keep this note in his pocket. Cosette would never know what had become of that man. All that there requires to be done is to let things take their own course. This man cannot escape. If he is not already dead, it is certain that he is about to die. What good fortune!

Having said all this to himself, he became gloomy.

Then he went downstairs and woke up the porter.

About an hour later, Jean Valjean went out in the complete costume of a National Guard, and with his arms. The porter had easily found in the neighborhood the wherewithal to complete his equipment. He had a loaded gun and a cartridge box filled with cartridges.

He strode off in the direction of the markets.

CHAPTER IV—GAVROCHE'S
EXCESS OF ZEAL

In the meantime, Gavroche had had an adventure.

Gavroche, after having conscientiously stoned the lantern in the Rue du Chaume, entered the Rue des Vielles-Haudriettes, and not seeing "even a cat" there, he thought the opportunity a good one to strike up all the song of which he was capable. His march, far from being retarded by his singing, was accelerated by it. He began to sow along the sleeping or terrified houses these incendiary couplets:

> "The bird slanders in the elms, and pretends that yesterday,
> Atala went off with a Russian, where fair maids go, lon la. My
> friend Pierrot, thou pratest, because Mila knocked at her pane
> the other day and called me. The jades are very charming,
> their poison which bewitched me would intoxicate Monsieur
> Orfila. I'm fond of love and its bickerings, I love Agnes, I love
> Pamela, Lise burned herself in setting me aflame. In former
> days when I saw the mantillas of Suzette and of Zeila, my soul
> mingled with their folds. Love, when thou gleamest in the dark
> thou crownest Lola with roses, I would lose my soul for that.
> Jeanne, at thy mirror thou deckest thyself! One fine day, my
> heart flew forth. I think that it is Jeanne who has it. At night,
> when I come from the quadrilles, I show Stella to the stars, and
> I say to them: 'Behold her.' Where fair maids go, lon la."

Gavroche, as he sang, was lavish of his pantomime. Gesture is the strong point of the refrain. His face, an inexhaustible repertory of masks, produced grimaces more convulsing and more fantastic than the rents of a cloth torn in a high gale. Unfortunately, as he was alone, and as it was night, this was neither seen nor even visible. Such wastes of riches do occur.

All at once, he stopped short.

"Let us interrupt the romance," said he.

His feline eye had just descried, in the recess of a carriage door, what is called in painting, an ensemble, that is to say, a person and a thing; the thing was a handcart, the person was a man from Auvergene who was sleeping therein.

The shafts of the cart rested on the pavement, and the Auvergnat's head was supported against the front of the cart. His body was coiled up on this inclined plane and his feet touched the ground.

Gavroche, with his experience of the things of this world, recognized a drunken man. He was some corner errand-man who had drunk too much and was sleeping too much.

"There now," thought Gavroche, "that's what the summer nights are good for. We'll take the cart for the Republic, and leave the Auvergnat for the Monarchy."

His mind had just been illuminated by this flash of light: "How bully that cart would look on our barricade!"

The Auvergnat was snoring.

Gavroche gently tugged at the cart from behind, and at the Auvergnat from the front, that is to say, by the feet, and at the expiration of another minute the imperturbable Auvergnat was reposing flat on the pavement.

The cart was free.

Gavroche, habituated to facing the unexpected in all quarters, had everything about him. He fumbled in one of his pockets, and pulled from it a scrap of paper and a bit of red pencil filched from some carpenter.

He wrote: "French Republic. Received thy cart." And he signed it: "GAVROCHE."

That done, he put the paper in the pocket of the still snoring Auvergnat's velvet vest, seized the cart shafts in both hands, and set off in the direction of the Halles, pushing the cart before him at a hard gallop with a glorious and triumphant uproar.

This was perilous. There was a post at the Royal Printing Establishment. Gavroche did not think of this. This post was occupied by the National Guards of the suburbs. The squad began to wake up, and heads were raised from camp beds. Two street lanterns broken in succession, that ditty sung at the top of the lungs. This was a great deal for those cowardly streets, which desire to go to sleep at sunset, and which put the extinguisher on their candles at such an early hour. For the last hour, that boy had been creating an uproar in that peaceable arrondissement, the uproar of a fly in a bottle. The sergeant of the banlieue lent an ear. He waited. He was a prudent man.

The mad rattle of the cart, filled to overflowing the possible measure of waiting, and decided the sergeant to make a reconnaissance.

"There's a whole band of them there!" said he, "let us proceed gently."

It was clear that the hydra of anarchy had emerged from its box and that it was stalking abroad through the quarter.

And the sergeant ventured out of the post with cautious tread.

All at once, Gavroche, pushing his cart in front of him, and at the very moment when he was about to turn into the Rue des Vielles-Haudriettes, found himself face to face with a uniform, a shako, a plume, and a gun.

For the second time, he stopped short.

"Hullo," said he, "it's him. Good day, public order."

Gavroche's amazement was always brief and speedily thawed.

"Where are you going, you rascal?" shouted the sergeant.

"Citizen," retorted Gavroche, "I haven't called you 'bourgeois' yet. Why do you insult me?"

"Where are you going, you rogue?"

"Monsieur," retorted Gavroche, "perhaps you were a man of wit yesterday, but you have degenerated this morning."

"I ask you where are you going, you villain?"

Gavroche replied, "You speak prettily. Really, no one would suppose you as old as you are. You ought to sell all your hair at a hundred francs apiece. That would yield you five hundred francs."

"Where are you going? Where are you going? Where are you going, bandit?"

Gavroche retorted again, "What villainous words! You must wipe your mouth better the first time that they give you suck."

The sergeant lowered his bayonet.

"Will you tell me where you are going, you wretch?"

"General," said Gavroche, "I'm on my way to look for a doctor for my wife who is in labor."

"To arms!" shouted the sergeant.

The masterstroke of strong men consists in saving themselves by the very means that have ruined them; Gavroche took in the whole situation at a glance. It was the cart that had told against him, it was the cart's place to protect him.

At the moment when the sergeant was on the point of making his descent on Gavroche, the cart, converted into a projectile and launched with all the latter's might, rolled down upon him furiously, and the sergeant, struck full in the stomach, tumbled over backward into the gutter while his gun went off in the air.

The men of the post had rushed out pell-mell at the sergeant's shout; the shot brought on a general random discharge, after which they reloaded their weapons and began again.

This blindman's buff musketry lasted for a quarter of an hour and killed several panes of glass.

In the meanwhile, Gavroche, who had retraced his steps at full speed, halted five or six streets distant and seated himself, panting, on the stone post that forms the corner of the Enfants-Rouges.

He listened.

After panting for a few minutes, he turned in the direction where the fusillade was raging, lifted his left hand to a level with his nose and thrust it forward three times, as he slapped the back of his head with his right hand; an imperious gesture in which Parisian street-urchindom has condensed French irony, and which is evidently efficacious, since it has already lasted half a century.

This gaiety was troubled by one bitter reflection.

"Yes," said he, "I'm splitting with laughter, I'm twisting with delight, I abound in joy, but I'm losing my way, I shall have to take a roundabout way. If I only reach the barricade in season!"

Thereupon he set out again on a run.

And as he ran, "Ah, by the way, where was I?" said he.

And he resumed his ditty, as he plunged rapidly through the streets, and this is what died away in the gloom: "But some prisons still remain, and I am going to put a stop to this sort of public order. Does anyone wish to play at skittles? The whole ancient world fell in ruin, when the big ball rolled. Good old folks, let us smash with our crutches that Louvre where the monarchy displayed itself in furbelows. We have forced its gates. On that day, King Charles X did not stick well and came unglued."

The post's recourse to arms was not without result. The cart was conquered, the drunken man was taken prisoner. The first was put in the pound, the second was later on somewhat harassed before the councils of war as an accomplice. The public ministry of the day proved its indefatigable zeal in the defense of society, in this instance.

Gavroche's adventure, which has lingered as a tradition in the quarters of the Temple, is one of the most terrible souvenirs of the elderly bourgeois of the Marais, and is entitled in their memories: "The nocturnal attack by the post of the Royal Printing Establishment."

VOLUME V: JEAN VALJEAN

BOOK FIRST: THE WAR BETWEEN FOUR WALLS

CHAPTER I—THE CHARYBDIS OF THE FAUBOURG SAINT ANTOINE AND THE SCYLLA OF THE FAUBOURG DU TEMPLE

The two most memorable barricades that the observer of social maladies can name do not belong to the period in which the action of this work is laid. These two barricades, both of them symbols, under two different aspects, of a redoubtable situation, sprang from the earth at the time of the fatal insurrection of June, 1848, the greatest war of the streets that history has ever beheld.

It sometimes happens that, even contrary to principles, even contrary to liberty, equality, and fraternity, even contrary to the universal vote, even contrary to the government, by all for all, from the depths of its anguish, of its discouragements and its destitutions, of its fevers, of its distresses, of its miasmas, of its ignorances, of its darkness, that great and despairing body, the rabble, protests against, and that the populace wages battle against, the people.

Beggars attack the common right; the ochlocracy rises against demos.

These are melancholy days; for there is always a certain amount of night even in this madness, there is suicide in this duel, and those words that are intended to be insults—beggars, canaille, ochlocracy, populace—exhibit, alas! Rather the fault of those who reign than the fault of those who suffer; rather the fault of the privileged than the fault of the disinherited.

For our own part, we never pronounce those words without pain and without respect, for when philosophy fathoms the facts to which they correspond, it often finds many a grandeur beside these miseries. Athens was an ochlocracy; the beggars were the making of Holland; the populace saved Rome more than once; and the rabble followed Jesus Christ.

There is no thinker who has not at times contemplated the magnificence of the lower classes.

It was of this rabble that Saint Jerome was thinking, no doubt, and of all these poor people and all these vagabonds and all these miserable people from which sprang the apostles and the martyrs, when he uttered this mysterious saying: "*Fex urbis, lex orbis*"—the dregs of the city, the law of the earth.

The exasperations of this crowd, which suffers and bleeds, its violences contrary to all sense, directed against the principles that are its life, its masterful deeds against the right, are its popular coups d'etat and should be repressed. The man of probity sacrifices himself, and out of his very love for this crowd, he combats it. But how excusable he feels it even while holding out against it! How he venerates it even while resisting it! This is one of those rare moments when, while doing that which it is one's duty to do, one feels something that disconcerts one, and that would dissuade one from proceeding further; one persists, it is necessary, but conscience, though satisfied, is sad, and the accomplishment of duty is complicated with a pain at the heart.

June 1848, let us hasten to say, was an exceptional fact, and almost impossible of classification, in the philosophy of history. All the words we have just uttered, must be discarded, when it becomes a question of this extraordinary revolt, in which one feels the holy anxiety of toil claiming its rights. It was necessary to combat it, and this was a duty, for it attacked the republic. But what was June 1848, at bottom? A revolt of the people against itself.

Where the subject is not lost sight of, there is no digression; may we, then, be permitted to arrest the reader's attention for a moment on the two absolutely unique barricades of which we have just spoken and that characterized this insurrection.

One blocked the entrance to the Faubourg Saint Antoine; the other defended the approach to the Faubourg du Temple; those before whom these two fearful masterpieces of civil war reared themselves beneath the brilliant blue sky of June, will never forget them.

The Saint-Antoine barricade was tremendous; it was three stories high, and seven hundred feet wide. It barred the vast opening of the Faubourg, that is to say, three streets, from angle to angle; ravined, jagged, cut up, divided, crenellated, with an immense rent, buttressed with piles that were bastions in themselves throwing out capes here and there, powerfully backed up by two great promontories of houses of the Faubourg, it reared itself like a cyclopean dike at the end of the formidable place that had seen the 14th of July. Nineteen barricades were ranged, one behind the other, in the depths of the streets behind this principal barricade. At the very sight of it, one felt the agonizing suffering in the immense Faubourg, which had reached that point of extremity when a distress may become a catastrophe. Of what was that barricade made? Of the ruins of three six-story houses demolished expressly, said some. Of the prodigy of all wraths, said others. It wore the lamentable aspect of all constructions of hatred, ruin. It might be asked: Who built this? It might also be said: Who destroyed this? It was the improvisation of the ebullition. Hold! Take this door! This grating! This penthouse! This mantle! This broken brazier! This cracked pot! Give all! Cast away all! Push this roll, dig, dismantle, overturn, ruin everything! It was the collaboration of the pavement, the block of stone, the beam, the bar of iron, the rag, the scrap, the broken pane, the unseated chair, the cabbage stalk, the tatter, the rag, and the malediction. It was grand and it was petty. It was the abyss parodied on the public place by hubbub. The mass beside the atom; the strip of ruined wall and the broken bowl, threatening fraternization of every sort of rubbish. Sisyphus had thrown his rock there and Job his potsherd. Terrible, in short. It was the acropolis of the barefooted. Overturned carts broke the uniformity of the slope; an immense dray was spread out there crossways, its axle pointing heavenward, and seemed a scar on that tumultuous facade; an omnibus hoisted gaily, by main force, to the very summit of the heap, as though the architects of this bit of savagery had wished to add a touch of the street urchin humor to their terror, presented its horseless, unharnessed pole to no one knows what horses of the air. This gigantic heap, the alluvium of the revolt, figured to the mind an Ossa on Pelion of all revolutions; '93 on '89, the 9th of Thermidor on the 10th of August, the 18th of Brumaire on the 11th of January, Vendemiaire on Prairial, 1848 on 1830. The situation deserved the trouble and this barricade was worthy to figure on the very spot from which the Bastille had disappeared. If the ocean made dikes, it is thus that it would build. The fury of the flood was stamped upon this shapeless mass. What flood? The crowd. One thought one beheld hubbub petrified. One thought one heard humming above this barricade as though there had been over their hive, enormous, dark bees of violent progress. Was it a thicket? Was it a bacchanalia? Was it a fortress? Vertigo seemed to have constructed it with blows of its wings. There was something of the cesspool in that redoubt and something Olympian in that confusion. One there beheld in a pellmell full of despair, the rafters of roofs, bits of garret windows with their figured paper, window sashes with their glass planted there in the ruins awaiting the cannon, wrecks of chimneys, cupboards, tables, benches, howling topsy turveydom, and those thousand poverty-stricken things, the very refuse of the mendicant, which contain at the same time fury and nothingness. One would have said that it was the tatters of a people, rags of wood, of iron, of bronze, of stone, and that the Faubourg Saint Antoine had thrust it there at its door, with a colossal flourish of the broom making of its misery its barricade. Blocks resembling headsman's blocks, dislocated chains, pieces of woodwork with brackets having the form of gibbets, horizontal wheels projecting from the rubbish, amalgamated with this edifice of anarchy the somber figure of the old tortures endured by the people. The barricade Saint Antoine converted everything into a weapon; everything that civil war could throw at the head of society proceeded thence; it was not combat, it was a paroxysm; the carbines that defended this redoubt, among which there were some blunderbusses, sent bits of earthenware bones, coat buttons, even the casters from night stands, dangerous projectiles on account of the brass. This barricade was furious; it hurled to the clouds an inexpressible clamor; at certain moments, when provoking the army, it was covered with throngs and tempest; a tumultuous crowd of flaming heads crowned it; a swarm filled it; it had a thorny crest of guns, of sabers, of cudgels, of axes, of pikes and of bayonets; a vast red flag flapped in the wind; shouts of command, songs of attack, the roll of drums, the sobs of women and bursts of gloomy laughter from the starving were to be heard there. It was huge and living, and, like the back of an electric beast, there proceeded from it little flashes of lightning. The spirit of revolution covered with its cloud this summit where rumbled that voice of the people that resembles the voice of God; a strange majesty was emitted by this titanic basket of rubbish. It was a heap of filth and it was Sinai.

As we have said previously, it attacked in the name of the revolution—what? The revolution. It—that barricade, chance, hazard, disorder, terror, misunderstanding, the unknown—had facing it the Constituent Assembly, the sovereignty of the people, universal suffrage, the nation, the republic; and it was the Carmagnole bidding defiance to the Marseillaise.

Immense but heroic defiance, for the old Faubourg is a hero.

The Faubourg and its redoubt lent each other assistance. The Faubourg shouldered the redoubt, the redoubt took its stand under cover of the Faubourg. The vast barricade spread out like a cliff against which the strategy of the African generals dashed itself. Its caverns, its excrescences, its warts, its gibbosities, grimaced, so to speak, and grinned beneath the smoke. The mitraille vanished in shapelessness; the bombs plunged into it; bullets only succeeded in making holes in it; what was the use of cannonading chaos? And the regiments, accustomed to the fiercest visions of war, gazed with uneasy eyes on that species of redoubt, a wild beast in its boarlike bristling and a mountain by its enormous size.

A quarter of a league away, from the corner of the Rue du Temple, that debouches on the boulevard near the Chateaud'Eau, if one thrust one's head bodily beyond the point formed by the front of the Dallemagne shop, one perceived in the distance, beyond the canal, in the street that mounts the slopes of Belleville at the culminating point of the rise, a strange wall reaching to the second story of the house fronts, a sort of hyphen between the houses on the right and the houses on the left, as though the street had folded back on itself its loftiest wall in order to close itself abruptly. This wall was built of pavingstones. It was straight, correct, cold, perpendicular, leveled with the square, laid out by rule and line. Cement was lacking, of course, but, as in the case of certain Roman walls, without interfering with its rigid architecture. The entablature was mathematically parallel with the base. From distance to distance, one could distinguish on the gray surface, almost invisible loopholes that resembled black threads. These loopholes were separated from each other by equal spaces. The street was deserted as far as the eye could reach. All windows and doors were closed. In the background rose this barrier, which made a blind thoroughfare of the street, a motionless and tranquil wall; no one was visible, nothing was audible; not a cry, not a sound, not a breath. A sepulchre.

The dazzling sun of June inundated this terrible thing with light.

It was the barricade of the Faubourg of the Temple.

As soon as one arrived on the spot, and caught sight of it, it was impossible, even for the boldest, not to become thoughtful before this mysterious apparition. It was adjusted, jointed, imbricated, rectilinear, symmetrical and funereal. Science and gloom met there. One felt that the chief of this barricade was a geometrician or a specter. One looked at it and spoke low.

From time to time, if some soldier, an officer or representative of the people, chanced to traverse the deserted highway, a faint, sharp whistle was heard, and the passerby fell dead or wounded, or, if he escaped the bullet, sometimes a biscaien was seen to ensconce itself in some closed shutter, in the interstice between two blocks of stone, or in the plaster of a wall. For the men in the barricade had made themselves two small cannons out of two cast iron lengths of gas pipe, plugged up at one end with tow and fireclay. There was no waste of useless powder. Nearly every shot told. There were corpses here and there, and pools of blood on the pavement. I remember a white butterfly that went and came in the street. Summer does not abdicate.

In the neighborhood, the spaces beneath the portes cocheres were encumbered with wounded.

One felt oneself aimed at by some person whom one did not see, and one understood that guns were leveled at the whole length of the street.

Massed behind the sort of sloping ridge that the vaulted canal forms at the entrance to the Faubourg du Temple, the soldiers of the attacking column, gravely and thoughtfully, watched this dismal redoubt, this immobility, this passivity, from which sprang death. Some crawled flat on their faces as far as the crest of the curve of the bridge, taking care that their shakos did not project beyond it.

The valiant Colonel Monteynard admired this barricade with a shudder. "How that is built!" he said to a Representative. "Not one paving stone projects beyond its neighbor. It is made of porcelain." At that moment, a bullet broke the cross on his breast, and he fell.

"The cowards!" people said. "Let them show themselves. Let us see them! They dare not! They are hiding!"

The barricade of the Faubourg du Temple, defended by eighty men, attacked by ten thousand, held out for three days. On the fourth, they did as at Zaatcha, as at Constantine, they pierced the houses, they came over the roofs, the barricade was taken. Not one of the eighty cowards thought of flight, all were killed there with the exception of the leader, Barthelemy, of whom we shall speak presently.

The Saint-Antoine barricade was the tumult of thunders; the barricade of the Temple was silence. The difference between these two redoubts was the difference between the formidable and the sinister. One seemed a maw; the other a mask.

Admitting that the gigantic and gloomy insurrection of June was composed of a wrath and of an enigma, one divined in the first barricade the dragon, and behind the second the sphinx.

These two fortresses had been erected by two men named, the one, Cournet, the other, Barthelemy. Cournet made the Saint-Antoine barricade; Barthelemy the barricade of the Temple. Each was the image of the man who had built it.

Cournet was a man of lofty stature; he had broad shoulders, a red face, a crushing fist, a bold heart, a loyal soul, a sincere and terrible eye. Intrepid, energetic, irascible, stormy; the most cordial of men, the most formidable of combatants. War, strife, conflict, were the very air he breathed and put him in a good humor. He had been an officer in the navy, and, from his gestures and his voice, one divined that he sprang from the ocean, and that he came from the tempest; he carried the hurricane on into battle. With the exception of the genius, there was in Cournet something of Danton, as, with the exception of the divinity, there was in Danton something of Hercules.

Barthelemy, thin, feeble, pale, taciturn, was a sort of tragic street urchin, who, having had his ears boxed by a policeman, lay in wait for him, and killed him, and at seventeen was sent to the galleys. He came out and made this barricade.

Later on, fatal circumstance, in London, proscribed by all, Barthelemy slew Cournet. It was a funereal duel. Some time afterward, caught in the gearing of one of those mysterious adventures in which passion plays a part, a catastrophe in which French justice sees extenuating circumstances, and in which English justice sees only death, Barthelemy was hanged. The somber social construction is so made that, thanks to material destitution, thanks to moral obscurity, that unhappy being who possessed an intelligence, certainly firm, possibly great, began in France with the galleys, and ended in England with the gallows. Barthelemy, on occasion, flew but one flag, the black flag.

CHAPTER II—WHAT IS TO BE DONE IN THE ABYSS IF ONE DOES NOT CONVERSE

Sixteen years count in the subterranean education of insurrection, and June 1848, knew a great deal more about it than June 1832. So the barricade of the Rue de la Chanvrerie was only an outline, and an embryo compared to the two colossal barricades that we have just sketched; but it was formidable for that epoch.

The insurgents under the eye of Enjolras, for Marius no longer looked after anything, had made good use of the night. The barricade had been not only repaired, but augmented. They had raised it two feet. Bars of iron planted in the pavement resembled lances in rest. All sorts of rubbish brought and added from all directions complicated the external confusion. The redoubt had been cleverly made over, into a wall on the inside and a thicket on the outside.

The staircase of pavingstones, which permitted one to mount it like the wall of a citadel, had been reconstructed.

The barricade had been put in order, the taproom disencumbered, the kitchen appropriated for the ambulance, the dressing of the wounded completed, the powder scattered on the ground and on the tables had been gathered up, bullets run, cartridges manufactured, lint scraped, the fallen weapons redistributed, the interior of the redoubt cleaned, the rubbish swept up, corpses removed.

They laid the dead in a heap in the Mondetour lane, of which they were still the masters. The pavement was red for a long time at that spot. Among the dead there were four National Guardsmen of the suburbs. Enjolras had their uniforms laid aside.

Enjolras had advised two hours of sleep. Advice from Enjolras was a command. Still, only three or four took advantage of it.

Feuilly employed these two hours in engraving this inscription on the wall that faced the tavern: LONG LIVE THE PEOPLES!

These four words, hollowed out in the rough stone with a nail, could be still read on the wall in 1848.

The three women had profited by the respite of the night to vanish definitely; that allowed the insurgents to breathe more freely.

They had found means of taking refuge in some neighboring house.

The greater part of the wounded were able, and wished, to fight still. On a litter of mattresses and trusses of straw in the kitchen, which had been converted into an ambulance, there were five men gravely wounded, two of whom were municipal guardsmen. The municipal guardsmen were attended to first.

In the taproom there remained only Mabeuf under his black cloth and Javert bound to his post.

"This is the hall of the dead," said Enjolras.

In the interior of this hall, barely lighted by a candle at one end, the mortuary table being behind the post like a horizontal bar, a sort of vast, vague cross resulted from Javert erect and Mabeuf lying prone.

The pole of the omnibus, although snapped off by the fusillade, was still sufficiently upright to admit of their fastening the flag to it.

Enjolras, who possessed that quality of a leader, of always doing what he said, attached to this staff the bullet-ridden and bloody coat of the old man's.

No repast had been possible. There was neither bread nor meat. The fifty men in the barricade had speedily exhausted the scanty provisions of the wine shop during the sixteen hours that they had passed there. At a given moment, every barricade inevitably becomes the raft of la Meduse. They were obliged to resign themselves to hunger. They had then reached the first hours of that Spartan day of the 6th of June when, in the barricade Saint-Merry, Jeanne, surrounded by the insurgents who demanded bread, replied to all combatants crying, "Something to eat!" with, "Why? It is three o'clock; at four we shall be dead."

As they could no longer eat, Enjolras forbade them to drink. He interdicted wine, and portioned out the brandy. They had found in the cellar fifteen full bottles hermetically sealed. Enjolras and Combeferre examined them. Combeferre when he came up again said, "It's the old stock of Father Hucheloup, who began business as a grocer." "It must be real wine," observed Bossuet. "It's lucky that Grantaire is asleep. If he were on foot, there would be a good deal of difficulty in saving those bottles." Enjolras, in spite of all murmurs, placed his veto on the fifteen bottles, and, in order that no one might touch them, he had them placed under the table on which Father Mabeuf was lying.

About two o'clock in the morning, they reckoned up their strength. There were still thirty-seven of them.

The day began to dawn. The torch, which had been replaced in its cavity in the pavement, had just been extinguished. The interior of the barricade, that species of tiny courtyard appropriated from the street, was bathed in shadows, and resembled, athwart the vague, twilight horror, the deck of a disabled ship. The combatants, as they went and came, moved about there like black forms. Above that terrible nesting place of gloom the stories of the mute houses were lividly outlined; at the very top, the chimneys stood palely out. The sky was of that charming, undecided hue, which may be white and may be blue. Birds flew about in it with cries of joy. The lofty house that formed the back of the barricade, being turned to the East, had upon its roof a rosy reflection. The morning breeze ruffled the gray hair on the head of the dead man at the third-story window.

"I am delighted that the torch has been extinguished," said Courfeyrac to Feuilly. "That torch flickering in the wind annoyed me. It had the appearance of being afraid. The light of torches resembles the wisdom of cowards; it gives a bad light because it trembles."

Dawn awakens minds as it does the birds; all began to talk.

Joly, perceiving a cat prowling on a gutter, extracted philosophy from it.

"What is the cat?" he exclaimed. "It is a corrective. The good God, having made the mouse, said, 'Hullo! I have committed a blunder.' And so he made the cat. The cat is the erratum of the mouse. The mouse, plus the cat, is the proof of creation revised and corrected."

Combeferre, surrounded by students and artisans, was speaking of the dead, of Jean Prouvaire, of Bahorel, of Mabeuf, and even of Cabuc, and of Enjolras's sad severity. He said, "Harmodius and Aristogiton, Brutus, Chereas, Stephanus, Cromwell, Charlotte Corday, Sand, have all had their moment of agony when it was too late. Our hearts quiver so, and human life is such a mystery that, even in the case of a civic murder, even in a murder for liberation, if there be such a thing, the remorse for having struck a man surpasses the joy of having served the human race."

And, such are the windings of the exchange of speech, that, a moment later, by a transition brought about through Jean Prouvaire's verses, Combeferre was comparing the translators of the Georgics, Raux with Cournand, Cournand with Delille, pointing out the passages translated by Malfilatre, particularly the prodigies of Caesar's death; and at that word, Caesar, the conversation reverted to Brutus.

"Caesar," said Combeferre, "fell justly. Cicero was severe toward Caesar, and he was right. That severity is not diatribe. When Zoilus insults Homer, when Maevius insults Virgil, when Vise insults Moliere, when Pope insults Shakespeare, when Frederic insults Voltaire, it is an old law of envy and hatred that is being carried out; genius attracts insult, great men are always more or less barked at. But Zoilus and Cicero are two different persons. Cicero is an arbiter in thought, just as Brutus is an arbiter by the sword. For my own part, I blame that last justice, the blade; but, antiquity admitted it. Caesar, the violator of the Rubicon, conferring, as though they came from him, the dignities that emanated from the people, not rising at the entrance of the senate, committed the acts of a king and almost of a tyrant, regia ac pene tyrannica. He was a great man; so much the worse, or so much the better; the lesson is but the more exalted. His twenty-three wounds touch me less than the spitting in the face of Jesus Christ. Caesar is stabbed by the senators; Christ is cuffed by lackeys. One feels the God through the greater outrage."

Bossuet, who towered above the interlocutors from the summit of a heap of pavingstones, exclaimed, rifle in hand, "Oh Cydathenaeum, Oh Myrrhinus, Oh Probalinthus, Oh graces of the AEantides! Oh! Who will grant me to pronounce the verses of Homer like a Greek of Laurium or of Edapteon?"

CHAPTER III—LIGHT AND SHADOW

Enjolras had been to make a reconnaissance. He had made his way out through Mondetour lane, gliding along close to the houses.

The insurgents, we will remark, were full of hope. The manner in which they had repulsed the attack of the preceding night had caused them to almost disdain in advance the attack at dawn. They waited for it with a smile. They had no more doubt as to their success than as to their cause. Moreover, succor was, evidently, on the way to them. They reckoned on it. With that facility of triumphant prophecy that is one of the sources of strength in the French combatant, they divided the day that was at hand into three distinct phases. At six o'clock in the morning a regiment "that had been labored with," would turn; at noon, the insurrection of all Paris; at sunset, revolution.

They heard the alarm bell of Saint-Merry, which had not been silent for an instant since the night before; a proof that the other barricade, the great one, Jeanne's, still held out.

All these hopes were exchanged between the different groups in a sort of gay and formidable whisper that resembled the warlike hum of a hive of bees.

Enjolras reappeared. He returned from his somber eagle flight into outer darkness. He listened for a moment to all this joy with folded arms, and one hand on his mouth. Then, fresh and rosy in the growing whiteness of the dawn, he said, "The whole army of Paris is to strike. A third of the army is bearing down upon the barricades in which you now are. There is the National Guard in addition. I have picked out the shakos of the fifth of the line, and the standard-bearers of the sixth legion. In one hour you will be attacked. As for the populace, it was seething yesterday, today it is not stirring. There is nothing to expect; nothing to hope for. Neither from a Faubourg nor from a regiment. You are abandoned."

These words fell upon the buzzing of the groups, and produced on them the effect caused on a swarm of bees by the first drops of a storm. A moment of indescribable silence ensued, in which death might have been heard flitting by.

This moment was brief.

A voice from the obscurest depths of the groups shouted to Enjolras:

"So be it. Let us raise the barricade to a height of twenty feet, and let us all remain in it. Citizens, let us offer the protests of corpses. Let us show that, if the people abandon the republicans, the republicans do not abandon the people."

These words freed the thought of all from the painful cloud of individual anxieties. It was hailed with an enthusiastic acclamation.

No one ever has known the name of the man who spoke thus; he was some unknown blouse-wearer, a stranger, a man forgotten, a passing hero, that great anonymous, always mingled in human crises and in social geneses who, at a given moment, utters in a supreme fashion the decisive word, and who vanishes into the shadows after having represented for a minute, in a lightning flash, the people and God.

This inexorable resolution so thoroughly impregnated the air of the 6th of

June 1832, that, almost at the very same hour, on the barricade Saint-Merry, the insurgents were raising that clamor, which has become a matter of history and that has been consigned to the documents in the case: "What matters it whether they come to our assistance or not? Let us get ourselves killed here, to the very last man."

As the reader sees, the two barricades, though materially isolated, were in communication with each other.

CHAPTER IV—MINUS FIVE, PLUS ONE

After the man who decreed the "protest of corpses" had spoken, and had given this formula of their common soul, there issued from all mouths a strangely satisfied and terrible cry, funereal in sense and triumphant in tone, "Long live death! Let us all remain here!"

"Why all?" said Enjolras.

"All! All!"

Enjolras resumed, "The position is good; the barricade is fine. Thirty men are enough. Why sacrifice forty?"

They replied, "Because not one will go away."

"Citizens," cried Enjolras, and there was an almost irritated vibration in his voice, "this republic is not rich enough in men to indulge in useless expenditure of them. Vainglory is waste. If the duty of some is to depart, that duty should be fulfilled like any other."

Enjolras, the man-principle, had over his coreligionists that sort of omnipotent power that emanates from the absolute. Still, great as was this omnipotence, a murmur arose. A leader to the very fingertips, Enjolras, seeing that they murmured, insisted. He resumed haughtily, "Let those who are afraid of not numbering more than thirty say so."

The murmurs redoubled.

"Besides," observed a voice in one group, "it is easy enough to talk about leaving. The barricade is hemmed in."

"Not on the side of the Halles," said Enjolras. "The Rue Mondetour is free, and through the Rue des Prêcheurs one can reach the Marche des Innocents."

"And there," went on another voice, "you would be captured. You would fall in with some grand guard of the line or the suburbs; they will spy a man passing in blouse and cap. 'From where come you? Don't you belong to the barricade?' And they will look at your hands. You smell of powder. Shot."

Enjolras, without making any reply, touched Combeferre's shoulder, and the two entered the taproom.

They emerged thence a moment later. Enjolras held in his outstretched hands the four uniforms that he had laid aside. Combeferre followed, carrying the shoulderbelts and the shakos.

"With this uniform," said Enjolras, "you can mingle with the ranks and escape; here is enough for four." And he flung on the ground, deprived of its pavement, the four uniforms.

No wavering took place in his stoical audience. Combeferre took the word.

"Come," said he, "you must have a little pity. Do you know what the question is here? It is a question of women. See here. Are there women or are there not? Are there children or are there not? Are there mothers, yes or no, who rock cradles with their foot and who have a lot of little ones around them? Let that man of you who has never beheld a nurse's breast raise his hand. Ah! You want to get yourselves killed, so do I—I, who am speaking to you; but I do not want to feel the phantoms of women wreathing their arms around me. Die, if you will, but don't make others die. Suicides like that, which is on the brink of accomplishment here, are sublime; but suicide is narrow, and does not admit of extension; and as soon as it touches your neighbors, suicide is murder. Think of the little blond heads; think of the white locks. Listen, Enjolras has just told me that he saw at the corner of the Rue du Cygne a lighted casement, a candle in a poor window, on the fifth floor, and on the pane the quivering shadow of the head of an old woman, who had the air of having spent the night in watching. Perhaps she is the mother of someone of you. Well, let that man go, and make haste, to say to his mother, 'Here I am, mother!' Let him feel at ease, the task here will be performed all the same. When one supports one's relatives by one's toil, one has not the right to sacrifice one's self. That is deserting one's family. And those who have daughters! What are you thinking of? You get yourselves killed, you are dead, that is well. And tomorrow? Young girls without bread—that is a terrible thing. Man begs, woman sells. Ah! Those charming and gracious beings, so gracious and so sweet, who have bonnets of flowers, who fill the house with purity, who sing and prattle, who are like a living perfume, who prove the existence of angels in heaven by the purity of virgins on earth, that Jeanne, that Lise, that Mimi, those adorable and honest creatures who are your blessings and your pride, ah! Good God, they will suffer hunger! What do you want me to say to you? There is a market for human flesh; and it is not with your shadowy hands, shuddering around them, that you will prevent them from entering it! Think of the street, think of the pavement covered with passersby, think of the shops past which women go and come with necks all bare, and through the mire. These women, too, were pure once. Think of your sisters, those of you who have them. Misery, prostitution, the police, Saint-Lazare—that is what those beautiful, delicate girls, those fragile marvels of modesty, gentleness and loveliness, fresher than lilacs in the month of May, will come to. Ah! You have got yourselves killed! You are no longer on hand! That is well; you have wished to release the people from Royalty, and you deliver over your daughters to the police. Friends, have a care, have mercy. Women, unhappy women, we are not in the habit of bestowing much thought on them. We trust to the women not having received a man's education, we prevent their reading, we prevent their thinking, we prevent their occupying themselves with politics; will you prevent them from going to the dead-house this evening, and recognizing your bodies? Let us see, those who have families must be tractable, and shake hands with us and take themselves off, and leave us here alone to attend to this affair. I know well that courage is required to leave, that it is hard; but the harder it is, the more meritorious. You say: 'I have a gun, I am at the barricade; so much the worse, I shall remain there.' So much the worse is easily said. My friends, there is a morrow; you will not be here tomorrow, but your families will; and what sufferings! See, here is a pretty, healthy child, with cheeks like an apple, who babbles, prattles, chatters, who laughs, who smells sweet beneath your kiss, and do you know what becomes of him when he is abandoned? I have seen one, a very small creature, no taller than that. His father was dead. Poor people had taken him in out of charity, but they had bread only for themselves. The child was always hungry. It was winter. He did not cry. You could see him approach the stove, in which there was never any fire, and whose pipe, you know, was of mastic and yellow clay. His breathing was hoarse, his face livid, his limbs flaccid, his belly prominent. He said nothing. If you spoke to him, he did not answer. He is dead. He was taken to the Necker Hospital, where I saw him. I was house surgeon in that hospital. Now, if there are any fathers among you, fathers whose happiness it is to stroll on Sundays holding their child's tiny hand in their robust hand, let each one of those fathers imagine that this child is his own. That poor brat, I remember, and I seem to see him now, when he lay nude on the dissecting table, how his ribs stood out on his skin like the graves beneath the grass in a cemetery. A sort of mud was found in his stomach. There were ashes in his teeth. Come, let us examine ourselves conscientiously and take counsel with our heart. Statistics show that the mortality among abandoned children is fifty-five percent. I repeat, it is a question of women, it concerns mothers, it concerns young girls, it concerns little children. Who is talking to you of yourselves? We know well what you are; we know well that you are all brave, parbleu! We know well that you all have in your souls the joy and the glory of giving your life for the great cause; we know well that you feel yourselves elected to die usefully and magnificently, and that each one of you clings to his share in the triumph. Very well. But you are not alone in this world. There are other beings of whom you must think. You must not be egoists."

All dropped their heads with a gloomy air.

Strange contradictions of the human heart at its most sublime moments. Combeferre, who spoke thus, was not an orphan. He recalled the mothers of other men, and forgot his own. He was about to get himself killed. He was "an egoist."

Marius, fasting, fevered, having emerged in succession from all hope, and having been stranded in grief, the most somber of shipwrecks, and saturated with violent emotions and conscious that the end was near, had plunged deeper and deeper into that visionary stupor that always precedes the fatal hour voluntarily accepted.

A physiologist might have studied in him the growing symptoms of that febrile absorption known to, and classified by, science, and that is to suffering what voluptuousness is to pleasure. Despair, also, has its ecstasy. Marius had reached this point. He looked on at everything as from without; as we have said, things that passed before him seemed far away; he made out the whole, but did not perceive the details. He beheld men going and coming as through a flame. He heard voices speaking as at the bottom of an abyss.

But this moved him. There was in this scene a point that pierced and roused even him. He had but one idea now, to die; and he did not wish to be turned aside from it, but he reflected, in his gloomy somnambulism, that while destroying himself, he was not prohibited from saving someone else.

He raised his voice.

"Enjolras and Combeferre are right," said he; "no unnecessary sacrifice. I join them, and you must make haste. Combeferre has said convincing things to you. There are some among you who have families, mothers, sisters, wives, children. Let such leave the ranks."

No one stirred.

"Married men and the supporters of families, step out of the ranks!" repeated Marius.

His authority was great. Enjolras was certainly the head of the barricade, but Marius was its savior.

"I order it," cried Enjolras.

"I entreat you," said Marius.

Then, touched by Combeferre's words, shaken by Enjolras's order, touched by Marius's entreaty, these heroic men began to denounce each other." It is true," said one young man to a full grown man, "you are the father of a family. Go." "It is your duty rather," retorted the man, "you have two sisters whom you maintain." And an unprecedented controversy broke forth. Each struggled to determine which should not allow himself to be placed at the door of the tomb.

"Make haste," said Courfeyrac, "in another quarter of an hour it will be too late."

"Citizens," pursued Enjolras, "this is the Republic, and universal suffrage reigns. Do you yourselves designate those who are to go."

They obeyed. After the expiration of a few minutes, five were unanimously selected and stepped out of the ranks.

"There are five of them!" exclaimed Marius.

There were only four uniforms.

"Well," began the five, "one must stay behind."

And then a struggle arose as to who should remain, and who should find reasons for the others not remaining. The generous quarrel began afresh.

"You have a wife who loves you." "You have your aged mother." "You have neither father nor mother, and what is to become of your three little brothers?" "You are the father of five children." "You have a right to live, you are only seventeen, it is too early for you to die."

These great revolutionary barricades were assembling points for heroism. The improbable was simple there. These men did not astonish each other.

"Be quick," repeated Courfeyrac.

Men shouted to Marius from the groups, "Do you designate who is to remain."

"Yes," said the five, "choose. We will obey you."

Marius did not believe that he was capable of another emotion. Still, at this idea, that of choosing a man for death, his blood rushed back to his heart. He would have turned pale, had it been possible for him to become any paler.

He advanced toward the five, who smiled upon him, and each, with his eyes full of that grand flame that one beholds in the depths of history hovering over Thermopylae, cried to him, "Me! Me! Me!"

And Marius stupidly counted them; there were still five of them! Then his glance dropped to the four uniforms.

At that moment, a fifth uniform fell, as if from heaven, upon the other four. The fifth man was saved.

Marius raised his eyes and recognized M. Fauchelevent.

Jean Valjean had just entered the barricade.

He had arrived by way of Mondetour lane, where by dint of inquiries made, or by instinct, or chance. Thanks to his dress of a National Guardsman, he had made his way without difficulty.

The sentinel stationed by the insurgents in the Rue Mondetour had no occasion to give the alarm for a single National Guardsman, and he had allowed the latter to entangle himself in the street, saying to himself, "Probably it is a reinforcement, in any case it is a prisoner." The moment was too grave to admit of the sentinel abandoning his duty and his post of observation.

At the moment when Jean Valjean entered the redoubt, no one had noticed him, all eyes being fixed on the five chosen men and the four uniforms. Jean Valjean also had seen and heard, and he had silently removed his coat and flung it on the pile with the rest.

The emotion aroused was indescribable.

"Who is this man?" demanded Bossuet.

"He is a man who saves others," replied Combeferre.

Marius added in a grave voice, "I know him."

This guarantee satisfied everyone.

Enjolras turned to Jean Valjean.

"Welcome, citizen."

And he added, "You know that we are about to die."

Jean Valjean, without replying, helped the insurgent whom he was saving to don his uniform.

CHAPTER V—THE HORIZON THAT ONE BEHOLDS FROM THE SUMMIT OF A BARRICADE

The situation of all in that fatal hour and that pitiless place, had as result and culminating point Enjolras's supreme melancholy.

Enjolras bore within him the plenitude of the revolution; he was incomplete, however, so far as the absolute can be so; he had too much of Saint-Just about him, and not enough of Anacharsis Cloots; still, his mind, in the society of the Friends of the A B C, had ended by undergoing a certain polarization from

Combeferre's ideas; for some time past, he had been gradually emerging from the narrow form of dogma, and had allowed himself to incline to the broadening influence of progress, and he had come to accept, as a definitive and magnificent evolution, the transformation of the great French Republic, into the immense human republic. As far as the immediate means were concerned, a violent situation being given, he wished to be violent; on that point, he never varied; and he remained of that epic and redoubtable school that is summed up in the words: "Eighty-three." Enjolras was standing erect on the staircase of pavingstones, one elbow resting on the stock of his gun. He was engaged in thought; he quivered, as at the passage of prophetic breaths; places where death is have these effects of tripods. A sort of stifled fire darted from his eyes, which were filled with an inward look. All at once he threw back his head, his blond locks fell back like those of an angel on the somber quadriga made of stars, they were like the mane of a startled lion in the flaming of an halo, and Enjolras cried, "Citizens, do you picture the future to yourselves? The streets of cities inundated with light, green branches on the thresholds, nations sisters, men just, old men blessing children, the past loving the present, thinkers entirely at liberty, believers on terms of full equality, for religion heaven, God the direct priest, human conscience become an altar, no more hatreds, the fraternity of the workshop and the school, for sole penalty and recompense fame, work for all, right for all, peace over all, no more bloodshed, no more wars, happy mothers! To conquer matter is the first step; to realize the ideal is the second. Reflect on what progress has already accomplished. Formerly, the first human races beheld with terror the hydra pass before their eyes, breathing on the waters, the dragon that vomited flame, the griffin who was the monster of the air, and who flew with the wings of an eagle and the talons of a tiger; fearful beasts that were above man. Man, nevertheless, spread his snares, consecrated by intelligence, and finally conquered these monsters. We have vanquished the hydra, and it is called the locomotive; we are on the point of vanquishing the griffin, we already grasp it, and it is called the balloon. On the day when this Promethean task shall be accomplished, and when man shall have definitely harnessed to his will the triple Chimera of antiquity, the hydra, the dragon and the griffin, he will be the master of water, fire, and of air, and he will be for the rest of animated creation that which the ancient gods formerly were to him. Courage, and onward! Citizens, where are we going? To science made government, to the force of things become the sole public force, to the natural law, having in itself its sanction and its penalty and promulgating itself by evidence, to a dawn of truth corresponding to a dawn of day. We are advancing to the union of peoples; we are advancing to the unity of man. No more fictions; no more parasites. The real governed by the true, that is the goal. Civilization will hold its assizes at the summit of Europe, and, later on, at the center of continents, in a grand parliament of the intelligence. Something similar has already been seen. The amphictyons had two sittings a year, one at Delphos the seat of the gods, the other at Thermopylae, the place of heroes. Europe will have her amphictyons; the globe will have its amphictyons. France bears this sublime future in her breast. This is the gestation of the nineteenth century. That which Greece sketched out is worthy of being finished by France. Listen to me, you, Feuilly, valiant artisan, man of the people. I revere you. Yes, you clearly behold the future, yes, you are right. You had neither father nor mother, Feuilly; you adopted humanity for your mother and right for your father. You are about to die, that is to say to triumph, here. Citizens, whatever happens today, through our defeat as well as through our victory, it is a revolution that we are about to create. As conflagrations light up a whole city, so revolutions illuminate the whole human race. And what is the revolution that we shall cause? I have just told you, the Revolution of the True. From a political point of view, there is but a single principle; the sovereignty of man over himself. This sovereignty of myself over myself is called Liberty. Where two or three of these sovereignties are combined, the state begins. But in that association there is no abdication. Each sovereignty concedes a certain quantity of itself, for the purpose of forming the common right. This quantity is the same for all of us. This identity of concession that each makes to all, is called Equality. Common right is nothing else than the protection of all beaming on the right of each. This protection of all over each is called Fraternity. The point of intersection of all these assembled sovereignties is called society. This intersection being a junction, this point is a knot. Hence what is called the social bond. Some say social contract—which is the same thing, the word contract being etymologically formed with the idea of a bond. Let us come to an understanding about equality; for, if liberty is the summit, equality is the base. Equality, citizens, is not wholly a surface vegetation, a society of great blades of grass and tiny oaks; a proximity of jealousies that render each other null and void; legally speaking, it is all aptitudes possessed of the same opportunity; politically, it is all votes possessed of the same weight; religiously, it is all consciences possessed of the same right. Equality has an organ: gratuitous and obligatory instruction. The right to the alphabet, that is where the beginning must be made. The primary school imposed on all, the secondary school offered to all, that is the law. From an identical school, an identical society will spring. Yes, instruction! Light! Light! Everything comes from light, and to it everything returns. Citizens, the nineteenth century is great, but the twentieth century will be happy. Then, there will be nothing more like the history of old, we shall no longer, as today, have to fear a conquest, an invasion, a usurpation, a rivalry of nations, arms in hand, an interruption of civilization depending on a marriage of kings, on a birth in hereditary tyrannies, a partition of peoples by a congress, a dismemberment because of the failure of a dynasty, a combat of two religions meeting face to face, like two bucks in the dark, on the bridge of the infinite; we shall no longer have to fear famine, farming out, prostitution arising from distress, misery from the failure of work and the scaffold and the sword, and battles and the ruffianism of chance in the forest of events. One might almost say: There will be no more events. We shall be happy. The human race will accomplish its law, as the terrestrial globe accomplishes its law; harmony will be reestablished between the soul and the star; the soul will gravitate around the truth, as the planet around the light. Friends, the present hour in which I am addressing you, is a gloomy hour; but these are terrible purchases of the future. A revolution is a toll. Oh! The human race will be delivered, raised up, consoled! We affirm it on this barrier. From where should proceed that cry of love, if not from the heights of sacrifice? Oh my brothers, this is the point of junction, of those who think and of those who suffer; this barricade is not made of pavingstones, nor of joists, nor of bits of iron; it is made of two heaps, a heap of ideas, and a heap of woes. Here misery meets the ideal. The day embraces the night, and says to it, 'I am about to die, and thou shalt be born again with me.' From the embrace of all desolations faith leaps forth. Sufferings bring hither their agony and ideas their immortality. This agony and this immortality are about to join and constitute our death. Brothers, he who dies here dies in the radiance of the future, and we are entering a tomb all flooded with the dawn."

Enjolras paused rather than became silent; his lips continued to move silently, as though he were talking to himself, which caused them all to gaze attentively at him, in the endeavor to hear more. There was no applause; but they whispered together for a long time. Speech being a breath, the rustling of intelligences resembles the rustling of leaves.

CHAPTER VI—MARIUS HAGGARD, JAVERT LACONIC

L et us narrate what was passing in Marius's thoughts.

Let the reader recall the state of his soul. We have just recalled it, everything was a vision to him now. His judgment was disturbed. Marius, let us insist on this point, was under the shadow of the great, dark wings that are spread over those in the death agony. He felt that he had entered the tomb, it seemed to him that he was already on the other side of the wall, and he no longer beheld the faces of the living except with the eyes of one dead.

How did M. Fauchelevent come there? Why was he there? What had he come there to do? Marius did not address all these questions to himself. Besides, since our despair has this peculiarity, that it envelops others as well as ourselves, it seemed logical to him that all the world should come there to die.

Only, he thought of Cosette with a pang at his heart.

However, M. Fauchelevent did not speak to him, did not look at him, and had not even the air of hearing him, when Marius raised his voice to say, "I know him."

As far as Marius was concerned, this attitude of M. Fauchelevent was comforting, and, if such a word can be used for such impressions, we should say that it pleased him. He had always felt the absolute impossibility of addressing that enigmatical man, who was, in his eyes, both equivocal and imposing. Moreover, it had been a long time since he had seen him; and this still further augmented the impossibility for Marius's timid and reserved nature.

The five chosen men left the barricade by way of Mondetour lane; they bore a perfect resemblance to members of the National Guard. One of them wept as he took his leave. Before setting out, they embraced those who remained.

When the five men sent back to life had taken their departure, Enjolras thought of the man who had been condemned to death.

He entered the taproom. Javert, still bound to the post, was engaged in meditation.

"Do you want anything?" Enjolras asked him.

Javert replied, "When are you going to kill me?"

"Wait. We need all our cartridges just at present."

"Then give me a drink," said Javert.

Enjolras himself offered him a glass of water, and, as Javert was pinioned, he helped him to drink.

"Is that all?" inquired Enjolras.

"I am uncomfortable against this post," replied Javert. "You are not tender to have left me to pass the night here. Bind me as you please, but you surely might lay me out on a table like that other man."

And with a motion of the head, he indicated the body of M. Mabeuf.

There was, as the reader will remember, a long, broad table at the end of the room, on which they had been running bullets and making cartridges. All the cartridges having been made, and all the powder used, this table was free.

At Enjolras's command, four insurgents unbound Javert from the post. While they were loosing him, a fifth held a bayonet against his breast.

Leaving his arms tied behind his back, they placed about his feet a slender but stout whipcord, as is done to men on the point of mounting the scaffold, which allowed him to take steps about fifteen inches in length, and made him walk to the table at the end of the room, where they laid him down, closely bound about the middle of the body.

By way of further security, and by means of a rope fastened to his neck, they added to the system of ligatures that rendered every attempt at escape impossible, the sort of bond that is called in prisons a martingale, which, starting at the neck, forks on the stomach, and meets the hands, after passing between the legs.

While they were binding Javert, a man standing on the threshold was surveying him with singular attention. The shadow cast by this man made Javert turn his head. He raised his eyes, and recognized Jean Valjean. He did not even start, but dropped his lids proudly and confined himself to the remark, "It is perfectly simple."

CHAPTER VII—THE SITUATION BECOMES AGGRAVATED

The daylight was increasing rapidly. Not a window was opened, not a door stood ajar; it was the dawn but not the awaking. The end of the Rue de la Chanvrerie, opposite the barricade, had been evacuated by the troops, as we have stated it seemed to be free, and presented itself to passersby with a sinister tranquillity. The Rue Saint-Denis was as dumb as the avenue of Sphinxes at Thebes. Not a living being in the crossroads, which gleamed white in the light of the sun. Nothing is so mournful as this light in deserted streets. Nothing was to be seen, but there was something to be heard. A mysterious movement was going on at a certain distance. It was evident that the critical moment was approaching. As on the previous evening, the sentinels had come in; but this time all had come.

The barricade was stronger than on the occasion of the first attack. Since the departure of the five, they had increased its height still further.

On the advice of the sentinel who had examined the region of the Halles, Enjolras, for fear of a surprise in the rear, came to a serious decision. He had the small gut of the Mondetour lane, which had been left open up to that time, barricaded. For this purpose, they tore up the pavement for the length of several houses more. In this manner, the barricade, walled on three streets, in front on the Rue de la Chanvrerie, to the left on the Rues du Cygne and de la Petite Truanderie, to the right on the Rue Mondetour, was really almost impregnable; it is true that they were fatally hemmed in there. It had three fronts, but no exit. "A fortress but a rat hole too," said Courfeyrac with a laugh.

Enjolras had about thirty paving stones "torn up in excess," said Bossuet, piled up near the door of the wine shop.

The silence was now so profound in the quarter from where the attack must needs come, that Enjolras had each man resume his post of battle.

An allowance of brandy was doled out to each.

Nothing is more curious than a barricade preparing for an assault. Each man selects his place as though at the theater. They jostle, and elbow and crowd each other. There are some who make stalls of pavingstones. Here is a corner of the wall that is in the way, it is removed; here is a redan, which may afford protection, they take shelter behind it. Left-handed men are precious; they take the places that are inconvenient to the rest. Many arrange to fight in a sitting posture. They wish to be at ease to kill, and to die comfortably. In the sad war of June, 1848, an insurgent who was a formidable marksman, and who was firing from the top of a terrace upon a roof, had a reclining chair brought there for his use; a charge of grapeshot found him out there.

As soon as the leader has given the order to clear the decks for action, all disorderly movements cease; there is no more pulling from one another; there are no more coteries; no more asides, there is no more holding aloof; everything in their spirits converges in, and changes into, a waiting for the assailants. A barricade before the arrival of danger is chaos; in danger, it is discipline itself. Peril produces order.

As soon as Enjolras had seized his double-barreled rifle, and had placed himself in a sort of embrasure he had reserved for himself, all the rest held their peace. A series of faint, sharp noises resounded confusedly along the wall of pavingstones. It was the men cocking their guns.

Moreover, their attitudes were prouder, more confident than ever; the excess of sacrifice strengthens; they no longer cherished any hope, but they had despair, despair, the last weapon, which sometimes gives victory; Virgil has said so. Supreme resources spring from extreme resolutions. To embark in death is sometimes the means of escaping a shipwreck; and the lid of the coffin becomes a plank of safety.

As on the preceding evening, the attention of all was directed, we might almost say leaned upon, the end of the street, now lighted up and visible.

They had not long to wait. A stir began distinctly in the Saint-Leu quarter, but it did not resemble the movement of the first attack. A clashing of chains, the uneasy jolting of a mass, the click of brass skipping along the pavement, a sort of solemn uproar, announced that some sinister construction of iron was approaching. There arose a tremor in the bosoms of these peaceful old streets, pierced and built for the fertile circulation of interests and ideas, and which are not made for the horrible rumble of the wheels of war.

The fixity of eye in all the combatants upon the extremity of the street became ferocious.

A cannon made its appearance.

Artillerymen were pushing the piece; it was in firing trim; the fore-carriage had been detached; two upheld the guncarriage, four were at the wheels; others followed with the caisson. They could see the smoke of the burning lintstock.

"Fire!" shouted Enjolras.

The whole barricade fired, the report was terrible; an avalanche of smoke covered and effaced both cannon and men; after a few seconds, the cloud dispersed, and the cannon and men re-appeared; the gun-crew had just finished rolling it slowly, correctly, without haste, into position facing the barricade. Not one of them had been struck. Then the captain of the piece, bearing down upon the breech in order to raise the muzzle, began to point the cannon with the gravity of an astronomer leveling a telescope.

"Bravo for the cannoneers!" cried Bossuet.

And the whole barricade clapped their hands.

A moment later, squarely planted in the very middle of the street, astride of the gutter, the piece was ready for action. A formidable pair of jaws yawned on the barricade.

"Come, merrily now!" ejaculated Courfeyrac. "That's the brutal part of it. After the fillip on the nose, the blow from the fist. The army is reaching out its big paw to us. The barricade is going to be severely shaken up. The fusillade tries, the cannon takes."

"It is a piece of eight, new model, brass," added Combeferre. "Those pieces are liable to burst as soon as the proportion of ten parts of tin to one hundred of brass is exceeded. The excess of tin renders them too tender. Then it comes to pass that they have caves and chambers when looked at from the vent hole. In order to obviate this danger, and to render it possible to force the charge, it may become necessary to return to the process of the fourteenth century, hooping, and to encircle the piece on the outside with a series of unwelded steel bands, from the breech to the trunnions. In the meantime, they remedy this defect as best they may; they manage to discover where the holes are located in the vent of a cannon, by means of a searcher. But there is a better method, with Gribeauval's movable star."

"In the sixteenth century," remarked Bossuet, "they used to rifle cannon."

"Yes," replied Combeferre, "that augments the projectile force, but diminishes the accuracy of the firing. In firing at short range, the trajectory is not as rigid as could be desired, the parabola is exaggerated, the line of the projectile is no longer sufficiently rectilinear to allow of its striking intervening objects, which is, nevertheless, a necessity of battle, the importance of which increases with the proximity of the enemy and the precipitation of the discharge. This defect of the tension of the curve of the projectile in the rifled cannon of the sixteenth century arose from the smallness of the charge; small charges for that sort of engine are imposed by the ballistic necessities, such, for instance, as the preservation of the gun-carriage. In short, that despot, the cannon, cannot do all that it desires; force is a great weakness. A cannonball only travels six hundred leagues an hour; light travels seventy thousand leagues a second. Such is the superiority of Jesus Christ over Napoleon."

"Reload your guns," said Enjolras.

How was the casing of the barricade going to behave under the cannonballs? Would they affect a breach? That was the question. While the insurgents were reloading their guns, the artillerymen were loading the cannon.

The anxiety in the redoubt was profound.

The shot sped the report burst forth.

"Present!" shouted a joyous voice.

And Gavroche flung himself into the barricade just as the ball dashed against it.

He came from the direction of the Rue du Cygne, and he had nimbly climbed over the auxiliary barricade that fronted on the labyrinth of the Rue de la Petite Truanderie.

Gavroche produced a greater sensation in the barricade than the cannonball.

The ball buried itself in the mass of rubbish. At the most there was an omnibus wheel broken, and the old Anceau cart was demolished. On seeing this, the barricade burst into a laugh.

"Go on!" shouted Bossuet to the artillerists.

CHAPTER VIII—THE ARTILLERY MEN COMPEL PEOPLE TO TAKE THEM SERIOUSLY

They flocked around Gavroche. But he had no time to tell anything. Marius drew him aside with a shudder.

"What are you doing here?"

"Hullo!" said the child. "What are you doing here yourself?"

And he stared at Marius intently with his epic effrontery. His eyes grew larger with the proud light within them.

It was with an accent of severity that Marius continued, "Who told you to come back? Did you deliver my letter at the address?"

Gavroche was not without some compunctions in the matter of that letter. In his haste to return to the barricade, he had got rid of it rather than delivered it. He was forced to acknowledge to himself that he had confided it rather lightly to that stranger whose face he had not been able to make out. It is true that the man was bareheaded, but that was not sufficient. In short, he had been administering to himself little inward remonstrances and he feared Marius's reproaches. In order to extricate himself from the predicament, he took the simplest course; he lied abominably.

"Citizen, I delivered the letter to the porter. The lady was asleep. She will have the letter when she wakes up."

Marius had had two objects in sending that letter: to bid farewell to Cosette and to save Gavroche. He was obliged to content himself with the half of his desire.

The despatch of his letter and the presence of M. Fauchelevent in the barricade, was a coincidence that occurred to him. He pointed out M. Fauchelevent to Gavroche.

"Do you know that man?"

"No," said Gavroche.

Gavroche had, in fact, as we have just mentioned, seen Jean Valjean only at night.

The troubled and unhealthy conjectures that had outlined themselves in Marius's mind were dissipated. Did he know M. Fauchelevent's opinions? Perhaps M. Fauchelevent was a republican. Hence his very natural presence in this combat.

In the meanwhile, Gavroche was shouting, at the other end of the barricade, "My gun!"

Courfeyrac had it returned to him.

Gavroche warned "his comrades" as he called them, that the barricade was blocked. He had had great difficulty in reaching it. A battalion of the line whose arms were piled in the Rue de la Petite Truanderie was on the watch on the side of the Rue du Cygne; on the opposite side, the municipal guard occupied the Rue des Prêcheurs. The bulk of the army was facing them in front.

This information given, Gavroche added, "I authorize you to hit 'em a tremendous whack."

Meanwhile, Enjolras was straining his ears and watching at his embrasure.

The assailants, dissatisfied, no doubt, with their shot, had not repeated it.

A company of infantry of the line had come up and occupied the end of the street behind the piece of ordnance. The soldiers were tearing up the pavement and constructing with the stones a small, low wall, a sort of side-work not more than eighteen inches high, and facing the barricade. In the angle at the left of this epaulement, there was visible the head of the column of a battalion from the suburbs massed in the Rue Saint-Denis.

Enjolras, on the watch, thought he distinguished the peculiar sound that is produced when the shells of grapeshot are drawn from the caissons, and he saw the commander of the piece change the elevation and incline the mouth of the cannon slightly to the left. Then the cannoneers began to load the piece. The chief seized the lintstock himself and lowered it to the vent.

"Down with your heads, hug the wall!" shouted Enjolras. "And all on your knees along the barricade!"

The insurgents who were straggling in front of the wine shop, and who had quitted their posts of combat on Gavroche's arrival, rushed pell-mell toward the barricade; but before Enjolras's order could be executed, the discharge took place with the terrifying rattle of a round of grapeshot. This is what it was, in fact.

The charge had been aimed at the cut in the redoubt, and had there rebounded from the wall; and this terrible rebound had produced two dead and three wounded.

If this were continued, the barricade was no longer tenable. The grapeshot made its way in.

A murmur of consternation arose.

"Let us prevent the second discharge," said Enjolras.

And, lowering his rifle, he took aim at the captain of the gun, who, at that moment, was bearing down on the breach of his gun and rectifying and definitely fixing its pointing.

The captain of the piece was a handsome sergeant of artillery, very young, blond, with a very gentle face, and the intelligent air peculiar to that predestined and redoubtable weapon that, by dint of perfecting itself in horror, must end in killing war.

Combeferre, who was standing beside Enjolras, scrutinized this young man.

"What a pity!" said Combeferre. "What hideous things these butcheries are! Come, when there are no more kings, there will be no more war. Enjolras, you are taking aim at that sergeant, you are not looking at him. Fancy, he is a charming young man; he is intrepid; it is evident that he is thoughtful; those young artillery men are very well educated; he has a father, a mother, a family; he is probably in love; he is not more than five and twenty at the most; he might be your brother."

"He is," said Enjolras.

"Yes," replied Combeferre, "he is mine too. Well, let us not kill him."

"Let me alone. It must be done."

And a tear trickled slowly down Enjolras's marble cheek.

At the same moment, he pressed the trigger of his rifle. The flame leaped forth. The artilleryman turned around twice, his arms extended in front of him, his head uplifted, as though for breath, then he fell with his side on the gun, and lay there motionless. They could see his back, from the center of which there flowed directly a stream of blood. The ball had traversed his breast from side to side. He was dead.

He had to be carried away and replaced by another. Several minutes were thus gained, in fact.

CHAPTER IX—EMPLOYMENT OF THE OLD TALENTS OF A POACHER AND THAT INFALLIBLE MARKSMANSHIP THAT INFLUENCED THE CONDEMNATION OF 1796

Opinions were exchanged in the barricade. The firing from the gun was about to begin again. Against that grapeshot, they could not hold out a quarter of an hour longer. It was absolutely necessary to deaden the blows.

Enjolras issued this command: "We must place a mattress there."

"We have none," said Combeferre, "the wounded are lying on them."

Jean Valjean, who was seated apart on a stone post, at the corner of the tavern, with his gun between his knees, had, up to that moment, taken no part in anything that was going on. He did not appear to hear the combatants saying around him, "Here is a gun that is doing nothing."

At the order issued by Enjolras, he rose.

It will be remembered that, on the arrival of the rabble in the Rue de la Chanvrerie, an old woman, foreseeing the bullets, had placed her mattress in front of her window. This window, an attic window, was on the roof of a six-story house situated a little beyond the barricade. The mattress, placed crosswise, supported at the bottom on two poles for drying linen, was upheld at the top by two ropes, which, at that distance, looked like two threads, and which were attached to two nails planted in the window frames. These ropes were distinctly visible, like hairs, against the sky.

"Can someone lend me a double-barreled rifle?" said Jean Valjean.

Enjolras, who had just reloaded his, handed it to him.

Jean Valjean took aim at the attic window and fired.

One of the mattress ropes was cut.

The mattress now hung by one thread only.

Jean Valjean fired the second charge. The second rope lashed the panes of the attic window. The mattress slipped between the two poles and fell into the street.

The barricade applauded.

All voices cried, "Here is a mattress!"

"Yes," said Combeferre, "but who will go and fetch it?"

The mattress had, in fact, fallen outside the barricade, between besiegers and besieged. Now, the death of the sergeant of artillery having exasperated the troop, the soldiers had, for several minutes, been lying flat on their stomachs behind the line of paving-stones they had erected, and, in order to supply the forced silence of the piece, which was quiet while its service was in course of reorganization, they had opened fire on the barricade. The insurgents did not reply to this musketry, in order to spare their ammunition. The fusillade broke against the barricade; but the street, which it filled, was terrible.

Jean Valjean stepped out of the cut, entered the street, traversed the storm of bullets, walked up to the mattress, hoisted it upon his back, and returned to the barricade.

He placed the mattress in the cut with his own hands. He fixed it there against the wall in such a manner that the artillerymen should not see it.

That done, they awaited the next discharge of grapeshot.

It was not long in coming.

The cannon vomited forth its package of buckshot with a roar. But there was no rebound. The effect they had foreseen had been attained. The barricade was saved.

"Citizen," said Enjolras to Jean Valjean, "the Republic thanks you."

Bossuet admired and laughed. He exclaimed, "It is immoral that a mattress should have so much power. Triumph of that which yields over that which strikes with lightning. But never mind, glory to the mattress which annuls a cannon!"

CHAPTER X—DAWN

At that moment, Cosette awoke.

Her chamber was narrow, neat, unobtrusive, with a long sash-window, facing the East on the back courtyard of the house.

Cosette knew nothing of what was going on in Paris. She had not been there on the preceding evening, and she had already retired to her chamber when Toussaint had said, "It appears that there is a row."

Cosette had slept only a few hours, but soundly. She had had sweet dreams, which possibly arose from the fact that her little bed was very white. Someone, who was Marius, had appeared to her in the light. She awoke with the sun in her eyes, which, at first, produced on her the effect of being a continuation of her dream. Her first thought on emerging from this dream was a smiling one. Cosette felt herself thoroughly reassured. Like Jean Valjean, she had, a few hours previously, passed through that reaction of the soul, which absolutely will not hear of unhappiness. She began to cherish hope, with all her might, without knowing why. Then she felt a pang at her heart. It was three days since she had seen Marius. But she said to herself that he must have received her letter, that he knew where she was, and that he was so clever that he would find means of reaching her. And that certainly today, and perhaps that very morning. It was broad daylight, but the rays of light were very horizontal; she thought that it was very early, but that she must rise, nevertheless, in order to receive Marius.

She felt that she could not live without Marius, and that, consequently, that was sufficient and that Marius would come. No objection was valid. All this was certain. It was monstrous enough already to have suffered for three days. Marius absent three days, this was horrible on the part of the good God. Now, this cruel teasing from on high had been gone through with. Marius was about to arrive, and he would bring good news. Youth is made thus; it quickly dries its eyes; it finds sorrow useless and does not accept it. Youth is the smile of the future in the presence of an unknown quantity, which is itself. It is natural to it to be happy. It seems as though its respiration were made of hope.

Moreover, Cosette could not remember what Marius had said to her on the subject of this absence, which was to last only one day, and what explanation of it he had given her. Everyone has noticed with what nimbleness a coin one has dropped on the ground rolls away and hides, and with what art it renders itself undiscoverable. There are thoughts that play us the same trick; they nestle away in a corner of our brain; that is the end of them; they are lost; it is impossible to lay the memory on them. Cosette was somewhat vexed at the useless little effort made by her memory. She told herself, that it was very naughty and very wicked of her, to have forgotten the words uttered by Marius.

She sprang out of bed and accomplished the two ablutions of soul and body, her prayers and her toilet.

One may, in a case of exigency, introduce the reader into a nuptial chamber, not into a virginal chamber. Verse would hardly venture it, prose must not.

It is the interior of a flower that is not yet unfolded, it is whiteness in the dark, it is the private cell of a closed lily, which must not be gazed upon by man so long as the sun has not gazed upon it. Woman in the bud is sacred. That innocent bud that opens, that adorable half-nudity that is afraid of itself, that white foot that takes refuge in a slipper, that throat that veils itself before a mirror as though a mirror were an eye, that chemise that makes haste to rise up and conceal the shoulder for a creaking bit of furniture or a passing vehicle, those cords tied, those clasps fastened, those laces drawn, those tremors, those shivers of cold and modesty, that exquisite affright in every movement, that almost winged uneasiness where there is no cause for alarm, the successive phases of dressing, as charming as the clouds of dawn, it is not fitting that all this should be narrated, and it is too much to have even called attention to it.

The eye of man must be more religious in the presence of the rising of a young girl than in the presence of the rising of a star. The possibility of hurting should inspire an augmentation of respect. The down on the peach, the bloom on the plum, the radiated crystal of the snow, the wing of the butterfly powdered with feathers, are coarse compared to that chastity, which does not even know that it is chaste. The young girl is only the flash of a dream, and is not yet a statue. Her bedchamber is hidden in the somber part of the ideal. The indiscreet touch of a glance brutalizes this vague penumbra. Here, contemplation is profanation.

We shall, therefore, show nothing of that sweet little flutter of Cosette's rising.

An oriental tale relates how the rose was made white by God, but that Adam looked upon her when she was unfolding, and she was ashamed and turned crimson. We are of the number who fall speechless in the presence of young girls and flowers, since we think them worthy of veneration.

Cosette dressed herself very hastily, combed and dressed her hair, which was a very simple matter in those days, when women did not swell out their curls and bands with cushions and puffs, and did not put crinoline in their locks. Then she opened the window and cast her eyes around her in every direction, hoping to descry some bit of the street, an angle of the house, an edge of pavement, so that she might be able to watch for Marius there. But no view of the outside was to be had. The back court was surrounded by tolerably high walls, and the outlook was only on several gardens. Cosette pronounced these gardens hideous: for the first time in her life, she found flowers ugly. The smallest scrap of the gutter of the street would have met her wishes better. She decided to gaze at the sky, as though she thought that Marius might come from that quarter.

All at once, she burst into tears. Not that this was fickleness of soul; but hopes cut in twain by dejection—that was her case. She had a confused consciousness of something horrible. Thoughts were rife in the air, in fact. She told herself that she was not sure of anything, that to withdraw herself from sight was to be lost; and the idea that Marius could return to her from heaven appeared to her no longer charming but mournful.

Then, as is the nature of these clouds, calm returned to her, and hope and a sort of unconscious smile, which yet indicated trust in God.

Everyone in the house was still asleep. A countrylike silence reigned. Not a shutter had been opened. The porter's lodge was closed. Toussaint had not risen, and Cosette, naturally, thought that her father was asleep. She must have suffered much, and she must have still been suffering greatly, for she said to herself, that her father had been unkind; but she counted on Marius. The eclipse of such a light was decidedly impossible. Now and then, she heard sharp shocks in the distance, and she said, "It is odd that people should be opening and shutting their carriage gates so early." They were the reports of the cannon battering the barricade.

A few feet below Cosette's window, in the ancient and perfectly black cornice of the wall, there was a martin's nest; the curve of this nest formed a little projection beyond the cornice, so that from above it was possible to look into this little paradise. The mother was there, spreading her wings like a fan over her brood; the father fluttered about, flew away, then came back, bearing in his beak food and kisses. The dawning day gilded this happy thing, the great law, "Multiply," lay there smiling and august, and that sweet mystery unfolded in the glory of the morning. Cosette, with her hair in the sunlight, her soul absorbed in chimeras, illuminated by love within and by the dawn without, bent over mechanically, and almost without daring to avow to herself that she was thinking at the same time of Marius, began to gaze at these birds, at this family, at that male and female, that mother and her little ones, with the profound trouble that a nest produces on a virgin.

CHAPTER XI—THE SHOT THAT MISSES NOTHING AND KILLS NO ONE

The assailants' fire continued. Musketry and grapeshot alternated, but without committing great ravages, to tell the truth. The top alone of the Corinthe facade suffered; the window on the first floor, and the attic window in the roof, riddled with buckshot and biscaiens, were slowly losing their shape. The combatants who had been posted there had been obliged to withdraw. However, this is according to the tactics of barricades; to fire for a long while, in order to exhaust the insurgents' ammunition, if they commit the mistake of replying. When it is perceived, from the slackening of their fire, that they have no more powder and ball, the assault is made. Enjolras had not fallen into this trap; the barricade did not reply.

At every discharge by platoons, Gavroche puffed out his cheek with his tongue, a sign of supreme disdain.

"Good for you," said he, "rip up the cloth. We want some lint."

Courfeyrac called the grapeshot to order for the little effect it produced, and said to the cannon, "You are growing diffuse, my good fellow."

One gets puzzled in battle, as at a ball. It is probable that this silence on the part of the redoubt began to render the besiegers uneasy, and to make them fear some unexpected incident, and that they felt the necessity of getting a clear view behind that heap of paving-stones, and of knowing what was going on behind that impassable wall that received blows without retorting. The insurgents suddenly perceived a helmet glittering in the sun on a neighboring roof. A fireman had placed his back against a tall chimney, and seemed to be acting as sentinel. His glance fell directly down into the barricade.

"There's an embarrassing watcher," said Enjolras.

Jean Valjean had returned Enjolras's rifle, but he had his own gun.

Without saying a word, he took aim at the fireman, and, a second later, the helmet, smashed by a bullet, rattled noisily into the street. The terrified soldier made haste to disappear. A second observer took his place. This one was an officer. Jean Valjean, who had reloaded his gun, took aim at the newcomer and sent the officer's casque to join the soldier's. The officer did not persist, and retired speedily. This time the warning was understood. No one made his appearance thereafter on that roof; and the idea of spying on the barricade was abandoned.

"Why did you not kill the man?" Bossuet asked Jean Valjean.

Jean Valjean made no reply.

CHAPTER XII—DISORDER A PARTISAN OF ORDER

Bossuet muttered in Combeferre's ear, "He did not answer my question."

"He is a man who does good by gunshots," said Combeferre.

Those who have preserved some memory of this already distant epoch know that the National Guard from the suburbs was valiant against insurrections. It was particularly zealous and intrepid in the days of June 1832. A certain good dramshop keeper of Pantin des Vertus or la Cunette, whose "establishment" had been closed by the riots, became leonine at the sight of his deserted dancehall, and got himself killed to preserve the order represented by a tea garden. In that bourgeois and heroic time, in the presence of ideas that had their knights, interests had their paladins. The prosiness of the originators detracted nothing from the bravery of the movement. The diminution of a pile of crowns made bankers sing the Marseillaise. They shed their blood lyrically for the countinghouse; and they defended the shop, that immense diminutive of the fatherland, with Lacedaemonian enthusiasm.

At bottom, we will observe, there was nothing in all this that was not extremely serious. It was social elements entering into strife, while awaiting the day when they should enter into equilibrium.

Another sign of the times was the anarchy mingled with governmentalism [the barbarous name of the correct party]. People were for order in combination with lack of discipline.

The drum suddenly beat capricious calls, at the command of such or such a Colonel of the National Guard; such and such a captain went into action through inspiration; such and such National Guardsmen fought, "for an idea," and on their own account. At critical moments, on "days" they took counsel less of their leaders than of their instincts. There existed in the army of order, veritable guerilleros, some of the sword, like Fannicot, others of the pen, like Henri Fonfrede.

Civilization, unfortunately, represented at this epoch rather by an aggregation of interests than by a group of principles, was or thought itself, in peril; it set up the cry of alarm; each, constituting himself a center, defended it, succored it, and protected it with his own head; and the first comer took it upon himself to save society.

Zeal sometimes proceeded to extermination. A platoon of the National Guard would constitute itself on its own authority a private council of war, and judge and execute a captured insurgent in five minutes. It was an improvisation of this sort that had slain Jean Prouvaire. Fierce Lynch law, with which no one party had any right to reproach the rest, for it has been applied by the Republic in America, as well as by the monarchy in Europe. This Lynch law was complicated with mistakes. On one day of rioting, a young poet, named Paul Aime Garnier, was pursued in the Place Royale, with a bayonet at his loins, and only escaped by taking refuge under the porte-cochère of No. 6. They shouted, "There's another of those Saint-Simonians!" and they wanted to kill him. Now, he had under his arm a volume of the memoirs of the Duc de Saint-Simon. A National Guard had read the words Saint-Simon on the book, and had shouted, "Death!"

On the 6th of June, 1832, a company of the National Guards from the suburbs, commanded by the Captain Fannicot, above mentioned, had itself decimated in the Rue de la Chanvrerie out of caprice and its own good pleasure. This fact, singular though it may seem, was proved at the judicial investigation opened in consequence of the insurrection of 1832. Captain Fannicot, a bold and impatient bourgeois, a sort of condottiere of the order of those whom we have just characterized, a fanatical and intractable governmentalist, could not resist the temptation to fire prematurely, and the ambition of capturing the barricade alone and unaided, that is to say, with his company. Exasperated by the successive apparition of the red flag and the old coat he took for the black flag, he loudly blamed the generals and chiefs of the corps, who were holding council and did not think that the moment for the decisive assault had arrived, and who were allowing "the insurrection to fry in its own fat," to use the celebrated expression of one of them. For his part, he thought the barricade ripe, and as that which is ripe ought to fall, he made the attempt.

He commanded men as resolute as himself, "raging fellows," as a witness said. His company, the same that had shot Jean Prouvaire the poet, was the first of the battalion posted at the angle of the street. At the moment when they were least expecting it, the captain launched his men against the barricade. This movement, executed with more good will than strategy, cost the Fannicot company dear. Before it had traversed two thirds of the street it was received by a general discharge from the barricade. Four, the most audacious, who were running on in front, were mown down point-blank at the very foot of the redoubt, and this courageous throng of National Guards, very brave men but lacking in military tenacity, were forced to fall back, after some hesitation, leaving fifteen corpses on the pavement. This momentary hesitation gave the insurgents time to reload their weapons, and a second and very destructive discharge struck the company before it could regain the corner of the street, its shelter. A moment more, and it was caught between two fires, and it received the volley from the battery piece that, not having received the order, had not discontinued its firing.

The intrepid and imprudent Fannicot was one of the dead from this grapeshot. He was killed by the cannon, that is to say, by order.

This attack, which was more furious than serious, irritated Enjolras. "The fools!" said he. "They are getting their own men killed and they are using up our ammunition for nothing."

Enjolras spoke like the real general of insurrection that he was. Insurrection and repression do not fight with equal weapons. Insurrection, which is speedily exhausted, has only a certain number of shots to fire and a certain number of combatants to expend. An empty cartridge box, a man killed, cannot be replaced. As repression has the army, it does not count its men, and, as it has Vincennes, it does not count its shots. Repression has as many regiments as the barricade has men, and as many arsenals as the barricade has cartridge-boxes. Thus they are struggles of one against a hundred, which always end in crushing the barricade; unless the revolution, uprising suddenly, flings into the balance its flaming archangel's sword. This does happen sometimes. Then everything rises, the pavements begin to seethe, popular redoubts abound. Paris quivers supremely, the quid divinum is given forth, a 10th of August is in the air, a 29th of July is in the air, a wonderful light appears, the yawning maw of force draws back, and the army, that lion, sees before it, erect and tranquil, that prophet, France.

CHAPTER XIII—PASSING GLEAMS

In the chaos of sentiments and passions that defend a barricade, there is a little of everything; there is bravery, there is youth, honor, enthusiasm, the ideal, conviction, the rage of the gambler, and, above all, intermittences of hope.

One of these intermittences, one of these vague quivers of hope suddenly traversed the barricade of the Rue de la Chanvrerie at the moment when it was least expected.

"Listen," suddenly cried Enjolras, who was still on the watch, "it seems to me that Paris is waking up."

It is certain that, on the morning of the 6th of June, the insurrection broke out afresh for an hour or two, to a certain extent. The obstinacy of the alarm peal of Saint-Merry reanimated some fancies. Barricades were begun in the Rue du Poirier and the Rue des Gravilliers. In front of the Porte Saint-Martin, a young man, armed with a rifle, attacked alone a squadron of cavalry. In plain sight, on the open boulevard, he placed one knee on the ground, shouldered his weapon, fired, killed the commander of the squadron, and turned away, saying, "There's another who will do us no more harm."

He was put to the sword. In the Rue Saint-Denis, a woman fired on the National Guard from behind a lowered blind. The slats of the blind could be seen to tremble at every shot. A child fourteen years of age was arrested in the Rue de la Cossonerie, with his pockets full of cartridges. Many posts were attacked. At the entrance to the Rue Bertin-Poiree, a very lively and utterly unexpected fusillade welcomed a regiment of cuirrassiers, at whose head marched Marshal General Cavaignac de Barague. In the Rue Planche-Mibray, they threw old pieces of pottery and household utensils down on the soldiers from the roofs; a bad sign; and when this matter was reported to Marshal Soult, Napoleon's old lieutenant grew thoughtful, as he recalled Suchet's saying at Saragossa, "We are lost when the old women empty their pots de chambre on our heads."

These general symptoms that presented themselves at the moment when it was thought that the uprising had been rendered local, this fever of wrath, these sparks that flew hither and there above those deep masses of combustibles that are called the faubourgs of Paris, all this, taken together, disturbed the military chiefs. They made haste to stamp out these beginnings of conflagration.

They delayed the attack on the barricades Maubuee, de la Chanvrerie and Saint-Merry until these sparks had been extinguished, in order that they might have to deal with the barricades only and be able to finish them at one blow. Columns were thrown into the streets where there was fermentation, sweeping the large, sounding the small, right and left, now slowly and cautiously, now at full charge. The troops broke in the doors of houses from which shots had been fired; at the same time, maneuvers by the cavalry dispersed the groups on the boulevards. This repression was not effected without some commotion, and without that tumultuous uproar peculiar to collisions between the army and the people. This was what Enjolras had caught in the intervals of the cannonade and the musketry. Moreover, he had seen wounded men passing the end of the street in litters, and he said to Courfeyrac, "Those wounded do not come from us."

Their hope did not last long; the gleam was quickly eclipsed. In less than half an hour, what was in the air vanished, it was a flash of lightning unaccompanied by thunder, and the insurgents felt that sort of leaden cope, which the indifference of the people casts over obstinate and deserted men, fall over them once more.

The general movement, which seemed to have assumed a vague outline, had miscarried; and the attention of the minister of war and the strategy of the generals could now be concentrated on the three or four barricades that still remained standing.

The sun was mounting above the horizon.

An insurgent hailed Enjolras.

"We are hungry here. Are we really going to die like this, without anything to eat?"

Enjolras, who was still leaning on his elbows at his embrasure, made an affirmative sign with his head, but without taking his eyes from the end of the street.

CHAPTER XIV—WHEREIN WILL APPEAR THE NAME OF ENJOLRAS'S MISTRESS

Courfeyrac, seated on a pavingstone beside Enjolras, continued to insult the cannon, and each time that that gloomy cloud of projectiles called grapeshot passed overhead with its terrible sound he assailed it with a burst of irony.

"You are wearing out your lungs, poor, brutal, old fellow, you pain me, you are wasting your row. That's not thunder, it's a cough."

And the bystanders laughed.

Courfeyrac and Bossuet, whose brave good humor increased with the peril, like Madame Scarron, replaced nourishment with pleasantry, and, as wine was lacking, they poured out gaiety to all.

"I admire Enjolras," said Bossuet. "His impassive temerity astounds me. He lives alone, which renders him a little sad, perhaps; Enjolras complains of his greatness, which binds him to widowhood. The rest of us have mistresses, more or less, who make us crazy, that is to say, brave. When a man is as much in love as a tiger, the least that he can do is to fight like a lion. That is one way of taking our revenge for the capers that mesdames our grisettes play on us. Roland gets himself killed for Angelique; all our heroism comes from our women. A man without a woman is a pistol without a trigger; it is the woman that sets the man off. Well, Enjolras has no woman. He is not in love, and yet he manages to be intrepid. It is a thing unheard of that a man should be as cold as ice and as bold as fire."

Enjolras did not appear to be listening, but had anyone been near him, that person would have heard him mutter in a low voice, "Patria."

Bossuet was still laughing when Courfeyrac exclaimed, "News!"

And assuming the tone of an usher making an announcement, he added, "My name is Eight-Pounder."

In fact, a new personage had entered on the scene. This was a second piece of ordnance.

The artillerymen rapidly performed their maneuvers in force and placed this second piece in line with the first.

This outlined the catastrophe.

A few minutes later, the two pieces, rapidly served, were firing point-blank at the redoubt; the platoon firing of the line and of the soldiers from the suburbs sustained the artillery.

Another cannonade was audible at some distance. At the same time that the two guns were furiously attacking the redoubt from the Rue de la Chanvrerie, two other cannons, trained one from the Rue Saint-Denis, the other from the Rue Aubry-le-Boucher, were riddling the Saint-Merry barricade. The four cannons echoed each other mournfully.

The barking of these somber dogs of war replied to each other.

One of the two pieces that was now battering the barricade on the Rue de la Chanvrerie was firing grapeshot, the other balls.

The piece that was firing balls was pointed a little high, and the aim was calculated so that the ball struck the extreme edge of the upper crest of the barricade, and crumbled the stone down upon the insurgents, mingled with bursts of grapeshot.

The object of this mode of firing was to drive the insurgents from the summit of the redoubt, and to compel them to gather close in the interior, that is to say, this announced the assault.

The combatants once driven from the crest of the barricade by balls, and from the windows of the cabaret by grapeshot, the attacking columns could venture into the street without being picked off, perhaps, even, without being seen, could briskly and suddenly scale the redoubt, as on the preceding evening, and, who knows? Take it by surprise.

"It is absolutely necessary that the inconvenience of those guns should be diminished," said Enjolras, and he shouted, "Fire on the artillery men!"

All were ready. The barricade, which had long been silent, poured forth a desperate fire; seven or eight discharges followed, with a sort of rage and joy; the street was filled with blinding smoke, and, at the end of a few minutes, athwart this mist all streaked with flame, two thirds of the gunners could be distinguished lying beneath the wheels of the cannons. Those who were left standing continued to serve the pieces with severe tranquillity, but the fire had slackened.

"Things are going well now," said Bossuet to Enjolras. "Success."

Enjolras shook his head and replied, "Another quarter of an hour of this success, and there will not be any cartridges left in the barricade."

It appears that Gavroche overheard this remark.

CHAPTER XV—GAVROCHE OUTSIDE

Courfeyrac suddenly caught sight of someone at the base of the barricade, outside in the street, amid the bullets.

Gavroche had taken a bottle basket from the wine shop, had made his way out through the cut, and was quietly engaged in emptying the full cartridge-boxes of the National Guardsmen who had been killed on the slope of the redoubt, into his basket.

"What are you doing there?" asked Courfeyrac.

Gavroche raised his face, "I'm filling my basket, citizen."

"Don't you see the grapeshot?"

Gavroche replied, "Well, it is raining. What then?"

Courfeyrac shouted, "Come in!"

"Instanter," said Gavroche.

And with a single bound he plunged into the street.

It will be remembered that Fannicot's company had left behind it a trail of bodies. Twenty corpses lay scattered here and there on the pavement, through the whole length of the street. Twenty cartouches for Gavroche meant a provision of cartridges for the barricade.

The smoke in the street was like a fog. Whoever has beheld a cloud that has fallen into a mountain gorge between two peaked escarpments can imagine this smoke rendered denser and thicker by two gloomy rows of lofty houses. It rose gradually and was incessantly renewed; hence a twilight that made even the broad daylight turn pale. The combatants could hardly see each other from one end of the street to the other, short as it was.

This obscurity, which had probably been desired and calculated on by the commanders who were to direct the assault on the barricade, was useful to Gavroche.

Beneath the folds of this veil of smoke, and thanks to his small size, he could advance tolerably far into the street without being seen. He rifled the first seven or eight cartridge-boxes without much danger.

He crawled flat on his belly, galloped on all fours, took his basket in his teeth, twisted, glided, undulated, wound from one dead body to another, and emptied the cartridge-box or cartouche as a monkey opens a nut.

They did not dare to shout to him to return from the barricade, which was quite near, for fear of attracting attention to him.

On one body, that of a corporal, he found a powderflask.

"For thirst," said he, putting it in his pocket.

By dint of advancing, he reached a point where the fog of the fusillade became transparent. So that the sharpshooters of the line ranged on the outlook behind their paving stone dike and the sharpshooters of the banlieue massed at the corner of the street suddenly pointed out to each other something moving through the smoke.

At the moment when Gavroche was relieving a sergeant, who was lying near a stone doorpost, of his cartridges, a bullet struck the body.

"Fichtre!" ejaculated Gavroche. "They are killing my dead men for me."

A second bullet struck a spark from the pavement beside him. A third overturned his basket.

Gavroche looked and saw that this came from the men of the banlieue.

He sprang to his feet, stood erect, with his hair flying in the wind, his hands on his hips, his eyes fixed on the National Guardsmen who were firing, and sang:

> "Men are ugly at Nanterre,
> 'Tis the fault of Voltaire;
> And dull at Palaiseau,
> 'Tis the fault of Rousseau."

Then he picked up his basket, replaced the cartridges that had fallen from it, without missing a single one, and, advancing toward the fusillade, set about plundering another cartridgebox. There a fourth bullet missed him, again. Gavroche sang,

> "I am not a notary,
> 'Tis the fault of Voltaire;
> I'm a little bird,
> 'Tis the fault of Rousseau."

A fifth bullet only succeeded in drawing from him a third couplet.

> "Joy is my character,
> 'Tis the fault of Voltaire;
> Misery is my trousseau,
> 'Tis the fault of Rousseau."

Thus it went on for some time. It was a charming and terrible sight.

Gavroche, though shot at, was teasing the fusillade. He had the air of being greatly diverted. It was the sparrow pecking at the sportsmen. To each discharge he retorted with a couplet. They aimed at him constantly, and always missed him. The National Guardsmen and the soldiers laughed as they took aim at him. He lay down, sprang to his feet, hid in the corner of a doorway, then made a bound, disappeared, reappeared, scampered away, returned, replied to the grapeshot with his thumb at his nose, and, all the while, went on pillaging the cartouches, emptying the cartridge-boxes, and filling his basket. The insurgents, panting with anxiety, followed him with their eyes. The barricade trembled; he sang. He was not a child, he was not a man; he was a strange gamin-fairy. He might have been called the invulnerable dwarf of the fray. The bullets flew after him, he was more nimble than they. He played a fearful game of hide and seek with death; every time that the flat-nosed face of the specter approached, the urchin administered to it a fillip.

One bullet, however, better aimed or more treacherous than the rest, finally struck the will-o'-the-wisp of a child. Gavroche was seen to stagger, then he sank to the earth. The whole barricade gave vent to a cry; but there was something of Antaeus in that pygmy; for the gamin to touch the pavement is the same as for the giant to touch the earth; Gavroche had fallen only to rise again; he remained in a sitting posture, a long thread of blood streaked his face, he raised both arms in the air, glanced in the direction from which the shot had come, and began to sing:

> "I have fallen to the earth,
> 'Tis the fault of Voltaire;
> With my nose in the gutter,
> 'Tis the fault of . . ."

He did not finish. A second bullet from the same marksman stopped him short. This time he fell face downward on the pavement, and moved no more. This grand little soul had taken its flight.

CHAPTER XVI—HOW FROM A BROTHER ONE BECOMES A FATHER

At that same moment, in the garden of the Luxembourg, for the gaze of the drama must be everywhere present, two children were holding each other by the hand. One might have been seven years old, the other five. The rain having soaked them, they were walking along the paths on the sunny side; the elder was leading the younger; they were pale and ragged; they had the air of wild birds. The smaller of them said, "I am very hungry."

The elder, who was already somewhat of a protector, was leading his brother with his left hand and in his right he carried a small stick.

They were alone in the garden. The garden was deserted, the gates had been closed by order of the police, on account of the insurrection. The troops who had been bivouacking there had departed for the exigencies of combat.

How did those children come there? Perhaps they had escaped from some guardhouse that stood ajar; perhaps there was in the vicinity, at the Barriere d'Enfer; or on the Esplanade de l'Observatoire, or in the neighboring carrefour, dominated by the pediment on which could be read: Invenerunt parvulum pannis involutum, some mountebank's booth from which they had fled; perhaps they had, on the preceding evening, escaped the eye of the inspectors of the garden at the hour of closing, and had passed the night in someone of those sentry boxes where people read the papers? The fact is, they were stray lambs and they seemed free. To be astray and to seem free is to be lost. These poor little creatures were, in fact, lost.

These two children were the same over whom Gavroche had been put to some trouble, as the reader will recollect. Children of the Thenardiers, leased out to Magnon, attributed to M. Gillenormand, and now leaves fallen from all these rootless branches, and swept over the ground by the wind. Their clothing, which had been clean in Magnon's day, and which had served her as a prospectus with M. Gillenormand, had been converted into rags.

Henceforth these beings belonged to the statistics as "Abandoned children," whom the police take note of, collect, mislay and find again on the pavements of Paris.

It required the disturbance of a day like that to account for these miserable little creatures being in that garden. If the superintendents had caught sight of them, they would have driven such rags forth. Poor little things do not enter public gardens; still, people should reflect that, as children, they have a right to flowers.

These children were there, thanks to the locked gates. They were there contrary to the regulations. They had slipped into the garden and there they remained. Closed gates do not dismiss the inspectors, oversight is supposed to continue, but it grows slack and reposes; and the inspectors, moved by the public anxiety and more occupied with the outside than the inside, no longer glanced into the garden, and had not seen the two delinquents.

It had rained the night before, and even a little in the morning. But in June, showers do not count for much. An hour after a storm, it can hardly be seen that the beautiful blonde day has wept. The earth, in summer, is as quickly dried as the cheek of a child. At that period of the solstice, the light of full noonday is, so to speak, poignant. It takes everything. It applies itself to the earth, and superposes itself with a sort of suction. One would say that the sun was thirsty. A shower is but a glass of water; a rainstorm is instantly drunk up. In the morning everything was dripping, in the afternoon everything is powdered over.

Nothing is so worthy of admiration as foliage washed by the rain and wiped by the rays of sunlight; it is warm freshness. The gardens and meadows, having water at their roots, and sun in their flowers, become perfuming-pans of incense, and smoke with all their odors at once. Everything smiles, sings and offers itself. One feels gently intoxicated. The springtime is a provisional paradise, the sun helps man to have patience.

There are beings who demand nothing further; mortals, who, having the azure of heaven, say, "It is enough!" dreamers absorbed in the wonderful, dipping into the idolatry of nature, indifferent to good and evil, contemplators of cosmos and radiantly forgetful of man, who do not understand how people can occupy themselves with the hunger of these, and the thirst of those, with the nudity of the poor in winter, with the lymphatic curvature of the little spinal column, with the pallet, the attic, the dungeon, and the rags of shivering young girls, when they can dream beneath the trees; peaceful and terrible spirits they, and pitilessly satisfied. Strange to say, the infinite suffices them. That great need of man, the finite, which admits of embrace, they ignore. The finite that admits of progress and sublime toil, they do not think about. The indefinite, which is born from the human and divine combination of the infinite and the finite, escapes them. Provided that they are face-to-face with immensity, they smile. Joy never, ecstasy forever. Their life lies in surrendering their personality in contemplation. The history of humanity is for them only a detailed plan. All is not there; the true All remains without; what is the use of busying oneself over that detail, man? Man suffers, that is quite possible; but look at Aldebaran rising! The mother has no more milk, the newborn babe is dying. I know nothing about that, but just look at this wonderful rosette that a slice of wood cells of the pine presents under the microscope! Compare the most beautiful Mechlin lace to that if you can! These thinkers forget to love. The zodiac thrives with them to such a point that it prevents their seeing the weeping child. God eclipses their souls. This is a family of minds that are, at once, great and petty. Horace was one of them; so was Goethe. La Fontaine perhaps; magnificent egoists of the infinite, tranquil spectators of sorrow, who do not behold Nero if the weather be fair, for whom the sun conceals the funeral pile, who would look on at an execution by the guillotine in the search for an effect of light, who hear neither the cry nor the sob, nor the death rattle, nor the alarm peal, for whom everything is well, since there is a month of May, who, so long as there are clouds of purple and gold above their heads, declare themselves content, and who are determined to be happy until the radiance of the stars and the songs of the birds are exhausted.

These are dark radiances. They have no suspicion that they are to be pitied. Certainly they are so. He who does not weep does not see. They are to be admired and pitied, as one would both pity and admire a being at once night and day, without eyes beneath his lashes but with a star on his brow.

The indifference of these thinkers, is, according to some, a superior philosophy. That may be; but in this superiority there is some infirmity. One may be immortal and yet limp: witness Vulcan. One may be more than man and less than man. There is incomplete immensity in nature. Who knows whether the sun is not a blind man?

But then, what? In whom can we trust? *Solem quis dicere falsum audeat?* Who shall dare to say that the sun is false? Thus certain geniuses, themselves, certain Very-Lofty mortals, man-stars, may be mistaken? That which is on high at the summit, at the crest, at the zenith, that which sends down so much light on the earth, sees but little, sees badly, sees not at all? Is not this a desperate state of things? No. But what is there, then, above the sun? The god.

On the 6th of June, 1832, about eleven o'clock in the morning, the Luxembourg, solitary and depopulated, was charming. The quincunxes and flowerbeds shed forth balm and dazzling beauty into the sunlight. The branches, wild with the brilliant glow of midday, seemed endeavoring to embrace. In the sycamores there was an uproar of linnets, sparrows triumphed, woodpeckers climbed along the chestnut trees, administering little pecks on the bark. The flowerbeds accepted the legitimate royalty of the lilies; the most august of perfumes is that which emanates from whiteness. The peppery odor of the carnations was perceptible. The old crows of Marie de Medici were amorous in the tall trees. The sun gilded, empurpled, set fire to and lighted up the tulips, which are nothing but all the varieties of flame made into flowers. All around the banks of tulips the bees, the sparks of these flame-flowers, hummed. All was grace and gaiety, even the impending rain; this relapse, by which the lilies of the valley and the honeysuckles were destined to profit, had nothing disturbing about it; the swallows indulged in the charming threat of flying low. He who was there aspired to happiness; life smelled good; all nature exhaled candor, help, assistance, paternity, caress, dawn. The thoughts that fell from heaven were as sweet as the tiny hand of a baby when one kisses it.

The statues under the trees, white and nude, had robes of shadow pierced with light; these goddesses were all tattered with sunlight; rays hung from them on all sides. Around the great fountain, the earth was already dried up to the point of being burnt. There was sufficient breeze to raise little insurrections of dust here and there. A few yellow leaves, left over from the autumn, chased each other merrily, and seemed to be playing tricks on each other.

This abundance of light had something indescribably reassuring about it. Life, sap, heat, odors overflowed; one was conscious, beneath creation, of the enormous size of the source; in all these breaths permeated with love, in this interchange of reverberations and reflections, in this marvelous expenditure of rays, in this infinite outpouring of liquid gold, one felt the prodigality of the inexhaustible; and, behind this splendor as behind a curtain of flame, one caught a glimpse of God, that millionaire of stars.

Thanks to the sand, there was not a speck of mud; thanks to the rain, there was not a grain of ashes. The clumps of blossoms had just been bathed; every sort of velvet, satin, gold and varnish, which springs from the earth in the form of flowers, was irreproachable. This magnificence was cleanly. The grand silence of happy nature filled the garden. A celestial silence that is compatible with a thousand sorts of music, the cooing of nests, the buzzing of swarms, the flutterings of the breeze. All the harmony of the season was complete in one gracious whole; the entrances and exits of spring took place in proper order; the lilacs ended; the jasmines began; some flowers were tardy, some insects in advance of their time; the vanguard of the red June butterflies fraternized with the rearguard of the white butterflies of May. The plantain trees were getting their new skins. The breeze hollowed out undulations in the magnificent enormity of the chestnut trees. It was splendid. A veteran from the neighboring barracks, who was gazing through the fence, said, "Here is the Spring presenting arms and in full uniform."

All nature was breakfasting; creation was at table; this was its hour; the great blue cloth was spread in the sky, and the great green cloth on earth; the sun lighted it all up brilliantly. God was serving the universal repast. Each creature had his pasture or his mess. The ringdove found his hempseed, the chaffinch found his millet, the goldfinch found chickweed, the redbreast found worms, the green finch found flies, the fly found infusoriae, the bee found flowers. They ate each other somewhat, it is true, which is the misery of evil mixed with good; but not a beast of them all had an empty stomach.

The two little abandoned creatures had arrived in the vicinity of the grand fountain, and, rather bewildered by all this light, they tried to hide themselves, the instinct of the poor and the weak in the presence of even impersonal magnificence; and they kept behind the swans' hutch.

Here and there, at intervals, when the wind blew, shouts, clamor, a sort of tumultuous death rattle, which was the firing, and dull blows, which were discharges of cannon, struck the ear confusedly. Smoke hung over the roofs in the direction of the Halles. A bell, which had the air of an appeal, was ringing in the distance.

These children did not appear to notice these noises. The little one repeated from time to time: "I am hungry."

Almost at the same instant with the children, another couple approached the great basin. They consisted of a goodman, about fifty years of age, who was leading by the hand a little fellow of six. No doubt, a father and his son. The little man of six had a big brioche.

At that epoch, certain houses abutting on the river, in the Rues Madame and d'Enfer, had keys to the Luxembourg garden, of which the lodgers enjoyed the use when the gates were shut, a privilege that was suppressed later on. This father and son came from one of these houses, no doubt.

The two poor little creatures watched "that gentleman" approaching, and hid themselves a little more thoroughly.

He was a bourgeois. The same person, perhaps, whom Marius had one day heard, through his love fever, near the same grand basin, counseling his son "to avoid excesses." He had an affable and haughty air, and a mouth that was always smiling, since it did not shut. This mechanical smile, produced by too much jaw and too little skin, shows the teeth rather than the soul. The child, with his brioche, which he had bitten into but had not finished eating, seemed satiated. The child was dressed as a National Guardsman, owing to the insurrection, and the father had remained clad as a bourgeois out of prudence.

Father and son halted near the fountain where two swans were sporting. This bourgeois appeared to cherish a special admiration for the swans. He resembled them in this sense, that he walked like them.

For the moment, the swans were swimming, which is their principal talent, and they were superb.

If the two poor little beings had listened and if they had been of an age to understand, they might have gathered the words of this grave man. The father was saying to his son, "The sage lives content with little. Look at me, my son. I do not love pomp. I am never seen in clothes decked with gold lace and stones; I leave that false splendor to badly organized souls."

Here the deep shouts that proceeded from the direction of the Halles burst out with fresh force of bell and uproar.

"What is that?" inquired the child.

The father replied, "It is the Saturnalia."

All at once, he caught sight of the two little ragged boys behind the green swanhutch.

"There is the beginning," said he.

And, after a pause, he added, "Anarchy is entering this garden."

In the meanwhile, his son took a bite of his brioche, spit it out, and, suddenly burst out crying.

"What are you crying about?" demanded his father.

"I am not hungry any more," said the child.

The father's smile became more accentuated.

"One does not need to be hungry in order to eat a cake."

"My cake tires me. It is stale."

"Don't you want any more of it?"

"No."

The father pointed to the swans.

"Throw it to those palmipeds."

The child hesitated. A person may not want any more of his cake; but that is no reason for giving it away.

The father went on, "Be humane. You must have compassion on animals."

And, taking the cake from his son, he flung it into the basin.

The cake fell very near the edge.

The swans were far away, in the center of the basin, and busy with some prey. They had seen neither the bourgeois nor the brioche.

The bourgeois, feeling that the cake was in danger of being wasted, and moved by this useless shipwreck, entered upon a telegraphic agitation, which finally attracted the attention of the swans.

They perceived something floating, steered for the edge like ships, as they are, and slowly directed their course toward the brioche, with the stupid majesty that befits white creatures.

"The swans understand signs," said the bourgeois, delighted to make a jest.

At that moment, the distant tumult of the city underwent another sudden increase. This time it was sinister. There are some gusts of wind that speak more distinctly than others. The one that was blowing at that moment brought clearly defined drumbeats, clamors, platoon firing, and the dismal replies of the tocsin and the cannon. This coincided with a black cloud that suddenly veiled the sun.

The swans had not yet reached the brioche.

"Let us return home," said the father, "they are attacking the Tuileries."

He grasped his son's hand again. Then he continued, "From the Tuileries to the Luxembourg, there is but the distance that separates Royalty from the peerage; that is not far. Shots will soon rain down."

He glanced at the cloud.

"Perhaps it is rain itself that is about to shower down; the sky is joining in; the younger branch is condemned. Let us return home quickly."

"I should like to see the swans eat the brioche," said the child.

The father replied, "That would be imprudent."

And he led his little bourgeois away.

The son, regretting the swans, turned his head back toward the basin until a corner of the quincunxes concealed it from him.

In the meanwhile, the two little waifs had approached the brioche at the same time as the swans. It was floating on the water. The smaller of them stared at the cake, the elder gazed after the retreating bourgeois.

Father and son entered the labyrinth of walks that leads to the grand flight of steps near the clump of trees on the side of the Rue Madame.

As soon as they had disappeared from view, the elder child hastily flung himself flat on his stomach on the rounding curb of the basin, and clinging to it with his left hand, and leaning over the water, on the verge of falling in, he stretched out his right hand with his stick toward the cake. The swans, perceiving the enemy, made haste, and in so doing, they produced an effect of their breasts that was of service to the little fisher; the water flowed back before the swans, and one of these gentle concentric undulations softly floated the brioche toward the child's wand. Just as the swans came up, the stick touched the cake. The child gave it a brisk rap, drew in the brioche, frightened away the swans, seized the cake, and sprang to his feet. The cake was wet; but they were hungry and thirsty. The elder broke the cake into two portions, a large one and a small one, took the small one for himself, gave the large one to his brother, and said to him, "Ram that into your muzzle."

CHAPTER XVII—MORTUUS PATER FILIUM MORITURUM EXPECTAT

Marius dashed out of the barricade, Combeferre followed him. But he was too late. Gavroche was dead. Combeferre brought back the basket of cartridges; Marius bore the child.

"Alas!" he thought. "That which the father had done for his father, he was requiting to the son; only, Thenardier had brought back his father alive; he was bringing back the child dead."

When Marius reentered the redoubt with Gavroche in his arms, his face, like the child, was inundated with blood.

At the moment when he had stooped to lift Gavroche, a bullet had grazed his head; he had not noticed it.

Courfeyrac untied his cravat and with it bandaged Marius's brow.

They laid Gavroche on the same table with Mabeuf, and spread over the two corpses the black shawl. There was enough of it for both the old man and the child.

Combeferre distributed the cartridges from the basket that he had brought in.

This gave each man fifteen rounds to fire.

Jean Valjean was still in the same place, motionless on his stone post. When Combeferre offered him his fifteen cartridges, he shook his head.

"Here's a rare eccentric," said Combeferre in a low voice to Enjolras. "He finds a way of not fighting in this barricade."

"Which does not prevent him from defending it," responded Enjolras.

"Heroism has its originals," resumed Combeferre.

And Courfeyrac, who had overheard, added, "He is another sort from Father Mabeuf."

One thing that must be noted is, that the fire that was battering the barricade hardly disturbed the interior. Those who have never traversed the whirlwind of this sort of war can form no idea of the singular moments of tranquillity mingled with these convulsions. Men go and come, they talk, they jest, they lounge. Someone whom we know heard a combatant say to him in the midst of the grapeshot, "We are here as at a bachelor breakfast." The redoubt of the Rue de la Chanvrerie, we repeat, seemed very calm within. All mutations and all phases had been, or were about to be, exhausted. The position, from critical, had become menacing, and, from menacing, was probably about to become desperate. In proportion as the situation grew gloomy, the glow of heroism empurpled the barricade more and more. Enjolras, who was grave, dominated it, in the attitude of a young Spartan sacrificing his naked sword to the somber genius, Epidotas.

Combeferre, wearing an apron, was dressing the wounds; Bossuet and Feuilly were making cartridges with the powder-flask picked up by Gavroche on the dead corporal, and Bossuet said to Feuilly, "We are soon to take the diligence for another planet"; Courfeyrac was disposing and arranging on some paving stones that he had reserved for himself near Enjolras, a complete arsenal, his sword-cane, his gun, two holster pistols, and a cudgel, with the care of a young girl setting a small dunkerque in order. Jean Valjean stared silently at the wall opposite him. An artisan was fastening Mother Hucheloup's big straw hat on his head with a string, "for fear of sunstroke," as he said. The young men from the Cougourde d'Aix were chatting merrily among themselves, as though eager to speak patois for the last time. Joly, who had taken Widow Hucheloup's mirror from the wall, was examining his tongue in it. Some combatants, having discovered a few crusts of rather mouldy bread, in a drawer, were eagerly devouring them. Marius was disturbed with regard to what his father was about to say to him.

CHAPTER XVIII—THE VULTURE BECOME PREY

We must insist upon one psychological fact peculiar to barricades. Nothing that is characteristic of that surprising war of the streets should be omitted.

Whatever may have been the singular inward tranquility we have just mentioned, the barricade, for those who are inside it, remains, nonetheless, a vision.

There is something of the apocalypse in civil war, all the mists of the unknown are commingled with fierce flashes, revolutions are sphinxes, and anyone who has passed through a barricade thinks he has traversed a dream.

The feelings to which one is subject in these places we have pointed out in the case of Marius, and we shall see the consequences; they are both more and less than life. On emerging from a barricade, one no longer knows what one has seen there. One has been terrible, but one knows it not. One has been surrounded with conflicting ideas that had human faces; one's head has been in the light of the future. There were corpses lying prone there, and phantoms standing erect. The hours were colossal and seemed hours of eternity. One has lived in death. Shadows have passed by. What were they?

One has beheld hands on which there was blood; there was a deafening horror; there was also a frightful silence; there were open mouths that shouted, and other open mouths that held their peace; one was in the midst of smoke, of night, perhaps. One fancied that one had touched the sinister ooze of unknown depths; one stares at something red on one's fingernails. One no longer remembers anything.

Let us return to the Rue de la Chanvrerie.

All at once, between two discharges, the distant sound of a clock striking the hour became audible.

"It is midday," said Combeferre.

The twelve strokes had not finished striking when Enjolras sprang to his feet, and from the summit of the barricade hurled this thundering shout, "Carry stones up into the houses; line the windowsills and the roofs with them. Half the men to their guns, the other half to the pavingstones. There is not a minute to be lost."

A squad of sappers and miners, ax on shoulder, had just made their appearance in battle array at the end of the street.

This could only be the head of a column; and of what column? The attacking column, evidently; the sappers charged with the demolition of the barricade must always precede the soldiers who are to scale it.

They were, evidently, on the brink of that moment that M. Clermont-Tonnerre, in 1822, called "the tug of war."

Enjolras's order was executed with the correct haste that is peculiar to ships and barricades, the only two scenes of combat where escape is impossible. In less than a minute, two-thirds of the stones that Enjolras had had piled up at the door of Corinthe had been carried up to the first floor and the attic, and before a second minute had elapsed, these stones, artistically set one upon the other, walled up the sash-window on the first floor and the windows in the roof to half their height. A few loopholes carefully planned by Feuilly, the principal architect, allowed of the passage of the gun barrels. This armament of the windows could be affected all the more easily since the firing of grapeshot had ceased. The two cannons were now discharging ball against the center of the barrier in order to make a hole there, and, if possible, a breach for the assault.

When the stones destined to the final defence were in place, Enjolras had the bottles that he had set under the table where Mabeuf lay, carried to the first floor.

"Who is to drink that?" Bossuet asked him.

"They," replied Enjolras.

Then they barricaded the window below, and held in readiness the iron crossbars that served to secure the door of the wine shop at night.

The fortress was complete. The barricade was the rampart, the wine shop was the dungeon. With the stones that remained, they stopped up the outlet.

As the defenders of a barricade are always obliged to be sparing of their ammunition, and as the assailants know this, the assailants combine their arrangements with a sort of irritating leisure, expose themselves to fire prematurely, though in appearance more than in reality, and take their ease. The preparations for attack are always made with a certain methodical deliberation; after which, the lightning strikes.

This deliberation permitted Enjolras to take a review of everything and to perfect everything. He felt that, since such men were to die, their death ought to be a masterpiece.

He said to Marius, "We are the two leaders. I will give the last orders inside. Do you remain outside and observe."

Marius posted himself on the lookout upon the crest of the barricade.

Enjolras had the door of the kitchen, which was the ambulance, as the reader will remember, nailed up.

"No splashing of the wounded," he said.

He issued his final orders in the taproom in a curt, but profoundly tranquil tone; Feuilly listened and replied in the name of all.

"On the first floor, hold your axes in readiness to cut the staircase. Have you them?"

"Yes," said Feuilly.

"How many?"

"Two axes and a poleax."

"That is good. There are now twenty-six combatants of us on foot. How many guns are there?"

"Thirty-four."

"Eight too many. Keep those eight guns loaded like the rest and at hand. Swords and pistols in your belts. Twenty men to the barricade. Six ambushed in the attic windows, and at the window on the first floor to fire on the assailants through the loopholes in the stones. Let not a single worker remain inactive here. Presently, when the drum beats the assault, let the twenty below stairs rush to the barricade. The first to arrive will have the best places."

These arrangements made, he turned to Javert and said, "I am not forgetting you."

And, laying a pistol on the table, he added, "The last man to leave this room will smash the skull of this spy."

"Here?" inquired a voice.

"No, let us not mix their corpses with our own. The little barricade of the Mondetour lane can be scaled. It is only four feet high. The man is well pinioned. He shall be taken there and put to death."

There was someone who was more impassive at that moment than Enjolras, it was Javert. Here Jean Valjean made his appearance.

He had been lost among the group of insurgents. He stepped forth and said to Enjolras, "You are the commander?"

"Yes."

"You thanked me a while ago."

"In the name of the Republic. The barricade has two saviors, Marius Pontmercy and yourself."

"Do you think that I deserve a recompense?"

"Certainly."

"Well, I request one."

"What is it?"

"That I may blow that man's brains out."

Javert raised his head, saw Jean Valjean, made an almost imperceptible movement, and said, "That is just."

As for Enjolras, he had begun to reload his rifle; he cut his eyes about him, "No objections."

And he turned to Jean Valjean, "Take the spy."

Jean Valjean did, in fact, take possession of Javert, by seating himself on the end of the table. He seized the pistol, and a faint click announced that he had cocked it.

Almost at the same moment, a blast of trumpets became audible.

"Take care!" shouted Marius from the top of the barricade.

Javert began to laugh with that noiseless laugh that was peculiar to him, and gazing intently at the insurgents, he said to them, "You are in no better case than I am."

"All out!" shouted Enjolras.

The insurgents poured out tumultuously, and, as they went, received in the back, may we be permitted the expression, this sally of Javert's, "We shall meet again shortly!"

CHAPTER XIX—JEAN VALJEAN
TAKES HIS REVENGE

When Jean Valjean was left alone with Javert, he untied the rope that fastened the prisoner across the middle of the body, and the knot of which was under the table. After this he made him a sign to rise.

Javert obeyed with that indefinable smile in which the supremacy of enchained authority is condensed.

Jean Valjean took Javert by the martingale, as one would take a beast of burden by the breast-band, and, dragging the latter after him, emerged from the wine shop slowly, because Javert, with his impeded limbs, could take only very short steps.

Jean Valjean had the pistol in his hand.

In this manner they crossed the inner trapezium of the barricade. The insurgents, all intent on the attack, which was imminent, had their backs turned to these two.

Marius alone, stationed on one side, at the extreme left of the barricade, saw them pass. This group of victim and executioner was illuminated by the sepulchral light that he bore in his own soul.

Jean Valjean with some difficulty, but without relaxing his hold for a single instant, made Javert, pinioned as he was, scale the little entrenchment in the Mondetour lane.

When they had crossed this barrier, they found themselves alone in the lane. No one saw them. Among the heap they could distinguish a livid face, streaming hair, a pierced hand and the half nude breast of a woman. It was Eponine. The corner of the houses hid them from the insurgents. The corpses carried away from the barricade formed a terrible pile a few paces distant.

Javert gazed askance at this body, and, profoundly calm, said in a low tone, "It strikes me that I know that girl."

Then he turned to Jean Valjean.

Jean Valjean thrust the pistol under his arm and fixed on Javert a look that it required no words to interpret, "Javert, it is I."

Javert replied, "Take your revenge."

Jean Valjean drew from his pocket a knife, and opened it.

"A clasp-knife!" exclaimed Javert, "you are right. That suits you better."

Jean Valjean cut the martingale that Javert had about his neck, then he cut the cords on his wrists, then, stooping down, he cut the cord on his feet; and, straightening himself up, he said to him, "You are free."

Javert was not easily astonished. Still, master of himself though he was, he could not repress a start. He remained open-mouthed and motionless.

Jean Valjean continued, "I do not think that I shall escape from this place. But if, by chance, I do, I live, under the name of Fauchelevent, in the Rue de l'Homme Arme, No. 7."

Javert snarled like a tiger, which made him half open one corner of his mouth, and he muttered between his teeth, "Have a care."

"Go," said Jean Valjean.

Javert began again, "Thou saidst Fauchelevent, Rue de l'Homme Arme?"

"Number 7."

Javert repeated in a low voice, "Number 7."

He buttoned up his coat once more, resumed the military stiffness between his shoulders, made a half turn, folded his arms and, supporting his chin on one of his hands, he set out in the direction of the Halles. Jean Valjean followed him with his eyes.

A few minutes later, Javert turned around and shouted to Jean Valjean, "You annoy me. Kill me, rather."

Javert himself did not notice that he no longer addressed Jean Valjean as "thou."

"Be off with you," said Jean Valjean.

Javert retreated slowly. A moment later he turned the corner of the Rue des Prêcheurs.

When Javert had disappeared, Jean Valjean fired his pistol in the air.

Then he returned to the barricade and said, "It is done."

In the meanwhile, this is what had taken place.

Marius, more intent on the outside than on the interior, had not, up to that time, taken a good look at the pinioned spy in the dark background of the taproom.

When he beheld him in broad daylight, striding over the barricade in order to proceed to his death, he recognized him. Something suddenly recurred to his mind. He recalled the inspector of the Rue de Pontoise, and the two pistols that the latter had handed to him and that he, Marius, had used in this very barricade, and not only did he recall his face, but his name as well.

This recollection was misty and troubled, however, like all his ideas.

It was not an affirmation that he made, but a question that he put to himself, "Is not that the inspector of police who told me that his name was Javert?"

Perhaps there was still time to intervene in behalf of that man. But, in the first place, he must know whether this was Javert.

Marius called to Enjolras, who had just stationed himself at the other extremity of the barricade, "Enjolras!"

"What?"

"What is the name of yonder man?"

"What man?"

"The police agent. Do you know his name?"

"Of course. He told us."

"What is it?"

"Javert."

Marius sprang to his feet.

At that moment, they heard the report of the pistol.

Jean Valjean re-appeared and cried: "It is done."

A gloomy chill traversed Marius's heart.

CHAPTER XX—THE DEAD ARE IN THE RIGHT AND THE LIVING ARE NOT IN THE WRONG

The death agony of the barricade was about to begin.

Everything contributed to its tragic majesty at that supreme moment; a thousand mysterious crashes in the air, the breath of armed masses set in movement in the streets that were not visible, the intermittent gallop of cavalry, the heavy shock of artillery on the march, the firing by squads, and the cannonades crossing each other in the labyrinth of Paris, the smokes of battle mounting all gilded above the roofs, indescribable and vaguely terrible cries, lightnings of menace everywhere, the tocsin of Saint-Merry, which now had the accents of a sob, the mildness of the weather, the splendor of the sky filled with sun and clouds, the beauty of the day, and the alarming silence of the houses.

For, since the preceding evening, the two rows of houses in the Rue de la Chanvrerie had become two walls; ferocious walls, doors closed, windows closed, shutters closed.

In those days, so different from those in which we live, when the hour was come, when the people wished to put an end to a situation, which had lasted too long, with a charter granted or with a legal country, when universal wrath was diffused in the atmosphere, when the city consented to the tearing up of the pavements, when insurrection made the bourgeoisie smile by whispering its password in its ear, then the inhabitant, thoroughly penetrated with the revolt, so to speak, was the auxiliary of the combatant, and the house fraternized with the improvised fortress that rested on it. When the situation was not ripe, when the insurrection was not decidedly admitted, when the masses disowned the movement, all was over with the combatants, the city was changed into a desert around the revolt, souls grew chilled, refuges were nailed up, and the street turned into a defile to help the army to take the barricade.

A people cannot be forced, through surprise, to walk more quickly than it chooses. Woe to whomsoever tries to force its hand! A people does not let itself go at random. Then it abandons the insurrection to itself. The insurgents become noxious, infected with the plague. A house is an escarpment, a door is a refusal, a facade is a wall. This wall hears, sees and will not. It might open and save you. No. This wall is a judge. It gazes at you and condemns you. What dismal things are closed houses. They seem dead, they are living. Life that is, as it were, suspended there, persists there. No one has gone out of them for four and twenty hours, but no one is missing from them. In the interior of that rock, people go and come, go to bed and rise again; they are a family party there; there they eat and drink; they are afraid, a terrible thing! Fear excuses this fearful lack of hospitality; terror is mixed with it, an extenuating circumstance. Sometimes, even, and this has been actually seen, fear turns to passion; fright may change into fury, as prudence does into rage; hence this wise saying, "The enraged moderates." There are outbursts of supreme terror, from which springs wrath like a mournful smoke. "What do these people want? What have they come there to do? Let them get out of the scrape. So much the worse for them. It is their fault. They are only getting what they deserve. It does not concern us. Here is our poor street all riddled with balls. They are a pack of rascals. Above all things, don't open the door." And the house assumes the air of a tomb. The insurgent is in the death-throes in front of that house; he sees the grapeshot and naked swords drawing near; if he cries, he knows that they are listening to him, and that no one will come; there stand walls that might protect him, there are men who might save him; and these walls have ears of flesh, and these men have bowels of stone.

Whom shall he reproach?

No one and everyone.

The incomplete times in which we live.

It is always at its own risk and peril that Utopia is converted into revolution, and from philosophical protest becomes an armed protest, and from Minerva turns to Pallas.

The Utopia that grows impatient and becomes revolt knows what awaits it; it almost always comes too soon. Then it becomes resigned, and stoically accepts catastrophe in lieu of triumph. It serves those who deny it without complaint, even excusing them, and even disculpates them, and its magnanimity consists in consenting to abandonment. It is indomitable in the face of obstacles and gentle toward ingratitude.

Is this ingratitude, however?

Yes, from the point of view of the human race.

No, from the point of view of the individual.

Progress is man's mode of existence. The general life of the human race is called Progress, the collective stride of the human race is called Progress. Progress advances; it makes the great human and terrestrial journey toward the celestial and the divine; it has its halting places where it rallies the laggard troop, it has its stations where it meditates, in the presence of some splendid Canaan suddenly unveiled on its horizon, it has its nights when it sleeps; and it is one of the poignant anxieties of the thinker that he sees the shadow resting on the human soul, and that he gropes in darkness without being able to awaken that slumbering Progress.

"God is dead, perhaps," said Gerard de Nerval one day to the writer of these lines, confounding progress with God, and taking the interruption of movement for the death of Being.

He who despairs is in the wrong. Progress infallibly awakes, and, in short, we may say that it marches on, even when it is asleep, for it has increased in size. When we behold it erect once more, we find it taller. To be always peaceful does not depend on progress any more than it does on the stream; erect no barriers, cast in no boulders; obstacles make water froth and humanity boil. Hence arise troubles; but after these troubles, we recognize the fact that ground has been gained. Until order, which is nothing else than universal peace, has been established, until harmony and unity reign, progress will have revolutions as its halting-places.

What, then, is progress? We have just enunciated it; the permanent life of the peoples.

Now, it sometimes happens, that the momentary life of individuals offers resistance to the eternal life of the human race.

Let us admit without bitterness, that the individual has his distinct interests, and can, without forfeiture, stipulate for his interest, and defend it; the present has its pardonable dose of egotism; momentary life has its rights, and is not bound to sacrifice itself constantly to the future. The generation that is passing in its turn over the earth, is not forced to abridge it for the sake of the generations, its equal, after all, who will have their turn later on. "I exist," murmurs that someone whose name is All. "I am young and in love, I am old and I wish to repose, I am the father of a family, I toil, I prosper, I am successful in business, I have houses to lease, I have money in the government funds, I am happy, I have a wife and children, I have all this, I desire to live, leave me in peace." Hence, at certain hours, a profound cold broods over the magnanimous vanguard of the human race.

Utopia, moreover, we must admit, quits its radiant sphere when it makes war. It, the truth of tomorrow, borrows its mode of procedure, battle, from the lie of yesterday. It, the future, behaves like the past. It, pure idea, becomes a deed of violence. It complicates its heroism with a violence for which it is just that it should be held to answer; a violence of occasion and expedient, contrary to principle, and for which it is fatally punished. The Utopia, insurrection, fights with the old military code in its fist; it shoots spies, it executes traitors; it suppresses living beings and flings them into unknown darkness. It makes use of death, a serious matter. It seems as though Utopia had no longer any faith in radiance, its irresistible and incorruptible force. It strikes with the sword. Now, no sword is simple. Every blade has two edges; he who wounds with the one is wounded with the other.

Having made this reservation, and made it with all severity, it is impossible for us not to admire, whether they succeed or not, those the glorious combatants of the future, the confessors of Utopia. Even when they miscarry, they are worthy of veneration; and it is, perhaps, in failure, that they possess the most majesty. Victory, when it is in accord with progress, merits the applause of the people; but a heroic defeat merits their tender compassion. The one is magnificent, the other sublime. For our own part, we prefer martyrdom to success. John Brown is greater than Washington, and Pisacane is greater than Garibaldi.

It certainly is necessary that someone should take the part of the vanquished.

We are unjust toward these great men who attempt the future, when they fail.

Revolutionists are accused of sowing fear abroad. Every barricade seems a crime. Their theories are incriminated, their aim suspected, their ulterior motive is feared, their conscience denounced. They are reproached with raising, erecting, and heaping up, against the reigning social state, a mass of miseries, of griefs, of iniquities, of wrongs, of despairs, and of tearing from the lowest depths blocks of shadow in order therein to embattle themselves and to combat. People shout to them, "You are tearing up the pavements of hell!" They might reply, "That is because our barricade is made of good intentions."

The best thing, assuredly, is the pacific solution. In short, let us agree that when we behold the pavement, we think of the bear, and it is a good will that renders society uneasy. But it depends on society to save itself, it is to its own good will that we make our appeal. No violent remedy is necessary. To study evil amiably, to prove its existence, then to cure it. It is to this that we invite it.

However that may be, even when fallen, above all when fallen, these men, who at every point of the universe, with their eyes fixed on France, are striving for the grand work with the inflexible logic of the ideal, are august; they give their life a free offering to progress; they accomplish the will of providence; they perform a religious act. At the appointed hour, with as much disinterestedness as an actor who answers to his cue, in obedience to the divine stage manager, they enter the tomb. And this hopeless combat, this stoical disappearance they accept in order to bring about the supreme and universal consequences, the magnificent and irresistibly human movement begun on the 14th of July, 1789; these soldiers are priests. The French revolution is an act of God.

Moreover, there are, and it is proper to add this distinction to the distinctions already pointed out in another chapter, there are accepted revolutions, revolutions that are called revolutions; there are refused revolutions, which are called riots.

An insurrection that breaks out, is an idea that is passing its examination before the people. If the people lets fall a black ball, the idea is dried fruit; the insurrection is a mere skirmish.

Waging war at every summons and every time that Utopia desires it, is not the thing for the peoples. Nations have not always and at every hour the temperament of heroes and martyrs.

They are positive. A priori, insurrection is repugnant to them, in the first place, because it often results in a catastrophe, in the second place, because it always has an abstraction as its point of departure.

Because, and this is a noble thing, it is always for the ideal, and for the ideal alone, that those who sacrifice themselves do thus sacrifice themselves. An insurrection is an enthusiasm. Enthusiasm may wax wroth; hence the appeal to arms. But every insurrection, which aims at a government or a regime, aims higher. Thus, for instance, and we insist upon it, what the chiefs of the insurrection of 1832, and, in particular, the young enthusiasts of the Rue de la Chanvrerie were combating, was not precisely Louis Philippe. The majority of them, when talking freely, did justice to this king who stood midway between monarchy and revolution; no one hated him. But they attacked the younger branch of the divine right in Louis Philippe as they had attacked its elder branch in Charles X; and that which they wished to overturn in overturning royalty in France, was, as we have explained, the usurpation of man over man, and of privilege over right in the entire universe. Paris without a king has as result the world without despots. This is the manner in which they reasoned. Their aim was distant no doubt, vague perhaps, and it retreated in the face of their efforts; but it was great.

Thus it is. And we sacrifice ourselves for these visions, which are almost always illusions for the sacrificed, but illusions with which, after all, the whole of human certainty is mingled. We throw ourselves into these tragic affairs and become intoxicated with that which we are about to do. Who knows? We may succeed. We are few in number, we have a whole army arrayed against us; but we are defending right, the natural law, the sovereignty of each one over himself from which no abdication is possible, justice and truth, and in case of need, we die like the three hundred Spartans. We do not think of Don Quixote but of Leonidas. And we march straight before us, and once pledged, we do not draw back, and we rush onward with head held low, cherishing as our hope an unprecedented victory, revolution completed, progress set free again, the aggrandizement of the human race, universal deliverance; and in the event of the worst, Thermopylae.

These passages of arms for the sake of progress often suffer shipwreck, and we have just explained why. The crowd is restive in the presence of the impulses of paladins. Heavy masses, the multitudes that are fragile because of their very weight, fear adventures; and there is a touch of adventure in the ideal.

Moreover, and we must not forget this, interests that are not very friendly to the ideal and the sentimental are in the way. Sometimes the stomach paralyzes the heart.

The grandeur and beauty of France lies in this, that she takes less from the stomach than other nations: she more easily knots the rope about her loins. She is the first awake, the last asleep. She marches forwards. She is a seeker.

This arises from the fact that she is an artist.

The ideal is nothing but the culminating point of logic, the same as the beautiful is nothing but the summit of the true. Artistic peoples are also consistent peoples. To love beauty is to see the light. That is why the torch of Europe, that is to say of civilization, was first borne by Greece, who passed it on to Italy, who handed it on to France. Divine, illuminating nations of scouts! Vitaelampada tradunt.

It is an admirable thing that the poetry of a people is the element of its progress. The amount of civilization is measured by the quantity of imagination. Only, a civilizing people should remain a manly people. Corinth, yes; Sybaris, no. Whoever becomes effeminate makes himself a bastard. He must be neither a dilettante nor a virtuoso: but he must be artistic. In the matter of civilization, he must not refine, but he must sublime. On this condition, one gives to the human race the pattern of the ideal.

The modern ideal has its type in art, and its means is science. It is through science that it will realize that august vision of the poets, the socially beautiful. Eden will be reconstructed by A+B. At the point that civilization has now reached, the exact is a necessary element of the splendid, and the artistic sentiment is not only served, but completed by the scientific organ; dreams must be calculated. Art, which is the conqueror, should have for support science, which is the walker; the solidity of the creature that is ridden is of importance. The modern spirit is the genius of Greece with the genius of India as its vehicle; Alexander on the elephant.

Races that are petrified in dogma or demoralized by lucre are unfit to guide civilization. Genuflection before the idol or before money wastes away the muscles that walk and the will that advances. Hieratic or mercantile absorption lessens a people's power of radiance, lowers its horizon by lowering its level, and deprives it of that intelligence, at once both human and divine of the universal goal, which makes missionaries of nations. Babylon has no ideal; Carthage has no ideal. Athens and Rome have and keep, throughout all the nocturnal darkness of the centuries, halos of civilization.

France is in the same quality of race as Greece and Italy. She is Athenian in the matter of beauty, and Roman in her greatness. Moreover, she is good. She gives herself. Oftener than is the case with other races, is she in the humor for self-devotion and sacrifice. Only, this humor seizes upon her, and again abandons her. And therein lies the great peril for those who run when she desires only to walk, or who walk on when she desires to halt. France has her relapses into materialism, and, at certain instants, the ideas that obstruct that sublime brain have no longer anything that recalls French greatness and are of the dimensions of a Missouri or a South Carolina. What is to be done in such a case? The giantess plays at being a dwarf; immense France has her freaks of pettiness. That is all.

To this there is nothing to say. Peoples, like planets, possess the right to an eclipse. And all is well, provided that the light returns and that the eclipse does not degenerate into night. Dawn and resurrection are synonymous. The reappearance of the light is identical with the persistence of the "I."

Let us state these facts calmly. Death on the barricade or the tomb in exile, is an acceptable occasion for devotion. The real name of devotion is disinterestedness. Let the abandoned allow themselves to be abandoned, let the exiled allow themselves to be exiled, and let us confine ourselves to entreating great nations not to retreat too far, when they do retreat. One must not push too far in descent under pretext of a return to reason.

Matter exists, the minute exists, interest exists, the stomach exists; but the stomach must not be the sole wisdom. The life of the moment has its rights, we admit, but permanent life has its rights also. Alas! The fact that one is mounted does not preclude a fall. This can be seen in history more frequently than is desirable. A nation is great, it tastes the ideal, then it bites the mire, and finds it good; and if it be asked how it happens that it has abandoned Socrates for Falstaff, it replies, "Because I love statesmen."

One word more before returning to our subject, the conflict.

A battle like the one we are engaged in describing is nothing else than a convulsion toward the ideal. Progress trammelled is sickly, and is subject to these tragic epilepsies. With that malady of progress, civil war, we have been obliged to come in contact in our passage. This is one of the fatal phases, at once act and entr'acte of that drama whose pivot is a social condemnation, and whose veritable title is Progress.

Progress!

The cry to which we frequently give utterance is our whole thought; and, at the point of this drama, which we have now reached, the idea that it contains having still more than one trial to undergo, it is, perhaps, permitted to us, if not to lift the veil from it, to at least allow its light to shine through.

The book that the reader has under his eye at this moment is, from one end to the other, as a whole and in detail, whatever may be its intermittences, exceptions and faults, the march from evil to good, from the unjust to the just, from night to day, from appetite to conscience, from rottenness to life, from hell to heaven, from nothingness to God. Point of departure: matter; point of arrival: the soul. The hydra at the beginning, the angel at the end.

CHAPTER XXI—THE HEROES

All at once, the drum beat the charge.

The attack was a hurricane. On the evening before, in the darkness, the barricade had been approached silently, as by a boa. Now, in broad daylight, in that widening street, surprise was decidedly impossible, rude force had, moreover, been unmasked, the cannon had begun the roar, the army hurled itself on the barricade. Fury now became skill. A powerful detachment of infantry of the line, broken at regular intervals, by the National Guard and the Municipal Guard on foot, and supported by serried masses that could be heard though not seen, debauched into the street at a run, with drums beating, trumpets braying, bayonets levelled, the sappers at their head, and, imperturbable under the projectiles, charged straight for the barricade with the weight of a brazen beam against a wall.

The wall held firm.

The insurgents fired impetuously. The barricade once scaled had a mane of lightning flashes. The assault was so furious, that for one moment, it was inundated with assailants; but it shook off the soldiers as the lion shakes off the dogs, and it was only covered with besiegers as the cliff is covered with foam, to reappear, a moment later, beetling, black and formidable.

The column, forced to retreat, remained massed in the street, unprotected but terrible, and replied to the redoubt with a terrible discharge of musketry. Anyone who has seen fireworks will recall the sheaf formed of interlacing lightnings that is called a bouquet. Let the reader picture to himself this bouquet, no longer vertical but horizontal, bearing a bullet, buck-shot or a biscaien at the tip of each one of its jets of flame, and picking off dead men one after another from its clusters of lightning. The barricade was underneath it.

On both sides, the resolution was equal. The bravery exhibited there was almost barbarous and was complicated with a sort of heroic ferocity that began by the sacrifice of self.

This was the epoch when a National Guardsman fought like a Zouave. The troop wished to make an end of it, insurrection was desirous of fighting. The acceptance of the death agony in the flower of youth and in the flush of health turns intrepidity into frenzy. In this fray, each one underwent the broadening growth of the death hour. The street was strewn with corpses.

The barricade had Enjolras at one of its extremities and Marius at the other. Enjolras, who carried the whole barricade in his head, reserved and sheltered himself; three soldiers fell, one after the other, under his embrasure, without having even seen him; Marius fought unprotected. He made himself a target. He stood with more than half his body above the breastworks. There is no more violent prodigal than the avaricious man who takes the bit in his teeth; there is no man more terrible in action than a dreamer. Marius was formidable and pensive. In battle he was as in a dream. One would have pronounced him a phantom engaged in firing a gun.

The insurgents' cartridges were giving out; but not their sarcasms. In this whirlwind of the sepulchre in which they stood, they laughed.

Courfeyrac was bareheaded.

"What have you done with your hat?" Bossuet asked him.

Courfeyrac replied, "They have finally taken it away from me with cannon balls."

Or they uttered haughty comments.

"Can anyone understand," exclaimed Feuilly bitterly, "those men, [and he cited names, well-known names, even celebrated names, some belonging to the old army]—who had promised to join us, and taken an oath to aid us, and who had pledged their honor to it, and who are our generals, and who abandon us!"

And Combeferre restricted himself to replying with a grave smile.

"There are people who observe the rules of honor as one observes the stars, from a great distance."

The interior of the barricade was so strewn with torn cartridges that one would have said that there had been a snowstorm.

The assailants had numbers in their favor; the insurgents had position. They were at the top of a wall, and they thundered point-blank upon the soldiers tripping over the dead and wounded and entangled in the escarpment. This barricade, constructed as it was and admirably buttressed, was really one of those situations where a handful of men hold a legion in check. Nevertheless, the attacking column, constantly recruited and enlarged under the shower of bullets, drew inexorably nearer, and now, little by little, step by step, but surely, the army closed in around the barricade as the vice grasps the wine press.

One assault followed another. The horror of the situation kept increasing.

Then there burst forth on that heap of paving stones, in that Rue de la Chanvrerie, a battle worthy of a wall of Troy. These haggard, ragged, exhausted men, who had had nothing to eat for four and twenty hours, who had not slept, who had but a few more rounds to fire, who were fumbling in their pockets that had been emptied of cartridges, nearly all of whom were wounded, with head or arm bandaged with black and blood-stained linen, with holes in their clothes from which the blood trickled, and who were hardly armed with poor guns and notched swords, became Titans. The barricade was ten times attacked, approached, assailed, scaled, and never captured.

In order to form an idea of this struggle, it is necessary to imagine fire set to a throng of terrible courages, and then to gaze at the conflagration. It was not a combat, it was the interior of a furnace; there mouths breathed the flame; there countenances were extraordinary. The human form seemed impossible there, the combatants flamed forth there, and it was formidable to behold the going and coming in that red glow of those salamanders of the fray.

The successive and simultaneous scenes of this grand slaughter we renounce all attempts at depicting. The epic alone has the right to fill twelve thousand verses with a battle.

One would have pronounced this that hell of Brahmanism, the most redoubtable of the seventeen abysses, which the Veda calls the Forest of Swords.

They fought hand to hand, foot to foot, with pistol shots, with blows of the sword, with their fists, at a distance, close at hand, from above, from below, from everywhere, from the roofs of the houses, from the windows of the wine shop, from the cellar windows, where some had crawled. They were one against sixty.

The facade of Corinthe, half demolished, was hideous. The window, tattooed with grapeshot, had lost glass and frame and was nothing now but a shapeless hole, tumultuously blocked with paving stones.

Bossuet was killed; Feuilly was killed; Courfeyrac was killed; Combeferre, transfixed by three blows from a bayonet in the breast at the moment when he was lifting up a wounded soldier, had only time to cast a glance to heaven when he expired.

Marius, still fighting, was so riddled with wounds, particularly in the head, that his countenance disappeared beneath the blood, and one would have said that his face was covered with a red kerchief.

Enjolras alone was not struck. When he had no longer any weapon, he reached out his hands to right and left and an insurgent thrust some arm or other into his fist. All he had left was the stumps of four swords; one more than Francois I at Marignan. Homer says, "Diomedes cuts the throat of Axylus, son of Teuthranis, who dwelled in happy Arisba; Euryalus, son of Mecistaeus, exterminates Dresos and Opheltios, Esepius, and that Pedasus whom the naiad Abarbarea bore to the blameless Bucolion; Ulysses overthrows Pidytes of Percosius; Antilochus, Ablerus; Polypaetes, Astyalus; Polydamas, Otos, of Cyllene; and Teucer, Aretaon. Meganthios dies under the blows of Euripylus' pike. Agamemnon, king of the heroes, flings to earth Elatos, born in the rocky city that is laved by the sounding river Satnois." In our old poems of exploits, Esplandian attacks the giant marquis Swantibore with a cobbler's shoulder-stick of fire, and the latter defends himself by stoning the hero with towers that he plucks up by the roots. Our ancient mural frescoes show us the two Dukes of Bretagne and Bourbon, armed, emblazoned and crested in warlike guise, on horseback and approaching each other, their battleaxes in hand, masked with iron, gloved with iron, booted with iron, the one caparisoned in ermine, the other draped in azure: Bretagne with his lion between the two horns of his crown, Bourbon helmeted with a monster fleur de lis on his visor. But, in order to be superb, it is not necessary to wear, like Yvon, the ducal morion, to have in the fist, like Esplandian, a living flame, or, like Phyles, father of Polydamas, to have brought back from Ephyra a good suit of mail, a present from the king of men, Euphetes; it suffices to give one's life for a conviction or a loyalty. This ingenuous little soldier, yesterday a peasant of Bauce or Limousin, who prowls with his clasp-knife by his side, around the children's nurses in the Luxembourg garden, this pale young student bent over a piece of anatomy or a book, a blond youth who shaves his beard with scissors, take both of them, breathe upon them with a breath of duty, place them face to face in the Carrefour Boucherat or in the blind alley Planche-Mibray, and let the one fight for his flag, and the other for his ideal, and let both of them imagine that they are fighting for their country; the struggle will be colossal; and the shadow that this raw recruit and this sawbones in conflict will produce in that grand epic field where humanity is striving, will equal the shadow cast by Megaryon, King of Lycia, tiger-filled, crushing in his embrace the immense body of Ajax, equal to the gods.

CHAPTER XXII—FOOT TO FOOT

When there were no longer any of the leaders left alive, except Enjolras and Marius at the two extremities of the barricade, the center, which had so long sustained Courfeyrac, Joly, Bossuet, Feuilly and Combeferre, gave way. The cannon, though it had not effected a practicable breach, had made a rather large hollow in the middle of the redoubt; there, the summit of the wall had disappeared before the balls, and had crumbled away; and the rubbish that had fallen, now inside, now outside, had, as it accumulated, formed two piles in the nature of slopes on the two sides of the barrier, one on the inside, the other on the outside. The exterior slope presented an inclined plane to the attack.

A final assault was there attempted, and this assault succeeded. The mass bristling with bayonets and hurled forward at a run, came up with irresistible force, and the serried front of battle of the attacking column made its appearance through the smoke on the crest of the battlements. This time, it was decisive. The group of insurgents who were defending the center retreated in confusion.

Then the gloomy love of life awoke once more in some of them. Many, finding themselves under the muzzles of this forest of guns, did not wish to die. This is a moment when the instinct of self-preservation emits howls, when the beast re-appears in men. They were hemmed in by the lofty, six-story house that formed the background of their redoubt. This house might prove their salvation. The building was barricaded, and walled, as it were, from top to bottom. Before the troops of the line had reached the interior of the redoubt, there was time for a door to open and shut, the space of a flash of lightning was sufficient for that, and the door of that house, suddenly opened a crack and closed again instantly, was life for these despairing men. Behind this house, there were streets, possible flight, space. They set to knocking at that door with the butts of their guns, and with kicks, shouting, calling, entreating, wringing their hands. No one opened. From the little window on the third floor, the head of the dead man gazed down upon them.

But Enjolras and Marius, and the seven or eight rallied about them, sprang forward and protected them. Enjolras had shouted to the soldiers, "Don't advance!" and as an officer had not obeyed, Enjolras had killed the officer. He was now in the little inner court of the redoubt, with his back planted against the Corinthe building, a sword in one hand, a rifle in the other, holding open the door of the wine shop that he barred against assailants. He shouted to the desperate men, "There is but one door open; this one." And shielding them with his body, and facing an entire battalion alone, he made them pass in behind him. All precipitated themselves there. Enjolras, executing with his rifle, which he now used like a cane, what single-stick players call a "covered rose" around his head, levelled the bayonets around and in front of him, and was the last to enter; and then ensued a horrible moment, when the soldiers tried to make their way in, and the insurgents strove to bar them out. The door was slammed with such violence, that, as it fell back into its frame, it showed the five fingers of a soldier who had been clinging to it, cut off and glued to the post.

Marius remained outside. A shot had just broken his collarbone, he felt that he was fainting and falling. At that moment, with eyes already shut, he felt the shock of a vigorous hand seizing him, and the swoon in which his senses vanished, hardly allowed him time for the thought, mingled with a last memory of Cosette,"I am taken prisoner. I shall be shot."

Enjolras, not seeing Marius among those who had taken refuge in the wine shop, had the same idea. But they had reached a moment when each man has not the time to meditate on his own death. Enjolras fixed the bar across the door, and bolted it, and double-locked it with key and chain, while those outside were battering furiously at it, the soldiers with the butts of their muskets, the sappers with their axes. The assailants were grouped about that door. The siege of the wine shop was now beginning.

The soldiers, we will observe, were full of wrath.

The death of the artillery-sergeant had enraged them, and then, a still more melancholy circumstance. During the few hours that had preceded the attack, it had been reported among them that the insurgents were mutilating their prisoners, and that there was the headless body of a soldier in the wine shop. This sort of fatal rumor is the usual accompaniment of civil wars, and it was a false report of this kind that, later on, produced the catastrophe of the Rue Transnonain.

When the door was barricaded, Enjolras said to the others, "Let us sell our lives dearly."

Then he approached the table on which lay Mabeuf and Gavroche. Beneath the black cloth two straight and rigid forms were visible, one large, the other small, and the two faces were vaguely outlined beneath the cold folds of the shroud. A hand projected from beneath the winding sheet and hung near the floor. It was that of the old man.

Enjolras bent down and kissed that venerable hand, just as he had kissed his brow on the preceding evening.

These were the only two kisses that he had bestowed in the course of his life.

Let us abridge the tale. The barricade had fought like a gate of Thebes; the wine shop fought like a house of Saragossa. These resistances are dogged. No quarter. No flag of truce possible. Men are willing to die, provided their opponent will kill them.

When Suchet says, "Capitulate," Palafox replies: "After the war with cannon, the war with knives." Nothing was lacking in the capture by assault of the Hucheloup wine shop; neither pavingstones raining from the windows and the roof on the besiegers and exasperating the soldiers by crushing them horribly, nor shots fired from the attic windows and the cellar, nor the fury of attack, nor, finally, when the door yielded, the frenzied madness of extermination. The assailants, rushing into the wine shop, their feet entangled in the panels of the door that had been beaten in and flung on the ground, found not a single combatant there. The spiral staircase, hewn asunder with the ax, lay in the middle of the taproom, a few wounded men were just breathing their last, everyone who was not killed was on the first floor, and from there, through the hole in the ceiling, which had formed the entrance of the stairs, a terrific fire burst forth. It was the last of their cartridges. When they were exhausted, when these formidable men on the point of death had no longer either powder or ball, each grasped in his hands two of the bottles that Enjolras had reserved, and of which we have spoken, and held the scaling party in check with these frightfully fragile clubs. They were bottles of aquafortis.

We relate these gloomy incidents of carnage as they occurred. The besieged man, alas! Converts everything into a weapon. Greek fire did not disgrace Archimedes, boiling pitch did not disgrace Bayard. All war is a thing of terror, and there is no choice in it. The musketry of the besiegers, though confined and embarrassed by being directed from below upwards, was deadly. The rim of the hole in the ceiling was speedily surrounded by heads of the slain, from which dripped long, red and smoking streams, the uproar was indescribable; a close and burning smoke almost produced night over this combat. Words are lacking to express horror when it has reached this pitch. There were no longer men in this conflict, which was now infernal. They were no longer giants matched with colossi. It resembled Milton and Dante rather than Homer. Demons attacked, spectres resisted.

It was heroism become monstrous.

CHAPTER XXIII—ORESTES FASTING AND PYLADES DRUNK

At length, by dint of mounting on each other's backs, aiding themselves with the skeleton of the staircase, climbing up the walls, clinging to the ceiling, slashing away at the very brink of the trapdoor, the last one who offered resistance, a score of assailants, soldiers, National Guardsmen, municipal guardsmen, in utter confusion, the majority disfigured by wounds in the face during that redoubtable ascent, blinded by blood, furious, rendered savage, made an irruption into the apartment on the first floor. There they found only one man still on his feet, Enjolras. Without cartridges, without sword, he had nothing in his hand now but the barrel of his gun whose stock he had broken over the head of those who were entering. He had placed the billiard table between his assailants and himself; he had retreated into the corner of the room, and there, with haughty eye, and head borne high, with this stump of a weapon in his hand, he was still so alarming as to speedily create an empty space around him. A cry arose, "He is the leader! It was he who slew the artilleryman. It is well that he has placed himself there. Let him remain there. Let us shoot him down on the spot."

"Shoot me," said Enjolras.

And flinging away his bit of gunbarrel, and folding his arms, he offered his breast.

The audacity of a fine death always affects men. As soon as Enjolras folded his arms and accepted his end, the din of strife ceased in the room, and this chaos suddenly stilled into a sort of sepulchral solemnity. The menacing majesty of Enjolras disarmed and motionless, appeared to oppress this tumult, and this young man, haughty, bloody, and charming, who alone had not a wound, who was as indifferent as an invulnerable being, seemed, by the authority of his tranquil glance, to constrain this sinister rabble to kill him respectfully. His beauty, at that moment augmented by his pride, was resplendent, and he was fresh and rosy after the fearful four and twenty hours that had just elapsed, as though he could no more be fatigued than wounded. It was of him, possibly, that a witness spoke afterward, before the council of war, "There was an insurgent whom I heard called Apollo." A National Guardsman who had taken aim at Enjolras, lowered his gun, saying, "It seems to me that I am about to shoot a flower."

Twelve men formed into a squad in the corner opposite Enjolras, and silently made ready their guns.

Then a sergeant shouted, "Take aim!"

An officer intervened.

"Wait."

And addressing Enjolras, "Do you wish to have your eyes bandaged?"

"No."

"Was it you who killed the artillery sergeant?"

"Yes."

Grantaire had waked up a few moments before.

Grantaire, it will be remembered, had been asleep ever since the preceding evening in the upper room of the wine shop, seated on a chair and leaning on the table.

He realized in its fullest sense the old metaphor of "dead drunk." The hideous potion of absinthe-porter and alcohol had thrown him into a lethargy. His table being small, and not suitable for the barricade, he had been left in possession of it. He was still in the same posture, with his breast bent over the table, his head lying flat on his arms, surrounded by glasses, beer jugs and bottles. His was the overwhelming slumber of the torpid bear and the satiated leech. Nothing had had any effect upon it, neither the fusillade, nor the cannonballs, nor the grapeshot that had made its way through the window into the room where he was. Nor the tremendous uproar of the assault. He merely replied to the cannonade, now and then, by a snore. He seemed to be waiting there for a bullet that should spare him the trouble of waking. Many corpses were strewn around him; and, at the first glance, there was nothing to distinguish him from those profound sleepers of death.

Noise does not rouse a drunken man; silence awakens him. The fall of everything around him only augmented Grantaire's prostration; the crumbling of all things was his lullaby. The sort of halt that the tumult underwent in the presence of Enjolras was a shock to this heavy slumber. It had the effect of a carriage going at full speed, which suddenly comes to a dead stop. The persons dozing within it wake up. Grantaire rose to his feet with a start, stretched out his arms, rubbed his eyes, stared, yawned, and understood.

A fit of drunkenness reaching its end resembles a curtain that is torn away. One beholds, at a single glance and as a whole, all that it has concealed. All suddenly presents itself to the memory; and the drunkard who has known nothing of what has been taking place during the last twenty-four hours, has no sooner opened his eyes than he is perfectly informed. Ideas recur to him with abrupt lucidity; the obliteration of intoxication, a sort of steam that has obscured the brain, is dissipated, and makes way for the clear and sharply outlined importunity of realities.

Relegated, as he was, to one corner, and sheltered behind the billiard table, the soldiers whose eyes were fixed on Enjolras, had not even noticed Grantaire, and the sergeant was preparing to repeat his order, "Take aim!" when all at once, they heard a strong voice shout beside them, "Long live the Republic! I'm one of them."

Grantaire had risen. The immense gleam of the whole combat that he had missed, and in which he had had no part, appeared in the brilliant glance of the transfigured drunken man.

He repeated, "Long live the Republic!" crossed the room with a firm stride and placed himself in front of the guns beside Enjolras.

"Finish both of us at one blow," said he.

And turning gently to Enjolras, he said to him, "Do you permit it?"

Enjolras pressed his hand with a smile.

This smile was not ended when the report resounded.

Enjolras, pierced by eight bullets, remained leaning against the wall, as though the balls had nailed him there. Only, his head was bowed.

Grantaire fell at his feet, as though struck by a thunderbolt.

A few moments later, the soldiers dislodged the last remaining insurgents, who had taken refuge at the top of the house. They fired into the attic through a wooden lattice. They fought under the very roof. They flung bodies, some of them still alive, out through the windows. Two light-infantrymen, who tried to lift the shattered omnibus, were slain by two shots fired from the attic. A man in a blouse was flung down from it, with a bayonet wound in the abdomen, and breathed his last on the ground. A soldier and an insurgent slipped together on the sloping slates of the roof, and, as they would not release each other, they fell, clasped in a ferocious embrace. A similar conflict went on in the cellar. Shouts, shots, a fierce trampling. Then silence. The barricade was captured.

The soldiers began to search the houses round about, and to pursue the fugitives.

CHAPTER XXIV—PRISONER

Marius was, in fact, a prisoner.

The hand that had seized him from behind and whose grasp he had felt at the moment of his fall and his loss of consciousness was that of Jean Valjean.

Jean Valjean had taken no other part in the combat than to expose himself in it. Had it not been for him, no one, in that supreme phase of agony, would have thought of the wounded. Thanks to him, everywhere present in the carnage, like a providence, those who fell were picked up, transported to the tap room, and cared for. In the intervals, he reappeared on the barricade. But nothing that could resemble a blow, an attack or even personal defence proceeded from his hands. He held his peace and lent succor. Moreover he had received only a few scratches. The bullets would have none of him. If suicide formed part of what he had meditated on coming to this sepulchre, to that spot, he had not succeeded. But we doubt whether he had thought of suicide, an irreligious act.

Jean Valjean, in the thick cloud of the combat, did not appear to see Marius; the truth is, that he never took his eyes from the latter. When a shot laid Marius low, Jean Valjean leaped forward with the agility of a tiger, fell upon him as on his prey, and bore him off.

The whirlwind of the attack was, at that moment, so violently concentrated upon Enjolras and upon the door of the wine shop, that no one saw Jean

Valjean sustaining the fainting Marius in his arms, traverse the unpaved field of the barricade and disappear behind the angle of the Corinthe building.

The reader will recall this angle that formed a sort of cape on the street; it afforded shelter from the bullets, the grapeshot, and all eyes, and a few square feet of space. There is sometimes a chamber that does not burn in the midst of a conflagration, and in the midst of raging seas, beyond a promontory or at the extremity of a blind alley of shoals, a tranquil nook. It was in this sort of fold in the interior trapezium of the barricade, that Eponine had breathed her last.

There Jean Valjean halted, let Marius slide to the ground, placed his back against the wall, and cast his eyes about him.

The situation was alarming.

For an instant, for two or three perhaps, this bit of wall was a shelter, but how was he to escape from this massacre? He recalled the anguish he had suffered in the Rue Polonceau eight years before, and in what manner he had contrived to make his escape; it was difficult then, today it was impossible. He had before him that deaf and implacable house, six stories in height, which appeared to be inhabited only by a dead man leaning out of his window; he had on his right the rather low barricade, which shut off the Rue de la Petite Truanderie; to pass this obstacle seemed easy, but beyond the crest of the barrier a line of bayonets was visible. The troops of the line were posted on the watch behind that barricade. It was evident, that to pass the barricade was to go in quest of the fire of the platoon, and that any head that should run the risk of lifting itself above the top of that wall of stones would serve as a target for sixty shots. On his left he had the field of battle. Death lurked around the corner of that wall.

What was to be done?

Only a bird could have extricated itself from this predicament.

And it was necessary to decide on the instant, to devise some expedient, to come to some decision. Fighting was going on a few paces away; fortunately, all were raging around a single point, the door of the wine shop; but if it should occur to one soldier, to one single soldier, to turn the corner of the house, or to attack him on the flank, all was over.

Jean Valjean gazed at the house facing him, he gazed at the barricade at one side of him, then he looked at the ground, with the violence of the last extremity, bewildered, and as though he would have liked to pierce a hole there with his eyes.

By dint of staring, something vaguely striking in such an agony began to assume form and outline at his feet, as though it had been a power of glance that made the thing desired unfold. A few paces distant he perceived, at the base of the small barrier so pitilessly guarded and watched on the exterior, beneath a disordered mass of paving stones that partly concealed it, an iron grating, placed flat and on a level with the soil. This grating, made of stout, transverse bars, was about two feet square. The frame of paving stones that supported it had been torn up, and it was, as it were, unfastened.

Through the bars a view could be had of a dark aperture, something like the flue of a chimney, or the pipe of a cistern. Jean Valjean darted forward. His old art of escape rose to his brain like an illumination. To thrust aside the stones, to raise the grating, to lift Marius, who was as inert as a dead body, upon his shoulders, to descend, with this burden on his loins, and with the aid of his elbows and knees into that sort of well, fortunately not very deep, to let the heavy trap, upon which the loosened stones rolled down afresh, fall into its place behind him, to gain his footing on a flagged surface three metres below the surface, all this was executed like that which one does in dreams, with the strength of a giant and the rapidity of an eagle; this took only a few minutes.

Jean Valjean found himself with Marius, who was still unconscious, in a sort of long, subterranean corridor.

There reigned profound peace, absolute silence, night.

The impression that he had formerly experienced when falling from the wall into the convent recurred to him. Only, what he was carrying today was not Cosette; it was Marius. He could barely hear the formidable tumult in the wine shop, taken by assault, like a vague murmur overhead.

BOOK SECOND: THE INTESTINE OF THE LEVIATHAN

CHAPTER I—THE LAND IMPOVERISHED BY THE SEA

Paris casts 25 million yearly into the water. And this without metaphor. How, and in what manner? Day and night. With what object? With no object. With what intention? With no intention. Why? For no reason. By means of what organ? By means of its intestine. What is its intestine? The sewer.

Twenty-five million is the most moderate approximative figure that the valuations of special science have set upon it.

Science, after having long groped about, now knows that the most fecundating and the most efficacious of fertilizers is human manure. The Chinese, let us confess it to our shame, knew it before us. Not a Chinese peasant—it is Eckberg who says this, goes to town without bringing back with him, at the two extremities of his bamboo pole, two full buckets of what we designate as filth. Thanks to human dung, the earth in China is still as young as in the days of Abraham. Chinese wheat yields a hundred fold of the seed. There is no guano comparable in fertility with the detritus of a capital. A great city is the most mighty of dungmakers. Certain success would attend the experiment of employing the city to manure the plain. If our gold is manure, our manure, on the other hand, is gold.

What is done with this golden manure? It is swept into the abyss.

Fleets of vessels are despatched, at great expense, to collect the dung of petrels and penguins at the South Pole, and the incalculable element of opulence we have on hand, we send to the sea. All the human and animal manure that the world wastes, restored to the land instead of being cast into the water, would suffice to nourish the world.

Those heaps of filth at the gate posts, those tumbrils of mud that jolt through the street by night, those terrible casks of the street department, those fetid drippings of subterranean mire, which the pavements hide from you, do you know what they are? They are the meadow in flower, the green grass, wild thyme, thyme and sage, they are game, they are cattle, they are the satisfied bellows of great oxen in the evening, they are perfumed hay, they are golden wheat, they are the bread on your table, they are the warm blood in your veins, they are health, they are joy, they are life. This is the will of that mysterious creation that is transformation on earth and transfiguration in heaven.

Restore this to the great crucible; your abundance will flow forth from it. The nutrition of the plains furnishes the nourishment of men.

You have it in your power to lose this wealth, and to consider me ridiculous to boot. This will form the masterpiece of your ignorance.

Statisticians have calculated that France alone makes a deposit of half a milliard every year, in the Atlantic, through the mouths of her rivers. Note this: with five hundred millions we could pay one quarter of the expenses of our budget. The cleverness of man is such that he prefers to get rid of these five hundred millions in the gutter. It is the very substance of the people that is carried off, here drop by drop, there wave after wave, the wretched outpour of our sewers into the rivers, and the gigantic collection of our rivers into the ocean. Every hiccough of our sewers costs us a thousand francs. From this spring two results, the land impoverished, and the water tainted. Hunger arising from the furrow, and disease from the stream.

It is notorious, for example, that at the present hour, the Thames is poisoning London.

So far as Paris is concerned, it has become indispensable of late, to transport the mouths of the sewers down stream, below the last bridge.

A double tubular apparatus, provided with valves and sluices, sucking up and driving back, a system of elementary drainage, simple as the lungs of a man, and that is already in full working order in many communities in England, would suffice to conduct the pure water of the fields into our cities, and to send back to the fields the rich water of the cities, and this easy exchange, the simplest in the world, would retain among us the five hundred millions now thrown away. People are thinking of other things.

The process actually in use does evil, with the intention of doing good. The intention is good, the result is melancholy. Thinking to purge the city, the population is blanched like plants raised in cellars. A sewer is a mistake. When drainage, everywhere, with its double function, restoring what it takes, shall have replaced the sewer, which is a simple impoverishing washing, then, this being combined with the data of a now social economy, the product of the earth will be increased tenfold, and the problem of misery will be singularly lightened. Add the suppression of parasitism, and it will be solved.

In the meanwhile, the public wealth flows away to the river, and leakage takes place. Leakage is the word. Europe is being ruined in this manner by exhaustion.

As for France, we have just cited its figures. Now, Paris contains one twenty-fifth of the total population of France, and Parisian guano being the richest of all, we understate the truth when we value the loss on the part of Paris at 25 million in the half milliard that France annually rejects. These twenty-five millions, employed in assistance and enjoyment, would double the splendor of Paris. The city spends them in sewers. So that we may say that Paris's great prodigality, its wonderful festival, its Beaujon folly, its orgy, its stream of gold from full hands, its pomp, its luxury, its magnificence, is its sewer system.

It is in this manner that, in the blindness of a poor political economy, we drown and allow to float down stream and to be lost in the gulfs the well-being of all. There should be nets at Saint-Cloud for the public fortune.

Economically considered, the matter can be summed up thus: Paris is a spendthrift. Paris, that model city, that patron of well-arranged capitals, of which every nation strives to possess a copy, that metropolis of the ideal, that august country of the initiative, of impulse and of effort, that center and that dwelling of minds, that nation-city, that hive of the future, that marvelous combination of Babylon and Corinth, would make a peasant of the Fo-Kian shrug his shoulders, from the point of view that we have just indicated.

Imitate Paris and you will ruin yourselves.

Moreover, and particularly in this immemorial and senseless waste, Paris is itself an imitator.

These surprising exhibitions of stupidity are not novel; this is no young folly. The ancients did like the moderns. "The sewers of Rome," says Liebig, "have absorbed all the well-being of the Roman peasant." When the Campagna of Rome was ruined by the Roman sewer, Rome exhausted Italy, and when she had put Italy in her sewer, she poured in Sicily, then Sardinia, then Africa. The sewer of Rome has engulfed the world. This cesspool offered its engulfment to the city and the universe. *Urbi et orbi.* Eternal city, unfathomable sewer.

Rome sets the example for these things as well as for others.

Paris follows this example with all the stupidity peculiar to intelligent towns.

For the requirements of the operation upon the subject of which we have just explained our views, Paris has beneath it another Paris; a Paris of sewers; which has its streets, its crossroads, its squares, its blind alleys, its arteries, and its circulation, which is of mire and minus the human form.

For nothing must be flattered, not even a great people; where there is everything there is also ignominy by the side of sublimity; and, if Paris contains Athens, the city of light, Tyre, the city of might, Sparta, the city of virtue, Nineveh, the city of marvels, it also contains Lutetia, the city of mud.

However, the stamp of its power is there also, and the titanic sink of Paris realizes, among monuments, that strange ideal realized in humanity by some men like Macchiavelli, Bacon and Mirabeau, grandiose vileness.

The subsoil of Paris, if the eye could penetrate its surface, would present the aspect of a colossal madrepore. A sponge has no more partitions and ducts than the mound of earth for a circuit of six leagues round about, on which rests the great and ancient city. Not to mention its catacombs, which are a separate cellar, not to mention the inextricable trelliswork of gas pipes, without reckoning the vast tubular system for the distribution of fresh water that ends in the pillar fountains, the sewers alone form a tremendous, shadowy network under the two banks; a labyrinth that has its slope for its guiding thread.

There appears, in the humid mist, the rat that seems the product to which Paris has given birth.

CHAPTER II—ANCIENT HISTORY OF THE SEWER

Let the reader imagine Paris lifted off like a cover, the subterranean network of sewers, from a bird's-eye view, will outline on the banks a species of large branch grafted on the river. On the right bank, the belt sewer will form the trunk of this branch, the secondary ducts will form the branches, and those without exit the twigs.

This figure is but a summary one and half exact, the right angle, which is the customary angle of this species of subterranean ramifications, being very rare in vegetation.

A more accurate image of this strange geometrical plan can be formed by supposing that one is viewing some eccentric oriental alphabet, as intricate as a thicket, against a background of shadows, and the misshapen letters should be welded one to another in apparent confusion, and as at haphazard, now by their angles, again by their extremities.

Sinks and sewers played a great part in the Middle Ages, in the Lower Empire and in the Orient of old. The masses regarded these beds of decomposition, these monstrous cradles of death, with a fear that was almost religious. The vermin ditch of Benares is no less conducive to giddiness than the lions' ditch of Babylon. Teglath-Phalasar, according to the rabbinical books, swore by the sink of Nineveh. It was from the sewer of Munster that John of Leyden produced his false moon, and it was from the cesspool of Kekscheb that oriental menalchme, Mokanna, the veiled prophet of Khorassan, caused his false sun to emerge.

The history of men is reflected in the history of sewers. The Germoniae* narrated Rome. The sewer of Paris has been an ancient and formidable thing. It has been a sepulchre, it has served as an asylum. Crime, intelligence, social protest, liberty of conscience, thought, theft, all that human laws persecute or have persecuted, is hidden in that hole; the maillotins in the fourteenth century, the tire-laine of the fifteenth, the Huguenots in the sixteenth, Morin's illuminated in the seventeenth, the chauffeurs [brigands] in the eighteenth.

---

* The steps of Aventine Hill, leading to the Tiber River where the bodies of executed criminals were disposed of.

A hundred years ago, the nocturnal blow of the dagger emerged thence, the pickpocket in danger slipped there; the forest had its cave, Paris had its sewer. Vagrancy, that Gallic picareria, accepted the sewer as the adjunct of the Cour des Miracles, and at evening, it returned there, fierce and sly, through the Maubuee outlet, as into a bedchamber.

It was quite natural, that those who had the blindalley Vide-Gousset (Empty Pocket) or the Rue Coupe-Gorge (Cut Throat), for the scene of their daily labor, should have for their domicile by night the culvert of the Chemin-Vert, or the catch basin of Hurepoix. Hence a throng of souvenirs. All sorts of phantoms haunt these long, solitary corridors; everywhere is putrescence and miasma; here and there are breathing-holes, where Villon within converses with Rabelais without.

The sewer in ancient Paris is the rendezvous of all exhaustions and of all attempts. Political economy therein spies a detritus, social philosophy there beholds a residuum.

The sewer is the conscience of the city. Everything there converges and confronts everything else. In that livid spot there are shades, but there are no longer any secrets. Each thing bears its true form, or at least, its definitive form. The mass of filth has this in its favor, that it is not a liar. Ingenuousness has taken refuge there. The mask of Basil is to be found there, but one beholds its cardboard and its strings and the inside as well as the outside, and it is accentuated by honest mud. Scapin's false nose is its next-door neighbor. All the uncleannesses of civilization, once past their use, fall into this trench of truth, where the immense social sliding ends. They are there engulfed, but they display themselves there. This mixture is a confession. There, no more false appearances, no plastering over is possible, filth removes its shirt, absolute denudation puts to the rout all illusions and mirages, there is nothing more except what really exists, presenting the sinister form of that which is coming to an end. There, the bottom of a bottle indicates drunkenness, a basket-handle tells a tale of domesticity; there the core of an apple that has entertained literary opinions becomes an applecore once more; the effigy on the big sou becomes frankly covered with verdigris, Caiphas's spittle meets Falstaff's puking, the louis-d'or that comes from the gaminghouse jostles the nail from which hangs the rope's end of the suicide. A livid fetus rolls along, enveloped in the spangles that danced at the Opera last Shrove Tuesday, a cap that has pronounced judgment on men wallows beside a mass of rottenness that was formerly Margoton's petticoat; it is more than fraternization, it is equivalent to addressing each other as thou. All that was formerly rouged, is washed free. The last veil is torn away. A sewer is a cynic. It tells everything.

The sincerity of foulness pleases us, and rests the soul. When one has passed one's time in enduring upon earth the spectacle of the great airs that reasons of state, the oath, political sagacity, human justice, professional probity, the austerities of situation, incorruptible robes all assume, it solaces one to enter a sewer and to behold the mire that befits it.

This is instructive at the same time. We have just said that history passes through the sewer. The Saint-Barthelemys filter through there, drop by drop, between the paving stones. Great public assassinations, political and religious butcheries, traverse this underground passage of civilization, and thrust their corpses there. For the eye of the thinker, all historic murderers are to be found there, in that hideous penumbra, on their knees, with a scrap of their winding-sheet for an apron, dismally sponging out their work. Louis XI is there with Tristan, Francois I with Duprat, Charles IX is there with his mother, Richelieu is there with Louis XIII, Louvois is there, Letellier is there, Hebert and Maillard are there, scratching the stones, and trying to make the traces of their actions disappear. Beneath these vaults one hears the brooms of spectres. One there breathes the enormous fetidness of social catastrophes. One beholds reddish reflections in the corners. There flows a terrible stream, in which bloody hands have been washed.

The social observer should enter these shadows. They form a part of his laboratory. Philosophy is the microscope of the thought. Everything desires to flee from it, but nothing escapes it. Tergiversation is useless. What side of oneself does one display in evasions? The shameful side. Philosophy pursues with its glance, probes the evil, and does not permit it to escape into nothingness. In the obliteration of things that disappear, in the watching of things that vanish, it recognizes all. It reconstructs the purple from the rag, and the woman from the scrap of her dress. From the cesspool, it reconstitutes the city; from mud, it reconstructs manners; from the potsherd it infers the amphora or the jug. By the imprint of a fingernail on a piece of parchment, it recognizes the difference that separates the Jewry of the Judengasse from the Jewry of the Ghetto. It rediscovers in what remains that which has been, good, evil, the true, the bloodstain of the palace, the inkblot of the cavern, the drop of sweat from the brothel, trials undergone, temptations welcomed, orgies cast forth, the turn that characters have taken as they became abased, the trace of prostitution in souls of which their grossness rendered them capable, and on the vesture of the porters of Rome the mark of Messalina's elbowing.

CHAPTER III—BRUNESEAU

The sewer of Paris in the Middle Ages was legendary. In the sixteenth century, Henri II attempted a bore, which failed. Not a hundred years ago, the cesspool, Mercier attests the fact, was abandoned to itself, and fared as best it might.

Such was this ancient Paris, delivered over to quarrels, to indecision, and to gropings. It was tolerably stupid for a long time. Later on, '89 showed how understanding comes to cities. But in the good, old times, the capital had not much head. It did not know how to manage its own affairs either morally or materially, and could not sweep out filth any better than it could abuses. Everything presented an obstacle, everything raised a question. The sewer, for example, was refractory to every itinerary. One could no more find one's bearings in the sewer than one could understand one's position in the city; above the unintelligible, below the inextricable; beneath the confusion of tongues there reigned the confusion of caverns; Daedalus backed up Babel.

Sometimes the Paris sewer took a notion to overflow, as though this misunderstood Nile were suddenly seized with a fit of rage. There occurred, infamous to relate, inundations of the sewer. At times, that stomach of civilization digested badly, the cesspool flowed back into the throat of the city, and Paris got an after-taste of her own filth. These resemblances of the sewer to remorse had their good points; they were warnings; very badly accepted, however; the city waxed indignant at the audacity of its mire, and did not admit that the filth should return. Drive it out better.

The inundation of 1802 is one of the actual memories of Parisians of the age of eighty. The mud spread in cross-form over the Place des Victoires, where stands the statue of Louis XIV; it entered the Rue Saint-Honore by the two mouths to the sewer in the Champs-Elysees, the Rue Saint-Florentin through the Saint-Florentin sewer, the Rue Pierre-a-Poisson through the sewer de la Sonnerie, the Rue Popincourt, through the sewer of the Chemin-Vert, the Rue de la Roquette, through the sewer of the Rue de Lappe; it covered the drain of the Rue des Champs-Elysees to the height of thirty-five centimeters; and, to the South, through the vent of the Seine, performing its functions in inverse sense, it penetrated the Rue Mazarine, the Rue de l'Echaude, and the Rue des Marais, where it stopped at a distance of one hundred and nine metres, a few paces distant from the house in which Racine had lived, respecting, in the seventeenth century, the poet more than the King. It attained its maximum depth in the Rue Saint-Pierre, where it rose to the height of three feet above the flagstones of the waterspout, and its maximum length in the Rue Saint-Sabin, where it spread out over a stretch two hundred and thirty-eight meters in length.

At the beginning of this century, the sewer of Paris was still a mysterious place. Mud can never enjoy a good fame; but in this case its evil renown reached the verge of the terrible. Paris knew, in a confused way, that she had under her a terrible cavern. People talked of it as of that monstrous bed of Thebes in which swarmed centipedes fifteen long feet in length, and which might have served Behemoth for a bathtub. The great boots of the sewermen never ventured further than certain well-known points. We were then very near the epoch when the scavenger's carts, from the summit of which Sainte-Foix fraternized with the Marquis de Crequi, discharged their loads directly into the sewer. As for cleaning out, that function was entrusted to the pouring rains that encumbered rather than swept away. Rome left some poetry to her sewer, and called it the Gemoniae; Paris insulted hers, and entitled it the Polypus-Hole. Science and superstition were in accord, in horror. The Polypus hole was no less repugnant to hygiene than to legend. The goblin was developed under the fetid covering of the Mouffetard sewer; the corpses of the Marmousets had been cast into the sewer de la Barillerie; Fagon attributed the redoubtable malignant fever of 1685 to the great hiatus of the sewer of the Marais, which remained yawning until 1833 in the Rue Saint-Louis, almost opposite the sign of the Gallant Messenger. The mouth of the sewer of the Rue de la Mortellerie was celebrated for the pestilences that had their source there; with its grating of iron, with points simulating a row of teeth, it was like a dragon's maw in that fatal street, breathing forth hell upon men. The popular imagination seasoned the somber Parisian sink with some indescribably hideous intermixture of the infinite. The sewer had no bottom. The sewer was the lower world. The idea of exploring these leprous regions did not even occur to the police. To try that unknown thing, to cast the plummet into that shadow, to set out on a voyage of discovery in that abyss—who would have dared? It was alarming. Nevertheless, someone did present himself. The cesspool had its Christopher Columbus.

One day, in 1805, during one of the rare apparitions that the Emperor made in Paris, the Minister of the Interior, some Decres or Cretet or other, came to the master's intimate levee. In the Carrousel there was audible the clanking of swords of all those extraordinary soldiers of the great Republic, and of the great Empire; then Napoleon's door was blocked with heroes; men from the

Rhine, from the Escaut, from the Adige, and from the Nile; companions of Joubert, of Desaix, of Marceau, of Hoche, of Kleber; the aerostiers of Fleurus, the grenadiers of Mayence, the pontoon-builders of Genoa, hussars whom the Pyramids had looked down upon, artillerists whom Junot's cannonball had spattered with mud, cuirassiers who had taken by assault the fleet lying at anchor in the Zuyderzee; some had followed Bonaparte upon the bridge of Lodi, others had accompanied Murat in the trenches of Mantua, others had preceded Lannes in the hollow road of Montebello. The whole army of that day was present there, in the courtyard of the Tuileries, represented by a squadron or a platoon, and guarding Napoleon in repose; and that was the splendid epoch when the grand army had Marengo behind it and Austerlitz before it. "Sire," said the Minister of the Interior to Napoleon, "yesterday I saw the most intrepid man in your Empire."

"What man is that?" said the Emperor brusquely, "and what has he done?"

"He wants to do something, Sire."

"What is it?"

"To visit the sewers of Paris."

This man existed and his name was Bruneseau.

CHAPTER IV—BRUNESEAU.

The visit took place. It was a formidable campaign; a nocturnal battle against pestilence and suffocation. It was, at the same time, a voyage of discovery. One of the survivors of this expedition, an intelligent workingman, who was very young at the time, related curious details with regard to it, several years ago, which Bruneseau thought himself obliged to omit in his report to the prefect of police, as unworthy of official style. The processes of disinfection were, at that epoch, extremely rudimentary. Hardly had Bruneseau crossed the first articulations of that subterranean network, when eight laborers out of the twenty refused to go any further. The operation was complicated; the visit entailed the necessity of cleaning; hence it was necessary to cleanse and at the same time, to proceed; to note the entrances of water, to count the gratings and the vents, to lay out in detail the branches, to indicate the currents at the point where they parted, to define the respective bounds of the divers basins, to sound the small sewers grafted on the principal sewer, to measure the height under the keystone of each drain, and the width, at the spring of the vaults as well as at the bottom, in order to determine the arrangements with regard to the level of each water-entrance, either of the bottom of the arch, or on the soil of the street. They advanced with toil. The lanterns pined away in the foul atmosphere. From time to time, a fainting sewerman was carried out. At certain points, there were precipices. The soil had given away, the pavement had crumbled, the sewer had changed into a bottomless well; they found nothing solid; a man disappeared suddenly; they had great difficulty in getting him out again. On the advice of Fourcroy, they lighted large cages filled with tow steeped in resin, from time to time, in spots that had been sufficiently disinfected. In some places, the wall was covered with misshapen fungi, one would have said tumors; the very stone seemed diseased within this unbreathable atmosphere.

Bruneseau, in his exploration, proceeded down hill. At the point of separation of the two water-conduits of the Grand-Hurleur, he deciphered upon a projecting stone the date of 1550; this stone indicated the limits where Philibert Delorme, charged by Henri II with visiting the subterranean drains of Paris, had halted. This stone was the mark of the sixteenth century on the sewer; Bruneseau found the handiwork of the seventeenth century once more in the Ponceau drain of the old Rue Vielle-du-Temple, vaulted between 1600 and 1650; and the handiwork of the eighteenth in the western section of the collecting canal, walled and vaulted in 1740. These two vaults, especially the less ancient, that of 1740, were more cracked and decrepit than the masonry of the belt sewer, which dated from 1412, an epoch when the brook of fresh water of Menilmontant was elevated to the dignity of the Grand Sewer of Paris, an advancement analogous to that of a peasant who should become first valet de chambre to the King; something like Gros-Jean transformed into Lebel.

Here and there, particularly beneath the Courthouse, they thought they recognized the hollows of ancient dungeons, excavated in the very sewer itself. Hideous in-pace. An iron neckcollar was hanging in one of these cells. They walled them all up. Some of their finds were singular; among others, the skeleton of an orangutan, who had disappeared from the Jardin des Plantes in 1800, a disappearance probably connected with the famous and indisputable apparition of the devil in the Rue des Bernardins, in the last year of the eighteenth century. The poor devil had ended by drowning himself in the sewer.

Beneath this long, arched drain, which terminated at the Arche-Marion, a perfectly preserved rag-picker's basket excited the admiration of all connoisseurs. Everywhere, the mire, which the sewermen came to handle with intrepidity, abounded in precious objects, jewels of gold and silver, precious stones, coins. If a giant had filtered this cesspool, he would have had the riches of centuries in his lair. At the point where the two branches of the Rue du Temple and of the Rue Sainte-Avoye separate, they picked up a singular Huguenot medal in copper, bearing on one side the pig hooded with a cardinal's hat, and on the other, a wolf with a tiara on his head.

The most surprising rencounter was at the entrance to the Grand Sewer. This entrance had formerly been closed by a grating of which nothing but the hinges remained. From one of these hinges hung a dirty and shapeless rag that, arrested there in its passage, no doubt, had floated there in the darkness and finished its process of being torn apart. Bruneseau held his lantern close to this rag and examined it. It was of very fine batiste, and in one of the corners, less frayed than the rest, they made out a heraldic coronet and embroidered above these seven letters: LAVBESP. The crown was the coronet of a Marquis, and the seven letters signified Laubespine. They recognized the fact, that what they had before their eyes was a morsel of the shroud of Marat. Marat in his youth had had amorous intrigues. This was when he was a member of the household of the Comte d'Artois, in the capacity of physician to the Stables. From these love affairs, historically proved, with a great lady, he had retained this sheet. As a waif or a souvenir. At his death, as this was the only linen of any fineness that he had in his house, they buried him in it. Some old women had shrouded him for the tomb in that swaddling-band in which the tragic Friend of the people had enjoyed voluptuousness. Bruneseau passed on. They left that rag where it hung; they did not put the finishing touch to it. Did this arise from scorn or from respect? Marat deserved both. And then, destiny was there sufficiently stamped to make them hesitate to touch it. Besides, the things of the sepulchre must be left in the spot they select. In short, the relic was a strange one. A Marquise had slept in it; Marat had rotted in it; it had traversed the Pantheon to end with the rats of the sewer. This chamber rag, of which Watteau would formerly have joyfully sketched every fold, had ended in becoming worthy of the fixed gaze of Dante.

The whole visit to the subterranean stream of filth of Paris lasted seven years, from 1805 to 1812. As he proceeded, Bruneseau drew, directed, and completed considerable works; in 1808 he lowered the arch of the Ponceau, and, everywhere creating new lines, he pushed the sewer, in 1809, under the Rue Saint-Denis as far as the fountain of the Innocents; in 1810, under the Rue Froidmanteau and under the Salpetriere; in 1811 under the Rue Neuve-des-Petits-Peres, under the Rue du Mail, under the Rue de l'Echarpe, under the Place Royale; in 1812, under the Rue de la Paix, and under the Chaussée d'Antin. At the same time, he had the whole network disinfected and rendered healthful. In the second year of his work, Bruneseau engaged the assistance of his son-in-law Nargaud.

It was thus that, at the beginning of the century, ancient society cleansed its double bottom, and performed the toilet of its sewer. There was that much clean, at all events.

Tortuous, cracked, unpaved, full of fissures, intersected by gullies, jolted by eccentric elbows, mounting and descending illogically, fetid, wild, fierce, submerged in obscurity, with cicatrices on its pavements and scars on its walls, terrible, such was, retrospectively viewed, the antique sewer of Paris. Ramifications in every direction, crossings, of trenches, branches, goose-feet, stars, as in military mines, coecum, blind alleys, vaults lined with saltpetre, pestiferous pools, scabby sweats, on the walls, drops dripping from the ceilings, darkness; nothing could equal the horror of this old, waste crypt, the digestive apparatus of Babylon, a cavern, ditch, gulf pierced with streets, a titanic mole-burrow, where the mind seems to behold that enormous blind mole, the past, prowling through the shadows, in the filth that has been splendor.

This, we repeat, was the sewer of the past.

CHAPTER V—PRESENT PROGRESS

Today the sewer is clean, cold, straight, correct. It almost realizes the ideal of what is understood in England by the word "respectable." It is proper and grayish; laid out by rule and line; one might almost say as though it came out of a bandbox. It resembles a tradesman who has become a counselor of state. One can almost see distinctly there. The mire there comports itself with decency. At first, one might readily mistake it for one of those subterranean corridors, which were so common in former days, and so useful in flights of monarchs and princes, in those good old times, "when the people loved their kings." The present sewer is a beautiful sewer; the pure style reigns there; the classical rectilinear alexandrine that, driven out of poetry, appears to have taken refuge in architecture, seems mingled with all the stones of that long, dark and whitish vault; each outlet is an arcade; the Rue de Rivoli serves as pattern even in the sewer. However, if the geometrical line is in place anywhere, it is certainly in the drainage trench of a great city. There, everything should be subordinated to the shortest road. The sewer has, nowadays, assumed a certain official aspect. The very police reports, of which it sometimes forms the subject, no longer are wanting in respect toward it. The words that characterize it in administrative language are sonorous and dignified. What used to be called a gut is now called a gallery; what used to be called a hole is now called a surveying orifice. Villon would no longer meet with his ancient temporary provisional lodging. This network of cellars has its immemorial population of prowlers, rodents, swarming in greater numbers than ever; from time to time, an aged and veteran rat risks his head at the window of the sewer and surveys the Parisians; but even these vermin grow tame, so satisfied are they with their subterranean palace. The cesspool no longer retains anything of its primitive ferocity. The rain, which in former days soiled the sewer, now washes it. Nevertheless, do not trust yourself too much to it. Miasmas still inhabit it. It is more hypocritical than irreproachable. The prefecture of police and the commission of health have done their best. But, in spite of all the processes of disinfection, it exhales, a vague, suspicious odor like Tartuffe after confession.

Let us confess, that, taking it all in all, this sweeping is a homage that the sewer pays to civilization, and as, from this point of view, Tartuffe's conscience is a progress over the Augean stables, it is certain that the sewers of Paris have been improved.

It is more than progress; it is transmutation. Between the ancient and the present sewer there is a revolution. What has affected this revolution?

The man whom all the world forgets, and whom we have mentioned, Bruneseau.

CHAPTER VI—FUTURE PROGRESS

The excavation of the sewer of Paris has been no slight task. The last ten centuries have toiled at it without being able to bring it to a termination, any more than they have been able to finish Paris. The sewer, in fact, receives all the countershocks of the growth of Paris. Within the bosom of the earth, it is a sort of mysterious polyp with a thousand antennae, which expands below as the city expands above. Every time that the city cuts a street, the sewer stretches out an arm. The old monarchy had constructed only twenty-three thousand three hundred metres of sewers; that was where Paris stood in this respect on the first of January 1806. Beginning with this epoch, of which we shall shortly speak, the work was usefully and energetically resumed and prosecuted; Napoleon built—the figures are curious—four thousand eight hundred and four meters; Louis XVIII, five thousand seven hundred and nine; Charles X, ten thousand eight hundred and thirty-six; Louis-Philippe, eighty-nine thousand and twenty; the Republic of 1848, twenty-three thousand three hundred and eighty-one; the present government, seventy thousand five hundred; in all, at the present time, two hundred and twenty-six thousand six hundred and ten metres; sixty leagues of sewers; the enormous entrails of Paris. An obscure ramification ever at work; a construction that is immense and ignored.

As the reader sees, the subterranean labyrinth of Paris is today more than ten times what it was at the beginning of the century. It is difficult to form any idea of all the perseverance and the efforts that have been required to bring this cesspool to the point of relative perfection in which it now is. It was with great difficulty that the ancient monarchical provostship and, during the last ten years of the eighteenth century, the revolutionary mayoralty, had succeeded in perforating the five leagues of sewer that existed previous to 1806. All sorts of obstacles hindered this operation, some peculiar to the soil, others inherent in the very prejudices of the laborious population of Paris. Paris is built upon a soil that is singularly rebellious to the pick, the hoe, the bore, and to human manipulation. There is nothing more difficult to pierce and to penetrate than the geological formation upon which is superposed the marvellous historical formation called Paris; as soon as work in any form whatsoever is begun and adventures upon this stretch of alluvium, subterranean resistances abound. There are liquid clays, springs, hard rocks, and those soft and deep quagmires that special science calls mustards. The pick advances laboriously through the calcareous layers alternating with very slender threads of clay, and schistose beds in plates incrusted with oyster shells, the contemporaries of the pre-Adamite oceans. Sometimes a rivulet suddenly bursts through a vault that has been begun, and inundates the laborers; or a layer of marl is laid bare, and rolls down with the fury of a cataract, breaking the stoutest supporting beams like glass. Quite recently, at Villette, when it became necessary to pass the collecting sewer under the Saint-Martin canal without interrupting navigation or emptying the canal, a fissure appeared in the basin of the canal, water suddenly became abundant in the subterranean tunnel, which was beyond the power of the pumping engines; it was necessary to send a diver to explore the fissure that had been made in the narrow entrance of the grand basin, and it was not without great difficulty that it was stopped up. Elsewhere near the Seine, and even at a considerable distance from the river, as for instance, at Belleville, Grand-Rue and Lumiere Passage, quicksands are encountered in which one sticks fast, and in which a man sinks visibly. Add suffocation by miasmas, burial by slides, and sudden crumbling of the earth. Add the typhus, with which the workmen become slowly impregnated. In our own day, after having excavated the gallery of Clichy, with a banquette to receive the principal water-conduit of Ourcq, a piece of work that was executed in a trench ten meters deep; after having, in the midst of landslides, and with the aid of excavations often putrid, and of shoring up, vaulted the Bievre from the Boulevard de l'Hopital, as far as the Seine; after having, in order to deliver Paris from the floods of Montmartre and in order to provide an outlet for that riverlike pool nine hectares in extent, which crouched near the Barriere des Martyrs, after having, let us state, constructed the line of sewers from the Barriere Blanche to the road of Aubervilliers, in four months, working day and night, at a depth of eleven metres; after having—a thing heretofore unseen—made a subterranean sewer in the Rue Barre-du-Bec, without a trench, six meters below the surface, the superintendent, Monnot, died. After having vaulted three thousand meters of sewer in all quarters of the city, from the Rue Traversiere-Saint-Antoine to the Rue de l'Ourcine, after having freed the Carrefour Censier-Mouffetard from inundations of rain by means of the branch of the Arbalete, after having built the Saint-Georges sewer, on rock and concrete in the fluid sands, after having directed the formidable lowering of the flooring of the vault timber in the Notre-Dame-de-Nazareth branch, Duleau the engineer died. There are no bulletins for such acts of bravery as these, which are more useful, nevertheless, than the brutal slaughter of the field of battle.

The sewers of Paris in 1832 were far from being what they are today. Bruneseau had given the impulse, but the cholera was required to bring about the vast reconstruction that took place later on. It is surprising to say, for example, that in 1821, a part of the belt sewer, called the Grand Canal, as in Venice, still stood stagnating uncovered to the sky, in the Rue des Gourdes. It was only in 1821 that the city of Paris found in its pocket the two hundred and 60,080 francs and six centimes required for covering this mass of filth. The three absorbing wells, of the Combat, the Cunette, and Saint-Mande, with their discharging mouths, their apparatus, their cesspools, and their depuratory branches, only date from 1836. The intestinal sewer of Paris has been made over anew, and, as we have said, it has been extended more than tenfold within the last quarter of a century.

Thirty years ago, at the epoch of the insurrection of the 5th and 6th of June, it was still, in many localities, nearly the same ancient sewer. A very great number of streets that are now convex were then sunken causeways. At the end of a slope, where the tributaries of a street or crossroads ended, there were often to be seen large, square gratings with heavy bars, whose iron, polished by the footsteps of the throng, gleamed dangerous and slippery for vehicles, and caused horses to fall. The official language of the Roads and Bridges gave to these gratings the expressive name of Cassis.[*]

In 1832, in a number of streets, in the Rue de l'Etoile, the Rue Saint-Louis, the Rue du Temple, the Rue Vielle-duTemple, the Rue Notre-Dame de Nazareth, the Rue Folie-Mericourt, the Quai aux Fleurs, the Rue du Petit-Muse, the Rue du Normandie, the Rue Pont-Aux-Biches, the Rue des Marais, the Faubourg Saint-Martin, the Rue Notre Dame des-Victoires, the Faubourg Montmartre, the Rue Grange-Bateliere, in the Champs-Elysees, the Rue Jacob, the Rue de Tournon, the ancient gothic sewer still cynically displayed its maw. It consisted of enormous voids of stone catchbasins sometimes surrounded by stone posts, with monumental effrontery.

Paris in 1806 still had nearly the same sewers numerically as stated in 1663; 5,300 fathoms. After Bruneseau, on the 1st of January 1832, it had forty thousand three hundred meters. Between 1806 and 1831, there had been built, on an average, 750 meters annually, afterward eight and even ten thousand meters of galleries were constructed every year, in masonry, of small stones, with hydraulic mortar that hardens underwater, on a cement foundation. At two hundred francs the meter, the sixty leagues of Paris' sewers of the present-day represent 48 million.

In addition to the economic progress that we have indicated at the beginning, grave problems of public hygiene are connected with that immense question: the sewers of Paris.

Paris is the center of two sheets, a sheet of water and a sheet of air. The sheet of water, lying at a tolerably great depth underground, but already sounded by two bores, is furnished by the layer of green clay situated between the chalk and the Jurassic limestone; this layer may be represented by a disk five and twenty leagues in circumference; a multitude of rivers and brooks ooze there; one drinks the Seine, the Marne, the Yonne, the Oise, the Aisne, the Cher, the Vienne and the Loire in a glass of water from the well of Grenelle. The sheet of water is healthy, it comes from heaven in the first place and next from the earth; the sheet of air is unhealthy, it comes from the sewer. All the miasms of the cesspool are mingled with the breath of the city; hence this bad breath. The air taken from above a dung-heap, as has been scientifically proved, is purer than the air taken from above Paris. In a given time, with the aid of progress, mechanisms become perfected, and as light increases, the sheet of water will be

---

[*] From *casser*, to break, ie, to break necks

employed to purify the sheet of air; that is to say, to wash the sewer. The reader knows, that by "washing the sewer" we mean: the restitution of the filth to the earth; the return to the soil of dung and of manure to the fields. Through this simple act, the entire social community will experience a diminution of misery and an augmentation of health. At the present hour, the radiation of diseases from Paris extends to fifty leagues around the Louvre, taken as the hub of this pestilential wheel.

We might say that, for ten centuries, the cesspool has been the disease of Paris. The sewer is the blemish that Paris has in her blood. The popular instinct has never been deceived in it. The occupation of sewermen was formerly almost as perilous, and almost as repugnant to the people, as the occupation of knacker, which was so long held in horror and handed over to the executioner. High wages were necessary to induce a mason to disappear in that fetid mine; the ladder of the cesspool cleaner hesitated to plunge into it; it was said, in proverbial form, "to descend into the sewer is to enter the grave;" and all sorts of hideous legends, as we have said, covered this colossal sink with terror; a dread sinkhole that bears the traces of the revolutions of the globe as of the revolutions of man, and where are to be found vestiges of all cataclysms from the shells of the Deluge to the rag of Marat.

BOOK THIRD: MUD BUT THE SOUL

CHAPTER I—THE SEWER AND ITS SURPRISES

It was in the sewers of Paris that Jean Valjean found himself.

Still another resemblance between Paris and the sea. As in the ocean, the diver may disappear there.

The transition was an unheard-of one. In the very heart of the city, Jean Valjean had escaped from the city, and, in the twinkling of an eye, in the time required to lift the cover and to replace it, he had passed from broad daylight to complete obscurity, from midday to midnight, from tumult to silence, from the whirlwind of thunders to the stagnation of the tomb, and, by a vicissitude far more tremendous even than that of the Rue Polonceau, from the most extreme peril to the most absolute obscurity.

An abrupt fall into a cavern; a disappearance into the secret trapdoor of Paris; to quit that street where death was on every side, for that sort of sepulchre where there was life, was a strange instant. He remained for several seconds as though bewildered; listening, stupefied. The waste-trap of safety had suddenly yawned beneath him. Celestial goodness had, in a manner, captured him by treachery. Adorable ambuscades of providence!

Only, the wounded man did not stir, and Jean Valjean did not know whether that which he was carrying in that grave was a living being or a dead corpse.

His first sensation was one of blindness. All of a sudden, he could see nothing. It seemed to him too, that, in one instant, he had become deaf. He no longer heard anything. The frantic storm of murder that had been let loose a few feet above his head did not reach him, thanks to the thickness of the earth that separated him from it, as we have said, otherwise than faintly and indistinctly, and like a rumbling, in the depths. He felt that the ground was solid under his feet; that was all; but that was enough. He extended one arm and then the other, touched the walls on both sides, and perceived that the passage was narrow; he slipped, and thus perceived that the pavement was wet. He cautiously put forward one foot, fearing a hole, a sink, some gulf; he discovered that the paving continued. A gust of fetidness informed him of the place in which he stood.

After the lapse of a few minutes, he was no longer blind. A little light fell through the manhole through which he had descended, and his eyes became accustomed to this cavern. He began to distinguish something. The passage in which he had burrowed—no other word can better express the situation—was walled in behind him. It was one of those blind alleys, which the special jargon terms branches. In front of him there was another wall, a wall like night. The light of the airhole died out ten or twelve paces from the point where Jean Valjean stood, and barely cast a wan pallor on a few meters of the damp walls of the sewer. Beyond, the opaqueness was massive; to penetrate there seemed horrible, an entrance into it appeared like an engulfment. A man could, however, plunge into that wall of fog and it was necessary so to do. Haste was even requisite. It occurred to Jean Valjean that the grating that he had caught sight of under the flagstones might also catch the eye of the soldiery, and that everything hung upon this chance. They also might descend into that well and search it. There was not a minute to be lost. He had deposited Marius on the ground, he picked him up again—that is the real word for it—placed him on his shoulders once more, and set out. He plunged resolutely into the gloom.

The truth is, that they were less safe than Jean Valjean fancied. Perils of another sort and no less serious were awaiting them, perchance. After the lightning-charged whirlwind of the combat, the cavern of miasmas and traps; after chaos, the sewer. Jean Valjean had fallen from one circle of hell into another.

When he had advanced fifty paces, he was obliged to halt. A problem presented itself. The passage terminated in another gut that he encountered across his path. There two ways presented themselves. Which should he take? Ought he to turn to the left or to the right? How was he to find his bearings in that black labyrinth? This labyrinth, to which we have already called the reader's attention, has a clue, which is its slope. To follow to the slope is to arrive at the river.

This Jean Valjean instantly comprehended.

He said to himself that he was probably in the sewer des Halles; that if he were to choose the path to the left and follow the slope, he would arrive, in less than a quarter of an hour, at some mouth on the Seine between the Pont au Change and the Pont-Neuf, that is to say, he would make his appearance in broad daylight on the most densely peopled spot in Paris. Perhaps he would come out on some manhole at the intersection of streets. Amazement of the passersby at beholding two bleeding men emerge from the earth at their feet. Arrival of the police, a call to arms of the neighboring post of guards. Thus they would be seized before they had even got out. It would be better to plunge into that labyrinth, to confide themselves to that black gloom, and to trust to Providence for the outcome.

He ascended the incline, and turned to the right.

When he had turned the angle of the gallery, the distant glimmer of an airhole disappeared, the curtain of obscurity fell upon him once more, and he became blind again. Nevertheless, he advanced as rapidly as possible. Marius's two arms were passed around his neck, and the former's feet dragged behind him. He held both these arms with one hand, and groped along the wall with the other. Marius's cheek touched his, and clung there, bleeding. He felt a warm stream that came from Marius trickling down upon him and making its way under his clothes. But a humid warmth near his ear, which the mouth of the wounded man touched, indicated respiration, and consequently, life. The passage along which Jean Valjean was now proceeding was not so narrow as the first. Jean Valjean walked through it with considerable difficulty. The rain of the preceding day had not, as yet, entirely run off, and it created a little torrent in the center of the bottom, and he was forced to hug the wall in order not to have his feet in the water.

Thus he proceeded in the gloom. He resembled the beings of the night groping in the invisible and lost beneath the earth in veins of shadow.

Still, little by little, whether it was that the distant airholes emitted a little wavering light in this opaque gloom, or whether his eyes had become accustomed to the obscurity, some vague vision returned to him, and he began once more to gain a confused idea, now of the wall that he touched, now of the vault beneath which he was passing. The pupil dilates in the dark, and the soul dilates in misfortune and ends by finding God there.

It was not easy to direct his course.

The line of the sewer reechoes, so to speak, the line of the streets that lie above it. There were then in Paris two thousand two hundred streets. Let the reader imagine himself beneath that forest of gloomy branches that is called the sewer. The system of sewers existing at that epoch, placed end to end, would have given a length of eleven leagues. We have said above, that the actual network, thanks to the special activity of the last thirty years, was no less than sixty leagues in extent.

Jean Valjean began by committing a blunder. He thought that he was beneath the Rue Saint-Denis, and it was a pity that it was not so. Under the Rue Saint-Denis there is an old stone sewer that dates from Louis XIII and that runs straight to the collecting sewer, called the Grand Sewer, with but a single elbow, on the right, on the elevation of the ancient Cour des Miracles, and a single branch, the Saint-Martin sewer, whose four arms describe a cross. But the gut of the Petite-Truanderie the entrance to which was in the vicinity of the Corinthe wine shop has never communicated with the sewer of the Rue Saint-Denis; it ended at the Montmartre sewer, and it was in this that Jean Valjean was entangled. There opportunities of losing oneself abound. The Montmartre sewer is one of the most labyrinthine of the ancient network. Fortunately, Jean Valjean had left behind him the sewer of the markets whose geometrical plan presents the appearance of a multitude of parrots' roosts piled on top of each other; but he had before him more than one embarrassing encounter and more than one street corner—for they are streets—presenting itself in the gloom like an interrogation point; first, on his left, the vast sewer of the Platriere, a sort of Chinese puzzle, thrusting out and entangling its chaos of Ts and Zs under the post office and under the rotunda of the Wheat Market, as far as the Seine, where it terminates in a Y; secondly, on his right, the curving corridor of the Rue du Cadran with its three teeth, which are also blind courts; thirdly, on his left, the branch of the Mail, complicated, almost at its inception, with a sort of fork, and proceeding from zigzag to zigzag until it ends in the grand crypt of the outlet of the Louvre, truncated and ramified in every direction; and lastly, the blind alley of a passage of the Rue des Jeuneurs, without counting little ducts here and there, before reaching the belt sewer, which alone could conduct him to some issue sufficiently distant to be safe.

Had Jean Valjean had any idea of all that we have here pointed out, he would speedily have perceived, merely by feeling the wall, that he was not in the subterranean gallery of the Rue Saint-Denis. Instead of the ancient stone, instead of the antique architecture, haughty and royal even in the sewer, with pavement and string courses of granite and mortar costing eight hundred livres the fathom, he would have felt under his hand contemporary cheapness, economical expedients, porous stone filled with mortar on a concrete foundation, which costs two hundred francs the meter, and the bourgeoise masonry known as a *petits materiaux*—small stuff; but of all this he knew nothing.

He advanced with anxiety, but with calmness, seeing nothing, knowing nothing, buried in chance, that is to say, engulfed in providence.

By degrees, we will admit, a certain horror seized upon him. The gloom that enveloped him penetrated his spirit. He walked in an enigma. This aqueduct of the sewer is formidable; it interlaces in a dizzy fashion. It is a melancholy thing to be caught in this Paris of shadows. Jean Valjean was obliged to find and even to invent his route without seeing it. In this unknown, every step that he risked might be his last. How was he to get out? Should he find an issue? Should he find it in time? Would that colossal subterranean sponge with its stone cavities, allow itself to be penetrated and pierced? Should he there encounter some unexpected knot in the darkness? Should he arrive at the inextricable and the impassable? Would Marius die there of hemorrhage and he of hunger? Should they end by both getting lost, and by furnishing two skeletons in a nook of that night? He did not know. He put all these questions to himself without replying to them. The intestines of Paris form a precipice. Like the prophet, he was in the belly of the monster.

All at once, he had a surprise. At the most unforeseen moment, and without having ceased to walk in a straight line, he perceived that he was no longer ascending; the water of the rivulet was beating against his heels, instead of meeting him at his toes. The sewer was now descending. Why? Was he about to arrive suddenly at the Seine? This danger was a great one, but the peril of retreating was still greater. He continued to advance.

It was not toward the Seine that he was proceeding. The ridge that the soil of Paris forms on its right bank empties one of its watersheds into the Seine and the other into the Grand Sewer. The crest of this ridge that determines the division of the waters describes a very capricious line. The culminating point, which is the point of separation of the currents, is in the Sainte-Avoye sewer, beyond the Rue Michelle-Comte, in the sewer of the Louvre, near the boulevards, and in the Montmartre sewer, near the Halles. It was this culminating point that Jean Valjean had reached. He was directing his course toward the belt sewer; he was on the right path. But he did not know it.

Every time that he encountered a branch, he felt of its angles, and if he found that the opening that presented itself was smaller than the passage in which he was, he did not enter but continued his route, rightly judging that every narrower way must needs terminate in a blind alley, and could only lead him further from his goal, that is to say, the outlet. Thus he avoided the quadruple trap that was set for him in the darkness by the four labyrinths that we have just enumerated.

At a certain moment, he perceived that he was emerging from beneath the Paris that was petrified by the uprising, where the barricades had suppressed circulation, and that he was entering beneath the living and normal Paris. Overhead he suddenly heard a noise as of thunder, distant but continuous. It was the rumbling of vehicles.

He had been walking for about half an hour, at least according to the calculation he made in his own mind, and he had not yet thought of rest; he had merely changed the hand with which he was holding Marius. The darkness was more profound than ever, but its very depth reassured him.

All at once, he saw his shadow in front of him. It was outlined on a faint, almost indistinct reddish glow, which vaguely empurpled the flooring vault underfoot, and the vault overhead, and gilded to his right and to his left the two viscous walls of the passage. Stupefied, he turned around.

Behind him, in the portion of the passage that he had just passed through, at a distance that appeared to him immense, piercing the dense obscurity, flamed a sort of horrible star that had the air of surveying him.

It was the gloomy star of the police that was rising in the sewer.

In the rear of that star eight or ten forms were moving about in a confused way, black, upright, indistinct, horrible.

CHAPTER II—EXPLANATION

On the day of the sixth of June, a battue of the sewers had been ordered. It was feared that the vanquished might have taken to them for refuge, and Prefect Gisquet was to search occult Paris while General Bugeaud swept public Paris; a double and connected operation that exacted a double strategy on the part of the public force, represented above by the army and below by the police. Three squads of agents and sewermen explored the subterranean drain of Paris, the first on the right bank, the second on the left bank, the third in the city. The agents of police were armed with carabines, with bludgeons, swords and poignards.

That which was directed at Jean Valjean at that moment, was the lantern of the patrol of the right bank.

This patrol had just visited the curving gallery and the three blind alleys that lie beneath the Rue du Cadran. While they were passing their lantern through the depths of these blind alleys, Jean Valjean had encountered on his path the entrance to the gallery, had perceived that it was narrower than the principal passage and had not penetrated there. He had passed on. The police, on emerging from the gallery du Cadran, had fancied that they heard the sound of footsteps in the direction of the belt sewer. They were, in fact, the steps of Jean Valjean. The sergeant in command of the patrol had raised his lantern, and the squad had begun to gaze into the mist in the direction from which the sound proceeded.

This was an indescribable moment for Jean Valjean.

Happily, if he saw the lantern well, the lantern saw him but ill. It was light and he was shadow. He was very far off, and mingled with the darkness of the place. He hugged the wall and halted. Moreover, he did not understand what it was that was moving behind him. The lack of sleep and food, and his emotions had caused him also to pass into the state of a visionary. He beheld a gleam, and around that gleam, forms. What was it? He did not comprehend.

Jean Valjean having paused, the sound ceased.

The men of the patrol listened, and heard nothing, they looked and saw nothing. They held a consultation.

There existed at that epoch at this point of the Montmartre sewer a sort of crossroads called *de service*, which was afterward suppressed, on account of the little interior lake that formed there, swallowing up the torrent of rain in heavy storms. The patrol could form a cluster in this open space. Jean Valjean saw these spectres form a sort of circle. These bulldogs' heads approached each other closely and whispered together.

The result of this council held by the watch dogs was, that they had been mistaken, that there had been no noise, that it was useless to get entangled in the belt sewer, that it would only be a waste of time, but that they ought to hasten toward Saint-Merry; that if there was anything to do, and any "bousingot" to track out, it was in that quarter.

From time to time, parties resole their old insults. In 1832 the word "bousingot" formed the interim between the word "jacobin," which had become obsolete, and the word "demagogue," which has since rendered such excellent service.

The sergeant gave orders to turn to the left, toward the watershed of the Seine.

If it had occurred to them to separate into two squads, and to go in both directions, Jean Valjean would have been captured. All hung on that thread. It is probable that the instructions of the prefecture, foreseeing a possibility of combat and insurgents in force, had forbidden the patrol to part company. The patrol resumed its march, leaving Jean Valjean behind it. Of all this movement, Jean Valjean perceived nothing, except the eclipse of the lantern that suddenly wheeled around.

Before taking his departure, the Sergeant, in order to acquit his policeman's conscience, discharged his gun in the direction of Jean Valjean. The detonation rolled from echo to echo in the crypt, like the rumbling of that titanic entrail. A bit of plaster that fell into the stream and splashed up the water a few paces away from Jean Valjean, warned him that the ball had struck the arch over his head.

Slow and measured steps resounded for some time on the timber work, gradually dying away as they retreated to a greater distance; the group of black forms vanished, a glimmer of light oscillated and floated, communicating to the vault a reddish glow that grew fainter, then disappeared; the silence became profound once more, the obscurity became complete, blindness and deafness resumed possession of the shadows; and Jean Valjean, not daring to stir as yet, remained for a long time leaning with his back against the wall, with straining ears, and dilated pupils, watching the disappearance of that phantom patrol.

CHAPTER III—THE "SPUN" MAN

This justice must be rendered to the police of that period, that even in the most serious public junctures, it imperturbably fulfilled its duties connected with the sewers and surveillance. A revolt was, in its eyes, no pretext for allowing malefactors to take the bit in their own mouths, and for neglecting society for the reason that the government was in peril. The ordinary service was performed correctly in company with the extraordinary service, and was not troubled by the latter. In the midst of an incalculable political event already begun, under the pressure of a possible revolution, a police agent, "spun" a thief without allowing himself to be distracted by insurrection and barricades.

It was something precisely parallel that took place on the afternoon of the 6th of June on the banks of the Seine, on the slope of the right shore, a little beyond the Pont des Invalides.

There is no longer any bank there now. The aspect of the locality has changed.

On that bank, two men, separated by a certain distance, seemed to be watching each other while mutually avoiding each other. The one who was in advance was trying to get away, the one in the rear was trying to overtake the other.

It was like a game of checkers played at a distance and in silence. Neither seemed to be in any hurry, and both walked slowly, as though each of them feared by too much haste to make his partner redouble his pace.

One would have said that it was an appetite following its prey, and purposely without wearing the air of doing so. The prey was crafty and on its guard.

The proper relations between the hunted polecat and the hunting dog were observed. The one who was seeking to escape had an insignificant mien and not an impressive appearance; the one who was seeking to seize him was rude of aspect, and must have been rude to encounter.

The first, conscious that he was the more feeble, avoided the second; but he avoided him in a manner that was deeply furious; anyone who could have observed him would have discerned in his eyes the sombre hostility of flight, and all the menace that fear contains.

The shore was deserted; there were no passersby; not even a boatman nor a lighter-man was in the skiffs that were moored here and there.

It was not easy to see these two men, except from the quay opposite, and to any person who had scrutinized them at that distance, the man who was in advance would have appeared like a bristling, tattered, and equivocal being, who was uneasy and trembling beneath a ragged blouse, and the other like a classic and official personage, wearing the frock-coat of authority buttoned to the chin.

Perchance the reader might recognize these two men, if he were to see them closer at hand.

What was the object of the second man?

Probably to succeed in clothing the first more warmly.

When a man clothed by the state pursues a man in rags, it is in order to make of him a man who is also clothed by the state. Only, the whole question lies in the color. To be dressed in blue is glorious; to be dressed in red is disagreeable.

There is a purple from below.

It is probably some unpleasantness and some purple of this sort that the first man is desirous of shirking.

If the other allowed him to walk on, and had not seized him as yet, it was, judging from all appearances, in the hope of seeing him lead up to some significant meeting place and to some group worth catching. This delicate operation is called "spinning."

What renders this conjecture entirely probable is that the buttoned-up man, on catching sight from the shore of a hackney-coach on the quay as it was passing along empty, made a sign to the driver; the driver understood, evidently recognized the person with whom he had to deal, turned about and began to follow the two men at the top of the quay, at a foot-pace. This was not observed by the slouching and tattered personage who was in advance.

The hackney-coach rolled along the trees of the Champs-Elysees. The bust of the driver, whip in hand, could be seen moving along above the parapet.

One of the secret instructions of the police authorities to their agents contains this article, "Always have on hand a hackney-coach, in case of emergency."

While these two men were maneuvring, each on his own side, with irreproachable strategy, they approached an inclined plane on the quay that descended to the shore, and that permitted cab drivers arriving from Passy to come to the river and water their horses. This inclined plane was suppressed later on, for the sake of symmetry; horses may die of thirst, but the eye is gratified.

It is probable that the man in the blouse had intended to ascend this inclined plane, with a view to making his escape into the Champs-Elysees, a place ornamented with trees, but, in return, much infested with policemen, and where the other could easily exercise violence.

This point on the quay is not very far distant from the house brought to Paris from Moret in 1824, by Colonel Brack, and designated as "the house of Francois I." A guardhouse is situated close at hand.

To the great surprise of his watcher, the man who was being tracked did not mount by the inclined plane for watering. He continued to advance along the quay on the shore.

His position was visibly becoming critical.

What was he intending to do, if not to throw himself into the Seine?

Henceforth, there existed no means of ascending to the quay; there was no other inclined plane, no staircase; and they were near the spot, marked by the bend in the Seine toward the Pont de Jena, where the bank, growing constantly narrower, ended in a slender tongue, and was lost in the water. There he would inevitably find himself blocked between the perpendicular wall on his right, the river on his left and in front of him, and the authorities on his heels.

It is true that this termination of the shore was hidden from sight by a heap of rubbish six or seven feet in height, produced by some demolition or other. But did this man hope to conceal himself effectually behind that heap of rubbish, which one need but skirt? The expedient would have been puerile. He certainly was not dreaming of such a thing. The innocence of thieves does not extend to that point.

The pile of rubbish formed a sort of projection at the water's edge, which was prolonged in a promontory as far as the wall of the quay.

The man who was being followed arrived at this little mound and went around it, so that he ceased to be seen by the other.

The latter, as he did not see, could not be seen; he took advantage of this fact to abandon all dissimulation and to walk very rapidly. In a few moments, he had reached the rubbish heap and passed around it. There he halted in sheer amazement. The man whom he had been pursuing was no longer there.

Total eclipse of the man in the blouse.

The shore, beginning with the rubbish heap, was only about thirty paces long, then it plunged into the water, which beat against the wall of the quay. The fugitive could not have thrown himself into the Seine without being seen by the man who was following him. What had become of him?

The man in the buttoned-up coat walked to the extremity of the shore, and remained there in thought for a moment, his fists clenched, his eyes searching. All at once he smote his brow. He had just perceived, at the point where the land came to an end and the water began, a large iron grating, low, arched, garnished with a heavy lock and with three massive hinges. This grating, a sort of door pierced at the base of the quay, opened on the river as well as on the shore. A blackish stream passed under it. This stream discharged into the Seine.

Beyond the heavy, rusty iron bars, a sort of dark and vaulted corridor could be descried. The man folded his arms and stared at the grating with an air of reproach.

As this gaze did not suffice, he tried to thrust it aside; he shook it, it resisted solidly. It is probable that it had just been opened, although no sound had been heard, a singular circumstance in so rusty a grating; but it is certain that it had been closed again. This indicated that the man before whom that door had just opened had not a hook but a key.

This evidence suddenly burst upon the mind of the man who was trying to move the grating, and evoked from him this indignant ejaculation, "That is too much! A government key!"

Then, immediately regaining his composure, he expressed a whole world of interior ideas by this outburst of monosyllables accented almost ironically, "Come! Come! Come! Come!"

That said, and in the hope of something or other, either that he should see the man emerge or other men enter, he posted himself on the watch behind a heap of rubbish, with the patient rage of a pointer.

The hackney-coach, which regulated all its movements on his, had, in its turn, halted on the quay above him, close to the parapet. The coachman, foreseeing a prolonged wait, encased his horses' muzzles in the bag of oats that is damp at the bottom, and that is so familiar to Parisians, to whom, be it said in parenthesis, the Government sometimes applies it. The rare passersby on the Pont de Jena turned their heads, before they pursued their way, to take a momentary glance at these two motionless items in the landscape, the man on the shore, the carriage on the quay.

CHAPTER IV—HE ALSO BEARS HIS CROSS

Jean Valjean had resumed his march and had not again paused.

This march became more and more laborious. The level of these vaults varies; the average height is about five feet, six inches, and has been calculated for the stature of a man; Jean Valjean was forced to bend over, in order not to strike Marius against the vault; at every step he had to bend, then to rise, and to feel incessantly of the wall. The moisture of the stones, and the viscous nature of the timber framework furnished but poor supports to which to cling, either for hand or foot. He stumbled along in the hideous dungheap of the city. The intermittent gleams from the airholes only appeared at very long intervals, and were so wan that the full sunlight seemed like the light of the moon; all the rest was mist, miasma, opaqueness, blackness. Jean Valjean was both hungry and thirsty; especially thirsty; and this, like the sea, was a place full of water where a man cannot drink. His strength, which was prodigious, as the reader knows, and which had been but little decreased by age, thanks to his chaste and sober life, began to give way, nevertheless. Fatigue began to gain on him; and as his strength decreased, it made the weight of his burden increase. Marius, who was, perhaps, dead, weighed him down as inert bodies weigh. Jean Valjean held him in such a manner that his chest was not oppressed, and so that respiration could proceed as well as possible. Between his legs he felt the rapid gliding of the rats. One of them was frightened to such a degree that he bit him. From time to time, a breath of fresh air reached him through the vent-holes of the mouths of the sewer, and reanimated him.

It might have been three hours past midday when he reached the belt-sewer.

He was, at first, astonished at this sudden widening. He found himself, all at once, in a gallery where his outstretched hands could not reach the two walls, and beneath a vault that his head did not touch. The Grand Sewer is, in fact, eight feet wide and seven feet high.

At the point where the Montmartre sewer joins the Grand Sewer, two other subterranean galleries, that of the Rue de Provence, and that of the Abattoir, form a square. Between these four ways, a less sagacious man would have remained undecided. Jean Valjean selected the broadest, that is to say, the belt-sewer. But here the question again came up—should he descend or ascend? He thought that the situation required haste, and that he must now gain the Seine at any risk. In other terms, he must descend. He turned to the left.

It was well that he did so, for it is an error to suppose that the belt-sewer has two outlets, the one in the direction of Bercy, the other toward Passy, and that it is, as its name indicates, the subterranean girdle of the Paris on the right bank. The Grand Sewer, which is, it must be remembered, nothing else than the old brook of Menilmontant, terminates, if one ascends it, in a blind sack, that is to say, at its ancient point of departure that was its source, at the foot of the knoll of Menilmontant. There is no direct communication with the branch that collects the waters of Paris beginning with the Quartier Popincourt, and that falls into the Seine through the Amelot sewer above the ancient Isle Louviers. This branch, which completes the collecting sewer, is separated from it, under the Rue Menilmontant itself, by a pile that marks the dividing point of the waters, between upstream and downstream. If Jean Valjean had ascended the gallery he would have arrived, after a thousand efforts, and broken down with fatigue, and in an expiring condition, in the gloom, at a wall. He would have been lost.

In case of necessity, by retracing his steps a little way, and entering the passage of the Filles-du-Calvaire, on condition that he did not hesitate at the subterranean crossing of the Carrefour Boucherat, and by taking the corridor Saint-Louis, then the Saint-Gilles gut on the left, then turning to the right and avoiding the Saint-Sebastian gallery, he might have reached the Amelot sewer, and thence, provided that he did not go astray in the sort of F that lies under the Bastille, he might have attained the outlet on the Seine near the Arsenal. But in order to do this, he must have been thoroughly familiar with the enormous madrepore of the sewer in all its ramifications and in all its openings. Now, we must again insist that he knew nothing of that frightful drain that he was traversing; and had anyone asked him in what he was, he would have answered, "In the night."

His instinct served him well. To descend was, in fact, possible safety.

He left on his right the two narrow passages that branch out in the form of a claw under the Rue Laffitte and the Rue Saint-Georges and the long, bifurcated corridor of the Chaussée d'Antin.

A little beyond an affluent, which was, probably, the Madeleine branch, he halted. He was extremely weary. A passably large airhole, probably the manhole in the Rue d'Anjou, furnished a light that was almost vivid. Jean Valjean, with the gentleness of movement that a brother would exercise toward his wounded brother, deposited Marius on the banquette of the sewer. Marius's bloodstained face appeared under the wan light of the airhole like the ashes at the bottom of a tomb. His eyes were closed, his hair was plastered down on his temples like a painter's brushes dried in red wash; his hands hung limp and dead. A clot of blood had collected in the knot of his cravat; his limbs were cold, and blood was clotted at the corners of his mouth; his shirt had thrust itself into his wounds, the cloth of his coat was chafing the yawning gashes in the living flesh. Jean Valjean, pushing aside the garments with the tips of his fingers, laid his hand upon Marius's breast; his heart was still beating. Jean Valjean tore up his shirt, bandaged the young man's wounds as well as he was able and stopped the flowing blood; then bending over Marius, who still lay unconscious and almost without breathing, in that half light, he gazed at him with inexpressible hatred.

On disarranging Marius's garments, he had found two things in his pockets, the roll that had been forgotten there on the preceding evening, and Marius's pocketbook. He ate the roll and opened the pocketbook. On the first page he found the four lines written by Marius. The reader will recall them: "My name is Marius Pontmercy. Carry my body to my grandfather, M. Gillenormand, Rue des Filles-du-Calvaire, No. 6, in the Marais."

Jean Valjean read these four lines by the light of the air-hole, and remained for a moment as though absorbed in thought, repeating in a low tone, "Rue des Filles-du-Calvaire, number 6, Monsieur Gillenormand." He replaced the pocketbook in Marius's pocket. He had eaten, his strength had returned to him; he took Marius up once more upon his back, placed the latter's head carefully on his right shoulder, and resumed his descent of the sewer.

The Grand Sewer, directed according to the course of the valley of Menilmontant, is about two leagues long. It is paved throughout a notable portion of its extent.

This torch of the names of the streets of Paris, with which we are illuminating for the reader Jean Valjean's subterranean march, Jean Valjean himself did not possess. Nothing told him what zone of the city he was traversing, nor what way he had made. Only the growing pallor of the pools of light that he encountered from time to time indicated to him that the sun was withdrawing from the pavement, and that the day would soon be over; and the rolling of vehicles overhead, having become intermittent instead of continuous, then having almost ceased, he concluded that he was no longer under central Paris, and that he was approaching some solitary region, in the vicinity of the outer boulevards, or the extreme outer quays. Where there are fewer houses and streets, the sewer has fewer airholes. The gloom deepened around Jean Valjean. Nevertheless, he continued to advance, groping his way in the dark.

Suddenly this darkness became terrible.

CHAPTER V—IN THE CASE OF SAND AS IN THAT OF WOMAN, THERE IS A FINENESS THAT IS TREACHEROUS

He felt that he was entering the water, and that he no longer had a pavement under his feet, but only mud.

It sometimes happens, that on certain shores of Bretagne or Scotland a man, either a traveler or a fisherman, while walking at low tide on the beach far from shore, suddenly notices that for several minutes past, he has been walking with some difficulty. The beach under foot is like pitch; his soles stick fast to it; it is no longer sand, it is birdlime. The strand is perfectly dry, but at every step that he takes, as soon as the foot is raised, the print is filled with water. The eye, however, has perceived no change; the immense beach is smooth and tranquil, all the sand has the same aspect, nothing distinguishes the soil that is solid from that which is not solid; the joyous little cloud of sand-lice continues to leap tumultuously under the feet of the passerby.

The man pursues his way, he walks on, turns toward the land, endeavors to approach the shore. He is not uneasy. Uneasy about what? Only he is conscious that the heaviness of his feet seems to be increasing at every step that he takes. All at once he sinks in. He sinks in two or three inches. Decidedly, he is not on the right road; he halts to get his bearings. Suddenly he glances at his feet; his feet have disappeared. The sand has covered them. He draws his feet out of the sand, he tries to retrace his steps, he turns back, he sinks in more deeply than before. The sand is up to his ankles, he tears himself free from it and flings himself to the left, the sand reaches to midleg, he flings himself to the right, the sand comes up to his knees. Then, with indescribable terror, he recognizes the fact that he is caught in a quicksand, and that he has beneath him that frightful medium in which neither man can walk nor fish can swim. He flings away his burden, if he have one, he lightens himself, like a ship in distress; it is too late, the sand is above his knees.

He shouts, he waves his hat, or his handkerchief, the sand continually gains on him; if the beach is deserted, if the land is too far away, if the bank of sand is too ill-famed, there is no hero in the neighborhood, all is over, he is condemned to be engulfed. He is condemned to that terrible interment, long, infallible, implacable, which it is impossible to either retard or hasten, which lasts for hours, which will not come to an end, which seizes you erect, free, in the flush of health, which drags you down by the feet, which, at every effort that you attempt, at every shout that you utter, draws you a little lower, which has the air of punishing you for your resistance by a redoubled grasp, which forces a man to return slowly to earth, while leaving him time to survey the horizon, the trees, the verdant country, the smoke of the villages on the plain, the sails of the ships on the sea, the birds that fly and sing, the sun and the sky. This engulfment is the sepulchre that assumes a tide, and that mounts from the depths of the earth toward a living man. Each minute is an inexorable layer-out of the dead. The wretched man tries to sit down, to lie down, to climb;

every movement that he makes buries him deeper; he straightens himself up, he sinks; he feels that he is being swallowed up; he shrieks, implores, cries to the clouds, wrings his hands, grows desperate. Behold him in the sand up to his belly, the sand reaches to his breast, he is only a bust now. He uplifts his hands, utters furious groans, clenches his nails on the beach, tries to cling fast to that ashes, supports himself on his elbows in order to raise himself from that soft sheath, and sobs frantically; the sand mounts higher. The sand has reached his shoulders, the sand reaches to his throat; only his face is visible now. His mouth cries aloud, the sand fills it; silence. His eyes still gaze forth, the sand closes them, night. Then his brow decreases, a little hair quivers above the sand; a hand projects, pierces the surface of the beach, waves and disappears. Sinister obliteration of a man.

Sometimes a rider is engulfed with his horse; sometimes the carter is swallowed up with his cart; all founders in that strand. It is shipwreck elsewhere than in the water. It is the earth drowning a man. The earth, permeated with the ocean, becomes a pitfall. It presents itself in the guise of a plain, and it yawns like a wave. The abyss is subject to these treacheries.

This melancholy fate, always possible on certain sea beaches, was also possible, thirty years ago, in the sewers of Paris.

Before the important works, undertaken in 1833, the subterranean drain of Paris was subject to these sudden slides.

The water filtered into certain subjacent strata, which were particularly friable; the footway, which was of flagstones, as in the ancient sewers, or of cement on concrete, as in the new galleries, having no longer an underpinning, gave way. A fold in a flooring of this sort means a crack, means crumbling. The framework crumbled away for a certain length. This crevice, the hiatus of a gulf of mire, was called a fontis, in the special tongue. What is a fontis? It is the quicksands of the seashore suddenly encountered under the surface of the earth; it is the beach of Mont Saint-Michel in a sewer. The soaked soil is in a state of fusion, as it were; all its molecules are in suspension in soft medium; it is not earth and it is not water. The depth is sometimes very great. Nothing can be more formidable than such an encounter. If the water predominates, death is prompt, the man is swallowed up; if earth predominates, death is slow.

Can anyone picture to himself such a death? If being swallowed by the earth is terrible on the seashore, what is it in a cesspool? Instead of the open air, the broad daylight, the clear horizon, those vast sounds, those free clouds that rain life, instead of those barks descried in the distance, of that hope under all sorts of forms, of probable passersby, of succor possible up to the very last moment, instead of all this, deafness, blindness, a black vault, the inside of a tomb already prepared, death in the mire beneath a cover! Slow suffocation by filth, a stone box where asphyxia opens its claw in the mire and clutches you by the throat; fetidness mingled with the death-rattle; slime instead of the strand, sulfuretted hydrogen in place of the hurricane, dung in place of the ocean! And to shout, to gnash one's teeth, and to writhe, and to struggle, and to agonize, with that enormous city that knows nothing of it all, over one's head!

Inexpressible is the horror of dying thus! Death sometimes redeems his atrocity by a certain terrible dignity. On the funeral pile, in shipwreck, one can be great; in the flames as in the foam, a superb attitude is possible; one there becomes transfigured as one perishes. But not here. Death is filthy. It is humiliating to expire. The supreme floating visions are abject. Mud is synonymous with shame. It is petty, ugly, infamous. To die in a butt of Malvoisie, like Clarence, is permissible; in the ditch of a scavenger, like Escoubleau, is horrible. To struggle therein is hideous; at the same time that one is going through the death agony, one is floundering about. There are shadows enough for hell, and mire enough to render it nothing but a slough, and the dying man knows not whether he is on the point of becoming a specter or a frog.

Everywhere else the sepulchre is sinister; here it is deformed.

The depth of the fontis varied, as well as their length and their density, according to the more or less bad quality of the subsoil. Sometimes a fontis was three or four feet deep, sometimes eight or ten; sometimes the bottom was unfathomable. Here the mire was almost solid, there almost liquid. In the Luniere fontis, it would have taken a man a day to disappear, while he would have been devoured in five minutes by the Philippeaux slough. The mire bears up more or less, according to its density. A child can escape where a man will perish. The first law of safety is to get rid of every sort of load. Every sewerman who felt the ground giving way beneath him began by flinging away his sack of tools, or his back-basket, or his hod.

The fontis were due to different causes: the friability of the soil; some landslip at a depth beyond the reach of man; the violent summer rains; the incessant flooding of winter; long, drizzling showers. Sometimes the weight of the surrounding houses on a marly or sandy soil forced out the vaults of the subterranean galleries and caused them to bend aside, or it chanced that a flooring vault burst and split under this crushing thrust. In this manner, the heaping up of the Parthenon, obliterated, a century ago, a portion of the vaults of Saint-Genevieve hill. When a sewer was broken in under the pressure of the houses, the mischief was sometimes betrayed in the street above by a sort of space, like the teeth of a saw, between the paving stones; this crevice was developed in an undulating line throughout the entire length of the cracked vault, and then, the evil being visible, the remedy could be promptly applied. It also frequently happened, that the interior ravages were not revealed by any external scar, and in that case, woe to the sewermen. When they entered without precaution into the sewer, they were liable to be lost. Ancient registers make mention of several scavengers who were buried in fontis in this manner. They give many names; among others, that of the sewerman who was swallowed up in a quagmire under the manhole of the Rue Careme-Prenant, a certain Blaise Poutrain; this Blaise Poutrain was the brother of Nicholas Poutrain, who was the last grave digger of the cemetery called the Charnier des Innocents, in 1785, the epoch when that cemetery expired.

There was also that young and charming Vicomte d'Escoubleau, of whom we have just spoken, one of the heroes of the siege of Lerida, where they delivered the assault in silk stockings, with violins at their head. D'Escoubleau, surprised one night at his cousin's, the Duchess de Sourdis, was drowned in a quagmire of the Beautreillis sewer, in which he had taken refuge in order to escape from the Duke. Madame de Sourdis, when informed of his death, demanded her smelling-bottle, and forgot to weep, through sniffling at her salts. In such cases, there is no love that holds fast; the sewer extinguishes it. Hero refuses to wash the body of Leander. Thisbe stops her nose in the presence of Pyramus and says, "Phew!"

CHAPTER VI—THE FONTIS

Jean Valjean found himself in the presence of a fontis.

This sort of quagmire was common at that period in the subsoil of the Champs-Elysees, difficult to handle in the hydraulic works and a bad preservative of the subterranean constructions, on account of its excessive fluidity. This fluidity exceeds even the inconsistency of the sands of the Quartier Saint-Georges, which could only be conquered by a stone construction on a concrete foundation, and the clayey strata, infected with gas, of the Quartier des Martyrs, which are so liquid that the only way in which a passage was effected under the gallery des Martyrs was by means of a cast-iron pipe. When, in 1836, the old stone sewer beneath the Faubourg Saint-Honore, in which we now see Jean Valjean, was demolished for the purpose of reconstructing it, the quicksand, which forms the subsoil of the Champs-Elysees as far as the Seine, presented such an obstacle, that the operation lasted nearly six months, to the great clamor of the dwellers on the riverside, particularly those who had hotels and carriages. The work was more than unhealthy; it was dangerous. It is true that they had four months and a half of rain, and three floods of the Seine.

The fontis that Jean Valjean had encountered was caused by the downpour of the preceding day. The pavement, badly sustained by the subjacent sand, had given way and had produced a stoppage of the water. Infiltration had taken place, a slip had followed. The dislocated bottom had sunk into the ooze. To what extent? Impossible to say. The obscurity was more dense there than elsewhere. It was a pit of mire in a cavern of night.

Jean Valjean felt the pavement vanishing beneath his feet. He entered this slime. There was water on the surface, slime at the bottom. He must pass it. To retrace his steps was impossible. Marius was dying, and Jean Valjean exhausted. Besides, where was he to go? Jean Valjean advanced. Moreover, the pit seemed, for the first few steps, not to be very deep. But in proportion as he advanced, his feet plunged deeper. Soon he had the slime up to his calves and water above his knees. He walked on, raising Marius in his arms, as far above the water as he could. The mire now reached to his knees, and the water to his waist. He could no longer retreat. This mud, dense enough for one man, could not, obviously, uphold two. Marius and Jean Valjean would have stood a chance of extricating themselves singly. Jean Valjean continued to advance, supporting the dying man, who was, perhaps, a corpse.

The water came up to his armpits; he felt that he was sinking; it was only with difficulty that he could move in the depth of ooze that he had now reached. The density, which was his support, was also an obstacle. He still held Marius on high, and with an unheard-of expenditure of force, he advanced still; but he was sinking. He had only his head above the water now and his two arms holding up Marius. In the old paintings of the deluge there is a mother holding her child thus.

He sank still deeper, he turned his face to the rear, to escape the water, and in order that he might be able to breathe; anyone who had seen him in that gloom would have thought that what he beheld was a mask floating on the shadows; he caught a faint glimpse above him of the drooping head and livid face of Marius; he made a desperate effort and launched his foot forward; his foot struck something solid; a point of support. It was high time.

He straightened himself up, and rooted himself upon that point of support with a sort of fury. This produced upon him the effect of the first step in a staircase leading back to life.

The point of support, thus encountered in the mire at the supreme moment, was the beginning of the other watershed of the pavement, which had bent but had not given way, and which had curved under the water like a plank and in a single piece. Well-built pavements form a vault and possess this sort of firmness. This fragment of the vaulting, partly submerged, but solid, was a veritable inclined plane, and, once on this plane, he was safe. Jean Valjean mounted this inclined plane and reached the other side of the quagmire.

As he emerged from the water, he came in contact with a stone and fell upon his knees. He reflected that this was but just, and he remained there for some time, with his soul absorbed in words addressed to God.

He rose to his feet, shivering, chilled, foul-smelling, bowed beneath the dying man whom he was dragging after him, all dripping with slime, and his soul filled with a strange light.

CHAPTER VII—ONE SOMETIMES RUNS AGROUND WHEN ONE FANCIES THAT ONE IS DISEMBARKING

He set out on his way once more.

However, although he had not left his life in the fontis, he seemed to have left his strength behind him there. That supreme effort had exhausted him. His lassitude was now such that he was obliged to pause for breath every three or four steps, and lean against the wall. Once he was forced to seat himself on the banquette in order to alter Marius's position, and he thought that he should have to remain there. But if his vigor was dead, his energy was not. He rose again.

He walked on desperately, almost fast, proceeded thus for a hundred paces, almost without drawing breath, and suddenly came in contact with the wall. He had reached an elbow of the sewer, and, arriving at the turn with head bent down, he had struck the wall. He raised his eyes, and at the extremity of the vault, far, very far away in front of him, he perceived a light. This time it was not that terrible light; it was good, white light. It was daylight. Jean Valjean saw the outlet.

A damned soul, who, in the midst of the furnace, should suddenly perceive the outlet of Gehenna, would experience what Jean Valjean felt. It would fly wildly with the stumps of its burned wings toward that radiant portal. Jean Valjean was no longer conscious of fatigue, he no longer felt Marius's weight, he found his legs once more of steel, he ran rather than walked. As he approached, the outlet became more and more distinctly defined. It was a pointed arch, lower than the vault, which gradually narrowed, and narrower than the gallery, which closed in as the vault grew lower. The tunnel ended like the interior of a funnel; a faulty construction, imitated from the wickets of penitentiaries, logical in a prison, illogical in a sewer, and which has since been corrected.

Jean Valjean reached the outlet.

There he halted.

It certainly was the outlet, but he could not get out.

The arch was closed by a heavy grating, and the grating, which, to all appearance, rarely swung on its rusty hinges, was clamped to its stone jamb by a thick lock, which, red with rust, seemed like an enormous brick. The keyhole could be seen, and the robust latch, deeply sunk in the iron staple. The door was plainly double-locked. It was one of those prison locks that old Paris was so fond of lavishing.

Beyond the grating was the open air, the river, the daylight, the shore, very narrow but sufficient for escape. The distant quays, Paris, that gulf in which one so easily hides oneself, the broad horizon, liberty. On the right, down stream, the bridge of Jena was discernible, on the left, upstream, the bridge of the Invalides; the place would have been a propitious one in which to await the night and to escape. It was one of the most solitary points in Paris; the shore that faces the Grand-Caillou. Flies were entering and emerging through the bars of the grating.

It might have been half-past eight o'clock in the evening. The day was declining.

Jean Valjean laid Marius down along the wall, on the dry portion of the vaulting, then he went to the grating and clenched both fists around the bars; the shock that he gave it was frenzied, but it did not move. The grating did not stir. Jean Valjean seized the bars one after the other, in the hope that he might be able to tear away the least solid, and to make of it a lever wherewith to raise the door or to break the lock. Not a bar stirred. The teeth of a tiger are not more firmly fixed in their sockets. No lever; no prying possible. The obstacle was invincible. There was no means of opening the gate.

Must he then stop there? What was he to do? What was to become of him? He had not the strength to retrace his steps, to recommence the journey he had already taken. Besides, how was he to again traverse that quagmire from which he had only extricated himself as by a miracle? And after the quagmire, was there not the police patrol, which assuredly could not be twice avoided? And then, where was he to go? What direction should he pursue? To follow the incline would not conduct him to his goal. If he were to reach another outlet, he would find it obstructed by a plug or a grating. Every outlet was, undoubtedly, closed in that manner. Chance had unsealed the grating through which he had entered, but it was evident that all the other sewer mouths were barred. He had only succeeded in escaping into a prison.

All was over. Everything that Jean Valjean had done was useless. Exhaustion had ended in failure.

They were both caught in the immense and gloomy web of death, and Jean Valjean felt the terrible spider running along those black strands and quivering in the shadows. He turned his back to the grating, and fell upon the pavement, hurled to earth rather than seated, close to Marius, who still made no movement, and with his head bent between his knees. This was the last drop of anguish.

Of what was he thinking during this profound depression? Neither of himself nor of Marius. He was thinking of Cosette.

CHAPTER VIII—THE TORN COATTAIL

In the midst of this prostration, a hand was laid on his shoulder, and a low voice said to him:, "Half-shares."

Some person in that gloom? Nothing so closely resembles a dream as despair. Jean Valjean thought that he was dreaming. He had heard no footsteps. Was it possible? He raised his eyes.

A man stood before him.

This man was clad in a blouse; his feet were bare; he held his shoes in his left hand; he had evidently removed them in order to reach Jean Valjean, without allowing his steps to be heard.

Jean Valjean did not hesitate for an instant. Unexpected as was this encounter, this man was known to him. The man was Thenardier.

Although awakened, so to speak, with a start, Jean Valjean, accustomed to alarms, and steeled to unforeseen shocks that must be promptly parried, instantly regained possession of his presence of mind. Moreover, the situation could not be made worse, a certain degree of distress is no longer capable of a crescendo, and Thenardier himself could add nothing to this blackness of this night.

A momentary pause ensued.

Thenardier, raising his right hand to a level with his forehead, formed with it a shade, then he brought his eyelashes together, by screwing up his eyes, a motion that, in connection with a slight contraction of the mouth, characterizes the sagacious attention of a man who is endeavoring to recognize another man. He did not succeed. Jean Valjean, as we have just stated, had his back turned to the light, and he was, moreover, so disfigured, so bemired, so bleeding that he would have been unrecognizable in full noonday. On the contrary, illuminated by the light from the grating, a cellar light, it is true, livid, yet precise in its lividness, Thenardier, as the energetic popular metaphor expresses it, immediately "leaped into" Jean Valjean's eyes. This inequality of conditions sufficed to assure some advantage to Jean Valjean in that mysterious duel that was on the point of beginning between the two situations and the two men. The encounter took place between Jean Valjean veiled and Thenardier unmasked.

Jean Valjean immediately perceived that Thenardier did not recognize him.

They surveyed each other for a moment in that half-gloom, as though taking each other's measure. Thenardier was the first to break the silence.

"How are you going to manage to get out?"

Jean Valjean made no reply. Thenardier continued, "It's impossible to pick the lock of that gate. But still you must get out of this."

"That is true," said Jean Valjean.

"Well, half-shares then."

"What do you mean by that?"

"You have killed that man; that's all right. I have the key."

Thenardier pointed to Marius. He went on, "I don't know you, but I want to help you. You must be a friend."

Jean Valjean began to comprehend. Thenardier took him for an assassin.

Thenardier resumed, "Listen, comrade. You didn't kill that man without looking to see what he had in his pockets. Give me my half. I'll open the door for you."

And half drawing from beneath his tattered blouse a huge key, he added, "Do you want to see how a key to liberty is made? Look here."

Jean Valjean "remained stupid"—the expression belongs to the elder Corneille—to such a degree that he doubted whether what he beheld was real. It was providence appearing in horrible guise, and his good angel springing from the earth in the form of Thenardier.

Thenardier thrust his fist into a large pocket concealed under his blouse, drew out a rope and offered it to Jean Valjean.

"Hold on," said he, "I'll give you the rope to boot."

"What is the rope for?"

"You will need a stone also, but you can find one outside. There's a heap of rubbish."

"What am I to do with a stone?"

"Idiot, you'll want to sling that stiff into the river, you'll need a stone and a rope, otherwise it would float on the water."

Jean Valjean took the rope. There is no one who does not occasionally accept in this mechanical way.

Thenardier snapped his fingers as though an idea had suddenly occurred to him.

"Ah, see here, comrade, how did you contrive to get out of that slough yonder? I haven't dared to risk myself in it. Phew! You don't smell good."

After a pause he added: "I'm asking you questions, but you're perfectly right not to answer. It's an apprenticeship against that cursed quarter of an hour before the examining magistrate. And then, when you don't talk at all, you run no risk of talking too loud. That's no matter, as I can't see your face and as I don't know your name, you are wrong in supposing that I don't know who you are and what you want. I twig. You've broken up that gentleman a bit; now you want to tuck him away somewhere. The river, that great hider of folly, is what you want. I'll get you out of your scrape. Helping a good fellow in a pinch is what suits me to a hair."

While expressing his approval of Jean Valjean's silence, he endeavored to force him to talk. He jostled his shoulder in an attempt to catch a sight of his profile, and he exclaimed, without, however, raising his tone, "Apropos of that quagmire, you're a hearty animal. Why didn't you toss the man in there?"

Jean Valjean preserved silence.

Thenardier resumed, pushing the rag that served him as a cravat to the level of his Adam's apple, a gesture that completes the capable air of a serious man: "After all, you acted wisely. The workmen, when they come tomorrow to stop up that hole, would certainly have found the stiff abandoned there, and it might have been possible, thread by thread, straw by straw, to pick up the scent and reach you. Someone has passed through the sewer. Who? Where did he get out? Was he seen to come out? The police are full of cleverness. The sewer is treacherous and tells tales of you. Such a find is a rarity, it attracts attention, very few people make use of the sewers for their affairs, while the river belongs to everybody. The river is the true grave. At the end of a month they fish up your man in the nets at Saint-Cloud. Well, what does one care for that? It's carrion! Who killed that man? Paris. And justice makes no inquiries. You have done well."

The more loquacious Thenardier became, the more mute was Jean Valjean.

Again Thenardier shook him by the shoulder.

"Now let's settle this business. Let's go shares. You have seen my key, show me your money."

Thenardier was haggard, fierce, suspicious, rather menacing, yet amicable.

There was one singular circumstance; Thenardier's manners were not simple; he had not the air of being wholly at his ease; while affecting an air of mystery, he spoke low; from time to time he laid his finger on his mouth, and muttered, "Hush!" It was difficult to divine why. There was no one there except themselves. Jean Valjean thought that other ruffians might possibly be concealed in some nook, not very far off, and that Thenardier did not care to share with them.

Thenardier resumed, "Let's settle up. How much did the stiff have in his bags?"

Jean Valjean searched his pockets.

It was his habit, as the reader will remember, to always have some money about him. The mournful life of expedients to which he had been condemned imposed this as a law upon him. On this occasion, however, he had been caught unprepared. When donning his uniform of a National Guardsman on the preceding evening, he had forgotten, dolefully absorbed as he was, to take his pocketbook. He had only some small change in his fob. He turned out his pocket, all soaked with ooze, and spread out on the banquette of the vault one louis d'or, two five-franc pieces, and five or six large sous.

Thenardier thrust out his lower lip with a significant twist of the neck.

"You knocked him over cheap," said he.

He set to feeling the pockets of Jean Valjean and Marius, with the greatest familiarity. Jean Valjean, who was chiefly concerned in keeping his back to the light, let him have his way.

While handling Marius's coat, Thenardier, with the skill of a pickpocket, and without being noticed by Jean Valjean, tore off a strip that he concealed under his blouse, probably thinking that this morsel of stuff might serve, later on, to identify the assassinated man and the assassin. However, he found no more than the thirty francs.

"That's true," said he, "both of you together have no more than that."

And, forgetting his motto, "half-shares," he took all.

He hesitated a little over the large sous. After due reflection, he took them also, muttering, "Never mind! You cut folks' throats too cheap altogether."

That done, he once more drew the big key from under his blouse.

"Now, my friend, you must leave. It's like the fair here, you pay when you go out. You have paid, now clear out."

And he began to laugh.

Had he, in lending to this stranger the aid of his key, and in making some other man than himself emerge from that portal, the pure and disinterested intention of rescuing an assassin? We may be permitted to doubt this.

Thenardier helped Jean Valjean to replace Marius on his shoulders, then he betook himself to the grating on tiptoe, and barefooted, making Jean Valjean a sign to follow him, looked out, laid his finger on his mouth, and remained for several seconds, as though in suspense; his inspection finished, he placed the key in the lock. The bolt slipped back and the gate swung open. It neither grated nor squeaked. It moved very softly.

It was obvious that this gate and those hinges, carefully oiled, were in the habit of opening more frequently than was supposed. This softness was suspicious; it hinted at furtive goings and comings, silent entrances and exits of nocturnal men, and the wolflike tread of crime.

The sewer was evidently an accomplice of some mysterious band. This taciturn grating was a receiver of stolen goods.

Thenardier opened the gate a little way, allowing just sufficient space for Jean Valjean to pass out, closed the grating again, gave the key a double turn in the lock and plunged back into the darkness, without making any more noise than a breath. He seemed to walk with the velvet paws of a tiger.

A moment later, that hideous providence had retreated into the invisibility. Jean Valjean found himself in the open air.

CHAPTER IX—MARIUS PRODUCES ON SOMEONE WHO IS A JUDGE OF THE MATTER, THE EFFECT OF BEING DEAD

He allowed Marius to slide down upon the shore. They were in the open air!

The miasmas, darkness, horror lay behind him. The pure, healthful, living, joyous air that was easy to breathe inundated him. Everywhere around him reigned silence, but that charming silence when the sun has set in an unclouded azure sky. Twilight had descended; night was drawing on, the great deliverer, the friend of all those who need a mantle of darkness that they may escape from an anguish. The sky presented itself in all directions like an enormous calm. The river flowed to his feet with the sound of a kiss. The aerial dialogue of the nests bidding each other good night in the elms of the Champs-Elysees was audible. A few stars, daintily piercing the pale blue of the zenith, and visible to revery alone, formed imperceptible little splendors amid the immensity. Evening was unfolding over the head of Jean Valjean all the sweetness of the infinite.

It was that exquisite and undecided hour, which says neither yes nor no. Night was already sufficiently advanced to render it possible to lose oneself at a little distance and yet there was sufficient daylight to permit of recognition at close quarters.

For several seconds, Jean Valjean was irresistibly overcome by that august and caressing serenity; such moments of oblivion do come to men; suffering refrains from harassing the unhappy wretch; everything is eclipsed in the thoughts; peace broods over the dreamer like night; and, beneath the twilight that beams and in imitation of the sky that is illuminated, the soul becomes studded with stars. Jean Valjean could not refrain from contemplating that vast, clear shadow that rested over him; thoughtfully he bathed in the sea of ecstasy and prayer in the majestic silence of the eternal heavens. Then he bent down swiftly to Marius, as though the sentiment of duty had returned to him, and, dipping up water in the hollow of his hand, he gently sprinkled a few drops on the latter's face. Marius's eyelids did not open; but his half-open mouth still breathed.

Jean Valjean was on the point of dipping his hand in the river once more, when, all at once, he experienced an indescribable embarrassment, such as a person feels when there is someone behind him whom he does not see.

We have already alluded to this impression, with which everyone is familiar. He turned around.

Someone was, in fact, behind him, as there had been a short while before.

A man of lofty stature, enveloped in a long coat, with folded arms, and bearing in his right fist a bludgeon of which the leaden head was visible, stood a few paces in the rear of the spot where Jean Valjean was crouching over Marius.

With the aid of the darkness, it seemed a sort of apparition. An ordinary man would have been alarmed because of the twilight, a thoughtful man on account of the bludgeon. Jean Valjean recognized Javert.

The reader has divined, no doubt, that Thenardier's pursuer was no other than Javert. Javert, after his unlooked-for escape from the barricade, had betaken himself to the prefecture of police, had rendered a verbal account to the Prefect in person in a brief audience, had then immediately gone on duty again, which implied—the note, the reader will recollect, which had been captured on his person—a certain surveillance of the shore on the right bank of the Seine near the Champs-Elysees, which had, for some time past, aroused the attention of the police. There he had caught sight of Thenardier and had followed him. The reader knows the rest.

Thus it will be easily understood that that grating, so obligingly opened to Jean Valjean, was a bit of cleverness on Thenardier's part. Thenardier intuitively felt that Javert was still there; the man spied upon has a scent that never deceives him; it was necessary to fling a bone to that sleuthhound. An assassin, what a godsend! Such an opportunity must never be allowed to slip. Thenardier, by putting Jean Valjean outside in his stead, provided a prey for the police, forced them to relinquish his scent, made them forget him in a bigger adventure, repaid Javert for his waiting, which always flatters a spy, earned thirty francs, and counted with certainty, so far as he himself was concerned, on escaping with the aid of this diversion.

Jean Valjean had fallen from one danger upon another.

These two encounters, this falling one after the other, from Thenardier upon Javert, was a rude shock.

Javert did not recognize Jean Valjean, who, as we have stated, no longer looked like himself. He did not unfold his arms, he made sure of his bludgeon in his fist, by an imperceptible movement, and said in a curt, calm voice, "Who are you?"

"I."

"Who is 'I'?"

"Jean Valjean."

Javert thrust his bludgeon between his teeth, bent his knees, inclined his body, laid his two powerful hands on the shoulders of Jean Valjean, which were clamped within them as in a couple of vices, scrutinized him, and recognized him. Their faces almost touched. Javert's look was terrible.

Jean Valjean remained inert beneath Javert's grasp, like a lion submitting to the claws of a lynx.

"Inspector Javert," said he, "you have me in your power. Moreover, I have regarded myself as your prisoner ever since this morning. I did not give you my address with any intention of escaping from you. Take me. Only grant me one favor."

Javert did not appear to hear him. He kept his eyes riveted on Jean Valjean. His chin being contracted, thrust his lips upwards toward his nose, a sign of savage revery. At length he released Jean Valjean, straightened himself stiffly up without bending, grasped his bludgeon again firmly, and, as though in a dream, he murmured rather than uttered this question, "What are you doing here? And who is this man?"

He still abstained from addressing Jean Valjean as thou.

Jean Valjean replied, and the sound of his voice appeared to rouse Javert, "It is with regard to him that I desire to speak to you. Dispose of me as you see fit; but first help me to carry him home. That is all that I ask of you."

Javert's face contracted as was always the case when anyone seemed to think him capable of making a concession. Nevertheless, he did not say "no."

Again he bent over, drew from his pocket a handkerchief, which he moistened in the water and with which he then wiped Marius's bloodstained brow.

"This man was at the barricade," said he in a low voice and as though speaking to himself. "He is the one they called Marius."

A spy of the first quality, who had observed everything, listened to everything, and taken in everything, even when he thought that he was to die; who had played the spy even in his agony, and who, with his elbows leaning on the first step of the sepulchre, had taken notes.

He seized Marius's hand and felt his pulse.

"He is wounded," said Jean Valjean.

"He is a dead man," said Javert.

Jean Valjean replied, "No. Not yet."

"So you have brought him there from the barricade?" remarked Javert.

His preoccupation must indeed have been very profound for him not to insist on this alarming rescue through the sewer, and for him not to even notice Jean Valjean's silence after his question.

Jean Valjean, on his side, seemed to have but one thought. He resumed, "He lives in the Marais, Rue des Filles-du-Calvaire, with his grandfather. I do not recollect his name."

Jean Valjean fumbled in Marius's coat, pulled out his pocketbook, opened it at the page Marius had pencilled, and held it out to Javert.

There was still sufficient light to admit of reading. Besides this, Javert possessed in his eye the feline phosphorescence of night birds. He deciphered the few lines written by Marius, and muttered, "Gillenormand, Rue des Filles-du Calvaire, No. 6."

Then he exclaimed, "Coachman!"

The reader will remember that the hackney-coach was waiting in case of need.

Javert kept Marius's pocketbook.

A moment later, the carriage, which had descended by the inclined plane of the wateringplace, was on the shore. Marius was laid upon the back seat, and Javert seated himself on the front seat beside Jean Valjean.

The door slammed, and the carriage drove rapidly away, ascending the quays in the direction of the Bastille.

They quitted the quays and entered the streets. The coachman, a black form on his box, whipped up his thin horses. A glacial silence reigned in the carriage. Marius, motionless, with his body resting in the corner, and his head drooping on his breast, his arms hanging, his legs stiff, seemed to be awaiting only a coffin; Jean Valjean seemed made of shadow, and Javert of stone, and in that vehicle full of night, whose interior, every time that it passed in front of a street lantern, appeared to be turned lividly wan, as by an intermittent flash of lightning, chance had united and seemed to be bringing face-to-face the three forms of tragic immobility, the corpse, the specter, and the statue.

CHAPTER X—RETURN OF THE SON WHO WAS PRODIGAL OF HIS LIFE

At every jolt over the pavement, a drop of blood trickled from Marius's hair.

Night had fully closed in when the carriage arrived at No. 6, Rue des Filles-du-Calvaire.

Javert was the first to alight; he made sure with one glance of the number on the carriage gate, and, raising the heavy knocker of beaten iron, embellished in the old style, with a male goat and a satyr confronting each other, he gave a violent peal. The gate opened a little way and Javert gave it a push. The porter half made his appearance yawning, vaguely awake, and with a candle in his hand.

Everyone in the house was asleep. People go to bed betimes in the Marais, especially on days when there is a revolt. This good, old quarter, terrified at the Revolution, takes refuge in slumber, as children, when they hear the Bugaboo coming, hide their heads hastily under their coverlet.

In the meantime Jean Valjean and the coachman had taken Marius out of the carriage, Jean Valjean supporting him under the armpits, and the coachman under the knees.

As they thus bore Marius, Jean Valjean slipped his hand under the latter's clothes, which were broadly rent, felt his breast, and assured himself that his heart was still beating. It was even beating a little less feebly, as though the movement of the carriage had brought about a certain fresh access of life.

Javert addressed the porter in a tone befitting the government, and the presence of the porter of a factious person.

"Some person whose name is Gillenormand?"

"Here. What do you want with him?"

"His son is brought back."

"His son?" said the porter stupidly.

"He is dead."

Jean Valjean, who, soiled and tattered, stood behind Javert, and whom the porter was surveying with some horror, made a sign to him with his head that this was not so.

The porter did not appear to understand either Javert's words or Jean Valjean's sign.

Javert continued, "He went to the barricade, and here he is."

"To the barricade?" ejaculated the porter.

"He has got himself killed. Go waken his father."

The porter did not stir.

"Go along with you!" repeated Javert.

And he added, "There will be a funeral here tomorrow."

For Javert, the usual incidents of the public highway were categorically classed, which is the beginning of foresight and surveillance, and each contingency had its own compartment; all possible facts were arranged in drawers, as it were, from which they emerged on occasion, in variable quantities; in the street, uproar, revolt, carnival, and funeral.

The porter contented himself with waking Basque. Basque woke Nicolette; Nicolette roused great-aunt Gillenormand.

As for the grandfather, they let him sleep on, thinking that he would hear about the matter early enough in any case.

Marius was carried up to the first floor, without anyone in the other parts of the house being aware of the fact, and deposited on an old sofa in M. Gillenormand's antechamber; and while Basque went in search of a physician, and while Nicolette opened the linen-presses, Jean Valjean felt Javert touch him on the shoulder. He understood and descended the stairs, having behind him the step of Javert who was following him.

The porter watched them take their departure as he had watched their arrival, in terrified somnolence.

They entered the carriage once more, and the coachman mounted his box.

"Inspector Javert," said Jean, "grant me yet another favor."

"What is it?" demanded Javert roughly.

"Let me go home for one instant. Then you shall do whatever you like with me."

Javert remained silent for a few moments, with his chin drawn back into the collar of his great-coat, then he lowered the glass and front.

"Driver," said he, "Rue de l'Homme Arme, No. 7."

CHAPTER XI—CONCUSSION
IN THE ABSOLUTE

They did not open their lips again during the whole space of their ride.

What did Jean Valjean want? To finish what he had begun; to warn Cosette, to tell her where Marius was, to give her, possibly, some other useful information, to take, if he could, certain final measures. As for himself, so far as he was personally concerned, all was over; he had been seized by Javert and had not resisted; any other man than himself in like situation would, perhaps, have had some vague thoughts connected with the rope that Thenardier had given him, and of the bars of the first cell that he should enter; but, let us impress it upon the reader, after the Bishop, there had existed in Jean Valjean a profound hesitation in the presence of any violence, even when directed against himself.

Suicide, that mysterious act of violence against the unknown, which may contain, in a measure, the death of the soul, was impossible to Jean Valjean.

At the entrance to the Rue de l'Homme Arme, the carriage halted, the way being too narrow to admit of the entrance of vehicles. Javert and Jean Valjean alighted.

The coachman humbly represented to "monsieur l'Inspecteur," that the Utrecht velvet of his carriage was all spotted with the blood of the assassinated man, and with mire from the assassin. That is the way he understood it. He added that an indemnity was due him. At the same time, drawing his certificate book from his pocket, he begged the inspector to have the goodness to write him "a bit of an attestation."

Javert thrust aside the book the coachman held out to him, and said, "How much do you want, including your time of waiting and the drive?"

"It comes to seven hours and a quarter," replied the man, "and my velvet was perfectly new. Eighty francs, Mr. Inspector."

Javert drew four napoleons from his pocket and dismissed the carriage.

Jean Valjean fancied that it was Javert's intention to conduct him on foot to the post of the Blancs-Manteaux or to the post of the Archives, both of which are close at hand.

They entered the street. It was deserted as usual. Javert followed Jean Valjean. They reached No. 7. Jean Valjean knocked. The door opened.

"It is well," said Javert. "Go upstairs."

He added with a strange expression, and as though he were exerting an effort in speaking in this manner, "I will wait for you here."

Jean Valjean looked at Javert. This mode of procedure was but little in accord with Javert's habits. However, he could not be greatly surprised that Javert should now have a sort of haughty confidence in him, the confidence of the cat that grants the mouse liberty to the length of its claws, seeing that Jean Valjean had made up his mind to surrender himself and to make an end of it. He pushed open the door, entered the house, called to the porter who was in bed and who had pulled the cord from his couch, "It is I!" and ascended the stairs.

On arriving at the first floor, he paused. All sorrowful roads have their stations. The window on the landing place, which was a sash-window, was open. As in many ancient houses, the staircase got its light from without and had a view on the street. The streetlantern, situated directly opposite, cast some light on the stairs, and thus affected some economy in illumination.

Jean Valjean, either for the sake of getting the air, or mechanically, thrust his head out of this window. He leaned out over the street. It is short, and the lantern lighted it from end to end. Jean Valjean was overwhelmed with amazement; there was no longer anyone there.

Javert had taken his departure.

CHAPTER XII—THE GRANDFATHER

Basque and the porter had carried Marius into the drawingroom, as he still lay stretched out, motionless, on the sofa upon which he had been placed on his arrival. The doctor who had been sent for had hastened there. Aunt Gillenormand had risen.

Aunt Gillenormand went and came, in affright, wringing her hands and incapable of doing anything but saying, "Heavens! is it possible?" At times she added, "Everything will be covered with blood." When her first horror had passed off, a certain philosophy of the situation penetrated her mind, and took form in the exclamation, "It was bound to end in this way!" She did not go so far as, "I told you so!" which is customary on this sort of occasion. At the physician's orders, a camp bed had been prepared beside the sofa. The doctor examined Marius, and after having found that his pulse was still beating, that the wounded man had no very deep wound on his breast, and that the blood on the corners of his lips proceeded from his nostrils, he had him placed flat on the bed, without a pillow, with his head on the same level as his body, and even a trifle lower, and with his bust bare in order to facilitate respiration. Mademoiselle Gillenormand, on perceiving that they were undressing Marius, withdrew. She set herself to telling her beads in her own chamber.

The trunk had not suffered any internal injury; a bullet, deadened by the pocketbook, had turned aside and made the tour of his ribs with a hideous laceration, which was of no great depth, and consequently, not dangerous. The long, underground journey had completed the dislocation of the broken collarbone, and the disorder there was serious. The arms had been slashed with sabre cuts. Not a single scar disfigured his face; but his head was fairly covered with cuts; what would be the result of these wounds on the head? Would they stop short at the hairy cuticle, or would they attack the brain? As yet, this could not be decided. A grave symptom was that they had caused a swoon, and that people do not always recover from such swoons. Moreover, the wounded man had been exhausted by hemorrhage. From the waist down, the barricade had protected the lower part of the body from injury.

Basque and Nicolette tore up linen and prepared bandages; Nicolette sewed them, Basque rolled them. As lint was lacking, the doctor, for the time being, arrested the bleeding with layers of wadding. Beside the bed, three candles burned on a table where the case of surgical instruments lay spread out. The doctor bathed Marius's face and hair with cold water. A full pail was reddened in an instant. The porter, candle in hand, lighted them.

The doctor seemed to be pondering sadly. From time to time, he made a negative sign with his head, as though replying to some question he had inwardly addressed to himself.

A bad sign for the sick man are these mysterious dialogues of the doctor with himself.

At the moment when the doctor was wiping Marius's face, and lightly touching his still closed eyes with his finger, a door opened at the end of the drawingroom, and a long, pallid figure made its appearance.

This was the grandfather.

The revolt had, for the past two days, deeply agitated, enraged and engrossed the mind of M. Gillenormand. He had not been able to sleep on the previous night, and he had been in a fever all day long. In the evening, he had gone to bed very early, recommending that everything in the house should be well barred, and he had fallen into a doze through sheer fatigue.

Old men sleep lightly; M. Gillenormand's chamber adjoined the drawingroom, and in spite of all the precautions that had been taken, the noise had awakened him. Surprised at the rift of light he saw under his door, he had risen from his bed, and had groped his way there.

He stood astonished on the threshold, one hand on the handle of the half-open door, with his head bent a little forward and quivering, his body wrapped in a white dressing-gown, which was straight and as destitute of folds as a winding-sheet; and he had the air of a phantom who is gazing into a tomb.

He saw the bed, and on the mattress that young man, bleeding, white with a waxen whiteness, with closed eyes and gaping mouth, and pallid lips, stripped to the waist, slashed all over with crimson wounds, motionless and brilliantly lighted up.

The grandfather trembled from head to foot as powerfully as ossified limbs can tremble, his eyes, whose corneae were yellow on account of his great age, were veiled in a sort of vitreous glitter, his whole face assumed in an instant the earthy angles of a skull, his arms fell pendent, as though a spring had broken, and his amazement was betrayed by the outspreading of the fingers of his two aged hands, which quivered all over, his knees formed an angle in front, allowing, through the opening in his dressing-gown, a view of his poor bare legs, all bristling with white hairs, and he murmured, "Marius!"

"Sir," said Basque, "Monsieur has just been brought back. He went to the barricade, and . . ."

"He is dead!" cried the old man in a terrible voice. "Ah! The rascal!"

Then a sort of sepulchral transformation straightened up this centenarian as erect as a young man.

"Sir," said he, "you are the doctor. Begin by telling me one thing. He is dead, is he not?"

The doctor, who was at the highest pitch of anxiety, remained silent.

M. Gillenormand wrung his hands with an outburst of terrible laughter.

"He is dead! He is dead! He is dead! He has got himself killed on the barricades! Out of hatred to me! He did that to spite me! Ah! You blood drinker! This is the way he returns to me! Misery of my life, he is dead!"

He went to the window, threw it wide open as though he were stifling, and, erect before the darkness, he began to talk into the street, to the night, "Pierced, sabred, exterminated, slashed, hacked in pieces! Just look at that, the villain! He knew well that I was waiting for him, and that I had had his room arranged, and that I had placed at the head of my bed his portrait taken when he was a little child! He knew well that he had only to come back, and that I had been recalling him for years, and that I remained by my fireside, with my hands on my knees, not knowing what to do, and that I was mad over it! You knew well, that you had but to return and to say: 'It is I,' and you would have been the master of the house, and that I should have obeyed you, and that you could have done whatever you pleased with your old numskull of a grandfather! You knew that well, and you said, 'No, he is a Royalist, I will not go!' And you went to the barricades, and you got yourself killed out of malice! To revenge yourself for what I said to you about Monsieur le Duc de Berry. It is infamous! Go to bed then and sleep tranquilly! He is dead, and this is my awakening."

The doctor, who was beginning to be uneasy in both quarters, quitted Marius for a moment, went to M. Gillenormand, and took his arm. The grandfather turned around, gazed at him with eyes that seemed exaggerated in size and bloodshot, and said to him calmly, "I thank you, Sir. I am composed, I am a man, I witnessed the death of Louis XVI, I know how to bear events. One thing is terrible and that is to think that it is your newspapers that do all the mischief. You will have scribblers, chatterers, lawyers, orators, tribunes, discussions, progress, enlightenment, the rights of man, the liberty of the press, and this is the way that your children will be brought home to you. Ah! Marius! It is abominable! Killed! Dead before me! A barricade! Ah, the scamp! Doctor, you live in this quarter, I believe? Oh! I know you well. I see your cabriolet pass my window. I am going to tell you. You are wrong to think that I am angry. One does not fly into a rage against a dead man. That would be stupid. This is a child whom I have reared. I was already old while he was very young. He played in the Tuileries garden with his little shovel and his little chair, and in order that the inspectors might not grumble, I stopped up the holes that he made in the earth with his shovel, with my cane. One day he exclaimed: Down with Louis XVIII! And off he went. It was no fault of mine. He was all rosy and blond. His mother is dead. Have you ever noticed that all little children are blond? Why is it so? He is the son of one of those brigands of the Loire, but children are innocent of their fathers' crimes. I remember when he was no higher than that. He could not manage to pronounce his Ds. He had a way of talking that was so sweet and indistinct that you would have thought it was a bird chirping. I remember that once, in front of the Hercules Farnese, people formed a circle to admire him and marvel at him, he was so handsome, was that child! He had a head such as you see in pictures. I talked in a deep voice, and I frightened him with my cane, but he knew very well that it was only to make him laugh. In the morning, when he entered my room, I grumbled, but he was like the sunlight to me, all the same. One cannot defend oneself against those brats. They take hold of you, they hold you fast, they never let you go again. The truth is, that there never was a cupid like that child. Now, what can you say for your Lafayettes, your Benjamin Constants, and your Tirecuir de Corcelles who have killed him? This cannot be allowed to pass in this fashion."

He approached Marius, who still lay livid and motionless, and to whom the physician had returned, and began once more to wring his hands. The old man's pallid lips moved as though mechanically, and permitted the passage of words that were barely audible, like breaths in the death agony, "Ah! Heartless lad! Ah! Clubbist! Ah! Wretch! Ah! Septembrist!"

Reproaches in the low voice of an agonizing man, addressed to a corpse.

Little by little, as it is always indispensable that internal eruptions should come to the light, the sequence of words returned, but the grandfather appeared no longer to have the strength to utter them, his voice was so weak, and extinct, that it seemed to come from the other side of an abyss, "It is all the same to me, I am going to die too, that I am. And to think that there is not a hussy in Paris who would not have been delighted to make this wretch happy! A scamp who, instead of amusing himself and enjoying life, went off to fight and get himself shot down like a brute! And for whom? Why? For the Republic! Instead of going to dance at the Chaumiere, as it is the duty of young folks to do! What's the use of being twenty years old? The Republic, a cursed pretty folly! Poor mothers, beget fine boys, do! Come, he is dead. That will make two funerals under the same carriage gate. So you have got yourself arranged like this for the sake of General Lamarque's handsome eyes! What had that General Lamarque done to you? A slasher! A chatterbox! To get oneself killed for a dead man! If that isn't enough to drive anyone mad! Just think of it! At twenty! And without so much as turning his head to see whether he was not leaving something behind him! That's the way poor, good old fellows are forced to die alone, nowadays. Perish in your corner, owl! Well, after all, so much the better, that is what I was hoping for, this will kill me on the spot. I am too old, I am a hundred years old, I am a hundred thousand years old, I ought, by rights, to have been dead long ago. This blow puts an end to it. So all is over, what happiness! What is the good of making him inhale ammonia and all that parcel of drugs? You are wasting your trouble, you fool of a doctor! Come, he's dead, completely dead. I know all about it, I am dead myself too. He hasn't done things by half. Yes, this age is infamous, infamous and that's what I think of you, of your ideas, of your systems, of your masters, of your oracles, of your doctors, of your scape-graces of writers, of your rascally philosophers, and of all the revolutions that, for the last sixty years, have been frightening the flocks of crows in the Tuileries! But you were pitiless in getting yourself killed like this, I shall not even grieve over your death, do you understand, you assassin?"

At that moment, Marius slowly opened his eyes, and his glance, still dimmed by lethargic wonder, rested on M. Gillenormand.

"Marius!" cried the old man. "Marius! My little Marius! My child! My well-beloved son! You open your eyes, you gaze upon me, you are alive, thanks!"

And he fell fainting.

BOOK FOURTH: JAVERT DERAILED

CHAPTER I—JAVERT

Javert passed slowly down the Rue de l'Homme Arme.

He walked with drooping head for the first time in his life, and likewise, for the first time in his life, with his hands behind his back.

Up to that day, Javert had borrowed from Napoleon's attitudes, only that which is expressive of resolution, with arms folded across the chest; that which is expressive of uncertainty—with the hands behind the back—had been unknown to him. Now, a change had taken place; his whole person, slow and sombre, was stamped with anxiety.

He plunged into the silent streets.

Nevertheless, he followed one given direction.

He took the shortest cut to the Seine, reached the Quai des Ormes, skirted the quay, passed the Greve, and halted at some distance from the post of the Place du Chatelet, at the angle of the Pont Notre-Dame. There, between the Notre-Dame and the Pont au Change on the one hand, and the Quai de la Megisserie and the Quai aux Fleurs on the other, the Seine forms a sort of square lake, traversed by a rapid.

This point of the Seine is dreaded by mariners. Nothing is more dangerous than this rapid, hemmed in, at that epoch, and irritated by the piles of the mill on the bridge, now demolished. The two bridges, situated thus close together, augment the peril; the water hurries in formidable wise through the arches. It rolls in vast and terrible waves; it accumulates and piles up there; the flood attacks the piles of the bridges as though in an effort to pluck them up with great liquid ropes. Men who fall in there never reappear; the best of swimmers are drowned there.

Javert leaned both elbows on the parapet, his chin resting in both hands, and, while his nails were mechanically twined in the abundance of his whiskers, he meditated.

A novelty, a revolution, a catastrophe had just taken place in the depths of his being; and he had something upon which to examine himself.

Javert was undergoing horrible suffering.

For several hours, Javert had ceased to be simple. He was troubled; that brain, so limpid in its blindness, had lost its transparency; that crystal was clouded. Javert felt duty divided within his conscience, and he could not conceal the fact from himself. When he had so unexpectedly encountered Jean Valjean on the banks of the Seine, there had been in him something of the wolf that regains his grip on his prey, and of the dog who finds his master again.

He beheld before him two paths, both equally straight, but he beheld two; and that terrified him; him, who had never in all his life known more than one straight line. And, the poignant anguish lay in this, that the two paths were contrary to each other. One of these straight lines excluded the other. Which of the two was the true one?

His situation was indescribable.

To owe his life to a malefactor, to accept that debt and to repay it; to be, in spite of himself, on a level with a fugitive from justice, and to repay his service with another service; to allow it to be said to him, "Go," and to say to the latter in his turn, "Be free"; to sacrifice to personal motives duty, that general obligation, and to be conscious, in those personal motives, of something that was also general, and, perchance, superior, to betray society in order to remain true to his conscience; that all these absurdities should be realized and should accumulate upon him, this was what overwhelmed him.

One thing had amazed him, this was that Jean Valjean should have done him a favor, and one thing petrified him, that he, Javert, should have done Jean Valjean a favor.

Where did he stand? He sought to comprehend his position, and could no longer find his bearings.

What was he to do now? To deliver up Jean Valjean was bad; to leave Jean Valjean at liberty was bad. In the first case, the man of authority fell lower than the man of the galleys, in the second, a convict rose above the law, and set his foot upon it. In both cases, dishonor for him, Javert. There was disgrace in any resolution at which he might arrive. Destiny has some extremities that rise perpendicularly from the impossible, and beyond which life is no longer anything but a precipice. Javert had reached one of those extremities.

One of his anxieties consisted in being constrained to think. The very violence of all these conflicting emotions forced him to it. Thought was something to which he was unused, and which was peculiarly painful.

In thought there always exists a certain amount of internal rebellion; and it irritated him to have that within him.

Thought on any subject whatever, outside of the restricted circle of his functions, would have been for him in any case useless and a fatigue; thought on the day that had just passed was a torture. Nevertheless, it was indispensable that he should take a look into his conscience, after such shocks, and render to himself an account of himself.

What he had just done made him shudder. He, Javert, had seen fit to decide, contrary to all the regulations of the police, contrary to the whole social and judicial organization, contrary to the entire code, upon a release; this had suited him; he had substituted his own affairs for the affairs of the public; was not this unjustifiable? Every time that he brought himself face to face with this deed without a name that he had committed, he trembled from head to foot. Upon what should he decide? One sole resource remained to him; to return in all haste to the Rue de l'Homme Arme, and commit Jean Valjean to prison. It was clear that that was what he ought to do. He could not.

Something barred his way in that direction.

Something? What? Is there in the world, anything outside of the tribunals, executory sentences, the police and the authorities? Javert was overwhelmed.

A galley slave sacred! A convict who could not be touched by the law! And that the deed of Javert!

Was it not a fearful thing that Javert and Jean Valjean, the man made to proceed with vigor, the man made to submit, that these two men who were both the things of the law, should have come to such a pass, that both of them had set themselves above the law? What then! Such enormities were to happen and no one was to be punished! Jean Valjean, stronger than the whole social order, was to remain at liberty, and he, Javert, was to go on eating the government's bread!

His revery gradually became terrible.

He might, athwart this revery, have also reproached himself on the subject of that insurgent who had been taken to the Rue des Filles-du-Calvaire; but he never even thought of that. The lesser fault was lost in the greater. Besides, that insurgent was, obviously, a dead man, and, legally, death puts an end to pursuit.

Jean Valjean was the load that weighed upon his spirit.

Jean Valjean disconcerted him. All the axioms that had served him as points of support all his life long, had crumbled away in the presence of this man. Jean Valjean's generosity toward him, Javert, crushed him. Other facts that he now recalled, and that he had formerly treated as lies and folly, now recurred to him as realities. M. Madeleine reappeared behind Jean Valjean, and the two figures were superposed in such fashion that they now formed but one, which was venerable. Javert felt that something terrible was penetrating his soul—admiration for a convict. Respect for a galley slave—is that a possible thing? He shuddered at it, yet could not escape from it. In vain did he struggle, he was reduced to confess, in his inmost heart, the sublimity of that wretch. This was odious.

A benevolent malefactor, merciful, gentle, helpful, clement, a convict, returning good for evil, giving back pardon for hatred, preferring pity to vengeance, preferring to ruin himself rather than to ruin his enemy, saving him who had smitten him, kneeling on the heights of virtue, more nearly akin to an angel than to a man. Javert was constrained to admit to himself that this monster existed.

Things could not go on in this manner.

Certainly, and we insist upon this point, he had not yielded without resistance to that monster, to that infamous angel, to that hideous hero, who enraged almost as much as he amazed him. Twenty times, as he sat in that carriage face to face with Jean Valjean, the legal tiger had roared within him. A score of times he had been tempted to fling himself upon Jean Valjean, to seize him and devour him, that is to say, to arrest him. What more simple, in fact? To cry out at the first post that they passed, "Here is a fugitive from justice, who has broken his ban!" to summon the gendarmes and say to them, "This man is yours!" then to go off, leaving that condemned man there, to ignore the rest and not to meddle further in the matter. This man is forever a prisoner of the law; the law may do with him what it will. What could be more just? Javert had said all this to himself; he had wished to pass beyond, to act, to apprehend the man, and then, as at present, he had not been able to do it; and every time that his arm had been raised convulsively toward Jean Valjean's collar, his hand had fallen back again, as beneath an enormous weight, and in the depths of his thought he had heard a voice, a strange voice crying to him, "It is well. Deliver up your savior. Then have the basin of Pontius Pilate brought and wash your claws."

Then his reflections reverted to himself and beside Jean Valjean glorified he beheld himself, Javert, degraded.

A convict was his benefactor!

But then, why had he permitted that man to leave him alive? He had the right to be killed in that barricade. He should have asserted that right. It would have been better to summon the other insurgents to his succor against Jean Valjean, to get himself shot by force.

His supreme anguish was the loss of certainty. He felt that he had been uprooted. The code was no longer anything more than a stump in his hand. He had to deal with scruples of an unknown species. There had taken place within him a sentimental revelation entirely distinct from legal affirmation, his only standard of measurement hitherto. To remain in his former uprightness did not suffice. A whole order of unexpected facts had cropped up and subjugated him. A whole new world was dawning on his soul: kindness accepted and repaid, devotion, mercy, indulgence, violences committed by pity on austerity, respect for persons, no more definitive condemnation, no more conviction, the possibility of a tear in the eye of the law, no one knows what justice according to God, running in inverse sense to justice according to men. He perceived amid the shadows the terrible rising of an unknown moral sun; it horrified and dazzled him. An owl forced to the gaze of an eagle.

He said to himself that it was true that there were exceptional cases, that authority might be put out of countenance, that the rule might be inadequate in the presence of a fact, that everything could not be framed within the text of the code, that the unforeseen compelled obedience, that the virtue of a convict might set a snare for the virtue of the functionary, that destiny did indulge in such ambushes, and he reflected with despair that he himself had not even been fortified against a surprise.

He was forced to acknowledge that goodness did exist. This convict had been good. And he himself, unprecedented circumstance, had just been good also. So he was becoming depraved.

He found that he was a coward. He conceived a horror of himself.

Javert's ideal, was not to be human, to be grand, to be sublime; it was to be irreproachable.

Now, he had just failed in this.

How had he come to such a pass? How had all this happened? He could not have told himself. He clasped his head in both hands, but in spite of all that he could do, he could not contrive to explain it to himself.

He had certainly always entertained the intention of restoring Jean Valjean to the law of which Jean Valjean was the captive, and of which he, Javert, was the slave. Not for a single instant while he held him in his grasp had he confessed to himself that he entertained the idea of releasing him. It was, in some sort, without his consciousness, that his hand had relaxed and had let him go free.

All sorts of interrogation points flashed before his eyes. He put questions to himself, and made replies to himself, and his replies frightened him. He asked himself: "What has that convict done, that desperate fellow, whom I have pursued even to persecution, and who has had me under his foot, and who could have avenged himself, and who owed it both to his rancor and to his safety, in leaving me my life, in showing mercy upon me? His duty? No. Something more. And I in showing mercy upon him in my turn—what have I done? My duty? No. Something more. So there is something beyond duty?" Here he took fright; his balance became disjointed; one of the scales fell into the abyss, the other rose heavenward, and Javert was no less terrified by the one that was on high than by the one that was below. Without being in the least in the world what is called Voltairian or a philosopher, or incredulous, being, on the contrary, respectful by instinct, toward the established church, he knew it only as an august fragment of the social whole; order was his dogma, and sufficed for him; ever since he had attained to man's estate and the rank of a functionary, he had centered nearly all his religion in the police. Being, and here we employ words without the least irony and in their most serious acceptation, being, as we have said, a spy as other men are priests. He had a superior, M. Gisquet; up to that day he had never dreamed of that other superior, God.

This new chief, God, he became unexpectedly conscious of, and he felt embarrassed by him. This unforeseen presence threw him off his bearings; he did not know what to do with this superior, he, who was not ignorant of the fact that the subordinate is bound always to bow, that he must not disobey, nor find fault, nor discuss, and that, in the presence of a superior who amazes him too greatly, the inferior has no other resource than that of handing in his resignation.

But how was he to set about handing in his resignation to God?

However things might stand—and it was to this point that he reverted constantly—one fact dominated everything else for him, and that was, that he had just committed a terrible infraction of the law. He had just shut his eyes on an escaped convict who had broken his ban. He had just set a galley slave at large. He had just robbed the laws of a man who belonged to them. That was what he had done. He no longer understood himself. The very reasons for his action escaped him; only their vertigo was left with him. Up to that moment he had lived with that blind faith that gloomy probity engenders. This faith had quitted him, this probity had deserted him. All that he had believed in melted away. Truths that he did not wish to recognize were besieging him, inexorably. Henceforth, he must be a different man. He was suffering from the strange pains of a conscience abruptly operated on for the cataract. He saw that which it was repugnant to him to behold. He felt himself emptied, useless, put out of joint with his past life, turned out, dissolved. Authority was dead within him. He had no longer any reason for existing.

A terrible situation! To be touched.

To be granite and to doubt! To be the statue of Chastisement cast in one piece in the mould of the law, and suddenly to become aware of the fact that one cherishes beneath one's breast of bronze something absurd and disobedient that almost resembles a heart! To come to the pass of returning good for good, although one has said to oneself up to that day that that good is evil! To be the watchdog, and to lick the intruder's hand! To be ice and melt! To be the pincers and to turn into a hand! To suddenly feel one's fingers opening! To relax one's grip, what a terrible thing!

The man-projectile no longer acquainted with his route and retreating!

To be obliged to confess this to oneself: infallibility is not infallible, there may exist error in the dogma, all has not been said when a code speaks, society is not perfect, authority is complicated with vacillation, a crack is possible in the immutable, judges are but men, the law may err, tribunals may make a mistake! To behold a rift in the immense blue pane of the firmament!

That which was passing in Javert was the Fampoux of a rectilinear conscience, the derailment of a soul, the crushing of a probity that had been irresistibly launched in a straight line and was breaking against God. It certainly was singular that the stoker of order, that the engineer of authority, mounted on the blind iron horse with its rigid road, could be unseated by a flash of light! That the immovable, the direct, the correct, the geometrical, the passive, the perfect, could bend! That there should exist for the locomotive a road to Damascus!

God, always within man, and refractory, He, the true conscience, to the false; a prohibition to the spark to die out; an order to the ray to remember the sun; an injunction to the soul to recognize the veritable absolute when confronted with the fictitious absolute, humanity that cannot be lost; the human heart indestructible; that splendid phenomenon, the finest, perhaps, of all our interior marvels, did Javert understand this? Did Javert penetrate it? Did Javert account for it to himself? Evidently he did not. But beneath the pressure of that incontestable incomprehensibility he felt his brain bursting.

He was less the man transfigured than the victim of this prodigy. In all this he perceived only the tremendous difficulty of existence. It seemed to him that, henceforth, his respiration was repressed forever. He was not accustomed to having something unknown hanging over his head.

Up to this point, everything above him had been, to his gaze, merely a smooth, limpid and simple surface; there was nothing incomprehensible, nothing obscure; nothing that was not defined, regularly disposed, linked, precise, circumscribed, exact, limited, closed, fully provided for; authority was a plane surface; there was no fall in it, no dizziness in its presence. Javert had never beheld the unknown except from below. The irregular, the unforeseen, the disordered opening of chaos, the possible slip over a precipice—this was the work of the lower regions, of rebels, of the wicked, of wretches. Now Javert threw himself back, and he was suddenly terrified by this unprecedented apparition: a gulf on high.

What! One was dismantled from top to bottom! One was disconcerted, absolutely! In what could one trust! That which had been agreed upon was giving way! What! The defect in society's armor could be discovered by a magnanimous wretch! What! An honest servitor of the law could suddenly find himself caught between two crimes—the crime of allowing a man to escape and the crime of arresting him! Everything was not settled in the orders given by the State to the functionary! There might be blind alleys in duty! What, all this was real! Was it true that an ex-ruffian, weighed down with convictions, could rise erect and end by being in the right? Was this credible? Were there cases in which the law should retire before transfigured crime, and stammer its excuses? Yes, that was the state of the case! And Javert saw it! And Javert had touched it! And not only could he not deny it, but he had taken part in it. These were realities. It was abominable that actual facts could reach such deformity. If facts did their duty, they would confine themselves to being proofs of the law; facts—it is God who sends them. Was anarchy, then, on the point of now descending from on high?

Thus, and in the exaggeration of anguish, and the optical illusion of consternation, all that might have corrected and restrained this impression was effaced, and society, and the human race, and the universe were, henceforth, summed up in his eyes, in one simple and terrible feature, thus the penal laws, the thing judged, the force due to legislation, the decrees of the sovereign courts, the magistracy, the government, prevention, repression, official cruelty, wisdom, legal infallibility, the principle of authority, all the dogmas on which rest political and civil security, sovereignty, justice, public truth, all this was rubbish, a shapeless mass, chaos; he himself, Javert, the spy of order, incorruptibility in the service of the police, the bulldog providence of society, vanquished and hurled to earth; and, erect, at the summit of all that ruin, a man with a green cap on his head and a halo around his brow; this was the astounding confusion to which he had come; this was the fearful vision that he bore within his soul.

Was this to be endured? No.

A violent state, if ever such existed. There were only two ways of escaping from it. One was to go resolutely to Jean Valjean, and restore to his cell the convict from the galleys. The other . . .

Javert quitted the parapet, and, with head erect this time, betook himself, with a firm tread, toward the station-house indicated by a lantern at one of the corners of the Place du Chatelet.

On arriving there, he saw through the window a sergeant of police, and he entered. Policemen recognize each other by the very way in which they open the door of a stationhouse. Javert mentioned his name, showed his card to the sergeant, and seated himself at the table of the post on which a candle was burning. On a table lay a pen, a leaden inkstand and paper, provided in the event of possible reports and the orders of the night patrols. This table, still completed by its straw-seated chair, is an institution; it exists in all police stations; it is invariably ornamented with a boxwood saucer filled with sawdust and a wafer box of cardboard filled with red wafers, and it forms the lowest stage of official style. It is there that the literature of the State has its beginning.

Javert took a pen and a sheet of paper, and began to write. This is what he wrote,

"A FEW OBSERVATIONS FOR THE GOOD OF THE SERVICE.

In the first place: I beg Monsieur le Prefet to cast his eyes on this. Secondly: prisoners, on arriving after examination, take off their shoes and stand barefoot on the flagstones while they are being searched. Many of them cough on their return to prison. This entails hospital expenses. Thirdly: the mode of keeping track of a man with relays of police agents from distance to distance, is good, but, on important occasions, it is requisite that at least two agents should never lose sight of each other, so that, in case one agent should, for any cause, grow weak in his service, the other may supervise him and take his place.

Fourthly: it is inexplicable why the special regulation of the prison of the Madelonettes interdicts the prisoner from having a chair, even by paying for it. Fifthly: in the Madelonettes there are only two bars to the canteen, so that the canteen woman can touch the prisoners with her hand. Sixthly: the prisoners called barkers, who summon the other prisoners to the parlor, force the prisoner to pay them two sous to call his name distinctly. This is a theft.

Seventhly: for a broken thread ten sous are withheld in the weaving shop; this is an abuse of the contractor, since the cloth is none the worse for it. Eighthly: it is annoying for visitors to La Force to be obliged to traverse the boys' court in order to reach the parlor of Sainte-Marie-l'Egyptienne. Ninthly: it is a fact that any day gendarmes can be overheard relating in the courtyard of the prefecture the interrogations put by the magistrates to prisoners. For a gendarme, who should be sworn to secrecy, to repeat what he has heard in the examination room is a grave disorder.

Tenthly: Mme. Henry is an honest woman; her canteen is very neat; but it is bad to have a woman keep the wicket to the mousetrap of the secret cells. This is unworthy of the Conciergerie of a great civilization."

Javert wrote these lines in his calmest and most correct chirography, not omitting a single comma, and making the paper screech under his pen. Below the last line he signed "JAVERT, Inspector of the 1st class. The Post of the Place du Chatelet. June 7th, 1832, about one o'clock in the morning."

Javert dried the fresh ink on the paper, folded it like a letter, sealed it, wrote on the back: Note for the administration, left it on the table, and quitted the post. The glazed and grated door fell to behind him.

Again he traversed the Place du Chatelet diagonally, regained the quay, and returned with automatic precision to the very point that he had abandoned a quarter of an hour previously, leaned on his elbows and found himself again in the same attitude on the same paving stone of the parapet. He did not appear to have stirred.

The darkness was complete. It was the sepulchral moment that follows midnight. A ceiling of clouds concealed the stars. Not a single light burned in the houses of the city; no one was passing; all of the streets and quays that could be seen were deserted; Notre-Dame and the towers of the courthouse seemed features of the night. A street lantern reddened the margin of the quay. The outlines of the bridges lay shapeless in the mist one behind the other. Recent rains had swollen the river.

The spot where Javert was leaning was, it will be remembered, situated precisely over the rapids of the Seine, perpendicularly above that formidable spiral of whirlpools that loose and knot themselves again like an endless screw.

Javert bent his head and gazed. All was black. Nothing was to be distinguished. A sound of foam was audible; but the river could not be seen. At moments, in that dizzy depth, a gleam of light appeared, and undulated vaguely, water possessing the power of taking light, no one knows from where, and converting it into a snake. The light vanished, and all became indistinct once more. Immensity seemed thrown open there. What lay below was not water, it was a gulf. The wall of the quay, abrupt, confused, mingled with the vapors, instantly concealed from sight, produced the effect of an escarpment of the infinite. Nothing was to be seen, but the hostile chill of the water and the stale odor of the wet stones could be felt. A fierce breath rose from this abyss. The flood in the river, divined rather than perceived, the tragic whispering of the waves, the melancholy vastness of the arches of the bridge, the imaginable fall into that gloomy void, into all that shadow was full of horror.

Javert remained motionless for several minutes, gazing at this opening of shadow; he considered the invisible with a fixity that resembled attention. The water roared. All at once he took off his hat and placed it on the edge of the quay. A moment later, a tall black figure, which a belated passerby in the distance might have taken for a phantom, appeared erect upon the parapet of the quay, bent over toward the Seine, then drew itself up again, and fell straight down into the shadows; a dull splash followed; and the shadow alone was in the secret of the convulsions of that obscure form that had disappeared beneath the water.

BOOK FIFTH: GRANDSON AND GRANDFATHER

CHAPTER I—IN WHICH THE TREE WITH THE ZINC PLASTER APPEARS AGAIN

Some time after the events we have just recorded, Sieur Boulatruelle experienced a lively emotion.

Sieur Boulatruelle was that road-mender of Montfermeil whom the reader has already seen in the gloomy parts of this book.

Boulatruelle, as the reader may, perchance, recall, was a man who was occupied with divers and troublesome matters. He broke stones and damaged travelers on the highway.

Road-mender and thief as he was, he cherished one dream; he believed in the treasures buried in the forest of Montfermeil. He hoped some day to find the money in the earth at the foot of a tree; in the meanwhile, he lived to search the pockets of passersby.

Nevertheless, for an instant, he was prudent. He had just escaped neatly. He had been, as the reader is aware, picked up in Jondrette's garret in company with the other ruffians. Utility of a vice: his drunkenness had been his salvation. The authorities had never been able to make out whether he had been there in the quality of a robber or a man who had been robbed. An order of nolle prosequi, founded on his well-authenticated state of intoxication on the evening of the ambush, had set him at liberty. He had taken to his heels. He had returned to his road from Gagny to Lagny, to make, under administrative supervision, broken stone for the good of the state, with downcast mien, in a very pensive mood, his ardor for theft somewhat cooled; but he was addicted nonetheless tenderly to the wine that had recently saved him.

As for the lively emotion that he had experienced a short time after his return to his roadmender's turf-thatched cot, here it is:

One morning, Boulatruelle, while on his way as was his wont, to his work, and possibly also to his ambush, a little before daybreak caught sight, through the branches of the trees, of a man, whose back alone he saw, but the shape of whose shoulders, as it seemed to him at that distance and in the early dusk, was not entirely unfamiliar to him. Boulatruelle, although intoxicated, had a correct and lucid memory, a defensive arm that is indispensable to anyone who is at all in conflict with legal order.

"Where the deuce have I seen something like that man yonder?" he said to himself. But he could make himself no answer, except that the man resembled someone of whom his memory preserved a confused trace.

However, apart from the identity that he could not manage to catch, Boulatruelle put things together and made calculations. This man did not belong in the countryside. He had just arrived there. On foot, evidently. No public conveyance passes through Montfermeil at that hour. He had walked all night. From where came he? Not from a very great distance; for he had neither haversack, nor bundle. From Paris, no doubt. Why was he in these woods? Why was he there at such an hour? What had he come there for?

Boulatruelle thought of the treasure. By dint of ransacking his memory, he recalled in a vague way that he had already, many years before, had a similar alarm in connection with a man who produced on him the effect that he might well be this very individual.

"By the deuce," said Boulatruelle, "I'll find him again. I'll discover the parish of that parishioner. This prowler of Patron-Minette has a reason, and I'll know it. People can't have secrets in my forest if I don't have a finger in the pie."

He took his pickax, which was very sharply pointed.

"There now," he grumbled, "is something that will search the earth and a man."

And, as one knots one thread to another thread, he took up the line of march at his best pace in the direction that the man must follow, and set out across the thickets.

When he had compassed a hundred strides, the day, which was already beginning to break, came to his assistance. Footprints stamped in the sand, weeds trodden down here and there, heather crushed, young branches in the brushwood bent and in the act of straightening themselves up again with the graceful deliberation of the arms of a pretty woman who stretches herself when she wakes, pointed out to him a sort of track. He followed it, then lost it. Time was flying. He plunged deeper into the woods and came to a sort of eminence. An early huntsman who was passing in the distance along a path, whistling the air of Guillery, suggested to him the idea of climbing a tree. Old as he was, he was agile. There stood close at hand a beech tree of great size, worthy of Tityrus and of Boulatruelle. Boulatruelle ascended the beech as high as he was able.

The idea was a good one. On scrutinizing the solitary waste on the side where the forest is thoroughly entangled and wild, Boulatruelle suddenly caught sight of his man.

Hardly had he got his eye upon him when he lost sight of him.

The man entered, or rather, glided into, an open glade, at a considerable distance, masked by large trees, but with which Boulatruelle was perfectly familiar, on account of having noticed, near a large pile of porous stones, an ailing chestnut tree bandaged with a sheet of zinc nailed directly upon the bark. This glade was the one that was formerly called the Blaru-bottom. The heap of stones, destined for no one knows what employment, which was visible there thirty years ago, is doubtless still there. Nothing equals a heap of stones in longevity, unless it is a board fence. They are temporary expedients. What a reason for lasting!

Boulatruelle, with the rapidity of joy, dropped rather than descended from the tree. The lair was unearthed, the question now was to seize the beast. That famous treasure of his dreams was probably there.

It was no small matter to reach that glade. By the beaten paths, which indulge in a thousand teasing zigzags, it required a good quarter of an hour. In a beeline, through the underbrush, which is peculiarly dense, very thorny, and very aggressive in that locality, a full half hour was necessary. Boulatruelle committed the error of not comprehending this. He believed in the straight line; a respectable optical illusion, which ruins many a man. The thicket, bristling as it was, struck him as the best road.

"Let's take to the wolves' Rue de Rivoli," said he.

Boulatruelle, accustomed to taking crooked courses, was on this occasion guilty of the fault of going straight.

He flung himself resolutely into the tangle of undergrowth.

He had to deal with holly bushes, nettles, hawthorns, eglantines, thistles, and very irascible brambles. He was much lacerated.

At the bottom of the ravine he found water that he was obliged to traverse.

At last he reached the Blaru-bottom, after the lapse of forty minutes, sweating, soaked, breathless, scratched, and ferocious.

There was no one in the glade. Boulatruelle rushed to the heap of stones. It was in its place. It had not been carried off.

As for the man, he had vanished in the forest. He had made his escape. Where? In what direction? Into what thicket? Impossible to guess.

And, heartrending to say, there, behind the pile of stones, in front of the tree with the sheet of zinc, was freshly turned earth, a pickax, abandoned or forgotten, and a hole.

The hole was empty.

"Thief!" shrieked Boulatruelle, shaking his fist at the horizon.

CHAPTER II—MARIUS, EMERGING FROM CIVIL WAR, MAKES READY FOR DOMESTIC WAR

For a long time, Marius was neither dead nor alive. For many weeks he lay in a fever accompanied by delirium, and by tolerably grave cerebral symptoms, caused more by the shocks of the wounds on the head than by the wounds themselves.

He repeated Cosette's name for whole nights in the melancholy loquacity of fever, and with the sombre obstinacy of agony. The extent of some of the lesions presented a serious danger, the suppuration of large wounds being always liable to become reabsorbed, and consequently, to kill the sick man, under certain atmospheric conditions; at every change of weather, at the slightest storm, the physician was uneasy.

"Above all things," he repeated, "let the wounded man be subjected to no emotion." The dressing of the wounds was complicated and difficult, the fixation of apparatus and bandages by cerecloths not having been invented as yet, at that epoch. Nicolette used up a sheet "as big as the ceiling," as she put it, for lint. It was not without difficulty that the chloruretted lotions and the nitrate of silver overcame the gangrene. As long as there was any danger, M. Gillenormand, seated in despair at his grandson's pillow, was, like Marius, neither alive nor dead.

Every day, sometimes twice a day, a very well dressed gentleman with white hair, such was the description given by the porter, came to inquire about the wounded man, and left a large package of lint for the dressings.

Finally, on the 7th of September, four months to a day, after the sorrowful night when he had been brought back to his grandfather in a dying condition, the doctor declared that he would answer for Marius. Convalescence began. But Marius was forced to remain for two months more stretched out on a long chair, on account of the results called up by the fracture of his collarbone. There always is a last wound like that which will not close, and which prolongs the dressings indefinitely, to the great annoyance of the sick person.

However, this long illness and this long convalescence saved him from all pursuit. In France, there is no wrath, not even of a public character, which six months will not extinguish. Revolts, in the present state of society, are so much the fault of everyone, that they are followed by a certain necessity of shutting the eyes.

Let us add, that the inexcusable Gisquet order, which enjoined doctors to lodge information against the wounded, having outraged public opinion, and not opinion alone, but the King first of all, the wounded were covered and protected by this indignation; and, with the exception of those who had been made prisoners in the very act of combat, the councils of war did not dare to trouble anyone. So Marius was left in peace.

M. Gillenormand first passed through all manner of anguish, and then through every form of ecstasy. It was found difficult to prevent his passing every night beside the wounded man; he had his big armchair carried to Marius's bedside; he required his daughter to take the finest linen in the house for compresses and bandages. Mademoiselle Gillenormand, like a sage and elderly person, contrived to spare the fine linen, while allowing the grandfather to think that he was obeyed. M. Gillenormand would not permit anyone to explain to him, that for the preparation of lint batiste is not nearly so good as coarse linen, nor new linen as old linen. He was present at all the dressings of the wounds from which Mademoiselle Gillenormand modestly absented herself. When the dead flesh was cut away with scissors, he said, "Aie! Aie!" Nothing was more touching than to see him with his gentle, senile palsy, offer the wounded man a cup of his cooling-draft. He overwhelmed the doctor with questions. He did not observe that he asked the same ones over and over again.

On the day when the doctor announced to him that Marius was out of danger, the goodman was in a delirium. He made his porter a present of three louis. That evening, on his return to his own chamber, he danced a gavotte, using his thumb and forefinger as castanets, and he sang the following song:

> "Jeanne was born at Fougere, a true shepherd's nest; I adore
> her petticoat, the rogue.
> Love, thou dwellest in her; for 'tis in her eyes that thou placest
> thy quiver, sly scamp!
> As for me, I sing her, and I love, more than Diana herself,
> Jeanne and her firm Breton breasts."

Then he knelt upon a chair, and Basque, who was watching him through the half-open door, made sure that he was praying.

Up to that time, he had not believed in God.

At each succeeding phase of improvement, which became more and more pronounced, the grandfather raved. He executed a multitude of mechanical actions full of joy; he ascended and descended the stairs, without knowing why. A pretty female neighbor was amazed one morning at receiving a big bouquet; it was M. Gillenormand who had sent it to her. The husband made a jealous scene. M. Gillenormand tried to draw Nicolette upon his knees. He called Marius, "M. le Baron." He shouted, "Long live the Republic!"

Every moment, he kept asking the doctor, "Is he no longer in danger?" He gazed upon Marius with the eyes of a grandmother. He brooded over him while he ate. He no longer knew himself, he no longer rendered himself an account of himself. Marius was the master of the house, there was abdication in his joy, he was the grandson of his grandson.

In the state of joy in which he then was, he was the most venerable of children. In his fear lest he might fatigue or annoy the convalescent, he stepped behind him to smile. He was content, joyous, delighted, charming, young. His white locks added a gentle majesty to the gay radiance of his visage. When grace is mingled with wrinkles, it is adorable. There is an indescribable aurora in beaming old age.

As for Marius, as he allowed them to dress his wounds and care for him, he had but one fixed idea: Cosette.

After the fever and delirium had left him, he did not again pronounce her name, and it might have been supposed that he no longer thought of her. He held his peace, precisely because his soul was there.

He did not know what had become of Cosette; the whole affair of the Rue de la Chanvrerie was like a cloud in his memory; shadows that were almost indistinct, floated through his mind, Eponine, Gavroche, Mabeuf, the Thenardiers, all his friends gloomily intermingled with the smoke of the barricade; the strange passage of M. Fauchelevent through that adventure produced on him the effect of a puzzle in a tempest; he understood nothing connected with his own life, he did not know how nor by whom he had been saved, and no one of those around him knew this; all that they had been able to tell him was, that he had been brought home at night in a hackneycoach, to the Rue des Filles-du-Calvaire; past, present, future were nothing more to him than the mist of a vague idea; but in that fog there was one immovable point, one clear and precise outline, something made of granite, a resolution, a will; to find Cosette once more. For him, the idea of life was not distinct from the idea of Cosette. He had decreed in his heart that he would not accept the one without the other, and he was immovably resolved to exact of any person whatever, who should desire to force him to live, from his grandfather, from fate, from hell—the restitution of his vanished Eden.

He did not conceal from himself the fact that obstacles existed.

Let us here emphasize one detail, he was not won over and was but little softened by all the solicitude and tenderness of his grandfather. In the first place, he was not in the secret; then, in his reveries of an invalid, which were still feverish, possibly, he distrusted this tenderness as a strange and novel thing, which had for its object his conquest. He remained cold. The grandfather absolutely wasted his poor old smile. Marius said to himself that it was all right so long as he, Marius, did not speak, and let things take their course; but that when it became a question of Cosette, he would find another face, and that his grandfather's true attitude would be unmasked. Then there would be an unpleasant scene; a recrudescence of family questions, a confrontation of positions, every sort of sarcasm and all manner of objections at one and the same time, Fauchelevent, Coupelevent, fortune, poverty, a stone about his neck, the future. Violent resistance; conclusion: a refusal. Marius stiffened himself in advance.

And then, in proportion as he regained life, the old ulcers of his memory opened once more, he reflected again on the past, Colonel Pontmercy placed himself once more between M. Gillenormand and him, Marius, he told himself that he had no true kindness to expect from a person who had been so unjust and so hard to his father. And with health, there returned to him a sort of harshness toward his grandfather. The old man was gently pained by this. M. Gillenormand, without however allowing it to appear, observed that Marius, ever since the latter had been brought back to him and had regained consciousness, had not once called him father. It is true that he did not say "monsieur" to him; but he contrived not to say either the one or the other, by means of a certain way of turning his phrases. Obviously, a crisis was approaching.

As almost always happens in such cases, Marius skirmished before giving battle, by way of proving himself. This is called "feeling the ground." One morning it came to pass that M. Gillenormand spoke slightingly of the Convention, apropos of a newspaper that had fallen into his hands, and gave vent to a Royalist harangue on Danton, Saint-Juste and Robespierre. "The men of '93 were giants," said Marius with severity. The old man held his peace, and uttered not a sound during the remainder of that day.

Marius, who had always present to his mind the inflexible grandfather of his early years, interpreted this silence as a profound concentration of wrath, augured from it a hot conflict, and augmented his preparations for the fray in the inmost recesses of his mind.

He decided that, in case of a refusal, he would tear off his bandages, dislocate his collarbone, that he would lay bare all the wounds that he had left, and would reject all food. His wounds were his munitions of war. He would have Cosette or die.

He awaited the propitious moment with the crafty patience of the sick.

That moment arrived.

CHAPTER III—MARIUS ATTACKED

One day, M. Gillenormand, while his daughter was putting in order the phials and cups on the marble of the commode, bent over Marius and said to him in his tenderest accents: "Look here, my little Marius, if I were in your place, I would eat meat now in preference to fish. A fried sole is excellent to begin a convalescence with, but a good cutlet is needed to put a sick man on his feet."

Marius, who had almost entirely recovered his strength, collected the whole of it, drew himself up into a sitting posture, laid his two clenched fists on the sheets of his bed, looked his grandfather in the face, assumed a terrible air, and said, "This leads me to say something to you."

"What is it?"

"That I wish to marry."

"Agreed," said his grandfather. And he burst out laughing.

"How agreed?"

"Yes, agreed. You shall have your little girl."

Marius, stunned and overwhelmed with the dazzling shock, trembled in every limb.

M. Gillenormand went on, "Yes, you shall have her, that pretty little girl of yours. She comes every day in the shape of an old gentleman to inquire after you. Ever since you were wounded, she has passed her time in weeping and making lint. I have made inquiries. She lives in the Rue de l'Homme Arme, No. 7. Ah! There we have it! Ah! So you want her! Well, you shall have her. You're caught. You had arranged your little plot, you had said to yourself, 'I'm going to signify this squarely to my grandfather, to that mummy of the Regency and of the Directory, to that ancient beau, to that Dorante turned Geronte; he has indulged in his frivolities also, that he has, and he has had his love affairs, and his grisettes and his Cosettes; he has made his rustle, he has had his wings, he has eaten of the bread of spring; he certainly must remember it.' Ah! You take the cockchafer by the horns. That's good. I offer you a cutlet and you answer me: 'By the way, I want to marry.' There's a transition for you! Ah! You reckoned on a bickering! You do not know that I am an old coward. What do you say to that? You are vexed? You did not expect to find your grandfather still more foolish than yourself, you are wasting the discourse that you meant to bestow upon me, Mr. Lawyer, and that's vexatious. Well, so much the worse, rage away. I'll do whatever you wish, and that cuts you short, imbecile! Listen. I have made my inquiries, I'm cunning too; she is charming, she is discreet, it is not true about the lancer, she has made heaps of lint, she's a jewel, she adores you, if you had died, there would have been three of us, her coffin would have accompanied mine. I have had an idea, ever since you have been better, of simply planting her at your bedside, but it is only in romances that young girls are brought to the bedsides of handsome young wounded men who interest them. It is not done. What would your aunt have said to it? You were nude three quarters of the time, my good fellow. Ask Nicolette, who has not left you for a moment, if there was any possibility of having a woman here. And then, what would the doctor have said? A pretty girl does not cure a man of fever. In short, it's all right, let us say no more about it, all's said, all's done, it's all settled, take her. Such is my ferocity. You see, I perceived that you did not love me. I said to myself: 'Here now, I have my little Cosette right under my hand, I'm going to give her to him, he will be obliged to love me a little then, or he must tell the reason why.' Ah! So you thought that the old man was going to storm, to put on a big voice, to shout no, and to lift his cane at all that aurora. Not a bit of it. Cosette, so be it; love, so be it; I ask nothing better. Pray take the trouble of getting married, sir. Be happy, my well-beloved child."

That said, the old man burst forth into sobs.

And he seized Marius's head, and pressed it with both arms against his breast, and both fell to weeping. This is one of the forms of supreme happiness.

"Father!" cried Marius.

"Ah, so you love me!" said the old man.

An ineffable moment ensued. They were choking and could not speak.

At length the old man stammered, "Come! his mouth is unstopped at last. He has said, 'Father,' to me."

Marius disengaged his head from his grandfather's arms, and said gently, "But, Father, now that I am quite well, it seems to me that I might see her."

"Agreed again, you shall see her tomorrow."

"Father!"

"What?"

"Why not today?"

"Well, today then. Let it be today. You have called me 'father' three times, and it is worth it. I will attend to it. She shall be brought here. Agreed, I tell you. It has already been put into verse. This is the ending of the elegy of the 'Jeune Malade' by Andre Chenier, by Andre Chenier whose throat was cut by the ras . . . by the giants of '93."

M. Gillenormand fancied that he detected a faint frown on the part of Marius, who, in truth, as we must admit, was no longer listening to him, and who was thinking far more of Cosette than of 1793.

The grandfather, trembling at having so inopportunely introduced Andre Chenier, resumed precipitately, "Cut his throat is not the word. The fact is that the great revolutionary geniuses, who were not malicious, that is incontestable, who were heroes, pardi! Found that Andre Chenier embarrassed them somewhat, and they had him guillot . . . that is to say, those great men on the 7th of Thermidor, besought Andre Chenier, in the interests of public safety, to be so good as to go . . ."

M. Gillenormand, clutched by the throat by his own phrase, could not proceed. Being able neither to finish it nor to retract it, while his daughter arranged the pillow behind Marius, who was overwhelmed with so many emotions, the old man rushed headlong, with as much rapidity as his age permitted, from the bedchamber, shut the door behind him, and, purple, choking and foaming at the mouth, his eyes starting from his head, he found himself nose to nose with honest Basque, who was blacking boots in the anteroom. He seized Basque by the collar, and shouted full in his face in fury:"By the hundred thousand Javottes of the devil, those ruffians did assassinate him!"

"Who, Sir?"

"Andre Chenier!"

"Yes, Sir," said Basque in alarm.

CHAPTER IV—MADEMOISELLE GILLENORMAND ENDS BY NO LONGER THINKING IT A BAD THING THAT M. FAUCHELEVENT SHOULD HAVE ENTERED WITH SOMETHING UNDER HIS ARM

Cosette and Marius beheld each other once more.

What that interview was like we decline to say. There are things that one must not attempt to depict; the sun is one of them.

The entire family, including Basque and Nicolette, were assembled in Marius's chamber at the moment when Cosette entered it.

Precisely at that moment, the grandfather was on the point of blowing his nose; he stopped short, holding his nose in his handkerchief, and gazing over it at Cosette.

She appeared on the threshold; it seemed to him that she was surrounded by a glory.

"Adorable!" he exclaimed.

Then he blew his nose noisily.

Cosette was intoxicated, delighted, frightened, in heaven. She was as thoroughly alarmed as anyone can be by happiness. She stammered all pale, yet flushed, she wanted to fling herself into Marius's arms, and dared not. Ashamed of loving in the presence of all these people. People are pitiless toward happy lovers; they remain when the latter most desire to be left alone. Lovers have no need of any people whatever.

With Cosette, and behind her, there had entered a man with white hair who was grave yet smiling, though with a vague and heartrending smile. It was "Monsieur Fauchelevent"; it was Jean Valjean.

He was very well dressed, as the porter had said, entirely in black, in perfectly new garments, and with a white cravat.

The porter was a thousand leagues from recognizing in this correct bourgeois, in this probable notary, the fear-inspiring bearer of the corpse, who had sprung up at his door on the night of the 7th of June, tattered, muddy, hideous, haggard, his face masked in blood and mire, supporting in his arms the fainting Marius; still, his porter's scent was aroused. When M.

Fauchelevent arrived with Cosette, the porter had not been able to refrain from communicating to his wife this aside: "I don't know why it is, but I can't help fancying that I've seen that face before."

M. Fauchelevent in Marius's chamber, remained apart near the door. He had under his arm, a package that bore considerable resemblance to an octavo volume enveloped in paper. The enveloping paper was of a greenish hue, and appeared to be mouldy.

"Does the gentleman always have books like that under his arm?" Mademoiselle Gillenormand, who did not like books, demanded in a low tone of Nicolette.

"Well," retorted M. Gillenormand, who had overheard her, in the same tone, "he's a learned man. What then? Is that his fault? Monsieur Boulard, one of my acquaintances, never walked out without a book under his arm either, and he always had some old volume hugged to his heart like that."

And, with a bow, he said aloud, "Monsieur Tranchelevent . . ."

Father Gillenormand did not do it intentionally, but inattention to proper names was an aristocratic habit of his.

"Monsieur Tranchelevent, I have the honor of asking you, on behalf of my grandson, Baron Marius Pontmercy, for the hand of Mademoiselle."

Monsieur Tranchelevent bowed.

"That's settled," said the grandfather.

And, turning to Marius and Cosette, with both arms extended in blessing, he cried, "Permission to adore each other!"

They did not require him to repeat it twice. So much the worse! The chirping began. They talked low. Marius, resting on his elbow on his reclining chair, Cosette standing beside him. "Oh, heavens!" murmured Cosette, "I see you once again! It is thou! It is you! The idea of going and fighting like that! But why? It is horrible. I have been dead for four months. Oh! How wicked it was of you to go to that battle! What had I done to you? I pardon you, but you will never do it again. A little while ago, when they came to tell us to come to you, I still thought that I was about to die, but it was from joy. I was so sad! I have not taken the time to dress myself, I must frighten people with my looks! What will your relatives say to see me in a crumpled collar? Do speak! You let me do all the talking. We are still in the Rue de l'Homme Arme. It seems that your shoulder was terrible. They told me that you could put your fist in it. And then, it seems that they cut your flesh with the scissors. That is frightful. I have cried till I have no eyes left. It is queer that a person can suffer like that. Your grandfather has a very kindly air. Don't disturb yourself, don't rise on your elbow, you will injure yourself. Oh! How happy I am! So our unhappiness is over! I am quite foolish. I had things to say to you, and I no longer know in the least what they were. Do you still love me? We live in the Rue de l'Homme Armé. There is no garden. I made lint all the time; stay, Sir, look, it is your fault, I have a callous on my fingers."

"Angel!" said Marius.

Angel is the only word in the language that cannot be worn out. No other word could resist the merciless use that lovers make of it.

Then as there were spectators, they paused and said not a word more, contenting themselves with softly touching each other's hands.

M. Gillenormand turned toward those who were in the room and cried, "Talk loud, the rest of you. Make a noise, you people behind the scenes. Come, a little uproar, the deuce! so that the children can chatter at their ease."

And, approaching Marius and Cosette, he said to them in a very low voice, "Call each other thou. Don't stand on ceremony."

Aunt Gillenormand looked on in amazement at this irruption of light in her elderly household. There was nothing aggressive about this amazement; it was not the least in the world like the scandalized and envious glance of an owl at two turtledoves, it was the stupid eye of a poor innocent seven and fifty years of age; it was a life that had been a failure gazing at that triumph, love.

"Mademoiselle Gillenormand senior," said her father to her, "I told you that this is what would happen to you."

He remained silent for a moment, and then added, "Look at the happiness of others."

Then he turned to Cosette.

"How pretty she is! How pretty she is! She's a Greuze. So you are going to have that all to yourself, you scamp! Ah! My rogue, you are getting off nicely with me, you are happy; if I were not fifteen years too old, we would fight with swords to see which of us should have her. Come now! I am in love with you, mademoiselle. It's perfectly simple. It is your right. You are in the right. Ah! What a sweet, charming little wedding this will make! Our parish is Saint-Denis du Saint Sacrament, but I will get a dispensation so that you can be married at Saint-Paul. The church is better. It was built by the Jesuits. It is more coquettish. It is opposite the fountain of Cardinal de Birague. The masterpiece of Jesuit architecture is at Namur. It is called Saint-Loup. You must go there after you are married. It is worth the journey. Mademoiselle, I am quite of your mind, I think girls ought to marry; that is what they are made for. There is a certain Sainte-Catherine whom I should always like to see uncoiffed.* It's a fine thing to remain a spinster, but it is chilly. The Bible says: Multiply. In order to save the people, Jeanne d'Arc is needed; but in order to make people, what is needed is Mother Goose. So, marry, my beauties. I really do not see the use in remaining a spinster! I know that they have their chapel apart in the church, and that they fall back on the Society of the Virgin; but, sapristi, a handsome husband, a fine fellow, and at the expiration of a year, a big, blond brat who nurses lustily, and who has fine rolls of fat on his thighs, and who musses up your breast in handfuls with his little rosy paws, laughing the while like the dawn, that's better than holding a candle at vespers, and chanting Turris eburnea!"

The grandfather executed a pirouette on his eighty-year-old heels, and began to talk again like a spring that has broken loose once more:

"Thus, hemming in the course of they musings, Alcippus, It is true that thou wilt wed ere long."

"By the way!"

"What is it, father?"

"Have not you an intimate friend?"

"Yes, Courfeyrac."

"What has become of him?"

"He is dead."

"That is good."

He seated himself near them, made Cosette sit down, and took their four hands in his aged and wrinkled hands, "She is exquisite, this darling. She's a masterpiece, this Cosette! She is a very little girl and a very great lady. She will only be a Baroness, which is a come down for her; she was born a Marquise. What eyelashes she has! Get it well fixed in your noddles, my children, that you are in the true road. Love each other. Be foolish about it. Love is the folly of men and the wit of God. Adore each other. Only," he added, suddenly becoming gloomy, "what a misfortune! It has just occurred to me! More than half of what I possess is swallowed up in an annuity; so long as I live, it will not matter, but after my death, a score of years hence, ah! My poor children, you will not have a sou! Your beautiful white hands, Madame la Baronne, will do the devil the honor of pulling him by the tail."

At this point they heard a grave and tranquil voice say, "Mademoiselle Euphrasie Fauchelevent possesses six hundred thousand francs."

It was the voice of Jean Valjean.

---

* unmarried

So far he had not uttered a single word, no one seemed to be aware that he was there, and he had remained standing erect and motionless, behind all these happy people.

"What has Mademoiselle Euphrasie to do with the question?" inquired the startled grandfather.

"I am she," replied Cosette.

"Six hundred thousand francs?" resumed M. Gillenormand.

"Minus fourteen or fifteen thousand francs, possibly," said Jean Valjean.

And he laid on the table the package that Mademoiselle Gillenormand had mistaken for a book.

Jean Valjean himself opened the package; it was a bundle of banknotes. They were turned over and counted. There were 500 notes for a thousand francs each, and 168 of five thousand. In all, 584,000 francs.

"This is a fine book," said M. Gillenormand.

"Five hundred and eighty-four thousand francs!" murmured the aunt.

"This arranges things well, does it not, Mademoiselle Gillenormand senior?" said the grandfather. "That devil of a Marius has ferreted out the nest of a millionaire grisette in his tree of dreams! Just trust to the love affairs of young folks now, will you! Students find studentesses with six hundred thousand francs. Cherubino works better than Rothschild."

"Five hundred and eighty-four thousand francs!" repeated Mademoiselle Gillenormand, in a low tone. "Five hundred and eighty-four! One might as well say six hundred thousand!"

As for Marius and Cosette, they were gazing at each other while this was going on; they hardly heeded this detail.

CHAPTER V—DEPOSIT YOUR MONEY IN A FOREST RATHER THAN WITH A NOTARY

The reader has, no doubt, understood, without necessitating a lengthy explanation, that Jean Valjean, after the Champmathieu affair, had been able, thanks to his first escape of a few days' duration, to come to Paris and to withdraw in season, from the hands of Laffitte, the sum earned by him, under the name of Monsieur Madeleine, at Montreuil-sur-Mer; and that fearing that he might be recaptured, that eventually happened—he had buried and hidden that sum in the forest of Montfermeil, in the locality known as the Blaru-bottom. The sum, six hundred and thirty thousand francs, all in bank-bills, was not very bulky, and was contained in a box; only, in order to preserve the box from dampness, he had placed it in a coffer filled with chestnut shavings. In the same coffer he had placed his other treasures, the Bishop's candlesticks. It will be remembered that he had carried off the candlesticks when he made his escape from Montreuil-sur-Mer. The man seen one evening for the first time by Boulatruelle, was Jean Valjean. Later on, every time that Jean Valjean needed money, he went to get it in the Blaru-bottom. Hence the absences we have mentioned. He had a pickax somewhere in the heather, in a hiding place known to himself alone. When he beheld Marius convalescent, feeling that the hour was at hand, when that money might prove of service, he had gone to get it; it was he again, whom Boulatruelle had seen in the woods, but on this occasion, in the morning instead of in the evening. Boulatreulle inherited his pickax.

The actual sum was five hundred and eighty-four thousand, five hundred francs. Jean Valjean withdrew the five hundred francs for himself. "We shall see hereafter," he thought.

The difference between that sum and the 630,000 francs withdrawn from Laffitte represented his expenditure in ten years, from 1823 to 1833. The five years of his stay in the convent had cost only five thousand francs.

Jean Valjean set the two candlesticks on the mantle, where they glittered to the great admiration of Toussaint.

Moreover, Jean Valjean knew that he was delivered from Javert. The story had been told in his presence, and he had verified the fact in the Moniteur, how a police inspector named Javert had been found drowned under a boat belonging to some laundresses, between the Pont au Change and the Pont-Neuf, and that a writing left by this man, otherwise irreproachable and highly esteemed by his superiors, pointed to a fit of mental aberration and a suicide. "In fact," thought Jean Valjean, "since he left me at liberty, once having got me in his power, he must have been already mad."

CHAPTER VI—THE TWO OLD MEN DO EVERYTHING, EACH ONE AFTER HIS OWN FASHION, TO RENDER COSETTE HAPPY

Everything was made ready for the wedding. The doctor, on being consulted, declared that it might take place in February. It was then December. A few ravishing weeks of perfect happiness passed.

The grandfather was not the least happy of them all. He remained for a quarter of an hour at a time gazing at Cosette.

"The wonderful, beautiful girl!" he exclaimed. "And she has so sweet and good an air! She is, without exception, the most charming girl that I have ever seen in my life. Later on, she'll have virtues with an odor of violets. How graceful! One cannot live otherwise than nobly with such a creature. Marius, my boy, you are a Baron, you are rich, don't go to pettifogging, I beg of you."

Cosette and Marius had passed abruptly from the sepulchre to paradise. The transition had not been softened, and they would have been stunned, had they not been dazzled by it.

"Do you understand anything about it?" said Marius to Cosette.

"No," replied Cosette, "but it seems to me that the good God is caring for us."

Jean Valjean did everything, smoothed away every difficulty, arranged everything, made everything easy. He hastened toward Cosette's happiness with as much ardor, and, apparently with as much joy, as Cosette herself.

As he had been a mayor, he understood how to solve that delicate problem, with the secret of which he alone was acquainted, Cosette's civil status. If he were to announce her origin bluntly, it might prevent the marriage, who knows? He extricated Cosette from all difficulties. He concocted for her a family of dead people, a sure means of not encountering any objections. Cosette was the only scion of an extinct family; Cosette was not his own daughter, but the daughter of the other Fauchelevent. Two brothers Fauchelevent had been gardeners to the convent of the Petit-Picpus. Inquiry was made at that convent; the very best information and the most respectable references abounded; the good nuns, not very apt and but little inclined to fathom questions of paternity, and not attaching any importance to the matter, had never understood exactly of which of the two Fauchelevents Cosette was the daughter. They said what was wanted and they said it with zeal. An acte de notoriete was drawn up. Cosette became in the eyes of the law, Mademoiselle Euphrasie Fauchelevent. She was declared an orphan, both father and mother being dead. Jean Valjean so arranged it that he was appointed, under the name of Fauchelevent, as Cosette's guardian, with M. Gillenormand as supervising guardian over him.

As for the five hundred and eighty thousand francs, they constituted a legacy bequeathed to Cosette by a dead person, who desired to remain unknown. The original legacy had consisted of five hundred and ninety-four thousand francs; but ten thousand francs had been expended on the education of Mademoiselle Euphrasie, five thousand francs of that amount having been paid to the convent. This legacy, deposited in the hands of a third party, was to be turned over to Cosette at her majority, or at the date of her marriage. This, taken as a whole, was very acceptable, as the reader will perceive, especially when the sum due was half a million. There were some peculiarities here and there, it is true, but they were not noticed; one of the interested parties had his eyes blindfolded by love, the others by the six hundred thousand francs.

Cosette learned that she was not the daughter of that old man whom she had so long called father. He was merely a kinsman; another Fauchelevent was her real father. At any other time this would have broken her heart. But at the ineffable moment that she was then passing through, it cast but a slight shadow, a faint cloud, and she was so full of joy that the cloud did not last long. She had Marius. The young man arrived, the old man was effaced; such is life.

And then, Cosette had, for long years, been habituated to seeing enigmas around her; every being who has had a mysterious childhood is always prepared for certain renunciations.

Nevertheless, she continued to call Jean Valjean: Father.

Cosette, happy as the angels, was enthusiastic over Father Gillenormand. It is true that he overwhelmed her with gallant compliments and presents. While Jean Valjean was building up for Cosette a normal situation in society and an unassailable status, M. Gillenormand was superintending the basket of wedding gifts. Nothing so amused him as being magnificent. He had given to Cosette a robe of Binche guipure that had descended to him from his own grandmother.

"These fashions come up again," said he, "ancient things are the rage, and the young women of my old age dress like the old women of my childhood."

He rifled his respectable chests of drawers in Coromandel lacquer, with swelling fronts, which had not been opened for years. "Let us hear the confession of these dowagers," he said, "let us see what they have in their paunches." He noisily violated the potbellied drawers of all his wives, of all his mistresses and of all his grandmothers. Pekins, damasks, lampas, painted moires, robes of shot gros de Tours, India kerchiefs embroidered in gold that could be washed, dauphines without a right or wrong side, in the piece, Genoa and Alencon point lace, parures in antique goldsmith's work, ivory bon-bon boxes ornamented with microscopic battles, gewgaws and ribbons— he lavished everything on Cosette. Cosette, amazed, desperately in love with Marius, and wild with gratitude toward M. Gillenormand, dreamed of a happiness without limit clothed in satin and velvet. Her wedding basket seemed to her to be upheld by seraphim. Her soul flew out into the azure depths, with wings of Mechlin lace.

The intoxication of the lovers was only equalled, as we have already said, by the ecstasy of the grandfather. A sort of flourish of trumpets went on in the Rue des Filles-du-Calvaire.

Every morning, a fresh offering of bric-a-brac from the grandfather to Cosette. All possible knickknacks glittered around her.

One day Marius, who was fond of talking gravely in the midst of his bliss, said, apropos of I know not what incident, "The men of the revolution are so great, that they have the prestige of the ages, like Cato and like Phocion, and each one of them seems to me an antique memory."

"Moire antique!" exclaimed the old gentleman. "Thanks, Marius. That is precisely the idea of which I was in search."

And on the following day, a magnificent dress of tearose colored moire antique was added to Cosette's wedding presents.

From these fripperies, the grandfather extracted a bit of wisdom.

"Love is all very well; but there must be something else to go with it. The useless must be mingled with happiness. Happiness is only the necessary. Season that enormously with the superfluous for me. A palace and her heart. Her heart and the Louvre. Her heart and the grand waterworks of Versailles. Give me my shepherdess and try to make her a duchess. Fetch me Phyllis crowned with cornflowers, and add a hundred thousand francs income. Open for me a bucolic perspective as far as you can see, beneath a marble colonnade. I consent to the bucolic and also to the fairy spectacle of marble and gold. Dry happiness resembles dry bread. One eats, but one does not dine. I want the superfluous, the useless, the extravagant, excess, that which serves no purpose. I remember to have seen, in the Cathedral of Strasburg, a clock, as tall as a three-story house that marked the hours, that had the kindness to indicate the hour, but that had not the air of being made for that; and that, after having

struck midday, or midnight, midday, the hour of the sun, or midnight, the hour
of love—or any other hour that you like—gave you the moon and the stars, the
earth and the sea, birds and fishes, Phoebus and Phoebe, and a host of things
that emerged from a niche, and the twelve apostles, and the Emperor Charles
the Fifth, and Eponine, and Sabinus, and a throng of little gilded goodmen,
who played on the trumpet to boot. Without reckoning delicious chimes that it
sprinkled through the air, on every occasion, without anyone's knowing why.
Is a petty bald clockface that merely tells the hour equal to that? For my part,
I am of the opinion of the big clock of Strasburg, and I prefer it to the cuckoo
clock from the Black Forest."

M. Gillenormand talked nonsense in connection with the wedding, and
all the fripperies of the eighteenth century passed pell-mell through his
dithyrambs.

"You are ignorant of the art of festivals. You do not know how to organize
a day of enjoyment in this age," he exclaimed. "Your nineteenth century is
weak. It lacks excess. It ignores the rich, it ignores the noble. In everything it
is clean-shaven. Your third estate is insipid, colorless, odorless, and shapeless.
The dreams of your bourgeois who set up, as they express it: a pretty boudoir
freshly decorated, violet, ebony and calico. Make way! Make way! The Sieur
Curmudgeon is marrying Mademoiselle Clutch-penny. Sumptuousness and
splendor. A louis d'or has been stuck to a candle. There's the epoch for you.
My demand is that I may flee from it beyond the Sarmatians. Ah! In 1787, I
predict that all was lost, from the day when I beheld the Duc de Rohan, Prince
de Leon, Duc de Chabot, Duc de Montbazon, Marquis de Sonbise, Vicomte
de Thouars, peer of France, go to Longchamps in a tapecu! That has borne
its fruits. In this century, men attend to business, they gamble on 'Change,
they win money, they are stingy. People take care of their surfaces and varnish
them; everyone is dressed as though just out of a band-box, washed, soaped,
scraped, shaved, combed, waked, smoothed, rubbed, brushed, cleaned on the
outside, irreproachable, polished as a pebble, discreet, neat, and at the same
time, death of my life, in the depths of their consciences they have dung-
heaps and cesspools that are enough to make a cow-herd who blows his nose
in his fingers, recoil. I grant to this age the device: 'Dirty Cleanliness.' Don't
be vexed, Marius, give me permission to speak; I say no evil of the people as
you see, I am always harping on your people, but do look favorably on my
dealing a bit of a slap to the bourgeoisie. I belong to it. He who loves well
lashes well. Thereupon, I say plainly, that nowadays people marry, but that
they no longer know how to marry. Ah! It is true, I regret the grace of the

ancient manners. I regret everything about them, their elegance, their chivalry, those courteous and delicate ways, that joyous luxury that everyone possessed, music forming part of the wedding, a symphony above stairs, a beating of drums below stairs, the dances, the joyous faces around the table, the fine-spun gallant compliments, the songs, the fireworks, the frank laughter, the devil's own row, the huge knots of ribbon. I regret the bride's garter. The bride's garter is cousin to the girdle of Venus. On what does the war of Troy turn? On Helen's garter, parbleu! Why did they fight, why did Diomed the divine break over the head of Meriones that great brazen helmet of ten points? Why did Achilles and Hector hew each other up with vast blows of their lances? Because Helen allowed Paris to take her garter. With Cosette's garter, Homer would construct the Iliad. He would put in his poem, a loquacious old fellow, like me, and he would call him Nestor. My friends, in bygone days, in those amiable days of yore, people married wisely; they had a good contract, and then they had a good carouse. As soon as Cujas had taken his departure, Gamacho entered. But, in sooth! The stomach is an agreeable beast that demands its due, and that wants to have its wedding also. People supped well, and had at table a beautiful neighbor without a guimpe so that her throat was only moderately concealed. Oh! The large laughing mouths, and how gay we were in those days! Youth was a bouquet; every young man terminated in a branch of lilacs or a tuft of roses; whether he was a shepherd or a warrior; and if, by chance, one was a captain of dragoons, one found means to call oneself Florian. People thought much of looking well. They embroidered and tinted themselves. A bourgeois had the air of a flower, a Marquis had the air of a precious stone. People had no straps to their boots, they had no boots. They were spruce, shining, waved, lustrous, fluttering, dainty, coquettish, which did not at all prevent their wearing swords by their sides. The hummingbird has beak and claws. That was the day of the Galland Indies. One of the sides of that century was delicate, the other was magnificent; and by the green cabbages! People amused themselves. Today, people are serious. The bourgeois is avaricious, the bourgeoise is a prude; your century is unfortunate. People would drive away the Graces as being too low in the neck. Alas! Beauty is concealed as though it were ugliness. Since the revolution, everything, including the ballet dancers, has had its trousers; a mountebank dancer must be grave; your rigadoons are doctrinarian. It is necessary to be majestic. People would be greatly annoyed if they did not carry their chins in their cravats. The ideal of an urchin of twenty when he marries, is to resemble M. Royer-Collard. And do you know what one arrives at with that majesty? At being petty. Learn this: joy is not only joyous;

it is great. But be in love gayly then, what the deuce! Marry, when you marry, with fever and giddiness, and tumult, and the uproar of happiness! Be grave in church, well and good. But, as soon as the Mass is finished, sarpejou! You must make a dream whirl around the bride. A marriage should be royal and chimerical; it should promenade its ceremony from the cathedral of Rheims to the pagoda of Chanteloup. I have a horror of a paltry wedding. *Ventregoulette!* Be in Olympus for that one day, at least. Be one of the gods. Ah! People might be sylphs. Games and Laughter, argiraspides; they are stupids. My friends, every recently made bridegroom ought to be Prince Aldobrandini. Profit by that unique minute in life to soar away to the empyrean with the swans and the eagles, even if you do have to fall back on the morrow into the bourgeoisie of the frogs. Don't economize on the nuptials, do not prune them of their splendors; don't scrimp on the day when you beam. The wedding is not the housekeeping. Oh! If I were to carry out my fancy, it would be gallant, violins would be heard under the trees. Here is my program: sky-blue and silver. I would mingle with the festival the rural divinities, I would convoke the Dryads and the Nereids. The nuptials of Amphitrite, a rosy cloud, nymphs with well dressed locks and entirely naked, an Academician offering quatrains to the goddess, a chariot drawn by marine monsters.

"Triton trotted on before, and drew from his conchshell sounds so rabishing that he delighted everyone."

—there's a festive program, there's a good one, or else I know nothing of such matters, deuce take it!"

While the grandfather, in full lyrical effusion, was listening to himself, Cosette and Marius grew intoxicated as they gazed freely at each other.

Aunt Gillenormand surveyed all this with her imperturbable placidity. Within the last five or six months she had experienced a certain amount of emotions. Marius returned, Marius brought back bleeding, Marius brought back from a barricade, Marius dead, then living, Marius reconciled, Marius betrothed, Marius wedding a poor girl, Marius wedding a millionairess. The six hundred thousand francs had been her last surprise. Then, her indifference of a girl taking her first communion returned to her. She went regularly to service, told her beads, read her euchology, mumbled Aves in one corner of the house, while I love you was being whispèred in the other, and she beheld Marius and Cosette in a vague way, like two shadows. The shadow was herself.

There is a certain state of inert asceticism in which the soul, neutralized by torpor, a stranger to that which may be designated as the business of living, receives no impressions, either human, or pleasant or painful, with the exception of earthquakes and catastrophes. This devotion, as Father Gillenormand said to his daughter, corresponds to a cold in the head. You smell nothing of life. Neither any bad, nor any good odor.

Moreover, the six hundred thousand francs had settled the elderly spinster's indecision. Her father had acquired the habit of taking her so little into account, that he had not consulted her in the matter of consent to Marius's marriage. He had acted impetuously, according to his wont, having, a despot-turned slave, but a single though—to satisfy Marius. As for the auny—it had not even occurred to him that the aunt existed, and that she could have an opinion of her own, and, sheep as she was, this had vexed her. Somewhat resentful in her inmost soul, but impassible externally, she had said to herself, "My father has settled the question of the marriage without reference to me; I shall settle the question of the inheritance without consulting him." She was rich, in fact, and her father was not. She had reserved her decision on this point. It is probable that, had the match been a poor one, she would have left him poor. "So much the worse for my nephew! He is wedding a beggar, let him be a beggar himself!" But Cosette's half-million pleased the aunt, and altered her inward situation so far as this pair of lovers were concerned. One owes some consideration to six hundred thousand francs, and it was evident that she could not do otherwise than leave her fortune to these young people, since they did not need it.

It was arranged that the couple should live with the grandfather—M. Gillenormand insisted on resigning to them his chamber, the finest in the house. "That will make me young again," he said. "It's an old plan of mine. I have always entertained the idea of having a wedding in my chamber."

He furnished this chamber with a multitude of elegant trifles. He had the ceiling and walls hung with an extraordinary stuff, which he had by him in the piece, and which he believed to have emanated from Utrecht with a buttercup-colored satin ground, covered with velvet auricula blossoms. "It was with that stuff," said he, "that the bed of the Duchesse d'Anville at la Roche-Guyon was draped." On the mantle, he set a little figure in Saxe porcelain, carrying a muff against her nude stomach.

M. Gillenormand's library became the lawyer's study, which Marius needed; a study, it will be remembered, being required by the council of the order.

CHAPTER VII—THE EFFECTS OF DREAMS MINGLED WITH HAPPINESS

The lovers saw each other every day. Cosette came with M. Fauchelevent. "This is reversing things," said Mademoiselle Gillenormand, "to have the bride come to the house to do the courting like this." But Marius's convalescence had caused the habit to become established, and the armchairs of the Rue des Filles-du-Calvaire, better adapted to interviews than the straw chairs of the Rue de l'Homme Arme, had rooted it. Marius and M. Fauchelevent saw each other, but did not address each other. It seemed as though this had been agreed upon. Every girl needs a chaperone. Cosette could not have come without M. Fauchelevent. In Marius's eyes, M. Fauchelevent was the condition attached to Cosette. He accepted it. By dint of discussing political matters, vaguely and without precision, from the point of view of the general amelioration of the fate of all men, they came to say a little more than "yes" and "no." Once, on the subject of education, which Marius wished to have free and obligatory, multiplied under all forms lavished on everyone, like the air and the sun in a word, respirable for the entire population, they were in unison, and they almost conversed. M. Fauchelevent talked well, and even with a certain loftiness of language—still he lacked something indescribable. M. Fauchelevent possessed something less and also something more, than a man of the world.

Marius, inwardly, and in the depths of his thought, surrounded with all sorts of mute questions this M. Fauchelevent, who was to him simply benevolent and cold. There were moments when doubts as to his own recollections occurred to him. There was a void in his memory, a black spot, an abyss excavated by four months of agony. Many things had been lost therein. He had come to the point of asking himself whether it were really a fact that he had seen M. Fauchelevent, so serious and so calm a man, in the barricade.

This was not, however, the only stupor that the apparitions and the disappearances of the past had left in his mind. It must not be supposed that he was delivered from all those obsessions of the memory that force us, even when happy, even when satisfied, to glance sadly behind us. The head that does not turn backward toward horizons that have vanished contains neither thought nor love. At times, Marius clasped his face between his hands, and the vague and tumultuous past traversed the twilight that reigned in his brain. Again he beheld Mabeuf fall, he heard Gavroche singing amid the grapeshot, he felt beneath his lips the cold brow of Eponine; Enjolras, Courfeyrac, Jean Prouvaire, Combeferre, Bossuet, Grantaire, all his friends rose erect before him, then dispersed into thin air. Were all those dear, sorrowful, valiant, charming or tragic beings merely dreams? Had they actually existed? The revolt had enveloped everything in its smoke. These great fevers create great dreams. He questioned himself; he felt himself; all these vanished realities made him dizzy. Where were they all then? Was it really true that all were dead? A fall into the shadows had carried off all except himself. It all seemed to him to have disappeared as though behind the curtain of a theater. There are curtains like this that drop in life. God passes on to the following act.

And he himself—was he actually the same man? He, the poor man, was rich; he, the abandoned, had a family; he, the despairing, was to marry Cosette. It seemed to him that he had traversed a tomb, and that he had entered into it black and had emerged from it white, and in that tomb the others had remained. At certain moments, all these beings of the past, returned and present, formed a circle around him, and overshadowed him; then he thought of Cosette, and recovered his serenity; but nothing less than this felicity could have sufficed to efface that catastrophe.

M. Fauchelevent almost occupied a place among these vanished beings. Marius hesitated to believe that the Fauchelevent of the barricade was the same as this Fauchelevent in flesh and blood, sitting so gravely beside Cosette. The first was, probably, one of those nightmares occasioned and brought back by his hours of delirium. However, the natures of both men were rigid, no question from Marius to M. Fauchelevent was possible. Such an idea had not even occurred to him. We have already indicated this characteristic detail.

Two men who have a secret in common, and who, by a sort of tacit agreement, exchange not a word on the subject, are less rare than is commonly supposed.

Once only, did Marius make the attempt. He introduced into the conversation the Rue de la Chanvrerie, and, turning to M. Fauchelevent, he said to him, "Of course, you are acquainted with that street?"

"What street?"

"The Rue de la Chanvrerie."

"I have no idea of the name of that street," replied M. Fauchelevent, in the most natural manner in the world.

The response that bore upon the name of the street and not upon the street itself, appeared to Marius to be more conclusive than it really was.

"Decidedly," thought he, "I have been dreaming. I have been subject to a hallucination. It was someone who resembled him. M. Fauchelevent was not there."'

CHAPTER VIII—TWO MEN
IMPOSSIBLE TO FIND

Marius's enchantment, great as it was, could not efface from his mind other preoccupations.

While the wedding was in preparation, and while awaiting the date fixed upon, he caused difficult and scrupulous retrospective researches to be made.

He owed gratitude in various quarters; he owed it on his father's account, he owed it on his own.

There was Thenardier; there was the unknown man who had brought him, Marius, back to M. Gillenormand.

Marius endeavored to find these two men, not intending to marry, to be happy, and to forget them, and fearing that, were these debts of gratitude not discharged, they would leave a shadow on his life, which promised so brightly for the future.

It was impossible for him to leave all these arrears of suffering behind him, and he wished, before entering joyously into the future, to obtain a quittance from the past.

That Thenardier was a villain detracted nothing from the fact that he had saved Colonel Pontmercy. Thenardier was a ruffian in the eyes of all the world except Marius.

And Marius, ignorant of the real scene in the battlefield of Waterloo, was not aware of the peculiar detail, that his father, so far as Thenardier was concerned was in the strange position of being indebted to the latter for his life, without being indebted to him for any gratitude.

None of the various agents whom Marius employed succeeded in discovering any trace of Thenardier. Obliteration appeared to be complete in that quarter. Madame Thenardier had died in prison pending the trial. Thenardier and his daughter Azelma, the only two remaining of that lamentable group, had plunged back into the gloom. The gulf of the social unknown had silently closed above those beings. On the surface there was not visible so much as that quiver, that trembling, those obscure concentric circles that announce that something has fallen in, and that the plummet may be dropped.

Madame Thenardier being dead, Boulatruelle being eliminated from the case, Claquesous having disappeared, the principal persons accused having escaped from prison, the trial connected with the ambush in the Gorbeau house had come to nothing.

That affair had remained rather obscure. The bench of Assizes had been obliged to content themselves with two subordinates. Panchaud, alias Printanier, alias Bigrenaille, and Demi-Liard, alias Deux-Milliards, who had been inconsistently condemned, after a hearing of both sides of the case, to ten years in the galleys. Hard labor for life had been the sentence pronounced against the escaped and contumacious accomplices.

Thenardier, the head and leader, had been, through contumacy, likewise condemned to death.

This sentence was the only information remaining about Thenardier, casting upon that buried name its sinister light like a candle beside a bier.

Moreover, by thrusting Thenardier back into the very remotest depths, through a fear of being recaptured, this sentence added to the density of the shadows that enveloped this man.

As for the other person, as for the unknown man who had saved Marius, the researches were at first to some extent successful, then came to an abrupt conclusion. They succeeded in finding the carriage that had brought Marius to the Rue des Filles-du-Calvaire on the evening of the 6th of June.

The coachman declared that, on the 6th of June, in obedience to the commands of a police agent, he had stood from three o'clock in the afternoon until nightfall on the Quai des Champs-Elysees, above the outlet of the Grand Sewer; that, toward nine o'clock in the evening, the grating of the sewer, which abuts on the bank of the river, had opened; that a man had emerged therefrom, bearing on his shoulders another man, who seemed to be dead; that the agent, who was on the watch at that point, had arrested the living man and had seized the dead man; that, at the order of the police agent, he, the coachman, had taken "all those folks" into his carriage; that they had first driven to the Rue des Filles-du-Calvaire; that they had there deposited the dead man; that the dead man was Monsieur Marius, and that he, the coachman, recognized him perfectly, although he was alive "this time"; that afterward, they had entered the vehicle again, that he had whipped up his horses; a few paces from the gate of the Archives, they had called to him to halt; that there, in the street, they had paid him and left him, and that the police agent had led the other man away; that he knew nothing more; that the night had been very dark.

Marius, as we have said, recalled nothing. He only remembered that he had been seized from behind by an energetic hand at the moment when he was falling backward into the barricade; then, everything vanished so far as he was concerned.

He had only regained consciousness at M. Gillenormand's.

He was lost in conjectures.

He could not doubt his own identity. Still, how had it come to pass that, having fallen in the Rue de la Chanvrerie, he had been picked up by the police agent on the banks of the Seine, near the Pont des Invalides?

Someone had carried him from the Quartier des Halles to the Champs-Elysees. And how? Through the sewer. Unheard-of devotion!

Someone? Who?

This was the man for whom Marius was searching.

Of this man, who was his savior, nothing; not a trace; not the faintest indication.

Marius, although forced to preserve great reserve, in that direction, pushed his inquiries as far as the prefecture of police. There, no more than elsewhere, did the information obtained lead to any enlightenment.

The prefecture knew less about the matter than did the hackneycoachman. They had no knowledge of any arrest having been made on the 6th of June at the mouth of the Grand Sewer.

No report of any agent had been received there upon this matter, which was regarded at the prefecture as a fable. The invention of this fable was attributed to the coachman.

A coachman who wants a gratuity is capable of anything, even of imagination. The fact was assured, nevertheless, and Marius could not doubt it, unless he doubted his own identity, as we have just said.

Everything about this singular enigma was inexplicable.

What had become of that man, that mysterious man, whom the coachman had seen emerge from the grating of the Grand Sewer bearing upon his back the unconscious Marius, and whom the police agent on the watch had arrested in the very act of rescuing an insurgent? What had become of the agent himself?

Why had this agent preserved silence? Had the man succeeded in making his escape? Had he bribed the agent? Why did this man give no sign of life to Marius, who owed everything to him? His disinterestedness was no less tremendous than his devotion. Why had not that man appeared again? Perhaps he was above compensation, but no one is above gratitude. Was he dead? Who was the man? What sort of a face had he? No one could tell him this.

The coachman answered, "The night was very dark." Basque and Nicolette, all in a flutter, had looked only at their young master all covered with blood.

The porter, whose candle had lighted the tragic arrival of Marius, had been the only one to take note of the man in question, and this is the description that he gave, "That man was terrible."

Marius had the bloodstained clothing he had worn when he had been brought back to his grandfather preserved, in the hope that it would prove of service in his researches.

On examining the coat, it was found that one skirt had been torn in a singular way. A piece was missing.

One evening, Marius was speaking in the presence of Cosette and Jean Valjean of the whole of that singular adventure, of the innumerable inquiries he had made, and of the fruitlessness of his efforts. The cold countenance of "Monsieur Fauchelevent" angered him.

He exclaimed, with a vivacity that had something of wrath in it, "Yes, that man, whoever he may have been, was sublime. Do you know what he did, Sir? He intervened like an archangel. He must have flung himself into the midst of the battle, have stolen me away, have opened the sewer, have dragged me into it and have carried me through it! He must have traversed more than a league and a half in those frightful subterranean galleries, bent over, weighed down, in the dark, in the cesspool, more than a league and a half, Sir, with a corpse upon his back! And with what object? With the sole object of saving the corpse. And that corpse I was. He said to himself, 'There may still be a glimpse of life there, perchance; I will risk my own existence for that miserable spark!' And his existence he risked not once but twenty times! And every step was a danger. The proof of it is, that on emerging from the sewer, he was arrested. Do you know, Sir, that that man did all this? And he had no recompense to expect. What was I? An insurgent. What was I? One of the conquered. Oh! If Cosette's six hundred thousand francs were mine . . ."

"They are yours," interrupted Jean Valjean.

"Well," resumed Marius, "I would give them all to find that man once more."

Jean Valjean remained silent.

BOOK SIXTH:
THE SLEEPLESS NIGHT

CHAPTER I—THE 16TH OF FEBRUARY, 1833

The night of the 16th to the 17th of February, 1833, was a blessed night. Above its shadows heaven stood open. It was the wedding night of Marius and Cosette.

The day had been adorable.

It had not been the grand festival dreamed by the grandfather, a fairy spectacle, with a confusion of cherubim and Cupids over the heads of the bridal pair, a marriage worthy to form the subject of a painting to be placed over a door; but it had been sweet and smiling.

The manner of marriage in 1833 was not the same as it is today. France had not yet borrowed from England that supreme delicacy of carrying off one's wife, of fleeing, on coming out of church, of hiding oneself with shame from one's happiness, and of combining the ways of a bankrupt with the delights of the Song of Songs. People had not yet grasped to the full the chastity, exquisiteness, and decency of jolting their paradise in a posting-chaise, of breaking up their mystery with clic-clacs, of taking for a nuptial bed the bed of an inn, and of leaving behind them, in a commonplace chamber, at so much a night, the most sacred of the souvenirs of life mingled pell-mell with the tête-à-tête of the conductor of the diligence and the maidservant of the inn.

In this second half of the nineteenth century in which we are now living, the mayor and his scarf, the priest and his chasuble, the law and God no longer suffice; they must be eked out by the Postilion de Lonjumeau; a blue waistcoat turned up with red, and with bell buttons, a plaque like a vantbrace, knee-breeches of green leather, oaths to the Norman horses with their tails knotted up, false galloons, varnished hat, long powdered locks, an enormous whip and tall boots. France does not yet carry elegance to the length of doing like the English nobility, and raining down on the post-chaise of the bridal pair a hail storm of slippers trodden down at heel and of worn-out shoes, in memory of Churchill, afterward Marlborough, or Malbrouck, who was assailed on his wedding day by the wrath of an aunt who brought him good luck. Old shoes and slippers do not, as yet, form a part of our nuptial celebrations; but patience, as good taste continues to spread, we shall come to that.

In 1833, a hundred years ago, marriage was not conducted at a full trot.

Strange to say, at that epoch, people still imagined that a wedding was a private and social festival, that a patriarchal banquet does not spoil a domestic solemnity, that gaiety, even in excess, provided it be honest, and decent, does happiness no harm, and that, in short, it is a good and a venerable thing that the fusion of these two destinies from which a family is destined to spring, should begin at home, and that the household should thenceforth have its nuptial chamber as its witness.

And people were so immodest as to marry in their own homes.

The marriage took place, therefore, in accordance with this now superannuated fashion, at M. Gillenormand's house.

Natural and commonplace as this matter of marrying is, the banns to publish, the papers to be drawn up, the mayoralty, and the church produce some complication. They could not get ready before the 16th of February.

Now, we note this detail, for the pure satisfaction of being exact, it chanced that the 16th fell on Shrove Tuesday. Hesitations, scruples, particularly on the part of Aunt Gillenormand.

"Shrove Tuesday!"* exclaimed the grandfather, "so much the better. There is a proverb: "A Shrove Tuesday marriage will have no ungrateful children.

Let us proceed. Here goes for the 16th! Do you want to delay, Marius?"

"No, certainly not!" replied the lover.

"Let us marry, then," cried the grandfather.

Accordingly, the marriage took place on the 16th, notwithstanding the public merrymaking. It rained that day, but there is always in the sky a tiny scrap of blue at the service of happiness, which lovers see, even when the rest of creation is under an umbrella.

On the preceding evening, Jean Valjean handed to Marius, in the presence of M. Gillenormand, the five hundred and eighty-four thousand francs.

As the marriage was taking place under the regime of community of property, the papers had been simple.

Henceforth, Toussaint was of no use to Jean Valjean; Cosette inherited her and promoted her to the rank of lady's maid.

As for Jean Valjean, a beautiful chamber in the Gillenormand house had been furnished expressly for him, and Cosette had said to him in such an irresistible manner, "Father, I entreat you," that she had almost persuaded him to promise that he would come and occupy it.

---

* Mardi Gras

A few days before that fixed on for the marriage, an accident happened to Jean Valjean; he crushed the thumb of his right hand. This was not a serious matter; and he had not allowed anyone to trouble himself about it, nor to dress it, nor even to see his hurt, not even Cosette. Nevertheless, this had forced him to swathe his hand in a linen bandage, and to carry his arm in a sling, and had prevented his signing. M. Gillenormand, in his capacity of Cosette's supervising-guardian, had supplied his place.

We will not conduct the reader either to the mayor's office or to the church. One does not follow a pair of lovers to that extent, and one is accustomed to turn one's back on the drama as soon as it puts a wedding nosegay in its buttonhole. We will confine ourselves to noting an incident that, though unnoticed by the wedding party, marked the transit from the Rue des Filles-du-Calvaire to the church of Saint-Paul.

At that epoch, the northern extremity of the Rue Saint-Louis was in process of repaving. It was barred off, beginning with the Rue du Pare-Royal. It was impossible for the wedding carriages to go directly to Saint-Paul. They were obliged to alter their course, and the simplest way was to turn through the boulevard. One of the invited guests observed that it was Shrove Tuesday, and that there would be a jam of vehicles. "Why?" asked M. Gillenormand. "Because of the maskers." "Capital," said the grandfather, "let us go that way. These young folks are on the way to be married; they are about to enter the serious part of life. This will prepare them for seeing a bit of the masquerade."

They went by way of the boulevard. The first wedding coach held Cosette and Aunt Gillenormand, M. Gillenormand and Jean Valjean. Marius, still separated from his betrothed according to usage, did not come until the second. The nuptial train, on emerging from the Rue des Filles-du-Calvaire, became entangled in a long procession of vehicles that formed an endless chain from the Madeleine to the Bastille, and from the Bastille to the Madeleine. Maskers abounded on the boulevard. In spite of the fact that it was raining at intervals, Merry-Andrew, Pantaloon and Clown persisted. In the good humor of that winter of 1833, Paris had disguised itself as Venice. Such Shrove Tuesdays are no longer to be seen nowadays. Everything that exists being a scattered Carnival, there is no longer any Carnival.

The sidewalks were overflowing with pedestrians and the windows with curious spectators. The terraces that crown the peristyles of the theatres were bordered with spectators. Besides the maskers, they stared at that procession—peculiar to Shrove Tuesday as to Longchamps—of vehicles of every description, citadines, tapissieres, carioles, cabriolets marching in order, rigorously riveted to each other by the police regulations, and locked into rails, as it were. Anyone in these vehicles is at once a spectator and a spectacle. Police sergeants maintained, on the sides of the boulevard, these two interminable parallel files, moving in contrary directions, and saw to it that nothing interfered with that double current, those two brooks of carriages, flowing, the one downstream, the other upstream, the one toward the Chaussée d'Antin, the other toward the Faubourg Saint-Antoine. The carriages of the peers of France and of the Ambassadors, emblazoned with coats of arms, held the middle of the way, going and coming freely. Certain joyous and magnificent trains, notably that of the Boeuf Gras, had the same privilege. In this gaiety of Paris, England cracked her whip; Lord Seymour's postchaise, harassed by a nickname from the populace, passed with great noise.

In the double file, along which the municipal guards galloped like sheepdogs, honest family coaches, loaded down with great-aunts and grandmothers, displayed at their doors fresh groups of children in disguise, Clowns of seven years of age, Columbines of six, ravishing little creatures, who felt that they formed an official part of the public mirth, who were imbued with the dignity of their harlequinade, and who possessed the gravity of functionaries.

From time to time, a hitch arose somewhere in the procession of vehicles; one or other of the two lateral files halted until the knot was disentangled; one carriage delayed sufficed to paralyze the whole line. Then they set out again on the march.

The wedding carriages were in the file proceeding toward the Bastille, and skirting the right side of the Boulevard. At the top of the Pont-aux-Choux, there was a stoppage. Nearly at the same moment, the other file, which was proceeding toward the Madeleine, halted also. At that point of the file there was a carriage-load of maskers.

These carriages, or to speak more correctly, these wagonloads of maskers are very familiar to Parisians. If they were missing on a Shrove Tuesday, or at the Mid-Lent, it would be taken in bad part, and people would say, "There's something behind that. Probably the ministry is about to undergo a change." A pile of Cassandras, Harlequins and Columbines, jolted along high above the passersby, all possible grotesquenesses, from the Turk to the savage, Hercules supporting Marquises, fishwives who would have made Rabelais stop up his ears just as the Maenads made Aristophanes drop his eyes, tow wigs, pink tights, dandified hats, spectacles of a grimacer, three-cornered hats of Janot tormented with a butterfly, shouts directed at pedestrians, fists on hips, bold attitudes, bare shoulders, immodesty unchained; a chaos of shamelessness driven by a coachman crowned with flowers; this is what that institution was like.

Greece stood in need of the chariot of Thespis, France stands in need of the hackney-coach of Vade.

Everything can be parodied, even parody. The Saturnalia, that grimace of antique beauty, ends, through exaggeration after exaggeration, in Shrove Tuesday; and the Bacchanal, formerly crowned with sprays of vine leaves and grapes, inundated with sunshine, displaying her marble breast in a divine semi-nudity, having at the present day lost her shape under the soaked rags of the North, has finally come to be called the Jack-pudding.

The tradition of carriageloads of maskers runs back to the most ancient days of the monarchy. The accounts of Louis XI allot to the bailiff of the palace "twenty sous, Tournois, for three coaches of mascarades in the crossroads." In our day, these noisy heaps of creatures are accustomed to have themselves driven in some ancient cuckoo carriage, whose imperial they load down, or they overwhelm a hired landau, with its top thrown back, with their tumultuous groups. Twenty of them ride in a carriage intended for six. They cling to the seats, to the rumble, on the cheeks of the hood, on the shafts. They even bestride the carriage lamps. They stand, sit, lie, with their knees drawn up in a knot, and their legs hanging. The women sit on the men's laps. Far away, above the throng of heads, their wild pyramid is visible. These carriage-loads form mountains of mirth in the midst of the rout. Colle, Panard and Piron flow from it, enriched with slang. This carriage, which has become colossal through its freight, has an air of conquest. Uproar reigns in front, tumult behind. People vociferate, shout, howl, there they break forth and writhe with enjoyment; gaiety roars; sarcasm flames forth, joviality is flaunted like a red flag; two jades there drag farce blossomed forth into an apotheosis; it is the triumphal car of laughter.

A laughter that is too cynical to be frank. In truth, this laughter is suspicious. This laughter has a mission. It is charged with proving the Carnival to the Parisians.

These fishwife vehicles, in which one feels one knows not what shadows, set the philosopher to thinking. There is government therein. There one lays one's finger on a mysterious affinity between public men and public women.

It certainly is sad that turpitude heaped up should give a sum total of gaiety, that by piling ignominy upon opprobrium the people should be enticed, that the system of spying, and serving as caryatids to prostitution should amuse the rabble when it confronts them, that the crowd loves to behold that monstrous living pile of tinsel rags, half dung, half light, roll by on four wheels howling and laughing, that they should clap their hands at this glory composed of all shames, that there would be no festival for the populace, did not the police promenade in their midst these sorts of twenty-headed hydras of joy. But what can be done about it? These beribboned and beflowered tumbrils of mire are insulted and pardoned by the laughter of the public. The laughter of all is the accomplice of universal degradation. Certain unhealthy festivals disaggregate the people and convert them into the populace. And populaces, like tyrants, require buffoons. The King has Roquelaure, the populace has the Merry-Andrew. Paris is a great, mad city on every occasion that it is a great sublime city. There the Carnival forms part of politics. Paris, let us confess it—willingly allows infamy to furnish it with comedy. She only demands of her masters—when she has masters—one thing: "Paint me the mud." Rome was of the same mind. She loved Nero. Nero was a titanic lighterman.

Chance ordained, as we have just said, that one of these shapeless clusters of masked men and women, dragged about on a vast calash, should halt on the left of the boulevard, while the wedding train halted on the right. The carriage-load of masks caught sight of the wedding carriage containing the bridal party opposite them on the other side of the boulevard.

"Hullo!" said a masker. "Here's a wedding."

"A sham wedding," retorted another. "We are the genuine article."

And, being too far off to accost the wedding party, and fearing also, the rebuke of the police, the two maskers turned their eyes elsewhere.

At the end of another minute, the carriage load of maskers had their hands full, the multitude set to yelling, which is the crowd's caress to masquerades; and the two maskers who had just spoken had to face the throng with their comrades, and did not find the entire repertory of projectiles of the fishmarkets too extensive to retort to the enormous verbal attacks of the populace. A frightful exchange of metaphors took place between the maskers and the crowd.

In the meanwhile, two other maskers in the same carriage, a Spaniard with an enormous nose, an elderly air, and huge black moustache, and a gaunt fishwife, who was quite a young girl, masked with a loup,* had also noticed the wedding, and while their companions and the passersby were exchanging insults, they had held a dialogue in a low voice.

Their aside was covered by the tumult and was lost in it. The gusts of rain had drenched the front of the vehicle, which was wide open; the breezes of

---

* a short mask

February are not warm; as the fishwife, clad in a low-necked gown, replied to the Spaniard, she shivered, laughed and coughed.

Here is their dialogue:

"Say, now."

"What, Daddy?"

"Do you see that old cove?"

"What old cove?"

"Yonder, in the first weddingcart, on our side."

"The one with his arm hung up in a black cravat?"

"Yes."

"Well?"

"I'm sure that I know him."

"Ah!"

"I'm willing that they should cut my throat, and I'm ready to swear that I never said either you, thou, or I, in my life, if I don't know that Parisian."

"Paris in Pantin today."

"Can you see the bride if you stoop down?"

"No."

"And the bridegroom?"

"There's no bridegroom in that trap."

"Bah!"

"Unless it's the old fellow."

"Try to get a sight of the bride by stooping very low."

"I can't."

"Never mind, that old cove who has something the matter with his paw I know, and that I'm positive."

"And what good does it do to know him?"

"No one can tell. Sometimes it does!"

"I don't care a hang for old fellows, that I don't!"

"I know him."

"Know him, if you want to."

"How the devil does he come to be one of the wedding party?"

"We are in it, too."

"Where does that wedding come from?"

"How should I know?"

"Listen."

"Well, what?"

"There's one thing you ought to do."

"What's that?"

"Get off of our trap and spin that wedding."

"What for?"

"To find out where it goes, and what it is. Hurry up and jump down, trot, my girl, your legs are young."

"I can't quit the vehicle."

"Why not?"

"I'm hired."

"Ah, the devil!"

"I owe my fishwife day to the prefecture."

"That's true."

"If I leave the cart, the first inspector who gets his eye on me will arrest me. You know that well enough."

"Yes, I do."

"I'm bought by the government for today."

"All the same, that old fellow bothers me."

"Do the old fellows bother you? But you're not a young girl."

"He's in the first carriage."

"Well?"

"In the bride's trap."

"What then?"

"So he is the father."

"What concern is that of mine?"

"I tell you that he's the father."

"As if he were the only father."

"Listen."

"What?"

"I can't go out otherwise than masked. Here I'm concealed, no one knows that I'm here. But tomorrow, there will be no more maskers. It's Ash Wednesday. I run the risk of being nabbed. I must sneak back into my hole. But you are free."

"Not particularly."

"More than I am, at any rate."

"Well, what of that?"

"You must try to find out where that wedding party went to."

"Where it went?"

"Yes."

"I know."

"Where is it going then?"

"To the Cadran-Bleu."

"In the first place, it's not in that direction."

"Well! To la Rapée."

"Or elsewhere."

"It's free. Wedding parties are at liberty."

"That's not the point at all. I tell you that you must try to learn for me what that wedding is, who that old cove belongs to, and where that wedding pair lives."

"I like that! That would be queer. It's so easy to find out a wedding party that passed through the street on a Shrove Tuesday, a week afterward. A pin in a haymow! It ain't possible!"

"That don't matter. You must try. You understand me, Azelma."

The two files resumed their movement on both sides of the boulevard, in opposite directions, and the carriage of the maskers lost sight of the "trap" of the bride.

CHAPTER II—JEAN VALJEAN STILL WEARS HIS ARM IN A SLING

To realize one's dream. To whom is this accorded? There must be elections for this in heaven; we are all candidates, unknown to ourselves; the angels vote. Cosette and Marius had been elected.

Cosette, both at the mayor's office and at church, was dazzling and touching. Toussaint, assisted by Nicolette, had dressed her.

Cosette wore over a petticoat of white taffeta, her robe of Binche guipure, a veil of English point, a necklace of fine pearls, a wreath of orange flowers; all this was white, and, from the midst of that whiteness she beamed forth. It was an exquisite candor expanding and becoming transfigured in the light. One would have pronounced her a virgin on the point of turning into a goddess.

Marius's handsome hair was lustrous and perfumed; here and there, beneath the thick curls, pale lines—the scars of the barricade—were visible.

The grandfather, haughty, with head held high, amalgamating more than ever in his toilet and his manners all the elegances of the epoch of Barras, escorted Cosette. He took the place of Jean Valjean, who, on account of his arm being still in a sling, could not give his hand to the bride.

Jean Valjean, dressed in black, followed them with a smile.

"Monsieur Fauchelevent," said the grandfather to him, "this is a fine day. I vote for the end of afflictions and sorrows. Henceforth, there must be no sadness anywhere. Pardieu, I decree joy! Evil has no right to exist. That there should be any unhappy men is, in sooth, a disgrace to the azure of the sky. Evil does not come from man, who is good at bottom. All human miseries have for their capital and central government hell, otherwise, known as the Devil's Tuileries. Good, here I am uttering demagogical words! As far as I am concerned, I have no longer any political opinions; let all me be rich, that is to say, mirthful, and I confine myself to that."

When, at the conclusion of all the ceremonies, after having pronounced before the mayor and before the priest all possible "yesses," after having signed the registers at the municipality and at the sacristy, after having exchanged their rings, after having knelt side by side under the pall of white moire in the smoke of the censer, they arrived, hand in hand, admired and envied by all, Marius in black, she in white, preceded by the suisse, with the epaulets of a colonel, tapping the pavement with his halberd, between two rows of astonished spectators, at the portals of the church, both leaves of which were thrown wide open, ready to enter their carriage again, and all being finished, Cosette still could not believe that it was real. She looked at Marius, she looked at the crowd, she looked at the sky: it seemed as though she feared that she should wake up from her dream. Her amazed and uneasy air added something indescribably enchanting to her beauty. They entered the same carriage to return home, Marius beside Cosette; M. Gillenormand and Jean Valjean sat opposite them; Aunt Gillenormand had withdrawn one degree, and was in the second vehicle.

"My children," said the grandfather, "here you are, Monsieur le Baron and Madame la Baronne, with an income of thirty thousand livres."

And Cosette, nestling close to Marius, caressed his ear with an angelic whisper, "So it is true. My name is Marius. I am Madame Thou."

These two creatures were resplendent. They had reached that irrevocable and irrecoverable moment, at the dazzling intersection of all youth and all joy. They realized the verses of Jean Prouvaire; they were forty years old taken together. It was marriage sublimated; these two children were two lilies. They did not see each other, they did not contemplate each other. Cosette perceived Marius in the midst of a glory; Marius perceived Cosette on an altar. And on that altar, and in that glory, the two apotheoses mingling, in the background, one knows not how, behind a cloud for Cosette, in a flash for Marius, there was the ideal thing, the real thing, the meeting of the kiss and the dream, the nuptial pillow. All the torments through which they had passed came back to them in intoxication. It seemed to them that their sorrows, their sleepless nights, their tears, their anguish, their terrors, their despair, converted into caresses and rays of light, rendered still more charming the charming hour that was approaching; and that their griefs were but so many handmaidens who were preparing the toilet of joy. How good it is to have suffered! Their unhappiness formed a halo around their happiness. The long agony of their love was terminating in an ascension.

It was the same enchantment in two souls, tinged with voluptuousness in Marius, and with modesty in Cosette. They said to each other in low tones, "We will go back to take a look at our little garden in the Rue Plumet." The folds of Cosette's gown lay across Marius.

Such a day is an ineffable mixture of dream and of reality. One possesses and one supposes. One still has time before one to divine. The emotion on that day, of being at midday and of dreaming of midnight is indescribable. The delights of these two hearts overflowed upon the crowd, and inspired the passersby with cheerfulness.

People halted in the Rue Saint-Antoine, in front of Saint-Paul, to gaze through the windows of the carriage at the orange-flowers quivering on Cosette's head.

Then they returned home to the Rue des Filles-du-Calvaire. Marius, triumphant and radiant, mounted side by side with Cosette the staircase up which he had been borne in a dying condition. The poor, who had trooped to the door, and who shared their purses, blessed them. There were flowers everywhere. The house was no less fragrant than the church; after the incense, roses. They thought they heard voices carolling in the infinite; they had God in their hearts; destiny appeared to them like a ceiling of stars; above their heads they beheld the light of a rising sun. All at once, the clock struck. Marius glanced at Cosette's charming bare arm, and at the rosy things that were vaguely visible through the lace of her bodice, and Cosette, intercepting Marius's glance, blushed to her very hair.

Quite a number of old family friends of the Gillenormand family had been invited; they pressed about Cosette. Each one vied with the rest in saluting her as Madame la Baronne.

The officer, Theodule Gillenormand, now a captain, had come from Chartres, where he was stationed in garrison, to be present at the wedding of his cousin Pontmercy. Cosette did not recognize him.

He, on his side, habituated as he was to have women consider him handsome, retained no more recollection of Cosette than of any other woman.

"How right I was not to believe in that story about the lancer!" said Father Gillenormand, to himself.

Cosette had never been more tender with Jean Valjean. She was in unison with Father Gillenormand; while he erected joy into aphorisms and maxims, she exhaled goodness like a perfume. Happiness desires that all the world should be happy.

She regained, for the purpose of addressing Jean Valjean, inflections of voice belonging to the time when she was a little girl. She caressed him with her smile.

A banquet had been spread in the dining room.

Illumination as brilliant as the daylight is the necessary seasoning of a great joy. Mist and obscurity are not accepted by the happy. They do not consent to be black. The night, yes; the shadows, no. If there is no sun, one must be made.

The dining room was full of gay things. In the center, above the white and glittering table, was a Venetian lustre with flat plates, with all sorts of colored birds, blue, violet, red, and green, perched amid the candles; around the chandelier, girandoles, on the walls, sconces with triple and quintuple branches; mirrors, silverware, glassware, plate, porcelain, faience, pottery, gold and silversmith's work, all was sparkling and gay. The empty spaces between the candelabra were filled in with bouquets, so that where there was not a light, there was a flower.

In the antechamber, three violins and a flute softly played quartettes by Haydn.

Jean Valjean had seated himself on a chair in the drawing room, behind the door, the leaf of which folded back upon him in such a manner as to nearly conceal him. A few moments before they sat down to table, Cosette came, as though inspired by a sudden whim, and made him a deep courtesy, spreading out her bridal toilet with both hands, and with a tenderly roguish glance, she asked him, "Father, are you satisfied?"

"Yes," said Jean Valjean, "I am content!"

"Well, then, laugh."

Jean Valjean began to laugh.

A few moments later, Basque announced that dinner was served.

The guests, preceded by M. Gillenormand with Cosette on his arm, entered the dining room, and arranged themselves in the proper order around the table.

Two large armchairs figured on the right and left of the bride, the first for

M. Gillenormand, the other for Jean Valjean. M. Gillenormand took his seat. The other armchair remained empty.

They looked about for M. Fauchelevent.

He was no longer there.

M. Gillenormand questioned Basque.

"Do you know where M. Fauchelevent is?"

"Sir," replied Basque, "I do, precisely. M. Fauchelevent told me to say to you, sir, that he was suffering, his injured hand was paining him somewhat, and that he could not dine with Monsieur le Baron and Madame la Baronne. That he begged to be excused, that he would come tomorrow. He has just taken his departure."

That empty armchair chilled the effusion of the wedding feast for a moment. But, if M. Fauchelevent was absent, M. Gillenormand was present, and the grandfather beamed for two. He affirmed that M. Fauchelevent had done well to retire early, if he were suffering, but that it was only a slight ailment. This declaration sufficed. Moreover, what is an obscure corner in such a submersion of joy? Cosette and Marius were passing through one of those egotistical and blessed moments when no other faculty is left to a person than that of receiving happiness. And then, an idea occurred to M. Gillenormand. "Pardieu, this armchair is empty. Come hither, Marius. Your aunt will permit it, although she has a right to you. This armchair is for you. That is legal and delightful. Fortunatus beside Fortunata." Applause from the whole table. Marius took Jean Valjean's place beside Cosette, and things fell out so that Cosette, who had, at first, been saddened by Jean Valjean's absence, ended by being satisfied with it. From the moment when Marius took his place, and was the substitute, Cosette would not have regretted God himself. She set her sweet little foot, shod in white satin, on Marius's foot.

The armchair being occupied, M. Fauchelevent was obliterated; and nothing was lacking.

And, five minutes afterward, the whole table from one end to the other, was laughing with all the animation of forgetfulness.

At dessert, M. Gillenormand, rising to his feet, with a glass of champagne in his hand—only half full so that the palsy of his eighty years might not cause an overflow, proposed the health of the married pair.

"You shall not escape two sermons," he exclaimed. "This morning you had one from the Curé, this evening you shall have one from your grandfather. Listen to me; I will give you a bit of advice: Adore each other. I do not make a pack of gyrations, I go straight to the mark, be happy. In all creation, only the turtle doves are wise. Philosophers say, 'Moderate your joys.' I say, 'Give rein to your joys.' Be as much smitten with each other as fiends. Be in a rage about it. The philosophers talk stuff and nonsense. I should like to stuff their philosophy down their gullets again. Can there be too many perfumes, too many open rosebuds, too many nightingales singing, too many green leaves, too much aurora in life? Can people love each other too much? Can people please each other too much? Take care, Estelle, thou art too pretty! Have a care, Nemorin, thou art too handsome! Fine stupidity, in sooth! Can people enchant each other too much, cajole each other too much, charm each other too much? Can one be too much alive, too happy? Moderate your joys. Ah, indeed! Down with the philosophers! Wisdom consists in jubilation. Make merry, let us make merry. Are we happy because we are good, or are we good because we are happy? Is the Sancy diamond called the Sancy because it belonged to Harley de Sancy, or because it weighs six hundred carats? I know nothing about it, life is full of such problems; the important point is to possess the Sancy and happiness. Let us be happy without quibbling and quirking. Let us obey the sun blindly. What is the sun? It is love. He who says love, says woman. Ah! Ah! Behold omnipotence—women. Ask that demagogue of a Marius if he is not the slave of that little tyrant of a Cosette. And of his own free will, too, the coward! Woman! There is no Robespierre who keeps his place but woman reigns. I am no longer Royalist except toward that royalty. What is Adam? The kingdom of Eve. No '89 for Eve. There has been the royal sceptre surmounted by a fleur-de-lis, there has been the imperial sceptre surmounted by a globe, there has been the scepter of Charlemagne, which was of iron, there has been the scepter of Louis the Great, which was of gold, the revolution twisted them between its thumb and forefinger, ha'penny straws; it is done with, it is broken, it lies on the earth, there is no longer any scepter, but make me a revolution against that little embroidered handkerchief, which smells of patchouli! I should like to see you do it. Try. Why is it so solid? Because it is a gewgaw. Ah! You are the nineteenth century? Well, what then? And we have been as foolish as you. Do not imagine that you have effected much change in the universe, because your trip-gallant is called the cholera morbus, and because your pourree is called the cachuca. In fact, the women must always be loved. I defy you to escape from that. These friends are our angels. Yes, love, woman, the kiss forms a circle from which I defy you to escape; and, for my own part, I should be only too happy to reenter it. Which of you has seen the planet Venus, the coquette of the abyss, the Celimene of the ocean, rise in the infinite, calming all here below? The ocean is a rough Alcestis. Well, grumble as he will, when Venus appears he is forced to smile. That brute beast submits. We are all made so. Wrath, tempest, claps of thunder, foam to the very ceiling. A woman enters on the scene, a planet rises; flat on your face! Marius was fighting six months ago; today he is married. That is well. Yes, Marius, yes, Cosette, you are in the right. Exist boldly for each other, make us burst with rage that we cannot do the same, idealize each other, catch in your beaks all the tiny blades of felicity that exist on earth, and arrange yourselves a nest for life. Pardi, to love, to be loved, what a fine miracle when one is young! Don't imagine that you have invented that. I, too, have had my dream, I, too, have meditated, I, too, have sighed; I, too, have had a moonlight soul. Love is a child six thousand years old. Love has the right to a long white beard. Methusalem is a street arab beside Cupid. For sixty centuries men and women have got out of their scrape by loving. The devil, who is cunning, took to hating man; man, who is still more cunning, took to loving woman. In this way he does more good than the devil does him harm. This craft was discovered in the days of the terrestrial paradise. The invention is old, my friends, but it is perfectly new. Profit by it. Be Daphnis and Chloe, while waiting to become Philemon and Baucis. Manage so that, when you are with each other, nothing shall be lacking to you, and that Cosette may be the sun for Marius, and that Marius may be the universe to Cosette. Cosette, let your fine weather be the smile of your husband; Marius, let your rain be your wife's tears. And let it never rain in your household. You have filched the winning number in the lottery; you have gained the great prize, guard it well, keep it under lock and key, do not squander it, adore each other and snap your fingers at all the rest. Believe what I say to you. It is good sense. And good sense cannot lie. Be a religion to each other. Each man has his own fashion of adoring God. Saperlotte! The best way to adore God is to love one's wife. I love thee! That's my catechism. He who loves is orthodox. The oath of Henri IV places sanctity somewhere between feasting and drunkenness. Ventre-saint-gris! I don't belong to the religion of that oath. Woman is forgotten in it. This astonishes me on the part of Henri IV. My friends, long live women! I am old, they say; it's astonishing how much I feel in the mood to be young. I should like to go and listen to the bagpipes in the woods. Children who contrive to be beautiful and contented, that intoxicates me. I would like greatly to get married, if anyone would have me. It is impossible to imagine that God could have made us for anything but this: to idolize, to coo, to preen ourselves, to be dovelike, to be dainty, to bill and coo our loves from morn to night, to gaze at one's image in one's little wife, to be proud, to be triumphant, to plume oneself; that is the aim of life. There, let not that displease you which we used to think in our day, when we were young folks. Ah! Vertu-bamboche! What charming women there were in those days, and what pretty little faces and what lovely lasses! I committed my ravages among them. Then love each other. If people did not love each other, I really do not see what use there would be in having any springtime; and for my own part, I should pray the good God to shut up all the beautiful things that he shows us, and to take away from us and put back in his box, the flowers, the birds, and the pretty maidens. My children, receive an old man's blessing."

The evening was gay, lively and agreeable. The grandfather's sovereign good humor gave the keynote to the whole feast, and each person regulated his conduct on that almost centenarian cordiality. They danced a little, they laughed a great deal; it was an amiable wedding. Goodman Days of Yore might have been invited to it. However, he was present in the person of Father Gillenormand.

There was a tumult, then silence.

The married pair disappeared.

A little after midnight, the Gillenormand house became a temple.

Here we pause. On the threshold of wedding nights stands a smiling angel with his finger on his lips.

The soul enters into contemplation before that sanctuary where the celebration of love takes place.

There should be flashes of light athwart such houses. The joy that they contain ought to make its escape through the stones of the walls in brilliancy, and vaguely illuminate the gloom. It is impossible that this sacred and fatal festival should not give off a celestial radiance to the infinite. Love is the sublime crucible wherein the fusion of the man and the woman takes place; the being one, the being triple, the being final, the human trinity proceeds from it. This birth of two souls into one, ought to be an emotion for the gloom. The lover is the priest; the ravished virgin is terrified. Something of that joy ascends to God. Where true marriage is, that is to say, where there is love, the ideal enters in. A nuptial bed makes a nook of dawn amid the shadows. If it were given to the eye of the flesh to scan the formidable and charming visions of the upper life, it is probable that we should behold the forms of night, the winged unknowns, the blue passers of the invisible, bend down, a throng of somber heads, around the luminous house, satisfied, showering benedictions, pointing out to each other the virgin wife gently alarmed, sweetly terrified, and bearing the reflection of human bliss upon their divine countenances. If at that supreme hour, the wedded pair, dazzled with voluptuousness and believing themselves alone, were to listen, they would hear in their chamber a confused rustling of wings. Perfect happiness implies a mutual understanding with the angels. That dark little chamber has all heaven for its ceiling. When two mouths, rendered sacred by love, approach to create, it is impossible that there should not be, above that ineffable kiss, a quivering throughout the immense mystery of stars.

These felicities are the true ones. There is no joy outside of these joys. Love is the only ecstasy. All the rest weeps.

To love, or to have loved, this suffices. Demand nothing more. There is no other pearl to be found in the shadowy folds of life. To love is a fulfilment.

CHAPTER III—THE INSEPARABLE

What had become of Jean Valjean?

Immediately after having laughed, at Cosette's graceful command, when no one was paying any heed to him, Jean Valjean had risen and had gained the antechamber unperceived. This was the very room that, eight months before, he had entered black with mud, with blood and powder, bringing back the grandson to the grandfather. The old wainscoting was garlanded with foliage and flowers; the musicians were seated on the sofa on which they had laid Marius down. Basque, in a black coat, knee breeches, white stockings and white gloves, was arranging roses around all of the dishes that were to be served. Jean Valjean pointed to his arm in its sling, charged Basque to explain his absence, and went away.

The long windows of the dining room opened on the street. Jean Valjean stood for several minutes, erect and motionless in the darkness, beneath those radiant windows. He listened. The confused sounds of the banquet reached his ear. He heard the loud, commanding tones of the grandfather, the violins, the clatter of the plates, the bursts of laughter, and through all that merry uproar, he distinguished Cosette's sweet and joyous voice.

He quitted the Rue des Filles-du-Calvaire, and returned to the Rue de l'Homme Arme.

In order to return there, he took the Rue Saint-Louis, the Rue Culture-Sainte-Catherine, and the Blancs-Manteaux; it was a little longer, but it was the road through which, for the last three months, he had become accustomed to pass every day on his way from the Rue de l'Homme Arme to the Rue des Filles-du-Calvaire, in order to avoid the obstructions and the mud in the Rue Vielle-du-Temple.

This road, through which Cosette had passed, excluded for him all possibility of any other itinerary.

Jean Valjean entered his lodgings. He lighted his candle and mounted the stairs. The apartment was empty. Even Toussaint was no longer there. Jean Valjean's step made more noise than usual in the chambers. All the cupboards stood open. He penetrated to Cosette's bedroom. There were no sheets on the bed. The pillow, covered with ticking, and without a case or lace, was laid on the blankets folded up on the foot of the mattress, whose covering was visible, and on which no one was ever to sleep again. All the little feminine objects that Cosette was attached to had been carried away; nothing remained except the heavy furniture and the four walls. Toussaint's bed was despoiled in like manner. One bed only was made up, and seemed to be waiting someone, and this was Jean Valjean's bed.

Jean Valjean looked at the walls, closed some of the cupboard doors, and went and came from one room to another.

Then he sought his own chamber once more, and set his candle on a table.

He had disengaged his arm from the sling, and he used his right hand as though it did not hurt him.

He approached his bed, and his eyes rested, was it by chance? Was it intentionally? On the inseparable of which Cosette had been jealous, on the little portmanteau that never left him. On his arrival in the Rue de l'Homme Armé, on the 4th of June, he had deposited it on a round table near the head of his bed. He went to this table with a sort of vivacity, took a key from his pocket, and opened the valise.

From it he slowly drew forth the garments in which, ten years before, Cosette had quitted Montfermeil; first the little gown, then the black fichu, then the stout, coarse child's shoes that Cosette might almost have worn still, so tiny were her feet, then the fustian bodice, which was very thick, then the knitted petticoat, next the apron with pockets, then the woollen stockings. These stockings, which still preserved the graceful form of a tiny leg, were no longer than Jean Valjean's hand. All this was black of hue. It was he who had brought those garments to Montfermeil for her. As he removed them from the valise, he laid them on the bed. He fell to thinking. He called up memories. It was in winter, in a very cold month of December, she was shivering, half-naked, in rags, her poor little feet were all red in their wooden shoes. He, Jean Valjean, had made her abandon those rags to clothe herself in these mourning habiliments. The mother must have felt pleased in her grave, to see her daughter wearing mourning for her, and, above all, to see that she was properly clothed, and that she was warm. He thought of that forest of Montfermeil; they had traversed it together, Cosette and he; he thought of what the weather had been, of the leafless trees, of the wood destitute of birds, of the sunless sky; it mattered not, it was charming. He arranged the tiny garments on the bed, the fichu next to the petticoat, the stockings beside the shoes, and he looked at them, one after the other. She was no taller than that, she had her big doll in her arms, she had put her louis d'or in the pocket of that apron, she had laughed, they walked hand in hand, she had no one in the world but him.

Then his venerable, white head fell forward on the bed, that stoical old heart broke, his face was engulfed, so to speak, in Cosette's garments, and if anyone had passed up the stairs at that moment, he would have heard frightful sobs.

CHAPTER IV—THE IMMORTAL LIVER[*]

The old and formidable struggle, of which we have already witnessed so many phases, began once more.

Jacob struggled with the angel but one night. Alas! How many times have we beheld Jean Valjean seized bodily by his conscience, in the darkness, and struggling desperately against it!

Unheard-of conflict! At certain moments the foot slips; at other moments the ground crumbles away underfoot. How many times had that conscience, mad for the good, clasped and overthrown him! How many times had the truth set her knee inexorably upon his breast! How many times, hurled to earth by the light, had he begged for mercy! How many times had that implacable spark, lighted within him, and upon him by the Bishop, dazzled him by force when he had wished to be blind! How many times had he risen to his feet in the combat, held fast to the rock, leaning against sophism, dragged in the dust, now getting the upper hand of his conscience, again overthrown by it! How many times, after an equivoque, after the specious and treacherous reasoning of egotism, had he heard his irritated conscience cry in his ear: "A trip! You wretch!" How many times had his refractory thoughts rattled convulsively in his throat, under the evidence of duty! Resistance to God. Funereal sweats. What secret wounds that he alone felt bleed! What excoriations in his lamentable existence! How many times he had risen bleeding, bruised, broken, enlightened, despair in his heart, serenity in his soul! And, vanquished, he had felt himself the conqueror. And, after having dislocated, broken, and rent his conscience with

---

[*] an allusion to the story of Prometheus

red-hot pincers, it had said to him, as it stood over him, formidable, luminous, and tranquil, "Now, go in peace!"

But on emerging from so melancholy a conflict, what a lugubrious peace, alas!

Nevertheless, that night Jean Valjean felt that he was passing through his final combat.

A heart-rending question presented itself.

Predestinations are not all direct; they do not open out in a straight avenue before the predestined man; they have blind courts, impassable alleys, obscure turns, disturbing crossroads offering the choice of many ways. Jean Valjean had halted at that moment at the most perilous of these crossroads.

He had come to the supreme crossing of good and evil. He had that gloomy intersection beneath his eyes. On this occasion once more, as had happened to him already in other sad vicissitudes, two roads opened out before him, the one tempting, the other alarming.

Which was he to take?

He was counseled to the one that alarmed him by that mysterious index finger that we all perceive whenever we fix our eyes on the darkness.

Once more, Jean Valjean had the choice between the terrible port and the smiling ambush.

Is it then true? the soul may recover; but not fate. Frightful thing! an incurable destiny!

This is the problem that presented itself to him:

In what manner was Jean Valjean to behave in relation to the happiness of Cosette and Marius? It was he who had willed that happiness, it was he who had brought it about; he had, himself, buried it in his entrails, and at that moment, when he reflected on it, he was able to enjoy the sort of satisfaction that an armorer would experience on recognizing his factory mark on a knife, on withdrawing it, all smoking, from his own breast.

Cosette had Marius, Marius possessed Cosette. They had everything, even riches. And this was his doing.

But what was he, Jean Valjean, to do with this happiness, now that it existed, now that it was there? Should he force himself on this happiness? Should he treat it as belonging to him? No doubt, Cosette did belong to another; but should he, Jean Valjean, retain of Cosette all that he could retain? Should he remain the sort of father, half seen but respected, which he had hitherto been? Should he, without saying a word, bring his past to that future? Should he present himself there, as though he had a right, and should he seat himself, veiled, at that luminous fireside? Should he take those innocent hands into his tragic hands, with a smile? Should he place upon the peaceful fender of the Gillenormand drawing room those feet of his, which dragged behind them the disgraceful shadow of the law? Should he enter into participation in the fair fortunes of Cosette and Marius? Should he render the obscurity on his brow and the cloud upon theirs still more dense? Should he place his catastrophe as a third associate in their felicity? Should he continue to hold his peace? In a word, should he be the sinister mute of destiny beside these two happy beings?

We must have become habituated to fatality and to encounters with it, in order to have the daring to raise our eyes when certain questions appear to us in all their horrible nakedness. Good or evil stands behind this severe interrogation point. "What are you going to do?" demands the sphinx.

This habit of trial Jean Valjean possessed. He gazed intently at the sphinx.

He examined the pitiless problem under all its aspects.

Cosette, that charming existence, was the raft of this shipwreck. What was he to do? To cling fast to it, or to let go his hold?

If he clung to it, he should emerge from disaster, he should ascend again into the sunlight, he should let the bitter water drip from his garments and his hair, he was saved, he should live.

And if he let go his hold?

Then the abyss.

Thus he took sad council with his thoughts. Or, to speak more correctly, he fought; he kicked furiously internally, now against his will, now against his conviction.

Happily for Jean Valjean that he had been able to weep. That relieved him, possibly. But the beginning was savage. A tempest, more furious than the one that had formerly driven him to Arras, broke loose within him. The past surged up before him facing the present; he compared them and sobbed. The silence of tears once opened, the despairing man writhed.

He felt that he had been stopped short.

Alas! In this fight to the death between our egotism and our duty, when we thus retreat step by step before our immutable ideal, bewildered, furious, exasperated at having to yield, disputing the ground, hoping for a possible flight, seeking an escape, what an abrupt and sinister resistance does the foot of the wall offer in our rear!

To feel the sacred shadow that forms an obstacle!

The invisible inexorable, what an obsession!

Then, one is never done with conscience. Make your choice, Brutus; make your choice, Cato. It is fathomless, since it is God. One flings into that well the labor of one's whole life, one flings in one's fortune, one flings in one's riches, one flings in one's success, one flings in one's liberty or fatherland, one flings in one's well-being, one flings in one's repose, one flings in one's joy! More! More! More! Empty the vase! Tip the urn! One must finish by flinging in one's heart.

Somewhere in the fog of the ancient hells, there is a tun like that.

Is not one pardonable, if one at last refuses! Can the inexhaustible have any right? Are not chains that are endless above human strength? Who would blame Sisyphus and Jean Valjean for saying: "It is enough!"

The obedience of matter is limited by friction; is there no limit to the obedience of the soul? If perpetual motion is impossible, can perpetual self-sacrifice be exacted?

The first step is nothing, it is the last that is difficult. What was the Champmathieu affair in comparison with Cosette's marriage and of that which it entailed? What is a reentrance into the galleys, compared to entrance into the void?

Oh, first step that must be descended, how somber art thou! Oh, second step, how black art thou!

How could he refrain from turning aside his head this time?

Martyrdom is sublimation, corrosive sublimation. It is a torture that consecrates. One can consent to it for the first hour; one seats oneself on the throne of glowing iron, one places on one's head the crown of hot iron, one accepts the globe of red hot iron, one takes the sceptre of red hot iron, but the mantle of flame still remains to be donned, and comes there not a moment when the miserable flesh revolts and when one abdicates from suffering?

At length, Jean Valjean entered into the peace of exhaustion.

He weighed, he reflected, he considered the alternatives, the mysterious balance of light and darkness.

Should he impose his galleys on those two dazzling children, or should he consummate his irremediable engulfment by himself? On one side lay the sacrifice of Cosette, on the other that of himself.

At what solution should he arrive? What decision did he come to?

What resolution did he take? What was his own inward definitive response to the unbribable interrogatory of fatality? What door did he decide to open? Which side of his life did he resolve upon closing and condemning? Among all the unfathomable precipices that surrounded him, which was his choice? What extremity did he accept? To which of the gulfs did he nod his head?

His dizzy revery lasted all night long.

He remained there until daylight, in the same attitude, bent double over that bed, prostrate beneath the enormity of fate, crushed, perchance, alas! With clenched fists, with arms outspread at right angles, like a man crucified who has been unnailed, and flung face down on the earth. There he remained for twelve hours, the twelve long hours of a long winter's night, ice-cold, without once raising his head, and without uttering a word. He was as motionless as a corpse, while his thoughts wallowed on the earth and soared, now like the hydra, now like the eagle. Anyone to behold him thus motionless would have pronounced him dead; all at once he shuddered convulsively, and his mouth, glued to Cosette's garments, kissed them; then it could be seen that he was alive.

Who could see? Since Jean Valjean was alone, and there was no one there.

The One who is in the shadows.

BOOK SEVENTH: THE LAST DRAUGHT FROM THE CUP

CHAPTER I—THE SEVENTH CIRCLE AND THE EIGHTH HEAVEN

The days that follow weddings are solitary. People respect the meditations of the happy pair. And also, their tardy slumbers, to some degree. The tumult of visits and congratulations only begins later on. On the morning of the 17th of February, it was a little past midday when Basque, with napkin and feather duster under his arm, busy in setting his antechamber to rights, heard a light tap at the door. There had been no ring, which was discreet on such a day. Basque opened the door, and beheld M. Fauchelevent. He introduced him into the drawing room, still encumbered and topsy-turvy, and which bore the air of a field of battle after the joys of the preceding evening.

"Dame, Sir," remarked Basque, "we all woke up late."

"Is your master up?" asked Jean Valjean.

"How is Monsieur's arm?" replied Basque.

"Better. Is your master up?"

"Which one? The old one or the new one?"

"Monsieur Pontmercy."

"Monsieur le Baron," said Basque, drawing himself up.

A man is a Baron most of all to his servants. He counts for something with them; they are what a philosopher would call, bespattered with the title, and that flatters them. Marius, be it said in passing, a militant republican as he had proved, was now a Baron in spite of himself. A small revolution had taken place in the family in connection with this title. It was now M. Gillenormand who clung to it, and Marius who detached himself from it. But Colonel Pontmercy had written, "My son will bear my title." Marius obeyed. And then, Cosette, in whom the woman was beginning to dawn, was delighted to be a Baroness.

"Monsieur le Baron?" repeated Basque. "I will go and see. I will tell him that M. Fauchelevent is here."

"No. Do not tell him that it is I. Tell him that someone wishes to speak to him in private, and mention no name."

"Ah!" ejaculated Basque.

"I wish to surprise him."

"Ah!" ejaculated Basque once more, emitting his second "Ah!" as an explanation of the first.

And he left the room.

Jean Valjean remained alone.

The drawing room, as we have just said, was in great disorder. It seemed as though, by lending an air, one might still hear the vague noise of the wedding. On the polished floor lay all sorts of flowers that had fallen from garlands and headdresses. The wax candles, burned to stumps, added stalactites of wax to the crystal drops of the chandeliers. Not a single piece of furniture was in its place. In the corners, three or four armchairs, drawn close together in a circle, had the appearance of continuing a conversation. The whole effect was cheerful. A certain grace still lingers around a dead feast. It has been a happy thing. On the chairs in disarray, among those fading flowers, beneath those extinct lights, people have thought of joy. The sun had succeeded to the chandelier, and made its way gayly into the drawing room.

Several minutes elapsed. Jean Valjean stood motionless on the spot where Basque had left him. He was very pale. His eyes were hollow, and so sunken in his head by sleeplessness that they nearly disappeared in their orbits. His black coat bore the weary folds of a garment that has been up all night. The elbows were whitened with the down that the friction of cloth against linen leaves behind it.

Jean Valjean stared at the window outlined on the polished floor at his feet by the sun.

There came a sound at the door, and he raised his eyes.

Marius entered, his head well up, his mouth smiling, an indescribable light on his countenance, his brow expanded, his eyes triumphant. He had not slept either.

"It is you, Father!" he exclaimed, on catching sight of Jean Valjean. "That idiot of a Basque had such a mysterious air! But you have come too early. It is only half past twelve. Cosette is asleep."

That word: "Father," said to M. Fauchelevent by Marius, signified supreme felicity. There had always existed, as the reader knows, a lofty wall, a coldness and a constraint between them; ice that must be broken or melted. Marius had reached that point of intoxication when the wall was lowered, when the ice dissolved, and when M. Fauchelevent was to him, as to Cosette, a father.

He continued: his words poured forth, as is the peculiarity of divine paroxysms of joy.

"How glad I am to see you! If you only knew how we missed you yesterday! Good morning, Father. How is your hand? Better, is it not?"

And, satisfied with the favorable reply, which he had made to himself, he pursued, "We have both been talking about you. Cosette loves you so dearly! You must not forget that you have a chamber here; we want nothing more to do with the Rue de l'Homme Arme. We will have no more of it at all. How could you go to live in a street like that, which is sickly, which is disagreeable, which is ugly, which has a barrier at one end, where one is cold, and into which one cannot enter? You are to come and install yourself here. And this very day. Or you will have to deal with Cosette. She means to lead us all by the nose, I warn you. You have your own chamber here, it is close to ours, it opens on the garden; the trouble with the clock has been attended to, the bed is made, it is all ready, you have only to take possession of it. Near your bed Cosette has placed a huge, old, easy chair covered with Utrecht velvet and she has said to it, 'Stretch out your arms to him.' A nightingale comes to the clump of acacias opposite your windows, every spring. In two months more you will have it. You will have its nest on your left and ours on your right. By night it will sing, and by day Cosette will prattle. Your chamber faces due South. Cosette will arrange your books for you, your *Voyages of Captain Cook* and the other, Vancouver's and all your affairs. I believe that there is a little valise to which you are attached, I have fixed upon a corner of honor for that. You have conquered my grandfather, you suit him. We will live together. Do you play whist? You will overwhelm my grandfather with delight if you play whist. It is you who shall take Cosette to walk on the days when I am at the courts, you shall give her your arm, you know, as you used to, in the Luxembourg.

We are absolutely resolved to be happy. And you shall be included in it, in our happiness, do you hear, father? Come, will you breakfast with us today?"

"Sir," said Jean Valjean, "I have something to say to you. I am an ex-convict."

The limit of shrill sounds perceptible can be overleaped, as well in the case of the mind as in that of the ear. These words, "I am an ex-convict," proceeding from the mouth of M. Fauchelevent and entering the ear of Marius overshot the possible. It seemed to him that something had just been said to him; but he did not know what. He stood with his mouth wide open.

Then he perceived that the man who was addressing him was frightful. Wholly absorbed in his own dazzled state, he had not, up to that moment, observed the other man's terrible pallor.

Jean Valjean untied the black cravat that supported his right arm, unrolled the linen from around his hand, bared his thumb and showed it to Marius.

"There is nothing the matter with my hand," said he.

Marius looked at the thumb.

"There has not been anything the matter with it," went on Jean Valjean.

There was, in fact, no trace of any injury.

Jean Valjean continued, "It was fitting that I should be absent from your marriage. I absented myself as much as was in my power. So I invented this injury in order that I might not commit a forgery, that I might not introduce a flaw into the marriage documents, in order that I might escape from signing."

Marius stammered.

"What is the meaning of this?"

"The meaning of it is," replied Jean Valjean, "that I have been in the galleys."

"You are driving me mad!" exclaimed Marius in terror.

"Monsieur Pontmercy," said Jean Valjean, "I was nineteen years in the galleys. For theft. Then, I was condemned for life for theft, for a second offense. At the present moment, I have broken my ban."

In vain did Marius recoil before the reality, refuse the fact, resist the evidence, he was forced to give way. He began to understand, and, as always happens in such cases, he understood too much. An inward shudder of hideous enlightenment flashed through him; an idea that made him quiver traversed his mind. He caught a glimpse of a wretched destiny for himself in the future.

"Say all, say all!" he cried. "You are Cosette's father!"

And he retreated a couple of paces with a movement of indescribable horror.

Jean Valjean elevated his head with so much majesty of attitude that he seemed to grow even to the ceiling.

"It is necessary that you should believe me here, Sir; although our oath to others may not be received in law . . ."

Here he paused, then, with a sort of sovereign and sepulchral authority, he added, articulating slowly, and emphasizing the syllables:

"You will believe me. I the father of Cosette! Before God, no. Monsieur le Baron Pontmercy, I am a peasant of Faverolles. I earned my living by pruning trees. My name is not Fauchelevent, but Jean Valjean. I am not related to Cosette. Reassure yourself."

Marius stammered, "Who will prove that to me?"

"I. Since I tell you so."

Marius looked at the man. He was melancholy yet tranquil. No lie could proceed from such a calm. That which is icy is sincere. The truth could be felt in that chill of the tomb.

"I believe you," said Marius.

Jean Valjean bent his head, as though taking note of this, and continued, "What am I to Cosette? A passerby. Ten years ago, I did not know that she was in existence. I love her, it is true. One loves a child whom one has seen when very young, being old oneself. When one is old, one feels oneself a grandfather toward all little children. You may, it seems to me, suppose that I have something that resembles a heart. She was an orphan. Without either father or mother. She needed me. That is why I began to love her. Children are so weak that the first-comer, even a man like me, can become their protector. I have fulfilled this duty toward Cosette. I do not think that so slight a thing can be called a good action; but if it be a good action, well, say that I have done it. Register this attenuating circumstance. Today, Cosette passes out of my life; our two roads part. Henceforth, I can do nothing for her. She is Madame Pontmercy. Her providence has changed. And Cosette gains by the change. All is well. As for the six hundred thousand francs, you do not mention them to me, but I forestall your thought, they are a deposit. How did that deposit come into my hands? What does that matter? I restore the deposit. Nothing more can be demanded of me. I complete the restitution by announcing my true name. That concerns me. I have a reason for desiring that you should know who I am."

And Jean Valjean looked Marius full in the face.

All that Marius experienced was tumultuous and incoherent. Certain gusts of destiny produce these billows in our souls.

We have all undergone moments of trouble in which everything within us is dispersed; we say the first things that occur to us, which are not always precisely those that should be said. There are sudden revelations that one cannot bear, and which intoxicate like baleful wine. Marius was stupefied by the novel situation that presented itself to him, to the point of addressing that man almost like a person who was angry with him for this avowal.

"But why," he exclaimed, "do you tell me all this? Who forces you to do so? You could have kept your secret to yourself. You are neither denounced, nor tracked nor pursued. You have a reason for wantonly making such a revelation. Conclude. There is something more. In what connection do you make this confession? What is your motive?"

"My motive?" replied Jean Valjean in a voice so low and dull that one would have said that he was talking to himself rather than to Marius. "From what motive, in fact, has this convict just said, 'I am a convict'? Well, yes! The motive is strange. It is out of honesty. Stay, the unfortunate point is that I have a thread in my heart, which keeps me fast. It is when one is old that that sort of thread is particularly solid. All life falls in ruin around one; one resists. Had I been able to tear out that thread, to break it, to undo the knot or to cut it, to go far away, I should have been safe. I had only to go away; there are diligences in the Rue Bouloy; you are happy; I am going. I have tried to break that thread, I have jerked at it, it would not break, I tore my heart with it. Then I said, 'I cannot live anywhere else than here.' I must stay. Well, yes, you are right, I am a fool, why not simply remain here? You offer me a chamber in this house, Madame Pontmercy is sincerely attached to me, she said to the armchair, 'Stretch out your arms to him,' your grandfather demands nothing better than to have me, I suit him, we shall live together, and take our meals in common, I shall give Cosette my arm . . . Madame Pontmercy, excuse me, it is a habit, we shall have but one roof, one table, one fire, the same chimney-corner in winter, the same promenade in summer, that is joy, that is happiness, that is everything. We shall live as one family. One family!"

At that word, Jean Valjean became wild. He folded his arms, glared at the floor beneath his feet as though he would have excavated an abyss therein, and his voice suddenly rose in thundering tones, "As one family! No. I belong to no family. I do not belong to yours. I do not belong to any family of men. In houses where people are among themselves, I am superfluous. There are families, but there is nothing of the sort for me. I am an unlucky wretch; I am left outside. Did I have a father and mother? I almost doubt it. On the day when I gave that child in marriage, all came to an end. I have seen her happy, and that she is with a man whom she loves, and that there exists here a kind old man, a household of two angels, and all joys in that house, and that it was well, I said to myself, 'Enter thou not.' I could have lied, it is true, have deceived you all, and remained Monsieur Fauchelevent. So long as it was for her, I could lie; but now it would be for myself, and I must not. It was sufficient for me to hold my peace, it is true, and all would go on. You ask me what has forced me to speak? A very odd thing; my conscience. To hold my peace was very easy, however. I passed the night in trying to persuade myself to it; you questioned me, and what I have just said to you is so extraordinary that you have the right to do it; well, yes, I have passed the night in alleging reasons to myself, and I gave myself very good reasons, I have done what I could. But there are two things in which I have not succeeded; in breaking the thread that holds me fixed, riveted and sealed here by the heart, or in silencing someone who speaks softly to me when I am alone. That is why I have come hither to tell you everything this morning. Everything or nearly everything. It is useless to tell you that which concerns only myself; I keep that to myself. You know the essential points. So I have taken my mystery and have brought it to you. And I have disemboweled my secret before your eyes. It was not a resolution that was easy to take. I struggled all night long. Ah! You think that I did not tell myself that this was no Champmathieu affair, that by concealing my name I was doing no one any injury, that the name of Fauchelevent had been given to me by Fauchelevent himself, out of gratitude for a service rendered to him, and that I might assuredly keep it, and that I should be happy in that chamber you offer me, that I should not be in anyone's way, that I should be in my own little corner, and that, while you would have Cosette, I should have the idea that I was in the same house with her. Each one of us would have had his share of happiness. If I continued to be Monsieur Fauchelevent, that would arrange everything. Yes, with the exception of my soul. There was joy everywhere upon my surface, but the bottom of my soul remained black. It is not enough to be happy, one must be content. Thus I should have remained Monsieur Fauchelevent, thus I should have concealed my true visage, thus, in the presence of your expansion, I should have had an enigma, thus, in the midst of your full noonday, I should have had shadows, thus, without crying "ware,' I should have simply introduced the galleys to your fireside, I should have taken my seat at your table with the thought that if you knew who I was, you would drive me from it, I should have allowed myself to be served by domestics who, had they known, would have said: 'How horrible!' I should have touched you with my elbow, which you have a right to dislike, I should have filched your clasps of the hand! There would have existed in your house a division of respect between venerable white locks and tainted white locks; at your most intimate hours, when all hearts thought themselves open to the very bottom to all the rest, when we four were together, your grandfather, you two and myself, a stranger would have been present! I should have been side by side with you in your existence, having for my only care not to disarrange the cover of my dreadful pit. Thus, I, a dead man, should have thrust myself upon you who are living beings. I should have condemned her to myself forever. You and Cosette and I would have had all three of our heads in the green cap! Does it not make you shudder? I am only the most crushed of men; I should have been the most monstrous of men. And I should have committed that crime every day! And I should have had that face of night upon my visage every day! Every day! And I should have communicated to you a share in my taint every day! Every day! To you, my dearly beloved, my children, to you, my innocent creatures! Is it nothing to hold one's peace? Is it a simple matter to keep silence? No, it is not simple. There is a silence that lies. And my lie, and my fraud and my indignity, and my cowardice and my treason and my crime, I should have drained drop by drop, I should have spit it out, then swallowed it again, I should have finished at midnight and have begun again at midday, and my 'good morning' would have lied, and my 'good night' would have lied, and I should have slept on it, I should have eaten it, with my bread, and I should have looked Cosette in the face, and I should have responded to the smile of the angel by the smile of the damned soul, and I should have been an abominable villain! Why should I do it? In order to be happy. In order to be happy. Have I the right to be happy? I stand outside of life, Sir."

Jean Valjean paused. Marius listened. Such chains of ideas and of anguishes cannot be interrupted. Jean Valjean lowered his voice once more, but it was no longer a dull voice—it was a sinister voice.

"You ask why I speak? I am neither denounced, nor pursued, nor tracked, you say. Yes! I am denounced! Yes! I am tracked! By whom? By myself. It is I who bar the passage to myself, and I drag myself, and I push myself, and I arrest myself, and I execute myself, and when one holds oneself, one is firmly held."

And, seizing a handful of his own coat by the nape of the neck and extending it toward Marius, "Do you see that fist?" he continued. "Don't you think that it holds that collar in such a wise as not to release it? Well! Conscience is another grasp! If one desires to be happy, Sir, one must never understand duty; for, as soon as one has comprehended it, it is implacable. One would say that it punished you for comprehending it; but no, it rewards you; for it places you in a hell, where you feel God beside you. One has no sooner lacerated his own entrails than he is at peace with himself."

And, with a poignant accent, he added, "Monsieur Pontmercy, this is not common sense, I am an honest man. It is by degrading myself in your eyes that I elevate myself in my own. This has happened to me once before, but it was less painful then; it was a mere nothing. Yes, an honest man. I should not be so if, through my fault, you had continued to esteem me; now that you despise me, I am so. I have that fatality hanging over me that, not being able to ever have anything but stolen consideration, that consideration humiliates me, and crushes me inwardly, and, in order that I may respect myself, it is necessary that I should be despised. Then I straighten up again. I am a galley slave who obeys his conscience. I know well that that is most improbable. But what would you have me do about it? It is the fact. I have entered into engagements with myself; I keep them. There are encounters that bind us, there are chances that involve us in duties. You see, Monsieur Pontmercy, various things have happened to me in the course of my life."

Again Jean Valjean paused, swallowing his saliva with an effort, as though his words had a bitter aftertaste, and then he went on, "When one has such a horror hanging over one, one has not the right to make others share it without their knowledge, one has not the right to make them slip over one's own precipice without their perceiving it, one has not the right to let one's red blouse drag upon them, one has no right to slyly encumber with one's misery the happiness of others. It is hideous to approach those who are healthy, and to touch them in the dark with one's ulcer. In spite of the fact that Fauchelevent lent me his name, I have no right to use it; he could give it to me, but I could not take it. A name is an I. You see, sir, that I have thought somewhat, I have read a little, although I am a peasant; and you see that I express myself properly. I understand things. I have procured myself an education. Well, yes, to abstract a name and to place oneself under it is dishonest. Letters of the alphabet can be filched, like a purse or a watch. To be a false signature in flesh and blood, to be a living false key, to enter the house of honest people by picking their lock, never more to look straightforward, to forever eye askance, to be infamous within the I, no! No! No! No! No! It is better to suffer, to bleed, to weep, to tear one's skin from the flesh with one's nails, to pass nights writhing in anguish, to devour oneself body and soul. That is why I have just told you all this. Wantonly, as you say."

He drew a painful breath, and hurled this final word, "In days gone by, I stole a loaf of bread in order to live; today, in order to live, I will not steal a name."

"To live!" interrupted Marius. "You do not need that name in order to live?"

"Ah! I understand the matter," said Jean Valjean, raising and lowering his head several times in succession.

A silence ensued. Both held their peace, each plunged in a gulf of thoughts. Marius was sitting near a table and resting the corner of his mouth on one of his fingers, which was folded back. Jean Valjean was pacing to and fro. He paused before a mirror, and remained motionless. Then, as though replying to some inward course of reasoning, he said, as he gazed at the mirror, which he did not see, "While, at present, I am relieved."

He took up his march again, and walked to the other end of the drawing room. At the moment when he turned around, he perceived that Marius was watching his walk. Then he said, with an inexpressible intonation, "I drag my leg a little. Now you understand why!"

Then he turned fully around toward Marius, "And now, Sir, imagine this: I have said nothing, I have remained Monsieur Fauchelevent, I have taken my place in your house, I am one of you, I am in my chamber, I come to breakfast in the morning in slippers, in the evening all three of us go to the play, I accompany Madame Pontmercy to the Tuileries, and to the Place Royale, we are together, you think me your equal; one fine day you are there, and I am there, we are conversing, we are laughing; all at once, you hear a voice shouting this name, 'Jean Valjean!' and behold, that terrible hand, the police, darts from the darkness, and abruptly tears off my mask!"

Again he paused; Marius had sprung to his feet with a shudder. Jean Valjean resumed, "What do you say to that?"

Marius's silence answered for him.

Jean Valjean continued, "You see that I am right in not holding my peace. Be happy, be in heaven, be the angel of an angel, exist in the sun, be content therewith, and do not trouble yourself about the means that a poor damned wretch takes to open his breast and force his duty to come forth; you have before you, sir, a wretched man."

Marius slowly crossed the room, and, when he was quite close to Jean Valjean, he offered the latter his hand.

But Marius was obliged to step up and take that hand that was not offered, Jean Valjean let him have his own way, and it seemed to Marius that he pressed a hand of marble.

"My grandfather has friends," said Marius; "I will procure your pardon."

"It is useless," replied Jean Valjean. "I am believed to be dead, and that suffices. The dead are not subjected to surveillance. They are supposed to rot in peace. Death is the same thing as pardon."

And, disengaging the hand Marius held, he added, with a sort of inexorable dignity, "Moreover, the friend to whom I have recourse is the doing of my duty; and I need but one pardon, that of my conscience."

At that moment, a door at the other end of the drawing room opened gently half way, and in the opening Cosette's head appeared. They saw only her sweet face, her hair was in charming disorder, her eyelids were still swollen with sleep. She made the movement of a bird, which thrusts its head out of its nest, glanced first at her husband, then at Jean Valjean, and cried to them with a smile, so that they seemed to behold a smile at the heart of a rose, "I will wager that you are talking politics. How stupid that is, instead of being with me!"

Jean Valjean shuddered.

"Cosette!" stammered Marius.

And he paused. One would have said that they were two criminals.

Cosette, who was radiant, continued to gaze at both of them. There was something in her eyes like gleams of paradise.

"I have caught you in the very act," said Cosette. "Just now, I heard my father Fauchelevent through the door saying: 'Conscience . . . doing my duty.' That is politics, indeed it is. I will not have it. People should not talk politics the very next day. It is not right."

"You are mistaken. Cosette," said Marius, "we are talking business. We are discussing the best investment of your six hundred thousand francs."

"That is not it at all," interrupted Cosette. "I am coming. Does any body want me here?"

And, passing resolutely through the door, she entered the drawing room. She was dressed in a voluminous white dressing-gown, with a thousand folds and large sleeves that, starting from the neck, fell to her feet. In the golden heavens of some ancient gothic pictures, there are these charming sacks fit to clothe the angels.

She contemplated herself from head to foot in a long mirror, then exclaimed, in an outburst of ineffable ecstasy, "There was once a King and a Queen. Oh! How happy I am!"

That said, she made a curtsey to Marius and to Jean Valjean.

"There," said she, "I am going to install myself near you in an easy chair, we breakfast in half an hour, you shall say anything you like, I know well that men must talk, and I will be very good."

Marius took her by the arm and said lovingly to her, "We are talking business."

"By the way," said Cosette, "I have opened my window, a flock of pierrots has arrived in the garde—birds, not maskers. Today is Ash Wednesday; but not for the birds."

"I tell you that we are talking business, go, my little Cosette, leave us alone for a moment. We are talking figures. That will bore you."

"You have a charming cravat on this morning, Marius. You are very dandified, monseigneur. No, it will not bore me."

"I assure you that it will bore you."

"No. Since it is you. I shall not understand you, but I shall listen to you. When one hears the voices of those whom one loves, one does not need to understand the words that they utter. That we should be here together—that is all that I desire. I shall remain with you, bah!"

"You are my beloved Cosette! Impossible."

"Impossible!"

"Yes."

"Very good," said Cosette. "I was going to tell you some news. I could have told you that your grandfather is still asleep, that your aunt is at mass, that the chimney in my father Fauchelevent's room smokes, that Nicolette has sent for the chimney-sweep, that Toussaint and Nicolette have already quarrelled, that Nicolette makes sport of Toussaint's stammer. Well, you shall know nothing. Ah! It is impossible? You shall see, gentlemen, that I, in my turn, can say: It is impossible. Then who will be caught? I beseech you, my little Marius, let me stay here with you two."

"I swear to you, that it is indispensable that we should be alone."

"Well, am I anybody?"

Jean Valjean had not uttered a single word. Cosette turned to him, "In the first place, Father, I want you to come and embrace me. What do you mean by not saying anything instead of taking my part? Who gave me such a father as that? You must perceive that my family life is very unhappy. My husband beats me. Come, embrace me instantly."

Jean Valjean approached.

Cosette turned toward Marius.

"As for you, I shall make a face at you."

Then she presented her brow to Jean Valjean.

Jean Valjean advanced a step toward her.

Cosette recoiled.

"Father, you are pale. Does your arm hurt you?"

"It is well," said Jean Valjean.

"Did you sleep badly?"

"No."

"Are you sad?"

"No."

"Embrace me if you are well, if you sleep well, if you are content, I will not scold you."

And again she offered him her brow.

Jean Valjean dropped a kiss upon that brow whereon rested a celestial gleam.

"Smile."

Jean Valjean obeyed. It was the smile of a specter.

"Now, defend me against my husband."

"Cosette! " ejaculated Marius.

"Get angry, Father. Say that I must stay. You can certainly talk before me. So you think me very silly. What you say is astonishing! Business, placing money in a bank a great matter truly. Men make mysteries out of nothing. I am very pretty this morning. Look at me, Marius."

And with an adorable shrug of the shoulders, and an indescribably exquisite pout, she glanced at Marius.

"I love you!" said Marius.

"I adore you!" said Cosette.

And they fell irresistibly into each other's arms.

"Now," said Cosette, adjusting a fold of her dressing gown, with a triumphant little grimace, "I shall stay."

"No, not that," said Marius, in a supplicating tone. "We have to finish something."

"Still no?"

Marius assumed a grave tone:, "I assure you, Cosette, that it is impossible."

"Ah! You put on your man's voice, Sir. That is well, I go. You, father, have not upheld me. Monsieur my father, monsieur my husband, you are tyrants. I shall go and tell grandpapa. If you think that I am going to return and talk platitudes to you, you are mistaken. I am proud. I shall wait for you now. You shall see, that it is you who are going to be bored without me. I am going, it is well."

And she left the room.

Two seconds later, the door opened once more, her fresh and rosy head was again thrust between the two leaves, and she cried to them, "I am very angry indeed."

The door closed again, and the shadows descended once more.

It was as though a ray of sunlight should have suddenly traversed the night, without itself being conscious of it.

Marius made sure that the door was securely closed.

"Poor Cosette!" he murmured. "When she finds out."

At that word Jean Valjean trembled in every limb. He fixed on Marius a bewildered eye.

"Cosette! Oh yes, it is true, you are going to tell Cosette about this. That is right. Stay, I had not thought of that. One has the strength for one thing, but not for another. Sir, I conjure you, I entreat now, Sir, give me your most sacred word of honor, that you will not tell her. Is it not enough that you should know it? I have been able to say it myself without being forced to it, I could have told it to the universe, to the whole world, it was all one to me. But she, she does not know what it is, it would terrify her. What, a convict! We should be obliged to explain matters to her, to say to her, 'He is a man who has been in the galleys.' She saw the chain gang pass by one day. Oh! My God!" He dropped into an armchair and hid his face in his hands.

His grief was not audible, but from the quivering of his shoulders it was evident that he was weeping. Silent tears, terrible tears.

There is something of suffocation in the sob. He was seized with a sort of convulsion, he threw himself against the back of the chair as though to gain breath, letting his arms fall, and allowing Marius to see his face inundated with tears, and Marius heard him murmur, so low that his voice seemed to issue from fathomless depths, "Oh! Would that I could die!"

"Be at your ease," said Marius, "I will keep your secret for myself alone." And, less touched, perhaps, than he ought to have been, but forced, for the last hour, to familiarize himself with something as unexpected as it was dreadful, gradually beholding the convict superposed before his very eyes, upon M. Fauchelevent, overcome, little by little, by that lugubrious reality, and led, by the natural inclination of the situation, to recognize the space that had just been placed between that man and himself, Marius added, "It is impossible that I should not speak a word to you with regard to the deposit, which you have so faithfully and honestly remitted. That is an act of probity. It is just that some recompense should be bestowed on you. Fix the sum yourself, it shall be counted out to you. Do not fear to set it very high."

"I thank you, Sir," replied Jean Valjean, gently.

He remained in thought for a moment, mechanically passing the tip of his forefinger across his thumbnail, then he lifted up his voice:, "All is nearly over. But one last thing remains for me . . ."

"What is it?"

Jean Valjean struggled with what seemed a last hesitation, and, without voice, without breath, he stammered rather than said, "Now that you know, do you think, Sir, you, who are the master, that I ought not to see Cosette any more?"

"I think that would be better," replied Marius coldly.

"I shall never see her more," murmured Jean Valjean. And he directed his steps toward the door.

He laid his hand on the knob, the latch yielded, the door opened. Jean Valjean pushed it open far enough to pass through, stood motionless for a second, then closed the door again and turned to Marius.

He was no longer pale, he was livid. There were no longer any tears in his eyes, but only a sort of tragic flame. His voice had regained a strange composure.

"Stay, Sir," he said. "If you will allow it, I will come to see her. I assure you that I desire it greatly. If I had not cared to see Cosette, I should not have made to you the confession that I have made, I should have gone away; but, as I desired to remain in the place where Cosette is, and to continue to see her, I had to tell you about it honestly. You follow my reasoning, do you not? It is a matter easily understood. You see, I have had her with me for more than nine years. We lived first in that hut on the boulevard, then in the convent, then near the Luxembourg. That was where you saw her for the first time. You remember her blue plush hat. Then we went to the Quartier des Invalides, where there was a railing on a garden, the Rue Plumet. I lived in a little back courtyard, from which I could hear her piano. That was my life. We never left each other. That lasted for nine years and some months. I was like her own father, and she was my child. I do not know whether you understand, Monsieur Pontmercy, but to go away now, never to see her again, never to speak to her again, to no longer have anything, would be hard. If you do not disapprove of it, I will come to see Cosette from time to time. I will not come often. I will not remain long. You shall give orders that I am to be received in the little waiting room. On the ground floor. I could enter perfectly well by the back door, but that might create surprise perhaps, and it would be better, I think, for me to enter by the usual door. Truly, Sir, I should like to see a little more of Cosette. As rarely as you please. Put yourself in my place, I have nothing left but that. And then, we must be cautious. If I no longer come at all, it would produce a bad effect, it would be considered singular. What I can do, by the way, is to come in the afternoon, when night is beginning to fall."

"You shall come every evening," said Marius, "and Cosette will be waiting for you."

"You are kind, Sir," said Jean Valjean.

Marius saluted Jean Valjean, happiness escorted despair to the door, and these two men parted.

CHAPTER II—THE OBSCURITIES THAT A REVELATION CAN CONTAIN

Marius was quite upset.

The sort of estrangement he had always felt toward the man beside whom he had seen Cosette was now explained to him. There was something enigmatic about that person, of which his instinct had warned him.

This enigma was the most hideous of disgraces, the galleys. This M. Fauchelevent was the convict Jean Valjean.

To abruptly find such a secret in the midst of one's happiness resembles the discovery of a scorpion in a nest of turtledoves.

Was the happiness of Marius and Cosette thenceforth condemned to such a neighborhood? Was this an accomplished fact? Did the acceptance of that man form a part of the marriage now consummated? Was there nothing to be done?

Had Marius wedded the convict as well?

In vain may one be crowned with light and joy, in vain may one taste the grand purple hour of life, happy love, such shocks would force even the archangel in his ecstasy, even the demigod in his glory, to shudder.

As is always the case in changes of view of this nature, Marius asked himself whether he had nothing with which to reproach himself. Had he been wanting in divination? Had he been wanting in prudence? Had he involuntarily dulled his wits? A little, perhaps. Had he entered upon this love affair, which had ended in his marriage to Cosette, without taking sufficient precautions to throw light upon the surroundings? He admitted—it is thus, by a series of successive admissions of ourselves in regard to ourselves, that life amends us, little by little—he admitted the chimerical and visionary side of his nature, a sort of internal cloud peculiar to many organizations, and which, in paroxysms of passion and sorrow, dilates as the temperature of the soul changes, and invades the entire man, to such a degree as to render him nothing more than a conscience bathed in a mist. We have more than once indicated this characteristic element of Marius's individuality.

He recalled that, in the intoxication of his love, in the Rue Plumet, during those six or seven ecstatic weeks, he had not even spoke to Cosette of that drama in the Gorbeau hovel, where the victim had taken up such a singular line of silence during the struggle and the ensuing flight. How had it happened that he had not mentioned this to Cosette? Yet it was so near and so terrible! How had it come to pass that he had not even named the Thenardiers, and, particularly, on the day when he had encountered Eponine? He now found it almost difficult to explain his silence of that time. Nevertheless, he could account for it. He recalled his benumbed state, his intoxication with Cosette, love absorbing everything, that catching away of each other into the ideal, and perhaps also, like the imperceptible quantity of reason mingled with this violent and charming state of the soul, a vague, dull instinct impelling him to conceal and abolish in his memory that redoubtable adventure, contact with which he dreaded, in which he did not wish to play any part, his agency in which he had kept secret, and in which he could be neither narrator nor witness without being an accuser.

Moreover, these few weeks had been a flash of lightning; there had been no time for anything except love.

In short, having weighed everything, turned everything over in his mind, examined everything, whatever might have been the consequences if he had told Cosette about the Gorbeau ambush, even if he had discovered that Jean Valjean was a convict, would that have changed him, Marius? Would that have changed her, Cosette? Would he have drawn back? Would he have adored her any the less? Would he have refrained from marrying her? No. Then there was nothing to regret, nothing with which he need reproach himself. All was well. There is a deity for those drunken men who are called lovers. Marius blind, had followed the path that he would have chosen had he been in full possession of his sight. Love had bandaged his eyes, in order to lead him where? To paradise.

But this paradise was henceforth complicated with an infernal accompaniment.

Marius's ancient estrangement toward this man, toward this Fauchelevent who had turned into Jean Valjean, was at present mingled with horror.

In this horror, let us state, there was some pity, and even a certain surprise.

This thief, this thief guilty of a second offense, had restored that deposit. And what a deposit! Six hundred thousand francs.

He alone was in the secret of that deposit. He might have kept it all, he had restored it all.

Moreover, he had himself revealed his situation. Nothing forced him to this. If anyone learned who he was, it was through himself. In this avowal there was something more than acceptance of humiliation, there was acceptance of peril. For a condemned man, a mask is not a mask, it is a shelter. A false name is security, and he had rejected that false name. He, the galley slave, might have hidden himself forever in an honest family; he had withstood this temptation. And with what motive? Through a conscientious scruple. He himself explained this with the irresistible accents of truth. In short, whatever this Jean Valjean might be, he was, undoubtedly, a conscience that was awakening. There existed some mysterious rehabilitation that had begun; and, to all appearances, scruples had for a long time already controlled this man. Such fits of justice and goodness are not characteristic of vulgar natures. An awakening of conscience is grandeur of soul.

Jean Valjean was sincere. This sincerity, visible, palpable, irrefragable, evident from the very grief that it caused him, rendered inquiries useless, and conferred authority on all that that man had said.

Here, for Marius, there was a strange reversal of situations. What breathed from M. Fauchelevent? distrust. What did Jean Valjean inspire? Confidence.

In the mysterious balance of this Jean Valjean, which the pensive Marius struck, he admitted the active principle, he admitted the passive principle, and he tried to reach a balance.

But all this went on as in a storm. Marius, while endeavoring to form a clear idea of this man, and while pursuing Jean Valjean, so to speak, in the depths of his thought, lost him and found him again in a fatal mist.

The deposit honestly restored, the probity of the confession—these were good. This produced a lightening of the cloud, then the cloud became black once more.

Troubled as were Marius's memories, a shadow of them returned to him.

After all, what was that adventure in the Jondrette attic? Why had that man taken to flight on the arrival of the police, instead of entering a complaint?

Here Marius found the answer. Because that man was a fugitive from justice, who had broken his ban.

Another question: Why had that man come to the barricade?

For Marius now once more distinctly beheld that recollection that had reappeared in his emotions like sympathetic ink at the application of heat. This man had been in the barricade. He had not fought there. What had he come there for? In the presence of this question a specter sprang up and replied, "Javert."

Marius recalled perfectly now that funereal sight of Jean Valjean dragging the pinioned Javert out of the barricade, and he still heard behind the corner of the little Rue Mondetour that frightful pistol shot. Obviously, there was hatred between that police spy and the galley slave. The one was in the other's way. Jean Valjean had gone to the barricade for the purpose of revenging himself. He had arrived late. He probably knew that Javert was a prisoner there. The Corsican vendetta has penetrated to certain lower strata and has become the law there; it is so simple that it does not astonish souls that are but half turned toward good; and those hearts are so constituted that a criminal, who is in the path of repentance, may be scrupulous in the matter of theft and unscrupulous in the matter of vengeance. Jean Valjean had killed Javert. At least, that seemed to be evident.

This was the final question, to be sure; but to this there was no reply. This question Marius felt like pincers. How had it come to pass that Jean Valjean's existence had elbowed that of Cosette for so long a period?

What melancholy sport of Providence was that which had placed that child in contact with that man? Are there then chains for two that are forged on high? And does God take pleasure in coupling the angel with the demon? So a crime and an innocence can be roommates in the mysterious galleys of wretchedness? In that defiling of condemned persons that is called human destiny, can two brows pass side by side, the one ingenuous, the other formidable, the one all bathed in the divine whiteness of dawn, the other forever blemished by the flash of an eternal lightning? Who could have arranged that inexplicable pairing off? In what manner, in consequence of what prodigy, had any community of life been established between this celestial little creature and that old criminal?

Who could have bound the lamb to the wolf, and, what was still more incomprehensible, have attached the wolf to the lamb? For the wolf loved the lamb, for the fierce creature adored the feeble one, for, during the space of nine years, the angel had had the monster as her point of support. Cosette's childhood and girlhood, her advent in the daylight, her virginal growth toward life and light, had been sheltered by that hideous devotion. Here questions exfoliated, so to speak, into innumerable enigmas, abysses yawned at the bottoms of abysses, and Marius could no longer bend over Jean Valjean without becoming dizzy. What was this man-precipice?

The old symbols of Genesis are eternal; in human society, such as it now exists, and until a broader day shall effect a change in it, there will always be two men, the one superior, the other subterranean; the one that is according to good is Abel; the other that is according to evil is Cain. What was this tender Cain? What was this ruffian religiously absorbed in the adoration of a virgin, watching over her, rearing her, guarding her, dignifying her, and enveloping her, impure as he was himself, with purity?

What was that cesspool that had venerated that innocence to such a point as not to leave upon it a single spot? What was this Jean Valjean educating Cosette? What was this figure of the shadows that had for its only object the preservation of the rising of a star from every shadow and from every cloud?

That was Jean Valjean's secret; that was also God's secret.

In the presence of this double secret, Marius recoiled. The one, in some sort, reassured him as to the other. God was as visible in this affair as was Jean Valjean. God has his instruments. He makes use of the tool that he wills. He is not responsible to men. Do we know how God sets about the work? Jean Valjean had labored over Cosette. He had, to some extent, made that soul. That was incontestable. Well, what then? The workman was horrible; but the work was admirable. God produces his miracles as seems good to him. He had constructed that charming Cosette, and he had employed Jean Valjean. It had pleased him to choose this strange collaborator for himself. What account have we to demand of him? Is this the first time that the dungheap has aided the spring to create the rose?

Marius made himself these replies, and declared to himself that they were good. He had not dared to press Jean Valjean on all the points that we have just indicated, but he did not confess to himself that he did not dare to do it. He adored Cosette, he possessed Cosette, Cosette was splendidly pure. That was sufficient for him. What enlightenment did he need? Cosette was a light. Does light require enlightenment? He had everything; what more could he desire? All, is not that enough? Jean Valjean's personal affairs did not concern him.

And bending over the fatal shadow of that man, he clung fast, convulsively, to the solemn declaration of that unhappy wretch: "I am nothing to Cosette. Ten years ago I did not know that she was in existence."

Jean Valjean was a passerby. He had said so himself. Well, he had passed. Whatever he was, his part was finished.

Henceforth, there remained Marius to fulfill the part of Providence to Cosette. Cosette had sought the azure in a person like herself, in her lover, her husband, her celestial male. Cosette, as she took her flight, winged and transfigured, left behind her on the earth her hideous and empty chrysalis, Jean Valjean.

In whatever circle of ideas Marius revolved, he always returned to a certain horror for Jean Valjean. A sacred horror, perhaps, for, as we have just pointed out, he felt a quid divinum in that man. But do what he would, and seek what extenuation he would, he was certainly forced to fall back upon this: the man was a convict; that is to say, a being who has not even a place in the social ladder, since he is lower than the very lowest rung. After the very last of men comes the convict. The convict is no longer, so to speak, in the semblance of the living. The law has deprived him of the entire quantity of humanity of which it can deprive a man.

Marius, on penal questions, still held to the inexorable system, though he was a democrat and he entertained all the ideas of the law on the subject of those whom the law strikes. He had not yet accomplished all progress, we admit. He had not yet come to distinguish between that which is written by man and that which is written by God, between law and right. He had not examined and weighed the right that man takes to dispose of the irrevocable and the irreparable. He was not shocked by the word vindicte. He found it quite simple that certain breaches of the written law should be followed by eternal suffering, and he accepted, as the process of civilization, social damnation. He still stood at this point, though safe to advance infallibly later on, since his nature was good, and, at bottom, wholly formed of latent progress.

In this stage of his ideas, Jean Valjean appeared to him hideous and repulsive. He was a man reproved, he was the convict. That word was for him like the sound of the trump on the Day of Judgment; and, after having reflected upon Jean Valjean for a long time, his final gesture had been to turn away his head. Vade retro.

Marius, if we must recognize and even insist upon the fact, while interrogating Jean Valjean to such a point that Jean Valjean had said, "You are confessing me," had not, nevertheless, put to him two or three decisive questions.

It was not that they had not presented themselves to his mind, but that he had been afraid of them. The Jondrette attic? The barricade? Javert? Who knows where these revelations would have stopped? Jean Valjean did not seem like a man who would draw back, and who knows whether Marius, after having urged him on, would not have himself desired to hold him back?

Has it not happened to all of us, in certain supreme conjunctures, to stop our ears in order that we may not hear the reply, after we have asked a question? It is especially when one loves that one gives way to these exhibitions of cowardice. It is not wise to question sinister situations to the last point, particularly when the indissoluble side of our life is fatally intermingled with them. What a terrible light might have proceeded from the despairing explanations of Jean Valjean, and who knows whether that hideous glare would not have darted forth as far as Cosette? Who knows whether a sort of infernal glow would not have lingered behind it on the brow of that angel? The spattering of a lightning flash is of the thunder also. Fatality has points of juncture where innocence itself is stamped with crime by the gloomy law of the reflections that give color. The purest figures may forever preserve the reflection of a horrible association. Rightly or wrongly, Marius had been afraid. He already knew too much. He sought to dull his senses rather than to gain further light.

In dismay he bore off Cosette in his arms and shut his eyes to Jean Valjean.

That man was the night, the living and horrible night. How should he dare to seek the bottom of it? It is a terrible thing to interrogate the shadow. Who knows what its reply will be? The dawn may be blackened forever by it.

In this state of mind the thought that that man would, henceforth, come into any contact whatever with Cosette was a heartrending perplexity to Marius.

He now almost reproached himself for not having put those formidable questions, before which he had recoiled, and from which an implacable and definitive decision might have sprung. He felt that he was too good, too gentle, too weak, if we must say the word. This weakness had led him to an imprudent concession. He had allowed himself to be touched. He had been in the wrong. He ought to have simply and purely rejected Jean Valjean. Jean Valjean played the part of fire, and that is what he should have done, and have freed his house from that man.

He was vexed with himself, he was angry with that whirlwind of emotions that had deafened, blinded, and carried him away. He was displeased with himself.

What was he to do now? Jean Valjean's visits were profoundly repugnant to him. What was the use in having that man in his house? What did the man want? Here, he became dismayed, he did not wish to dig down, he did not wish to penetrate deeply; he did not wish to sound himself. He had promised, he had allowed himself to be drawn into a promise; Jean Valjean held his promise; one must keep one's word even to a convict, above all to a convict. Still, his first duty was to Cosette. In short, he was carried away by the repugnance that dominated him.

Marius turned over all this confusion of ideas in his mind, passing from one to the other, and moved by all of them. Hence arose a profound trouble.

It was not easy for him to hide this trouble from Cosette, but love is a talent, and Marius succeeded in doing it.

However, without any apparent object, he questioned Cosette, who was as candid as a dove is white and who suspected nothing; he talked of her childhood and her youth, and he became more and more convinced that that convict had been everything good, paternal, and respectable that a man can be toward Cosette. All that Marius had caught a glimpse of and had surmised was real. That sinister nettle had loved and protected that lily.

BOOK EIGHTH: FADING AWAY OF THE TWILIGHT

CHAPTER I—THE LOWER CHAMBER

On the following day, at nightfall, Jean Valjean knocked at the carriage gate of the Gillenormand house. It was Basque who received him. Basque was in the courtyard at the appointed hour, as though he had received his orders. It sometimes happens that one says to a servant, "You will watch for Mr. So and So, when he arrives."

Basque addressed Jean Valjean without waiting for the latter to approach him, "Monsieur le Baron has charged me to inquire whether monsieur desires to go upstairs or to remain below?"

"I will remain below," replied Jean Valjean.

Basque, who was perfectly respectful, opened the door of the waiting room and said, "I will go and inform Madame."

The room that Jean Valjean entered was a damp, vaulted room on the ground floor, which served as a cellar on occasion, which opened on the street, was paved with red squares and was badly lighted by a grated window.

This chamber was not one of those that are harassed by the feather duster, the pope's head brush, and the broom. The dust rested tranquilly there. Persecution of the spiders was not organized there. A fine web, which spread far and wide, and was very black and ornamented with dead flies, formed a wheel on one of the window panes. The room, which was small and low-ceiled, was furnished with a heap of empty bottles piled up in one corner.

The wall, which was daubed with an ochre yellow wash, was scaling off in large flakes. At one end there was a mantle painted in black with a narrow shelf. A fire was burning there; which indicated that Jean Valjean's reply: "I will remain below," had been foreseen.

Two armchairs were placed at the two corners of the fireplace. Between the chairs an old bedside rug, which displayed more foundation thread than wool, had been spread by way of a carpet.

The chamber was lighted by the fire on the hearth and the twilight falling through the window.

Jean Valjean was fatigued. For days he had neither eaten nor slept. He threw himself into one of the armchairs.

Basque returned, set a lighted candle on the mantle and retired. Jean Valjean, his head drooping and his chin resting on his breast, perceived neither Basque nor the candle.

All at once, he drew himself up with a start. Cosette was standing beside him.

He had not seen her enter, but he had felt that she was there.

He turned around. He gazed at her. She was adorably lovely. But what he was contemplating with that profound gaze was not her beauty but her soul.

"Well," exclaimed Cosette, "father, I knew that you were peculiar, but I never should have expected this. What an idea! Marius told me that you wish me to receive you here."

"Yes, it is my wish."

"I expected that reply. Good. I warn you that I am going to make a scene for you. Let us begin at the beginning. Embrace me, father."

And she offered him her cheek.

Jean Valjean remained motionless.

"You do not stir. I take note of it. Attitude of guilt. But never mind, I pardon you. Jesus Christ said, 'Offer the other cheek.' Here it is."

And she presented her other cheek.

Jean Valjean did not move. It seemed as though his feet were nailed to the pavement.

"This is becoming serious," said Cosette. "What have I done to you? I declare that I am perplexed. You owe me reparation. You will dine with us."

"I have dined."

"That is not true. I will get M. Gillenormand to scold you. Grandfathers are made to reprimand fathers. Come. Go upstairs with me to the drawing room. Immediately."

"Impossible."

Here Cosette lost ground a little. She ceased to command and passed to questioning.

"But why? And you choose the ugliest chamber in the house in which to see me. It's horrible here."

"Thou knowest . . ."

Jean Valjean caught himself up.

"You know, madame, that I am peculiar, I have my freaks."

Cosette struck her tiny hands together.

"Madame! . . . You know! . . . More novelties! What is the meaning of this?"

Jean Valjean directed upon her that heartrending smile to which he occasionally had recourse, "You wished to be Madame. You are so."

"Not for you, Father."

"Do not call me Father."

"What?"

"Call me 'Monsieur Jean.' 'Jean,' if you like."

"You are no longer my father? I am no longer Cosette? 'Monsieur Jean'? What does this mean? Why, these are revolutions, aren't they? What has taken place? Come, look me in the face. And you won't live with us! And you won't have my chamber! What have I done to you? Has anything happened?"

"Nothing."

"Well then?"

"Everything is as usual."

"Why do you change your name?"

"You have changed yours, surely."

He smiled again with the same smile as before and added, "Since you are Madame Pontmercy, I certainly can be Monsieur Jean."

"I don't understand anything about it. All this is idiotic. I shall ask permission of my husband for you to be 'Monsieur Jean.' I hope that he will not consent to it. You cause me a great deal of pain. One does have freaks, but one does not cause one's little Cosette grief. That is wrong. You have no right to be wicked, you who are so good."

He made no reply.

She seized his hands with vivacity, and raising them to her face with an irresistible movement, she pressed them against her neck beneath her chin, which is a gesture of profound tenderness.

"Oh!" she said to him. "Be good!"

And she went on, "This is what I call being good: being nice and coming and living here—there are birds here as there are in the Rue Plumet—living with us, quitting that hole of a Rue de l'Homme Arme, not giving us riddles to guess, being like all the rest of the world, dining with us, breakfasting with us, being my father."

He loosed her hands.

"You no longer need a father, you have a husband."

Cosette became angry.

"I no longer need a father! One really does not know what to say to things like that, which are not common sense!"

"If Toussaint were here," resumed Jean Valjean, like a person who is driven to seek authorities, and who clutches at every branch, "she would be the first to agree that it is true that I have always had ways of my own. There is nothing new in this. I always have loved my black corner."

"But it is cold here. One cannot see distinctly. It is abominable, that it is, to wish to be Monsieur Jean! I will not have you say 'you' to me."

"Just now, as I was coming hither," replied Jean Valjean, "I saw a piece of furniture in the Rue Saint Louis. It was at a cabinet maker's. If I were a pretty woman, I would treat myself to that bit of furniture. A very neat toilet table in the reigning style. What you call rosewood, I think. It is inlaid. The mirror is quite large. There are drawers. It is pretty."

"Hou! The villainous bear!" replied Cosette.

And with supreme grace, setting her teeth and drawing back her lips, she blew at Jean Valjean. She was a Grace copying a cat.

"I am furious," she resumed. "Ever since yesterday, you have made me rage, all of you. I am greatly vexed. I don't understand. You do not defend me against Marius. Marius will not uphold me against you. I am all alone. I arrange a chamber prettily. If I could have put the good God there I would have done it. My chamber is left on my hands. My lodger sends me into bankruptcy. I order a nice little dinner of Nicolette. We will have nothing to do with your dinner, Madame. And my father Fauchelevent wants me to call him 'Monsieur Jean,' and to receive him in a frightful, old, ugly cellar, where the walls have beards, and where the crystal consists of empty bottles, and the curtains are of spiders' webs! You are singular, I admit, that is your style, but people who get married are granted a truce. You ought not to have begun being singular again instantly. So you are going to be perfectly contented in your abominable Rue de l'Homme Arme. I was very desperate indeed there, that I was. What have you against me? You cause me a great deal of grief. Fi!"

And, becoming suddenly serious, she gazed intently at Jean Valjean and added, "Are you angry with me because I am happy?"

Ingenuousness sometimes unconsciously penetrates deep. This question, which was simple for Cosette, was profound for Jean Valjean. Cosette had meant to scratch, and she lacerated.

Jean Valjean turned pale.

He remained for a moment without replying, then, with an inexpressible intonation, and speaking to himself, he murmured, "Her happiness was the object of my life. Now God may sign my dismissal. Cosette, thou art happy; my day is over."

"Ah, you have said thou to me!" exclaimed Cosette.

And she sprang to his neck.

Jean Valjean, in bewilderment, strained her wildly to his breast. It almost seemed to him as though he were taking her back.

"Thanks, father!" said Cosette.

This enthusiastic impulse was on the point of becoming poignant for Jean Valjean. He gently removed Cosette's arms, and took his hat.

"Well?" said Cosette.

"I leave you, Madame, they are waiting for you."

And, from the threshold, he added, "I have said thou to you. Tell your husband that this shall not happen again. Pardon me."

Jean Valjean quitted the room, leaving Cosette stupefied at this enigmatical farewell.

CHAPTER II—ANOTHER STEP BACKWARD

On the following day, at the same hour, Jean Valjean came.

Cosette asked him no questions, was no longer astonished, no longer exclaimed that she was cold, no longer spoke of the drawing room, she avoided saying either "father" or "Monsieur Jean." She allowed herself to be addressed as you. She allowed herself to be called Madame. Only, her joy had undergone a certain diminution. She would have been sad, if sadness had been possible to her.

It is probable that she had had with Marius one of those conversations in which the beloved man says what he pleases, explains nothing, and satisfies the beloved woman. The curiosity of lovers does not extend very far beyond their own love.

The lower room had made a little toilet. Basque had suppressed the bottles, and Nicolette the spiders.

All the days that followed brought Jean Valjean at the same hour. He came every day, because he had not the strength to take Marius's words otherwise than literally. Marius arranged matters so as to be absent at the hours when Jean Valjean came. The house grew accustomed to the novel ways of M. Fauchelevent. Toussaint helped in this direction: "Monsieur has always been like that," she repeated. The grandfather issued this decree: "He's an original." And all was said. Moreover, at the age of ninety-six, no bond is any longer possible, all is merely juxtaposition; a newcomer is in the way. There is no longer any room; all habits are acquired. M. Fauchelevent, M. Tranchelevent, Father Gillenormand asked nothing better than to be relieved from "that gentleman." He added, "Nothing is more common than those originals. They do all sorts of queer things. They have no reason. The Marquis de Canaples was still worse. He bought a palace that he might lodge in the garret. These are fantastic appearances that people affect."

No one caught a glimpse of the sinister foundation. And moreover, who could have guessed such a thing? There are marshes of this description in India. The water seems extraordinary, inexplicable, rippling though there is no wind, and agitated where it should be calm. One gazes at the surface of these causeless ebullitions; one does not perceive the hydra that crawls on the bottom.

Many men have a secret monster in this same manner, a dragon that gnaws them, a despair that inhabits their night. Such a man resembles other men, he goes and comes. No one knows that he bears within him a frightful parasitic pain with a thousand teeth, which lives within the unhappy man, and of which he is dying. No one knows that this man is a gulf. He is stagnant but deep. From time to time, a trouble of which the onlooker understands nothing appears on his surface. A mysterious wrinkle is formed, then vanishes, then reappears; an air bubble rises and bursts. It is the breathing of the unknown beast.

Certain strange habits: arriving at the hour when other people are taking their leave, keeping in the background when other people are displaying themselves, preserving on all occasions what may be designated as the wall-colored mantle, seeking the solitary walk, preferring the deserted street, avoiding any share in conversation, avoiding crowds and festivals, seeming at one's ease and living poorly, having one's key in one's pocket, and one's candle at the porter's lodge, however rich one may be, entering by the side door, ascending the private staircase—all these insignificant singularities—fugitive folds on the surface, often proceed from a formidable foundation.

Many weeks passed in this manner. A new life gradually took possession of Cosette: the relations that marriage creates, visits, the care of the house, pleasures, great matters. Cosette's pleasures were not costly, they consisted in one thing: being with Marius. The great occupation of her life was to go out with him, to remain with him. It was for them a joy that was always fresh, to go out arm in arm, in the face of the sun, in the open street, without hiding themselves, before the whole world, both of them completely alone.

Cosette had one vexation. Toussaint could not get on with Nicolette, the soldering of two elderly maids being impossible, and she went away. The grandfather was well; Marius argued a case here and there; Aunt Gillenormand peacefully led that life aside, which sufficed for her, beside the new household. Jean Valjean came every day.

The address as thou disappeared, the you, the "Madame," the "Monsieur Jean," rendered him another person to Cosette. The care he had himself taken to detach her from him was succeeding. She became more and more gay and less and less tender. Yet she still loved him sincerely, and he felt it.

One day she said to him suddenly, "You used to be my father, you are no longer my father, you were my uncle, you are no longer my uncle, you were Monsieur Fauchelevent, you are Jean. Who are you then? I don't like all this. If I did not know how good you are, I should be afraid of you."

He still lived in the Rue de l'Homme Arme, because he could not make up his mind to remove to a distance from the quarter where Cosette dwelled.

At first, he only remained a few minutes with Cosette, and then went away.

Little by little he acquired the habit of making his visits less brief. One would have said that he was taking advantage of the authorization of the days, which were lengthening, he arrived earlier and departed later.

One day Cosette chanced to say "father" to him. A flash of joy illuminated Jean Valjean's melancholy old countenance. He caught her up, "Say Jean."

"Ah! Truly," she replied with a burst of laughter. "Monsieur Jean."

"That is right," said he. And he turned aside so that she might not see him wipe his eyes.

CHAPTER III—THEY RECALL THE GARDEN OF THE RUE PLUMET

This was the last time. After that last flash of light, complete extinction ensued. No more familiarity, no more good morning with a kiss, never more that word so profoundly sweet, "My father!" He was at his own request and through his own complicity driven out of all his happinesses one after the other; and he had this sorrow, that after having lost Cosette wholly in one day, he was afterward obliged to lose her again in detail.

The eye eventually becomes accustomed to the light of a cellar. In short, it sufficed for him to have an apparition of Cosette every day. His whole life was concentrated in that one hour.

He seated himself close to her, he gazed at her in silence, or he talked to her of years gone by, of her childhood, of the convent, of her little friends of those bygone days.

One afternoon—it was on one of those early days in April, already warm and fresh, the moment of the sun's great gaiety, the gardens that surrounded the windows of Marius and Cosette felt the emotion of waking, the hawthorn was on the point of budding, a jewelled garniture of gillyflowers spread over the ancient walls, snapdragons yawned through the crevices of the stones, amid the grass there was a charming beginning of daisies, and buttercups, the white butterflies of the year were making their first appearance, the wind, that minstrel of the eternal wedding, was trying in the trees the first notes of that grand, auroral symphony that the old poets called the springtide—Marius said to Cosette, "We said that we would go back to take a look at our garden in the Rue Plumet. Let us go there. We must not be ungrateful." And away they flitted, like two swallows toward the spring. This garden of the Rue Plumet produced on them the effect of the dawn. They already had behind them in life something that was like the springtime of their love. The house in the Rue Plumet being held on a lease, still belonged to Cosette. They went to that garden and that house. There they found themselves again, there they forgot themselves. That evening, at the usual hour, Jean Valjean came to the Rue des Filles-du-Calvaire. "Madame went out with Monsieur and has not yet returned," Basque said to him. He seated himself in silence, and waited an hour. Cosette did not return. He departed with drooping head.

Cosette was so intoxicated with her walk to "their garden," and so joyous at having "lived a whole day in her past," that she talked of nothing else on the morrow. She did not notice that she had not seen Jean Valjean.

"In what way did you go there?" Jean Valjean asked her.

"On foot."

"And how did you return?"

"In a hackney carriage."

For some time, Jean Valjean had noticed the economical life led by the young people. He was troubled by it. Marius's economy was severe, and that word had its absolute meaning for Jean Valjean. He hazarded a query: "Why do you not have a carriage of your own? A pretty coupe would only cost you five hundred francs a month. You are rich."

"I don't know," replied Cosette.

"It is like Toussaint," resumed Jean Valjean. "She is gone. You have not replaced her. Why?"

"Nicolette suffices."

"But you ought to have a maid."

"Have I not Marius?"

"You ought to have a house of your own, your own servants, a carriage, a box at the theater. There is nothing too fine for you. Why not profit by your riches? Wealth adds to happiness."

Cosette made no reply.

Jean Valjean's visits were not abridged. Far from it. When it is the heart that is slipping, one does not halt on the downward slope.

When Jean Valjean wished to prolong his visit and to induce forgetfulness of the hour, he sang the praises of Marius; he pronounced him handsome, noble, courageous, witty, eloquent, good. Cosette outdid him. Jean Valjean began again. They were never weary. Marius—that word was inexhaustible; those six letters contained volumes. In this manner, Jean Valjean contrived to remain a long time.

It was so sweet to see Cosette, to forget by her side! It alleviated his wounds. It frequently happened that Basque came twice to announce, "M. Gillenormand sends me to remind Madame la Baronne that dinner is served."

On those days, Jean Valjean was very thoughtful on his return home.

Was there, then, any truth in that comparison of the chrysalis that had presented itself to the mind of Marius? Was Jean Valjean really a chrysalis who would persist, and who would come to visit his butterfly?

One day he remained still longer than usual. On the following day he observed that there was no fire on the hearth. "Hello!" he thought. "No fire." And he furnished the explanation for himself. "It is perfectly simple. It is April. The cold weather has ceased."

"Heavens! How cold it is here!" exclaimed Cosette when she entered.

"Why, no," said Jean Valjean.

"Was it you who told Basque not to make a fire then?"

"Yes, since we are now in the month of May."

"But we have a fire until June. One is needed all the year in this cellar."

"I thought that a fire was unnecessary."

"That is exactly like one of your ideas!" retorted Cosette.

On the following day there was a fire. But the two armchairs were arranged at the other end of the room near the door. "What is the meaning of this?" thought Jean Valjean.

He went for the armchairs and restored them to their ordinary place near the hearth.

This fire lighted once more encouraged him, however. He prolonged the conversation even beyond its customary limits. As he rose to take his leave, Cosette said to him, "My husband said a queer thing to me yesterday."

"What was it?"

"He said to me, 'Cosette, we have an income of thirty thousand livres. Twenty-seven that you own, and three that my grandfather gives me.' I replied, 'That makes thirty.' He went on, 'Would you have the courage to live on the three thousand?' I answered, 'Yes, on nothing. Provided that it was with you.' And then I asked, 'Why do you say that to me?' He replied, 'I wanted to know.'"

Jean Valjean found not a word to answer. Cosette probably expected some explanation from him; he listened in gloomy silence. He went back to the Rue de l'Homme Armé; he was so deeply absorbed that he mistook the door and instead of entering his own house, he entered the adjoining dwelling. It was only after having ascended nearly two stories that he perceived his error and went down again.

His mind was swarming with conjectures. It was evident that Marius had his doubts as to the origin of the six hundred thousand francs, that he feared some source that was not pure, who knows? That he had even, perhaps, discovered that the money came from him, Jean Valjean, that he hesitated before this suspicious fortune, and was disinclined to take it as his own, preferring that both he and Cosette should remain poor, rather than that they should be rich with wealth that was not clean.

Moreover, Jean Valjean began vaguely to surmise that he was being shown the door.

On the following day, he underwent something like a shock on entering the ground-floor room. The armchairs had disappeared. There was not a single chair of any sort.

"Ah, what's this!" exclaimed Cosette as she entered. "No chairs! Where are the armchairs?"

"They are no longer here," replied Jean Valjean.

"This is too much!"

Jean Valjean stammered, "It was I who told Basque to remove them."

"And your reason?"

"I have only a few minutes to stay today."

"A brief stay is no reason for remaining standing."

"I think that Basque needed the chairs for the drawing room."

"Why?"

"You have company this evening, no doubt."

"We expect no one."

Jean Valjean had not another word to say.

Cosette shrugged her shoulders.

"To have the chairs carried off! The other day you had the fire put out. How odd you are!"

"Adieu!" murmured Jean Valjean.

He did not say, "Adieu, Cosette." But he had not the strength to say, "Adieu, Madame."

He went away utterly overwhelmed.

This time he had understood.

On the following day he did not come. Cosette only observed the fact in the evening.

"Why," said she, "Monsieur Jean has not been here today."

And she felt a slight twinge at her heart, but she hardly perceived it, being immediately diverted by a kiss from Marius.

On the following day he did not come.

Cosette paid no heed to this, passed her evening and slept well that night, as usual, and thought of it only when she woke. She was so happy! She speedily despatched Nicolette to M. Jean's house to inquire whether he were ill, and why he had not come on the previous evening. Nicolette brought back the reply of M. Jean that he was not ill. He was busy. He would come soon. As soon as he was able. Moreover, he was on the point of taking a little journey. Madame must remember that it was his custom to take trips from time to time. They were not to worry about him. They were not to think of him.

Nicolette on entering M. Jean's had repeated to him her mistress' very words. That Madame had sent her to inquire why M. Jean bad not come on the preceding evening. "It is two days since I have been there," said Jean Valjean gently.

But the remark passed unnoticed by Nicolette, who did not report it to Cosette.

CHAPTER IV—ATTRACTION
AND EXTINCTION

During the last months of spring and the first months of summer in 1833, the rare passersby in the Marais, the petty shopkeepers, the loungers on thresholds, noticed an old man neatly clad in black, who emerged every day at the same hour, toward nightfall, from the Rue de l'Homme Arme, on the side of the Rue Sainte-Croix-de-la-Bretonnerie, passed in front of the Blancs Manteaux, gained the Rue Culture-Sainte-Catherine, and, on arriving at the Rue de l'Echarpe, turned to the left, and entered the Rue Saint-Louis.

There he walked at a slow pace, with his head strained forward, seeing nothing, hearing nothing, his eye immovably fixed on a point that seemed to be a star to him, that never varied, and that was no other than the corner of the Rue des Filles-du-Calvaire. The nearer he approached the corner of the street the more his eye lighted up; a sort of joy illuminated his pupils like an inward aurora, he had a fascinated and much affected air, his lips indulged in obscure movements, as though he were talking to someone whom he did not see, he smiled vaguely and advanced as slowly as possible. One would have said that, while desirous of reaching his destination, he feared the moment when he should be close at hand. When only a few houses remained between him and that street that appeared to attract him his pace slackened, to such a degree that, at times, one might have thought that he was no longer advancing at all. The vacillation of his head and the fixity of his eyeballs suggested the thought of the magnetic needle seeking the pole. Whatever time he spent on arriving, he was obliged to arrive at last; he reached the Rue des Filles-du-Calvaire; then he halted, he trembled, he thrust his head with a sort of melancholy timidity around the corner of the last house, and gazed into that street, and there was in that tragic look something that resembled the dazzling light of the impossible, and the reflection from a paradise that was closed to him. Then a tear, which had slowly gathered in the corner of his lids, and had become large enough to fall, trickled down his cheek, and sometimes stopped at his mouth. The old man tasted its bitter flavor. Thus he remained for several minutes as though made of stone, then he returned by the same road and with the same step, and, in proportion as he retreated, his glance died out.

Little by little, this old man ceased to go as far as the corner of the Rue des Filles-du-Calvaire; he halted half way in the Rue Saint-Louis; sometimes a little further off, sometimes a little nearer.

One day he stopped at the corner of the Rue Culture-Sainte-Catherine and looked at the Rue des Filles-du-Calvaire from a distance. Then he shook his head slowly from right to left, as though refusing himself something, and retraced his steps.

Soon he no longer came as far as the Rue Saint-Louis. He got as far as the Rue Pavee, shook his head and turned back; then he went no further than the Rue des Trois-Pavillons; then he did not overstep the Blancs-Manteaux. One would have said that he was a pendulum that was no longer wound up, and whose oscillations were growing shorter before ceasing altogether.

Every day he emerged from his house at the same hour, he undertook the same trip, but he no longer completed it, and, perhaps without himself being aware of the fact, he constantly shortened it. His whole countenance expressed this single idea: What is the use?—His eye was dim; no more radiance. His tears were also exhausted; they no longer collected in the corner of his eyelid; that thoughtful eye was dry. The old man's head was still craned forward; his chin moved at times; the folds in his gaunt neck were painful to behold. Sometimes, when the weather was bad, he had an umbrella under his arm, but he never opened it.

The good women of the quarter said, "He is an innocent." The children followed him and laughed.

BOOK NINTH: SUPREME SHADOW, SUPREME DAWN

CHAPTER I—PITY FOR THE UNHAPPY, BUT INDULGENCE FOR THE HAPPY

It is a terrible thing to be happy! How content one is! How all-sufficient one finds it! How, being in possession of the false object of life, happiness, one forgets the true object, duty!

Let us say, however, that the reader would do wrong were he to blame Marius.

Marius, as we have explained, before his marriage, had put no questions to M. Fauchelevent, and, since that time, he had feared to put any to Jean Valjean. He had regretted the promise into which he had allowed himself to be drawn.

He had often said to himself that he had done wrong in making that concession to despair. He had confined himself to gradually estranging Jean Valjean from his house and to effacing him, as much as possible, from Cosette's mind. He had, in a manner, always placed himself between Cosette and Jean Valjean, sure that, in this way, she would not perceive nor think of the latter. It was more than effacement, it was an eclipse.

Marius did what he considered necessary and just. He thought that he had serious reasons that the reader has already seen, and others, which will be seen later on, for getting rid of Jean Valjean without harshness, but without weakness.

Chance having ordained that he should encounter, in a case which he had argued, a former employee of the Laffitte establishment, he had acquired mysterious information, without seeking it, which he had not been able, it is true, to probe, out of respect for the secret that he had promised to guard, and out of consideration for Jean Valjean's perilous position. He believed at that moment that he had a grave duty to perform: the restitution of the six hundred thousand francs to someone whom he sought with all possible discretion. In the meanwhile, he abstained from touching that money.

As for Cosette, she had not been initiated into any of these secrets; but it would be harsh to condemn her also.

There existed between Marius and her an all-powerful magnetism, which caused her to do, instinctively and almost mechanically, what Marius wished. She was conscious of Marius's will in the direction of "Monsieur Jean," she conformed to it. Her husband had not been obliged to say anything to her; she yielded to the vague but clear pressure of his tacit intentions, and obeyed blindly. Her obedience in this instance consisted in not remembering what Marius forgot. She was not obliged to make any effort to accomplish this. Without her knowing why herself, and without his having any cause to accuse her of it, her soul had become so wholly her husband's that which was shrouded in gloom in Marius's mind became overcast in hers.

Let us not go too far, however; in what concerns Jean Valjean, this forgetfulness and obliteration were merely superficial. She was rather heedless than forgetful. At bottom, she was sincerely attached to the man whom she had so long called her father; but she loved her husband still more dearly. This was what had somewhat disturbed the balance of her heart, which leaned to one side only.

It sometimes happened that Cosette spoke of Jean Valjean and expressed her surprise. Then Marius calmed her, "He is absent, I think. Did not he say that he was setting out on a journey?"

"That is true," thought Cosette. "He had a habit of disappearing in this fashion. But not for so long." Two or three times she despatched Nicolette to inquire in the Rue de l'Homme Arme whether M. Jean had returned from his journey. Jean Valjean caused the answer "no" to be given.

Cosette asked nothing more, since she had but one need on earth, Marius.

Let us also say that, on their side, Cosette and Marius had also been absent. They had been to Vernon. Marius had taken Cosette to his father's grave.

Marius gradually won Cosette away from Jean Valjean. Cosette allowed it.

Moreover that which is called, far too harshly in certain cases, the ingratitude of children, is not always a thing so deserving of reproach as it is supposed. It is the ingratitude of nature. Nature, as we have elsewhere said, "looks before her." Nature divides living beings into those who are arriving and those who are departing. Those who are departing are turned toward the shadows, those who are arriving toward the light. Hence a gulf that is fatal on the part of the old, and involuntary on the part of the young. This breach, at first insensible, increases slowly, like all separations of branches. The boughs, without becoming detached from the trunk, grow away from it. It is no fault of theirs. Youth goes where there is joy, festivals, vivid lights, love. Old age goes toward the end. They do not lose sight of each other, but there is no longer a close connection. Young people feel the cooling off of life; old people, that of the tomb. Let us not blame these poor children.

CHAPTER II—LAST FLICKERINGS OF A LAMP WITHOUT OIL

One day, Jean Valjean descended his staircase, took three steps in the street, seated himself on a post, on that same stone post where Gavroche had found him meditating on the night between the 5th and the 6th of June; he remained there a few moments, then went upstairs again. This was the last oscillation of the pendulum. On the following day he did not leave his apartment. On the day after that, he did not leave his bed.

His portress, who prepared his scanty repasts, a few cabbages or potatoes with bacon, glanced at the brown earthenware plate and exclaimed, "But you ate nothing yesterday, poor, dear man!"

"Certainly I did," replied Jean Valjean.

"The plate is quite full."

"Look at the water jug. It is empty."

"That proves that you have drunk; it does not prove that you have eaten."

"Well," said Jean Valjean, "what if I felt hungry only for water?"

"That is called thirst, and, when one does not eat at the same time, it is called fever."

"I will eat tomorrow."

"Or at Trinity day. Why not today? Is it the thing to say, 'I will eat tomorrow?' The idea of leaving my platter without even touching it! My ladyfinger potatoes were so good!"

Jean Valjean took the old woman's hand, "I promise you that I will eat them," he said, in his benevolent voice.

"I am not pleased with you," replied the portress.

Jean Valjean saw no other human creature than this good woman. There are streets in Paris through which no one ever passes, and houses to which no one ever comes. He was in one of those streets and one of those houses.

While he still went out, he had purchased of a coppersmith, for a few sous, a little copper crucifix that he had hung up on a nail opposite his bed. That gibbet is always good to look at.

A week passed, and Jean Valjean had not taken a step in his room. He still remained in bed. The portress said to her husband, "The goodman upstairs yonder does not get up, he no longer eats, he will not last long. That man has his sorrows, that he has. You won't get it out of my head that his daughter has made a bad marriage."

The porter replied, with the tone of marital sovereignty, "If he's rich, let him have a doctor. If he is not rich, let him go without. If he has no doctor he will die."

"And if he has one?"

"He will die," said the porter.

The portress set to scraping away the grass from what she called her pavement, with an old knife, and, as she tore out the blades, she grumbled, "It's a shame. Such a neat old man! He's as white as a chicken."

She caught sight of the doctor of the quarter as he passed the end of the street; she took it upon herself to request him to come upstairs.

"It's on the second floor," said she. "You have only to enter. As the goodman no longer stirs from his bed, the door is always unlocked."

The doctor saw Jean Valjean and spoke with him.

When he came down again the portress interrogated him, "Well, doctor?"

"Your sick man is very ill indeed."

"What is the matter with him?"

"Everything and nothing. He is a man who, to all appearances, has lost some person who is dear to him. People die of that."

"What did he say to you?"

"He told me that he was in good health."

"Shall you come again, doctor?"

"Yes," replied the doctor. "But someone else besides must come."

CHAPTER III—A PEN IS HEAVY TO THE MAN WHO LIFTED THE FAUCHELEVENT'S CART

One evening Jean Valjean found difficulty in raising himself on his elbow; he felt of his wrist and could not find his pulse; his breath was short and halted at times; he recognized the fact that he was weaker than he had ever been before. Then, no doubt under the pressure of some supreme preoccupation, he made an effort, drew himself up into a sitting posture and dressed himself. He put on his old workingman's clothes. As he no longer went out, he had returned to them and preferred them. He was obliged to pause many times while dressing himself; merely putting his arms through his waistcoat made the perspiration trickle from his forehead.

Since he had been alone, he had placed his bed in the antechamber, in order to inhabit that deserted apartment as little as possible.

He opened the valise and drew from it Cosette's outfit.

He spread it out on his bed.

The Bishop's candlesticks were in their place on the mantle. He took from a drawer two wax candles and put them in the candlesticks. Then, although it was still broad daylight, it was summer, he lighted them. In the same way candles are to be seen lighted in broad daylight in chambers where there is a corpse.

Every step that he took in going from one piece of furniture to another exhausted him, and he was obliged to sit down. It was not ordinary fatigue that expends the strength only to renew it; it was the remnant of all movement possible to him, it was life drained that flows away drop by drop in overwhelming efforts and that will never be renewed.

The chair into which he allowed himself to fall was placed in front of that mirror, so fatal for him, so providential for Marius, in which he had read

Cosette's reversed writing on the blotting book. He caught sight of himself in this mirror, and did not recognize himself. He was eighty years old; before Marius's marriage, he would have hardly been taken for fifty; that year had counted for thirty. What he bore on his brow was no longer the wrinkles of age, it was the mysterious mark of death. The hollowing of that pitiless nail could be felt there. His cheeks were pendulous; the skin of his face had the color that would lead one to think that it already had earth upon it; the corners of his mouth drooped as in the mask that the ancients sculptured on tombs. He gazed into space with an air of reproach; one would have said that he was one of those grand tragic beings who have cause to complain of someone.

He was in that condition, the last phase of dejection, in which sorrow no longer flows; it is coagulated, so to speak; there is something on the soul like a clot of despair.

Night had come. He laboriously dragged a table and the old armchair to the fireside, and placed upon the table a pen, some ink and some paper.

That done, he had a fainting fit. When he recovered consciousness, he was thirsty. As he could not lift the jug, he tipped it over painfully toward his mouth, and swallowed a draft.

As neither the pen nor the ink had been used for a long time, the point of the pen had curled up, the ink had dried away, he was forced to rise and put a few drops of water in the ink, which he did not accomplish without pausing and sitting down two or three times, and he was compelled to write with the back of the pen. He wiped his brow from time to time.

Then he turned toward the bed, and, still seated, for he could not stand, he gazed at the little black gown and all those beloved objects.

These contemplations lasted for hours that seemed minutes.

All at once he shivered, he felt that a child was taking possession of him; he rested his elbows on the table, which was illuminated by the Bishop's candles and took up the pen. His hand trembled. He wrote slowly the few following lines:

"Cosette, I bless thee. I am going to explain to thee. Thy husband was right in giving me to understand that I ought to go away; but there is a little error in what he believed, though he was in the right. He is excellent. Love him well even after I am dead. Monsieur Pontmercy, love my darling child well. Cosette, this paper will be found; this is what I wish to say to thee, thou wilt see the figures, if I have the strength to recall them, listen well, this money is really thine. Here is the whole matter: White jet comes from Norway, black jet comes from England, black glass jewellery comes from Germany. Jet is the lightest, the most precious, the most costly. Imitations can be made in France as well as in Germany. What is needed is a little anvil two inches square, and a lamp burning spirits of wine to soften the wax. The wax was formerly made with resin and lampblack, and cost four livres the pound. I invented a way of making it with gum shellac and turpentine. It does not cost more than thirty sous, and is much better. Buckles are made with a violet glass that is stuck fast, by means of this wax, to a little framework of black iron. The glass must be violet for iron jewelery, and black for gold jewelery. Spain buys a great deal of it. It is the country of jet . . ."

Here he paused, the pen fell from his fingers, he was seized by one of those sobs that at times welled up from the very depths of his being; the poor man clasped his head in both hands, and meditated.

"Oh!" he exclaimed within himself [lamentable cries, heard by God alone], "all is over. I shall never see her more. She is a smile that passed over me. I am about to plunge into the night without even seeing her again. Oh! One minute, one instant, to hear her voice, to touch her dress, to gaze upon her, upon her, the angel! And then to die! It is nothing to die, what is frightful is to die without seeing her. She would smile on me, she would say a word to me, would that do any harm to anyone? No, all is over, and forever. Here I am all alone. My God! My God! I shall never see her again!" At that moment there came a knock at the door.

CHAPTER IV—A BOTTLE OF INK THAT ONLY SUCCEEDED IN WHITENING

That same day, or to speak more accurately, that same evening, as Marius left the table, and was on the point of withdrawing to his study, having a case to look over, Basque handed him a letter saying, "The person who wrote the letter is in the antechamber."

Cosette had taken the grandfather's arm and was strolling in the garden.

A letter, like a man, may have an unprepossessing exterior. Coarse paper, coarsely folded—the very sight of certain missives is displeasing.

The letter that Basque had brought was of this sort.

Marius took it. It smelled of tobacco. Nothing evokes a memory like an odor. Marius recognized that tobacco. He looked at the superscription: "To Monsieur, Monsieur le Baron Pommerci. At his hotel." The recognition of the tobacco caused him to recognize the writing as well. It may be said that amazement has its lightning flashes.

Marius was, as it were, illuminated by one of these flashes.

The sense of smell, that mysterious aid to memory, had just revived a whole world within him. This was certainly the paper, the fashion of folding, the dull tint of ink; it was certainly the well-known handwriting, especially was it the same tobacco.

The Jondrette garret rose before his mind.

Thus, strange freak of chance! One of the two scents that he had so diligently sought, the one in connection with which he had lately again exerted so many efforts and that he supposed to be forever lost, had come and presented itself to him of its own accord.

He eagerly broke the seal, and read:

"Monsieur le Baron: If the Supreme Being had given me the talents, I might have been baron Thenard, member of the Institute [Academy of Sciences], but I am not. I only bear the same as him, happy if this memory recommends me to the eccellence of your kindnesses. The benefit with which you will honor me will be reciprocle. I am in possession of a secret concerning an individual. This individual concerns you. I hold the secret at your disposal desiring to have the honor to be huseful to you. I will furnish you with the simple means of driving from your honorabel family that individual who has no right there, madame la baronne being of lofty birth. The sanctuary of virtue cannot cohabit longer with crime without abdicating. I awate in the entichamber the orders of Monsieur le Baron. With respect."

The letter was signed "Thenard."

This signature was not false. It was merely a trifle abridged.

Moreover, the rigmarole and the orthography completed the revelation. The certificate of origin was complete.

Marius's emotion was profound. After a start of surprise, he underwent a feeling of happiness. If he could now but find that other man of whom he was in search, the man who had saved him, Marius, there would be nothing left for him to desire.

He opened the drawer of his secretary, took out several banknotes, put them in his pocket, closed the secretary again, and rang the bell. Basque half opened the door.

"Show the man in," said Marius.

Basque announced, "Monsieur Thenard."

A man entered.

A fresh surprise for Marius. The man who entered was an utter stranger to him.

This man, who was old, moreover, had a thick nose, his chin swathed in a cravat, green spectacles with a double screen of green taffeta over his eyes, and his hair was plastered and flattened down on his brow on a level with his eyebrows like the wigs of English coachmen in "high life." His hair was gray. He was dressed in black from head to foot, in garments that were very threadbare but clean; a bunch of seals depending from his fob suggested the idea of a watch. He held in his hand an old hat! He walked in a bent attitude, and the curve in his spine augmented the profundity of his bow.

The first thing that struck the observer was, that this personage's coat, which was too ample although carefully buttoned, had not been made for him.

Here a short digression becomes necessary.

There was in Paris at that epoch, in a low-lived old lodging in the Rue Beautreillis, near the Arsenal, an ingenious Jew whose profession was to change villains into honest men. Not for too long, which might have proved embarrassing for the villain. The change was on sight, for a day or two, at the rate of thirty sous a day, by means of a costume that resembled the honesty of the world in general as nearly as possible. This costumer was called "the Changer;" the pickpockets of Paris had given him this name and knew him by no other. He had a tolerably complete wardrobe. The rags with which he tricked out people were almost probable. He had specialties and categories; on each nail of his shop hung a social status, threadbare and worn; here the suit of a magistrate, there the outfit of a Curé, beyond the outfit of a banker, in one corner the costume of a retired military man, elsewhere the habiliments of a man of letters, and further on the dress of a statesman.

This creature was the costumer of the immense drama that knavery plays in Paris. His lair was the green room from which theft emerged, and into which roguery retreated. A tattered knave arrived at this dressing room, deposited his thirty sous and selected, according to the part that he wished to play, the costume that suited him, and on descending the stairs once more, the knave was a somebody. On the following day, the clothes were faithfully returned, and the Changer, who trusted the thieves with everything, was never robbed. There was one inconvenience about these clothes, they "did not fit"; not having been made for those who wore them, they were too tight for one, too loose for another and did not adjust themselves to anyone. Every pickpocket who exceeded or fell short of the human average was ill at his ease in the Changer's costumes. It was necessary that one should not be either too fat or too lean. The changer had foreseen only ordinary men. He had taken the measure of the species from the first rascal who came to hand, who is neither stout nor thin, neither tall nor short. Hence adaptations that were sometimes difficult and from which the Changer's clients extricated themselves as best they might. So much the worse for the exceptions! The suit of the statesman, for instance, black from head to foot, and consequently proper, would have been too large for Pitt and too small for Castelcicala. The costume of a statesman was designated as follows in the Changer's catalogue; we copy:

"A coat of black cloth, trousers of black wool, a silk waistcoat, boots and linen." On the margin there stood: ex-ambassador, and a note that we also copy: "In a separate box, a neatly frizzed peruke, green glasses, seals, and two small quills an inch long, wrapped in cotton." All this belonged to the statesman, the ex-ambassador. This whole costume was, if we may so express ourselves, debilitated; the seams were white, a vague buttonhole yawned at one of the elbows; moreover, one of the coat buttons was missing on the breast; but this was only detail; as the hand of the statesman should always be thrust into his coat and laid upon his heart, its function was to conceal the absent button.

If Marius had been familiar with the occult institutions of Paris, he would instantly have recognized upon the back of the visitor whom Basque had just shown in, the statesman's suit borrowed from the pick-me-down-that shop of the Changer.

Marius's disappointment on beholding another man than the one whom he expected to see turned to the newcomer's disadvantage.

He surveyed him from head to foot, while that personage made exaggerated bows, and demanded in a curt tone, "What do you want?"

The man replied with an amiable grin of which the caressing smile of a crocodile will furnish some idea, "It seems to me impossible that I should not have already had the honor of seeing Monsieur le Baron in society. I think I actually did meet monsieur personally, several years ago, at the house of Madame la Princesse Bagration and in the drawing rooms of his Lordship the Vicomte Dambray, peer of France."

It is always a good bit of tactics in knavery to pretend to recognize someone whom one does not know.

Marius paid attention to the manner of this man's speech. He spied on his accent and gesture, but his disappointment increased; the pronunciation was nasal and absolutely unlike the dry, shrill tone that he had expected.

He was utterly routed.

"I know neither Madame Bagration nor M. Dambray," said he. "I have never set foot in the house of either of them in my life."

The reply was ungracious. The personage, determined to be gracious at any cost, insisted.

"Then it must have been at Chateaubriand's that I have seen Monsieur! I know Chateaubriand very well. He is very affable. He sometimes says to me: 'Thenard, my friend . . . won't you drink a glass of wine with me?'"

Marius's brow grew more and more severe. "I have never had the honor of being received by M. de Chateaubriand. Let us cut it short. What do you want?"

The man bowed lower at that harsh voice.

"Monsieur le Baron, deign to listen to me. There is in America, in a district near Panama, a village called la Joya. That village is composed of a single house, a large, square house of three stories, built of bricks dried in the sun, each side of the square five hundred feet in length, each story retreating twelve feet back of the story below, in such a manner as to leave in front a terrace that makes the circuit of the edifice, in the center an inner court where the provisions and munitions are kept; no windows, loopholes, no doors, ladders, ladders to mount from the ground to the first terrace, and from the first to the second, and from the second to the third, ladders to descend into the inner court, no doors to the chambers, trap doors, no staircases to the chambers, ladders; in the evening the traps are closed, the ladders are withdrawn carbines and blunderbusses trained from the loopholes; no means of entering, a house by day, a citadel by night, eight hundred inhabitants—that is the village. Why so many precautions? Because the country is dangerous; it is full of cannibals. Then why do people go there? Because the country is marvelous; gold is found there."

"What are you driving at?" interrupted Marius, who had passed from disappointment to impatience.

"At this, Monsieur le Baron. I am an old and weary diplomat. Ancient civilization has thrown me on my own devices. I want to try savages."

"Well?"

"Monsieur le Baron, egotism is the law of the world. The proletarian peasant woman, who toils by the day, turns around when the diligence passes by, the peasant proprietress, who toils in her field, does not turn around. The dog of the poor man barks at the rich man, the dog of the rich man barks at the poor man. Each one for himself. Self-interest—that's the object of men. Gold, that's the loadstone."

"What then? Finish."

"I should like to go and establish myself at la Joya. There are three of us. I have my spouse and my young lady; a very beautiful girl. The journey is long and costly. I need a little money."

"What concern is that of mine?" demanded Marius.

The stranger stretched his neck out of his cravat, a gesture characteristic of the vulture, and replied with an augmented smile.

"Has not Monsieur le Baron perused my letter?"

There was some truth in this. The fact is, that the contents of the epistle had slipped Marius's mind. He had seen the writing rather than read the letter. He could hardly recall it. But a moment ago a fresh start had been given him. He had noted that detail: "my spouse and my young lady."

He fixed a penetrating glance on the stranger. An examining judge could not have done the look better. He almost lay in wait for him.

He confined himself to replying, "State the case precisely."

The stranger inserted his two hands in both his fobs, drew himself up without straightening his dorsal column, but scrutinizing Marius in his turn, with the green gaze of his spectacles.

"So be it, Monsieur le Baron. I will be precise. I have a secret to sell to you."

"A secret?"

"A secret."

"Which concerns me?"

"Somewhat."

"What is the secret?"

Marius scrutinized the man more and more as he listened to him.

"I commence gratis," said the stranger. "You will see that I am interesting."

"Speak."

"Monsieur le Baron, you have in your house a thief and an assassin."

Marius shuddered.

"In my house? No," said he.

The imperturbable stranger brushed his hat with his elbow and went on, "An assassin and a thief. Remark, Monsieur le Baron, that I do not here speak of ancient deeds, deeds of the past that have lapsed, which can be effaced by limitation before the law and by repentance before God. I speak of recent deeds, of actual facts as still unknown to justice at this hour. I continue. This man has insinuated himself into your confidence, and almost into your family under a false name. I am about to tell you his real name. And to tell it to you for nothing."

"I am listening."

"His name is Jean Valjean."

"I know it."

"I am going to tell you, equally for nothing, who he is."

"Say on."

"He is an ex-convict."

"I know it."

"You know it since I have had the honor of telling you."

"No. I knew it before."

Marius's cold tone, that double reply of "I know it," his laconicism, which was not favorable to dialogue, stirred up some smouldering wrath in the stranger. He launched a furious glance on the sly at Marius, which was instantly extinguished. Rapid as it was, this glance was of the kind that a man recognizes when he has once beheld it; it did not escape Marius. Certain flashes can only proceed from certain souls; the eye, that vent hole of the thought, glows with it; spectacles hide nothing; try putting a pane of glass over hell!

The stranger resumed with a smile, "I will not permit myself to contradict Monsieur le Baron. In any case, you ought to perceive that I am well informed. Now what I have to tell you is known to myself alone. This concerns the fortune of Madame la Baronne. It is an extraordinary secret. It is for sale—I make you the first offer of it. Cheap. Twenty thousand francs."

"I know that secret as well as the others," said Marius.

The personage felt the necessity of lowering his price a trifle.

"Monsieur le Baron, say ten thousand francs and I will speak."

"I repeat to you that there is nothing that you can tell me. I know what you wish to say to me."

A fresh flash gleamed in the man's eye. He exclaimed, "But I must dine today, nevertheless. It is an extraordinary secret, I tell you. Monsieur le Baron, I will speak. I speak. Give me twenty francs."

Marius gazed intently at him. "I know your extraordinary secret, just as I knew Jean Valjean's name, just as I know your name."

"My name?"

"Yes."

"That is not difficult, Monsieur le Baron. I had the honor to write to you and to tell it to you. Thenard."

"—Dier."

"Hey?"

"Thenardier."

"Who's that?"

In danger the porcupine bristles up, the beetle feigns death, the old guard forms in a square; this man burst into laughter.

Then he flicked a grain of dust from the sleeve of his coat with a fillip.

Marius continued, "You are also Jondrette the workman, Fabantou the comedian, Genflot the poet, Don Alvares the Spaniard, and Mistress Balizard."

"Mistress what?"

"And you kept a pot-house at Montfermeil."

"A pot-house! Never."

"And I tell you that your name is Thenardier."

"I deny it."

"And that you are a rascal. Here."

And Marius drew a banknote from his pocket and flung it in his face.

"Thanks! Pardon me! Five hundred francs! Monsieur le Baron!"

And the man, overcome, bowed, seized the note, and examined it.

"Five hundred francs!" he began again, taken aback. And he stammered in a low voice: "An honest rustler." Then brusquely, "Well, so be it!" he exclaimed. "Let us put ourselves at our ease."

And with the agility of a monkey, flinging back his hair, tearing off his spectacles, and withdrawing from his nose by sleight of hand the two quills of which mention was recently made, and which the reader has also met with on another page of this book, he took off his face as the man takes off his hat.

His eye lighted up; his uneven brow, with hollows in some places and bumps in others, hideously wrinkled at the top, was laid bare, his nose had become as sharp as a beak; the fierce and sagacious profile of the man of prey reappeared.

"Monsieur le Baron is infallible," he said in a clear voice from which all nasal twang had disappeared, "I am Thenardier."

And he straightened up his crooked back.

Thenardier, for it was really he, was strangely surprised; he would have been troubled, had he been capable of such a thing. He had come to bring astonishment, and it was he who had received it. This humiliation had been worth five hundred francs to him, and, taking it all in all, he accepted it; but he was nonetheless bewildered.

He beheld this Baron Pontmercy for the first time, and, in spite of his disguise, this Baron Pontmercy recognized him, and recognized him thoroughly. And not only was this Baron perfectly informed as to Thenardier, but he seemed well posted as to Jean Valjean. Who was this almost beardless young man, who was so glacial and so generous, who knew people's names, who knew all their names, and who opened his purse to them, who bullied rascals like a judge, and who paid them like a dupe?

Thenardier, the reader will remember, although he had been Marius's neighbor, had never seen him, which is not unusual in Paris; he had formerly, in a vague way, heard his daughters talk of a very poor young man named Marius who lived in the house. He had written to him, without knowing him, the letter with which the reader is acquainted.

No connection between that Marius and M. le Baron Pontmercy was possible in his mind.

As for the name Pontmercy, it will be recalled that, on the battlefield of Waterloo, he had only heard the last two syllables, for which he always entertained the legitimate scorn that one owes to what is merely an expression of thanks.

However, through his daughter Azelma, who had started on the scent of the married pair on the 16th of February, and through his own personal researches, he had succeeded in learning many things, and, from the depths of his own gloom, he had contrived to grasp more than one mysterious clew. He had discovered, by dint of industry, or, at least, by dint of induction, he had guessed who the man was whom he had encountered on a certain day in the Grand Sewer. From the man he had easily reached the name. He knew that Madame la Baronne Pontmercy was Cosette. But he meant to be discreet in that quarter.

Who was Cosette? He did not know exactly himself. He did, indeed, catch an inkling of illegitimacy, the history of Fantine had always seemed to him equivocal; but what was the use of talking about that? In order to cause himself to be paid for his silence? He had, or thought he had, better wares than that for sale. And, according to all appearances, if he were to come and make to the Baron Pontmercy this revelation—and without proof: "Your wife is a bastard," the only result would be to attract the boot of the husband toward the loins of the revealer.

From Thenardier's point of view, the conversation with Marius had not yet begun. He ought to have drawn back, to have modified his strategy, to have abandoned his position, to have changed his front; but nothing essential had been compromised as yet, and he had five hundred francs in his pocket. Moreover, he had something decisive to say, and, even against this very well informed and well-armed Baron Pontmercy, he felt himself strong. For men of Thenardier's nature, every dialogue is a combat. In the one in which he was about to engage, what was his situation? He did not know to whom he was speaking, but he did know of what he was speaking, he made this rapid review of his inner forces, and after having said, "I am Thenardier," he waited.

Marius had become thoughtful. So he had hold of Thenardier at last. That man whom he had so greatly desired to find was before him. He could honor Colonel Pontmercy's recommendation.

He felt humiliated that that hero should have owned anything to this villain, and that the letter of change drawn from the depths of the tomb by his father upon him, Marius, had been protested up to that day. It also seemed to him, in the complex state of his mind toward Thenardier, that there was occasion to avenge the Colonel for the misfortune of having been saved by such a rascal. In any case, he was content. He was about to deliver the Colonel's shade from this unworthy creditor at last, and it seemed to him that he was on the point of rescuing his father's memory from the debtors' prison. By the side of this duty there was another—to elucidate, if possible, the source of Cosette's fortune. The opportunity appeared to present itself. Perhaps Thenardier knew something. It might prove useful to see the bottom of this man.

He commenced with this.

Thenardier had caused the "honest rustler" to disappear in his fob, and was gazing at Marius with a gentleness that was almost tender.

Marius broke the silence.

"Thenardier, I have told you your name. Now, would you like to have me tell you your secret—the one that you came here to reveal to me? I have information of my own, also. You shall see that I know more about it than you do. Jean Valjean, as you have said, is an assassin and a thief. A thief, because he robbed a wealthy manufacturer, whose ruin he brought about. An assassin, because he assassinated police-agent Javert."

"I don't understand, sir," ejaculated Thenardier.

"I will make myself intelligible. In a certain arrondissement of the Pas de Calais, there was, in 1822, a man who had fallen out with justice, and who, under the name of M. Madeleine, had regained his status and rehabilitated himself. This man had become a just man in the full force of the term. In a trade, the manufacture of black glass goods, he made the fortune of an entire city. As far as his personal fortune was concerned he made that also, but as a secondary matter, and in some sort, by accident. He was the foster-father of the poor. He founded hospitals, opened schools, visited the sick, dowered young girls, supported widows, and adopted orphans; he was like the guardian angel of the country. He refused the cross, he was appointed Mayor. A liberated convict knew the secret of a penalty incurred by this man in former days; he denounced him, and had him arrested, and profited by the arrest to come to Paris and cause the banker Laffitte—I have the fact from the cashier himself—by means of a false signature, to hand over to him the sum of over half a million that belonged to M. Madeleine. This convict who robbed M. Madeleine was Jean Valjean. As for the other fact, you have nothing to tell me about it either. Jean Valjean killed the agent Javert; he shot him with a pistol. I, the person who is speaking to you, was present."

Thenardier cast upon Marius the sovereign glance of a conquered man who lays his hand once more upon the victory, and who has just regained, in one instant, all the ground he has lost. But the smile returned instantly. The inferior's triumph in the presence of his superior must be wheedling.

Thenardier contented himself with saying to Marius, "Monsieur le Baron, we are on the wrong track."

And he emphasized this phrase by making his bunch of seals execute an expressive whirl.

"What!" broke forth Marius, "do you dispute that? These are facts."

"They are chimeras. The confidence with which Monsieur le Baron honors me renders it my duty to tell him so. Truth and justice before all things. I do not like to see folks accused unjustly. Monsieur le Baron, Jean Valjean did not rob M. Madeleine and Jean Valjean did not kill Javert."

"This is too much! How is this?"

"For two reasons."

"What are they? Speak."

"This is the first: he did not rob M. Madeleine, because it is Jean Valjean himself who was M. Madeleine."

"What tale are you telling me?"

"And this is the second: he did not assassinate Javert, because the person who killed Javert was Javert."

"What do you mean to say?"

"That Javert committed suicide."

"Prove it! Prove it!" cried Marius beside himself.

Thenardier resumed, scanning his phrase after the manner of the ancient Alexandrine measure:

"Police-agent-Ja-vert-was-found-drowned-un-der-a-boat-of-the-Pont-au-Change."

"But prove it!"

Thenardier drew from his pocket a large envelope of gray paper, which seemed to contain sheets folded in different sizes.

"I have my papers," he said calmly.

And he added, "Monsieur le Baron, in your interests I desired to know Jean Valjean thoroughly. I say that Jean Valjean and M. Madeleine are one and the same man, and I say that Javert had no other assassin than Javert. If I speak, it is because I have proofs. Not manuscript proofs—writing is suspicious, handwriting is complaisant, but printed proofs."

As he spoke, Thenardier extracted from the envelope two copies of newspapers, yellow, faded, and strongly saturated with tobacco. One of these two newspapers, broken at every fold and falling into rags, seemed much older than the other.

"Two facts, two proofs," remarked Thenardier. And he offered the two newspapers, unfolded, to Marius.

The reader is acquainted with these two papers. One, the most ancient, a number of the Drapeau Blanc of the 25th of July, 1823, the text of which can be seen in the first volume, established the identity of M. Madeleine and Jean Valjean.

The other, a Moniteur of the 15th of June, 1832, announced the suicide of Javert, adding that it appeared from a verbal report of Javert to the prefect that, having been taken prisoner in the barricade of the Rue de la Chanvrerie, he had owed his life to the magnanimity of an insurgent who, holding him under his pistol, had fired into the air, instead of blowing out his brains.

Marius read. He had evidence, a certain date, irrefragable proof, these two newspapers had not been printed expressly for the purpose of backing up Thenardier's statements; the note printed in the Moniteur had been an administrative communication from the Prefecture of Police. Marius could not doubt.

The information of the cashier-clerk had been false, and he himself had been deceived.

Jean Valjean, who had suddenly grown grand, emerged from his cloud. Marius could not repress a cry of joy.

"Well, then this unhappy wretch is an admirable man! The whole of that fortune really belonged to him! He is Madeleine, the providence of a whole countryside! He is Jean Valjean, Javert's savior! He is a hero! He is a saint!"

"He's not a saint, and he's not a hero!" said Thenardier. "He's an assassin and a robber."

And he added, in the tone of a man who begins to feel that he possesses some authority, "Let us be calm."

Robber, assassin—those words that Marius thought had disappeared and that returned, fell upon him like an ice-cold shower-bath.

"Again!" said he.

"Always," ejaculated Thenardier. "Jean Valjean did not rob Madeleine, but he is a thief. He did not kill Javert, but he is a murderer."

"Will you speak," retorted Marius, "of that miserable theft, committed forty years ago, and expiated, as your own newspapers prove, by a whole life of repentance, of self-abnegation, and of virtue?"

"I say assassination and theft, Monsieur le Baron, and I repeat that I am speaking of actual facts. What I have to reveal to you is absolutely unknown. It belongs to unpublished matter. And perhaps you will find in it the source of the fortune so skilfully presented to Madame la Baronne by Jean Valjean. I say skilfully, because, by a gift of that nature it would not be so very unskilful to slip into an honorable house whose comforts one would then share, and, at the same stroke, to conceal one's crime, and to enjoy one's theft, to bury one's name, and to create for oneself a family."

"I might interrupt you at this point," said Marius, "but go on."

"Monsieur le Baron, I will tell you all, leaving the recompense to your generosity. This secret is worth massive gold. You will say to me, 'Why do not you apply to Jean Valjean?' For a very simple reason; I know that he has stripped himself, and stripped himself in your favor, and I consider the combination ingenious; but he has no longer a son, he would show me his empty hands, and, since I am in need of some money for my trip to la Joya, I prefer you, you who have it all, to him who has nothing. I am a little fatigued, permit me to take a chair."

Marius seated himself and motioned to him to do the same.

Thenardier installed himself on a tufted chair, picked up his two newspapers, thrust them back into their envelope, and murmured as he pecked at the Drapeau Blanc with his nail, "It cost me a good deal of trouble to get this one."

That done he crossed his legs and stretched himself out on the back of the chair, an attitude characteristic of people who are sure of what they are saying, then he entered upon his subject gravely, emphasizing his words, "Monsieur le Baron, on the 6th of June, 1832, about a year ago, on the day of the insurrection, a man was in the Grand Sewer of Paris, at the point where the sewer enters the Seine, between the Pont des Invalides and the Pont de Jena."

Marius abruptly drew his chair closer to that of Thenardier. Thenardier noticed this movement and continued with the deliberation of an orator who holds his interlocutor and who feels his adversary palpitating under his words, "This man, forced to conceal himself, and for reasons, moreover, which are foreign to politics, had adopted the sewer as his domicile and had a key to it. It was, I repeat, on the 6th of June; it might have been eight o'clock in the evening. The man hears a noise in the sewer. Greatly surprised, he hides himself and lies in wait. It was the sound of footsteps, someone was walking in the dark, and coming in his direction. Strange to say, there was another man in the sewer besides himself. The grating of the outlet from the sewer was not far off. A little light that fell through it permitted him to recognize the newcomer, and to see that the man was carrying something on his back. He was walking in a bent attitude. The man who was walking in a bent attitude was an ex-convict, and what he was dragging on his shoulders was a corpse. Assassination caught in the very act, if ever there was such a thing. As for the theft, that is understood; one does not kill a man gratis. This convict was on his way to fling the body into the river. One fact is to be noticed, that before reaching the exit grating, this convict, who had come a long distance in the sewer, must, necessarily, have encountered a frightful quagmire where it seems as though he might have left the body, but the sewermen would have found the assassinated man the very next day, while at work on the quagmire, and that did not suit the assassin's plans. He had preferred to traverse that quagmire with his burden, and his exertions must have been terrible, for it is impossible to risk one's life more completely; I don't understand how he could have come out of that alive."

Marius's chair approached still nearer. Thenardier took advantage of this to draw a long breath. He went on, "Monsieur le Baron, a sewer is not the Champ de Mars. One lacks everything there, even room. When two men are there, they must meet. That is what happened. The man domiciled there and the passerby were forced to bid each other good-day, greatly to the regret of both. The passerby said to the inhabitant, "You see what I have on my back, I must get out, you have the key, give it to me." That convict was a man of terrible strength. There was no way of refusing. Nevertheless, the man who had the key parleyed, simply to gain time. He examined the dead man, but he could see nothing, except that the latter was young, well dressed, with the air of being rich, and all disfigured with blood. While talking, the man contrived to tear and pull off behind, without the assassin perceiving it, a bit of the assassinated man's coat. A document for conviction, you understand; a means of recovering the trace of things and of bringing home the crime to the criminal. He put this document for conviction in his pocket. After which he opened the grating, made the man go out with his embarrassment on his back, closed the grating again, and ran off, not caring to be mixed up with the remainder of the adventure and above all, not wishing to be present when the assassin threw the assassinated man into the river. Now you comprehend. The man who was carrying the corpse was Jean Valjean; the one who had the key is speaking to you at this moment; and the piece of the coat . . ."

Thenardier completed his phrase by drawing from his pocket, and holding, on a level with his eyes, nipped between his two thumbs and his two forefingers, a strip of torn black cloth, all covered with dark spots.

Marius had sprung to his feet, pale, hardly able to draw his breath, with his eyes riveted on the fragment of black cloth, and, without uttering a word, without taking his eyes from that fragment, he retreated to the wall and fumbled with his right hand along the wall for a key that was in the lock of a cupboard near the chimney.

He found the key, opened the cupboard, plunged his arm into it without looking, and without his frightened gaze quitting the rag Thenardier still held outspread.

But Thenardier continued, "Monsieur le Baron, I have the strongest of reasons for believing that the assassinated young man was an opulent stranger lured into a trap by Jean Valjean, and the bearer of an enormous sum of money."

"The young man was myself, and here is the coat!" cried Marius, and he flung upon the floor an old black coat all covered with blood.

Then, snatching the fragment from the hands of Thenardier, he crouched down over the coat, and laid the torn morsel against the tattered skirt. The rent fitted exactly, and the strip completed the coat.

Thenardier was petrified.

This is what he thought: "I'm struck all of a heap."

Marius rose to his feet trembling, despairing, radiant.

He fumbled in his pocket and stalked furiously to Thenardier, presenting to him and almost thrusting in his face his fist filled with banknotes for five hundred and a thousand francs.

"You are an infamous wretch! You are a liar, a calumniator, a villain. You came to accuse that man, you have only justified him; you wanted to ruin him, you have only succeeded in glorifying him. And it is you who are the thief! And it is you who are the assassin! I saw you, Thenardier Jondrette, in that lair on the Rue de l'Hopital. I know enough about you to send you to the galleys and even further if I choose. Here are a thousand francs, bully that you are!"

And he flung a thousand franc note at Thenardier.

"Ah! Jondrette Thenardier, vile rascal! Let this serve you as a lesson, you dealer in secondhand secrets, merchant of mysteries, rummager of the shadows, wretch! Take these five hundred francs and get out of here! Waterloo protects you."

"Waterloo!" growled Thenardier, pocketing the five hundred francs along with the thousand.

"Yes, assassin! You there saved the life of a Colonel. . ."

"Of a General," said Thenardier, elevating his head.

"Of a Colonel!" repeated Marius in a rage. "I wouldn't give a ha'penny for a general. And you come here to commit infamies! I tell you that you have committed all crimes. Go! Disappear! Only be happy, that is all that I desire. Ah! Monster! Here are three thousand francs more. Take them. You will depart tomorrow, for America, with your daughter; for your wife is dead, you abominable liar. I shall watch over your departure, you ruffian, and at that moment I will count out to you twenty thousand francs. Go get yourself hung elsewhere!"

"Monsieur le Baron!" replied Thenardier, bowing to the very earth, "eternal gratitude." And Thenardier left the room, understanding nothing, stupefied and delighted with this sweet crushing beneath sacks of gold, and with that thunder that had burst forth over his head in bankbills.

Struck by lightning he was, but he was also content; and he would have been greatly angered had he had a lightning rod to ward off such lightning as that.

Let us finish with this man at once.

Two days after the events that we are at this moment narrating, he set out, thanks to Marius's care, for America under a false name, with his daughter Azelma, furnished with a draft on New York for twenty thousand francs.

The moral wretchedness of Thenardier, the bourgeois who had missed his vocation, was irremediable. He was in America what he had been in Europe. Contact with an evil man sometimes suffices to corrupt a good action and to cause evil things to spring from it. With Marius's money, Thenardier set up as a slave dealer.

As soon as Thenardier had left the house, Marius rushed to the garden, where Cosette was still walking.

"Cosette! Cosette!" he cried. "Come! Come quick! Let us go. Basque, a carriage! Cosette, come. Ah! My God! It was he who saved my life! Let us not lose a minute! Put on your shawl."

Cosette thought him mad and obeyed.

He could not breathe, he laid his hand on his heart to restrain its throbbing. He paced back and forth with huge strides, he embraced Cosette, "Ah! Cosette! I am an unhappy wretch!" said he.

Marius was bewildered. He began to catch a glimpse in Jean Valjean of some indescribably lofty and melancholy figure. An unheard-of virtue, supreme and sweet, humble in its immensity, appeared to him. The convict was transfigured into Christ.

Marius was dazzled by this prodigy. He did not know precisely what he beheld, but it was grand.

In an instant, a hackney carriage stood in front of the door.

Marius helped Cosette in and darted in himself.

"Driver," said he, "Rue de l'Homme Arme, Number 7."

The carriage drove off.

"Ah! What happiness!" ejaculated Cosette. "Rue de l'Homme Arme, I did not dare to speak to you of that. We are going to see M. Jean."

"Thy father! Cosette, thy father more than ever. Cosette, I guess it. You told me that you had never received the letter that I sent you by Gavroche. It must have fallen into his hands. Cosette, he went to the barricade to save me. As it is a necessity with him to be an angel, he saved others also; he saved Javert. He rescued me from that gulf to give me to you. He carried me on his back through that frightful sewer. Ah! I am a monster of ingratitude. Cosette, after having been your providence, he became mine. Just imagine, there was a terrible quagmire enough to drown one a hundred times over, to drown one in mire. Cosette! He made me traverse it. I was unconscious; I saw nothing, I heard nothing, I could know nothing of my own adventure. We are going to bring him back, to take him with us, whether he is willing or not, he shall never leave us again. If only he is at home! Provided only that we can find him, I will pass the rest of my life in venerating him. Yes, that is how it should be, do you see, Cosette? Gavroche must have delivered my letter to him. All is explained. You understand."

Cosette did not understand a word.

"You are right," she said to him.

Meanwhile the carriage rolled on.

CHAPTER V—A NIGHT BEHIND WHICH THERE IS DAY

Jean Valjean turned around at the knock that he heard on his door.

"Come in," he said feebly.

The door opened.

Cosette and Marius made their appearance.

Cosette rushed into the room.

Marius remained on the threshold, leaning against the jamb of the door.

"Cosette!" said Jean Valjean.

And he sat erect in his chair, his arms outstretched and trembling, haggard, livid, gloomy, an immense joy in his eyes.

Cosette, stifling with emotion, fell upon Jean Valjean's breast.

"Father!" said she.

Jean Valjean, overcome, stammered, "Cosette! She! You! Madame! It is thou! Ah! My God!"

And, pressed close in Cosette's arms, he exclaimed, "It is thou! Thou art here! Thou dost pardon me then!"

Marius, lowering his eyelids, in order to keep his tears from flowing, took a step forward and murmured between lips convulsively contracted to repress his sobs, "My father!"

"And you also, you pardon me!" Jean Valjean said to him.

Marius could find no words, and Jean Valjean added, "Thanks."

Cosette tore off her shawl and tossed her hat on the bed.

"It embarrasses me," said she.

And, seating herself on the old man's knees, she put aside his white locks with an adorable movement, and kissed his brow.

Jean Valjean, bewildered, let her have her own way.

Cosette, who only understood in a very confused manner, redoubled her caresses, as though she desired to pay Marius's debt.

Jean Valjean stammered, "How stupid people are! I thought that I should never see her again. Imagine, Monsieur Pontmercy, at the very moment when you entered, I was saying to myself, 'All is over. Here is her little gown, I am a miserable man, I shall never see Cosette again,' and I was saying that at the very moment when you were mounting the stairs. Was not I an idiot? Just see how idiotic one can be! One reckons without the good God. The good God says, 'You fancy that you are about to be abandoned, stupid! No. No, things will not go so. Come, there is a goodman yonder who is in need of an angel.' And the angel comes, and one sees one's Cosette again! And one sees one's little Cosette once more! Ah! I was very unhappy."

For a moment he could not speak, then he went on, "I really needed to see Cosette a little bit now and then. A heart needs a bone to gnaw. But I was perfectly conscious that I was in the way. I gave myself reasons: 'They do not want you, keep in your own course, one has not the right to cling eternally.' Ah! God be praised, I see her once more! Dost thou know, Cosette, thy husband is very handsome? Ah! What a pretty embroidered collar thou hast on, luckily. I am fond of that pattern. It was thy husband who chose it, was it not? And then, thou shouldst have some cashmere shawls. Let me call her thou, Monsieur Pontmercy. It will not be for long."

And Cosette began again, "How wicked of you to have left us like that! Where did you go? Why have you stayed away so long? Formerly your journeys only lasted three or four days. I sent Nicolette, the answer always was, 'He is absent.' How long have you been back? Why did you not let us know? Do you know that you are very much changed? Ah! What a naughty father! He has been ill, and we have not known it! Stay, Marius, feel how cold his hand is!"

"So you are here! Monsieur Pontmercy, you pardon me!" repeated Jean Valjean.

At that word, which Jean Valjean had just uttered once more, all that was swelling Marius's heart found vent.

He burst forth, "Cosette, do you hear? He has come to that! He asks my forgiveness! And do you know what he has done for me, Cosette? He has saved my life. He has done more—he has given you to me. And after having saved me, and after having given you to me, Cosette, what has he done with himself? He has sacrificed himself. Behold the man. And he says to me the ingrate, to me the forgetful, to me the pitiless, to me the guilty one, 'Thanks!' Cosette, my whole life passed at the feet of this man would be too little. That barricade, that sewer, that furnace, that cesspool—all that he traversed for me, for thee, Cosette! He carried me away through all the deaths that he put aside before me, and accepted for himself. Every courage, every virtue, every heroism, every sanctity he possesses! Cosette, that man is an angel!"

"Hush! Hush!" said Jean Valjean in a low voice. "Why tell all that?"

"But you!" cried Marius with a wrath in which there was veneration. "Why did you not tell it to me? It is your own fault, too. You save people's lives, and you conceal it from them! You do more, under the pretext of unmasking yourself, you calumniate yourself. It is frightful."

"I told the truth," replied Jean Valjean.

"No," retorted Marius, "the truth is the whole truth; and that you did not tell. You were Monsieur Madeleine, why not have said so? You saved Javert, why not have said so? I owed my life to you, why not have said so?"

"Because I thought as you do. I thought that you were in the right. It was necessary that I should go away. If you had known about that affair, of the sewer, you would have made me remain near you. I was therefore forced to hold my peace. If I had spoken, it would have caused embarrassment in every way."

"It would have embarrassed what? Embarrassed whom?" retorted Marius. "Do you think that you are going to stay here? We shall carry you off. Ah!

Good heavens! When I reflect that it was by an accident that I have learned all this. You form a part of ourselves. You are her father, and mine. You shall not pass another day in this dreadful house. Do not imagine that you will be here tomorrow."

"Tomorrow," said Jean Valjean, "I shall not be here, but I shall not be with you."

"What do you mean?" replied Marius. "Ah! Come now, we are not going to permit any more journeys. You shall never leave us again. You belong to us. We shall not loose our hold of you."

"This time it is for good," added Cosette. "We have a carriage at the door. I shall run away with you. If necessary, I shall employ force."

And she laughingly made a movement to lift the old man in her arms.

"Your chamber still stands ready in our house," she went on. "If you only knew how pretty the garden is now! The azaleas are doing very well there. The walks are sanded with river sand; there are tiny violet shells. You shall eat my strawberries. I water them myself. And no more 'madame,' no more 'Monsieur Jean,' we are living under a Republic, everybody says thou, don't they, Marius? The program is changed. If you only knew, father, I have had a sorrow, there was a robin redbreast that had made her nest in a hole in the wall, and a horrible cat ate her. My poor, pretty, little robin redbreast, which used to put her head out of her window and look at me! I cried over it. I should have liked to kill the cat. But now nobody cries any more. Everybody laughs, everybody is happy. You are going to come with us. How delighted grandfather will be! You shall have your plot in the garden, you shall cultivate it, and we shall see whether your strawberries are as fine as mine. And, then, I shall do everything that you wish, and then, you will obey me prettily."

Jean Valjean listened to her without hearing her. He heard the music of her voice rather than the sense of her words; one of those large tears that are the sombre pearls of the soul welled up slowly in his eyes.

He murmured, "The proof that God is good is that she is here."

"Father!" said Cosette.

Jean Valjean continued, "It is quite true that it would be charming for us to live together. Their trees are full of birds. I would walk with Cosette. It is sweet to be among living people who bid each other 'good-day,' who call to each other in the garden. People see each other from early morning. We should each cultivate our own little corner. She would make me eat her strawberries. I would make her gather my roses. That would be charming. Only . . ." He paused and said gently, "It is a pity."

The tear did not fall, it retreated, and Jean Valjean replaced it with a smile. Cosette took both the old man's hands in hers.

"My God!" said she, "your hands are still colder than before. Are you ill? Do you suffer?"

"I? No," replied Jean Valjean. "I am very well. Only . . ."

He paused.

"Only what?"

"I am going to die presently."

Cosette and Marius shuddered.

"To die!" exclaimed Marius.

"Yes, but that is nothing," said Jean Valjean.

He took breath, smiled, and resumed, "Cosette, thou wert talking to me, go on, so thy little robin redbreast is dead? Speak, so that I may hear thy voice."

Marius gazed at the old man in amazement.

Cosette uttered a heartrending cry.

"Father! My father! You will live. You are going to live. I insist upon your living, do you hear?"

Jean Valjean raised his head toward her with adoration.

"Oh! Yes, forbid me to die. Who knows? Perhaps I shall obey. I was on the verge of dying when you came. That stopped me, it seemed to me that I was born again."

"You are full of strength and life," cried Marius. "Do you imagine that a person can die like this? You have had sorrow, you shall have no more. It is I who ask your forgiveness, and on my knees! You are going to live, and to live with us, and to live a long time. We take possession of you once more. There are two of us here who will henceforth have no other thought than your happiness."

"You see," resumed Cosette, all bathed in tears, "that Marius says that you shall not die."

Jean Valjean continued to smile.

"Even if you were to take possession of me, Monsieur Pontmercy, would that make me other than I am? No, God has thought like you and myself, and he does not change his mind; it is useful for me to go. Death is a good arrangement. God knows better than we what we need. May you be happy, may Monsieur Pontmercy have Cosette, may youth wed the morning, may there be around you, my children, lilacs and nightingales; may your life be a beautiful, sunny lawn, may all the enchantments of heaven fill your souls, and now let me, who am good for nothing, die; it is certain that all this is right.

Come, be reasonable, nothing is possible now, I am fully conscious that all is over. And then, last night, I drank that whole jug of water. How good thy husband is, Cosette! Thou art much better off with him than with me."

A noise became audible at the door.

It was the doctor entering.

"Good day, and farewell, doctor," said Jean Valjean. "Here are my poor children."

Marius stepped up to the doctor. He addressed to him only this single word, "Monsieur?" But his manner of pronouncing it contained a complete question.

The doctor replied to the question by an expressive glance.

"Because things are not agreeable," said Jean Valjean, "that is no reason for being unjust toward God."

A silence ensued.

All breasts were oppressed.

Jean Valjean turned to Cosette. He began to gaze at her as though he wished to retain her features for eternity.

In the depths of the shadow into which he had already descended, ecstasy was still possible to him when gazing at Cosette. The reflection of that sweet face lighted up his pale visage.

The doctor felt of his pulse.

"Ah! It was you that he wanted!" he murmured, looking at Cosette and Marius.

And bending down to Marius's ear, he added in a very low voice:

"Too late."

Jean Valjean surveyed the doctor and Marius serenely, almost without ceasing to gaze at Cosette.

These barely articulate words were heard to issue from his mouth, "It is nothing to die; it is dreadful not to live."

All at once he rose to his feet. These accesses of strength are sometimes the sign of the death agony. He walked with a firm step to the wall, thrusting aside Marius and the doctor who tried to help him, detached from the wall a little copper crucifix that was suspended there, and returned to his seat with all the freedom of movement of perfect health, and said in a loud voice, as he laid the crucifix on the table, "Behold the great martyr."

Then his chest sank in, his head wavered, as though the intoxication of the tomb were seizing hold upon him.

His hands, which rested on his knees, began to press their nails into the stuff of his trousers.

Cosette supported his shoulders, and sobbed, and tried to speak to him, but could not.

Among the words mingled with that mournful saliva that accompanies tears, they distinguished like the following, "Father, do not leave us. Is it possible that we have found you only to lose you again?"

It might be said that agony writhes. It goes, comes, advances toward the sepulchre, and returns toward life. There is groping in the action of dying.

Jean Valjean rallied after this semi-swoon, shook his brow as though to make the shadows fall away from it and became almost perfectly lucid once more.

He took a fold of Cosette's sleeve and kissed it.

"He is coming back! Doctor, he is coming back," cried Marius.

"You are good, both of you," said Jean Valjean. "I am going to tell you what has caused me pain. What has pained me, Monsieur Pontmercy, is that you have not been willing to touch that money. That money really belongs to your wife. I will explain to you, my children, and for that reason, also, I am glad to see you. Black jet comes from England, white jet comes from Norway. All this is in this paper, which you will read. For bracelets, I invented a way of substituting for slides of soldered sheet iron, slides of iron laid together. It is prettier, better, and less costly. You will understand how much money can be made in that way. So Cosette's fortune is really hers. I give you these details, in order that your mind may be set at rest."

The portress had come upstairs and was gazing in at the half-open door. The doctor dismissed her.

But he could not prevent this zealous woman from exclaiming to the dying man before she disappeared, "Would you like a priest?"

"I have had one," replied Jean Valjean.

And with his finger he seemed to indicate a point above his head where one would have said that he saw someone.

It is probable, in fact, that the Bishop was present at this death agony.

Cosette gently slipped a pillow under his loins.

Jean Valjean resumed, "Have no fear, Monsieur Pontmercy, I adjure you. The six hundred thousand francs really belong to Cosette. My life will have been wasted if you do not enjoy them! We managed to do very well with those glass goods. We rivaled what is called Berlin jewellery. However, we could not equal the black glass of England. A gross, which contains twelve hundred very well cut grains, only costs three francs."

When a being who is dear to us is on the point of death, we gaze upon him with a look that clings convulsively to him and that would fain hold him back.

Cosette gave her hand to Marius, and both, mute with anguish, not knowing what to say to the dying man, stood trembling and despairing before him.

Jean Valjean sank moment by moment. He was failing; he was drawing near to the gloomy horizon.

His breath had become intermittent; a little rattling interrupted it. He found some difficulty in moving his forearm, his feet had lost all movement, and in proportion as the wretchedness of limb and feebleness of body increased, all the majesty of his soul was displayed and spread over his brow. The light of the unknown world was already visible in his eyes.

His face paled and smiled. Life was no longer there, it was something else.

His breath sank, his glance grew grander. He was a corpse on which the wings could be felt.

He made a sign to Cosette to draw near, then to Marius; the last minute of the last hour had, evidently, arrived.

He began to speak to them in a voice so feeble that it seemed to come from a distance, and one would have said that a wall now rose between them and him.

"Draw near, draw near, both of you. I love you dearly. Oh! How good it is to die like this! And thou lovest me also, my Cosette. I knew well that thou still felt friendly toward thy poor old man. How kind it was of thee to place that pillow under my loins! Thou wilt weep for me a little, wilt thou not? Not too much. I do not wish thee to have any real griefs. You must enjoy yourselves a great deal, my children. I forgot to tell you that the profit was greater still on the buckles without tongues than on all the rest. A gross of a dozen dozens cost ten francs and sold for sixty. It really was a good business. So there is no occasion for surprise at the six hundred thousand francs, Monsieur Pontmercy. It is honest money. You may be rich with a tranquil mind. Thou must have a carriage, a box at the theatres now and then, and handsome ball dresses, my Cosette, and then, thou must give good dinners to thy friends, and be very happy. I was writing to Cosette a while ago. She will find my letter. I bequeath to her the two candlesticks that stand on the mantle. They are of silver, but to me they are gold, they are diamonds; they change candles that are placed in them into wax tapers. I do not know whether the person who gave them to me is pleased with me yonder on high. I have done what I could. My children, you will not forget that I am a poor man, you will have me buried in the first plot of earth that you find, under a stone to mark the spot. This is my wish. No name on the stone. If Cosette cares to come for a little while now and then, it will give me pleasure. And you too, Monsieur Pontmercy. I must admit that I have not always loved you. I ask your pardon for that. Now she and you form but one for me. I feel very grateful to you. I am sure that you make Cosette happy. If you only knew, Monsieur Pontmercy, her pretty rosy cheeks were my delight; when I saw her in the least pale, I was sad. In the chest of drawers, there is a bankbill for five hundred francs. I have not touched it. It is for the poor. Cosette, dost thou see thy little gown yonder on the bed? Dost thou recognize it? That was ten years ago, however. How time flies! We have been very happy. All is over. Do not weep, my children, I am not going very far, I shall see you from there, you will only have to look at night, and you will see me smile. Cosette, dost thou remember Montfermeil? Thou wert in the forest, thou wert greatly terrified; dost thou remember how I took hold of the handle of the water bucket? That was the first time that I touched thy poor, little hand. It was so cold! Ah! Your hands were red then, mademoiselle, they are very white now. And the big doll! Dost thou remember? Thou didst call her Catherine. Thou regrettedest not having taken her to the convent! How thou didst make me laugh sometimes, my sweet angel! When it had been raining, thou didst float bits of straw on the gutters, and watch them pass away. One day I gave thee a willow battledore and a shuttlecock with yellow, blue, and green feathers. Thou hast forgotten it. Thou wert roguish so young! Thou didst play. Thou didst put cherries in thy ears. Those are things of the past. The forests through which one has passed with one's child, the trees under which one has strolled, the convents where one has concealed oneself, the games, the hearty laughs of childhood, are shadows. I imagined that all that belonged to me. In that lay my stupidity. Those Thenardiers were wicked. Thou must forgive them. Cosette, the moment has come to tell thee the name of thy mother. She was called Fantine. Remember that name—Fantine. Kneel whenever thou utterest it. She suffered much. She loved thee dearly. She had as much unhappiness as thou hast had happiness. That is the way God apportions things. He is there on high, he sees us all, and he knows what he does in the midst of his great stars. I am on the verge of departure, my children. Love each other well and always. There is nothing else but that in the world: love for each other. You will think sometimes of the poor old man who died here. Oh my Cosette, it is not my fault, indeed, that I have not seen thee all this time, it cut me to the heart; I went as far as the corner of the street, I must have produced a queer effect on the people who saw me pass, I was like a madman, I once went out without my hat. I no longer see clearly, my children, I had still other things to say, but never mind. Think a little of me. Come still nearer. I die happy. Give me your dear and well-beloved heads, so that I may lay my hands upon them."

Cosette and Marius fell on their knees, in despair, suffocating with tears, each beneath one of Jean Valjean's hands. Those august hands no longer moved.

He had fallen backward, the light of the candles illuminated him.

His white face looked up to heaven, he allowed Cosette and Marius to cover his hands with kisses.

He was dead.

The night was starless and extremely dark. No doubt, in the gloom, some immense angel stood erect with wings outspread, awaiting that soul.

CHAPTER VI—THE GRASS COVERS AND THE RAIN EFFACES

In the cemetery of Pere-Lachaise, in the vicinity of the common grave, far from the elegant quarter of that city of sepulchres, far from all the tombs of fancy that display in the presence of eternity all the hideous fashions of death, in a deserted corner, beside an old wall, beneath a great yew tree over which climbs the wild convolvulus, amid dandelions and mosses, there lies a stone. That stone is no more exempt than others from the leprosy of time, of dampness, of the lichens and from the defilement of the birds. The water turns it green, the air blackens it. It is not near any path, and people are not fond of walking in that direction, because the grass is high and their feet are immediately wet. When there is a little sunshine, the lizards come there. All around there is a quivering of weeds. In the spring, linnets warble in the trees.

This stone is perfectly plain. In cutting it the only thought was the requirements of the tomb, and no other care was taken than to make the stone long enough and narrow enough to cover a man.

No name is to be read there.

Only, many years ago, a hand wrote upon it in pencil these four lines, which have become gradually illegible beneath the rain and the dust, and which are, today, probably effaced:

> "He sleeps. Although his fate was very strange, he lived.
> He died when he had no longer his angel.
> The things came to pass simply, of itself,
> as the night comes when day is gone."